THE ANNE OF GREEN GABLES COLLECTION: SIX NOVELS IN ONE VOLUME

By

Lucy Maud Montgomery

CK

Cover Photograph: Smudge 9000

ISBN: 978-1-78139-344-4

Contents

ANNE OF GREEN GABLES

ANNE OF AVONLEA

ANNE OF THE ISLAND

ANNE'S HOUSE OF DREAMS

RAINBOW VALLEY

RILLA OF INGLESIDE

ANNE OF GREEN GABLES

CHAPTER I. Mrs. Rachel Lynde is Surprised

Mrs. Rachel Lynde lived just where the Avonlea main road dipped down into a little hollow, fringed with alders and ladies' eardrops and traversed by a brook that had its source away back in the woods of the old Cuthbert place; it was reputed to be an intricate, headlong brook in its earlier course through those woods, with dark secrets of pool and cascade; but by the time it reached Lynde's Hollow it was a quiet, well-conducted little stream, for not even a brook could run past Mrs. Rachel Lynde's door without due regard for decency and decorum; it probably was conscious that Mrs. Rachel was sitting at her window, keeping a sharp eye on everything that passed, from brooks and children up, and that if she noticed anything odd or out of place she would never rest until she had ferreted out the whys and wherefores thereof.

There are plenty of people in Avonlea and out of it, who can attend closely to their neighbor's business by dint of neglecting their own; but Mrs. Rachel Lynde was one of those capable creatures who can manage their own concerns and those of other folks into the bargain. She was a notable housewife; her work was always done and well done; she "ran" the Sewing Circle, helped run the Sunday-school, and was the strongest prop of the Church Aid Society and Foreign Missions Auxiliary. Yet with all this Mrs. Rachel found abundant time to sit for hours at her kitchen window, knitting "cotton warp" quilts—she had knitted sixteen of them, as Avonlea housekeepers were wont to tell in awed voices—and keeping a sharp eye on the main road that crossed the hollow and wound up the steep red hill beyond. Since Avonlea occupied a little triangular peninsula jutting out into the Gulf of St. Lawrence with water on two sides of it, anybody who went out of it or into it had to pass over that hill road and so run the unseen gauntlet of Mrs. Rachel's all-seeing eye.

She was sitting there one afternoon in early June. The sun was coming in at the window warm and bright; the orchard on the slope below the house was in a bridal flush of pinky-white bloom, hummed over by a myriad of bees. Thomas Lynde—a meek little man whom Avonlea people called "Rachel Lynde's husband"—was sowing his late turnip seed on the hill field beyond the barn; and Matthew Cuthbert ought to have been sowing his on the big red brook field away over by Green Gables. Mrs. Rachel knew that he ought because she had heard him tell Peter Morrison the evening before in William J. Blair's store over at Carmody that he meant to sow his turnip seed the next afternoon. Peter had asked him, of course, for Matthew Cuthbert had never been known to volunteer information about anything in his whole life.

And yet here was Matthew Cuthbert, at half-past three on the afternoon of a busy day, placidly driving over the hollow and up the hill; moreover, he wore a white collar and his best suit of clothes, which was plain proof that he was going out of Avonlea; and he had the buggy and the sorrel mare, which betokened that he was going a considerable distance. Now, where was Matthew Cuthbert going and why was he going there?

Had it been any other man in Avonlea, Mrs. Rachel, deftly putting this and that together, might have given a pretty good guess as to both questions. But Matthew so rarely went from home that it must be something pressing and unusual which was taking him; he was the shyest man alive and hated to have to go among strangers or to any place where he might have to talk. Matthew, dressed up with a white collar and driving in a buggy, was something that didn't happen often. Mrs. Rachel, ponder as she might, could make nothing of it and her afternoon's enjoyment was spoiled.

"I'll just step over to Green Gables after tea and find out from Marilla where he's gone and why," the worthy woman finally concluded. "He doesn't generally go to town this time of year and he NEVER visits; if he'd run out of turnip seed he wouldn't dress up and take the buggy to go for more; he wasn't driving fast enough to be going for a doctor. Yet something must have happened since last night to start him off. I'm clean puzzled, that's what, and I won't know a minute's peace of mind or conscience until I know what has taken Matthew Cuthbert out of Avonlea today."

Accordingly after tea Mrs. Rachel set out; she had not far to go; the big, rambling, orchard-embowered house where the Cuthberts lived was a scant quarter of a mile up the road from Lynde's Hollow. To be sure, the long lane made it a good deal further. Matthew Cuthbert's father, as shy and silent as his son after him, had got as far away as he possibly could from his fellow men without actually retreating into the woods when he founded his homestead. Green Gables was built at the furthest edge of his cleared land and there it was to this day, barely visible from the main road along which all the other Avonlea houses were so sociably situated. Mrs. Rachel Lynde did not call living in such a place LIVING at all.

"It's just STAYING, that's what," she said as she stepped along the deep-rutted, grassy lane bordered with wild rose bushes. "It's no wonder Matthew and Marilla are both a little odd, living away back here by themselves. Trees aren't much company, though dear knows if they were there'd be enough of them. I'd ruther look at people. To be sure, they seem contented enough; but then, I suppose, they're used to it. A body can get used to anything, even to being hanged, as the Irishman said."

With this Mrs. Rachel stepped out of the lane into the backyard of Green Gables. Very green and neat and precise was that yard, set about on one side with great patriarchal willows and the other with prim Lombardies. Not a stray stick nor stone was to be seen, for Mrs. Rachel would have seen it if there had been. Privately she was of the opinion that Marilla Cuthbert swept that yard over as often as she swept her house. One could have eaten a meal off the ground without overbrimming the proverbial peck of dirt.

Mrs. Rachel rapped smartly at the kitchen door and stepped in when bidden to do so. The kitchen at Green Gables was a cheerful apartment—or would have been cheerful if it had not been so painfully clean as to give it something of the appearance of an unused parlor. Its windows looked east and west; through the west one, looking out on the back yard, came a flood of mellow June sunlight; but the east one, whence you got a glimpse of the bloom white cherry-trees in the left orchard and nodding, slender birches down in the hollow by the brook, was greened over by a tangle of vines. Here sat Marilla Cuthbert, when she sat at all, always slightly distrustful of sunshine, which seemed to her too dancing and irresponsible a thing for a world which was meant to be taken seriously; and here she sat now, knitting, and the table behind her was laid for supper.

Mrs. Rachel, before she had fairly closed the door, had taken a mental note of everything that was on that table. There were three plates laid, so that Marilla must be expecting some one home with Matthew to tea; but the dishes were everyday dishes and there was only crab-apple preserves and one kind of cake, so that the expected company could not be any particular company. Yet what of Matthew's white collar and the sorrel mare? Mrs. Rachel was getting fairly dizzy with this unusual mystery about quiet, unmysterious Green Gables.

"Good evening, Rachel," Marilla said briskly. "This is a real fine evening, isn't it? Won't you sit down? How are all your folks?"

Something that for lack of any other name might be called friendship existed and always had existed between Marilla Cuthbert and Mrs. Rachel, in spite of—or perhaps because of—their dissimilarity.

Marilla was a tall, thin woman, with angles and without curves; her dark hair showed some gray streaks and was always twisted up in a hard little knot behind with two wire hairpins stuck aggressively through it. She looked like a woman of narrow experience and rigid conscience, which she was; but there was a saving something about her mouth which, if it had been ever so slightly developed, might have been considered indicative of a sense of humor.

"We're all pretty well," said Mrs. Rachel. "I was kind of afraid YOU weren't, though, when I saw Matthew starting off today. I thought maybe he was going to the doctor's."

Marilla's lips twitched understandingly. She had expected Mrs. Rachel up; she had known that the sight of Matthew jaunting off so unaccountably would be too much for her neighbor's curiosity.

"Oh, no, I'm quite well although I had a bad headache yesterday," she said. "Matthew went to Bright River. We're getting a little boy from an orphan asylum in Nova Scotia and he's coming on the train tonight."

If Marilla had said that Matthew had gone to Bright River to meet a kangaroo from Australia Mrs. Rachel could not have been more astonished. She was actually stricken dumb for five seconds. It was unsupposable that Marilla was making fun of her, but Mrs. Rachel was almost forced to suppose it.

"Are you in earnest, Marilla?" she demanded when voice returned to her.

"Yes, of course," said Marilla, as if getting boys from orphan asylums in Nova Scotia were part of the usual spring work on any well-regulated Avonlea farm instead of being an unheard of innovation.

Mrs. Rachel felt that she had received a severe mental jolt. She thought in exclamation points. A boy! Marilla and Matthew Cuthbert of all people adopting a boy! From an orphan asylum! Well, the world was certainly turning upside down! She would be surprised at nothing after this! Nothing!

"What on earth put such a notion into your head?" she demanded disapprovingly.

This had been done without her advice being asked, and must perforce be disapproved.

"Well, we've been thinking about it for some time—all winter in fact," returned Marilla. "Mrs. Alexander Spencer was up here one day before Christmas and she said she was going to get a little girl from the asylum over in Hopeton in the spring. Her cousin lives there and Mrs. Spencer has visited here and knows all about it. So Matthew and I have talked it over off and on ever since. We thought we'd get a boy. Matthew is getting up in years, you know—he's sixty—and he isn't so spry as he once was. His heart troubles him a good deal. And you know how desperate hard it's got to be to get hired help. There's never anybody to be had but those stupid, half-grown little French boys; and as soon as you do get one broke into your ways and taught something he's up and off to the lobster canneries or the States. At first Matthew suggested getting a Home boy. But I said 'no' flat to that. 'They may be all right—I'm not saying they're not—but no London street Arabs for me,' I said. 'Give me a native born at least. There'll be a risk, no matter who we get. But I'll feel easier in my mind and sleep sounder at nights if we get a born Canadian.' So in the end we decided to ask Mrs. Spencer to pick us out one when she went over to get her little girl. We heard last week she was going, so we sent her word by Richard Spencer's folks at Carmody to bring us a smart, likely boy of about ten or eleven. We decided that would be the best age—old enough to be of some use in doing chores right off and young enough to be trained up proper. We mean to give him a good home and schooling. We had a telegram from Mrs. Alexander Spencer today—the mail-man brought it from the station—saying they were coming on the five-thirty train tonight. So Matthew went to Bright River to meet him. Mrs. Spencer will drop him off there. Of course she goes on to White Sands station herself."

Mrs. Rachel prided herself on always speaking her mind; she proceeded to speak it now, having adjusted her mental attitude to this amazing piece of news.

"Well, Marilla, I'll just tell you plain that I think you're doing a mighty foolish thing—a risky thing, that's what. You don't know what you're getting. You're bringing a strange child into your house and home and you don't know a single thing about him nor what his disposition is like nor what sort of parents he had nor how he's likely to turn out. Why, it was only last week I read in the paper how a man and his wife up west of the Island took a boy out of an orphan asylum and he set fire to the house at night—set it ON PURPOSE, Marilla—and nearly burnt them to a crisp in their beds. And I know another case where an adopted boy used to suck the eggs—they couldn't break him of it. If you had asked my advice in the matter—which you didn't do, Marilla—I'd have said for mercy's sake not to think of such a thing, that's what."

This Job's comforting seemed neither to offend nor to alarm Marilla. She knitted steadily on.

"I don't deny there's something in what you say, Rachel. I've had some qualms myself. But Matthew was terrible set on it. I could see that, so I gave in. It's so seldom Matthew sets his mind on anything that when he does I always feel it's my duty to give in. And as for the risk, there's risks in pretty near everything a body does in this world. There's risks in people's having children of their own if it comes to that—they don't always turn out well. And then Nova Scotia is right close to the Island. It isn't as if we were getting him from England or the States. He can't be much different from ourselves."

"Well, I hope it will turn out all right," said Mrs. Rachel in a tone that plainly indicated her painful doubts. "Only don't say I didn't warn you if he burns Green Gables down or puts strychnine in the well—I heard of a case over in New Brunswick where an orphan asylum child did that and the whole family died in fearful agonies. Only, it was a girl in that instance."

"Well, we're not getting a girl," said Marilla, as if poisoning wells were a purely feminine accomplishment and not to be dreaded in the case of a boy. "I'd never dream of taking a girl to bring up. I wonder at Mrs. Alexander Spencer for doing it. But there, SHE wouldn't shrink from adopting a whole orphan asylum if she took it into her head."

Mrs. Rachel would have liked to stay until Matthew came home with his imported orphan. But reflecting that it would be a good two hours at least before his arrival she concluded to go up the road to Robert Bell's and tell the news. It would certainly make a sensation second to none, and Mrs. Rachel dearly loved to make a sensation. So she took herself away, somewhat to Marilla's relief, for the latter felt her doubts and fears reviving under the influence of Mrs. Rachel's pessimism.

"Well, of all things that ever were or will be!" ejaculated Mrs. Rachel when she was safely out in the lane. "It does really seem as if I must be dreaming. Well, I'm sorry for that poor young one and no mistake. Matthew and Marilla don't know anything about children and they'll expect him to be wiser and steadier that his own grandfather, if so be's he ever had a grandfather, which is doubtful. It seems uncanny to think of a child at Green Gables somehow; there's never been one there, for Matthew and Marilla were grown up when the new house was built—if they ever WERE children, which is hard to believe when one looks at them. I wouldn't be in that orphan's shoes for anything. My, but I pity him, that's what."

So said Mrs. Rachel to the wild rose bushes out of the fulness of her heart; but if she could have seen the child who was waiting patiently at the Bright River station at that very moment her pity would have been still deeper and more profound.

CHAPTER II. Matthew Cuthbert is surprised

Matthew Cuthbert and the sorrel mare jogged comfortably over the eight miles to Bright River. It was a pretty road, running along between snug farmsteads, with now and again a bit of balsamy fir wood to drive through or a hollow where wild plums hung out their filmy bloom. The air was sweet with the breath of many apple orchards and the meadows sloped away in the distance to horizon mists of pearl and purple; while

> "The little birds sang as if it were
> The one day of summer in all the year."

Matthew enjoyed the drive after his own fashion, except during the moments when he met women and had to nod to them—for in Prince Edward island you are supposed to nod to all and sundry you meet on the road whether you know them or not.

Matthew dreaded all women except Marilla and Mrs. Rachel; he had an uncomfortable feeling that the mysterious creatures were secretly laughing at him. He may have been quite right in thinking so, for he was an odd-looking personage, with an ungainly figure and long iron-gray hair that touched his stooping shoulders, and a full, soft brown beard which he had worn ever since he was twenty. In fact, he had looked at twenty very much as he looked at sixty, lacking a little of the grayness.

When he reached Bright River there was no sign of any train; he thought he was too early, so he tied his horse in the yard of the small Bright River hotel and went over to the station house. The long platform was almost deserted; the only living creature in sight being a girl who was sitting on a pile of shingles at the extreme end. Matthew, barely noting that it WAS a girl, sidled past her as quickly as possible without looking at her. Had he looked he could hardly have failed to notice the tense rigidity and expectation of her attitude and expression. She was sitting there waiting for something or somebody and, since sitting and waiting was the only thing to do just then, she sat and waited with all her might and main.

Matthew encountered the stationmaster locking up the ticket office preparatory to going home for supper, and asked him if the five-thirty train would soon be along.

"The five-thirty train has been in and gone half an hour ago," answered that brisk official. "But there was a passenger dropped off for you—a little girl. She's sitting out there on the shingles. I asked her to go into the ladies' waiting room, but she informed me gravely that she preferred to stay outside. 'There was more scope for imagination,' she said. She's a case, I should say."

"I'm not expecting a girl," said Matthew blankly. "It's a boy I've come for. He should be here. Mrs. Alexander Spencer was to bring him over from Nova Scotia for me."

The stationmaster whistled.

"Guess there's some mistake," he said. "Mrs. Spencer came off the train with that girl and gave her into my charge. Said you and your sister were adopting her from an orphan asylum and that you would be along for her presently. That's all I know about it—and I haven't got any more orphans concealed hereabouts."

"I don't understand," said Matthew helplessly, wishing that Marilla was at hand to cope with the situation.

"Well, you'd better question the girl," said the station-master carelessly. "I dare say she'll be able to explain—she's got a tongue of her own, that's certain. Maybe they were out of boys of the brand you wanted."

He walked jauntily away, being hungry, and the unfortunate Matthew was left to do that which was harder for him than bearding a lion in its den—walk up to a girl—a strange girl—an orphan girl—and demand of her why she wasn't a boy. Matthew groaned in spirit as he turned about and shuffled gently down the platform towards her.

She had been watching him ever since he had passed her and she had her eyes on him now. Matthew was not looking at her and would not have seen what she was really like if he had been, but an ordinary observer would have seen this: A child of about eleven, garbed in a very short, very tight, very ugly dress of yellowish-gray wincey. She wore a faded brown sailor hat and beneath the hat, extending down her back, were two braids of very thick, decidedly red hair. Her face was small, white and thin, also much freckled; her mouth was large and so were her eyes, which looked green in some lights and moods and gray in others.

So far, the ordinary observer; an extraordinary observer might have seen that the chin was very pointed and pronounced; that the big eyes were full of spirit and vivacity; that the mouth was sweet-lipped and expressive; that the forehead was broad and full; in short, our discerning extraordinary observer might have concluded that no commonplace soul inhabited the body of this stray woman-child of whom shy Matthew Cuthbert was so ludicrously afraid.

Matthew, however, was spared the ordeal of speaking first, for as soon as she concluded that he was coming to her she stood up, grasping with one thin brown hand the handle of a shabby, old-fashioned carpet-bag; the other she held out to him.

"I suppose you are Mr. Matthew Cuthbert of Green Gables?" she said in a peculiarly clear, sweet voice. "I'm very glad to see you. I was beginning to be afraid you weren't coming for me and I was imagining all the things that might have happened to prevent you. I had made up my mind that if you didn't come for me to-night I'd go down the track to that big wild cherry-tree at the bend, and climb up into it to stay all night. I wouldn't be a bit afraid, and it would be lovely to sleep in a wild cherry-tree all white with bloom in the moonshine, don't you think? You could imagine you were dwelling in marble halls, couldn't you? And I was quite sure you would come for me in the morning, if you didn't to-night."

Matthew had taken the scrawny little hand awkwardly in his; then and there he decided what to do. He could not tell this child with the glowing eyes that there had been a mistake; he would take her home and let Marilla do that. She couldn't be left at Bright River anyhow, no matter what mistake had been made, so all questions and explanations might as well be deferred until he was safely back at Green Gables.

"I'm sorry I was late," he said shyly. "Come along. The horse is over in the yard. Give me your bag."

"Oh, I can carry it," the child responded cheerfully. "It isn't heavy. I've got all my worldly goods in it, but it isn't heavy. And if it isn't carried in just a certain way the handle pulls out—so I'd better keep it because I know the exact knack of it. It's an extremely old carpet-bag. Oh, I'm very glad you've come, even if it would have been nice to sleep in a wild cherry-tree. We've got to drive a long piece, haven't we? Mrs. Spencer said it was eight miles. I'm glad because I love driving. Oh, it seems so wonderful that I'm going to live with you and belong to you. I've never belonged to anybody—not really. But the asylum was the worst. I've only been in it four months, but that was enough. I don't suppose you ever were an orphan in an asylum, so you can't possibly understand what it is like. It's worse than anything you could imagine. Mrs. Spencer said it was wicked of me to talk like that, but I didn't mean to be wicked. It's so easy to be wicked without knowing it, isn't it? They were good, you know—the asylum people. But there is so little scope for the imagination in an asylum—only just in the other orphans. It was pretty interesting to imagine things about them—to imagine that perhaps the girl who sat next to you was really the daughter of a belted earl, who had been stolen away from her parents in her infancy by a cruel nurse who died before she could confess. I used to lie awake at nights and imagine things like that, because I didn't have time in the day. I guess that's why I'm so thin—I AM dreadful thin, ain't I? There isn't a pick on my bones. I do love to imagine I'm nice and plump, with dimples in my elbows."

With this Matthew's companion stopped talking, partly because she was out of breath and partly because they had reached the buggy. Not another word did she say until they had left the village and were driving down a steep little hill, the road part of which had been cut so deeply into the soft soil, that the banks, fringed with blooming wild cherry-trees and slim white birches, were several feet above their heads.

The child put out her hand and broke off a branch of wild plum that brushed against the side of the buggy.

"Isn't that beautiful? What did that tree, leaning out from the bank, all white and lacy, make you think of?" she asked.

"Well now, I dunno," said Matthew.

"Why, a bride, of course—a bride all in white with a lovely misty veil. I've never seen one, but I can imagine what she would look like. I don't ever expect to be a bride myself. I'm so homely nobody will ever want to marry me—unless it might be a foreign missionary. I suppose a foreign missionary mightn't be very particular. But I do hope that some day I shall have a white dress. That is my highest ideal of earthly bliss. I just love pretty clothes. And I've never had a pretty dress in my life that I can remember—but of course it's all the more to look for-ward to, isn't it? And then I can imagine that I'm dressed gorgeously. This morning when I left the asylum I felt so ashamed because I had to wear this horrid old wincey dress. All the orphans had to wear them, you know. A merchant in Hopeton last winter donated three hundred yards of wincey to the asylum. Some people said it was because he couldn't sell it, but I'd rather believe that it was out of the kindness of his heart, wouldn't you? When we got on the train I felt as if everybody must be looking at me and pitying me. But I just went to work and im-agined that I had on the most beautiful pale blue silk dress—because when you ARE imagining you might as well imagine something worth while—and a big hat all flowers and nodding plumes, and a gold watch, and kid gloves and boots. I felt cheered up right away and I enjoyed my trip to the Island with all my might. I wasn't a bit sick coming over in the boat. Neither was Mrs. Spencer although she generally is. She said she hadn't time to get sick, watching to see that I didn't fall overboard. She said she never saw the beat of me for prowling about. But if it kept her from being seasick it's a mercy I did prowl, isn't it? And I wanted to see everything that was to be seen on that boat, because I didn't know whether I'd ever have another opportunity. Oh, there are a lot more cherry-trees all in bloom! This Island is the bloomiest place. I just love it already, and I'm so glad I'm going to live here. I've always heard that Prince Edward Island was the prettiest place in the world, and I used to imagine I was living here, but I never really expected I would. It's delightful when your imaginations come true, isn't it? But those red roads are so funny. When we got into the train at Charlottetown and the red roads began to flash past I asked Mrs. Spencer what made them red and she said she didn't know and for pity's sake not to ask her any more questions. She said I must have asked her a thousand already. I suppose I had, too, but how you going to find out about things if you don't ask questions? And what DOES make the roads red?"

"Well now, I dunno," said Matthew.

"Well, that is one of the things to find out sometime. Isn't it splendid to think of all the things there are to find out about? It just makes me feel glad to be alive—it's such an interesting world. It wouldn't be half so interesting if we know all about everything, would it? There'd be no scope for imagination then, would there? But am I talking too much? People are always telling me I do. Would you rather I didn't talk? If you say so I'll stop. I can STOP when I make up my mind to it, although it's difficult."

Matthew, much to his own surprise, was enjoying himself. Like most quiet folks he liked talkative people when they were willing to do the talking themselves and did not expect him to keep up his end of it. But he had never expected to enjoy the society of a little girl. Women were bad enough in all conscience, but little girls were worse. He detested the way they had of sidling past him timidly, with sidewise glances, as if they expected him to gobble them up at a mouthful if they ventured to say a word. That was the Avonlea type of well-bred little girl. But this freckled witch was very different, and although he found it rather difficult for his slower intelligence to keep up with her brisk mental processes he thought that he "kind of liked her chatter." So he said as shyly as usual:

"Oh, you can talk as much as you like. I don't mind."

"Oh, I'm so glad. I know you and I are going to get along together fine. It's such a relief to talk when one wants to and not be told that children should be seen and not heard. I've had that said to me a million times if I have once. And people laugh at me because I use big words. But if you have big ideas you have to use big words to express them, haven't you?"

"Well now, that seems reasonable," said Matthew.

"Mrs. Spencer said that my tongue must be hung in the middle. But it isn't—it's firmly fastened at one end. Mrs. Spencer said your place was named Green Gables. I asked her all about it. And she said there were trees all around it. I was gladder than ever. I just love trees. And there weren't any at all about the asylum, only a few poor weeny-teeny things out in front with little whitewashed cagey things about them. They just looked like orphans themselves, those trees did. It used to make me want to cry to look at them. I used to say to them, 'Oh, you POOR little things! If you were out in a great big woods with other trees all around you and little mosses and Junebells growing over your roots and a brook not far away and birds singing in you branches, you could grow, couldn't you? But you can't where you are. I know just exactly how you feel, little trees.' I felt sorry to leave them behind this morning. You do get so attached to things like that, don't you? Is there a brook anywhere near Green Gables? I forgot to ask Mrs. Spencer that."

"Well now, yes, there's one right below the house."

"Fancy. It's always been one of my dreams to live near a brook. I never expected I would, though. Dreams don't often come true, do they? Wouldn't it be nice if they did? But just now I feel pretty nearly perfectly happy. I can't feel exactly perfectly happy because—well, what color would you call this?"

She twitched one of her long glossy braids over her thin shoulder and held it up before Matthew's eyes. Matthew was not used to deciding on the tints of ladies' tresses, but in this case there couldn't be much doubt.

"It's red, ain't it?" he said.

The girl let the braid drop back with a sigh that seemed to come from her very toes and to exhale forth all the sorrows of the ages.

"Yes, it's red," she said resignedly. "Now you see why I can't be perfectly happy. Nobody could who has red hair. I don't mind the other things so much—the freckles and the green eyes and my skinniness. I can imagine them away. I can imagine that I have a beautiful rose-leaf complexion and lovely starry violet eyes. But I CANNOT imagine that red hair away. I do my best. I think to myself, 'Now my hair is a glorious black, black as the raven's wing.' But all the time I KNOW it is just plain red and it breaks my heart. It will be my lifelong sorrow. I read of a girl once in a novel who had a lifelong sorrow but it wasn't red hair. Her hair was pure gold rippling back from her alabaster brow. What is an alabaster brow? I never could find out. Can you tell me?"

"Well now, I'm afraid I can't," said Matthew, who was getting a little dizzy. He felt as he had once felt in his rash youth when another boy had enticed him on the merry-go-round at a picnic.

"Well, whatever it was it must have been something nice because she was divinely beautiful. Have you ever imagined what it must feel like to be divinely beautiful?"

"Well now, no, I haven't," confessed Matthew ingenuously.

"I have, often. Which would you rather be if you had the choice—divinely beautiful or dazzlingly clever or angelically good?"

"Well now, I—I don't know exactly."

"Neither do I. I can never decide. But it doesn't make much real difference for it isn't likely I'll ever be either. It's certain I'll never be angelically good. Mrs. Spencer says—oh, Mr. Cuthbert! Oh, Mr. Cuthbert!! Oh, Mr. Cuthbert!!!"

That was not what Mrs. Spencer had said; neither had the child tumbled out of the buggy nor had Matthew done anything astonishing. They had simply rounded a curve in the road and found themselves in the "Avenue."

The "Avenue," so called by the Newbridge people, was a stretch of road four or five hundred yards long, completely arched over with huge, wide-spreading apple-trees, planted years ago by an eccentric old farmer. Overhead was one long canopy of snowy fragrant bloom. Below the boughs the air was full of a purple twilight and far ahead a glimpse of painted sunset sky shone like a great rose window at the end of a cathedral aisle.

Its beauty seemed to strike the child dumb. She leaned back in the buggy, her thin hands clasped before her, her face lifted rapturously to the white splendor above. Even when they had passed out and were driving down the long slope to Newbridge she never moved or spoke. Still with rapt face she gazed afar into the sunset west, with eyes that saw visions trooping splendidly across that glowing background. Through Newbridge, a bustling little village where dogs barked at them and small boys hooted and curious faces peered from the windows, they drove, still in silence. When three more miles had dropped away behind them the child had not spoken. She could keep silence, it was evident, as energetically as she could talk.

"I guess you're feeling pretty tired and hungry," Matthew ventured to say at last, accounting for her long visitation of dumbness with the only reason he could think of. "But we haven't very far to go now—only another mile."

She came out of her reverie with a deep sigh and looked at him with the dreamy gaze of a soul that had been wondering afar, star-led.

"Oh, Mr. Cuthbert," she whispered, "that place we came through—that white place—what was it?"

"Well now, you must mean the Avenue," said Matthew after a few moments' profound reflection. "It is a kind of pretty place."

"Pretty? Oh, PRETTY doesn't seem the right word to use. Nor beautiful, either. They don't go far enough. Oh, it was wonderful—wonderful. It's the first thing I ever saw that couldn't be improved upon by imagination. It just satisfies me here"—she put one hand on her breast—"it made a queer funny ache and yet it was a pleasant ache. Did you ever have an ache like that, Mr. Cuthbert?"

"Well now, I just can't recollect that I ever had."

"I have it lots of time—whenever I see anything royally beautiful. But they shouldn't call that lovely place the Avenue. There is no meaning in a name like that. They should call it—let me see—the White Way of Delight. Isn't that a nice imaginative name? When I don't like the name of a place or a person I always imagine a new one and always think of them so. There was a girl at the asylum whose name was Hepzibah Jenkins, but I always imagined her as Rosalia DeVere. Other people may call that place the Avenue, but I shall always call it the White Way of Delight. Have we really only another mile to go before we get home? I'm glad and I'm sorry. I'm sorry because this drive has been so pleasant and I'm always sorry when pleasant things end. Something still pleasanter may come after, but you can never be sure. And it's so often the case that it isn't pleasanter. That has been my experience anyhow. But I'm glad to think of getting home. You see, I've never had a real home since I can remember. It gives me that pleasant ache again just to think of coming to a really truly home. Oh, isn't that pretty!"

They had driven over the crest of a hill. Below them was a pond, looking almost like a river so long and winding was it. A bridge spanned it midway and from there to its lower end, where an amber-hued belt of sand-hills shut it in from the dark blue gulf beyond, the water was a glory of many shifting hues—the most spiritual shadings of crocus and rose and ethereal green, with other elusive tintings for which no name has ever been found. Above the bridge the pond ran up into fringing groves of fir and maple and lay all darkly translucent in their wavering shadows. Here and there a wild plum leaned out from the bank like a white-clad girl tip-toeing to her own reflection. From the marsh at the head of the pond came the clear, mournfully-sweet chorus of the frogs. There was a little gray house peering around a white apple orchard on a slope beyond and, although it was not yet quite dark, a light was shining from one of its windows.

"That's Barry's pond," said Matthew.

"Oh, I don't like that name, either. I shall call it—let me see—the Lake of Shining Waters. Yes, that is the right name for it. I know because of the thrill.

When I hit on a name that suits exactly it gives me a thrill. Do things ever give you a thrill?"

Matthew ruminated.

"Well now, yes. It always kind of gives me a thrill to see them ugly white grubs that spade up in the cucumber beds. I hate the look of them."

"Oh, I don't think that can be exactly the same kind of a thrill. Do you think it can? There doesn't seem to be much connection between grubs and lakes of shining waters, does there? But why do other people call it Barry's pond?"

"I reckon because Mr. Barry lives up there in that house. Orchard Slope's the name of his place. If it wasn't for that big bush behind it you could see Green Gables from here. But we have to go over the bridge and round by the road, so it's near half a mile further."

"Has Mr. Barry any little girls? Well, not so very little either—about my size."

"He's got one about eleven. Her name is Diana."

"Oh!" with a long indrawing of breath. "What a perfectly lovely name!"

"Well now, I dunno. There's something dreadful heathenish about it, seems to me. I'd ruther Jane or Mary or some sensible name like that. But when Diana was born there was a schoolmaster boarding there and they gave him the naming of her and he called her Diana."

"I wish there had been a schoolmaster like that around when I was born, then. Oh, here we are at the bridge. I'm going to shut my eyes tight. I'm always afraid going over bridges. I can't help imagining that perhaps just as we get to the middle, they'll crumple up like a jack-knife and nip us. So I shut my eyes. But I always have to open them for all when I think we're getting near the middle. Because, you see, if the bridge DID crumple up I'd want to SEE it crumple. What a jolly rumble it makes! I always like the rumble part of it. Isn't it splendid there are so many things to like in this world? There we're over. Now I'll look back. Good night, dear Lake of Shining Waters. I always say good night to the things I love, just as I would to people. I think they like it. That water looks as if it was smiling at me."

When they had driven up the further hill and around a corner Matthew said:

"We're pretty near home now. That's Green Gables over—"

"Oh, don't tell me," she interrupted breathlessly, catching at his partially raised arm and shutting her eyes that she might not see his gesture. "Let me guess. I'm sure I'll guess right."

She opened her eyes and looked about her. They were on the crest of a hill. The sun had set some time since, but the landscape was still clear in the mellow afterlight. To the west a dark church spire rose up against a marigold sky. Below was a little valley and beyond a long, gently-rising slope with snug farmsteads scattered along it. From one to another the child's eyes darted, eager and wistful. At last they lingered on one away to the left, far back from the road, dimly white with blossoming trees in the twilight of the surrounding woods. Over it, in the stainless southwest sky, a great crystal-white star was shining like a lamp of guidance and promise.

"That's it, isn't it?" she said, pointing.

Matthew slapped the reins on the sorrel's back delightedly.

"Well now, you've guessed it! But I reckon Mrs. Spencer described it so's you could tell."

"No, she didn't—really she didn't. All she said might just as well have been about most of those other places. I hadn't any real idea what it looked like. But just as soon as I saw it I felt it was home. Oh, it seems as if I must be in a dream. Do you know, my arm must be black and blue from the elbow up, for I've pinched myself so many times today. Every little while a horrible sickening feeling would come over me and I'd be so afraid it was all a dream. Then I'd pinch myself to see if it was real—until suddenly I remembered that even supposing it was only a dream I'd better go on dreaming as long as I could; so I stopped pinching. But it IS real and we're nearly home."

With a sigh of rapture she relapsed into silence. Matthew stirred uneasily. He felt glad that it would be Marilla and not he who would have to tell this waif of the world that the home she longed for was not to be hers after all. They drove over Lynde's Hollow, where it was already quite dark, but not so dark that Mrs. Rachel could not see them from her window vantage, and up the hill and into the long lane of Green Gables. By the time they arrived at the house Matthew was shrinking from the approaching revelation with an energy he did not understand. It was not of Marilla or himself he was thinking of the trouble this mistake was probably going to make for them, but of the child's disappointment. When he thought of that rapt light being quenched in her eyes he had an uncomfortable feeling that he was going to assist at murdering something—much the same feeling that came over him when he had to kill a lamb or calf or any other innocent little creature.

The yard was quite dark as they turned into it and the poplar leaves were rustling silkily all round it.

"Listen to the trees talking in their sleep," she whispered, as he lifted her to the ground. "What nice dreams they must have!"

Then, holding tightly to the carpet-bag which contained "all her worldly goods," she followed him into the house.

CHAPTER III. Marilla Cuthbert is Surprised

Marilla came briskly forward as Matthew opened the door. But when her eyes fell of the odd little figure in the stiff, ugly dress, with the long braids of red hair and the eager, luminous eyes, she stopped short in amazement.

"Matthew Cuthbert, who's that?" she ejaculated. "Where is the boy?"

"There wasn't any boy," said Matthew wretchedly. "There was only HER."

He nodded at the child, remembering that he had never even asked her name.

"No boy! But there MUST have been a boy," insisted Marilla. "We sent word to Mrs. Spencer to bring a boy."

"Well, she didn't. She brought HER. I asked the station-master. And I had to bring her home. She couldn't be left there, no matter where the mistake had come in."

"Well, this is a pretty piece of business!" ejaculated Marilla.

During this dialogue the child had remained silent, her eyes roving from one to the other, all the animation fading out of her face. Suddenly she seemed to grasp the full meaning of what had been said. Dropping her precious carpet-bag she sprang forward a step and clasped her hands.

"You don't want me!" she cried. "You don't want me because I'm not a boy! I might have expected it. Nobody ever did want me. I might have known it was all too beautiful to last. I might have known nobody really did want me. Oh, what shall I do? I'm going to burst into tears!"

Burst into tears she did. Sitting down on a chair by the table, flinging her arms out upon it, and burying her face in them, she proceeded to cry stormily. Marilla and Matthew looked at each other deprecatingly across the stove. Neither of them knew what to say or do. Finally Marilla stepped lamely into the breach.

"Well, well, there's no need to cry so about it."

"Yes, there IS need!" The child raised her head quickly, revealing a tear-stained face and trembling lips. "YOU would cry, too, if you were an orphan and had come to a place you thought was going to be home and found that they didn't want you because you weren't a boy. Oh, this is the most TRAGICAL thing that ever happened to me!"

Something like a reluctant smile, rather rusty from long disuse, mellowed Marilla's grim expression.

"Well, don't cry any more. We're not going to turn you out-of-doors to-night. You'll have to stay here until we investigate this affair. What's your name?"

The child hesitated for a moment.

"Will you please call me Cordelia?" she said eagerly.

"CALL you Cordelia? Is that your name?"

"No-o-o, it's not exactly my name, but I would love to be called Cordelia. It's such a perfectly elegant name."

"I don't know what on earth you mean. If Cordelia isn't your name, what is?"

"Anne Shirley," reluctantly faltered forth the owner of that name, "but, oh, please do call me Cordelia. It can't matter much to you what you call me if I'm only going to be here a little while, can it? And Anne is such an unromantic name."

"Unromantic fiddlesticks!" said the unsympathetic Marilla. "Anne is a real good plain sensible name. You've no need to be ashamed of it."

"Oh, I'm not ashamed of it," explained Anne, "only I like Cordelia better. I've always imagined that my name was Cordelia—at least, I always have of late years. When I was young I used to imagine it was Geraldine, but I like Cordelia better now. But if you call me Anne please call me Anne spelled with an E."

"What difference does it make how it's spelled?" asked Marilla with another rusty smile as she picked up the teapot.

"Oh, it makes SUCH a difference. It LOOKS so much nicer. When you hear a name pronounced can't you always see it in your mind, just as if it was printed out? I can; and A-n-n looks dreadful, but A-n-n-e looks so much more distinguished. If you'll only call me Anne spelled with an E I shall try to reconcile myself to not being called Cordelia."

"Very well, then, Anne spelled with an E, can you tell us how this mistake came to be made? We sent word to Mrs. Spencer to bring us a boy. Were there no boys at the asylum?"

"Oh, yes, there was an abundance of them. But Mrs. Spencer said DISTINCTLY that you wanted a girl about eleven years old. And the matron said she thought I would do. You don't know how delighted I was. I couldn't sleep all last night for joy. Oh," she added reproachfully, turning to Matthew, "why didn't you tell me at the station that you didn't want me and leave me there? If I hadn't seen the White Way of Delight and the Lake of Shining Waters it wouldn't be so hard."

"What on earth does she mean?" demanded Marilla, staring at Matthew.

"She—she's just referring to some conversation we had on the road," said Matthew hastily. "I'm going out to put the mare in, Marilla. Have tea ready when I come back."

"Did Mrs. Spencer bring anybody over besides you?" continued Marilla when Matthew had gone out.

"She brought Lily Jones for herself. Lily is only five years old and she is very beautiful and had nut-brown hair. If I was very beautiful and had nut-brown hair would you keep me?"

"No. We want a boy to help Matthew on the farm. A girl would be of no use to us. Take off your hat. I'll lay it and your bag on the hall table."

Anne took off her hat meekly. Matthew came back presently and they sat down to supper. But Anne could not eat. In vain she nibbled at the bread and butter and pecked at the crab-apple preserve out of the little scalloped glass dish by her plate. She did not really make any headway at all.

"You're not eating anything," said Marilla sharply, eying her as if it were a serious shortcoming. Anne sighed.

"I can't. I'm in the depths of despair. Can you eat when you are in the depths of despair?"

"I've never been in the depths of despair, so I can't say," responded Marilla.

"Weren't you? Well, did you ever try to IMAGINE you were in the depths of despair?"

"No, I didn't."

"Then I don't think you can understand what it's like. It's very uncomfortable feeling indeed. When you try to eat a lump comes right up in your throat and you can't swallow anything, not even if it was a chocolate caramel. I had one chocolate caramel once two years ago and it was simply delicious. I've often dreamed since then that I had a lot of chocolate caramels, but I always wake up just when I'm going to eat them. I do hope you won't be offended because I can't eat. Everything is extremely nice, but still I cannot eat."

"I guess she's tired," said Matthew, who hadn't spoken since his return from the barn. "Best put her to bed, Marilla."

Marilla had been wondering where Anne should be put to bed. She had prepared a couch in the kitchen chamber for the desired and expected boy. But, although it was neat and clean, it did not seem quite the thing to put a girl there somehow. But the spare room was out of the question for such a stray waif, so there remained only the east gable room. Marilla lighted a candle and told Anne to follow her, which Anne spiritlessly did, taking her hat and carpet-bag from the hall table as she passed. The hall was fearsomely clean; the little gable chamber in which she presently found herself seemed still cleaner.

Marilla set the candle on a three-legged, three-cornered table and turned down the bedclothes.

"I suppose you have a nightgown?" she questioned.

Anne nodded.

"Yes, I have two. The matron of the asylum made them for me. They're fearfully skimpy. There is never enough to go around in an asylum, so things are always skimpy—at least in a poor asylum like ours. I hate skimpy night-dresses. But one can dream just as well in them as in lovely trailing ones, with frills around the neck, that's one consolation."

"Well, undress as quick as you can and go to bed. I'll come back in a few minutes for the candle. I daren't trust you to put it out yourself. You'd likely set the place on fire."

CHAPTER III. Marilla Cuthbert is Surprised

When Marilla had gone Anne looked around her wistfully. The whitewashed walls were so painfully bare and staring that she thought they must ache over their own bareness. The floor was bare, too, except for a round braided mat in the middle such as Anne had never seen before. In one corner was the bed, a high, old-fashioned one, with four dark, low-turned posts. In the other corner was the aforesaid three-corner table adorned with a fat, red velvet pin-cushion hard enough to turn the point of the most adventurous pin. Above it hung a little six-by-eight mirror. Midway between table and bed was the window, with an icy white muslin frill over it, and opposite it was the wash-stand. The whole apartment was of a rigidity not to be described in words, but which sent a shiver to the very marrow of Anne's bones. With a sob she hastily discarded her garments, put on the skimpy nightgown and sprang into bed where she burrowed face downward into the pillow and pulled the clothes over her head. When Marilla came up for the light various skimpy articles of raiment scattered most untidily over the floor and a certain tempestuous appearance of the bed were the only indications of any presence save her own.

She deliberately picked up Anne's clothes, placed them neatly on a prim yellow chair, and then, taking up the candle, went over to the bed.

"Good night," she said, a little awkwardly, but not unkindly.

Anne's white face and big eyes appeared over the bedclothes with a startling suddenness.

"How can you call it a GOOD night when you know it must be the very worst night I've ever had?" she said reproachfully.

Then she dived down into invisibility again.

Marilla went slowly down to the kitchen and proceeded to wash the supper dishes. Matthew was smoking—a sure sign of perturbation of mind. He seldom smoked, for Marilla set her face against it as a filthy habit; but at certain times and seasons he felt driven to it and them Marilla winked at the practice, realizing that a mere man must have some vent for his emotions.

"Well, this is a pretty kettle of fish," she said wrathfully. "This is what comes of sending word instead of going ourselves. Richard Spencer's folks have twisted that message somehow. One of us will have to drive over and see Mrs. Spencer tomorrow, that's certain. This girl will have to be sent back to the asylum."

"Yes, I suppose so," said Matthew reluctantly.

"You SUPPOSE so! Don't you know it?"

"Well now, she's a real nice little thing, Marilla. It's kind of a pity to send her back when she's so set on staying here."

"Matthew Cuthbert, you don't mean to say you think we ought to keep her!"

Marilla's astonishment could not have been greater if Matthew had expressed a predilection for standing on his head.

"Well, now, no, I suppose not—not exactly," stammered Matthew, uncomfortably driven into a corner for his precise meaning. "I suppose—we could hardly be expected to keep her."

"I should say not. What good would she be to us?"

"We might be some good to her," said Matthew suddenly and unexpectedly.

"Matthew Cuthbert, I believe that child has bewitched you! I can see as plain as plain that you want to keep her."

"Well now, she's a real interesting little thing," persisted Matthew. "You should have heard her talk coming from the station."

"Oh, she can talk fast enough. I saw that at once. It's nothing in her favour, either. I don't like children who have so much to say. I don't want an orphan girl and if I did she isn't the style I'd pick out. There's something I don't understand about her. No, she's got to be despatched straight-way back to where she came from."

"I could hire a French boy to help me," said Matthew, "and she'd be company for you."

"I'm not suffering for company," said Marilla shortly. "And I'm not going to keep her."

"Well now, it's just as you say, of course, Marilla," said Matthew rising and putting his pipe away. "I'm going to bed."

To bed went Matthew. And to bed, when she had put her dishes away, went Marilla, frowning most resolutely. And up-stairs, in the east gable, a lonely, heart-hungry, friendless child cried herself to sleep.

CHAPTER IV. Morning at Green Gables

It was broad daylight when Anne awoke and sat up in bed, staring confusedly at the window through which a flood of cheery sunshine was pouring and outside of which something white and feathery waved across glimpses of blue sky.

For a moment she could not remember where she was. First came a delightful thrill, as something very pleasant; then a horrible remembrance. This was Green Gables and they didn't want her because she wasn't a boy!

But it was morning and, yes, it was a cherry-tree in full bloom outside of her window. With a bound she was out of bed and across the floor. She pushed up the sash—it went up stiffly and creakily, as if it hadn't been opened for a long time, which was the case; and it stuck so tight that nothing was needed to hold it up.

Anne dropped on her knees and gazed out into the June morning, her eyes glistening with delight. Oh, wasn't it beautiful? Wasn't it a lovely place? Suppose she wasn't really going to stay here! She would imagine she was. There was scope for imagination here.

A huge cherry-tree grew outside, so close that its boughs tapped against the house, and it was so thick-set with blossoms that hardly a leaf was to be seen. On both sides of the house was a big orchard, one of apple-trees and one of cherry-trees, also showered over with blossoms; and their grass was all sprinkled with dandelions. In the garden below were lilac-trees purple with flowers, and their dizzily sweet fragrance drifted up to the window on the morning wind.

Below the garden a green field lush with clover sloped down to the hollow where the brook ran and where scores of white birches grew, upspringing airily out of an undergrowth suggestive of delightful possibilities in ferns and mosses and woodsy things generally. Beyond it was a hill, green and feathery with spruce and fir; there was a gap in it where the gray gable end of the little house she had seen from the other side of the Lake of Shining Waters was visible.

Off to the left were the big barns and beyond them, away down over green, low-sloping fields, was a sparkling blue glimpse of sea.

Anne's beauty-loving eyes lingered on it all, taking everything greedily in. She had looked on so many unlovely places in her life, poor child; but this was as lovely as anything she had ever dreamed.

She knelt there, lost to everything but the loveliness around her, until she was startled by a hand on her shoulder. Marilla had come in unheard by the small dreamer.

"It's time you were dressed," she said curtly.

Marilla really did not know how to talk to the child, and her uncomfortable ignorance made her crisp and curt when she did not mean to be.

Anne stood up and drew a long breath.

"Oh, isn't it wonderful?" she said, waving her hand comprehensively at the good world outside.

"It's a big tree," said Marilla, "and it blooms great, but the fruit don't amount to much never—small and wormy."

"Oh, I don't mean just the tree; of course it's lovely—yes, it's RADIANTLY lovely—it blooms as if it meant it—but I meant everything, the garden and the orchard and the brook and the woods, the whole big dear world. Don't you feel as if you just loved the world on a morning like this? And I can hear the brook laughing all the way up here. Have you ever noticed what cheerful things brooks are? They're always laughing. Even in winter-time I've heard them under the ice. I'm so glad there's a brook near Green Gables. Perhaps you think it doesn't make any difference to me when you're not going to keep me, but it does. I shall always like to remember that there is a brook at Green Gables even if I never see it again. If there wasn't a brook I'd be HAUNTED by the uncomfortable feeling that there ought to be one. I'm not in the depths of despair this morning. I never can be in the morning. Isn't it a splendid thing that there are mornings? But I feel very sad. I've just been imagining that it was really me you wanted after all and that I was to stay here for ever and ever. It was a great comfort while it lasted. But the worst of imagining things is that the time comes when you have to stop and that hurts."

"You'd better get dressed and come down-stairs and never mind your imaginings," said Marilla as soon as she could get a word in edgewise. "Breakfast is waiting. Wash your face and comb your hair. Leave the window up and turn your bedclothes back over the foot of the bed. Be as smart as you can."

Anne could evidently be smart to some purpose for she was down-stairs in ten minutes' time, with her clothes neatly on, her hair brushed and braided, her face washed, and a comfortable consciousness pervading her soul that she had fulfilled all Marilla's requirements. As a matter of fact, however, she had forgotten to turn back the bedclothes.

"I'm pretty hungry this morning," she announced as she slipped into the chair Marilla placed for her. "The world doesn't seem such a howling wilderness as it did last night. I'm so glad it's a sunshiny morning. But I like rainy mornings real well, too. All sorts of mornings are interesting, don't you think? You don't know what's going to happen through the day, and there's so much scope for imagination. But I'm glad it's not rainy today because it's easier to be cheerful and bear up under affliction on a sunshiny day. I feel that I have a good deal to bear up under. It's all very well to read about sorrows and imagine yourself living through them heroically, but it's not so nice when you really come to have them, is it?"

"For pity's sake hold your tongue," said Marilla. "You talk entirely too much for a little girl."

Thereupon Anne held her tongue so obediently and thoroughly that her continued silence made Marilla rather nervous, as if in the presence of something not exactly natural. Matthew also held his tongue,—but this was natural,—so that the meal was a very silent one.

As it progressed Anne became more and more abstracted, eating mechanically, with her big eyes fixed unswervingly and unseeingly on the sky outside the window. This made Marilla more nervous than ever; she had an uncomfortable feeling that while this odd child's body might be there at the table her spirit was far away in some remote airy cloudland, borne aloft on the wings of imagination. Who would want such a child about the place?

Yet Matthew wished to keep her, of all unaccountable things! Marilla felt that he wanted it just as much this morning as he had the night before, and that he would go on wanting it. That was Matthew's way—take a whim into his head and cling to it with the most amazing silent persistency—a persistency ten times more potent and effectual in its very silence than if he had talked it out.

When the meal was ended Anne came out of her reverie and offered to wash the dishes.

"Can you wash dishes right?" asked Marilla distrustfully.

"Pretty well. I'm better at looking after children, though. I've had so much experience at that. It's such a pity you haven't any here for me to look after."

"I don't feel as if I wanted any more children to look after than I've got at present. YOU'RE problem enough in all conscience. What's to be done with you I don't know. Matthew is a most ridiculous man."

"I think he's lovely," said Anne reproachfully. "He is so very sympathetic. He didn't mind how much I talked—he seemed to like it. I felt that he was a kindred spirit as soon as ever I saw him."

"You're both queer enough, if that's what you mean by kindred spirits," said Marilla with a sniff. "Yes, you may wash the dishes. Take plenty of hot water, and be sure you dry them well. I've got enough to attend to this morning for I'll have to drive over to White Sands in the afternoon and see Mrs. Spencer. You'll come with me and we'll settle what's to be done with you. After you've finished the dishes go up-stairs and make your bed."

Anne washed the dishes deftly enough, as Marilla who kept a sharp eye on the process, discerned. Later on she made her bed less successfully, for she had never learned the art of wrestling with a feather tick. But is was done somehow and smoothed down; and then Marilla, to get rid of her, told her she might go out-of-doors and amuse herself until dinner time.

Anne flew to the door, face alight, eyes glowing. On the very threshold she stopped short, wheeled about, came back and sat down by the table, light and glow as effectually blotted out as if some one had clapped an extinguisher on her.

"What's the matter now?" demanded Marilla.

"I don't dare go out," said Anne, in the tone of a martyr relinquishing all earthly joys. "If I can't stay here there is no use in my loving Green Gables. And if I go out there and get acquainted with all those trees and flowers and the orchard and the brook I'll not be able to help loving it. It's hard enough now, so I won't make it any harder. I want to go out so much—everything seems to be calling to me, 'Anne, Anne, come out to us. Anne, Anne, we want a playmate'—but it's better not. There is no use in loving things if you have to be torn from them, is there? And it's so hard to keep from loving things, isn't it? That was why I was so glad when I thought I was going to live here. I thought I'd have so many things to love and nothing to hinder me. But that brief dream is over. I am resigned to my fate now, so I don't think I'll go out for fear I'll get unresigned again. What is the name of that geranium on the window-sill, please?"

"That's the apple-scented geranium."

"Oh, I don't mean that sort of a name. I mean just a name you gave it yourself. Didn't you give it a name? May I give it one then? May I call it—let me see—Bonny would do—may I call it Bonny while I'm here? Oh, do let me!"

"Goodness, I don't care. But where on earth is the sense of naming a geranium?"

"Oh, I like things to have handles even if they are only geraniums. It makes them seem more like people. How do you know but that it hurts a geranium's feelings just to be called a geranium and nothing else? You wouldn't like to be called nothing but a woman all the time. Yes, I shall call it Bonny. I named that cherry-tree outside my bedroom window this morning. I called it Snow Queen because it was so white. Of course, it won't always be in blossom, but one can imagine that it is, can't one?"

"I never in all my life saw or heard anything to equal her," muttered Marilla, beating a retreat down to the cellar after potatoes. "She is kind of interesting as Matthew says. I can feel already that I'm wondering what on earth she'll say next. She'll be casting a spell over me, too. She's cast it over Matthew. That look he gave me when he went out said everything he said or hinted last night over again. I wish he was like other men and would talk things out. A body could answer back then and argue him into reason. But what's to be done with a man who just LOOKS?"

Anne had relapsed into reverie, with her chin in her hands and her eyes on the sky, when Marilla returned from her cellar pilgrimage. There Marilla left her until the early dinner was on the table.

"I suppose I can have the mare and buggy this afternoon, Matthew?" said Marilla.

Matthew nodded and looked wistfully at Anne. Marilla intercepted the look and said grimly:

"I'm going to drive over to White Sands and settle this thing. I'll take Anne with me and Mrs. Spencer will probably make arrangements to send her back to Nova Scotia at once. I'll set your tea out for you and I'll be home in time to milk the cows."

Still Matthew said nothing and Marilla had a sense of having wasted words and breath. There is nothing more aggravating than a man who won't talk back—unless it is a woman who won't.

Matthew hitched the sorrel into the buggy in due time and Marilla and Anne set off. Matthew opened the yard gate for them and as they drove slowly through, he said, to nobody in particular as it seemed:

"Little Jerry Buote from the Creek was here this morning, and I told him I guessed I'd hire him for the summer."

Marilla made no reply, but she hit the unlucky sorrel such a vicious clip with the whip that the fat mare, unused to such treatment, whizzed indignantly down the lane at an alarming pace. Marilla looked back once as the buggy bounced along and saw that aggravating Matthew leaning over the gate, looking wistfully after them.

CHAPTER V. Anne's History

"Do you know," said Anne confidentially, "I've made up my mind to enjoy this drive. It's been my experience that you can nearly always enjoy things if you make up your mind firmly that you will. Of course, you must make it up FIRMLY. I am not going to think about going back to the asylum while we're having our drive. I'm just going to think about the drive. Oh, look, there's one little early wild rose out! Isn't it lovely? Don't you think it must be glad to be a rose? Wouldn't it be nice if roses could talk? I'm sure they could tell us such lovely things. And isn't pink the most bewitching color in the world? I love it, but I can't wear it. Redheaded people can't wear pink, not even in imagination. Did you ever know of anybody whose hair was red when she was young, but got to be another color when she grew up?"

"No, I don't know as I ever did," said Marilla mercilessly, "and I shouldn't think it likely to happen in your case either."

Anne sighed.

"Well, that is another hope gone. 'My life is a perfect graveyard of buried hopes.' That's a sentence I read in a book once, and I say it over to comfort myself whenever I'm disappointed in anything."

"I don't see where the comforting comes in myself," said Marilla.

"Why, because it sounds so nice and romantic, just as if I were a heroine in a book, you know. I am so fond of romantic things, and a graveyard full of buried hopes is about as romantic a thing as one can imagine isn't it? I'm rather glad I have one. Are we going across the Lake of Shining Waters today?"

"We're not going over Barry's pond, if that's what you mean by your Lake of Shining Waters. We're going by the shore road."

"Shore road sounds nice," said Anne dreamily. "Is it as nice as it sounds? Just when you said 'shore road' I saw it in a picture in my mind, as quick as that! And White Sands is a pretty name, too; but I don't like it as well as Avonlea. Avonlea is a lovely name. It just sounds like music. How far is it to White Sands?"

"It's five miles; and as you're evidently bent on talking you might as well talk to some purpose by telling me what you know about yourself."

"Oh, what I KNOW about myself isn't really worth telling," said Anne eagerly. "If you'll only let me tell you what I IMAGINE about myself you'll think it ever so much more interesting."

"No, I don't want any of your imaginings. Just you stick to bald facts. Begin at the beginning. Where were you born and how old are you?"

"I was eleven last March," said Anne, resigning herself to bald facts with a little sigh. "And I was born in Bolingbroke, Nova Scotia. My father's name was Walter Shirley, and he was a teacher in the Bolingbroke High School. My mother's name was Bertha Shirley. Aren't Walter and Bertha lovely names? I'm so glad my parents had nice names. It would be a real disgrace to have a father named— well, say Jedediah, wouldn't it?"

"I guess it doesn't matter what a person's name is as long as he behaves himself," said Marilla, feeling herself called upon to inculcate a good and useful moral.

"Well, I don't know." Anne looked thoughtful. "I read in a book once that a rose by any other name would smell as sweet, but I've never been able to believe it. I don't believe a rose WOULD be as nice if it was called a thistle or a skunk cabbage. I suppose my father could have been a good man even if he had been called Jedediah; but I'm sure it would have been a cross. Well, my mother was a teacher in the High school, too, but when she married father she gave up teaching, of course. A husband was enough responsibility. Mrs. Thomas said that they were a pair of babies and as poor as church mice. They went to live in a weeny-teeny little yellow house in Bolingbroke. I've never seen that house, but I've imagined it thousands of times. I think it must have had honeysuckle over the parlor window and lilacs in the front yard and lilies of the valley just inside the gate. Yes, and muslin curtains in all the windows. Muslin curtains give a house such an air. I was born in that house. Mrs. Thomas said I was the homeliest baby she ever saw, I was so scrawny and tiny and nothing but eyes, but that mother thought I was perfectly beautiful. I should think a mother would be a better judge than a poor woman who came in to scrub, wouldn't you? I'm glad she was satisfied with me anyhow, I would feel so sad if I thought I was a disappointment to her—because she didn't live very long after that, you see. She died of fever when I was just three months old. I do wish she'd lived long enough for me to remember calling her mother. I think it would be so sweet to say 'mother,' don't you? And father died four days afterwards from fever too. That left me an orphan and folks were at their wits' end, so Mrs. Thomas said, what to do with me. You see, nobody wanted me even then. It seems to be my fate. Father and mother had both come from places far away and it was well known they hadn't any relatives living. Finally Mrs. Thomas said she'd take me, though she was poor and had a drunken husband. She brought me up by hand. Do you know if there is anything in being brought up by hand that ought to make people who are brought up that way better than other people? Because whenever I was naughty Mrs. Thomas would ask me how I could be such a bad girl when she had brought me up by hand— reproachful-like.

"Mr. and Mrs. Thomas moved away from Bolingbroke to Marysville, and I lived with them until I was eight years old. I helped look after the Thomas children—there were four of them younger than me—and I can tell you they took a lot of looking after. Then Mr. Thomas was killed falling under a train and his mother offered to take Mrs. Thomas and the children, but she didn't want me. Mrs. Thomas was at HER wits' end, so she said, what to do with me. Then Mrs. Hammond from up the river came down and said she'd take me, seeing I was handy with children, and I went up the river to live with her in a little clearing among the stumps. It was a very lonesome place. I'm sure I could never have lived there if I hadn't had an imagination. Mr. Hammond worked a little sawmill up there, and Mrs. Hammond had eight children. She had twins three times. I like babies in moderation, but twins three times in succession is TOO MUCH. I told Mrs. Hammond so firmly, when the last pair came. I used to get so dreadfully tired carrying them about.

"I lived up river with Mrs. Hammond over two years, and then Mr. Hammond died and Mrs. Hammond broke up housekeeping. She divided her children among her relatives and went to the States. I had to go to the asylum at Hopeton, because nobody would take me. They didn't want me at the asylum, either; they said they were over-crowded as it was. But they had to take me and I was there four months until Mrs. Spencer came."

Anne finished up with another sigh, of relief this time. Evidently she did not like talking about her experiences in a world that had not wanted her.

"Did you ever go to school?" demanded Marilla, turning the sorrel mare down the shore road.

"Not a great deal. I went a little the last year I stayed with Mrs. Thomas. When I went up river we were so far from a school that I couldn't walk it in winter and there was a vacation in summer, so I could only go in the spring and fall. But of course I went while I was at the asylum. I can read pretty well and I know ever so many pieces of poetry off by heart—'The Battle of Hohenlinden' and 'Edinburgh after Flodden,' and 'Bingen of the Rhine,' and most of the 'Lady of the Lake' and most of 'The Seasons' by James Thompson. Don't you just love poetry that gives you a crinkly feeling up and down your back? There is a piece in the Fifth Reader—'The Downfall of Poland'—that is just full of thrills. Of course, I wasn't in the Fifth Reader—I was only in the Fourth—but the big girls used to lend me theirs to read."

"Were those women—Mrs. Thomas and Mrs. Hammond—good to you?" asked Marilla, looking at Anne out of the corner of her eye.

"O-o-o-h," faltered Anne. Her sensitive little face suddenly flushed scarlet and embarrassment sat on her brow. "Oh, they MEANT to be—I know they meant to be just as good and kind as possible. And when people mean to be good to you, you don't mind very much when they're not quite—always. They had a good deal to worry them, you know. It's very trying to have a drunken husband, you see; and it must be very trying to have twins three times in succession, don't you think? But I feel sure they meant to be good to me."

Marilla asked no more questions. Anne gave herself up to a silent rapture over the shore road and Marilla guided the sorrel abstractedly while she pondered deeply. Pity was suddenly stirring in her heart for the child. What a starved, unloved life she had had—a life of drudgery and poverty and neglect; for Marilla was shrewd enough to read between the lines of Anne's history and divine the truth. No wonder she had been so delighted at the prospect of a real home. It was a pity she had to be sent back. What if she, Marilla, should indulge Matthew's un-accountable whim and let her stay? He was set on it; and the child seemed a nice, teachable little thing.

"She's got too much to say," thought Marilla, "but she might be trained out of that. And there's nothing rude or slangy in what she does say. She's ladylike. It's likely her people were nice folks."

The shore road was "woodsy and wild and lonesome." On the right hand, scrub firs, their spirits quite unbroken by long years of tussle with the gulf winds, grew thickly. On the left were the steep red sandstone cliffs, so near the track in places that a mare of less steadiness than the sorrel might have tried the nerves of the people behind her. Down at the base of the cliffs were heaps of surf-worn rocks or little sandy coves inlaid with pebbles as with ocean jewels; beyond lay the sea, shimmering and blue, and over it soared the gulls, their pinions flashing silvery in the sunlight.

"Isn't the sea wonderful?" said Anne, rousing from a long, wide-eyed silence. "Once, when I lived in Marysville, Mr. Thomas hired an express wagon and took us all to spend the day at the shore ten miles away. I enjoyed every moment of that day, even if I had to look after the children all the time. I lived it over in hap-py dreams for years. But this shore is nicer than the Marysville shore. Aren't those gulls splendid? Would you like to be a gull? I think I would—that is, if I couldn't be a human girl. Don't you think it would be nice to wake up at sunrise and swoop down over the water and away out over that lovely blue all day; and then at night to fly back to one's nest? Oh, I can just imagine myself doing it. What big house is that just ahead, please?"

"That's the White Sands Hotel. Mr. Kirke runs it, but the season hasn't begun yet. There are heaps of Americans come there for the summer. They think this shore is just about right."

"I was afraid it might be Mrs. Spencer's place," said Anne mournfully. "I don't want to get there. Somehow, it will seem like the end of everything."

CHAPTER VI. Marilla Makes Up Her Mind

Get there they did, however, in due season. Mrs. Spencer lived in a big yellow house at White Sands Cove, and she came to the door with surprise and welcome mingled on her benevolent face.

"Dear, dear," she exclaimed, "you're the last folks I was looking for today, but I'm real glad to see you. You'll put your horse in? And how are you, Anne?"

"I'm as well as can be expected, thank you," said Anne smilelessly. A blight seemed to have descended on her.

"I suppose we'll stay a little while to rest the mare," said Marilla, "but I promised Matthew I'd be home early. The fact is, Mrs. Spencer, there's been a queer mistake somewhere, and I've come over to see where it is. We send word, Matthew and I, for you to bring us a boy from the asylum. We told your brother Robert to tell you we wanted a boy ten or eleven years old."

"Marilla Cuthbert, you don't say so!" said Mrs. Spencer in distress. "Why, Robert sent word down by his daughter Nancy and she said you wanted a girl—didn't she Flora Jane?" appealing to her daughter who had come out to the steps.

"She certainly did, Miss Cuthbert," corroborated Flora Jane earnestly.

"I'm dreadful sorry," said Mrs. Spencer. "It's too bad; but it certainly wasn't my fault, you see, Miss Cuthbert. I did the best I could and I thought I was following your instructions. Nancy is a terrible flighty thing. I've often had to scold her well for her heedlessness."

"It was our own fault," said Marilla resignedly. "We should have come to you ourselves and not left an important message to be passed along by word of mouth in that fashion. Anyhow, the mistake has been made and the only thing to do is to set it right. Can we send the child back to the asylum? I suppose they'll take her back, won't they?"

"I suppose so," said Mrs. Spencer thoughtfully, "but I don't think it will be necessary to send her back. Mrs. Peter Blewett was up here yesterday, and she was saying to me how much she wished she'd sent by me for a little girl to help her. Mrs. Peter has a large family, you know, and she finds it hard to get help. Anne will be the very girl for you. I call it positively providential."

Marilla did not look as if she thought Providence had much to do with the matter. Here was an unexpectedly good chance to get this unwelcome orphan off her hands, and she did not even feel grateful for it.

She knew Mrs. Peter Blewett only by sight as a small, shrewish-faced woman without an ounce of superfluous flesh on her bones. But she had heard of her. "A terrible worker and driver," Mrs. Peter was said to be; and discharged servant girls told fearsome tales of her temper and stinginess, and her family of pert, quarrelsome children. Marilla felt a qualm of conscience at the thought of handing Anne over to her tender mercies.

"Well, I'll go in and we'll talk the matter over," she said.

"And if there isn't Mrs. Peter coming up the lane this blessed minute!" exclaimed Mrs. Spencer, bustling her guests through the hall into the parlor, where a deadly chill struck on them as if the air had been strained so long through dark green, closely drawn blinds that it had lost every particle of warmth it had ever possessed. "That is real lucky, for we can settle the matter right away. Take the armchair, Miss Cuthbert. Anne, you sit here on the ottoman and don't wiggle. Let me take your hats. Flora Jane, go out and put the kettle on. Good afternoon, Mrs. Blewett. We were just saying how fortunate it was you happened along. Let me introduce you two ladies. Mrs. Blewett, Miss Cuthbert. Please excuse me for just a moment. I forgot to tell Flora Jane to take the buns out of the oven."

Mrs. Spencer whisked away, after pulling up the blinds. Anne sitting mutely on the ottoman, with her hands clasped tightly in her lap, stared at Mrs Blewett as one fascinated. Was she to be given into the keeping of this sharp-faced, sharp-eyed woman? She felt a lump coming up in her throat and her eyes smarted painfully. She was beginning to be afraid she couldn't keep the tears back when Mrs. Spencer returned, flushed and beaming, quite capable of taking any and every difficulty, physical, mental or spiritual, into consideration and settling it out of hand.

"It seems there's been a mistake about this little girl, Mrs. Blewett," she said. "I was under the impression that Mr. and Miss Cuthbert wanted a little girl to adopt. I was certainly told so. But it seems it was a boy they wanted. So if you're still of the same mind you were yesterday, I think she'll be just the thing for you."

Mrs. Blewett darted her eyes over Anne from head to foot.

"How old are you and what's your name?" she demanded.

"Anne Shirley," faltered the shrinking child, not daring to make any stipulations regarding the spelling thereof, "and I'm eleven years old."

"Humph! You don't look as if there was much to you. But you're wiry. I don't know but the wiry ones are the best after all. Well, if I take you you'll have to be a good girl, you know—good and smart and respectful. I'll expect you to earn your keep, and no mistake about that. Yes, I suppose I might as well take her off your hands, Miss Cuthbert. The baby's awful fractious, and I'm clean worn out attending to him. If you like I can take her right home now."

Marilla looked at Anne and softened at sight of the child's pale face with its look of mute misery—the misery of a helpless little creature who finds itself once more caught in the trap from which it had escaped. Marilla felt an uncomfortable conviction that, if she denied the appeal of that look, it would haunt her to her dying day. More-over, she did not fancy Mrs. Blewett. To hand a sensitive, "high-strung" child over to such a woman! No, she could not take the responsibility of doing that!

"Well, I don't know," she said slowly. "I didn't say that Matthew and I had absolutely decided that we wouldn't keep her. In fact I may say that Matthew is disposed to keep her. I just came over to find out how the mistake had occurred. I think I'd better take her home again and talk it over with Matthew. I feel that I oughtn't to decide on anything without consulting him. If we make up our mind not to keep her we'll bring or send her over to you tomorrow night. If we don't you may know that she is going to stay with us. Will that suit you, Mrs. Blewett?"

"I suppose it'll have to," said Mrs. Blewett ungraciously.

During Marilla's speech a sunrise had been dawning on Anne's face. First the look of despair faded out; then came a faint flush of hope; her eyes grew deep and bright as morning stars. The child was quite transfigured; and, a moment later, when Mrs. Spencer and Mrs. Blewett went out in quest of a recipe the latter had come to borrow she sprang up and flew across the room to Marilla.

"Oh, Miss Cuthbert, did you really say that perhaps you would let me stay at Green Gables?" she said, in a breathless whisper, as if speaking aloud might shatter the glorious possibility. "Did you really say it? Or did I only imagine that you did?"

"I think you'd better learn to control that imagination of yours, Anne, if you can't distinguish between what is real and what isn't," said Marilla crossly. "Yes, you did hear me say just that and no more. It isn't decided yet and perhaps we will conclude to let Mrs. Blewett take you after all. She certainly needs you much more than I do."

"I'd rather go back to the asylum than go to live with her," said Anne passionately. "She looks exactly like a—like a gimlet."

Marilla smothered a smile under the conviction that Anne must be reproved for such a speech.

"A little girl like you should be ashamed of talking so about a lady and a stranger," she said severely. "Go back and sit down quietly and hold your tongue and behave as a good girl should."

"I'll try to do and be anything you want me, if you'll only keep me," said Anne, returning meekly to her ottoman.

When they arrived back at Green Gables that evening Matthew met them in the lane. Marilla from afar had noted him prowling along it and guessed his motive. She was prepared for the relief she read in his face when he saw that she had at least brought back Anne back with her. But she said nothing, to him, relative to the affair, until they were both out in the yard behind the barn milking the cows. Then she briefly told him Anne's history and the result of the interview with Mrs. Spencer.

"I wouldn't give a dog I liked to that Blewett woman," said Matthew with unusual vim.

"I don't fancy her style myself," admitted Marilla, "but it's that or keeping her ourselves, Matthew. And since you seem to want her, I suppose I'm willing—or have to be. I've been thinking over the idea until I've got kind of used to it. It seems a sort of duty. I've never brought up a child, especially a girl, and I dare say I'll make a terrible mess of it. But I'll do my best. So far as I'm concerned, Matthew, she may stay."

Matthew's shy face was a glow of delight.

"Well now, I reckoned you'd come to see it in that light, Marilla," he said. "She's such an interesting little thing."

"It'd be more to the point if you could say she was a useful little thing," retorted Marilla, "but I'll make it my business to see she's trained to be that. And mind, Matthew, you're not to go interfering with my methods. Perhaps an old maid doesn't know much about bringing up a child, but I guess she knows more than an old bachelor. So you just leave me to manage her. When I fail it'll be time enough to put your oar in."

"There, there, Marilla, you can have your own way," said Matthew reassuringly. "Only be as good and kind to her as you can without spoiling her. I kind of think she's one of the sort you can do anything with if you only get her to love you."

Marilla sniffed, to express her contempt for Matthew's opinions concerning anything feminine, and walked off to the dairy with the pails.

"I won't tell her tonight that she can stay," she reflected, as she strained the milk into the creamers. "She'd be so excited that she wouldn't sleep a wink. Marilla Cuthbert, you're fairly in for it. Did you ever suppose you'd see the day when you'd be adopting an orphan girl? It's surprising enough; but not so surprising as that Matthew should be at the bottom of it, him that always seemed to have such a mortal dread of little girls. Anyhow, we've decided on the experiment and goodness only knows what will come of it."

CHAPTER VII. Anne Says Her Prayers

When Marilla took Anne up to bed that night she said stiffly:

"Now, Anne, I noticed last night that you threw your clothes all about the floor when you took them off. That is a very untidy habit, and I can't allow it at all. As soon as you take off any article of clothing fold it neatly and place it on the chair. I haven't any use at all for little girls who aren't neat."

"I was so harrowed up in my mind last night that I didn't think about my clothes at all," said Anne. "I'll fold them nicely tonight. They always made us do that at the asylum. Half the time, though, I'd forget, I'd be in such a hurry to get into bed nice and quiet and imagine things."

"You'll have to remember a little better if you stay here," admonished Marilla. "There, that looks something like. Say your prayers now and get into bed."

"I never say any prayers," announced Anne.

Marilla looked horrified astonishment.

"Why, Anne, what do you mean? Were you never taught to say your prayers? God always wants little girls to say their prayers. Don't you know who God is, Anne?"

"'God is a spirit, infinite, eternal and unchangeable, in His being, wisdom, power, holiness, justice, goodness, and truth,'" responded Anne promptly and glibly.

Marilla looked rather relieved.

"So you do know something then, thank goodness! You're not quite a heathen. Where did you learn that?"

"Oh, at the asylum Sunday-school. They made us learn the whole catechism. I liked it pretty well. There's something splendid about some of the words. 'Infinite, eternal and unchangeable.' Isn't that grand? It has such a roll to it—just like a big organ playing. You couldn't quite call it poetry, I suppose, but it sounds a lot like it, doesn't it?"

"We're not talking about poetry, Anne—we are talking about saying your prayers. Don't you know it's a terrible wicked thing not to say your prayers every night? I'm afraid you are a very bad little girl."

"You'd find it easier to be bad than good if you had red hair," said Anne reproachfully. "People who haven't red hair don't know what trouble is. Mrs. Thomas told me that God made my hair red ON PURPOSE, and I've never cared about Him since. And anyhow I'd always be too tired at night to bother saying prayers. People who have to look after twins can't be expected to say their prayers. Now, do you honestly think they can?"

Marilla decided that Anne's religious training must be begun at once. Plainly there was no time to be lost.

"You must say your prayers while you are under my roof, Anne."

"Why, of course, if you want me to," assented Anne cheerfully. "I'd do anything to oblige you. But you'll have to tell me what to say for this once. After I get into bed I'll imagine out a real nice prayer to say always. I believe that it will be quite interesting, now that I come to think of it."

"You must kneel down," said Marilla in embarrassment.

Anne knelt at Marilla's knee and looked up gravely.

"Why must people kneel down to pray? If I really wanted to pray I'll tell you what I'd do. I'd go out into a great big field all alone or into the deep, deep, woods, and I'd look up into the sky—up—up—up—into that lovely blue sky that looks as if there was no end to its blueness. And then I'd just FEEL a prayer. Well, I'm ready. What am I to say?"

Marilla felt more embarrassed than ever. She had intended to teach Anne the childish classic, "Now I lay me down to sleep." But she had, as I have told you, the glimmerings of a sense of humor—which is simply another name for a sense of fitness of things; and it suddenly occurred to her that that simple little prayer, sacred to white-robed childhood lisping at motherly knees, was entirely unsuited to this freckled witch of a girl who knew and cared nothing bout God's love, since she had never had it translated to her through the medium of human love.

"You're old enough to pray for yourself, Anne," she said finally. "Just thank God for your blessings and ask Him humbly for the things you want."

"Well, I'll do my best," promised Anne, burying her face in Marilla's lap. "Gracious heavenly Father—that's the way the ministers say it in church, so I suppose it's all right in private prayer, isn't it?" she interjected, lifting her head for a moment.

"Gracious heavenly Father, I thank Thee for the White
Way of Delight and the Lake of Shining Waters and Bonny
and the Snow Queen. I'm really extremely grateful for
them. And that's all the blessings I can think of just
now to thank Thee for. As for the things I want,
they're so numerous that it would take a great deal of
time to name them all so I will only mention the two
most important. Please let me stay at Green Gables;
and please let me be good-looking when I grow up.
I remain,
"Yours respectfully,
Anne Shirley.

"There, did I do all right?" she asked eagerly, getting up. "I could have made it much more flowery if I'd had a little more time to think it over."

Poor Marilla was only preserved from complete collapse by remembering that it was not irreverence, but simply spiritual ignorance on the part of Anne that was responsible for this extraordinary petition. She tucked the child up in bed, mentally vowing that she should be taught a prayer the very next day, and was leaving the room with the light when Anne called her back.

"I've just thought of it now. I should have said, 'Amen' in place of 'yours respectfully,' shouldn't I?—the way the ministers do. I'd forgotten it, but I felt a prayer should be finished off in some way, so I put in the other. Do you suppose it will make any difference?"

"I—I don't suppose it will," said Marilla. "Go to sleep now like a good child. Good night."

"I can only say good night tonight with a clear conscience," said Anne, cuddling luxuriously down among her pillows.

Marilla retreated to the kitchen, set the candle firmly on the table, and glared at Matthew.

"Matthew Cuthbert, it's about time somebody adopted that child and taught her something. She's next door to a perfect heathen. Will you believe that she never said a prayer in her life till tonight? I'll send her to the manse tomorrow and borrow the Peep of the Day series, that's what I'll do. And she shall go to Sunday-school just as soon as I can get some suitable clothes made for her. I foresee that I shall have my hands full. Well, well, we can't get through this world without our share of trouble. I've had a pretty easy life of it so far, but my time has come at last and I suppose I'll just have to make the best of it."

CHAPTER VIII. Anne's Bringing-up Is Begun

For reasons best known to herself, Marilla did not tell Anne that she was to stay at Green Gables until the next afternoon. During the forenoon she kept the child busy with various tasks and watched over her with a keen eye while she did them. By noon she had concluded that Anne was smart and obedient, willing to work and quick to learn; her most serious shortcoming seemed to be a tendency to fall into daydreams in the middle of a task and forget all about it until such time as she was sharply recalled to earth by a reprimand or a catastrophe.

When Anne had finished washing the dinner dishes she suddenly confronted Marilla with the air and expression of one desperately determined to learn the worst. Her thin little body trembled from head to foot; her face flushed and her eyes dilated until they were almost black; she clasped her hands tightly and said in an imploring voice:

"Oh, please, Miss Cuthbert, won't you tell me if you are going to send me away or not? I've tried to be patient all the morning, but I really feel that I cannot bear not knowing any longer. It's a dreadful feeling. Please tell me."

"You haven't scalded the dishcloth in clean hot water as I told you to do," said Marilla immovably. "Just go and do it before you ask any more questions, Anne."

Anne went and attended to the dishcloth. Then she returned to Marilla and fastened imploring eyes of the latter's face. "Well," said Marilla, unable to find any excuse for deferring her explanation longer, "I suppose I might as well tell you. Matthew and I have decided to keep you—that is, if you will try to be a good little girl and show yourself grateful. Why, child, whatever is the matter?"

"I'm crying," said Anne in a tone of bewilderment. "I can't think why. I'm glad as glad can be. Oh, GLAD doesn't seem the right word at all. I was glad about the White Way and the cherry blossoms—but this! Oh, it's something more than glad. I'm so happy. I'll try to be so good. It will be uphill work, I expect, for Mrs. Thomas often told me I was desperately wicked. However, I'll do my very best. But can you tell me why I'm crying?"

"I suppose it's because you're all excited and worked up," said Marilla disapprovingly. "Sit down on that chair and try to calm yourself. I'm afraid you both cry and laugh far too easily. Yes, you can stay here and we will try to do right by you. You must go to school; but it's only a fortnight till vacation so it isn't worth while for you to start before it opens again in September."

"What am I to call you?" asked Anne. "Shall I always say Miss Cuthbert? Can I call you Aunt Marilla?"

"No; you'll call me just plain Marilla. I'm not used to being called Miss Cuthbert and it would make me nervous."

"It sounds awfully disrespectful to just say Marilla," protested Anne.

"I guess there'll be nothing disrespectful in it if you're careful to speak respectfully. Everybody, young and old, in Avonlea calls me Marilla except the minister. He says Miss Cuthbert—when he thinks of it."

"I'd love to call you Aunt Marilla," said Anne wistfully. "I've never had an aunt or any relation at all—not even a grandmother. It would make me feel as if I really belonged to you. Can't I call you Aunt Marilla?"

"No. I'm not your aunt and I don't believe in calling people names that don't belong to them."

"But we could imagine you were my aunt."

"I couldn't," said Marilla grimly.

"Do you never imagine things different from what they really are?" asked Anne wide-eyed.

"No."

"Oh!" Anne drew a long breath. "Oh, Miss—Marilla, how much you miss!"

"I don't believe in imagining things different from what they really are," retorted Marilla. "When the Lord puts us in certain circumstances He doesn't mean for us to imagine them away. And that reminds me. Go into the sitting room, Anne—be sure your feet are clean and don't let any flies in—and bring me out the illustrated card that's on the mantelpiece. The Lord's Prayer is on it and you'll devote your spare time this afternoon to learning it off by heart. There's to be no more of such praying as I heard last night."

"I suppose I was very awkward," said Anne apologetically, "but then, you see, I'd never had any practice. You couldn't really expect a person to pray very well the first time she tried, could you? I thought out a splendid prayer after I went to bed, just as I promised you I would. It was nearly as long as a minister's and so poetical. But would you believe it? I couldn't remember one word when I woke up this morning. And I'm afraid I'll never be able to think out another one as good. Somehow, things never are so good when they're thought out a second time. Have you ever noticed that?"

"Here is something for you to notice, Anne. When I tell you to do a thing I want you to obey me at once and not stand stock-still and discourse about it. Just you go and do as I bid you."

Anne promptly departed for the sitting-room across the hall; she failed to return; after waiting ten minutes Marilla laid down her knitting and marched after her with a grim expression. She found Anne standing motionless before a picture hanging on the wall between the two windows, with her eyes astar with dreams. The white and green light strained through apple trees and clustering vines outside fell over the rapt little figure with a half-unearthly radiance.

"Anne, whatever are you thinking of?" demanded Marilla sharply.

Anne came back to earth with a start.

"That," she said, pointing to the picture—a rather vivid chromo entitled, "Christ Blessing Little Children"—"and I was just imagining I was one of them—that I was the little girl in the blue dress, standing off by herself in the corner as if she didn't belong to anybody, like me. She looks lonely and sad, don't you think? I guess she hadn't any father or mother of her own. But she wanted to be blessed, too, so she just crept shyly up on the outside of the crowd, hoping nobody would notice her—except Him. I'm sure I know just how she felt. Her heart must have beat and her hands must have got cold, like mine did when I asked you if I could stay. She was afraid He mightn't notice her. But it's likely He did, don't you think? I've been trying to imagine it all out—her edging a little nearer all the time until she was quite close to Him; and then He would look at her and put His hand on her hair and oh, such a thrill of joy as would run over her! But I wish the artist hadn't painted Him so sorrowful looking. All His pictures are like that, if you've noticed. But I don't believe He could really have looked so sad or the children would have been afraid of Him."

"Anne," said Marilla, wondering why she had not broken into this speech long before, "you shouldn't talk that way. It's irreverent—positively irreverent."

Anne's eyes marveled.

"Why, I felt just as reverent as could be. I'm sure I didn't mean to be irreverent."

"Well I don't suppose you did—but it doesn't sound right to talk so familiarly about such things. And another thing, Anne, when I send you after something you're to bring it at once and not fall into mooning and imagining before pictures. Remember that. Take that card and come right to the kitchen. Now, sit down in the corner and learn that prayer off by heart."

Anne set the card up against the jugful of apple blossoms she had brought in to decorate the dinner-table—Marilla had eyed that decoration askance, but had said nothing—propped her chin on her hands, and fell to studying it intently for several silent minutes.

"I like this," she announced at length. "It's beautiful. I've heard it before—I heard the superintendent of the asylum Sunday school say it over once. But I didn't like it then. He had such a cracked voice and he prayed it so mournfully. I really felt sure he thought praying was a disagreeable duty. This isn't poetry, but it makes me feel just the same way poetry does. 'Our Father who art in heaven hallowed be Thy name.' That is just like a line of music. Oh, I'm so glad you thought of making me learn this, Miss—Marilla."

"Well, learn it and hold your tongue," said Marilla shortly.

Anne tipped the vase of apple blossoms near enough to bestow a soft kiss on a pink-cupped bud, and then studied diligently for some moments longer.

"Marilla," she demanded presently, "do you think that I shall ever have a bosom friend in Avonlea?"

"A—a what kind of friend?"

"A bosom friend—an intimate friend, you know—a really kindred spirit to whom I can confide my inmost soul. I've dreamed of meeting her all my life. I never really supposed I would, but so many of my loveliest dreams have come true all at once that perhaps this one will, too. Do you think it's possible?"

"Diana Barry lives over at Orchard Slope and she's about your age. She's a very nice little girl, and perhaps she will be a playmate for you when she comes home. She's visiting her aunt over at Carmody just now. You'll have to be careful how you behave yourself, though. Mrs. Barry is a very particular woman. She won't let Diana play with any little girl who isn't nice and good."

Anne looked at Marilla through the apple blossoms, her eyes aglow with interest.

"What is Diana like? Her hair isn't red, is it? Oh, I hope not. It's bad enough to have red hair myself, but I positively couldn't endure it in a bosom friend."

"Diana is a very pretty little girl. She has black eyes and hair and rosy cheeks. And she is good and smart, which is better than being pretty."

Marilla was as fond of morals as the Duchess in Wonderland, and was firmly convinced that one should be tacked on to every remark made to a child who was being brought up.

But Anne waved the moral inconsequently aside and seized only on the delightful possibilities before it.

"Oh, I'm so glad she's pretty. Next to being beautiful oneself—and that's impossible in my case—it would be best to have a beautiful bosom friend. When I lived with Mrs. Thomas she had a bookcase in her sitting room with glass doors. There weren't any books in it; Mrs. Thomas kept her best china and her preserves there—when she had any preserves to keep. One of the doors was broken. Mr. Thomas smashed it one night when he was slightly intoxicated. But the other was whole and I used to pretend that my reflection in it was another little girl who lived in it. I called her Katie Maurice, and we were very intimate. I used to talk to her by the hour, especially on Sunday, and tell her everything. Katie was the comfort and consolation of my life. We used to pretend that the bookcase was enchanted and that if I only knew the spell I could open the door and step right into the room where Katie Maurice lived, instead of into Mrs. Thomas' shelves of preserves and china. And then Katie Maurice would have taken me by the hand and led me out into a wonderful place, all flowers and sunshine and fairies, and we would have lived there happy for ever after. When I went to live with Mrs. Hammond it just broke my heart to leave Katie Maurice. She felt it dreadfully, too, I know she did, for she was crying when she kissed me good-bye through the bookcase door. There was no bookcase at Mrs. Hammond's. But just up the river a little way from the house there was a long green little valley, and the loveliest echo lived there. It echoed back every word you said, even if you didn't talk a bit loud. So I imagined that it was a little girl called Violetta and we were great friends and I loved her almost as well as I loved Katie Maurice—not quite, but almost, you know. The night before I went to the asylum I said good-bye to Violetta, and oh, her good-bye came back to me in such sad, sad tones. I had become so attached to her that I hadn't the heart to imagine a bosom friend at the asylum, even if there had been any scope for imagination there."

"I think it's just as well there wasn't," said Marilla drily. "I don't approve of such goings-on. You seem to half believe your own imaginations. It will be well for you to have a real live friend to put such nonsense out of your head. But don't let Mrs. Barry hear you talking about your Katie Maurices and your Violettas or she'll think you tell stories."

"Oh, I won't. I couldn't talk of them to everybody—their memories are too sacred for that. But I thought I'd like to have you know about them. Oh, look, here's a big bee just tumbled out of an apple blossom. Just think what a lovely place to live—in an apple blossom! Fancy going to sleep in it when the wind was rocking it. If I wasn't a human girl I think I'd like to be a bee and live among the flowers."

"Yesterday you wanted to be a sea gull," sniffed Marilla. "I think you are very fickle minded. I told you to learn that prayer and not talk. But it seems impossible for you to stop talking if you've got anybody that will listen to you. So go up to your room and learn it."

"Oh, I know it pretty nearly all now—all but just the last line."

"Well, never mind, do as I tell you. Go to your room and finish learning it well, and stay there until I call you down to help me get tea."

"Can I take the apple blossoms with me for company?" pleaded Anne.

"No; you don't want your room cluttered up with flowers. You should have left them on the tree in the first place."

"I did feel a little that way, too," said Anne. "I kind of felt I shouldn't shorten their lovely lives by picking them—I wouldn't want to be picked if I were an apple blossom. But the temptation was IRRESISTIBLE. What do you do when you meet with an irresistible temptation?"

"Anne, did you hear me tell you to go to your room?"

Anne sighed, retreated to the east gable, and sat down in a chair by the window.

"There—I know this prayer. I learned that last sentence coming upstairs. Now I'm going to imagine things into this room so that they'll always stay imagined. The floor is covered with a white velvet carpet with pink roses all over it and there are pink silk curtains at the windows. The walls are hung with gold and silver brocade tapestry. The furniture is mahogany. I never saw any mahogany, but it does sound SO luxurious. This is a couch all heaped with gorgeous silken cushions, pink and blue and crimson and gold, and I am reclining gracefully on it. I can see my reflection in that splendid big mirror hanging on the wall. I am tall and regal, clad in a gown of trailing white lace, with a pearl cross on my breast and pearls in my hair. My hair is of midnight darkness and my skin is a clear ivory pallor. My name is the Lady Cordelia Fitzgerald. No, it isn't—I can't make THAT seem real."

She danced up to the little looking-glass and peered into it. Her pointed freckled face and solemn gray eyes peered back at her.

"You're only Anne of Green Gables," she said earnestly, "and I see you, just as you are looking now, whenever I try to imagine I'm the Lady Cordelia. But it's a million times nicer to be Anne of Green Gables than Anne of nowhere in particular, isn't it?"

She bent forward, kissed her reflection affectionately, and betook herself to the open window.

"Dear Snow Queen, good afternoon. And good afternoon dear birches down in the hollow. And good afternoon, dear gray house up on the hill. I wonder if Diana is to be my bosom friend. I hope she will, and I shall love her very much. But I must never quite forget Katie Maurice and Violetta. They would feel so hurt if I did and I'd hate to hurt anybody's feelings, even a little bookcase girl's or a little echo girl's. I must be careful to remember them and send them a kiss every day."

Anne blew a couple of airy kisses from her fingertips past the cherry blossoms and then, with her chin in her hands, drifted luxuriously out on a sea of day-dreams.

CHAPTER IX. Mrs. Rachel Lynde Is Properly Horrified

Anne had been a fortnight at Green Gables before Mrs. Lynde arrived to inspect her. Mrs. Rachel, to do her justice, was not to blame for this. A severe and unseasonable attack of grippe had confined that good lady to her house ever since the occasion of her last visit to Green Gables. Mrs. Rachel was not often sick and had a well-defined contempt for people who were; but grippe, she asserted, was like no other illness on earth and could only be interpreted as one of the special visitations of Providence. As soon as her doctor allowed her to put her foot out-of-doors she hurried up to Green Gables, bursting with curiosity to see Matthew and Marilla's orphan, concerning whom all sorts of stories and suppositions had gone abroad in Avonlea.

Anne had made good use of every waking moment of that fortnight. Already she was acquainted with every tree and shrub about the place. She had discovered that a lane opened out below the apple orchard and ran up through a belt of woodland; and she had explored it to its furthest end in all its delicious vagaries of brook and bridge, fir coppice and wild cherry arch, corners thick with fern, and branching byways of maple and mountain ash.

She had made friends with the spring down in the hollow—that wonderful deep, clear icy-cold spring; it was set about with smooth red sandstones and rimmed in by great palm-like clumps of water fern; and beyond it was a log bridge over the brook.

That bridge led Anne's dancing feet up over a wooded hill beyond, where perpetual twilight reigned under the straight, thick-growing firs and spruces; the only flowers there were myriads of delicate "June bells," those shyest and sweetest of woodland blooms, and a few pale, aerial starflowers, like the spirits of last year's blossoms. Gossamers glimmered like threads of silver among the trees and the fir boughs and tassels seemed to utter friendly speech.

All these raptured voyages of exploration were made in the odd half hours which she was allowed for play, and Anne talked Matthew and Marilla half-deaf over her discoveries. Not that Matthew complained, to be sure; he listened to it all with a wordless smile of enjoyment on his face; Marilla permitted the "chatter" until she found herself becoming too interested in it, whereupon she always promptly quenched Anne by a curt command to hold her tongue.

Anne was out in the orchard when Mrs. Rachel came, wandering at her own sweet will through the lush, tremulous grasses splashed with ruddy evening sunshine; so that good lady had an excellent chance to talk her illness fully over, describing every ache and pulse beat with such evident enjoyment that Marilla thought even grippe must bring its compensations. When details were exhausted Mrs. Rachel introduced the real reason of her call.

"I've been hearing some surprising things about you and Matthew."

"I don't suppose you are any more surprised than I am myself," said Marilla. "I'm getting over my surprise now."

"It was too bad there was such a mistake," said Mrs. Rachel sympathetically. "Couldn't you have sent her back?"

"I suppose we could, but we decided not to. Matthew took a fancy to her. And I must say I like her myself—although I admit she has her faults. The house seems a different place already. She's a real bright little thing."

Marilla said more than she had intended to say when she began, for she read disapproval in Mrs. Rachel's expression.

"It's a great responsibility you've taken on yourself," said that lady gloomily, "especially when you've never had any experience with children. You don't know much about her or her real disposition, I suppose, and there's no guessing how a child like that will turn out. But I don't want to discourage you I'm sure, Marilla."

"I'm not feeling discouraged," was Marilla's dry response, "when I make up my mind to do a thing it stays made up. I suppose you'd like to see Anne. I'll call her in."

Anne came running in presently, her face sparkling with the delight of her orchard rovings; but, abashed at finding the delight herself in the unexpected presence of a stranger, she halted confusedly inside the door. She certainly was an odd-looking little creature in the short tight wincey dress she had worn from the asylum, below which her thin legs seemed ungracefully long. Her freckles were more numerous and obtrusive than ever; the wind had ruffled her hatless hair into over-brilliant disorder; it had never looked redder than at that moment.

"Well, they didn't pick you for your looks, that's sure and certain," was Mrs. Rachel Lynde's emphatic comment. Mrs. Rachel was one of those delightful and popular people who pride themselves on speaking their mind without fear or favor. "She's terrible skinny and homely, Marilla. Come here, child, and let me have a look at you. Lawful heart, did any one ever see such freckles? And hair as red as carrots! Come here, child, I say."

Anne "came there," but not exactly as Mrs. Rachel expected. With one bound she crossed the kitchen floor and stood before Mrs. Rachel, her face scarlet with anger, her lips quivering, and her whole slender form trembling from head to foot.

"I hate you," she cried in a choked voice, stamping her foot on the floor. "I hate you—I hate you—I hate you—" a louder stamp with each assertion of hatred.

"How dare you call me skinny and ugly? How dare you say I'm freckled and red-headed? You are a rude, impolite, unfeeling woman!"

"Anne!" exclaimed Marilla in consternation.

But Anne continued to face Mrs. Rachel undauntedly, head up, eyes blazing, hands clenched, passionate indignation exhaling from her like an atmosphere.

"How dare you say such things about me?" she repeated vehemently. "How would you like to have such things said about you? How would you like to be told that you are fat and clumsy and probably hadn't a spark of imagination in you? I don't care if I do hurt your feelings by saying so! I hope I hurt them. You have hurt mine worse than they were ever hurt before even by Mrs. Thomas' intoxicated husband. And I'll NEVER forgive you for it, never, never!"

Stamp! Stamp!

"Did anybody ever see such a temper!" exclaimed the horrified Mrs. Rachel.

"Anne go to your room and stay there until I come up," said Marilla, recovering her powers of speech with difficulty.

Anne, bursting into tears, rushed to the hall door, slammed it until the tins on the porch wall outside rattled in sympathy, and fled through the hall and up the stairs like a whirlwind. A subdued slam above told that the door of the east gable had been shut with equal vehemence.

"Well, I don't envy you your job bringing THAT up, Marilla," said Mrs. Rachel with unspeakable solemnity.

Marilla opened her lips to say she knew not what of apology or deprecation. What she did say was a surprise to herself then and ever afterwards.

"You shouldn't have twitted her about her looks, Rachel."

"Marilla Cuthbert, you don't mean to say that you are upholding her in such a terrible display of temper as we've just seen?" demanded Mrs. Rachel indignantly.

"No," said Marilla slowly, "I'm not trying to excuse her. She's been very naughty and I'll have to give her a talking to about it. But we must make allowances for her. She's never been taught what is right. And you WERE too hard on her, Rachel."

Marilla could not help tacking on that last sentence, although she was again surprised at herself for doing it. Mrs. Rachel got up with an air of offended dignity.

"Well, I see that I'll have to be very careful what I say after this, Marilla, since the fine feelings of orphans, brought from goodness knows where, have to be considered before anything else. Oh, no, I'm not vexed—don't worry yourself. I'm too sorry for you to leave any room for anger in my mind. You'll have your own troubles with that child. But if you'll take my advice—which I suppose you won't do, although I've brought up ten children and buried two—you'll do that 'talking to' you mention with a fair-sized birch switch. I should think THAT would be the most effective language for that kind of a child. Her temper matches her hair I guess. Well, good evening, Marilla. I hope you'll come down to see me often as usual. But you can't expect me to visit here again in a hurry, if I'm liable to be flown at and insulted in such a fashion. It's something new in MY experience."

Whereat Mrs. Rachel swept out and away—if a fat woman who always waddled COULD be said to sweep away—and Marilla with a very solemn face betook herself to the east gable.

On the way upstairs she pondered uneasily as to what she ought to do. She felt no little dismay over the scene that had just been enacted. How unfortunate that Anne should have displayed such temper before Mrs. Rachel Lynde, of all people! Then Marilla suddenly became aware of an uncomfortable and rebuking consciousness that she felt more humiliation over this than sorrow over the discovery of such a serious defect in Anne's disposition. And how was she to punish her? The amiable suggestion of the birch switch—to the efficiency of which all of Mrs. Rachel's own children could have borne smarting testimony—did not appeal to Marilla. She did not believe she could whip a child. No, some other method of punishment must be found to bring Anne to a proper realization of the enormity of her offense.

Marilla found Anne face downward on her bed, crying bitterly, quite oblivious of muddy boots on a clean counterpane.

"Anne," she said not ungently.

No answer.

"Anne," with greater severity, "get off that bed this minute and listen to what I have to say to you."

Anne squirmed off the bed and sat rigidly on a chair beside it, her face swollen and tear-stained and her eyes fixed stubbornly on the floor.

"This is a nice way for you to behave. Anne! Aren't you ashamed of yourself?"

"She hadn't any right to call me ugly and redheaded," retorted Anne, evasive and defiant.

"You hadn't any right to fly into such a fury and talk the way you did to her, Anne. I was ashamed of you—thoroughly ashamed of you. I wanted you to behave nicely to Mrs. Lynde, and instead of that you have disgraced me. I'm sure I don't know why you should lose your temper like that just because Mrs. Lynde said you were red-haired and homely. You say it yourself often enough."

"Oh, but there's such a difference between saying a thing yourself and hearing other people say it," wailed Anne. "You may know a thing is so, but you can't help hoping other people don't quite think it is. I suppose you think I have an awful temper, but I couldn't help it. When she said those things something just rose right up in me and choked me. I HAD to fly out at her."

"Well, you made a fine exhibition of yourself I must say. Mrs. Lynde will have a nice story to tell about you everywhere—and she'll tell it, too. It was a dreadful thing for you to lose your temper like that, Anne."

"Just imagine how you would feel if somebody told you to your face that you were skinny and ugly," pleaded Anne tearfully.

An old remembrance suddenly rose up before Marilla. She had been a very small child when she had heard one aunt say of her to another, "What a pity she is such a dark, homely little thing." Marilla was every day of fifty before the sting had gone out of that memory.

"I don't say that I think Mrs. Lynde was exactly right in saying what she did to you, Anne," she admitted in a softer tone. "Rachel is too outspoken. But that is no excuse for such behavior on your part. She was a stranger and an elderly person and my visitor—all three very good reasons why you should have been respectful to her. You were rude and saucy and"—Marilla had a saving inspiration of punishment—"you must go to her and tell her you are very sorry for your bad temper and ask her to forgive you."

"I can never do that," said Anne determinedly and darkly. "You can punish me in any way you like, Marilla. You can shut me up in a dark, damp dungeon inhabited by snakes and toads and feed me only on bread and water and I shall not complain. But I cannot ask Mrs. Lynde to forgive me."

"We're not in the habit of shutting people up in dark damp dungeons," said Marilla drily, "especially as they're rather scarce in Avonlea. But apologize to Mrs. Lynde you must and shall and you'll stay here in your room until you can tell me you're willing to do it."

"I shall have to stay here forever then," said Anne mournfully, "because I can't tell Mrs. Lynde I'm sorry I said those things to her. How can I? I'm NOT sorry. I'm sorry I've vexed you; but I'm GLAD I told her just what I did. It was a great satisfaction. I can't say I'm sorry when I'm not, can I? I can't even IMAGINE I'm sorry."

"Perhaps your imagination will be in better working order by the morning," said Marilla, rising to depart. "You'll have the night to think over your conduct in and come to a better frame of mind. You said you would try to be a very good girl if we kept you at Green Gables, but I must say it hasn't seemed very much like it this evening."

Leaving this Parthian shaft to rankle in Anne's stormy bosom, Marilla descended to the kitchen, grievously troubled in mind and vexed in soul. She was as angry with herself as with Anne, because, whenever she recalled Mrs. Rachel's dumbfounded countenance her lips twitched with amusement and she felt a most reprehensible desire to laugh.

CHAPTER X. Anne's Apology

Marilla said nothing to Matthew about the affair that evening; but when Anne proved still refractory the next morning an explanation had to be made to account for her absence from the breakfast table. Marilla told Matthew the whole story, taking pains to impress him with a due sense of the enormity of Anne's behavior.

"It's a good thing Rachel Lynde got a calling down; she's a meddlesome old gossip," was Matthew's consolatory rejoinder.

"Matthew Cuthbert, I'm astonished at you. You know that Anne's behavior was dreadful, and yet you take her part! I suppose you'll be saying next thing that she oughtn't to be punished at all!"

"Well now—no—not exactly," said Matthew uneasily. "I reckon she ought to be punished a little. But don't be too hard on her, Marilla. Recollect she hasn't ever had anyone to teach her right. You're—you're going to give her something to eat, aren't you?"

"When did you ever hear of me starving people into good behavior?" demanded Marilla indignantly. "She'll have her meals regular, and I'll carry them up to her myself. But she'll stay up there until she's willing to apologize to Mrs. Lynde, and that's final, Matthew."

Breakfast, dinner, and supper were very silent meals—for Anne still remained obdurate. After each meal Marilla carried a well-filled tray to the east gable and brought it down later on not noticeably depleted. Matthew eyed its last descent with a troubled eye. Had Anne eaten anything at all?

When Marilla went out that evening to bring the cows from the back pasture, Matthew, who had been hanging about the barns and watching, slipped into the house with the air of a burglar and crept upstairs. As a general thing Matthew gravitated between the kitchen and the little bedroom off the hall where he slept; once in a while he ventured uncomfortably into the parlor or sitting room when the minister came to tea. But he had never been upstairs in his own house since the spring he helped Marilla paper the spare bedroom, and that was four years ago.

He tiptoed along the hall and stood for several minutes outside the door of the east gable before he summoned courage to tap on it with his fingers and then open the door to peep in.

CHAPTER X. Anne's Apology

Anne was sitting on the yellow chair by the window gazing mournfully out into the garden. Very small and unhappy she looked, and Matthew's heart smote him. He softly closed the door and tiptoed over to her.

"Anne," he whispered, as if afraid of being overheard, "how are you making it, Anne?"

Anne smiled wanly.

"Pretty well. I imagine a good deal, and that helps to pass the time. Of course, it's rather lonesome. But then, I may as well get used to that."

Anne smiled again, bravely facing the long years of solitary imprisonment before her.

Matthew recollected that he must say what he had come to say without loss of time, lest Marilla return prematurely. "Well now, Anne, don't you think you'd better do it and have it over with?" he whispered. "It'll have to be done sooner or later, you know, for Marilla's a dreadful deter-mined woman—dreadful determined, Anne. Do it right off, I say, and have it over."

"Do you mean apologize to Mrs. Lynde?"

"Yes—apologize—that's the very word," said Matthew eagerly. "Just smooth it over so to speak. That's what I was trying to get at."

"I suppose I could do it to oblige you," said Anne thoughtfully. "It would be true enough to say I am sorry, because I AM sorry now. I wasn't a bit sorry last night. I was mad clear through, and I stayed mad all night. I know I did because I woke up three times and I was just furious every time. But this morning it was over. I wasn't in a temper anymore—and it left a dreadful sort of goneness, too. I felt so ashamed of myself. But I just couldn't think of going and telling Mrs. Lynde so. It would be so humiliating. I made up my mind I'd stay shut up here forever rather than do that. But still—I'd do anything for you—if you really want me to—"

"Well now, of course I do. It's terrible lonesome downstairs without you. Just go and smooth things over—that's a good girl."

"Very well," said Anne resignedly. "I'll tell Marilla as soon as she comes in I've repented."

"That's right—that's right, Anne. But don't tell Marilla I said anything about it. She might think I was putting my oar in and I promised not to do that."

"Wild horses won't drag the secret from me," promised Anne solemnly. "How would wild horses drag a secret from a person anyhow?"

But Matthew was gone, scared at his own success. He fled hastily to the remotest corner of the horse pasture lest Marilla should suspect what he had been up to. Marilla herself, upon her return to the house, was agreeably surprised to hear a plaintive voice calling, "Marilla" over the banisters.

"Well?" she said, going into the hall.

"I'm sorry I lost my temper and said rude things, and I'm willing to go and tell Mrs. Lynde so."

"Very well." Marilla's crispness gave no sign of her relief. She had been wondering what under the canopy she should do if Anne did not give in. "I'll take you down after milking."

Accordingly, after milking, behold Marilla and Anne walking down the lane, the former erect and triumphant, the latter drooping and dejected. But halfway down Anne's dejection vanished as if by enchantment. She lifted her head and stepped lightly along, her eyes fixed on the sunset sky and an air of subdued exhilaration about her. Marilla beheld the change disapprovingly. This was no meek penitent such as it behooved her to take into the presence of the offended Mrs. Lynde.

"What are you thinking of, Anne?" she asked sharply.

"I'm imagining out what I must say to Mrs. Lynde," answered Anne dreamily.

This was satisfactory—or should have been so. But Marilla could not rid herself of the notion that something in her scheme of punishment was going askew. Anne had no business to look so rapt and radiant.

Rapt and radiant Anne continued until they were in the very presence of Mrs. Lynde, who was sitting knitting by her kitchen window. Then the radiance vanished. Mournful penitence appeared on every feature. Before a word was spoken Anne suddenly went down on her knees before the astonished Mrs. Rachel and held out her hands beseechingly.

"Oh, Mrs. Lynde, I am so extremely sorry," she said with a quiver in her voice. "I could never express all my sorrow, no, not if I used up a whole dictionary. You must just imagine it. I behaved terribly to you—and I've disgraced the dear friends, Matthew and Marilla, who have let me stay at Green Gables although I'm not a boy. I'm a dreadfully wicked and ungrateful girl, and I deserve to be punished and cast out by respectable people forever. It was very wicked of me to fly into a temper because you told me the truth. It WAS the truth; every word you said was true. My hair is red and I'm freckled and skinny and ugly. What I said to you was true, too, but I shouldn't have said it. Oh, Mrs. Lynde, please, please, forgive me. If you refuse it will be a lifelong sorrow on a poor little orphan girl, would you, even if she had a dreadful temper? Oh, I am sure you wouldn't. Please say you forgive me, Mrs. Lynde."

Anne clasped her hands together, bowed her head, and waited for the word of judgment.

There was no mistaking her sincerity—it breathed in every tone of her voice. Both Marilla and Mrs. Lynde recognized its unmistakable ring. But the former under-stood in dismay that Anne was actually enjoying her valley of humiliation—was reveling in the thoroughness of her abasement. Where was the wholesome punishment upon which she, Marilla, had plumed herself? Anne had turned it into a species of positive pleasure.

Good Mrs. Lynde, not being overburdened with perception, did not see this. She only perceived that Anne had made a very thorough apology and all resentment vanished from her kindly, if somewhat officious, heart.

CHAPTER X. Anne's Apology

"There, there, get up, child," she said heartily. "Of course I forgive you. I guess I was a little too hard on you, anyway. But I'm such an outspoken person. You just mustn't mind me, that's what. It can't be denied your hair is terrible red; but I knew a girl once—went to school with her, in fact—whose hair was every mite as red as yours when she was young, but when she grew up it darkened to a real handsome auburn. I wouldn't be a mite surprised if yours did, too—not a mite."

"Oh, Mrs. Lynde!" Anne drew a long breath as she rose to her feet. "You have given me a hope. I shall always feel that you are a benefactor. Oh, I could endure anything if I only thought my hair would be a handsome auburn when I grew up. It would be so much easier to be good if one's hair was a handsome auburn, don't you think? And now may I go out into your garden and sit on that bench under the apple-trees while you and Marilla are talking? There is so much more scope for imagination out there."

"Laws, yes, run along, child. And you can pick a bouquet of them white June lilies over in the corner if you like."

As the door closed behind Anne Mrs. Lynde got briskly up to light a lamp.

"She's a real odd little thing. Take this chair, Marilla; it's easier than the one you've got; I just keep that for the hired boy to sit on. Yes, she certainly is an odd child, but there is something kind of taking about her after all. I don't feel so surprised at you and Matthew keeping her as I did—nor so sorry for you, either. She may turn out all right. Of course, she has a queer way of expressing herself—a little too—well, too kind of forcible, you know; but she'll likely get over that now that she's come to live among civilized folks. And then, her temper's pretty quick, I guess; but there's one comfort, a child that has a quick temper, just blaze up and cool down, ain't never likely to be sly or deceitful. Preserve me from a sly child, that's what. On the whole, Marilla, I kind of like her."

When Marilla went home Anne came out of the fragrant twilight of the orchard with a sheaf of white narcissi in her hands.

"I apologized pretty well, didn't I?" she said proudly as they went down the lane. "I thought since I had to do it I might as well do it thoroughly."

"You did it thoroughly, all right enough," was Marilla's comment. Marilla was dismayed at finding herself inclined to laugh over the recollection. She had also an uneasy feeling that she ought to scold Anne for apologizing so well; but then, that was ridiculous! She compromised with her conscience by saying severely:

"I hope you won't have occasion to make many more such apologies. I hope you'll try to control your temper now, Anne."

"That wouldn't be so hard if people wouldn't twit me about my looks," said Anne with a sigh. "I don't get cross about other things; but I'm SO tired of being twitted about my hair and it just makes me boil right over. Do you suppose my hair will really be a handsome auburn when I grow up?"

"You shouldn't think so much about your looks, Anne. I'm afraid you are a very vain little girl."

"How can I be vain when I know I'm homely?" protested Anne. "I love pretty things; and I hate to look in the glass and see something that isn't pretty. It makes me feel so sorrowful—just as I feel when I look at any ugly thing. I pity it because it isn't beautiful."

"Handsome is as handsome does," quoted Marilla. "I've had that said to me before, but I have my doubts about it," remarked skeptical Anne, sniffing at her narcissi. "Oh, aren't these flowers sweet! It was lovely of Mrs. Lynde to give them to me. I have no hard feelings against Mrs. Lynde now. It gives you a lovely, comfortable feeling to apologize and be forgiven, doesn't it? Aren't the stars bright tonight? If you could live in a star, which one would you pick? I'd like that lovely clear big one away over there above that dark hill."

"Anne, do hold your tongue," said Marilla, thoroughly worn out trying to follow the gyrations of Anne's thoughts.

Anne said no more until they turned into their own lane. A little gypsy wind came down it to meet them, laden with the spicy perfume of young dew-wet ferns. Far up in the shadows a cheerful light gleamed out through the trees from the kitchen at Green Gables. Anne suddenly came close to Marilla and slipped her hand into the older woman's hard palm.

"It's lovely to be going home and know it's home," she said. "I love Green Gables already, and I never loved any place before. No place ever seemed like home. Oh, Marilla, I'm so happy. I could pray right now and not find it a bit hard."

Something warm and pleasant welled up in Marilla's heart at touch of that thin little hand in her own—a throb of the maternity she had missed, perhaps. Its very unaccustomedness and sweetness disturbed her. She hastened to restore her sensations to their normal calm by inculcating a moral.

"If you'll be a good girl you'll always be happy, Anne. And you should never find it hard to say your prayers."

"Saying one's prayers isn't exactly the same thing as praying," said Anne meditatively. "But I'm going to imagine that I'm the wind that is blowing up there in those tree tops. When I get tired of the trees I'll imagine I'm gently waving down here in the ferns—and then I'll fly over to Mrs. Lynde's garden and set the flowers dancing—and then I'll go with one great swoop over the clover field—and then I'll blow over the Lake of Shining Waters and ripple it all up into little sparkling waves. Oh, there's so much scope for imagination in a wind! So I'll not talk any more just now, Marilla."

"Thanks be to goodness for that," breathed Marilla in devout relief.

CHAPTER XI. Anne's Impressions of Sunday-School

"Well, how do you like them?" said Marilla.

Anne was standing in the gable room, looking solemnly at three new dresses spread out on the bed. One was of snuffy colored gingham which Marilla had been tempted to buy from a peddler the preceding summer because it looked so serviceable; one was of black-and-white checkered sateen which she had picked up at a bargain counter in the winter; and one was a stiff print of an ugly blue shade which she had purchased that week at a Carmody store.

She had made them up herself, and they were all made alike—plain skirts fulled tightly to plain waists, with sleeves as plain as waist and skirt and tight as sleeves could be.

"I'll imagine that I like them," said Anne soberly.

"I don't want you to imagine it," said Marilla, offended. "Oh, I can see you don't like the dresses! What is the matter with them? Aren't they neat and clean and new?"

"Yes."

"Then why don't you like them?"

"They're—they're not—pretty," said Anne reluctantly.

"Pretty!" Marilla sniffed. "I didn't trouble my head about getting pretty dresses for you. I don't believe in pampering vanity, Anne, I'll tell you that right off. Those dresses are good, sensible, serviceable dresses, without any frills or furbelows about them, and they're all you'll get this summer. The brown gingham and the blue print will do you for school when you begin to go. The sateen is for church and Sunday school. I'll expect you to keep them neat and clean and not to tear them. I should think you'd be grateful to get most anything after those skimpy wincey things you've been wearing."

"Oh, I AM grateful," protested Anne. "But I'd be ever so much gratefuller if—if you'd made just one of them with puffed sleeves. Puffed sleeves are so fashionable now. It would give me such a thrill, Marilla, just to wear a dress with puffed sleeves."

"Well, you'll have to do without your thrill. I hadn't any material to waste on puffed sleeves. I think they are ridiculous-looking things anyhow. I prefer the plain, sensible ones."

"But I'd rather look ridiculous when everybody else does than plain and sensible all by myself," persisted Anne mournfully.

"Trust you for that! Well, hang those dresses carefully up in your closet, and then sit down and learn the Sunday school lesson. I got a quarterly from Mr. Bell for you and you'll go to Sunday school tomorrow," said Marilla, disappearing downstairs in high dudgeon.

Anne clasped her hands and looked at the dresses.

"I did hope there would be a white one with puffed sleeves," she whispered disconsolately. "I prayed for one, but I didn't much expect it on that account. I didn't suppose God would have time to bother about a little orphan girl's dress. I knew I'd just have to depend on Marilla for it. Well, fortunately I can imagine that one of them is of snow-white muslin with lovely lace frills and three-puffed sleeves."

The next morning warnings of a sick headache prevented Marilla from going to Sunday-school with Anne.

"You'll have to go down and call for Mrs. Lynde, Anne," she said. "She'll see that you get into the right class. Now, mind you behave yourself properly. Stay to preaching afterwards and ask Mrs. Lynde to show you our pew. Here's a cent for collection. Don't stare at people and don't fidget. I shall expect you to tell me the text when you come home."

Anne started off irreproachable, arrayed in the stiff black-and-white sateen, which, while decent as regards length and certainly not open to the charge of skimpiness, contrived to emphasize every corner and angle of her thin figure. Her hat was a little, flat, glossy, new sailor, the extreme plainness of which had likewise much disappointed Anne, who had permitted herself secret visions of ribbon and flowers. The latter, however, were supplied before Anne reached the main road, for being confronted halfway down the lane with a golden frenzy of wind-stirred buttercups and a glory of wild roses, Anne promptly and liberally garlanded her hat with a heavy wreath of them. Whatever other people might have thought of the result it satisfied Anne, and she tripped gaily down the road, holding her ruddy head with its decoration of pink and yellow very proudly.

When she had reached Mrs. Lynde's house she found that lady gone. Nothing daunted, Anne proceeded onward to the church alone. In the porch she found a crowd of little girls, all more or less gaily attired in whites and blues and pinks, and all staring with curious eyes at this stranger in their midst, with her extraordinary head adornment. Avonlea little girls had already heard queer stories about Anne. Mrs. Lynde said she had an awful temper; Jerry Buote, the hired boy at Green Gables, said she talked all the time to herself or to the trees and flowers like a crazy girl. They looked at her and whispered to each other behind their quarterlies. Nobody made any friendly advances, then or later on when the opening exercises were over and Anne found herself in Miss Rogerson's class.

CHAPTER XI. Anne's Impressions of Sunday-School

Miss Rogerson was a middle-aged lady who had taught a Sunday-school class for twenty years. Her method of teaching was to ask the printed questions from the quarterly and look sternly over its edge at the particular little girl she thought ought to answer the question. She looked very often at Anne, and Anne, thanks to Marilla's drilling, answered promptly; but it may be questioned if she understood very much about either question or answer.

She did not think she liked Miss Rogerson, and she felt very miserable; every other little girl in the class had puffed sleeves. Anne felt that life was really not worth living without puffed sleeves.

"Well, how did you like Sunday school?" Marilla wanted to know when Anne came home. Her wreath having faded, Anne had discarded it in the lane, so Marilla was spared the knowledge of that for a time.

"I didn't like it a bit. It was horrid."

"Anne Shirley!" said Marilla rebukingly.

Anne sat down on the rocker with a long sigh, kissed one of Bonny's leaves, and waved her hand to a blossoming fuchsia.

"They might have been lonesome while I was away," she explained. "And now about the Sunday school. I behaved well, just as you told me. Mrs. Lynde was gone, but I went right on myself. I went into the church, with a lot of other little girls, and I sat in the corner of a pew by the window while the opening exercises went on. Mr. Bell made an awfully long prayer. I would have been dreadfully tired before he got through if I hadn't been sitting by that window. But it looked right out on the Lake of Shining Waters, so I just gazed at that and imagined all sorts of splendid things."

"You shouldn't have done anything of the sort. You should have listened to Mr. Bell."

"But he wasn't talking to me," protested Anne. "He was talking to God and he didn't seem to be very much interested in it, either. I think he thought God was too far off though. There was a long row of white birches hanging over the lake and the sunshine fell down through them, 'way, 'way down, deep into the water. Oh, Marilla, it was like a beautiful dream! It gave me a thrill and I just said, 'Thank you for it, God,' two or three times."

"Not out loud, I hope," said Marilla anxiously.

"Oh, no, just under my breath. Well, Mr. Bell did get through at last and they told me to go into the classroom with Miss Rogerson's class. There were nine other girls in it. They all had puffed sleeves. I tried to imagine mine were puffed, too, but I couldn't. Why couldn't I? It was as easy as could be to imagine they were puffed when I was alone in the east gable, but it was awfully hard there among the others who had really truly puffs."

"You shouldn't have been thinking about your sleeves in Sunday school. You should have been attending to the lesson. I hope you knew it."

"Oh, yes; and I answered a lot of questions. Miss Rogerson asked ever so many. I don't think it was fair for her to do all the asking. There were lots I wanted to ask her, but I didn't like to because I didn't think she was a kindred spirit.

Then all the other little girls recited a paraphrase. She asked me if I knew any. I told her I didn't, but I could recite, 'The Dog at His Master's Grave' if she liked. That's in the Third Royal Reader. It isn't a really truly religious piece of poetry, but it's so sad and melancholy that it might as well be. She said it wouldn't do and she told me to learn the nineteenth paraphrase for next Sunday. I read it over in church afterwards and it's splendid. There are two lines in particular that just thrill me.

> "'Quick as the slaughtered squadrons fell
> In Midian's evil day.'

"I don't know what 'squadrons' means nor 'Midian,' either, but it sounds SO tragical. I can hardly wait until next Sunday to recite it. I'll practice it all the week. After Sunday school I asked Miss Rogerson—because Mrs. Lynde was too far away—to show me your pew. I sat just as still as I could and the text was Revelations, third chapter, second and third verses. It was a very long text. If I was a minister I'd pick the short, snappy ones. The sermon was awfully long, too. I suppose the minister had to match it to the text. I didn't think he was a bit interesting. The trouble with him seems to be that he hasn't enough imagination. I didn't listen to him very much. I just let my thoughts run and I thought of the most surprising things."

Marilla felt helplessly that all this should be sternly reproved, but she was hampered by the undeniable fact that some of the things Anne had said, especially about the minister's sermons and Mr. Bell's prayers, were what she herself had really thought deep down in her heart for years, but had never given expression to. It almost seemed to her that those secret, unuttered, critical thoughts had suddenly taken visible and accusing shape and form in the person of this outspoken morsel of neglected humanity.

CHAPTER XII. A Solemn Vow and Promise

It was not until the next Friday that Marilla heard the story of the flower-wreathed hat. She came home from Mrs. Lynde's and called Anne to account.

"Anne, Mrs. Rachel says you went to church last Sunday with your hat rigged out ridiculous with roses and buttercups. What on earth put you up to such a caper? A pretty-looking object you must have been!"

"Oh. I know pink and yellow aren't becoming to me," began Anne.

"Becoming fiddlesticks! It was putting flowers on your hat at all, no matter what color they were, that was ridiculous. You are the most aggravating child!"

"I don't see why it's any more ridiculous to wear flowers on your hat than on your dress," protested Anne. "Lots of little girls there had bouquets pinned on their dresses. What's the difference?"

Marilla was not to be drawn from the safe concrete into dubious paths of the abstract.

"Don't answer me back like that, Anne. It was very silly of you to do such a thing. Never let me catch you at such a trick again. Mrs. Rachel says she thought she would sink through the floor when she saw you come in all rigged out like that. She couldn't get near enough to tell you to take them off till it was too late. She says people talked about it something dreadful. Of course they would think I had no better sense than to let you go decked out like that."

"Oh, I'm so sorry," said Anne, tears welling into her eyes. "I never thought you'd mind. The roses and buttercups were so sweet and pretty I thought they'd look lovely on my hat. Lots of the little girls had artificial flowers on their hats. I'm afraid I'm going to be a dreadful trial to you. Maybe you'd better send me back to the asylum. That would be terrible; I don't think I could endure it; most likely I would go into consumption; I'm so thin as it is, you see. But that would be better than being a trial to you."

"Nonsense," said Marilla, vexed at herself for having made the child cry. "I don't want to send you back to the asylum, I'm sure. All I want is that you should behave like other little girls and not make yourself ridiculous. Don't cry any more. I've got some news for you. Diana Barry came home this afternoon. I'm going up to see if I can borrow a skirt pattern from Mrs. Barry, and if you like you can come with me and get acquainted with Diana."

Anne rose to her feet, with clasped hands, the tears still glistening on her cheeks; the dish towel she had been hemming slipped unheeded to the floor.

"Oh, Marilla, I'm frightened—now that it has come I'm actually frightened. What if she shouldn't like me! It would be the most tragical disappointment of my life."

"Now, don't get into a fluster. And I do wish you wouldn't use such long words. It sounds so funny in a little girl. I guess Diana'll like you well enough. It's her mother you've got to reckon with. If she doesn't like you it won't matter how much Diana does. If she has heard about your outburst to Mrs. Lynde and going to church with buttercups round your hat I don't know what she'll think of you. You must be polite and well behaved, and don't make any of your startling speeches. For pity's sake, if the child isn't actually trembling!"

Anne WAS trembling. Her face was pale and tense.

"Oh, Marilla, you'd be excited, too, if you were going to meet a little girl you hoped to be your bosom friend and whose mother mightn't like you," she said as she hastened to get her hat.

They went over to Orchard Slope by the short cut across the brook and up the firry hill grove. Mrs. Barry came to the kitchen door in answer to Marilla's knock. She was a tall black-eyed, black-haired woman, with a very resolute mouth. She had the reputation of being very strict with her children.

"How do you do, Marilla?" she said cordially. "Come in. And this is the little girl you have adopted, I suppose?"

"Yes, this is Anne Shirley," said Marilla.

"Spelled with an E," gasped Anne, who, tremulous and excited as she was, was determined there should be no misunderstanding on that important point.

Mrs. Barry, not hearing or not comprehending, merely shook hands and said kindly:

"How are you?"

"I am well in body although considerable rumpled up in spirit, thank you ma'am," said Anne gravely. Then aside to Marilla in an audible whisper, "There wasn't anything startling in that, was there, Marilla?"

Diana was sitting on the sofa, reading a book which she dropped when the callers entered. She was a very pretty little girl, with her mother's black eyes and hair, and rosy cheeks, and the merry expression which was her inheritance from her father.

"This is my little girl Diana," said Mrs. Barry. "Diana, you might take Anne out into the garden and show her your flowers. It will be better for you than straining your eyes over that book. She reads entirely too much—" this to Marilla as the little girls went out—"and I can't prevent her, for her father aids and abets her. She's always poring over a book. I'm glad she has the prospect of a play-mate—perhaps it will take her more out-of-doors."

Outside in the garden, which was full of mellow sunset light streaming through the dark old firs to the west of it, stood Anne and Diana, gazing bashfully at each other over a clump of gorgeous tiger lilies.

CHAPTER XII. A Solemn Vow and Promise

The Barry garden was a bowery wilderness of flowers which would have delighted Anne's heart at any time less fraught with destiny. It was encircled by huge old willows and tall firs, beneath which flourished flowers that loved the shade. Prim, right-angled paths neatly bordered with clamshells, intersected it like moist red ribbons and in the beds between old-fashioned flowers ran riot. There were rosy bleeding-hearts and great splendid crimson peonies; white, fragrant narcissi and thorny, sweet Scotch roses; pink and blue and white columbines and lilac-tinted Bouncing Bets; clumps of southernwood and ribbon grass and mint; purple Adam-and-Eve, daffodils, and masses of sweet clover white with its delicate, fragrant, feathery sprays; scarlet lightning that shot its fiery lances over prim white musk-flowers; a garden it was where sunshine lingered and bees hummed, and winds, beguiled into loitering, purred and rustled.

"Oh, Diana," said Anne at last, clasping her hands and speaking almost in a whisper, "oh, do you think you can like me a little—enough to be my bosom friend?"

Diana laughed. Diana always laughed before she spoke.

"Why, I guess so," she said frankly. "I'm awfully glad you've come to live at Green Gables. It will be jolly to have somebody to play with. There isn't any other girl who lives near enough to play with, and I've no sisters big enough."

"Will you swear to be my friend forever and ever?" demanded Anne eagerly.

Diana looked shocked.

"Why it's dreadfully wicked to swear," she said rebukingly.

"Oh no, not my kind of swearing. There are two kinds, you know."

"I never heard of but one kind," said Diana doubtfully.

"There really is another. Oh, it isn't wicked at all. It just means vowing and promising solemnly."

"Well, I don't mind doing that," agreed Diana, relieved. "How do you do it?"

"We must join hands—so," said Anne gravely. "It ought to be over running water. We'll just imagine this path is running water. I'll repeat the oath first. I solemnly swear to be faithful to my bosom friend, Diana Barry, as long as the sun and moon shall endure. Now you say it and put my name in."

Diana repeated the "oath" with a laugh fore and aft. Then she said:

"You're a queer girl, Anne. I heard before that you were queer. But I believe I'm going to like you real well."

When Marilla and Anne went home Diana went with them as for as the log bridge. The two little girls walked with their arms about each other. At the brook they parted with many promises to spend the next afternoon together.

"Well, did you find Diana a kindred spirit?" asked Marilla as they went up through the garden of Green Gables.

"Oh yes," sighed Anne, blissfully unconscious of any sarcasm on Marilla's part. "Oh Marilla, I'm the happiest girl on Prince Edward Island this very moment. I assure you I'll say my prayers with a right good-will tonight. Diana and I are going to build a playhouse in Mr. William Bell's birch grove tomorrow. Can I have those broken pieces of china that are out in the woodshed? Diana's birthday is in February and mine is in March. Don't you think that is a very strange coincidence? Diana is going to lend me a book to read. She says it's perfectly splendid and tremendously exciting. She's going to show me a place back in the woods where rice lilies grow. Don't you think Diana has got very soulful eyes? I wish I had soulful eyes. Diana is going to teach me to sing a song called 'Nelly in the Hazel Dell.' She's going to give me a picture to put up in my room; it's a perfectly beautiful picture, she says—a lovely lady in a pale blue silk dress. A sewing-machine agent gave it to her. I wish I had something to give Diana. I'm an inch taller than Diana, but she is ever so much fatter; she says she'd like to be thin because it's so much more graceful, but I'm afraid she only said it to soothe my feelings. We're going to the shore some day to gather shells. We have agreed to call the spring down by the log bridge the Dryad's Bubble. Isn't that a perfectly elegant name? I read a story once about a spring called that. A dryad is sort of a grown-up fairy, I think."

"Well, all I hope is you won't talk Diana to death," said Marilla. "But remember this in all your planning, Anne. You're not going to play all the time nor most of it. You'll have your work to do and it'll have to be done first."

Anne's cup of happiness was full, and Matthew caused it to overflow. He had just got home from a trip to the store at Carmody, and he sheepishly produced a small parcel from his pocket and handed it to Anne, with a deprecatory look at Marilla.

"I heard you say you liked chocolate sweeties, so I got you some," he said.

"Humph," sniffed Marilla. "It'll ruin her teeth and stomach. There, there, child, don't look so dismal. You can eat those, since Matthew has gone and got them. He'd better have brought you peppermints. They're wholesomer. Don't sicken yourself eating all them at once now."

"Oh, no, indeed, I won't," said Anne eagerly. "I'll just eat one tonight, Marilla. And I can give Diana half of them, can't I? The other half will taste twice as sweet to me if I give some to her. It's delightful to think I have something to give her."

"I will say it for the child," said Marilla when Anne had gone to her gable, "she isn't stingy. I'm glad, for of all faults I detest stinginess in a child. Dear me, it's only three weeks since she came, and it seems as if she'd been here always. I can't imagine the place without her. Now, don't be looking I told-you-so, Matthew. That's bad enough in a woman, but it isn't to be endured in a man. I'm perfectly willing to own up that I'm glad I consented to keep the child and that I'm getting fond of her, but don't you rub it in, Matthew Cuthbert."

CHAPTER XIII. The Delights of Anticipation

"It's time Anne was in to do her sewing," said Marilla, glancing at the clock and then out into the yellow August afternoon where everything drowsed in the heat. "She stayed playing with Diana more than half an hour more'n I gave her leave to; and now she's perched out there on the woodpile talking to Matthew, nineteen to the dozen, when she knows perfectly well she ought to be at her work. And of course he's listening to her like a perfect ninny. I never saw such an infatuated man. The more she talks and the odder the things she says, the more he's delighted evidently. Anne Shirley, you come right in here this minute, do you hear me!"

A series of staccato taps on the west window brought Anne flying in from the yard, eyes shining, cheeks faintly flushed with pink, unbraided hair streaming behind her in a torrent of brightness.

"Oh, Marilla," she exclaimed breathlessly, "there's going to be a Sunday-school picnic next week—in Mr. Harmon Andrews's field, right near the lake of Shining Waters. And Mrs. Superintendent Bell and Mrs. Rachel Lynde are going to make ice cream—think of it, Marilla—ICE CREAM! And, oh, Marilla, can I go to it?"

"Just look at the clock, if you please, Anne. What time did I tell you to come in?"

"Two o'clock—but isn't it splendid about the picnic, Marilla? Please can I go? Oh, I've never been to a picnic—I've dreamed of picnics, but I've never—"

"Yes, I told you to come at two o'clock. And it's a quarter to three. I'd like to know why you didn't obey me, Anne."

"Why, I meant to, Marilla, as much as could be. But you have no idea how fascinating Idlewild is. And then, of course, I had to tell Matthew about the picnic. Matthew is such a sympathetic listener. Please can I go?"

"You'll have to learn to resist the fascination of Idle-whatever-you-call-it. When I tell you to come in at a certain time I mean that time and not half an hour later. And you needn't stop to discourse with sympathetic listeners on your way, either. As for the picnic, of course you can go. You're a Sunday-school scholar, and it's not likely I'd refuse to let you go when all the other little girls are going."

"But—but," faltered Anne, "Diana says that everybody must take a basket of things to eat. I can't cook, as you know, Marilla, and—and—I don't mind going to a picnic without puffed sleeves so much, but I'd feel terribly humiliated if I had to go without a basket. It's been preying on my mind ever since Diana told me."

"Well, it needn't prey any longer. I'll bake you a basket."

"Oh, you dear good Marilla. Oh, you are so kind to me. Oh, I'm so much obliged to you."

Getting through with her "ohs" Anne cast herself into Marilla's arms and rapturously kissed her sallow cheek. It was the first time in her whole life that childish lips had voluntarily touched Marilla's face. Again that sudden sensation of startling sweetness thrilled her. She was secretly vastly pleased at Anne's impulsive caress, which was probably the reason why she said brusquely:

"There, there, never mind your kissing nonsense. I'd sooner see you doing strictly as you're told. As for cooking, I mean to begin giving you lessons in that some of these days. But you're so featherbrained, Anne, I've been waiting to see if you'd sober down a little and learn to be steady before I begin. You've got to keep your wits about you in cooking and not stop in the middle of things to let your thoughts rove all over creation. Now, get out your patchwork and have your square done before teatime."

"I do NOT like patchwork," said Anne dolefully, hunting out her workbasket and sitting down before a little heap of red and white diamonds with a sigh. "I think some kinds of sewing would be nice; but there's no scope for imagination in patchwork. It's just one little seam after another and you never seem to be getting anywhere. But of course I'd rather be Anne of Green Gables sewing patchwork than Anne of any other place with nothing to do but play. I wish time went as quick sewing patches as it does when I'm playing with Diana, though. Oh, we do have such elegant times, Marilla. I have to furnish most of the imagination, but I'm well able to do that. Diana is simply perfect in every other way. You know that little piece of land across the brook that runs up between our farm and Mr. Barry's. It belongs to Mr. William Bell, and right in the corner there is a little ring of white birch trees—the most romantic spot, Marilla. Diana and I have our playhouse there. We call it Idlewild. Isn't that a poetical name? I assure you it took me some time to think it out. I stayed awake nearly a whole night before I invented it. Then, just as I was dropping off to sleep, it came like an inspiration. Diana was ENRAPTURED when she heard it. We have got our house fixed up elegantly. You must come and see it, Marilla—won't you? We have great big stones, all covered with moss, for seats, and boards from tree to tree for shelves. And we have all our dishes on them. Of course, they're all broken but it's the easiest thing in the world to imagine that they are whole. There's a piece of a plate with a spray of red and yellow ivy on it that is especially beautiful. We keep it in the parlor and we have the fairy glass there, too. The fairy glass is as lovely as a dream. Diana found it out in the woods behind their chicken house. It's all full of rainbows—just little young rainbows that haven't grown big yet—and Diana's mother told her it was broken off a hanging lamp they once had. But it's nice to imagine the fairies lost it one night when they had a ball, so we call it the fairy glass. Matthew is going to make us a table. Oh, we have named that little round pool over in Mr. Barry's field Willowmere. I got that name out of the book Diana lent me. That was a thrilling book, Marilla. The heroine had five lovers. I'd be satisfied with one, wouldn't you? She was very handsome and she went through great tribulations. She could faint as easy as anything. I'd love to be able to faint, wouldn't you, Marilla? It's so romantic. But I'm really very healthy for all I'm so thin. I believe I'm getting fatter, though. Don't you think I am? I look at my elbows every morning when I get up to see if any dimples are coming. Diana is having a new dress made with elbow sleeves. She is going to wear it to the picnic. Oh, I do hope it will be fine next Wednesday. I don't feel that I could endure the disappointment if anything happened to prevent me from getting to the picnic. I suppose I'd live through it, but I'm certain it would be a lifelong sorrow. It wouldn't matter if I got to a hundred picnics in after years; they wouldn't make up for missing this one. They're going to have boats on the Lake of Shining Waters—and ice cream, as I told you. I have never tasted ice cream. Diana tried to explain what it was like, but I guess ice cream is one of those things that are beyond imagination."

"Anne, you have talked even on for ten minutes by the clock," said Marilla. "Now, just for curiosity's sake, see if you can hold your tongue for the same length of time."

Anne held her tongue as desired. But for the rest of the week she talked picnic and thought picnic and dreamed picnic. On Saturday it rained and she worked herself up into such a frantic state lest it should keep on raining until and over Wednesday that Marilla made her sew an extra patchwork square by way of steadying her nerves.

On Sunday Anne confided to Marilla on the way home from church that she grew actually cold all over with excitement when the minister announced the picnic from the pulpit.

"Such a thrill as went up and down my back, Marilla! I don't think I'd ever really believed until then that there was honestly going to be a picnic. I couldn't help fearing I'd only imagined it. But when a minister says a thing in the pulpit you just have to believe it."

"You set your heart too much on things, Anne," said Marilla, with a sigh. "I'm afraid there'll be a great many disappointments in store for you through life."

"Oh, Marilla, looking forward to things is half the pleasure of them," exclaimed Anne. "You mayn't get the things themselves; but nothing can prevent you from having the fun of looking forward to them. Mrs. Lynde says, 'Blessed are they who expect nothing for they shall not be disappointed.' But I think it would be worse to expect nothing than to be disappointed."

Marilla wore her amethyst brooch to church that day as usual. Marilla always wore her amethyst brooch to church. She would have thought it rather sacrilegious to leave it off—as bad as forgetting her Bible or her collection dime. That amethyst brooch was Marilla's most treasured possession. A seafaring uncle had given it to her mother who in turn had bequeathed it to Marilla. It was an old-fashioned oval, containing a braid of her mother's hair, surrounded by a border of very fine amethysts. Marilla knew too little about precious stones to realize how fine the amethysts actually were; but she thought them very beautiful and was always pleasantly conscious of their violet shimmer at her throat, above her good brown satin dress, even although she could not see it.

Anne had been smitten with delighted admiration when she first saw that brooch.

"Oh, Marilla, it's a perfectly elegant brooch. I don't know how you can pay attention to the sermon or the prayers when you have it on. I couldn't, I know. I think amethysts are just sweet. They are what I used to think diamonds were like. Long ago, before I had ever seen a diamond, I read about them and I tried to imagine what they would be like. I thought they would be lovely glimmering purple stones. When I saw a real diamond in a lady's ring one day I was so disappointed I cried. Of course, it was very lovely but it wasn't my idea of a diamond. Will you let me hold the brooch for one minute, Marilla? Do you think amethysts can be the souls of good violets?"

CHAPTER XIV. Anne's Confession

ON the Monday evening before the picnic Marilla came down from her room with a troubled face.

"Anne," she said to that small personage, who was shelling peas by the spotless table and singing, "Nelly of the Hazel Dell" with a vigor and expression that did credit to Diana's teaching, "did you see anything of my amethyst brooch? I thought I stuck it in my pincushion when I came home from church yesterday evening, but I can't find it anywhere."

"I—I saw it this afternoon when you were away at the Aid Society," said Anne, a little slowly. "I was passing your door when I saw it on the cushion, so I went in to look at it."

"Did you touch it?" said Marilla sternly.

"Y-e-e-s," admitted Anne, "I took it up and I pinned it on my breast just to see how it would look."

"You had no business to do anything of the sort. It's very wrong in a little girl to meddle. You shouldn't have gone into my room in the first place and you shouldn't have touched a brooch that didn't belong to you in the second. Where did you put it?"

"Oh, I put it back on the bureau. I hadn't it on a minute. Truly, I didn't mean to meddle, Marilla. I didn't think about its being wrong to go in and try on the brooch; but I see now that it was and I'll never do it again. That's one good thing about me. I never do the same naughty thing twice."

"You didn't put it back," said Marilla. "That brooch isn't anywhere on the bureau. You've taken it out or something, Anne."

"I did put it back," said Anne quickly—pertly, Marilla thought. "I don't just remember whether I stuck it on the pincushion or laid it in the china tray. But I'm perfectly certain I put it back."

"I'll go and have another look," said Marilla, determining to be just. "If you put that brooch back it's there still. If it isn't I'll know you didn't, that's all!"

Marilla went to her room and made a thorough search, not only over the bureau but in every other place she thought the brooch might possibly be. It was not to be found and she returned to the kitchen.

"Anne, the brooch is gone. By your own admission you were the last person to handle it. Now, what have you done with it? Tell me the truth at once. Did you take it out and lose it?"

"No, I didn't," said Anne solemnly, meeting Marilla's angry gaze squarely. "I never took the brooch out of your room and that is the truth, if I was to be led to the block for it—although I'm not very certain what a block is. So there, Marilla."

Anne's "so there" was only intended to emphasize her assertion, but Marilla took it as a display of defiance.

"I believe you are telling me a falsehood, Anne," she said sharply. "I know you are. There now, don't say anything more unless you are prepared to tell the whole truth. Go to your room and stay there until you are ready to confess."

"Will I take the peas with me?" said Anne meekly.

"No, I'll finish shelling them myself. Do as I bid you."

When Anne had gone Marilla went about her evening tasks in a very disturbed state of mind. She was worried about her valuable brooch. What if Anne had lost it? And how wicked of the child to deny having taken it, when anybody could see she must have! With such an innocent face, too!

"I don't know what I wouldn't sooner have had happen," thought Marilla, as she nervously shelled the peas. "Of course, I don't suppose she meant to steal it or anything like that. She's just taken it to play with or help along that imagination of hers. She must have taken it, that's clear, for there hasn't been a soul in that room since she was in it, by her own story, until I went up tonight. And the brooch is gone, there's nothing surer. I suppose she has lost it and is afraid to own up for fear she'll be punished. It's a dreadful thing to think she tells falsehoods. It's a far worse thing than her fit of temper. It's a fearful responsibility to have a child in your house you can't trust. Slyness and untruthfulness—that's what she has displayed. I declare I feel worse about that than about the brooch. If she'd only have told the truth about it I wouldn't mind so much."

Marilla went to her room at intervals all through the evening and searched for the brooch, without finding it. A bedtime visit to the east gable produced no result. Anne persisted in denying that she knew anything about the brooch but Marilla was only the more firmly convinced that she did.

She told Matthew the story the next morning. Matthew was confounded and puzzled; he could not so quickly lose faith in Anne but he had to admit that circumstances were against her.

"You're sure it hasn't fell down behind the bureau?" was the only suggestion he could offer.

"I've moved the bureau and I've taken out the drawers and I've looked in every crack and cranny" was Marilla's positive answer. "The brooch is gone and that child has taken it and lied about it. That's the plain, ugly truth, Matthew Cuthbert, and we might as well look it in the face."

"Well now, what are you going to do about it?" Matthew asked forlornly, feeling secretly thankful that Marilla and not he had to deal with the situation. He felt no desire to put his oar in this time.

CHAPTER XIV. Anne's Confession

"She'll stay in her room until she confesses," said Marilla grimly, remembering the success of this method in the former case. "Then we'll see. Perhaps we'll be able to find the brooch if she'll only tell where she took it; but in any case she'll have to be severely punished, Matthew."

"Well now, you'll have to punish her," said Matthew, reaching for his hat. "I've nothing to do with it, remember. You warned me off yourself."

Marilla felt deserted by everyone. She could not even go to Mrs. Lynde for advice. She went up to the east gable with a very serious face and left it with a face more serious still. Anne steadfastly refused to confess. She persisted in asserting that she had not taken the brooch. The child had evidently been crying and Marilla felt a pang of pity which she sternly repressed. By night she was, as she expressed it, "beat out."

"You'll stay in this room until you confess, Anne. You can make up your mind to that," she said firmly.

"But the picnic is tomorrow, Marilla," cried Anne. "You won't keep me from going to that, will you? You'll just let me out for the afternoon, won't you? Then I'll stay here as long as you like AFTERWARDS cheerfully. But I MUST go to the picnic."

"You'll not go to picnics nor anywhere else until you've confessed, Anne."

"Oh, Marilla," gasped Anne.

But Marilla had gone out and shut the door.

Wednesday morning dawned as bright and fair as if expressly made to order for the picnic. Birds sang around Green Gables; the Madonna lilies in the garden sent out whiffs of perfume that entered in on viewless winds at every door and window, and wandered through halls and rooms like spirits of benediction. The birches in the hollow waved joyful hands as if watching for Anne's usual morning greeting from the east gable. But Anne was not at her window. When Marilla took her breakfast up to her she found the child sitting primly on her bed, pale and resolute, with tight-shut lips and gleaming eyes.

"Marilla, I'm ready to confess."

"Ah!" Marilla laid down her tray. Once again her method had succeeded; but her success was very bitter to her. "Let me hear what you have to say then, Anne."

"I took the amethyst brooch," said Anne, as if repeating a lesson she had learned. "I took it just as you said. I didn't mean to take it when I went in. But it did look so beautiful, Marilla, when I pinned it on my breast that I was overcome by an irresistible temptation. I imagined how perfectly thrilling it would be to take it to Idlewild and play I was the Lady Cordelia Fitzgerald. It would be so much easier to imagine I was the Lady Cordelia if I had a real amethyst brooch on. Diana and I make necklaces of roseberries but what are roseberries compared to amethysts? So I took the brooch. I thought I could put it back before you came home. I went all the way around by the road to lengthen out the time. When I was going over the bridge across the Lake of Shining Waters I took the brooch off to have another look at it. Oh, how it did shine in the sunlight! And then, when I was leaning over the bridge, it just slipped through my fingers—so—and went down—down—down, all purply-sparkling, and sank forevermore beneath the Lake of Shining Waters. And that's the best I can do at confessing, Marilla."

Marilla felt hot anger surge up into her heart again. This child had taken and lost her treasured amethyst brooch and now sat there calmly reciting the details thereof without the least apparent compunction or repentance.

"Anne, this is terrible," she said, trying to speak calmly. "You are the very wickedest girl I ever heard of."

"Yes, I suppose I am," agreed Anne tranquilly. "And I know I'll have to be punished. It'll be your duty to punish me, Marilla. Won't you please get it over right off because I'd like to go to the picnic with nothing on my mind."

"Picnic, indeed! You'll go to no picnic today, Anne Shirley. That shall be your punishment. And it isn't half severe enough either for what you've done!"

"Not go to the picnic!" Anne sprang to her feet and clutched Marilla's hand. "But you PROMISED me I might! Oh, Marilla, I must go to the picnic. That was why I confessed. Punish me any way you like but that. Oh, Marilla, please, please, let me go to the picnic. Think of the ice cream! For anything you know I may never have a chance to taste ice cream again."

Marilla disengaged Anne's clinging hands stonily.

"You needn't plead, Anne. You are not going to the picnic and that's final. No, not a word."

Anne realized that Marilla was not to be moved. She clasped her hands together, gave a piercing shriek, and then flung herself face downward on the bed, crying and writhing in an utter abandonment of disappointment and despair.

"For the land's sake!" gasped Marilla, hastening from the room. "I believe the child is crazy. No child in her senses would behave as she does. If she isn't she's utterly bad. Oh dear, I'm afraid Rachel was right from the first. But I've put my hand to the plow and I won't look back."

That was a dismal morning. Marilla worked fiercely and scrubbed the porch floor and the dairy shelves when she could find nothing else to do. Neither the shelves nor the porch needed it—but Marilla did. Then she went out and raked the yard.

When dinner was ready she went to the stairs and called Anne. A tear-stained face appeared, looking tragically over the banisters.

"Come down to your dinner, Anne."

"I don't want any dinner, Marilla," said Anne, sobbingly. "I couldn't eat anything. My heart is broken. You'll feel remorse of conscience someday, I expect, for breaking it, Marilla, but I forgive you. Remember when the time comes that I forgive you. But please don't ask me to eat anything, especially boiled pork and greens. Boiled pork and greens are so unromantic when one is in affliction."

Exasperated, Marilla returned to the kitchen and poured out her tale of woe to Matthew, who, between his sense of justice and his unlawful sympathy with Anne, was a miserable man.

"Well now, she shouldn't have taken the brooch, Marilla, or told stories about it," he admitted, mournfully surveying his plateful of unromantic pork and greens as if he, like Anne, thought it a food unsuited to crises of feeling, "but she's such a little thing—such an interesting little thing. Don't you think it's pretty rough not to let her go to the picnic when she's so set on it?"

"Matthew Cuthbert, I'm amazed at you. I think I've let her off entirely too easy. And she doesn't appear to realize how wicked she's been at all—that's what worries me most. If she'd really felt sorry it wouldn't be so bad. And you don't seem to realize it, neither; you're making excuses for her all the time to yourself—I can see that."

"Well now, she's such a little thing," feebly reiterated Matthew. "And there should be allowances made, Marilla. You know she's never had any bringing up."

"Well, she's having it now" retorted Marilla.

The retort silenced Matthew if it did not convince him. That dinner was a very dismal meal. The only cheerful thing about it was Jerry Buote, the hired boy, and Marilla resented his cheerfulness as a personal insult.

When her dishes were washed and her bread sponge set and her hens fed Marilla remembered that she had noticed a small rent in her best black lace shawl when she had taken it off on Monday afternoon on returning from the Ladies' Aid.

She would go and mend it. The shawl was in a box in her trunk. As Marilla lifted it out, the sunlight, falling through the vines that clustered thickly about the window, struck upon something caught in the shawl—something that glittered and sparkled in facets of violet light. Marilla snatched at it with a gasp. It was the amethyst brooch, hanging to a thread of the lace by its catch!

"Dear life and heart," said Marilla blankly, "what does this mean? Here's my brooch safe and sound that I thought was at the bottom of Barry's pond. Whatever did that girl mean by saying she took it and lost it? I declare I believe Green Gables is bewitched. I remember now that when I took off my shawl Monday afternoon I laid it on the bureau for a minute. I suppose the brooch got caught in it somehow. Well!"

Marilla betook herself to the east gable, brooch in hand. Anne had cried herself out and was sitting dejectedly by the window.

"Anne Shirley," said Marilla solemnly, "I've just found my brooch hanging to my black lace shawl. Now I want to know what that rigmarole you told me this morning meant."

"Why, you said you'd keep me here until I confessed," returned Anne wearily, "and so I decided to confess because I was bound to get to the picnic. I thought out a confession last night after I went to bed and made it as interesting as I could. And I said it over and over so that I wouldn't forget it. But you wouldn't let me go to the picnic after all, so all my trouble was wasted."

Marilla had to laugh in spite of herself. But her conscience pricked her.

"Anne, you do beat all! But I was wrong—I see that now. I shouldn't have doubted your word when I'd never known you to tell a story. Of course, it wasn't right for you to confess to a thing you hadn't done—it was very wrong to do so. But I drove you to it. So if you'll forgive me, Anne, I'll forgive you and we'll start square again. And now get yourself ready for the picnic."

Anne flew up like a rocket.

"Oh, Marilla, isn't it too late?"

"No, it's only two o'clock. They won't be more than well gathered yet and it'll be an hour before they have tea. Wash your face and comb your hair and put on your gingham. I'll fill a basket for you. There's plenty of stuff baked in the house. And I'll get Jerry to hitch up the sorrel and drive you down to the picnic ground."

"Oh, Marilla," exclaimed Anne, flying to the washstand. "Five minutes ago I was so miserable I was wishing I'd never been born and now I wouldn't change places with an angel!"

That night a thoroughly happy, completely tired-out Anne returned to Green Gables in a state of beatification impossible to describe.

"Oh, Marilla, I've had a perfectly scrumptious time. Scrumptious is a new word I learned today. I heard Mary Alice Bell use it. Isn't it very expressive? Everything was lovely. We had a splendid tea and then Mr. Harmon Andrews took us all for a row on the Lake of Shining Waters—six of us at a time. And Jane Andrews nearly fell overboard. She was leaning out to pick water lilies and if Mr. Andrews hadn't caught her by her sash just in the nick of time she'd fallen in and prob'ly been drowned. I wish it had been me. It would have been such a romantic experience to have been nearly drowned. It would be such a thrilling tale to tell. And we had the ice cream. Words fail me to describe that ice cream. Marilla, I assure you it was sublime."

That evening Marilla told the whole story to Matthew over her stocking basket.

"I'm willing to own up that I made a mistake," she concluded candidly, "but I've learned a lesson. I have to laugh when I think of Anne's 'confession,' although I suppose I shouldn't for it really was a falsehood. But it doesn't seem as bad as the other would have been, somehow, and anyhow I'm responsible for it. That child is hard to understand in some respects. But I believe she'll turn out all right yet. And there's one thing certain, no house will ever be dull that she's in."

CHAPTER XV. A Tempest in the School Teapot

"What a splendid day!" said Anne, drawing a long breath. "Isn't it good just to be alive on a day like this? I pity the people who aren't born yet for missing it. They may have good days, of course, but they can never have this one. And it's splendider still to have such a lovely way to go to school by, isn't it?"

"It's a lot nicer than going round by the road; that is so dusty and hot," said Diana practically, peeping into her dinner basket and mentally calculating if the three juicy, toothsome, raspberry tarts reposing there were divided among ten girls how many bites each girl would have.

The little girls of Avonlea school always pooled their lunches, and to eat three raspberry tarts all alone or even to share them only with one's best chum would have forever and ever branded as "awful mean" the girl who did it. And yet, when the tarts were divided among ten girls you just got enough to tantalize you.

The way Anne and Diana went to school WAS a pretty one. Anne thought those walks to and from school with Diana couldn't be improved upon even by imagination. Going around by the main road would have been so unromantic; but to go by Lover's Lane and Willowmere and Violet Vale and the Birch Path was romantic, if ever anything was.

Lover's Lane opened out below the orchard at Green Gables and stretched far up into the woods to the end of the Cuthbert farm. It was the way by which the cows were taken to the back pasture and the wood hauled home in winter. Anne had named it Lover's Lane before she had been a month at Green Gables.

"Not that lovers ever really walk there," she explained to Marilla, "but Diana and I are reading a perfectly magnificent book and there's a Lover's Lane in it. So we want to have one, too. And it's a very pretty name, don't you think? So romantic! We can't imagine the lovers into it, you know. I like that lane because you can think out loud there without people calling you crazy."

Anne, starting out alone in the morning, went down Lover's Lane as far as the brook. Here Diana met her, and the two little girls went on up the lane under the leafy arch of maples—"maples are such sociable trees," said Anne; "they're always rustling and whispering to you"—until they came to a rustic bridge. Then they left the lane and walked through Mr. Barry's back field and past Willowmere. Beyond Willowmere came Violet Vale—a little green dimple in the shadow of Mr. Andrew Bell's big woods. "Of course there are no violets there now," Anne told Marilla, "but Diana says there are millions of them in spring. Oh, Marilla, can't you just imagine you see them? It actually takes away my breath. I named it Violet Vale. Diana says she never saw the beat of me for hitting on fancy names for places. It's nice to be clever at something, isn't it? But Diana named the Birch Path. She wanted to, so I let her; but I'm sure I could have found something more poetical than plain Birch Path. Anybody can think of a name like that. But the Birch Path is one of the prettiest places in the world, Marilla."

It was. Other people besides Anne thought so when they stumbled on it. It was a little narrow, twisting path, winding down over a long hill straight through Mr. Bell's woods, where the light came down sifted through so many emerald screens that it was as flawless as the heart of a diamond. It was fringed in all its length with slim young birches, white stemmed and lissom boughed; ferns and starflowers and wild lilies-of-the-valley and scarlet tufts of pigeonberries grew thickly along it; and always there was a delightful spiciness in the air and music of bird calls and the murmur and laugh of wood winds in the trees overhead. Now and then you might see a rabbit skipping across the road if you were quiet—which, with Anne and Diana, happened about once in a blue moon. Down in the valley the path came out to the main road and then it was just up the spruce hill to the school.

The Avonlea school was a whitewashed building, low in the eaves and wide in the windows, furnished inside with comfortable substantial old-fashioned desks that opened and shut, and were carved all over their lids with the initials and hieroglyphics of three generations of school children. The schoolhouse was set back from the road and behind it was a dusky fir wood and a brook where all the children put their bottles of milk in the morning to keep cool and sweet until dinner hour.

Marilla had seen Anne start off to school on the first day of September with many secret misgivings. Anne was such an odd girl. How would she get on with the other children? And how on earth would she ever manage to hold her tongue during school hours?

Things went better than Marilla feared, however. Anne came home that evening in high spirits.

"I think I'm going to like school here," she announced. "I don't think much of the master, through. He's all the time curling his mustache and making eyes at Prissy Andrews. Prissy is grown up, you know. She's sixteen and she's studying for the entrance examination into Queen's Academy at Charlottetown next year. Tillie Boulter says the master is DEAD GONE on her. She's got a beautiful complexion and curly brown hair and she does it up so elegantly. She sits in the long seat at the back and he sits there, too, most of the time—to explain her lessons, he says. But Ruby Gillis says she saw him writing something on her slate and when Prissy read it she blushed as red as a beet and giggled; and Ruby Gillis says she doesn't believe it had anything to do with the lesson."

"Anne Shirley, don't let me hear you talking about your teacher in that way again," said Marilla sharply. "You don't go to school to criticize the master. I guess he can teach YOU something, and it's your business to learn. And I want you to understand right off that you are not to come home telling tales about him. That is something I won't encourage. I hope you were a good girl."

"Indeed I was," said Anne comfortably. "It wasn't so hard as you might imagine, either. I sit with Diana. Our seat is right by the window and we can look down to the Lake of Shining Waters. There are a lot of nice girls in school and we had scrumptious fun playing at dinnertime. It's so nice to have a lot of little girls to play with. But of course I like Diana best and always will. I ADORE Diana. I'm dreadfully far behind the others. They're all in the fifth book and I'm only in the fourth. I feel that it's kind of a disgrace. But there's not one of them has such an imagination as I have and I soon found that out. We had reading and geography and Canadian history and dictation today. Mr. Phillips said my spelling was disgraceful and he held up my slate so that everybody could see it, all marked over. I felt so mortified, Marilla; he might have been politer to a stranger, I think. Ruby Gillis gave me an apple and Sophia Sloane lent me a lovely pink card with 'May I see you home?' on it. I'm to give it back to her tomorrow. And Tillie Boulter let me wear her bead ring all the afternoon. Can I have some of those pearl beads off the old pincushion in the garret to make myself a ring? And oh, Marilla, Jane Andrews told me that Minnie MacPherson told her that she heard Prissy Andrews tell Sara Gillis that I had a very pretty nose. Marilla, that is the first compliment I have ever had in my life and you can't imagine what a strange feeling it gave me. Marilla, have I really a pretty nose? I know you'll tell me the truth."

"Your nose is well enough," said Marilla shortly. Secretly she thought Anne's nose was a remarkable pretty one; but she had no intention of telling her so.

That was three weeks ago and all had gone smoothly so far. And now, this crisp September morning, Anne and Diana were tripping blithely down the Birch Path, two of the happiest little girls in Avonlea.

"I guess Gilbert Blythe will be in school today," said Diana. "He's been visiting his cousins over in New Brunswick all summer and he only came home Saturday night. He's AW'FLY handsome, Anne. And he teases the girls something terrible. He just torments our lives out."

Diana's voice indicated that she rather liked having her life tormented out than not.

"Gilbert Blythe?" said Anne. "Isn't his name that's written up on the porch wall with Julia Bell's and a big 'Take Notice' over them?"

"Yes," said Diana, tossing her head, "but I'm sure he doesn't like Julia Bell so very much. I've heard him say he studied the multiplication table by her freckles."

"Oh, don't speak about freckles to me," implored Anne. "It isn't delicate when I've got so many. But I do think that writing take-notices up on the wall about the boys and girls is the silliest ever. I should just like to see anybody dare to write my name up with a boy's. Not, of course," she hastened to add, "that anybody would."

Anne sighed. She didn't want her name written up. But it was a little humiliating to know that there was no danger of it.

"Nonsense," said Diana, whose black eyes and glossy tresses had played such havoc with the hearts of Avonlea schoolboys that her name figured on the porch walls in half a dozen take-notices. "It's only meant as a joke. And don't you be too sure your name won't ever be written up. Charlie Sloane is DEAD GONE on you. He told his mother—his MOTHER, mind you—that you were the smartest girl in school. That's better than being good looking."

"No, it isn't," said Anne, feminine to the core. "I'd rather be pretty than clever. And I hate Charlie Sloane, I can't bear a boy with goggle eyes. If anyone wrote my name up with his I'd never GET over it, Diana Barry. But it IS nice to keep head of your class."

"You'll have Gilbert in your class after this," said Diana, "and he's used to being head of his class, I can tell you. He's only in the fourth book although he's nearly fourteen. Four years ago his father was sick and had to go out to Alberta for his health and Gilbert went with him. They were there three years and Gilbert didn't go to school hardly any until they came back. You won't find it so easy to keep head after this, Anne."

"I'm glad," said Anne quickly. "I couldn't really feel proud of keeping head of little boys and girls of just nine or ten. I got up yesterday spelling 'ebullition.' Josie Pye was head and, mind you, she peeped in her book. Mr. Phillips didn't see her—he was looking at Prissy Andrews—but I did. I just swept her a look of freezing scorn and she got as red as a beet and spelled it wrong after all."

"Those Pye girls are cheats all round," said Diana indignantly, as they climbed the fence of the main road. "Gertie Pye actually went and put her milk bottle in my place in the brook yesterday. Did you ever? I don't speak to her now."

When Mr. Phillips was in the back of the room hearing Prissy Andrews's Latin, Diana whispered to Anne,

"That's Gilbert Blythe sitting right across the aisle from you, Anne. Just look at him and see if you don't think he's handsome."

Anne looked accordingly. She had a good chance to do so, for the said Gilbert Blythe was absorbed in stealthily pinning the long yellow braid of Ruby Gillis, who sat in front of him, to the back of her seat. He was a tall boy, with curly brown hair, roguish hazel eyes, and a mouth twisted into a teasing smile. Presently Ruby Gillis started up to take a sum to the master; she fell back into her seat with a little shriek, believing that her hair was pulled out by the roots. Everybody looked at her and Mr. Phillips glared so sternly that Ruby began to cry. Gilbert had whisked the pin out of sight and was studying his history with the soberest face in the world; but when the commotion subsided he looked at Anne and winked with inexpressible drollery.

"I think your Gilbert Blythe IS handsome," confided Anne to Diana, "but I think he's very bold. It isn't good manners to wink at a strange girl."

But it was not until the afternoon that things really began to happen.

Mr. Phillips was back in the corner explaining a problem in algebra to Prissy Andrews and the rest of the scholars were doing pretty much as they pleased eating green apples, whispering, drawing pictures on their slates, and driving crickets harnessed to strings, up and down aisle. Gilbert Blythe was trying to make Anne Shirley look at him and failing utterly, because Anne was at that moment totally oblivious not only to the very existence of Gilbert Blythe, but of every other scholar in Avonlea school itself. With her chin propped on her hands and her eyes fixed on the blue glimpse of the Lake of Shining Waters that the west window afforded, she was far away in a gorgeous dreamland hearing and seeing nothing save her own wonderful visions.

Gilbert Blythe wasn't used to putting himself out to make a girl look at him and meeting with failure. She SHOULD look at him, that red-haired Shirley girl with the little pointed chin and the big eyes that weren't like the eyes of any other girl in Avonlea school.

Gilbert reached across the aisle, picked up the end of Anne's long red braid, held it out at arm's length and said in a piercing whisper:

"Carrots! Carrots!"

Then Anne looked at him with a vengeance!

She did more than look. She sprang to her feet, her bright fancies fallen into cureless ruin. She flashed one indignant glance at Gilbert from eyes whose angry sparkle was swiftly quenched in equally angry tears.

"You mean, hateful boy!" she exclaimed passionately. "How dare you!"

And then—thwack! Anne had brought her slate down on Gilbert's head and cracked it—slate not head—clear across.

Avonlea school always enjoyed a scene. This was an especially enjoyable one. Everybody said "Oh" in horrified delight. Diana gasped. Ruby Gillis, who was inclined to be hysterical, began to cry. Tommy Sloane let his team of crickets escape him altogether while he stared open-mouthed at the tableau.

Mr. Phillips stalked down the aisle and laid his hand heavily on Anne's shoulder.

"Anne Shirley, what does this mean?" he said angrily. Anne returned no answer. It was asking too much of flesh and blood to expect her to tell before the whole school that she had been called "carrots." Gilbert it was who spoke up stoutly.

"It was my fault Mr. Phillips. I teased her."

Mr. Phillips paid no heed to Gilbert.

"I am sorry to see a pupil of mine displaying such a temper and such a vindictive spirit," he said in a solemn tone, as if the mere fact of being a pupil of his ought to root out all evil passions from the hearts of small imperfect mortals. "Anne, go and stand on the platform in front of the blackboard for the rest of the afternoon."

Anne would have infinitely preferred a whipping to this punishment under which her sensitive spirit quivered as from a whiplash. With a white, set face she obeyed. Mr. Phillips took a chalk crayon and wrote on the blackboard above her head.

"Ann Shirley has a very bad temper. Ann Shirley must learn to control her temper," and then read it out loud so that even the primer class, who couldn't read writing, should understand it.

Anne stood there the rest of the afternoon with that legend above her. She did not cry or hang her head. Anger was still too hot in her heart for that and it sustained her amid all her agony of humiliation. With resentful eyes and passion-red cheeks she confronted alike Diana's sympathetic gaze and Charlie Sloane's indignant nods and Josie Pye's malicious smiles. As for Gilbert Blythe, she would not even look at him. She would NEVER look at him again! She would never speak to him!!

When school was dismissed Anne marched out with her red head held high. Gilbert Blythe tried to intercept her at the porch door.

"I'm awfully sorry I made fun of your hair, Anne," he whispered contritely. "Honest I am. Don't be mad for keeps, now."

Anne swept by disdainfully, without look or sign of hearing. "Oh how could you, Anne?" breathed Diana as they went down the road half reproachfully, half admiringly. Diana felt that SHE could never have resisted Gilbert's plea.

"I shall never forgive Gilbert Blythe," said Anne firmly. "And Mr. Phillips spelled my name without an e, too. The iron has entered into my soul, Diana."

Diana hadn't the least idea what Anne meant but she understood it was something terrible.

"You mustn't mind Gilbert making fun of your hair," she said soothingly. "Why, he makes fun of all the girls. He laughs at mine because it's so black. He's called me a crow a dozen times; and I never heard him apologize for anything before, either."

"There's a great deal of difference between being called a crow and being called carrots," said Anne with dignity. "Gilbert Blythe has hurt my feelings EXCRUCIATINGLY, Diana."

It is possible the matter might have blown over without more excruciation if nothing else had happened. But when things begin to happen they are apt to keep on.

Avonlea scholars often spent noon hour picking gum in Mr. Bell's spruce grove over the hill and across his big pasture field. From there they could keep an eye on Eben Wright's house, where the master boarded. When they saw Mr. Phillips emerging therefrom they ran for the schoolhouse; but the distance being about three times longer than Mr. Wright's lane they were very apt to arrive there, breathless and gasping, some three minutes too late.

On the following day Mr. Phillips was seized with one of his spasmodic fits of reform and announced before going home to dinner, that he should expect to find all the scholars in their seats when he returned. Anyone who came in late would be punished.

All the boys and some of the girls went to Mr. Bell's spruce grove as usual, fully intending to stay only long enough to "pick a chew." But spruce groves are seductive and yellow nuts of gum beguiling; they picked and loitered and strayed;

and as usual the first thing that recalled them to a sense of the flight of time was Jimmy Glover shouting from the top of a patriarchal old spruce "Master's coming."

The girls who were on the ground, started first and managed to reach the schoolhouse in time but without a second to spare. The boys, who had to wriggle hastily down from the trees, were later; and Anne, who had not been picking gum at all but was wandering happily in the far end of the grove, waist deep among the bracken, singing softly to herself, with a wreath of rice lilies on her hair as if she were some wild divinity of the shadowy places, was latest of all. Anne could run like a deer, however; run she did with the impish result that she overtook the boys at the door and was swept into the schoolhouse among them just as Mr. Phillips was in the act of hanging up his hat.

Mr. Phillips's brief reforming energy was over; he didn't want the bother of punishing a dozen pupils; but it was necessary to do something to save his word, so he looked about for a scapegoat and found it in Anne, who had dropped into her seat, gasping for breath, with a forgotten lily wreath hanging askew over one ear and giving her a particularly rakish and disheveled appearance.

"Anne Shirley, since you seem to be so fond of the boys' company we shall indulge your taste for it this afternoon," he said sarcastically. "Take those flowers out of your hair and sit with Gilbert Blythe."

The other boys snickered. Diana, turning pale with pity, plucked the wreath from Anne's hair and squeezed her hand. Anne stared at the master as if turned to stone.

"Did you hear what I said, Anne?" queried Mr. Phillips sternly.

"Yes, sir," said Anne slowly "but I didn't suppose you really meant it."

"I assure you I did"—still with the sarcastic inflection which all the children, and Anne especially, hated. It flicked on the raw. "Obey me at once."

For a moment Anne looked as if she meant to disobey. Then, realizing that there was no help for it, she rose haughtily, stepped across the aisle, sat down beside Gilbert Blythe, and buried her face in her arms on the desk. Ruby Gillis, who got a glimpse of it as it went down, told the others going home from school that she'd "acksually never seen anything like it—it was so white, with awful little red spots in it."

To Anne, this was as the end of all things. It was bad enough to be singled out for punishment from among a dozen equally guilty ones; it was worse still to be sent to sit with a boy, but that that boy should be Gilbert Blythe was heaping insult on injury to a degree utterly unbearable. Anne felt that she could not bear it and it would be of no use to try. Her whole being seethed with shame and anger and humiliation.

At first the other scholars looked and whispered and giggled and nudged. But as Anne never lifted her head and as Gilbert worked fractions as if his whole soul was absorbed in them and them only, they soon returned to their own tasks and Anne was forgotten. When Mr. Phillips called the history class out Anne should have gone, but Anne did not move, and Mr. Phillips, who had been writing some verses "To Priscilla" before he called the class, was thinking about an obstinate rhyme still and never missed her. Once, when nobody was looking, Gilbert took from his desk a little pink candy heart with a gold motto on it, "You are sweet," and slipped it under the curve of Anne's arm. Whereupon Anne arose, took the pink heart gingerly between the tips of her fingers, dropped it on the floor, ground it to powder beneath her heel, and resumed her position without deigning to bestow a glance on Gilbert.

When school went out Anne marched to her desk, ostentatiously took out everything therein, books and writing tablet, pen and ink, testament and arithmetic, and piled them neatly on her cracked slate.

"What are you taking all those things home for, Anne?" Diana wanted to know, as soon as they were out on the road. She had not dared to ask the question before.

"I am not coming back to school any more," said Anne. Diana gasped and stared at Anne to see if she meant it.

"Will Marilla let you stay home?" she asked.

"She'll have to," said Anne. "I'll NEVER go to school to that man again."

"Oh, Anne!" Diana looked as if she were ready to cry. "I do think you're mean. What shall I do? Mr. Phillips will make me sit with that horrid Gertie Pye—I know he will because she is sitting alone. Do come back, Anne."

"I'd do almost anything in the world for you, Diana," said Anne sadly. "I'd let myself be torn limb from limb if it would do you any good. But I can't do this, so please don't ask it. You harrow up my very soul."

"Just think of all the fun you will miss," mourned Diana. "We are going to build the loveliest new house down by the brook; and we'll be playing ball next week and you've never played ball, Anne. It's tremendously exciting. And we're going to learn a new song—Jane Andrews is practicing it up now; and Alice Andrews is going to bring a new Pansy book next week and we're all going to read it out loud, chapter about, down by the brook. And you know you are so fond of reading out loud, Anne."

Nothing moved Anne in the least. Her mind was made up. She would not go to school to Mr. Phillips again; she told Marilla so when she got home.

"Nonsense," said Marilla.

"It isn't nonsense at all," said Anne, gazing at Marilla with solemn, reproachful eyes. "Don't you understand, Marilla? I've been insulted."

"Insulted fiddlesticks! You'll go to school tomorrow as usual."

"Oh, no." Anne shook her head gently. "I'm not going back, Marilla. I'll learn my lessons at home and I'll be as good as I can be and hold my tongue all the time if it's possible at all. But I will not go back to school, I assure you."

Marilla saw something remarkably like unyielding stubbornness looking out of Anne's small face. She understood that she would have trouble in overcoming it; but she re-solved wisely to say nothing more just then. "I'll run down and see Rachel about it this evening," she thought. "There's no use reasoning with Anne now. She's too worked up and I've an idea she can be awful stubborn if she takes the notion. Far as I can make out from her story, Mr. Phillips has been carrying matters with a rather high hand. But it would never do to say so to her. I'll just talk it over with Rachel. She's sent ten children to school and she ought to know something about it. She'll have heard the whole story, too, by this time."

Marilla found Mrs. Lynde knitting quilts as industriously and cheerfully as usual.

"I suppose you know what I've come about," she said, a little shamefacedly.

Mrs. Rachel nodded.

"About Anne's fuss in school, I reckon," she said. "Tillie Boulter was in on her way home from school and told me about it." "I don't know what to do with her," said Marilla. "She declares she won't go back to school. I never saw a child so worked up. I've been expecting trouble ever since she started to school. I knew things were going too smooth to last. She's so high strung. What would you advise, Rachel?"

"Well, since you've asked my advice, Marilla," said Mrs. Lynde amiably— Mrs. Lynde dearly loved to be asked for advice—"I'd just humor her a little at first, that's what I'd do. It's my belief that Mr. Phillips was in the wrong. Of course, it doesn't do to say so to the children, you know. And of course he did right to punish her yesterday for giving way to temper. But today it was different. The others who were late should have been punished as well as Anne, that's what. And I don't believe in making the girls sit with the boys for punishment. It isn't modest. Tillie Boulter was real indignant. She took Anne's part right through and said all the scholars did too. Anne seems real popular among them, somehow. I never thought she'd take with them so well."

"Then you really think I'd better let her stay home," said Marilla in amazement.

"Yes. That is I wouldn't say school to her again until she said it herself. Depend upon it, Marilla, she'll cool off in a week or so and be ready enough to go back of her own accord, that's what, while, if you were to make her go back right off, dear knows what freak or tantrum she'd take next and make more trouble than ever. The less fuss made the better, in my opinion. She won't miss much by not going to school, as far as THAT goes. Mr. Phillips isn't any good at all as a teacher. The order he keeps is scandalous, that's what, and he neglects the young fry and puts all his time on those big scholars he's getting ready for Queen's. He'd never have got the school for another year if his uncle hadn't been a trustee—THE trustee, for he just leads the other two around by the nose, that's what. I declare, I don't know what education in this Island is coming to."

Mrs. Rachel shook her head, as much as to say if she were only at the head of the educational system of the Province things would be much better managed.

Marilla took Mrs. Rachel's advice and not another word was said to Anne about going back to school. She learned her lessons at home, did her chores, and played with Diana in the chilly purple autumn twilights; but when she met Gilbert Blythe on the road or encountered him in Sunday school she passed him by with an icy contempt that was no whit thawed by his evident desire to appease her.

Even Diana's efforts as a peacemaker were of no avail. Anne had evidently made up her mind to hate Gilbert Blythe to the end of life.

As much as she hated Gilbert, however, did she love Diana, with all the love of her passionate little heart, equally intense in its likes and dislikes. One evening Marilla, coming in from the orchard with a basket of apples, found Anne sitting along by the east window in the twilight, crying bitterly.

"Whatever's the matter now, Anne?" she asked.

"It's about Diana," sobbed Anne luxuriously. "I love Diana so, Marilla. I cannot ever live without her. But I know very well when we grow up that Diana will get married and go away and leave me. And oh, what shall I do? I hate her husband—I just hate him furiously. I've been imagining it all out—the wedding and everything—Diana dressed in snowy garments, with a veil, and looking as beautiful and regal as a queen; and me the bridesmaid, with a lovely dress too, and puffed sleeves, but with a breaking heart hid beneath my smiling face. And then bidding Diana goodbye-e-e—" Here Anne broke down entirely and wept with increasing bitterness.

Marilla turned quickly away to hide her twitching face; but it was no use; she collapsed on the nearest chair and burst into such a hearty and unusual peal of laughter that Matthew, crossing the yard outside, halted in amazement. When had he heard Marilla laugh like that before?

"Well, Anne Shirley," said Marilla as soon as she could speak, "if you must borrow trouble, for pity's sake borrow it handier home. I should think you had an imagination, sure enough."

CHAPTER XVI. Diana Is Invited to Tea with Tragic Results

OCTOBER was a beautiful month at Green Gables, when the birches in the hollow turned as golden as sunshine and the maples behind the orchard were royal crimson and the wild cherry trees along the lane put on the loveliest shades of dark red and bronzy green, while the fields sunned themselves in aftermaths.

Anne reveled in the world of color about her.

"Oh, Marilla," she exclaimed one Saturday morning, coming dancing in with her arms full of gorgeous boughs, "I'm so glad I live in a world where there are Octobers. It would be terrible if we just skipped from September to November, wouldn't it? Look at these maple branches. Don't they give you a thrill—several thrills? I'm going to decorate my room with them."

"Messy things," said Marilla, whose aesthetic sense was not noticeably developed. "You clutter up your room entirely too much with out-of-doors stuff, Anne. Bedrooms were made to sleep in."

"Oh, and dream in too, Marilla. And you know one can dream so much better in a room where there are pretty things. I'm going to put these boughs in the old blue jug and set them on my table."

"Mind you don't drop leaves all over the stairs then. I'm going on a meeting of the Aid Society at Carmody this afternoon, Anne, and I won't likely be home before dark. You'll have to get Matthew and Jerry their supper, so mind you don't forget to put the tea to draw until you sit down at the table as you did last time."

"It was dreadful of me to forget," said Anne apologetically, "but that was the afternoon I was trying to think of a name for Violet Vale and it crowded other things out. Matthew was so good. He never scolded a bit. He put the tea down himself and said we could wait awhile as well as not. And I told him a lovely fairy story while we were waiting, so he didn't find the time long at all. It was a beautiful fairy story, Marilla. I forgot the end of it, so I made up an end for it myself and Matthew said he couldn't tell where the join came in."

"Matthew would think it all right, Anne, if you took a notion to get up and have dinner in the middle of the night. But you keep your wits about you this time. And—I don't really know if I'm doing right—it may make you more addlepated than ever—but you can ask Diana to come over and spend the afternoon with you and have tea here."

"Oh, Marilla!" Anne clasped her hands. "How perfectly lovely! You ARE able to imagine things after all or else you'd never have understood how I've longed for that very thing. It will seem so nice and grown-uppish. No fear of my forgetting to put the tea to draw when I have company. Oh, Marilla, can I use the rosebud spray tea set?"

"No, indeed! The rosebud tea set! Well, what next? You know I never use that except for the minister or the Aids. You'll put down the old brown tea set. But you can open the little yellow crock of cherry preserves. It's time it was being used anyhow—I believe it's beginning to work. And you can cut some fruit cake and have some of the cookies and snaps."

"I can just imagine myself sitting down at the head of the table and pouring out the tea," said Anne, shutting her eyes ecstatically. "And asking Diana if she takes sugar! I know she doesn't but of course I'll ask her just as if I didn't know. And then pressing her to take another piece of fruit cake and another helping of preserves. Oh, Marilla, it's a wonderful sensation just to think of it. Can I take her into the spare room to lay off her hat when she comes? And then into the parlor to sit?"

"No. The sitting room will do for you and your company. But there's a bottle half full of raspberry cordial that was left over from the church social the other night. It's on the second shelf of the sitting-room closet and you and Diana can have it if you like, and a cooky to eat with it along in the afternoon, for I daresay Matthew'll be late coming in to tea since he's hauling potatoes to the vessel."

Anne flew down to the hollow, past the Dryad's Bubble and up the spruce path to Orchard Slope, to ask Diana to tea. As a result just after Marilla had driven off to Carmody, Diana came over, dressed in HER second-best dress and looking exactly as it is proper to look when asked out to tea. At other times she was wont to run into the kitchen without knocking; but now she knocked primly at the front door. And when Anne, dressed in her second best, as primly opened it, both little girls shook hands as gravely as if they had never met before. This unnatural solemnity lasted until after Diana had been taken to the east gable to lay off her hat and then had sat for ten minutes in the sitting room, toes in position.

"How is your mother?" inquired Anne politely, just as if she had not seen Mrs. Barry picking apples that morning in excellent health and spirits.

"She is very well, thank you. I suppose Mr. Cuthbert is hauling potatoes to the LILY SANDS this afternoon, is he?" said Diana, who had ridden down to Mr. Harmon Andrews's that morning in Matthew's cart.

"Yes. Our potato crop is very good this year. I hope your father's crop is good too."

"It is fairly good, thank you. Have you picked many of your apples yet?"

"Oh, ever so many," said Anne forgetting to be dignified and jumping up quickly. "Let's go out to the orchard and get some of the Red Sweetings, Diana. Marilla says we can have all that are left on the tree. Marilla is a very generous woman. She said we could have fruit cake and cherry preserves for tea. But it isn't good manners to tell your company what you are going to give them to eat, so I won't tell you what she said we could have to drink. Only it begins with an R and a C and it's bright red color. I love bright red drinks, don't you? They taste twice as good as any other color."

The orchard, with its great sweeping boughs that bent to the ground with fruit, proved so delightful that the little girls spent most of the afternoon in it, sitting in a grassy corner where the frost had spared the green and the mellow autumn sunshine lingered warmly, eating apples and talking as hard as they could. Diana had much to tell Anne of what went on in school. She had to sit with Gertie Pye and she hated it; Gertie squeaked her pencil all the time and it just made her— Diana's—blood run cold; Ruby Gillis had charmed all her warts away, true's you live, with a magic pebble that old Mary Joe from the Creek gave her. You had to rub the warts with the pebble and then throw it away over your left shoulder at the time of the new moon and the warts would all go. Charlie Sloane's name was written up with Em White's on the porch wall and Em White was AWFUL MAD about it; Sam Boulter had "sassed" Mr. Phillips in class and Mr. Phillips whipped him and Sam's father came down to the school and dared Mr. Phillips to lay a hand on one of his children again; and Mattie Andrews had a new red hood and a blue crossover with tassels on it and the airs she put on about it were perfectly sickening; and Lizzie Wright didn't speak to Mamie Wilson because Mamie Wilson's grown-up sister had cut out Lizzie Wright's grown-up sister with her beau; and everybody missed Anne so and wished she's come to school again; and Gilbert Blythe—

But Anne didn't want to hear about Gilbert Blythe. She jumped up hurriedly and said suppose they go in and have some raspberry cordial.

Anne looked on the second shelf of the room pantry but there was no bottle of raspberry cordial there. Search revealed it away back on the top shelf. Anne put it on a tray and set it on the table with a tumbler.

"Now, please help yourself, Diana," she said politely. "I don't believe I'll have any just now. I don't feel as if I wanted any after all those apples."

Diana poured herself out a tumblerful, looked at its bright-red hue admiringly, and then sipped it daintily.

"That's awfully nice raspberry cordial, Anne," she said. "I didn't know raspberry cordial was so nice."

"I'm real glad you like it. Take as much as you want. I'm going to run out and stir the fire up. There are so many responsibilities on a person's mind when they're keeping house, isn't there?"

When Anne came back from the kitchen Diana was drinking her second glassful of cordial; and, being entreated thereto by Anne, she offered no particular objection to the drinking of a third. The tumblerfuls were generous ones and the raspberry cordial was certainly very nice.

"The nicest I ever drank," said Diana. "It's ever so much nicer than Mrs. Lynde's, although she brags of hers so much. It doesn't taste a bit like hers."

"I should think Marilla's raspberry cordial would prob'ly be much nicer than Mrs. Lynde's," said Anne loyally. "Marilla is a famous cook. She is trying to teach me to cook but I assure you, Diana, it is uphill work. There's so little scope for imagination in cookery. You just have to go by rules. The last time I made a cake I forgot to put the flour in. I was thinking the loveliest story about you and me, Diana. I thought you were desperately ill with smallpox and everybody deserted you, but I went boldly to your bedside and nursed you back to life; and then I took the smallpox and died and I was buried under those poplar trees in the graveyard and you planted a rosebush by my grave and watered it with your tears; and you never, never forgot the friend of your youth who sacrificed her life for you. Oh, it was such a pathetic tale, Diana. The tears just rained down over my cheeks while I mixed the cake. But I forgot the flour and the cake was a dismal failure. Flour is so essential to cakes, you know. Marilla was very cross and I don't wonder. I'm a great trial to her. She was terribly mortified about the pudding sauce last week. We had a plum pudding for dinner on Tuesday and there was half the pudding and a pitcherful of sauce left over. Marilla said there was enough for another dinner and told me to set it on the pantry shelf and cover it. I meant to cover it just as much as could be, Diana, but when I carried it in I was imagining I was a nun—of course I'm a Protestant but I imagined I was a Catholic—taking the veil to bury a broken heart in cloistered seclusion; and I forgot all about covering the pudding sauce. I thought of it next morning and ran to the pantry. Diana, fancy if you can my extreme horror at finding a mouse drowned in that pudding sauce! I lifted the mouse out with a spoon and threw it out in the yard and then I washed the spoon in three waters. Marilla was out milking and I fully intended to ask her when she came in if I'd give the sauce to the pigs; but when she did come in I was imagining that I was a frost fairy going through the woods turning the trees red and yellow, whichever they wanted to be, so I never thought about the pudding sauce again and Marilla sent me out to pick apples. Well, Mr. and Mrs. Chester Ross from Spencervale came here that morning. You know they are very stylish people, especially Mrs. Chester Ross. When Marilla called me in dinner was all ready and everybody was at the table. I tried to be as polite and dignified as I could be, for I wanted Mrs. Chester Ross to think I was a ladylike little girl even if I wasn't pretty. Everything went right until I saw Marilla coming with the plum pudding in one hand and the pitcher of pudding sauce WARMED UP, in the other. Diana, that was a terrible moment. I remembered everything and I just stood up in my place and shrieked out 'Marilla, you mustn't use that pudding sauce. There was a mouse drowned in it. I forgot to tell you before.' Oh, Diana, I shall never forget that awful moment if I live to be a hundred. Mrs. Chester Ross just LOOKED at me and I thought I would sink through the floor with mortification. She is such a perfect housekeeper and fancy what she must have thought of us. Marilla turned red as fire but she never said a word—then. She just carried that sauce and pudding out and brought in some strawberry preserves. She even offered me some, but I couldn't swallow a mouthful. It was like heaping coals of fire on my head. After Mrs. Chester Ross went away, Marilla gave me a dreadful scolding. Why, Diana, what is the matter?"

Diana had stood up very unsteadily; then she sat down again, putting her hands to her head.

"I'm—I'm awful sick," she said, a little thickly. "I—I—must go right home."

"Oh, you mustn't dream of going home without your tea," cried Anne in distress. "I'll get it right off—I'll go and put the tea down this very minute."

"I must go home," repeated Diana, stupidly but determinedly.

"Let me get you a lunch anyhow," implored Anne. "Let me give you a bit of fruit cake and some of the cherry preserves. Lie down on the sofa for a little while and you'll be better. Where do you feel bad?"

"I must go home," said Diana, and that was all she would say. In vain Anne pleaded.

"I never heard of company going home without tea," she mourned. "Oh, Diana, do you suppose that it's possible you're really taking the smallpox? If you are I'll go and nurse you, you can depend on that. I'll never forsake you. But I do wish you'd stay till after tea. Where do you feel bad?"

"I'm awful dizzy," said Diana.

And indeed, she walked very dizzily. Anne, with tears of disappointment in her eyes, got Diana's hat and went with her as far as the Barry yard fence. Then she wept all the way back to Green Gables, where she sorrowfully put the remainder of the raspberry cordial back into the pantry and got tea ready for Matthew and Jerry, with all the zest gone out of the performance.

The next day was Sunday and as the rain poured down in torrents from dawn till dusk Anne did not stir abroad from Green Gables. Monday afternoon Marilla sent her down to Mrs. Lynde's on an errand. In a very short space of time Anne came flying back up the lane with tears rolling down her cheeks. Into the kitchen she dashed and flung herself face downward on the sofa in an agony.

"Whatever has gone wrong now, Anne?" queried Marilla in doubt and dismay. "I do hope you haven't gone and been saucy to Mrs. Lynde again."

No answer from Anne save more tears and stormier sobs!

"Anne Shirley, when I ask you a question I want to be answered. Sit right up this very minute and tell me what you are crying about."

Anne sat up, tragedy personified.

"Mrs. Lynde was up to see Mrs. Barry today and Mrs. Barry was in an awful state," she wailed. "She says that I set Diana DRUNK Saturday and sent her home in a disgraceful condition. And she says I must be a thoroughly bad, wicked little girl and she's never, never going to let Diana play with me again. Oh, Marilla, I'm just overcome with woe."

Marilla stared in blank amazement.

"Set Diana drunk!" she said when she found her voice. "Anne are you or Mrs. Barry crazy? What on earth did you give her?"

"Not a thing but raspberry cordial," sobbed Anne. "I never thought raspberry cordial would set people drunk, Marilla—not even if they drank three big tumblerfuls as Diana did. Oh, it sounds so—so—like Mrs. Thomas's husband! But I didn't mean to set her drunk."

"Drunk fiddlesticks!" said Marilla, marching to the sitting room pantry. There on the shelf was a bottle which she at once recognized as one containing some of her three-year-old homemade currant wine for which she was celebrated in Avonlea, although certain of the stricter sort, Mrs. Barry among them, disapproved strongly of it. And at the same time Marilla recollected that she had put the bottle of raspberry cordial down in the cellar instead of in the pantry as she had told Anne.

She went back to the kitchen with the wine bottle in her hand. Her face was twitching in spite of herself.

"Anne, you certainly have a genius for getting into trouble. You went and gave Diana currant wine instead of raspberry cordial. Didn't you know the difference yourself?"

"I never tasted it," said Anne. "I thought it was the cordial. I meant to be so—so—hospitable. Diana got awfully sick and had to go home. Mrs. Barry told Mrs. Lynde she was simply dead drunk. She just laughed silly-like when her mother asked her what was the matter and went to sleep and slept for hours. Her mother smelled her breath and knew she was drunk. She had a fearful headache all day yesterday. Mrs. Barry is so indignant. She will never believe but what I did it on purpose."

"I should think she would better punish Diana for being so greedy as to drink three glassfuls of anything," said Marilla shortly. "Why, three of those big glasses would have made her sick even if it had only been cordial. Well, this story will be a nice handle for those folks who are so down on me for making currant wine, although I haven't made any for three years ever since I found out that the minister didn't approve. I just kept that bottle for sickness. There, there, child, don't cry. I can't see as you were to blame although I'm sorry it happened so."

"I must cry," said Anne. "My heart is broken. The stars in their courses fight against me, Marilla. Diana and I are parted forever. Oh, Marilla, I little dreamed of this when first we swore our vows of friendship."

"Don't be foolish, Anne. Mrs. Barry will think better of it when she finds you're not to blame. I suppose she thinks you've done it for a silly joke or something of that sort. You'd best go up this evening and tell her how it was."

"My courage fails me at the thought of facing Diana's injured mother," sighed Anne. "I wish you'd go, Marilla. You're so much more dignified than I am. Likely she'd listen to you quicker than to me."

"Well, I will," said Marilla, reflecting that it would probably be the wiser course. "Don't cry any more, Anne. It will be all right."

Marilla had changed her mind about it being all right by the time she got back from Orchard Slope. Anne was watching for her coming and flew to the porch door to meet her.

"Oh, Marilla, I know by your face that it's been no use," she said sorrowfully. "Mrs. Barry won't forgive me?"

"Mrs. Barry indeed!" snapped Marilla. "Of all the unreasonable women I ever saw she's the worst. I told her it was all a mistake and you weren't to blame, but she just simply didn't believe me. And she rubbed it well in about my currant wine and how I'd always said it couldn't have the least effect on anybody. I just told her plainly that currant wine wasn't meant to be drunk three tumblerfuls at a time and that if a child I had to do with was so greedy I'd sober her up with a right good spanking."

Marilla whisked into the kitchen, grievously disturbed, leaving a very much distracted little soul in the porch behind her. Presently Anne stepped out bareheaded into the chill autumn dusk; very determinedly and steadily she took her way down through the sere clover field over the log bridge and up through the spruce grove, lighted by a pale little moon hanging low over the western woods. Mrs. Barry, coming to the door in answer to a timid knock, found a white-lipped eager-eyed suppliant on the doorstep.

Her face hardened. Mrs. Barry was a woman of strong prejudices and dislikes, and her anger was of the cold, sullen sort which is always hardest to overcome. To do her justice, she really believed Anne had made Diana drunk out of sheer malice prepense, and she was honestly anxious to preserve her little daughter from the contamination of further intimacy with such a child.

"What do you want?" she said stiffly.

Anne clasped her hands.

"Oh, Mrs. Barry, please forgive me. I did not mean to—to—intoxicate Diana. How could I? Just imagine if you were a poor little orphan girl that kind people had adopted and you had just one bosom friend in all the world. Do you think you would intoxicate her on purpose? I thought it was only raspberry cordial. I was firmly convinced it was raspberry cordial. Oh, please don't say that you won't let Diana play with me any more. If you do you will cover my life with a dark cloud of woe."

This speech which would have softened good Mrs. Lynde's heart in a twinkling, had no effect on Mrs. Barry except to irritate her still more. She was suspicious of Anne's big words and dramatic gestures and imagined that the child was making fun of her. So she said, coldly and cruelly:

"I don't think you are a fit little girl for Diana to associate with. You'd better go home and behave yourself."

Anne's lips quivered.

"Won't you let me see Diana just once to say farewell?" she implored.

"Diana has gone over to Carmody with her father," said Mrs. Barry, going in and shutting the door.

Anne went back to Green Gables calm with despair.

"My last hope is gone," she told Marilla. "I went up and saw Mrs. Barry myself and she treated me very insultingly. Marilla, I do NOT think she is a well-bred woman. There is nothing more to do except to pray and I haven't much hope that that'll do much good because, Marilla, I do not believe that God Himself can do very much with such an obstinate person as Mrs. Barry."

"Anne, you shouldn't say such things" rebuked Marilla, striving to overcome that unholy tendency to laughter which she was dismayed to find growing upon her. And indeed, when she told the whole story to Matthew that night, she did laugh heartily over Anne's tribulations.

But when she slipped into the east gable before going to bed and found that Anne had cried herself to sleep an unaccustomed softness crept into her face.

"Poor little soul," she murmured, lifting a loose curl of hair from the child's tear-stained face. Then she bent down and kissed the flushed cheek on the pillow.

CHAPTER XVII. A New Interest in Life

THE next afternoon Anne, bending over her patchwork at the kitchen window, happened to glance out and beheld Diana down by the Dryad's Bubble beckoning mysteriously. In a trice Anne was out of the house and flying down to the hollow, astonishment and hope struggling in her expressive eyes. But the hope faded when she saw Diana's dejected countenance.

"Your mother hasn't relented?" she gasped.

Diana shook her head mournfully.

"No; and oh, Anne, she says I'm never to play with you again. I've cried and cried and I told her it wasn't your fault, but it wasn't any use. I had ever such a time coaxing her to let me come down and say good-bye to you. She said I was only to stay ten minutes and she's timing me by the clock."

"Ten minutes isn't very long to say an eternal farewell in," said Anne tearfully. "Oh, Diana, will you promise faithfully never to forget me, the friend of your youth, no matter what dearer friends may caress thee?"

"Indeed I will," sobbed Diana, "and I'll never have another bosom friend—I don't want to have. I couldn't love anybody as I love you."

"Oh, Diana," cried Anne, clasping her hands, "do you LOVE me?"

"Why, of course I do. Didn't you know that?"

"No." Anne drew a long breath. "I thought you LIKED me of course but I never hoped you LOVED me. Why, Diana, I didn't think anybody could love me. Nobody ever has loved me since I can remember. Oh, this is wonderful! It's a ray of light which will forever shine on the darkness of a path severed from thee, Diana. Oh, just say it once again."

"I love you devotedly, Anne," said Diana stanchly, "and I always will, you may be sure of that."

"And I will always love thee, Diana," said Anne, solemnly extending her hand. "In the years to come thy memory will shine like a star over my lonely life, as that last story we read together says. Diana, wilt thou give me a lock of thy jet-black tresses in parting to treasure forevermore?"

"Have you got anything to cut it with?" queried Diana, wiping away the tears which Anne's affecting accents had caused to flow afresh, and returning to practicalities.

"Yes. I've got my patchwork scissors in my apron pocket fortunately," said Anne. She solemnly clipped one of Diana's curls. "Fare thee well, my beloved friend. Henceforth we must be as strangers though living side by side. But my heart will ever be faithful to thee."

Anne stood and watched Diana out of sight, mournfully waving her hand to the latter whenever she turned to look back. Then she returned to the house, not a little consoled for the time being by this romantic parting.

"It is all over," she informed Marilla. "I shall never have another friend. I'm really worse off than ever before, for I haven't Katie Maurice and Violetta now. And even if I had it wouldn't be the same. Somehow, little dream girls are not satisfying after a real friend. Diana and I had such an affecting farewell down by the spring. It will be sacred in my memory forever. I used the most pathetic language I could think of and said 'thou' and 'thee.' 'Thou' and 'thee' seem so much more romantic than 'you.' Diana gave me a lock of her hair and I'm going to sew it up in a little bag and wear it around my neck all my life. Please see that it is buried with me, for I don't believe I'll live very long. Perhaps when she sees me lying cold and dead before her Mrs. Barry may feel remorse for what she has done and will let Diana come to my funeral."

"I don't think there is much fear of your dying of grief as long as you can talk, Anne," said Marilla unsympathetically.

The following Monday Anne surprised Marilla by coming down from her room with her basket of books on her arm and hip and her lips primmed up into a line of determination.

"I'm going back to school," she announced. "That is all there is left in life for me, now that my friend has been ruthlessly torn from me. In school I can look at her and muse over days departed."

"You'd better muse over your lessons and sums," said Marilla, concealing her delight at this development of the situation. "If you're going back to school I hope we'll hear no more of breaking slates over people's heads and such carryings on. Behave yourself and do just what your teacher tells you."

"I'll try to be a model pupil," agreed Anne dolefully. "There won't be much fun in it, I expect. Mr. Phillips said Minnie Andrews was a model pupil and there isn't a spark of imagination or life in her. She is just dull and poky and never seems to have a good time. But I feel so depressed that perhaps it will come easy to me now. I'm going round by the road. I couldn't bear to go by the Birch Path all alone. I should weep bitter tears if I did."

Anne was welcomed back to school with open arms. Her imagination had been sorely missed in games, her voice in the singing and her dramatic ability in the perusal aloud of books at dinner hour. Ruby Gillis smuggled three blue plums over to her during testament reading; Ella May MacPherson gave her an enormous yellow pansy cut from the covers of a floral catalogue—a species of desk decoration much prized in Avonlea school. Sophia Sloane offered to teach her a perfectly elegant new pattern of knit lace, so nice for trimming aprons. Katie Boulter gave her a perfume bottle to keep slate water in, and Julia Bell copied carefully on a piece of pale pink paper scalloped on the edges the following effusion:

> When twilight drops her curtain down
> And pins it with a star
> Remember that you have a friend
> Though she may wander far.

"It's so nice to be appreciated," sighed Anne rapturously to Marilla that night.

The girls were not the only scholars who "appreciated" her. When Anne went to her seat after dinner hour—she had been told by Mr. Phillips to sit with the model Minnie Andrews—she found on her desk a big luscious "strawberry apple." Anne caught it up all ready to take a bite when she remembered that the only place in Avonlea where strawberry apples grew was in the old Blythe orchard on the other side of the Lake of Shining Waters. Anne dropped the apple as if it were a red-hot coal and ostentatiously wiped her fingers on her handkerchief. The apple lay untouched on her desk until the next morning, when little Timothy Andrews, who swept the school and kindled the fire, annexed it as one of his perquisites. Charlie Sloane's slate pencil, gorgeously bedizened with striped red and yellow paper, costing two cents where ordinary pencils cost only one, which he sent up to her after dinner hour, met with a more favorable reception. Anne was graciously pleased to accept it and rewarded the donor with a smile which exalted that infatuated youth straightway into the seventh heaven of delight and caused him to make such fearful errors in his dictation that Mr. Phillips kept him in after school to rewrite it.

But as,

> The Caesar's pageant shorn of Brutus' bust
> Did but of Rome's best son remind her more,

so the marked absence of any tribute or recognition from Diana Barry who was sitting with Gertie Pye embittered Anne's little triumph.

"Diana might just have smiled at me once, I think," she mourned to Marilla that night. But the next morning a note most fearfully and wonderfully twisted and folded, and a small parcel were passed across to Anne.

Dear Anne (ran the former)

Mother says I'm not to play with you or talk to you even in school. It isn't my fault and don't be cross at me, because I love you as much as ever. I miss you awfully to tell all my secrets to and I don't like Gertie Pye one bit. I made you one of the new bookmarkers out of red tissue paper. They are awfully fashionable now and only three girls in school know how to make them. When you look at it remember

Your true friend

Diana Barry.

Anne read the note, kissed the bookmark, and dispatched a prompt reply back to the other side of the school.

My own darling Diana:—

Of course I am not cross at you because you have to obey your mother. Our spirits can commune. I shall keep your lovely present forever. Minnie Andrews is a very nice little girl—although she has no imagination—but after having been Diana's busum friend I cannot be Minnie's. Please excuse mistakes because my spelling isn't very good yet, although much improoved.

Yours until death us do part

Anne or Cordelia Shirley.

P.S. I shall sleep with your letter under my pillow tonight. A. OR C.S.

Marilla pessimistically expected more trouble since Anne had again begun to go to school. But none developed. Perhaps Anne caught something of the "model" spirit from Minnie Andrews; at least she got on very well with Mr. Phillips thenceforth. She flung herself into her studies heart and soul, determined not to be outdone in any class by Gilbert Blythe. The rivalry between them was soon apparent; it was entirely good natured on Gilbert's side; but it is much to be feared that the same thing cannot be said of Anne, who had certainly an unpraiseworthy tenacity for holding grudges. She was as intense in her hatreds as in her loves. She would not stoop to admit that she meant to rival Gilbert in schoolwork, because that would have been to acknowledge his existence which Anne persistently ignored; but the rivalry was there and honors fluctuated between them. Now Gilbert was head of the spelling class; now Anne, with a toss of her long red braids, spelled him down. One morning Gilbert had all his sums done correctly and had his name written on the blackboard on the roll of honor; the next morning Anne, having wrestled wildly with decimals the entire evening before, would be first. One awful day they were ties and their names were written up together. It was almost as bad as a take-notice and Anne's mortification was as evident as Gilbert's satisfaction. When the written examinations at the end of each month were held the suspense was terrible. The first month Gilbert came out three marks ahead. The second Anne beat him by five. But her triumph was marred by the fact that Gilbert congratulated her heartily before the whole school. It would have been ever so much sweeter to her if he had felt the sting of his defeat.

Mr. Phillips might not be a very good teacher; but a pupil so inflexibly determined on learning as Anne was could hardly escape making progress under any kind of teacher. By the end of the term Anne and Gilbert were both promoted into the fifth class and allowed to begin studying the elements of "the branches"—by which Latin, geometry, French, and algebra were meant. In geometry Anne met her Waterloo.

"It's perfectly awful stuff, Marilla," she groaned. "I'm sure I'll never be able to make head or tail of it. There is no scope for imagination in it at all. Mr. Phillips says I'm the worst dunce he ever saw at it. And Gil—I mean some of the others are so smart at it. It is extremely mortifying, Marilla.

"Even Diana gets along better than I do. But I don't mind being beaten by Diana. Even although we meet as strangers now I still love her with an INEXTINGUISHABLE love. It makes me very sad at times to think about her.

CHAPTER XVII. A New Interest in Life

But really, Marilla, one can't stay sad very long in such an interesting world, can one?"

CHAPTER XVIII. Anne to the Rescue

ALL things great are wound up with all things little. At first glance it might not seem that the decision of a certain Canadian Premier to include Prince Edward Island in a political tour could have much or anything to do with the fortunes of little Anne Shirley at Green Gables. But it had.

It was a January the Premier came, to address his loyal supporters and such of his nonsupporters as chose to be present at the monster mass meeting held in Charlottetown. Most of the Avonlea people were on Premier's side of politics; hence on the night of the meeting nearly all the men and a goodly proportion of the women had gone to town thirty miles away. Mrs. Rachel Lynde had gone too. Mrs. Rachel Lynde was a red-hot politician and couldn't have believed that the political rally could be carried through without her, although she was on the opposite side of politics. So she went to town and took her husband—Thomas would be useful in looking after the horse—and Marilla Cuthbert with her. Marilla had a sneaking interest in politics herself, and as she thought it might be her only chance to see a real live Premier, she promptly took it, leaving Anne and Matthew to keep house until her return the following day.

Hence, while Marilla and Mrs. Rachel were enjoying themselves hugely at the mass meeting, Anne and Matthew had the cheerful kitchen at Green Gables all to themselves. A bright fire was glowing in the old-fashioned Waterloo stove and blue-white frost crystals were shining on the windowpanes. Matthew nodded over a FARMERS' ADVOCATE on the sofa and Anne at the table studied her lessons with grim determination, despite sundry wistful glances at the clock shelf, where lay a new book that Jane Andrews had lent her that day. Jane had assured her that it was warranted to produce any number of thrills, or words to that effect, and Anne's fingers tingled to reach out for it. But that would mean Gilbert Blythe's triumph on the morrow. Anne turned her back on the clock shelf and tried to imagine it wasn't there.

"Matthew, did you ever study geometry when you went to school?"

"Well now, no, I didn't," said Matthew, coming out of his doze with a start.

"I wish you had," sighed Anne, "because then you'd be able to sympathize with me. You can't sympathize properly if you've never studied it. It is casting a cloud over my whole life. I'm such a dunce at it, Matthew."

"Well now, I dunno," said Matthew soothingly. "I guess you're all right at any-thing. Mr. Phillips told me last week in Blair's store at Carmody that you was the smartest scholar in school and was making rapid progress. 'Rapid progress' was his very words. There's them as runs down Teddy Phillips and says he ain't much of a teacher, but I guess he's all right."

Matthew would have thought anyone who praised Anne was "all right."

"I'm sure I'd get on better with geometry if only he wouldn't change the let-ters," complained Anne. "I learn the proposition off by heart and then he draws it on the blackboard and puts different letters from what are in the book and I get all mixed up. I don't think a teacher should take such a mean advantage, do you? We're studying agriculture now and I've found out at last what makes the roads red. It's a great comfort. I wonder how Marilla and Mrs. Lynde are enjoying themselves. Mrs. Lynde says Canada is going to the dogs the way things are being run at Ottawa and that it's an awful warning to the electors. She says if women were allowed to vote we would soon see a blessed change. What way do you vote, Matthew?"

"Conservative," said Matthew promptly. To vote Conservative was part of Matthew's religion.

"Then I'm Conservative too," said Anne decidedly. "I'm glad because Gil— because some of the boys in school are Grits. I guess Mr. Phillips is a Grit too because Prissy Andrews's father is one, and Ruby Gillis says that when a man is courting he always has to agree with the girl's mother in religion and her father in politics. Is that true, Matthew?"

"Well now, I dunno," said Matthew.

"Did you ever go courting, Matthew?"

"Well now, no, I dunno's I ever did," said Matthew, who had certainly never thought of such a thing in his whole existence.

Anne reflected with her chin in her hands.

"It must be rather interesting, don't you think, Matthew? Ruby Gillis says when she grows up she's going to have ever so many beaus on the string and have them all crazy about her; but I think that would be too exciting. I'd rather have just one in his right mind. But Ruby Gillis knows a great deal about such matters be-cause she has so many big sisters, and Mrs. Lynde says the Gillis girls have gone off like hot cakes. Mr. Phillips goes up to see Prissy Andrews nearly every even-ing. He says it is to help her with her lessons but Miranda Sloane is studying for Queen's too, and I should think she needed help a lot more than Prissy because she's ever so much stupider, but he never goes to help her in the evenings at all. There are a great many things in this world that I can't understand very well, Mat-thew."

"Well now, I dunno as I comprehend them all myself," acknowledged Mat-thew.

"Well, I suppose I must finish up my lessons. I won't allow myself to open that new book Jane lent me until I'm through. But it's a terrible temptation, Matthew. Even when I turn my back on it I can see it there just as plain. Jane said she cried herself sick over it. I love a book that makes me cry. But I think I'll carry that book into the sitting room and lock it in the jam closet and give you the key. And you must NOT give it to me, Matthew, until my lessons are done, not even if I implore you on my bended knees. It's all very well to say resist temptation, but it's ever so much easier to resist it if you can't get the key. And then shall I run down the cellar and get some russets, Matthew? Wouldn't you like some russets?"

"Well now, I dunno but what I would," said Matthew, who never ate russets but knew Anne's weakness for them.

Just as Anne emerged triumphantly from the cellar with her plateful of russets came the sound of flying footsteps on the icy board walk outside and the next moment the kitchen door was flung open and in rushed Diana Barry, white faced and breathless, with a shawl wrapped hastily around her head. Anne promptly let go of her candle and plate in her surprise, and plate, candle, and apples crashed together down the cellar ladder and were found at the bottom embedded in melted grease, the next day, by Marilla, who gathered them up and thanked mercy the house hadn't been set on fire.

"Whatever is the matter, Diana?" cried Anne. "Has your mother relented at last?"

"Oh, Anne, do come quick," implored Diana nervously. "Minnie May is awful sick—she's got croup. Young Mary Joe says—and Father and Mother are away to town and there's nobody to go for the doctor. Minnie May is awful bad and Young Mary Joe doesn't know what to do—and oh, Anne, I'm so scared!"

Matthew, without a word, reached out for cap and coat, slipped past Diana and away into the darkness of the yard.

"He's gone to harness the sorrel mare to go to Carmody for the doctor," said Anne, who was hurrying on hood and jacket. "I know it as well as if he'd said so. Matthew and I are such kindred spirits I can read his thoughts without words at all."

"I don't believe he'll find the doctor at Carmody," sobbed Diana. "I know that Dr. Blair went to town and I guess Dr. Spencer would go too. Young Mary Joe never saw anybody with croup and Mrs. Lynde is away. Oh, Anne!"

"Don't cry, Di," said Anne cheerily. "I know exactly what to do for croup. You forget that Mrs. Hammond had twins three times. When you look after three pairs of twins you naturally get a lot of experience. They all had croup regularly. Just wait till I get the ipecac bottle—you mayn't have any at your house. Come on now."

The two little girls hastened out hand in hand and hurried through Lover's Lane and across the crusted field beyond, for the snow was too deep to go by the shorter wood way. Anne, although sincerely sorry for Minnie May, was far from being insensible to the romance of the situation and to the sweetness of once more sharing that romance with a kindred spirit.

The night was clear and frosty, all ebony of shadow and silver of snowy slope; big stars were shining over the silent fields; here and there the dark pointed firs stood up with snow powdering their branches and the wind whistling through them. Anne thought it was truly delightful to go skimming through all this mystery and loveliness with your bosom friend who had been so long estranged.

Minnie May, aged three, was really very sick. She lay on the kitchen sofa feverish and restless, while her hoarse breathing could be heard all over the house. Young Mary Joe, a buxom, broad-faced French girl from the creek, whom Mrs. Barry had engaged to stay with the children during her absence, was helpless and bewildered, quite incapable of thinking what to do, or doing it if she thought of it.

Anne went to work with skill and promptness.

"Minnie May has croup all right; she's pretty bad, but I've seen them worse. First we must have lots of hot water. I declare, Diana, there isn't more than a cupful in the kettle! There, I've filled it up, and, Mary Joe, you may put some wood in the stove. I don't want to hurt your feelings but it seems to me you might have thought of this before if you'd any imagination. Now, I'll undress Minnie May and put her to bed and you try to find some soft flannel cloths, Diana. I'm going to give her a dose of ipecac first of all."

Minnie May did not take kindly to the ipecac but Anne had not brought up three pairs of twins for nothing. Down that ipecac went, not only once, but many times during the long, anxious night when the two little girls worked patiently over the suffering Minnie May, and Young Mary Joe, honestly anxious to do all she could, kept up a roaring fire and heated more water than would have been needed for a hospital of croupy babies.

It was three o'clock when Matthew came with a doctor, for he had been obliged to go all the way to Spencervale for one. But the pressing need for assistance was past. Minnie May was much better and was sleeping soundly.

"I was awfully near giving up in despair," explained Anne. "She got worse and worse until she was sicker than ever the Hammond twins were, even the last pair. I actually thought she was going to choke to death. I gave her every drop of ipecac in that bottle and when the last dose went down I said to myself—not to Diana or Young Mary Joe, because I didn't want to worry them any more than they were worried, but I had to say it to myself just to relieve my feelings—'This is the last lingering hope and I fear, tis a vain one.' But in about three minutes she coughed up the phlegm and began to get better right away. You must just imagine my relief, doctor, because I can't express it in words. You know there are some things that cannot be expressed in words."

"Yes, I know," nodded the doctor. He looked at Anne as if he were thinking some things about her that couldn't be expressed in words. Later on, however, he expressed them to Mr. and Mrs. Barry.

"That little redheaded girl they have over at Cuthbert's is as smart as they make 'em. I tell you she saved that baby's life, for it would have been too late by the time I got there. She seems to have a skill and presence of mind perfectly wonderful in a child of her age. I never saw anything like the eyes of her when she was explaining the case to me."

Anne had gone home in the wonderful, white-frosted winter morning, heavy eyed from loss of sleep, but still talking unweariedly to Matthew as they crossed the long white field and walked under the glittering fairy arch of the Lover's Lane maples.

"Oh, Matthew, isn't it a wonderful morning? The world looks like something God had just imagined for His own pleasure, doesn't it? Those trees look as if I could blow them away with a breath—pouf! I'm so glad I live in a world where there are white frosts, aren't you? And I'm so glad Mrs. Hammond had three pairs of twins after all. If she hadn't I mightn't have known what to do for Minnie May. I'm real sorry I was ever cross with Mrs. Hammond for having twins. But, oh, Matthew, I'm so sleepy. I can't go to school. I just know I couldn't keep my eyes open and I'd be so stupid. But I hate to stay home, for Gil—some of the others will get head of the class, and it's so hard to get up again—although of course the harder it is the more satisfaction you have when you do get up, haven't you?"

"Well now, I guess you'll manage all right," said Matthew, looking at Anne's white little face and the dark shadows under her eyes. "You just go right to bed and have a good sleep. I'll do all the chores."

Anne accordingly went to bed and slept so long and soundly that it was well on in the white and rosy winter afternoon when she awoke and descended to the kitchen where Marilla, who had arrived home in the meantime, was sitting knitting.

"Oh, did you see the Premier?" exclaimed Anne at once. "What did he look like Marilla?"

"Well, he never got to be Premier on account of his looks," said Marilla. "Such a nose as that man had! But he can speak. I was proud of being a Conservative. Rachel Lynde, of course, being a Liberal, had no use for him. Your dinner is in the oven, Anne, and you can get yourself some blue plum preserve out of the pantry. I guess you're hungry. Matthew has been telling me about last night. I must say it was fortunate you knew what to do. I wouldn't have had any idea myself, for I never saw a case of croup. There now, never mind talking till you've had your dinner. I can tell by the look of you that you're just full up with speeches, but they'll keep."

Marilla had something to tell Anne, but she did not tell it just then for she knew if she did Anne's consequent excitement would lift her clear out of the region of such material matters as appetite or dinner. Not until Anne had finished her saucer of blue plums did Marilla say:

"Mrs. Barry was here this afternoon, Anne. She wanted to see you, but I wouldn't wake you up. She says you saved Minnie May's life, and she is very sorry she acted as she did in that affair of the currant wine. She says she knows now you didn't mean to set Diana drunk, and she hopes you'll forgive her and be good friends with Diana again. You're to go over this evening if you like for Diana can't stir outside the door on account of a bad cold she caught last night. Now, Anne Shirley, for pity's sake don't fly up into the air."

The warning seemed not unnecessary, so uplifted and aerial was Anne's expression and attitude as she sprang to her feet, her face irradiated with the flame of her spirit.

"Oh, Marilla, can I go right now—without washing my dishes? I'll wash them when I come back, but I cannot tie myself down to anything so unromantic as dishwashing at this thrilling moment."

"Yes, yes, run along," said Marilla indulgently. "Anne Shirley—are you crazy? Come back this instant and put something on you. I might as well call to the wind. She's gone without a cap or wrap. Look at her tearing through the orchard with her hair streaming. It'll be a mercy if she doesn't catch her death of cold."

Anne came dancing home in the purple winter twilight across the snowy places. Afar in the southwest was the great shimmering, pearl-like sparkle of an evening star in a sky that was pale golden and ethereal rose over gleaming white spaces and dark glens of spruce. The tinkles of sleigh bells among the snowy hills came like elfin chimes through the frosty air, but their music was not sweeter than the song in Anne's heart and on her lips.

"You see before you a perfectly happy person, Marilla," she announced. "I'm perfectly happy—yes, in spite of my red hair. Just at present I have a soul above red hair. Mrs. Barry kissed me and cried and said she was so sorry and she could never repay me. I felt fearfully embarrassed, Marilla, but I just said as politely as I could, 'I have no hard feelings for you, Mrs. Barry. I assure you once for all that I did not mean to intoxicate Diana and henceforth I shall cover the past with the mantle of oblivion.' That was a pretty dignified way of speaking wasn't it, Marilla?"

"I felt that I was heaping coals of fire on Mrs. Barry's head. And Diana and I had a lovely afternoon. Diana showed me a new fancy crochet stitch her aunt over at Carmody taught her. Not a soul in Avonlea knows it but us, and we pledged a solemn vow never to reveal it to anyone else. Diana gave me a beautiful card with a wreath of roses on it and a verse of poetry:

"If you love me as I love you
Nothing but death can part us two.

"And that is true, Marilla. We're going to ask Mr. Phillips to let us sit together in school again, and Gertie Pye can go with Minnie Andrews. We had an elegant tea. Mrs. Barry had the very best china set out, Marilla, just as if I was real company. I can't tell you what a thrill it gave me. Nobody ever used their very best china on my account before. And we had fruit cake and pound cake and doughnuts and two kinds of preserves, Marilla. And Mrs. Barry asked me if I took tea and said 'Pa, why don't you pass the biscuits to Anne?' It must be lovely to be grown up, Marilla, when just being treated as if you were is so nice."

"I don't know about that," said Marilla, with a brief sigh.

"Well, anyway, when I am grown up," said Anne decidedly, "I'm always going to talk to little girls as if they were too, and I'll never laugh when they use big words. I know from sorrowful experience how that hurts one's feelings. After tea Diana and I made taffy. The taffy wasn't very good, I suppose because neither Diana nor I had ever made any before. Diana left me to stir it while she buttered the plates and I forgot and let it burn; and then when we set it out on the platform to cool the cat walked over one plate and that had to be thrown away. But the making of it was splendid fun. Then when I came home Mrs. Barry asked me to come over as often as I could and Diana stood at the window and threw kisses to me all the way down to Lover's Lane. I assure you, Marilla, that I feel like praying tonight and I'm going to think out a special brand-new prayer in honor of the occasion."

CHAPTER XIX. A Concert a Catastrophe and a Confession

"MARILLA, can I go over to see Diana just for a minute?" asked Anne, running breathlessly down from the east gable one February evening.

"I don't see what you want to be traipsing about after dark for," said Marilla shortly. "You and Diana walked home from school together and then stood down there in the snow for half an hour more, your tongues going the whole blessed time, clickety-clack. So I don't think you're very badly off to see her again."

"But she wants to see me," pleaded Anne. "She has something very important to tell me."

"How do you know she has?"

"Because she just signaled to me from her window. We have arranged a way to signal with our candles and cardboard. We set the candle on the window sill and make flashes by passing the cardboard back and forth. So many flashes mean a certain thing. It was my idea, Marilla."

"I'll warrant you it was," said Marilla emphatically. "And the next thing you'll be setting fire to the curtains with your signaling nonsense."

"Oh, we're very careful, Marilla. And it's so interesting. Two flashes mean, 'Are you there?' Three mean 'yes' and four 'no.' Five mean, 'Come over as soon as possible, because I have something important to reveal.' Diana has just signaled five flashes, and I'm really suffering to know what it is."

"Well, you needn't suffer any longer," said Marilla sarcastically. "You can go, but you're to be back here in just ten minutes, remember that."

Anne did remember it and was back in the stipulated time, although probably no mortal will ever know just what it cost her to confine the discussion of Diana's important communication within the limits of ten minutes. But at least she had made good use of them.

"Oh, Marilla, what do you think? You know tomorrow is Diana's birthday. Well, her mother told her she could ask me to go home with her from school and stay all night with her. And her cousins are coming over from Newbridge in a big pung sleigh to go to the Debating Club concert at the hall tomorrow night. And they are going to take Diana and me to the concert—if you'll let me go, that is. You will, won't you, Marilla? Oh, I feel so excited."

"You can calm down then, because you're not going. You're better at home in your own bed, and as for that club concert, it's all nonsense, and little girls should not be allowed to go out to such places at all."

"I'm sure the Debating Club is a most respectable affair," pleaded Anne.

"I'm not saying it isn't. But you're not going to begin gadding about to concerts and staying out all hours of the night. Pretty doings for children. I'm surprised at Mrs. Barry's letting Diana go."

"But it's such a very special occasion," mourned Anne, on the verge of tears. "Diana has only one birthday in a year. It isn't as if birthdays were common things, Marilla. Prissy Andrews is going to recite 'Curfew Must Not Ring To-night.' That is such a good moral piece, Marilla, I'm sure it would do me lots of good to hear it. And the choir are going to sing four lovely pathetic songs that are pretty near as good as hymns. And oh, Marilla, the minister is going to take part; yes, indeed, he is; he's going to give an address. That will be just about the same thing as a sermon. Please, mayn't I go, Marilla?"

"You heard what I said, Anne, didn't you? Take off your boots now and go to bed. It's past eight."

"There's just one more thing, Marilla," said Anne, with the air of producing the last shot in her locker. "Mrs. Barry told Diana that we might sleep in the spare-room bed. Think of the honor of your little Anne being put in the spare-room bed."

"It's an honor you'll have to get along without. Go to bed, Anne, and don't let me hear another word out of you."

When Anne, with tears rolling over her cheeks, had gone sorrowfully upstairs, Matthew, who had been apparently sound asleep on the lounge during the whole dialogue, opened his eyes and said decidedly:

"Well now, Marilla, I think you ought to let Anne go."

"I don't then," retorted Marilla. "Who's bringing this child up, Matthew, you or me?"

"Well now, you," admitted Matthew.

"Don't interfere then."

"Well now, I ain't interfering. It ain't interfering to have your own opinion. And my opinion is that you ought to let Anne go."

"You'd think I ought to let Anne go to the moon if she took the notion, I've no doubt" was Marilla's amiable rejoinder. "I might have let her spend the night with Diana, if that was all. But I don't approve of this concert plan. She'd go there and catch cold like as not, and have her head filled up with nonsense and excitement. It would unsettle her for a week. I understand that child's disposition and what's good for it better than you, Matthew."

"I think you ought to let Anne go," repeated Matthew firmly. Argument was not his strong point, but holding fast to his opinion certainly was. Marilla gave a gasp of helplessness and took refuge in silence. The next morning, when Anne was washing the breakfast dishes in the pantry, Matthew paused on his way out to the barn to say to Marilla again:

"I think you ought to let Anne go, Marilla."

For a moment Marilla looked things not lawful to be uttered. Then she yielded to the inevitable and said tartly:

"Very well, she can go, since nothing else'll please you."

Anne flew out of the pantry, dripping dishcloth in hand.

"Oh, Marilla, Marilla, say those blessed words again."

"I guess once is enough to say them. This is Matthew's doings and I wash my hands of it. If you catch pneumonia sleeping in a strange bed or coming out of that hot hall in the middle of the night, don't blame me, blame Matthew. Anne Shirley, you're dripping greasy water all over the floor. I never saw such a careless child."

"Oh, I know I'm a great trial to you, Marilla," said Anne repentantly. "I make so many mistakes. But then just think of all the mistakes I don't make, although I might. I'll get some sand and scrub up the spots before I go to school. Oh, Marilla, my heart was just set on going to that concert. I never was to a concert in my life, and when the other girls talk about them in school I feel so out of it. You didn't know just how I felt about it, but you see Matthew did. Matthew understands me, and it's so nice to be understood, Marilla."

Anne was too excited to do herself justice as to lessons that morning in school. Gilbert Blythe spelled her down in class and left her clear out of sight in mental arithmetic. Anne's consequent humiliation was less than it might have been, however, in view of the concert and the spare-room bed. She and Diana talked so constantly about it all day that with a stricter teacher than Mr. Phillips dire disgrace must inevitably have been their portion.

Anne felt that she could not have borne it if she had not been going to the concert, for nothing else was discussed that day in school. The Avonlea Debating Club, which met fortnightly all winter, had had several smaller free entertainments; but this was to be a big affair, admission ten cents, in aid of the library. The Avonlea young people had been practicing for weeks, and all the scholars were especially interested in it by reason of older brothers and sisters who were going to take part. Everybody in school over nine years of age expected to go, except Carrie Sloane, whose father shared Marilla's opinions about small girls going out to night concerts. Carrie Sloane cried into her grammar all the afternoon and felt that life was not worth living.

For Anne the real excitement began with the dismissal of school and increased therefrom in crescendo until it reached to a crash of positive ecstasy in the concert itself. They had a "perfectly elegant tea;" and then came the delicious occupation of dressing in Diana's little room upstairs. Diana did Anne's front hair in the new pompadour style and Anne tied Diana's bows with the especial knack she possessed; and they experimented with at least half a dozen different ways of arranging their back hair. At last they were ready, cheeks scarlet and eyes glowing with excitement.

True, Anne could not help a little pang when she contrasted her plain black tam and shapeless, tight-sleeved, homemade gray-cloth coat with Diana's jaunty fur cap and smart little jacket. But she remembered in time that she had an imagination and could use it.

Then Diana's cousins, the Murrays from Newbridge, came; they all crowded into the big pung sleigh, among straw and furry robes. Anne reveled in the drive to the hall, slipping along over the satin-smooth roads with the snow crisping under the runners. There was a magnificent sunset, and the snowy hills and deep-blue water of the St. Lawrence Gulf seemed to rim in the splendor like a huge bowl of pearl and sapphire brimmed with wine and fire. Tinkles of sleigh bells and distant laughter, that seemed like the mirth of wood elves, came from every quarter.

"Oh, Diana," breathed Anne, squeezing Diana's mittened hand under the fur robe, "isn't it all like a beautiful dream? Do I really look the same as usual? I feel so different that it seems to me it must show in my looks."

"You look awfully nice," said Diana, who having just received a compliment from one of her cousins, felt that she ought to pass it on. "You've got the loveliest color."

The program that night was a series of "thrills" for at least one listener in the audience, and, as Anne assured Diana, every succeeding thrill was thrillier than the last. When Prissy Andrews, attired in a new pink-silk waist with a string of pearls about her smooth white throat and real carnations in her hair—rumor whispered that the master had sent all the way to town for them for her—"climbed the slimy ladder, dark without one ray of light," Anne shivered in luxurious sympathy; when the choir sang "Far Above the Gentle Daisies" Anne gazed at the ceiling as if it were frescoed with angels; when Sam Sloane proceeded to explain and illustrate "How Sockery Set a Hen" Anne laughed until people sitting near her laughed too, more out of sympathy with her than with amusement at a selection that was rather threadbare even in Avonlea; and when Mr. Phillips gave Mark Antony's oration over the dead body of Caesar in the most heart-stirring tones—looking at Prissy Andrews at the end of every sentence—Anne felt that she could rise and mutiny on the spot if but one Roman citizen led the way.

Only one number on the program failed to interest her. When Gilbert Blythe recited "Bingen on the Rhine" Anne picked up Rhoda Murray's library book and read it until he had finished, when she sat rigidly stiff and motionless while Diana clapped her hands until they tingled.

It was eleven when they got home, sated with dissipation, but with the exceeding sweet pleasure of talking it all over still to come. Everybody seemed asleep and the house was dark and silent. Anne and Diana tiptoed into the parlor, a long narrow room out of which the spare room opened. It was pleasantly warm and dimly lighted by the embers of a fire in the grate.

"Let's undress here," said Diana. "It's so nice and warm."

"Hasn't it been a delightful time?" sighed Anne rapturously. "It must be splendid to get up and recite there. Do you suppose we will ever be asked to do it, Diana?"

"Yes, of course, someday. They're always wanting the big scholars to recite. Gilbert Blythe does often and he's only two years older than us. Oh, Anne, how could you pretend not to listen to him? When he came to the line,

"THERE'S ANOTHER, not A SISTER,

he looked right down at you."

"Diana," said Anne with dignity, "you are my bosom friend, but I cannot allow even you to speak to me of that person. Are you ready for bed? Let's run a race and see who'll get to the bed first."

The suggestion appealed to Diana. The two little white-clad figures flew down the long room, through the spare-room door, and bounded on the bed at the same moment. And then—something—moved beneath them, there was a gasp and a cry—and somebody said in muffled accents:

"Merciful goodness!"

Anne and Diana were never able to tell just how they got off that bed and out of the room. They only knew that after one frantic rush they found themselves tiptoeing shiveringly upstairs.

"Oh, who was it—WHAT was it?" whispered Anne, her teeth chattering with cold and fright.

"It was Aunt Josephine," said Diana, gasping with laughter. "Oh, Anne, it was Aunt Josephine, however she came to be there. Oh, and I know she will be furious. It's dreadful—it's really dreadful—but did you ever know anything so funny, Anne?"

"Who is your Aunt Josephine?"

"She's father's aunt and she lives in Charlottetown. She's awfully old—seventy anyhow—and I don't believe she was EVER a little girl. We were expecting her out for a visit, but not so soon. She's awfully prim and proper and she'll scold dreadfully about this, I know. Well, we'll have to sleep with Minnie May—and you can't think how she kicks."

Miss Josephine Barry did not appear at the early breakfast the next morning. Mrs. Barry smiled kindly at the two little girls.

"Did you have a good time last night? I tried to stay awake until you came home, for I wanted to tell you Aunt Josephine had come and that you would have to go upstairs after all, but I was so tired I fell asleep. I hope you didn't disturb your aunt, Diana."

Diana preserved a discreet silence, but she and Anne exchanged furtive smiles of guilty amusement across the table. Anne hurried home after breakfast and so remained in blissful ignorance of the disturbance which presently resulted in the Barry household until the late afternoon, when she went down to Mrs. Lynde's on an errand for Marilla.

"So you and Diana nearly frightened poor old Miss Barry to death last night?" said Mrs. Lynde severely, but with a twinkle in her eye. "Mrs. Barry was here a few minutes ago on her way to Carmody. She's feeling real worried over it. Old Miss Barry was in a terrible temper when she got up this morning—and Josephine Barry's temper is no joke, I can tell you that. She wouldn't speak to Diana at all."

"It wasn't Diana's fault," said Anne contritely. "It was mine. I suggested racing to see who would get into bed first."

"I knew it!" said Mrs. Lynde, with the exultation of a correct guesser. "I knew that idea came out of your head. Well, it's made a nice lot of trouble, that's what. Old Miss Barry came out to stay for a month, but she declares she won't stay another day and is going right back to town tomorrow, Sunday and all as it is. She'd have gone today if they could have taken her. She had promised to pay for a quarter's music lessons for Diana, but now she is determined to do nothing at all for such a tomboy. Oh, I guess they had a lively time of it there this morning. The Barrys must feel cut up. Old Miss Barry is rich and they'd like to keep on the good side of her. Of course, Mrs. Barry didn't say just that to me, but I'm a pretty good judge of human nature, that's what."

"I'm such an unlucky girl," mourned Anne. "I'm always getting into scrapes myself and getting my best friends—people I'd shed my heart's blood for—into them too. Can you tell me why it is so, Mrs. Lynde?"

"It's because you're too heedless and impulsive, child, that's what. You never stop to think—whatever comes into your head to say or do you say or do it without a moment's reflection."

"Oh, but that's the best of it," protested Anne. "Something just flashes into your mind, so exciting, and you must out with it. If you stop to think it over you spoil it all. Haven't you never felt that yourself, Mrs. Lynde?"

No, Mrs. Lynde had not. She shook her head sagely.

"You must learn to think a little, Anne, that's what. The proverb you need to go by is 'Look before you leap'—especially into spare-room beds."

Mrs. Lynde laughed comfortably over her mild joke, but Anne remained pensive. She saw nothing to laugh at in the situation, which to her eyes appeared very serious. When she left Mrs. Lynde's she took her way across the crusted fields to Orchard Slope. Diana met her at the kitchen door.

"Your Aunt Josephine was very cross about it, wasn't she?" whispered Anne.

"Yes," answered Diana, stifling a giggle with an apprehensive glance over her shoulder at the closed sitting-room door. "She was fairly dancing with rage, Anne. Oh, how she scolded. She said I was the worst-behaved girl she ever saw and that my parents ought to be ashamed of the way they had brought me up. She says she won't stay and I'm sure I don't care. But Father and Mother do."

"Why didn't you tell them it was my fault?" demanded Anne.

"It's likely I'd do such a thing, isn't it?" said Diana with just scorn. "I'm no telltale, Anne Shirley, and anyhow I was just as much to blame as you."

"Well, I'm going in to tell her myself," said Anne resolutely.

Diana stared.

"Anne Shirley, you'd never! why—she'll eat you alive!"

"Don't frighten me any more than I am frightened," implored Anne. "I'd rather walk up to a cannon's mouth. But I've got to do it, Diana. It was my fault and I've got to confess. I've had practice in confessing, fortunately."

"Well, she's in the room," said Diana. "You can go in if you want to. I wouldn't dare. And I don't believe you'll do a bit of good."

With this encouragement Anne bearded the lion in its den—that is to say, walked resolutely up to the sitting-room door and knocked faintly. A sharp "Come in" followed.

Miss Josephine Barry, thin, prim, and rigid, was knitting fiercely by the fire, her wrath quite unappeased and her eyes snapping through her gold-rimmed glasses. She wheeled around in her chair, expecting to see Diana, and beheld a white-faced girl whose great eyes were brimmed up with a mixture of desperate courage and shrinking terror.

"Who are you?" demanded Miss Josephine Barry, without ceremony.

"I'm Anne of Green Gables," said the small visitor tremulously, clasping her hands with her characteristic gesture, "and I've come to confess, if you please."

"Confess what?"

"That it was all my fault about jumping into bed on you last night. I suggested it. Diana would never have thought of such a thing, I am sure. Diana is a very ladylike girl, Miss Barry. So you must see how unjust it is to blame her."

"Oh, I must, hey? I rather think Diana did her share of the jumping at least. Such carryings on in a respectable house!"

"But we were only in fun," persisted Anne. "I think you ought to forgive us, Miss Barry, now that we've apologized. And anyhow, please forgive Diana and let her have her music lessons. Diana's heart is set on her music lessons, Miss Barry, and I know too well what it is to set your heart on a thing and not get it. If you must be cross with anyone, be cross with me. I've been so used in my early days to having people cross at me that I can endure it much better than Diana can."

Much of the snap had gone out of the old lady's eyes by this time and was replaced by a twinkle of amused interest. But she still said severely:

"I don't think it is any excuse for you that you were only in fun. Little girls never indulged in that kind of fun when I was young. You don't know what it is to be awakened out of a sound sleep, after a long and arduous journey, by two great girls coming bounce down on you."

"I don't KNOW, but I can IMAGINE," said Anne eagerly. "I'm sure it must have been very disturbing. But then, there is our side of it too. Have you any imagination, Miss Barry? If you have, just put yourself in our place. We didn't know there was anybody in that bed and you nearly scared us to death. It was simply awful the way we felt. And then we couldn't sleep in the spare room after being promised. I suppose you are used to sleeping in spare rooms. But just imagine what you would feel like if you were a little orphan girl who had never had such an honor."

All the snap had gone by this time. Miss Barry actually laughed—a sound which caused Diana, waiting in speechless anxiety in the kitchen outside, to give a great gasp of relief.

"I'm afraid my imagination is a little rusty—it's so long since I used it," she said. "I dare say your claim to sympathy is just as strong as mine. It all depends on the way we look at it. Sit down here and tell me about yourself."

"I am very sorry I can't," said Anne firmly. "I would like to, because you seem like an interesting lady, and you might even be a kindred spirit although you don't look very much like it. But it is my duty to go home to Miss Marilla Cuthbert. Miss Marilla Cuthbert is a very kind lady who has taken me to bring up properly. She is doing her best, but it is very discouraging work. You must not blame her because I jumped on the bed. But before I go I do wish you would tell me if you will forgive Diana and stay just as long as you meant to in Avonlea."

"I think perhaps I will if you will come over and talk to me occasionally," said Miss Barry.

That evening Miss Barry gave Diana a silver bangle bracelet and told the senior members of the household that she had unpacked her valise.

"I've made up my mind to stay simply for the sake of getting better acquainted with that Anne-girl," she said frankly. "She amuses me, and at my time of life an amusing person is a rarity."

Marilla's only comment when she heard the story was, "I told you so." This was for Matthew's benefit.

Miss Barry stayed her month out and over. She was a more agreeable guest than usual, for Anne kept her in good humor. They became firm friends.

When Miss Barry went away she said:

"Remember, you Anne-girl, when you come to town you're to visit me and I'll put you in my very sparest spare-room bed to sleep."

"Miss Barry was a kindred spirit, after all," Anne confided to Marilla. "You wouldn't think so to look at her, but she is. You don't find it right out at first, as in Matthew's case, but after a while you come to see it. Kindred spirits are not so scarce as I used to think. It's splendid to find out there are so many of them in the world."

CHAPTER XX. A Good Imagination Gone Wrong

Spring had come once more to Green Gables—the beautiful capricious, reluctant Canadian spring, lingering along through April and May in a succession of sweet, fresh, chilly days, with pink sunsets and miracles of resurrection and growth. The maples in Lover's Lane were red budded and little curly ferns pushed up around the Dryad's Bubble. Away up in the barrens, behind Mr. Silas Sloane's place, the Mayflowers blossomed out, pink and white stars of sweetness under their brown leaves. All the school girls and boys had one golden afternoon gathering them, coming home in the clear, echoing twilight with arms and baskets full of flowery spoil.

"I'm so sorry for people who live in lands where there are no Mayflowers," said Anne. "Diana says perhaps they have something better, but there couldn't be anything better than Mayflowers, could there, Marilla? And Diana says if they don't know what they are like they don't miss them. But I think that is the saddest thing of all. I think it would be TRAGIC, Marilla, not to know what Mayflowers are like and NOT to miss them. Do you know what I think Mayflowers are, Marilla? I think they must be the souls of the flowers that died last summer and this is their heaven. But we had a splendid time today, Marilla. We had our lunch down in a big mossy hollow by an old well—such a ROMANTIC spot. Charlie Sloane dared Arty Gillis to jump over it, and Arty did because he wouldn't take a dare. Nobody would in school. It is very FASHIONABLE to dare. Mr. Phillips gave all the Mayflowers he found to Prissy Andrews and I heard him to say 'sweets to the sweet.' He got that out of a book, I know; but it shows he has some imagination. I was offered some Mayflowers too, but I rejected them with scorn. I can't tell you the person's name because I have vowed never to let it cross my lips. We made wreaths of the Mayflowers and put them on our hats; and when the time came to go home we marched in procession down the road, two by two, with our bouquets and wreaths, singing 'My Home on the Hill.' Oh, it was so thrilling, Marilla. All Mr. Silas Sloane's folks rushed out to see us and everybody we met on the road stopped and stared after us. We made a real sensation."

"Not much wonder! Such silly doings!" was Marilla's response.

After the Mayflowers came the violets, and Violet Vale was empurpled with them. Anne walked through it on her way to school with reverent steps and worshiping eyes, as if she trod on holy ground.

"Somehow," she told Diana, "when I'm going through here I don't really care whether Gil—whether anybody gets ahead of me in class or not. But when I'm up in school it's all different and I care as much as ever. There's such a lot of different Annes in me. I sometimes think that is why I'm such a troublesome person. If I was just the one Anne it would be ever so much more comfortable, but then it wouldn't be half so interesting."

One June evening, when the orchards were pink blossomed again, when the frogs were singing silverly sweet in the marshes about the head of the Lake of Shining Waters, and the air was full of the savor of clover fields and balsamic fir woods, Anne was sitting by her gable window. She had been studying her lessons, but it had grown too dark to see the book, so she had fallen into wide-eyed reverie, looking out past the boughs of the Snow Queen, once more bestarred with its tufts of blossom.

In all essential respects the little gable chamber was unchanged. The walls were as white, the pincushion as hard, the chairs as stiffly and yellowly upright as ever. Yet the whole character of the room was altered. It was full of a new vital, pulsing personality that seemed to pervade it and to be quite independent of schoolgirl books and dresses and ribbons, and even of the cracked blue jug full of apple blossoms on the table. It was as if all the dreams, sleeping and waking, of its vivid occupant had taken a visible although unmaterial form and had tapestried the bare room with splendid filmy tissues of rainbow and moonshine. Presently Marilla came briskly in with some of Anne's freshly ironed school aprons. She hung them over a chair and sat down with a short sigh. She had had one of her headaches that afternoon, and although the pain had gone she felt weak and "tuckered out," as she expressed it. Anne looked at her with eyes limpid with sympathy.

"I do truly wish I could have had the headache in your place, Marilla. I would have endured it joyfully for your sake."

"I guess you did your part in attending to the work and letting me rest," said Marilla. "You seem to have got on fairly well and made fewer mistakes than usual. Of course it wasn't exactly necessary to starch Matthew's handkerchiefs! And most people when they put a pie in the oven to warm up for dinner take it out and eat it when it gets hot instead of leaving it to be burned to a crisp. But that doesn't seem to be your way evidently."

Headaches always left Marilla somewhat sarcastic.

"Oh, I'm so sorry," said Anne penitently. "I never thought about that pie from the moment I put it in the oven till now, although I felt INSTINCTIVELY that there was something missing on the dinner table. I was firmly resolved, when you left me in charge this morning, not to imagine anything, but keep my thoughts on facts. I did pretty well until I put the pie in, and then an irresistible temptation came to me to imagine I was an enchanted princess shut up in a lonely tower with a handsome knight riding to my rescue on a coal-black steed. So that is how I came to forget the pie. I didn't know I starched the handkerchiefs. All the time I was ironing I was trying to think of a name for a new island Diana and I have discovered up the brook. It's the most ravishing spot, Marilla. There are two maple trees on it and the brook flows right around it. At last it struck me that it would be splendid to call it Victoria Island because we found it on the Queen's birthday. Both Diana and I are very loyal. But I'm sorry about that pie and the handkerchiefs. I wanted to be extra good today because it's an anniversary. Do you remember what happened this day last year, Marilla?"

"No, I can't think of anything special."

"Oh, Marilla, it was the day I came to Green Gables. I shall never forget it. It was the turning point in my life. Of course it wouldn't seem so important to you. I've been here for a year and I've been so happy. Of course, I've had my troubles, but one can live down troubles. Are you sorry you kept me, Marilla?"

"No, I can't say I'm sorry," said Marilla, who sometimes wondered how she could have lived before Anne came to Green Gables, "no, not exactly sorry. If you've finished your lessons, Anne, I want you to run over and ask Mrs. Barry if she'll lend me Diana's apron pattern."

"Oh—it's—it's too dark," cried Anne.

"Too dark? Why, it's only twilight. And goodness knows you've gone over often enough after dark."

"I'll go over early in the morning," said Anne eagerly. "I'll get up at sunrise and go over, Marilla."

"What has got into your head now, Anne Shirley? I want that pattern to cut out your new apron this evening. Go at once and be smart too."

"I'll have to go around by the road, then," said Anne, taking up her hat reluctantly.

"Go by the road and waste half an hour! I'd like to catch you!"

"I can't go through the Haunted Wood, Marilla," cried Anne desperately.

Marilla stared.

"The Haunted Wood! Are you crazy? What under the canopy is the Haunted Wood?"

"The spruce wood over the brook," said Anne in a whisper.

"Fiddlesticks! There is no such thing as a haunted wood anywhere. Who has been telling you such stuff?"

"Nobody," confessed Anne. "Diana and I just imagined the wood was haunted. All the places around here are so—so—COMMONPLACE. We just got this up for our own amusement. We began it in April. A haunted wood is so very romantic, Marilla. We chose the spruce grove because it's so gloomy. Oh, we have imagined the most harrowing things. There's a white lady walks along the brook just about this time of the night and wrings her hands and utters wailing cries. She appears when there is to be a death in the family. And the ghost of a little murdered child haunts the corner up by Idlewild; it creeps up behind you and lays its cold fingers on your hand—so. Oh, Marilla, it gives me a shudder to think of it. And there's a headless man stalks up and down the path and skeletons glower at you between the boughs. Oh, Marilla, I wouldn't go through the Haunted Wood after dark now for anything. I'd be sure that white things would reach out from behind the trees and grab me."

"Did ever anyone hear the like!" ejaculated Marilla, who had listened in dumb amazement. "Anne Shirley, do you mean to tell me you believe all that wicked nonsense of your own imagination?"

"Not believe EXACTLY," faltered Anne. "At least, I don't believe it in daylight. But after dark, Marilla, it's different. That is when ghosts walk."

"There are no such things as ghosts, Anne."

"Oh, but there are, Marilla," cried Anne eagerly. "I know people who have seen them. And they are respectable people. Charlie Sloane says that his grandmother saw his grandfather driving home the cows one night after he'd been buried for a year. You know Charlie Sloane's grandmother wouldn't tell a story for anything. She's a very religious woman. And Mrs. Thomas's father was pursued home one night by a lamb of fire with its head cut off hanging by a strip of skin. He said he knew it was the spirit of his brother and that it was a warning he would die within nine days. He didn't, but he died two years after, so you see it was really true. And Ruby Gillis says—"

"Anne Shirley," interrupted Marilla firmly, "I never want to hear you talking in this fashion again. I've had my doubts about that imagination of yours right along, and if this is going to be the outcome of it, I won't countenance any such doings. You'll go right over to Barry's, and you'll go through that spruce grove, just for a lesson and a warning to you. And never let me hear a word out of your head about haunted woods again."

Anne might plead and cry as she liked—and did, for her terror was very real. Her imagination had run away with her and she held the spruce grove in mortal dread after nightfall. But Marilla was inexorable. She marched the shrinking ghost-seer down to the spring and ordered her to proceed straightaway over the bridge and into the dusky retreats of wailing ladies and headless specters beyond.

"Oh, Marilla, how can you be so cruel?" sobbed Anne. "What would you feel like if a white thing did snatch me up and carry me off?"

"I'll risk it," said Marilla unfeelingly. "You know I always mean what I say. I'll cure you of imagining ghosts into places. March, now."

Anne marched. That is, she stumbled over the bridge and went shuddering up the horrible dim path beyond. Anne never forgot that walk. Bitterly did she repent the license she had given to her imagination. The goblins of her fancy lurked in every shadow about her, reaching out their cold, fleshless hands to grasp the terrified small girl who had called them into being. A white strip of birch bark blowing up from the hollow over the brown floor of the grove made her heart stand still. The long-drawn wail of two old boughs rubbing against each other brought out the perspiration in beads on her forehead. The swoop of bats in the darkness over her was as the wings of unearthly creatures. When she reached Mr. William Bell's field she fled across it as if pursued by an army of white things, and arrived at the Barry kitchen door so out of breath that she could hardly gasp out her request for the apron pattern. Diana was away so that she had no excuse to linger. The dreadful return journey had to be faced. Anne went back over it with shut eyes, preferring to take the risk of dashing her brains out among the boughs to that of seeing a white thing. When she finally stumbled over the log bridge she drew one long shivering breath of relief.

"Well, so nothing caught you?" said Marilla unsympathetically.

"Oh, Mar—Marilla," chattered Anne, "I'll b-b-be contt-tented with c-c-commonplace places after this."

CHAPTER XXI. A New Departure in Flavorings

"Dear me, there is nothing but meetings and partings in this world, as Mrs. Lynde says," remarked Anne plaintively, putting her slate and books down on the kitchen table on the last day of June and wiping her red eyes with a very damp handkerchief. "Wasn't it fortunate, Marilla, that I took an extra handkerchief to school today? I had a presentiment that it would be needed."

"I never thought you were so fond of Mr. Phillips that you'd require two hand-kerchiefs to dry your tears just because he was going away," said Marilla.

"I don't think I was crying because I was really so very fond of him," reflected Anne. "I just cried because all the others did. It was Ruby Gillis started it. Ruby Gillis has always declared she hated Mr. Phillips, but just as soon as he got up to make his farewell speech she burst into tears. Then all the girls began to cry, one after the other. I tried to hold out, Marilla. I tried to remember the time Mr. Phillips made me sit with Gil—with a, boy; and the time he spelled my name without an e on the blackboard; and how he said I was the worst dunce he ever saw at geometry and laughed at my spelling; and all the times he had been so horrid and sarcastic; but somehow I couldn't, Marilla, and I just had to cry too. Jane Andrews has been talking for a month about how glad she'd be when Mr. Phillips went away and she declared she'd never shed a tear. Well, she was worse than any of us and had to borrow a handkerchief from her brother—of course the boys didn't cry—because she hadn't brought one of her own, not expecting to need it. Oh, Marilla, it was heartrending. Mr. Phillips made such a beautiful farewell speech beginning, 'The time has come for us to part.' It was very affecting. And he had tears in his eyes too, Marilla. Oh, I felt dreadfully sorry and remorseful for all the times I'd talked in school and drawn pictures of him on my slate and made fun of him and Prissy. I can tell you I wished I'd been a model pupil like Minnie Andrews. She hadn't anything on her conscience. The girls cried all the way home from school. Carrie Sloane kept saying every few minutes, 'The time has come for us to part,' and that would start us off again whenever we were in any danger of cheering up. I do feel dreadfully sad, Marilla. But one can't feel quite in the depths of despair with two months' vacation before them, can they, Marilla? And besides, we met the new minister and his wife coming from the station. For all I was feeling so bad about Mr. Phillips going away I couldn't help taking a little interest in a new minister, could I? His wife is very pretty. Not exactly regally lovely, of course—it wouldn't do, I suppose, for a minister to have a regally love-ly wife, because it might set a bad example. Mrs. Lynde says the minister's wife over at Newbridge sets a very bad example because she dresses so fashionably. Our new minister's wife was dressed in blue muslin with lovely puffed sleeves and a hat trimmed with roses. Jane Andrews said she thought puffed sleeves were too worldly for a minister's wife, but I didn't make any such uncharitable remark, Marilla, because I know what it is to long for puffed sleeves. Besides, she's only been a minister's wife for a little while, so one should make allowances, shouldn't they? They are going to board with Mrs. Lynde until the manse is ready."

If Marilla, in going down to Mrs. Lynde's that evening, was actuated by any motive save her avowed one of returning the quilting frames she had borrowed the preceding winter, it was an amiable weakness shared by most of the Avonlea people. Many a thing Mrs. Lynde had lent, sometimes never expecting to see it again, came home that night in charge of the borrowers thereof. A new minister, and moreover a minister with a wife, was a lawful object of curiosity in a quiet little country settlement where sensations were few and far between.

Old Mr. Bentley, the minister whom Anne had found lacking in imagination, had been pastor of Avonlea for eighteen years. He was a widower when he came, and a widower he remained, despite the fact that gossip regularly married him to this, that, or the other one, every year of his sojourn. In the preceding February he had resigned his charge and departed amid the regrets of his people, most of whom had the affection born of long intercourse for their good old minister in spite of his shortcomings as an orator. Since then the Avonlea church had enjoyed a variety of religious dissipation in listening to the many and various candidates and "supplies" who came Sunday after Sunday to preach on trial. These stood or fell by the judgment of the fathers and mothers in Israel; but a certain small, red-haired girl who sat meekly in the corner of the old Cuthbert pew also had her opinions about them and discussed the same in full with Matthew, Marilla always declining from principle to criticize ministers in any shape or form.

"I don't think Mr. Smith would have done, Matthew" was Anne's final sum-ming up. "Mrs. Lynde says his delivery was so poor, but I think his worst fault was just like Mr. Bentley's—he had no imagination. And Mr. Terry had too much; he let it run away with him just as I did mine in the matter of the Haunted Wood. Besides, Mrs. Lynde says his theology wasn't sound. Mr. Gresham was a very good man and a very religious man, but he told too many funny stories and made the people laugh in church; he was undignified, and you must have some dignity about a minister, mustn't you, Matthew? I thought Mr. Marshall was decidedly attractive; but Mrs. Lynde says he isn't married, or even engaged, because she made special inquiries about him, and she says it would never do to have a young unmarried minister in Avonlea, because he might marry in the congregation and that would make trouble. Mrs. Lynde is a very farseeing woman, isn't she, Mat-thew? I'm very glad they've called Mr. Allan. I liked him because his sermon was interesting and he prayed as if he meant it and not just as if he did it because he was in the habit of it. Mrs. Lynde says he isn't perfect, but she says she supposes we couldn't expect a perfect minister for seven hundred and fifty dollars a year, and anyhow his theology is sound because she questioned him thoroughly on all the points of doctrine. And she knows his wife's people and they are most respectable and the women are all good housekeepers. Mrs. Lynde says that sound doctrine in the man and good housekeeping in the woman make an ideal combination for a minister's family."

The new minister and his wife were a young, pleasant-faced couple, still on their honeymoon, and full of all good and beautiful enthusiasms for their chosen lifework. Avonlea opened its heart to them from the start. Old and young liked the frank, cheerful young man with his high ideals, and the bright, gentle little lady who assumed the mistress-ship of the manse. With Mrs. Allan Anne fell promptly and wholeheartedly in love. She had discovered another kindred spirit.

"Mrs. Allan is perfectly lovely," she announced one Sunday afternoon. "She's taken our class and she's a splendid teacher. She said right away she didn't think it was fair for the teacher to ask all the questions, and you know, Marilla, that is exactly what I've always thought. She said we could ask her any question we liked and I asked ever so many. I'm good at asking questions, Marilla."

"I believe you" was Marilla's emphatic comment.

"Nobody else asked any except Ruby Gillis, and she asked if there was to be a Sunday-school picnic this summer. I didn't think that was a very proper question to ask because it hadn't any connection with the lesson—the lesson was about Daniel in the lions' den—but Mrs. Allan just smiled and said she thought there would be. Mrs. Allan has a lovely smile; she has such EXQUISITE dimples in her cheeks. I wish I had dimples in my cheeks, Marilla. I'm not half so skinny as I was when I came here, but I have no dimples yet. If I had perhaps I could influence people for good. Mrs. Allan said we ought always to try to influence other people for good. She talked so nice about everything. I never knew before that religion was such a cheerful thing. I always thought it was kind of melancholy, but Mrs. Allan's isn't, and I'd like to be a Christian if I could be one like her. I wouldn't want to be one like Mr. Superintendent Bell."

"It's very naughty of you to speak so about Mr. Bell," said Marilla severely. "Mr. Bell is a real good man."

"Oh, of course he's good," agreed Anne, "but he doesn't seem to get any comfort out of it. If I could be good I'd dance and sing all day because I was glad of it. I suppose Mrs. Allan is too old to dance and sing and of course it wouldn't be dignified in a minister's wife. But I can just feel she's glad she's a Christian and that she'd be one even if she could get to heaven without it."

"I suppose we must have Mr. and Mrs. Allan up to tea someday soon," said Marilla reflectively. "They've been most everywhere but here. Let me see. Next Wednesday would be a good time to have them. But don't say a word to Matthew about it, for if he knew they were coming he'd find some excuse to be away that day. He'd got so used to Mr. Bentley he didn't mind him, but he's going to find it hard to get acquainted with a new minister, and a new minister's wife will frighten him to death."

"I'll be as secret as the dead," assured Anne. "But oh, Marilla, will you let me make a cake for the occasion? I'd love to do something for Mrs. Allan, and you know I can make a pretty good cake by this time."

"You can make a layer cake," promised Marilla.

Monday and Tuesday great preparations went on at Green Gables. Having the minister and his wife to tea was a serious and important undertaking, and Marilla was determined not to be eclipsed by any of the Avonlea housekeepers. Anne was wild with excitement and delight. She talked it all over with Diana Tuesday night in the twilight, as they sat on the big red stones by the Dryad's Bubble and made rainbows in the water with little twigs dipped in fir balsam.

"Everything is ready, Diana, except my cake which I'm to make in the morning, and the baking-powder biscuits which Marilla will make just before teatime. I assure you, Diana, that Marilla and I have had a busy two days of it. It's such a responsibility having a minister's family to tea. I never went through such an experience before. You should just see our pantry. It's a sight to behold. We're going to have jellied chicken and cold tongue. We're to have two kinds of jelly, red and yellow, and whipped cream and lemon pie, and cherry pie, and three kinds of cookies, and fruit cake, and Marilla's famous yellow plum preserves that she keeps especially for ministers, and pound cake and layer cake, and biscuits as aforesaid; and new bread and old both, in case the minister is dyspeptic and can't eat new. Mrs. Lynde says ministers are dyspeptic, but I don't think Mr. Allan has been a minister long enough for it to have had a bad effect on him. I just grow cold when I think of my layer cake. Oh, Diana, what if it shouldn't be good! I dreamed last night that I was chased all around by a fearful goblin with a big layer cake for a head."

"It'll be good, all right," assured Diana, who was a very comfortable sort of friend. "I'm sure that piece of the one you made that we had for lunch in Idlewild two weeks ago was perfectly elegant."

"Yes; but cakes have such a terrible habit of turning out bad just when you especially want them to be good," sighed Anne, setting a particularly well-balsamed twig afloat. "However, I suppose I shall just have to trust to Providence and be careful to put in the flour. Oh, look, Diana, what a lovely rainbow! Do you suppose the dryad will come out after we go away and take it for a scarf?"

"You know there is no such thing as a dryad," said Diana. Diana's mother had found out about the Haunted Wood and had been decidedly angry over it. As a result Diana had abstained from any further imitative flights of imagination and did not think it prudent to cultivate a spirit of belief even in harmless dryads.

"But it's so easy to imagine there is," said Anne. "Every night before I go to bed, I look out of my window and wonder if the dryad is really sitting here, combing her locks with the spring for a mirror. Sometimes I look for her footprints in the dew in the morning. Oh, Diana, don't give up your faith in the dryad!"

Wednesday morning came. Anne got up at sunrise because she was too excited to sleep. She had caught a severe cold in the head by reason of her dabbling in the spring on the preceding evening; but nothing short of absolute pneumonia could have quenched her interest in culinary matters that morning. After breakfast she proceeded to make her cake. When she finally shut the oven door upon it she drew a long breath.

"I'm sure I haven't forgotten anything this time, Marilla. But do you think it will rise? Just suppose perhaps the baking powder isn't good? I used it out of the new can. And Mrs. Lynde says you can never be sure of getting good baking powder nowadays when everything is so adulterated. Mrs. Lynde says the Government ought to take the matter up, but she says we'll never see the day when a Tory Government will do it. Marilla, what if that cake doesn't rise?"

"We'll have plenty without it" was Marilla's unimpassioned way of looking at the subject.

The cake did rise, however, and came out of the oven as light and feathery as golden foam. Anne, flushed with delight, clapped it together with layers of ruby jelly and, in imagination, saw Mrs. Allan eating it and possibly asking for another piece!

"You'll be using the best tea set, of course, Marilla," she said. "Can I fix the table with ferns and wild roses?"

"I think that's all nonsense," sniffed Marilla. "In my opinion it's the eatables that matter and not flummery decorations."

"Mrs. Barry had HER table decorated," said Anne, who was not entirely guilt-less of the wisdom of the serpent, "and the minister paid her an elegant compliment. He said it was a feast for the eye as well as the palate."

"Well, do as you like," said Marilla, who was quite determined not to be surpassed by Mrs. Barry or anybody else. "Only mind you leave enough room for the dishes and the food."

Anne laid herself out to decorate in a manner and after a fashion that should leave Mrs. Barry's nowhere. Having abundance of roses and ferns and a very artistic taste of her own, she made that tea table such a thing of beauty that when the minister and his wife sat down to it they exclaimed in chorus over it loveliness.

"It's Anne's doings," said Marilla, grimly just; and Anne felt that Mrs. Allan's approving smile was almost too much happiness for this world.

Matthew was there, having been inveigled into the party only goodness and Anne knew how. He had been in such a state of shyness and nervousness that Marilla had given him up in despair, but Anne took him in hand so successfully that he now sat at the table in his best clothes and white collar and talked to the minister not uninterestingly. He never said a word to Mrs. Allan, but that perhaps was not to be expected.

All went merry as a marriage bell until Anne's layer cake was passed. Mrs. Allan, having already been helped to a bewildering variety, declined it. But Marilla, seeing the disappointment on Anne's face, said smilingly:

"Oh, you must take a piece of this, Mrs. Allan. Anne made it on purpose for you."

"In that case I must sample it," laughed Mrs. Allan, helping herself to a plump triangle, as did also the minister and Marilla.

Mrs. Allan took a mouthful of hers and a most peculiar expression crossed her face; not a word did she say, however, but steadily ate away at it. Marilla saw the expression and hastened to taste the cake.

"Anne Shirley!" she exclaimed, "what on earth did you put into that cake?"

"Nothing but what the recipe said, Marilla," cried Anne with a look of anguish. "Oh, isn't it all right?"

"All right! It's simply horrible. Mr. Allan, don't try to eat it. Anne, taste it yourself. What flavoring did you use?"

"Vanilla," said Anne, her face scarlet with mortification after tasting the cake. "Only vanilla. Oh, Marilla, it must have been the baking powder. I had my suspicions of that bak—"

"Baking powder fiddlesticks! Go and bring me the bottle of vanilla you used."

Anne fled to the pantry and returned with a small bottle partially filled with a brown liquid and labeled yellowly, "Best Vanilla."

Marilla took it, uncorked it, smelled it.

"Mercy on us, Anne, you've flavored that cake with ANODYNE LINIMENT. I broke the liniment bottle last week and poured what was left into an old empty vanilla bottle. I suppose it's partly my fault—I should have warned you—but for pity's sake why couldn't you have smelled it?"

Anne dissolved into tears under this double disgrace.

"I couldn't—I had such a cold!" and with this she fairly fled to the gable chamber, where she cast herself on the bed and wept as one who refuses to be comforted.

Presently a light step sounded on the stairs and somebody entered the room.

"Oh, Marilla," sobbed Anne, without looking up, "I'm disgraced forever. I shall never be able to live this down. It will get out—things always do get out in Avonlea. Diana will ask me how my cake turned out and I shall have to tell her the truth. I shall always be pointed at as the girl who flavored a cake with anodyne liniment. Gil—the boys in school will never get over laughing at it. Oh, Marilla, if you have a spark of Christian pity don't tell me that I must go down and wash the dishes after this. I'll wash them when the minister and his wife are gone, but I cannot ever look Mrs. Allan in the face again. Perhaps she'll think I tried to poison her. Mrs. Lynde says she knows an orphan girl who tried to poison her benefactor. But the liniment isn't poisonous. It's meant to be taken internally—although not in cakes. Won't you tell Mrs. Allan so, Marilla?"

"Suppose you jump up and tell her so yourself," said a merry voice.

Anne flew up, to find Mrs. Allan standing by her bed, surveying her with laughing eyes.

"My dear little girl, you mustn't cry like this," she said, genuinely disturbed by Anne's tragic face. "Why, it's all just a funny mistake that anybody might make."

"Oh, no, it takes me to make such a mistake," said Anne forlornly. "And I wanted to have that cake so nice for you, Mrs. Allan."

"Yes, I know, dear. And I assure you I appreciate your kindness and thoughtfulness just as much as if it had turned out all right. Now, you mustn't cry any more, but come down with me and show me your flower garden. Miss Cuthbert tells me you have a little plot all your own. I want to see it, for I'm very much interested in flowers."

Anne permitted herself to be led down and comforted, reflecting that it was really providential that Mrs. Allan was a kindred spirit. Nothing more was said about the liniment cake, and when the guests went away Anne found that she had enjoyed the evening more than could have been expected, considering that terrible incident. Nevertheless, she sighed deeply.

"Marilla, isn't it nice to think that tomorrow is a new day with no mistakes in it yet?"

"I'll warrant you'll make plenty in it," said Marilla. "I never saw your beat for making mistakes, Anne."

"Yes, and well I know it," admitted Anne mournfully. "But have you ever noticed one encouraging thing about me, Marilla? I never make the same mistake twice."

"I don't know as that's much benefit when you're always making new ones."

"Oh, don't you see, Marilla? There must be a limit to the mistakes one person can make, and when I get to the end of them, then I'll be through with them. That's a very comforting thought."

"Well, you'd better go and give that cake to the pigs," said Marilla. "It isn't fit for any human to eat, not even Jerry Boute."

CHAPTER XXII. Anne is Invited Out to Tea

"And what are your eyes popping out of your head about. Now?" asked Marilla, when Anne had just come in from a run to the post office. "Have you discovered another kindred spirit?" Excitement hung around Anne like a garment, shone in her eyes, kindled in every feature. She had come dancing up the lane, like a wind-blown sprite, through the mellow sunshine and lazy shadows of the August evening.

"No, Marilla, but oh, what do you think? I am invited to tea at the manse tomorrow afternoon! Mrs. Allan left the letter for me at the post office. Just look at it, Marilla. 'Miss Anne Shirley, Green Gables.' That is the first time I was ever called 'Miss.' Such a thrill as it gave me! I shall cherish it forever among my choicest treasures."

"Mrs. Allan told me she meant to have all the members of her Sunday-school class to tea in turn," said Marilla, regarding the wonderful event very coolly. "You needn't get in such a fever over it. Do learn to take things calmly, child."

For Anne to take things calmly would have been to change her nature. All "spirit and fire and dew," as she was, the pleasures and pains of life came to her with trebled intensity. Marilla felt this and was vaguely troubled over it, realizing that the ups and downs of existence would probably bear hardly on this impulsive soul and not sufficiently understanding that the equally great capacity for delight might more than compensate. Therefore Marilla conceived it to be her duty to drill Anne into a tranquil uniformity of disposition as impossible and alien to her as to a dancing sunbeam in one of the brook shallows. She did not make much headway, as she sorrowfully admitted to herself. The downfall of some dear hope or plan plunged Anne into "deeps of affliction." The fulfillment thereof exalted her to dizzy realms of delight. Marilla had almost begun to despair of ever fashioning this waif of the world into her model little girl of demure manners and prim deportment. Neither would she have believed that she really liked Anne much better as she was.

Anne went to bed that night speechless with misery because Matthew had said the wind was round northeast and he feared it would be a rainy day tomorrow. The rustle of the poplar leaves about the house worried her, it sounded so like pattering raindrops, and the full, faraway roar of the gulf, to which she listened delightedly at other times, loving its strange, sonorous, haunting rhythm, now seemed like a prophecy of storm and disaster to a small maiden who particularly wanted a fine day. Anne thought that the morning would never come.

But all things have an end, even nights before the day on which you are invited to take tea at the manse. The morning, in spite of Matthew's predictions, was fine and Anne's spirits soared to their highest. "Oh, Marilla, there is something in me today that makes me just love everybody I see," she exclaimed as she washed the breakfast dishes. "You don't know how good I feel! Wouldn't it be nice if it could last? I believe I could be a model child if I were just invited out to tea every day. But oh, Marilla, it's a solemn occasion too. I feel so anxious. What if I shouldn't behave properly? You know I never had tea at a manse before, and I'm not sure that I know all the rules of etiquette, although I've been studying the rules given in the Etiquette Department of the Family Herald ever since I came here. I'm so afraid I'll do something silly or forget to do something I should do. Would it be good manners to take a second helping of anything if you wanted to VERY much?"

"The trouble with you, Anne, is that you're thinking too much about yourself. You should just think of Mrs. Allan and what would be nicest and most agreeable to her," said Marilla, hitting for once in her life on a very sound and pithy piece of advice. Anne instantly realized this.

"You are right, Marilla. I'll try not to think about myself at all."

Anne evidently got through her visit without any serious breach of "etiquette," for she came home through the twilight, under a great, high-sprung sky gloried over with trails of saffron and rosy cloud, in a beatified state of mind and told Marilla all about it happily, sitting on the big red-sandstone slab at the kitchen door with her tired curly head in Marilla's gingham lap.

A cool wind was blowing down over the long harvest fields from the rims of firry western hills and whistling through the poplars. One clear star hung over the orchard and the fireflies were flitting over in Lover's Lane, in and out among the ferns and rustling boughs. Anne watched them as she talked and somehow felt that wind and stars and fireflies were all tangled up together into something unutterably sweet and enchanting.

"Oh, Marilla, I've had a most FASCINATING time. I feel that I have not lived in vain and I shall always feel like that even if I should never be invited to tea at a manse again. When I got there Mrs. Allan met me at the door. She was dressed in the sweetest dress of pale-pink organdy, with dozens of frills and elbow sleeves, and she looked just like a seraph. I really think I'd like to be a minister's wife when I grow up, Marilla. A minister mightn't mind my red hair because he wouldn't be thinking of such worldly things. But then of course one would have to be naturally good and I'll never be that, so I suppose there's no use in thinking about it. Some people are naturally good, you know, and others are not. I'm one of the others. Mrs. Lynde says I'm full of original sin. No matter how hard I try to be good I can never make such a success of it as those who are naturally good. It's a good deal like geometry, I expect. But don't you think the trying so hard ought to count for something? Mrs. Allan is one of the naturally good people. I love her passionately. You know there are some people, like Matthew and Mrs. Allan that you can love right off without any trouble. And there are others, like Mrs. Lynde, that you have to try very hard to love. You know you OUGHT to love them because they know so much and are such active workers in the church, but you have to keep reminding yourself of it all the time or else you forget. There was another little girl at the manse to tea, from the White Sands Sunday school. Her name was Laurette Bradley, and she was a very nice little girl. Not exactly a kindred spirit, you know, but still very nice. We had an elegant tea, and I think I kept all the rules of etiquette pretty well. After tea Mrs. Allan played and sang and she got Lauretta and me to sing too. Mrs. Allan says I have a good voice and she says I must sing in the Sunday-school choir after this. You can't think how I was thrilled at the mere thought. I've longed so to sing in the Sunday-school choir, as Diana does, but I feared it was an honor I could never aspire to. Lauretta had to go home early because there is a big concert in the White Sands Hotel tonight and her sister is to recite at it. Lauretta says that the Americans at the hotel give a concert every fortnight in aid of the Charlottetown hospital, and they ask lots of the White Sands people to recite. Lauretta said she expected to be asked herself someday. I just gazed at her in awe. After she had gone Mrs. Allan and I had a heart-to-heart talk. I told her everything—about Mrs. Thomas and the twins and Katie Maurice and Violetta and coming to Green Gables and my troubles over geometry. And would you believe it, Marilla? Mrs. Allan told me she was a dunce at geometry too. You don't know how that encouraged me. Mrs. Lynde came to the manse just before I left, and what do you think, Marilla? The trustees have hired a new teacher and it's a lady. Her name is Miss Muriel Stacy. Isn't that a romantic name? Mrs. Lynde says they've never had a female teacher in Avonlea before and she thinks it is a dangerous innovation. But I think it will be splendid to have a lady teacher, and I really don't see how I'm going to live through the two weeks before school begins. I'm so impatient to see her."

CHAPTER XXIII. Anne Comes to Grief in an Affair of Honor

Anne had to live through more than two weeks, as it happened. Almost a month having elapsed since the liniment cake episode, it was high time for her to get into fresh trouble of some sort, little mistakes, such as absentmindedly emptying a pan of skim milk into a basket of yarn balls in the pantry instead of into the pigs' bucket, and walking clean over the edge of the log bridge into the brook while wrapped in imaginative reverie, not really being worth counting.

A week after the tea at the manse Diana Barry gave a party.

"Small and select," Anne assured Marilla. "Just the girls in our class."

They had a very good time and nothing untoward happened until after tea, when they found themselves in the Barry garden, a little tired of all their games and ripe for any enticing form of mischief which might present itself. This presently took the form of "daring."

Daring was the fashionable amusement among the Avonlea small fry just then. It had begun among the boys, but soon spread to the girls, and all the silly things that were done in Avonlea that summer because the doers thereof were "dared" to do them would fill a book by themselves.

First of all Carrie Sloane dared Ruby Gillis to climb to a certain point in the huge old willow tree before the front door; which Ruby Gillis, albeit in mortal dread of the fat green caterpillars with which said tree was infested and with the fear of her mother before her eyes if she should tear her new muslin dress, nimbly did, to the discomfiture of the aforesaid Carrie Sloane. Then Josie Pye dared Jane Andrews to hop on her left leg around the garden without stopping once or putting her right foot to the ground; which Jane Andrews gamely tried to do, but gave out at the third corner and had to confess herself defeated.

Josie's triumph being rather more pronounced than good taste permitted, Anne Shirley dared her to walk along the top of the board fence which bounded the garden to the east. Now, to "walk" board fences requires more skill and steadiness of head and heel than one might suppose who has never tried it. But Josie Pye, if deficient in some qualities that make for popularity, had at least a natural and inborn gift, duly cultivated, for walking board fences. Josie walked the Barry fence with an airy unconcern which seemed to imply that a little thing like that wasn't worth a "dare." Reluctant admiration greeted her exploit, for most of the other girls could appreciate it, having suffered many things themselves in their efforts to walk fences. Josie descended from her perch, flushed with victory, and darted a defiant glance at Anne.

Anne tossed her red braids.

"I don't think it's such a very wonderful thing to walk a little, low, board fence," she said. "I knew a girl in Marysville who could walk the ridgepole of a roof."

"I don't believe it," said Josie flatly. "I don't believe anybody could walk a ridgepole. YOU couldn't, anyhow."

"Couldn't I?" cried Anne rashly.

"Then I dare you to do it," said Josie defiantly. "I dare you to climb up there and walk the ridgepole of Mr. Barry's kitchen roof."

Anne turned pale, but there was clearly only one thing to be done. She walked toward the house, where a ladder was leaning against the kitchen roof. All the fifth-class girls said, "Oh!" partly in excitement, partly in dismay.

"Don't you do it, Anne," entreated Diana. "You'll fall off and be killed. Never mind Josie Pye. It isn't fair to dare anybody to do anything so dangerous."

"I must do it. My honor is at stake," said Anne solemnly. "I shall walk that ridgepole, Diana, or perish in the attempt. If I am killed you are to have my pearl bead ring."

Anne climbed the ladder amid breathless silence, gained the ridgepole, balanced herself uprightly on that precarious footing, and started to walk along it, dizzily conscious that she was uncomfortably high up in the world and that walking ridgepoles was not a thing in which your imagination helped you out much. Nevertheless, she managed to take several steps before the catastrophe came. Then she swayed, lost her balance, stumbled, staggered, and fell, sliding down over the sun-baked roof and crashing off it through the tangle of Virginia creeper beneath—all before the dismayed circle below could give a simultaneous, terrified shriek.

If Anne had tumbled off the roof on the side up which she had ascended Diana would probably have fallen heir to the pearl bead ring then and there. Fortunately she fell on the other side, where the roof extended down over the porch so nearly to the ground that a fall therefrom was a much less serious thing. Nevertheless, when Diana and the other girls had rushed frantically around the house—except Ruby Gillis, who remained as if rooted to the ground and went into hysterics—they found Anne lying all white and limp among the wreck and ruin of the Virginia creeper.

"Anne, are you killed?" shrieked Diana, throwing herself on her knees beside her friend. "Oh, Anne, dear Anne, speak just one word to me and tell me if you're killed."

To the immense relief of all the girls, and especially of Josie Pye, who, in spite of lack of imagination, had been seized with horrible visions of a future branded as the girl who was the cause of Anne Shirley's early and tragic death, Anne sat dizzily up and answered uncertainly:

"No, Diana, I am not killed, but I think I am rendered unconscious."

"Where?" sobbed Carrie Sloane. "Oh, where, Anne?" Before Anne could answer Mrs. Barry appeared on the scene. At sight of her Anne tried to scramble to her feet, but sank back again with a sharp little cry of pain.

"What's the matter? Where have you hurt yourself?" demanded Mrs. Barry.

"My ankle," gasped Anne. "Oh, Diana, please find your father and ask him to take me home. I know I can never walk there. And I'm sure I couldn't hop so far on one foot when Jane couldn't even hop around the garden."

Marilla was out in the orchard picking a panful of summer apples when she saw Mr. Barry coming over the log bridge and up the slope, with Mrs. Barry beside him and a whole procession of little girls trailing after him. In his arms he carried Anne, whose head lay limply against his shoulder.

At that moment Marilla had a revelation. In the sudden stab of fear that pierced her very heart she realized what Anne had come to mean to her. She would have admitted that she liked Anne—nay, that she was very fond of Anne. But now she knew as she hurried wildly down the slope that Anne was dearer to her than anything else on earth.

"Mr. Barry, what has happened to her?" she gasped, more white and shaken than the self-contained, sensible Marilla had been for many years.

Anne herself answered, lifting her head.

"Don't be very frightened, Marilla. I was walking the ridgepole and I fell off. I expect I have sprained my ankle. But, Marilla, I might have broken my neck. Let us look on the bright side of things."

"I might have known you'd go and do something of the sort when I let you go to that party," said Marilla, sharp and shrewish in her very relief. "Bring her in here, Mr. Barry, and lay her on the sofa. Mercy me, the child has gone and fainted!"

It was quite true. Overcome by the pain of her injury, Anne had one more of her wishes granted to her. She had fainted dead away.

Matthew, hastily summoned from the harvest field, was straightway dispatched for the doctor, who in due time came, to discover that the injury was more serious than they had supposed. Anne's ankle was broken.

That night, when Marilla went up to the east gable, where a white-faced girl was lying, a plaintive voice greeted her from the bed.

"Aren't you very sorry for me, Marilla?"

"It was your own fault," said Marilla, twitching down the blind and lighting a lamp.

"And that is just why you should be sorry for me," said Anne, "because the thought that it is all my own fault is what makes it so hard. If I could blame it on anybody I would feel so much better. But what would you have done, Marilla, if you had been dared to walk a ridgepole?"

"I'd have stayed on good firm ground and let them dare away. Such absurdity!" said Marilla.

Anne sighed.

"But you have such strength of mind, Marilla. I haven't. I just felt that I couldn't bear Josie Pye's scorn. She would have crowed over me all my life. And I think I have been punished so much that you needn't be very cross with me, Marilla. It's not a bit nice to faint, after all. And the doctor hurt me dreadfully when he was setting my ankle. I won't be able to go around for six or seven weeks and I'll miss the new lady teacher. She won't be new any more by the time I'm able to go to school. And Gil—everybody will get ahead of me in class. Oh, I am an afflicted mortal. But I'll try to bear it all bravely if only you won't be cross with me, Marilla."

"There, there, I'm not cross," said Marilla. "You're an unlucky child, there's no doubt about that; but as you say, you'll have the suffering of it. Here now, try and eat some supper."

"Isn't it fortunate I've got such an imagination?" said Anne. "It will help me through splendidly, I expect. What do people who haven't any imagination do when they break their bones, do you suppose, Marilla?"

Anne had good reason to bless her imagination many a time and oft during the tedious seven weeks that followed. But she was not solely dependent on it. She had many visitors and not a day passed without one or more of the schoolgirls dropping in to bring her flowers and books and tell her all the happenings in the juvenile world of Avonlea.

"Everybody has been so good and kind, Marilla," sighed Anne happily, on the day when she could first limp across the floor. "It isn't very pleasant to be laid up; but there is a bright side to it, Marilla. You find out how many friends you have. Why, even Superintendent Bell came to see me, and he's really a very fine man. Not a kindred spirit, of course; but still I like him and I'm awfully sorry I ever criticized his prayers. I believe now he really does mean them, only he has got into the habit of saying them as if he didn't. He could get over that if he'd take a little trouble. I gave him a good broad hint. I told him how hard I tried to make my own little private prayers interesting. He told me all about the time he broke his ankle when he was a boy. It does seem so strange to think of Superintendent Bell ever being a boy. Even my imagination has its limits, for I can't imagine THAT. When I try to imagine him as a boy I see him with gray whiskers and spectacles, just as he looks in Sunday school, only small. Now, it's so easy to imagine Mrs. Allan as a little girl. Mrs. Allan has been to see me fourteen times. Isn't that something to be proud of, Marilla? When a minister's wife has so many claims on her time! She is such a cheerful person to have visit you, too. She never tells you it's your own fault and she hopes you'll be a better girl on account of it. Mrs. Lynde always told me that when she came to see me; and she said it in a kind of way that made me feel she might hope I'd be a better girl but didn't really believe I would. Even Josie Pye came to see me. I received her as politely as I could, because I think she was sorry she dared me to walk a ridgepole. If I had been killed she would had to carry a dark burden of remorse all her life. Diana has been a faithful friend. She's been over every day to cheer my lonely pillow. But oh, I shall be so glad when I can go to school for I've heard such exciting things about the new teacher. The girls all think she is perfectly sweet. Diana says she has the loveliest fair curly hair and such fascinating eyes. She dresses beautifully, and her sleeve puffs are bigger than anybody else's in Avonlea. Every other Friday afternoon she has recitations and everybody has to say a piece or take part in a dialogue. Oh, it's just glorious to think of it. Josie Pye says she hates it but that is just because Josie has so little imagination. Diana and Ruby Gillis and Jane Andrews are preparing a dialogue, called 'A Morning Visit,' for next Friday. And the Friday afternoons they don't have recitations Miss Stacy takes them all to the woods for a 'field' day and they study ferns and flowers and birds. And they have physical culture exercises every morning and evening. Mrs. Lynde says she never heard of such goings on and it all comes of having a lady teacher. But I think it must be splendid and I believe I shall find that Miss Stacy is a kindred spirit."

"There's one thing plain to be seen, Anne," said Marilla, "and that is that your fall off the Barry roof hasn't injured your tongue at all."

CHAPTER XXIV. Miss Stacy and Her Pupils Get Up a Concert

It was October again when Anne was ready to go back to school—a glorious October, all red and gold, with mellow mornings when the valleys were filled with delicate mists as if the spirit of autumn had poured them in for the sun to drain—amethyst, pearl, silver, rose, and smoke-blue. The dews were so heavy that the fields glistened like cloth of silver and there were such heaps of rustling leaves in the hollows of many-stemmed woods to run crisply through. The Birch Path was a canopy of yellow and the ferns were sear and brown all along it. There was a tang in the very air that inspired the hearts of small maidens tripping, unlike snails, swiftly and willingly to school; and it WAS jolly to be back again at the little brown desk beside Diana, with Ruby Gillis nodding across the aisle and Carrie Sloane sending up notes and Julia Bell passing a "chew" of gum down from the back seat. Anne drew a long breath of happiness as she sharpened her pencil and arranged her picture cards in her desk. Life was certainly very interesting.

In the new teacher she found another true and helpful friend. Miss Stacy was a bright, sympathetic young woman with the happy gift of winning and holding the affections of her pupils and bringing out the best that was in them mentally and morally. Anne expanded like a flower under this wholesome influence and carried home to the admiring Matthew and the critical Marilla glowing accounts of schoolwork and aims.

"I love Miss Stacy with my whole heart, Marilla. She is so ladylike and she has such a sweet voice. When she pronounces my name I feel INSTINCTIVELY that she's spelling it with an E. We had recitations this afternoon. I just wish you could have been there to hear me recite 'Mary, Queen of Scots.' I just put my whole soul into it. Ruby Gillis told me coming home that the way I said the line, 'Now for my father's arm,' she said, 'my woman's heart farewell,' just made her blood run cold."

"Well now, you might recite it for me some of these days, out in the barn," suggested Matthew.

"Of course I will," said Anne meditatively, "but I won't be able to do it so well, I know. It won't be so exciting as it is when you have a whole schoolful before you hanging breathlessly on your words. I know I won't be able to make your blood run cold."

"Mrs. Lynde says it made HER blood run cold to see the boys climbing to the very tops of those big trees on Bell's hill after crows' nests last Friday," said Marilla. "I wonder at Miss Stacy for encouraging it."

"But we wanted a crow's nest for nature study," explained Anne. "That was on our field afternoon. Field afternoons are splendid, Marilla. And Miss Stacy explains everything so beautifully. We have to write compositions on our field afternoons and I write the best ones."

"It's very vain of you to say so then. You'd better let your teacher say it."

"But she DID say it, Marilla. And indeed I'm not vain about it. How can I be, when I'm such a dunce at geometry? Although I'm really beginning to see through it a little, too. Miss Stacy makes it so clear. Still, I'll never be good at it and I assure you it is a humbling reflection. But I love writing compositions. Mostly Miss Stacy lets us choose our own subjects; but next week we are to write a composition on some remarkable person. It's hard to choose among so many remarkable people who have lived. Mustn't it be splendid to be remarkable and have compositions written about you after you're dead? Oh, I would dearly love to be remarkable. I think when I grow up I'll be a trained nurse and go with the Red Crosses to the field of battle as a messenger of mercy. That is, if I don't go out as a foreign missionary. That would be very romantic, but one would have to be very good to be a missionary, and that would be a stumbling block. We have physical culture exercises every day, too. They make you graceful and promote digestion."

"Promote fiddlesticks!" said Marilla, who honestly thought it was all nonsense.

But all the field afternoons and recitation Fridays and physical culture contortions paled before a project which Miss Stacy brought forward in November. This was that the scholars of Avonlea school should get up a concert and hold it in the hall on Christmas Night, for the laudable purpose of helping to pay for a schoolhouse flag. The pupils one and all taking graciously to this plan, the preparations for a program were begun at once. And of all the excited performers-elect none was so excited as Anne Shirley, who threw herself into the undertaking heart and soul, hampered as she was by Marilla's disapproval. Marilla thought it all rank foolishness.

"It's just filling your heads up with nonsense and taking time that ought to be put on your lessons," she grumbled. "I don't approve of children's getting up concerts and racing about to practices. It makes them vain and forward and fond of gadding."

"But think of the worthy object," pleaded Anne. "A flag will cultivate a spirit of patriotism, Marilla."

"Fudge! There's precious little patriotism in the thoughts of any of you. All you want is a good time."

"Well, when you can combine patriotism and fun, isn't it all right? Of course it's real nice to be getting up a concert. We're going to have six choruses and Diana is to sing a solo. I'm in two dialogues—'The Society for the Suppression of

Gossip' and 'The Fairy Queen.' The boys are going to have a dialogue too. And I'm to have two recitations, Marilla. I just tremble when I think of it, but it's a nice thrilly kind of tremble. And we're to have a tableau at the last—'Faith, Hope and Charity.' Diana and Ruby and I are to be in it, all draped in white with flowing hair. I'm to be Hope, with my hands clasped—so—and my eyes uplifted. I'm going to practice my recitations in the garret. Don't be alarmed if you hear me groaning. I have to groan heartrendingly in one of them, and it's really hard to get up a good artistic groan, Marilla. Josie Pye is sulky because she didn't get the part she wanted in the dialogue. She wanted to be the fairy queen. That would have been ridiculous, for who ever heard of a fairy queen as fat as Josie? Fairy queens must be slender. Jane Andrews is to be the queen and I am to be one of her maids of honor. Josie says she thinks a red-haired fairy is just as ridiculous as a fat one, but I do not let myself mind what Josie says. I'm to have a wreath of white roses on my hair and Ruby Gillis is going to lend me her slippers because I haven't any of my own. It's necessary for fairies to have slippers, you know. You couldn't imagine a fairy wearing boots, could you? Especially with copper toes? We are going to decorate the hall with creeping spruce and fir mottoes with pink tissue-paper roses in them. And we are all to march in two by two after the audience is seated, while Emma White plays a march on the organ. Oh, Marilla, I know you are not so enthusiastic about it as I am, but don't you hope your little Anne will distinguish herself?"

"All I hope is that you'll behave yourself. I'll be heartily glad when all this fuss is over and you'll be able to settle down. You are simply good for nothing just now with your head stuffed full of dialogues and groans and tableaus. As for your tongue, it's a marvel it's not clean worn out."

Anne sighed and betook herself to the back yard, over which a young new moon was shining through the leafless poplar boughs from an apple-green western sky, and where Matthew was splitting wood. Anne perched herself on a block and talked the concert over with him, sure of an appreciative and sympathetic listener in this instance at least.

"Well now, I reckon it's going to be a pretty good concert. And I expect you'll do your part fine," he said, smiling down into her eager, vivacious little face. Anne smiled back at him. Those two were the best of friends and Matthew thanked his stars many a time and oft that he had nothing to do with bringing her up. That was Marilla's exclusive duty; if it had been his he would have been worried over frequent conflicts between inclination and said duty. As it was, he was free to, "spoil Anne"—Marilla's phrasing—as much as he liked. But it was not such a bad arrangement after all; a little "appreciation" sometimes does quite as much good as all the conscientious "bringing up" in the world.

CHAPTER XXV. Matthew Insists on Puffed Sleeves

Matthew was having a bad ten minutes of it. He had come into the kitchen, in the twilight of a cold, gray December evening, and had sat down in the woodbox corner to take off his heavy boots, unconscious of the fact that Anne and a bevy of her schoolmates were having a practice of "The Fairy Queen" in the sitting room. Presently they came trooping through the hall and out into the kitchen, laughing and chattering gaily. They did not see Matthew, who shrank bashfully back into the shadows beyond the woodbox with a boot in one hand and a bootjack in the other, and he watched them shyly for the aforesaid ten minutes as they put on caps and jackets and talked about the dialogue and the concert. Anne stood among them, bright eyed and animated as they; but Matthew suddenly became conscious that there was something about her different from her mates. And what worried Matthew was that the difference impressed him as being something that should not exist. Anne had a brighter face, and bigger, starrier eyes, and more delicate features than the other; even shy, unobservant Matthew had learned to take note of these things; but the difference that disturbed him did not consist in any of these respects. Then in what did it consist?

Matthew was haunted by this question long after the girls had gone, arm in arm, down the long, hard-frozen lane and Anne had betaken herself to her books. He could not refer it to Marilla, who, he felt, would be quite sure to sniff scornfully and remark that the only difference she saw between Anne and the other girls was that they sometimes kept their tongues quiet while Anne never did. This, Matthew felt, would be no great help.

He had recourse to his pipe that evening to help him study it out, much to Marilla's disgust. After two hours of smoking and hard reflection Matthew arrived at a solution of his problem. Anne was not dressed like the other girls!

The more Matthew thought about the matter the more he was convinced that Anne never had been dressed like the other girls—never since she had come to Green Gables. Marilla kept her clothed in plain, dark dresses, all made after the same unvarying pattern. If Matthew knew there was such a thing as fashion in dress it was as much as he did; but he was quite sure that Anne's sleeves did not look at all like the sleeves the other girls wore. He recalled the cluster of little girls he had seen around her that evening—all gay in waists of red and blue and pink and white—and he wondered why Marilla always kept her so plainly and soberly gowned.

Of course, it must be all right. Marilla knew best and Marilla was bringing her up. Probably some wise, inscrutable motive was to be served thereby. But surely it would do no harm to let the child have one pretty dress—something like Diana Barry always wore. Matthew decided that he would give her one; that surely could not be objected to as an unwarranted putting in of his oar. Christmas was only a fortnight off. A nice new dress would be the very thing for a present. Matthew, with a sigh of satisfaction, put away his pipe and went to bed, while Marilla opened all the doors and aired the house.

The very next evening Matthew betook himself to Carmody to buy the dress, determined to get the worst over and have done with it. It would be, he felt assured, no trifling ordeal. There were some things Matthew could buy and prove himself no mean bargainer; but he knew he would be at the mercy of shopkeepers when it came to buying a girl's dress.

After much cogitation Matthew resolved to go to Samuel Lawson's store instead of William Blair's. To be sure, the Cuthberts always had gone to William Blair's; it was almost as much a matter of conscience with them as to attend the Presbyterian church and vote Conservative. But William Blair's two daughters frequently waited on customers there and Matthew held them in absolute dread. He could contrive to deal with them when he knew exactly what he wanted and could point it out; but in such a matter as this, requiring explanation and consultation, Matthew felt that he must be sure of a man behind the counter. So he would go to Lawson's, where Samuel or his son would wait on him.

Alas! Matthew did not know that Samuel, in the recent expansion of his business, had set up a lady clerk also; she was a niece of his wife's and a very dashing young person indeed, with a huge, drooping pompadour, big, rolling brown eyes, and a most extensive and bewildering smile. She was dressed with exceeding smartness and wore several bangle bracelets that glittered and rattled and tinkled with every movement of her hands. Matthew was covered with confusion at finding her there at all; and those bangles completely wrecked his wits at one fell swoop.

"What can I do for you this evening, Mr. Cuthbert?" Miss Lucilla Harris inquired, briskly and ingratiatingly, tapping the counter with both hands.

"Have you any—any—any—well now, say any garden rakes?" stammered Matthew.

Miss Harris looked somewhat surprised, as well she might, to hear a man inquiring for garden rakes in the middle of December.

"I believe we have one or two left over," she said, "but they're upstairs in the lumber room. I'll go and see." During her absence Matthew collected his scattered senses for another effort.

When Miss Harris returned with the rake and cheerfully inquired: "Anything else tonight, Mr. Cuthbert?" Matthew took his courage in both hands and replied:

"Well now, since you suggest it, I might as well—take—that is—look at—buy some—some hayseed."

Miss Harris had heard Matthew Cuthbert called odd. She now concluded that he was entirely crazy.

"We only keep hayseed in the spring," she explained loftily. "We've none on hand just now."

"Oh, certainly—certainly—just as you say," stammered unhappy Matthew, seizing the rake and making for the door. At the threshold he recollected that he had not paid for it and he turned miserably back. While Miss Harris was counting out his change he rallied his powers for a final desperate attempt.

"Well now—if it isn't too much trouble—I might as well—that is—I'd like to look at—at—some sugar."

"White or brown?" queried Miss Harris patiently.

"Oh—well now—brown," said Matthew feebly.

"There's a barrel of it over there," said Miss Harris, shaking her bangles at it. "It's the only kind we have."

"I'll—I'll take twenty pounds of it," said Matthew, with beads of perspiration standing on his forehead.

Matthew had driven halfway home before he was his own man again. It had been a gruesome experience, but it served him right, he thought, for committing the heresy of going to a strange store. When he reached home he hid the rake in the tool house, but the sugar he carried in to Marilla.

"Brown sugar!" exclaimed Marilla. "Whatever possessed you to get so much? You know I never use it except for the hired man's porridge or black fruit cake. Jerry's gone and I've made my cake long ago. It's not good sugar, either—it's coarse and dark—William Blair doesn't usually keep sugar like that."

"I—I thought it might come in handy sometime," said Matthew, making good his escape.

When Matthew came to think the matter over he decided that a woman was required to cope with the situation. Marilla was out of the question. Matthew felt sure she would throw cold water on his project at once. Remained only Mrs. Lynde; for of no other woman in Avonlea would Matthew have dared to ask advice. To Mrs. Lynde he went accordingly, and that good lady promptly took the matter out of the harassed man's hands.

"Pick out a dress for you to give Anne? To be sure I will. I'm going to Carmody tomorrow and I'll attend to it. Have you something particular in mind? No? Well, I'll just go by my own judgment then. I believe a nice rich brown would just suit Anne, and William Blair has some new gloria in that's real pretty. Perhaps you'd like me to make it up for her, too, seeing that if Marilla was to make it Anne would probably get wind of it before the time and spoil the surprise? Well, I'll do it. No, it isn't a mite of trouble. I like sewing. I'll make it to fit my niece, Jenny Gillis, for she and Anne are as like as two peas as far as figure goes."

"Well now, I'm much obliged," said Matthew, "and—and—I dunno—but I'd like—I think they make the sleeves different nowadays to what they used to be. If it wouldn't be asking too much I—I'd like them made in the new way."

"Puffs? Of course. You needn't worry a speck more about it, Matthew. I'll make it up in the very latest fashion," said Mrs. Lynde. To herself she added when Matthew had gone:

"It'll be a real satisfaction to see that poor child wearing something decent for once. The way Marilla dresses her is positively ridiculous, that's what, and I've ached to tell her so plainly a dozen times. I've held my tongue though, for I can see Marilla doesn't want advice and she thinks she knows more about bringing children up than I do for all she's an old maid. But that's always the way. Folks that has brought up children know that there's no hard and fast method in the world that'll suit every child. But them as never have think it's all as plain and easy as Rule of Three—just set your three terms down so fashion, and the sum'll work out correct. But flesh and blood don't come under the head of arithmetic and that's where Marilla Cuthbert makes her mistake. I suppose she's trying to cultivate a spirit of humility in Anne by dressing her as she does; but it's more likely to cultivate envy and discontent. I'm sure the child must feel the difference between her clothes and the other girls'. But to think of Matthew taking notice of it! That man is waking up after being asleep for over sixty years."

Marilla knew all the following fortnight that Matthew had something on his mind, but what it was she could not guess, until Christmas Eve, when Mrs. Lynde brought up the new dress. Marilla behaved pretty well on the whole, although it is very likely she distrusted Mrs. Lynde's diplomatic explanation that she had made the dress because Matthew was afraid Anne would find out about it too soon if Marilla made it.

"So this is what Matthew has been looking so mysterious over and grinning about to himself for two weeks, is it?" she said a little stiffly but tolerantly. "I knew he was up to some foolishness. Well, I must say I don't think Anne needed any more dresses. I made her three good, warm, serviceable ones this fall, and anything more is sheer extravagance. There's enough material in those sleeves alone to make a waist, I declare there is. You'll just pamper Anne's vanity, Matthew, and she's as vain as a peacock now. Well, I hope she'll be satisfied at last, for I know she's been hankering after those silly sleeves ever since they came in, although she never said a word after the first. The puffs have been getting bigger and more ridiculous right along; they're as big as balloons now. Next year anybody who wears them will have to go through a door sideways."

Christmas morning broke on a beautiful white world. It had been a very mild December and people had looked forward to a green Christmas; but just enough snow fell softly in the night to transfigure Avonlea. Anne peeped out from her frosted gable window with delighted eyes. The firs in the Haunted Wood were all feathery and wonderful; the birches and wild cherry trees were outlined in pearl; the plowed fields were stretches of snowy dimples; and there was a crisp tang in the air that was glorious. Anne ran downstairs singing until her voice reechoed through Green Gables.

"Merry Christmas, Marilla! Merry Christmas, Matthew! Isn't it a lovely Christmas? I'm so glad it's white. Any other kind of Christmas doesn't seem real, does it? I don't like green Christmases. They're not green—they're just nasty faded browns and grays. What makes people call them green? Why—why—Matthew, is that for me? Oh, Matthew!"

Matthew had sheepishly unfolded the dress from its paper swathings and held it out with a deprecatory glance at Marilla, who feigned to be contemptuously filling the teapot, but nevertheless watched the scene out of the corner of her eye with a rather interested air.

Anne took the dress and looked at it in reverent silence. Oh, how pretty it was—a lovely soft brown gloria with all the gloss of silk; a skirt with dainty frills and shirrings; a waist elaborately pintucked in the most fashionable way, with a little ruffle of filmy lace at the neck. But the sleeves—they were the crowning glory! Long elbow cuffs, and above them two beautiful puffs divided by rows of shirring and bows of brown-silk ribbon.

"That's a Christmas present for you, Anne," said Matthew shyly. "Why— why—Anne, don't you like it? Well now—well now."

For Anne's eyes had suddenly filled with tears.

"Like it! Oh, Matthew!" Anne laid the dress over a chair and clasped her hands. "Matthew, it's perfectly exquisite. Oh, I can never thank you enough. Look at those sleeves! Oh, it seems to me this must be a happy dream."

"Well, well, let us have breakfast," interrupted Marilla. "I must say, Anne, I don't think you needed the dress; but since Matthew has got it for you, see that you take good care of it. There's a hair ribbon Mrs. Lynde left for you. It's brown, to match the dress. Come now, sit in."

"I don't see how I'm going to eat breakfast," said Anne rapturously. "Breakfast seems so commonplace at such an exciting moment. I'd rather feast my eyes on that dress. I'm so glad that puffed sleeves are still fashionable. It did seem to me that I'd never get over it if they went out before I had a dress with them. I'd never have felt quite satisfied, you see. It was lovely of Mrs. Lynde to give me the ribbon too. I feel that I ought to be a very good girl indeed. It's at times like this I'm sorry I'm not a model little girl; and I always resolve that I will be in future. But somehow it's hard to carry out your resolutions when irresistible temptations come. Still, I really will make an extra effort after this."

When the commonplace breakfast was over Diana appeared, crossing the white log bridge in the hollow, a gay little figure in her crimson ulster. Anne flew down the slope to meet her.

"Merry Christmas, Diana! And oh, it's a wonderful Christmas. I've something splendid to show you. Matthew has given me the loveliest dress, with SUCH sleeves. I couldn't even imagine any nicer."

"I've got something more for you," said Diana breathlessly. "Here—this box. Aunt Josephine sent us out a big box with ever so many things in it—and this is for you. I'd have brought it over last night, but it didn't come until after dark, and I never feel very comfortable coming through the Haunted Wood in the dark now."

Anne opened the box and peeped in. First a card with "For the Anne-girl and Merry Christmas," written on it; and then, a pair of the daintiest little kid slippers, with beaded toes and satin bows and glistening buckles.

"Oh," said Anne, "Diana, this is too much. I must be dreaming."

"I call it providential," said Diana. "You won't have to borrow Ruby's slippers now, and that's a blessing, for they're two sizes too big for you, and it would be awful to hear a fairy shuffling. Josie Pye would be delighted. Mind you, Rob Wright went home with Gertie Pye from the practice night before last. Did you ever hear anything equal to that?"

All the Avonlea scholars were in a fever of excitement that day, for the hall had to be decorated and a last grand rehearsal held.

The concert came off in the evening and was a pronounced success. The little hall was crowded; all the performers did excellently well, but Anne was the bright particular star of the occasion, as even envy, in the shape of Josie Pye, dared not deny.

"Oh, hasn't it been a brilliant evening?" sighed Anne, when it was all over and she and Diana were walking home together under a dark, starry sky.

"Everything went off very well," said Diana practically. "I guess we must have made as much as ten dollars. Mind you, Mr. Allan is going to send an account of it to the Charlottetown papers."

"Oh, Diana, will we really see our names in print? It makes me thrill to think of it. Your solo was perfectly elegant, Diana. I felt prouder than you did when it was encored. I just said to myself, 'It is my dear bosom friend who is so honored.'"

"Well, your recitations just brought down the house, Anne. That sad one was simply splendid."

"Oh, I was so nervous, Diana. When Mr. Allan called out my name I really cannot tell how I ever got up on that platform. I felt as if a million eyes were looking at me and through me, and for one dreadful moment I was sure I couldn't begin at all. Then I thought of my lovely puffed sleeves and took courage. I knew that I must live up to those sleeves, Diana. So I started in, and my voice seemed to be coming from ever so far away. I just felt like a parrot. It's providential that I practiced those recitations so often up in the garret, or I'd never have been able to get through. Did I groan all right?"

"Yes, indeed, you groaned lovely," assured Diana.

"I saw old Mrs. Sloane wiping away tears when I sat down. It was splendid to think I had touched somebody's heart. It's so romantic to take part in a concert, isn't it? Oh, it's been a very memorable occasion indeed."

"Wasn't the boys' dialogue fine?" said Diana. "Gilbert Blythe was just splendid. Anne, I do think it's awful mean the way you treat Gil. Wait till I tell you. When you ran off the platform after the fairy dialogue one of your roses fell out of your hair. I saw Gil pick it up and put it in his breast pocket. There now. You're so romantic that I'm sure you ought to be pleased at that."

"It's nothing to me what that person does," said Anne loftily. "I simply never waste a thought on him, Diana."

That night Marilla and Matthew, who had been out to a concert for the first time in twenty years, sat for a while by the kitchen fire after Anne had gone to bed.

"Well now, I guess our Anne did as well as any of them," said Matthew proudly.

"Yes, she did," admitted Marilla. "She's a bright child, Matthew. And she looked real nice too. I've been kind of opposed to this concert scheme, but I suppose there's no real harm in it after all. Anyhow, I was proud of Anne tonight, although I'm not going to tell her so."

"Well now, I was proud of her and I did tell her so 'fore she went upstairs," said Matthew. "We must see what we can do for her some of these days, Marilla. I guess she'll need something more than Avonlea school by and by."

"There's time enough to think of that," said Marilla. "She's only thirteen in March. Though tonight it struck me she was growing quite a big girl. Mrs. Lynde made that dress a mite too long, and it makes Anne look so tall. She's quick to learn and I guess the best thing we can do for her will be to send her to Queen's after a spell. But nothing need be said about that for a year or two yet."

"Well now, it'll do no harm to be thinking it over off and on," said Matthew. "Things like that are all the better for lots of thinking over."

CHAPTER XXVI. The Story Club Is Formed

Junior Avonlea found it hard to settle down to humdrum existence again. To Anne in particular things seemed fearfully flat, stale, and unprofitable after the goblet of excitement she had been sipping for weeks. Could she go back to the former quiet pleasures of those faraway days before the concert? At first, as she told Diana, she did not really think she could.

"I'm positively certain, Diana, that life can never be quite the same again as it was in those olden days," she said mournfully, as if referring to a period of at least fifty years back. "Perhaps after a while I'll get used to it, but I'm afraid concerts spoil people for everyday life. I suppose that is why Marilla disapproves of them. Marilla is such a sensible woman. It must be a great deal better to be sensible; but still, I don't believe I'd really want to be a sensible person, because they are so unromantic. Mrs. Lynde says there is no danger of my ever being one, but you can never tell. I feel just now that I may grow up to be sensible yet. But perhaps that is only because I'm tired. I simply couldn't sleep last night for ever so long. I just lay awake and imagined the concert over and over again. That's one splendid thing about such affairs—it's so lovely to look back to them."

Eventually, however, Avonlea school slipped back into its old groove and took up its old interests. To be sure, the concert left traces. Ruby Gillis and Emma White, who had quarreled over a point of precedence in their platform seats, no longer sat at the same desk, and a promising friendship of three years was broken up. Josie Pye and Julia Bell did not "speak" for three months, because Josie Pye had told Bessie Wright that Julia Bell's bow when she got up to recite made her think of a chicken jerking its head, and Bessie told Julia. None of the Sloanes would have any dealings with the Bells, because the Bells had declared that the Sloanes had too much to do in the program, and the Sloanes had retorted that the Bells were not capable of doing the little they had to do properly. Finally, Charlie Sloane fought Moody Spurgeon MacPherson, because Moody Spurgeon had said that Anne Shirley put on airs about her recitations, and Moody Spurgeon was "licked"; consequently Moody Spurgeon's sister, Ella May, would not "speak" to Anne Shirley all the rest of the winter. With the exception of these trifling frictions, work in Miss Stacy's little kingdom went on with regularity and smoothness.

The winter weeks slipped by. It was an unusually mild winter, with so little snow that Anne and Diana could go to school nearly every day by way of the Birch Path. On Anne's birthday they were tripping lightly down it, keeping eyes and ears alert amid all their chatter, for Miss Stacy had told them that they must soon write a composition on "A Winter's Walk in the Woods," and it behooved them to be observant.

"Just think, Diana, I'm thirteen years old today," remarked Anne in an awed voice. "I can scarcely realize that I'm in my teens. When I woke this morning it seemed to me that everything must be different. You've been thirteen for a month, so I suppose it doesn't seem such a novelty to you as it does to me. It makes life seem so much more interesting. In two more years I'll be really grown up. It's a great comfort to think that I'll be able to use big words then without being laughed at."

"Ruby Gillis says she means to have a beau as soon as she's fifteen," said Diana.

"Ruby Gillis thinks of nothing but beaus," said Anne disdainfully. "She's actually delighted when anyone writes her name up in a take-notice for all she pretends to be so mad. But I'm afraid that is an uncharitable speech. Mrs. Allan says we should never make uncharitable speeches; but they do slip out so often before you think, don't they? I simply can't talk about Josie Pye without making an uncharitable speech, so I never mention her at all. You may have noticed that. I'm trying to be as much like Mrs. Allan as I possibly can, for I think she's perfect. Mr. Allan thinks so too. Mrs. Lynde says he just worships the ground she treads on and she doesn't really think it right for a minister to set his affections so much on a mortal being. But then, Diana, even ministers are human and have their besetting sins just like everybody else. I had such an interesting talk with Mrs. Allan about besetting sins last Sunday afternoon. There are just a few things it's proper to talk about on Sundays and that is one of them. My besetting sin is imagining too much and forgetting my duties. I'm striving very hard to overcome it and now that I'm really thirteen perhaps I'll get on better."

"In four more years we'll be able to put our hair up," said Diana. "Alice Bell is only sixteen and she is wearing hers up, but I think that's ridiculous. I shall wait until I'm seventeen."

"If I had Alice Bell's crooked nose," said Anne decidedly, "I wouldn't—but there! I won't say what I was going to because it was extremely uncharitable. Besides, I was comparing it with my own nose and that's vanity. I'm afraid I think too much about my nose ever since I heard that compliment about it long ago. It really is a great comfort to me. Oh, Diana, look, there's a rabbit. That's something to remember for our woods composition. I really think the woods are just as lovely in winter as in summer. They're so white and still, as if they were asleep and dreaming pretty dreams."

"I won't mind writing that composition when its time comes," sighed Diana. "I can manage to write about the woods, but the one we're to hand in Monday is terrible. The idea of Miss Stacy telling us to write a story out of our own heads!"

CHAPTER XXVI. The Story Club Is Formed

"Why, it's as easy as wink," said Anne.

"It's easy for you because you have an imagination," retorted Diana, "but what would you do if you had been born without one? I suppose you have your composition all done?"

Anne nodded, trying hard not to look virtuously complacent and failing miserably.

"I wrote it last Monday evening. It's called 'The Jealous Rival; or In Death Not Divided.' I read it to Marilla and she said it was stuff and nonsense. Then I read it to Matthew and he said it was fine. That is the kind of critic I like. It's a sad, sweet story. I just cried like a child while I was writing it. It's about two beautiful maidens called Cordelia Montmorency and Geraldine Seymour who lived in the same village and were devotedly attached to each other. Cordelia was a regal brunette with a coronet of midnight hair and duskly flashing eyes. Geraldine was a queenly blonde with hair like spun gold and velvety purple eyes."

"I never saw anybody with purple eyes," said Diana dubiously.

"Neither did I. I just imagined them. I wanted something out of the common. Geraldine had an alabaster brow too. I've found out what an alabaster brow is. That is one of the advantages of being thirteen. You know so much more than you did when you were only twelve."

"Well, what became of Cordelia and Geraldine?" asked Diana, who was beginning to feel rather interested in their fate.

"They grew in beauty side by side until they were sixteen. Then Bertram DeVere came to their native village and fell in love with the fair Geraldine. He saved her life when her horse ran away with her in a carriage, and she fainted in his arms and he carried her home three miles; because, you understand, the carriage was all smashed up. I found it rather hard to imagine the proposal because I had no experience to go by. I asked Ruby Gillis if she knew anything about how men proposed because I thought she'd likely be an authority on the subject, having so many sisters married. Ruby told me she was hid in the hall pantry when Malcolm Andres proposed to her sister Susan. She said Malcolm told Susan that his dad had given him the farm in his own name and then said, 'What do you say, darling pet, if we get hitched this fall?' And Susan said, 'Yes—no—I don't know—let me see'—and there they were, engaged as quick as that. But I didn't think that sort of a proposal was a very romantic one, so in the end I had to imagine it out as well as I could. I made it very flowery and poetical and Bertram went on his knees, although Ruby Gillis says it isn't done nowadays. Geraldine accepted him in a speech a page long. I can tell you I took a lot of trouble with that speech. I rewrote it five times and I look upon it as my masterpiece. Bertram gave her a diamond ring and a ruby necklace and told her they would go to Europe for a wedding tour, for he was immensely wealthy. But then, alas, shadows began to darken over their path. Cordelia was secretly in love with Bertram herself and when Geraldine told her about the engagement she was simply furious, especially when she saw the necklace and the diamond ring. All her affection for Geraldine turned to bitter hate and she vowed that she should never marry Bertram. But she pretended to be Geraldine's friend the same as ever. One evening they were standing on the bridge over a rushing turbulent stream and Cordelia, thinking they were alone, pushed Geraldine over the brink with a wild, mocking, 'Ha, ha, ha.' But Bertram saw it all and he at once plunged into the current, exclaiming, 'I will save thee, my peerless Geraldine.' But alas, he had forgotten he couldn't swim, and they were both drowned, clasped in each other's arms. Their bodies were washed ashore soon afterwards. They were buried in the one grave and their funeral was most imposing, Diana. It's so much more romantic to end a story up with a funeral than a wedding. As for Cordelia, she went insane with remorse and was shut up in a lunatic asylum. I thought that was a poetical retribution for her crime."

"How perfectly lovely!" sighed Diana, who belonged to Matthew's school of critics. "I don't see how you can make up such thrilling things out of your own head, Anne. I wish my imagination was as good as yours."

"It would be if you'd only cultivate it," said Anne cheeringly. "I've just thought of a plan, Diana. Let you and me have a story club all our own and write stories for practice. I'll help you along until you can do them by yourself. You ought to cultivate your imagination, you know. Miss Stacy says so. Only we must take the right way. I told her about the Haunted Wood, but she said we went the wrong way about it in that."

This was how the story club came into existence. It was limited to Diana and Anne at first, but soon it was extended to include Jane Andrews and Ruby Gillis and one or two others who felt that their imaginations needed cultivating. No boys were allowed in it—although Ruby Gillis opined that their admission would make it more exciting—and each member had to produce one story a week.

"It's extremely interesting," Anne told Marilla. "Each girl has to read her story out loud and then we talk it over. We are going to keep them all sacredly and have them to read to our descendants. We each write under a nom-de-plume. Mine is Rosamond Montmorency. All the girls do pretty well. Ruby Gillis is rather sentimental. She puts too much lovemaking into her stories and you know too much is worse than too little. Jane never puts any because she says it makes her feel so silly when she had to read it out loud. Jane's stories are extremely sensible. Then Diana puts too many murders into hers. She says most of the time she doesn't know what to do with the people so she kills them off to get rid of them. I mostly always have to tell them what to write about, but that isn't hard for I've millions of ideas."

"I think this story-writing business is the foolishest yet," scoffed Marilla. "You'll get a pack of nonsense into your heads and waste time that should be put on your lessons. Reading stories is bad enough but writing them is worse."

"But we're so careful to put a moral into them all, Marilla," explained Anne. "I insist upon that. All the good people are rewarded and all the bad ones are suitably punished. I'm sure that must have a wholesome effect. The moral is the great thing. Mr. Allan says so. I read one of my stories to him and Mrs. Allan and they both agreed that the moral was excellent. Only they laughed in the wrong places. I like it better when people cry. Jane and Ruby almost always cry when I come to the pathetic parts. Diana wrote her Aunt Josephine about our club and her Aunt Josephine wrote back that we were to send her some of our stories. So we copied out four of our very best and sent them. Miss Josephine Barry wrote back that she had never read anything so amusing in her life. That kind of puzzled us because the stories were all very pathetic and almost everybody died. But I'm glad Miss Barry liked them. It shows our club is doing some good in the world. Mrs. Allan says that ought to be our object in everything. I do really try to make it my object but I forget so often when I'm having fun. I hope I shall be a little like Mrs. Allan when I grow up. Do you think there is any prospect of it, Marilla?"

"I shouldn't say there was a great deal" was Marilla's encouraging answer. "I'm sure Mrs. Allan was never such a silly, forgetful little girl as you are."

"No; but she wasn't always so good as she is now either," said Anne seriously. "She told me so herself—that is, she said she was a dreadful mischief when she was a girl and was always getting into scrapes. I felt so encouraged when I heard that. Is it very wicked of me, Marilla, to feel encouraged when I hear that other people have been bad and mischievous? Mrs. Lynde says it is. Mrs. Lynde says she always feels shocked when she hears of anyone ever having been naughty, no matter how small they were. Mrs. Lynde says she once heard a minister confess that when he was a boy he stole a strawberry tart out of his aunt's pantry and she never had any respect for that minister again. Now, I wouldn't have felt that way. I'd have thought that it was real noble of him to confess it, and I'd have thought what an encouraging thing it would be for small boys nowadays who do naughty things and are sorry for them to know that perhaps they may grow up to be ministers in spite of it. That's how I'd feel, Marilla."

"The way I feel at present, Anne," said Marilla, "is that it's high time you had those dishes washed. You've taken half an hour longer than you should with all your chattering. Learn to work first and talk afterwards."

CHAPTER XXVII. Vanity and Vexation of Spirit

Marilla, walking home one late April evening from an Aid meeting, realized that the winter was over and gone with the thrill of delight that spring never fails to bring to the oldest and saddest as well as to the youngest and merriest. Marilla was not given to subjective analysis of her thoughts and feelings. She probably imagined that she was thinking about the Aids and their missionary box and the new carpet for the vestry room, but under these reflections was a harmonious consciousness of red fields smoking into pale-purply mists in the declining sun, of long, sharp-pointed fir shadows falling over the meadow beyond the brook, of still, crimson-budded maples around a mirrorlike wood pool, of a wakening in the world and a stir of hidden pulses under the gray sod. The spring was abroad in the land and Marilla's sober, middle-aged step was lighter and swifter because of its deep, primal gladness.

Her eyes dwelt affectionately on Green Gables, peering through its network of trees and reflecting the sunlight back from its windows in several little coruscations of glory. Marilla, as she picked her steps along the damp lane, thought that it was really a satisfaction to know that she was going home to a briskly snapping wood fire and a table nicely spread for tea, instead of to the cold comfort of old Aid meeting evenings before Anne had come to Green Gables.

Consequently, when Marilla entered her kitchen and found the fire black out, with no sign of Anne anywhere, she felt justly disappointed and irritated. She had told Anne to be sure and have tea ready at five o'clock, but now she must hurry to take off her second-best dress and prepare the meal herself against Matthew's return from plowing.

"I'll settle Miss Anne when she comes home," said Marilla grimly, as she shaved up kindlings with a carving knife and with more vim than was strictly necessary. Matthew had come in and was waiting patiently for his tea in his corner. "She's gadding off somewhere with Diana, writing stories or practicing dialogues or some such tomfoolery, and never thinking once about the time or her duties. She's just got to be pulled up short and sudden on this sort of thing. I don't care if Mrs. Allan does say she's the brightest and sweetest child she ever knew. She may be bright and sweet enough, but her head is full of nonsense and there's never any knowing what shape it'll break out in next. Just as soon as she grows out of one freak she takes up with another. But there! Here I am saying the very thing I was so riled with Rachel Lynde for saying at the Aid today. I was real glad when Mrs. Allan spoke up for Anne, for if she hadn't I know I'd have said something too sharp to Rachel before everybody. Anne's got plenty of faults, goodness knows, and far be it from me to deny it. But I'm bringing her up and not Rachel Lynde, who'd pick faults in the Angel Gabriel himself if he lived in Avonlea. Just the same, Anne has no business to leave the house like this when I told her she was to stay home this afternoon and look after things. I must say, with all her faults, I never found her disobedient or untrustworthy before and I'm real sorry to find her so now."

"Well now, I dunno," said Matthew, who, being patient and wise and, above all, hungry, had deemed it best to let Marilla talk her wrath out unhindered, having learned by experience that she got through with whatever work was on hand much quicker if not delayed by untimely argument. "Perhaps you're judging her too hasty, Marilla. Don't call her untrustworthy until you're sure she has disobeyed you. Mebbe it can all be explained—Anne's a great hand at explaining."

"She's not here when I told her to stay," retorted Marilla. "I reckon she'll find it hard to explain THAT to my satisfaction. Of course I knew you'd take her part, Matthew. But I'm bringing her up, not you."

It was dark when supper was ready, and still no sign of Anne, coming hurriedly over the log bridge or up Lover's Lane, breathless and repentant with a sense of neglected duties. Marilla washed and put away the dishes grimly. Then, wanting a candle to light her way down the cellar, she went up to the east gable for the one that generally stood on Anne's table. Lighting it, she turned around to see Anne herself lying on the bed, face downward among the pillows.

"Mercy on us," said astonished Marilla, "have you been asleep, Anne?"

"No," was the muffled reply.

"Are you sick then?" demanded Marilla anxiously, going over to the bed.

Anne cowered deeper into her pillows as if desirous of hiding herself forever from mortal eyes.

"No. But please, Marilla, go away and don't look at me. I'm in the depths of despair and I don't care who gets head in class or writes the best composition or sings in the Sunday-school choir any more. Little things like that are of no importance now because I don't suppose I'll ever be able to go anywhere again. My career is closed. Please, Marilla, go away and don't look at me."

"Did anyone ever hear the like?" the mystified Marilla wanted to know. "Anne Shirley, whatever is the matter with you? What have you done? Get right up this minute and tell me. This minute, I say. There now, what is it?"

Anne had slid to the floor in despairing obedience.

"Look at my hair, Marilla," she whispered.

Accordingly, Marilla lifted her candle and looked scrutinizingly at Anne's hair, flowing in heavy masses down her back. It certainly had a very strange appearance.

"Anne Shirley, what have you done to your hair? Why, it's GREEN!"

Green it might be called, if it were any earthly color—a queer, dull, bronzy green, with streaks here and there of the original red to heighten the ghastly effect. Never in all her life had Marilla seen anything so grotesque as Anne's hair at that moment.

"Yes, it's green," moaned Anne. "I thought nothing could be as bad as red hair. But now I know it's ten times worse to have green hair. Oh, Marilla, you little know how utterly wretched I am."

"I little know how you got into this fix, but I mean to find out," said Marilla. "Come right down to the kitchen—it's too cold up here—and tell me just what you've done. I've been expecting something queer for some time. You haven't got into any scrape for over two months, and I was sure another one was due. Now, then, what did you do to your hair?"

"I dyed it."

"Dyed it! Dyed your hair! Anne Shirley, didn't you know it was a wicked thing to do?"

"Yes, I knew it was a little wicked," admitted Anne. "But I thought it was worth while to be a little wicked to get rid of red hair. I counted the cost, Marilla. Besides, I meant to be extra good in other ways to make up for it."

"Well," said Marilla sarcastically, "if I'd decided it was worth while to dye my hair I'd have dyed it a decent color at least. I wouldn't have dyed it green."

"But I didn't mean to dye it green, Marilla," protested Anne dejectedly. "If I was wicked I meant to be wicked to some purpose. He said it would turn my hair a beautiful raven black—he positively assured me that it would. How could I doubt his word, Marilla? I know what it feels like to have your word doubted. And Mrs. Allan says we should never suspect anyone of not telling us the truth unless we have proof that they're not. I have proof now—green hair is proof enough for anybody. But I hadn't then and I believed every word he said IMPLICITLY."

"Who said? Who are you talking about?"

"The peddler that was here this afternoon. I bought the dye from him."

"Anne Shirley, how often have I told you never to let one of those Italians in the house! I don't believe in encouraging them to come around at all."

"Oh, I didn't let him in the house. I remembered what you told me, and I went out, carefully shut the door, and looked at his things on the step. Besides, he wasn't an Italian—he was a German Jew. He had a big box full of very interesting things and he told me he was working hard to make enough money to bring his wife and children out from Germany. He spoke so feelingly about them that it touched my heart. I wanted to buy something from him to help him in such a worthy object. Then all at once I saw the bottle of hair dye. The peddler said it was warranted to dye any hair a beautiful raven black and wouldn't wash off. In a trice I saw myself with beautiful raven-black hair and the temptation was irresistible. But the price of the bottle was seventy-five cents and I had only fifty cents left out of my chicken money. I think the peddler had a very kind heart, for he said that, seeing it was me, he'd sell it for fifty cents and that was just giving it away. So I bought it, and as soon as he had gone I came up here and applied it with an old hairbrush as the directions said. I used up the whole bottle, and oh, Marilla, when I saw the dreadful color it turned my hair I repented of being wicked, I can tell you. And I've been repenting ever since."

"Well, I hope you'll repent to good purpose," said Marilla severely, "and that you've got your eyes opened to where your vanity has led you, Anne. Goodness knows what's to be done. I suppose the first thing is to give your hair a good washing and see if that will do any good."

Accordingly, Anne washed her hair, scrubbing it vigorously with soap and water, but for all the difference it made she might as well have been scouring its original red. The peddler had certainly spoken the truth when he declared that the dye wouldn't wash off, however his veracity might be impeached in other respects.

"Oh, Marilla, what shall I do?" questioned Anne in tears. "I can never live this down. People have pretty well forgotten my other mistakes—the liniment cake and setting Diana drunk and flying into a temper with Mrs. Lynde. But they'll never forget this. They will think I am not respectable. Oh, Marilla, 'what a tangled web we weave when first we practice to deceive.' That is poetry, but it is true. And oh, how Josie Pye will laugh! Marilla, I CANNOT face Josie Pye. I am the unhappiest girl in Prince Edward Island."

Anne's unhappiness continued for a week. During that time she went nowhere and shampooed her hair every day. Diana alone of outsiders knew the fatal secret, but she promised solemnly never to tell, and it may be stated here and now that she kept her word. At the end of the week Marilla said decidedly:

"It's no use, Anne. That is fast dye if ever there was any. Your hair must be cut off; there is no other way. You can't go out with it looking like that."

Anne's lips quivered, but she realized the bitter truth of Marilla's remarks. With a dismal sigh she went for the scissors.

"Please cut it off at once, Marilla, and have it over. Oh, I feel that my heart is broken. This is such an unromantic affliction. The girls in books lose their hair in fevers or sell it to get money for some good deed, and I'm sure I wouldn't mind losing my hair in some such fashion half so much. But there is nothing comforting in having your hair cut off because you've dyed it a dreadful color, is there? I'm going to weep all the time you're cutting it off, if it won't interfere. It seems such a tragic thing."

Anne wept then, but later on, when she went upstairs and looked in the glass, she was calm with despair. Marilla had done her work thoroughly and it had been necessary to shingle the hair as closely as possible. The result was not becoming, to state the case as mildly as may be. Anne promptly turned her glass to the wall.

"I'll never, never look at myself again until my hair grows," she exclaimed passionately.

Then she suddenly righted the glass.

"Yes, I will, too. I'd do penance for being wicked that way. I'll look at myself every time I come to my room and see how ugly I am. And I won't try to imagine it away, either. I never thought I was vain about my hair, of all things, but now I know I was, in spite of its being red, because it was so long and thick and curly. I expect something will happen to my nose next."

Anne's clipped head made a sensation in school on the following Monday, but to her relief nobody guessed the real reason for it, not even Josie Pye, who, however, did not fail to inform Anne that she looked like a perfect scarecrow.

"I didn't say anything when Josie said that to me," Anne confided that evening to Marilla, who was lying on the sofa after one of her headaches, "because I thought it was part of my punishment and I ought to bear it patiently. It's hard to be told you look like a scarecrow and I wanted to say something back. But I didn't. I just swept her one scornful look and then I forgave her. It makes you feel very virtuous when you forgive people, doesn't it? I mean to devote all my energies to being good after this and I shall never try to be beautiful again. Of course it's better to be good. I know it is, but it's sometimes so hard to believe a thing even when you know it. I do really want to be good, Marilla, like you and Mrs. Allan and Miss Stacy, and grow up to be a credit to you. Diana says when my hair begins to grow to tie a black velvet ribbon around my head with a bow at one side. She says she thinks it will be very becoming. I will call it a snood—that sounds so romantic. But am I talking too much, Marilla? Does it hurt your head?"

"My head is better now. It was terrible bad this afternoon, though. These headaches of mine are getting worse and worse. I'll have to see a doctor about them. As for your chatter, I don't know that I mind it—I've got so used to it."

Which was Marilla's way of saying that she liked to hear it.

CHAPTER XXVIII. An Unfortunate Lily Maid

"OF course you must be Elaine, Anne," said Diana. "I could never have the courage to float down there."

"Nor I," said Ruby Gillis, with a shiver. "I don't mind floating down when there's two or three of us in the flat and we can sit up. It's fun then. But to lie down and pretend I was dead—I just couldn't. I'd die really of fright."

"Of course it would be romantic," conceded Jane Andrews, "but I know I couldn't keep still. I'd be popping up every minute or so to see where I was and if I wasn't drifting too far out. And you know, Anne, that would spoil the effect."

"But it's so ridiculous to have a redheaded Elaine," mourned Anne. "I'm not afraid to float down and I'd love to be Elaine. But it's ridiculous just the same. Ruby ought to be Elaine because she is so fair and has such lovely long golden hair—Elaine had 'all her bright hair streaming down,' you know. And Elaine was the lily maid. Now, a red-haired person cannot be a lily maid."

"Your complexion is just as fair as Ruby's," said Diana earnestly, "and your hair is ever so much darker than it used to be before you cut it."

"Oh, do you really think so?" exclaimed Anne, flushing sensitively with delight. "I've sometimes thought it was myself—but I never dared to ask anyone for fear she would tell me it wasn't. Do you think it could be called auburn now, Diana?"

"Yes, and I think it is real pretty," said Diana, looking admiringly at the short, silky curls that clustered over Anne's head and were held in place by a very jaunty black velvet ribbon and bow.

They were standing on the bank of the pond, below Orchard Slope, where a little headland fringed with birches ran out from the bank; at its tip was a small wooden platform built out into the water for the convenience of fishermen and duck hunters. Ruby and Jane were spending the midsummer afternoon with Diana, and Anne had come over to play with them.

Anne and Diana had spent most of their playtime that summer on and about the pond. Idlewild was a thing of the past, Mr. Bell having ruthlessly cut down the little circle of trees in his back pasture in the spring. Anne had sat among the stumps and wept, not without an eye to the romance of it; but she was speedily consoled, for, after all, as she and Diana said, big girls of thirteen, going on fourteen, were too old for such childish amusements as playhouses, and there were more fascinating sports to be found about the pond. It was splendid to fish for trout over the bridge and the two girls learned to row themselves about in the little flat-bottomed dory Mr. Barry kept for duck shooting.

It was Anne's idea that they dramatize Elaine. They had studied Tennyson's poem in school the preceding winter, the Superintendent of Education having pre-scribed it in the English course for the Prince Edward Island schools. They had analyzed and parsed it and torn it to pieces in general until it was a wonder there was any meaning at all left in it for them, but at least the fair lily maid and Lance-lot and Guinevere and King Arthur had become very real people to them, and Anne was devoured by secret regret that she had not been born in Camelot. Those days, she said, were so much more romantic than the present.

Anne's plan was hailed with enthusiasm. The girls had discovered that if the flat were pushed off from the landing place it would drift down with the current under the bridge and finally strand itself on another headland lower down which ran out at a curve in the pond. They had often gone down like this and nothing could be more convenient for playing Elaine.

"Well, I'll be Elaine," said Anne, yielding reluctantly, for, although she would have been delighted to play the principal character, yet her artistic sense demand-ed fitness for it and this, she felt, her limitations made impossible. "Ruby, you must be King Arthur and Jane will be Guinevere and Diana must be Lancelot. But first you must be the brothers and the father. We can't have the old dumb servitor because there isn't room for two in the flat when one is lying down. We must pall the barge all its length in blackest samite. That old black shawl of your mother's will be just the thing, Diana."

The black shawl having been procured, Anne spread it over the flat and then lay down on the bottom, with closed eyes and hands folded over her breast.

"Oh, she does look really dead," whispered Ruby Gillis nervously, watching the still, white little face under the flickering shadows of the birches. "It makes me feel frightened, girls. Do you suppose it's really right to act like this? Mrs. Lynde says that all play-acting is abominably wicked."

"Ruby, you shouldn't talk about Mrs. Lynde," said Anne severely. "It spoils the effect because this is hundreds of years before Mrs. Lynde was born. Jane, you arrange this. It's silly for Elaine to be talking when she's dead."

Jane rose to the occasion. Cloth of gold for coverlet there was none, but an old piano scarf of yellow Japanese crepe was an excellent substitute. A white lily was not obtainable just then, but the effect of a tall blue iris placed in one of Anne's folded hands was all that could be desired.

"Now, she's all ready," said Jane. "We must kiss her quiet brows and, Diana, you say, 'Sister, farewell forever,' and Ruby, you say, 'Farewell, sweet sister,' both of you as sorrowfully as you possibly can. Anne, for goodness sake smile a little. You know Elaine 'lay as though she smiled.' That's better. Now push the flat off."

The flat was accordingly pushed off, scraping roughly over an old embedded stake in the process. Diana and Jane and Ruby only waited long enough to see it caught in the current and headed for the bridge before scampering up through the woods, across the road, and down to the lower headland where, as Lancelot and Guinevere and the King, they were to be in readiness to receive the lily maid.

For a few minutes Anne, drifting slowly down, enjoyed the romance of her situation to the full. Then something happened not at all romantic. The flat began to leak. In a very few moments it was necessary for Elaine to scramble to her feet, pick up her cloth of gold coverlet and pall of blackest samite and gaze blankly at a big crack in the bottom of her barge through which the water was literally pouring. That sharp stake at the landing had torn off the strip of batting nailed on the flat. Anne did not know this, but it did not take her long to realize that she was in a dangerous plight. At this rate the flat would fill and sink long before it could drift to the lower headland. Where were the oars? Left behind at the landing!

Anne gave one gasping little scream which nobody ever heard; she was white to the lips, but she did not lose her self-possession. There was one chance—just one.

"I was horribly frightened," she told Mrs. Allan the next day, "and it seemed like years while the flat was drifting down to the bridge and the water rising in it every moment. I prayed, Mrs. Allan, most earnestly, but I didn't shut my eyes to pray, for I knew the only way God could save me was to let the flat float close enough to one of the bridge piles for me to climb up on it. You know the piles are just old tree trunks and there are lots of knots and old branch stubs on them. It was proper to pray, but I had to do my part by watching out and right well I knew it. I just said, 'Dear God, please take the flat close to a pile and I'll do the rest,' over and over again. Under such circumstances you don't think much about making a flowery prayer. But mine was answered, for the flat bumped right into a pile for a minute and I flung the scarf and the shawl over my shoulder and scrambled up on a big providential stub. And there I was, Mrs. Allan, clinging to that slippery old pile with no way of getting up or down. It was a very unromantic position, but I didn't think about that at the time. You don't think much about romance when you have just escaped from a watery grave. I said a grateful prayer at once and then I gave all my attention to holding on tight, for I knew I should probably have to depend on human aid to get back to dry land."

The flat drifted under the bridge and then promptly sank in midstream. Ruby, Jane, and Diana, already awaiting it on the lower headland, saw it disappear before their very eyes and had not a doubt but that Anne had gone down with it. For a moment they stood still, white as sheets, frozen with horror at the tragedy; then, shrieking at the tops of their voices, they started on a frantic run up through the woods, never pausing as they crossed the main road to glance the way of the bridge. Anne, clinging desperately to her precarious foothold, saw their flying forms and heard their shrieks. Help would soon come, but meanwhile her position was a very uncomfortable one.

The minutes passed by, each seeming an hour to the unfortunate lily maid. Why didn't somebody come? Where had the girls gone? Suppose they had fainted, one and all! Suppose nobody ever came! Suppose she grew so tired and cramped that she could hold on no longer! Anne looked at the wicked green depths below her, wavering with long, oily shadows, and shivered. Her imagination began to suggest all manner of gruesome possibilities to her.

Then, just as she thought she really could not endure the ache in her arms and wrists another moment, Gilbert Blythe came rowing under the bridge in Harmon Andrews's dory!

Gilbert glanced up and, much to his amazement, beheld a little white scornful face looking down upon him with big, frightened but also scornful gray eyes.

"Anne Shirley! How on earth did you get there?" he exclaimed.

Without waiting for an answer he pulled close to the pile and extended his hand. There was no help for it; Anne, clinging to Gilbert Blythe's hand, scrambled down into the dory, where she sat, drabbled and furious, in the stern with her arms full of dripping shawl and wet crepe. It was certainly extremely difficult to be dignified under the circumstances!

"What has happened, Anne?" asked Gilbert, taking up his oars. "We were playing Elaine" explained Anne frigidly, without even looking at her rescuer, "and I had to drift down to Camelot in the barge—I mean the flat. The flat began to leak and I climbed out on the pile. The girls went for help. Will you be kind enough to row me to the landing?"

Gilbert obligingly rowed to the landing and Anne, disdaining assistance, sprang nimbly on shore.

"I'm very much obliged to you," she said haughtily as she turned away. But Gilbert had also sprung from the boat and now laid a detaining hand on her arm.

"Anne," he said hurriedly, "look here. Can't we be good friends? I'm awfully sorry I made fun of your hair that time. I didn't mean to vex you and I only meant it for a joke. Besides, it's so long ago. I think your hair is awfully pretty now— honest I do. Let's be friends."

For a moment Anne hesitated. She had an odd, newly awakened consciousness under all her outraged dignity that the half-shy, half-eager expression in Gilbert's hazel eyes was something that was very good to see. Her heart gave a quick, queer little beat. But the bitterness of her old grievance promptly stiffened up her wavering determination. That scene of two years before flashed back into her rec- ollection as vividly as if it had taken place yesterday. Gilbert had called her "carrots" and had brought about her disgrace before the whole school. Her re- sentment, which to other and older people might be as laughable as its cause, was in no whit allayed and softened by time seemingly. She hated Gilbert Blythe! She would never forgive him!

"No," she said coldly, "I shall never be friends with you, Gilbert Blythe; and I don't want to be!"

"All right!" Gilbert sprang into his skiff with an angry color in his cheeks. "I'll never ask you to be friends again, Anne Shirley. And I don't care either!"

He pulled away with swift defiant strokes, and Anne went up the steep, ferny little path under the maples. She held her head very high, but she was conscious of an odd feeling of regret. She almost wished she had answered Gilbert different- ly. Of course, he had insulted her terribly, but still—! Altogether, Anne rather thought it would be a relief to sit down and have a good cry. She was really quite unstrung, for the reaction from her fright and cramped clinging was making itself felt.

Halfway up the path she met Jane and Diana rushing back to the pond in a state narrowly removed from positive frenzy. They had found nobody at Orchard Slope, both Mr. and Mrs. Barry being away. Here Ruby Gillis had succumbed to hysterics, and was left to recover from them as best she might, while Jane and Diana flew through the Haunted Wood and across the brook to Green Gables. There they had found nobody either, for Marilla had gone to Carmody and Matthew was making hay in the back field.

"Oh, Anne," gasped Diana, fairly falling on the former's neck and weeping with relief and delight, "oh, Anne—we thought—you were—drowned—and we felt like murderers—because we had made—you be—Elaine. And Ruby is in hysterics—oh, Anne, how did you escape?"

"I climbed up on one of the piles," explained Anne wearily, "and Gilbert Blythe came along in Mr. Andrews's dory and brought me to land."

"Oh, Anne, how splendid of him! Why, it's so romantic!" said Jane, finding breath enough for utterance at last. "Of course you'll speak to him after this."

"Of course I won't," flashed Anne, with a momentary return of her old spirit. "And I don't want ever to hear the word 'romantic' again, Jane Andrews. I'm awfully sorry you were so frightened, girls. It is all my fault. I feel sure I was born under an unlucky star. Everything I do gets me or my dearest friends into a scrape. We've gone and lost your father's flat, Diana, and I have a presentiment that we'll not be allowed to row on the pond any more."

Anne's presentiment proved more trustworthy than presentiments are apt to do. Great was the consternation in the Barry and Cuthbert households when the events of the afternoon became known.

"Will you ever have any sense, Anne?" groaned Marilla.

"Oh, yes, I think I will, Marilla," returned Anne optimistically. A good cry, indulged in the grateful solitude of the east gable, had soothed her nerves and restored her to her wonted cheerfulness. "I think my prospects of becoming sensible are brighter now than ever."

"I don't see how," said Marilla.

"Well," explained Anne, "I've learned a new and valuable lesson today. Ever since I came to Green Gables I've been making mistakes, and each mistake has helped to cure me of some great shortcoming. The affair of the amethyst brooch cured me of meddling with things that didn't belong to me. The Haunted Wood mistake cured me of letting my imagination run away with me. The liniment cake mistake cured me of carelessness in cooking. Dyeing my hair cured me of vanity. I never think about my hair and nose now—at least, very seldom. And today's mistake is going to cure me of being too romantic. I have come to the conclusion that it is no use trying to be romantic in Avonlea. It was probably easy enough in towered Camelot hundreds of years ago, but romance is not appreciated now. I feel quite sure that you will soon see a great improvement in me in this respect, Marilla."

"I'm sure I hope so," said Marilla skeptically.

But Matthew, who had been sitting mutely in his corner, laid a hand on Anne's shoulder when Marilla had gone out.

"Don't give up all your romance, Anne," he whispered shyly, "a little of it is a good thing—not too much, of course—but keep a little of it, Anne, keep a little of it."

CHAPTER XXIX. An Epoch in Anne's Life

Anne was bringing the cows home from the back pasture by way of Lover's Lane. It was a September evening and all the gaps and clearings in the woods were brimmed up with ruby sunset light. Here and there the lane was splashed with it, but for the most part it was already quite shadowy beneath the maples, and the spaces under the firs were filled with a clear violet dusk like airy wine. The winds were out in their tops, and there is no sweeter music on earth than that which the wind makes in the fir trees at evening.

The cows swung placidly down the lane, and Anne followed them dreamily, repeating aloud the battle canto from MARMION—which had also been part of their English course the preceding winter and which Miss Stacy had made them learn off by heart—and exulting in its rushing lines and the clash of spears in its imagery. When she came to the lines:

> The stubborn spearsmen still made good
> Their dark impenetrable wood,

she stopped in ecstasy to shut her eyes that she might the better fancy herself one of that heroic ring. When she opened them again it was to behold Diana coming through the gate that led into the Barry field and looking so important that Anne instantly divined there was news to be told. But betray too eager curiosity she would not.

"Isn't this evening just like a purple dream, Diana? It makes me so glad to be alive. In the mornings I always think the mornings are best; but when evening comes I think it's lovelier still."

"It's a very fine evening," said Diana, "but oh, I have such news, Anne. Guess. You can have three guesses."

"Charlotte Gillis is going to be married in the church after all and Mrs. Allan wants us to decorate it," cried Anne.

"No. Charlotte's beau won't agree to that, because nobody ever has been married in the church yet, and he thinks it would seem too much like a funeral. It's too mean, because it would be such fun. Guess again."

"Jane's mother is going to let her have a birthday party?"

Diana shook her head, her black eyes dancing with merriment.

"I can't think what it can be," said Anne in despair, "unless it's that Moody Spurgeon MacPherson saw you home from prayer meeting last night. Did he?"

"I should think not," exclaimed Diana indignantly. "I wouldn't be likely to boast of it if he did, the horrid creature! I knew you couldn't guess it. Mother had a letter from Aunt Josephine today, and Aunt Josephine wants you and me to go to town next Tuesday and stop with her for the Exhibition. There!"

"Oh, Diana," whispered Anne, finding it necessary to lean up against a maple tree for support, "do you really mean it? But I'm afraid Marilla won't let me go. She will say that she can't encourage gadding about. That was what she said last week when Jane invited me to go with them in their double-seated buggy to the American concert at the White Sands Hotel. I wanted to go, but Marilla said I'd be better at home learning my lessons and so would Jane. I was bitterly disappointed, Diana. I felt so heartbroken that I wouldn't say my prayers when I went to bed. But I repented of that and got up in the middle of the night and said them."

"I'll tell you," said Diana, "we'll get Mother to ask Marilla. She'll be more likely to let you go then; and if she does we'll have the time of our lives, Anne. I've never been to an Exhibition, and it's so aggravating to hear the other girls talking about their trips. Jane and Ruby have been twice, and they're going this year again."

"I'm not going to think about it at all until I know whether I can go or not," said Anne resolutely. "If I did and then was disappointed, it would be more than I could bear. But in case I do go I'm very glad my new coat will be ready by that time. Marilla didn't think I needed a new coat. She said my old one would do very well for another winter and that I ought to be satisfied with having a new dress. The dress is very pretty, Diana—navy blue and made so fashionably. Marilla always makes my dresses fashionably now, because she says she doesn't intend to have Matthew going to Mrs. Lynde to make them. I'm so glad. It is ever so much easier to be good if your clothes are fashionable. At least, it is easier for me. I suppose it doesn't make such a difference to naturally good people. But Matthew said I must have a new coat, so Marilla bought a lovely piece of blue broadcloth, and it's being made by a real dressmaker over at Carmody. It's to be done Saturday night, and I'm trying not to imagine myself walking up the church aisle on Sunday in my new suit and cap, because I'm afraid it isn't right to imagine such things. But it just slips into my mind in spite of me. My cap is so pretty. Matthew bought it for me the day we were over at Carmody. It is one of those little blue velvet ones that are all the rage, with gold cord and tassels. Your new hat is elegant, Diana, and so becoming. When I saw you come into church last Sunday my heart swelled with pride to think you were my dearest friend. Do you suppose it's wrong for us to think so much about our clothes? Marilla says it is very sinful. But it is such an interesting subject, isn't it?"

Marilla agreed to let Anne go to town, and it was arranged that Mr. Barry should take the girls in on the following Tuesday. As Charlottetown was thirty miles away and Mr. Barry wished to go and return the same day, it was necessary to make a very early start. But Anne counted it all joy, and was up before sunrise on Tuesday morning. A glance from her window assured her that the day would be fine, for the eastern sky behind the firs of the Haunted Wood was all silvery and cloudless. Through the gap in the trees a light was shining in the western gable of Orchard Slope, a token that Diana was also up.

Anne was dressed by the time Matthew had the fire on and had the breakfast ready when Marilla came down, but for her own part was much too excited to eat. After breakfast the jaunty new cap and jacket were donned, and Anne hastened over the brook and up through the firs to Orchard Slope. Mr. Barry and Diana were waiting for her, and they were soon on the road.

It was a long drive, but Anne and Diana enjoyed every minute of it. It was delightful to rattle along over the moist roads in the early red sunlight that was creeping across the shorn harvest fields. The air was fresh and crisp, and little smoke-blue mists curled through the valleys and floated off from the hills. Sometimes the road went through woods where maples were beginning to hang out scarlet banners; sometimes it crossed rivers on bridges that made Anne's flesh cringe with the old, half-delightful fear; sometimes it wound along a harbor shore and passed by a little cluster of weather-gray fishing huts; again it mounted to hills whence a far sweep of curving upland or misty-blue sky could be seen; but wherever it went there was much of interest to discuss. It was almost noon when they reached town and found their way to "Beechwood." It was quite a fine old mansion, set back from the street in a seclusion of green elms and branching beeches. Miss Barry met them at the door with a twinkle in her sharp black eyes.

"So you've come to see me at last, you Anne-girl," she said. "Mercy, child, how you have grown! You're taller than I am, I declare. And you're ever so much better looking than you used to be, too. But I dare say you know that without being told."

"Indeed I didn't," said Anne radiantly. "I know I'm not so freckled as I used to be, so I've much to be thankful for, but I really hadn't dared to hope there was any other improvement. I'm so glad you think there is, Miss Barry." Miss Barry's house was furnished with "great magnificence," as Anne told Marilla afterward. The two little country girls were rather abashed by the splendor of the parlor where Miss Barry left them when she went to see about dinner.

"Isn't it just like a palace?" whispered Diana. "I never was in Aunt Josephine's house before, and I'd no idea it was so grand. I just wish Julia Bell could see this—she puts on such airs about her mother's parlor."

"Velvet carpet," sighed Anne luxuriously, "and silk curtains! I've dreamed of such things, Diana. But do you know I don't believe I feel very comfortable with them after all. There are so many things in this room and all so splendid that there is no scope for imagination. That is one consolation when you are poor—there are so many more things you can imagine about."

Their sojourn in town was something that Anne and Diana dated from for years. From first to last it was crowded with delights.

On Wednesday Miss Barry took them to the Exhibition grounds and kept them there all day.

"It was splendid," Anne related to Marilla later on. "I never imagined anything so interesting. I don't really know which department was the most interesting. I think I liked the horses and the flowers and the fancywork best. Josie Pye took first prize for knitted lace. I was real glad she did. And I was glad that I felt glad, for it shows I'm improving, don't you think, Marilla, when I can rejoice in Josie's success? Mr. Harmon Andrews took second prize for Gravenstein apples and Mr. Bell took first prize for a pig. Diana said she thought it was ridiculous for a Sunday-school superintendent to take a prize in pigs, but I don't see why. Do you? She said she would always think of it after this when he was praying so solemnly. Clara Louise MacPherson took a prize for painting, and Mrs. Lynde got first prize for homemade butter and cheese. So Avonlea was pretty well represented, wasn't it? Mrs. Lynde was there that day, and I never knew how much I really liked her until I saw her familiar face among all those strangers. There were thousands of people there, Marilla. It made me feel dreadfully insignificant. And Miss Barry took us up to the grandstand to see the horse races. Mrs. Lynde wouldn't go; she said horse racing was an abomination and, she being a church member, thought it her bounden duty to set a good example by staying away. But there were so many there I don't believe Mrs. Lynde's absence would ever be noticed. I don't think, though, that I ought to go very often to horse races, because they ARE awfully fascinating. Diana got so excited that she offered to bet me ten cents that the red horse would win. I didn't believe he would, but I refused to bet, because I wanted to tell Mrs. Allan all about everything, and I felt sure it wouldn't do to tell her that. It's always wrong to do anything you can't tell the minister's wife. It's as good as an extra conscience to have a minister's wife for your friend. And I was very glad I didn't bet, because the red horse DID win, and I would have lost ten cents. So you see that virtue was its own reward. We saw a man go up in a balloon. I'd love to go up in a balloon, Marilla; it would be simply thrilling; and we saw a man selling fortunes. You paid him ten cents and a little bird picked out your fortune for you. Miss Barry gave Diana and me ten cents each to have our fortunes told. Mine was that I would marry a dark-complected man who was very wealthy, and I would go across water to live. I looked carefully at all the dark men I saw after that, but I didn't care much for any of them, and anyhow I suppose it's too early to be looking out for him yet. Oh, it was a never-to-be-forgotten day, Marilla. I was so tired I couldn't sleep at night. Miss Barry put us in the spare room, according to promise. It was an elegant room, Marilla, but somehow sleeping in a spare room isn't what I used to think it was. That's the worst of growing up, and I'm beginning to realize it. The things you wanted so much when you were a child don't seem half so wonderful to you when you get them."

Thursday the girls had a drive in the park, and in the evening Miss Barry took them to a concert in the Academy of Music, where a noted prima donna was to sing. To Anne the evening was a glittering vision of delight.

"Oh, Marilla, it was beyond description. I was so excited I couldn't even talk, so you may know what it was like. I just sat in enraptured silence. Madame Selitsky was perfectly beautiful, and wore white satin and diamonds. But when she began to sing I never thought about anything else. Oh, I can't tell you how I felt. But it seemed to me that it could never be hard to be good any more. I felt like I do when I look up to the stars. Tears came into my eyes, but, oh, they were such happy tears. I was so sorry when it was all over, and I told Miss Barry I didn't see how I was ever to return to common life again. She said she thought if we went over to the restaurant across the street and had an ice cream it might help me. That sounded so prosaic; but to my surprise I found it true. The ice cream was delicious, Marilla, and it was so lovely and dissipated to be sitting there eating it at eleven o'clock at night. Diana said she believed she was born for city life. Miss Barry asked me what my opinion was, but I said I would have to think it over very seriously before I could tell her what I really thought. So I thought it over after I went to bed. That is the best time to think things out. And I came to the conclusion, Marilla, that I wasn't born for city life and that I was glad of it. It's nice to be eating ice cream at brilliant restaurants at eleven o'clock at night once in a while; but as a regular thing I'd rather be in the east gable at eleven, sound asleep, but kind of knowing even in my sleep that the stars were shining outside and that the wind was blowing in the firs across the brook. I told Miss Barry so at breakfast the next morning and she laughed. Miss Barry generally laughed at anything I said, even when I said the most solemn things. I don't think I liked it, Marilla, because I wasn't trying to be funny. But she is a most hospitable lady and treated us royally."

Friday brought going-home time, and Mr. Barry drove in for the girls.

"Well, I hope you've enjoyed yourselves," said Miss Barry, as she bade them good-bye.

"Indeed we have," said Diana.

"And you, Anne-girl?"

"I've enjoyed every minute of the time," said Anne, throwing her arms impulsively about the old woman's neck and kissing her wrinkled cheek. Diana would never have dared to do such a thing and felt rather aghast at Anne's freedom. But Miss Barry was pleased, and she stood on her veranda and watched the buggy out of sight. Then she went back into her big house with a sigh. It seemed very lonely, lacking those fresh young lives. Miss Barry was a rather selfish old lady, if the truth must be told, and had never cared much for anybody but herself. She valued people only as they were of service to her or amused her. Anne had amused her, and consequently stood high in the old lady's good graces. But Miss Barry found herself thinking less about Anne's quaint speeches than of her fresh enthusiasms, her transparent emotions, her little winning ways, and the sweetness of her eyes and lips.

"I thought Marilla Cuthbert was an old fool when I heard she'd adopted a girl out of an orphan asylum," she said to herself, "but I guess she didn't make much of a mistake after all. If I'd a child like Anne in the house all the time I'd be a better and happier woman."

Anne and Diana found the drive home as pleasant as the drive in—pleasanter, indeed, since there was the delightful consciousness of home waiting at the end of it. It was sunset when they passed through White Sands and turned into the shore road. Beyond, the Avonlea hills came out darkly against the saffron sky. Behind them the moon was rising out of the sea that grew all radiant and transfigured in her light. Every little cove along the curving road was a marvel of dancing ripples. The waves broke with a soft swish on the rocks below them, and the tang of the sea was in the strong, fresh air.

"Oh, but it's good to be alive and to be going home," breathed Anne.

When she crossed the log bridge over the brook the kitchen light of Green Gables winked her a friendly welcome back, and through the open door shone the hearth fire, sending out its warm red glow athwart the chilly autumn night. Anne ran blithely up the hill and into the kitchen, where a hot supper was waiting on the table.

"So you've got back?" said Marilla, folding up her knitting.

"Yes, and oh, it's so good to be back," said Anne joyously. "I could kiss everything, even to the clock. Marilla, a broiled chicken! You don't mean to say you cooked that for me!"

"Yes, I did," said Marilla. "I thought you'd be hungry after such a drive and need something real appetizing. Hurry and take off your things, and we'll have supper as soon as Matthew comes in. I'm glad you've got back, I must say. It's been fearful lonesome here without you, and I never put in four longer days."

After supper Anne sat before the fire between Matthew and Marilla, and gave them a full account of her visit.

"I've had a splendid time," she concluded happily, "and I feel that it marks an epoch in my life. But the best of it all was the coming home."

CHAPTER XXX. The Queens Class Is Organized

Marilla laid her knitting on her lap and leaned back in her chair. Her eyes were tired, and she thought vaguely that she must see about having her glasses changed the next time she went to town, for her eyes had grown tired very often of late.

It was nearly dark, for the full November twilight had fallen around Green Gables, and the only light in the kitchen came from the dancing red flames in the stove.

Anne was curled up Turk-fashion on the hearthrug, gazing into that joyous glow where the sunshine of a hundred summers was being distilled from the maple cordwood. She had been reading, but her book had slipped to the floor, and now she was dreaming, with a smile on her parted lips. Glittering castles in Spain were shaping themselves out of the mists and rainbows of her lively fancy; adventures wonderful and enthralling were happening to her in cloudland—adventures that always turned out triumphantly and never involved her in scrapes like those of actual life.

Marilla looked at her with a tenderness that would never have been suffered to reveal itself in any clearer light than that soft mingling of fireshine and shadow. The lesson of a love that should display itself easily in spoken word and open look was one Marilla could never learn. But she had learned to love this slim, gray-eyed girl with an affection all the deeper and stronger from its very undemonstrativeness. Her love made her afraid of being unduly indulgent, indeed. She had an uneasy feeling that it was rather sinful to set one's heart so intensely on any human creature as she had set hers on Anne, and perhaps she performed a sort of unconscious penance for this by being stricter and more critical than if the girl had been less dear to her. Certainly Anne herself had no idea how Marilla loved her. She sometimes thought wistfully that Marilla was very hard to please and distinctly lacking in sympathy and understanding. But she always checked the thought reproachfully, remembering what she owed to Marilla.

"Anne," said Marilla abruptly, "Miss Stacy was here this afternoon when you were out with Diana."

Anne came back from her other world with a start and a sigh.

"Was she? Oh, I'm so sorry I wasn't in. Why didn't you call me, Marilla? Diana and I were only over in the Haunted Wood. It's lovely in the woods now. All the little wood things—the ferns and the satin leaves and the crackerberries—have gone to sleep, just as if somebody had tucked them away until spring under a blanket of leaves. I think it was a little gray fairy with a rainbow scarf that came tiptoeing along the last moonlight night and did it. Diana wouldn't say much about that, though. Diana has never forgotten the scolding her mother gave her about imagining ghosts into the Haunted Wood. It had a very bad effect on Diana's imagination. It blighted it. Mrs. Lynde says Myrtle Bell is a blighted being. I asked Ruby Gillis why Myrtle was blighted, and Ruby said she guessed it was because her young man had gone back on her. Ruby Gillis thinks of nothing but young men, and the older she gets the worse she is. Young men are all very well in their place, but it doesn't do to drag them into everything, does it? Diana and I are thinking seriously of promising each other that we will never marry but be nice old maids and live together forever. Diana hasn't quite made up her mind though, because she thinks perhaps it would be nobler to marry some wild, dashing, wicked young man and reform him. Diana and I talk a great deal about serious subjects now, you know. We feel that we are so much older than we used to be that it isn't becoming to talk of childish matters. It's such a solemn thing to be almost fourteen, Marilla. Miss Stacy took all us girls who are in our teens down to the brook last Wednesday, and talked to us about it. She said we couldn't be too careful what habits we formed and what ideals we acquired in our teens, because by the time we were twenty our characters would be developed and the foundation laid for our whole future life. And she said if the foundation was shaky we could never build anything really worth while on it. Diana and I talked the matter over coming home from school. We felt extremely solemn, Marilla. And we decided that we would try to be very careful indeed and form respectable habits and learn all we could and be as sensible as possible, so that by the time we were twenty our characters would be properly developed. It's perfectly appalling to think of being twenty, Marilla. It sounds so fearfully old and grown up. But why was Miss Stacy here this afternoon?"

"That is what I want to tell you, Anne, if you'll ever give me a chance to get a word in edgewise. She was talking about you."

"About me?" Anne looked rather scared. Then she flushed and exclaimed:

"Oh, I know what she was saying. I meant to tell you, Marilla, honestly I did, but I forgot. Miss Stacy caught me reading Ben Hur in school yesterday afternoon when I should have been studying my Canadian history. Jane Andrews lent it to me. I was reading it at dinner hour, and I had just got to the chariot race when school went in. I was simply wild to know how it turned out—although I felt sure Ben Hur must win, because it wouldn't be poetical justice if he didn't—so I spread the history open on my desk lid and then tucked Ben Hur between the desk and my knee. I just looked as if I were studying Canadian history, you know, while all the while I was reveling in Ben Hur. I was so interested in it that I never noticed Miss Stacy coming down the aisle until all at once I just looked up and there she was looking down at me, so reproachful-like. I can't tell you how ashamed I felt, Marilla, especially when I heard Josie Pye giggling. Miss Stacy took Ben Hur away, but she never said a word then. She kept me in at recess and talked to me.

She said I had done very wrong in two respects. First, I was wasting the time I ought to have put on my studies; and secondly, I was deceiving my teacher in trying to make it appear I was reading a history when it was a storybook instead. I had never realized until that moment, Marilla, that what I was doing was deceitful. I was shocked. I cried bitterly, and asked Miss Stacy to forgive me and I'd never do such a thing again; and I offered to do penance by never so much as looking at Ben Hur for a whole week, not even to see how the chariot race turned out. But Miss Stacy said she wouldn't require that, and she forgave me freely. So I think it wasn't very kind of her to come up here to you about it after all."

"Miss Stacy never mentioned such a thing to me, Anne, and its only your guilty conscience that's the matter with you. You have no business to be taking storybooks to school. You read too many novels anyhow. When I was a girl I wasn't so much as allowed to look at a novel."

"Oh, how can you call Ben Hur a novel when it's really such a religious book?" protested Anne. "Of course it's a little too exciting to be proper reading for Sunday, and I only read it on weekdays. And I never read ANY book now unless either Miss Stacy or Mrs. Allan thinks it is a proper book for a girl thirteen and three-quarters to read. Miss Stacy made me promise that. She found me reading a book one day called, The Lurid Mystery of the Haunted Hall. It was one Ruby Gillis had lent me, and, oh, Marilla, it was so fascinating and creepy. It just curdled the blood in my veins. But Miss Stacy said it was a very silly, unwholesome book, and she asked me not to read any more of it or any like it. I didn't mind promising not to read any more like it, but it was AGONIZING to give back that book without knowing how it turned out. But my love for Miss Stacy stood the test and I did. It's really wonderful, Marilla, what you can do when you're truly anxious to please a certain person."

"Well, I guess I'll light the lamp and get to work," said Marilla. "I see plainly that you don't want to hear what Miss Stacy had to say. You're more interested in the sound of your own tongue than in anything else."

"Oh, indeed, Marilla, I do want to hear it," cried Anne contritely. "I won't say another word—not one. I know I talk too much, but I am really trying to overcome it, and although I say far too much, yet if you only knew how many things I want to say and don't, you'd give me some credit for it. Please tell me, Marilla."

"Well, Miss Stacy wants to organize a class among her advanced students who mean to study for the entrance examination into Queen's. She intends to give them extra lessons for an hour after school. And she came to ask Matthew and me if we would like to have you join it. What do you think about it yourself, Anne? Would you like to go to Queen's and pass for a teacher?"

"Oh, Marilla!" Anne straightened to her knees and clasped her hands. "It's been the dream of my life—that is, for the last six months, ever since Ruby and Jane began to talk of studying for the Entrance. But I didn't say anything about it, because I supposed it would be perfectly useless. I'd love to be a teacher. But won't it be dreadfully expensive? Mr. Andrews says it cost him one hundred and fifty dollars to put Prissy through, and Prissy wasn't a dunce in geometry."

"I guess you needn't worry about that part of it. When Matthew and I took you to bring up we resolved we would do the best we could for you and give you a good education. I believe in a girl being fitted to earn her own living whether she ever has to or not. You'll always have a home at Green Gables as long as Matthew and I are here, but nobody knows what is going to happen in this uncertain world, and it's just as well to be prepared. So you can join the Queen's class if you like, Anne."

"Oh, Marilla, thank you." Anne flung her arms about Marilla's waist and looked up earnestly into her face. "I'm extremely grateful to you and Matthew. And I'll study as hard as I can and do my very best to be a credit to you. I warn you not to expect much in geometry, but I think I can hold my own in anything else if I work hard."

"I dare say you'll get along well enough. Miss Stacy says you are bright and diligent." Not for worlds would Marilla have told Anne just what Miss Stacy had said about her; that would have been to pamper vanity. "You needn't rush to any extreme of killing yourself over your books. There is no hurry. You won't be ready to try the Entrance for a year and a half yet. But it's well to begin in time and be thoroughly grounded, Miss Stacy says."

"I shall take more interest than ever in my studies now," said Anne blissfully, "because I have a purpose in life. Mr. Allan says everybody should have a purpose in life and pursue it faithfully. Only he says we must first make sure that it is a worthy purpose. I would call it a worthy purpose to want to be a teacher like Miss Stacy, wouldn't you, Marilla? I think it's a very noble profession."

The Queen's class was organized in due time. Gilbert Blythe, Anne Shirley, Ruby Gillis, Jane Andrews, Josie Pye, Charlie Sloane, and Moody Spurgeon MacPherson joined it. Diana Barry did not, as her parents did not intend to send her to Queen's. This seemed nothing short of a calamity to Anne. Never, since the night on which Minnie May had had the croup, had she and Diana been separated in anything. On the evening when the Queen's class first remained in school for the extra lessons and Anne saw Diana go slowly out with the others, to walk home alone through the Birch Path and Violet Vale, it was all the former could do to keep her seat and refrain from rushing impulsively after her chum. A lump came into her throat, and she hastily retired behind the pages of her uplifted Latin grammar to hide the tears in her eyes. Not for worlds would Anne have had Gilbert Blythe or Josie Pye see those tears.

"But, oh, Marilla, I really felt that I had tasted the bitterness of death, as Mr. Allan said in his sermon last Sunday, when I saw Diana go out alone," she said mournfully that night. "I thought how splendid it would have been if Diana had only been going to study for the Entrance, too. But we can't have things perfect in this imperfect world, as Mrs. Lynde says. Mrs. Lynde isn't exactly a comforting person sometimes, but there's no doubt she says a great many very true things. And I think the Queen's class is going to be extremely interesting. Jane and Ruby are just going to study to be teachers. That is the height of their ambition. Ruby says she will only teach for two years after she gets through, and then she intends to be married. Jane says she will devote her whole life to teaching, and never, never marry, because you are paid a salary for teaching, but a husband won't pay you anything, and growls if you ask for a share in the egg and butter money. I expect Jane speaks from mournful experience, for Mrs. Lynde says that her father is a perfect old crank, and meaner than second skimmings. Josie Pye says she is just going to college for education's sake, because she won't have to earn her own living; she says of course it is different with orphans who are living on charity—THEY have to hustle. Moody Spurgeon is going to be a minister. Mrs. Lynde says he couldn't be anything else with a name like that to live up to. I hope it isn't wicked of me, Marilla, but really the thought of Moody Spurgeon being a minister makes me laugh. He's such a funny-looking boy with that big fat face, and his little blue eyes, and his ears sticking out like flaps. But perhaps he will be more intellectual looking when he grows up. Charlie Sloane says he's going to go into politics and be a member of Parliament, but Mrs. Lynde says he'll never succeed at that, because the Sloanes are all honest people, and it's only rascals that get on in politics nowadays."

"What is Gilbert Blythe going to be?" queried Marilla, seeing that Anne was opening her Caesar.

"I don't happen to know what Gilbert Blythe's ambition in life is—if he has any," said Anne scornfully.

There was open rivalry between Gilbert and Anne now. Previously the rivalry had been rather onesided, but there was no longer any doubt that Gilbert was as determined to be first in class as Anne was. He was a foeman worthy of her steel. The other members of the class tacitly acknowledged their superiority, and never dreamed of trying to compete with them.

Since the day by the pond when she had refused to listen to his plea for forgiveness, Gilbert, save for the aforesaid determined rivalry, had evinced no recognition whatever of the existence of Anne Shirley. He talked and jested with the other girls, exchanged books and puzzles with them, discussed lessons and plans, sometimes walked home with one or the other of them from prayer meeting or Debating Club. But Anne Shirley he simply ignored, and Anne found out that it is not pleasant to be ignored. It was in vain that she told herself with a toss of her head that she did not care. Deep down in her wayward, feminine little heart she knew that she did care, and that if she had that chance of the Lake of Shining Waters again she would answer very differently. All at once, as it seemed, and to her secret dismay, she found that the old resentment she had cherished against him was gone—gone just when she most needed its sustaining power. It was in vain that she recalled every incident and emotion of that memorable occasion and tried to feel the old satisfying anger. That day by the pond had witnessed its last spasmodic flicker. Anne realized that she had forgiven and forgotten without knowing it. But it was too late.

And at least neither Gilbert nor anybody else, not even Diana, should ever suspect how sorry she was and how much she wished she hadn't been so proud and horrid! She determined to "shroud her feelings in deepest oblivion," and it may be stated here and now that she did it, so successfully that Gilbert, who possibly was not quite so indifferent as he seemed, could not console himself with any belief that Anne felt his retaliatory scorn. The only poor comfort he had was that she snubbed Charlie Sloane, unmercifully, continually, and undeservedly.

Otherwise the winter passed away in a round of pleasant duties and studies. For Anne the days slipped by like golden beads on the necklace of the year. She was happy, eager, interested; there were lessons to be learned and honor to be won; delightful books to read; new pieces to be practiced for the Sunday-school choir; pleasant Saturday afternoons at the manse with Mrs. Allan; and then, almost before Anne realized it, spring had come again to Green Gables and all the world was abloom once more.

Studies palled just a wee bit then; the Queen's class, left behind in school while the others scattered to green lanes and leafy wood cuts and meadow byways, looked wistfully out of the windows and discovered that Latin verbs and French exercises had somehow lost the tang and zest they had possessed in the crisp winter months. Even Anne and Gilbert lagged and grew indifferent. Teacher and taught were alike glad when the term was ended and the glad vacation days stretched rosily before them.

"But you've done good work this past year," Miss Stacy told them on the last evening, "and you deserve a good, jolly vacation. Have the best time you can in the out-of-door world and lay in a good stock of health and vitality and ambition to carry you through next year. It will be the tug of war, you know—the last year before the Entrance."

"Are you going to be back next year, Miss Stacy?" asked Josie Pye.

Josie Pye never scrupled to ask questions; in this instance the rest of the class felt grateful to her; none of them would have dared to ask it of Miss Stacy, but all wanted to, for there had been alarming rumors running at large through the school for some time that Miss Stacy was not coming back the next year—that she had been offered a position in the grade school of her own home district and meant to accept. The Queen's class listened in breathless suspense for her answer.

"Yes, I think I will," said Miss Stacy. "I thought of taking another school, but I have decided to come back to Avonlea. To tell the truth, I've grown so interested in my pupils here that I found I couldn't leave them. So I'll stay and see you through."

"Hurrah!" said Moody Spurgeon. Moody Spurgeon had never been so carried away by his feelings before, and he blushed uncomfortably every time he thought about it for a week.

"Oh, I'm so glad," said Anne, with shining eyes. "Dear Stacy, it would be perfectly dreadful if you didn't come back. I don't believe I could have the heart to go on with my studies at all if another teacher came here."

When Anne got home that night she stacked all her textbooks away in an old trunk in the attic, locked it, and threw the key into the blanket box.

"I'm not even going to look at a schoolbook in vacation," she told Marilla. "I've studied as hard all the term as I possibly could and I've pored over that geometry until I know every proposition in the first book off by heart, even when the letters ARE changed. I just feel tired of everything sensible and I'm going to let my imagination run riot for the summer. Oh, you needn't be alarmed, Marilla. I'll only let it run riot within reasonable limits. But I want to have a real good jolly time this summer, for maybe it's the last summer I'll be a little girl. Mrs. Lynde says that if I keep stretching out next year as I've done this I'll have to put on longer skirts. She says I'm all running to legs and eyes. And when I put on longer skirts I shall feel that I have to live up to them and be very dignified. It won't even do to believe in fairies then, I'm afraid; so I'm going to believe in them with all my whole heart this summer. I think we're going to have a very gay vacation. Ruby Gillis is going to have a birthday party soon and there's the Sunday school picnic and the missionary concert next month. And Mr. Barry says that some evening he'll take Diana and me over to the White Sands Hotel and have dinner there. They have dinner there in the evening, you know. Jane Andrews was over once last summer and she says it was a dazzling sight to see the electric lights and the flowers and all the lady guests in such beautiful dresses. Jane says it was her first glimpse into high life and she'll never forget it to her dying day."

Mrs. Lynde came up the next afternoon to find out why Marilla had not been at the Aid meeting on Thursday. When Marilla was not at Aid meeting people knew there was something wrong at Green Gables.

"Matthew had a bad spell with his heart Thursday," Marilla explained, "and I didn't feel like leaving him. Oh, yes, he's all right again now, but he takes them spells oftener than he used to and I'm anxious about him. The doctor says he must be careful to avoid excitement. That's easy enough, for Matthew doesn't go about looking for excitement by any means and never did, but he's not to do any very heavy work either and you might as well tell Matthew not to breathe as not to work. Come and lay off your things, Rachel. You'll stay to tea?"

"Well, seeing you're so pressing, perhaps I might as well, stay" said Mrs. Rachel, who had not the slightest intention of doing anything else.

Mrs. Rachel and Marilla sat comfortably in the parlor while Anne got the tea and made hot biscuits that were light and white enough to defy even Mrs. Rachel's criticism.

"I must say Anne has turned out a real smart girl," admitted Mrs. Rachel, as Marilla accompanied her to the end of the lane at sunset. "She must be a great help to you."

"She is," said Marilla, "and she's real steady and reliable now. I used to be afraid she'd never get over her featherbrained ways, but she has and I wouldn't be afraid to trust her in anything now."

"I never would have thought she'd have turned out so well that first day I was here three years ago," said Mrs. Rachel. "Lawful heart, shall I ever forget that tantrum of hers! When I went home that night I says to Thomas, says I, 'Mark my words, Thomas, Marilla Cuthbert'll live to rue the step she's took.' But I was mistaken and I'm real glad of it. I ain't one of those kind of people, Marilla, as can never be brought to own up that they've made a mistake. No, that never was my way, thank goodness. I did make a mistake in judging Anne, but it weren't no wonder, for an odder, unexpecteder witch of a child there never was in this world, that's what. There was no ciphering her out by the rules that worked with other children. It's nothing short of wonderful how she's improved these three years, but especially in looks. She's a real pretty girl got to be, though I can't say I'm overly partial to that pale, big-eyed style myself. I like more snap and color, like Diana Barry has or Ruby Gillis. Ruby Gillis's looks are real showy. But somehow—I don't know how it is but when Anne and them are together, though she ain't half as handsome, she makes them look kind of common and overdone—something like them white June lilies she calls narcissus alongside of the big, red peonies, that's what."

CHAPTER XXXI. Where the Brook and River Meet

Anne had her "good" summer and enjoyed it wholeheartedly. She and Diana fairly lived outdoors, reveling in all the delights that Lover's Lane and the Dryad's Bubble and Willowmere and Victoria Island afforded. Marilla offered no objections to Anne's gypsyings. The Spencervale doctor who had come the night Minnie May had the croup met Anne at the house of a patient one afternoon early in vacation, looked her over sharply, screwed up his mouth, shook his head, and sent a message to Marilla Cuthbert by another person. It was:

"Keep that redheaded girl of yours in the open air all summer and don't let her read books until she gets more spring into her step."

This message frightened Marilla wholesomely. She read Anne's death warrant by consumption in it unless it was scrupulously obeyed. As a result, Anne had the golden summer of her life as far as freedom and frolic went. She walked, rowed, berried, and dreamed to her heart's content; and when September came she was bright-eyed and alert, with a step that would have satisfied the Spencervale doctor and a heart full of ambition and zest once more.

"I feel just like studying with might and main," she declared as she brought her books down from the attic. "Oh, you good old friends, I'm glad to see your honest faces once more—yes, even you, geometry. I've had a perfectly beautiful summer, Marilla, and now I'm rejoicing as a strong man to run a race, as Mr. Allan said last Sunday. Doesn't Mr. Allan preach magnificent sermons? Mrs. Lynde says he is improving every day and the first thing we know some city church will gobble him up and then we'll be left and have to turn to and break in another green preacher. But I don't see the use of meeting trouble halfway, do you, Marilla? I think it would be better just to enjoy Mr. Allan while we have him. If I were a man I think I'd be a minister. They can have such an influence for good, if their theology is sound; and it must be thrilling to preach splendid sermons and stir your hearers' hearts. Why can't women be ministers, Marilla? I asked Mrs. Lynde that and she was shocked and said it would be a scandalous thing. She said there might be female ministers in the States and she believed there was, but thank goodness we hadn't got to that stage in Canada yet and she hoped we never would. But I don't see why. I think women would make splendid ministers. When there is a social to be got up or a church tea or anything else to raise money the women have to turn to and do the work. I'm sure Mrs. Lynde can pray every bit as well as Superintendent Bell and I've no doubt she could preach too with a little practice."

"Yes, I believe she could," said Marilla dryly. "She does plenty of unofficial preaching as it is. Nobody has much of a chance to go wrong in Avonlea with Rachel to oversee them."

"Marilla," said Anne in a burst of confidence, "I want to tell you something and ask you what you think about it. It has worried me terribly—on Sunday afternoons, that is, when I think specially about such matters. I do really want to be good; and when I'm with you or Mrs. Allan or Miss Stacy I want it more than ever and I want to do just what would please you and what you would approve of. But mostly when I'm with Mrs. Lynde I feel desperately wicked and as if I wanted to go and do the very thing she tells me I oughtn't to do. I feel irresistibly tempted to do it. Now, what do you think is the reason I feel like that? Do you think it's because I'm really bad and unregenerate?"

Marilla looked dubious for a moment. Then she laughed.

"If you are I guess I am too, Anne, for Rachel often has that very effect on me. I sometimes think she'd have more of an influence for good, as you say yourself, if she didn't keep nagging people to do right. There should have been a special commandment against nagging. But there, I shouldn't talk so. Rachel is a good Christian woman and she means well. There isn't a kinder soul in Avonlea and she never shirks her share of work."

"I'm very glad you feel the same," said Anne decidedly. "It's so encouraging. I shan't worry so much over that after this. But I dare say there'll be other things to worry me. They keep coming up new all the time—things to perplex you, you know. You settle one question and there's another right after. There are so many things to be thought over and decided when you're beginning to grow up. It keeps me busy all the time thinking them over and deciding what is right. It's a serious thing to grow up, isn't it, Marilla? But when I have such good friends as you and Matthew and Mrs. Allan and Miss Stacy I ought to grow up successfully, and I'm sure it will be my own fault if I don't. I feel it's a great responsibility because I have only the one chance. If I don't grow up right I can't go back and begin over again. I've grown two inches this summer, Marilla. Mr. Gillis measured me at Ruby's party. I'm so glad you made my new dresses longer. That dark-green one is so pretty and it was sweet of you to put on the flounce. Of course I know it wasn't really necessary, but flounces are so stylish this fall and Josie Pye has flounces on all her dresses. I know I'll be able to study better because of mine. I shall have such a comfortable feeling deep down in my mind about that flounce."

"It's worth something to have that," admitted Marilla.

Miss Stacy came back to Avonlea school and found all her pupils eager for work once more. Especially did the Queen's class gird up their loins for the fray, for at the end of the coming year, dimly shadowing their pathway already, loomed up that fateful thing known as "the Entrance," at the thought of which one and all felt their hearts sink into their very shoes. Suppose they did not pass! That thought was doomed to haunt Anne through the waking hours of that winter, Sunday afternoons inclusive, to the almost entire exclusion of moral and theological problems. When Anne had bad dreams she found herself staring miserably at pass lists of the Entrance exams, where Gilbert Blythe's name was blazoned at the top and in which hers did not appear at all.

But it was a jolly, busy, happy swift-flying winter. Schoolwork was as interesting, class rivalry as absorbing, as of yore. New worlds of thought, feeling, and ambition, fresh, fascinating fields of unexplored knowledge seemed to be opening out before Anne's eager eyes.

"Hills peeped o'er hill and Alps on Alps arose."

Much of all this was due to Miss Stacy's tactful, careful, broadminded guidance. She led her class to think and explore and discover for themselves and encouraged straying from the old beaten paths to a degree that quite shocked Mrs. Lynde and the school trustees, who viewed all innovations on established methods rather dubiously.

Apart from her studies Anne expanded socially, for Marilla, mindful of the Spencervale doctor's dictum, no longer vetoed occasional outings. The Debating Club flourished and gave several concerts; there were one or two parties almost verging on grown-up affairs; there were sleigh drives and skating frolics galore.

Betweentimes Anne grew, shooting up so rapidly that Marilla was astonished one day, when they were standing side by side, to find the girl was taller than herself.

"Why, Anne, how you've grown!" she said, almost unbelievingly. A sigh followed on the words. Marilla felt a queer regret over Anne's inches. The child she had learned to love had vanished somehow and here was this tall, serious-eyed girl of fifteen, with the thoughtful brows and the proudly poised little head, in her place. Marilla loved the girl as much as she had loved the child, but she was conscious of a queer sorrowful sense of loss. And that night, when Anne had gone to prayer meeting with Diana, Marilla sat alone in the wintry twilight and indulged in the weakness of a cry. Matthew, coming in with a lantern, caught her at it and gazed at her in such consternation that Marilla had to laugh through her tears.

"I was thinking about Anne," she explained. "She's got to be such a big girl—and she'll probably be away from us next winter. I'll miss her terrible."

"She'll be able to come home often," comforted Matthew, to whom Anne was as yet and always would be the little, eager girl he had brought home from Bright River on that June evening four years before. "The branch railroad will be built to Carmody by that time."

"It won't be the same thing as having her here all the time," sighed Marilla gloomily, determined to enjoy her luxury of grief uncomforted. "But there—men can't understand these things!"

There were other changes in Anne no less real than the physical change. For one thing, she became much quieter. Perhaps she thought all the more and dreamed as much as ever, but she certainly talked less. Marilla noticed and commented on this also.

"You don't chatter half as much as you used to, Anne, nor use half as many big words. What has come over you?"

Anne colored and laughed a little, as she dropped her book and looked dreamily out of the window, where big fat red buds were bursting out on the creeper in response to the lure of the spring sunshine.

"I don't know—I don't want to talk as much," she said, denting her chin thoughtfully with her forefinger. "It's nicer to think dear, pretty thoughts and keep them in one's heart, like treasures. I don't like to have them laughed at or wondered over. And somehow I don't want to use big words any more. It's almost a pity, isn't it, now that I'm really growing big enough to say them if I did want to. It's fun to be almost grown up in some ways, but it's not the kind of fun I expected, Marilla. There's so much to learn and do and think that there isn't time for big words. Besides, Miss Stacy says the short ones are much stronger and better. She makes us write all our essays as simply as possible. It was hard at first. I was so used to crowding in all the fine big words I could think of—and I thought of any number of them. But I've got used to it now and I see it's so much better."

"What has become of your story club? I haven't heard you speak of it for a long time."

"The story club isn't in existence any longer. We hadn't time for it—and anyhow I think we had got tired of it. It was silly to be writing about love and murder and elopements and mysteries. Miss Stacy sometimes has us write a story for training in composition, but she won't let us write anything but what might happen in Avonlea in our own lives, and she criticizes it very sharply and makes us criticize our own too. I never thought my compositions had so many faults until I began to look for them myself. I felt so ashamed I wanted to give up altogether, but Miss Stacy said I could learn to write well if I only trained myself to be my own severest critic. And so I am trying to."

"You've only two more months before the Entrance," said Marilla. "Do you think you'll be able to get through?"

Anne shivered.

"I don't know. Sometimes I think I'll be all right—and then I get horribly afraid. We've studied hard and Miss Stacy has drilled us thoroughly, but we mayn't get through for all that. We've each got a stumbling block. Mine is geometry of course, and Jane's is Latin, and Ruby and Charlie's is algebra, and Josie's is arithmetic. Moody Spurgeon says he feels it in his bones that he is going to fail in English history. Miss Stacy is going to give us examinations in June just as hard as we'll have at the Entrance and mark us just as strictly, so we'll have some idea. I wish it was all over, Marilla. It haunts me. Sometimes I wake up in the night and wonder what I'll do if I don't pass."

"Why, go to school next year and try again," said Marilla unconcernedly.

"Oh, I don't believe I'd have the heart for it. It would be such a disgrace to fail, especially if Gil—if the others passed. And I get so nervous in an examination that I'm likely to make a mess of it. I wish I had nerves like Jane Andrews. Nothing rattles her."

CHAPTER XXXI. Where the Brook and River Meet

Anne sighed and, dragging her eyes from the witcheries of the spring world, the beckoning day of breeze and blue, and the green things upspringing in the garden, buried herself resolutely in her book. There would be other springs, but if she did not succeed in passing the Entrance, Anne felt convinced that she would never recover sufficiently to enjoy them.

CHAPTER XXXII. The Pass List Is Out

With the end of June came the close of the term and the close of Miss Stacy's rule in Avonlea school. Anne and Diana walked home that evening feeling very sober indeed. Red eyes and damp handkerchiefs bore convincing testimony to the fact that Miss Stacy's farewell words must have been quite as touching as Mr. Phillips's had been under similar circumstances three years before. Diana looked back at the schoolhouse from the foot of the spruce hill and sighed deeply.

"It does seem as if it was the end of everything, doesn't it?" she said dismally.

"You oughtn't to feel half as badly as I do," said Anne, hunting vainly for a dry spot on her handkerchief. "You'll be back again next winter, but I suppose I've left the dear old school forever—if I have good luck, that is."

"It won't be a bit the same. Miss Stacy won't be there, nor you nor Jane nor Ruby probably. I shall have to sit all alone, for I couldn't bear to have another deskmate after you. Oh, we have had jolly times, haven't we, Anne? It's dreadful to think they're all over."

Two big tears rolled down by Diana's nose.

"If you would stop crying I could," said Anne imploringly. "Just as soon as I put away my hanky I see you brimming up and that starts me off again. As Mrs. Lynde says, 'If you can't be cheerful, be as cheerful as you can.' After all, I dare say I'll be back next year. This is one of the times I KNOW I'm not going to pass. They're getting alarmingly frequent."

"Why, you came out splendidly in the exams Miss Stacy gave."

"Yes, but those exams didn't make me nervous. When I think of the real thing you can't imagine what a horrid cold fluttery feeling comes round my heart. And then my number is thirteen and Josie Pye says it's so unlucky. I am NOT superstitious and I know it can make no difference. But still I wish it wasn't thirteen."

"I do wish I was going in with you," said Diana. "Wouldn't we have a perfectly elegant time? But I suppose you'll have to cram in the evenings."

"No; Miss Stacy has made us promise not to open a book at all. She says it would only tire and confuse us and we are to go out walking and not think about the exams at all and go to bed early. It's good advice, but I expect it will be hard to follow; good advice is apt to be, I think. Prissy Andrews told me that she sat up half the night every night of her Entrance week and crammed for dear life; and I had determined to sit up AT LEAST as long as she did. It was so kind of your Aunt Josephine to ask me to stay at Beechwood while I'm in town."

"You'll write to me while you're in, won't you?"

"I'll write Tuesday night and tell you how the first day goes," promised Anne.

"I'll be haunting the post office Wednesday," vowed Diana.

Anne went to town the following Monday and on Wednesday Diana haunted the post office, as agreed, and got her letter.

"Dearest Diana" [wrote Anne],

"Here it is Tuesday night and I'm writing this in the library at Beechwood. Last night I was horribly lonesome all alone in my room and wished so much you were with me. I couldn't "cram" because I'd promised Miss Stacy not to, but it was as hard to keep from opening my history as it used to be to keep from reading a story before my lessons were learned.

"This morning Miss Stacy came for me and we went to the Academy, calling for Jane and Ruby and Josie on our way. Ruby asked me to feel her hands and they were as cold as ice. Josie said I looked as if I hadn't slept a wink and she didn't believe I was strong enough to stand the grind of the teacher's course even if I did get through. There are times and seasons even yet when I don't feel that I've made any great headway in learning to like Josie Pye!

"When we reached the Academy there were scores of students there from all over the Island. The first person we saw was Moody Spurgeon sitting on the steps and muttering away to himself. Jane asked him what on earth he was doing and he said he was repeating the multiplication table over and over to steady his nerves and for pity's sake not to interrupt him, because if he stopped for a moment he got frightened and forgot everything he ever knew, but the multiplication table kept all his facts firmly in their proper place!

"When we were assigned to our rooms Miss Stacy had to leave us. Jane and I sat together and Jane was so composed that I envied her. No need of the multiplication table for good, steady, sensible Jane! I wondered if I looked as I felt and if they could hear my heart thumping clear across the room. Then a man came in and began distributing the English examination sheets. My hands grew cold then and my head fairly whirled around as I picked it up. Just one awful moment—Diana, I felt exactly as I did four years ago when I asked Marilla if I might stay at Green Gables—and then everything cleared up in my mind and my heart began beating again—I forgot to say that it had stopped altogether!—for I knew I could do something with THAT paper anyhow.

"At noon we went home for dinner and then back again for history in the afternoon. The history was a pretty hard paper and I got dreadfully mixed up in the dates. Still, I think I did fairly well today. But oh, Diana, tomorrow the geometry exam comes off and when I think of it it takes every bit of determination I possess to keep from opening my Euclid. If I thought the multiplication table would help me any I would recite it from now till tomorrow morning.

"I went down to see the other girls this evening. On my way I met Moody Spurgeon wandering distractedly around. He said he knew he had failed in history and he was born to be a disappointment to his parents and he was going home on the morning train; and it would be easier to be a carpenter than a minister, anyhow. I cheered him up and persuaded him to stay to the end because it would be unfair to Miss Stacy if he didn't. Sometimes I have wished I was born a boy, but when I see Moody Spurgeon I'm always glad I'm a girl and not his sister.

"Ruby was in hysterics when I reached their boardinghouse; she had just discovered a fearful mistake she had made in her English paper. When she recovered we went uptown and had an ice cream. How we wished you had been with us.

"Oh, Diana, if only the geometry examination were over! But there, as Mrs. Lynde would say, the sun will go on rising and setting whether I fail in geometry or not. That is true but not especially comforting. I think I'd rather it didn't go on if I failed!

"Yours devotedly,

"Anne"

The geometry examination and all the others were over in due time and Anne arrived home on Friday evening, rather tired but with an air of chastened triumph about her. Diana was over at Green Gables when she arrived and they met as if they had been parted for years.

"You old darling, it's perfectly splendid to see you back again. It seems like an age since you went to town and oh, Anne, how did you get along?"

"Pretty well, I think, in everything but the geometry. I don't know whether I passed in it or not and I have a creepy, crawly presentiment that I didn't. Oh, how good it is to be back! Green Gables is the dearest, loveliest spot in the world."

"How did the others do?"

"The girls say they know they didn't pass, but I think they did pretty well. Josie says the geometry was so easy a child of ten could do it! Moody Spurgeon still thinks he failed in history and Charlie says he failed in algebra. But we don't really know anything about it and won't until the pass list is out. That won't be for a fortnight. Fancy living a fortnight in such suspense! I wish I could go to sleep and never wake up until it is over."

Diana knew it would be useless to ask how Gilbert Blythe had fared, so she merely said:

"Oh, you'll pass all right. Don't worry."

"I'd rather not pass at all than not come out pretty well up on the list," flashed Anne, by which she meant—and Diana knew she meant—that success would be incomplete and bitter if she did not come out ahead of Gilbert Blythe.

With this end in view Anne had strained every nerve during the examinations. So had Gilbert. They had met and passed each other on the street a dozen times without any sign of recognition and every time Anne had held her head a little higher and wished a little more earnestly that she had made friends with Gilbert when he asked her, and vowed a little more determinedly to surpass him in the examination. She knew that all Avonlea junior was wondering which would come out first; she even knew that Jimmy Glover and Ned Wright had a bet on the question and that Josie Pye had said there was no doubt in the world that Gilbert would be first; and she felt that her humiliation would be unbearable if she failed.

But she had another and nobler motive for wishing to do well. She wanted to "pass high" for the sake of Matthew and Marilla—especially Matthew. Matthew had declared to her his conviction that she "would beat the whole Island." That, Anne felt, was something it would be foolish to hope for even in the wildest dreams. But she did hope fervently that she would be among the first ten at least, so that she might see Matthew's kindly brown eyes gleam with pride in her achievement. That, she felt, would be a sweet reward indeed for all her hard work and patient grubbing among unimaginative equations and conjugations.

At the end of the fortnight Anne took to "haunting" the post office also, in the distracted company of Jane, Ruby, and Josie, opening the Charlottetown dailies with shaking hands and cold, sinkaway feelings as bad as any experienced during the Entrance week. Charlie and Gilbert were not above doing this too, but Moody Spurgeon stayed resolutely away.

"I haven't got the grit to go there and look at a paper in cold blood," he told Anne. "I'm just going to wait until somebody comes and tells me suddenly whether I've passed or not."

When three weeks had gone by without the pass list appearing Anne began to feel that she really couldn't stand the strain much longer. Her appetite failed and her interest in Avonlea doings languished. Mrs. Lynde wanted to know what else you could expect with a Tory superintendent of education at the head of affairs, and Matthew, noting Anne's paleness and indifference and the lagging steps that bore her home from the post office every afternoon, began seriously to wonder if he hadn't better vote Grit at the next election.

But one evening the news came. Anne was sitting at her open window, for the time forgetful of the woes of examinations and the cares of the world, as she drank in the beauty of the summer dusk, sweet-scented with flower breaths from the garden below and sibilant and rustling from the stir of poplars. The eastern sky above the firs was flushed faintly pink from the reflection of the west, and Anne was wondering dreamily if the spirit of color looked like that, when she saw Diana come flying down through the firs, over the log bridge, and up the slope, with a fluttering newspaper in her hand.

Anne sprang to her feet, knowing at once what that paper contained. The pass list was out! Her head whirled and her heart beat until it hurt her. She could not move a step. It seemed an hour to her before Diana came rushing along the hall and burst into the room without even knocking, so great was her excitement.

"Anne, you've passed," she cried, "passed the VERY FIRST—you and Gilbert both—you're ties—but your name is first. Oh, I'm so proud!"

Diana flung the paper on the table and herself on Anne's bed, utterly breathless and incapable of further speech. Anne lighted the lamp, oversetting the match safe and using up half a dozen matches before her shaking hands could accomplish the task. Then she snatched up the paper. Yes, she had passed—there was her name at the very top of a list of two hundred! That moment was worth living for.

"You did just splendidly, Anne," puffed Diana, recovering sufficiently to sit up and speak, for Anne, starry eyed and rapt, had not uttered a word. "Father brought the paper home from Bright River not ten minutes ago—it came out on the afternoon train, you know, and won't be here till tomorrow by mail—and when I saw the pass list I just rushed over like a wild thing. You've all passed, every one of you, Moody Spurgeon and all, although he's conditioned in history. Jane and Ruby did pretty well—they're halfway up—and so did Charlie. Josie just scraped through with three marks to spare, but you'll see she'll put on as many airs as if she'd led. Won't Miss Stacy be delighted? Oh, Anne, what does it feel like to see your name at the head of a pass list like that? If it were me I know I'd go crazy with joy. I am pretty near crazy as it is, but you're as calm and cool as a spring evening."

"I'm just dazzled inside," said Anne. "I want to say a hundred things, and I can't find words to say them in. I never dreamed of this—yes, I did too, just once! I let myself think ONCE, 'What if I should come out first?' quakingly, you know, for it seemed so vain and presumptuous to think I could lead the Island. Excuse me a minute, Diana. I must run right out to the field to tell Matthew. Then we'll go up the road and tell the good news to the others."

They hurried to the hayfield below the barn where Matthew was coiling hay, and, as luck would have it, Mrs. Lynde was talking to Marilla at the lane fence.

"Oh, Matthew," exclaimed Anne, "I've passed and I'm first—or one of the first! I'm not vain, but I'm thankful."

"Well now, I always said it," said Matthew, gazing at the pass list delightedly. "I knew you could beat them all easy."

"You've done pretty well, I must say, Anne," said Marilla, trying to hide her extreme pride in Anne from Mrs. Rachel's critical eye. But that good soul said heartily:

"I just guess she has done well, and far be it from me to be backward in saying it. You're a credit to your friends, Anne, that's what, and we're all proud of you."

That night Anne, who had wound up the delightful evening with a serious little talk with Mrs. Allan at the manse, knelt sweetly by her open window in a great sheen of moonshine and murmured a prayer of gratitude and aspiration that came straight from her heart. There was in it thankfulness for the past and reverent petition for the future; and when she slept on her white pillow her dreams were as fair and bright and beautiful as maidenhood might desire.

CHAPTER XXXIII. The Hotel Concert

"Put on your white organdy, by all means, Anne," advised Diana decidedly.

They were together in the east gable chamber; outside it was only twilight—a lovely yellowish-green twilight with a clear-blue cloudless sky. A big round moon, slowly deepening from her pallid luster into burnished silver, hung over the Haunted Wood; the air was full of sweet summer sounds—sleepy birds twittering, freakish breezes, faraway voices and laughter. But in Anne's room the blind was drawn and the lamp lighted, for an important toilet was being made.

The east gable was a very different place from what it had been on that night four years before, when Anne had felt its bareness penetrate to the marrow of her spirit with its inhospitable chill. Changes had crept in, Marilla conniving at them resignedly, until it was as sweet and dainty a nest as a young girl could desire.

The velvet carpet with the pink roses and the pink silk curtains of Anne's early visions had certainly never materialized; but her dreams had kept pace with her growth, and it is not probable she lamented them. The floor was covered with a pretty matting, and the curtains that softened the high window and fluttered in the vagrant breezes were of pale-green art muslin. The walls, hung not with gold and silver brocade tapestry, but with a dainty apple-blossom paper, were adorned with a few good pictures given Anne by Mrs. Allan. Miss Stacy's photograph occupied the place of honor, and Anne made a sentimental point of keeping fresh flowers on the bracket under it. Tonight a spike of white lilies faintly perfumed the room like the dream of a fragrance. There was no "mahogany furniture," but there was a white-painted bookcase filled with books, a cushioned wicker rocker, a toilet table befrilled with white muslin, a quaint, gilt-framed mirror with chubby pink Cupids and purple grapes painted over its arched top, that used to hang in the spare room, and a low white bed.

Anne was dressing for a concert at the White Sands Hotel. The guests had got it up in aid of the Charlottetown hospital, and had hunted out all the available amateur talent in the surrounding districts to help it along. Bertha Sampson and Pearl Clay of the White Sands Baptist choir had been asked to sing a duet; Milton Clark of Newbridge was to give a violin solo; Winnie Adella Blair of Carmody was to sing a Scotch ballad; and Laura Spencer of Spencervale and Anne Shirley of Avonlea were to recite.

As Anne would have said at one time, it was "an epoch in her life," and she was deliciously athrill with the excitement of it. Matthew was in the seventh heaven of gratified pride over the honor conferred on his Anne and Marilla was not far behind, although she would have died rather than admit it, and said she didn't think it was very proper for a lot of young folks to be gadding over to the hotel without any responsible person with them.

Anne and Diana were to drive over with Jane Andrews and her brother Billy in their double-seated buggy; and several other Avonlea girls and boys were going too. There was a party of visitors expected out from town, and after the concert a supper was to be given to the performers.

"Do you really think the organdy will be best?" queried Anne anxiously. "I don't think it's as pretty as my blue-flowered muslin—and it certainly isn't so fashionable."

"But it suits you ever so much better," said Diana. "It's so soft and frilly and clinging. The muslin is stiff, and makes you look too dressed up. But the organdy seems as if it grew on you."

Anne sighed and yielded. Diana was beginning to have a reputation for notable taste in dressing, and her advice on such subjects was much sought after. She was looking very pretty herself on this particular night in a dress of the lovely wild-rose pink, from which Anne was forever debarred; but she was not to take any part in the concert, so her appearance was of minor importance. All her pains were bestowed upon Anne, who, she vowed, must, for the credit of Avonlea, be dressed and combed and adorned to the Queen's taste.

"Pull out that frill a little more—so; here, let me tie your sash; now for your slippers. I'm going to braid your hair in two thick braids, and tie them halfway up with big white bows—no, don't pull out a single curl over your forehead—just have the soft part. There is no way you do your hair suits you so well, Anne, and Mrs. Allan says you look like a Madonna when you part it so. I shall fasten this little white house rose just behind your ear. There was just one on my bush, and I saved it for you."

"Shall I put my pearl beads on?" asked Anne. "Matthew brought me a string from town last week, and I know he'd like to see them on me."

Diana pursed up her lips, put her black head on one side critically, and finally pronounced in favor of the beads, which were thereupon tied around Anne's slim milk-white throat.

"There's something so stylish about you, Anne," said Diana, with unenvious admiration. "You hold your head with such an air. I suppose it's your figure. I am just a dumpling. I've always been afraid of it, and now I know it is so. Well, I suppose I shall just have to resign myself to it."

"But you have such dimples," said Anne, smiling affectionately into the pretty, vivacious face so near her own. "Lovely dimples, like little dents in cream. I have given up all hope of dimples. My dimple-dream will never come true; but so many of my dreams have that I mustn't complain. Am I all ready now?"

"All ready," assured Diana, as Marilla appeared in the doorway, a gaunt figure with grayer hair than of yore and no fewer angles, but with a much softer face. "Come right in and look at our elocutionist, Marilla. Doesn't she look lovely?"

Marilla emitted a sound between a sniff and a grunt.

"She looks neat and proper. I like that way of fixing her hair. But I expect she'll ruin that dress driving over there in the dust and dew with it, and it looks most too thin for these damp nights. Organdy's the most unserviceable stuff in the world anyhow, and I told Matthew so when he got it. But there is no use in saying anything to Matthew nowadays. Time was when he would take my advice, but now he just buys things for Anne regardless, and the clerks at Carmody know they can palm anything off on him. Just let them tell him a thing is pretty and fashionable, and Matthew plunks his money down for it. Mind you keep your skirt clear of the wheel, Anne, and put your warm jacket on."

Then Marilla stalked downstairs, thinking proudly how sweet Anne looked, with that

"One moonbeam from the forehead to the crown"

and regretting that she could not go to the concert herself to hear her girl recite.

"I wonder if it IS too damp for my dress," said Anne anxiously.

"Not a bit of it," said Diana, pulling up the window blind. "It's a perfect night, and there won't be any dew. Look at the moonlight."

"I'm so glad my window looks east into the sunrising," said Anne, going over to Diana. "It's so splendid to see the morning coming up over those long hills and glowing through those sharp fir tops. It's new every morning, and I feel as if I washed my very soul in that bath of earliest sunshine. Oh, Diana, I love this little room so dearly. I don't know how I'll get along without it when I go to town next month."

"Don't speak of your going away tonight," begged Diana. "I don't want to think of it, it makes me so miserable, and I do want to have a good time this evening. What are you going to recite, Anne? And are you nervous?"

"Not a bit. I've recited so often in public I don't mind at all now. I've decided to give 'The Maiden's Vow.' It's so pathetic. Laura Spencer is going to give a comic recitation, but I'd rather make people cry than laugh."

"What will you recite if they encore you?"

"They won't dream of encoring me," scoffed Anne, who was not without her own secret hopes that they would, and already visioned herself telling Matthew all about it at the next morning's breakfast table. "There are Billy and Jane now—I hear the wheels. Come on."

Billy Andrews insisted that Anne should ride on the front seat with him, so she unwillingly climbed up. She would have much preferred to sit back with the girls, where she could have laughed and chattered to her heart's content. There was not much of either laughter or chatter in Billy. He was a big, fat, stolid youth of twenty, with a round, expressionless face, and a painful lack of conversational gifts.

But he admired Anne immensely, and was puffed up with pride over the prospect of driving to White Sands with that slim, upright figure beside him.

Anne, by dint of talking over her shoulder to the girls and occasionally passing a sop of civility to Billy—who grinned and chuckled and never could think of any reply until it was too late—contrived to enjoy the drive in spite of all. It was a night for enjoyment. The road was full of buggies, all bound for the hotel, and laughter, silver clear, echoed and reechoed along it. When they reached the hotel it was a blaze of light from top to bottom. They were met by the ladies of the concert committee, one of whom took Anne off to the performers' dressing room which was filled with the members of a Charlottetown Symphony Club, among whom Anne felt suddenly shy and frightened and countrified. Her dress, which, in the east gable, had seemed so dainty and pretty, now seemed simple and plain—too simple and plain, she thought, among all the silks and laces that glistened and rustled around her. What were her pearl beads compared to the diamonds of the big, handsome lady near her? And how poor her one wee white rose must look beside all the hothouse flowers the others wore! Anne laid her hat and jacket away, and shrank miserably into a corner. She wished herself back in the white room at Green Gables.

It was still worse on the platform of the big concert hall of the hotel, where she presently found herself. The electric lights dazzled her eyes, the perfume and hum bewildered her. She wished she were sitting down in the audience with Diana and Jane, who seemed to be having a splendid time away at the back. She was wedged in between a stout lady in pink silk and a tall, scornful-looking girl in a white-lace dress. The stout lady occasionally turned her head squarely around and surveyed Anne through her eyeglasses until Anne, acutely sensitive of being so scrutinized, felt that she must scream aloud; and the white-lace girl kept talking audibly to her next neighbor about the "country bumpkins" and "rustic belles" in the audience, languidly anticipating "such fun" from the displays of local talent on the program. Anne believed that she would hate that white-lace girl to the end of life.

Unfortunately for Anne, a professional elocutionist was staying at the hotel and had consented to recite. She was a lithe, dark-eyed woman in a wonderful gown of shimmering gray stuff like woven moonbeams, with gems on her neck and in her dark hair. She had a marvelously flexible voice and wonderful power of expression; the audience went wild over her selection. Anne, forgetting all about herself and her troubles for the time, listened with rapt and shining eyes; but when the recitation ended she suddenly put her hands over her face. She could never get up and recite after that—never. Had she ever thought she could recite? Oh, if she were only back at Green Gables!

At this unpropitious moment her name was called. Somehow Anne—who did not notice the rather guilty little start of surprise the white-lace girl gave, and would not have understood the subtle compliment implied therein if she had—got on her feet, and moved dizzily out to the front. She was so pale that Diana and Jane, down in the audience, clasped each other's hands in nervous sympathy.

Anne was the victim of an overwhelming attack of stage fright. Often as she had recited in public, she had never before faced such an audience as this, and the sight of it paralyzed her energies completely. Everything was so strange, so brilliant, so bewildering—the rows of ladies in evening dress, the critical faces, the whole atmosphere of wealth and culture about her. Very different this from the plain benches at the Debating Club, filled with the homely, sympathetic faces of friends and neighbors. These people, she thought, would be merciless critics. Perhaps, like the white-lace girl, they anticipated amusement from her "rustic" efforts. She felt hopelessly, helplessly ashamed and miserable. Her knees trembled, her heart fluttered, a horrible faintness came over her; not a word could she utter, and the next moment she would have fled from the platform despite the humiliation which, she felt, must ever after be her portion if she did so.

But suddenly, as her dilated, frightened eyes gazed out over the audience, she saw Gilbert Blythe away at the back of the room, bending forward with a smile on his face—a smile which seemed to Anne at once triumphant and taunting. In reality it was nothing of the kind. Gilbert was merely smiling with appreciation of the whole affair in general and of the effect produced by Anne's slender white form and spiritual face against a background of palms in particular. Josie Pye, whom he had driven over, sat beside him, and her face certainly was both triumphant and taunting. But Anne did not see Josie, and would not have cared if she had. She drew a long breath and flung her head up proudly, courage and determination tingling over her like an electric shock. She WOULD NOT fail before Gilbert Blythe—he should never be able to laugh at her, never, never! Her fright and nervousness vanished; and she began her recitation, her clear, sweet voice reaching to the farthest corner of the room without a tremor or a break. Self-possession was fully restored to her, and in the reaction from that horrible moment of powerlessness she recited as she had never done before. When she finished there were bursts of honest applause. Anne, stepping back to her seat, blushing with shyness and delight, found her hand vigorously clasped and shaken by the stout lady in pink silk.

"My dear, you did splendidly," she puffed. "I've been crying like a baby, actually I have. There, they're encoring you—they're bound to have you back!"

"Oh, I can't go," said Anne confusedly. "But yet—I must, or Matthew will be disappointed. He said they would encore me."

"Then don't disappoint Matthew," said the pink lady, laughing.

Smiling, blushing, limpid eyed, Anne tripped back and gave a quaint, funny little selection that captivated her audience still further. The rest of the evening was quite a little triumph for her.

When the concert was over, the stout, pink lady—who was the wife of an American millionaire—took her under her wing, and introduced her to everybody; and everybody was very nice to her. The professional elocutionist, Mrs. Evans, came and chatted with her, telling her that she had a charming voice and "interpreted" her selections beautifully. Even the white-lace girl paid her a languid little compliment. They had supper in the big, beautifully decorated dining room; Diana and Jane were invited to partake of this, also, since they had come with Anne, but Billy was nowhere to be found, having decamped in mortal fear of some such invitation. He was in waiting for them, with the team, however, when it was all over, and the three girls came merrily out into the calm, white moonshine radiance. Anne breathed deeply, and looked into the clear sky beyond the dark boughs of the firs.

Oh, it was good to be out again in the purity and silence of the night! How great and still and wonderful everything was, with the murmur of the sea sounding through it and the darkling cliffs beyond like grim giants guarding enchanted coasts.

"Hasn't it been a perfectly splendid time?" sighed Jane, as they drove away. "I just wish I was a rich American and could spend my summer at a hotel and wear jewels and low-necked dresses and have ice cream and chicken salad every blessed day. I'm sure it would be ever so much more fun than teaching school. Anne, your recitation was simply great, although I thought at first you were never going to begin. I think it was better than Mrs. Evans's."

"Oh, no, don't say things like that, Jane," said Anne quickly, "because it sounds silly. It couldn't be better than Mrs. Evans's, you know, for she is a professional, and I'm only a schoolgirl, with a little knack of reciting. I'm quite satisfied if the people just liked mine pretty well."

"I've a compliment for you, Anne," said Diana. "At least I think it must be a compliment because of the tone he said it in. Part of it was anyhow. There was an American sitting behind Jane and me—such a romantic-looking man, with coal-black hair and eyes. Josie Pye says he is a distinguished artist, and that her mother's cousin in Boston is married to a man that used to go to school with him. Well, we heard him say—didn't we, Jane?—'Who is that girl on the platform with the splendid Titian hair? She has a face I should like to paint.' There now, Anne. But what does Titian hair mean?"

"Being interpreted it means plain red, I guess," laughed Anne. "Titian was a very famous artist who liked to paint red-haired women."

"DID you see all the diamonds those ladies wore?" sighed Jane. "They were simply dazzling. Wouldn't you just love to be rich, girls?"

"We ARE rich," said Anne staunchly. "Why, we have sixteen years to our credit, and we're happy as queens, and we've all got imaginations, more or less. Look at that sea, girls—all silver and shadow and vision of things not seen. We couldn't enjoy its loveliness any more if we had millions of dollars and ropes of diamonds. You wouldn't change into any of those women if you could. Would you want to be that white-lace girl and wear a sour look all your life, as if you'd been born turning up your nose at the world? Or the pink lady, kind and nice as she is, so stout and short that you'd really no figure at all? Or even Mrs. Evans, with that sad, sad look in her eyes? She must have been dreadfully unhappy sometime to have such a look. You KNOW you wouldn't, Jane Andrews!"

"I DON'T know—exactly," said Jane unconvinced. "I think diamonds would comfort a person for a good deal."

CHAPTER XXXIII. The Hotel Concert

"Well, I don't want to be anyone but myself, even if I go uncomforted by diamonds all my life," declared Anne. "I'm quite content to be Anne of Green Gables, with my string of pearl beads. I know Matthew gave me as much love with them as ever went with Madame the Pink Lady's jewels."

CHAPTER XXXIV. A Queen's Girl

The next three weeks were busy ones at Green Gables, for Anne was getting ready to go to Queen's, and there was much sewing to be done, and many things to be talked over and arranged. Anne's outfit was ample and pretty, for Matthew saw to that, and Marilla for once made no objections whatever to anything he purchased or suggested. More—one evening she went up to the east gable with her arms full of a delicate pale green material.

"Anne, here's something for a nice light dress for you. I don't suppose you really need it; you've plenty of pretty waists; but I thought maybe you'd like something real dressy to wear if you were asked out anywhere of an evening in town, to a party or anything like that. I hear that Jane and Ruby and Josie have got 'evening dresses,' as they call them, and I don't mean you shall be behind them. I got Mrs. Allan to help me pick it in town last week, and we'll get Emily Gillis to make it for you. Emily has got taste, and her fits aren't to be equaled."

"Oh, Marilla, it's just lovely," said Anne. "Thank you so much. I don't believe you ought to be so kind to me—it's making it harder every day for me to go away."

The green dress was made up with as many tucks and frills and shirrings as Emily's taste permitted. Anne put it on one evening for Matthew's and Marilla's benefit, and recited "The Maiden's Vow" for them in the kitchen. As Marilla watched the bright, animated face and graceful motions her thoughts went back to the evening Anne had arrived at Green Gables, and memory recalled a vivid picture of the odd, frightened child in her preposterous yellowish-brown wincey dress, the heartbreak looking out of her tearful eyes. Something in the memory brought tears to Marilla's own eyes.

"I declare, my recitation has made you cry, Marilla," said Anne gaily stooping over Marilla's chair to drop a butterfly kiss on that lady's cheek. "Now, I call that a positive triumph."

"No, I wasn't crying over your piece," said Marilla, who would have scorned to be betrayed into such weakness by any poetry stuff. "I just couldn't help thinking of the little girl you used to be, Anne. And I was wishing you could have stayed a little girl, even with all your queer ways. You've grown up now and you're going away; and you look so tall and stylish and so—so—different altogether in that dress—as if you didn't belong in Avonlea at all—and I just got lonesome thinking it all over."

"Marilla!" Anne sat down on Marilla's gingham lap, took Marilla's lined face between her hands, and looked gravely and tenderly into Marilla's eyes. "I'm not a bit changed—not really. I'm only just pruned down and branched out. The real ME—back here—is just the same. It won't make a bit of difference where I go or how much I change outwardly; at heart I shall always be your little Anne, who will love you and Matthew and dear Green Gables more and better every day of her life."

Anne laid her fresh young cheek against Marilla's faded one, and reached out a hand to pat Matthew's shoulder. Marilla would have given much just then to have possessed Anne's power of putting her feelings into words; but nature and habit had willed it otherwise, and she could only put her arms close about her girl and hold her tenderly to her heart, wishing that she need never let her go.

Matthew, with a suspicious moisture in his eyes, got up and went out-of-doors. Under the stars of the blue summer night he walked agitatedly across the yard to the gate under the poplars.

"Well now, I guess she ain't been much spoiled," he muttered, proudly. "I guess my putting in my oar occasional never did much harm after all. She's smart and pretty, and loving, too, which is better than all the rest. She's been a blessing to us, and there never was a luckier mistake than what Mrs. Spencer made—if it WAS luck. I don't believe it was any such thing. It was Providence, because the Almighty saw we needed her, I reckon."

The day finally came when Anne must go to town. She and Matthew drove in one fine September morning, after a tearful parting with Diana and an untearful practical one—on Marilla's side at least—with Marilla. But when Anne had gone Diana dried her tears and went to a beach picnic at White Sands with some of her Carmody cousins, where she contrived to enjoy herself tolerably well; while Marilla plunged fiercely into unnecessary work and kept at it all day long with the bitterest kind of heartache—the ache that burns and gnaws and cannot wash itself away in ready tears. But that night, when Marilla went to bed, acutely and miserably conscious that the little gable room at the end of the hall was untenanted by any vivid young life and unstirred by any soft breathing, she buried her face in her pillow, and wept for her girl in a passion of sobs that appalled her when she grew calm enough to reflect how very wicked it must be to take on so about a sinful fellow creature.

Anne and the rest of the Avonlea scholars reached town just in time to hurry off to the Academy. That first day passed pleasantly enough in a whirl of excitement, meeting all the new students, learning to know the professors by sight and being assorted and organized into classes. Anne intended taking up the Second Year work being advised to do so by Miss Stacy; Gilbert Blythe elected to do the same. This meant getting a First Class teacher's license in one year instead of two, if they were successful; but it also meant much more and harder work. Jane, Ruby, Josie, Charlie, and Moody Spurgeon, not being troubled with the stirrings of ambition, were content to take up the Second Class work. Anne was conscious of a pang of loneliness when she found herself in a room with fifty other students, not one of whom she knew, except the tall, brown-haired boy across the room; and knowing him in the fashion she did, did not help her much, as she reflected pessimistically. Yet she was undeniably glad that they were in the same class; the old rivalry could still be carried on, and Anne would hardly have known what to do if it had been lacking.

"I wouldn't feel comfortable without it," she thought. "Gilbert looks awfully determined. I suppose he's making up his mind, here and now, to win the medal. What a splendid chin he has! I never noticed it before. I do wish Jane and Ruby had gone in for First Class, too. I suppose I won't feel so much like a cat in a strange garret when I get acquainted, though. I wonder which of the girls here are going to be my friends. It's really an interesting speculation. Of course I promised Diana that no Queen's girl, no matter how much I liked her, should ever be as dear to me as she is; but I've lots of second-best affections to bestow. I like the look of that girl with the brown eyes and the crimson waist. She looks vivid and red-rosy; there's that pale, fair one gazing out of the window. She has lovely hair, and looks as if she knew a thing or two about dreams. I'd like to know them both—know them well—well enough to walk with my arm about their waists, and call them nicknames. But just now I don't know them and they don't know me, and probably don't want to know me particularly. Oh, it's lonesome!"

It was lonesomer still when Anne found herself alone in her hall bedroom that night at twilight. She was not to board with the other girls, who all had relatives in town to take pity on them. Miss Josephine Barry would have liked to board her, but Beechwood was so far from the Academy that it was out of the question; so Miss Barry hunted up a boarding-house, assuring Matthew and Marilla that it was the very place for Anne.

"The lady who keeps it is a reduced gentlewoman," explained Miss Barry. "Her husband was a British officer, and she is very careful what sort of boarders she takes. Anne will not meet with any objectionable persons under her roof. The table is good, and the house is near the Academy, in a quiet neighborhood."

All this might be quite true, and indeed, proved to be so, but it did not materially help Anne in the first agony of homesickness that seized upon her. She looked dismally about her narrow little room, with its dull-papered, pictureless walls, its small iron bedstead and empty book-case; and a horrible choke came into her throat as she thought of her own white room at Green Gables, where she would have the pleasant consciousness of a great green still outdoors, of sweet peas growing in the garden, and moonlight falling on the orchard, of the brook below the slope and the spruce boughs tossing in the night wind beyond it, of a vast starry sky, and the light from Diana's window shining out through the gap in the trees. Here there was nothing of this; Anne knew that outside of her window was a hard street, with a network of telephone wires shutting out the sky, the tramp of alien feet, and a thousand lights gleaming on stranger faces. She knew that she was going to cry, and fought against it.

CHAPTER XXXIV. A Queen's Girl

"I WON'T cry. It's silly—and weak—there's the third tear splashing down by my nose. There are more coming! I must think of something funny to stop them. But there's nothing funny except what is connected with Avonlea, and that only makes things worse—four—five—I'm going home next Friday, but that seems a hundred years away. Oh, Matthew is nearly home by now—and Marilla is at the gate, looking down the lane for him—six—seven—eight—oh, there's no use in counting them! They're coming in a flood presently. I can't cheer up—I don't WANT to cheer up. It's nicer to be miserable!"

The flood of tears would have come, no doubt, had not Josie Pye appeared at that moment. In the joy of seeing a familiar face Anne forgot that there had never been much love lost between her and Josie. As a part of Avonlea life even a Pye was welcome.

"I'm so glad you came up," Anne said sincerely.

"You've been crying," remarked Josie, with aggravating pity. "I suppose you're homesick—some people have so little self-control in that respect. I've no intention of being homesick, I can tell you. Town's too jolly after that poky old Avonlea. I wonder how I ever existed there so long. You shouldn't cry, Anne; it isn't becoming, for your nose and eyes get red, and then you seem ALL red. I'd a perfectly scrumptious time in the Academy today. Our French professor is simply a duck. His moustache would give you kerwollowps of the heart. Have you anything eatable around, Anne? I'm literally starving. Ah, I guessed likely Marilla'd load you up with cake. That's why I called round. Otherwise I'd have gone to the park to hear the band play with Frank Stockley. He boards same place as I do, and he's a sport. He noticed you in class today, and asked me who the red-headed girl was. I told him you were an orphan that the Cuthberts had adopted, and nobody knew very much about what you'd been before that."

Anne was wondering if, after all, solitude and tears were not more satisfactory than Josie Pye's companionship when Jane and Ruby appeared, each with an inch of Queen's color ribbon—purple and scarlet—pinned proudly to her coat. As Josie was not "speaking" to Jane just then she had to subside into comparative harmlessness.

"Well," said Jane with a sigh, "I feel as if I'd lived many moons since the morning. I ought to be home studying my Virgil—that horrid old professor gave us twenty lines to start in on tomorrow. But I simply couldn't settle down to study tonight. Anne, methinks I see the traces of tears. If you've been crying DO own up. It will restore my self-respect, for I was shedding tears freely before Ruby came along. I don't mind being a goose so much if somebody else is goosey, too. Cake? You'll give me a teeny piece, won't you? Thank you. It has the real Avonlea flavor."

Ruby, perceiving the Queen's calendar lying on the table, wanted to know if Anne meant to try for the gold medal.

Anne blushed and admitted she was thinking of it.

"Oh, that reminds me," said Josie, "Queen's is to get one of the Avery scholarships after all. The word came today. Frank Stockley told me—his uncle is one of

191

the board of governors, you know. It will be announced in the Academy tomorrow."

An Avery scholarship! Anne felt her heart beat more quickly, and the horizons of her ambition shifted and broadened as if by magic. Before Josie had told the news Anne's highest pinnacle of aspiration had been a teacher's provincial license, First Class, at the end of the year, and perhaps the medal! But now in one moment Anne saw herself winning the Avery scholarship, taking an Arts course at Redmond College, and graduating in a gown and mortar board, before the echo of Josie's words had died away. For the Avery scholarship was in English, and Anne felt that here her foot was on native heath.

A wealthy manufacturer of New Brunswick had died and left part of his fortune to endow a large number of scholarships to be distributed among the various high schools and academies of the Maritime Provinces, according to their respective standings. There had been much doubt whether one would be allotted to Queen's, but the matter was settled at last, and at the end of the year the graduate who made the highest mark in English and English Literature would win the scholarship—two hundred and fifty dollars a year for four years at Redmond College. No wonder that Anne went to bed that night with tingling cheeks!

"I'll win that scholarship if hard work can do it," she resolved. "Wouldn't Matthew be proud if I got to be a B.A.? Oh, it's delightful to have ambitions. I'm so glad I have such a lot. And there never seems to be any end to them—that's the best of it. Just as soon as you attain to one ambition you see another one glittering higher up still. It does make life so interesting."

CHAPTER XXXV. The Winter at Queen's

Anne's homesickness wore off, greatly helped in the wearing by her weekend visits home. As long as the open weather lasted the Avonlea students went out to Carmody on the new branch railway every Friday night. Diana and several other Avonlea young folks were generally on hand to meet them and they all walked over to Avonlea in a merry party. Anne thought those Friday evening gypsyings over the autumnal hills in the crisp golden air, with the homelights of Avonlea twinkling beyond, were the best and dearest hours in the whole week.

Gilbert Blythe nearly always walked with Ruby Gillis and carried her satchel for her. Ruby was a very handsome young lady, now thinking herself quite as grown up as she really was; she wore her skirts as long as her mother would let her and did her hair up in town, though she had to take it down when she went home. She had large, bright-blue eyes, a brilliant complexion, and a plump showy figure. She laughed a great deal, was cheerful and good-tempered, and enjoyed the pleasant things of life frankly.

"But I shouldn't think she was the sort of girl Gilbert would like," whispered Jane to Anne. Anne did not think so either, but she would not have said so for the Avery scholarship. She could not help thinking, too, that it would be very pleasant to have such a friend as Gilbert to jest and chatter with and exchange ideas about books and studies and ambitions. Gilbert had ambitions, she knew, and Ruby Gillis did not seem the sort of person with whom such could be profitably discussed.

There was no silly sentiment in Anne's ideas concerning Gilbert. Boys were to her, when she thought about them at all, merely possible good comrades. If she and Gilbert had been friends she would not have cared how many other friends he had nor with whom he walked. She had a genius for friendship; girl friends she had in plenty; but she had a vague consciousness that masculine friendship might also be a good thing to round out one's conceptions of companionship and furnish broader standpoints of judgment and comparison. Not that Anne could have put her feelings on the matter into just such clear definition. But she thought that if Gilbert had ever walked home with her from the train, over the crisp fields and along the ferny byways, they might have had many and merry and interesting conversations about the new world that was opening around them and their hopes and ambitions therein. Gilbert was a clever young fellow, with his own thoughts about things and a determination to get the best out of life and put the best into it.

Ruby Gillis told Jane Andrews that she didn't understand half the things Gilbert Blythe said; he talked just like Anne Shirley did when she had a thoughtful fit on and for her part she didn't think it any fun to be bothering about books and that sort of thing when you didn't have to. Frank Stockley had lots more dash and go, but then he wasn't half as good-looking as Gilbert and she really couldn't decide which she liked best!

In the Academy Anne gradually drew a little circle of friends about her, thoughtful, imaginative, ambitious students like herself. With the "rose-red" girl, Stella Maynard, and the "dream girl," Priscilla Grant, she soon became intimate, finding the latter pale spiritual-looking maiden to be full to the brim of mischief and pranks and fun, while the vivid, black-eyed Stella had a heartful of wistful dreams and fancies, as aerial and rainbow-like as Anne's own.

After the Christmas holidays the Avonlea students gave up going home on Fridays and settled down to hard work. By this time all the Queen's scholars had gravitated into their own places in the ranks and the various classes had assumed distinct and settled shadings of individuality. Certain facts had become generally accepted. It was admitted that the medal contestants had practically narrowed down to three—Gilbert Blythe, Anne Shirley, and Lewis Wilson; the Avery scholarship was more doubtful, any one of a certain six being a possible winner. The bronze medal for mathematics was considered as good as won by a fat, funny little up-country boy with a bumpy forehead and a patched coat.

Ruby Gillis was the handsomest girl of the year at the Academy; in the Second Year classes Stella Maynard carried off the palm for beauty, with small but critical minority in favor of Anne Shirley. Ethel Marr was admitted by all competent judges to have the most stylish modes of hair-dressing, and Jane Andrews—plain, plodding, conscientious Jane—carried off the honors in the domestic science course. Even Josie Pye attained a certain preeminence as the sharpest-tongued young lady in attendance at Queen's. So it may be fairly stated that Miss Stacy's old pupils held their own in the wider arena of the academical course.

Anne worked hard and steadily. Her rivalry with Gilbert was as intense as it had ever been in Avonlea school, although it was not known in the class at large, but somehow the bitterness had gone out of it. Anne no longer wished to win for the sake of defeating Gilbert; rather, for the proud consciousness of a well-won victory over a worthy foeman. It would be worth while to win, but she no longer thought life would be insupportable if she did not.

In spite of lessons the students found opportunities for pleasant times. Anne spent many of her spare hours at Beechwood and generally ate her Sunday dinners there and went to church with Miss Barry. The latter was, as she admitted, growing old, but her black eyes were not dim nor the vigor of her tongue in the least abated. But she never sharpened the latter on Anne, who continued to be a prime favorite with the critical old lady.

"That Anne-girl improves all the time," she said. "I get tired of other girls— there is such a provoking and eternal sameness about them. Anne has as many shades as a rainbow and every shade is the prettiest while it lasts. I don't know that she is as amusing as she was when she was a child, but she makes me love her and I like people who make me love them. It saves me so much trouble in making myself love them."

Then, almost before anybody realized it, spring had come; out in Avonlea the Mayflowers were peeping pinkly out on the sere barrens where snow-wreaths lingered; and the "mist of green" was on the woods and in the valleys. But in Charlottetown harassed Queen's students thought and talked only of examinations.

"It doesn't seem possible that the term is nearly over," said Anne. "Why, last fall it seemed so long to look forward to—a whole winter of studies and classes. And here we are, with the exams looming up next week. Girls, sometimes I feel as if those exams meant everything, but when I look at the big buds swelling on those chestnut trees and the misty blue air at the end of the streets they don't seem half so important."

Jane and Ruby and Josie, who had dropped in, did not take this view of it. To them the coming examinations were constantly very important indeed—far more important than chestnut buds or Maytime hazes. It was all very well for Anne, who was sure of passing at least, to have her moments of belittling them, but when your whole future depended on them—as the girls truly thought theirs did— you could not regard them philosophically.

"I've lost seven pounds in the last two weeks," sighed Jane. "It's no use to say don't worry. I WILL worry. Worrying helps you some—it seems as if you were doing something when you're worrying. It would be dreadful if I failed to get my license after going to Queen's all winter and spending so much money."

"*I* don't care," said Josie Pye. "If I don't pass this year I'm coming back next. My father can afford to send me. Anne, Frank Stockley says that Professor Tremaine said Gilbert Blythe was sure to get the medal and that Emily Clay would likely win the Avery scholarship."

"That may make me feel badly tomorrow, Josie," laughed Anne, "but just now I honestly feel that as long as I know the violets are coming out all purple down in the hollow below Green Gables and that little ferns are poking their heads up in Lovers' Lane, it's not a great deal of difference whether I win the Avery or not. I've done my best and I begin to understand what is meant by the 'joy of the strife.' Next to trying and winning, the best thing is trying and failing. Girls, don't talk about exams! Look at that arch of pale green sky over those houses and picture to yourself what it must look like over the purply-dark beech-woods back of Avonlea."

"What are you going to wear for commencement, Jane?" asked Ruby practically.

Jane and Josie both answered at once and the chatter drifted into a side eddy of fashions. But Anne, with her elbows on the window sill, her soft cheek laid against her clasped hands, and her eyes filled with visions, looked out unheedingly across city roof and spire to that glorious dome of sunset sky and wove her dreams of a possible future from the golden tissue of youth's own optimism. All the Beyond was hers with its possibilities lurking rosily in the oncoming years—each year a rose of promise to be woven into an immortal chaplet.

CHAPTER XXXVI. The Glory and the Dream

On the morning when the final results of all the examinations were to be posted on the bulletin board at Queen's, Anne and Jane walked down the street together. Jane was smiling and happy; examinations were over and she was comfortably sure she had made a pass at least; further considerations troubled Jane not at all; she had no soaring ambitions and consequently was not affected with the unrest attendant thereon. For we pay a price for everything we get or take in this world; and although ambitions are well worth having, they are not to be cheaply won, but exact their dues of work and self-denial, anxiety and discouragement. Anne was pale and quiet; in ten more minutes she would know who had won the medal and who the Avery. Beyond those ten minutes there did not seem, just then, to be anything worth being called Time.

"Of course you'll win one of them anyhow," said Jane, who couldn't understand how the faculty could be so unfair as to order it otherwise.

"I have not hope of the Avery," said Anne. "Everybody says Emily Clay will win it. And I'm not going to march up to that bulletin board and look at it before everybody. I haven't the moral courage. I'm going straight to the girls' dressing room. You must read the announcements and then come and tell me, Jane. And I implore you in the name of our old friendship to do it as quickly as possible. If I have failed just say so, without trying to break it gently; and whatever you do DON'T sympathize with me. Promise me this, Jane."

Jane promised solemnly; but, as it happened, there was no necessity for such a promise. When they went up the entrance steps of Queen's they found the hall full of boys who were carrying Gilbert Blythe around on their shoulders and yelling at the tops of their voices, "Hurrah for Blythe, Medalist!"

For a moment Anne felt one sickening pang of defeat and disappointment. So she had failed and Gilbert had won! Well, Matthew would be sorry—he had been so sure she would win.

And then!

Somebody called out:

"Three cheers for Miss Shirley, winner of the Avery!"

"Oh, Anne," gasped Jane, as they fled to the girls' dressing room amid hearty cheers. "Oh, Anne I'm so proud! Isn't it splendid?"

And then the girls were around them and Anne was the center of a laughing, congratulating group. Her shoulders were thumped and her hands shaken vigorously. She was pushed and pulled and hugged and among it all she managed to whisper to Jane:

"Oh, won't Matthew and Marilla be pleased! I must write the news home right away."

Commencement was the next important happening. The exercises were held in the big assembly hall of the Academy. Addresses were given, essays read, songs sung, the public award of diplomas, prizes and medals made.

Matthew and Marilla were there, with eyes and ears for only one student on the platform—a tall girl in pale green, with faintly flushed cheeks and starry eyes, who read the best essay and was pointed out and whispered about as the Avery winner.

"Reckon you're glad we kept her, Marilla?" whispered Matthew, speaking for the first time since he had entered the hall, when Anne had finished her essay.

"It's not the first time I've been glad," retorted Marilla. "You do like to rub things in, Matthew Cuthbert."

Miss Barry, who was sitting behind them, leaned forward and poked Marilla in the back with her parasol.

"Aren't you proud of that Anne-girl? I am," she said.

Anne went home to Avonlea with Matthew and Marilla that evening. She had not been home since April and she felt that she could not wait another day. The apple blossoms were out and the world was fresh and young. Diana was at Green Gables to meet her. In her own white room, where Marilla had set a flowering house rose on the window sill, Anne looked about her and drew a long breath of happiness.

"Oh, Diana, it's so good to be back again. It's so good to see those pointed firs coming out against the pink sky—and that white orchard and the old Snow Queen. Isn't the breath of the mint delicious? And that tea rose—why, it's a song and a hope and a prayer all in one. And it's GOOD to see you again, Diana!"

"I thought you liked that Stella Maynard better than me," said Diana reproachfully. "Josie Pye told me you did. Josie said you were INFATUATED with her."

Anne laughed and pelted Diana with the faded "June lilies" of her bouquet.

"Stella Maynard is the dearest girl in the world except one and you are that one, Diana," she said. "I love you more than ever—and I've so many things to tell you. But just now I feel as if it were joy enough to sit here and look at you. I'm tired, I think—tired of being studious and ambitious. I mean to spend at least two hours tomorrow lying out in the orchard grass, thinking of absolutely nothing."

"You've done splendidly, Anne. I suppose you won't be teaching now that you've won the Avery?"

"No. I'm going to Redmond in September. Doesn't it seem wonderful? I'll have a brand new stock of ambition laid in by that time after three glorious, golden months of vacation. Jane and Ruby are going to teach. Isn't it splendid to think we all got through even to Moody Spurgeon and Josie Pye?"

"The Newbridge trustees have offered Jane their school already," said Diana. "Gilbert Blythe is going to teach, too. He has to. His father can't afford to send him to college next year, after all, so he means to earn his own way through. I expect he'll get the school here if Miss Ames decides to leave."

Anne felt a queer little sensation of dismayed surprise. She had not known this; she had expected that Gilbert would be going to Redmond also. What would she do without their inspiring rivalry? Would not work, even at a coeducational college with a real degree in prospect, be rather flat without her friend the enemy?

The next morning at breakfast it suddenly struck Anne that Matthew was not looking well. Surely he was much grayer than he had been a year before.

"Marilla," she said hesitatingly when he had gone out, "is Matthew quite well?"

"No, he isn't," said Marilla in a troubled tone. "He's had some real bad spells with his heart this spring and he won't spare himself a mite. I've been real worried about him, but he's some better this while back and we've got a good hired man, so I'm hoping he'll kind of rest and pick up. Maybe he will now you're home. You always cheer him up."

Anne leaned across the table and took Marilla's face in her hands.

"You are not looking as well yourself as I'd like to see you, Marilla. You look tired. I'm afraid you've been working too hard. You must take a rest, now that I'm home. I'm just going to take this one day off to visit all the dear old spots and hunt up my old dreams, and then it will be your turn to be lazy while I do the work."

Marilla smiled affectionately at her girl.

"It's not the work—it's my head. I've got a pain so often now—behind my eyes. Doctor Spencer's been fussing with glasses, but they don't do me any good. There is a distinguished oculist coming to the Island the last of June and the doctor says I must see him. I guess I'll have to. I can't read or sew with any comfort now. Well, Anne, you've done real well at Queen's I must say. To take First Class License in one year and win the Avery scholarship—well, well, Mrs. Lynde says pride goes before a fall and she doesn't believe in the higher education of women at all; she says it unfits them for woman's true sphere. I don't believe a word of it. Speaking of Rachel reminds me—did you hear anything about the Abbey Bank lately, Anne?"

"I heard it was shaky," answered Anne. "Why?"

"That is what Rachel said. She was up here one day last week and said there was some talk about it. Matthew felt real worried. All we have saved is in that bank—every penny. I wanted Matthew to put it in the Savings Bank in the first place, but old Mr. Abbey was a great friend of father's and he'd always banked with him. Matthew said any bank with him at the head of it was good enough for anybody."

"I think he has only been its nominal head for many years," said Anne. "He is a very old man; his nephews are really at the head of the institution."

"Well, when Rachel told us that, I wanted Matthew to draw our money right out and he said he'd think of it. But Mr. Russell told him yesterday that the bank was all right."

Anne had her good day in the companionship of the outdoor world. She never forgot that day; it was so bright and golden and fair, so free from shadow and so lavish of blossom. Anne spent some of its rich hours in the orchard; she went to the Dryad's Bubble and Willowmere and Violet Vale; she called at the manse and had a satisfying talk with Mrs. Allan; and finally in the evening she went with Matthew for the cows, through Lovers' Lane to the back pasture. The woods were all gloried through with sunset and the warm splendor of it streamed down through the hill gaps in the west. Matthew walked slowly with bent head; Anne, tall and erect, suited her springing step to his.

"You've been working too hard today, Matthew," she said reproachfully. "Why won't you take things easier?"

"Well now, I can't seem to," said Matthew, as he opened the yard gate to let the cows through. "It's only that I'm getting old, Anne, and keep forgetting it. Well, well, I've always worked pretty hard and I'd rather drop in harness."

"If I had been the boy you sent for," said Anne wistfully, "I'd be able to help you so much now and spare you in a hundred ways. I could find it in my heart to wish I had been, just for that."

"Well now, I'd rather have you than a dozen boys, Anne," said Matthew patting her hand. "Just mind you that—rather than a dozen boys. Well now, I guess it wasn't a boy that took the Avery scholarship, was it? It was a girl—my girl—my girl that I'm proud of."

He smiled his shy smile at her as he went into the yard. Anne took the memory of it with her when she went to her room that night and sat for a long while at her open window, thinking of the past and dreaming of the future. Outside the Snow Queen was mistily white in the moonshine; the frogs were singing in the marsh beyond Orchard Slope. Anne always remembered the silvery, peaceful beauty and fragrant calm of that night. It was the last night before sorrow touched her life; and no life is ever quite the same again when once that cold, sanctifying touch has been laid upon it.

CHAPTER XXXVII. The Reaper Whose Name Is Death

"Matthew—Matthew—what is the matter? Matthew, are you sick?"

It was Marilla who spoke, alarm in every jerky word. Anne came through the hall, her hands full of white narcissus,—it was long before Anne could love the sight or odor of white narcissus again,—in time to hear her and to see Matthew standing in the porch doorway, a folded paper in his hand, and his face strangely drawn and gray. Anne dropped her flowers and sprang across the kitchen to him at the same moment as Marilla. They were both too late; before they could reach him Matthew had fallen across the threshold.

"He's fainted," gasped Marilla. "Anne, run for Martin—quick, quick! He's at the barn."

Martin, the hired man, who had just driven home from the post office, started at once for the doctor, calling at Orchard Slope on his way to send Mr. and Mrs. Barry over. Mrs. Lynde, who was there on an errand, came too. They found Anne and Marilla distractedly trying to restore Matthew to consciousness.

Mrs. Lynde pushed them gently aside, tried his pulse, and then laid her ear over his heart. She looked at their anxious faces sorrowfully and the tears came into her eyes.

"Oh, Marilla," she said gravely. "I don't think—we can do anything for him."

"Mrs. Lynde, you don't think—you can't think Matthew is—is—" Anne could not say the dreadful word; she turned sick and pallid.

"Child, yes, I'm afraid of it. Look at his face. When you've seen that look as often as I have you'll know what it means."

Anne looked at the still face and there beheld the seal of the Great Presence.

When the doctor came he said that death had been instantaneous and probably painless, caused in all likelihood by some sudden shock. The secret of the shock was discovered to be in the paper Matthew had held and which Martin had brought from the office that morning. It contained an account of the failure of the Abbey Bank.

The news spread quickly through Avonlea, and all day friends and neighbors thronged Green Gables and came and went on errands of kindness for the dead and living. For the first time shy, quiet Matthew Cuthbert was a person of central importance; the white majesty of death had fallen on him and set him apart as one crowned.

When the calm night came softly down over Green Gables the old house was hushed and tranquil. In the parlor lay Matthew Cuthbert in his coffin, his long gray hair framing his placid face on which there was a little kindly smile as if he but slept, dreaming pleasant dreams. There were flowers about him—sweet old-fashioned flowers which his mother had planted in the homestead garden in her bridal days and for which Matthew had always had a secret, wordless love. Anne had gathered them and brought them to him, her anguished, tearless eyes burning in her white face. It was the last thing she could do for him.

The Barrys and Mrs. Lynde stayed with them that night. Diana, going to the east gable, where Anne was standing at her window, said gently:

"Anne dear, would you like to have me sleep with you tonight?"

"Thank you, Diana." Anne looked earnestly into her friend's face. "I think you won't misunderstand me when I say I want to be alone. I'm not afraid. I haven't been alone one minute since it happened—and I want to be. I want to be quite silent and quiet and try to realize it. I can't realize it. Half the time it seems to me that Matthew can't be dead; and the other half it seems as if he must have been dead for a long time and I've had this horrible dull ache ever since."

Diana did not quite understand. Marilla's impassioned grief, breaking all the bounds of natural reserve and lifelong habit in its stormy rush, she could comprehend better than Anne's tearless agony. But she went away kindly, leaving Anne alone to keep her first vigil with sorrow.

Anne hoped that the tears would come in solitude. It seemed to her a terrible thing that she could not shed a tear for Matthew, whom she had loved so much and who had been so kind to her, Matthew who had walked with her last evening at sunset and was now lying in the dim room below with that awful peace on his brow. But no tears came at first, even when she knelt by her window in the darkness and prayed, looking up to the stars beyond the hills—no tears, only the same horrible dull ache of misery that kept on aching until she fell asleep, worn out with the day's pain and excitement.

In the night she awakened, with the stillness and the darkness about her, and the recollection of the day came over her like a wave of sorrow. She could see Matthew's face smiling at her as he had smiled when they parted at the gate that last evening—she could hear his voice saying, "My girl—my girl that I'm proud of." Then the tears came and Anne wept her heart out. Marilla heard her and crept in to comfort her.

"There—there—don't cry so, dearie. It can't bring him back. It—it—isn't right to cry so. I knew that today, but I couldn't help it then. He'd always been such a good, kind brother to me—but God knows best."

"Oh, just let me cry, Marilla," sobbed Anne. "The tears don't hurt me like that ache did. Stay here for a little while with me and keep your arm round me—so. I couldn't have Diana stay, she's good and kind and sweet—but it's not her sorrow—she's outside of it and she couldn't come close enough to my heart to help me. It's our sorrow—yours and mine. Oh, Marilla, what will we do without him?"

"We've got each other, Anne. I don't know what I'd do if you weren't here—if you'd never come. Oh, Anne, I know I've been kind of strict and harsh with you maybe—but you mustn't think I didn't love you as well as Matthew did, for all that. I want to tell you now when I can. It's never been easy for me to say things out of my heart, but at times like this it's easier. I love you as dear as if you were my own flesh and blood and you've been my joy and comfort ever since you came to Green Gables."

Two days afterwards they carried Matthew Cuthbert over his homestead threshold and away from the fields he had tilled and the orchards he had loved and the trees he had planted; and then Avonlea settled back to its usual placidity and even at Green Gables affairs slipped into their old groove and work was done and duties fulfilled with regularity as before, although always with the aching sense of "loss in all familiar things." Anne, new to grief, thought it almost sad that it could be so—that they COULD go on in the old way without Matthew. She felt something like shame and remorse when she discovered that the sunrises behind the firs and the pale pink buds opening in the garden gave her the old inrush of gladness when she saw them—that Diana's visits were pleasant to her and that Diana's merry words and ways moved her to laughter and smiles—that, in brief, the beautiful world of blossom and love and friendship had lost none of its power to please her fancy and thrill her heart, that life still called to her with many insistent voices.

"It seems like disloyalty to Matthew, somehow, to find pleasure in these things now that he has gone," she said wistfully to Mrs. Allan one evening when they were together in the manse garden. "I miss him so much—all the time—and yet, Mrs. Allan, the world and life seem very beautiful and interesting to me for all. Today Diana said something funny and I found myself laughing. I thought when it happened I could never laugh again. And it somehow seems as if I oughtn't to."

"When Matthew was here he liked to hear you laugh and he liked to know that you found pleasure in the pleasant things around you," said Mrs. Allan gently. "He is just away now; and he likes to know it just the same. I am sure we should not shut our hearts against the healing influences that nature offers us. But I can understand your feeling. I think we all experience the same thing. We resent the thought that anything can please us when someone we love is no longer here to share the pleasure with us, and we almost feel as if we were unfaithful to our sorrow when we find our interest in life returning to us."

"I was down to the graveyard to plant a rosebush on Matthew's grave this afternoon," said Anne dreamily. "I took a slip of the little white Scotch rosebush his mother brought out from Scotland long ago; Matthew always liked those roses the best—they were so small and sweet on their thorny stems. It made me feel glad that I could plant it by his grave—as if I were doing something that must please him in taking it there to be near him. I hope he has roses like them in heaven. Perhaps the souls of all those little white roses that he has loved so many summers were all there to meet him. I must go home now. Marilla is all alone and she gets lonely at twilight."

"She will be lonelier still, I fear, when you go away again to college," said Mrs. Allan.

Anne did not reply; she said good night and went slowly back to green Gables. Marilla was sitting on the front door-steps and Anne sat down beside her. The door was open behind them, held back by a big pink conch shell with hints of sea sunsets in its smooth inner convolutions.

Anne gathered some sprays of pale-yellow honeysuckle and put them in her hair. She liked the delicious hint of fragrance, as some aerial benediction, above her every time she moved.

"Doctor Spencer was here while you were away," Marilla said. "He says that the specialist will be in town tomorrow and he insists that I must go in and have my eyes examined. I suppose I'd better go and have it over. I'll be more than thankful if the man can give me the right kind of glasses to suit my eyes. You won't mind staying here alone while I'm away, will you? Martin will have to drive me in and there's ironing and baking to do."

"I shall be all right. Diana will come over for company for me. I shall attend to the ironing and baking beautifully—you needn't fear that I'll starch the handker-chiefs or flavor the cake with liniment."

Marilla laughed.

"What a girl you were for making mistakes in them days, Anne. You were al-ways getting into scrapes. I did use to think you were possessed. Do you mind the time you dyed your hair?"

"Yes, indeed. I shall never forget it," smiled Anne, touching the heavy braid of hair that was wound about her shapely head. "I laugh a little now sometimes when I think what a worry my hair used to be to me—but I don't laugh MUCH, because it was a very real trouble then. I did suffer terribly over my hair and my freckles. My freckles are really gone; and people are nice enough to tell me my hair is au-burn now—all but Josie Pye. She informed me yesterday that she really thought it was redder than ever, or at least my black dress made it look redder, and she asked me if people who had red hair ever got used to having it. Marilla, I've al-most decided to give up trying to like Josie Pye. I've made what I would once have called a heroic effort to like her, but Josie Pye won't BE liked."

"Josie is a Pye," said Marilla sharply, "so she can't help being disagreeable. I suppose people of that kind serve some useful purpose in society, but I must say I don't know what it is any more than I know the use of thistles. Is Josie going to teach?"

"No, she is going back to Queen's next year. So are Moody Spurgeon and Charlie Sloane. Jane and Ruby are going to teach and they have both got schools—Jane at Newbridge and Ruby at some place up west."

"Gilbert Blythe is going to teach too, isn't he?"

"Yes"—briefly.

"What a nice-looking fellow he is," said Marilla absently. "I saw him in church last Sunday and he seemed so tall and manly. He looks a lot like his father did at the same age. John Blythe was a nice boy. We used to be real good friends, he and I. People called him my beau."

Anne looked up with swift interest.

"Oh, Marilla—and what happened?—why didn't you—"

"We had a quarrel. I wouldn't forgive him when he asked me to. I meant to, after awhile—but I was sulky and angry and I wanted to punish him first. He never came back—the Blythes were all mighty independent. But I always felt—rather sorry. I've always kind of wished I'd forgiven him when I had the chance."

"So you've had a bit of romance in your life, too," said Anne softly.

"Yes, I suppose you might call it that. You wouldn't think so to look at me, would you? But you never can tell about people from their outsides. Everybody has forgot about me and John. I'd forgotten myself. But it all came back to me when I saw Gilbert last Sunday."

CHAPTER XXXVIII. The Bend in the road

Marilla went to town the next day and returned in the evening. Anne had gone over to Orchard Slope with Diana and came back to find Marilla in the kitchen, sitting by the table with her head leaning on her hand. Something in her dejected attitude struck a chill to Anne's heart. She had never seen Marilla sit limply inert like that.

"Are you very tired, Marilla?"

"Yes—no—I don't know," said Marilla wearily, looking up. "I suppose I am tired but I haven't thought about it. It's not that."

"Did you see the oculist? What did he say?" asked Anne anxiously.

"Yes, I saw him. He examined my eyes. He says that if I give up all reading and sewing entirely and any kind of work that strains the eyes, and if I'm careful not to cry, and if I wear the glasses he's given me he thinks my eyes may not get any worse and my headaches will be cured. But if I don't he says I'll certainly be stone-blind in six months. Blind! Anne, just think of it!"

For a minute Anne, after her first quick exclamation of dismay, was silent. It seemed to her that she could NOT speak. Then she said bravely, but with a catch in her voice:

"Marilla, DON'T think of it. You know he has given you hope. If you are careful you won't lose your sight altogether; and if his glasses cure your headaches it will be a great thing."

"I don't call it much hope," said Marilla bitterly. "What am I to live for if I can't read or sew or do anything like that? I might as well be blind—or dead. And as for crying, I can't help that when I get lonesome. But there, it's no good talking about it. If you'll get me a cup of tea I'll be thankful. I'm about done out. Don't say anything about this to any one for a spell yet, anyway. I can't bear that folks should come here to question and sympathize and talk about it."

When Marilla had eaten her lunch Anne persuaded her to go to bed. Then Anne went herself to the east gable and sat down by her window in the darkness alone with her tears and her heaviness of heart. How sadly things had changed since she had sat there the night after coming home! Then she had been full of hope and joy and the future had looked rosy with promise. Anne felt as if she had lived years since then, but before she went to bed there was a smile on her lips and peace in her heart. She had looked her duty courageously in the face and found it a friend—as duty ever is when we meet it frankly.

One afternoon a few days later Marilla came slowly in from the front yard where she had been talking to a caller—a man whom Anne knew by sight as Sadler from Carmody. Anne wondered what he could have been saying to bring that look to Marilla's face.

"What did Mr. Sadler want, Marilla?"

Marilla sat down by the window and looked at Anne. There were tears in her eyes in defiance of the oculist's prohibition and her voice broke as she said:

"He heard that I was going to sell Green Gables and he wants to buy it."

"Buy it! Buy Green Gables?" Anne wondered if she had heard aright. "Oh, Marilla, you don't mean to sell Green Gables!"

"Anne, I don't know what else is to be done. I've thought it all over. If my eyes were strong I could stay here and make out to look after things and manage, with a good hired man. But as it is I can't. I may lose my sight altogether; and anyway I'll not be fit to run things. Oh, I never thought I'd live to see the day when I'd have to sell my home. But things would only go behind worse and worse all the time, till nobody would want to buy it. Every cent of our money went in that bank; and there's some notes Matthew gave last fall to pay. Mrs. Lynde advises me to sell the farm and board somewhere—with her I suppose. It won't bring much—it's small and the buildings are old. But it'll be enough for me to live on I reckon. I'm thankful you're provided for with that scholarship, Anne. I'm sorry you won't have a home to come to in your vacations, that's all, but I suppose you'll manage somehow."

Marilla broke down and wept bitterly.

"You mustn't sell Green Gables," said Anne resolutely.

"Oh, Anne, I wish I didn't have to. But you can see for yourself. I can't stay here alone. I'd go crazy with trouble and loneliness. And my sight would go—I know it would."

"You won't have to stay here alone, Marilla. I'll be with you. I'm not going to Redmond."

"Not going to Redmond!" Marilla lifted her worn face from her hands and looked at Anne. "Why, what do you mean?"

"Just what I say. I'm not going to take the scholarship. I decided so the night after you came home from town. You surely don't think I could leave you alone in your trouble, Marilla, after all you've done for me. I've been thinking and planning. Let me tell you my plans. Mr. Barry wants to rent the farm for next year. So you won't have any bother over that. And I'm going to teach. I've applied for the school here—but I don't expect to get it for I understand the trustees have promised it to Gilbert Blythe. But I can have the Carmody school—Mr. Blair told me so last night at the store. Of course that won't be quite as nice or convenient as if I had the Avonlea school. But I can board home and drive myself over to Carmody and back, in the warm weather at least. And even in winter I can come home Fridays. We'll keep a horse for that. Oh, I have it all planned out, Marilla. And I'll read to you and keep you cheered up. You sha'n't be dull or lonesome. And we'll be real cozy and happy here together, you and I."

Marilla had listened like a woman in a dream.

"Oh, Anne, I could get on real well if you were here, I know. But I can't let you sacrifice yourself so for me. It would be terrible."

"Nonsense!" Anne laughed merrily. "There is no sacrifice. Nothing could be worse than giving up Green Gables—nothing could hurt me more. We must keep the dear old place. My mind is quite made up, Marilla. I'm NOT going to Redmond; and I AM going to stay here and teach. Don't you worry about me a bit."

"But your ambitions—and—"

"I'm just as ambitious as ever. Only, I've changed the object of my ambitions. I'm going to be a good teacher—and I'm going to save your eyesight. Besides, I mean to study at home here and take a little college course all by myself. Oh, I've dozens of plans, Marilla. I've been thinking them out for a week. I shall give life here my best, and I believe it will give its best to me in return. When I left Queen's my future seemed to stretch out before me like a straight road. I thought I could see along it for many a milestone. Now there is a bend in it. I don't know what lies around the bend, but I'm going to believe that the best does. It has a fascination of its own, that bend, Marilla. I wonder how the road beyond it goes—what there is of green glory and soft, checkered light and shadows—what new landscapes—what new beauties—what curves and hills and valleys further on."

"I don't feel as if I ought to let you give it up," said Marilla, referring to the scholarship.

"But you can't prevent me. I'm sixteen and a half, 'obstinate as a mule,' as Mrs. Lynde once told me," laughed Anne. "Oh, Marilla, don't you go pitying me. I don't like to be pitied, and there is no need for it. I'm heart glad over the very thought of staying at dear Green Gables. Nobody could love it as you and I do—so we must keep it."

"You blessed girl!" said Marilla, yielding. "I feel as if you'd given me new life. I guess I ought to stick out and make you go to college—but I know I can't, so I ain't going to try. I'll make it up to you though, Anne."

When it became noised abroad in Avonlea that Anne Shirley had given up the idea of going to college and intended to stay home and teach there was a good deal of discussion over it. Most of the good folks, not knowing about Marilla's eyes, thought she was foolish. Mrs. Allan did not. She told Anne so in approving words that brought tears of pleasure to the girl's eyes. Neither did good Mrs. Lynde. She came up one evening and found Anne and Marilla sitting at the front door in the warm, scented summer dusk. They liked to sit there when the twilight came down and the white moths flew about in the garden and the odor of mint filled the dewy air.

Mrs. Rachel deposited her substantial person upon the stone bench by the door, behind which grew a row of tall pink and yellow hollyhocks, with a long breath of mingled weariness and relief.

"I declare I'm getting glad to sit down. I've been on my feet all day, and two hundred pounds is a good bit for two feet to carry round. It's a great blessing not to be fat, Marilla. I hope you appreciate it. Well, Anne, I hear you've given up your notion of going to college. I was real glad to hear it. You've got as much education now as a woman can be comfortable with. I don't believe in girls going to college with the men and cramming their heads full of Latin and Greek and all that nonsense."

"But I'm going to study Latin and Greek just the same, Mrs. Lynde," said Anne laughing. "I'm going to take my Arts course right here at Green Gables, and study everything that I would at college."

Mrs. Lynde lifted her hands in holy horror.

"Anne Shirley, you'll kill yourself."

"Not a bit of it. I shall thrive on it. Oh, I'm not going to overdo things. As 'Josiah Allen's wife,' says, I shall be 'mejum'. But I'll have lots of spare time in the long winter evenings, and I've no vocation for fancy work. I'm going to teach over at Carmody, you know."

"I don't know it. I guess you're going to teach right here in Avonlea. The trustees have decided to give you the school."

"Mrs. Lynde!" cried Anne, springing to her feet in her surprise. "Why, I thought they had promised it to Gilbert Blythe!"

"So they did. But as soon as Gilbert heard that you had applied for it he went to them—they had a business meeting at the school last night, you know—and told them that he withdrew his application, and suggested that they accept yours. He said he was going to teach at White Sands. Of course he knew how much you wanted to stay with Marilla, and I must say I think it was real kind and thoughtful in him, that's what. Real self-sacrificing, too, for he'll have his board to pay at White Sands, and everybody knows he's got to earn his own way through college. So the trustees decided to take you. I was tickled to death when Thomas came home and told me."

"I don't feel that I ought to take it," murmured Anne. "I mean—I don't think I ought to let Gilbert make such a sacrifice for—for me."

"I guess you can't prevent him now. He's signed papers with the White Sands trustees. So it wouldn't do him any good now if you were to refuse. Of course you'll take the school. You'll get along all right, now that there are no Pyes going. Josie was the last of them, and a good thing she was, that's what. There's been some Pye or other going to Avonlea school for the last twenty years, and I guess their mission in life was to keep school teachers reminded that earth isn't their home. Bless my heart! What does all that winking and blinking at the Barry gable mean?"

"Diana is signaling for me to go over," laughed Anne. "You know we keep up the old custom. Excuse me while I run over and see what she wants."

Anne ran down the clover slope like a deer, and disappeared in the firry shadows of the Haunted Wood. Mrs. Lynde looked after her indulgently.

"There's a good deal of the child about her yet in some ways."

"There's a good deal more of the woman about her in others," retorted Marilla, with a momentary return of her old crispness.

But crispness was no longer Marilla's distinguishing characteristic. As Mrs. Lynde told her Thomas that night.

"Marilla Cuthbert has got MELLOW. That's what."

Anne went to the little Avonlea graveyard the next evening to put fresh flowers on Matthew's grave and water the Scotch rosebush. She lingered there until dusk, liking the peace and calm of the little place, with its poplars whose rustle was like low, friendly speech, and its whispering grasses growing at will among the graves. When she finally left it and walked down the long hill that sloped to the Lake of Shining Waters it was past sunset and all Avonlea lay before her in a dreamlike afterlight—"a haunt of ancient peace." There was a freshness in the air as of a wind that had blown over honey-sweet fields of clover. Home lights twinkled out here and there among the homestead trees. Beyond lay the sea, misty and purple, with its haunting, unceasing murmur. The west was a glory of soft mingled hues, and the pond reflected them all in still softer shadings. The beauty of it all thrilled Anne's heart, and she gratefully opened the gates of her soul to it.

"Dear old world," she murmured, "you are very lovely, and I am glad to be alive in you."

Halfway down the hill a tall lad came whistling out of a gate before the Blythe homestead. It was Gilbert, and the whistle died on his lips as he recognized Anne. He lifted his cap courteously, but he would have passed on in silence, if Anne had not stopped and held out her hand.

"Gilbert," she said, with scarlet cheeks, "I want to thank you for giving up the school for me. It was very good of you—and I want you to know that I appreciate it."

Gilbert took the offered hand eagerly.

"It wasn't particularly good of me at all, Anne. I was pleased to be able to do you some small service. Are we going to be friends after this? Have you really forgiven me my old fault?"

Anne laughed and tried unsuccessfully to withdraw her hand.

"I forgave you that day by the pond landing, although I didn't know it. What a stubborn little goose I was. I've been—I may as well make a complete confession—I've been sorry ever since."

"We are going to be the best of friends," said Gilbert, jubilantly. "We were born to be good friends, Anne. You've thwarted destiny enough. I know we can help each other in many ways. You are going to keep up your studies, aren't you? So am I. Come, I'm going to walk home with you."

Marilla looked curiously at Anne when the latter entered the kitchen.

"Who was that came up the lane with you, Anne?"

"Gilbert Blythe," answered Anne, vexed to find herself blushing. "I met him on Barry's hill."

"I didn't think you and Gilbert Blythe were such good friends that you'd stand for half an hour at the gate talking to him," said Marilla with a dry smile.

"We haven't been—we've been good enemies. But we have decided that it will be much more sensible to be good friends in the future. Were we really there half an hour? It seemed just a few minutes. But, you see, we have five years' lost conversations to catch up with, Marilla."

Anne sat long at her window that night companioned by a glad content. The wind purred softly in the cherry boughs, and the mint breaths came up to her. The stars twinkled over the pointed firs in the hollow and Diana's light gleamed through the old gap.

Anne's horizons had closed in since the night she had sat there after coming home from Queen's; but if the path set before her feet was to be narrow she knew that flowers of quiet happiness would bloom along it. The joy of sincere work and worthy aspiration and congenial friendship were to be hers; nothing could rob her of her birthright of fancy or her ideal world of dreams. And there was always the bend in the road!

"'God's in his heaven, all's right with the world,'" whispered Anne softly. softly.

ANNE OF AVONLEA

To
MY FORMER TEACHER
HATTIE GORDON SMITH
IN GRATEFUL REMEMBRANCE OF HER
SYMPATHY AND ENCOURAGEMENT.

Flowers spring to blossom where she walks
The careful ways of duty,
Our hard, stiff lines of life with her
Are flowing curves of beauty.
—WHITTIER

I - An Irate Neighbor

A tall, slim girl, "half-past sixteen," with serious gray eyes and hair which her friends called auburn, had sat down on the broad red sandstone doorstep of a Prince Edward Island farmhouse one ripe afternoon in August, firmly resolved to construe so many lines of Virgil.

But an August afternoon, with blue hazes scarfing the harvest slopes, little winds whispering elfishly in the poplars, and a dancing slendor of red poppies outflaming against the dark coppice of young firs in a corner of the cherry orchard, was fitter for dreams than dead languages. The Virgil soon slipped unheeded to the ground, and Anne, her chin propped on her clasped hands, and her eyes on the splendid mass of fluffy clouds that were heaping up just over Mr. J. A. Harrison's house like a great white mountain, was far away in a delicious world where a certain schoolteacher was doing a wonderful work, shaping the destinies of future statesmen, and inspiring youthful minds and hearts with high and lofty ambitions.

To be sure, if you came down to harsh facts . . . which, it must be confessed, Anne seldom did until she had to . . . it did not seem likely that there was much promising material for celebrities in Avonlea school; but you could never tell what might happen if a teacher used her influence for good. Anne had certain rose-tinted ideals of what a teacher might accomplish if she only went the right way about it; and she was in the midst of a delightful scene, forty years hence, with a famous personage . . . just exactly what he was to be famous for was left in convenient haziness, but Anne thought it would be rather nice to have him a college president or a Canadian premier . . . bowing low over her wrinkled hand and assuring her that it was she who had first kindled his ambition, and that all his success in life was due to the lessons she had instilled so long ago in Avonlea school. This pleasant vision was shattered by a most unpleasant interruption.

A demure little Jersey cow came scuttling down the lane and five seconds later Mr. Harrison arrived . . . if "arrived" be not too mild a term to describe the manner of his irruption into the yard.

He bounced over the fence without waiting to open the gate, and angrily confronted astonished Anne, who had risen to her feet and stood looking at him in some bewilderment. Mr. Harrison was their new righthand neighbor and she had never met him before, although she had seen him once or twice.

In early April, before Anne had come home from Queen's, Mr. Robert Bell, whose farm adjoined the Cuthbert place on the west, had sold out and moved to Charlottetown. His farm had been bought by a certain Mr. J. A. Harrison, whose name, and the fact that he was a New Brunswick man, were all that was known about him. But before he had been a month in Avonlea he had won the reputation of being an odd person . . . "a crank," Mrs. Rachel Lynde said. Mrs. Rachel was an outspoken lady, as those of you who may have already made her acquaintance will remember. Mr. Harrison was certainly different from other people . . . and that is the essential characteristic of a crank, as everybody knows.

In the first place he kept house for himself and had publicly stated that he wanted no fools of women around his diggings. Feminine Avonlea took its revenge by the gruesome tales it related about his house-keeping and cooking. He had hired little John Henry Carter of White Sands and John Henry started the stories. For one thing, there was never any stated time for meals in the Harrison establishment. Mr. Harrison "got a bite" when he felt hungry, and if John Henry were around at the time, he came in for a share, but if he were not, he had to wait until Mr. Harrison's next hungry spell. John Henry mournfully averred that he would have starved to death if it wasn't that he got home on Sundays and got a good filling up, and that his mother always gave him a basket of "grub" to take back with him on Monday mornings.

As for washing dishes, Mr. Harrison never made any pretence of doing it unless a rainy Sunday came. Then he went to work and washed them all at once in the rainwater hogshead, and left them to drain dry.

Again, Mr. Harrison was "close." When he was asked to subscribe to the Rev. Mr. Allan's salary he said he'd wait and see how many dollars' worth of good he got out of his preaching first . . . he didn't believe in buying a pig in a poke. And when Mrs. Lynde went to ask for a contribution to missions . . . and incidentally to see the inside of the house . . . he told her there were more heathens among the old woman gossips in Avonlea than anywhere else he knew of, and he'd cheerfully contribute to a mission for Christianizing them if she'd undertake it. Mrs. Rachel got herself away and said it was a mercy poor Mrs. Robert Bell was safe in her grave, for it would have broken her heart to see the state of her house in which she used to take so much pride.

"Why, she scrubbed the kitchen floor every second day," Mrs. Lynde told Marilla Cuthbert indignantly, "and if you could see it now! I had to hold up my skirts as I walked across it."

Finally, Mr. Harrison kept a parrot called Ginger. Nobody in Avonlea had ever kept a parrot before; consequently that proceeding was considered barely respectable. And such a parrot! If you took John Henry Carter's word for it, never was such an unholy bird. It swore terribly. Mrs. Carter would have taken John Henry away at once if she had been sure she could get another place for him. Besides, Ginger had bitten a piece right out of the back of John Henry's neck one day when he had stooped down too near the cage. Mrs. Carter showed everybody the mark when the luckless John Henry went home on Sundays.

I - An Irate Neighbor

All these things flashed through Anne's mind as Mr. Harrison stood, quite speechless with wrath apparently, before her. In his most amiable mood Mr. Harrison could not have been considered a handsome man; he was short and fat and bald; and now, with his round face purple with rage and his prominent blue eyes almost sticking out of his head, Anne thought he was really the ugliest person she had ever seen.

All at once Mr. Harrison found his voice.

"I'm not going to put up with this," he spluttered, "not a day longer, do you hear, miss. Bless my soul, this is the third time, miss . . . the third time! Patience has ceased to be a virtue, miss. I warned your aunt the last time not to let it occur again . . . and she's let it . . . she's done it . . . what does she mean by it, that is what I want to know. That is what I'm here about, miss."

"Will you explain what the trouble is?" asked Anne, in her most dignified manner. She had been practicing it considerably of late to have it in good working order when school began; but it had no apparent effect on the irate J. A. Harrison.

"Trouble, is it? Bless my soul, trouble enough, I should think. The trouble is, miss, that I found that Jersey cow of your aunt's in my oats again, not half an hour ago. The third time, mark you. I found her in last Tuesday and I found her in yesterday. I came here and told your aunt not to let it occur again. She has let it occur again. Where's your aunt, miss? I just want to see her for a minute and give her a piece of my mind . . . a piece of J. A. Harrison's mind, miss."

"If you mean Miss Marilla Cuthbert, she is not my aunt, and she has gone down to East Grafton to see a distant relative of hers who is very ill," said Anne, with due increase of dignity at every word. "I am very sorry that my cow should have broken into your oats . . . she is my cow and not Miss Cuthbert's . . . Matthew gave her to me three years ago when she was a little calf and he bought her from Mr. Bell."

"Sorry, miss! Sorry isn't going to help matters any. You'd better go and look at the havoc that animal has made in my oats . . . trampled them from center to circumference, miss."

"I am very sorry," repeated Anne firmly, "but perhaps if you kept your fences in better repair Dolly might not have broken in. It is your part of the line fence that separates your oatfield from our pasture and I noticed the other day that it was not in very good condition."

"My fence is all right," snapped Mr. Harrison, angrier than ever at this carrying of the war into the enemy's country. "The jail fence couldn't keep a demon of a cow like that out. And I can tell you, you redheaded snippet, that if the cow is yours, as you say, you'd be better employed in watching her out of other people's grain than in sitting round reading yellow-covered novels," . . . with a scathing glance at the innocent tan-colored Virgil by Anne's feet.

Something at that moment was red besides Anne's hair . . . which had always been a tender point with her.

"I'd rather have red hair than none at all, except a little fringe round my ears," she flashed.

The shot told, for Mr. Harrison was really very sensitive about his bald head. His anger choked him up again and he could only glare speechlessly at Anne, who recovered her temper and followed up her advantage.

"I can make allowance for you, Mr. Harrison, because I have an imagination. I can easily imagine how very trying it must be to find a cow in your oats and I shall not cherish any hard feelings against you for the things you've said. I promise you that Dolly shall never break into your oats again. I give you my word of honor on THAT point."

"Well, mind you she doesn't," muttered Mr. Harrison in a somewhat subdued tone; but he stamped off angrily enough and Anne heard him growling to himself until he was out of earshot.

Grievously disturbed in mind, Anne marched across the yard and shut the naughty Jersey up in the milking pen.

"She can't possibly get out of that unless she tears the fence down," she reflected. "She looks pretty quiet now. I daresay she has sickened herself on those oats. I wish I'd sold her to Mr. Shearer when he wanted her last week, but I thought it was just as well to wait until we had the auction of the stock and let them all go together. I believe it is true about Mr. Harrison being a crank. Certainly there's nothing of the kindred spirit about HIM."

Anne had always a weather eye open for kindred spirits.

Marilla Cuthbert was driving into the yard as Anne returned from the house, and the latter flew to get tea ready. They discussed the matter at the tea table.

"I'll be glad when the auction is over," said Marilla. "It is too much responsibility having so much stock about the place and nobody but that unreliable Martin to look after them. He has never come back yet and he promised that he would certainly be back last night if I'd give him the day off to go to his aunt's funeral. I don't know how many aunts he has got, I am sure. That's the fourth that's died since he hired here a year ago. I'll be more than thankful when the crop is in and Mr. Barry takes over the farm. We'll have to keep Dolly shut up in the pen till Martin comes, for she must be put in the back pasture and the fences there have to be fixed. I declare, it is a world of trouble, as Rachel says. Here's poor Mary Keith dying and what is to become of those two children of hers is more than I know. She has a brother in British Columbia and she has written to him about them, but she hasn't heard from him yet."

"What are the children like? How old are they?"

"Six past . . . they're twins."

"Oh, I've always been especially interested in twins ever since Mrs. Hammond had so many," said Anne eagerly. "Are they pretty?"

"Goodness, you couldn't tell . . . they were too dirty. Davy had been out making mud pies and Dora went out to call him in. Davy pushed her headfirst into the biggest pie and then, because she cried, he got into it himself and wallowed in it to show her it was nothing to cry about. Mary said Dora was really a very good child but that Davy was full of mischief. He has never had any bringing up you might say. His father died when he was a baby and Mary has been sick almost ever since."

"I'm always sorry for children that have no bringing up," said Anne soberly. "You know *I* hadn't any till you took me in hand. I hope their uncle will look after them. Just what relation is Mrs. Keith to you?"

"Mary? None in the world. It was her husband . . . he was our third cousin. There's Mrs. Lynde coming through the yard. I thought she'd be up to hear about Mary."

"Don't tell her about Mr. Harrison and the cow," implored Anne.

Marilla promised; but the promise was quite unnecessary, for Mrs. Lynde was no sooner fairly seated than she said,

"I saw Mr. Harrison chasing your Jersey out of his oats today when I was coming home from Carmody. I thought he looked pretty mad. Did he make much of a rumpus?"

Anne and Marilla furtively exchanged amused smiles. Few things in Avonlea ever escaped Mrs. Lynde. It was only that morning Anne had said,

"If you went to your own room at midnight, locked the door, pulled down the blind, and SNEEZED, Mrs. Lynde would ask you the next day how your cold was!"

"I believe he did," admitted Marilla. "I was away. He gave Anne a piece of his mind."

"I think he is a very disagreeable man," said Anne, with a resentful toss of her ruddy head.

"You never said a truer word," said Mrs. Rachel solemnly. "I knew there'd be trouble when Robert Bell sold his place to a New Brunswick man, that's what. I don't know what Avonlea is coming to, with so many strange people rushing into it. It'll soon not be safe to go to sleep in our beds."

"Why, what other strangers are coming in?" asked Marilla.

"Haven't you heard? Well, there's a family of Donnells, for one thing. They've rented Peter Sloane's old house. Peter has hired the man to run his mill. They belong down east and nobody knows anything about them. Then that shiftless Timothy Cotton family are going to move up from White Sands and they'll simply be a burden on the public. He is in consumption . . . when he isn't stealing . . . and his wife is a slack-twisted creature that can't turn her hand to a thing. She washes her dishes SITTING DOWN. Mrs. George Pye has taken her husband's orphan nephew, Anthony Pye. He'll be going to school to you, Anne, so you may expect trouble, that's what. And you'll have another strange pupil, too. Paul Irving is coming from the States to live with his grandmother. You remember his father, Marilla . . . Stephen Irving, him that jilted Lavendar Lewis over at Grafton?"

"I don't think he jilted her. There was a quarrel . . . I suppose there was blame on both sides."

"Well, anyway, he didn't marry her, and she's been as queer as possible ever since, they say . . . living all by herself in that little stone house she calls Echo Lodge. Stephen went off to the States and went into business with his uncle and married a Yankee. He's never been home since, though his mother has been up to see him once or twice. His wife died two years ago and he's sending the boy home to his mother for a spell. He's ten years old and I don't know if he'll be a very desirable pupil. You can never tell about those Yankees."

Mrs Lynde looked upon all people who had the misfortune to be born or brought up elsewhere than in Prince Edward Island with a decided can-any-good-thing-come-out-of-Nazareth air. They MIGHT be good people, of course; but you were on the safe side in doubting it. She had a special prejudice against "Yankees." Her husband had been cheated out of ten dollars by an employer for whom he had once worked in Boston and neither angels nor principalities nor powers could have convinced Mrs. Rachel that the whole United States was not responsible for it.

"Avonlea school won't be the worse for a little new blood," said Marilla drily, "and if this boy is anything like his father he'll be all right. Steve Irving was the nicest boy that was ever raised in these parts, though some people did call him proud. I should think Mrs. Irving would be very glad to have the child. She has been very lonesome since her husband died."

"Oh, the boy may be well enough, but he'll be different from Avonlea children," said Mrs. Rachel, as if that clinched the matter. Mrs. Rachel's opinions concerning any person, place, or thing, were always warranted to wear. "What's this I hear about your going to start up a Village Improvement Society, Anne?"

"I was just talking it over with some of the girls and boys at the last Debating Club," said Anne, flushing. "They thought it would be rather nice . . . and so do Mr. and Mrs. Allan. Lots of villages have them now."

"Well, you'll get into no end of hot water if you do. Better leave it alone, Anne, that's what. People don't like being improved."

"Oh, we are not going to try to improve the PEOPLE. It is Avonlea itself. There are lots of things which might be done to make it prettier. For instance, if we could coax Mr. Levi Boulter to pull down that dreadful old house on his upper farm wouldn't that be an improvement?"

"It certainly would," admitted Mrs. Rachel. "That old ruin has been an eyesore to the settlement for years. But if you Improvers can coax Levi Boulter to do anything for the public that he isn't to be paid for doing, may I be there to see and hear the process, that's what. I don't want to discourage you, Anne, for there may be something in your idea, though I suppose you did get it out of some rubbishy Yankee magazine; but you'll have your hands full with your school and I advise you as a friend not to bother with your improvements, that's what. But there, I know you'll go ahead with it if you've set your mind on it. You were always one to carry a thing through somehow."

Something about the firm outlines of Anne's lips told that Mrs. Rachel was not far astray in this estimate. Anne's heart was bent on forming the Improvement Society. Gilbert Blythe, who was to teach in White Sands but would always be home from Friday night to Monday morning, was enthusiastic about it; and most of the other folks were willing to go in for anything that meant occasional meetings and consequently some "fun." As for what the "improvements" were to be, nobody had any very clear idea except Anne and Gilbert. They had talked them over and planned them out until an ideal Avonlea existed in their minds, if nowhere else.

Mrs. Rachel had still another item of news.

"They've given the Carmody school to a Priscilla Grant. Didn't you go to Queen's with a girl of that name, Anne?"

"Yes, indeed. Priscilla to teach at Carmody! How perfectly lovely!" exclaimed Anne, her gray eyes lighting up until they looked like evening stars, causing Mrs. Lynde to wonder anew if she would ever get it settled to her satisfaction whether Anne Shirley were really a pretty girl or not.

II - Selling in Haste and Repenting at Leisure

Anne drove over to Carmody on a shopping expedition the next afternoon and took Diana Barry with her. Diana was, of course, a pledged member of the Improvement Society, and the two girls talked about little else all the way to Carmody and back.

"The very first thing we ought to do when we get started is to have that hall painted," said Diana, as they drove past the Avonlea hall, a rather shabby building set down in a wooded hollow, with spruce trees hooding it about on all sides. "It's a disgraceful looking place and we must attend to it even before we try to get Mr. Levi Boulder to pull his house down. Father says we'll never succeed in DOING that. Levi Boulter is too mean to spend the time it would take."

"Perhaps he'll let the boys take it down if they promise to haul the boards and split them up for him for kindling wood," said Anne hopefully. "We must do our best and be content to go slowly at first. We can't expect to improve everything all at once. We'll have to educate public sentiment first, of course."

Diana wasn't exactly sure what educating public sentiment meant; but it sounded fine and she felt rather proud that she was going to belong to a society with such an aim in view.

"I thought of something last night that we could do, Anne. You know that three-cornered piece of ground where the roads from Carmody and Newbridge and White Sands meet? It's all grown over with young spruce; but wouldn't it be nice to have them all cleared out, and just leave the two or three birch trees that are on it?"

"Splendid," agreed Anne gaily. "And have a rustic seat put under the birches. And when spring comes we'll have a flower-bed made in the middle of it and plant geraniums."

"Yes; only we'll have to devise some way of getting old Mrs. Hiram Sloane to keep her cow off the road, or she'll eat our geraniums up," laughed Diana. "I begin to see what you mean by educating public sentiment, Anne. There's the old Boulter house now. Did you ever see such a rookery? And perched right close to the road too. An old house with its windows gone always makes me think of something dead with its eyes picked out."

"I think an old, deserted house is such a sad sight," said Anne dreamily. "It always seems to me to be thinking about its past and mourning for its old-time joys.

Marilla says that a large family was raised in that old house long ago, and that it was a real pretty place, with a lovely garden and roses climbing all over it. It was full of little children and laughter and songs; and now it is empty, and nothing ever wanders through it but the wind. How lonely and sorrowful it must feel! Perhaps they all come back on moonlit nights . . . the ghosts of the little children of long ago and the roses and the songs . . . and for a little while the old house can dream it is young and joyous again."

Diana shook her head.

"I never imagine things like that about places now, Anne. Don't you remember how cross mother and Marilla were when we imagined ghosts into the Haunted Wood? To this day I can't go through that bush comfortably after dark; and if I began imagining such things about the old Boulter house I'd be frightened to pass it too. Besides, those children aren't dead. They're all grown up and doing well . . . and one of them is a butcher. And flowers and songs couldn't have ghosts anyhow."

Anne smothered a little sigh. She loved Diana dearly and they had always been good comrades. But she had long ago learned that when she wandered into the realm of fancy she must go alone. The way to it was by an enchanted path where not even her dearest might follow her.

A thunder-shower came up while the girls were at Carmody; it did not last long, however, and the drive home, through lanes where the raindrops sparkled on the boughs and little leafy valleys where the drenched ferns gave out spicy odors, was delightful. But just as they turned into the Cuthbert lane Anne saw something that spoiled the beauty of the landscape for her.

Before them on the right extended Mr. Harrison's broad, gray-green field of late oats, wet and luxuriant; and there, standing squarely in the middle of it, up to her sleek sides in the lush growth, and blinking at them calmly over the intervening tassels, was a Jersey cow!

Anne dropped the reins and stood up with a tightening of the lips that boded no good to the predatory quadruped. Not a word said she, but she climbed nimbly down over the wheels, and whisked across the fence before Diana understood what had happened.

"Anne, come back," shrieked the latter, as soon as she found her voice. "You'll ruin your dress in that wet grain . . . ruin it. She doesn't hear me! Well, she'll never get that cow out by herself. I must go and help her, of course."

Anne was charging through the grain like a mad thing. Diana hopped briskly down, tied the horse securely to a post, turned the skirt of her pretty gingham dress over her shoulders, mounted the fence, and started in pursuit of her frantic friend. She could run faster than Anne, who was hampered by her clinging and drenched skirt, and soon overtook her. Behind them they left a trail that would break Mr. Harrison's heart when he should see it.

"Anne, for mercy's sake, stop," panted poor Diana. "I'm right out of breath and you are wet to the skin."

"I must . . . get . . . that cow . . . out . . . before . . . Mr. Harrison . . . sees her," gasped Anne. "I don't . . . care . . . if I'm . . . drowned . . . if we . . . can . . . only . . . do that."

But the Jersey cow appeared to see no good reason for being hustled out of her luscious browsing ground. No sooner had the two breathless girls got near her than she turned and bolted squarely for the opposite corner of the field.

"Head her off," screamed Anne. "Run, Diana, run."

Diana did run. Anne tried to, and the wicked Jersey went around the field as if she were possessed. Privately, Diana thought she was. It was fully ten minutes before they headed her off and drove her through the corner gap into the Cuthbert lane.

There is no denying that Anne was in anything but an angelic temper at that precise moment. Nor did it soothe her in the least to behold a buggy halted just outside the lane, wherein sat Mr. Shearer of Carmody and his son, both of whom wore a broad smile.

"I guess you'd better have sold me that cow when I wanted to buy her last week, Anne," chuckled Mr. Shearer.

"I'll sell her to you now, if you want her," said her flushed and disheveled owner. "You may have her this very minute."

"Done. I'll give you twenty for her as I offered before, and Jim here can drive her right over to Carmody. She'll go to town with the rest of the shipment this evening. Mr. Reed of Brighton wants a Jersey cow."

Five minutes later Jim Shearer and the Jersey cow were marching up the road, and impulsive Anne was driving along the Green Gables lane with her twenty dollars.

"What will Marilla say?" asked Diana.

"Oh, she won't care. Dolly was my own cow and it isn't likely she'd bring more than twenty dollars at the auction. But oh dear, if Mr. Harrison sees that grain he will know she has been in again, and after my giving him my word of honor that I'd never let it happen! Well, it has taught me a lesson not to give my word of honor about cows. A cow that could jump over or break through our milk-pen fence couldn't be trusted anywhere."

Marilla had gone down to Mrs. Lynde's, and when she returned knew all about Dolly's sale and transfer, for Mrs. Lynde had seen most of the transaction from her window and guessed the rest.

"I suppose it's just as well she's gone, though you DO do things in a dreadful headlong fashion, Anne. I don't see how she got out of the pen, though. She must have broken some of the boards off."

"I didn't think of looking," said Anne, "but I'll go and see now. Martin has never come back yet. Perhaps some more of his aunts have died. I think it's something like Mr. Peter Sloane and the octogenarians. The other evening Mrs. Sloane was reading a newspaper and she said to Mr. Sloane, 'I see here that another octogenarian has just died. What is an octogenarian, Peter?' And Mr. Sloane said he didn't know, but they must be very sickly creatures, for you never heard tell of them but they were dying. That's the way with Martin's aunts."

"Martin's just like all the rest of those French," said Marilla in disgust. "You can't depend on them for a day." Marilla was looking over Anne's Carmody purchases when she heard a shrill shriek in the barnyard. A minute later Anne dashed into the kitchen, wringing her hands.

"Anne Shirley, what's the matter now?"

"Oh, Marilla, whatever shall I do? This is terrible. And it's all my fault. Oh, will I EVER learn to stop and reflect a little before doing reckless things? Mrs. Lynde always told me I would do something dreadful some day, and now I've done it!"

"Anne, you are the most exasperating girl! WHAT is it you've done?"

"Sold Mr. Harrison's Jersey cow . . . the one he bought from Mr. Bell . . . to Mr. Shearer! Dolly is out in the milking pen this very minute."

"Anne Shirley, are you dreaming?"

"I only wish I were. There's no dream about it, though it's very like a nightmare. And Mr. Harrison's cow is in Charlottetown by this time. Oh, Marilla, I thought I'd finished getting into scrapes, and here I am in the very worst one I ever was in in my life. What can I do?"

"Do? There's nothing to do, child, except go and see Mr. Harrison about it. We can offer him our Jersey in exchange if he doesn't want to take the money. She is just as good as his."

"I'm sure he'll be awfully cross and disagreeable about it, though," moaned Anne.

"I daresay he will. He seems to be an irritable sort of a man. I'll go and explain to him if you like."

"No, indeed, I'm not as mean as that," exclaimed Anne. "This is all my fault and I'm certainly not going to let you take my punishment. I'll go myself and I'll go at once. The sooner it's over the better, for it will be terribly humiliating."

Poor Anne got her hat and her twenty dollars and was passing out when she happened to glance through the open pantry door. On the table reposed a nut cake which she had baked that morning . . . a particularly toothsome concoction iced with pink icing and adorned with walnuts. Anne had intended it for Friday evening, when the youth of Avonlea were to meet at Green Gables to organize the Improvement Society. But what were they compared to the justly offended Mr. Harrison? Anne thought that cake ought to soften the heart of any man, especially one who had to do his own cooking, and she promptly popped it into a box. She would take it to Mr. Harrison as a peace offering.

"That is, if he gives me a chance to say anything at all," she thought ruefully, as she climbed the lane fence and started on a short cut across the fields, golden in the light of the dreamy August evening. "I know now just how people feel who are being led to execution."

III - Mr. Harrison at Home

Mr. Harrison's house was an old-fashioned, low-eaved, whitewashed structure, set against a thick spruce grove.

Mr. Harrison himself was sitting on his vineshaded veranda, in his shirt sleeves, enjoying his evening pipe. When he realized who was coming up the path he sprang suddenly to his feet, bolted into the house, and shut the door. This was merely the uncomfortable result of his surprise, mingled with a good deal of shame over his outburst of temper the day before. But it nearly swept the remnant of her courage from Anne's heart.

"If he's so cross now what will he be when he hears what I've done," she reflected miserably, as she rapped at the door.

But Mr. Harrison opened it, smiling sheepishly, and invited her to enter in a tone quite mild and friendly, if somewhat nervous. He had laid aside his pipe and donned his coat; he offered Anne a very dusty chair very politely, and her reception would have passed off pleasantly enough if it had not been for the telltale of a parrot who was peering through the bars of his cage with wicked golden eyes. No sooner had Anne seated herself than Ginger exclaimed,

"Bless my soul, what's that redheaded snippet coming here for?"

It would be hard to say whose face was the redder, Mr. Harrison's or Anne's.

"Don't you mind that parrot," said Mr. Harrison, casting a furious glance at Ginger. "He's . . . he's always talking nonsense. I got him from my brother who was a sailor. Sailors don't always use the choicest language, and parrots are very imitative birds."

"So I should think," said poor Anne, the remembrance of her errand quelling her resentment. She couldn't afford to snub Mr. Harrison under the circumstances, that was certain. When you had just sold a man's Jersey cow offhand, without his knowledge or consent you must not mind if his parrot repeated uncomplimentary things. Nevertheless, the "redheaded snippet" was not quite so meek as she might otherwise have been.

"I've come to confess something to you, Mr. Harrison," she said resolutely. "It's . . . it's about . . . that Jersey cow."

"Bless my soul," exclaimed Mr. Harrison nervously, "has she gone and broken into my oats again? Well, never mind . . . never mind if she has. It's no difference

. . . none at all, I . . . I was too hasty yesterday, that's a fact. Never mind if she has."

"Oh, if it were only that," sighed Anne. "But it's ten times worse. I don't . . ."

"Bless my soul, do you mean to say she's got into my wheat?"

"No . . . no . . . not the wheat. But . . ."

"Then it's the cabbages! She's broken into my cabbages that I was raising for Exhibition, hey?"

"It's NOT the cabbages, Mr. Harrison. I'll tell you everything . . . that is what I came for—but please don't interrupt me. It makes me so nervous. Just let me tell my story and don't say anything till I get through—and then no doubt you'll say plenty," Anne concluded, but in thought only.

"I won't say another word," said Mr. Harrison, and he didn't. But Ginger was not bound by any contract of silence and kept ejaculating, "Redheaded snippet" at intervals until Anne felt quite wild.

"I shut my Jersey cow up in our pen yesterday. This morning I went to Carmody and when I came back I saw a Jersey cow in your oats. Diana and I chased her out and you can't imagine what a hard time we had. I was so dreadfully wet and tired and vexed—and Mr. Shearer came by that very minute and offered to buy the cow. I sold her to him on the spot for twenty dollars. It was wrong of me. I should have waited and consulted Marilla, of course. But I'm dreadfully given to doing things without thinking—everybody who knows me will tell you that. Mr. Shearer took the cow right away to ship her on the afternoon train."

"Redheaded snippet," quoted Ginger in a tone of profound contempt.

At this point Mr. Harrison arose and, with an expression that would have struck terror into any bird but a parrot, carried Ginger's cage into an adjoining room and shut the door. Ginger shrieked, swore, and otherwise conducted himself in keeping with his reputation, but finding himself left alone, relapsed into sulky silence.

"Excuse me and go on," said Mr. Harrison, sitting down again. "My brother the sailor never taught that bird any manners."

"I went home and after tea I went out to the milking pen. Mr. Harrison," . . . Anne leaned forward, clasping her hands with her old childish gesture, while her big gray eyes gazed imploringly into Mr. Harrison's embarrassed face . . . "I found my cow still shut up in the pen. It was YOUR cow I had sold to Mr. Shearer."

"Bless my soul," exclaimed Mr. Harrison, in blank amazement at this unlooked-for conclusion. "What a VERY extraordinary thing!"

"Oh, it isn't in the least extraordinary that I should be getting myself and other people into scrapes," said Anne mournfully. "I'm noted for that. You might suppose I'd have grown out of it by this time . . . I'll be seventeen next March . . . but it seems that I haven't. Mr. Harrison, is it too much to hope that you'll forgive me? I'm afraid it's too late to get your cow back, but here is the money for her . . . or you can have mine in exchange if you'd rather. She's a very good cow. And I can't express how sorry I am for it all."

"Tut, tut," said Mr. Harrison briskly, "don't say another word about it, miss. It's of no consequence . . . no consequence whatever. Accidents will happen. I'm too hasty myself sometimes, miss . . . far too hasty. But I can't help speaking out just what I think and folks must take me as they find me. If that cow had been in my cabbages now . . . but never mind, she wasn't, so it's all right. I think I'd rather have your cow in exchange, since you want to be rid of her."

"Oh, thank you, Mr. Harrison. I'm so glad you are not vexed. I was afraid you would be."

"And I suppose you were scared to death to come here and tell me, after the fuss I made yesterday, hey? But you mustn't mind me, I'm a terrible outspoken old fellow, that's all . . . awful apt to tell the truth, no matter if it is a bit plain."

"So is Mrs. Lynde," said Anne, before she could prevent herself.

"Who? Mrs. Lynde? Don't you tell me I'm like that old gossip," said Mr. Harrison irritably. "I'm not . . . not a bit. What have you got in that box?"

"A cake," said Anne archly. In her relief at Mr. Harrison's unexpected amiability her spirits soared upward feather-light. "I brought it over for you . . . I thought perhaps you didn't have cake very often."

"I don't, that's a fact, and I'm mighty fond of it, too. I'm much obliged to you. It looks good on top. I hope it's good all the way through."

"It is," said Anne, gaily confident. "I have made cakes in my time that were NOT, as Mrs. Allan could tell you, but this one is all right. I made it for the Improvement Society, but I can make another for them."

"Well, I'll tell you what, miss, you must help me eat it. I'll put the kettle on and we'll have a cup of tea. How will that do?"

"Will you let me make the tea?" said Anne dubiously.

Mr. Harrison chuckled.

"I see you haven't much confidence in my ability to make tea. You're wrong . . . I can brew up as good a jorum of tea as you ever drank. But go ahead yourself. Fortunately it rained last Sunday, so there's plenty of clean dishes."

Anne hopped briskly up and went to work. She washed the teapot in several waters before she put the tea to steep. Then she swept the stove and set the table, bringing the dishes out of the pantry. The state of that pantry horrified Anne, but she wisely said nothing. Mr. Harrison told her where to find the bread and butter and a can of peaches. Anne adorned the table with a bouquet from the garden and shut her eyes to the stains on the tablecloth. Soon the tea was ready and Anne found herself sitting opposite Mr. Harrison at his own table, pouring his tea for him, and chatting freely to him about her school and friends and plans. She could hardly believe the evidence of her senses.

Mr. Harrison had brought Ginger back, averring that the poor bird would be lonesome; and Anne, feeling that she could forgive everybody and everything, offered him a walnut. But Ginger's feelings had been grievously hurt and he rejected all overtures of friendship. He sat moodily on his perch and ruffled his feathers up until he looked like a mere ball of green and gold.

"Why do you call him Ginger?" asked Anne, who liked appropriate names and thought Ginger accorded not at all with such gorgeous plumage.

"My brother the sailor named him. Maybe it had some reference to his temper. I think a lot of that bird though . . . you'd be surprised if you knew how much. He has his faults of course. That bird has cost me a good deal one way and another. Some people object to his swearing habits but he can't be broken of them. I've tried . . . other people have tried. Some folks have prejudices against parrots. Silly, ain't it? I like them myself. Ginger's a lot of company to me. Nothing would induce me to give that bird up . . . nothing in the world, miss."

Mr. Harrison flung the last sentence at Anne as explosively as if he suspected her of some latent design of persuading him to give Ginger up. Anne, however, was beginning to like the queer, fussy, fidgety little man, and before the meal was over they were quite good friends. Mr. Harrison found out about the Improvement Society and was disposed to approve of it.

"That's right. Go ahead. There's lots of room for improvement in this settlement . . . and in the people too."

"Oh, I don't know," flashed Anne. To herself, or to her particular cronies, she might admit that there were some small imperfections, easily removable, in Avonlea and its inhabitants. But to hear a practical outsider like Mr. Harrison saying it was an entirely different thing. "I think Avonlea is a lovely place; and the people in it are very nice, too."

"I guess you've got a spice of temper," commented Mr. Harrison, surveying the flushed cheeks and indignant eyes opposite him. "It goes with hair like yours, I reckon. Avonlea is a pretty decent place or I wouldn't have located here; but I suppose even you will admit that it has SOME faults?"

"I like it all the better for them," said loyal Anne. "I don't like places or people either that haven't any faults. I think a truly perfect person would be very uninteresting. Mrs. Milton White says she never met a perfect person, but she's heard enough about one . . . her husband's first wife. Don't you think it must be very uncomfortable to be married to a man whose first wife was perfect?"

"It would be more uncomfortable to be married to the perfect wife," declared Mr. Harrison, with a sudden and inexplicable warmth.

When tea was over Anne insisted on washing the dishes, although Mr. Harrison assured her that there were enough in the house to do for weeks yet. She would dearly have loved to sweep the floor also, but no broom was visible and she did not like to ask where it was for fear there wasn't one at all.

"You might run across and talk to me once in a while," suggested Mr. Harrison when she was leaving. "'Tisn't far and folks ought to be neighborly. I'm kind of interested in that society of yours. Seems to me there'll be some fun in it. Who are you going to tackle first?"

"We are not going to meddle with PEOPLE . . . it is only PLACES we mean to improve," said Anne, in a dignified tone. She rather suspected that Mr. Harrison was making fun of the project.

When she had gone Mr. Harrison watched her from the window . . . a lithe, girlish shape, tripping lightheartedly across the fields in the sunset afterglow.

"I'm a crusty, lonesome, crabbed old chap," he said aloud, "but there's something about that little girl makes me feel young again . . . and it's such a pleasant sensation I'd like to have it repeated once in a while."

"Redheaded snippet," croaked Ginger mockingly.

Mr. Harrison shook his fist at the parrot.

"You ornery bird," he muttered, "I almost wish I'd wrung your neck when my brother the sailor brought you home. Will you never be done getting me into trouble?"

Anne ran home blithely and recounted her adventures to Marilla, who had been not a little alarmed by her long absence and was on the point of starting out to look for her.

"It's a pretty good world, after all, isn't it, Marilla?" concluded Anne happily. "Mrs. Lynde was complaining the other day that it wasn't much of a world. She said whenever you looked forward to anything pleasant you were sure to be more or less disappointed . . . perhaps that is true. But there is a good side to it too. The bad things don't always come up to your expectations either . . . they nearly always turn out ever so much better than you think. I looked forward to a dreadfully unpleasant experience when I went over to Mr. Harrison's tonight; and instead he was quite kind and I had almost a nice time. I think we're going to be real good friends if we make plenty of allowances for each other, and everything has turned out for the best. But all the same, Marilla, I shall certainly never again sell a cow before making sure to whom she belongs. And I do NOT like parrots!"

IV - Different Opinions

One evening at sunset, Jane Andrews, Gilbert Blythe, and Anne Shirley were lingering by a fence in the shadow of gently swaying spruce boughs, where a wood cut known as the Birch Path joined the main road. Jane had been up to spend the afternoon with Anne, who walked part of the way home with her; at the fence they met Gilbert, and all three were now talking about the fateful morrow; for that morrow was the first of September and the schools would open. Jane would go to Newbridge and Gilbert to White Sands.

"You both have the advantage of me," sighed Anne. "You're going to teach children who don't know you, but I have to teach my own old schoolmates, and Mrs. Lynde says she's afraid they won't respect me as they would a stranger unless I'm very cross from the first. But I don't believe a teacher should be cross. Oh, it seems to me such a responsibility!"

"I guess we'll get on all right," said Jane comfortably. Jane was not troubled by any aspirations to be an influence for good. She meant to earn her salary fairly, please the trustees, and get her name on the School Inspector's roll of honor. Further ambitions Jane had none. "The main thing will be to keep order and a teacher has to be a little cross to do that. If my pupils won't do as I tell them I shall punish them."

"How?"

"Give them a good whipping, of course."

"Oh, Jane, you wouldn't," cried Anne, shocked. "Jane, you COULDN'T!"

"Indeed, I could and would, if they deserved it," said Jane decidedly.

"I could NEVER whip a child," said Anne with equal decision. "I don't believe in it AT ALL. Miss Stacy never whipped any of us and she had perfect order; and Mr. Phillips was always whipping and he had no order at all. No, if I can't get along without whipping I shall not try to teach school. There are better ways of managing. I shall try to win my pupils' affections and then they will WANT to do what I tell them."

"But suppose they don't?" said practical Jane.

"I wouldn't whip them anyhow. I'm sure it wouldn't do any good. Oh, don't whip your pupils, Jane dear, no matter what they do."

"What do you think about it, Gilbert?" demanded Jane. "Don't you think there are some children who really need a whipping now and then?"

"Don't you think it's a cruel, barbarous thing to whip a child . . . ANY child?" exclaimed Anne, her face flushing with earnestness.

"Well," said Gilbert slowly, torn between his real convictions and his wish to measure up to Anne's ideal, "there's something to be said on both sides. I don't believe in whipping children MUCH. I think, as you say, Anne, that there are better ways of managing as a rule, and that corporal punishment should be a last resort. But on the other hand, as Jane says, I believe there is an occasional child who can't be influenced in any other way and who, in short, needs a whipping and would be improved by it. Corporal punishment as a last resort is to be my rule."

Gilbert, having tried to please both sides, succeeded, as is usual and eminently right, in pleasing neither. Jane tossed her head.

"I'll whip my pupils when they're naughty. It's the shortest and easiest way of convincing them."

Anne gave Gilbert a disappointed glance.

"I shall never whip a child," she repeated firmly. "I feel sure it isn't either right or necessary."

"Suppose a boy sauced you back when you told him to do something?" said Jane.

"I'd keep him in after school and talk kindly and firmly to him," said Anne. "There is some good in every person if you can find it. It is a teacher's duty to find and develop it. That is what our School Management professor at Queen's told us, you know. Do you suppose you could find any good in a child by whipping him? It's far more important to influence the children aright than it is even to teach them the three R's, Professor Rennie says."

"But the Inspector examines them in the three R's, mind you, and he won't give you a good report if they don't come up to his standard," protested Jane.

"I'd rather have my pupils love me and look back to me in after years as a real helper than be on the roll of honor," asserted Anne decidedly.

"Wouldn't you punish children at all, when they misbehaved?" asked Gilbert.

"Oh, yes, I suppose I shall have to, although I know I'll hate to do it. But you can keep them in at recess or stand them on the floor or give them lines to write."

"I suppose you won't punish the girls by making them sit with the boys?" said Jane slyly.

Gilbert and Anne looked at each other and smiled rather foolishly. Once upon a time, Anne had been made to sit with Gilbert for punishment and sad and bitter had been the consequences thereof.

"Well, time will tell which is the best way," said Jane philosophically as they parted.

Anne went back to Green Gables by way of Birch Path, shadowy, rustling, fern-scented, through Violet Vale and past Willowmere, where dark and light kissed each other under the firs, and down through Lover's Lane . . . spots she and Diana had so named long ago. She walked slowly, enjoying the sweetness of wood and field and the starry summer twilight, and thinking soberly about the new duties she was to take up on the morrow. When she reached the yard at

Green Gables Mrs. Lynde's loud, decided tones floated out through the open kitchen window.

"Mrs. Lynde has come up to give me good advice about tomorrow," thought Anne with a grimace, "but I don't believe I'll go in. Her advice is much like pepper, I think . . . excellent in small quantities but rather scorching in her doses. I'll run over and have a chat with Mr. Harrison instead."

This was not the first time Anne had run over and chatted with Mr. Harrison since the notable affair of the Jersey cow. She had been there several evenings and Mr. Harrison and she were very good friends, although there were times and seasons when Anne found the outspokenness on which he prided himself rather trying. Ginger still continued to regard her with suspicion, and never failed to greet her sarcastically as "redheaded snippet." Mr. Harrison had tried vainly to break him of the habit by jumping excitedly up whenever he saw Anne coming and exclaiming,

"Bless my soul, here's that pretty little girl again," or something equally flattering. But Ginger saw through the scheme and scorned it. Anne was never to know how many compliments Mr. Harrison paid her behind her back. He certainly never paid her any to her face.

"Well, I suppose you've been back in the woods laying in a supply of switches for tomorrow?" was his greeting as Anne came up the veranda steps.

"No, indeed," said Anne indignantly. She was an excellent target for teasing because she always took things so seriously. "I shall never have a switch in my school, Mr. Harrison. Of course, I shall have to have a pointer, but I shall use it for pointing ONLY."

"So you mean to strap them instead? Well, I don't know but you're right. A switch stings more at the time but the strap smarts longer, that's a fact."

"I shall not use anything of the sort. I'm not going to whip my pupils."

"Bless my soul," exclaimed Mr. Harrison in genuine astonishment, "how do you lay out to keep order then?"

"I shall govern by affection, Mr. Harrison."

"It won't do," said Mr. Harrison, "won't do at all, Anne. 'Spare the rod and spoil the child.' When I went to school the master whipped me regular every day because he said if I wasn't in mischief just then I was plotting it."

"Methods have changed since your schooldays, Mr. Harrison."

"But human nature hasn't. Mark my words, you'll never manage the young fry unless you keep a rod in pickle for them. The thing is impossible."

"Well, I'm going to try my way first," said Anne, who had a fairly strong will of her own and was apt to cling very tenaciously to her theories.

"You're pretty stubborn, I reckon," was Mr. Harrison's way of putting it. "Well, well, we'll see. Someday when you get riled up . . . and people with hair like yours are desperate apt to get riled . . . you'll forget all your pretty little notions and give some of them a whaling. You're too young to be teaching anyhow . . . far too young and childish."

Altogether, Anne went to bed that night in a rather pessimistic mood. She slept poorly and was so pale and tragic at breakfast next morning that Marilla was alarmed and insisted on making her take a cup of scorching ginger tea. Anne sipped it patiently, although she could not imagine what good ginger tea would do. Had it been some magic brew, potent to confer age and experience, Anne would have swallowed a quart of it without flinching.

"Marilla, what if I fail!"

"You'll hardly fail completely in one day and there's plenty more days coming," said Marilla. "The trouble with you, Anne, is that you'll expect to teach those children everything and reform all their faults right off, and if you can't you'll think you've failed."

V - A Full-fledged Schoolma'am

When Anne reached the school that morning . . . for the first time in her life she had traversed the Birch Path deaf and blind to its beauties . . . all was quiet and still. The preceding teacher had trained the children to be in their places at her arrival, and when Anne entered the schoolroom she was confronted by prim rows of "shining morning faces" and bright, inquisitive eyes. She hung up her hat and faced her pupils, hoping that she did not look as frightened and foolish as she felt and that they would not perceive how she was trembling.

She had sat up until nearly twelve the preceding night composing a speech she meant to make to her pupils upon opening the school. She had revised and improved it painstakingly, and then she had learned it off by heart. It was a very good speech and had some very fine ideas in it, especially about mutual help and earnest striving after knowledge. The only trouble was that she could not now remember a word of it.

After what seemed to her a year . . . about ten seconds in reality . . . she said faintly, "Take your Testaments, please," and sank breathlessly into her chair under cover of the rustle and clatter of desk lids that followed. While the children read their verses Anne marshalled her shaky wits into order and looked over the array of little pilgrims to the Grownup Land.

Most of them were, of course, quite well known to her. Her own classmates had passed out in the preceding year but the rest had all gone to school with her, excepting the primer class and ten newcomers to Avonlea. Anne secretly felt more interest in these ten than in those whose possibilities were already fairly well mapped out to her. To be sure, they might be just as commonplace as the rest; but on the other hand there MIGHT be a genius among them. It was a thrilling idea.

Sitting by himself at a corner desk was Anthony Pye. He had a dark, sullen little face, and was staring at Anne with a hostile expression in his black eyes. Anne instantly made up her mind that she would win that boy's affection and discomfit the Pyes utterly.

In the other corner another strange boy was sitting with Arty Sloane. . . a jolly looking little chap, with a snub nose, freckled face, and big, light blue eyes, fringed with whitish lashes . . . probably the DonNELL boy; and if resemblance went for anything, his sister was sitting across the aisle with Mary Bell. Anne wondered what sort of mother the child had, to send her to school dressed as she was. She wore a faded pink silk dress, trimmed with a great deal of cotton lace, soiled white kid slippers, and silk stockings. Her sandy hair was tortured into innumerable kinky and unnatural curls, surmounted by a flamboyant bow of pink ribbon bigger than her head. Judging from her expression she was very well satisfied with herself.

A pale little thing, with smooth ripples of fine, silky, fawn-colored hair flowing over her shoulders, must, Anne thought, be Annetta Bell, whose parents had formerly lived in the Newbridge school district, but, by reason of hauling their house fifty yards north of its old site were now in Avonlea. Three pallid little girls crowded into one seat were certainly Cottons; and there was no doubt that the small beauty with the long brown curls and hazel eyes, who was casting coquettish looks at Jack Gills over the edge of her Testament, was Prillie Rogerson, whose father had recently married a second wife and brought Prillie home from her grandmother's in Grafton. A tall, awkward girl in a back seat, who seemed to have too many feet and hands, Anne could not place at all, but later on discovered that her name was Barbara Shaw and that she had come to live with an Avonlea aunt. She was also to find that if Barbara ever managed to walk down the aisle without falling over her own or somebody else's feet the Avonlea scholars wrote the unusual fact up on the porch wall to commemorate it.

But when Anne's eyes met those of the boy at the front desk facing her own, a queer little thrill went over her, as if she had found her genius. She knew this must be Paul Irving and that Mrs. Rachel Lynde had been right for once when she prophesied that he would be unlike the Avonlea children. More than that, Anne realized that he was unlike other children anywhere, and that there was a soul subtly akin to her own gazing at her out of the very dark blue eyes that were watching her so intently.

She knew Paul was ten but he looked no more than eight. He had the most beautiful little face she had ever seen in a child . . . features of exquisite delicacy and refinement, framed in a halo of chestnut curls. His mouth was delicious, being full without pouting, the crimson lips just softly touching and curving into finely finished little corners that narrowly escaped being dimpled. He had a sober, grave, meditative expression, as if his spirit was much older than his body; but when Anne smiled softly at him it vanished in a sudden answering smile, which seemed an illumination of his whole being, as if some lamp had suddenly kindled into flame inside of him, irradiating him from top to toe. Best of all, it was involuntary, born of no external effort or motive, but simply the outflashing of a hidden personality, rare and fine and sweet. With a quick interchange of smiles Anne and Paul were fast friends forever before a word had passed between them.

The day went by like a dream. Anne could never clearly recall it afterwards. It almost seemed as if it were not she who was teaching but somebody else. She heard classes and worked sums and set copies mechanically. The children behaved quite well; only two cases of discipline occurred. Morley Andrews was caught driving a pair of trained crickets in the aisle. Anne stood Morley on the platform for an hour and . . . which Morley felt much more keenly . . . confiscated his crickets. She put them in a box and on the way from school set them free in Violet Vale; but Morley believed, then and ever afterwards, that she took them home and kept them for her own amusement.

The other culprit was Anthony Pye, who poured the last drops of water from his slate bottle down the back of Aurelia Clay's neck. Anne kept Anthony in at recess and talked to him about what was expected of gentlemen, admonishing him that they never poured water down ladies' necks. She wanted all her boys to be gentlemen, she said. Her little lecture was quite kind and touching; but unfortunately Anthony remained absolutely untouched. He listened to her in silence, with the same sullen expression, and whistled scornfully as he went out. Anne sighed; and then cheered herself up by remembering that winning a Pye's affections, like the building of Rome, wasn't the work of a day. In fact, it was doubtful whether some of the Pyes had any affections to win; but Anne hoped better things of Anthony, who looked as if he might be a rather nice boy if one ever got behind his sullenness.

When school was dismissed and the children had gone Anne dropped wearily into her chair. Her head ached and she felt woefully discouraged. There was no real reason for discouragement, since nothing very dreadful had occurred; but Anne was very tired and inclined to believe that she would never learn to like teaching. And how terrible it would be to be doing something you didn't like every day for . . . well, say forty years. Anne was of two minds whether to have her cry out then and there, or wait till she was safely in her own white room at home. Before she could decide there was a click of heels and a silken swish on the porch floor, and Anne found herself confronted by a lady whose appearance made her recall a recent criticism of Mr. Harrison's on an overdressed female he had seen in a Charlottetown store. "She looked like a head-on collision between a fashion plate and a nightmare."

The newcomer was gorgeously arrayed in a pale blue summer silk, puffed, frilled, and shirred wherever puff, frill, or shirring could possibly be placed. Her head was surmounted by a huge white chiffon hat, bedecked with three long but rather stringy ostrich feathers. A veil of pink chiffon, lavishly sprinkled with huge black dots, hung like a flounce from the hat brim to her shoulders and floated off in two airy streamers behind her. She wore all the jewelry that could be crowded on one small woman, and a very strong odor of perfume attended her.

"I am Mrs. DonNELL . . . Mrs. H. B. DonNELL," announced this vision, "and I have come in to see you about something Clarice Almira told me when she came home to dinner today. It annoyed me EXCESSIVELY."

"I'm sorry," faltered Anne, vainly trying to recollect any incident of the morning connected with the Donnell children.

"Clarice Almira told me that you pronounced our name DONnell. Now, Miss Shirley, the correct pronunciation of our name is DonNELL . . . accent on the last syllable. I hope you'll remember this in future."

"I'll try to," gasped Anne, choking back a wild desire to laugh. "I know by experience that it's very unpleasant to have one's name SPELLED wrong and I suppose it must be even worse to have it pronounced wrong."

"Certainly it is. And Clarice Almira also informed me that you call my son Jacob."

"He told me his name was Jacob," protested Anne.

"I might well have expected that," said Mrs. H. B. Donnell, in a tone which implied that gratitude in children was not to be looked for in this degenerate age. "That boy has such plebeian tastes, Miss Shirley. When he was born I wanted to call him St. Clair . . . it sounds SO aristocratic, doesn't it? But his father insisted he should be called Jacob after his uncle. I yielded, because Uncle Jacob was a rich old bachelor. And what do you think, Miss Shirley? When our innocent boy was five years old Uncle Jacob actually went and got married and now he has three boys of his own. Did you ever hear of such ingratitude? The moment the invitation to the wedding . . . for he had the impertinence to send us an invitation, Miss Shirley . . . came to the house I said, 'No more Jacobs for me, thank you.' From that day I called my son St. Clair and St. Clair I am determined he shall be called. His father obstinately continues to call him Jacob, and the boy himself has a perfectly unaccountable preference for the vulgar name. But St. Clair he is and St. Clair he shall remain. You will kindly remember this, Miss Shirley, will you not? THANK you. I told Clarice Almira that I was sure it was only a misunderstanding and that a word would set it right. Donnell. . . accent on the last syllable . . . and St. Clair . . . on no account Jacob. You'll remember? THANK you."

When Mrs. H. B. DonNELL had skimmed away Anne locked the school door and went home. At the foot of the hill she found Paul Irving by the Birch Path. He held out to her a cluster of the dainty little wild orchids which Avonlea children called "rice lillies."

"Please, teacher, I found these in Mr. Wright's field," he said shyly, "and I came back to give them to you because I thought you were the kind of lady that would like them, and because . . ." he lifted his big beautiful eyes . . . "I like you, teacher."

"You darling," said Anne, taking the fragrant spikes. As if Paul's words had been a spell of magic, discouragement and weariness passed from her spirit, and hope upwelled in her heart like a dancing fountain. She went through the Birch Path light-footedly, attended by the sweetness of her orchids as by a benediction.

"Well, how did you get along?" Marilla wanted to know.

"Ask me that a month later and I may be able to tell you. I can't now . . . I don't know myself . . . I'm too near it. My thoughts feel as if they had been all stirred up until they were thick and muddy. The only thing I feel really sure of having accomplished today is that I taught Cliffie Wright that A is A. He never knew it before. Isn't it something to have started a soul along a path that may end in Shakespeare and Paradise Lost?"

Mrs. Lynde came up later on with more encouragement. That good lady had waylaid the schoolchildren at her gate and demanded of them how they liked their new teacher.

"And every one of them said they liked you splendid, Anne, except Anthony Pye. I must admit he didn't. He said you 'weren't any good, just like all girl teachers.' There's the Pye leaven for you. But never mind."

"I'm not going to mind," said Anne quietly, "and I'm going to make Anthony Pye like me yet. Patience and kindness will surely win him."

"Well, you can never tell about a Pye," said Mrs. Rachel cautiously. "They go by contraries, like dreams, often as not. As for that DonNELL woman, she'll get no DonNELLing from me, I can assure you. The name is DONnell and always has been. The woman is crazy, that's what. She has a pug dog she calls Queenie and it has its meals at the table along with the family, eating off a china plate. I'd be afraid of a judgment if I was her. Thomas says Donnell himself is a sensible, hard-working man, but he hadn't much gumption when he picked out a wife, that's what."

VI - All Sorts and Conditions of Men . . . and women

A September day on Prince Edward Island hills; a crisp wind blowing up over the sand dunes from the sea; a long red road, winding through fields and woods, now looping itself about a corner of thick set spruces, now threading a plantation of young maples with great feathery sheets of ferns beneath them, now dipping down into a hollow where a brook flashed out of the woods and into them again, now basking in open sunshine between ribbons of golden-rod and smoke-blue asters; air athrill with the pipings of myriads of crickets, those glad little pensioners of the summer hills; a plump brown pony ambling along the road; two girls behind him, full to the lips with the simple, priceless joy of youth and life.

"Oh, this is a day left over from Eden, isn't it, Diana?" . . . and Anne sighed for sheer happiness. "The air has magic in it. Look at the purple in the cup of the harvest valley, Diana. And oh, do smell the dying fir! It's coming up from that little sunny hollow where Mr. Eben Wright has been cutting fence poles. Bliss is it on such a day to be alive; but to smell dying fir is very heaven. That's two thirds Wordsworth and one third Anne Shirley. It doesn't seem possible that there should be dying fir in heaven, does it? And yet it doesn't seem to me that heaven would be quite perfect if you couldn't get a whiff of dead fir as you went through its woods. Perhaps we'll have the odor there without the death. Yes, I think that will be the way. That delicious aroma must be the souls of the firs . . . and of course it will be just souls in heaven."

"Trees haven't souls," said practical Diana, "but the smell of dead fir is certainly lovely. I'm going to make a cushion and fill it with fir needles. You'd better make one too, Anne."

"I think I shall . . . and use it for my naps. I'd be certain to dream I was a dryad or a woodnymph then. But just this minute I'm well content to be Anne Shirley, Avonlea schoolma'am, driving over a road like this on such a sweet, friendly day."

"It's a lovely day but we have anything but a lovely task before us," sighed Diana. "Why on earth did you offer to canvass this road, Anne? Almost all the cranks in Avonlea live along it, and we'll probably be treated as if we were begging for ourselves. It's the very worst road of all."

"That is why I chose it. Of course Gilbert and Fred would have taken this road if we had asked them. But you see, Diana, I feel myself responsible for the

A.V.I.S., since I was the first to suggest it, and it seems to me that I ought to do the most disagreeable things. I'm sorry on your account; but you needn't say a word at the cranky places. I'll do all the talking . . . Mrs. Lynde would say I was well able to. Mrs. Lynde doesn't know whether to approve of our enterprise or not. She inclines to, when she remembers that Mr. and Mrs. Allan are in favor of it; but the fact that village improvement societies first originated in the States is a count against it. So she is halting between two opinions and only success will justify us in Mrs. Lynde's eyes. Priscilla is going to write a paper for our next Improvement meeting, and I expect it will be good, for her aunt is such a clever writer and no doubt it runs in the family. I shall never forget the thrill it gave me when I found out that Mrs. Charlotte E. Morgan was Priscilla's aunt. It seemed so wonderful that I was a friend of the girl whose aunt wrote 'Edgewood Days' and 'The Rosebud Garden.'"

"Where does Mrs. Morgan live?"

"In Toronto. And Priscilla says she is coming to the Island for a visit next summer, and if it is possible Priscilla is going to arrange to have us meet her. That seems almost too good to be true—but it's something pleasant to imagine after you go to bed."

The Avonlea Village Improvement Society was an organized fact. Gilbert Blythe was president, Fred Wright vice-president, Anne Shirley secretary, and Diana Barry treasurer. The "Improvers," as they were promptly christened, were to meet once a fortnight at the homes of the members. It was admitted that they could not expect to affect many improvements so late in the season; but they meant to plan the next summer's campaign, collect and discuss ideas, write and read papers, and, as Anne said, educate the public sentiment generally.

There was some disapproval, of course, and . . . which the Improvers felt much more keenly . . . a good deal of ridicule. Mr. Elisha Wright was reported to have said that a more appropriate name for the organization would be Courting Club. Mrs. Hiram Sloane declared she had heard the Improvers meant to plough up all the roadsides and set them out with geraniums. Mr. Levi Boulter warned his neighbors that the Improvers would insist that everybody pull down his house and rebuild it after plans approved by the society. Mr. James Spencer sent them word that he wished they would kindly shovel down the church hill. Eben Wright told Anne that he wished the Improvers could induce old Josiah Sloane to keep his whiskers trimmed. Mr. Lawrence Bell said he would whitewash his barns if nothing else would please them but he would NOT hang lace curtains in the cowstable windows. Mr. Major Spencer asked Clifton Sloane, an Improver who drove the milk to the Carmody cheese factory, if it was true that everybody would have to have his milk-stand hand-painted next summer and keep an embroidered centerpiece on it.

In spite of . . . or perhaps, human nature being what it is, because of . . . this, the Society went gamely to work at the only improvement they could hope to bring about that fall. At the second meeting, in the Barry parlor, Oliver Sloane moved that they start a subscription to re-shingle and paint the hall; Julia Bell seconded it, with an uneasy feeling that she was doing something not exactly lady-like. Gilbert put the motion, it was carried unanimously, and Anne gravely recorded it in her minutes. The next thing was to appoint a committee, and Gertie Pye, determined not to let Julia Bell carry off all the laurels, boldly moved that Miss Jane Andrews be chairman of said committee. This motion being also duly seconded and carried, Jane returned the compliment by appointing Gertie on the committee, along with Gilbert, Anne, Diana, and Fred Wright. The committee chose their routes in private conclave. Anne and Diana were told off for the New-bridge road, Gilbert and Fred for the White Sands road, and Jane and Gertie for the Carmody road.

"Because," explained Gilbert to Anne, as they walked home together through the Haunted Wood, "the Pyes all live along that road and they won't give a cent unless one of themselves canvasses them."

The next Saturday Anne and Diana started out. They drove to the end of the road and canvassed homeward, calling first on the "Andrew girls."

"If Catherine is alone we may get something," said Diana, "but if Eliza is there we won't."

Eliza was there . . . very much so . . . and looked even grimmer than usual. Miss Eliza was one of those people who give you the impression that life is indeed a vale of tears, and that a smile, never to speak of a laugh, is a waste of nervous energy truly reprehensible. The Andrew girls had been "girls" for fifty odd years and seemed likely to remain girls to the end of their earthly pilgrimage. Catherine, it was said, had not entirely given up hope, but Eliza, who was born a pessimist, had never had any. They lived in a little brown house built in a sunny corner scooped out of Mark Andrew's beech woods. Eliza complained that it was terrible hot in summer, but Catherine was wont to say it was lovely and warm in winter.

Eliza was sewing patchwork, not because it was needed but simply as a protest against the frivolous lace Catherine was crocheting. Eliza listened with a frown and Catherine with a smile, as the girls explained their errand. To be sure, when-ever Catherine caught Eliza's eye she discarded the smile in guilty confusion; but it crept back the next moment.

"If I had money to waste," said Eliza grimly, "I'd burn it up and have the fun of seeing a blaze maybe; but I wouldn't give it to that hall, not a cent. It's no benefit to the settlement . . . just a place for young folks to meet and carry on when they's better be home in their beds."

"Oh, Eliza, young folks must have some amusement," protested Catherine.

"I don't see the necessity. We didn't gad about to halls and places when we were young, Catherine Andrews. This world is getting worse every day."

"I think it's getting better," said Catherine firmly.

"YOU think!" Miss Eliza's voice expressed the utmost contempt. "It doesn't signify what you THINK, Catherine Andrews. Facts is facts."

"Well, I always like to look on the bright side, Eliza."

"There isn't any bright side."

"Oh, indeed there is," cried Anne, who couldn't endure such heresy in silence. "Why, there are ever so many bright sides, Miss Andrews. It's really a beautiful world."

"You won't have such a high opinion of it when you've lived as long in it as I have," retorted Miss Eliza sourly, "and you won't be so enthusiastic about improving it either. How is your mother, Diana? Dear me, but she has failed of late. She looks terrible run down. And how long is it before Marilla expects to be stone blind, Anne?"

"The doctor thinks her eyes will not get any worse if she is very careful," faltered Anne.

Eliza shook her head.

"Doctors always talk like that just to keep people cheered up. I wouldn't have much hope if I was her. It's best to be prepared for the worst."

"But oughtn't we be prepared for the best too?" pleaded Anne. "It's just as likely to happen as the worst."

"Not in my experience, and I've fifty-seven years to set against your sixteen," retorted Eliza. "Going, are you? Well, I hope this new society of yours will be able to keep Avonlea from running any further down hill but I haven't much hope of it."

Anne and Diana got themselves thankfully out, and drove away as fast as the fat pony could go. As they rounded the curve below the beech wood a plump figure came speeding over Mr. Andrews' pasture, waving to them excitedly. It was Catherine Andrews and she was so out of breath that she could hardly speak, but she thrust a couple of quarters into Anne's hand.

"That's my contribution to painting the hall," she gasped. "I'd like to give you a dollar but I don't dare take more from my egg money for Eliza would find it out if I did. I'm real interested in your society and I believe you're going to do a lot of good. I'm an optimist. I HAVE to be, living with Eliza. I must hurry back before she misses me . . . she thinks I'm feeding the hens. I hope you'll have good luck canvassing, and don't be cast down over what Eliza said. The world IS getting better . . . it certainly is."

The next house was Daniel Blair's.

"Now, it all depends on whether his wife is home or not," said Diana, as they jolted along a deep-rutted lane. "If she is we won't get a cent. Everybody says Dan Blair doesn't dare have his hair cut without asking her permission; and it's certain she's very close, to state it moderately. She says she has to be just before she's generous. But Mrs. Lynde says she's so much 'before' that generosity never catches up with her at all."

Anne related their experience at the Blair place to Marilla that evening.

"We tied the horse and then rapped at the kitchen door. Nobody came but the door was open and we could hear somebody in the pantry, going on dreadfully. We couldn't make out the words but Diana says she knows they were swearing by the sound of them. I can't believe that of Mr. Blair, for he is always so quiet and meek; but at least he had great provocation, for Marilla, when that poor man came to the door, red as a beet, with perspiration streaming down his face, he had on one of his wife's big gingham aprons. 'I can't get this durned thing off,' he said, 'for the strings are tied in a hard knot and I can't bust 'em, so you'll have to excuse me, ladies.' We begged him not to mention it and went in and sat down. Mr. Blair sat down too; he twisted the apron around to his back and rolled it up, but he did look so ashamed and worried that I felt sorry for him, and Diana said she feared we had called at an inconvenient time. 'Oh, not at all,' said Mr. Blair, trying to smile . . . you know he is always very polite . . . 'I'm a little busy . . . getting ready to bake a cake as it were. My wife got a telegram today that her sister from Montreal is coming tonight and she's gone to the train to meet her and left orders for me to make a cake for tea. She writ out the recipe and told me what to do but I've clean forgot half the directions already. And it says, 'flavor according to taste.' What does that mean? How can you tell? And what if my taste doesn't happen to be other people's taste? Would a tablespoon of vanilla be enough for a small layer cake?"

"I felt sorrier than ever for the poor man. He didn't seem to be in his proper sphere at all. I had heard of henpecked husbands and now I felt that I saw one. It was on my lips to say, 'Mr. Blair, if you'll give us a subscription for the hall I'll mix up your cake for you.' But I suddenly thought it wouldn't be neighborly to drive too sharp a bargain with a fellow creature in distress. So I offered to mix the cake for him without any conditions at all. He just jumped at my offer. He said he'd been used to making his own bread before he was married but he feared cake was beyond him, and yet he hated to disappoint his wife. He got me another apron, and Diana beat the eggs and I mixed the cake. Mr. Blair ran about and got us the materials. He had forgotten all about his apron and when he ran it streamed out behind him and Diana said she thought she would die to see it. He said he could bake the cake all right . . . he was used to that . . . and then he asked for our list and he put down four dollars. So you see we were rewarded. But even if he hadn't given a cent I'd always feel that we had done a truly Christian act in helping him."

Theodore White's was the next stopping place. Neither Anne nor Diana had ever been there before, and they had only a very slight acquaintance with Mrs. Theodore, who was not given to hospitality. Should they go to the back or front door? While they held a whispered consultation Mrs. Theodore appeared at the front door with an armful of newspapers. Deliberately she laid them down one by one on the porch floor and the porch steps, and then down the path to the very feet of her mystified callers.

"Will you please wipe your feet carefully on the grass and then walk on these papers?" she said anxiously. "I've just swept the house all over and I can't have any more dust tracked in. The path's been real muddy since the rain yesterday."

"Don't you dare laugh," warned Anne in a whisper, as they marched along the newspapers. "And I implore you, Diana, not to look at me, no matter what she says, or I shall not be able to keep a sober face."

The papers extended across the hall and into a prim, fleckless parlor. Anne and Diana sat down gingerly on the nearest chairs and explained their errand. Mrs. White heard them politely, interrupting only twice, once to chase out an adventurous fly, and once to pick up a tiny wisp of grass that had fallen on the carpet from Anne's dress. Anne felt wretchedly guilty; but Mrs. White subscribed two dollars and paid the money down . . . "to prevent us from having to go back for it," Diana said when they got away. Mrs. White had the newspapers gathered up before they had their horse untied and as they drove out of the yard they saw her busily wielding a broom in the hall.

"I've always heard that Mrs. Theodore White was the neatest woman alive and I'll believe it after this," said Diana, giving way to her suppressed laughter as soon as it was safe.

"I am glad she has no children," said Anne solemnly. "It would be dreadful beyond words for them if she had."

At the Spencers' Mrs. Isabella Spencer made them miserable by saying something ill-natured about everyone in Avonlea. Mr. Thomas Boulter refused to give anything because the hall, when it had been built, twenty years before, hadn't been built on the site he recommended. Mrs. Esther Bell, who was the picture of health, took half an hour to detail all her aches and pains, and sadly put down fifty cents because she wouldn't be there that time next year to do it . . . no, she would be in her grave.

Their worst reception, however, was at Simon Fletcher's. When they drove into the yard they saw two faces peering at them through the porch window. But although they rapped and waited patiently and persistently nobody came to the door. Two decidedly ruffled and indignant girls drove away from Simon Fletcher's. Even Anne admitted that she was beginning to feel discouraged. But the tide turned after that. Several Sloane homesteads came next, where they got liberal subscriptions, and from that to the end they fared well, with only an occasional snub. Their last place of call was at Robert Dickson's by the pond bridge. They stayed to tea here, although they were nearly home, rather than risk offending Mrs. Dickson, who had the reputation of being a very "touchy" woman.

While they were there old Mrs. James White called in.

"I've just been down to Lorenzo's," she announced. "He's the proudest man in Avonlea this minute. What do you think? There's a brand new boy there . . . and after seven girls that's quite an event, I can tell you." Anne pricked up her ears, and when they drove away she said.

"I'm going straight to Lorenzo White's."

"But he lives on the White Sands road and it's quite a distance out of our way," protested Diana. "Gilbert and Fred will canvass him."

"They are not going around until next Saturday and it will be too late by then," said Anne firmly. "The novelty will be worn off. Lorenzo White is dreadfully mean but he will subscribe to ANYTHING just now. We mustn't let such a golden opportunity slip, Diana." The result justified Anne's foresight. Mr. White met them in the yard, beaming like the sun upon an Easter day. When Anne asked for a subscription he agreed enthusiastically.

"Certain, certain. Just put me down for a dollar more than the highest subscription you've got."

"That will be five dollars . . . Mr. Daniel Blair put down four," said Anne, half afraid. But Lorenzo did not flinch.

"Five it is . . . and here's the money on the spot. Now, I want you to come into the house. There's something in there worth seeing . . . something very few people have seen as yet. Just come in and pass YOUR opinion."

"What will we say if the baby isn't pretty?" whispered Diana in trepidation as they followed the excited Lorenzo into the house.

"Oh, there will certainly be something else nice to say about it," said Anne easily. "There always is about a baby."

The baby WAS pretty, however, and Mr. White felt that he got his five dollars' worth of the girls' honest delight over the plump little newcomer. But that was the first, last, and only time that Lorenzo White ever subscribed to anything.

Anne, tired as she was, made one more effort for the public weal that night, slipping over the fields to interview Mr. Harrison, who was as usual smoking his pipe on the veranda with Ginger beside him. Strickly speaking he was on the Carmody road; but Jane and Gertie, who were not acquainted with him save by doubtful report, had nervously begged Anne to canvass him.

Mr. Harrison, however, flatly refused to subscribe a cent, and all Anne's wiles were in vain.

"But I thought you approved of our society, Mr. Harrison," she mourned.

"So I do . . . so I do . . . but my approval doesn't go as deep as my pocket, Anne."

"A few more experiences such as I have had today would make me as much of a pessimist as Miss Eliza Andrews," Anne told her reflection in the east gable mirror at bedtime.

VII - The Pointing of Duty

Anne leaned back in her chair one mild October evening and sighed. She was sitting at a table covered with text books and exercises, but the closely written sheets of paper before her had no apparent connection with studies or school work.

"What is the matter?" asked Gilbert, who had arrived at the open kitchen door just in time to hear the sigh.

Anne colored, and thrust her writing out of sight under some school compositions.

"Nothing very dreadful. I was just trying to write out some of my thoughts, as Professor Hamilton advised me, but I couldn't get them to please me. They seem so still and foolish directly they're written down on white paper with black ink. Fancies are like shadows . . . you can't cage them, they're such wayward, dancing things. But perhaps I'll learn the secret some day if I keep on trying. I haven't a great many spare moments, you know. By the time I finish correcting school exercises and compositions, I don't always feel like writing any of my own."

"You are getting on splendidly in school, Anne. All the children like you," said Gilbert, sitting down on the stone step.

"No, not all. Anthony Pye doesn't and WON'T like me. What is worse, he doesn't respect me . . . no, he doesn't. He simply holds me in contempt and I don't mind confessing to you that it worries me miserably. It isn't that he is so very bad . . . he is only rather mischievous, but no worse than some of the others. He seldom disobeys me; but he obeys with a scornful air of toleration as if it wasn't worthwhile disputing the point or he would . . . and it has a bad effect on the others. I've tried every way to win him but I'm beginning to fear I never shall. I want to, for he's rather a cute little lad, if he IS a Pye, and I could like him if he'd let me."

"Probably it's merely the effect of what he hears at home."

"Not altogether. Anthony is an independent little chap and makes up his own mind about things. He has always gone to men before and he says girl teachers are no good. Well, we'll see what patience and kindness will do. I like overcoming difficulties and teaching is really very interesting work. Paul Irving makes up for all that is lacking in the others. That child is a perfect darling, Gilbert, and a genius into the bargain. I'm persuaded the world will hear of him some day," concluded Anne in a tone of conviction.

"I like teaching, too," said Gilbert. "It's good training, for one thing. Why, Anne, I've learned more in the weeks I've been teaching the young ideas of White Sands than I learned in all the years I went to school myself. We all seem to be getting on pretty well. The Newbridge people like Jane, I hear; and I think White Sands is tolerably satisfied with your humble servant . . . all except Mr. Andrew Spencer. I met Mrs. Peter Blewett on my way home last night and she told me she thought it her duty to inform me that Mr. Spencer didn't approve of my methods."

"Have you ever noticed," asked Anne reflectively, "that when people say it is their duty to tell you a certain thing you may prepare for something disagreeable? Why is it that they never seem to think it a duty to tell you the pleasant things they hear about you? Mrs. H. B. DonNELL called at the school again yesterday and told me she thought it HER duty to inform me that Mrs. Harmon Andrew didn't approve of my reading fairy tales to the children, and that Mr. Rogerson thought Prillie wasn't coming on fast enough in arithmetic. If Prillie would spend less time making eyes at the boys over her slate she might do better. I feel quite sure that Jack Gillis works her class sums for her, though I've never been able to catch him red-handed."

"Have you succeeded in reconciling Mrs. DonNELL's hopeful son to his saintly name?"

"Yes," laughed Anne, "but it was really a difficult task. At first, when I called him 'St. Clair' he would not take the least notice until I'd spoken two or three times; and then, when the other boys nudged him, he would look up with such an aggrieved air, as if I'd called him John or Charlie and he couldn't be expected to know I meant him. So I kept him in after school one night and talked kindly to him. I told him his mother wished me to call him St. Clair and I couldn't go against her wishes. He saw it when it was all explained out . . . he's really a very reasonable little fellow . . . and he said *I* could call him St. Clair but that he'd 'lick the stuffing' out of any of the boys that tried it. Of course, I had to rebuke him again for using such shocking language. Since then *I* call him St. Clair and the boys call him Jake and all goes smoothly. He informs me that he means to be a carpenter, but Mrs. DonNELL says I am to make a college professor out of him."

The mention of college gave a new direction to Gilbert's thoughts, and they talked for a time of their plans and wishes . . . gravely, earnestly, hopefully, as youth loves to talk, while the future is yet an untrodden path full of wonderful possibilities.

Gilbert had finally made up his mind that he was going to be a doctor.

"It's a splendid profession," he said enthusiastically. "A fellow has to fight something all through life . . . didn't somebody once define man as a fighting animal? . . . and I want to fight disease and pain and ignorance . . . which are all members one of another. I want to do my share of honest, real work in the world, Anne . . . add a little to the sum of human knowledge that all the good men have been accumulating since it began. The folks who lived before me have done so much for me that I want to show my gratitude by doing something for the folks who will live after me. It seems to me that is the only way a fellow can get square with his obligations to the race."

"I'd like to add some beauty to life," said Anne dreamily. "I don't exactly want to make people KNOW more . . . though I know that IS the noblest ambition . . . but I'd love to make them have a pleasanter time because of me . . . to have some little joy or happy thought that would never have existed if I hadn't been born."

"I think you're fulfilling that ambition every day," said Gilbert admiringly.

And he was right. Anne was one of the children of light by birthright. After she had passed through a life with a smile or a word thrown across it like a gleam of sunshine the owner of that life saw it, for the time being at least, as hopeful and lovely and of good report.

Finally Gilbert rose regretfully.

"Well, I must run up to MacPhersons'. Moody Spurgeon came home from Queen's today for Sunday and he was to bring me out a book Professor Boyd is lending me."

"And I must get Marilla's tea. She went to see Mrs. Keith this evening and she will soon be back."

Anne had tea ready when Marilla came home; the fire was crackling cheerily, a vase of frost-bleached ferns and ruby-red maple leaves adorned the table, and delectable odors of ham and toast pervaded the air. But Marilla sank into her chair with a deep sigh.

"Are your eyes troubling you? Does your head ache?" queried Anne anxiously.

"No. I'm only tired . . . and worried. It's about Mary and those children . . . Mary is worse . . . she can't last much longer. And as for the twins, *I* don't know what is to become of them."

"Hasn't their uncle been heard from?"

"Yes, Mary had a letter from him. He's working in a lumber camp and 'shacking it,' whatever that means. Anyway, he says he can't possibly take the children till the spring. He expects to be married then and will have a home to take them to; but he says she must get some of the neighbors to keep them for the winter. She says she can't bear to ask any of them. Mary never got on any too well with the East Grafton people and that's a fact. And the long and short of it is, Anne, that I'm sure Mary wants me to take those children . . . she didn't say so but she LOOKED it."

"Oh!" Anne clasped her hands, all athrill with excitement. "And of course you will, Marilla, won't you?"

"I haven't made up my mind," said Marilla rather tartly. "I don't rush into things in your headlong way, Anne. Third cousinship is a pretty slim claim. And it will be a fearful responsibility to have two children of six years to look after . . . twins, at that."

Marilla had an idea that twins were just twice as bad as single children.

"Twins are very interesting . . . at least one pair of them," said Anne. "It's only when there are two or three pairs that it gets monotonous. And I think it would be real nice for you to have something to amuse you when I'm away in school."

"I don't reckon there'd be much amusement in it . . . more worry and bother than anything else, I should say. It wouldn't be so risky if they were even as old as you were when I took you. I wouldn't mind Dora so much . . . she seems good and quiet. But that Davy is a limb."

Anne was fond of children and her heart yearned over the Keith twins. The remembrance of her own neglected childhood was very vivid with her still. She knew that Marilla's only vulnerable point was her stern devotion to what she believed to be her duty, and Anne skillfully marshalled her arguments along this line.

"If Davy is naughty it's all the more reason why he should have good training, isn't it, Marilla? If we don't take them we don't know who will, nor what kind of influences may surround them. Suppose Mrs. Keith's next door neighbors, the Sprotts, were to take them. Mrs. Lynde says Henry Sprott is the most profane man that ever lived and you can't believe a word his children say. Wouldn't it be dreadful to have the twins learn anything like that? Or suppose they went to the Wiggins'. Mrs. Lynde says that Mr. Wiggins sells everything off the place that can be sold and brings his family up on skim milk. You wouldn't like your relations to be starved, even if they were only third cousins, would you? It seems to me, Marilla, that it is our duty to take them."

"I suppose it is," assented Marilla gloomily. "I daresay I'll tell Mary I'll take them. You needn't look so delighted, Anne. It will mean a good deal of extra work for you. I can't sew a stitch on account of my eyes, so you'll have to see to the making and mending of their clothes. And you don't like sewing."

"I hate it," said Anne calmly, "but if you are willing to take those children from a sense of duty surely I can do their sewing from a sense of duty. It does people good to have to do things they don't like . . . in moderation."

VIII - Marilla Adopts Twins

Mrs. Rachel Lynde was sitting at her kitchen window, knitting a quilt, just as she had been sitting one evening several years previously when Matthew Cuthbert had driven down over the hill with what Mrs. Rachel called "his imported orphan." But that had been in springtime; and this was late autumn, and all the woods were leafless and the fields sere and brown. The sun was just setting with a great deal of purple and golden pomp behind the dark woods west of Avonlea when a buggy drawn by a comfortable brown nag came down the hill. Mrs. Rachel peered at it eagerly.

"There's Marilla getting home from the funeral," she said to her husband, who was lying on the kitchen lounge. Thomas Lynde lay more on the lounge nowadays than he had been used to do, but Mrs. Rachel, who was so sharp at noticing anything beyond her own household, had not as yet noticed this. "And she's got the twins with her, . . . yes, there's Davy leaning over the dashboard grabbing at the pony's tail and Marilla jerking him back. Dora's sitting up on the seat as prim as you please. She always looks as if she'd just been starched and ironed. Well, poor Marilla is going to have her hands full this winter and no mistake. Still, I don't see that she could do anything less than take them, under the circumstances, and she'll have Anne to help her. Anne's tickled to death over the whole business, and she has a real knacky way with children, I must say. Dear me, it doesn't seem a day since poor Matthew brought Anne herself home and everybody laughed at the idea of Marilla bringing up a child. And now she has adopted twins. You're never safe from being surprised till you're dead."

The fat pony jogged over the bridge in Lynde's Hollow and along the Green Gables lane. Marilla's face was rather grim. It was ten miles from East Grafton and Davy Keith seemed to be possessed with a passion for perpetual motion. It was beyond Marilla's power to make him sit still and she had been in an agony the whole way lest he fall over the back of the wagon and break his neck, or tumble over the dashboard under the pony's heels. In despair she finally threatened to whip him soundly when she got him home. Whereupon Davy climbed into her lap, regardless of the reins, flung his chubby arms about her neck and gave her a bear-like hug.

"I don't believe you mean it," he said, smacking her wrinkled cheek affectionately. "You don't LOOK like a lady who'd whip a little boy just 'cause he couldn't keep still. Didn't you find it awful hard to keep still when you was only 's old as me?"

"No, I always kept still when I was told," said Marilla, trying to speak sternly, albeit she felt her heart waxing soft within her under Davy's impulsive caresses.

"Well, I s'pose that was 'cause you was a girl," said Davy, squirming back to his place after another hug. "You WAS a girl once, I s'pose, though it's awful funny to think of it. Dora can sit still . . . but there ain't much fun in it *I* don't think. Seems to me it must be slow to be a girl. Here, Dora, let me liven you up a bit."

Davy's method of "livening up" was to grasp Dora's curls in his fingers and give them a tug. Dora shrieked and then cried.

"How can you be such a naughty boy and your poor mother just laid in her grave this very day?" demanded Marilla despairingly.

"But she was glad to die," said Davy confidentially. "I know, 'cause she told me so. She was awful tired of being sick. We'd a long talk the night before she died. She told me you was going to take me and Dora for the winter and I was to be a good boy. I'm going to be good, but can't you be good running round just as well as sitting still? And she said I was always to be kind to Dora and stand up for her, and I'm going to."

"Do you call pulling her hair being kind to her?"

"Well, I ain't going to let anybody else pull it," said Davy, doubling up his fists and frowning. "They'd just better try it. I didn't hurt her much . . . she just cried 'cause she's a girl. I'm glad I'm a boy but I'm sorry I'm a twin. When Jimmy Sprott's sister conterdicks him he just says, 'I'm oldern you, so of course I know better,' and that settles HER. But I can't tell Dora that, and she just goes on thinking diffrunt from me. You might let me drive the gee-gee for a spell, since I'm a man."

Altogether, Marilla was a thankful woman when she drove into her own yard, where the wind of the autumn night was dancing with the brown leaves. Anne was at the gate to meet them and lift the twins out. Dora submitted calmly to be kissed, but Davy responded to Anne's welcome with one of his hearty hugs and the cheerful announcement, "I'm Mr. Davy Keith."

At the supper table Dora behaved like a little lady, but Davy's manners left much to be desired.

"I'm so hungry I ain't got time to eat p'litely," he said when Marilla reproved him. "Dora ain't half as hungry as I am. Look at all the ex'cise I took on the road here. That cake's awful nice and plummy. We haven't had any cake at home for ever'n ever so long, 'cause mother was too sick to make it and Mrs. Sprott said it was as much as she could do to bake our bread for us. And Mrs. Wiggins never puts any plums in HER cakes. Catch her! Can I have another piece?"

Marilla would have refused but Anne cut a generous second slice. However, she reminded Davy that he ought to say "Thank you" for it. Davy merely grinned at her and took a huge bite. When he had finished the slice he said,

"If you'll give me ANOTHER piece I'll say thank you for IT."

"No, you have had plenty of cake," said Marilla in a tone which Anne knew and Davy was to learn to be final.

Davy winked at Anne, and then, leaning over the table, snatched Dora's first piece of cake, from which she had just taken one dainty little bite, out of her very fingers and, opening his mouth to the fullest extent, crammed the whole slice in. Dora's lip trembled and Marilla was speechless with horror. Anne promptly exclaimed, with her best "schoolma'am" air,

"Oh, Davy, gentlemen don't do things like that."

"I know they don't," said Davy, as soon as he could speak, "but I ain't a gemplum."

"But don't you want to be?" said shocked Anne.

"Course I do. But you can't be a gemplum till you grow up."

"Oh, indeed you can," Anne hastened to say, thinking she saw a chance to sow good seed betimes. "You can begin to be a gentleman when you are a little boy. And gentlemen NEVER snatch things from ladies . . . or forget to say thank you . . . or pull anybody's hair."

"They don't have much fun, that's a fact," said Davy frankly. "I guess I'll wait till I'm grown up to be one."

Marilla, with a resigned air, had cut another piece of cake for Dora. She did not feel able to cope with Davy just then. It had been a hard day for her, what with the funeral and the long drive. At that moment she looked forward to the future with a pessimism that would have done credit to Eliza Andrews herself.

The twins were not noticeably alike, although both were fair. Dora had long sleek curls that never got out of order. Davy had a crop of fuzzy little yellow ringlets all over his round head. Dora's hazel eyes were gentle and mild; Davy's were as roguish and dancing as an elf's. Dora's nose was straight, Davy's a positive snub; Dora had a "prunes and prisms" mouth, Davy's was all smiles; and besides, he had a dimple in one cheek and none in the other, which gave him a dear, comical, lopsided look when he laughed. Mirth and mischief lurked in every corner of his little face.

"They'd better go to bed," said Marilla, who thought it was the easiest way to dispose of them. "Dora will sleep with me and you can put Davy in the west gable. You're not afraid to sleep alone, are you, Davy?"

"No; but I ain't going to bed for ever so long yet," said Davy comfortably.

"Oh, yes, you are." That was all the much-tried Marilla said, but something in her tone squelched even Davy. He trotted obediently upstairs with Anne.

"When I'm grown up the very first thing I'm going to do is stay up ALL night just to see what it would be like," he told her confidentially.

In after years Marilla never thought of that first week of the twins' sojourn at Green Gables without a shiver. Not that it really was so much worse than the weeks that followed it; but it seemed so by reason of its novelty. There was seldom a waking minute of any day when Davy was not in mischief or devising it; but his first notable exploit occurred two days after his arrival, on Sunday morning . . . a fine, warm day, as hazy and mild as September. Anne dressed him for church while Marilla attended to Dora. Davy at first objected strongly to having his face washed.

"Marilla washed it yesterday . . . and Mrs. Wiggins scoured me with hard soap the day of the funeral. That's enough for one week. I don't see the good of being so awful clean. It's lots more comfable being dirty."

"Paul Irving washes his face every day of his own accord," said Anne astutely.

Davy had been an inmate of Green Gables for little over forty-eight hours; but he already worshipped Anne and hated Paul Irving, whom he had heard Anne praising enthusiastically the day after his arrival. If Paul Irving washed his face every day, that settled it. He, Davy Keith, would do it too, if it killed him. The same consideration induced him to submit meekly to the other details of his toilet, and he was really a handsome little lad when all was done. Anne felt an almost maternal pride in him as she led him into the old Cuthbert pew.

Davy behaved quite well at first, being occupied in casting covert glances at all the small boys within view and wondering which was Paul Irving. The first two hymns and the Scripture reading passed off uneventfully. Mr. Allan was praying when the sensation came.

Lauretta White was sitting in front of Davy, her head slightly bent and her fair hair hanging in two long braids, between which a tempting expanse of white neck showed, encased in a loose lace frill. Lauretta was a fat, placid-looking child of eight, who had conducted herself irreproachably in church from the very first day her mother carried her there, an infant of six months.

Davy thrust his hand into his pocket and produced . . . a caterpillar, a furry, squirming caterpillar. Marilla saw and clutched at him but she was too late. Davy dropped the caterpillar down Lauretta's neck.

Right into the middle of Mr. Allan's prayer burst a series of piercing shrieks. The minister stopped appalled and opened his eyes. Every head in the congregation flew up. Lauretta White was dancing up and down in her pew, clutching frantically at the back of her dress.

"Ow . . . mommer . . . mommer . . . ow . . . take it off . . . ow . . . get it out . . . ow . . . that bad boy put it down my neck . . . ow . . . mommer . . . it's going further down . . . ow . . . ow . . . ow. . . ."

Mrs. White rose and with a set face carried the hysterical, writhing Lauretta out of church. Her shrieks died away in the distance and Mr. Allan proceeded with the service. But everybody felt that it was a failure that day. For the first time in her life Marilla took no notice of the text and Anne sat with scarlet cheeks of mortification.

When they got home Marilla put Davy to bed and made him stay there for the rest of the day. She would not give him any dinner but allowed him a plain tea of bread and milk. Anne carried it to him and sat sorrowfully by him while he ate it with an unrepentant relish. But Anne's mournful eyes troubled him.

"I s'pose," he said reflectively, "that Paul Irving wouldn't have dropped a caterpillar down a girl's neck in church, would he?"

"Indeed he wouldn't," said Anne sadly.

"Well, I'm kind of sorry I did it, then," conceded Davy. "But it was such a jolly big caterpillar . . . I picked him up on the church steps just as we went in. It seemed a pity to waste him. And say, wasn't it fun to hear that girl yell?"

Tuesday afternoon the Aid Society met at Green Gables. Anne hurried home from school, for she knew that Marilla would need all the assistance she could give. Dora, neat and proper, in her nicely starched white dress and black sash, was sitting with the members of the Aid in the parlor, speaking demurely when spoken to, keeping silence when not, and in every way comporting herself as a model child. Davy, blissfully dirty, was making mud pies in the barnyard.

"I told him he might," said Marilla wearily. "I thought it would keep him out of worse mischief. He can only get dirty at that. We'll have our teas over before we call him to his. Dora can have hers with us, but I would never dare to let Davy sit down at the table with all the Aids here."

When Anne went to call the Aids to tea she found that Dora was not in the parlor. Mrs. Jasper Bell said Davy had come to the front door and called her out. A hasty consultation with Marilla in the pantry resulted in a decision to let both children have their teas together later on.

Tea was half over when the dining room was invaded by a forlorn figure. Marilla and Anne stared in dismay, the Aids in amazement. Could that be Dora . . . that sobbing nondescript in a drenched, dripping dress and hair from which the water was streaming on Marilla's new coin-spot rug?

"Dora, what has happened to you?" cried Anne, with a guilty glance at Mrs. Jasper Bell, whose family was said to be the only one in the world in which accidents never occurred.

"Davy made me walk the pigpen fence," wailed Dora. "I didn't want to but he called me a fraid-cat. And I fell off into the pigpen and my dress got all dirty and the pig runned right over me. My dress was just awful but Davy said if I'd stand under the pump he'd wash it clean, and I did and he pumped water all over me but my dress ain't a bit cleaner and my pretty sash and shoes is all spoiled."

Anne did the honors of the table alone for the rest of the meal while Marilla went upstairs and redressed Dora in her old clothes. Davy was caught and sent to bed without any supper. Anne went to his room at twilight and talked to him seriously . . . a method in which she had great faith, not altogether unjustified by results. She told him she felt very badly over his conduct.

"I feel sorry now myself," admitted Davy, "but the trouble is I never feel sorry for doing things till after I've did them. Dora wouldn't help me make pies, cause she was afraid of messing her clo'es and that made me hopping mad. I s'pose Paul Irving wouldn't have made HIS sister walk a pigpen fence if he knew she'd fall in?"

"No, he would never dream of such a thing. Paul is a perfect little gentleman."

Davy screwed his eyes tight shut and seemed to meditate on this for a time. Then he crawled up and put his arms about Anne's neck, snuggling his flushed little face down on her shoulder.

"Anne, don't you like me a little bit, even if I ain't a good boy like Paul?"

"Indeed I do," said Anne sincerely. Somehow, it was impossible to help liking Davy. "But I'd like you better still if you weren't so naughty."

"I . . . did something else today," went on Davy in a muffled voice. "I'm sorry now but I'm awful scared to tell you. You won't be very cross, will you? And you won't tell Marilla, will you?"

"I don't know, Davy. Perhaps I ought to tell her. But I think I can promise you I won't if you promise me that you will never do it again, whatever it is."

"No, I never will. Anyhow, it's not likely I'd find any more of them this year. I found this one on the cellar steps."

"Davy, what is it you've done?"

"I put a toad in Marilla's bed. You can go and take it out if you like. But say, Anne, wouldn't it be fun to leave it there?"

"Davy Keith!" Anne sprang from Davy's clinging arms and flew across the hall to Marilla's room. The bed was slightly rumpled. She threw back the blankets in nervous haste and there in very truth was the toad, blinking at her from under a pillow.

"How can I carry that awful thing out?" moaned Anne with a shudder. The fire shovel suggested itself to her and she crept down to get it while Marilla was busy in the pantry. Anne had her own troubles carrying that toad downstairs, for it hopped off the shovel three times and once she thought she had lost it in the hall. When she finally deposited it in the cherry orchard she drew a long breath of relief.

"If Marilla knew she'd never feel safe getting into bed again in her life. I'm so glad that little sinner repented in time. There's Diana signaling to me from her window. I'm glad . . . I really feel the need of some diversion, for what with Anthony Pye in school and Davy Keith at home my nerves have had about all they can endure for one day."

IX - A Question of Color

"That old nuisance of a Rachel Lynde was here again today, pestering me for a subscription towards buying a carpet for the vestry room," said Mr. Harrison wrathfully. "I detest that woman more than anybody I know. She can put a whole sermon, text, comment, and application, into six words, and throw it at you like a brick."

Anne, who was perched on the edge of the veranda, enjoying the charm of a mild west wind blowing across a newly ploughed field on a gray November twilight and piping a quaint little melody among the twisted firs below the garden, turned her dreamy face over her shoulder.

"The trouble is, you and Mrs. Lynde don't understand one another," she explained. "That is always what is wrong when people don't like each other. I didn't like Mrs. Lynde at first either; but as soon as I came to understand her I learned to."

"Mrs. Lynde may be an acquired taste with some folks; but I didn't keep on eating bananas because I was told I'd learn to like them if I did," growled Mr. Harrison. "And as for understanding her, I understand that she is a confirmed busybody and I told her so."

"Oh, that must have hurt her feelings very much," said Anne reproachfully. "How could you say such a thing? I said some dreadful things to Mrs. Lynde long ago but it was when I had lost my temper. I couldn't say them DELIBERATELY."

"It was the truth and I believe in telling the truth to everybody."

"But you don't tell the whole truth," objected Anne. "You only tell the disagreeable part of the truth. Now, you've told me a dozen times that my hair was red, but you've never once told me that I had a nice nose."

"I daresay you know it without any telling," chuckled Mr. Harrison.

"I know I have red hair too . . . although it's MUCH darker than it used to be . . . so there's no need of telling me that either."

"Well, well, I'll try and not mention it again since you're so sensitive. You must excuse me, Anne. I've got a habit of being outspoken and folks mustn't mind it."

"But they can't help minding it. And I don't think it's any help that it's your habit. What would you think of a person who went about sticking pins and needles into people and saying, 'Excuse me, you mustn't mind it . . . it's just a habit I've got.' You'd think he was crazy, wouldn't you? And as for Mrs. Lynde being a busybody, perhaps she is. But did you tell her she had a very kind heart and always helped the poor, and never said a word when Timothy Cotton stole a crock of butter out of her dairy and told his wife he'd bought it from her? Mrs. Cotton cast it up to her the next time they met that it tasted of turnips and Mrs. Lynde just said she was sorry it had turned out so poorly."

"I suppose she has some good qualities," conceded Mr. Harrison grudgingly. "Most folks have. I have some myself, though you might never suspect it. But anyhow I ain't going to give anything to that carpet. Folks are everlasting begging for money here, it seems to me. How's your project of painting the hall coming on?"

"Splendidly. We had a meeting of the A.V.I.S. last Friday night and found that we had plenty of money subscribed to paint the hall and shingle the roof too. MOST people gave very liberally, Mr. Harrison."

Anne was a sweet-souled lass, but she could instill some venom into innocent italics when occasion required.

"What color are you going to have it?"

"We have decided on a very pretty green. The roof will be dark red, of course. Mr. Roger Pye is going to get the paint in town today."

"Who's got the job?"

"Mr. Joshua Pye of Carmody. He has nearly finished the shingling. We had to give him the contract, for every one of the Pyes . . . and there are four families, you know . . . said they wouldn't give a cent unless Joshua got it. They had subscribed twelve dollars between them and we thought that was too much to lose, although some people think we shouldn't have given in to the Pyes. Mrs. Lynde says they try to run everything."

"The main question is will this Joshua do his work well. If he does I don't see that it matters whether his name is Pye or Pudding."

"He has the reputation of being a good workman, though they say he's a very peculiar man. He hardly ever talks."

"He's peculiar enough all right then," said Mr. Harrison drily. "Or at least, folks here will call him so. I never was much of a talker till I came to Avonlea and then I had to begin in self-defense or Mrs. Lynde would have said I was dumb and started a subscription to have me taught sign language. You're not going yet, Anne?"

"I must. I have some sewing to do for Dora this evening. Besides, Davy is probably breaking Marilla's heart with some new mischief by this time. This morning the first thing he said was, 'Where does the dark go, Anne? I want to know.' I told him it went around to the other side of the world but after breakfast he declared it didn't . . . that it went down the well. Marilla says she caught him hanging over the well-box four times today, trying to reach down to the dark."

"He's a limb," declared Mr. Harrison. "He came over here yesterday and pulled six feathers out of Ginger's tail before I could get in from the barn. The poor bird has been moping ever since. Those children must be a sight of trouble to you folks."

"Everything that's worth having is some trouble," said Anne, secretly resolving to forgive Davy's next offence, whatever it might be, since he had avenged her on Ginger.

Mr. Roger Pye brought the hall paint home that night and Mr. Joshua Pye, a surly, taciturn man, began painting the next day. He was not disturbed in his task. The hall was situated on what was called "the lower road." In late autumn this road was always muddy and wet, and people going to Carmody traveled by the longer "upper" road. The hall was so closely surrounded by fir woods that it was invisible unless you were near it. Mr. Joshua Pye painted away in the solitude and independence that were so dear to his unsociable heart.

Friday afternoon he finished his job and went home to Carmody. Soon after his departure Mrs. Rachel Lynde drove by, having braved the mud of the lower road out of curiosity to see what the hall looked like in its new coat of paint. When she rounded the spruce curve she saw.

The sight affected Mrs. Lynde oddly. She dropped the reins, held up her hands, and said "Gracious Providence!" She stared as if she could not believe her eyes. Then she laughed almost hysterically.

"There must be some mistake . . . there must. I knew those Pyes would make a mess of things."

Mrs. Lynde drove home, meeting several people on the road and stopping to tell them about the hall. The news flew like wildfire. Gilbert Blythe, poring over a text book at home, heard it from his father's hired boy at sunset, and rushed breathlessly to Green Gables, joined on the way by Fred Wright. They found Diana Barry, Jane Andrews, and Anne Shirley, despair personified, at the yard gate of Green Gables, under the big leafless willows.

"It isn't true surely, Anne?" exclaimed Gilbert.

"It is true," answered Anne, looking like the muse of tragedy. "Mrs. Lynde called on her way from Carmody to tell me. Oh, it is simply dreadful! What is the use of trying to improve anything?"

"What is dreadful?" asked Oliver Sloane, arriving at this moment with a band-box he had brought from town for Marilla.

"Haven't you heard?" said Jane wrathfully. "Well, its simply this. . . Joshua Pye has gone and painted the hall blue instead of green. . . a deep, brilliant blue, the shade they use for painting carts and wheelbarrows. And Mrs. Lynde says it is the most hideous color for a building, especially when combined with a red roof, that she ever saw or imagined. You could simply have knocked me down with a feather when I heard it. It's heartbreaking, after all the trouble we've had."

"How on earth could such a mistake have happened?" wailed Diana.

The blame of this unmerciful disaster was eventually narrowed down to the Pyes. The Improvers had decided to use Morton-Harris paints and the Morton-Harris paint cans were numbered according to a color card. A purchaser chose his shade on the card and ordered by the accompanying number. Number 147 was the shade of green desired and when Mr. Roger Pye sent word to the Improvers by his son, John Andrew, that he was going to town and would get their paint for them, the Improvers told John Andrew to tell his father to get 147. John Andrew always averred that he did so, but Mr. Roger Pye as stanchly declared that John Andrew told him 157; and there the matter stands to this day.

That night there was blank dismay in every Avonlea house where an Improver lived. The gloom at Green Gables was so intense that it quenched even Davy. Anne wept and would not be comforted.

"I must cry, even if I am almost seventeen, Marilla," she sobbed. "It is so mortifying. And it sounds the death knell of our society. We'll simply be laughed out of existence."

In life, as in dreams, however, things often go by contraries. The Avonlea people did not laugh; they were too angry. Their money had gone to paint the hall and consequently they felt themselves bitterly aggrieved by the mistake. Public indignation centered on the Pyes. Roger Pye and John Andrew had bungled the matter between them; and as for Joshua Pye, he must be a born fool not to suspect there was something wrong when he opened the cans and saw the color of the paint. Joshua Pye, when thus animadverted upon, retorted that the Avonlea taste in colors was no business of his, whatever his private opinion might be; he had been hired to paint the hall, not to talk about it; and he meant to have his money for it.

The Improvers paid him his money in bitterness of spirit, after consulting Mr. Peter Sloane, who was a magistrate.

"You'll have to pay it," Peter told him. "You can't hold him responsible for the mistake, since he claims he was never told what the color was supposed to be but just given the cans and told to go ahead. But it's a burning shame and that hall certainly does look awful."

The luckless Improvers expected that Avonlea would be more prejudiced than ever against them; but instead, public sympathy veered around in their favor. People thought the eager, enthusiastic little band who had worked so hard for their object had been badly used. Mrs. Lynde told them to keep on and show the Pyes that there really were people in the world who could do things without making a muddle of them. Mr. Major Spencer sent them word that he would clean out all the stumps along the road front of his farm and seed it down with grass at his own expense; and Mrs. Hiram Sloane called at the school one day and beckoned Anne mysteriously out into the porch to tell her that if the "Sassiety" wanted to make a geranium bed at the crossroads in the spring they needn't be afraid of her cow, for she would see that the marauding animal was kept within safe bounds. Even Mr. Harrison chuckled, if he chuckled at all, in private, and was all sympathy outwardly.

"Never mind, Anne. Most paints fade uglier every year but that blue is as ugly as it can be to begin with, so it's bound to fade prettier. And the roof is shingled and painted all right. Folks will be able to sit in the hall after this without being leaked on. You've accomplished so much anyhow."

IX - A Question of Color

"But Avonlea's blue hall will be a byword in all the neighboring settlements from this time out," said Anne bitterly.

And it must be confessed that it was.

X - Davy in Search of a Sensation

Anne, walking home from school through the Birch Path one November after-noon, felt convinced afresh that life was a very wonderful thing. The day had been a good day; all had gone well in her little kingdom. St. Clair Donnell had not fought any of the other boys over the question of his name; Prillie Rogerson's face had been so puffed up from the effects of toothache that she did not once try to coquette with the boys in her vicinity. Barbara Shaw had met with only ONE ac-cident . . . spilling a dipper of water over the floor . . . and Anthony Pye had not been in school at all.

"What a nice month this November has been!" said Anne, who had never quite got over her childish habit of talking to herself. "November is usually such a disa-greeable month . . . as if the year had suddenly found out that she was growing old and could do nothing but weep and fret over it. This year is growing old gracefully . . . just like a stately old lady who knows she can be charming even with gray hair and wrinkles. We've had lovely days and delicious twilights. This last fortnight has been so peaceful, and even Davy has been almost well-behaved. I really think he is improving a great deal. How quiet the woods are today . . . not a murmur except that soft wind purring in the treetops! It sounds like surf on a faraway shore. How dear the woods are! You beautiful trees! I love every one of you as a friend."

Anne paused to throw her arm about a slim young birch and kiss its cream-white trunk. Diana, rounding a curve in the path, saw her and laughed.

"Anne Shirley, you're only pretending to be grown up. I believe when you're alone you're as much a little girl as you ever were."

"Well, one can't get over the habit of being a little girl all at once," said Anne gaily. "You see, I was little for fourteen years and I've only been grown-uppish for scarcely three. I'm sure I shall always feel like a child in the woods. These walks home from school are almost the only time I have for dreaming . . . except the half-hour or so before I go to sleep. I'm so busy with teaching and studying and helping Marilla with the twins that I haven't another moment for imagining things. You don't know what splendid adventures I have for a little while after I go to bed in the east gable every night. I always imagine I'm something very bril-liant and triumphant and splendid . . . a great prima donna or a Red Cross nurse or a queen. Last night I was a queen. It's really splendid to imagine you are a queen.

You have all the fun of it without any of the inconveniences and you can stop being a queen whenever you want to, which you couldn't in real life. But here in the woods I like best to imagine quite different things . . . I'm a dryad living in an old pine, or a little brown wood-elf hiding under a crinkled leaf. That white birch you caught me kissing is a sister of mine. The only difference is, she's a tree and I'm a girl, but that's no real difference. Where are you going, Diana?"

"Down to the Dicksons. I promised to help Alberta cut out her new dress. Can't you walk down in the evening, Anne, and come home with me?"

"I might . . . since Fred Wright is away in town," said Anne with a rather too innocent face.

Diana blushed, tossed her head, and walked on. She did not look offended, however.

Anne fully intended to go down to the Dicksons' that evening, but she did not. When she arrived at Green Gables she found a state of affairs which banished every other thought from her mind. Marilla met her in the yard . . . a wild-eyed Marilla.

"Anne, Dora is lost!"

"Dora! Lost!" Anne looked at Davy, who was swinging on the yard gate, and detected merriment in his eyes. "Davy, do you know where she is?"

"No, I don't," said Davy stoutly. "I haven't seen her since dinner time, cross my heart."

"I've been away ever since one o'clock," said Marilla. "Thomas Lynde took sick all of a sudden and Rachel sent up for me to go at once. When I left here Dora was playing with her doll in the kitchen and Davy was making mud pies behind the barn. I only got home half an hour ago . . . and no Dora to be seen. Davy declares he never saw her since I left."

"Neither I did," avowed Davy solemnly.

"She must be somewhere around," said Anne. "She would never wander far away alone . . . you know how timid she is. Perhaps she has fallen asleep in one of the rooms."

Marilla shook her head.

"I've hunted the whole house through. But she may be in some of the buildings."

A thorough search followed. Every corner of house, yard, and outbuildings was ransacked by those two distracted people. Anne roved the orchards and the Haunted Wood, calling Dora's name. Marilla took a candle and explored the cellar. Davy accompanied each of them in turn, and was fertile in thinking of places where Dora could possibly be. Finally they met again in the yard.

"It's a most mysterious thing," groaned Marilla.

"Where can she be?" said Anne miserably

"Maybe she's tumbled into the well," suggested Davy cheerfully.

Anne and Marilla looked fearfully into each other's eyes. The thought had been with them both through their entire search but neither had dared to put it into words.

"She . . . she might have," whispered Marilla.

Anne, feeling faint and sick, went to the wellbox and peered over. The bucket sat on the shelf inside. Far down below was a tiny glimmer of still water. The Cuthbert well was the deepest in Avonlea. If Dora. . . but Anne could not face the idea. She shuddered and turned away.

"Run across for Mr. Harrison," said Marilla, wringing her hands.

"Mr. Harrison and John Henry are both away . . . they went to town today. I'll go for Mr. Barry."

Mr. Barry came back with Anne, carrying a coil of rope to which was attached a claw-like instrument that had been the business end of a grubbing fork. Marilla and Anne stood by, cold and shaken with horror and dread, while Mr. Barry dragged the well, and Davy, astride the gate, watched the group with a face indicative of huge enjoyment.

Finally Mr. Barry shook his head, with a relieved air.

"She can't be down there. It's a mighty curious thing where she could have got to, though. Look here, young man, are you sure you've no idea where your sister is?"

"I've told you a dozen times that I haven't," said Davy, with an injured air. "Maybe a tramp come and stole her."

"Nonsense," said Marilla sharply, relieved from her horrible fear of the well. "Anne, do you suppose she could have strayed over to Mr. Harrison's? She has always been talking about his parrot ever since that time you took her over."

"I can't believe Dora would venture so far alone but I'll go over and see," said Anne.

Nobody was looking at Davy just then or it would have been seen that a very decided change came over his face. He quietly slipped off the gate and ran, as fast as his fat legs could carry him, to the barn.

Anne hastened across the fields to the Harrison establishment in no very hopeful frame of mind. The house was locked, the window shades were down, and there was no sign of anything living about the place. She stood on the veranda and called Dora loudly.

Ginger, in the kitchen behind her, shrieked and swore with sudden fierceness; but between his outbursts Anne heard a plaintive cry from the little building in the yard which served Mr. Harrison as a toolhouse. Anne flew to the door, unhasped it, and caught up a small mortal with a tearstained face who was sitting forlornly on an upturned nail keg.

"Oh, Dora, Dora, what a fright you have given us! How came you to be here?"

"Davy and I came over to see Ginger," sobbed Dora, "but we couldn't see him after all, only Davy made him swear by kicking the door. And then Davy brought me here and run out and shut the door; and I couldn't get out. I cried and cried, I was frightened, and oh, I'm so hungry and cold; and I thought you'd never come, Anne."

"Davy?" But Anne could say no more. She carried Dora home with a heavy heart. Her joy at finding the child safe and sound was drowned out in the pain caused by Davy's behavior. The freak of shutting Dora up might easily have been pardoned. But Davy had told falsehoods . . . downright coldblooded falsehoods about it. That was the ugly fact and Anne could not shut her eyes to it. She could have sat down and cried with sheer disappointment. She had grown to love Davy dearly . . . how dearly she had not known until this minute . . . and it hurt her unbearably to discover that he was guilty of deliberate falsehood.

Marilla listened to Anne's tale in a silence that boded no good Davy-ward; Mr. Barry laughed and advised that Davy be summarily dealt with. When he had gone home Anne soothed and warmed the sobbing, shivering Dora, got her her supper and put her to bed. Then she returned to the kitchen, just as Marilla came grimly in, leading, or rather pulling, the reluctant, cobwebby Davy, whom she had just found hidden away in the darkest corner of the stable.

She jerked him to the mat on the middle of the floor and then went and sat down by the east window. Anne was sitting limply by the west window. Between them stood the culprit. His back was toward Marilla and it was a meek, subdued, frightened back; but his face was toward Anne and although it was a little shamefaced there was a gleam of comradeship in Davy's eyes, as if he knew he had done wrong and was going to be punished for it, but could count on a laugh over it all with Anne later on.

But no half hidden smile answered him in Anne's gray eyes, as there might have done had it been only a question of mischief. There was something else . . . something ugly and repulsive.

"How could you behave so, Davy?" she asked sorrowfully.

Davy squirmed uncomfortably.

"I just did it for fun. Things have been so awful quiet here for so long that I thought it would be fun to give you folks a big scare. It was, too."

In spite of fear and a little remorse Davy grinned over the recollection.

"But you told a falsehood about it, Davy," said Anne, more sorrowfully than ever.

Davy looked puzzled.

"What's a falsehood? Do you mean a whopper?"

"I mean a story that was not true."

"Course I did," said Davy frankly. "If I hadn't you wouldn't have been scared. I HAD to tell it."

Anne was feeling the reaction from her fright and exertions. Davy's impenitent attitude gave the finishing touch. Two big tears brimmed up in her eyes.

"Oh, Davy, how could you?" she said, with a quiver in her voice. "Don't you know how wrong it was?"

Davy was aghast. Anne crying . . . he had made Anne cry! A flood of real remorse rolled like a wave over his warm little heart and engulfed it. He rushed to Anne, hurled himself into her lap, flung his arms around her neck, and burst into tears.

"I didn't know it was wrong to tell whoppers," he sobbed. "How did you expect me to know it was wrong? All Mr. Sprott's children told them REGULAR every day, and cross their hearts too. I s'pose Paul Irving never tells whoppers and here I've been trying awful hard to be as good as him, but now I s'pose you'll never love me again. But I think you might have told me it was wrong. I'm awful sorsorry I've made you cry, Anne, and I'll never tell a whopper again."

Davy buried his face in Anne's shoulder and cried stormily. Anne, in a sudden glad flash of understanding, held him tight and looked over his curly thatch at Marilla.

"He didn't know it was wrong to tell falsehoods, Marilla. I think we must forgive him for that part of it this time if he will promise never to say what isn't true again."

"I never will, now that I know it's bad," asseverated Davy between sobs. "If you ever catch me telling a whopper again you can . . ." Davy groped mentally for a suitable penance . . . "you can skin me alive, Anne."

"Don't say 'whopper,' Davy . . . say 'falsehood,'" said the schoolma'am.

"Why?" queried Davy, settling comfortably down and looking up with a tearstained, investigating face. "Why ain't whopper as good as falsehood? I want to know. It's just as big a word."

"It's slang; and it's wrong for little boys to use slang."

"There's an awful lot of things it's wrong to do," said Davy with a sigh. "I never s'posed there was so many. I'm sorry it's wrong to tell whop . . . falsehoods, 'cause it's awful handy, but since it is I'm never going to tell any more. What are you going to do to me for telling them this time? I want to know." Anne looked beseechingly at Marilla.

"I don't want to be too hard on the child," said Marilla. "I daresay nobody ever did tell him it was wrong to tell lies, and those Sprott children were no fit companions for him. Poor Mary was too sick to train him properly and I presume you couldn't expect a six-year-old child to know things like that by instinct. I suppose we'll just have to assume he doesn't know ANYTHING right and begin at the beginning. But he'll have to be punished for shutting Dora up, and I can't think of any way except to send him to bed without his supper and we've done that so often. Can't you suggest something else, Anne? I should think you ought to be able to, with that imagination you're always talking of."

"But punishments are so horrid and I like to imagine only pleasant things," said Anne, cuddling Davy. "There are so many unpleasant things in the world already that there is no use in imagining any more."

In the end Davy was sent to bed, as usual, there to remain until noon next day. He evidently did some thinking, for when Anne went up to her room a little later she heard him calling her name softly. Going in, she found him sitting up in bed, with his elbows on his knees and his chin propped on his hands.

"Anne," he said solemnly, "is it wrong for everybody to tell whop . . . falsehoods? I want to know?"

"Yes, indeed."

"Is it wrong for a grown-up person?"

"Yes."

"Then," said Davy decidedly, "Marilla is bad, for SHE tells them. And she's worse'n me, for I didn't know it was wrong but she does."

"Davy Keith, Marilla never told a story in her life," said Anne indignantly.

"She did so. She told me last Tuesday that something dreadful WOULD happen to me if I didn't say my prayers every night. And I haven't said them for over a week, just to see what would happen . . . and nothing has," concluded Davy in an aggrieved tone.

Anne choked back a mad desire to laugh with the conviction that it would be fatal, and then earnestly set about saving Marilla's reputation.

"Why, Davy Keith," she said solemnly, "something dreadful HAS happened to you this very day."

Davy looked sceptical.

"I s'pose you mean being sent to bed without any supper," he said scornfully, "but THAT isn't dreadful. Course, I don't like it, but I've been sent to bed so much since I come here that I'm getting used to it. And you don't save anything by making me go without supper either, for I always eat twice as much for breakfast."

"I don't mean your being sent to bed. I mean the fact that you told a falsehood today. And, Davy," . . . Anne leaned over the footboard of the bed and shook her finger impressively at the culprit . . . "for a boy to tell what isn't true is almost the worst thing that could HAPPEN to him . . . almost the very worst. So you see Marilla told you the truth."

"But I thought the something bad would be exciting," protested Davy in an injured tone.

"Marilla isn't to blame for what you thought. Bad things aren't always exciting. They're very often just nasty and stupid."

"It was awful funny to see Marilla and you looking down the well, though," said Davy, hugging his knees.

Anne kept a sober face until she got downstairs and then she collapsed on the sitting room lounge and laughed until her sides ached.

"I wish you'd tell me the joke," said Marilla, a little grimly. "I haven't seen much to laugh at today."

"You'll laugh when you hear this," assured Anne. And Marilla did laugh, which showed how much her education had advanced since the adoption of Anne. But she sighed immediately afterwards.

"I suppose I shouldn't have told him that, although I heard a minister say it to a child once. But he did aggravate me so. It was that night you were at the Carmody concert and I was putting him to bed. He said he didn't see the good of praying until he got big enough to be of some importance to God. Anne, I do not know what we are going to do with that child. I never saw his beat. I'm feeling clean discouraged."

"Oh, don't say that, Marilla. Remember how bad I was when I came here."

"Anne, you never were bad . . . NEVER. I see that now, when I've learned what real badness is. You were always getting into terrible scrapes, I'll admit, but your motive was always good. Davy is just bad from sheer love of it."

"Oh, no, I don't think it is real badness with him either," pleaded Anne. "It's just mischief. And it is rather quiet for him here, you know. He has no other boys to play with and his mind has to have something to occupy it. Dora is so prim and proper she is no good for a boy's playmate. I really think it would be better to let them go to school, Marilla."

"No," said Marilla resolutely, "my father always said that no child should be cooped up in the four walls of a school until it was seven years old, and Mr. Allan says the same thing. The twins can have a few lessons at home but go to school they shan't till they're seven."

"Well, we must try to reform Davy at home then," said Anne cheerfully. "With all his faults he's really a dear little chap. I can't help loving him. Marilla, it may be a dreadful thing to say, but honestly, I like Davy better than Dora, for all she's so good."

"I don't know but that I do, myself," confessed Marilla, "and it isn't fair, for Dora isn't a bit of trouble. There couldn't be a better child and you'd hardly know she was in the house."

"Dora is too good," said Anne. "She'd behave just as well if there wasn't a soul to tell her what to do. She was born already brought up, so she doesn't need us; and I think," concluded Anne, hitting on a very vital truth, "that we always love best the people who need us. Davy needs us badly."

"He certainly needs something," agreed Marilla. "Rachel Lynde would say it was a good spanking."

XI - Facts and Fancies

"Teaching is really very interesting work," wrote Anne to a Queen's Academy chum. "Jane says she thinks it is monotonous but I don't find it so. Something funny is almost sure to happen every day, and the children say such amusing things. Jane says she punishes her pupils when they make funny speeches, which is probably why she finds teaching monotonous. This afternoon little Jimmy Andrews was trying to spell 'speckled' and couldn't manage it. 'Well,' he said finally, 'I can't spell it but I know what it means.'

"'What?' I asked.

"'St. Clair Donnell's face, miss.'

"St. Clair is certainly very much freckled, although I try to prevent the others from commenting on it . . . for I was freckled once and well do I remember it. But I don't think St. Clair minds. It was because Jimmy called him 'St. Clair' that St. Clair pounded him on the way home from school. I heard of the pounding, but not officially, so I don't think I'll take any notice of it.

"Yesterday I was trying to teach Lottie Wright to do addition. I said, 'If you had three candies in one hand and two in the other, how many would you have altogether?' 'A mouthful,' said Lottie. And in the nature study class, when I asked them to give me a good reason why toads shouldn't be killed, Benjie Sloane gravely answered, 'Because it would rain the next day.'

"It's so hard not to laugh, Stella. I have to save up all my amusement until I get home, and Marilla says it makes her nervous to hear wild shrieks of mirth proceeding from the east gable without any apparent cause. She says a man in Grafton went insane once and that was how it began.

"Did you know that Thomas a Becket was canonized as a SNAKE? Rose Bell says he was . . . also that William Tyndale WROTE the New Testament. Claude White says a 'glacier' is a man who puts in window frames!

"I think the most difficult thing in teaching, as well as the most interesting, is to get the children to tell you their real thoughts about things. One stormy day last week I gathered them around me at dinner hour and tried to get them to talk to me just as if I were one of themselves. I asked them to tell me the things they most wanted. Some of the answers were commonplace enough . . . dolls, ponies, and skates. Others were decidedly original. Hester Boulter wanted 'to wear her Sunday dress every day and eat in the sitting room.' Hannah Bell wanted 'to be good without having to take any trouble about it.' Marjory White, aged ten, wanted to be a WIDOW. Questioned why, she gravely said that if you weren't married people called you an old maid, and if you were your husband bossed you; but if you were a widow there'd be no danger of either. The most remarkable wish was Sally Bell's. She wanted a 'honeymoon.' I asked her if she knew what it was and she said she thought it was an extra nice kind of bicycle because her cousin in Montreal went on a honeymoon when he was married and he had always had the very latest in bicycles!

"Another day I asked them all to tell me the naughtiest thing they had ever done. I couldn't get the older ones to do so, but the third class answered quite freely. Eliza Bell had 'set fire to her aunt's carded rolls.' Asked if she meant to do it she said, 'not altogether.' She just tried a little end to see how it would burn and the whole bundle blazed up in a jiffy. Emerson Gillis had spent ten cents for candy when he should have put it in his missionary box. Annetta Bell's worst crime was 'eating some blueberries that grew in the graveyard.' Willie White had 'slid down the sheephouse roof a lot of times with his Sunday trousers on.' 'But I was punished for it 'cause I had to wear patched pants to Sunday School all summer, and when you're punished for a thing you don't have to repent of it,' declared Willie.

"I wish you could see some of their compositions . . . so much do I wish it that I'll send you copies of some written recently. Last week I told the fourth class I wanted them to write me letters about anything they pleased, adding by way of suggestion that they might tell me of some place they had visited or some interesting thing or person they had seen. They were to write the letters on real note paper, seal them in an envelope, and address them to me, all without any assistance from other people. Last Friday morning I found a pile of letters on my desk and that evening I realized afresh that teaching has its pleasures as well as its pains. Those compositions would atone for much. Here is Ned Clay's, address, spelling, and grammar as originally penned.

"'Miss teacher ShiRley
Green gabels.
p.e. Island can
birds

"'Dear teacher I think I will write you a composition about birds. birds is very useful animals. my cat catches birds. His name is William but pa calls him tom. he is oll striped and he got one of his ears froz of last winter. only for that he would be a good-looking cat. My unkle has adopted a cat. it come to his house one day and woudent go away and unkle says it has forgot more than most people ever knowed. he lets it sleep on his rocking chare and my aunt says he thinks more of it than he does of his children. that is not right. we ought to be kind to cats and give them new milk but we ought not be better to them than to our children. this is oll I can think of so no more at present from
edward blake ClaY.'"

"St. Clair Donnell's is, as usual, short and to the point. St. Clair never wastes words. I do not think he chose his subject or added the postscript out of malice aforethought. It is just that he has not a great deal of tact or imagination."

"'Dear Miss Shirley

"'You told us to describe something strange we have seen. I will describe the Avonlea Hall. It has two doors, an inside one and an outside one. It has six windows and a chimney. It has two ends and two sides. It is painted blue. That is what makes it strange. It is built on the lower Carmody road. It is the third most important building in Avonlea. The others are the church and the blacksmith shop. They hold debating clubs and lectures in it and concerts.

"'Yours truly,

"'Jacob Donnell.

"'P.S. The hall is a very bright blue.'"

"Annetta Bell's letter was quite long, which surprised me, for writing essays is not Annetta's forte, and hers are generally as brief as St. Clair's. Annetta is a quiet little puss and a model of good behavior, but there isn't a shadow of orginality in her. Here is her letter.—

"'Dearest teacher,

""I think I will write you a letter to tell you how much I love you. I love you with my whole heart and soul and mind . . . with all there is of me to love . . . and I want to serve you for ever. It would be my highest privilege. That is why I try so hard to be good in school and learn my lessuns.

"'You are so beautiful, my teacher. Your voice is like music and your eyes are like pansies when the dew is on them. You are like a tall stately queen. Your hair is like rippling gold. Anthony Pye says it is red, but you needn't pay any attention to Anthony.

"'I have only known you for a few months but I cannot realize that there was ever a time when I did not know you . . . when you had not come into my life to bless and hallow it. I will always look back to this year as the most wonderful in my life because it brought you to me. Besides, it's the year we moved to Avonlea from Newbridge. My love for you has made my life very rich and it has kept me from much of harm and evil. I owe this all to you, my sweetest teacher.

"'I shall never forget how sweet you looked the last time I saw you in that black dress with flowers in your hair. I shall see you like that for ever, even when we are both old and gray. You will always be young and fair to me, dearest teacher. I am thinking of you all the time. . . in the morning and at the noontide and at the twilight. I love you when you laugh and when you sigh . . . even when you look disdainful. I never saw you look cross though Anthony Pye says you always look so but I don't wonder you look cross at him for he deserves it. I love you in every dress . . . you seem more adorable in each new dress than the last.

"'Dearest teacher, good night. The sun has set and the stars are shining . . . stars that are as bright and beautiful as your eyes. I kiss your hands and face, my sweet. May God watch over you and protect you from all harm.

""Your afecksionate pupil,

"'Annetta Bell.'"

"This extraordinary letter puzzled me not a little. I knew Annetta couldn't have composed it any more than she could fly. When I went to school the next day I took her for a walk down to the brook at recess and asked her to tell me the truth about the letter. Annetta cried and 'fessed up freely. She said she had never written a letter and she didn't know how to, or what to say, but there was bundle of love letters in her mother's top bureau drawer which had been written to her by an old 'beau.'

"'It wasn't father,' sobbed Annetta, 'it was someone who was studying for a minister, and so he could write lovely letters, but ma didn't marry him after all. She said she couldn't make out what he was driving at half the time. But I thought the letters were sweet and that I'd just copy things out of them here and there to write you. I put "teacher" where he put "lady" and I put in something of my own when I could think of it and I changed some words. I put "dress" in place of "mood." I didn't know just what a "mood" was but I s'posed it was something to wear. I didn't s'pose you'd know the difference. I don't see how you found out it wasn't all mine. You must be awful clever, teacher.'

"I told Annetta it was very wrong to copy another person's letter and pass it off as her own. But I'm afraid that all Annetta repented of was being found out.

"'And I do love you, teacher,' she sobbed. 'It was all true, even if the minister wrote it first. I do love you with all my heart.'

"It's very difficult to scold anybody properly under such circumstances.

"Here is Barbara Shaw's letter. I can't reproduce the blots of the original.

"'Dear teacher,

""You said we might write about a visit. I never visited but once. It was at my Aunt Mary's last winter. My Aunt Mary is a very particular woman and a great housekeeper. The first night I was there we were at tea. I knocked over a jug and broke it. Aunt Mary said she had had that jug ever since she was married and nobody had ever broken it before. When we got up I stepped on her dress and all the gathers tore out of the skirt. The next morning when I got up I hit the pitcher against the basin and cracked them both and I upset a cup of tea on the tablecloth at breakfast. When I was helping Aunt Mary with the dinner dishes I dropped a china plate and it smashed. That evening I fell downstairs and sprained my ankle and had to stay in bed for a week. I heard Aunt Mary tell Uncle Joseph it was a mercy or I'd have broken everything in the house. When I got better it was time to go home. I don't like visiting very much. I like going to school better, especially since I came to Avonlea.

"'Yours respectfully,

""Barbara Shaw.'"

"Willie White's began,

""Respected Miss,

""I want to tell you about my Very Brave Aunt. She lives in Ontario and one day she went out to the barn and saw a dog in the yard. The dog had no business there so she got a stick and whacked him hard and drove him into the barn and shut him up. Pretty soon a man came looking for an inaginary lion' (Query;—Did Willie mean a menagerie lion?) 'that had run away from a circus. And it turned out that the dog was a lion and my Very Brave Aunt had druv him into the barn with a stick. It was a wonder she was not et up but she was very brave. Emerson Gillis says if she thought it was a dog she wasn't any braver than if it really was a dog. But Emerson is jealous because he hasn't got a Brave Aunt himself, nothing but uncles.'

"'I have kept the best for the last. You laugh at me because I think Paul is a genius but I am sure his letter will convince you that he is a very uncommon child. Paul lives away down near the shore with his grandmother and he has no playmates . . . no real playmates. You remember our School Management professor told us that we must not have 'favorites' among our pupils, but I can't help loving Paul Irving the best of all mine. I don't think it does any harm, though, for everybody loves Paul, even Mrs. Lynde, who says she could never have believed she'd get so fond of a Yankee. The other boys in school like him too. There is nothing weak or girlish about him in spite of his dreams and fancies. He is very manly and can hold his own in all games. He fought St. Clair Donnell recently because St. Clair said the Union Jack was away ahead of the Stars and Stripes as a flag. The result was a drawn battle and a mutual agreement to respect each other's patriotism henceforth. St. Clair says he can hit the HARDEST but Paul can hit the OFTENEST.'"

"Paul's Letter.

"'My dear teacher,

"'You told us we might write you about some interesting people we knew. I think the most interesting people I know are my rock people and I mean to tell you about them. I have never told anybody about them except grandma and father but I would like to have you know about them because you understand things. There are a great many people who do not understand things so there is no use in telling them.'

"'My rock people live at the shore. I used to visit them almost every evening before the winter came. Now I can't go till spring, but they will be there, for people like that never change . . . that is the splendid thing about them. Nora was the first one of them I got acquainted with and so I think I love her the best. She lives in Andrews' Cove and she has black hair and black eyes, and she knows all about the mermaids and the water kelpies. You ought to hear the stories she can tell. Then there are the Twin Sailors. They don't live anywhere, they sail all the time, but they often come ashore to talk to me. They are a pair of jolly tars and they have seen everything in the world. . . and more than what is in the world. Do you know what happened to the youngest Twin Sailor once? He was sailing and he sailed right into a moonglade. A moonglade is the track the full moon makes on the water when it is rising from the sea, you know, teacher. Well, the youngest Twin Sailor sailed along the moonglade till he came right up to the moon, and there was a little golden door in the moon and he opened it and sailed right through. He had some wonderful adventures in the moon but it would make this letter too long to tell them.'

"'Then there is the Golden Lady of the cave. One day I found a big cave down on the shore and I went away in and after a while I found the Golden Lady. She has golden hair right down to her feet and her dress is all glittering and glistening like gold that is alive. And she has a golden harp and plays on it all day long . . . you can hear the music any time along shore if you listen carefully but most people would think it was only the wind among the rocks. I've never told Nora about the Golden Lady. I was afraid it might hurt her feelings. It even hurt her feelings if I talked too long with the Twin Sailors.'

"'I always met the Twin Sailors at the Striped Rocks. The youngest Twin Sailor is very good-tempered but the oldest Twin Sailor can look dreadfully fierce at times. I have my suspicions about that oldest Twin. I believe he'd be a pirate if he dared. There's really something very mysterious about him. He swore once and I told him if he ever did it again he needn't come ashore to talk to me because I'd promised grandmother I'd never associate with anybody that swore. He was pretty well scared, I can tell you, and he said if I would forgive him he would take me to the sunset. So the next evening when I was sitting on the Striped Rocks the oldest Twin came sailing over the sea in an enchanted boat and I got in her. The boat was all pearly and rainbowy, like the inside of the mussel shells, and her sail was like moonshine. Well, we sailed right across to the sunset. Think of that, teacher, I've been in the sunset. And what do you suppose it is? The sunset is a land all flowers. We sailed into a great garden, and the clouds are beds of flowers. We sailed into a great harbor, all the color of gold, and I stepped right out of the boat on a big meadow all covered with buttercups as big as roses. I stayed there for ever so long. It seemed nearly a year but the Oldest Twin says it was only a few minutes. You see, in the sunset land the time is ever so much longer than it is here.'

"'Your loving pupil Paul Irving.'

"'P. S. of course, this letter isn't really true, teacher. P.I.'"

XII - A Jonah Day

It really began the night before with a restless, wakeful vigil of grumbling toothache. When Anne arose in the dull, bitter winter morning she felt that life was flat, stale, and unprofitable.

She went to school in no angelic mood. Her cheek was swollen and her face ached. The schoolroom was cold and smoky, for the fire refused to burn and the children were huddled about it in shivering groups. Anne sent them to their seats with a sharper tone than she had ever used before. Anthony Pye strutted to his with his usual impertinent swagger and she saw him whisper something to his seat-mate and then glance at her with a grin.

Never, so it seemed to Anne, had there been so many squeaky pencils as there were that morning; and when Barbara Shaw came up to the desk with a sum she tripped over the coal scuttle with disastrous results. The coal rolled to every part of the room, her slate was broken into fragments, and when she picked herself up, her face, stained with coal dust, sent the boys into roars of laughter.

Anne turned from the second reader class which she was hearing.

"Really, Barbara," she said icily, "if you cannot move without falling over something you'd better remain in your seat. It is positively disgraceful for a girl of your age to be so awkward."

Poor Barbara stumbled back to her desk, her tears combining with the coal dust to produce an effect truly grotesque. Never before had her beloved, sympathetic teacher spoken to her in such a tone or fashion, and Barbara was heartbroken. Anne herself felt a prick of conscience but it only served to increase her mental irritation, and the second reader class remember that lesson yet, as well as the unmerciful infliction of arithmetic that followed. Just as Anne was snapping the sums out St. Clair Donnell arrived breathlessly.

"You are half an hour late, St. Clair," Anne reminded him frigidly. "Why is this?"

"Please, miss, I had to help ma make a pudding for dinner 'cause we're expecting company and Clarice Almira's sick," was St. Clair's answer, given in a perfectly respectful voice but nevertheless provocative of great mirth among his mates.

"Take your seat and work out the six problems on page eighty-four of your arithmetic for punishment," said Anne. St. Clair looked rather amazed at her tone but he went meekly to his desk and took out his slate. Then he stealthily passed a small parcel to Joe Sloane across the aisle. Anne caught him in the act and jumped to a fatal conclusion about that parcel.

Old Mrs. Hiram Sloane had lately taken to making and selling "nut cakes" by way of adding to her scanty income. The cakes were specially tempting to small boys and for several weeks Anne had had not a little trouble in regard to them. On their way to school the boys would invest their spare cash at Mrs. Hiram's, bring the cakes along with them to school, and, if possible, eat them and treat their mates during school hours. Anne had warned them that if they brought any more cakes to school they would be confiscated; and yet here was St. Clair Donnell coolly passing a parcel of them, wrapped up in the blue and white striped paper Mrs. Hiram used, under her very eyes.

"Joseph," said Anne quietly, "bring that parcel here."

Joe, startled and abashed, obeyed. He was a fat urchin who always blushed and stuttered when he was frightened. Never did anybody look more guilty than poor Joe at that moment.

"Throw it into the fire," said Anne.

Joe looked very blank.

"P . . . p . . . p . . . lease, m . . . m . . . miss," he began.

"Do as I tell you, Joseph, without any words about it."

"B . . . b . . . but m . . . m . . . miss . . . th . . . th . . . they're . . ." gasped Joe in desperation.

"Joseph, are you going to obey me or are you NOT?" said Anne.

A bolder and more self-possessed lad than Joe Sloane would have been over-awed by her tone and the dangerous flash of her eyes. This was a new Anne whom none of her pupils had ever seen before. Joe, with an agonized glance at St. Clair, went to the stove, opened the big, square front door, and threw the blue and white parcel in, before St. Clair, who had sprung to his feet, could utter a word. Then he dodged back just in time.

For a few moments the terrified occupants of Avonlea school did not know whether it was an earthquake or a volcanic explosion that had occurred. The inno-cent looking parcel which Anne had rashly supposed to contain Mrs. Hiram's nut cakes really held an assortment of firecrackers and pinwheels for which Warren Sloane had sent to town by St. Clair Donnell's father the day before, intending to have a birthday celebration that evening. The crackers went off in a thunderclap of noise and the pinwheels bursting out of the door spun madly around the room, hissing and spluttering. Anne dropped into her chair white with dismay and all the girls climbed shrieking upon their desks. Joe Sloane stood as one transfixed in the midst of the commotion and St. Clair, helpless with laughter, rocked to and fro in the aisle. Prillie Rogerson fainted and Annetta Bell went into hysterics.

It seemed a long time, although it was really only a few minutes, before the last pinwheel subsided. Anne, recovering herself, sprang to open doors and win-dows and let out the gas and smoke which filled the room. Then she helped the girls carry the unconscious Prillie into the porch, where Barbara Shaw, in an agony of desire to be useful, poured a pailful of half frozen water over Prillie's face and shoulders before anyone could stop her.

It was a full hour before quiet was restored . . . but it was a quiet that might be felt. Everybody realized that even the explosion had not cleared the teacher's mental atmosphere. Nobody, except Anthony Pye, dared whisper a word. Ned Clay accidentally squeaked his pencil while working a sum, caught Anne's eye and wished the floor would open and swallow him up. The geography class were whisked through a continent with a speed that made them dizzy. The grammar class were parsed and analyzed within an inch of their lives. Chester Sloane, spelling "odoriferous" with two f's, was made to feel that he could never live down the disgrace of it, either in this world or that which is to come.

Anne knew that she had made herself ridiculous and that the incident would be laughed over that night at a score of tea-tables, but the knowledge only angered her further. In a calmer mood she could have carried off the situation with a laugh but now that was impossible; so she ignored it in icy disdain.

When Anne returned to the school after dinner all the children were as usual in their seats and every face was bent studiously over a desk except Anthony Pye's. He peered across his book at Anne, his black eyes sparkling with curiosity and mockery. Anne twitched open the drawer of her desk in search of chalk and under her very hand a lively mouse sprang out of the drawer, scampered over the desk, and leaped to the floor.

Anne screamed and sprang back, as if it had been a snake, and Anthony Pye laughed aloud.

Then a silence fell . . . a very creepy, uncomfortable silence. Annetta Bell was of two minds whether to go into hysterics again or not, especially as she didn't know just where the mouse had gone. But she decided not to. Who could take any comfort out of hysterics with a teacher so white-faced and so blazing-eyed standing before one?

"Who put that mouse in my desk?" said Anne. Her voice was quite low but it made a shiver go up and down Paul Irving's spine. Joe Sloane caught her eye, felt responsible from the crown of his head to the sole of his feet, but stuttered out wildly,

"N . . . n . . . not m . . . m . . . me t . . . t . . . teacher, n . . . n . . . not m . . . m . . . me."

Anne paid no attention to the wretched Joseph. She looked at Anthony Pye, and Anthony Pye looked back unabashed and unashamed.

"Anthony, was it you?"

"Yes, it was," said Anthony insolently.

Anne took her pointer from her desk. It was a long, heavy hardwood pointer.

"Come here, Anthony."

It was far from being the most severe punishment Anthony Pye had ever undergone. Anne, even the stormy-souled Anne she was at that moment, could not have punished any child cruelly. But the pointer nipped keenly and finally Anthony's bravado failed him; he winced and the tears came to his eyes.

Anne, conscience-stricken, dropped the pointer and told Anthony to go to his seat. She sat down at her desk feeling ashamed, repentant, and bitterly mortified. Her quick anger was gone and she would have given much to have been able to seek relief in tears. So all her boasts had come to this . . . she had actually whipped one of her pupils. How Jane would triumph! And how Mr. Harrison would chuckle! But worse than this, bitterest thought of all, she had lost her last chance of winning Anthony Pye. Never would he like her now.

Anne, by what somebody has called "a Herculaneum effort," kept back her tears until she got home that night. Then she shut herself in the east gable room and wept all her shame and remorse and disappointment into her pillows . . . wept so long that Marilla grew alarmed, invaded the room, and insisted on knowing what the trouble was.

"The trouble is, I've got things the matter with my conscience," sobbed Anne. "Oh, this has been such a Jonah day, Marilla. I'm so ashamed of myself. I lost my temper and whipped Anthony Pye."

"I'm glad to hear it," said Marilla with decision. "It's what you should have done long ago."

"Oh, no, no, Marilla. And I don't see how I can ever look those children in the face again. I feel that I have humiliated myself to the very dust. You don't know how cross and hateful and horrid I was. I can't forget the expression in Paul Irving's eyes . . . he looked so surprised and disappointed. Oh, Marilla, I HAVE tried so hard to be patient and to win Anthony's liking . . . and now it has all gone for nothing."

Marilla passed her hard work-worn hand over the girl's glossy, tumbled hair with a wonderful tenderness. When Anne's sobs grew quieter she said, very gently for her,

"You take things too much to heart, Anne. We all make mistakes . . . but people forget them. And Jonah days come to everybody. As for Anthony Pye, why need you care if he does dislike you? He is the only one."

"I can't help it. I want everybody to love me and it hurts me so when anybody doesn't. And Anthony never will now. Oh, I just made an idiot of myself today, Marilla. I'll tell you the whole story."

Marilla listened to the whole story, and if she smiled at certain parts of it Anne never knew. When the tale was ended she said briskly,

"Well, never mind. This day's done and there's a new one coming tomorrow, with no mistakes in it yet, as you used to say yourself. Just come downstairs and have your supper. You'll see if a good cup of tea and those plum puffs I made today won't hearten you up."

"Plum puffs won't minister to a mind diseased," said Anne disconsolately; but Marilla thought it a good sign that she had recovered sufficiently to adapt a quotation.

The cheerful supper table, with the twins' bright faces, and Marilla's matchless plum puffs . . . of which Davy ate four . . . did "hearten her up" considerably after all. She had a good sleep that night and awakened in the morning to find herself and the world transformed. It had snowed softly and thickly all through the hours of darkness and the beautiful whiteness, glittering in the frosty sunshine, looked like a mantle of charity cast over all the mistakes and humiliations of the past.

> "Every morn is a fresh beginning,
> Every morn is the world made new,"

sang Anne, as she dressed.

Owing to the snow she had to go around by the road to school and she thought it was certainly an impish coincidence that Anthony Pye should come ploughing along just as she left the Green Gables lane. She felt as guilty as if their positions were reversed; but to her unspeakable astonishment Anthony not only lifted his cap . . . which he had never done before . . . but said easily,

"Kind of bad walking, ain't it? Can I take those books for you, teacher?"

Anne surrendered her books and wondered if she could possibly be awake. Anthony walked on in silence to the school, but when Anne took her books she smiled down at him . . . not the stereotyped "kind" smile she had so persistently assumed for his benefit but a sudden outflashing of good comradeship. Anthony smiled . . . no, if the truth must be told, Anthony GRINNED back. A grin is not generally supposed to be a respectful thing; yet Anne suddenly felt that if she had not yet won Anthony's liking she had, somehow or other, won his respect.

Mrs. Rachel Lynde came up the next Saturday and confirmed this.

"Well, Anne, I guess you've won over Anthony Pye, that's what. He says he believes you are some good after all, even if you are a girl. Says that whipping you gave him was 'just as good as a man's.'"

"I never expected to win him by whipping him, though," said Anne, a little mournfully, feeling that her ideals had played her false somewhere. "It doesn't seem right. I'm sure my theory of kindness can't be wrong."

"No, but the Pyes are an exception to every known rule, that's what," declared Mrs. Rachel with conviction.

Mr. Harrison said, "Thought you'd come to it," when he heard it, and Jane rubbed it in rather unmercifully.

XIII - A Golden Picnic

Anne, on her way to Orchard Slope, met Diana, bound for Green Gables, just where the mossy old log bridge spanned the brook below the Haunted Wood, and they sat down by the margin of the Dryad's Bubble, where tiny ferns were unrolling like curly-headed green pixy folk wakening up from a nap.

"I was just on my way over to invite you to help me celebrate my birthday on Saturday," said Anne.

"Your birthday? But your birthday was in March!"

"That wasn't my fault," laughed Anne. "If my parents had consulted me it would never have happened then. I should have chosen to be born in spring, of course. It must be delightful to come into the world with the mayflowers and violets. You would always feel that you were their foster sister. But since I didn't, the next best thing is to celebrate my birthday in the spring. Priscilla is coming over Saturday and Jane will be home. We'll all four start off to the woods and spend a golden day making the acquaintance of the spring. We none of us really know her yet, but we'll meet her back there as we never can anywhere else. I want to explore all those fields and lonely places anyhow. I have a conviction that there are scores of beautiful nooks there that have never really been SEEN although they may have been LOOKED at. We'll make friends with wind and sky and sun, and bring home the spring in our hearts."

"It SOUNDS awfully nice," said Diana, with some inward distrust of Anne's magic of words. "But won't it be very damp in some places yet?"

"Oh, we'll wear rubbers," was Anne's concession to practicalities. "And I want you to come over early Saturday morning and help me prepare lunch. I'm going to have the daintiest things possible . . . things that will match the spring, you understand . . . little jelly tarts and lady fingers, and drop cookies frosted with pink and yellow icing, and buttercup cake. And we must have sandwiches too, though they're NOT very poetical."

Saturday proved an ideal day for a picnic . . . a day of breeze and blue, warm, sunny, with a little rollicking wind blowing across meadow and orchard. Over every sunlit upland and field was a delicate, flower-starred green.

Mr. Harrison, harrowing at the back of his farm and feeling some of the spring witch-work even in his sober, middle-aged blood, saw four girls, basket laden, tripping across the end of his field where it joined a fringing woodland of birch and fir. Their blithe voices and laughter echoed down to him.

"It's so easy to be happy on a day like this, isn't it?" Anne was saying, with true Anneish philosophy. "Let's try to make this a really golden day, girls, a day to which we can always look back with delight. We're to seek for beauty and refuse to see anything else. 'Begone, dull care!' Jane, you are thinking of something that went wrong in school yesterday."

"How do you know?" gasped Jane, amazed.

"Oh, I know the expression . . . I've felt it often enough on my own face. But put it out of your mind, there's a dear. It will keep till Monday . . . or if it doesn't so much the better. Oh, girls, girls, see that patch of violets! There's something for memory's picture gallery. When I'm eighty years old . . . if I ever am . . . I shall shut my eyes and see those violets just as I see them now. That's the first good gift our day has given us."

"If a kiss could be seen I think it would look like a violet," said Priscilla.

Anne glowed.

"I'm so glad you SPOKE that thought, Priscilla, instead of just thinking it and keeping it to yourself. This world would be a much more interesting place . . . although it IS very interesting anyhow . . . if people spoke out their real thoughts."

"It would be too hot to hold some folks," quoted Jane sagely.

"I suppose it might be, but that would be their own faults for thinking nasty things. Anyhow, we can tell all our thoughts today because we are going to have nothing but beautiful thoughts. Everybody can say just what comes into her head. THAT is conversation. Here's a little path I never saw before. Let's explore it."

The path was a winding one, so narrow that the girls walked in single file and even then the fir boughs brushed their faces. Under the firs were velvety cushions of moss, and further on, where the trees were smaller and fewer, the ground was rich in a variety of green growing things.

"What a lot of elephant's ears," exclaimed Diana. "I'm going to pick a big bunch, they're so pretty."

"How did such graceful feathery things ever come to have such a dreadful name?" asked Priscilla.

"Because the person who first named them either had no imagination at all or else far too much," said Anne, "Oh, girls, look at that!"

"That" was a shallow woodland pool in the center of a little open glade where the path ended. Later on in the season it would be dried up and its place filled with a rank growth of ferns; but now it was a glimmering placid sheet, round as a saucer and clear as crystal. A ring of slender young birches encircled it and little ferns fringed its margin.

"HOW sweet!" said Jane.

"Let us dance around it like wood-nymphs," cried Anne, dropping her basket and extending her hands.

But the dance was not a success for the ground was boggy and Jane's rubbers came off.

"You can't be a wood-nymph if you have to wear rubbers," was her decision.

"Well, we must name this place before we leave it," said Anne, yielding to the indisputable logic of facts. "Everybody suggest a name and we'll draw lots. Diana?"

"Birch Pool," suggested Diana promptly.

"Crystal Lake," said Jane.

Anne, standing behind them, implored Priscilla with her eyes not to perpetrate another such name and Priscilla rose to the occasion with "Glimmer-glass." Anne's selection was "The Fairies' Mirror."

The names were written on strips of birch bark with a pencil Schoolma'am Jane produced from her pocket, and placed in Anne's hat. Then Priscilla shut her eyes and drew one. "Crystal Lake," read Jane triumphantly. Crystal Lake it was, and if Anne thought that chance had played the pool a shabby trick she did not say so.

Pushing through the undergrowth beyond, the girls came out to the young green seclusion of Mr. Silas Sloane's back pasture. Across it they found the entrance to a lane striking up through the woods and voted to explore it also. It rewarded their quest with a succession of pretty surprises. First, skirting Mr. Sloane's pasture, came an archway of wild cherry trees all in bloom. The girls swung their hats on their arms and wreathed their hair with the creamy, fluffy blossoms. Then the lane turned at right angles and plunged into a spruce wood so thick and dark that they walked in a gloom as of twilight, with not a glimpse of sky or sunlight to be seen.

"This is where the bad wood elves dwell," whispered Anne. "They are impish and malicious but they can't harm us, because they are not allowed to do evil in the spring. There was one peeping at us around that old twisted fir; and didn't you see a group of them on that big freckly toadstool we just passed? The good fairies always dwell in the sunshiny places."

"I wish there really were fairies," said Jane. "Wouldn't it be nice to have three wishes granted you . . . or even only one? What would you wish for, girls, if you could have a wish granted? I'd wish to be rich and beautiful and clever."

"I'd wish to be tall and slender," said Diana.

"I would wish to be famous," said Priscilla. Anne thought of her hair and then dismissed the thought as unworthy.

"I'd wish it might be spring all the time and in everybody's heart and all our lives," she said.

"But that," said Priscilla, "would be just wishing this world were like heaven."

"Only like a part of heaven. In the other parts there would be summer and autumn . . . yes, and a bit of winter, too. I think I want glittering snowy fields and white frosts in heaven sometimes. Don't you, Jane?"

"I . . . I don't know," said Jane uncomfortably. Jane was a good girl, a member of the church, who tried conscientiously to live up to her profession and believed everything she had been taught. But she never thought about heaven any more than she could help, for all that.

"Minnie May asked me the other day if we would wear our best dresses every day in heaven," laughed Diana.

"And didn't you tell her we would?" asked Anne.

"Mercy, no! I told her we wouldn't be thinking of dresses at all there."

"Oh, I think we will . . . a LITTLE," said Anne earnestly. "There'll be plenty of time in all eternity for it without neglecting more important things. I believe we'll all wear beautiful dresses . . . or I suppose RAIMENT would be a more suitable way of speaking. I shall want to wear pink for a few centuries at first . . . it would take me that long to get tired of it, I feel sure. I do love pink so and I can never wear it in THIS world."

Past the spruces the lane dipped down into a sunny little open where a log bridge spanned a brook; and then came the glory of a sunlit beechwood where the air was like transparent golden wine, and the leaves fresh and green, and the wood floor a mosaic of tremulous sunshine. Then more wild cherries, and a little valley of lissome firs, and then a hill so steep that the girls lost their breath climbing it; but when they reached the top and came out into the open the prettiest surprise of all awaited them.

Beyond were the "back fields" of the farms that ran out to the upper Carmody road. Just before them, hemmed in by beeches and firs but open to the south, was a little corner and in it a garden . . . or what had once been a garden. A tumble-down stone dyke, overgrown with mosses and grass, surrounded it. Along the eastern side ran a row of garden cherry trees, white as a snowdrift. There were traces of old paths still and a double line of rosebushes through the middle; but all the rest of the space was a sheet of yellow and white narcissi, in their airiest, most lavish, wind-swayed bloom above the lush green grasses.

"Oh, how perfectly lovely!" three of the girls cried. Anne only gazed in eloquent silence.

"How in the world does it happen that there ever was a garden back here?" said Priscilla in amazement.

"It must be Hester Gray's garden," said Diana. "I've heard mother speak of it but I never saw it before, and I wouldn't have supposed that it could be in existence still. You've heard the story, Anne?"

"No, but the name seems familiar to me."

"Oh, you've seen it in the graveyard. She is buried down there in the poplar corner. You know the little brown stone with the opening gates carved on it and 'Sacred to the memory of Hester Gray, aged twenty-two.' Jordan Gray is buried right beside her but there's no stone to him. It's a wonder Marilla never told you about it, Anne. To be sure, it happened thirty years ago and everybody has forgotten."

"Well, if there's a story we must have it," said Anne. "Let's sit right down here among the narcissi and Diana will tell it. Why, girls, there are hundreds of them . . . they've spread over everything. It looks as if the garden were carpeted with moonshine and sunshine combined. This is a discovery worth making. To think that I've lived within a mile of this place for six years and have never seen it before! Now, Diana."

"Long ago," began Diana, "this farm belonged to old Mr. David Gray. He didn't live on it . . . he lived where Silas Sloane lives now. He had one son, Jordan, and he went up to Boston one winter to work and while he was there he fell in love with a girl named Hester Murray. She was working in a store and she hated it. She'd been brought up in the country and she always wanted to get back. When Jordan asked her to marry him she said she would if he'd take her away to some quiet spot where she'd see nothing but fields and trees. So he brought her to Avonlea. Mrs. Lynde said he was taking a fearful risk in marrying a Yankee, and it's certain that Hester was very delicate and a very poor housekeeper; but mother says she was very pretty and sweet and Jordan just worshipped the ground she walked on. Well, Mr. Gray gave Jordan this farm and he built a little house back here and Jordan and Hester lived in it for four years. She never went out much and hardly anybody went to see her except mother and Mrs. Lynde. Jordan made her this garden and she was crazy about it and spent most of her time in it. She wasn't much of a housekeeper but she had a knack with flowers. And then she got sick. Mother says she thinks she was in consumption before she ever came here. She never really laid up but just grew weaker and weaker all the time. Jordan wouldn't have anybody to wait on her. He did it all himself and mother says he was as tender and gentle as a woman. Every day he'd wrap her in a shawl and carry her out to the garden and she'd lie there on a bench quite happy. They say she used to make Jordan kneel down by her every night and morning and pray with her that she might die out in the garden when the time came. And her prayer was answered. One day Jordan carried her out to the bench and then he picked all the roses that were out and heaped them over her; and she just smiled up at him . . . and closed her eyes . . . and that," concluded Diana softly, "was the end."

"Oh, what a dear story," sighed Anne, wiping away her tears.

"What became of Jordan?" asked Priscilla.

"He sold the farm after Hester died and went back to Boston. Mr. Jabez Sloane bought the farm and hauled the little house out to the road. Jordan died about ten years after and he was brought home and buried beside Hester."

"I can't understand how she could have wanted to live back here, away from everything," said Jane.

"Oh, I can easily understand THAT," said Anne thoughtfully. "I wouldn't want it myself for a steady thing, because, although I love the fields and woods, I love people too. But I can understand it in Hester. She was tired to death of the noise of the big city and the crowds of people always coming and going and caring nothing for her. She just wanted to escape from it all to some still, green, friendly place where she could rest. And she got just what she wanted, which is something very few people do, I believe. She had four beautiful years before she died. . . four years of perfect happiness, so I think she was to be envied more than pitied. And then to shut your eyes and fall asleep among roses, with the one you loved best on earth smiling down at you . . . oh, I think it was beautiful!"

"She set out those cherry trees over there," said Diana. "She told mother she'd never live to eat their fruit, but she wanted to think that something she had planted would go on living and helping to make the world beautiful after she was dead."

"I'm so glad we came this way," said Anne, the shining-eyed. "This is my adopted birthday, you know, and this garden and its story is the birthday gift it has given me. Did your mother ever tell you what Hester Gray looked like, Diana?"

"No . . . only just that she was pretty."

"I'm rather glad of that, because I can imagine what she looked like, without being hampered by facts. I think she was very slight and small, with softly curling dark hair and big, sweet, timid brown eyes, and a little wistful, pale face."

The girls left their baskets in Hester's garden and spent the rest of the afternoon rambling in the woods and fields surrounding it, discovering many pretty nooks and lanes. When they got hungry they had lunch in the prettiest spot of all . . . on the steep bank of a gurgling brook where white birches shot up out of long feathery grasses. The girls sat down by the roots and did full justice to Anne's dainties, even the unpoetical sandwiches being greatly appreciated by hearty, un-spoiled appetites sharpened by all the fresh air and exercise they had enjoyed. Anne had brought glasses and lemonade for her guests, but for her own part drank cold brook water from a cup fashioned out of birch bark. The cup leaked, and the water tasted of earth, as brook water is apt to do in spring; but Anne thought it more appropriate to the occasion than lemonade.

"Look do you see that poem?" she said suddenly, pointing.

"Where?" Jane and Diana stared, as if expecting to see Runic rhymes on the birch trees.

"There . . . down in the brook . . . that old green, mossy log with the water flowing over it in those smooth ripples that look as if they'd been combed, and that single shaft of sunshine falling right athwart it, far down into the pool. Oh, it's the most beautiful poem I ever saw."

"I should rather call it a picture," said Jane. "A poem is lines and verses."

"Oh dear me, no." Anne shook her head with its fluffy wild cherry coronal positively. "The lines and verses are only the outward garments of the poem and are no more really it than your ruffles and flounces are YOU, Jane. The real poem is the soul within them . . . and that beautiful bit is the soul of an unwritten poem. It is not every day one sees a soul . . . even of a poem."

"I wonder what a soul . . . a person's soul . . . would look like," said Priscilla dreamily.

"Like that, I should think," answered Anne, pointing to a radiance of sifted sunlight streaming through a birch tree. "Only with shape and features of course. I like to fancy souls as being made of light. And some are all shot through with rosy stains and quivers . . . and some have a soft glitter like moonlight on the sea . . . and some are pale and transparent like mist at dawn."

"I read somewhere once that souls were like flowers," said Priscilla.

"Then your soul is a golden narcissus," said Anne, "and Diana's is like a red, red rose. Jane's is an apple blossom, pink and wholesome and sweet."

"And your own is a white violet, with purple streaks in its heart," finished Priscilla.

Jane whispered to Diana that she really could not understand what they were talking about. Could she?

The girls went home by the light of a calm golden sunset, their baskets filled with narcissus blossoms from Hester's garden, some of which Anne carried to the cemetery next day and laid upon Hester's grave. Minstrel robins were whistling in the firs and the frogs were singing in the marshes. All the basins among the hills were brimmed with topaz and emerald light.

"Well, we have had a lovely time after all," said Diana, as if she had hardly expected to have it when she set out.

"It has been a truly golden day," said Priscilla.

"I'm really awfully fond of the woods myself," said Jane.

Anne said nothing. She was looking afar into the western sky and thinking of little Hester Gray.

XIV - A Danger Averted

Anne, walking home from the post office one Friday evening, was joined by Mrs. Lynde, who was as usual cumbered with all the cares of church and state.

"I've just been down to Timothy Cotton's to see if I could get Alice Louise to help me for a few days," she said. "I had her last week, for, though she's too slow to stop quick, she's better than nobody. But she's sick and can't come. Timothy's sitting there, too, coughing and complaining. He's been dying for ten years and he'll go on dying for ten years more. That kind can't even die and have done with it . . . they can't stick to anything, even to being sick, long enough to finish it. They're a terrible shiftless family and what is to become of them I don't know, but perhaps Providence does."

Mrs. Lynde sighed as if she rather doubted the extent of Providential knowledge on the subject.

"Marilla was in about her eyes again Tuesday, wasn't she? What did the specialist think of them?" she continued.

"He was much pleased," said Anne brightly. "He says there is a great improvement in them and he thinks the danger of her losing her sight completely is past. But he says she'll never be able to read much or do any fine hand-work again. How are your preparations for your bazaar coming on?"

The Ladies' Aid Society was preparing for a fair and supper, and Mrs. Lynde was the head and front of the enterprise.

"Pretty well . . . and that reminds me. Mrs. Allan thinks it would be nice to fix up a booth like an old-time kitchen and serve a supper of baked beans, doughnuts, pie, and so on. We're collecting old-fashioned fixings everywhere. Mrs. Simon Fletcher is going to lend us her mother's braided rugs and Mrs. Levi Boulter some old chairs and Aunt Mary Shaw will lend us her cupboard with the glass doors. I suppose Marilla will let us have her brass candlesticks? And we want all the old dishes we can get. Mrs. Allan is specially set on having a real blue willow ware platter if we can find one. But nobody seems to have one. Do you know where we could get one?"

"Miss Josephine Barry has one. I'll write and ask her if she'll lend it for the occasion," said Anne.

"Well, I wish you would. I guess we'll have the supper in about a fortnight's time. Uncle Abe Andrews is prophesying rain and storms for about that time; and that's a pretty sure sign we'll have fine weather."

The said "Uncle Abe," it may be mentioned, was at least like other prophets in that he had small honor in his own country. He was, in fact, considered in the light of a standing joke, for few of his weather predictions were ever fulfilled. Mr. Elisha Wright, who labored under the impression that he was a local wit, used to say that nobody in Avonlea ever thought of looking in the Charlottetown dailies for weather probabilities. No; they just asked Uncle Abe what it was going to be tomorrow and expected the opposite. Nothing daunted, Uncle Abe kept on prophesying.

"We want to have the fair over before the election comes off," continued Mrs. Lynde, "for the candidates will be sure to come and spend lots of money. The Tories are bribing right and left, so they might as well be given a chance to spend their money honestly for once."

Anne was a red-hot Conservative, out of loyalty to Matthew's memory, but she said nothing. She knew better than to get Mrs. Lynde started on politics. She had a letter for Marilla, postmarked from a town in British Columbia.

"It's probably from the children's uncle," she said excitedly, when she got home. "Oh, Marilla, I wonder what he says about them."

"The best plan might be to open it and see," said Marilla curtly. A close observer might have thought that she was excited also, but she would rather have died than show it.

Anne tore open the letter and glanced over the somewhat untidy and poorly written contents.

"He says he can't take the children this spring . . . he's been sick most of the winter and his wedding is put off. He wants to know if we can keep them till the fall and he'll try and take them then. We will, of course, won't we Marilla?"

"I don't see that there is anything else for us to do," said Marilla rather grimly, although she felt a secret relief. "Anyhow they're not so much trouble as they were . . . or else we've got used to them. Davy has improved a great deal."

"His MANNERS are certainly much better," said Anne cautiously, as if she were not prepared to say as much for his morals.

Anne had come home from school the previous evening, to find Marilla away at an Aid meeting, Dora asleep on the kitchen sofa, and Davy in the sitting room closet, blissfully absorbing the contents of a jar of Marilla's famous yellow plum preserves . . . "company jam," Davy called it . . . which he had been forbidden to touch. He looked very guilty when Anne pounced on him and whisked him out of the closet.

"Davy Keith, don't you know that it is very wrong of you to be eating that jam, when you were told never to meddle with anything in THAT closet?"

"Yes, I knew it was wrong," admitted Davy uncomfortably, "but plum jam is awful nice, Anne. I just peeped in and it looked so good I thought I'd take just a weeny taste. I stuck my finger in . . ." Anne groaned . . . "and licked it clean. And it was so much gooder than I'd ever thought that I got a spoon and just SAILED IN."

Anne gave him such a serious lecture on the sin of stealing plum jam that Davy became conscience stricken and promised with repentant kisses never to do it again.

"Anyhow, there'll be plenty of jam in heaven, that's one comfort," he said complacently.

Anne nipped a smile in the bud.

"Perhaps there will . . . if we want it," she said, "But what makes you think so?"

"Why, it's in the catechism," said Davy.

"Oh, no, there is nothing like THAT in the catechism, Davy."

"But I tell you there is," persisted Davy. "It was in that question Marilla taught me last Sunday. 'Why should we love God?' It says, 'Because He makes preserves, and redeems us.' Preserves is just a holy way of saying jam."

"I must get a drink of water," said Anne hastily. When she came back it cost her some time and trouble to explain to Davy that a certain comma in the said catechism question made a great deal of difference in the meaning.

"Well, I thought it was too good to be true," he said at last, with a sigh of disappointed conviction. "And besides, I didn't see when He'd find time to make jam if it's one endless Sabbath day, as the hymn says. I don't believe I want to go to heaven. Won't there ever be any Saturdays in heaven, Anne?"

"Yes, Saturdays, and every other kind of beautiful days. And every day in heaven will be more beautiful than the one before it, Davy," assured Anne, who was rather glad that Marilla was not by to be shocked. Marilla, it is needless to say, was bringing the twins up in the good old ways of theology and discouraged all fanciful speculations thereupon. Davy and Dora were taught a hymn, a catechism question, and two Bible verses every Sunday. Dora learned meekly and recited like a little machine, with perhaps as much understanding or interest as if she were one. Davy, on the contrary, had a lively curiosity, and frequently asked questions which made Marilla tremble for his fate.

"Chester Sloane says we'll do nothing all the time in heaven but walk around in white dresses and play on harps; and he says he hopes he won't have to go till he's an old man, 'cause maybe he'll like it better then. And he thinks it will be horrid to wear dresses and I think so too. Why can't men angels wear trousers, Anne? Chester Sloane is interested in those things, 'cause they're going to make a minister of him. He's got to be a minister 'cause his grandmother left the money to send him to college and he can't have it unless he is a minister. She thought a minister was such a 'spectable thing to have in a family. Chester says he doesn't mind much . . . though he'd rather be a blacksmith . . . but he's bound to have all the fun he can before he begins to be a minister, 'cause he doesn't expect to have much afterwards. I ain't going to be a minister. I'm going to be a storekeeper, like Mr. Blair, and keep heaps of candy and bananas. But I'd rather like going to your kind of a heaven if they'd let me play a mouth organ instead of a harp. Do you s'pose they would?"

"Yes, I think they would if you wanted it," was all Anne could trust herself to say.

The A.V.I.S. met at Mr. Harmon Andrews' that evening and a full attendance had been requested, since important business was to be discussed. The A.V.I.S. was in a flourishing condition, and had already accomplished wonders. Early in the spring Mr. Major Spencer had redeemed his promise and had stumped, graded, and seeded down all the road front of his farm. A dozen other men, some prompted by a determination not to let a Spencer get ahead of them, others goaded into action by Improvers in their own households, had followed his example. The result was that there were long strips of smooth velvet turf where once had been unsightly undergrowth or brush. The farm fronts that had not been done looked so badly by contrast that their owners were secretly shamed into resolving to see what they could do another spring. The triangle of ground at the cross roads had also been cleared and seeded down, and Anne's bed of geraniums, unharmed by any marauding cow, was already set out in the center.

Altogether, the Improvers thought that they were getting on beautifully, even if Mr. Levi Boulter, tactfully approached by a carefully selected committee in regard to the old house on his upper farm, did bluntly tell them that he wasn't going to have it meddled with.

At this especial meeting they intended to draw up a petition to the school trustees, humbly praying that a fence be put around the school grounds; and a plan was also to be discussed for planting a few ornamental trees by the church, if the funds of the society would permit of it . . . for, as Anne said, there was no use in starting another subscription as long as the hall remained blue. The members were assembled in the Andrews' parlor and Jane was already on her feet to move the appointment of a committee which should find out and report on the price of said trees, when Gertie Pye swept in, pompadoured and frilled within an inch of her life. Gertie had a habit of being late . . . "to make her entrance more effective," spiteful people said. Gertie's entrance in this instance was certainly effective, for she paused dramatically on the middle of the floor, threw up her hands, rolled her eyes, and exclaimed, "I've just heard something perfectly awful. What DO you think? Mr. Judson Parker IS GOING TO RENT ALL THE ROAD FENCE OF HIS FARM TO A PATENT MEDICINE COMPANY TO PAINT ADVERTISEMENTS ON."

For once in her life Gertie Pye made all the sensation she desired. If she had thrown a bomb among the complacent Improvers she could hardly have made more.

"It CAN'T be true," said Anne blankly.

"That's just what *I* said when I heard it first, don't you know," said Gertie, who was enjoying herself hugely. "*I* said it couldn't be true . . . that Judson Parker wouldn't have the HEART to do it, don't you know. But father met him this afternoon and asked him about it and he said it WAS true. Just fancy! His farm is side-on to the Newbridge road and how perfectly awful it will look to see advertisements of pills and plasters all along it, don't you know?"

The Improvers DID know, all too well. Even the least imaginative among them could picture the grotesque effect of half a mile of board fence adorned with such advertisements. All thought of church and school grounds vanished before this new danger. Parliamentary rules and regulations were forgotten, and Anne, in despair, gave up trying to keep minutes at all. Everybody talked at once and fearful was the hubbub.

"Oh, let us keep calm," implored Anne, who was the most excited of them all, "and try to think of some way of preventing him."

"I don't know how you're going to prevent him," exclaimed Jane bitterly. "Everybody knows what Judson Parker is. He'd do ANYTHING for money. He hasn't a SPARK of public spirit or ANY sense of the beautiful."

The prospect looked rather unpromising. Judson Parker and his sister were the only Parkers in Avonlea, so that no leverage could be exerted by family connections. Martha Parker was a lady of all too certain age who disapproved of young people in general and the Improvers in particular. Judson was a jovial, smooth-spoken man, so uniformly goodnatured and bland that it was surprising how few friends he had. Perhaps he had got the better in too many business transactions. . . which seldom makes for popularity. He was reputed to be very "sharp" and it was the general opinion that he "hadn't much principle."

"If Judson Parker has a chance to 'turn an honest penny,' as he says himself, he'll never lose it," declared Fred Wright.

"Is there NOBODY who has any influence over him?" asked Anne despairingly.

"He goes to see Louisa Spencer at White Sands," suggested Carrie Sloane. "Perhaps she could coax him not to rent his fences."

"Not she," said Gilbert emphatically. "I know Louisa Spencer well. She doesn't 'believe' in Village Improvement Societies, but she DOES believe in dollars and cents. She'd be more likely to urge Judson on than to dissuade him."

"The only thing to do is to appoint a committee to wait on him and protest," said Julia Bell, "and you must send girls, for he'd hardly be civil to boys . . . but *I* won't go, so nobody need nominate me."

"Better send Anne alone," said Oliver Sloane. "She can talk Judson over if anybody can."

Anne protested. She was willing to go and do the talking; but she must have others with her "for moral support." Diana and Jane were therefore appointed to support her morally and the Improvers broke up, buzzing like angry bees with indignation. Anne was so worried that she didn't sleep until nearly morning, and then she dreamed that the trustees had put a fence around the school and painted "Try Purple Pills" all over it.

The committee waited on Judson Parker the next afternoon. Anne pleaded eloquently against his nefarious design and Jane and Diana supported her morally and valiantly. Judson was sleek, suave, flattering; paid them several compliments of the delicacy of sunflowers; felt real bad to refuse such charming young ladies . . . but business was business; couldn't afford to let sentiment stand in the way these hard times.

"But I'll tell what I WILL do," he said, with a twinkle in his light, full eyes. "I'll tell the agent he must use only handsome, tasty colors . . . red and yellow and so on. I'll tell him he mustn't paint the ads BLUE on any account."

The vanquished committee retired, thinking things not lawful to be uttered.

"We have done all we can do and must simply trust the rest to Providence," said Jane, with an unconscious imitation of Mrs. Lynde's tone and manner.

"I wonder if Mr. Allan could do anything," reflected Diana.

Anne shook her head.

"No, it's no use to worry Mr. Allan, especially now when the baby's so sick. Judson would slip away from him as smoothly as from us, although he HAS taken to going to church quite regularly just now. That is simply because Louisa Spencer's father is an elder and very particular about such things."

"Judson Parker is the only man in Avonlea who would dream of renting his fences," said Jane indignantly. "Even Levi Boulter or Lorenzo White would never stoop to that, tightfisted as they are. They would have too much respect for public opinion."

Public opinion was certainly down on Judson Parker when the facts became known, but that did not help matters much. Judson chuckled to himself and defied it, and the Improvers were trying to reconcile themselves to the prospect of seeing the prettiest part of the Newbridge road defaced by advertisements, when Anne rose quietly at the president's call for reports of committees on the occasion of the next meeting of the Society, and announced that Mr. Judson Parker had instructed her to inform the Society that he was NOT going to rent his fences to the Patent Medicine Company.

Jane and Diana stared as if they found it hard to believe their ears. Parliamentary etiquette, which was generally very strictly enforced in the A.V.I.S., forbade them giving instant vent to their curiosity, but after the Society adjourned Anne was besieged for explanations. Anne had no explanation to give. Judson Parker had overtaken her on the road the preceding evening and told her that he had decided to humor the A.V.I.S. in its peculiar prejudice against patent medicine advertisements. That was all Anne would say, then or ever afterwards, and it was the simple truth; but when Jane Andrews, on her way home, confided to Oliver Sloane her firm belief that there was more behind Judson Parker's mysterious change of heart than Anne Shirley had revealed, she spoke the truth also.

Anne had been down to old Mrs. Irving's on the shore road the preceding evening and had come home by a short cut which led her first over the low-lying shore fields, and then through the beech wood below Robert Dickson's, by a little footpath that ran out to the main road just above the Lake of Shining Waters . . . known to unimaginative people as Barry's pond.

Two men were sitting in their buggies, reined off to the side of the road, just at the entrance of the path. One was Judson Parker; the other was Jerry Corcoran, a

Newbridge man against whom, as Mrs. Lynde would have told you in eloquent italics, nothing shady had ever been PROVED. He was an agent for agricultural implements and a prominent personage in matters political. He had a finger . . . some people said ALL his fingers . . . in every political pie that was cooked; and as Canada was on the eve of a general election Jerry Corcoran had been a busy man for many weeks, canvassing the county in the interests of his party's candidate. Just as Anne emerged from under the overhanging beech boughs she heard Corcoran say, "If you'll vote for Amesbury, Parker . . . well, I've a note for that pair of harrows you've got in the spring. I suppose you wouldn't object to having it back, eh?"

"We . . . ll, since you put it in that way," drawled Judson with a grin, "I reckon I might as well do it. A man must look out for his own interests in these hard times."

Both saw Anne at this moment and conversation abruptly ceased. Anne bowed frostily and walked on, with her chin slightly more tilted than usual. Soon Judson Parker overtook her.

"Have a lift, Anne?" he inquired genially.

"Thank you, no," said Anne politely, but with a fine, needle-like disdain in her voice that pierced even Judson Parker's none too sensitive consciousness. His face reddened and he twitched his reins angrily; but the next second prudential considerations checked him. He looked uneasily at Anne, as she walked steadily on, glancing neither to the right nor to the left. Had she heard Corcoran's unmistakable offer and his own too plain acceptance of it? Confound Corcoran! If he couldn't put his meaning into less dangerous phrases he'd get into trouble some of these long-come-shorts. And confound redheaded school-ma'ams with a habit of popping out of beechwoods where they had no business to be. If Anne had heard, Judson Parker, measuring her corn in his own half bushel, as the country saying went, and cheating himself thereby, as such people generally do, believed that she would tell it far and wide. Now, Judson Parker, as has been seen, was not overly regardful of public opinion; but to be known as having accepted a bribe would be a nasty thing; and if it ever reached Isaac Spencer's ears farewell forever to all hope of winning Louisa Jane with her comfortable prospects as the heiress of a well-to-do farmer. Judson Parker knew that Mr. Spencer looked somewhat askance at him as it was; he could not afford to take any risks.

"Ahem . . . Anne, I've been wanting to see you about that little matter we were discussing the other day. I've decided not to let my fences to that company after all. A society with an aim like yours ought to be encouraged."

Anne thawed out the merest trifle.

"Thank you," she said.

"And . . . and . . . you needn't mention that little conversation of mine with Jerry."

"I have no intention of mentioning it in any case," said Anne icily, for she would have seen every fence in Avonlea painted with advertisements before she would have stooped to bargain with a man who would sell his vote.

"Just so . . . just so," agreed Judson, imagining that they understood each other beautifully. "I didn't suppose you would. Of course, I was only stringing Jerry . . . he thinks he's so all-fired cute and smart. I've no intention of voting for Amesbury. I'm going to vote for Grant as I've always done . . . you'll see that when the election comes off. I just led Jerry on to see if he would commit himself. And it's all right about the fence . . . you can tell the Improvers that."

"It takes all sorts of people to make a world, as I've often heard, but I think there are some who could be spared," Anne told her reflection in the east gable mirror that night. "I wouldn't have mentioned the disgraceful thing to a soul anyhow, so my conscience is clear on THAT score. I really don't know who or what is to be thanked for this. *I* did nothing to bring it about, and it's hard to believe that Providence ever works by means of the kind of politics men like Judson Parker and Jerry Corcoran have."

XV - The Beginning of Vacation

Anne locked the schoolhouse door on a still, yellow evening, when the winds were purring in the spruces around the playground, and the shadows were long and lazy by the edge of the woods. She dropped the key into her pocket with a sigh of satisfaction. The school year was ended, she had been reengaged for the next, with many expressions of satisfaction. . . . only Mr. Harmon Andrews told her she ought to use the strap oftener . . . and two delightful months of a well-earned vacation beckoned her invitingly. Anne felt at peace with the world and herself as she walked down the hill with her basket of flowers in her hand. Since the earliest mayflowers Anne had never missed her weekly pilgrimage to Matthew's grave. Everyone else in Avonlea, except Marilla, had already forgotten quiet, shy, unimportant Matthew Cuthbert; but his memory was still green in Anne's heart and always would be. She could never forget the kind old man who had been the first to give her the love and sympathy her starved childhood had craved.

At the foot of the hill a boy was sitting on the fence in the shadow of the spruces . . . a boy with big, dreamy eyes and a beautiful, sensitive face. He swung down and joined Anne, smiling; but there were traces of tears on his cheeks.

"I thought I'd wait for you, teacher, because I knew you were going to the graveyard," he said, slipping his hand into hers. "I'm going there, too . . . I'm taking this bouquet of geraniums to put on Grandpa Irving's grave for grandma. And look, teacher, I'm going to put this bunch of white roses beside Grandpa's grave in memory of my little mother. . . because I can't go to her grave to put it there. But don't you think she'll know all about it, just the same?"

"Yes, I am sure she will, Paul."

"You see, teacher, it's just three years today since my little mother died. It's such a long, long time but it hurts just as much as ever . . . and I miss her just as much as ever. Sometimes it seems to me that I just can't bear it, it hurts so."

Paul's voice quivered and his lip trembled. He looked down at his roses, hoping that his teacher would not notice the tears in his eyes.

"And yet," said Anne, very softly, "you wouldn't want it to stop hurting . . . you wouldn't want to forget your little mother even if you could."

"No, indeed, I wouldn't . . . that's just the way I feel. You're so good at understanding, teacher. Nobody else understands so well . . . not even grandma, although she's so good to me. Father understood pretty well, but still I couldn't talk much to him about mother, because it made him feel so bad. When he put his hand over his face I always knew it was time to stop. Poor father, he must be dreadfully lonesome without me; but you see he has nobody but a housekeeper now and he thinks housekeepers are no good to bring up little boys, especially when he has to be away from home so much on business. Grandmothers are better, next to mothers. Someday, when I'm brought up, I'll go back to father and we're never going to be parted again."

Paul had talked so much to Anne about his mother and father that she felt as if she had known them. She thought his mother must have been very like what he was himself, in temperament and disposition; and she had an idea that Stephen Irving was a rather reserved man with a deep and tender nature which he kept hidden scrupulously from the world.

"Father's not very easy to get acquainted with," Paul had said once. "I never got really acquainted with him until after my little mother died. But he's splendid when you do get to know him. I love him the best in all the world, and Grandma Irving next, and then you, teacher. I'd love you next to father if it wasn't my DUTY to love Grandma Irving best, because she's doing so much for me. YOU know, teacher. I wish she would leave the lamp in my room till I go to sleep, though. She takes it right out as soon as she tucks me up because she says I mustn't be a coward. I'm NOT scared, but I'd RATHER have the light. My little mother used always to sit beside me and hold my hand till I went to sleep. I expect she spoiled me. Mothers do sometimes, you know."

No, Anne did not know this, although she might imagine it. She thought sadly of HER "little mother," the mother who had thought her so "perfectly beautiful" and who had died so long ago and was buried beside her boyish husband in that unvisited grave far away. Anne could not remember her mother and for this reason she almost envied Paul.

"My birthday is next week," said Paul, as they walked up the long red hill, basking in the June sunshine, "and father wrote me that he is sending me something that he thinks I'll like better than anything else he could send. I believe it has come already, for Grandma is keeping the bookcase drawer locked and that is something new. And when I asked her why, she just looked mysterious and said little boys mustn't be too curious. It's very exciting to have a birthday, isn't it? I'll be eleven. You'd never think it to look at me, would you? Grandma says I'm very small for my age and that it's all because I don't eat enough porridge. I do my very best, but Grandma gives such generous platefuls . . . there's nothing mean about Grandma, I can tell you. Ever since you and I had that talk about praying going home from Sunday School that day, teacher . . . when you said we ought to pray about all our difficulties . . . I've prayed every night that God would give me enough grace to enable me to eat every bit of my porridge in the mornings. But I've never been able to do it yet, and whether it's because I have too little grace or too much porridge I really can't decide. Grandma says father was brought up on porridge, and it certainly did work well in his case, for you ought to see the shoulders he has. But sometimes," concluded Paul with a sigh and a meditative air "I really think porridge will be the death of me."

Anne permitted herself a smile, since Paul was not looking at her. All Avonlea knew that old Mrs. Irving was bringing her grandson up in accordance with the good, old-fashioned methods of diet and morals.

"Let us hope not, dear," she said cheerfully. "How are your rock people coming on? Does the oldest Twin still continue to behave himself?"

"He HAS to," said Paul emphatically. "He knows I won't associate with him if he doesn't. He is really full of wickedness, I think."

"And has Nora found out about the Golden Lady yet?"

"No; but I think she suspects. I'm almost sure she watched me the last time I went to the cave. *I* don't mind if she finds out . . . it is only for HER sake I don't want her to . . . so that her feelings won't be hurt. But if she is DETERMINED to have her feelings hurt it can't be helped."

"If I were to go to the shore some night with you do you think I could see your rock people too?"

Paul shook his head gravely.

"No, I don't think you could see MY rock people. I'm the only person who can see them. But you could see rock people of your own. You're one of the kind that can. We're both that kind. YOU know, teacher," he added, squeezing her hand chummily. "Isn't it splendid to be that kind, teacher?"

"Splendid," Anne agreed, gray shining eyes looking down into blue shining ones. Anne and Paul both knew

> "How fair the realm
> Imagination opens to the view,"

and both knew the way to that happy land. There the rose of joy bloomed immortal by dale and stream; clouds never darkened the sunny sky; sweet bells never jangled out of tune; and kindred spirits abounded. The knowledge of that land's geography . . . "east o' the sun, west o' the moon" . . . is priceless lore, not to be bought in any market place. It must be the gift of the good fairies at birth and the years can never deface it or take it away. It is better to possess it, living in a garret, than to be the inhabitant of palaces without it.

The Avonlea graveyard was as yet the grass-grown solitude it had always been. To be sure, the Improvers had an eye on it, and Priscilla Grant had read a paper on cemeteries before the last meeting of the Society. At some future time the Improvers meant to have the lichened, wayward old board fence replaced by a neat wire railing, the grass mown and the leaning monuments straightened up.

Anne put on Matthew's grave the flowers she had brought for it, and then went over to the little poplar shaded corner where Hester Gray slept. Ever since the day of the spring picnic Anne had put flowers on Hester's grave when she visited Matthew's. The evening before she had made a pilgrimage back to the little deserted garden in the woods and brought therefrom some of Hester's own white roses.

"I thought you would like them better than any others, dear," she said softly.

Anne was still sitting there when a shadow fell over the grass and she looked up to see Mrs. Allan. They walked home together.

Mrs. Allan's face was not the face of the girlbride whom the minister had brought to Avonlea five years before. It had lost some of its bloom and youthful curves, and there were fine, patient lines about eyes and mouth. A tiny grave in that very cemetery accounted for some of them; and some new ones had come during the recent illness, now happily over, of her little son. But Mrs. Allan's dimples were as sweet and sudden as ever, her eyes as clear and bright and true; and what her face lacked of girlish beauty was now more than atoned for in added tenderness and strength.

"I suppose you are looking forward to your vacation, Anne?" she said, as they left the graveyard.

Anne nodded.

"Yes. . . . I could roll the word as a sweet morsel under my tongue. I think the summer is going to be lovely. For one thing, Mrs. Morgan is coming to the Island in July and Priscilla is going to bring her up. I feel one of my old 'thrills' at the mere thought."

"I hope you'll have a good time, Anne. You've worked very hard this past year and you have succeeded."

"Oh, I don't know. I've come so far short in so many things. I haven't done what I meant to do when I began to teach last fall. I haven't lived up to my ideals."

"None of us ever do," said Mrs. Allan with a sigh. "But then, Anne, you know what Lowell says, 'Not failure but low aim is crime.' We must have ideals and try to live up to them, even if we never quite succeed. Life would be a sorry business without them. With them it's grand and great. Hold fast to your ideals, Anne."

"I shall try. But I have to let go most of my theories," said Anne, laughing a little. "I had the most beautiful set of theories you ever knew when I started out as a schoolma'am, but every one of them has failed me at some pinch or another."

"Even the theory on corporal punishment," teased Mrs. Allan.

But Anne flushed.

"I shall never forgive myself for whipping Anthony."

"Nonsense, dear, he deserved it. And it agreed with him. You have had no trouble with him since and he has come to think there's nobody like you. Your kindness won his love after the idea that a 'girl was no good' was rooted out of his stubborn mind."

"He may have deserved it, but that is not the point. If I had calmly and deliber-ately decided to whip him because I thought it a just punishment for him I would not feel over it as I do. But the truth is, Mrs. Allan, that I just flew into a temper and whipped him because of that. I wasn't thinking whether it was just or unjust . . . even if he hadn't deserved it I'd have done it just the same. That is what humili-ates me."

"Well, we all make mistakes, dear, so just put it behind you. We should regret our mistakes and learn from them, but never carry them forward into the future with us. There goes Gilbert Blythe on his wheel . . . home for his vacation too, I suppose. How are you and he getting on with your studies?"

"Pretty well. We plan to finish the Virgil tonight . . . there are only twenty lines to do. Then we are not going to study any more until September."

"Do you think you will ever get to college?"

"Oh, I don't know." Anne looked dreamily afar to the opal-tinted horizon. "Marilla's eyes will never be much better than they are now, although we are so thankful to think that they will not get worse. And then there are the twins . . . somehow I don't believe their uncle will ever really send for them. Perhaps college may be around the bend in the road, but I haven't got to the bend yet and I don't think much about it lest I might grow discontented."

"Well, I should like to see you go to college, Anne; but if you never do, don't be discontented about it. We make our own lives wherever we are, after all . . . college can only help us to do it more easily. They are broad or narrow according to what we put into them, not what we get out. Life is rich and full here . . . everywhere . . . if we can only learn how to open our whole hearts to its richness and fulness."

"I think I understand what you mean," said Anne thoughtfully, "and I know I have so much to feel thankful for . . . oh, so much . . . my work, and Paul Irving, and the dear twins, and all my friends. Do you know, Mrs. Allan, I'm so thankful for friendship. It beautifies life so much."

"True friendship is a very helpful thing indeed," said Mrs. Allan, "and we should have a very high ideal of it, and never sully it by any failure in truth and sincerity. I fear the name of friendship is often degraded to a kind of intimacy that has nothing of real friendship in it."

"Yes . . . like Gertie Pye's and Julia Bell's. They are very intimate and go everywhere together; but Gertie is always saying nasty things of Julia behind her back and everybody thinks she is jealous of her because she is always so pleased when anybody criticizes Julia. I think it is desecration to call that friendship. If we have friends we should look only for the best in them and give them the best that is in us, don't you think? Then friendship would be the most beautiful thing in the world."

"Friendship IS very beautiful," smiled Mrs. Allan, "but some day . . ."

Then she paused abruptly. In the delicate, white-browed face beside her, with its candid eyes and mobile features, there was still far more of the child than of the woman. Anne's heart so far harbored only dreams of friendship and ambition, and Mrs. Allan did not wish to brush the bloom from her sweet unconsciousness. So she left her sentence for the future years to finish.

XVI - The Substance of Things Hoped For

"Anne," said Davy appealingly, scrambling up on the shiny, leather-covered sofa in the Green Gables kitchen, where Anne sat, reading a letter, "Anne, I'm AWFUL hungry. You've no idea."

"I'll get you a piece of bread and butter in a minute," said Anne absently. Her letter evidently contained some exciting news, for her cheeks were as pink as the roses on the big bush outside, and her eyes were as starry as only Anne's eyes could be.

"But I ain't bread and butter hungry," said Davy in a disgusted tone. "I'm plum cake hungry."

"Oh," laughed Anne, laying down her letter and putting her arm about Davy to give him a squeeze, "that's a kind of hunger that can be endured very comfortably, Davy-boy. You know it's one of Marilla's rules that you can't have anything but bread and butter between meals."

"Well, gimme a piece then . . . please."

Davy had been at last taught to say "please," but he generally tacked it on as an afterthought. He looked with approval at the generous slice Anne presently brought to him. "You always put such a nice lot of butter on it, Anne. Marilla spreads it pretty thin. It slips down a lot easier when there's plenty of butter."

The slice "slipped down" with tolerable ease, judging from its rapid disappearance. Davy slid head first off the sofa, turned a double somersault on the rug, and then sat up and announced decidedly,

"Anne, I've made up my mind about heaven. I don't want to go there."

"Why not?" asked Anne gravely.

"Cause heaven is in Simon Fletcher's garret, and I don't like Simon Fletcher."

"Heaven in . . . Simon Fletcher's garret!" gasped Anne, too amazed even to laugh. "Davy Keith, whatever put such an extraordinary idea into your head?"

"Milty Boulter says that's where it is. It was last Sunday in Sunday School. The lesson was about Elijah and Elisha, and I up and asked Miss Rogerson where heaven was. Miss Rogerson looked awful offended. She was cross anyhow, because when she'd asked us what Elijah left Elisha when he went to heaven Milty Boulter said, 'His old clo'es,' and us fellows all laughed before we thought. I wish you could think first and do things afterwards, 'cause then you wouldn't do them. But Milty didn't mean to be disrespeckful. He just couldn't think of the name of the thing. Miss Rogerson said heaven was where God was and I wasn't to ask questions like that. Milty nudged me and said in a whisper, 'Heaven's in Uncle Simon's garret and I'll esplain about it on the road home.' So when we was coming home he esplained. Milty's a great hand at esplaining things. Even if he don't know anything about a thing he'll make up a lot of stuff and so you get it esplained all the same. His mother is Mrs. Simon's sister and he went with her to the funeral when his cousin, Jane Ellen, died. The minister said she'd gone to heaven, though Milty says she was lying right before them in the coffin. But he s'posed they carried the coffin to the garret afterwards. Well, when Milty and his mother went upstairs after it was all over to get her bonnet he asked her where heaven was that Jane Ellen had gone to, and she pointed right to the ceiling and said, 'Up there.' Milty knew there wasn't anything but the garret over the ceiling, so that's how HE found out. And he's been awful scared to go to his Uncle Simon's ever since."

Anne took Davy on her knee and did her best to straighten out this theological tangle also. She was much better fitted for the task than Marilla, for she remembered her own childhood and had an instinctive understanding of the curious ideas that seven-year-olds sometimes get about matters that are, of course, very plain and simple to grown up people. She had just succeeded in convincing Davy that heaven was NOT in Simon Fletcher's garret when Marilla came in from the garden, where she and Dora had been picking peas. Dora was an industrious little soul and never happier than when "helping" in various small tasks suited to her chubby fingers. She fed chickens, picked up chips, wiped dishes, and ran errands galore. She was neat, faithful and observant; she never had to be told how to do a thing twice and never forgot any of her little duties. Davy, on the other hand, was rather heedless and forgetful; but he had the born knack of winning love, and even yet Anne and Marilla liked him the better.

While Dora proudly shelled the peas and Davy made boats of the pods, with masts of matches and sails of paper, Anne told Marilla about the wonderful contents of her letter.

"Oh, Marilla, what do you think? I've had a letter from Priscilla and she says that Mrs. Morgan is on the Island, and that if it is fine Thursday they are going to drive up to Avonlea and will reach here about twelve. They will spend the afternoon with us and go to the hotel at White Sands in the evening, because some of Mrs. Morgan's American friends are staying there. Oh, Marilla, isn't it wonderful? I can hardly believe I'm not dreaming."

"I daresay Mrs. Morgan is a lot like other people," said Marilla drily, although she did feel a trifle excited herself. Mrs. Morgan was a famous woman and a visit from her was no commonplace occurrence. "They'll be here to dinner, then?"

"Yes; and oh, Marilla, may I cook every bit of the dinner myself? I want to feel that I can do something for the author of 'The Rosebud Garden,' if it is only to cook a dinner for her. You won't mind, will you?"

"Goodness, I'm not so fond of stewing over a hot fire in July that it would vex me very much to have someone else do it. You're quite welcome to the job."

"Oh, thank you," said Anne, as if Marilla had just conferred a tremendous favor, "I'll make out the menu this very night."

"You'd better not try to put on too much style," warned Marilla, a little alarmed by the high-flown sound of 'menu.' "You'll likely come to grief if you do."

"Oh, I'm not going to put on any 'style,' if you mean trying to do or have things we don't usually have on festal occasions," assured Anne. "That would be affectation, and, although I know I haven't as much sense and steadiness as a girl of seventeen and a schoolteacher ought to have, I'm not so silly as THAT. But I want to have everything as nice and dainty as possible. Davy-boy, don't leave those peapods on the back stairs . . . someone might slip on them. I'll have a light soup to begin with . . . you know I can make lovely cream-of-onion soup . . . and then a couple of roast fowls. I'll have the two white roosters. I have real affection for those roosters and they've been pets ever since the gray hen hatched out just the two of them . . . little balls of yellow down. But I know they would have to be sacrificed sometime, and surely there couldn't be a worthier occasion than this. But oh, Marilla, *I* cannot kill them . . . not even for Mrs. Morgan's sake. I'll have to ask John Henry Carter to come over and do it for me."

"I'll do it," volunteered Davy, "if Marilla'll hold them by the legs, 'cause I guess it'd take both my hands to manage the axe. It's awful jolly fun to see them hopping about after their heads are cut off."

"Then I'll have peas and beans and creamed potatoes and a lettuce salad, for vegetables," resumed Anne, "and for dessert, lemon pie with whipped cream, and coffee and cheese and lady fingers. I'll make the pies and lady fingers tomorrow and do up my white muslin dress. And I must tell Diana tonight, for she'll want to do up hers. Mrs. Morgan's heroines are nearly always dressed in white muslin, and Diana and I have always resolved that that was what we would wear if we ever met her. It will be such a delicate compliment, don't you think? Davy, dear, you mustn't poke peapods into the cracks of the floor. I must ask Mr. and Mrs. Allan and Miss Stacy to dinner, too, for they're all very anxious to meet Mrs. Morgan. It's so fortunate she's coming while Miss Stacy is here. Davy dear, don't sail the peapods in the water bucket . . . go out to the trough. Oh, I do hope it will be fine Thursday, and I think it will, for Uncle Abe said last night when he called at Mr. Harrison's, that it was going to rain most of this week."

"That's a good sign," agreed Marilla.

Anne ran across to Orchard Slope that evening to tell the news to Diana, who was also very much excited over it, and they discussed the matter in the hammock swung under the big willow in the Barry garden.

"Oh, Anne, mayn't I help you cook the dinner?" implored Diana. "You know I can make splendid lettuce salad."

"Indeed you, may" said Anne unselfishly. "And I shall want you to help me decorate too. I mean to have the parlor simply a BOWER of blossoms . . . and the dining table is to be adorned with wild roses. Oh, I do hope everything will go smoothly. Mrs. Morgan's heroines NEVER get into scrapes or are taken at a disadvantage, and they are always so selfpossessed and such good housekeepers. They seem to be BORN good housekeepers. You remember that Gertrude in 'Edgewood Days' kept house for her father when she was only eight years old. When I was eight years old I hardly knew how to do a thing except bring up children. Mrs. Morgan must be an authority on girls when she has written so much about them, and I do want her to have a good opinion of us. I've imagined it all out a dozen different ways . . . what she'll look like, and what she'll say, and what I'll say. And I'm so anxious about my nose. There are seven freckles on it, as you can see. They came at the A.V.I S. picnic, when I went around in the sun without my hat. I suppose it's ungrateful of me to worry over them, when I should be thankful they're not spread all over my face as they once were; but I do wish they hadn't come . . . all Mrs. Morgan's heroines have such perfect complexions. I can't recall a freckled one among them."

"Yours are not very noticeable," comforted Diana. "Try a little lemon juice on them tonight."

The next day Anne made her pies and lady fingers, did up her muslin dress, and swept and dusted every room in the house . . . a quite unnecessary proceeding, for Green Gables was, as usual, in the apple pie order dear to Marilla's heart. But Anne felt that a fleck of dust would be a desecration in a house that was to be honored by a visit from Charlotte E. Morgan. She even cleaned out the "catch-all" closet under the stairs, although there was not the remotest possibility of Mrs. Morgan's seeing its interior.

"But I want to FEEL that it is in perfect order, even if she isn't to see it," Anne told Marilla. "You know, in her book 'Golden Keys,' she makes her two heroines Alice and Louisa take for their motto that verse of Longfellow's,

> 'In the elder days of art
> Builders wrought with greatest care
> Each minute and unseen part,
> For the gods see everywhere,'

and so they always kept their cellar stairs scrubbed and never forgot to sweep under the beds. I should have a guilty conscience if I thought this closet was in disorder when Mrs. Morgan was in the house. Ever since we read 'Golden Keys,' last April, Diana and I have taken that verse for our motto too."

That night John Henry Carter and Davy between them contrived to execute the two white roosters, and Anne dressed them, the usually distasteful task glorified in her eyes by the destination of the plump birds.

"I don't like picking fowls," she told Marilla, "but isn't it fortunate we don't have to put our souls into what our hands may be doing? I've been picking chickens with my hands but in imagination I've been roaming the Milky Way."

"I thought you'd scattered more feathers over the floor than usual," remarked Marilla.

Then Anne put Davy to bed and made him promise that he would behave perfectly the next day.

"If I'm as good as good can be all day tomorrow will you let me be just as bad as I like all the next day?" asked Davy.

"I couldn't do that," said Anne discreetly, "but I'll take you and Dora for a row in the flat right to the bottom of the pond, and we'll go ashore on the sandhills and have a picnic."

"It's a bargain," said Davy. "I'll be good, you bet. I meant to go over to Mr. Harrison's and fire peas from my new popgun at Ginger but another day'll do as well. I espect it will be just like Sunday, but a picnic at the shore'll make up for THAT."

XVII - A Chapter of Accidents

Anne woke three times in the night and made pilgrimages to her window to make sure that Uncle Abe's prediction was not coming true. Finally the morning dawned pearly and lustrous in a sky full of silver sheen and radiance, and the wonderful day had arrived.

Diana appeared soon after breakfast, with a basket of flowers over one arm and HER muslin dress over the other . . . for it would not do to don it until all the dinner preparations were completed. Meanwhile she wore her afternoon pink print and a lawn apron fearfully and wonderfully ruffled and frilled; and very neat and pretty and rosy she was.

"You look simply sweet," said Anne admiringly.

Diana sighed.

"But I've had to let out every one of my dresses AGAIN. I weigh four pounds more than I did in July. Anne, WHERE will this end? Mrs. Morgan's heroines are all tall and slender."

"Well, let's forget our troubles and think of our mercies," said Anne gaily. "Mrs. Allan says that whenever we think of anything that is a trial to us we should also think of something nice that we can set over against it. If you are slightly too plump you've got the dearest dimples; and if I have a freckled nose the SHAPE of it is all right. Do you think the lemon juice did any good?"

"Yes, I really think it did," said Diana critically; and, much elated, Anne led the way to the garden, which was full of airy shadows and wavering golden lights.

"We'll decorate the parlor first. We have plenty of time, for Priscilla said they'd be here about twelve or half past at the latest, so we'll have dinner at one."

There may have been two happier and more excited girls somewhere in Canada or the United States at that moment, but I doubt it. Every snip of the scissors, as rose and peony and bluebell fell, seemed to chirp, "Mrs. Morgan is coming today." Anne wondered how Mr. Harrison COULD go on placidly mowing hay in the field across the lane, just as if nothing were going to happen.

The parlor at Green Gables was a rather severe and gloomy apartment, with rigid horsehair furniture, stiff lace curtains, and white antimacassars that were always laid at a perfectly correct angle, except at such times as they clung to unfortunate people's buttons. Even Anne had never been able to infuse much grace into it, for Marilla would not permit any alterations. But it is wonderful what flowers can accomplish if you give them a fair chance; when Anne and Diana finished with the room you would not have recognized it.

A great blue bowlful of snowballs overflowed on the polished table. The shining black mantelpiece was heaped with roses and ferns. Every shelf of the whatnot held a sheaf of bluebells; the dark corners on either side of the grate were lighted up with jars full of glowing crimson peonies, and the grate itself was aflame with yellow poppies. All this splendor and color, mingled with the sunshine falling through the honeysuckle vines at the windows in a leafy riot of dancing shadows over walls and floor, made of the usually dismal little room the veritable "bower" of Anne's imagination, and even extorted a tribute of admiration from Marilla, who came in to criticize and remained to praise.

"Now, we must set the table," said Anne, in the tone of a priestess about to perform some sacred rite in honor of a divinity. "We'll have a big vaseful of wild roses in the center and one single rose in front of everybody's plate—and a special bouquet of rosebuds only by Mrs. Morgan's—an allusion to 'The Rosebud Garden' you know."

The table was set in the sitting room, with Marilla's finest linen and the best china, glass, and silver. You may be perfectly certain that every article placed on it was polished or scoured to the highest possible perfection of gloss and glitter.

Then the girls tripped out to the kitchen, which was filled with appetizing odors emanating from the oven, where the chickens were already sizzling splendidly. Anne prepared the potatoes and Diana got the peas and beans ready. Then, while Diana shut herself into the pantry to compound the lettuce salad, Anne, whose cheeks were already beginning to glow crimson, as much with excitement as from the heat of the fire, prepared the bread sauce for the chickens, minced her onions for the soup, and finally whipped the cream for her lemon pies.

And what about Davy all this time? Was he redeeming his promise to be good? He was, indeed. To be sure, he insisted on remaining in the kitchen, for his curiosity wanted to see all that went on. But as he sat quietly in a corner, busily engaged in untying the knots in a piece of herring net he had brought home from his last trip to the shore, nobody objected to this.

At half past eleven the lettuce salad was made, the golden circles of the pies were heaped with whipped cream, and everything was sizzling and bubbling that ought to sizzle and bubble.

"We'd better go and dress now," said Anne, "for they may be here by twelve. We must have dinner at sharp one, for the soup must be served as soon as it's done."

Serious indeed were the toilet rites presently performed in the east gable. Anne peered anxiously at her nose and rejoiced to see that its freckles were not at all prominent, thanks either to the lemon juice or to the unusual flush on her cheeks. When they were ready they looked quite as sweet and trim and girlish as ever did any of "Mrs. Morgan's heroines."

"I do hope I'll be able to say something once in a while, and not sit like a mute," said Diana anxiously. "All Mrs. Morgan's heroines converse so beautifully. But I'm afraid I'll be tongue-tied and stupid. And I'll be sure to say 'I seen.' I haven't often said it since Miss Stacy taught here; but in moments of excitement it's sure to pop out. Anne, if I were to say 'I seen' before Mrs. Morgan I'd die of mortification. And it would be almost as bad to have nothing to say."

"I'm nervous about a good many things," said Anne, "but I don't think there is much fear that I won't be able to talk."

And, to do her justice, there wasn't.

Anne shrouded her muslin glories in a big apron and went down to concoct her soup. Marilla had dressed herself and the twins, and looked more excited than she had ever been known to look before. At half past twelve the Allans and Miss Stacy came. Everything was going well but Anne was beginning to feel nervous. It was surely time for Priscilla and Mrs. Morgan to arrive. She made frequent trips to the gate and looked as anxiously down the lane as ever her namesake in the Bluebeard story peered from the tower casement.

"Suppose they don't come at all?" she said piteously.

"Don't suppose it. It would be too mean," said Diana, who, however, was beginning to have uncomfortable misgivings on the subject.

"Anne," said Marilla, coming out from the parlor, "Miss Stacy wants to see Miss Barry's willowware platter."

Anne hastened to the sitting room closet to get the platter. She had, in accordance with her promise to Mrs. Lynde, written to Miss Barry of Charlottetown, asking for the loan of it. Miss Barry was an old friend of Anne's, and she promptly sent the platter out, with a letter exhorting Anne to be very careful of it, for she had paid twenty dollars for it. The platter had served its purpose at the Aid bazaar and had then been returned to the Green Gables closet, for Anne would not trust anybody but herself to take it back to town.

She carried the platter carefully to the front door where her guests were enjoying the cool breeze that blew up from the brook. It was examined and admired; then, just as Anne had taken it back into her own hands, a terrific crash and clatter sounded from the kitchen pantry. Marilla, Diana, and Anne fled out, the latter pausing only long enough to set the precious platter hastily down on the second step of the stairs.

When they reached the pantry a truly harrowing spectacle met their eyes . . . a guilty looking small boy scrambling down from the table, with his clean print blouse liberally plastered with yellow filling, and on the table the shattered remnants of what had been two brave, becreamed lemon pies.

Davy had finished ravelling out his herring net and had wound the twine into a ball. Then he had gone into the pantry to put it up on the shelf above the table, where he already kept a score or so of similar balls, which, so far as could be discovered, served no useful purpose save to yield the joy of possession. Davy had to climb on the table and reach over to the shelf at a dangerous angle . . . something he had been forbidden by Marilla to do, as he had come to grief once before in the experiment. The result in this instance was disastrous. Davy slipped and came sprawling squarely down on the lemon pies. His clean blouse was ruined for that time and the pies for all time. It is, however, an ill wind that blows nobody good, and the pig was eventually the gainer by Davy's mischance.

"Davy Keith," said Marilla, shaking him by the shoulder, "didn't I forbid you to climb up on that table again? Didn't I?"

"I forgot," whimpered Davy. "You've told me not to do such an awful lot of things that I can't remember them all."

"Well, you march upstairs and stay there till after dinner. Perhaps you'll get them sorted out in your memory by that time. No, Anne, never you mind interceding for him. I'm not punishing him because he spoiled your pies . . . that was an accident. I'm punishing him for his disobedience. Go, Davy, I say."

"Ain't I to have any dinner?" wailed Davy.

"You can come down after dinner is over and have yours in the kitchen."

"Oh, all right," said Davy, somewhat comforted. "I know Anne'll save some nice bones for me, won't you, Anne? 'Cause you know I didn't mean to fall on the pies. Say, Anne, since they ARE spoiled can't I take some of the pieces upstairs with me?"

"No, no lemon pie for you, Master Davy," said Marilla, pushing him toward the hall.

"What shall we do for dessert?" asked Anne, looking regretfully at the wreck and ruin.

"Get out a crock of strawberry preserves," said Marilla consolingly. "There's plenty of whipped cream left in the bowl for it."

One o'clock came . . . but no Priscilla or Mrs. Morgan. Anne was in an agony. Everything was done to a turn and the soup was just what soup should be, but couldn't be depended on to remain so for any length of time.

"I don't believe they're coming after all," said Marilla crossly.

Anne and Diana sought comfort in each other's eyes.

At half past one Marilla again emerged from the parlor.

"Girls, we MUST have dinner. Everybody is hungry and it's no use waiting any longer. Priscilla and Mrs. Morgan are not coming, that's plain, and nothing is being improved by waiting."

Anne and Diana set about lifting the dinner, with all the zest gone out of the performance.

"I don't believe I'll be able to eat a mouthful," said Diana dolefully.

"Nor I. But I hope everything will be nice for Miss Stacy's and Mr. and Mrs. Allan's sakes," said Anne listlessly.

When Diana dished the peas she tasted them and a very peculiar expression crossed her face.

"Anne, did YOU put sugar in these peas?"

"Yes," said Anne, mashing the potatoes with the air of one expected to do her duty. "I put a spoonful of sugar in. We always do. Don't you like it?"

"But *I* put a spoonful in too, when I set them on the stove," said Diana.

Anne dropped her masher and tasted the peas also. Then she made a grimace.

"How awful! I never dreamed you had put sugar in, because I knew your mother never does. I happened to think of it, for a wonder . . . I'm always forgetting it . . . so I popped a spoonful in."

"It's a case of too many cooks, I guess," said Marilla, who had listened to this dialogue with a rather guilty expression. "I didn't think you'd remember about the sugar, Anne, for I'm perfectly certain you never did before . . . so *I* put in a spoonful."

The guests in the parlor heard peal after peal of laughter from the kitchen, but they never knew what the fun was about. There were no green peas on the dinner table that day, however.

"Well," said Anne, sobering down again with a sigh of recollection, "we have the salad anyhow and I don't think anything has happened to the beans. Let's carry the things in and get it over."

It cannot be said that that dinner was a notable success socially. The Allans and Miss Stacy exerted themselves to save the situation and Marilla's customary placidity was not noticeably ruffled. But Anne and Diana, between their disappointment and the reaction from their excitement of the forenoon, could neither talk nor eat. Anne tried heroically to bear her part in the conversation for the sake of her guests; but all the sparkle had been quenched in her for the time being, and, in spite of her love for the Allans and Miss Stacy, she couldn't help thinking how nice it would be when everybody had gone home and she could bury her weariness and disappointment in the pillows of the east gable.

There is an old proverb that really seems at times to be inspired . . . "it never rains but it pours." The measure of that day's tribulations was not yet full. Just as Mr. Allan had finished returning thanks there arose a strange, ominous sound on the stairs, as of some hard, heavy object bounding from step to step, finishing up with a grand smash at the bottom. Everybody ran out into the hall. Anne gave a shriek of dismay.

At the bottom of the stairs lay a big pink conch shell amid the fragments of what had been Miss Barry's platter; and at the top of the stairs knelt a terrified Davy, gazing down with wide-open eyes at the havoc.

"Davy," said Marilla ominously, "did you throw that conch down ON PURPOSE?"

"No, I never did," whimpered Davy. "I was just kneeling here, quiet as quiet, to watch you folks through the bannisters, and my foot struck that old thing and pushed it off . . . and I'm awful hungry . . . and I do wish you'd lick a fellow and have done with it, instead of always sending him upstairs to miss all the fun."

"Don't blame Davy," said Anne, gathering up the fragments with trembling fingers. "It was my fault. I set that platter there and forgot all about it. I am properly punished for my carelessness; but oh, what will Miss Barry say?"

"Well, you know she only bought it, so it isn't the same as if it was an heirloom," said Diana, trying to console.

The guests went away soon after, feeling that it was the most tactful thing to do, and Anne and Diana washed the dishes, talking less than they had ever been known to do before. Then Diana went home with a headache and Anne went with another to the east gable, where she stayed until Marilla came home from the post office at sunset, with a letter from Priscilla, written the day before. Mrs. Morgan had sprained her ankle so severely that she could not leave her room.

"And oh, Anne dear," wrote Priscilla, "I'm so sorry, but I'm afraid we won't get up to Green Gables at all now, for by the time Aunty's ankle is well she will have to go back to Toronto. She has to be there by a certain date."

"Well," sighed Anne, laying the letter down on the red sandstone step of the back porch, where she was sitting, while the twilight rained down out of a dappled sky, "I always thought it was too good to be true that Mrs. Morgan should really come. But there . . . that speech sounds as pessimistic as Miss Eliza Andrews and I'm ashamed of making it. After all, it was NOT too good to be true . . . things just as good and far better are coming true for me all the time. And I suppose the events of today have a funny side too. Perhaps when Diana and I are old and gray we shall be able to laugh over them. But I feel that I can't expect to do it before then, for it has truly been a bitter disappointment."

"You'll probably have a good many more and worse disappointments than that before you get through life," said Marilla, who honestly thought she was making a comforting speech. "It seems to me, Anne, that you are never going to outgrow your fashion of setting your heart so on things and then crashing down into despair because you don't get them."

"I know I'm too much inclined that, way" agreed Anne ruefully. "When I think something nice is going to happen I seem to fly right up on the wings of anticipation; and then the first thing I realize I drop down to earth with a thud. But really, Marilla, the flying part IS glorious as long as it lasts . . . it's like soaring through a sunset. I think it almost pays for the thud."

"Well, maybe it does," admitted Marilla. "I'd rather walk calmly along and do without both flying and thud. But everybody has her own way of living . . . I used to think there was only one right way . . . but since I've had you and the twins to bring up I don't feel so sure of it. What are you going to do about Miss Barry's platter?"

"Pay her back the twenty dollars she paid for it, I suppose. I'm so thankful it wasn't a cherished heirloom because then no money could replace it."

"Maybe you could find one like it somewhere and buy it for her."

"I'm afraid not. Platters as old as that are very scarce. Mrs. Lynde couldn't find one anywhere for the supper. I only wish I could, for of course Miss Barry would just as soon have one platter as another, if both were equally old and genuine. Marilla, look at that big star over Mr. Harrison's maple grove, with all that holy hush of silvery sky about it. It gives me a feeling that is like a prayer. After all, when one can see stars and skies like that, little disappointments and accidents can't matter so much, can they?"

"Where's Davy?" said Marilla, with an indifferent glance at the star.

"In bed. I've promised to take him and Dora to the shore for a picnic tomorrow. Of course, the original agreement was that he must be good. But he TRIED to be good . . . and I hadn't the heart to disappoint him."

"You'll drown yourself or the twins, rowing about the pond in that flat," grumbled Marilla. "I've lived here for sixty years and I've never been on the pond yet."

"Well, it's never too late to mend," said Anne roguishly. "Suppose you come with us tomorrow. We'll shut Green Gables up and spend the whole day at the shore, daffing the world aside."

"No, thank you," said Marilla, with indignant emphasis. "I'd be a nice sight, wouldn't I, rowing down the pond in a flat? I think I hear Rachel pronouncing on it. There's Mr. Harrison driving away somewhere. Do you suppose there is any truth in the gossip that Mr. Harrison is going to see Isabella Andrews?"

"No, I'm sure there isn't. He just called there one evening on business with Mr. Harmon Andrews and Mrs. Lynde saw him and said she knew he was courting because he had a white collar on. I don't believe Mr. Harrison will ever marry. He seems to have a prejudice against marriage."

"Well, you can never tell about those old bachelors. And if he had a white collar on I'd agree with Rachel that it looks suspicious, for I'm sure he never was seen with one before."

"I think he only put it on because he wanted to conclude a business deal with Harmon Andrews," said Anne. "I've heard him say that's the only time a man needs to be particular about his appearance, because if he looks prosperous the party of the second part won't be so likely to try to cheat him. I really feel sorry for Mr. Harrison; I don't believe he feels satisfied with his life. It must be very lonely to have no one to care about except a parrot, don't you think? But I notice Mr. Harrison doesn't like to be pitied. Nobody does, I imagine."

"There's Gilbert coming up the lane," said Marilla. "If he wants you to go for a row on the pond mind you put on your coat and rubbers. There's a heavy dew tonight."

XVIII - An Adventure on the Tory Road

"Anne," said Davy, sitting up in bed and propping his chin on his hands, "Anne, where is sleep? People go to sleep every night, and of course I know it's the place where I do the things I dream, but I want to know WHERE it is and how I get there and back without knowing anything about it . . . and in my nighty too. Where is it?"

Anne was kneeling at the west gable window watching the sunset sky that was like a great flower with petals of crocus and a heart of fiery yellow. She turned her head at Davy's question and answered dreamily,

> "'Over the mountains of the moon,
> Down the valley of the shadow.'"

Paul Irving would have known the meaning of this, or made a meaning out of it for himself, if he didn't; but practical Davy, who, as Anne often despairingly remarked, hadn't a particle of imagination, was only puzzled and disgusted.

"Anne, I believe you're just talking nonsense."

"Of course, I was, dear boy. Don't you know that it is only very foolish folk who talk sense all the time?"

"Well, I think you might give a sensible answer when I ask a sensible question," said Davy in an injured tone.

"Oh, you are too little to understand," said Anne. But she felt rather ashamed of saying it; for had she not, in keen remembrance of many similar snubs administered in her own early years, solemnly vowed that she would never tell any child it was too little to understand? Yet here she was doing it . . . so wide sometimes is the gulf between theory and practice.

"Well, I'm doing my best to grow," said Davy, "but it's a thing you can't hurry much. If Marilla wasn't so stingy with her jam I believe I'd grow a lot faster."

"Marilla is not stingy, Davy," said Anne severely. "It is very ungrateful of you to say such a thing."

"There's another word that means the same thing and sounds a lot better, but I don't just remember it," said Davy, frowning intently. "I heard Marilla say she was it, herself, the other day."

"If you mean ECONOMICAL, it's a VERY different thing from being stingy. It is an excellent trait in a person if she is economical. If Marilla had been stingy she wouldn't have taken you and Dora when your mother died. Would you have liked to live with Mrs. Wiggins?"

"You just bet I wouldn't!" Davy was emphatic on that point. "Nor I don't want to go out to Uncle Richard neither. I'd far rather live here, even if Marilla is that long-tailed word when it comes to jam, 'cause YOU'RE here, Anne. Say, Anne, won't you tell me a story 'fore I go to sleep? I don't want a fairy story. They're all right for girls, I s'pose, but I want something exciting . . . lots of killing and shooting in it, and a house on fire, and in'trusting things like that."

Fortunately for Anne, Marilla called out at this moment from her room.

"Anne, Diana's signaling at a great rate. You'd better see what she wants."

Anne ran to the east gable and saw flashes of light coming through the twilight from Diana's window in groups of five, which meant, according to their old childish code, "Come over at once for I have something important to reveal." Anne threw her white shawl over her head and hastened through the Haunted Wood and across Mr. Bell's pasture corner to Orchard Slope.

"I've good news for you, Anne," said Diana. "Mother and I have just got home from Carmody, and I saw Mary Sentner from Spencer vale in Mr. Blair's store. She says the old Copp girls on the Tory Road have a willow-ware platter and she thinks it's exactly like the one we had at the supper. She says they'll likely sell it, for Martha Copp has never been known to keep anything she COULD sell; but if they won't there's a platter at Wesley Keyson's at Spencervale and she knows they'd sell it, but she isn't sure it's just the same kind as Aunt Josephine's."

"I'll go right over to Spencervale after it tomorrow," said Anne resolutely, "and you must come with me. It will be such a weight off my mind, for I have to go to town day after tomorrow and how can I face your Aunt Josephine without a willow-ware platter? It would be even worse than the time I had to confess about jumping on the spare room bed."

Both girls laughed over the old memory . . . concerning which, if any of my readers are ignorant and curious, I must refer them to Anne's earlier history.

The next afternoon the girls fared forth on their platter hunting expedition. It was ten miles to Spencervale and the day was not especially pleasant for traveling. It was very warm and windless, and the dust on the road was such as might have been expected after six weeks of dry weather.

"Oh, I do wish it would rain soon," sighed Anne. "Everything is so parched up. The poor fields just seem pitiful to me and the trees seem to be stretching out their hands pleading for rain. As for my garden, it hurts me every time I go into it. I suppose I shouldn't complain about a garden when the farmers' crops are suffering so. Mr. Harrison says his pastures are so scorched up that his poor cows can hardly get a bite to eat and he feels guilty of cruelty to animals every time he meets their eyes."

After a wearisome drive the girls reached Spencervale and turned down the "Tory" Road . . . a green, solitary highway where the strips of grass between the wheel tracks bore evidence to lack of travel. Along most of its extent it was lined with thick-set young spruces crowding down to the roadway, with here and there a break where the back field of a Spencervale farm came out to the fence or an expanse of stumps was aflame with fireweed and goldenrod.

"Why is it called the Tory Road?" asked Anne.

"Mr. Allan says it is on the principle of calling a place a grove because there are no trees in it," said Diana, "for nobody lives along the road except the Copp girls and old Martin Bovyer at the further end, who is a Liberal. The Tory government ran the road through when they were in power just to show they were doing something."

Diana's father was a Liberal, for which reason she and Anne never discussed politics. Green Gables folk had always been Conservatives.

Finally the girls came to the old Copp homestead . . . a place of such exceeding external neatness that even Green Gables would have suffered by contrast. The house was a very old-fashioned one, situated on a slope, which fact had necessitated the building of a stone basement under one end. The house and outbuildings were all whitewashed to a condition of blinding perfection and not a weed was visible in the prim kitchen garden surrounded by its white paling.

"The shades are all down," said Diana ruefully. "I believe that nobody is home."

This proved to be the case. The girls looked at each other in perplexity.

"I don't know what to do," said Anne. "If I were sure the platter was the right kind I would not mind waiting until they came home. But if it isn't it may be too late to go to Wesley Keyson's afterward."

Diana looked at a certain little square window over the basement.

"That is the pantry window, I feel sure," she said, "because this house is just like Uncle Charles' at Newbridge, and that is their pantry window. The shade isn't down, so if we climbed up on the roof of that little house we could look into the pantry and might be able to see the platter. Do you think it would be any harm?"

"No, I don't think so," decided Anne, after due reflection, "since our motive is not idle curiosity."

This important point of ethics being settled, Anne prepared to mount the aforesaid "little house," a construction of lathes, with a peaked roof, which had in times past served as a habitation for ducks. The Copp girls had given up keeping ducks . . . "because they were such untidy birds". . . and the house had not been in use for some years, save as an abode of correction for setting hens. Although scrupulously whitewashed it had become somewhat shaky, and Anne felt rather dubious as she scrambled up from the vantage point of a keg placed on a box.

"I'm afraid it won't bear my weight," she said as she gingerly stepped on the roof.

"Lean on the window sill," advised Diana, and Anne accordingly leaned. Much to her delight, she saw, as she peered through the pane, a willow-ware platter, exactly such as she was in quest of, on the shelf in front of the window. So much she saw before the catastrophe came. In her joy Anne forgot the precarious nature of her footing, incautiously ceased to lean on the window sill, gave an impulsive little hop of pleasure . . . and the next moment she had crashed through the roof up to her armpits, and there she hung, quite unable to extricate herself. Diana dashed into the duck house and, seizing her unfortunate friend by the waist, tried to draw her down.

"Ow . . . don't," shrieked poor Anne. "There are some long splinters sticking into me. See if you can put something under my feet . . . then perhaps I can draw myself up."

Diana hastily dragged in the previously mentioned keg and Anne found that it was just sufficiently high to furnish a secure resting place for her feet. But she could not release herself.

"Could I pull you out if I crawled up?" suggested Diana.

Anne shook her head hopelessly.

"No . . . the splinters hurt too badly. If you can find an axe you might chop me out, though. Oh dear, I do really begin to believe that I was born under an ill-omened star."

Diana searched faithfully but no axe was to be found.

"I'll have to go for help," she said, returning to the prisoner.

"No, indeed, you won't," said Anne vehemently. "If you do the story of this will get out everywhere and I shall be ashamed to show my face. No, we must just wait until the Copp girls come home and bind them to secrecy. They'll know where the axe is and get me out. I'm not uncomfortable, as long as I keep perfectly still . . . not uncomfortable in BODY I mean. I wonder what the Copp girls value this house at. I shall have to pay for the damage I've done, but I wouldn't mind that if I were only sure they would understand my motive in peeping in at their pantry window. My sole comfort is that the platter is just the kind I want and if Miss Copp will only sell it to me I shall be resigned to what has happened."

"What if the Copp girls don't come home until after night . . . or till tomorrow?" suggested Diana.

"If they're not back by sunset you'll have to go for other assistance, I suppose," said Anne reluctantly, "but you mustn't go until you really have to. Oh dear, this is a dreadful predicament. I wouldn't mind my misfortunes so much if they were romantic, as Mrs. Morgan's heroines' always are, but they are always just simply ridiculous. Fancy what the Copp girls will think when they drive into their yard and see a girl's head and shoulders sticking out of the roof of one of their outhouses. Listen . . . is that a wagon? No, Diana, I believe it is thunder."

Thunder it was undoubtedly, and Diana, having made a hasty pilgrimage around the house, returned to announce that a very black cloud was rising rapidly in the northwest.

"I believe we're going to have a heavy thunder-shower," she exclaimed in dismay, "Oh, Anne, what will we do?"

"We must prepare for it," said Anne tranquilly. A thunderstorm seemed a trifle in comparison with what had already happened. "You'd better drive the horse and buggy into that open shed. Fortunately my parasol is in the buggy. Here . . . take my hat with you. Marilla told me I was a goose to put on my best hat to come to the Tory Road and she was right, as she always is."

Diana untied the pony and drove into the shed, just as the first heavy drops of rain fell. There she sat and watched the resulting downpour, which was so thick and heavy that she could hardly see Anne through it, holding the parasol bravely over her bare head. There was not a great deal of thunder, but for the best part of an hour the rain came merrily down. Occasionally Anne slanted back her parasol and waved an encouraging hand to her friend; But conversation at that distance was quite out of the question. Finally the rain ceased, the sun came out, and Diana ventured across the puddles of the yard.

"Did you get very wet?" she asked anxiously.

"Oh, no," returned Anne cheerfully. "My head and shoulders are quite dry and my skirt is only a little damp where the rain beat through the lathes. Don't pity me, Diana, for I haven't minded it at all. I kept thinking how much good the rain will do and how glad my garden must be for it, and imagining what the flowers and buds would think when the drops began to fall. I imagined out a most interesting dialogue between the asters and the sweet peas and the wild canaries in the lilac bush and the guardian spirit of the garden. When I go home I mean to write it down. I wish I had a pencil and paper to do it now, because I daresay I'll forget the best parts before I reach home."

Diana the faithful had a pencil and discovered a sheet of wrapping paper in the box of the buggy. Anne folded up her dripping parasol, put on her hat, spread the wrapping paper on a shingle Diana handed up, and wrote out her garden idyl under conditions that could hardly be considered as favorable to literature. Nevertheless, the result was quite pretty, and Diana was "enraptured" when Anne read it to her.

"Oh, Anne, it's sweet . . . just sweet. DO send it to the 'Canadian Woman.'"

Anne shook her head.

"Oh, no, it wouldn't be suitable at all. There is no PLOT in it, you see. It's just a string of fancies. I like writing such things, but of course nothing of the sort would ever do for publication, for editors insist on plots, so Priscilla says. Oh, there's Miss Sarah Copp now. PLEASE, Diana, go and explain."

Miss Sarah Copp was a small person, garbed in shabby black, with a hat chosen less for vain adornment than for qualities that would wear well. She looked as amazed as might be expected on seeing the curious tableau in her yard, but when she heard Diana's explanation she was all sympathy. She hurriedly unlocked the back door, produced the axe, and with a few skillfull blows set Anne free. The latter, somewhat tired and stiff, ducked down into the interior of her prison and thankfully emerged into liberty once more.

"Miss Copp," she said earnestly. "I assure you I looked into your pantry window only to discover if you had a willow-ware platter. I didn't see anything else—I didn't LOOK for anything else."

"Bless you, that's all right," said Miss Sarah amiably. "You needn't worry—there's no harm done. Thank goodness, we Copps keep our pantries presentable at all times and don't care who sees into them. As for that old duckhouse, I'm glad it's smashed, for maybe now Martha will agree to having it taken down. She never would before for fear it might come in handy sometime and I've had to whitewash it every spring. But you might as well argue with a post as with Martha. She went to town today—I drove her to the station. And you want to buy my platter. Well, what will you give for it?"

"Twenty dollars," said Anne, who was never meant to match business wits with a Copp, or she would not have offered her price at the start.

"Well, I'll see," said Miss Sarah cautiously. "That platter is mine fortunately, or I'd never dare to sell it when Martha wasn't here. As it is, I daresay she'll raise a fuss. Martha's the boss of this establishment I can tell you. I'm getting awful tired of living under another woman's thumb. But come in, come in. You must be real tired and hungry. I'll do the best I can for you in the way of tea but I warn you not to expect anything but bread and butter and some cowcumbers. Martha locked up all the cake and cheese and preserves afore she went. She always does, because she says I'm too extravagant with them if company comes."

The girls were hungry enough to do justice to any fare, and they enjoyed Miss Sarah's excellent bread and butter and "cowcumbers" thoroughly. When the meal was over Miss Sarah said,

"I don't know as I mind selling the platter. But it's worth twenty-five dollars. It's a very old platter."

Diana gave Anne's foot a gentle kick under the table, meaning, "Don't agree—she'll let it go for twenty if you hold out." But Anne was not minded to take any chances in regard to that precious platter. She promptly agreed to give twenty-five and Miss Sarah looked as if she felt sorry she hadn't asked for thirty.

"Well, I guess you may have it. I want all the money I can scare up just now. The fact is—" Miss Sarah threw up her head importantly, with a proud flush on her thin cheeks—"I'm going to be married—to Luther Wallace. He wanted me twenty years ago. I liked him real well but he was poor then and father packed him off. I s'pose I shouldn't have let him go so meek but I was timid and frightened of father. Besides, I didn't know men were so skurse."

When the girls were safely away, Diana driving and Anne holding the coveted platter carefully on her lap, the green, rain-freshened solitudes of the Tory Road were enlivened by ripples of girlish laughter.

"I'll amuse your Aunt Josephine with the 'strange eventful history' of this afternoon when I go to town tomorrow. We've had a rather trying time but it's over now. I've got the platter, and that rain has laid the dust beautifully. So 'all's well that ends well.'"

"We're not home yet," said Diana rather pessimistically, "and there's no telling what may happen before we are. You're such a girl to have adventures, Anne."

"Having adventures comes natural to some people," said Anne serenely. "You just have a gift for them or you haven't."

XIX - Just a Happy Day

"After all," Anne had said to Marilla once, "I believe the nicest and sweetest days are not those on which anything very splendid or wonderful or exciting happens but just those that bring simple little pleasures, following one another softly, like pearls slipping off a string."

Life at Green Gables was full of just such days, for Anne's adventures and misadventures, like those of other people, did not all happen at once, but were sprinkled over the year, with long stretches of harmless, happy days between, filled with work and dreams and laughter and lessons. Such a day came late in August. In the forenoon Anne and Diana rowed the delighted twins down the pond to the sandshore to pick "sweet grass" and paddle in the surf, over which the wind was harping an old lyric learned when the world was young.

In the afternoon Anne walked down to the old Irving place to see Paul. She found him stretched out on the grassy bank beside the thick fir grove that sheltered the house on the north, absorbed in a book of fairy tales. He sprang up radiantly at sight of her.

"Oh, I'm so glad you've come, teacher," he said eagerly, "because Grandma's away. You'll stay and have tea with me, won't you? It's so lonesome to have tea all by oneself. YOU know, teacher. I've had serious thoughts of asking Young Mary Joe to sit down and eat her tea with me, but I expect Grandma wouldn't approve. She says the French have to be kept in their place. And anyhow, it's difficult to talk with Young Mary Joe. She just laughs and says, 'Well, yous do beat all de kids I ever knowed.' That isn't my idea of conversation."

"Of course I'll stay to tea," said Anne gaily. "I was dying to be asked. My mouth has been watering for some more of your grandma's delicious shortbread ever since I had tea here before."

Paul looked very sober.

"If it depended on me, teacher," he said, standing before Anne with his hands in his pockets and his beautiful little face shadowed with sudden care, "You should have shortbread with a right good will. But it depends on Mary Joe. I heard Grandma tell her before she left that she wasn't to give me any shortcake because it was too rich for little boys' stomachs. But maybe Mary Joe will cut some for you if I promise I won't eat any. Let us hope for the best."

"Yes, let us," agreed Anne, whom this cheerful philosophy suited exactly, "and if Mary Joe proves hard-hearted and won't give me any shortbread it doesn't matter in the least, so you are not to worry over that."

"You're sure you won't mind if she doesn't?" said Paul anxiously.

"Perfectly sure, dear heart."

"Then I won't worry," said Paul, with a long breath of relief, "especially as I really think Mary Joe will listen to reason. She's not a naturally unreasonable person, but she has learned by experience that it doesn't do to disobey Grandma's orders. Grandma is an excellent woman but people must do as she tells them. She was very much pleased with me this morning because I managed at last to eat all my plateful of porridge. It was a great effort but I succeeded. Grandma says she thinks she'll make a man of me yet. But, teacher, I want to ask you a very important question. You will answer it truthfully, won't you?"

"I'll try," promised Anne.

"Do you think I'm wrong in my upper story?" asked Paul, as if his very existence depended on her reply.

"Goodness, no, Paul," exclaimed Anne in amazement. "Certainly you're not. What put such an idea into your head?"

"Mary Joe . . . but she didn't know I heard her. Mrs. Peter Sloane's hired girl, Veronica, came to see Mary Joe last evening and I heard them talking in the kitchen as I was going through the hall. I heard Mary Joe say, 'Dat Paul, he is de queeres' leetle boy. He talks dat queer. I tink dere's someting wrong in his upper story.' I couldn't sleep last night for ever so long, thinking of it, and wondering if Mary Joe was right. I couldn't bear to ask Grandma about it somehow, but I made up my mind I'd ask you. I'm so glad you think I'm all right in my upper story."

"Of course you are. Mary Joe is a silly, ignorant girl, and you are never to worry about anything she says," said Anne indignantly, secretly resolving to give Mrs. Irving a discreet hint as to the advisability of restraining Mary Joe's tongue.

"Well, that's a weight off my mind," said Paul. "I'm perfectly happy now, teacher, thanks to you. It wouldn't be nice to have something wrong in your upper story, would it, teacher? I suppose the reason Mary Joe imagines I have is because I tell her what I think about things sometimes."

"It is a rather dangerous practice," admitted Anne, out of the depths of her own experience.

"Well, by and by I'll tell you the thoughts I told Mary Joe and you can see for yourself if there's anything queer in them," said Paul, "but I'll wait till it begins to get dark. That is the time I ache to tell people things, and when nobody else is handy I just HAVE to tell Mary Joe. But after this I won't, if it makes her imagine I'm wrong in my upper story. I'll just ache and bear it."

"And if the ache gets too bad you can come up to Green Gables and tell me your thoughts," suggested Anne, with all the gravity that endeared her to children, who so dearly love to be taken seriously.

"Yes, I will. But I hope Davy won't be there when I go because he makes faces at me. I don't mind VERY much because he is such a little boy and I am quite a big one, but still it is not pleasant to have faces made at you. And Davy makes such terrible ones. Sometimes I am frightened he will never get his face straightened out again. He makes them at me in church when I ought to be thinking of sacred things. Dora likes me though, and I like her, but not so well as I did before she told Minnie May Barry that she meant to marry me when I grew up. I may marry somebody when I grow up but I'm far too young to be thinking of it yet, don't you think, teacher?"

"Rather young," agreed teacher.

"Speaking of marrying, reminds me of another thing that has been troubling me of late," continued Paul. "Mrs. Lynde was down here one day last week having tea with Grandma, and Grandma made me show her my little mother's picture . . . the one father sent me for my birthday present. I didn't exactly want to show it to Mrs. Lynde. Mrs. Lynde is a good, kind woman, but she isn't the sort of person you want to show your mother's picture to. YOU know, teacher. But of course I obeyed Grandma. Mrs. Lynde said she was very pretty but kind of actressy looking, and must have been an awful lot younger than father. Then she said, 'Some of these days your pa will be marrying again likely. How will you like to have a new ma, Master Paul?' Well, the idea almost took my breath away, teacher, but I wasn't going to let Mrs. Lynde see THAT. I just looked her straight in the face . . . like this . . . and I said, 'Mrs. Lynde, father made a pretty good job of picking out my first mother and I could trust him to pick out just as good a one the second time.' And I CAN trust him, teacher. But still, I hope, if he ever does give me a new mother, he'll ask my opinion about her before it's too late. There's Mary Joe coming to call us to tea. I'll go and consult with her about the shortbread."

As a result of the "consultation," Mary Joe cut the shortbread and added a dish of preserves to the bill of fare. Anne poured the tea and she and Paul had a very merry meal in the dim old sitting room whose windows were open to the gulf breezes, and they talked so much "nonsense" that Mary Joe was quite scandalized and told Veronica the next evening that "de school mees" was as queer as Paul. After tea Paul took Anne up to his room to show her his mother's picture, which had been the mysterious birthday present kept by Mrs. Irving in the bookcase. Paul's little low-ceilinged room was a soft whirl of ruddy light from the sun that was setting over the sea and swinging shadows from the fir trees that grew close to the square, deep-set window. From out this soft glow and glamor shone a sweet, girlish face, with tender mother eyes, that was hanging on the wall at the foot of the bed.

"That's my little mother," said Paul with loving pride. "I got Grandma to hang it there where I'd see it as soon as I opened my eyes in the morning. I never mind not having the light when I go to bed now, because it just seems as if my little mother was right here with me. Father knew just what I would like for a birthday present, although he never asked me. Isn't it wonderful how much fathers DO know?"

"Your mother was very lovely, Paul, and you look a little like her. But her eyes and hair are darker than yours."

"My eyes are the same color as father's," said Paul, flying about the room to heap all available cushions on the window seat, "but father's hair is gray. He has lots of it, but it is gray. You see, father is nearly fifty. That's ripe old age, isn't it? But it's only OUTSIDE he's old. INSIDE he's just as young as anybody. Now, teacher, please sit here; and I'll sit at your feet. May I lay my head against your knee? That's the way my little mother and I used to sit. Oh, this is real splendid, I think."

"Now, I want to hear those thoughts which Mary Joe pronounces so queer," said Anne, patting the mop of curls at her side. Paul never needed any coaxing to tell his thoughts . . . at least, to congenial souls.

"I thought them out in the fir grove one night," he said dreamily. "Of course I didn't BELIEVE them but I THOUGHT them. YOU know, teacher. And then I wanted to tell them to somebody and there was nobody but Mary Joe. Mary Joe was in the pantry setting bread and I sat down on the bench beside her and I said, 'Mary Joe, do you know what I think? I think the evening star is a lighthouse on the land where the fairies dwell.' And Mary Joe said, 'Well, yous are de queer one. Dare ain't no such ting as fairies.' I was very much provoked. Of course, I knew there are no fairies; but that needn't prevent my thinking there is. You know, teacher. But I tried again quite patiently. I said, 'Well then, Mary Joe, do you know what I think? I think an angel walks over the world after the sun sets . . . a great, tall, white angel, with silvery folded wings . . . and sings the flowers and birds to sleep. Children can hear him if they know how to listen.' Then Mary Joe held up her hands all over flour and said, 'Well, yous are de queer leetle boy. Yous make me feel scare.' And she really did looked scared. I went out then and whispered the rest of my thoughts to the garden. There was a little birch tree in the garden and it died. Grandma says the salt spray killed it; but I think the dryad belonging to it was a foolish dryad who wandered away to see the world and got lost. And the little tree was so lonely it died of a broken heart."

"And when the poor, foolish little dryad gets tired of the world and comes back to her tree HER heart will break," said Anne.

"Yes; but if dryads are foolish they must take the consequences, just as if they were real people," said Paul gravely. "Do you know what I think about the new moon, teacher? I think it is a little golden boat full of dreams."

"And when it tips on a cloud some of them spill out and fall into your sleep."

"Exactly, teacher. Oh, you DO know. And I think the violets are little snips of the sky that fell down when the angels cut out holes for the stars to shine through. And the buttercups are made out of old sunshine; and I think the sweet peas will be butterflies when they go to heaven. Now, teacher, do you see anything so very queer about those thoughts?"

"No, laddie dear, they are not queer at all; they are strange and beautiful thoughts for a little boy to think, and so people who couldn't think anything of the sort themselves, if they tried for a hundred years, think them queer. But keep on thinking them, Paul . . . some day you are going to be a poet, I believe."

When Anne reached home she found a very different type of boyhood waiting to be put to bed. Davy was sulky; and when Anne had undressed him he bounced into bed and buried his face in the pillow.

"Davy, you have forgotten to say your prayers," said Anne rebukingly.

"No, I didn't forget," said Davy defiantly, "but I ain't going to say my prayers any more. I'm going to give up trying to be good, 'cause no matter how good I am you'd like Paul Irving better. So I might as well be bad and have the fun of it."

"I don't like Paul Irving BETTER," said Anne seriously. "I like you just as well, only in a different way."

"But I want you to like me the same way," pouted Davy.

"You can't like different people the same way. You don't like Dora and me the same way, do you?"

Davy sat up and reflected.

"No . . . o . . . o," he admitted at last, "I like Dora because she's my sister but I like you because you're YOU."

"And I like Paul because he is Paul and Davy because he is Davy," said Anne gaily.

"Well, I kind of wish I'd said my prayers then," said Davy, convinced by this logic. "But it's too much bother getting out now to say them. I'll say them twice over in the morning, Anne. Won't that do as well?"

No, Anne was positive it would not do as well. So Davy scrambled out and knelt down at her knee. When he had finished his devotions he leaned back on his little, bare, brown heels and looked up at her.

"Anne, I'm gooder than I used to be."

"Yes, indeed you are, Davy," said Anne, who never hesitated to give credit where credit was due.

"I KNOW I'm gooder," said Davy confidently, "and I'll tell you how I know it. Today Marilla give me two pieces of bread and jam, one for me and one for Dora. One was a good deal bigger than the other and Marilla didn't say which was mine. But I give the biggest piece to Dora. That was good of me, wasn't it?"

"Very good, and very manly, Davy."

"Of course," admitted Davy, "Dora wasn't very hungry and she only et half her slice and then she give the rest to me. But I didn't know she was going to do that when I give it to her, so I WAS good, Anne."

In the twilight Anne sauntered down to the Dryad's Bubble and saw Gilbert Blythe coming down through the dusky Haunted Wood. She had a sudden realization that Gilbert was a schoolboy no longer. And how manly he looked—the tall, frank-faced fellow, with the clear, straightforward eyes and the broad shoulders. Anne thought Gilbert was a very handsome lad, even though he didn't look at all like her ideal man. She and Diana had long ago decided what kind of a man they admired and their tastes seemed exactly similar. He must be very tall and distinguished looking, with melancholy, inscrutable eyes, and a melting, sympathetic voice. There was nothing either melancholy or inscrutable in Gilbert's physiognomy, but of course that didn't matter in friendship!

Gilbert stretched himself out on the ferns beside the Bubble and looked approvingly at Anne. If Gilbert had been asked to describe his ideal woman the description would have answered point for point to Anne, even to those seven tiny freckles whose obnoxious presence still continued to vex her soul. Gilbert was as yet little more than a boy; but a boy has his dreams as have others, and in Gilbert's future there was always a girl with big, limpid gray eyes, and a face as fine and delicate as a flower. He had made up his mind, also, that his future must be worthy of its goddess. Even in quiet Avonlea there were temptations to be met and faced. White Sands youth were a rather "fast" set, and Gilbert was popular wherever he went. But he meant to keep himself worthy of Anne's friendship and perhaps some distant day her love; and he watched over word and thought and deed as jealously as if her clear eyes were to pass in judgment on it. She held over him the unconscious influence that every girl, whose ideals are high and pure, wields over her friends; an influence which would endure as long as she was faithful to those ideals and which she would as certainly lose if she were ever false to them. In Gilbert's eyes Anne's greatest charm was the fact that she never stooped to the petty practices of so many of the Avonlea girls—the small jealousies, the little deceits and rivalries, the palpable bids for favor. Anne held herself apart from all this, not consciously or of design, but simply because anything of the sort was utterly foreign to her transparent, impulsive nature, crystal clear in its motives and aspirations.

But Gilbert did not attempt to put his thoughts into words, for he had already too good reason to know that Anne would mercilessly and frostily nip all attempts at sentiment in the bud—or laugh at him, which was ten times worse.

"You look like a real dryad under that birch tree," he said teasingly.

"I love birch trees," said Anne, laying her cheek against the creamy satin of the slim bole, with one of the pretty, caressing gestures that came so natural to her.

"Then you'll be glad to hear that Mr. Major Spencer has decided to set out a row of white birches all along the road front of his farm, by way of encouraging the A.V.I.S.," said Gilbert. "He was talking to me about it today. Major Spencer is the most progressive and public-spirited man in Avonlea. And Mr. William Bell is going to set out a spruce hedge along his road front and up his lane. Our Society is getting on splendidly, Anne. It is past the experimental stage and is an accepted fact. The older folks are beginning to take an interest in it and the White Sands people are talking of starting one too. Even Elisha Wright has come around since that day the Americans from the hotel had the picnic at the shore. They praised our roadsides so highly and said they were so much prettier than in any other part of the Island. And when, in due time, the other farmers follow Mr. Spencer's good example and plant ornamental trees and hedges along their road fronts Avonlea will be the prettiest settlement in the province."

"The Aids are talking of taking up the graveyard," said Anne, "and I hope they will, because there will have to be a subscription for that, and it would be no use for the Society to try it after the hall affair. But the Aids would never have stirred in the matter if the Society hadn't put it into their thoughts unofficially. Those trees we planted on the church grounds are flourishing, and the trustees have promised me that they will fence in the school grounds next year. If they do I'll have an arbor day and every scholar shall plant a tree; and we'll have a garden in the corner by the road."

"We've succeeded in almost all our plans so far, except in getting the old Boulter house removed," said Gilbert, "and I've given THAT up in despair. Levi won't have it taken down just to vex us. There's a contrary streak in all the Boulters and it's strongly developed in him."

"Julia Bell wants to send another committee to him, but I think the better way will just be to leave him severely alone," said Anne sagely.

"And trust to Providence, as Mrs. Lynde says," smiled Gilbert. "Certainly, no more committees. They only aggravate him. Julia Bell thinks you can do anything, if you only have a committee to attempt it. Next spring, Anne, we must start an agitation for nice lawns and grounds. We'll sow good seed betimes this winter. I've a treatise here on lawns and lawnmaking and I'm going to prepare a paper on the subject soon. Well, I suppose our vacation is almost over. School opens Monday. Has Ruby Gillis got the Carmody school?"

"Yes; Priscilla wrote that she had taken her own home school, so the Carmody trustees gave it to Ruby. I'm sorry Priscilla is not coming back, but since she can't I'm glad Ruby has got the school. She will be home for Saturdays and it will seem like old times, to have her and Jane and Diana and myself all together again."

Marilla, just home from Mrs. Lynde's, was sitting on the back porch step when Anne returned to the house.

"Rachel and I have decided to have our cruise to town tomorrow," she said. "Mr. Lynde is feeling better this week and Rachel wants to go before he has another sick spell."

"I intend to get up extra early tomorrow morning, for I've ever so much to do," said Anne virtuously. "For one thing, I'm going to shift the feathers from my old bedtick to the new one. I ought to have done it long ago but I've just kept putting it off . . . it's such a detestable task. It's a very bad habit to put off disagreeable things, and I never mean to again, or else I can't comfortably tell my pupils not to do it. That would be inconsistent. Then I want to make a cake for Mr. Harrison and finish my paper on gardens for the A.V.I.S., and write Stella, and wash and starch my muslin dress, and make Dora's new apron."

"You won't get half done," said Marilla pessimistically. "I never yet planned to do a lot of things but something happened to prevent me."

XX - The Way It Often Happens

Anne rose betimes the next morning and blithely greeted the fresh day, when the banners of the sunrise were shaken triumphantly across the pearly skies. Green Gables lay in a pool of sunshine, flecked with the dancing shadows of poplar and willow. Beyond the land was Mr. Harrison's wheatfield, a great, windrippled expanse of pale gold. The world was so beautiful that Anne spent ten blissful minutes hanging idly over the garden gate drinking the loveliness in.

After breakfast Marilla made ready for her journey. Dora was to go with her, having been long promised this treat.

"Now, Davy, you try to be a good boy and don't bother Anne," she straitly charged him. "If you are good I'll bring you a striped candy cane from town."

For alas, Marilla had stooped to the evil habit of bribing people to be good!

"I won't be bad on purpose, but s'posen I'm bad zacksidentally?" Davy wanted to know.

"You'll have to guard against accidents," admonished Marilla. "Anne, if Mr. Shearer comes today get a nice roast and some steak. If he doesn't you'll have to kill a fowl for dinner tomorrow."

Anne nodded.

"I'm not going to bother cooking any dinner for just Davy and myself today," she said. "That cold ham bone will do for noon lunch and I'll have some steak fried for you when you come home at night."

"I'm going to help Mr. Harrison haul dulse this morning," announced Davy. "He asked me to, and I guess he'll ask me to dinner too. Mr. Harrison is an awful kind man. He's a real sociable man. I hope I'll be like him when I grow up. I mean BEHAVE like him . . . I don't want to LOOK like him. But I guess there's no danger, for Mrs. Lynde says I'm a very handsome child. Do you s'pose it'll last, Anne? I want to know?"

"I daresay it will," said Anne gravely. "You ARE a handsome boy, Davy," . . . Marilla looked volumes of disapproval . . . "but you must live up to it and be just as nice and gentlemanly as you look to be."

"And you told Minnie May Barry the other day, when you found her crying 'cause some one said she was ugly, that if she was nice and kind and loving people wouldn't mind her looks," said Davy discontentedly. "Seems to me you can't get out of being good in this world for some reason or 'nother. You just HAVE to behave."

"Don't you want to be good?" asked Marilla, who had learned a great deal but had not yet learned the futility of asking such questions.

"Yes, I want to be good but not TOO good," said Davy cautiously. "You don't have to be very good to be a Sunday School superintendent. Mr. Bell's that, and he's a real bad man."

"Indeed he's not," said Marilla indignantly.

"He is . . . he says he is himself," asseverated Davy. "He said it when he prayed in Sunday School last Sunday. He said he was a vile worm and a miserable sinner and guilty of the blackest 'niquity. What did he do that was so bad, Marilla? Did he kill anybody? Or steal the collection cents? I want to know."

Fortunately Mrs. Lynde came driving up the lane at this moment and Marilla made off, feeling that she had escaped from the snare of the fowler, and wishing devoutly that Mr. Bell were not quite so highly figurative in his public petitions, especially in the hearing of small boys who were always "wanting to know."

Anne, left alone in her glory, worked with a will. The floor was swept, the beds made, the hens fed, the muslin dress washed and hung out on the line. Then Anne prepared for the transfer of feathers. She mounted to the garret and donned the first old dress that came to hand . . . a navy blue cashmere she had worn at fourteen. It was decidedly on the short side and as "skimpy" as the notable wincey Anne had worn upon the occasion of her debut at Green Gables; but at least it would not be materially injured by down and feathers. Anne completed her toilet by tying a big red and white spotted handkerchief that had belonged to Matthew over her head, and, thus accoutred, betook herself to the kitchen chamber, whither Marilla, before her departure, had helped her carry the feather bed.

A cracked mirror hung by the chamber window and in an unlucky moment Anne looked into it. There were those seven freckles on her nose, more rampant than ever, or so it seemed in the glare of light from the unshaded window.

"Oh, I forgot to rub that lotion on last night," she thought. "I'd better run down to the pantry and do it now."

Anne had already suffered many things trying to remove those freckles. On one occasion the entire skin had peeled off her nose but the freckles remained. A few days previously she had found a recipe for a freckle lotion in a magazine and, as the ingredients were within her reach, she straightway compounded it, much to the disgust of Marilla, who thought that if Providence had placed freckles on your nose it was your bounden duty to leave them there.

Anne scurried down to the pantry, which, always dim from the big willow growing close to the window, was now almost dark by reason of the shade drawn to exclude flies. Anne caught the bottle containing the lotion from the shelf and copiously anointed her nose therewith by means of a little sponge sacred to the purpose. This important duty done, she returned to her work. Any one who has ever shifted feathers from one tick to another will not need to be told that when Anne finished she was a sight to behold. Her dress was white with down and fluff, and her front hair, escaping from under the handkerchief, was adorned with a veritable halo of feathers. At this auspicious moment a knock sounded at the kitchen door.

"That must be Mr. Shearer," thought Anne. "I'm in a dreadful mess but I'll have to run down as I am, for he's always in a hurry."

Down flew Anne to the kitchen door. If ever a charitable floor did open to swallow up a miserable, befeathered damsel the Green Gables porch floor should promptly have engulfed Anne at that moment. On the doorstep were standing Priscilla Grant, golden and fair in silk attire, a short, stout gray-haired lady in a tweed suit, and another lady, tall stately, wonderfully gowned, with a beautiful, highbred face and large, black-lashed violet eyes, whom Anne "instinctively felt," as she would have said in her earlier days, to be Mrs. Charlotte E. Morgan.

In the dismay of the moment one thought stood out from the confusion of Anne's mind and she grasped at it as at the proverbial straw. All Mrs. Morgan's heroines were noted for "rising to the occasion." No matter what their troubles were, they invariably rose to the occasion and showed their superiority over all ills of time, space, and quantity. Anne therefore felt it was HER duty to rise to the occasion and she did it, so perfectly that Priscilla afterward declared she never admired Anne Shirley more than at that moment. No matter what her outraged feelings were she did not show them. She greeted Priscilla and was introduced to her companions as calmly and composedly as if she had been arrayed in purple and fine linen. To be sure, it was somewhat of a shock to find that the lady she had instinctively felt to be Mrs. Morgan was not Mrs. Morgan at all, but an unknown Mrs. Pendexter, while the stout little gray-haired woman was Mrs. Morgan; but in the greater shock the lesser lost its power. Anne ushered her guests to the spare room and thence into the parlor, where she left them while she hastened out to help Priscilla unharness her horse.

"It's dreadful to come upon you so unexpectedly as this," apologized Priscilla, "but I did not know till last night that we were coming. Aunt Charlotte is going away Monday and she had promised to spend today with a friend in town. But last night her friend telephoned to her not to come because they were quarantined for scarlet fever. So I suggested we come here instead, for I knew you were longing to see her. We called at the White Sands Hotel and brought Mrs. Pendexter with us. She is a friend of aunt's and lives in New York and her husband is a millionaire. We can't stay very long, for Mrs. Pendexter has to be back at the hotel by five o'clock."

Several times while they were putting away the horse Anne caught Priscilla looking at her in a furtive, puzzled way.

"She needn't stare at me so," Anne thought a little resentfully. "If she doesn't KNOW what it is to change a feather bed she might IMAGINE it."

When Priscilla had gone to the parlor, and before Anne could escape upstairs, Diana walked into the kitchen. Anne caught her astonished friend by the arm.

"Diana Barry, who do you suppose is in that parlor at this very moment? Mrs. Charlotte E. Morgan . . . and a New York millionaire's wife . . . and here I am like

THIS . . . and NOT A THING IN THE HOUSE FOR DINNER BUT A COLD HAM BONE, Diana!"

By this time Anne had become aware that Diana was staring at her in precisely the same bewildered fashion as Priscilla had done. It was really too much.

"Oh, Diana, don't look at me so," she implored. "YOU, at least, must know that the neatest person in the world couldn't empty feathers from one tick into another and remain neat in the process."

"It . . . it . . . isn't the feathers," hesitated Diana. "It's . . . it's . . . your nose, Anne."

"My nose? Oh, Diana, surely nothing has gone wrong with it!"

Anne rushed to the little looking glass over the sink. One glance revealed the fatal truth. Her nose was a brilliant scarlet!

Anne sat down on the sofa, her dauntless spirit subdued at last.

"What is the matter with it?" asked Diana, curiosity overcoming delicacy.

"I thought I was rubbing my freckle lotion on it, but I must have used that red dye Marilla has for marking the pattern on her rugs," was the despairing response. "What shall I do?"

"Wash it off," said Diana practically.

"Perhaps it won't wash off. First I dye my hair; then I dye my nose. Marilla cut my hair off when I dyed it but that remedy would hardly be practicable in this case. Well, this is another punishment for vanity and I suppose I deserve it . . . though there's not much comfort in THAT. It is really almost enough to make one believe in ill-luck, though Mrs. Lynde says there is no such thing, because everything is foreordained."

Fortunately the dye washed off easily and Anne, somewhat consoled, betook herself to the east gable while Diana ran home. Presently Anne came down again, clothed and in her right mind. The muslin dress she had fondly hoped to wear was bobbing merrily about on the line outside, so she was forced to content herself with her black lawn. She had the fire on and the tea steeping when Diana returned; the latter wore HER muslin, at least, and carried a covered platter in her hand.

"Mother sent you this," she said, lifting the cover and displaying a nicely carved and jointed chicken to Anne's greatful eyes.

The chicken was supplemented by light new bread, excellent butter and cheese, Marilla's fruit cake and a dish of preserved plums, floating in their golden syrup as in congealed summer sunshine. There was a big bowlful of pink-and-white asters also, by way of decoration; yet the spread seemed very meager beside the elaborate one formerly prepared for Mrs. Morgan.

Anne's hungry guests, however, did not seem to think anything was lacking and they ate the simple viands with apparent enjoyment. But after the first few moments Anne thought no more of what was or was not on her bill of fare. Mrs. Morgan's appearance might be somewhat disappointing, as even her loyal worshippers had been forced to admit to each other; but she proved to be a delightful conversationalist. She had traveled extensively and was an excellent storyteller.

She had seen much of men and women, and crystalized her experiences into witty little sentences and epigrams which made her hearers feel as if they were listening to one of the people in clever books. But under all her sparkle there was a strongly felt undercurrent of true, womanly sympathy and kindheartedness which won affection as easily as her brilliancy won admiration. Nor did she monopolize the conversation. She could draw others out as skillfully and fully as she could talk herself, and Anne and Diana found themselves chattering freely to her. Mrs. Pendexter said little; she merely smiled with her lovely eyes and lips, and ate chicken and fruit cake and preserves with such exquisite grace that she conveyed the impression of dining on ambrosia and honeydew. But then, as Anne said to Diana later on, anybody so divinely beautiful as Mrs. Pendexter didn't need to talk; it was enough for her just to LOOK.

After dinner they all had a walk through Lover's Lane and Violet Vale and the Birch Path, then back through the Haunted Wood to the Dryad's Bubble, where they sat down and talked for a delightful last half hour. Mrs. Morgan wanted to know how the Haunted Wood came by its name, and laughed until she cried when she heard the story and Anne's dramatic account of a certain memorable walk through it at the witching hour of twilight.

"It has indeed been a feast of reason and flow of soul, hasn't it?" said Anne, when her guests had gone and she and Diana were alone again. "I don't know which I enjoyed more . . . listening to Mrs. Morgan or gazing at Mrs. Pendexter. I believe we had a nicer time than if we'd known they were coming and been cumbered with much serving. You must stay to tea with me, Diana, and we'll talk it all over."

"Priscilla says Mrs. Pendexter's husband's sister is married to an English earl; and yet she took a second helping of the plum preserves," said Diana, as if the two facts were somehow incompatible.

"I daresay even the English earl himself wouldn't have turned up his aristocratic nose at Marilla's plum preserves," said Anne proudly.

Anne did not mention the misfortune which had befallen HER nose when she related the day's history to Marilla that evening. But she took the bottle of freckle lotion and emptied it out of the window.

"I shall never try any beautifying messes again," she said, darkly resolute. "They may do for careful, deliberate people; but for anyone so hopelessly given over to making mistakes as I seem to be it's tempting fate to meddle with them."

XXI - Sweet Miss Lavendar

School opened and Anne returned to her work, with fewer theories but considerably more experience. She had several new pupils, six- and seven-year-olds just venturing, round-eyed, into a world of wonder. Among them were Davy and Dora. Davy sat with Milty Boulter, who had been going to school for a year and was therefore quite a man of the world. Dora had made a compact at Sunday School the previous Sunday to sit with Lily Sloane; but Lily Sloane not coming the first day, she was temporarily assigned to Mirabel Cotton, who was ten years old and therefore, in Dora's eyes, one of the "big girls."

"I think school is great fun," Davy told Marilla when he got home that night. "You said I'd find it hard to sit still and I did . . . you mostly do tell the truth, I notice . . . but you can wriggle your legs about under the desk and that helps a lot. It's splendid to have so many boys to play with. I sit with Milty Boulter and he's fine. He's longer than me but I'm wider. It's nicer to sit in the back seats but you can't sit there till your legs grow long enough to touch the floor. Milty drew a picture of Anne on his slate and it was awful ugly and I told him if he made pictures of Anne like that I'd lick him at recess. I thought first I'd draw one of him and put horns and a tail on it, but I was afraid it would hurt his feelings, and Anne says you should never hurt anyone's feelings. It seems it's dreadful to have your feelings hurt. It's better to knock a boy down than hurt his feelings if you MUST do something. Milty said he wasn't scared of me but he'd just as soon call it somebody else to 'blige me, so he rubbed out Anne's name and printed Barbara Shaw's under it. Milty doesn't like Barbara 'cause she calls him a sweet little boy and once she patted him on his head."

Dora said primly that she liked school; but she was very quiet, even for her; and when at twilight Marilla bade her go upstairs to bed she hesitated and began to cry.

"I'm . . . I'm frightened," she sobbed. "I . . . I don't want to go upstairs alone in the dark."

"What notion have you got into your head now?" demanded Marilla. "I'm sure you've gone to bed alone all summer and never been frightened before."

Dora still continued to cry, so Anne picked her up, cuddled her sympathetically, and whispered,

"Tell Anne all about it, sweetheart. What are you frightened of?"

"Of . . . of Mirabel Cotton's uncle," sobbed Dora. "Mirabel Cotton told me all about her family today in school. Nearly everybody in her family has died . . . all her grandfathers and grandmothers and ever so many uncles and aunts. They have a habit of dying, Mirabel says. Mirabel's awful proud of having so many dead relations, and she told me what they all died of, and what they said, and how they looked in their coffins. And Mirabel says one of her uncles was seen walking around the house after he was buried. Her mother saw him. I don't mind the rest so much but I can't help thinking about that uncle."

Anne went upstairs with Dora and sat by her until she fell asleep. The next day Mirabel Cotton was kept in at recess and "gently but firmly" given to understand that when you were so unfortunate as to possess an uncle who persisted in walking about houses after he had been decently interred it was not in good taste to talk about that eccentric gentleman to your deskmate of tender years. Mirabel thought this very harsh. The Cottons had not much to boast of. How was she to keep up her prestige among her schoolmates if she were forbidden to make capital out of the family ghost?

September slipped by into a gold and crimson graciousness of October. One Friday evening Diana came over.

"I'd a letter from Ella Kimball today, Anne, and she wants us to go over to tea tomorrow afternoon to meet her cousin, Irene Trent, from town. But we can't get one of our horses to go, for they'll all be in use tomorrow, and your pony is lame . . . so I suppose we can't go."

"Why can't we walk?" suggested Anne. "If we go straight back through the woods we'll strike the West Grafton road not far from the Kimball place. I was through that way last winter and I know the road. It's no more than four miles and we won't have to walk home, for Oliver Kimball will be sure to drive us. He'll be only too glad of the excuse, for he goes to see Carrie Sloane and they say his father will hardly ever let him have a horse."

It was accordingly arranged that they should walk, and the following afternoon they set out, going by way of Lover's Lane to the back of the Cuthbert farm, where they found a road leading into the heart of acres of glimmering beech and maple woods, which were all in a wondrous glow of flame and gold, lying in a great purple stillness and peace.

"It's as if the year were kneeling to pray in a vast cathedral full of mellow stained light, isn't it?" said Anne dreamily. "It doesn't seem right to hurry through it, does it? It seems irreverent, like running in a church."

"We MUST hurry though," said Diana, glancing at her watch. "We've left ourselves little enough time as it is."

"Well, I'll walk fast but don't ask me to talk," said Anne, quickening her pace. "I just want to drink the day's loveliness in . . . I feel as if she were holding it out to my lips like a cup of airy wine and I'll take a sip at every step."

Perhaps it was because she was so absorbed in "drinking it in" that Anne took the left turning when they came to a fork in the road. She should have taken the right, but ever afterward she counted it the most fortunate mistake of her life.

They came out finally to a lonely, grassy road, with nothing in sight along it but ranks of spruce saplings.

"Why, where are we?" exclaimed Diana in bewilderment. "This isn't the West Grafton road."

"No, it's the base line road in Middle Grafton," said Anne, rather shamefacedly. "I must have taken the wrong turning at the fork. I don't know where we are exactly, but we must be all of three miles from Kimballs' still."

"Then we can't get there by five, for it's half past four now," said Diana, with a despairing look at her watch. "We'll arrive after they have had their tea, and they'll have all the bother of getting ours over again."

"We'd better turn back and go home," suggested Anne humbly. But Diana, after consideration, vetoed this.

"No, we may as well go and spend the evening, since we have come this far."

A few yards further on the girls came to a place where the road forked again.

"Which of these do we take?" asked Diana dubiously.

Anne shook her head.

"I don't know and we can't afford to make any more mistakes. Here is a gate and a lane leading right into the wood. There must be a house at the other side. Let us go down and inquire."

"What a romantic old lane this it," said Diana, as they walked along its twists and turns. It ran under patriarchal old firs whose branches met above, creating a perpetual gloom in which nothing except moss could grow. On either hand were brown wood floors, crossed here and there by fallen lances of sunlight. All was very still and remote, as if the world and the cares of the world were far away.

"I feel as if we were walking through an enchanted forest," said Anne in a hushed tone. "Do you suppose we'll ever find our way back to the real world again, Diana? We shall presently come to a palace with a spellbound princess in it, I think."

Around the next turn they came in sight, not indeed of a palace, but of a little house almost as surprising as a palace would have been in this province of conventional wooden farmhouses, all as much alike in general characteristics as if they had grown from the same seed. Anne stopped short in rapture and Diana exclaimed, "Oh, I know where we are now. That is the little stone house where Miss Lavendar Lewis lives . . . Echo Lodge, she calls it, I think. I've often heard of it but I've never seen it before. Isn't it a romantic spot?"

"It's the sweetest, prettiest place I ever saw or imagined," said Anne delightedly. "It looks like a bit out of a story book or a dream."

The house was a low-eaved structure built of undressed blocks of red Island sandstone, with a little peaked roof out of which peered two dormer windows, with quaint wooden hoods over them, and two great chimneys. The whole house was covered with a luxuriant growth of ivy, finding easy foothold on the rough stonework and turned by autumn frosts to most beautiful bronze and wine-red tints.

Before the house was an oblong garden into which the lane gate where the girls were standing opened. The house bounded it on one side; on the three others it was enclosed by an old stone dyke, so overgrown with moss and grass and ferns that it looked like a high, green bank. On the right and left the tall, dark spruces spread their palm-like branches over it; but below it was a little meadow, green with clover aftermath, sloping down to the blue loop of the Grafton River. No other house or clearing was in sight . . . nothing but hills and valleys covered with feathery young firs.

"I wonder what sort of a person Miss Lewis is," speculated Diana as they opened the gate into the garden. "They say she is very peculiar."

"She'll be interesting then," said Anne decidedly. "Peculiar people are always that at least, whatever else they are or are not. Didn't I tell you we would come to an enchanted palace? I knew the elves hadn't woven magic over that lane for nothing."

"But Miss Lavendar Lewis is hardly a spellbound princess," laughed Diana. "She's an old maid . . . she's forty-five and quite gray, I've heard."

"Oh, that's only part of the spell," asserted Anne confidently. "At heart she's young and beautiful still . . . and if we only knew how to unloose the spell she would step forth radiant and fair again. But we don't know how . . . it's always and only the prince who knows that . . . and Miss Lavendar's prince hasn't come yet. Perhaps some fatal mischance has befallen him . . . though THAT'S against the law of all fairy tales."

"I'm afraid he came long ago and went away again," said Diana. "They say she used to be engaged to Stephan Irving . . . Paul's father . . . when they were young. But they quarreled and parted."

"Hush," warned Anne. "The door is open."

The girls paused in the porch under the tendrils of ivy and knocked at the open door. There was a patter of steps inside and a rather odd little personage presented herself . . . a girl of about fourteen, with a freckled face, a snub nose, a mouth so wide that it did really seem as if it stretched "from ear to ear," and two long braids of fair hair tied with two enormous bows of blue ribbon.

"Is Miss Lewis at home?" asked Diana.

"Yes, ma'am. Come in, ma'am. I'll tell Miss Lavendar you're here, ma'am. She's upstairs, ma'am."

With this the small handmaiden whisked out of sight and the girls, left alone, looked about them with delighted eyes. The interior of this wonderful little house was quite as interesting as its exterior.

The room had a low ceiling and two square, small-paned windows, curtained with muslin frills. All the furnishings were old-fashioned, but so well and daintily kept that the effect was delicious. But it must be candidly admitted that the most attractive feature, to two healthy girls who had just tramped four miles through autumn air, was a table, set out with pale blue china and laden with delicacies, while little golden-hued ferns scattered over the cloth gave it what Anne would have termed "a festal air."

"Miss Lavendar must be expecting company to tea," she whispered. "There are six places set. But what a funny little girl she has. She looked like a messenger from pixy land. I suppose she could have told us the road, but I was curious to see Miss Lavendar. S . . . s . . . sh, she's coming."

And with that Miss Lavendar Lewis was standing in the doorway. The girls were so surprised that they forgot good manners and simply stared. They had unconsciously been expecting to see the usual type of elderly spinster as known to their experience . . . a rather angular personage, with prim gray hair and spectacles. Nothing more unlike Miss Lavendar could possibly be imagined.

She was a little lady with snow-white hair beautifully wavy and thick, and carefully arranged in becoming puffs and coils. Beneath it was an almost girlish face, pink cheeked and sweet lipped, with big soft brown eyes and dimples . . . actually dimples. She wore a very dainty gown of cream muslin with pale-hued roses on it . . . a gown which would have seemed ridiculously juvenile on most women of her age, but which suited Miss Lavendar so perfectly that you never thought about it at all.

"Charlotta the Fourth says that you wished to see me," she said, in a voice that matched her appearance.

"We wanted to ask the right road to West Grafton," said Diana. "We are invited to tea at Mr. Kimball's, but we took the wrong path coming through the woods and came out to the base line instead of the West Grafton road. Do we take the right or left turning at your gate?"

"The left," said Miss Lavendar, with a hesitating glance at her tea table. Then she exclaimed, as if in a sudden little burst of resolution,

"But oh, won't you stay and have tea with me? Please, do. Mr. Kimball's will have tea over before you get there. And Charlotta the Fourth and I will be so glad to have you."

Diana looked mute inquiry at Anne.

"We'd like to stay," said Anne promptly, for she had made up her mind that she wanted to know more of this surprising Miss Lavendar, "if it won't inconvenience you. But you are expecting other guests, aren't you?"

Miss Lavendar looked at her tea table again, and blushed.

"I know you'll think me dreadfully foolish," she said. "I AM foolish . . . and I'm ashamed of it when I'm found out, but never unless I AM found out. I'm not expecting anybody . . . I was just pretending I was. You see, I was so lonely. I love company . . . that is, the right kind of company.. .but so few people ever come here because it is so far out of the way. Charlotta the Fourth was lonely too. So I just pretended I was going to have a tea party. I cooked for it . . . and decorated the table for it.. . and set it with my mother's wedding china . . . and I dressed up for it." Diana secretly thought Miss Lavendar quite as peculiar as report had pictured her. The idea of a woman of forty-five playing at having a tea party, just as if she were a little girl! But Anne of the shining eyes exclaimed joyfuly, "Oh, do YOU imagine things too?"

That "too" revealed a kindred spirit to Miss Lavendar.

"Yes, I do," she confessed, boldly. "Of course it's silly in anybody as old as I am. But what is the use of being an independent old maid if you can't be silly when you want to, and when it doesn't hurt anybody? A person must have some compensations. I don't believe I could live at times if I didn't pretend things. I'm not often caught at it though, and Charlotta the Fourth never tells. But I'm glad to be caught today, for you have really come and I have tea all ready for you. Will you go up to the spare room and take off your hats? It's the white door at the head of the stairs. I must run out to the kitchen and see that Charlotta the Fourth isn't letting the tea boil. Charlotta the Fourth is a very good girl but she WILL let the tea boil."

Miss Lavendar tripped off to the kitchen on hospitable thoughts intent and the girls found their way up to the spare room, an apartment as white as its door, lighted by the ivy-hung dormer window and looking, as Anne said, like the place where happy dreams grew.

"This is quite an adventure, isn't it?" said Diana. "And isn't Miss Lavendar sweet, if she IS a little odd? She doesn't look a bit like an old maid."

"She looks just as music sounds, I think," answered Anne.

When they went down Miss Lavendar was carrying in the teapot, and behind her, looking vastly pleased, was Charlotta the Fourth, with a plate of hot biscuits.

"Now, you must tell me your names," said Miss Lavendar. "I'm so glad you are young girls. I love young girls. It's so easy to pretend I'm a girl myself when I'm with them. I do hate" . . . with a little grimace . . . "to believe I'm old. Now, who are you . . . just for convenience' sake? Diana Barry? And Anne Shirley? May I pretend that I've known you for a hundred years and call you Anne and Diana right away?"

"You, may" the girls said both together.

"Then just let's sit comfily down and eat everything," said Miss Lavendar happily. "Charlotta, you sit at the foot and help with the chicken. It is so fortunate that I made the sponge cake and doughnuts. Of course, it was foolish to do it for imaginary guests . . . I know Charlotta the Fourth thought so, didn't you, Charlotta? But you see how well it has turned out. Of course they wouldn't have been wasted, for Charlotta the Fourth and I could have eaten them through time. But sponge cake is not a thing that improves with time."

That was a merry and memorable meal; and when it was over they all went out to the garden, lying in the glamor of sunset.

"I do think you have the loveliest place here," said Diana, looking round her admiringly.

"Why do you call it Echo Lodge?" asked Anne.

"Charlotta," said Miss Lavendar, "go into the house and bring out the little tin horn that is hanging over the clock shelf."

Charlotta the Fourth skipped off and returned with the horn.

"Blow it, Charlotta," commanded Miss Lavendar.

Charlotta accordingly blew, a rather raucous, strident blast. There was moment's stillness . . . and then from the woods over the river came a multitude of fairy echoes, sweet, elusive, silvery, as if all the "horns of elfland" were blowing against the sunset. Anne and Diana exclaimed in delight.

"Now laugh, Charlotta . . . laugh loudly."

Charlotta, who would probably have obeyed if Miss Lavendar had told her to stand on her head, climbed upon the stone bench and laughed loud and heartily. Back came the echoes, as if a host of pixy people were mimicking her laughter in the purple woodlands and along the fir-fringed points.

"People always admire my echoes very much," said Miss Lavendar, as if the echoes were her personal property. "I love them myself. They are very good company . . . with a little pretending. On calm evenings Charlotta the Fourth and I often sit out here and amuse ourselves with them. Charlotta, take back the horn and hang it carefully in its place."

"Why do you call her Charlotta the Fourth?" asked Diana, who was bursting with curiosity on this point.

"Just to keep her from getting mixed up with other Charlottas in my thoughts," said Miss Lavendar seriously. "They all look so much alike there's no telling them apart. Her name isn't really Charlotta at all. It is . . . let me see . . . what is it? I THINK it's Leonora . . . yes, it IS Leonora. You see, it is this way. When mother died ten years ago I couldn't stay here alone . . . and I couldn't afford to pay the wages of a grown-up girl. So I got little Charlotta Bowman to come and stay with me for board and clothes. Her name really was Charlotta . . . she was Charlotta the First. She was just thirteen. She stayed with me till she was sixteen and then she went away to Boston, because she could do better there. Her sister came to stay with me then. Her name was Julietta . . . Mrs. Bowman had a weakness for fancy names I think . . . but she looked so like Charlotta that I kept calling her that all the time . . .and she didn't mind. So I just gave up trying to remember her right name. She was Charlotta the Second, and when she went away Evelina came and she was Charlotta the Third. Now I have Charlotta the Fourth; but when she is sixteen . . . she's fourteen now . . . she will want to go to Boston too, and what I shall do then I really do not know. Charlotta the Fourth is the last of the Bowman girls, and the best. The other Charlottas always let me see that they thought it silly of me to pretend things but Charlotta the Fourth never does, no matter what she may really think. I don't care what people think about me if they don't let me see it."

"Well," said Diana looking regretfully at the setting sun. "I suppose we must go if we want to get to Mr. Kimball's before dark. We've had a lovely time, Miss Lewis."

"Won't you come again to see me?" pleaded Miss Lavendar.

Tall Anne put her arm about the little lady.

"Indeed we shall," she promised. "Now that we have discovered you we'll wear out our welcome coming to see you. Yes, we must go . . . 'we must tear ourselves away,' as Paul Irving says every time he comes to Green Gables."

"Paul Irving?" There was a subtle change in Miss Lavendar's voice. "Who is he? I didn't think there was anybody of that name in Avonlea."

Anne felt vexed at her own heedlessness. She had forgotten about Miss Lavendar's old romance when Paul's name slipped out.

"He is a little pupil of mine," she explained slowly. "He came from Boston last year to live with his grandmother, Mrs. Irving of the shore road."

"Is he Stephen Irving's son?" Miss Lavendar asked, bending over her name-sake border so that her face was hidden.

"Yes."

"I'm going to give you girls a bunch of lavendar apiece," said Miss Lavendar brightly, as if she had not heard the answer to her question. "It's very sweet, don't you think? Mother always loved it. She planted these borders long ago. Father named me Lavendar because he was so fond of it. The very first time he saw mother was when he visited her home in East Grafton with her brother. He fell in love with her at first sight; and they put him in the spare room bed to sleep and the sheets were scented with lavendar and he lay awake all night and thought of her. He always loved the scent of lavendar after that . . . and that was why he gave me the name. Don't forget to come back soon, girls dear. We'll be looking for you, Charlotta the Fourth and I."

She opened the gate under the firs for them to pass through. She looked suddenly old and tired; the glow and radiance had faded from her face; her parting smile was as sweet with ineradicable youth as ever, but when the girls looked back from the first curve in the lane they saw her sitting on the old stone bench under the silver poplar in the middle of the garden with her head leaning wearily on her hand.

"She does look lonely," said Diana softly. "We must come often to see her."

"I think her parents gave her the only right and fitting name that could possibly be given her," said Anne. "If they had been so blind as to name her Elizabeth or Nellie or Muriel she must have been called Lavendar just the same, I think. It's so suggestive of sweetness and old-fashioned graces and 'silk attire.' Now, my name just smacks of bread and butter, patchwork and chores."

"Oh, I don't think so," said Diana. "Anne seems to me real stately and like a queen. But I'd like Kerrenhappuch if it happened to be your name. I think people make their names nice or ugly just by what they are themselves. I can't bear Josie or Gertie for names now but before I knew the Pye girls I thought them real pretty."

"That's a lovely idea, Diana," said Anne enthusiastically. "Living so that you beautify your name, even if it wasn't beautiful to begin with . . . making it stand in people's thoughts for something so lovely and pleasant that they never think of it by itself. Thank you, Diana."

XXII - Odds and Ends

"So you had tea at the stone house with Lavendar Lewis?" said Marilla at the breakfast table next morning. "What is she like now? It's over fifteen years since I saw her last . . . it was one Sunday in Grafton church. I suppose she has changed a great deal. Davy Keith, when you want something you can't reach, ask to have it passed and don't spread yourself over the table in that fashion. Did you ever see Paul Irving doing that when he was here to meals?"

"But Paul's arms are longer'n mine," brumbled Davy. "They've had eleven years to grow and mine've only had seven. 'Sides, I DID ask, but you and Anne was so busy talking you didn't pay any 'tention. 'Sides, Paul's never been here to any meal escept tea, and it's easier to be p'lite at tea than at breakfast. You ain't half as hungry. It's an awful long while between supper and breakfast. Now, Anne, that spoonful ain't any bigger than it was last year and I'M ever so much bigger."

"Of course, I don't know what Miss Lavendar used to look like but I don't fancy somehow that she has changed a great deal," said Anne, after she had helped Davy to maple syrup, giving him two spoonfuls to pacify him. "Her hair is snow-white but her face is fresh and almost girlish, and she has the sweetest brown eyes . . . such a pretty shade of wood-brown with little golden glints in them . . . and her voice makes you think of white satin and tinkling water and fairy bells all mixed up together."

"She was reckoned a great beauty when she was a girl," said Marilla. "I never knew her very well but I liked her as far as I did know her. Some folks thought her peculiar even then. DAVY, if ever I catch you at such a trick again you'll be made to wait for your meals till everyone else is done, like the French."

Most conversations between Anne and Marilla in the presence of the twins, were punctuated by these rebukes Davy-ward. In this instance, Davy, sad to relate, not being able to scoop up the last drops of his syrup with his spoon, had solved the difficulty by lifting his plate in both hands and applying his small pink tongue to it. Anne looked at him with such horrified eyes that the little sinner turned red and said, half shamefacedly, half defiantly,

"There ain't any wasted that way."

"People who are different from other people are always called peculiar," said Anne. "And Miss Lavendar is certainly different, though it's hard to say just where the difference comes in. Perhaps it is because she is one of those people who never grow old."

"One might as well grow old when all your generation do," said Marilla, rather reckless of her pronouns. "If you don't, you don't fit in anywhere. Far as I can learn Lavendar Lewis has just dropped out of everything. She's lived in that out of the way place until everybody has forgotten her. That stone house is one of the oldest on the Island. Old Mr. Lewis built it eighty years ago when he came out from England. Davy, stop joggling Dora's elbow. Oh, I saw you! You needn't try to look innocent. What does make you behave so this morning?"

"Maybe I got out of the wrong side of the bed," suggested Davy. "Milty Boulter says if you do that things are bound to go wrong with you all day. His grandmother told him. But which is the right side? And what are you to do when your bed's against the wall? I want to know."

"I've always wondered what went wrong between Stephen Irving and Lavendar Lewis," continued Marilla, ignoring Davy. "They were certainly engaged twenty-five years ago and then all at once it was broken off. I don't know what the trouble was but it must have been something terrible, for he went away to the States and never come home since."

"Perhaps it was nothing very dreadful after all. I think the little things in life often make more trouble than the big things," said Anne, with one of those flashes of insight which experience could not have bettered. "Marilla, please don't say anything about my being at Miss Lavendar's to Mrs. Lynde. She'd be sure to ask a hundred questions and somehow I wouldn't like it . . . nor Miss Lavendar either if she knew, I feel sure."

"I daresay Rachel would be curious," admitted Marilla, "though she hasn't as much time as she used to have for looking after other people's affairs. She's tied home now on account of Thomas; and she's feeling pretty downhearted, for I think she's beginning to lose hope of his ever getting better. Rachel will be left pretty lonely if anything happens to him, with all her children settled out west, except Eliza in town; and she doesn't like her husband."

Marilla's pronouns slandered Eliza, who was very fond of her husband.

"Rachel says if he'd only brace up and exert his will power he'd get better. But what is the use of asking a jellyfish to sit up straight?" continued Marilla. "Thomas Lynde never had any will power to exert. His mother ruled him till he married and then Rachel carried it on. It's a wonder he dared to get sick without asking her permission. But there, I shouldn't talk so. Rachel has been a good wife to him. He'd never have amounted to anything without her, that's certain. He was born to be ruled; and it's well he fell into the hands of a clever, capable manager like Rachel. He didn't mind her way. It saved him the bother of ever making up his own mind about anything. Davy, do stop squirming like an eel."

"I've nothing else to do," protested Davy. "I can't eat any more, and it's no fun watching you and Anne eat."

"Well, you and Dora go out and give the hens their wheat," said Marilla. "And don't you try to pull any more feathers out of the white rooster's tail either."

"I wanted some feathers for an Injun headdress," said Davy sulkily. "Milty Boulter has a dandy one, made out of the feathers his mother give him when she killed their old white gobbler. You might let me have some. That rooster's got ever so many more'n he wants."

"You may have the old feather duster in the garret," said Anne, "and I'll dye them green and red and yellow for you."

"You do spoil that boy dreadfully," said Marilla, when Davy, with a radiant face, had followed prim Dora out. Marilla's education had made great strides in the past six years; but she had not yet been able to rid herself of the idea that it was very bad for a child to have too many of its wishes indulged.

"All the boys of his class have Indian headdresses, and Davy wants one too," said Anne. "*I* know how it feels . . . I'll never forget how I used to long for puffed sleeves when all the other girls had them. And Davy isn't being spoiled. He is improving every day. Think what a difference there is in him since he came here a year ago."

"He certainly doesn't get into as much mischief since he began to go to school," acknowledged Marilla. "I suppose he works off the tendency with the other boys. But it's a wonder to me we haven't heard from Richard Keith before this. Never a word since last May."

"I'll be afraid to hear from him," sighed Anne, beginning to clear away the dishes. "If a letter should come I'd dread opening it, for fear it would tell us to send the twins to him."

A month later a letter did come. But it was not from Richard Keith. A friend of his wrote to say that Richard Keith had died of consumption a fortnight previously. The writer of the letter was the executor of his will and by that will the sum of two thousand dollars was left to Miss Marilla Cuthbert in trust for David and Dora Keith until they came of age or married. In the meantime the interest was to be used for their maintenance.

"It seems dreadful to be glad of anything in connection with a death," said Anne soberly. "I'm sorry for poor Mr. Keith; but I AM glad that we can keep the twins."

"It's a very good thing about the money," said Marilla practically. "I wanted to keep them but I really didn't see how I could afford to do it, especially when they grew older. The rent of the farm doesn't do any more than keep the house and I was bound that not a cent of your money should be spent on them. You do far too much for them as it is. Dora didn't need that new hat you bought her any more than a cat needs two tails. But now the way is made clear and they are provided for."

Davy and Dora were delighted when they heard that they were to live at Green Gables, "for good." The death of an uncle whom they had never seen could not weigh a moment in the balance against that. But Dora had one misgiving.

"Was Uncle Richard buried?" she whispered to Anne.

"Yes, dear, of course."

"He . . . he . . . isn't like Mirabel Cotton's uncle, is he?" in a still more agitated whisper. "He won't walk about houses after being buried, will he, Anne?"

XXIII - Miss Lavendar's Romance

"I think I'll take a walk through to Echo Lodge this evening," said Anne, one Friday afternoon in December.

"It looks like snow," said Marilla dubiously.

"I'll be there before the snow comes and I mean to stay all night. Diana can't go because she has company, and I'm sure Miss Lavendar will be looking for me tonight. It's a whole fortnight since I was there."

Anne had paid many a visit to Echo Lodge since that October day. Sometimes she and Diana drove around by the road; sometimes they walked through the woods. When Diana could not go Anne went alone. Between her and Miss Lavendar had sprung up one of those fervent, helpful friendships possible only between a woman who has kept the freshness of youth in her heart and soul, and a girl whose imagination and intuition supplied the place of experience. Anne had at last discovered a real "kindred spirit," while into the little lady's lonely, seques- tered life of dreams Anne and Diana came with the wholesome joy and exhilaration of the outer existence, which Miss Lavendar, "the world forgetting, by the world forgot," had long ceased to share; they brought an atmosphere of youth and reality to the little stone house. Charlotta the Fourth always greeted them with her very widest smile . . . and Charlotta's smiles WERE fearfully wide . . . loving them for the sake of her adored mistress as well as for their own. Never had there been such "high jinks" held in the little stone house as were held there that beautiful, late-lingering autumn, when November seemed October over again, and even December aped the sunshine and hazes of summer.

But on this particular day it seemed as if December had remembered that it was time for winter and had turned suddenly dull and brooding, with a windless hush predictive of coming snow. Nevertheless, Anne keenly enjoyed her walk through the great gray maze of the beechlands; though alone she never found it lonely; her imagination peopled her path with merry companions, and with these she carried on a gay, pretended conversation that was wittier and more fascinating than conversations are apt to be in real life, where people sometimes fail most lamentably to talk up to the requirements. In a "make believe" assembly of choice spirits everybody says just the thing you want her to say and so gives you the chance to say just what YOU want to say. Attended by this invisible company,

Anne traversed the woods and arrived at the fir lane just as broad, feathery flakes began to flutter down softly.

At the first bend she came upon Miss Lavendar, standing under a big, broad-branching fir. She wore a gown of warm, rich red, and her head and shoulders were wrapped in a silvery gray silk shawl.

"You look like the queen of the fir wood fairies," called Anne merrily.

"I thought you would come tonight, Anne," said Miss Lavendar, running forward. "And I'm doubly glad, for Charlotta the Fourth is away. Her mother is sick and she had to go home for the night. I should have been very lonely if you hadn't come . . . even the dreams and the echoes wouldn't have been enough company. Oh, Anne, how pretty you are," she added suddenly, looking up at the tall, slim girl with the soft rose-flush of walking on her face. "How pretty and how young! It's so delightful to be seventeen, isn't it? I do envy you," concluded Miss Lavendar candidly.

"But you are only seventeen at heart," smiled Anne.

"No, I'm old . . . or rather middle-aged, which is far worse," sighed Miss Lavendar. "Sometimes I can pretend I'm not, but at other times I realize it. And I can't reconcile myself to it as most women seem to. I'm just as rebellious as I was when I discovered my first gray hair. Now, Anne, don't look as if you were trying to understand. Seventeen CAN'T understand. I'm going to pretend right away that I am seventeen too, and I can do it, now that you're here. You always bring youth in your hand like a gift. We're going to have a jolly evening. Tea first . . . what do you want for tea? We'll have whatever you like. Do think of something nice and indigestible."

There were sounds of riot and mirth in the little stone house that night. What with cooking and feasting and making candy and laughing and "pretending," it is quite true that Miss Lavendar and Anne comported themselves in a fashion entirely unsuited to the dignity of a spinster of forty-five and a sedate schoolma'am. Then, when they were tired, they sat down on the rug before the grate in the parlor, lighted only by the soft fireshine and perfumed deliciously by Miss Lavendar's open rose-jar on the mantel. The wind had risen and was sighing and wailing around the eaves and the snow was thudding softly against the windows, as if a hundred storm sprites were tapping for entrance.

"I'm so glad you're here, Anne," said Miss Lavendar, nibbling at her candy. "If you weren't I should be blue . . . very blue . . . almost navy blue. Dreams and make-believes are all very well in the daytime and the sunshine, but when dark and storm come they fail to satisfy. One wants real things then. But you don't know this . . . seventeen never knows it. At seventeen dreams DO satisfy because you think the realities are waiting for you further on. When I was seventeen, Anne, I didn't think forty-five would find me a white-haired little old maid with nothing but dreams to fill my life."

"But you aren't an old maid," said Anne, smiling into Miss Lavendar's wistful woodbrown eyes. "Old maids are BORN . . . they don't BECOME."

"Some are born old maids, some achieve old maidenhood, and some have old maidenhood thrust upon them," parodied Miss Lavendar whimsically.

"You are one of those who have achieved it then," laughed Anne, "and you've done it so beautifully that if every old maid were like you they would come into the fashion, I think."

"I always like to do things as well as possible," said Miss Lavendar meditatively, "and since an old maid I had to be I was determined to be a very nice one. People say I'm odd; but it's just because I follow my own way of being an old maid and refuse to copy the traditional pattern. Anne, did anyone ever tell you anything about Stephen Irving and me?"

"Yes," said Anne candidly, "I've heard that you and he were engaged once."

"So we were . . . twenty-five years ago . . . a lifetime ago. And we were to have been married the next spring. I had my wedding dress made, although nobody but mother and Stephen ever knew THAT. We'd been engaged in a way almost all our lives, you might say. When Stephen was a little boy his mother would bring him here when she came to see my mother; and the second time he ever came . . . he was nine and I was six . . . he told me out in the garden that he had pretty well made up his mind to marry me when he grew up. I remember that I said 'Thank you'; and when he was gone I told mother very gravely that there was a great weight off my mind, because I wasn't frightened any more about having to be an old maid. How poor mother laughed!"

"And what went wrong?" asked Anne breathlessly.

"We had just a stupid, silly, commonplace quarrel. So commonplace that, if you'll believe me, I don't even remember just how it began. I hardly know who was the more to blame for it. Stephen did really begin it, but I suppose I provoked him by some foolishness of mine. He had a rival or two, you see. I was vain and coquettish and liked to tease him a little. He was a very high-strung, sensitive fellow. Well, we parted in a temper on both sides. But I thought it would all come right; and it would have if Stephen hadn't come back too soon. Anne, my dear, I'm sorry to say" . . . Miss Lavendar dropped her voice as if she were about to confess a predilection for murdering people, "that I am a dreadfully sulky person. Oh, you needn't smile, . . . it's only too true. I DO sulk; and Stephen came back before I had finished sulking. I wouldn't listen to him and I wouldn't forgive him; and so he went away for good. He was too proud to come again. And then I sulked because he didn't come. I might have sent for him perhaps, but I couldn't humble myself to do that. I was just as proud as he was . . . pride and sulkiness make a very bad combination, Anne. But I could never care for anybody else and I didn't want to. I knew I would rather be an old maid for a thousand years than marry anybody who wasn't Stephen Irving. Well, it all seems like a dream now, of course. How sympathetic you look, Anne . . . as sympathetic as only seventeen can look. But don't overdo it. I'm really a very happy, contented little person in spite of my broken heart. My heart did break, if ever a heart did, when I realized that Stephen Irving was not coming back. But, Anne, a broken heart in real life isn't half as dreadful as it is in books. It's a good deal like a bad tooth . . . though you won't think THAT a very romantic simile. It takes spells of aching and gives you a sleepless night now and then, but between times it lets you enjoy life and dreams and echoes and peanut candy as if there were nothing the matter with it. And now you're looking disappointed. You don't think I'm half as interesting a person as you did five minutes ago when you believed I was always the prey of a tragic memory bravely hidden beneath external smiles. That's the worst . . . or the best . . . of real life, Anne. It WON'T let you be miserable. It keeps on trying to make you comfortable . . . and succeeding...even when you're determined to be unhappy and romantic. Isn't this candy scrumptious? I've eaten far more than is good for me already but I'm going to keep recklessly on."

After a little silence Miss Lavendar said abruptly,

"It gave me a shock to hear about Stephen's son that first day you were here, Anne. I've never been able to mention him to you since, but I've wanted to know all about him. What sort of a boy is he?"

"He is the dearest, sweetest child I ever knew, Miss Lavendar . . . and he pretends things too, just as you and I do."

"I'd like to see him," said Miss Lavendar softly, as if talking to herself. "I wonder if he looks anything like the little dream-boy who lives here with me . . . MY little dream-boy."

"If you would like to see Paul I'll bring him through with me sometime," said Anne.

"I would like it . . . but not too soon. I want to get used to the thought. There might be more pain than pleasure in it . . . if he looked too much like Stephen . . . or if he didn't look enough like him. In a month's time you may bring him."

Accordingly, a month later Anne and Paul walked through the woods to the stone house, and met Miss Lavendar in the lane. She had not been expecting them just then and she turned very pale.

"So this is Stephen's boy," she said in a low tone, taking Paul's hand and looking at him as he stood, beautiful and boyish, in his smart little fur coat and cap. "He . . . he is very like his father."

"Everybody says I'm a chip off the old block," remarked Paul, quite at his ease.

Anne, who had been watching the little scene, drew a relieved breath. She saw that Miss Lavendar and Paul had "taken" to each other, and that there would be no constraint or stiffness. Miss Lavendar was a very sensible person, in spite of her dreams and romance, and after that first little betrayal she tucked her feelings out of sight and entertained Paul as brightly and naturally as if he were anybody's son who had come to see her. They all had a jolly afternoon together and such a feast of fat things by way of supper as would have made old Mrs. Irving hold up her hands in horror, believing that Paul's digestion would be ruined for ever.

"Come again, laddie," said Miss Lavendar, shaking hands with him at parting.

"You may kiss me if you like," said Paul gravely.

Miss Lavendar stooped and kissed him.

"How did you know I wanted to?" she whispered.

"Because you looked at me just as my little mother used to do when she wanted to kiss me. As a rule, I don't like to be kissed. Boys don't. You know, Miss Lewis. But I think I rather like to have you kiss me. And of course I'll come to see you again. I think I'd like to have you for a particular friend of mine, if you don't object."

"I . . . I don't think I shall object," said Miss Lavendar. She turned and went in very quickly; but a moment later she was waving a gay and smiling good-bye to them from the window.

"I like Miss Lavendar," announced Paul, as they walked through the beech woods. "I like the way she looked at me, and I like her stone house, and I like Charlotta the Fourth. I wish Grandma Irving had a Charlotta the Fourth instead of a Mary Joe. I feel sure Charlotta the Fourth wouldn't think I was wrong in my upper story when I told her what I think about things. Wasn't that a splendid tea we had, teacher? Grandma says a boy shouldn't be thinking about what he gets to eat, but he can't help it sometimes when he is real hungry. YOU know, teacher. I don't think Miss Lavendar would make a boy eat porridge for breakfast if he didn't like it. She'd get things for him he did like. But of course" . . . Paul was nothing if not fair-minded . . . "that mightn't be very good for him. It's very nice for a change though, teacher. YOU know."

XXIV - A Prophet in His Own Country

One May day Avonlea folks were mildly excited over some "Avonlea Notes," signed "Observer," which appeared in the Charlottetown 'Daily Enterprise.' Gossip ascribed the authorship thereof to Charlie Sloane, partly because the said Charlie had indulged in similar literary flights in times past, and partly because one of the notes seemed to embody a sneer at Gilbert Blythe. Avonlea juvenile society persisted in regarding Gilbert Blythe and Charlie Sloane as rivals in the good graces of a certain damsel with gray eyes and an imagination.

Gossip, as usual, was wrong. Gilbert Blythe, aided and abetted by Anne, had written the notes, putting in the one about himself as a blind. Only two of the notes have any bearing on this history:

"Rumor has it that there will be a wedding in our village ere the daisies are in bloom. A new and highly respected citizen will lead to the hymeneal altar one of our most popular ladies.

"Uncle Abe, our well-known weather prophet, predicts a violent storm of thunder and lightning for the evening of the twenty-third of May, beginning at seven o'clock sharp. The area of the storm will extend over the greater part of the Province. People traveling that evening will do well to take umbrellas and mackintoshes with them."

"Uncle Abe really has predicted a storm for sometime this spring," said Gilbert, "but do you suppose Mr. Harrison really does go to see Isabella Andrews?"

"No," said Anne, laughing, "I'm sure he only goes to play checkers with Mr. Harrison Andrews, but Mrs. Lynde says she knows Isabella Andrews must be going to get married, she's in such good spirits this spring."

Poor old Uncle Abe felt rather indignant over the notes. He suspected that "Observer" was making fun of him. He angrily denied having assigned any particular date for his storm but nobody believed him.

Life in Avonlea continued on the smooth and even tenor of its way. The "planting" was put in; the Improvers celebrated an Arbor Day. Each Improver set out, or caused to be set out, five ornamental trees. As the society now numbered forty members, this meant a total of two hundred young trees. Early oats greened over the red fields; apple orchards flung great blossoming arms about the farmhouses and the Snow Queen adorned itself as a bride for her husband. Anne liked to sleep with her window open and let the cherry fragrance blow over her face all night. She thought it very poetical. Marilla thought she was risking her life.

"Thanksgiving should be celebrated in the spring," said Anne one evening to Marilla, as they sat on the front door steps and listened to the silver-sweet chorus of the frogs. "I think it would be ever so much better than having it in November when everything is dead or asleep. Then you have to remember to be thankful; but in May one simply can't help being thankful . . . that they are alive, if for nothing else. I feel exactly as Eve must have felt in the garden of Eden before the trouble began. IS that grass in the hollow green or golden? It seems to me, Marilla, that a pearl of a day like this, when the blossoms are out and the winds don't know where to blow from next for sheer crazy delight must be pretty near as good as heaven."

Marilla looked scandalized and glanced apprehensively around to make sure the twins were not within earshot. They came around the corner of the house just then.

"Ain't it an awful nice-smelling evening?" asked Davy, sniffing delightedly as he swung a hoe in his grimy hands. He had been working in his garden. That spring Marilla, by way of turning Davy's passion for reveling in mud and clay into useful channels, had given him and Dora a small plot of ground for a garden. Both had eagerly gone to work in a characteristic fashion. Dora planted, weeded, and watered carefully, systematically, and dispassionately. As a result, her plot was already green with prim, orderly little rows of vegetables and annuals. Davy, however, worked with more zeal than discretion; he dug and hoed and raked and watered and transplanted so energetically that his seeds had no chance for their lives.

"How is your garden coming on, Davy-boy?" asked Anne.

"Kind of slow," said Davy with a sigh. "I don't know why the things don't grow better. Milty Boulter says I must have planted them in the dark of the moon and that's the whole trouble. He says you must never sow seeds or kill pork or cut your hair or do any 'portant thing in the wrong time of the moon. Is that true, Anne? I want to know."

"Maybe if you didn't pull your plants up by the roots every other day to see how they're getting on 'at the other end,' they'd do better," said Marilla sarcastically.

"I only pulled six of them up," protested Davy. "I wanted to see if there was grubs at the roots. Milty Boulter said if it wasn't the moon's fault it must be grubs. But I only found one grub. He was a great big juicy curly grub. I put him on a stone and got another stone and smashed him flat. He made a jolly SQUISH I tell you. I was sorry there wasn't more of them. Dora's garden was planted same time's mine and her things are growing all right. It CAN'T be the moon," Davy concluded in a reflective tone.

"Marilla, look at that apple tree," said Anne. "Why, the thing is human. It is reaching out long arms to pick its own pink skirts daintily up and provoke us to admiration."

"Those Yellow Duchess trees always bear well," said Marilla complacently. "That tree'll be loaded this year. I'm real glad. . . they're great for pies."

But neither Marilla nor Anne nor anybody else was fated to make pies out of Yellow Duchess apples that year.

The twenty-third of May came . . . an unseasonably warm day, as none realized more keenly than Anne and her little beehive of pupils, sweltering over fractions and syntax in the Avonlea schoolroom. A hot breeze blew all the forenoon; but after noon hour it died away into a heavy stillness. At half past three Anne heard a low rumble of thunder. She promptly dismissed school at once, so that the children might get home before the storm came.

As they went out to the playground Anne perceived a certain shadow and gloom over the world in spite of the fact that the sun was still shining brightly. Annetta Bell caught her hand nervously.

"Oh, teacher, look at that awful cloud!"

Anne looked and gave an exclamation of dismay. In the northwest a mass of cloud, such as she had never in all her life beheld before, was rapidly rolling up. It was dead black, save where its curled and fringed edges showed a ghastly, livid white. There was something about it indescribably menacing as it gloomed up in the clear blue sky; now and again a bolt of lightning shot across it, followed by a savage growl. It hung so low that it almost seemed to be touching the tops of the wooded hills.

Mr. Harmon Andrews came clattering up the hill in his truck wagon, urging his team of grays to their utmost speed. He pulled them to a halt opposite the school.

"Guess Uncle Abe's hit it for once in his life, Anne," he shouted. "His storm's coming a leetle ahead of time. Did ye ever see the like of that cloud? Here, all you young ones, that are going my way, pile in, and those that ain't scoot for the post office if ye've more'n a quarter of a mile to go, and stay there till the shower's over."

Anne caught Davy and Dora by the hands and flew down the hill, along the Birch Path, and past Violet Vale and Willowmere, as fast as the twins' fat legs could go. They reached Green Gables not a moment too soon and were joined at the door by Marilla, who had been hustling her ducks and chickens under shelter. As they dashed into the kitchen the light seemed to vanish, as if blown out by some mighty breath; the awful cloud rolled over the sun and a darkness as of late twilight fell across the world. At the same moment, with a crash of thunder and a blinding glare of lightning, the hail swooped down and blotted the landscape out in one white fury.

Through all the clamor of the storm came the thud of torn branches striking the house and the sharp crack of breaking glass. In three minutes every pane in the west and north windows was broken and the hail poured in through the apertures covering the floor with stones, the smallest of which was as big as a hen's egg. For three quarters of an hour the storm raged unabated and no one who underwent it ever forgot it. Marilla, for once in her life shaken out of her composure by sheer terror, knelt by her rocking chair in a corner of the kitchen, gasping and sobbing between the deafening thunder peals. Anne, white as paper, had dragged the sofa away from the window and sat on it with a twin on either side. Davy at the first crash had howled, "Anne, Anne, is it the Judgment Day? Anne, Anne, I never meant to be naughty," and then had buried his face in Anne's lap and kept it there, his little body quivering. Dora, somewhat pale but quite composed, sat with her hand clasped in Anne's, quiet and motionless. It is doubtful if an earthquake would have disturbed Dora.

Then, almost as suddenly as it began, the storm ceased. The hail stopped, the thunder rolled and muttered away to the eastward, and the sun burst out merry and radiant over a world so changed that it seemed an absurd thing to think that a scant three quarters of an hour could have effected such a transformation.

Marilla rose from her knees, weak and trembling, and dropped on her rocker. Her face was haggard and she looked ten years older.

"Have we all come out of that alive?" she asked solemnly.

"You bet we have," piped Davy cheerfully, quite his own man again. "I wasn't a bit scared either . . . only just at the first. It come on a fellow so sudden. I made up my mind quick as a wink that I wouldn't fight Teddy Sloane Monday as I'd promised; but now maybe I will. Say, Dora, was you scared?"

"Yes, I was a little scared," said Dora primly, "but I held tight to Anne's hand and said my prayers over and over again."

"Well, I'd have said my prayers too if I'd have thought of it," said Davy; "but," he added triumphantly, "you see I came through just as safe as you for all I didn't say them."

Anne got Marilla a glassful of her potent currant wine . . . HOW potent it was Anne, in her earlier days, had had all too good reason to know . . . and then they went to the door to look out on the strange scene.

Far and wide was a white carpet, knee deep, of hailstones; drifts of them were heaped up under the eaves and on the steps. When, three or four days later, those hailstones melted, the havoc they had wrought was plainly seen, for every green growing thing in the field or garden was cut off. Not only was every blossom stripped from the apple trees but great boughs and branches were wrenched away. And out of the two hundred trees set out by the Improvers by far the greater number were snapped off or torn to shreds.

"Can it possibly be the same world it was an hour ago?" asked Anne, dazedly. "It MUST have taken longer than that to play such havoc."

"The like of this has never been known in Prince Edward Island," said Marilla, "never. I remember when I was a girl there was a bad storm, but it was nothing to this. We'll hear of terrible destruction, you may be sure."

"I do hope none of the children were caught out in it," murmured Anne anxiously. As it was discovered later, none of the children had been, since all those who had any distance to go had taken Mr. Andrews' excellent advice and sought refuge at the post office.

"There comes John Henry Carter," said Marilla.

John Henry came wading through the hailstones with a rather scared grin.

"Oh, ain't this awful, Miss Cuthbert? Mr. Harrison sent me over to see if yous had come out all right."

"We're none of us killed," said Marilla grimly, "and none of the buildings was struck. I hope you got off equally well."

"Yas'm. Not quite so well, ma'am. We was struck. The lightning knocked over the kitchen chimbly and come down the flue and knocked over Ginger's cage and tore a hole in the floor and went into the sullar. Yas'm."

"Was Ginger hurt?" queried Anne.

"Yas'm. He was hurt pretty bad. He was killed." Later on Anne went over to comfort Mr. Harrison. She found him sitting by the table, stroking Ginger's gay dead body with a trembling hand.

"Poor Ginger won't call you any more names, Anne," he said mournfully.

Anne could never have imagined herself crying on Ginger's account, but the tears came into her eyes.

"He was all the company I had, Anne . . . and now he's dead. Well, well, I'm an old fool to care so much. I'll let on I don't care. I know you're going to say something sympathetic as soon as I stop talking . . . but don't. If you did I'd cry like a baby. Hasn't this been a terrible storm? I guess folks won't laugh at Uncle Abe's predictions again. Seems as if all the storms that he's been prophesying all his life that never happened came all at once. Beats all how he struck the very day though, don't it? Look at the mess we have here. I must hustle round and get some boards to patch up that hole in the floor."

Avonlea folks did nothing the next day but visit each other and compare damages. The roads were impassable for wheels by reason of the hailstones, so they walked or rode on horseback. The mail came late with ill tidings from all over the province. Houses had been struck, people killed and injured; the whole telephone and telegraph system had been disorganized, and any number of young stock exposed in the fields had perished.

Uncle Abe waded out to the blacksmith's forge early in the morning and spent the whole day there. It was Uncle Abe's hour of triumph and he enjoyed it to the full. It would be doing Uncle Abe an injustice to say that he was glad the storm had happened; but since it had to be he was very glad he had predicted it . . . to the very day, too. Uncle Abe forgot that he had ever denied setting the day. As for the trifling discrepancy in the hour, that was nothing.

Gilbert arrived at Green Gables in the evening and found Marilla and Anne busily engaged in nailing strips of oilcloth over the broken windows.

"Goodness only knows when we'll get glass for them," said Marilla. "Mr. Barry went over to Carmody this afternoon but not a pane could he get for love or money. Lawson and Blair were cleaned out by the Carmody people by ten o'clock. Was the storm bad at White Sands, Gilbert?"

"I should say so. I was caught in the school with all the children and I thought some of them would go mad with fright. Three of them fainted, and two girls took hysterics, and Tommy Blewett did nothing but shriek at the top of his voice the whole time."

"I only squealed once," said Davy proudly. "My garden was all smashed flat," he continued mournfully, "but so was Dora's," he added in a tone which indicated that there was yet balm in Gilead.

Anne came running down from the west gable.

"Oh, Gilbert, have you heard the news? Mr. Levi Boulter's old house was struck and burned to the ground. It seems to me that I'm dreadfully wicked to feel glad over THAT, when so much damage has been done. Mr. Boulter says he believes the A.V.I.S. magicked up that storm on purpose."

"Well, one thing is certain," said Gilbert, laughing, "'Observer' has made Uncle Abe's reputation as a weather prophet. 'Uncle Abe's storm' will go down in local history. It is a most extraordinary coincidence that it should have come on the very day we selected. I actually have a half guilty feeling, as if I really had 'magicked' it up. We may as well rejoice over the old house being removed, for there's not much to rejoice over where our young trees are concerned. Not ten of them have escaped."

"Ah, well, we'll just have to plant them over again next spring," said Anne philosophically. "That is one good thing about this world . . . there are always sure to be more springs."

XXV - An Avonlea Scandal

One blithe June morning, a fortnight after Uncle Abe's storm, Anne came slowly through the Green Gables yard from the garden, carrying in her hands two blighted stalks of white narcissus.

"Look, Marilla," she said sorrowfully, holding up the flowers before the eyes of a grim lady, with her hair coifed in a green gingham apron, who was going into the house with a plucked chicken, "these are the only buds the storm spared . . . and even they are imperfect. I'm so sorry . . . I wanted some for Matthew's grave. He was always so fond of June lilies."

"I kind of miss them myself," admitted Marilla, "though it doesn't seem right to lament over them when so many worse things have happened. . . all the crops destroyed as well as the fruit."

"But people have sown their oats over again," said Anne comfortingly, "and Mr. Harrison says he thinks if we have a good summer they will come out all right though late. And my annuals are all coming up again . . . but oh, nothing can replace the June lilies. Poor little Hester Gray will have none either. I went all the way back to her garden last night but there wasn't one. I'm sure she'll miss them."

"I don't think it's right for you to say such things, Anne, I really don't," said Marilla severely. "Hester Gray has been dead for thirty years and her spirit is in heaven . . . I hope."

"Yes, but I believe she loves and remembers her garden here still," said Anne. "I'm sure no matter how long I'd lived in heaven I'd like to look down and see somebody putting flowers on my grave. If I had had a garden here like Hester Gray's it would take me more than thirty years, even in heaven, to forget being homesick for it by spells."

"Well, don't let the twins hear you talking like that," was Marilla's feeble protest, as she carried her chicken into the house.

Anne pinned her narcissi on her hair and went to the lane gate, where she stood for awhile sunning herself in the June brightness before going in to attend to her Saturday morning duties. The world was growing lovely again; old Mother Nature was doing her best to remove the traces of the storm, and, though she was not to succeed fully for many a moon, she was really accomplishing wonders.

"I wish I could just be idle all day today," Anne told a bluebird, who was singing and swinging on a willow bough, "but a schoolma'am, who is also helping to bring up twins, can't indulge in laziness, birdie. How sweet you are singing, little bird. You are just putting the feelings of my heart into song ever so much better than I could myself. Why, who is coming?"

An express wagon was jolting up the lane, with two people on the front seat and a big trunk behind. When it drew near Anne recognized the driver as the son of the station agent at Bright River; but his companion was a stranger . . . a scrap of a woman who sprang nimbly down at the gate almost before the horse came to a standstill. She was a very pretty little person, evidently nearer fifty than forty, but with rosy cheeks, sparkling black eyes, and shining black hair, surmounted by a wonderful beflowered and beplumed bonnet. In spite of having driven eight miles over a dusty road she was as neat as if she had just stepped out of the pro-verbial bandbox.

"Is this where Mr. James A. Harrison lives?" she inquired briskly.

"No, Mr. Harrison lives over there," said Anne, quite lost in astonishment.

"Well, I DID think this place seemed too tidy . . . MUCH too tidy for James A. to be living here, unless he has greatly changed since I knew him," chirped the little lady. "Is it true that James A. is going to be married to some woman living in this settlement?"

"No, oh no," cried Anne, flushing so guiltily that the stranger looked curiously at her, as if she half suspected her of matrimonial designs on Mr. Harrison.

"But I saw it in an Island paper," persisted the Fair Unknown. "A friend sent a marked copy to me . . . friends are always so ready to do such things. James A.'s name was written in over 'new citizen.'"

"Oh, that note was only meant as a joke," gasped Anne. "Mr. Harrison has no intention of marrying ANYBODY. I assure you he hasn't."

"I'm very glad to hear it," said the rosy lady, climbing nimbly back to her seat in the wagon, "because he happens to be married already. *I* am his wife. Oh, you may well look surprised. I suppose he has been masquerading as a bachelor and breaking hearts right and left. Well, well, James A.," nodding vigorously over the fields at the long white house, "your fun is over. I am here . . . though I wouldn't have bothered coming if I hadn't thought you were up to some mischief. I sup-pose," turning to Anne, "that parrot of his is as profane as ever?"

"His parrot . . . is dead . . . I THINK," gasped poor Anne, who couldn't have felt sure of her own name at that precise moment.

"Dead! Everything will be all right then," cried the rosy lady jubilantly. "I can manage James A. if that bird is out of the way."

With which cryptic utterance she went joyfully on her way and Anne flew to the kitchen door to meet Marilla.

"Anne, who was that woman?"

"Marilla," said Anne solemnly, but with dancing eyes, "do I look as if I were crazy?"

"Not more so than usual," said Marilla, with no thought of being sarcastic.

"Well then, do you think I am awake?"

"Anne, what nonsense has got into you? Who was that woman, I say?"

"Marilla, if I'm not crazy and not asleep she can't be such stuff as dreams are made of . . . she must be real. Anyway, I'm sure I couldn't have imagined such a bonnet. She says she is Mr. Harrison's wife, Marilla."

Marilla stared in her turn.

"His wife! Anne Shirley! Then what has he been passing himself off as an unmarried man for?"

"I don't suppose he did, really," said Anne, trying to be just. "He never said he wasn't married. People simply took it for granted. Oh Marilla, what will Mrs. Lynde say to this?"

They found out what Mrs. Lynde had to say when she came up that evening. Mrs. Lynde wasn't surprised! Mrs. Lynde had always expected something of the sort! Mrs. Lynde had always known there was SOMETHING about Mr. Harrison!

"To think of his deserting his wife!" she said indignantly. "It's like something you'd read of in the States, but who would expect such a thing to happen right here in Avonlea?"

"But we don't know that he deserted her," protested Anne, determined to believe her friend innocent till he was proved guilty. "We don't know the rights of it at all."

"Well, we soon will. I'm going straight over there," said Mrs. Lynde, who had never learned that there was such a word as delicacy in the dictionary. "I'm not supposed to know anything about her arrival, and Mr. Harrison was to bring some medicine for Thomas from Carmody today, so that will be a good excuse. I'll find out the whole story and come in and tell you on the way back."

Mrs. Lynde rushed in where Anne had feared to tread. Nothing would have induced the latter to go over to the Harrison place; but she had her natural and proper share of curiosity and she felt secretly glad that Mrs. Lynde was going to solve the mystery. She and Marilla waited expectantly for that good lady's return, but waited in vain. Mrs. Lynde did not revisit Green Gables that night. Davy, arriving home at nine o'clock from the Boulter place, explained why.

"I met Mrs. Lynde and some strange woman in the Hollow," he said, "and gracious, how they were talking both at once! Mrs. Lynde said to tell you she was sorry it was too late to call tonight. Anne, I'm awful hungry. We had tea at Milty's at four and I think Mrs. Boulter is real mean. She didn't give us any preserves or cake . . . and even the bread was skurce."

"Davy, when you go visiting you must never criticize anything you are given to eat," said Anne solemnly. "It is very bad manners."

"All right . . . I'll only think it," said Davy cheerfully. "Do give a fellow some supper, Anne."

Anne looked at Marilla, who followed her into the pantry and shut the door cautiously.

"You can give him some jam on his bread, I know what tea at Levi Boulter's is apt to be."

Davy took his slice of bread and jam with a sigh.

"It's a kind of disappointing world after all," he remarked. "Milty has a cat that takes fits . . . she's took a fit regular every day for three weeks. Milty says it's awful fun to watch her. I went down today on purpose to see her have one but the mean old thing wouldn't take a fit and just kept healthy as healthy, though Milty and me hung round all the afternoon and waited. But never mind" . . . Davy brightened up as the insidious comfort of the plum jam stole into his soul . . . "maybe I'll see her in one sometime yet. It doesn't seem likely she'd stop having them all at once when she's been so in the habit of it, does it? This jam is awful nice."

Davy had no sorrows that plum jam could not cure.

Sunday proved so rainy that there was no stirring abroad; but by Monday everybody had heard some version of the Harrison story. The school buzzed with it and Davy came home, full of information.

"Marilla, Mr. Harrison has a new wife . . . well, not ezackly new, but they've stopped being married for quite a spell, Milty says. I always s'posed people had to keep on being married once they'd begun, but Milty says no, there's ways of stopping if you can't agree. Milty says one way is just to start off and leave your wife, and that's what Mr. Harrison did. Milty says Mr. Harrison left his wife because she throwed things at him . . . HARD things . . . and Arty Sloane says it was because she wouldn't let him smoke, and Ned Clay says it was 'cause she never let up scolding him. I wouldn't leave MY wife for anything like that. I'd just put my foot down and say, 'Mrs. Davy, you've just got to do what'll please ME 'cause I'm a MAN.' THAT'D settle her pretty quick I guess. But Annetta Clay says SHE left HIM because he wouldn't scrape his boots at the door and she doesn't blame her. I'm going right over to Mr. Harrison's this minute to see what she's like."

Davy soon returned, somewhat cast down.

"Mrs. Harrison was away . . . she's gone to Carmody with Mrs. Rachel Lynde to get new paper for the parlor. And Mr. Harrison said to tell Anne to go over and see him 'cause he wants to have a talk with her. And say, the floor is scrubbed, and Mr. Harrison is shaved, though there wasn't any preaching yesterday."

The Harrison kitchen wore a very unfamiliar look to Anne. The floor was indeed scrubbed to a wonderful pitch of purity and so was every article of furniture in the room; the stove was polished until she could see her face in it; the walls were whitewashed and the window panes sparkled in the sunlight. By the table sat Mr. Harrison in his working clothes, which on Friday had been noted for sundry rents and tatters but which were now neatly patched and brushed. He was sprucely shaved and what little hair he had was carefully trimmed.

"Sit down, Anne, sit down," said Mr. Harrison in a tone but two degrees removed from that which Avonlea people used at funerals. "Emily's gone over to Carmody with Rachel Lynde . . . she's struck up a lifelong friendship already with Rachel Lynde. Beats all how contrary women are. Well, Anne, my easy times are over . . . all over. It's neatness and tidiness for me for the rest of my natural life, I suppose."

Mr. Harrison did his best to speak dolefully, but an irrepressible twinkle in his eye betrayed him.

"Mr. Harrison, you are glad your wife is come back," cried Anne, shaking her finger at him. "You needn't pretend you're not, because I can see it plainly."

Mr. Harrison relaxed into a sheepish smile.

"Well . . . well . . . I'm getting used to it," he conceded. "I can't say I was sorry to see Emily. A man really needs some protection in a community like this, where he can't play a game of checkers with a neighbor without being accused of wanting to marry that neighbor's sister and having it put in the paper."

"Nobody would have supposed you went to see Isabella Andrews if you hadn't pretended to be unmarried," said Anne severely.

"I didn't pretend I was. If anybody'd have asked me if I was married I'd have said I was. But they just took it for granted. I wasn't anxious to talk about the matter . . . I was feeling too sore over it. It would have been nuts for Mrs. Rachel Lynde if she had known my wife had left me, wouldn't it now?"

"But some people say that you left her."

"She started it, Anne, she started it. I'm going to tell you the whole story, for I don't want you to think worse of me than I deserve . . . nor of Emily neither. But let's go out on the veranda. Everything is so fearful neat in here that it kind of makes me homesick. I suppose I'll get used to it after awhile but it eases me up to look at the yard. Emily hasn't had time to tidy it up yet."

As soon as they were comfortably seated on the veranda Mr. Harrison began his tale of woe.

"I lived in Scottsford, New Brunswick, before I came here, Anne. My sister kept house for me and she suited me fine; she was just reasonably tidy and she let me alone and spoiled me . . . so Emily says. But three years ago she died. Before she died she worried a lot about what was to become of me and finally she got me to promise I'd get married. She advised me to take Emily Scott because Emily had money of her own and was a pattern housekeeper. I said, says I, 'Emily Scott wouldn't look at me.' 'You ask her and see,' says my sister; and just to ease her mind I promised her I would . . . and I did. And Emily said she'd have me. Never was so surprised in my life, Anne . . . a smart pretty little woman like her and an old fellow like me. I tell you I thought at first I was in luck. Well, we were married and took a little wedding trip to St. John for a fortnight and then we went home. We got home at ten o'clock at night, and I give you my word, Anne, that in half an hour that woman was at work housecleaning. Oh, I know you're thinking my house needed it . . . you've got a very expressive face, Anne; your thoughts just come out on it like print . . . but it didn't, not that bad. It had got pretty mixed up while I was keeping bachelor's hall, I admit, but I'd got a woman to come in and clean it up before I was married and there'd been considerable painting and fixing done. I tell you if you took Emily into a brand new white marble palace she'd be into the scrubbing as soon as she could get an old dress on. Well, she cleaned house till one o'clock that night and at four she was up and at it again. And she kept on that way . . . far's I could see she never stopped. It was scour and sweep and dust everlasting, except on Sundays, and then she was just longing for Monday to begin again. But it was her way of amusing herself and I could have reconciled myself to it if she'd left me alone. But that she wouldn't do. She'd set out to make me over but she hadn't caught me young enough. I wasn't allowed to come into the house unless I changed my boots for slippers at the door. I darsn't smoke a pipe for my life unless I went to the barn. And I didn't use good enough grammar. Emily'd been a schoolteacher in her early life and she'd never got over it. Then she hated to see me eating with my knife. Well, there it was, pick and nag everlasting. But I s'pose, Anne, to be fair, *I* was cantankerous too. I didn't try to improve as I might have done . . . I just got cranky and disagreeable when she found fault. I told her one day she hadn't complained of my grammar when I proposed to her. It wasn't an overly tactful thing to say. A woman would forgive a man for beating her sooner than for hinting she was too much pleased to get him. Well, we bickered along like that and it wasn't exactly pleasant, but we might have got used to each other after a spell if it hadn't been for Ginger. Ginger was the rock we split on at last. Emily didn't like parrots and she couldn't stand Ginger's profane habits of speech. I was attached to the bird for my brother the sailor's sake. My brother the sailor was a pet of mine when we were little tads and he'd sent Ginger to me when he was dying. I didn't see any sense in getting worked up over his swearing. There's nothing I hate worse'n profanity in a human being, but in a parrot, that's just repeating what it's heard with no more understanding of it than I'd have of Chinese, allowances might be made. But Emily couldn't see it that way. Women ain't logical. She tried to break Ginger of swearing but she hadn't any better success than she had in trying to make me stop saying 'I seen' and 'them things.' Seemed as if the more she tried the worse Ginger got, same as me.

"Well, things went on like this, both of us getting raspier, till the CLIMAX came. Emily invited our minister and his wife to tea, and another minister and HIS wife that was visiting them. I'd promised to put Ginger away in some safe place where nobody would hear him . . . Emily wouldn't touch his cage with a ten-foot pole . . . and I meant to do it, for I didn't want the ministers to hear anything unpleasant in my house. But it slipped my mind . . . Emily was worrying me so much about clean collars and grammar that it wasn't any wonder . . . and I never thought of that poor parrot till we sat down to tea. Just as minister number one was in the very middle of saying grace, Ginger, who was on the veranda outside the dining room window, lifted up HIS voice. The gobbler had come into view in the yard and the sight of a gobbler always had an unwholesome effect on Ginger. He surpassed himself that time. You can smile, Anne, and I don't deny I've chuckled some over it since myself, but at the time I felt almost as much mortified as Emily. I went out and carried Ginger to the barn. I can't say I enjoyed the meal. I knew by the look of Emily that there was trouble brewing for Ginger and James A. When the folks went away I started for the cow pasture and on the way I did some thinking. I felt sorry for Emily and kind of fancied I hadn't been so thoughtful of her as I might; and besides, I wondered if the ministers would think that

Ginger had learned his vocabulary from me. The long and short of it was, I decided that Ginger would have to be mercifully disposed of and when I'd druv the cows home I went in to tell Emily so. But there was no Emily and there was a letter on the table . . . just according to the rule in story books. Emily writ that I'd have to choose between her and Ginger; she'd gone back to her own house and there she would stay till I went and told her I'd got rid of that parrot.

"I was all riled up, Anne, and I said she might stay till doomsday if she waited for that; and I stuck to it. I packed up her belongings and sent them after her. It made an awful lot of talk . . . Scottsford was pretty near as bad as Avonlea for gossip . . . and everybody sympathized with Emily. It kept me all cross and cantankerous and I saw I'd have to get out or I'd never have any peace. I concluded I'd come to the Island. I'd been here when I was a boy and I liked it; but Emily had always said she wouldn't live in a place where folks were scared to walk out after dark for fear they'd fall off the edge. So, just to be contrary, I moved over here. And that's all there is to it. I hadn't ever heard a word from or about Emily till I come home from the back field Saturday and found her scrubbing the floor but with the first decent dinner I'd had since she left me all ready on the table. She told me to eat it first and then we'd talk . . . by which I concluded that Emily had learned some lessons about getting along with a man. So she's here and she's going to stay . . . seeing that Ginger's dead and the Island's some bigger than she thought. There's Mrs. Lynde and her now. No, don't go, Anne. Stay and get acquainted with Emily. She took quite a notion to you Saturday . . . wanted to know who that handsome redhaired girl was at the next house."

Mrs. Harrison welcomed Anne radiantly and insisted on her staying to tea.

"James A. has been telling me all about you and how kind you've been, making cakes and things for him," she said. "I want to get acquainted with all my new neighbors just as soon as possible. Mrs. Lynde is a lovely woman, isn't she? So friendly."

When Anne went home in the sweet June dusk, Mrs. Harrison went with her across the fields where the fireflies were lighting their starry lamps.

"I suppose," said Mrs. Harrison confidentially, "that James A. has told you our story?"

"Yes."

"Then I needn't tell it, for James A. is a just man and he would tell the truth. The blame was far from being all on his side. I can see that now. I wasn't back in my own house an hour before I wished I hadn't been so hasty but I wouldn't give in. I see now that I expected too much of a man. And I was real foolish to mind his bad grammar. It doesn't matter if a man does use bad grammar so long as he is a good provider and doesn't go poking round the pantry to see how much sugar you've used in a week. I feel that James A. and I are going to be real happy now. I wish I knew who 'Observer' is, so that I could thank him. I owe him a real debt of gratitude."

Anne kept her own counsel and Mrs. Harrison never knew that her gratitude found its way to its object. Anne felt rather bewildered over the far-reaching consequences of those foolish "notes." They had reconciled a man to his wife and made the reputation of a prophet.

Mrs. Lynde was in the Green Gables kitchen. She had been telling the whole story to Marilla.

"Well, and how do you like Mrs. Harrison?" she asked Anne.

"Very much. I think she's a real nice little woman."

"That's exactly what she is," said Mrs. Rachel with emphasis, "and as I've just been sayin' to Marilla, I think we ought all to overlook Mr. Harrison's peculiarities for her sake and try to make her feel at home here, that's what. Well, I must get back. Thomas'll be wearying for me. I get out a little since Eliza came and he's seemed a lot better these past few days, but I never like to be long away from him. I hear Gilbert Blythe has resigned from White Sands. He'll be off to college in the fall, I suppose."

Mrs. Rachel looked sharply at Anne, but Anne was bending over a sleepy Davy nodding on the sofa and nothing was to be read in her face. She carried Davy away, her oval girlish cheek pressed against his curly yellow head. As they went up the stairs Davy flung a tired arm about Anne's neck and gave her a warm hug and a sticky kiss.

"You're awful nice, Anne. Milty Boulter wrote on his slate today and showed it to Jennie Sloane,

"'Roses red and vi'lets blue,
Sugar's sweet, and so are you'

and that 'spresses my feelings for you ezackly, Anne."

XXVI - Around the Bend

Thomas Lynde faded out of life as quietly and unobtrusively as he had lived it. His wife was a tender, patient, unwearied nurse. Sometimes Rachel had been a little hard on her Thomas in health, when his slowness or meekness had provoked her; but when he became ill no voice could be lower, no hand more gently skillful, no vigil more uncomplaining.

"You've been a good wife to me, Rachel," he once said simply, when she was sitting by him in the dusk, holding his thin, blanched old hand in her work-hardened one. "A good wife. I'm sorry I ain't leaving you better off; but the children will look after you. They're all smart, capable children, just like their mother. A good mother . . . a good woman . . . ."

He had fallen asleep then, and the next morning, just as the white dawn was creeping up over the pointed firs in the hollow, Marilla went softly into the east gable and wakened Anne.

"Anne, Thomas Lynde is gone . . . their hired boy just brought the word. I'm going right down to Rachel."

On the day after Thomas Lynde's funeral Marilla went about Green Gables with a strangely preoccupied air. Occasionally she looked at Anne, seemed on the point of saying something, then shook her head and buttoned up her mouth. After tea she went down to see Mrs. Rachel; and when she returned she went to the east gable, where Anne was correcting school exercises.

"How is Mrs. Lynde tonight?" asked the latter.

"She's feeling calmer and more composed," answered Marilla, sitting down on Anne's bed . . . a proceeding which betokened some unusual mental excitement, for in Marilla's code of household ethics to sit on a bed after it was made up was an unpardonable offense. "But she's very lonely. Eliza had to go home today . . . her son isn't well and she felt she couldn't stay any longer."

"When I've finished these exercises I'll run down and chat awhile with Mrs. Lynde," said Anne. "I had intended to study some Latin composition tonight but it can wait."

"I suppose Gilbert Blythe is going to college in the fall," said Marilla jerkily. "How would you like to go too, Anne?"

Anne looked up in astonishment.

"I would like it, of course, Marilla. But it isn't possible."

"I guess it can be made possible. I've always felt that you should go. I've never felt easy to think you were giving it all up on my account."

"But Marilla, I've never been sorry for a moment that I stayed home. I've been so happy . . . Oh, these past two years have just been delightful."

"Oh, yes, I know you've been contented enough. But that isn't the question exactly. You ought to go on with your education. You've saved enough to put you through one year at Redmond and the money the stock brought in will do for another year . . . and there's scholarships and things you might win."

"Yes, but I can't go, Marilla. Your eyes are better, of course; but I can't leave you alone with the twins. They need so much looking after."

"I won't be alone with them. That's what I meant to discuss with you. I had a long talk with Rachel tonight. Anne, she's feeling dreadful bad over a good many things. She's not left very well off. It seems they mortgaged the farm eight years ago to give the youngest boy a start when he went west; and they've never been able to pay much more than the interest since. And then of course Thomas' illness has cost a good deal, one way or another. The farm will have to be sold and Rachel thinks there'll be hardly anything left after the bills are settled. She says she'll have to go and live with Eliza and it's breaking her heart to think of leaving Avonlea. A woman of her age doesn't make new friends and interests easy. And, Anne, as she talked about it the thought came to me that I would ask her to come and live with me, but I thought I ought to talk it over with you first before I said anything to her. If I had Rachel living with me you could go to college. How do you feel about it?"

"I feel . . . as if . . . somebody . . . had handed me . . . the moon . . . and I didn't know . . . exactly . . . what to do . . . with it," said Anne dazedly. "But as for asking Mrs. Lynde to come here, that is for you to decide, Marilla. Do you think . . . are you sure . . . you would like it? Mrs. Lynde is a good woman and a kind neighbor, but . . . but . . ."

"But she's got her faults, you mean to say? Well, she has, of course; but I think I'd rather put up with far worse faults than see Rachel go away from Avonlea. I'd miss her terrible. She's the only close friend I've got here and I'd be lost without her. We've been neighbors for forty-five years and we've never had a quarrel . . . though we came rather near it that time you flew at Mrs. Rachel for calling you homely and redhaired. Do you remember, Anne?"

"I should think I do," said Anne ruefully. "People don't forget things like that. How I hated poor Mrs. Rachel at that moment!"

"And then that 'apology' you made her. Well, you were a handful, in all conscience, Anne. I did feel so puzzled and bewildered how to manage you. Matthew understood you better."

"Matthew understood everything," said Anne softly, as she always spoke of him.

"Well, I think it could be managed so that Rachel and I wouldn't clash at all. It always seemed to me that the reason two women can't get along in one house is that they try to share the same kitchen and get in each other's way. Now, if Rachel came here, she could have the north gable for her bedroom and the spare room for a kitchen as well as not, for we don't really need a spare room at all. She could put her stove there and what furniture she wanted to keep, and be real comfortable and independent. She'll have enough to live on of course...her children'll see to that...so all I'd be giving her would be house room. Yes, Anne, far as I'm concerned I'd like it."

"Then ask her," said Anne promptly. "I'd be very sorry myself to see Mrs. Rachel go away."

"And if she comes," continued Marilla, "You can go to college as well as not. She'll be company for me and she'll do for the twins what I can't do, so there's no reason in the world why you shouldn't go."

Anne had a long meditation at her window that night. Joy and regret struggled together in her heart. She had come at last . . . suddenly and unexpectedly . . . to the bend in the road; and college was around it, with a hundred rainbow hopes and visions; but Anne realized as well that when she rounded that curve she must leave many sweet things behind. . . all the little simple duties and interests which had grown so dear to her in the last two years and which she had glorified into beauty and delight by the enthusiasm she had put into them. She must give up her school . . . and she loved every one of her pupils, even the stupid and naughty ones. The mere thought of Paul Irving made her wonder if Redmond were such a name to conjure with after all.

"I've put out a lot of little roots these two years," Anne told the moon, "and when I'm pulled up they're going to hurt a great deal. But it's best to go, I think, and, as Marilla says, there's no good reason why I shouldn't. I must get out all my ambitions and dust them."

Anne sent in her resignation the next day; and Mrs. Rachel, after a heart to heart talk with Marilla, gratefully accepted the offer of a home at Green Gables. She elected to remain in her own house for the summer, however; the farm was not to be sold until the fall and there were many arrangements to be made.

"I certainly never thought of living as far off the road as Green Gables," sighed Mrs. Rachel to herself. "But really, Green Gables doesn't seem as out of the world as it used to do . . . Anne has lots of company and the twins make it real lively. And anyhow, I'd rather live at the bottom of a well than leave Avonlea."

These two decisions being noised abroad speedily ousted the arrival of Mrs. Harrison in popular gossip. Sage heads were shaken over Marilla Cuthbert's rash step in asking Mrs. Rachel to live with her. People opined that they wouldn't get on together. They were both "too fond of their own way," and many doleful predictions were made, none of which disturbed the parties in question at all. They had come to a clear and distinct understanding of the respective duties and rights of their new arrangements and meant to abide by them.

"I won't meddle with you nor you with me," Mrs. Rachel had said decidedly, "and as for the twins, I'll be glad to do all I can for them; but I won't undertake to answer Davy's questions, that's what. I'm not an encyclopedia, neither am I a Philadelphia lawyer. You'll miss Anne for that."

"Sometimes Anne's answers were about as queer as Davy's questions," said Marilla drily. "The twins will miss her and no mistake; but her future can't be sacrificed to Davy's thirst for information. When he asks questions I can't answer I'll just tell him children should be seen and not heard. That was how I was brought up, and I don't know but what it was just as good a way as all these new-fangled notions for training children."

"Well, Anne's methods seem to have worked fairly well with Davy," said Mrs. Lynde smilingly. "He is a reformed character, that's what."

"He isn't a bad little soul," conceded Marilla. "I never expected to get as fond of those children as I have. Davy gets round you somehow . . . and Dora is a lovely child, although she is . . . kind of . . . well, kind of . . ."

"Monotonous? Exactly," supplied Mrs. Rachel. "Like a book where every page is the same, that's what. Dora will make a good, reliable woman but she'll never set the pond on fire. Well, that sort of folks are comfortable to have round, even if they're not as interesting as the other kind."

Gilbert Blythe was probably the only person to whom the news of Anne's resignation brought unmixed pleasure. Her pupils looked upon it as a sheer catastrophe. Annetta Bell had hysterics when she went home. Anthony Pye fought two pitched and unprovoked battles with other boys by way of relieving his feelings. Barbara Shaw cried all night. Paul Irving defiantly told his grandmother that she needn't expect him to eat any porridge for a week.

"I can't do it, Grandma," he said. "I don't really know if I can eat ANYTHING. I feel as if there was a dreadful lump in my throat. I'd have cried coming home from school if Jake Donnell hadn't been watching me. I believe I will cry after I go to bed. It wouldn't show on my eyes tomorrow, would it? And it would be such a relief. But anyway, I can't eat porridge. I'm going to need all my strength of mind to bear up against this, Grandma, and I won't have any left to grapple with porridge. Oh Grandma, I don't know what I'll do when my beautiful teacher goes away. Milty Boulter says he bets Jane Andrews will get the school. I suppose Miss Andrews is very nice. But I know she won't understand things like Miss Shirley."

Diana also took a very pessimistic view of affairs.

"It will be horribly lonesome here next winter," she mourned, one twilight when the moonlight was raining "airy silver" through the cherry boughs and filling the east gable with a soft, dream-like radiance in which the two girls sat and talked, Anne on her low rocker by the window, Diana sitting Turkfashion on the bed. "You and Gilbert will be gone . . . and the Allans too. They are going to call Mr. Allan to Charlottetown and of course he'll accept. It's too mean. We'll be vacant all winter, I suppose, and have to listen to a long string of candidates . . . and half of them won't be any good."

"I hope they won't call Mr. Baxter from East Grafton here, anyhow," said Anne decidedly. "He wants the call but he does preach such gloomy sermons. Mr. Bell says he's a minister of the old school, but Mrs. Lynde says there's nothing whatever the matter with him but indigestion. His wife isn't a very good cook, it seems, and Mrs. Lynde says that when a man has to eat sour bread two weeks out of three his theology is bound to get a kink in it somewhere. Mrs. Allan feels very badly about going away. She says everybody has been so kind to her since she came here as a bride that she feels as if she were leaving lifelong friends. And then, there's the baby's grave, you know. She says she doesn't see how she can go away and leave that . . . it was such a little mite of a thing and only three months old, and she says she is afraid it will miss its mother, although she knows better and wouldn't say so to Mr. Allan for anything. She says she has slipped through the birch grove back of the manse nearly every night to the graveyard and sung a little lullaby to it. She told me all about it last evening when I was up putting some of those early wild roses on Matthew's grave. I promised her that as long as I was in Avonlea I would put flowers on the baby's grave and when I was away I felt sure that . . ."

"That I would do it," supplied Diana heartily. "Of course I will. And I'll put them on Matthew's grave too, for your sake, Anne."

"Oh, thank you. I meant to ask you to if you would. And on little Hester Gray's too? Please don't forget hers. Do you know, I've thought and dreamed so much about little Hester Gray that she has become strangely real to me. I think of her, back there in her little garden in that cool, still, green corner; and I have a fancy that if I could steal back there some spring evening, just at the magic time 'twixt light and dark, and tiptoe so softly up the beech hill that my footsteps could not frighten her, I would find the garden just as it used to be, all sweet with June lilies and early roses, with the tiny house beyond it all hung with vines; and little Hester Gray would be there, with her soft eyes, and the wind ruffling her dark hair, wandering about, putting her fingertips under the chins of the lilies and whispering secrets with the roses; and I would go forward, oh, so softly, and hold out my hands and say to her, 'Little Hester Gray, won't you let me be your playmate, for I love the roses too?' And we would sit down on the old bench and talk a little and dream a little, or just be beautifully silent together. And then the moon would rise and I would look around me . . . and there would be no Hester Gray and no little vine-hung house, and no roses . . . only an old waste garden starred with June lilies amid the grasses, and the wind sighing, oh, so sorrowfully in the cherry trees. And I would not know whether it had been real or if I had just imagined it all."

Diana crawled up and got her back against the headboard of the bed. When your companion of twilight hour said such spooky things it was just as well not to be able to fancy there was anything behind you.

"I'm afraid the Improvement Society will go down when you and Gilbert are both gone," she remarked dolefully.

"Not a bit of fear of it," said Anne briskly, coming back from dreamland to the affairs of practical life. "It is too firmly established for that, especially since the older people are becoming so enthusiastic about it. Look what they are doing this summer for their lawns and lanes. Besides, I'll be watching for hints at Redmond and I'll write a paper for it next winter and send it over. Don't take such a gloomy view of things, Diana. And don't grudge me my little hour of gladness and jubilation now. Later on, when I have to go away, I'll feel anything but glad."

"It's all right for you to be glad . . . you're going to college and you'll have a jolly time and make heaps of lovely new friends."

"I hope I shall make new friends," said Anne thoughtfully. "The possibilities of making new friends help to make life very fascinating. But no matter how many friends I make they'll never be as dear to me as the old ones . . . especially a certain girl with black eyes and dimples. Can you guess who she is, Diana?"

"But there'll be so many clever girls at Redmond," sighed Diana, "and I'm only a stupid little country girl who says 'I seen' sometimes. . . though I really know better when I stop to think. Well, of course these past two years have really been too pleasant to last. I know SOMEBODY who is glad you are going to Redmond anyhow. Anne, I'm going to ask you a question . . . a serious question. Don't be vexed and do answer seriously. Do you care anything for Gilbert?"

"Ever so much as a friend and not a bit in the way you mean," said Anne calmly and decidedly; she also thought she was speaking sincerely.

Diana sighed. She wished, somehow, that Anne had answered differently.

"Don't you mean EVER to be married, Anne?"

"Perhaps . . . some day . . . when I meet the right one," said Anne, smiling dreamily up at the moonlight.

"But how can you be sure when you do meet the right one?" persisted Diana.

"Oh, I should know him . . . SOMETHING would tell me. You know what my ideal is, Diana."

"But people's ideals change sometimes."

"Mine won't. And I COULDN'T care for any man who didn't fulfill it."

"What if you never meet him?"

"Then I shall die an old maid," was the cheerful response. "I daresay it isn't the hardest death by any means."

"Oh, I suppose the dying would be easy enough; it's the living an old maid I shouldn't like," said Diana, with no intention of being humorous. "Although I wouldn't mind being an old maid VERY much if I could be one like Miss Lavendar. But I never could be. When I'm forty-five I'll be horribly fat. And while there might be some romance about a thin old maid there couldn't possibly be any about a fat one. Oh, mind you, Nelson Atkins proposed to Ruby Gillis three weeks ago. Ruby told me all about it. She says she never had any intention of taking him, because any one who married him will have to go in with the old folks; but Ruby says that he made such a perfectly beautiful and romantic proposal that it simply swept her off her feet. But she didn't want to do anything rash so she asked for a week to consider; and two days later she was at a meeting of the Sewing Circle at his mother's and there was a book called 'The Complete Guide to Etiquette,' lying on the parlor table. Ruby said she simply couldn't describe her feelings when in a section of it headed, 'The Deportment of Courtship and Marriage,' she found the very proposal Nelson had made, word for word. She went home and wrote him a perfectly scathing refusal; and she says his father and mother have taken turns watching him ever since for fear he'll drown himself in the river; but Ruby says they needn't be afraid; for in the Deportment of Courtship and Marriage it told how a rejected lover should behave and there's nothing about drowning in THAT. And she says Wilbur Blair is literally pining away for her but she's perfectly helpless in the matter."

Anne made an impatient movement.

"I hate to say it . . . it seems so disloyal . . . but, well, I don't like Ruby Gillis now. I liked her when we went to school and Queen's together . . . though not so well as you and Jane of course. But this last year at Carmody she seems so different . . . so . . . so . . ."

"I know," nodded Diana. "It's the Gillis coming out in her . . . she can't help it. Mrs. Lynde says that if ever a Gillis girl thought about anything but the boys she never showed it in her walk and conversation. She talks about nothing but boys and what compliments they pay her, and how crazy they all are about her at Carmody. And the strange thing is, they ARE, too . . ." Diana admitted this somewhat resentfully. "Last night when I saw her in Mr. Blair's store she whispered to me that she'd just made a new 'mash.' I wouldn't ask her who it was, because I knew she was dying to BE asked. Well, it's what Ruby always wanted, I suppose. You remember even when she was little she always said she meant to have dozens of beaus when she grew up and have the very gayest time she could before she settled down. She's so different from Jane, isn't she? Jane is such a nice, sensible, lady-like girl."

"Dear old Jane is a jewel," agreed Anne, "but," she added, leaning forward to bestow a tender pat on the plump, dimpled little hand hanging over her pillow, "there's nobody like my own Diana after all. Do you remember that evening we first met, Diana, and 'swore' eternal friendship in your garden? We've kept that 'oath,' I think . . . we've never had a quarrel nor even a coolness. I shall never forget the thrill that went over me the day you told me you loved me. I had had such a lonely, starved heart all through my childhood. I'm just beginning to realize how starved and lonely it really was. Nobody cared anything for me or wanted to be bothered with me. I should have been miserable if it hadn't been for that strange little dream-life of mine, wherein I imagined all the friends and love I craved. But when I came to Green Gables everything was changed. And then I met you. You don't know what your friendship meant to me. I want to thank you here and now, dear, for the warm and true affection you've always given me."

"And always, always will," sobbed Diana. "I shall NEVER love anybody . . . any GIRL . . . half as well as I love you. And if I ever do marry and have a little girl of my own I'm going to name her ANNE."

XXVII - An Afternoon at the Stone House

"Where are you going, all dressed up, Anne?" Davy wanted to know. "You look bully in that dress."

Anne had come down to dinner in a new dress of pale green muslin . . . the first color she had worn since Matthew's death. It became her perfectly, bringing out all the delicate, flower-like tints of her face and the gloss and burnish of her hair.

"Davy, how many times have I told you that you mustn't use that word," she rebuked. "I'm going to Echo Lodge."

"Take me with you," entreated Davy.

"I would if I were driving. But I'm going to walk and it's too far for your eight-year-old legs. Besides, Paul is going with me and I fear you don't enjoy yourself in his company."

"Oh, I like Paul lots better'n I did," said Davy, beginning to make fearful in-roads into his pudding. "Since I've got pretty good myself I don't mind his being gooder so much. If I can keep on I'll catch up with him some day, both in legs and goodness. 'Sides, Paul's real nice to us second primer boys in school. He won't let the other big boys meddle with us and he shows us lots of games."

"How came Paul to fall into the brook at noon hour yesterday?" asked Anne. "I met him on the playground, such a dripping figure that I sent him promptly home for clothes without waiting to find out what had happened."

"Well, it was partly a zacksident," explained Davy. "He stuck his head in on purpose but the rest of him fell in zacksidentally. We was all down at the brook and Prillie Rogerson got mad at Paul about something . . . she's awful mean and horrid anyway, if she IS pretty . . . and said that his grandmother put his hair up in curl rags every night. Paul wouldn't have minded what she said, I guess, but Gracie Andrews laughed, and Paul got awful red, 'cause Gracie's his girl, you know. He's CLEAN GONE on her . . . brings her flowers and carries her books as far as the shore road. He got as red as a beet and said his grandmother didn't do any such thing and his hair was born curly. And then he laid down on the bank and stuck his head right into the spring to show them. Oh, it wasn't the spring we drink out of . . ." seeing a horrified look on Marilla's face . . . "it was the little one lower down. But the bank's awful slippy and Paul went right in. I tell you he made a bully splash. Oh, Anne, Anne, I didn't mean to say that . . . it just slipped out before I thought. He made a SPLENDID splash. But he looked so funny when he crawled out, all wet and muddy. The girls laughed more'n ever, but Gracie didn't laugh. She looked sorry. Gracie's a nice girl but she's got a snub nose. When I get big enough to have a girl I won't have one with a snub nose . . . I'll pick one with a pretty nose like yours, Anne."

"A boy who makes such a mess of syrup all over his face when he is eating his pudding will never get a girl to look at him," said Marilla severely.

"But I'll wash my face before I go courting," protested Davy, trying to improve matters by rubbing the back of his hand over the smears. "And I'll wash behind my ears too, without being told. I remembered to this morning, Marilla. I don't forget half as often as I did. But . . ." and Davy sighed . . . "there's so many corners about a fellow that it's awful hard to remember them all. Well, if I can't go to Miss Lavendar's I'll go over and see Mrs. Harrison. Mrs. Harrison's an awful nice woman, I tell you. She keeps a jar of cookies in her pantry a-purpose for little boys, and she always gives me the scrapings out of a pan she's mixed up a plum cake in. A good many plums stick to the sides, you see. Mr. Harrison was always a nice man, but he's twice as nice since he got married over again. I guess getting married makes folks nicer. Why don't YOU get married, Marilla? I want to know."

Marilla's state of single blessedness had never been a sore point with her, so she answered amiably, with an exchange of significant looks with Anne, that she supposed it was because nobody would have her.

"But maybe you never asked anybody to have you," protested Davy.

"Oh, Davy," said Dora primly, shocked into speaking without being spoken to, "it's the MEN that have to do the asking."

"I don't know why they have to do it ALWAYS," grumbled Davy. "Seems to me everything's put on the men in this world. Can I have some more pudding, Marilla?"

"You've had as much as was good for you," said Marilla; but she gave him a moderate second helping.

"I wish people could live on pudding. Why can't they, Marilla? I want to know."

"Because they'd soon get tired of it."

"I'd like to try that for myself," said skeptical Davy. "But I guess it's better to have pudding only on fish and company days than none at all. They never have any at Milty Boulter's. Milty says when company comes his mother gives them cheese and cuts it herself . . . one little bit apiece and one over for manners."

"If Milty Boulter talks like that about his mother at least you needn't repeat it," said Marilla severely.

"Bless my soul," . . . Davy had picked this expression up from Mr. Harrison and used it with great gusto . . . "Milty meant it as a compelment. He's awful proud of his mother, cause folks say she could scratch a living on a rock."

"I . . . I suppose them pesky hens are in my pansy bed again," said Marilla, rising and going out hurriedly.

The slandered hens were nowhere near the pansy bed and Marilla did not even glance at it. Instead, she sat down on the cellar hatch and laughed until she was ashamed of herself.

When Anne and Paul reached the stone house that afternoon they found Miss Lavendar and Charlotta the Fourth in the garden, weeding, raking, clipping, and trimming as if for dear life. Miss Lavendar herself, all gay and sweet in the frills and laces she loved, dropped her shears and ran joyously to meet her guests, while Charlotta the Fourth grinned cheerfully.

"Welcome, Anne. I thought you'd come today. You belong to the afternoon so it brought you. Things that belong together are sure to come together. What a lot of trouble that would save some people if they only knew it. But they don't . . . and so they waste beautiful energy moving heaven and earth to bring things together that DON'T belong. And you, Paul . . . why, you've grown! You're half a head taller than when you were here before."

"Yes, I've begun to grow like pigweed in the night, as Mrs. Lynde says," said Paul, in frank delight over the fact. "Grandma says it's the porridge taking effect at last. Perhaps it is. Goodness knows . . ." Paul sighed deeply . . . "I've eaten enough to make anyone grow. I do hope, now that I've begun, I'll keep on till I'm as tall as father. He is six feet, you know, Miss Lavendar."

Yes, Miss Lavendar did know; the flush on her pretty cheeks deepened a little; she took Paul's hand on one side and Anne's on the other and walked to the house in silence.

"Is it a good day for the echoes, Miss Lavendar?" queried Paul anxiously. The day of his first visit had been too windy for echoes and Paul had been much disappointed.

"Yes, just the best kind of a day," answered Miss Lavendar, rousing herself from her reverie. "But first we are all going to have something to eat. I know you two folks didn't walk all the way back here through those beechwoods without getting hungry, and Charlotta the Fourth and I can eat any hour of the day . . . we have such obliging appetites. So we'll just make a raid on the pantry. Fortunately it's lovely and full. I had a presentiment that I was going to have company today and Charlotta the Fourth and I prepared."

"I think you are one of the people who always have nice things in their pantry," declared Paul. "Grandma's like that too. But she doesn't approve of snacks between meals. I wonder," he added meditatively, "if I OUGHT to eat them away from home when I know she doesn't approve."

"Oh, I don't think she would disapprove after you have had a long walk. That makes a difference," said Miss Lavendar, exchanging amused glances with Anne over Paul's brown curls. "I suppose that snacks ARE extremely unwholesome. That is why we have them so often at Echo Lodge. We. . . Charlotta the Fourth and I . . . live in defiance of every known law of diet. We eat all sorts of indigestible things whenever we happen to think of it, by day or night; and we flourish like green bay trees. We are always intending to reform. When we read any article in a paper warning us against something we like we cut it out and pin it up on the kitchen wall so that we'll remember it. But we never can somehow . . . until after we've gone and eaten that very thing. Nothing has ever killed us yet; but Charlotta the Fourth has been known to have bad dreams after we had eaten doughnuts and mince pie and fruit cake before we went to bed."

"Grandma lets me have a glass of milk and a slice of bread and butter before I go to bed; and on Sunday nights she puts jam on the bread," said Paul. "So I'm always glad when it's Sunday night . . . for more reasons than one. Sunday is a very long day on the shore road. Grandma says it's all too short for her and that father never found Sundays tiresome when he was a little boy. It wouldn't seem so long if I could talk to my rock people but I never do that because Grandma doesn't approve of it on Sundays. I think a good deal; but I'm afraid my thoughts are worldly. Grandma says we should never think anything but religious thoughts on Sundays. But teacher here said once that every really beautiful thought was religious, no matter what it was about, or what day we thought it on. But I feel sure Grandma thinks that sermons and Sunday School lessons are the only things you can think truly religious thoughts about. And when it comes to a difference of opinion between Grandma and teacher I don't know what to do. In my heart" . . . Paul laid his hand on his breast and raised very serious blue eyes to Miss Lavendar's immediately sympathetic face . . . "I agree with teacher. But then, you see, Grandma has brought father up HER way and made a brilliant success of him; and teacher has never brought anybody up yet, though she's helping with Davy and Dora. But you can't tell how they'll turn out till they ARE grown up. So sometimes I feel as if it might be safer to go by Grandma's opinions."

"I think it would," agreed Anne solemnly. "Anyway, I daresay that if your Grandma and I both got down to what we really do mean, under our different ways of expressing it, we'd find out we both meant much the same thing. You'd better go by her way of expressing it, since it's been the result of experience. We'll have to wait until we see how the twins do turn out before we can be sure that my way is equally good." After lunch they went back to the garden, where Paul made the acquaintance of the echoes, to his wonder and delight, while Anne and Miss Lavendar sat on the stone bench under the poplar and talked.

"So you are going away in the fall?" said Miss Lavendar wistfully. "I ought to be glad for your sake, Anne . . . but I'm horribly, selfishly sorry. I shall miss you so much. Oh, sometimes, I think it is of no use to make friends. They only go out of your life after awhile and leave a hurt that is worse than the emptiness before they came."

"That sounds like something Miss Eliza Andrews might say but never Miss Lavendar," said Anne. "NOTHING is worse than emptiness . . . and I'm not going out of your life. There are such things as letters and vacations. Dearest, I'm afraid you're looking a little pale and tired."

"Oh . . . hoo . . . hoo . . . hoo," went Paul on the dyke, where he had been making noises diligently . . . not all of them melodious in the making, but all coming back transmuted into the very gold and silver of sound by the fairy alchemists over the river. Miss Lavendar made an impatient movement with her pretty hands.

"I'm just tired of everything . . . even of the echoes. There is nothing in my life but echoes . . . echoes of lost hopes and dreams and joys. They're beautiful and mocking. Oh Anne, it's horrid of me to talk like this when I have company. It's just that I'm getting old and it doesn't agree with me. I know I'll be fearfully cranky by the time I'm sixty. But perhaps all I need is a course of blue pills." At this moment Charlotta the Fourth, who had disappeared after lunch, returned, and announced that the northeast corner of Mr. John Kimball's pasture was red with early strawberries, and wouldn't Miss Shirley like to go and pick some.

"Early strawberries for tea!" exclaimed Miss Lavendar. "Oh, I'm not so old as I thought . . . and I don't need a single blue pill! Girls, when you come back with your strawberries we'll have tea out here under the silver poplar. I'll have it all ready for you with home-grown cream."

Anne and Charlotta the Fourth accordingly betook themselves back to Mr. Kimball's pasture, a green remote place where the air was as soft as velvet and fragrant as a bed of violets and golden as amber.

"Oh, isn't it sweet and fresh back here?" breathed Anne. "I just feel as if I were drinking in the sunshine."

"Yes, ma'am, so do I. That's just exactly how I feel too, ma'am," agreed Charlotta the Fourth, who would have said precisely the same thing if Anne had remarked that she felt like a pelican of the wilderness. Always after Anne had visited Echo Lodge Charlotta the Fourth mounted to her little room over the kitchen and tried before her looking glass to speak and look and move like Anne. Charlotta could never flatter herself that she quite succeeded; but practice makes perfect, as Charlotta had learned at school, and she fondly hoped that in time she might catch the trick of that dainty uplift of chin, that quick, starry outflashing of eyes, that fashion of walking as if you were a bough swaying in the wind. It seemed so easy when you watched Anne. Charlotta the Fourth admired Anne wholeheartedly. It was not that she thought her so very handsome. Diana Barry's beauty of crimson cheek and black curls was much more to Charlotta the Fourth's taste than Anne's moonshine charm of luminous gray eyes and the pale, everchanging roses of her cheeks.

"But I'd rather look like you than be pretty," she told Anne sincerely.

Anne laughed, sipped the honey from the tribute, and cast away the sting. She was used to taking her compliments mixed. Public opinion never agreed on Anne's looks. People who had heard her called handsome met her and were disappointed. People who had heard her called plain saw her and wondered where other people's eyes were. Anne herself would never believe that she had any claim to beauty. When she looked in the glass all she saw was a little pale face with seven freckles on the nose thereof. Her mirror never revealed to her the elusive, ever-varying play of feeling that came and went over her features like a rosy illuminating flame, or the charm of dream and laughter alternating in her big eyes.

While Anne was not beautiful in any strictly defined sense of the word she possessed a certain evasive charm and distinction of appearance that left beholders with a pleasurable sense of satisfaction in that softly rounded girlhood of hers, with all its strongly felt potentialities. Those who knew Anne best felt, without realizing that they felt it, that her greatest attraction was the aura of possibility surrounding her. . . the power of future development that was in her. She seemed to walk in an atmosphere of things about to happen.

As they picked, Charlotta the Fourth confided to Anne her fears regarding Miss Lavendar. The warm-hearted little handmaiden was honestly worried over her adored mistress' condition.

"Miss Lavendar isn't well, Miss Shirley, ma'am. I'm sure she isn't, though she never complains. She hasn't seemed like herself this long while, ma'am . . . not since that day you and Paul were here together before. I feel sure she caught cold that night, ma'am. After you and him had gone she went out and walked in the garden for long after dark with nothing but a little shawl on her. There was a lot of snow on the walks and I feel sure she got a chill, ma'am. Ever since then I've noticed her acting tired and lonesome like. She don't seem to take an interest in anything, ma'am. She never pretends company's coming, nor fixes up for it, nor nothing, ma'am. It's only when you come she seems to chirk up a bit. And the worst sign of all, Miss Shirley, ma'am . . ." Charlotta the Fourth lowered her voice as if she were about to tell some exceedingly weird and awful symptom indeed . . . "is that she never gets cross now when I breaks things. Why, Miss Shirley, ma'am, yesterday I bruk her green and yaller bowl that's always stood on the bookcase. Her grandmother brought it out from England and Miss Lavendar was awful choice of it. I was dusting it just as careful, Miss Shirley, ma'am, and it slipped out, so fashion, afore I could grab holt of it, and bruk into about forty millyun pieces. I tell you I was sorry and scared. I thought Miss Lavendar would scold me awful, ma'am; and I'd ruther she had than take it the way she did. She just come in and hardly looked at it and said, 'It's no matter, Charlotta. Take up the pieces and throw them away.' Just like that, Miss Shirley, ma'am . . . 'take up the pieces and throw them away,' as if it wasn't her grandmother's bowl from England. Oh, she isn't well and I feel awful bad about it. She's got nobody to look after her but me."

Charlotta the Fourth's eyes brimmed up with tears. Anne patted the little brown paw holding the cracked pink cup sympathetically.

"I think Miss Lavendar needs a change, Charlotta. She stays here alone too much. Can't we induce her to go away for a little trip?"

Charlotta shook her head, with its rampant bows, disconsolately.

"I don't think so, Miss Shirley, ma'am. Miss Lavendar hates visiting. She's only got three relations she ever visits and she says she just goes to see them as a family duty. Last time when she come home she said she wasn't going to visit for family duty no more. 'I've come home in love with loneliness, Charlotta,' she says to me, 'and I never want to stray from my own vine and fig tree again. My relations try so hard to make an old lady of me and it has a bad effect on me.' Just like that, Miss Shirley, ma'am. 'It has a very bad effect on me.' So I don't think it would do any good to coax her to go visiting."

"We must see what can be done," said Anne decidedly, as she put the last possible berry in her pink cup. "Just as soon as I have my vacation I'll come through and spend a whole week with you. We'll have a picnic every day and pretend all sorts of interesting things, and see if we can't cheer Miss Lavendar up."

"That will be the very thing, Miss Shirley, ma'am," exclaimed Charlotta the Fourth in rapture. She was glad for Miss Lavendar's sake and for her own too. With a whole week in which to study Anne constantly she would surely be able to learn how to move and behave like her.

When the girls got back to Echo Lodge they found that Miss Lavendar and Paul had carried the little square table out of the kitchen to the garden and had everything ready for tea. Nothing ever tasted so delicious as those strawberries and cream, eaten under a great blue sky all curdled over with fluffy little white clouds, and in the long shadows of the wood with its lispings and its murmurings. After tea Anne helped Charlotta wash the dishes in the kitchen, while Miss Lavendar sat on the stone bench with Paul and heard all about his rock people. She was a good listener, this sweet Miss Lavendar, but just at the last it struck Paul that she had suddenly lost interest in the Twin Sailors.

"Miss Lavendar, why do you look at me like that?" he asked gravely.

"How do I look, Paul?"

"Just as if you were looking through me at somebody I put you in mind of," said Paul, who had such occasional flashes of uncanny insight that it wasn't quite safe to have secrets when he was about.

"You do put me in mind of somebody I knew long ago," said Miss Lavendar dreamily.

"When you were young?"

"Yes, when I was young. Do I seem very old to you, Paul?"

"Do you know, I can't make up my mind about that," said Paul confidentially. "Your hair looks old . . . I never knew a young person with white hair. But your eyes are as young as my beautiful teacher's when you laugh. I tell you what, Miss Lavendar" . . . Paul's voice and face were as solemn as a judge's . . . "I think you would make a splendid mother. You have just the right look in your eyes . . . the look my little mother always had. I think it's a pity you haven't any boys of your own."

"I have a little dream boy, Paul."

"Oh, have you really? How old is he?"

"About your age I think. He ought to be older because I dreamed him long before you were born. But I'll never let him get any older than eleven or twelve; because if I did some day he might grow up altogether and then I'd lose him."

"I know," nodded Paul. "That's the beauty of dream-people . . . they stay any age you want them. You and my beautiful teacher and me myself are the only folks in the world that I know of that have dream-people. Isn't it funny and nice we should all know each other? But I guess that kind of people always find each other out. Grandma never has dream-people and Mary Joe thinks I'm wrong in the upper story because I have them. But I think it's splendid to have them. YOU know, Miss Lavendar. Tell me all about your little dream-boy."

"He has blue eyes and curly hair. He steals in and wakens me with a kiss every morning. Then all day he plays here in the garden . . . and I play with him. Such games as we have. We run races and talk with the echoes; and I tell him stories. And when twilight comes . . ."

"I know," interrupted Paul eagerly. "He comes and sits beside you . . . SO . . . because of course at twelve he'd be too big to climb into your lap . . . and lays his head on your shoulder . . . SO . . . and you put your arms about him and hold him tight, tight, and rest your cheek on his head . . . yes, that's the very way. Oh, you DO know, Miss Lavendar."

Anne found the two of them there when she came out of the stone house, and something in Miss Lavendar's face made her hate to disturb them.

"I'm afraid we must go, Paul, if we want to get home before dark. Miss Lavendar, I'm going to invite myself to Echo Lodge for a whole week pretty soon."

"If you come for a week I'll keep you for two," threatened Miss Lavendar.

XXVIII - The Prince Comes Back to the Enchanted Palace

The last day of school came and went. A triumphant "semi-annual examination" was held and Anne's pupils acquitted themselves splendidly. At the close they gave her an address and a writing desk. All the girls and ladies present cried, and some of the boys had it cast up to them later on that they cried too, although they always denied it.

Mrs. Harmon Andrews, Mrs. Peter Sloane, and Mrs. William Bell walked home together and talked things over.

"I do think it is such a pity Anne is leaving when the children seem so much attached to her," sighed Mrs. Peter Sloane, who had a habit of sighing over everything and even finished off her jokes that way. "To be sure," she added hastily, "we all know we'll have a good teacher next year too."

"Jane will do her duty, I've no doubt," said Mrs. Andrews rather stiffly. "I don't suppose she'll tell the children quite so many fairy tales or spend so much time roaming about the woods with them. But she has her name on the Inspector's Roll of Honor and the Newbridge people are in a terrible state over her leaving."

"I'm real glad Anne is going to college," said Mrs. Bell. "She has always wanted it and it will be a splendid thing for her."

"Well, I don't know." Mrs. Andrews was determined not to agree fully with anybody that day. "I don't see that Anne needs any more education. She'll probably be marrying Gilbert Blythe, if his infatuation for her lasts till he gets through college, and what good will Latin and Greek do her then? If they taught you at college how to manage a man there might be some sense in her going."

Mrs. Harmon Andrews, so Avonlea gossip whispered, had never learned how to manage her "man," and as a result the Andrews household was not exactly a model of domestic happiness.

"I see that the Charlottetown call to Mr. Allan is up before the Presbytery," said Mrs. Bell. "That means we'll be losing him soon, I suppose."

"They're not going before September," said Mrs. Sloane. "It will be a great loss to the community . . . though I always did think that Mrs. Allan dressed rather too gay for a minister's wife. But we are none of us perfect. Did you notice how neat and snug Mr. Harrison looked today? I never saw such a changed man. He goes to church every Sunday and has subscribed to the salary."

"Hasn't that Paul Irving grown to be a big boy?" said Mrs. Andrews. "He was such a mite for his age when he came here. I declare I hardly knew him today. He's getting to look a lot like his father."

"He's a smart boy," said Mrs. Bell.

"He's smart enough, but" . . . Mrs. Andrews lowered her voice . . . "I believe he tells queer stories. Gracie came home from school one day last week with the greatest rigmarole he had told her about people who lived down at the shore . . . stories there couldn't be a word of truth in, you know. I told Gracie not to believe them, and she said Paul didn't intend her to. But if he didn't what did he tell them to her for?"

"Anne says Paul is a genius," said Mrs. Sloane.

"He may be. You never know what to expect of them Americans," said Mrs. Andrews. Mrs. Andrews' only acquaintance with the word "genius" was derived from the colloquial fashion of calling any eccentric individual "a queer genius." She probably thought, with Mary Joe, that it meant a person with something wrong in his upper story.

Back in the schoolroom Anne was sitting alone at her desk, as she had sat on the first day of school two years before, her face leaning on her hand, her dewy eyes looking wistfully out of the window to the Lake of Shining Waters. Her heart was so wrung over the parting with her pupils that for a moment college had lost all its charm. She still felt the clasp of Annetta Bell's arms about her neck and heard the childish wail, "I'll NEVER love any teacher as much as you, Miss Shirley, never, never."

For two years she had worked earnestly and faithfully, making many mistakes and learning from them. She had had her reward. She had taught her scholars something, but she felt that they had taught her much more . . . lessons of tenderness, self-control, innocent wisdom, lore of childish hearts. Perhaps she had not succeeded in "inspiring" any wonderful ambitions in her pupils, but she had taught them, more by her own sweet personality than by all her careful precepts, that it was good and necessary in the years that were before them to live their lives finely and graciously, holding fast to truth and courtesy and kindness, keeping aloof from all that savored of falsehood and meanness and vulgarity. They were, perhaps, all unconscious of having learned such lessons; but they would remember and practice them long after they had forgotten the capital of Afghanistan and the dates of the Wars of the Roses.

"Another chapter in my life is closed," said Anne aloud, as she locked her desk. She really felt very sad over it; but the romance in the idea of that "closed chapter" did comfort her a little.

Anne spent a fortnight at Echo Lodge early in her vacation and everybody concerned had a good time.

She took Miss Lavendar on a shopping expedition to town and persuaded her to buy a new organdy dress; then came the excitement of cutting and making it together, while the happy Charlotta the Fourth basted and swept up clippings. Miss Lavendar had complained that she could not feel much interest in anything, but the sparkle came back to her eyes over her pretty dress.

"What a foolish, frivolous person I must be," she sighed. "I'm wholesomely ashamed to think that a new dress . . . even it is a forget-me-not organdy . . . should exhilarate me so, when a good conscience and an extra contribution to Foreign Missions couldn't do it."

Midway in her visit Anne went home to Green Gables for a day to mend the twins' stockings and settle up Davy's accumulated store of questions. In the evening she went down to the shore road to see Paul Irving. As she passed by the low, square window of the Irving sitting room she caught a glimpse of Paul on somebody's lap; but the next moment he came flying through the hall.

"Oh, Miss Shirley," he cried excitedly, "you can't think what has happened! Something so splendid. Father is here . . . just think of that! Father is here! Come right in. Father, this is my beautiful teacher. YOU know, father."

Stephen Irving came forward to meet Anne with a smile. He was a tall, handsome man of middle age, with iron-gray hair, deep-set, dark blue eyes, and a strong, sad face, splendidly modeled about chin and brow. Just the face for a hero of romance, Anne thought with a thrill of intense satisfaction. It was so disappointing to meet someone who ought to be a hero and find him bald or stooped, or otherwise lacking in manly beauty. Anne would have thought it dreadful if the object of Miss Lavendar's romance had not looked the part.

"So this is my little son's 'beautiful teacher,' of whom I have heard so much," said Mr. Irving with a hearty handshake. "Paul's letters have been so full of you, Miss Shirley, that I feel as if I were pretty well acquainted with you already. I want to thank you for what you have done for Paul. I think that your influence has been just what he needed. Mother is one of the best and dearest of women; but her robust, matter-of-fact Scotch common sense could not always understand a temperament like my laddie's. What was lacking in her you have supplied. Between you, I think Paul's training in these two past years has been as nearly ideal as a motherless boy's could be."

Everybody likes to be appreciated. Under Mr. Irving's praise Anne's face "burst flower like into rosy bloom," and the busy, weary man of the world, looking at her, thought he had never seen a fairer, sweeter slip of girlhood than this little "down east" schoolteacher with her red hair and wonderful eyes.

Paul sat between them blissfully happy.

"I never dreamed father was coming," he said radiantly. "Even Grandma didn't know it. It was a great surprise. As a general thing . . ." Paul shook his brown curls gravely . . . "I don't like to be surprised. You lose all the fun of expecting things when you're surprised. But in a case like this it is all right. Father came last night after I had gone to bed. And after Grandma and Mary Joe had stopped being surprised he and Grandma came upstairs to look at me, not meaning to wake me up till morning. But I woke right up and saw father. I tell you I just sprang at him."

"With a hug like a bear's," said Mr. Irving, putting his arms around Paul's shoulder smilingly. "I hardly knew my boy, he had grown so big and brown and sturdy."

"I don't know which was the most pleased to see father, Grandma or I," continued Paul. "Grandma's been in kitchen all day making the things father likes to eat. She wouldn't trust them to Mary Joe, she says. That's HER way of showing gladness. *I* like best just to sit and talk to father. But I'm going to leave you for a little while now if you'll excuse me. I must get the cows for Mary Joe. That is one of my daily duties."

When Paul had scampered away to do his "daily duty" Mr. Irving talked to Anne of various matters. But Anne felt that he was thinking of something else underneath all the time. Presently it came to the surface.

"In Paul's last letter he spoke of going with you to visit an old . . . friend of mine . . . Miss Lewis at the stone house in Grafton. Do you know her well?"

"Yes, indeed, she is a very dear friend of mine," was Anne's demure reply, which gave no hint of the sudden thrill that tingled over her from head to foot at Mr. Irving's question. Anne "felt instinctively" that romance was peeping at her around a corner.

Mr. Irving rose and went to the window, looking out on a great, golden, billowing sea where a wild wind was harping. For a few moments there was silence in the little dark-walled room. Then he turned and looked down into Anne's sympathetic face with a smile, half-whimsical, half-tender.

"I wonder how much you know," he said.

"I know all about it," replied Anne promptly. "You see," she explained hastily, "Miss Lavendar and I are very intimate. She wouldn't tell things of such a sacred nature to everybody. We are kindred spirits."

"Yes, I believe you are. Well, I am going to ask a favor of you. I would like to go and see Miss Lavendar if she will let me. Will you ask her if I may come?"

Would she not? Oh, indeed she would! Yes, this was romance, the very, the real thing, with all the charm of rhyme and story and dream. It was a little belated, perhaps, like a rose blooming in October which should have bloomed in June; but none the less a rose, all sweetness and fragrance, with the gleam of gold in its heart. Never did Anne's feet bear her on a more willing errand than on that walk through the beechwoods to Grafton the next morning. She found Miss Lavendar in the garden. Anne was fearfully excited. Her hands grew cold and her voice trembled.

"Miss Lavendar, I have something to tell you . . . something very important. Can you guess what it is?"

Anne never supposed that Miss Lavendar could GUESS; but Miss Lavendar's face grew very pale and Miss Lavendar said in a quiet, still voice, from which all the color and sparkle that Miss Lavendar's voice usually suggested had faded.

"Stephen Irving is home?"

"How did you know? Who told you?" cried Anne disappointedly, vexed that her great revelation had been anticipated.

"Nobody. I knew that must be it, just from the way you spoke."

"He wants to come and see you," said Anne. "May I send him word that he may?"

"Yes, of course," fluttered Miss Lavendar. "There is no reason why he shouldn't. He is only coming as any old friend might."

Anne had her own opinion about that as she hastened into the house to write a note at Miss Lavendar's desk.

"Oh, it's delightful to be living in a storybook," she thought gaily. "It will come out all right of course . . . it must . . . and Paul will have a mother after his own heart and everybody will be happy. But Mr. Irving will take Miss Lavendar away . . . and dear knows what will happen to the little stone house . . . and so there are two sides to it, as there seems to be to everything in this world." The important note was written and Anne herself carried it to the Grafton post office, where she waylaid the mail carrier and asked him to leave it at the Avonlea office.

"It's so very important," Anne assured him anxiously. The mail carrier was a rather grumpy old personage who did not at all look the part of a messenger of Cupid; and Anne was none too certain that his memory was to be trusted. But he said he would do his best to remember and she had to be contented with that.

Charlotta the Fourth felt that some mystery pervaded the stone house that afternoon . . . a mystery from which she was excluded. Miss Lavendar roamed about the garden in a distracted fashion. Anne, too, seemed possessed by a demon of unrest, and walked to and fro and went up and down. Charlotta the Fourth endured it till patience ceased to be a virtue; then she confronted Anne on the occasion of that romantic young person's third aimless peregrination through the kitchen.

"Please, Miss Shirley, ma'am," said Charlotta the Fourth, with an indignant toss of her very blue bows, "it's plain to be seen you and Miss Lavendar have got a secret and I think, begging your pardon if I'm too forward, Miss Shirley, ma'am, that it's real mean not to tell me when we've all been such chums."

"Oh, Charlotta dear, I'd have told you all about it if it were my secret . . . but it's Miss Lavendar's, you see. However, I'll tell you this much . . . and if nothing comes of it you must never breathe a word about it to a living soul. You see, Prince Charming is coming tonight. He came long ago, but in a foolish moment went away and wandered afar and forgot the secret of the magic pathway to the enchanted castle, where the princess was weeping her faithful heart out for him. But at last he remembered it again and the princess is waiting still . . . because nobody but her own dear prince could carry her off."

"Oh, Miss Shirley, ma'am, what is that in prose?" gasped the mystified Charlotta.

Anne laughed.

"In prose, an old friend of Miss Lavendar's is coming to see her tonight."

"Do you mean an old beau of hers?" demanded the literal Charlotta.

"That is probably what I do mean . . . in prose," answered Anne gravely. "It is Paul's father . . . Stephen Irving. And goodness knows what will come of it, but let us hope for the best, Charlotta."

"I hope that he'll marry Miss Lavendar," was Charlotta's unequivocal response. "Some women's intended from the start to be old maids, and I'm afraid I'm one of them, Miss Shirley, ma'am, because I've awful little patience with the men. But Miss Lavendar never was. And I've been awful worried, thinking what on earth she'd do when I got so big I'd HAVE to go to Boston. There ain't any more girls in our family and dear knows what she'd do if she got some stranger that might laugh at her pretendings and leave things lying round out of their place and not be willing to be called Charlotta the Fifth. She might get someone who wouldn't be as unlucky as me in breaking dishes but she'd never get anyone who'd love her better."

And the faithful little handmaiden dashed to the oven door with a sniff.

They went through the form of having tea as usual that night at Echo Lodge; but nobody really ate anything. After tea Miss Lavendar went to her room and put on her new forget-me-not organdy, while Anne did her hair for her. Both were dreadfully excited; but Miss Lavendar pretended to be very calm and indifferent.

"I must really mend that rent in the curtain tomorrow," she said anxiously, inspecting it as if it were the only thing of any importance just then. "Those curtains have not worn as well as they should, considering the price I paid. Dear me, Charlotta has forgotten to dust the stair railing AGAIN. I really MUST speak to her about it."

Anne was sitting on the porch steps when Stephen Irving came down the lane and across the garden.

"This is the one place where time stands still," he said, looking around him with delighted eyes. "There is nothing changed about this house or garden since I was here twenty-five years ago. It makes me feel young again."

"You know time always does stand still in an enchanted palace," said Anne seriously. "It is only when the prince comes that things begin to happen."

Mr. Irving smiled a little sadly into her uplifted face, all astar with its youth and promise.

"Sometimes the prince comes too late," he said. He did not ask Anne to translate her remark into prose. Like all kindred spirits he "understood."

"Oh, no, not if he is the real prince coming to the true princess," said Anne, shaking her red head decidedly, as she opened the parlor door. When he had gone in she shut it tightly behind him and turned to confront Charlotta the Fourth, who was in the hall, all "nods and becks and wreathed smiles."

"Oh, Miss Shirley, ma'am," she breathed, "I peeked from the kitchen window . . . and he's awful handsome . . . and just the right age for Miss Lavendar. And oh, Miss Shirley, ma'am, do you think it would be much harm to listen at the door?"

"It would be dreadful, Charlotta," said Anne firmly, "so just you come away with me out of the reach of temptation."

"I can't do anything, and it's awful to hang round just waiting," sighed Charlotta. "What if he don't propose after all, Miss Shirley, ma'am? You can never be sure of them men. My older sister, Charlotta the First, thought she was engaged to one once. But it turned out HE had a different opinion and she says she'll never trust one of them again. And I heard of another case where a man thought he wanted one girl awful bad when it was really her sister he wanted all the time. When a man don't know his own mind, Miss Shirley, ma'am, how's a poor woman going to be sure of it?"

"We'll go to the kitchen and clean the silver spoons," said Anne. "That's a task which won't require much thinking fortunately . . . for I COULDN'T think tonight. And it will pass the time."

It passed an hour. Then, just as Anne laid down the last shining spoon, they heard the front door shut. Both sought comfort fearfully in each other's eyes.

"Oh, Miss Shirley, ma'am," gasped Charlotta, "if he's going away this early there's nothing into it and never will be." They flew to the window. Mr. Irving had no intention of going away. He and Miss Lavendar were strolling slowly down the middle path to the stone bench.

"Oh, Miss Shirley, ma'am, he's got his arm around her waist," whispered Charlotta the Fourth delightedly. "He must have proposed to her or she'd never allow it."

Anne caught Charlotta the Fourth by her own plump waist and danced her around the kitchen until they were both out of breath.

"Oh, Charlotta," she cried gaily, "I'm neither a prophetess nor the daughter of a prophetess but I'm going to make a prediction. There'll be a wedding in this old stone house before the maple leaves are red. Do you want that translated into prose, Charlotta?"

"No, I can understand that," said Charlotta. "A wedding ain't poetry. Why, Miss Shirley, ma'am, you're crying! What for?"

"Oh, because it's all so beautiful . . . and story bookish . . . and romantic . . . and sad," said Anne, winking the tears out of her eyes. "It's all perfectly lovely . . . but there's a little sadness mixed up in it too, somehow."

"Oh, of course there's a resk in marrying anybody," conceded Charlotta the Fourth, "but, when all's said and done, Miss Shirley, ma'am, there's many a worse thing than a husband."

XXIX - Poetry and Prose

For the next month Anne lived in what, for Avonlea, might be called a whirl of excitement. The preparation of her own modest outfit for Redmond was of secondary importance. Miss Lavendar was getting ready to be married and the stone house was the scene of endless consultations and plannings and discussions, with Charlotta the Fourth hovering on the outskirts of things in agitated delight and wonder. Then the dressmaker came, and there was the rapture and wretchedness of choosing fashions and being fitted. Anne and Diana spent half their time at Echo Lodge and there were nights when Anne could not sleep for wondering whether she had done right in advising Miss Lavendar to select brown rather than navy blue for her traveling dress, and to have her gray silk made princess.

Everybody concerned in Miss Lavendar's story was very happy. Paul Irving rushed to Green Gables to talk the news over with Anne as soon as his father had told him.

"I knew I could trust father to pick me out a nice little second mother," he said proudly. "It's a fine thing to have a father you can depend on, teacher. I just love Miss Lavendar. Grandma is pleased, too. She says she's real glad father didn't pick out an American for his second wife, because, although it turned out all right the first time, such a thing wouldn't be likely to happen twice. Mrs. Lynde says she thoroughly approves of the match and thinks its likely Miss Lavendar will give up her queer notions and be like other people, now that she's going to be married. But I hope she won't give her queer notions up, teacher, because I like them. And I don't want her to be like other people. There are too many other people around as it is. YOU know, teacher."

Charlotta the Fourth was another radiant person.

"Oh, Miss Shirley, ma'am, it has all turned out so beautiful. When Mr. Irving and Miss Lavendar come back from their tower I'm to go up to Boston and live with them . . . and me only fifteen, and the other girls never went till they were sixteen. Ain't Mr. Irving splendid? He just worships the ground she treads on and it makes me feel so queer sometimes to see the look in his eyes when he's watching her. It beggars description, Miss Shirley, ma'am. I'm awful thankful they're so fond of each other. It's the best way, when all's said and done, though some folks can get along without it. I've got an aunt who has been married three times and says she married the first time for love and the last two times for strictly business, and was happy with all three except at the times of the funerals. But I think she took a resk, Miss Shirley, ma'am."

"Oh, it's all so romantic," breathed Anne to Marilla that night. "If I hadn't taken the wrong path that day we went to Mr. Kimball's I'd never have known Miss Lavendar; and if I hadn't met her I'd never have taken Paul there . . . and he'd never have written to his father about visiting Miss Lavendar just as Mr. Irving was starting for San Francisco. Mr. Irving says whenever he got that letter he made up his mind to send his partner to San Francisco and come here instead. He hadn't heard anything of Miss Lavendar for fifteen years. Somebody had told him then that she was to be married and he thought she was and never asked anybody anything about her. And now everything has come right. And I had a hand in bringing it about. Perhaps, as Mrs. Lynde says, everything is foreordained and it was bound to happen anyway. But even so, it's nice to think one was an instrument used by predestination. Yes indeed, it's very romantic."

"I can't see that it's so terribly romantic at all," said Marilla rather crisply. Marilla thought Anne was too worked up about it and had plenty to do with getting ready for college without "traipsing" to Echo Lodge two days out of three helping Miss Lavendar. "In the first place two young fools quarrel and turn sulky; then Steve Irving goes to the States and after a spell gets married up there and is perfectly happy from all accounts. Then his wife dies and after a decent interval he thinks he'll come home and see if his first fancy'll have him. Meanwhile, she's been living single, probably because nobody nice enough came along to want her, and they meet and agree to be married after all. Now, where is the romance in all that?"

"Oh, there isn't any, when you put it that way," gasped Anne, rather as if somebody had thrown cold water over her. "I suppose that's how it looks in prose. But it's very different if you look at it through poetry . . . and *I* think it's nicer . . ." Anne recovered herself and her eyes shone and her cheeks flushed . . . "to look at it through poetry."

Marilla glanced at the radiant young face and refrained from further sarcastic comments. Perhaps some realization came to her that after all it was better to have, like Anne, "the vision and the faculty divine" . . . that gift which the world cannot bestow or take away, of looking at life through some transfiguring . . . or revealing? . . . medium, whereby everything seemed apparelled in celestial light, wearing a glory and a freshness not visible to those who, like herself and Charlotta the Fourth, looked at things only through prose.

"When's the wedding to be?" she asked after a pause.

"The last Wednesday in August. They are to be married in the garden under the honeysuckle trellis . . . the very spot where Mr. Irving proposed to her twenty-five years ago. Marilla, that IS romantic, even in prose. There's to be nobody there except Mrs. Irving and Paul and Gilbert and Diana and I, and Miss Lavendar's cousins. And they will leave on the six o'clock train for a trip to the Pacific coast. When they come back in the fall Paul and Charlotta the Fourth are to go up to Boston to live with them. But Echo Lodge is to be left just as it is. . . only of course they'll sell the hens and cow, and board up the windows . . . and every summer they're coming down to live in it. I'm so glad. It would have hurt me dreadfully next winter at Redmond to think of that dear stone house all stripped and deserted, with empty rooms . . . or far worse still, with other people living in it. But I can think of it now, just as I've always seen it, waiting happily for the summer to bring life and laughter back to it again."

There was more romance in the world than that which had fallen to the share of the middle-aged lovers of the stone house. Anne stumbled suddenly on it one evening when she went over to Orchard Slope by the wood cut and came out into the Barry garden. Diana Barry and Fred Wright were standing together under the big willow. Diana was leaning against the gray trunk, her lashes cast down on very crimson cheeks. One hand was held by Fred, who stood with his face bent toward her, stammering something in low earnest tones. There were no other people in the world except their two selves at that magic moment; so neither of them saw Anne, who, after one dazed glance of comprehension, turned and sped noiselessly back through the spruce wood, never stopping till she gained her own gable room, where she sat breathlessly down by her window and tried to collect her scattered wits.

"Diana and Fred are in love with each other," she gasped. "Oh, it does seem so . . . so . . . so HOPELESSLY grown up."

Anne, of late, had not been without her suspicions that Diana was proving false to the melancholy Byronic hero of her early dreams. But as "things seen are mightier than things heard," or suspected, the realization that it was actually so came to her with almost the shock of perfect surprise. This was succeeded by a queer, little lonely feeling . . . as if, somehow, Diana had gone forward into a new world, shutting a gate behind her, leaving Anne on the outside.

"Things are changing so fast it almost frightens me," Anne thought, a little sadly. "And I'm afraid that this can't help making some difference between Diana and me. I'm sure I can't tell her all my secrets after this . . . she might tell Fred. And what CAN she see in Fred? He's very nice and jolly . . . but he's just Fred Wright."

It is always a very puzzling question . . . what can somebody see in somebody else? But how fortunate after all that it is so, for if everybody saw alike . . . well, in that case, as the old Indian said, "Everybody would want my squaw." It was plain that Diana DID see something in Fred Wright, however Anne's eyes might be holden. Diana came to Green Gables the next evening, a pensive, shy young lady, and told Anne the whole story in the dusky seclusion of the east gable. Both girls cried and kissed and laughed.

"I'm so happy," said Diana, "but it does seem ridiculous to think of me being engaged."

"What is it really like to be engaged?" asked Anne curiously.

"Well, that all depends on who you're engaged to," answered Diana, with that maddening air of superior wisdom always assumed by those who are engaged over those who are not. "It's perfectly lovely to be engaged to Fred . . . but I think it would be simply horrid to be engaged to anyone else."

"There's not much comfort for the rest of us in that, seeing that there is only one Fred," laughed Anne.

"Oh, Anne, you don't understand," said Diana in vexation. "I didn't mean THAT . . . it's so hard to explain. Never mind, you'll understand sometime, when your own turn comes."

"Bless you, dearest of Dianas, I understand now. What is an imagination for if not to enable you to peep at life through other people's eyes?"

"You must be my bridesmaid, you know, Anne. Promise me that . . . wherever you may be when I'm married."

"I'll come from the ends of the earth if necessary," promised Anne solemnly.

"Of course, it won't be for ever so long yet," said Diana, blushing. "Three years at the very least . . . for I'm only eighteen and mother says no daughter of hers shall be married before she's twenty-one. Besides, Fred's father is going to buy the Abraham Fletcher farm for him and he says he's got to have it two thirds paid for before he'll give it to him in his own name. But three years isn't any too much time to get ready for housekeeping, for I haven't a speck of fancy work made yet. But I'm going to begin crocheting doilies tomorrow. Myra Gillis had thirty-seven doilies when she was married and I'm determined I shall have as many as she had."

"I suppose it would be perfectly impossible to keep house with only thirty-six doilies," conceded Anne, with a solemn face but dancing eyes.

Diana looked hurt.

"I didn't think you'd make fun of me, Anne," she said reproachfully.

"Dearest, I wasn't making fun of you," cried Anne repentantly. "I was only teasing you a bit. I think you'll make the sweetest little housekeeper in the world. And I think it's perfectly lovely of you to be planning already for your home o'dreams."

Anne had no sooner uttered the phrase, "home o'dreams," than it captivated her fancy and she immediately began the erection of one of her own. It was, of course, tenanted by an ideal master, dark, proud, and melancholy; but oddly enough, Gilbert Blythe persisted in hanging about too, helping her arrange pictures, lay out gardens, and accomplish sundry other tasks which a proud and melancholy hero evidently considered beneath his dignity. Anne tried to banish Gilbert's image from her castle in Spain but, somehow, he went on being there, so Anne, being in a hurry, gave up the attempt and pursued her aerial architecture with such success that her "home o'dreams" was built and furnished before Diana spoke again.

"I suppose, Anne, you must think it's funny I should like Fred so well when he's so different from the kind of man I've always said I would marry . . . the tall, slender kind? But somehow I wouldn't want Fred to be tall and slender . . . because, don't you see, he wouldn't be Fred then. Of course," added Diana rather dolefully, "we will be a dreadfully pudgy couple. But after all that's better than one of us being short and fat and the other tall and lean, like Morgan Sloane and his wife. Mrs. Lynde says it always makes her think of the long and short of it when she sees them together."

"Well," said Anne to herself that night, as she brushed her hair before her gilt framed mirror, "I am glad Diana is so happy and satisfied. But when my turn comes . . . if it ever does . . . I do hope there'll be something a little more thrilling about it. But then Diana thought so too, once. I've heard her say time and again she'd never get engaged any poky commonplace way . . . he'd HAVE to do something splendid to win her. But she has changed. Perhaps I'll change too. But I won't . . . and I'm determined I won't. Oh, I think these engagements are dreadfully unsettling things when they happen to your intimate friends."

XXX - A Wedding at the Stone House

The last week in August came. Miss Lavendar was to be married in it. Two weeks later Anne and Gilbert would leave for Redmond College. In a week's time Mrs. Rachel Lynde would move to Green Gables and set up her lares and penates in the erstwhile spare room, which was already prepared for her coming. She had sold all her superfluous household plenishings by auction and was at present reveling in the congenial occupation of helping the Allans pack up. Mr. Allan was to preach his farewell sermon the next Sunday. The old order was changing rapidly to give place to the new, as Anne felt with a little sadness threading all her excitement and happiness.

"Changes ain't totally pleasant but they're excellent things," said Mr. Harrison philosophically. "Two years is about long enough for things to stay exactly the same. If they stayed put any longer they might grow mossy."

Mr. Harrison was smoking on his veranda. His wife had self-sacrificingly told that he might smoke in the house if he took care to sit by an open window. Mr. Harrison rewarded this concession by going outdoors altogether to smoke in fine weather, and so mutual goodwill reigned.

Anne had come over to ask Mrs. Harrison for some of her yellow dahlias. She and Diana were going through to Echo Lodge that evening to help Miss Lavendar and Charlotta the Fourth with their final preparations for the morrow's bridal. Miss Lavendar herself never had dahlias; she did not like them and they would not have suited the fine retirement of her old-fashioned garden. But flowers of any kind were rather scarce in Avonlea and the neighboring districts that summer, thanks to Uncle Abe's storm; and Anne and Diana thought that a certain old cream-colored stone jug, usually kept sacred to doughnuts, brimmed over with yellow dahlias, would be just the thing to set in a dim angle of the stone house stairs, against the dark background of red hall paper.

"I s'pose you'll be starting off for college in a fortnight's time?" continued Mr. Harrison. "Well, we're going to miss you an awful lot, Emily and me. To be sure, Mrs. Lynde'll be over there in your place. There ain't nobody but a substitute can be found for them."

The irony of Mr. Harrison's tone is quite untransferable to paper. In spite of his wife's intimacy with Mrs. Lynde, the best that could be said of the relationship between her and Mr. Harrison even under the new regime, was that they preserved an armed neutrality.

"Yes, I'm going," said Anne. "I'm very glad with my head . . . and very sorry with my heart."

"I s'pose you'll be scooping up all the honors that are lying round loose at Redmond."

"I may try for one or two of them," confessed Anne, "but I don't care so much for things like that as I did two years ago. What I want to get out of my college course is some knowledge of the best way of living life and doing the most and best with it. I want to learn to understand and help other people and myself."

Mr. Harrison nodded.

"That's the idea exactly. That's what college ought to be for, instead of for turning out a lot of B.A.'s, so chock full of book-learning and vanity that there ain't room for anything else. You're all right. College won't be able to do you much harm, I reckon."

Diana and Anne drove over to Echo Lodge after tea, taking with them all the flowery spoil that several predatory expeditions in their own and their neighbors' gardens had yielded. They found the stone house agog with excitement. Charlotta the Fourth was flying around with such vim and briskness that her blue bows seemed really to possess the power of being everywhere at once. Like the helmet of Navarre, Charlotta's blue bows waved ever in the thickest of the fray.

"Praise be to goodness you've come," she said devoutly, "for there's heaps of things to do . . . and the frosting on that cake WON'T harden . . . and there's all the silver to be rubbed up yet . . . and the horsehair trunk to be packed . . . and the roosters for the chicken salad are running out there beyant the henhouse yet, crowing, Miss Shirley, ma'am. And Miss Lavendar ain't to be trusted to do a thing. I was thankful when Mr. Irving came a few minutes ago and took her off for a walk in the woods. Courting's all right in its place, Miss Shirley, ma'am, but if you try to mix it up with cooking and scouring everything's spoiled. That's MY opinion, Miss Shirley, ma'am."

Anne and Diana worked so heartily that by ten o'clock even Charlotta the Fourth was satisfied. She braided her hair in innumerable plaits and took her weary little bones off to bed.

"But I'm sure I shan't sleep a blessed wink, Miss Shirley, ma'am, for fear that something'll go wrong at the last minute . . . the cream won't whip . . . or Mr. Irving'll have a stroke and not be able to come."

"He isn't in the habit of having strokes, is he?" asked Diana, the dimpled corners of her mouth twitching. To Diana, Charlotta the Fourth was, if not exactly a thing of beauty, certainly a joy forever.

"They're not things that go by habit," said Charlotta the Fourth with dignity. "They just HAPPEN . . . and there you are. ANYBODY can have a stroke. You don't have to learn how. Mr. Irving looks a lot like an uncle of mine that had one once just as he was sitting down to dinner one day. But maybe everything'll go all right. In this world you've just got to hope for the best and prepare for the worst and take whatever God sends."

"The only thing I'm worried about is that it won't be fine tomorrow," said Diana. "Uncle Abe predicted rain for the middle of the week, and ever since the big storm I can't help believing there's a good deal in what Uncle Abe says."

Anne, who knew better than Diana just how much Uncle Abe had to do with the storm, was not much disturbed by this. She slept the sleep of the just and weary, and was roused at an unearthly hour by Charlotta the Fourth.

"Oh, Miss Shirley, ma'am, it's awful to call you so early," came wailing through the keyhole, "but there's so much to do yet . . . and oh, Miss Shirley, ma'am, I'm skeered it's going to rain and I wish you'd get up and tell me you think it ain't." Anne flew to the window, hoping against hope that Charlotta the Fourth was saying this merely by way of rousing her effectually. But alas, the morning did look unpropitious. Below the window Miss Lavendar's garden, which should have been a glory of pale virgin sunshine, lay dim and windless; and the sky over the firs was dark with moody clouds.

"Isn't it too mean!" said Diana.

"We must hope for the best," said Anne determinedly. "If it only doesn't actually rain, a cool, pearly gray day like this would really be nicer than hot sunshine."

"But it will rain," mourned Charlotta, creeping into the room, a figure of fun, with her many braids wound about her head, the ends, tied up with white thread, sticking out in all directions. "It'll hold off till the last minute and then pour cats and dogs. And all the folks will get sopping . . . and track mud all over the house . . . and they won't be able to be married under the honeysuckle . . . and it's awful unlucky for no sun to shine on a bride, say what you will, Miss Shirley, ma'am. *I* knew things were going too well to last."

Charlotta the Fourth seemed certainly to have borrowed a leaf out of Miss Eliza Andrews' book.

It did not rain, though it kept on looking as if it meant to. By noon the rooms were decorated, the table beautifully laid; and upstairs was waiting a bride, "adorned for her husband."

"You do look sweet," said Anne rapturously.

"Lovely," echoed Diana.

"Everything's ready, Miss Shirley, ma'am, and nothing dreadful has happened YET," was Charlotta's cheerful statement as she betook herself to her little back room to dress. Out came all the braids; the resultant rampant crinkliness was plaited into two tails and tied, not with two bows alone, but with four, of brand-new ribbon, brightly blue. The two upper bows rather gave the impression of overgrown wings sprouting from Charlotta's neck, somewhat after the fashion of Raphael's cherubs. But Charlotta the Fourth thought them very beautiful, and after she had rustled into a white dress, so stiffly starched that it could stand alone, she surveyed herself in her glass with great satisfaction . . . a satisfaction which lasted until she went out in the hall and caught a glimpse through the spare room door of a tall girl in some softly clinging gown, pinning white, star-like flowers on the smooth ripples of her ruddy hair.

"Oh, I'll NEVER be able to look like Miss Shirley," thought poor Charlotta despairingly. "You just have to be born so, I guess . . . don't seem's if any amount of practice could give you that AIR."

By one o'clock the guests had come, including Mr. and Mrs. Allan, for Mr. Allan was to perform the ceremony in the absence of the Grafton minister on his vacation. There was no formality about the marriage. Miss Lavendar came down the stairs to meet her bridegroom at the foot, and as he took her hand she lifted her big brown eyes to his with a look that made Charlotta the Fourth, who intercepted it, feel queerer than ever. They went out to the honeysuckle arbor, where Mr. Allan was awaiting them. The guests grouped themselves as they pleased. Anne and Diana stood by the old stone bench, with Charlotta the Fourth between them, desperately clutching their hands in her cold, tremulous little paws.

Mr. Allan opened his blue book and the ceremony proceeded. Just as Miss Lavendar and Stephen Irving were pronounced man and wife a very beautiful and symbolic thing happened. The sun suddenly burst through the gray and poured a flood of radiance on the happy bride. Instantly the garden was alive with dancing shadows and flickering lights.

"What a lovely omen," thought Anne, as she ran to kiss the bride. Then the three girls left the rest of the guests laughing around the bridal pair while they flew into the house to see that all was in readiness for the feast.

"Thanks be to goodness, it's over, Miss Shirley, ma'am," breathed Charlotta the Fourth, "and they're married safe and sound, no matter what happens now. The bags of rice are in the pantry, ma'am, and the old shoes are behind the door, and the cream for whipping is on the sullar steps."

At half past two Mr. and Mrs. Irving left, and everybody went to Bright River to see them off on the afternoon train. As Miss Lavendar . . . I beg her pardon, Mrs. Irving . . . stepped from the door of her old home Gilbert and the girls threw the rice and Charlotta the Fourth hurled an old shoe with such excellent aim that she struck Mr. Allan squarely on the head. But it was reserved for Paul to give the prettiest send-off. He popped out of the porch ringing furiously a huge old brass dinner bell which had adorned the dining room mantel. Paul's only motive was to make a joyful noise; but as the clangor died away, from point and curve and hill across the river came the chime of "fairy wedding bells," ringing clearly, sweetly, faintly and more faint, as if Miss Lavendar's beloved echoes were bidding her greeting and farewell. And so, amid this benediction of sweet sounds, Miss Lavendar drove away from the old life of dreams and make-believes to a fuller life of realities in the busy world beyond.

Two hours later Anne and Charlotta the Fourth came down the lane again. Gilbert had gone to West Grafton on an errand and Diana had to keep an engagement at home. Anne and Charlotta had come back to put things in order and lock up the little stone house. The garden was a pool of late golden sunshine, with butterflies hovering and bees booming; but the little house had already that indefinable air of desolation which always follows a festivity.

"Oh dear me, don't it look lonesome?" sniffed Charlotta the Fourth, who had been crying all the way home from the station. "A wedding ain't much cheerfuller than a funeral after all, when it's all over, Miss Shirley, ma'am."

A busy evening followed. The decorations had to be removed, the dishes washed, the uneaten delicacies packed into a basket for the delectation of Charlotta the Fourth's young brothers at home. Anne would not rest until everything was in apple-pie order; after Charlotta had gone home with her plunder Anne went over the still rooms, feeling like one who trod alone some banquet hall deserted, and closed the blinds. Then she locked the door and sat down under the silver poplar to wait for Gilbert, feeling very tired but still unweariedly thinking "long, long thoughts."

"What are you thinking of, Anne?" asked Gilbert, coming down the walk. He had left his horse and buggy out at the road.

"Of Miss Lavendar and Mr. Irving," answered Anne dreamily. "Isn't it beautiful to think how everything has turned out . . . how they have come together again after all the years of separation and misunderstanding?"

"Yes, it's beautiful," said Gilbert, looking steadily down into Anne's uplifted face, "but wouldn't it have been more beautiful still, Anne, if there had been NO separation or misunderstanding . . . if they had come hand in hand all the way through life, with no memories behind them but those which belonged to each other?"

For a moment Anne's heart fluttered queerly and for the first time her eyes faltered under Gilbert's gaze and a rosy flush stained the paleness of her face. It was as if a veil that had hung before her inner consciousness had been lifted, giving to her view a revelation of unsuspected feelings and realities. Perhaps, after all, romance did not come into one's life with pomp and blare, like a gay knight riding down; perhaps it crept to one's side like an old friend through quiet ways; perhaps it revealed itself in seeming prose, until some sudden shaft of illumination flung athwart its pages betrayed the rhythm and the music, perhaps . . . perhaps . . . love unfolded naturally out of a beautiful friendship, as a golden-hearted rose slipping from its green sheath.

Then the veil dropped again; but the Anne who walked up the dark lane was not quite the same Anne who had driven gaily down it the evening before. The page of girlhood had been turned, as by an unseen finger, and the page of womanhood was before her with all its charm and mystery, its pain and gladness.

Gilbert wisely said nothing more; but in his silence he read the history of the next four years in the light of Anne's remembered blush. Four years of earnest, happy work . . . and then the guerdon of a useful knowledge gained and a sweet heart won.

Behind them in the garden the little stone house brooded among the shadows. It was lonely but not forsaken. It had not yet done with dreams and laughter and the joy of life; there were to be future summers for the little stone house; meanwhile, it could wait. And over the river in purple durance the echoes bided their time.

ANNE OF THE ISLAND

TO
ALL THE GIRLS
ALL OVER THE WORLD
WHO HAVE "WANTED MORE"
ABOUT ANNE

All precious things discovered late
To those that seek them issue forth,
For Love in sequel works with Fate,
And draws the veil from hidden worth.
—TENNYSON

Chapter I - The Shadow of Change

"Harvest is ended and summer is gone," quoted Anne Shirley, gazing across the shorn fields dreamily. She and Diana Barry had been picking apples in the Green Gables orchard, but were now resting from their labors in a sunny corner, where airy fleets of thistledown drifted by on the wings of a wind that was still summer-sweet with the incense of ferns in the Haunted Wood.

But everything in the landscape around them spoke of autumn. The sea was roaring hollowly in the distance, the fields were bare and sere, scarfed with golden rod, the brook valley below Green Gables overflowed with asters of ethereal purple, and the Lake of Shining Waters was blue—blue—blue; not the changeful blue of spring, nor the pale azure of summer, but a clear, steadfast, serene blue, as if the water were past all moods and tenses of emotion and had settled down to a tranquility unbroken by fickle dreams.

"It has been a nice summer," said Diana, twisting the new ring on her left hand with a smile. "And Miss Lavendar's wedding seemed to come as a sort of crown to it. I suppose Mr. and Mrs. Irving are on the Pacific coast now."

"It seems to me they have been gone long enough to go around the world," sighed Anne.

"I can't believe it is only a week since they were married. Everything has changed. Miss Lavendar and Mr. and Mrs. Allan gone—how lonely the manse looks with the shutters all closed! I went past it last night, and it made me feel as if everybody in it had died."

"We'll never get another minister as nice as Mr. Allan," said Diana, with gloomy conviction. "I suppose we'll have all kinds of supplies this winter, and half the Sundays no preaching at all. And you and Gilbert gone—it will be awfully dull."

"Fred will be here," insinuated Anne slyly.

"When is Mrs. Lynde going to move up?" asked Diana, as if she had not heard Anne's remark.

"Tomorrow. I'm glad she's coming—but it will be another change. Marilla and I cleared everything out of the spare room yesterday. Do you know, I hated to do it? Of course, it was silly—but it did seem as if we were committing sacrilege. That old spare room has always seemed like a shrine to me. When I was a child I thought it the most wonderful apartment in the world. You remember what a consuming desire I had to sleep in a spare room bed—but not the Green Gables spare room. Oh, no, never there! It would have been too terrible—I couldn't have slept a wink from awe. I never WALKED through that room when Marilla sent me in on an errand—no, indeed, I tiptoed through it and held my breath, as if I were in church, and felt relieved when I got out of it. The pictures of George Whitefield and the Duke of Wellington hung there, one on each side of the mirror, and frowned so sternly at me all the time I was in, especially if I dared peep in the mirror, which was the only one in the house that didn't twist my face a little. I always wondered how Marilla dared houseclean that room. And now it's not only cleaned but stripped bare. George Whitefield and the Duke have been relegated to the upstairs hall. 'So passes the glory of this world,'" concluded Anne, with a laugh in which there was a little note of regret. It is never pleasant to have our old shrines desecrated, even when we have outgrown them.

"I'll be so lonesome when you go," moaned Diana for the hundredth time. "And to think you go next week!"

"But we're together still," said Anne cheerily. "We mustn't let next week rob us of this week's joy. I hate the thought of going myself—home and I are such good friends. Talk of being lonesome! It's I who should groan. YOU'LL be here with any number of your old friends—AND Fred! While I shall be alone among strangers, not knowing a soul!"

"EXCEPT Gilbert—AND Charlie Sloane," said Diana, imitating Anne's italics and slyness.

"Charlie Sloane will be a great comfort, of course," agreed Anne sarcastically; whereupon both those irresponsible damsels laughed. Diana knew exactly what Anne thought of Charlie Sloane; but, despite sundry confidential talks, she did not know just what Anne thought of Gilbert Blythe. To be sure, Anne herself did not know that.

"The boys may be boarding at the other end of Kingsport, for all I know," Anne went on. "I am glad I'm going to Redmond, and I am sure I shall like it after a while. But for the first few weeks I know I won't. I shan't even have the comfort of looking forward to the weekend visit home, as I had when I went to Queen's. Christmas will seem like a thousand years away."

"Everything is changing—or going to change," said Diana sadly. "I have a feeling that things will never be the same again, Anne."

"We have come to a parting of the ways, I suppose," said Anne thoughtfully. "We had to come to it. Do you think, Diana, that being grown-up is really as nice as we used to imagine it would be when we were children?"

"I don't know—there are SOME nice things about it," answered Diana, again caressing her ring with that little smile which always had the effect of making Anne feel suddenly left out and inexperienced. "But there are so many puzzling things, too. Sometimes I feel as if being grown-up just frightened me—and then I would give anything to be a little girl again."

"I suppose we'll get used to being grownup in time," said Anne cheerfully. "There won't be so many unexpected things about it by and by—though, after all,

I fancy it's the unexpected things that give spice to life. We're eighteen, Diana. In two more years we'll be twenty. When I was ten I thought twenty was a green old age. In no time you'll be a staid, middle-aged matron, and I shall be nice, old maid Aunt Anne, coming to visit you on vacations. You'll always keep a corner for me, won't you, Di darling? Not the spare room, of course—old maids can't aspire to spare rooms, and I shall be as 'umble as Uriah Heep, and quite content with a little over-the-porch or off-the-parlor cubby hole."

"What nonsense you do talk, Anne," laughed Diana. "You'll marry somebody splendid and handsome and rich—and no spare room in Avonlea will be half gorgeous enough for you—and you'll turn up your nose at all the friends of your youth."

"That would be a pity; my nose is quite nice, but I fear turning it up would spoil it," said Anne, patting that shapely organ. "I haven't so many good features that I could afford to spoil those I have; so, even if I should marry the King of the Cannibal Islands, I promise you I won't turn up my nose at you, Diana."

With another gay laugh the girls separated, Diana to return to Orchard Slope, Anne to walk to the Post Office. She found a letter awaiting her there, and when Gilbert Blythe overtook her on the bridge over the Lake of Shining Waters she was sparkling with the excitement of it.

"Priscilla Grant is going to Redmond, too," she exclaimed. "Isn't that splendid? I hoped she would, but she didn't think her father would consent. He has, however, and we're to board together. I feel that I can face an army with banners—or all the professors of Redmond in one fell phalanx—with a chum like Priscilla by my side."

"I think we'll like Kingsport," said Gilbert. "It's a nice old burg, they tell me, and has the finest natural park in the world. I've heard that the scenery in it is magnificent."

"I wonder if it will be—can be—any more beautiful than this," murmured Anne, looking around her with the loving, enraptured eyes of those to whom "home" must always be the loveliest spot in the world, no matter what fairer lands may lie under alien stars.

They were leaning on the bridge of the old pond, drinking deep of the enchantment of the dusk, just at the spot where Anne had climbed from her sinking Dory on the day Elaine floated down to Camelot. The fine, empurpling dye of sunset still stained the western skies, but the moon was rising and the water lay like a great, silver dream in her light. Remembrance wove a sweet and subtle spell over the two young creatures.

"You are very quiet, Anne," said Gilbert at last.

"I'm afraid to speak or move for fear all this wonderful beauty will vanish just like a broken silence," breathed Anne.

Gilbert suddenly laid his hand over the slender white one lying on the rail of the bridge. His hazel eyes deepened into darkness, his still boyish lips opened to say something of the dream and hope that thrilled his soul. But Anne snatched her hand away and turned quickly. The spell of the dusk was broken for her.

"I must go home," she exclaimed, with a rather overdone carelessness. "Marilla had a headache this afternoon, and I'm sure the twins will be in some dreadful mischief by this time. I really shouldn't have stayed away so long."

She chattered ceaselessly and inconsequently until they reached the Green Gables lane. Poor Gilbert hardly had a chance to get a word in edgewise. Anne felt rather relieved when they parted. There had been a new, secret self-consciousness in her heart with regard to Gilbert, ever since that fleeting moment of revelation in the garden of Echo Lodge. Something alien had intruded into the old, perfect, school-day comradeship—something that threatened to mar it.

"I never felt glad to see Gilbert go before," she thought, half-resentfully, half-sorrowfully, as she walked alone up the lane. "Our friendship will be spoiled if he goes on with this nonsense. It mustn't be spoiled—I won't let it. Oh, WHY can't boys be just sensible!"

Anne had an uneasy doubt that it was not strictly "sensible" that she should still feel on her hand the warm pressure of Gilbert's, as distinctly as she had felt it for the swift second his had rested there; and still less sensible that the sensation was far from being an unpleasant one—very different from that which had attended a similar demonstration on Charlie Sloane's part, when she had been sitting out a dance with him at a White Sands party three nights before. Anne shivered over the disagreeable recollection. But all problems connected with infatuated swains vanished from her mind when she entered the homely, unsentimental atmosphere of the Green Gables kitchen where an eight-year-old boy was crying grievously on the sofa.

"What is the matter, Davy?" asked Anne, taking him up in her arms. "Where are Marilla and Dora?"

"Marilla's putting Dora to bed," sobbed Davy, "and I'm crying 'cause Dora fell down the outside cellar steps, heels over head, and scraped all the skin off her nose, and—"

"Oh, well, don't cry about it, dear. Of course, you are sorry for her, but crying won't help her any. She'll be all right tomorrow. Crying never helps any one, Davy-boy, and—"

"I ain't crying 'cause Dora fell down cellar," said Davy, cutting short Anne's wellmeant preachment with increasing bitterness. "I'm crying, cause I wasn't there to see her fall. I'm always missing some fun or other, seems to me."

"Oh, Davy!" Anne choked back an unholy shriek of laughter. "Would you call it fun to see poor little Dora fall down the steps and get hurt?"

"She wasn't MUCH hurt," said Davy, defiantly. "'Course, if she'd been killed I'd have been real sorry, Anne. But the Keiths ain't so easy killed. They're like the Blewetts, I guess. Herb Blewett fell off the hayloft last Wednesday, and rolled right down through the turnip chute into the box stall, where they had a fearful wild, cross horse, and rolled right under his heels. And still he got out alive, with only three bones broke. Mrs. Lynde says there are some folks you can't kill with a meat-axe. Is Mrs. Lynde coming here tomorrow, Anne?"

"Yes, Davy, and I hope you'll be always very nice and good to her."

"I'll be nice and good. But will she ever put me to bed at nights, Anne?"

"Perhaps. Why?"

"'Cause," said Davy very decidedly, "if she does I won't say my prayers before her like I do before you, Anne."

"Why not?"

"'Cause I don't think it would be nice to talk to God before strangers, Anne. Dora can say hers to Mrs. Lynde if she likes, but *I* won't. I'll wait till she's gone and then say 'em. Won't that be all right, Anne?"

"Yes, if you are sure you won't forget to say them, Davy-boy."

"Oh, I won't forget, you bet. I think saying my prayers is great fun. But it won't be as good fun saying them alone as saying them to you. I wish you'd stay home, Anne. I don't see what you want to go away and leave us for."

"I don't exactly WANT to, Davy, but I feel I ought to go."

"If you don't want to go you needn't. You're grown up. When *I'm* grown up I'm not going to do one single thing I don't want to do, Anne."

"All your life, Davy, you'll find yourself doing things you don't want to do."

"I won't," said Davy flatly. "Catch me! I have to do things I don't want to now 'cause you and Marilla'll send me to bed if I don't. But when I grow up you can't do that, and there'll be nobody to tell me not to do things. Won't I have the time! Say, Anne, Milty Boulter says his mother says you're going to college to see if you can catch a man. Are you, Anne? I want to know."

For a second Anne burned with resentment. Then she laughed, reminding herself that Mrs. Boulter's crude vulgarity of thought and speech could not harm her.

"No, Davy, I'm not. I'm going to study and grow and learn about many things."

"What things?"

> "'Shoes and ships and sealing wax
> And cabbages and kings,'"

quoted Anne.

"But if you DID want to catch a man how would you go about it? I want to know," persisted Davy, for whom the subject evidently possessed a certain fascination.

"You'd better ask Mrs. Boulter," said Anne thoughtlessly. "I think it's likely she knows more about the process than I do."

"I will, the next time I see her," said Davy gravely.

"Davy! If you do!" cried Anne, realizing her mistake.

"But you just told me to," protested Davy aggrieved.

"It's time you went to bed," decreed Anne, by way of getting out of the scrape.

After Davy had gone to bed Anne wandered down to Victoria Island and sat there alone, curtained with fine-spun, moonlit gloom, while the water laughed around her in a duet of brook and wind. Anne had always loved that brook. Many a dream had she spun over its sparkling water in days gone by. She forgot love-lorn youths, and the cayenne speeches of malicious neighbors, and all the problems of her girlish existence. In imagination she sailed over storied seas that wash the distant shining shores of "faery lands forlorn," where lost Atlantis and

Elysium lie, with the evening star for pilot, to the land of Heart's Desire. And she was richer in those dreams than in realities; for things seen pass away, but the things that are unseen are eternal.

Chapter II - Garlands of Autumn

The following week sped swiftly, crowded with innumerable "last things," as Anne called them. Good-bye calls had to be made and received, being pleasant or otherwise, according to whether callers and called-upon were heartily in sympathy with Anne's hopes, or thought she was too much puffed-up over going to college and that it was their duty to "take her down a peg or two."

The A.V.I.S. gave a farewell party in honor of Anne and Gilbert one evening at the home of Josie Pye, choosing that place, partly because Mr. Pye's house was large and convenient, partly because it was strongly suspected that the Pye girls would have nothing to do with the affair if their offer of the house for the party was not accepted. It was a very pleasant little time, for the Pye girls were gracious, and said and did nothing to mar the harmony of the occasion—which was not according to their wont. Josie was unusually amiable—so much so that she even remarked condescendingly to Anne,

"Your new dress is rather becoming to you, Anne. Really, you look ALMOST PRETTY in it."

"How kind of you to say so," responded Anne, with dancing eyes. Her sense of humor was developing, and the speeches that would have hurt her at fourteen were becoming merely food for amusement now. Josie suspected that Anne was laughing at her behind those wicked eyes; but she contented herself with whispering to Gertie, as they went downstairs, that Anne Shirley would put on more airs than ever now that she was going to college—you'd see!

All the "old crowd" was there, full of mirth and zest and youthful lightheartedness. Diana Barry, rosy and dimpled, shadowed by the faithful Fred; Jane Andrews, neat and sensible and plain; Ruby Gillis, looking her handsomest and brightest in a cream silk blouse, with red geraniums in her golden hair; Gilbert Blythe and Charlie Sloane, both trying to keep as near the elusive Anne as possible; Carrie Sloane, looking pale and melancholy because, so it was reported, her father would not allow Oliver Kimball to come near the place; Moody Spurgeon MacPherson, whose round face and objectionable ears were as round and objectionable as ever; and Billy Andrews, who sat in a corner all the evening, chuckled when any one spoke to him, and watched Anne Shirley with a grin of pleasure on his broad, freckled countenance.

Anne had known beforehand of the party, but she had not known that she and Gilbert were, as the founders of the Society, to be presented with a very complimentary "address" and "tokens of respect"—in her case a volume of Shakespeare's plays, in Gilbert's a fountain pen. She was so taken by surprise and pleased by the nice things said in the address, read in Moody Spurgeon's most solemn and ministerial tones, that the tears quite drowned the sparkle of her big gray eyes. She had worked hard and faithfully for the A.V.I.S., and it warmed the cockles of her heart that the members appreciated her efforts so sincerely. And they were all so nice and friendly and jolly—even the Pye girls had their merits; at that moment Anne loved all the world.

She enjoyed the evening tremendously, but the end of it rather spoiled all. Gilbert again made the mistake of saying something sentimental to her as they ate their supper on the moonlit verandah; and Anne, to punish him, was gracious to Charlie Sloane and allowed the latter to walk home with her. She found, however, that revenge hurts nobody quite so much as the one who tries to inflict it. Gilbert walked airily off with Ruby Gillis, and Anne could hear them laughing and talking gaily as they loitered along in the still, crisp autumn air. They were evidently having the best of good times, while she was horribly bored by Charlie Sloane, who talked unbrokenly on, and never, even by accident, said one thing that was worth listening to. Anne gave an occasional absent "yes" or "no," and thought how beautiful Ruby had looked that night, how very goggly Charlie's eyes were in the moonlight—worse even than by daylight—and that the world, somehow, wasn't quite such a nice place as she had believed it to be earlier in the evening.

"I'm just tired out—that is what is the matter with me," she said, when she thankfully found herself alone in her own room. And she honestly believed it was. But a certain little gush of joy, as from some secret, unknown spring, bubbled up in her heart the next evening, when she saw Gilbert striding down through the Haunted Wood and crossing the old log bridge with that firm, quick step of his. So Gilbert was not going to spend this last evening with Ruby Gillis after all!

"You look tired, Anne," he said.

"I am tired, and, worse than that, I'm disgruntled. I'm tired because I've been packing my trunk and sewing all day. But I'm disgruntled because six women have been here to say good-bye to me, and every one of the six managed to say something that seemed to take the color right out of life and leave it as gray and dismal and cheerless as a November morning."

"Spiteful old cats!" was Gilbert's elegant comment.

"Oh, no, they weren't," said Anne seriously. "That is just the trouble. If they had been spiteful cats I wouldn't have minded them. But they are all nice, kind, motherly souls, who like me and whom I like, and that is why what they said, or hinted, had such undue weight with me. They let me see they thought I was crazy going to Redmond and trying to take a B.A., and ever since I've been wondering if I am. Mrs. Peter Sloane sighed and said she hoped my strength would hold out till I got through; and at once I saw myself a hopeless victim of nervous prostration at the end of my third year; Mrs. Eben Wright said it must cost an awful lot to put in four years at Redmond; and I felt all over me that it was unpardonable of me to squander Marilla's money and my own on such a folly. Mrs. Jasper Bell said she hoped I wouldn't let college spoil me, as it did some people; and I felt in my bones that the end of my four Redmond years would see me a most insufferable creature, thinking I knew it all, and looking down on everything and everybody in Avonlea; Mrs. Elisha Wright said she understood that Redmond girls, especially those who belonged to Kingsport, were 'dreadful dressy and stuck-up,' and she guessed I wouldn't feel much at home among them; and I saw myself, a snubbed, dowdy, humiliated country girl, shuffling through Redmond's classic halls in coppertoned boots."

Anne ended with a laugh and a sigh commingled. With her sensitive nature all disapproval had weight, even the disapproval of those for whose opinions she had scant respect. For the time being life was savorless, and ambition had gone out like a snuffed candle.

"You surely don't care for what they said," protested Gilbert. "You know exactly how narrow their outlook on life is, excellent creatures though they are. To do anything THEY have never done is anathema maranatha. You are the first Avonlea girl who has ever gone to college; and you know that all pioneers are considered to be afflicted with moonstruck madness."

"Oh, I know. But FEELING is so different from KNOWING. My common sense tells me all you can say, but there are times when common sense has no power over me. Common nonsense takes possession of my soul. Really, after Mrs. Elisha went away I hardly had the heart to finish packing."

"You're just tired, Anne. Come, forget it all and take a walk with me—a ramble back through the woods beyond the marsh. There should be something there I want to show you."

"Should be! Don't you know if it is there?"

"No. I only know it should be, from something I saw there in spring. Come on. We'll pretend we are two children again and we'll go the way of the wind."

They started gaily off. Anne, remembering the unpleasantness of the preceding evening, was very nice to Gilbert; and Gilbert, who was learning wisdom, took care to be nothing save the schoolboy comrade again. Mrs. Lynde and Marilla watched them from the kitchen window.

"That'll be a match some day," Mrs. Lynde said approvingly.

Marilla winced slightly. In her heart she hoped it would, but it went against her grain to hear the matter spoken of in Mrs. Lynde's gossipy matter-of-fact way.

"They're only children yet," she said shortly.

Mrs. Lynde laughed good-naturedly.

"Anne is eighteen; I was married when I was that age. We old folks, Marilla, are too much given to thinking children never grow up, that's what. Anne is a young woman and Gilbert's a man, and he worships the ground she walks on, as any one can see. He's a fine fellow, and Anne can't do better. I hope she won't get any romantic nonsense into her head at Redmond. I don't approve of them coeducational places and never did, that's what. I don't believe," concluded Mrs. Lynde solemnly, "that the students at such colleges ever do much else than flirt."

"They must study a little," said Marilla, with a smile.

"Precious little," sniffed Mrs. Rachel. "However, I think Anne will. She never was flirtatious. But she doesn't appreciate Gilbert at his full value, that's what. Oh, I know girls! Charlie Sloane is wild about her, too, but I'd never advise her to marry a Sloane. The Sloanes are good, honest, respectable people, of course. But when all's said and done, they're SLOANES."

Marilla nodded. To an outsider, the statement that Sloanes were Sloanes might not be very illuminating, but she understood. Every village has such a family; good, honest, respectable people they may be, but SLOANES they are and must ever remain, though they speak with the tongues of men and angels.

Gilbert and Anne, happily unconscious that their future was thus being settled by Mrs. Rachel, were sauntering through the shadows of the Haunted Wood. Beyond, the harvest hills were basking in an amber sunset radiance, under a pale, aerial sky of rose and blue. The distant spruce groves were burnished bronze, and their long shadows barred the upland meadows. But around them a little wind sang among the fir tassels, and in it there was the note of autumn.

"This wood really is haunted now—by old memories," said Anne, stooping to gather a spray of ferns, bleached to waxen whiteness by frost. "It seems to me that the little girls Diana and I used to be play here still, and sit by the Dryad's Bubble in the twilights, trysting with the ghosts. Do you know, I can never go up this path in the dusk without feeling a bit of the old fright and shiver? There was one especially horrifying phantom which we created—the ghost of the murdered child that crept up behind you and laid cold fingers on yours. I confess that, to this day, I cannot help fancying its little, furtive footsteps behind me when I come here after nightfall. I'm not afraid of the White Lady or the headless man or the skeletons, but I wish I had never imagined that baby's ghost into existence. How angry Marilla and Mrs. Barry were over that affair," concluded Anne, with reminiscent laughter.

The woods around the head of the marsh were full of purple vistas, threaded with gossamers. Past a dour plantation of gnarled spruces and a maple-fringed, sun-warm valley they found the "something" Gilbert was looking for.

"Ah, here it is," he said with satisfaction.

"An apple tree—and away back here!" exclaimed Anne delightedly.

"Yes, a veritable apple-bearing apple tree, too, here in the very midst of pines and beeches, a mile away from any orchard. I was here one day last spring and found it, all white with blossom. So I resolved I'd come again in the fall and see if it had been apples. See, it's loaded. They look good, too—tawny as russets but with a dusky red cheek. Most wild seedlings are green and uninviting."

"I suppose it sprang years ago from some chance-sown seed," said Anne dreamily. "And how it has grown and flourished and held its own here all alone among aliens, the brave determined thing!"

"Here's a fallen tree with a cushion of moss. Sit down, Anne—it will serve for a woodland throne. I'll climb for some apples. They all grow high—the tree had to reach up to the sunlight."

The apples proved to be delicious. Under the tawny skin was a white, white flesh, faintly veined with red; and, besides their own proper apple taste, they had a certain wild, delightful tang no orchard-grown apple ever possessed.

"The fatal apple of Eden couldn't have had a rarer flavor," commented Anne. "But it's time we were going home. See, it was twilight three minutes ago and now it's moonlight. What a pity we couldn't have caught the moment of transformation. But such moments never are caught, I suppose."

"Let's go back around the marsh and home by way of Lover's Lane. Do you feel as disgruntled now as when you started out, Anne?"

"Not I. Those apples have been as manna to a hungry soul. I feel that I shall love Redmond and have a splendid four years there."

"And after those four years—what?"

"Oh, there's another bend in the road at their end," answered Anne lightly. "I've no idea what may be around it—I don't want to have. It's nicer not to know."

Lover's Lane was a dear place that night, still and mysteriously dim in the pale radiance of the moonlight. They loitered through it in a pleasant chummy silence, neither caring to talk.

"If Gilbert were always as he has been this evening how nice and simple everything would be," reflected Anne.

Gilbert was looking at Anne, as she walked along. In her light dress, with her slender delicacy, she made him think of a white iris.

"I wonder if I can ever make her care for me," he thought, with a pang of self-distrust.

Chapter III - Greeting and Farewell

Charlie Sloane, Gilbert Blythe and Anne Shirley left Avonlea the following Monday morning. Anne had hoped for a fine day. Diana was to drive her to the station and they wanted this, their last drive together for some time, to be a pleasant one. But when Anne went to bed Sunday night the east wind was moaning around Green Gables with an ominous prophecy which was fulfilled in the morning. Anne awoke to find raindrops pattering against her window and shadowing the pond's gray surface with widening rings; hills and sea were hidden in mist, and the whole world seemed dim and dreary. Anne dressed in the cheerless gray dawn, for an early start was necessary to catch the boat train; she struggled against the tears that WOULD well up in her eyes in spite of herself. She was leaving the home that was so dear to her, and something told her that she was leaving it forever, save as a holiday refuge. Things would never be the same again; coming back for vacations would not be living there. And oh, how dear and beloved everything was—that little white porch room, sacred to the dreams of girlhood, the old Snow Queen at the window, the brook in the hollow, the Dryad's Bubble, the Haunted Woods, and Lover's Lane—all the thousand and one dear spots where memories of the old years bided. Could she ever be really happy anywhere else?

Breakfast at Green Gables that morning was a rather doleful meal. Davy, for the first time in his life probably, could not eat, but blubbered shamelessly over his porridge. Nobody else seemed to have much appetite, save Dora, who tucked away her rations comfortably. Dora, like the immortal and most prudent Charlotte, who "went on cutting bread and butter" when her frenzied lover's body had been carried past on a shutter, was one of those fortunate creatures who are seldom disturbed by anything. Even at eight it took a great deal to ruffle Dora's placidity. She was sorry Anne was going away, of course, but was that any reason why she should fail to appreciate a poached egg on toast? Not at all. And, seeing that Davy could not eat his, Dora ate it for him.

Promptly on time Diana appeared with horse and buggy, her rosy face glowing above her raincoat. The good-byes had to be said then somehow. Mrs. Lynde came in from her quarters to give Anne a hearty embrace and warn her to be careful of her health, whatever she did. Marilla, brusque and tearless, pecked Anne's cheek and said she supposed they'd hear from her when she got settled. A casual observer might have concluded that Anne's going mattered very little to her—unless said observer had happened to get a good look in her eyes. Dora kissed Anne primly and squeezed out two decorous little tears; but Davy, who had been crying on the back porch step ever since they rose from the table, refused to say good-bye at all. When he saw Anne coming towards him he sprang to his feet, bolted up the back stairs, and hid in a clothes closet, out of which he would not come. His muffled howls were the last sounds Anne heard as she left Green Gables.

It rained heavily all the way to Bright River, to which station they had to go, since the branch line train from Carmody did not connect with the boat train. Charlie and Gilbert were on the station platform when they reached it, and the train was whistling. Anne had just time to get her ticket and trunk check, say a hurried farewell to Diana, and hasten on board. She wished she were going back with Diana to Avonlea; she knew she was going to die of homesickness. And oh, if only that dismal rain would stop pouring down as if the whole world were weeping over summer vanished and joys departed! Even Gilbert's presence brought her no comfort, for Charlie Sloane was there, too, and Sloanishness could be tolerated only in fine weather. It was absolutely insufferable in rain.

But when the boat steamed out of Charlottetown harbor things took a turn for the better. The rain ceased and the sun began to burst out goldenly now and again between the rents in the clouds, burnishing the gray seas with copper-hued radiance, and lighting up the mists that curtained the Island's red shores with gleams of gold foretokening a fine day after all. Besides, Charlie Sloane promptly became so seasick that he had to go below, and Anne and Gilbert were left alone on deck.

"I am very glad that all the Sloanes get seasick as soon as they go on water," thought Anne mercilessly. "I am sure I couldn't take my farewell look at the 'ould sod' with Charlie standing there pretending to look sentimentally at it, too."

"Well, we're off," remarked Gilbert unsentimentally.

"Yes, I feel like Byron's 'Childe Harold'—only it isn't really my 'native shore' that I'm watching," said Anne, winking her gray eyes vigorously. "Nova Scotia is that, I suppose. But one's native shore is the land one loves the best, and that's good old P.E.I. for me. I can't believe I didn't always live here. Those eleven years before I came seem like a bad dream. It's seven years since I crossed on this boat—the evening Mrs. Spencer brought me over from Hopetown. I can see myself, in that dreadful old wincey dress and faded sailor hat, exploring decks and cabins with enraptured curiosity. It was a fine evening; and how those red Island shores did gleam in the sunshine. Now I'm crossing the strait again. Oh, Gilbert, I do hope I'll like Redmond and Kingsport, but I'm sure I won't!"

"Where's all your philosophy gone, Anne?"

"It's all submerged under a great, swamping wave of loneliness and homesickness. I've longed for three years to go to Redmond—and now I'm going—and I wish I weren't! Never mind! I shall be cheerful and philosophical again after I have just one good cry. I MUST have that, 'as a went'—and I'll have to wait until I get into my boardinghouse bed tonight, wherever it may be, before I can have it. Then Anne will be herself again. I wonder if Davy has come out of the closet yet."

It was nine that night when their train reached Kingsport, and they found themselves in the blue-white glare of the crowded station. Anne felt horribly bewildered, but a moment later she was seized by Priscilla Grant, who had come to Kingsport on Saturday.

"Here you are, beloved! And I suppose you're as tired as I was when I got here Saturday night."

"Tired! Priscilla, don't talk of it. I'm tired, and green, and provincial, and only about ten years old. For pity's sake take your poor, broken-down chum to some place where she can hear herself think."

"I'll take you right up to our boardinghouse. I've a cab ready outside."

"It's such a blessing you're here, Prissy. If you weren't I think I should just sit down on my suitcase, here and now, and weep bitter tears. What a comfort one familiar face is in a howling wilderness of strangers!"

"Is that Gilbert Blythe over there, Anne? How he has grown up this past year! He was only a schoolboy when I taught in Carmody. And of course that's Charlie Sloane. HE hasn't changed—couldn't! He looked just like that when he was born, and he'll look like that when he's eighty. This way, dear. We'll be home in twenty minutes."

"Home!" groaned Anne. "You mean we'll be in some horrible boardinghouse, in a still more horrible hall bedroom, looking out on a dingy back yard."

"It isn't a horrible boardinghouse, Anne-girl. Here's our cab. Hop in—the driver will get your trunk. Oh, yes, the boardinghouse—it's really a very nice place of its kind, as you'll admit tomorrow morning when a good night's sleep has turned your blues rosy pink. It's a big, old-fashioned, gray stone house on St. John Street, just a nice little constitutional from Redmond. It used to be the 'residence' of great folk, but fashion has deserted St. John Street and its houses only dream now of better days. They're so big that people living in them have to take boarders just to fill up. At least, that is the reason our landladies are very anxious to impress on us. They're delicious, Anne—our landladies, I mean."

"How many are there?"

"Two. Miss Hannah Harvey and Miss Ada Harvey. They were born twins about fifty years ago."

"I can't get away from twins, it seems," smiled Anne. "Wherever I go they confront me."

"Oh, they're not twins now, dear. After they reached the age of thirty they never were twins again. Miss Hannah has grown old, not too gracefully, and Miss Ada has stayed thirty, less gracefully still. I don't know whether Miss Hannah can smile or not; I've never caught her at it so far, but Miss Ada smiles all the time and that's worse. However, they're nice, kind souls, and they take two boarders every year because Miss Hannah's economical soul cannot bear to 'waste room space'—not because they need to or have to, as Miss Ada has told me seven times since Saturday night. As for our rooms, I admit they are hall bedrooms, and mine does look out on the back yard. Your room is a front one and looks out on Old St. John's graveyard, which is just across the street."

"That sounds gruesome," shivered Anne. "I think I'd rather have the back yard view."

"Oh, no, you wouldn't. Wait and see. Old St. John's is a darling place. It's been a graveyard so long that it's ceased to be one and has become one of the sights of Kingsport. I was all through it yesterday for a pleasure exertion. There's a big stone wall and a row of enormous trees all around it, and rows of trees all through it, and the queerest old tombstones, with the queerest and quaintest inscriptions. You'll go there to study, Anne, see if you don't. Of course, nobody is ever buried there now. But a few years ago they put up a beautiful monument to the memory of Nova Scotian soldiers who fell in the Crimean War. It is just opposite the entrance gates and there's 'scope for imagination' in it, as you used to say. Here's your trunk at last—and the boys coming to say good night. Must I really shake hands with Charlie Sloane, Anne? His hands are always so cold and fishy-feeling. We must ask them to call occasionally. Miss Hannah gravely told me we could have 'young gentlemen callers' two evenings in the week, if they went away at a reasonable hour; and Miss Ada asked me, smiling, please to be sure they didn't sit on her beautiful cushions. I promised to see to it; but goodness knows where else they CAN sit, unless they sit on the floor, for there are cushions on EVERYTHING. Miss Ada even has an elaborate Battenburg one on top of the piano."

Anne was laughing by this time. Priscilla's gay chatter had the intended effect of cheering her up; homesickness vanished for the time being, and did not even return in full force when she finally found herself alone in her little bedroom. She went to her window and looked out. The street below was dim and quiet. Across it the moon was shining above the trees in Old St. John's, just behind the great dark head of the lion on the monument. Anne wondered if it could have been only that morning that she had left Green Gables. She had the sense of a long passage of time which one day of change and travel gives.

"I suppose that very moon is looking down on Green Gables now," she mused. "But I won't think about it—that way homesickness lies. I'm not even going to have my good cry. I'll put that off to a more convenient season, and just now I'll go calmly and sensibly to bed and to sleep."

Chapter IV - April's Lady

Kingsport is a quaint old town, hearking back to early Colonial days, and wrapped in its ancient atmosphere, as some fine old dame in garments fashioned like those of her youth. Here and there it sprouts out into modernity, but at heart it is still unspoiled; it is full of curious relics, and haloed by the romance of many legends of the past. Once it was a mere frontier station on the fringe of the wilderness, and those were the days when Indians kept life from being monotonous to the settlers. Then it grew to be a bone of contention between the British and the French, being occupied now by the one and now by the other, emerging from each occupation with some fresh scar of battling nations branded on it.

It has in its park a martello tower, autographed all over by tourists, a dismantled old French fort on the hills beyond the town, and several antiquated cannon in its public squares. It has other historic spots also, which may be hunted out by the curious, and none is more quaint and delightful than Old St. John's Cemetery at the very core of the town, with streets of quiet, old-time houses on two sides, and busy, bustling, modern thoroughfares on the others. Every citizen of Kingsport feels a thrill of possessive pride in Old St. John's, for, if he be of any pretensions at all, he has an ancestor buried there, with a queer, crooked slab at his head, or else sprawling protectively over the grave, on which all the main facts of his history are recorded. For the most part no great art or skill was lavished on those old tombstones. The larger number are of roughly chiselled brown or gray native stone, and only in a few cases is there any attempt at ornamentation. Some are adorned with skull and cross-bones, and this grizzly decoration is frequently coupled with a cherub's head. Many are prostrate and in ruins. Into almost all Time's tooth has been gnawing, until some inscriptions have been completely effaced, and others can only be deciphered with difficulty. The graveyard is very full and very bowery, for it is surrounded and intersected by rows of elms and willows, beneath whose shade the sleepers must lie very dreamlessly, forever crooned to by the winds and leaves over them, and quite undisturbed by the clamor of traffic just beyond.

Anne took the first of many rambles in Old St. John's the next afternoon. She and Priscilla had gone to Redmond in the forenoon and registered as students, after which there was nothing more to do that day. The girls gladly made their escape, for it was not exhilarating to be surrounded by crowds of strangers, most of whom had a rather alien appearance, as if not quite sure where they belonged.

The "freshettes" stood about in detached groups of two or three, looking askance at each other; the "freshies," wiser in their day and generation, had banded themselves together on the big staircase of the entrance hall, where they were shouting out glees with all the vigor of youthful lungs, as a species of defiance to their traditional enemies, the Sophomores, a few of whom were prowling loftily about, looking properly disdainful of the "unlicked cubs" on the stairs. Gilbert and Charlie were nowhere to be seen.

"Little did I think the day would ever come when I'd be glad of the sight of a Sloane," said Priscilla, as they crossed the campus, "but I'd welcome Charlie's goggle eyes almost ecstatically. At least, they'd be familiar eyes."

"Oh," sighed Anne. "I can't describe how I felt when I was standing there, waiting my turn to be registered—as insignificant as the teeniest drop in a most enormous bucket. It's bad enough to feel insignificant, but it's unbearable to have it grained into your soul that you will never, can never, be anything but insignificant, and that is how I did feel—as if I were invisible to the naked eye and some of those Sophs might step on me. I knew I would go down to my grave unwept, unhonored and unsung."

"Wait till next year," comforted Priscilla. "Then we'll be able to look as bored and sophisticated as any Sophomore of them all. No doubt it is rather dreadful to feel insignificant; but I think it's better than to feel as big and awkward as I did— as if I were sprawled all over Redmond. That's how I felt—I suppose because I was a good two inches taller than any one else in the crowd. I wasn't afraid a Soph might walk over me; I was afraid they'd take me for an elephant, or an overgrown sample of a potato-fed Islander."

"I suppose the trouble is we can't forgive big Redmond for not being little Queen's," said Anne, gathering about her the shreds of her old cheerful philosophy to cover her nakedness of spirit. "When we left Queen's we knew everybody and had a place of our own. I suppose we have been unconsciously expecting to take life up at Redmond just where we left off at Queen's, and now we feel as if the ground had slipped from under our feet. I'm thankful that neither Mrs. Lynde nor Mrs. Elisha Wright know, or ever will know, my state of mind at present. They would exult in saying 'I told you so,' and be convinced it was the beginning of the end. Whereas it is just the end of the beginning."

"Exactly. That sounds more Anneish. In a little while we'll be acclimated and acquainted, and all will be well. Anne, did you notice the girl who stood alone just outside the door of the coeds' dressing room all the morning—the pretty one with the brown eyes and crooked mouth?"

"Yes, I did. I noticed her particularly because she seemed the only creature there who LOOKED as lonely and friendless as I FELT. I had YOU, but she had no one."

"I think she felt pretty all-by-herselfish, too. Several times I saw her make a motion as if to cross over to us, but she never did it—too shy, I suppose. I wished she would come. If I hadn't felt so much like the aforesaid elephant I'd have gone to her. But I couldn't lumber across that big hall with all those boys howling on the stairs. She was the prettiest freshette I saw today, but probably favor is deceitful and even beauty is vain on your first day at Redmond," concluded Priscilla with a laugh.

"I'm going across to Old St. John's after lunch," said Anne. "I don't know that a graveyard is a very good place to go to get cheered up, but it seems the only get-at-able place where there are trees, and trees I must have. I'll sit on one of those old slabs and shut my eyes and imagine I'm in the Avonlea woods."

Anne did not do that, however, for she found enough of interest in Old St. John's to keep her eyes wide open. They went in by the entrance gates, past the simple, massive, stone arch surmounted by the great lion of England.

> "'And on Inkerman yet the wild bramble is gory,
> And those bleak heights henceforth shall be famous in story,'"

quoted Anne, looking at it with a thrill. They found themselves in a dim, cool, green place where winds were fond of purring. Up and down the long grassy aisles they wandered, reading the quaint, voluminous epitaphs, carved in an age that had more leisure than our own.

"'Here lieth the body of Albert Crawford, Esq.,'" read Anne from a worn, gray slab, "'for many years Keeper of His Majesty's Ordnance at Kingsport. He served in the army till the peace of 1763, when he retired from bad health. He was a brave officer, the best of husbands, the best of fathers, the best of friends. He died October 29th, 1792, aged 84 years.' There's an epitaph for you, Prissy. There is certainly some 'scope for imagination' in it. How full such a life must have been of adventure! And as for his personal qualities, I'm sure human eulogy couldn't go further. I wonder if they told him he was all those best things while he was alive."

"Here's another," said Priscilla. "Listen—

'To the memory of Alexander Ross, who died on the 22nd of September, 1840, aged 43 years. This is raised as a tribute of affection by one whom he served so faithfully for 27 years that he was regarded as a friend, deserving the fullest confidence and attachment.'"

"A very good epitaph," commented Anne thoughtfully. "I wouldn't wish a better. We are all servants of some sort, and if the fact that we are faithful can be truthfully inscribed on our tombstones nothing more need be added. Here's a sorrowful little gray stone, Prissy—'to the memory of a favorite child.' And here is another 'erected to the memory of one who is buried elsewhere.' I wonder where that unknown grave is. Really, Pris, the graveyards of today will never be as interesting as this. You were right—I shall come here often. I love it already. I see we're not alone here—there's a girl down at the end of this avenue."

"Yes, and I believe it's the very girl we saw at Redmond this morning. I've been watching her for five minutes. She has started to come up the avenue exactly half a dozen times, and half a dozen times has she turned and gone back. Either she's dreadfully shy or she has got something on her conscience. Let's go and meet her. It's easier to get acquainted in a graveyard than at Redmond, I believe."

They walked down the long grassy arcade towards the stranger, who was sitting on a gray slab under an enormous willow. She was certainly very pretty, with a vivid, irregular, bewitching type of prettiness. There was a gloss as of brown nuts on her satin-smooth hair and a soft, ripe glow on her round cheeks. Her eyes were big and brown and velvety, under oddly-pointed black brows, and her crooked mouth was rose-red. She wore a smart brown suit, with two very modish little shoes peeping from beneath it; and her hat of dull pink straw, wreathed with golden-brown poppies, had the indefinable, unmistakable air which pertains to the "creation" of an artist in millinery. Priscilla had a sudden stinging consciousness that her own hat had been trimmed by her village store milliner, and Anne wondered uncomfortably if the blouse she had made herself, and which Mrs. Lynde had fitted, looked VERY countrified and home-made besides the stranger's smart attire. For a moment both girls felt like turning back.

But they had already stopped and turned towards the gray slab. It was too late to retreat, for the brown-eyed girl had evidently concluded that they were coming to speak to her. Instantly she sprang up and came forward with outstretched hand and a gay, friendly smile in which there seemed not a shadow of either shyness or burdened conscience.

"Oh, I want to know who you two girls are," she exclaimed eagerly. "I've been DYING to know. I saw you at Redmond this morning. Say, wasn't it AWFUL there? For the time I wished I had stayed home and got married."

Anne and Priscilla both broke into unconstrained laughter at this unexpected conclusion. The brown-eyed girl laughed, too.

"I really did. I COULD have, you know. Come, let's all sit down on this gravestone and get acquainted. It won't be hard. I know we're going to adore each other—I knew it as soon as I saw you at Redmond this morning. I wanted so much to go right over and hug you both."

"Why didn't you?" asked Priscilla.

"Because I simply couldn't make up my mind to do it. I never can make up my mind about anything myself—I'm always afflicted with indecision. Just as soon as I decide to do something I feel in my bones that another course would be the correct one. It's a dreadful misfortune, but I was born that way, and there is no use in blaming me for it, as some people do. So I couldn't make up my mind to go and speak to you, much as I wanted to."

"We thought you were too shy," said Anne.

"No, no, dear. Shyness isn't among the many failings—or virtues—of Philippa Gordon—Phil for short. Do call me Phil right off. Now, what are your handles?"

"She's Priscilla Grant," said Anne, pointing.

"And SHE'S Anne Shirley," said Priscilla, pointing in turn.

"And we're from the Island," said both together.

"I hail from Bolingbroke, Nova Scotia," said Philippa.

"Bolingbroke!" exclaimed Anne. "Why, that is where I was born."

"Do you really mean it? Why, that makes you a Bluenose after all."

"No, it doesn't," retorted Anne. "Wasn't it Dan O'Connell who said that if a man was born in a stable it didn't make him a horse? I'm Island to the core."

"Well, I'm glad you were born in Bolingbroke anyway. It makes us kind of neighbors, doesn't it? And I like that, because when I tell you secrets it won't be as if I were telling them to a stranger. I have to tell them. I can't keep secrets—it's no use to try. That's my worst failing—that, and indecision, as aforesaid. Would you believe it?—it took me half an hour to decide which hat to wear when I was coming here—HERE, to a graveyard! At first I inclined to my brown one with the feather; but as soon as I put it on I thought this pink one with the floppy brim would be more becoming. When I got IT pinned in place I liked the brown one better. At last I put them close together on the bed, shut my eyes, and jabbed with a hat pin. The pin speared the pink one, so I put it on. It is becoming, isn't it? Tell me, what do you think of my looks?"

At this naive demand, made in a perfectly serious tone, Priscilla laughed again. But Anne said, impulsively squeezing Philippa's hand,

"We thought this morning that you were the prettiest girl we saw at Redmond."

Philippa's crooked mouth flashed into a bewitching, crooked smile over very white little teeth.

"I thought that myself," was her next astounding statement, "but I wanted some one else's opinion to bolster mine up. I can't decide even on my own appearance. Just as soon as I've decided that I'm pretty I begin to feel miserably that I'm not. Besides, have a horrible old great-aunt who is always saying to me, with a mournful sigh, 'You were such a pretty baby. It's strange how children change when they grow up.' I adore aunts, but I detest great-aunts. Please tell me quite often that I am pretty, if you don't mind. I feel so much more comfortable when I can believe I'm pretty. And I'll be just as obliging to you if you want me to—I CAN be, with a clear conscience."

"Thanks," laughed Anne, "but Priscilla and I are so firmly convinced of our own good looks that we don't need any assurance about them, so you needn't trouble."

"Oh, you're laughing at me. I know you think I'm abominably vain, but I'm not. There really isn't one spark of vanity in me. And I'm never a bit grudging about paying compliments to other girls when they deserve them. I'm so glad I know you folks. I came up on Saturday and I've nearly died of homesickness ever since. It's a horrible feeling, isn't it? In Bolingbroke I'm an important personage, and in Kingsport I'm just nobody! There were times when I could feel my soul turning a delicate blue. Where do you hang out?"

"Thirty-eight St. John's Street."

"Better and better. Why, I'm just around the corner on Wallace Street. I don't like my boardinghouse, though. It's bleak and lonesome, and my room looks out on such an unholy back yard. It's the ugliest place in the world. As for cats—well, surely ALL the Kingsport cats can't congregate there at night, but half of them must. I adore cats on hearth rugs, snoozing before nice, friendly fires, but cats in back yards at midnight are totally different animals. The first night I was here I cried all night, and so did the cats. You should have seen my nose in the morning. How I wished I had never left home!"

"I don't know how you managed to make up your mind to come to Redmond at all, if you are really such an undecided person," said amused Priscilla.

"Bless your heart, honey, I didn't. It was father who wanted me to come here. His heart was set on it—why, I don't know. It seems perfectly ridiculous to think of me studying for a B.A. degree, doesn't it? Not but what I can do it, all right. I have heaps of brains."

"Oh!" said Priscilla vaguely.

"Yes. But it's such hard work to use them. And B.A.'s are such learned, digni-fied, wise, solemn creatures—they must be. No, *I* didn't want to come to Redmond. I did it just to oblige father. He IS such a duck. Besides, I knew if I stayed home I'd have to get married. Mother wanted that—wanted it decidedly. Mother has plenty of decision. But I really hated the thought of being married for a few years yet. I want to have heaps of fun before I settle down. And, ridiculous as the idea of my being a B.A. is, the idea of my being an old married woman is still more absurd, isn't it? I'm only eighteen. No, I concluded I would rather come to Redmond than be married. Besides, how could I ever have made up my mind which man to marry?"

"Were there so many?" laughed Anne.

"Heaps. The boys like me awfully—they really do. But there were only two that mattered. The rest were all too young and too poor. I must marry a rich man, you know."

"Why must you?"

"Honey, you couldn't imagine ME being a poor man's wife, could you? I can't do a single useful thing, and I am VERY extravagant. Oh, no, my husband must have heaps of money. So that narrowed them down to two. But I couldn't decide between two any easier than between two hundred. I knew perfectly well that whichever one I chose I'd regret all my life that I hadn't married the other."

"Didn't you—love—either of them?" asked Anne, a little hesitatingly. It was not easy for her to speak to a stranger of the great mystery and transformation of life.

"Goodness, no. *I* couldn't love anybody. It isn't in me. Besides I wouldn't want to. Being in love makes you a perfect slave, *I* think. And it would give a man such power to hurt you. I'd be afraid. No, no, Alec and Alonzo are two dear boys, and I like them both so much that I really don't know which I like the better. That is the trouble. Alec is the best looking, of course, and I simply couldn't marry a man who wasn't handsome. He is good-tempered too, and has lovely, curly, black hair. He's rather too perfect—I don't believe I'd like a perfect husband—somebody I could never find fault with."

"Then why not marry Alonzo?" asked Priscilla gravely.

"Think of marrying a name like Alonzo!" said Phil dolefully. "I don't believe I could endure it. But he has a classic nose, and it WOULD be a comfort to have a nose in the family that could be depended on. I can't depend on mine. So far, it takes after the Gordon pattern, but I'm so afraid it will develop Byrne tendencies as I grow older. I examine it every day anxiously to make sure it's still Gordon. Mother was a Byrne and has the Byrne nose in the Byrnest degree. Wait till you see it. I adore nice noses. Your nose is awfully nice, Anne Shirley. Alonzo's nose nearly turned the balance in his favor. But ALONZO! No, I couldn't decide. If I could have done as I did with the hats—stood them both up together, shut my eyes, and jabbed with a hatpin—it would have been quite easy."

"What did Alec and Alonzo feel like when you came away?" queried Priscilla.

"Oh, they still have hope. I told them they'd have to wait till I could make up my mind. They're quite willing to wait. They both worship me, you know. Meanwhile, I intend to have a good time. I expect I shall have heaps of beaux at Redmond. I can't be happy unless I have, you know. But don't you think the freshmen are fearfully homely? I saw only one really handsome fellow among them. He went away before you came. I heard his chum call him Gilbert. His chum had eyes that stuck out THAT FAR. But you're not going yet, girls? Don't go yet."

"I think we must," said Anne, rather coldly. "It's getting late, and I've some work to do."

"But you'll both come to see me, won't you?" asked Philippa, getting up and putting an arm around each. "And let me come to see you. I want to be chummy with you. I've taken such a fancy to you both. And I haven't quite disgusted you with my frivolity, have I?"

"Not quite," laughed Anne, responding to Phil's squeeze, with a return of cordiality.

"Because I'm not half so silly as I seem on the surface, you know. You just accept Philippa Gordon, as the Lord made her, with all her faults, and I believe you'll come to like her. Isn't this graveyard a sweet place? I'd love to be buried here. Here's a grave I didn't see before—this one in the iron railing—oh, girls, look, see—the stone says it's the grave of a middy who was killed in the fight between the Shannon and the Chesapeake. Just fancy!"

Anne paused by the railing and looked at the worn stone, her pulses thrilling with sudden excitement. The old graveyard, with its over-arching trees and long aisles of shadows, faded from her sight. Instead, she saw the Kingsport Harbor of nearly a century agone. Out of the mist came slowly a great frigate, brilliant with "the meteor flag of England." Behind her was another, with a still, heroic form, wrapped in his own starry flag, lying on the quarter deck—the gallant Lawrence. Time's finger had turned back his pages, and that was the Shannon sailing triumphant up the bay with the Chesapeake as her prize.

"Come back, Anne Shirley—come back," laughed Philippa, pulling her arm. "You're a hundred years away from us. Come back."

Anne came back with a sigh; her eyes were shining softly.

"I've always loved that old story," she said, "and although the English won that victory, I think it was because of the brave, defeated commander I love it. This grave seems to bring it so near and make it so real. This poor little middy was only eighteen. He 'died of desperate wounds received in gallant action'—so reads his epitaph. It is such as a soldier might wish for."

Before she turned away, Anne unpinned the little cluster of purple pansies she wore and dropped it softly on the grave of the boy who had perished in the great sea-duel.

"Well, what do you think of our new friend?" asked Priscilla, when Phil had left them.

"I like her. There is something very lovable about her, in spite of all her nonsense. I believe, as she says herself, that she isn't half as silly as she sounds. She's a dear, kissable baby—and I don't know that she'll ever really grow up."

"I like her, too," said Priscilla, decidedly. "She talks as much about boys as Ruby Gillis does. But it always enrages or sickens me to hear Ruby, whereas I just wanted to laugh good-naturedly at Phil. Now, what is the why of that?"

"There is a difference," said Anne meditatively. "I think it's because Ruby is really so CONSCIOUS of boys. She plays at love and love-making. Besides, you feel, when she is boasting of her beaux that she is doing it to rub it well into you that you haven't half so many. Now, when Phil talks of her beaux it sounds as if she was just speaking of chums. She really looks upon boys as good comrades, and she is pleased when she has dozens of them tagging round, simply because she likes to be popular and to be thought popular. Even Alex and Alonzo—I'll never be able to think of those two names separately after this—are to her just two playfellows who want her to play with them all their lives. I'm glad we met her, and I'm glad we went to Old St. John's. I believe I've put forth a tiny soul-root into Kingsport soil this afternoon. I hope so. I hate to feel transplanted."

Chapter V - Letters from Home

For the next three weeks Anne and Priscilla continued to feel as strangers in a strange land. Then, suddenly, everything seemed to fall into focus—Redmond, professors, classes, students, studies, social doings. Life became homogeneous again, instead of being made up of detached fragments. The Freshmen, instead of being a collection of unrelated individuals, found themselves a class, with a class spirit, a class yell, class interests, class antipathies and class ambitions. They won the day in the annual "Arts Rush" against the Sophomores, and thereby gained the respect of all the classes, and an enormous, confidence-giving opinion of themselves. For three years the Sophomores had won in the "rush"; that the victory of this year perched upon the Freshmen's banner was attributed to the strategic generalship of Gilbert Blythe, who marshalled the campaign and originated certain new tactics, which demoralized the Sophs and swept the Freshmen to triumph. As a reward of merit he was elected president of the Freshman Class, a position of honor and responsibility—from a Fresh point of view, at least—coveted by many. He was also invited to join the "Lambs"—Redmondese for Lamba Theta—a compliment rarely paid to a Freshman. As a preparatory initiation ordeal he had to parade the principal business streets of Kingsport for a whole day wearing a sunbonnet and a voluminous kitchen apron of gaudily flowered calico. This he did cheerfully, doffing his sunbonnet with courtly grace when he met ladies of his acquaintance. Charlie Sloane, who had not been asked to join the Lambs, told Anne he did not see how Blythe could do it, and HE, for his part, could never humiliate himself so.

"Fancy Charlie Sloane in a 'caliker' apron and a 'sunbunnit,'" giggled Priscilla. "He'd look exactly like his old Grandmother Sloane. Gilbert, now, looked as much like a man in them as in his own proper habiliments."

Anne and Priscilla found themselves in the thick of the social life of Redmond. That this came about so speedily was due in great measure to Philippa Gordon. Philippa was the daughter of a rich and well-known man, and belonged to an old and exclusive "Bluenose" family. This, combined with her beauty and charm—a charm acknowledged by all who met her—promptly opened the gates of all cliques, clubs and classes in Redmond to her; and where she went Anne and Priscilla went, too. Phil "adored" Anne and Priscilla, especially Anne. She was a loyal little soul, crystal-free from any form of snobbishness. "Love me, love my friends" seemed to be her unconscious motto. Without effort, she took them with her into her ever widening circle of acquaintanceship, and the two Avonlea girls found their social pathway at Redmond made very easy and pleasant for them, to the envy and wonderment of the other freshettes, who, lacking Philippa's sponsorship, were doomed to remain rather on the fringe of things during their first college year.

To Anne and Priscilla, with their more serious views of life, Phil remained the amusing, lovable baby she had seemed on their first meeting. Yet, as she said herself, she had "heaps" of brains. When or where she found time to study was a mystery, for she seemed always in demand for some kind of "fun," and her home evenings were crowded with callers. She had all the "beaux" that heart could desire, for nine-tenths of the Freshmen and a big fraction of all the other classes were rivals for her smiles. She was naively delighted over this, and gleefully recounted each new conquest to Anne and Priscilla, with comments that might have made the unlucky lover's ears burn fiercely.

"Alec and Alonzo don't seem to have any serious rival yet," remarked Anne, teasingly.

"Not one," agreed Philippa. "I write them both every week and tell them all about my young men here. I'm sure it must amuse them. But, of course, the one I like best I can't get. Gilbert Blythe won't take any notice of me, except to look at me as if I were a nice little kitten he'd like to pat. Too well I know the reason. I owe you a grudge, Queen Anne. I really ought to hate you and instead I love you madly, and I'm miserable if I don't see you every day. You're different from any girl I ever knew before. When you look at me in a certain way I feel what an insignificant, frivolous little beast I am, and I long to be better and wiser and stronger. And then I make good resolutions; but the first nice-looking mannie who comes my way knocks them all out of my head. Isn't college life magnificent? It's so funny to think I hated it that first day. But if I hadn't I might never got really acquainted with you. Anne, please tell me over again that you like me a little bit. I yearn to hear it."

"I like you a big bit—and I think you're a dear, sweet, adorable, velvety, clawless, little—kitten," laughed Anne, "but I don't see when you ever get time to learn your lessons."

Phil must have found time for she held her own in every class of her year. Even the grumpy old professor of Mathematics, who detested coeds, and had bitterly opposed their admission to Redmond, couldn't floor her. She led the freshettes everywhere, except in English, where Anne Shirley left her far behind. Anne herself found the studies of her Freshman year very easy, thanks in great part to the steady work she and Gilbert had put in during those two past years in Avonlea. This left her more time for a social life which she thoroughly enjoyed. But never for a moment did she forget Avonlea and the friends there. To her, the happiest moments in each week were those in which letters came from home. It was not until she had got her first letters that she began to think she could ever like Kingsport or feel at home there. Before they came, Avonlea had seemed thousands of miles away; those letters brought it near and linked the old life to the new so closely that they began to seem one and the same, instead of two hopelessly segregated existences. The first batch contained six letters, from Jane Andrews, Ruby Gillis, Diana Barry, Marilla, Mrs. Lynde and Davy. Jane's was a copperplate production, with every "t" nicely crossed and every "i" precisely dotted, and not an interesting sentence in it. She never mentioned the school, concerning which Anne was avid to hear; she never answered one of the questions Anne had asked in her letter. But she told Anne how many yards of lace she had recently crocheted, and the kind of weather they were having in Avonlea, and how she intended to have her new dress made, and the way she felt when her head ached. Ruby Gillis wrote a gushing epistle deploring Anne's absence, assuring her she was horribly missed in everything, asking what the Redmond "fellows" were like, and filling the rest with accounts of her own harrowing experiences with her numerous admirers. It was a silly, harmless letter, and Anne would have laughed over it had it not been for the postscript. "Gilbert seems to be enjoying Redmond, judging from his letters," wrote Ruby. "I don't think Charlie is so stuck on it."

So Gilbert was writing to Ruby! Very well. He had a perfect right to, of course. Only—!! Anne did not know that Ruby had written the first letter and that Gilbert had answered it from mere courtesy. She tossed Ruby's letter aside contemptuously. But it took all Diana's breezy, newsy, delightful epistle to banish the sting of Ruby's postscript. Diana's letter contained a little too much Fred, but was otherwise crowded and crossed with items of interest, and Anne almost felt herself back in Avonlea while reading it. Marilla's was a rather prim and colorless epistle, severely innocent of gossip or emotion. Yet somehow it conveyed to Anne a whiff of the wholesome, simple life at Green Gables, with its savor of ancient peace, and the steadfast abiding love that was there for her. Mrs. Lynde's letter was full of church news. Having broken up housekeeping, Mrs. Lynde had more time than ever to devote to church affairs and had flung herself into them heart and soul. She was at present much worked up over the poor "supplies" they were having in the vacant Avonlea pulpit.

"I don't believe any but fools enter the ministry nowadays," she wrote bitterly. "Such candidates as they have sent us, and such stuff as they preach! Half of it ain't true, and, what's worse, it ain't sound doctrine. The one we have now is the worst of the lot. He mostly takes a text and preaches about something else. And he says he doesn't believe all the heathen will be eternally lost. The idea! If they won't all the money we've been giving to Foreign Missions will be clean wasted, that's what! Last Sunday night he announced that next Sunday he'd preach on the axe-head that swam. I think he'd better confine himself to the Bible and leave sensational subjects alone. Things have come to a pretty pass if a minister can't find enough in Holy Writ to preach about, that's what. What church do you attend, Anne? I hope you go regularly. People are apt to get so careless about churchgoing away from home, and I understand college students are great sinners in this respect. I'm told many of them actually study their lessons on Sunday. I hope you'll never sink that low, Anne. Remember how you were brought up. And be very careful what friends you make. You never know what sort of creatures are in them colleges. Outwardly they may be as whited sepulchers and inwardly as ravening wolves, that's what. You'd better not have anything to say to any young man who isn't from the Island.

"I forgot to tell you what happened the day the minister called here. It was the funniest thing I ever saw. I said to Marilla, 'If Anne had been here wouldn't she have had a laugh?' Even Marilla laughed. You know he's a very short, fat little man with bow legs. Well, that old pig of Mr. Harrison's—the big, tall one—had wandered over here that day again and broke into the yard, and it got into the back porch, unbeknowns to us, and it was there when the minister appeared in the doorway. It made one wild bolt to get out, but there was nowhere to bolt to except between them bow legs. So there it went, and, being as it was so big and the minister so little, it took him clean off his feet and carried him away. His hat went one way and his cane another, just as Marilla and I got to the door. I'll never forget the look of him. And that poor pig was near scared to death. I'll never be able to read that account in the Bible of the swine that rushed madly down the steep place into the sea without seeing Mr. Harrison's pig careering down the hill with that minister. I guess the pig thought he had the Old Boy on his back instead of inside of him. I was thankful the twins weren't about. It wouldn't have been the right thing for them to have seen a minister in such an undignified predicament. Just before they got to the brook the minister jumped off or fell off. The pig rushed through the brook like mad and up through the woods. Marilla and I run down and helped the minister get up and brush his coat. He wasn't hurt, but he was mad. He seemed to hold Marilla and me responsible for it all, though we told him the pig didn't belong to us, and had been pestering us all summer. Besides, what did he come to the back door for? You'd never have caught Mr. Allan doing that. It'll be a long time before we get a man like Mr. Allan. But it's an ill wind that blows no good. We've never seen hoof or hair of that pig since, and it's my belief we never will.

"Things is pretty quiet in Avonlea. I don't find Green Gables as lonesome as I expected. I think I'll start another cotton warp quilt this winter. Mrs. Silas Sloane has a handsome new apple-leaf pattern.

"When I feel that I must have some excitement I read the murder trials in that Boston paper my niece sends me. I never used to do it, but they're real interesting. The States must be an awful place. I hope you'll never go there, Anne. But the way girls roam over the earth now is something terrible. It always makes me think of Satan in the Book of Job, going to and fro and walking up and down. I don't believe the Lord ever intended it, that's what.

"Davy has been pretty good since you went away. One day he was bad and Marilla punished him by making him wear Dora's apron all day, and then he went and cut all Dora's aprons up. I spanked him for that and then he went and chased my rooster to death.

"The MacPhersons have moved down to my place. She's a great housekeeper and very particular. She's rooted all my June lilies up because she says they make a garden look so untidy. Thomas set them lilies out when we were married. Her husband seems a nice sort of a man, but she can't get over being an old maid, that's what.

"Don't study too hard, and be sure and put your winter underclothes on as soon as the weather gets cool. Marilla worries a lot about you, but I tell her you've got a lot more sense than I ever thought you would have at one time, and that you'll be all right."

Davy's letter plunged into a grievance at the start.

"Dear anne, please write and tell marilla not to tie me to the rale of the bridge when I go fishing the boys make fun of me when she does. Its awful lonesome here without you but grate fun in school. Jane andrews is crosser than you. I scared mrs. lynde with a jacky lantern last nite. She was offel mad and she was mad cause I chased her old rooster round the yard till he fell down ded. I didn't mean to make him fall down ded. What made him die, anne, I want to know. mrs. lynde threw him into the pig pen she mite of sold him to mr. blair. mr. blair is giving 50 sense apeace for good ded roosters now. I herd mrs. lynde asking the minister to pray for her. What did she do that was so bad, anne, I want to know. I've got a kite with a magnificent tail, anne. Milty bolter told me a grate story in school yesterday. it is troo. old Joe Mosey and Leon were playing cards one nite last week in the woods. The cards were on a stump and a big black man bigger than the trees come along and grabbed the cards and the stump and disapered with a noys like thunder. Ill bet they were skared. Milty says the black man was the old harry. was he, anne, I want to know. Mr. kimball over at spenservale is very sick and will have to go to the hospitable. please excuse me while I ask marilla if thats spelled rite. Marilla says its the silem he has to go to not the other place. He thinks he has a snake inside of him. whats it like to have a snake inside of you, anne. I want to know. mrs. lawrence bell is sick to. mrs. lynde says that all that is the matter with her is that she thinks too much about her insides."

"I wonder," said Anne, as she folded up her letters, "what Mrs. Lynde would think of Philippa."

Chapter VI - In the Park

"What are you going to do with yourselves today, girls?" asked Philippa, popping into Anne's room one Saturday afternoon.

"We are going for a walk in the park," answered Anne. "I ought to stay in and finish my blouse. But I couldn't sew on a day like this. There's something in the air that gets into my blood and makes a sort of glory in my soul. My fingers would twitch and I'd sew a crooked seam. So it's ho for the park and the pines."

"Does 'we' include any one but yourself and Priscilla?"

"Yes, it includes Gilbert and Charlie, and we'll be very glad if it will include you, also."

"But," said Philippa dolefully, "if I go I'll have to be gooseberry, and that will be a new experience for Philippa Gordon."

"Well, new experiences are broadening. Come along, and you'll be able to sympathize with all poor souls who have to play gooseberry often. But where are all the victims?"

"Oh, I was tired of them all and simply couldn't be bothered with any of them today. Besides, I've been feeling a little blue—just a pale, elusive azure. It isn't serious enough for anything darker. I wrote Alec and Alonzo last week. I put the letters into envelopes and addressed them, but I didn't seal them up. That evening something funny happened. That is, Alec would think it funny, but Alonzo wouldn't be likely to. I was in a hurry, so I snatched Alec's letter—as I thought—out of the envelope and scribbled down a postscript. Then I mailed both letters. I got Alonzo's reply this morning. Girls, I had put that postscript to his letter and he was furious. Of course he'll get over it—and I don't care if he doesn't—but it spoiled my day. So I thought I'd come to you darlings to get cheered up. After the football season opens I won't have any spare Saturday afternoons. I adore football. I've got the most gorgeous cap and sweater striped in Redmond colors to wear to the games. To be sure, a little way off I'll look like a walking barber's pole. Do you know that that Gilbert of yours has been elected Captain of the Freshman football team?"

"Yes, he told us so last evening," said Priscilla, seeing that outraged Anne would not answer. "He and Charlie were down. We knew they were coming, so we painstakingly put out of sight or out of reach all Miss Ada's cushions. That very elaborate one with the raised embroidery I dropped on the floor in the corner behind the chair it was on. I thought it would be safe there. But would you believe it? Charlie Sloane made for that chair, noticed the cushion behind it, solemnly fished it up, and sat on it the whole evening. Such a wreck of a cushion as it was! Poor Miss Ada asked me today, still smiling, but oh, so reproachfully, why I had allowed it to be sat upon. I told her I hadn't—that it was a matter of predestination coupled with inveterate Sloanishness and I wasn't a match for both combined."

"Miss Ada's cushions are really getting on my nerves," said Anne. "She finished two new ones last week, stuffed and embroidered within an inch of their lives. There being absolutely no other cushionless place to put them she stood them up against the wall on the stair landing. They topple over half the time and if we come up or down the stairs in the dark we fall over them. Last Sunday, when Dr. Davis prayed for all those exposed to the perils of the sea, I added in thought 'and for all those who live in houses where cushions are loved not wisely but too well!' There! we're ready, and I see the boys coming through Old St. John's. Do you cast in your lot with us, Phil?"

"I'll go, if I can walk with Priscilla and Charlie. That will be a bearable degree of gooseberry. That Gilbert of yours is a darling, Anne, but why does he go around so much with Goggle-eyes?"

Anne stiffened. She had no great liking for Charlie Sloane; but he was of Avonlea, so no outsider had any business to laugh at him.

"Charlie and Gilbert have always been friends," she said coldly. "Charlie is a nice boy. He's not to blame for his eyes."

"Don't tell me that! He is! He must have done something dreadful in a previous existence to be punished with such eyes. Pris and I are going to have such sport with him this afternoon. We'll make fun of him to his face and he'll never know it."

Doubtless, "the abandoned P's," as Anne called them, did carry out their amiable intentions. But Sloane was blissfully ignorant; he thought he was quite a fine fellow to be walking with two such coeds, especially Philippa Gordon, the class beauty and belle. It must surely impress Anne. She would see that some people appreciated him at his real value.

Gilbert and Anne loitered a little behind the others, enjoying the calm, still beauty of the autumn afternoon under the pines of the park, on the road that climbed and twisted round the harbor shore.

"The silence here is like a prayer, isn't it?" said Anne, her face upturned to the shining sky. "How I love the pines! They seem to strike their roots deep into the romance of all the ages. It is so comforting to creep away now and then for a good talk with them. I always feel so happy out here."

> "'And so in mountain solitudes o'ertaken
> As by some spell divine,
> Their cares drop from them like the needles shaken
> From out the gusty pine,'"

quoted Gilbert.

"They make our little ambitions seem rather petty, don't they, Anne?"

"I think, if ever any great sorrow came to me, I would come to the pines for comfort," said Anne dreamily.

"I hope no great sorrow ever will come to you, Anne," said Gilbert, who could not connect the idea of sorrow with the vivid, joyous creature beside him, unwitting that those who can soar to the highest heights can also plunge to the deepest depths, and that the natures which enjoy most keenly are those which also suffer most sharply.

"But there must—sometime," mused Anne. "Life seems like a cup of glory held to my lips just now. But there must be some bitterness in it—there is in every cup. I shall taste mine some day. Well, I hope I shall be strong and brave to meet it. And I hope it won't be through my own fault that it will come. Do you remember what Dr. Davis said last Sunday evening—that the sorrows God sent us brought comfort and strength with them, while the sorrows we brought on ourselves, through folly or wickedness, were by far the hardest to bear? But we mustn't talk of sorrow on an afternoon like this. It's meant for the sheer joy of living, isn't it?"

"If I had my way I'd shut everything out of your life but happiness and pleasure, Anne," said Gilbert in the tone that meant "danger ahead."

"Then you would be very unwise," rejoined Anne hastily. "I'm sure no life can be properly developed and rounded out without some trial and sorrow—though I suppose it is only when we are pretty comfortable that we admit it. Come—the others have got to the pavilion and are beckoning to us."

They all sat down in the little pavilion to watch an autumn sunset of deep red fire and pallid gold. To their left lay Kingsport, its roofs and spires dim in their shroud of violet smoke. To their right lay the harbor, taking on tints of rose and copper as it stretched out into the sunset. Before them the water shimmered, satin smooth and silver gray, and beyond, clean shaven William's Island loomed out of the mist, guarding the town like a sturdy bulldog. Its lighthouse beacon flared through the mist like a baleful star, and was answered by another in the far horizon.

"Did you ever see such a strong-looking place?" asked Philippa. "I don't want William's Island especially, but I'm sure I couldn't get it if I did. Look at that sentry on the summit of the fort, right beside the flag. Doesn't he look as if he had stepped out of a romance?"

"Speaking of romance," said Priscilla, "we've been looking for heather—but, of course, we couldn't find any. It's too late in the season, I suppose."

"Heather!" exclaimed Anne. "Heather doesn't grow in America, does it?"

"There are just two patches of it in the whole continent," said Phil, "one right here in the park, and one somewhere else in Nova Scotia, I forget where. The famous Highland Regiment, the Black Watch, camped here one year, and, when the men shook out the straw of their beds in the spring, some seeds of heather took root."

"Oh, how delightful!" said enchanted Anne.

"Let's go home around by Spofford Avenue," suggested Gilbert. "We can see all 'the handsome houses where the wealthy nobles dwell.' Spofford Avenue is the finest residential street in Kingsport. Nobody can build on it unless he's a millionaire."

"Oh, do," said Phil. "There's a perfectly killing little place I want to show you, Anne. IT wasn't built by a millionaire. It's the first place after you leave the park, and must have grown while Spofford Avenue was still a country road. It DID grow—it wasn't built! I don't care for the houses on the Avenue. They're too brand new and plateglassy. But this little spot is a dream—and its name—but wait till you see it."

They saw it as they walked up the pine-fringed hill from the park. Just on the crest, where Spofford Avenue petered out into a plain road, was a little white frame house with groups of pines on either side of it, stretching their arms protectingly over its low roof. It was covered with red and gold vines, through which its green-shuttered windows peeped. Before it was a tiny garden, surrounded by a low stone wall. October though it was, the garden was still very sweet with dear, old-fashioned, unworldly flowers and shrubs—sweet may, southern-wood, lemon verbena, alyssum, petunias, marigolds and chrysanthemums. A tiny brick wall, in herring-bone pattern, led from the gate to the front porch. The whole place might have been transplanted from some remote country village; yet there was something about it that made its nearest neighbor, the big lawn-encircled palace of a tobacco king, look exceedingly crude and showy and ill-bred by contrast. As Phil said, it was the difference between being born and being made.

"It's the dearest place I ever saw," said Anne delightedly. "It gives me one of my old, delightful funny aches. It's dearer and quainter than even Miss Lavendar's stone house."

"It's the name I want you to notice especially," said Phil. "Look—in white letters, around the archway over the gate. 'Patty's Place.' Isn't that killing? Especially on this Avenue of Pinehursts and Elmwolds and Cedarcrofts? 'Patty's Place,' if you please! I adore it."

"Have you any idea who Patty is?" asked Priscilla.

"Patty Spofford is the name of the old lady who owns it, I've discovered. She lives there with her niece, and they've lived there for hundreds of years, more or less—maybe a little less, Anne. Exaggeration is merely a flight of poetic fancy. I understand that wealthy folk have tried to buy the lot time and again—it's really worth a small fortune now, you know—but 'Patty' won't sell upon any consideration. And there's an apple orchard behind the house in place of a back yard—you'll see it when we get a little past—a real apple orchard on Spofford Avenue!"

"I'm going to dream about 'Patty's Place' tonight," said Anne. "Why, I feel as if I belonged to it. I wonder if, by any chance, we'll ever see the inside of it."

"It isn't likely," said Priscilla.

Anne smiled mysteriously.

"No, it isn't likely. But I believe it will happen. I have a queer, creepy, crawly feeling—you can call it a presentiment, if you like—that 'Patty's Place' and I are going to be better acquainted yet."

Chapter VII - Home Again

Those first three weeks at Redmond had seemed long; but the rest of the term flew by on wings of wind. Before they realized it the Redmond students found themselves in the grind of Christmas examinations, emerging therefrom more or less triumphantly. The honor of leading in the Freshman classes fluctuated between Anne, Gilbert and Philippa; Priscilla did very well; Charlie Sloane scraped through respectably, and comported himself as complacently as if he had led in everything.

"I can't really believe that this time tomorrow I'll be in Green Gables," said Anne on the night before departure. "But I shall be. And you, Phil, will be in Bolingbroke with Alec and Alonzo."

"I'm longing to see them," admitted Phil, between the chocolate she was nibbling. "They really are such dear boys, you know. There's to be no end of dances and drives and general jamborees. I shall never forgive you, Queen Anne, for not coming home with me for the holidays."

"'Never' means three days with you, Phil. It was dear of you to ask me—and I'd love to go to Bolingbroke some day. But I can't go this year—I MUST go home. You don't know how my heart longs for it."

"You won't have much of a time," said Phil scornfully. "There'll be one or two quilting parties, I suppose; and all the old gossips will talk you over to your face and behind your back. You'll die of lonesomeness, child."

"In Avonlea?" said Anne, highly amused.

"Now, if you'd come with me you'd have a perfectly gorgeous time. Bolingbroke would go wild over you, Queen Anne—your hair and your style and, oh, everything! You're so DIFFERENT. You'd be such a success—and I would bask in reflected glory—'not the rose but near the rose.' Do come, after all, Anne."

"Your picture of social triumphs is quite fascinating, Phil, but I'll paint one to offset it. I'm going home to an old country farmhouse, once green, rather faded now, set among leafless apple orchards. There is a brook below and a December fir wood beyond, where I've heard harps swept by the fingers of rain and wind. There is a pond nearby that will be gray and brooding now. There will be two oldish ladies in the house, one tall and thin, one short and fat; and there will be two twins, one a perfect model, the other what Mrs. Lynde calls a 'holy terror.' There will be a little room upstairs over the porch, where old dreams hang thick, and a big, fat, glorious feather bed which will almost seem the height of luxury after a boardinghouse mattress. How do you like my picture, Phil?"

"It seems a very dull one," said Phil, with a grimace.

"Oh, but I've left out the transforming thing," said Anne softly. "There'll be love there, Phil—faithful, tender love, such as I'll never find anywhere else in the world—love that's waiting for me. That makes my picture a masterpiece, doesn't it, even if the colors are not very brilliant?"

Phil silently got up, tossed her box of chocolates away, went up to Anne, and put her arms about her.

"Anne, I wish I was like you," she said soberly.

Diana met Anne at the Carmody station the next night, and they drove home together under silent, star-sown depths of sky. Green Gables had a very festal appearance as they drove up the lane. There was a light in every window, the glow breaking out through the darkness like flame-red blossoms swung against the dark background of the Haunted Wood. And in the yard was a brave bonfire with two gay little figures dancing around it, one of which gave an unearthly yell as the buggy turned in under the poplars.

"Davy means that for an Indian war-whoop," said Diana. "Mr. Harrison's hired boy taught it to him, and he's been practicing it up to welcome you with. Mrs. Lynde says it has worn her nerves to a frazzle. He creeps up behind her, you know, and then lets go. He was determined to have a bonfire for you, too. He's been piling up branches for a fortnight and pestering Marilla to be let pour some kerosene oil over it before setting it on fire. I guess she did, by the smell, though Mrs. Lynde said up to the last that Davy would blow himself and everybody else up if he was let."

Anne was out of the buggy by this time, and Davy was rapturously hugging her knees, while even Dora was clinging to her hand.

"Isn't that a bully bonfire, Anne? Just let me show you how to poke it—see the sparks? I did it for you, Anne, 'cause I was so glad you were coming home."

The kitchen door opened and Marilla's spare form darkened against the inner light. She preferred to meet Anne in the shadows, for she was horribly afraid that she was going to cry with joy—she, stern, repressed Marilla, who thought all display of deep emotion unseemly. Mrs. Lynde was behind her, sonsy, kindly, matronly, as of yore. The love that Anne had told Phil was waiting for her surrounded her and enfolded her with its blessing and its sweetness. Nothing, after all, could compare with old ties, old friends, and old Green Gables! How starry Anne's eyes were as they sat down to the loaded supper table, how pink her cheeks, how silver-clear her laughter! And Diana was going to stay all night, too. How like the dear old times it was! And the rose-bud tea-set graced the table! With Marilla the force of nature could no further go.

"I suppose you and Diana will now proceed to talk all night," said Marilla sarcastically, as the girls went upstairs. Marilla was always sarcastic after any self-betrayal.

"Yes," agreed Anne gaily, "but I'm going to put Davy to bed first. He insists on that."

"You bet," said Davy, as they went along the hall. "I want somebody to say my prayers to again. It's no fun saying them alone."

"You don't say them alone, Davy. God is always with you to hear you."

"Well, I can't see Him," objected Davy. "I want to pray to somebody I can see, but I WON'T say them to Mrs. Lynde or Marilla, there now!"

Nevertheless, when Davy was garbed in his gray flannel nighty, he did not seem in a hurry to begin. He stood before Anne, shuffling one bare foot over the other, and looked undecided.

"Come, dear, kneel down," said Anne.

Davy came and buried his head in Anne's lap, but he did not kneel down.

"Anne," he said in a muffled voice. "I don't feel like praying after all. I haven't felt like it for a week now. I—I DIDN'T pray last night nor the night before."

"Why not, Davy?" asked Anne gently.

"You—you won't be mad if I tell you?" implored Davy.

Anne lifted the little gray-flannelled body on her knee and cuddled his head on her arm.

"Do I ever get 'mad' when you tell me things, Davy?"

"No-o-o, you never do. But you get sorry, and that's worse. You'll be awful sorry when I tell you this, Anne—and you'll be 'shamed of me, I s'pose."

"Have you done something naughty, Davy, and is that why you can't say your prayers?"

"No, I haven't done anything naughty—yet. But I want to do it."

"What is it, Davy?"

"I—I want to say a bad word, Anne," blurted out Davy, with a desperate effort. "I heard Mr. Harrison's hired boy say it one day last week, and ever since I've been wanting to say it ALL the time—even when I'm saying my prayers."

"Say it then, Davy."

Davy lifted his flushed face in amazement.

"But, Anne, it's an AWFUL bad word."

"SAY IT!"

Davy gave her another incredulous look, then in a low voice he said the dreadful word. The next minute his face was burrowing against her.

"Oh, Anne, I'll never say it again—never. I'll never WANT to say it again. I knew it was bad, but I didn't s'pose it was so—so—I didn't s'pose it was like THAT."

"No, I don't think you'll ever want to say it again, Davy—or think it, either. And I wouldn't go about much with Mr. Harrison's hired boy if I were you."

"He can make bully war-whoops," said Davy a little regretfully.

"But you don't want your mind filled with bad words, do you, Davy—words that will poison it and drive out all that is good and manly?"

"No," said Davy, owl-eyed with introspection.

"Then don't go with those people who use them. And now do you feel as if you could say your prayers, Davy?"

"Oh, yes," said Davy, eagerly wriggling down on his knees, "I can say them now all right. I ain't scared now to say 'if I should die before I wake,' like I was when I was wanting to say that word."

Probably Anne and Diana did empty out their souls to each other that night, but no record of their confidences has been preserved. They both looked as fresh and bright-eyed at breakfast as only youth can look after unlawful hours of revelry and confession. There had been no snow up to this time, but as Diana crossed the old log bridge on her homeward way the white flakes were beginning to flutter down over the fields and woods, russet and gray in their dreamless sleep. Soon the far-away slopes and hills were dim and wraith-like through their gauzy scarfing, as if pale autumn had flung a misty bridal veil over her hair and was waiting for her wintry bridegroom. So they had a white Christmas after all, and a very pleasant day it was. In the forenoon letters and gifts came from Miss Lavendar and Paul; Anne opened them in the cheerful Green Gables kitchen, which was filled with what Davy, sniffing in ecstasy, called "pretty smells."

"Miss Lavendar and Mr. Irving are settled in their new home now," reported Anne. "I am sure Miss Lavendar is perfectly happy—I know it by the general tone of her letter—but there's a note from Charlotta the Fourth. She doesn't like Boston at all, and she is fearfully homesick. Miss Lavendar wants me to go through to Echo Lodge some day while I'm home and light a fire to air it, and see that the cushions aren't getting moldy. I think I'll get Diana to go over with me next week, and we can spend the evening with Theodora Dix. I want to see Theodora. By the way, is Ludovic Speed still going to see her?"

"They say so," said Marilla, "and he's likely to continue it. Folks have given up expecting that that courtship will ever arrive anywhere."

"I'd hurry him up a bit, if I was Theodora, that's what," said Mrs. Lynde. And there is not the slightest doubt but that she would.

There was also a characteristic scrawl from Philippa, full of Alec and Alonzo, what they said and what they did, and how they looked when they saw her.

"But I can't make up my mind yet which to marry," wrote Phil. "I do wish you had come with me to decide for me. Some one will have to. When I saw Alec my heart gave a great thump and I thought, 'He might be the right one.' And then, when Alonzo came, thump went my heart again. So that's no guide, though it should be, according to all the novels I've ever read. Now, Anne, YOUR heart wouldn't thump for anybody but the genuine Prince Charming, would it? There must be something radically wrong with mine. But I'm having a perfectly gorgeous time. How I wish you were here! It's snowing today, and I'm rapturous. I was so afraid we'd have a green Christmas and I loathe them. You know, when Christmas is a dirty grayey-browney affair, looking as if it had been left over a hundred years ago and had been in soak ever since, it is called a GREEN Christmas! Don't ask me why. As Lord Dundreary says, 'there are thome thingth no fellow can underthtand.'

"Anne, did you ever get on a street car and then discover that you hadn't any money with you to pay your fare? I did, the other day. It's quite awful. I had a nickel with me when I got on the car. I thought it was in the left pocket of my coat. When I got settled down comfortably I felt for it. It wasn't there. I had a cold chill. I felt in the other pocket. Not there. I had another chill. Then I felt in a little inside pocket. All in vain. I had two chills at once.

"I took off my gloves, laid them on the seat, and went over all my pockets again. It was not there. I stood up and shook myself, and then looked on the floor. The car was full of people, who were going home from the opera, and they all stared at me, but I was past caring for a little thing like that.

"But I could not find my fare. I concluded I must have put it in my mouth and swallowed it inadvertently.

"I didn't know what to do. Would the conductor, I wondered, stop the car and put me off in ignominy and shame? Was it possible that I could convince him that I was merely the victim of my own absentmindedness, and not an unprincipled creature trying to obtain a ride upon false pretenses? How I wished that Alec or Alonzo were there. But they weren't because I wanted them. If I HADN'T wanted them they would have been there by the dozen. And I couldn't decide what to say to the conductor when he came around. As soon as I got one sentence of explanation mapped out in my mind I felt nobody could believe it and I must compose another. It seemed there was nothing to do but trust in Providence, and for all the comfort that gave me I might as well have been the old lady who, when told by the captain during a storm that she must put her trust in the Almighty exclaimed, 'Oh, Captain, is it as bad as that?'

"Just at the conventional moment, when all hope had fled, and the conductor was holding out his box to the passenger next to me, I suddenly remembered where I had put that wretched coin of the realm. I hadn't swallowed it after all. I meekly fished it out of the index finger of my glove and poked it in the box. I smiled at everybody and felt that it was a beautiful world."

The visit to Echo Lodge was not the least pleasant of many pleasant holiday outings. Anne and Diana went back to it by the old way of the beech woods, carrying a lunch basket with them. Echo Lodge, which had been closed ever since Miss Lavendar's wedding, was briefly thrown open to wind and sunshine once more, and firelight glimmered again in the little rooms. The perfume of Miss Lavendar's rose bowl still filled the air. It was hardly possible to believe that Miss Lavendar would not come tripping in presently, with her brown eyes a-star with welcome, and that Charlotta the Fourth, blue of bow and wide of smile, would not pop through the door. Paul, too, seemed hovering around, with his fairy fancies.

"It really makes me feel a little bit like a ghost revisiting the old time glimpses of the moon," laughed Anne. "Let's go out and see if the echoes are at home. Bring the old horn. It is still behind the kitchen door."

The echoes were at home, over the white river, as silver-clear and multitudinous as ever; and when they had ceased to answer the girls locked up Echo Lodge again and went away in the perfect half hour that follows the rose and saffron of a winter sunset.

Chapter VIII - Anne's First Proposal

The old year did not slip away in a green twilight, with a pinky-yellow sunset. Instead, it went out with a wild, white bluster and blow. It was one of the nights when the storm-wind hurtles over the frozen meadows and black hollows, and moans around the eaves like a lost creature, and drives the snow sharply against the shaking panes.

"Just the sort of night people like to cuddle down between their blankets and count their mercies," said Anne to Jane Andrews, who had come up to spend the afternoon and stay all night. But when they were cuddled between their blankets, in Anne's little porch room, it was not her mercies of which Jane was thinking.

"Anne," she said very solemnly, "I want to tell you something. May I"

Anne was feeling rather sleepy after the party Ruby Gillis had given the night before. She would much rather have gone to sleep than listen to Jane's confidences, which she was sure would bore her. She had no prophetic inkling of what was coming. Probably Jane was engaged, too; rumor averred that Ruby Gillis was engaged to the Spencervale schoolteacher, about whom all the girls were said to be quite wild.

"I'll soon be the only fancy-free maiden of our old quartet," thought Anne, drowsily. Aloud she said, "Of course."

"Anne," said Jane, still more solemnly, "what do you think of my brother Billy?"

Anne gasped over this unexpected question, and floundered helplessly in her thoughts. Goodness, what DID she think of Billy Andrews? She had never thought ANYTHING about him—round-faced, stupid, perpetually smiling, good-natured Billy Andrews. Did ANYBODY ever think about Billy Andrews?

"I—I don't understand, Jane," she stammered. "What do you mean—exactly?"

"Do you like Billy?" asked Jane bluntly.

"Why—why—yes, I like him, of course," gasped Anne, wondering if she were telling the literal truth. Certainly she did not DISlike Billy. But could the indifferent tolerance with which she regarded him, when he happened to be in her range of vision, be considered positive enough for liking? WHAT was Jane trying to elucidate?

"Would you like him for a husband?" asked Jane calmly.

"A husband!" Anne had been sitting up in bed, the better to wrestle with the problem of her exact opinion of Billy Andrews. Now she fell flatly back on her pillows, the very breath gone out of her. "Whose husband?"

"Yours, of course," answered Jane. "Billy wants to marry you. He's always been crazy about you—and now father has given him the upper farm in his own name and there's nothing to prevent him from getting married. But he's so shy he couldn't ask you himself if you'd have him, so he got me to do it. I'd rather not have, but he gave me no peace till I said I would, if I got a good chance. What do you think about it, Anne?"

Was it a dream? Was it one of those nightmare things in which you find yourself engaged or married to some one you hate or don't know, without the slightest idea how it ever came about? No, she, Anne Shirley, was lying there, wide awake, in her own bed, and Jane Andrews was beside her, calmly proposing for her brother Billy. Anne did not know whether she wanted to writhe or laugh; but she could do neither, for Jane's feelings must not be hurt.

"I—I couldn't marry Bill, you know, Jane," she managed to gasp. "Why, such an idea never occurred to me—never!"

"I don't suppose it did," agreed Jane. "Billy has always been far too shy to think of courting. But you might think it over, Anne. Billy is a good fellow. I must say that, if he is my brother. He has no bad habits and he's a great worker, and you can depend on him. 'A bird in the hand is worth two in the bush.' He told me to tell you he'd be quite willing to wait till you got through college, if you insisted, though he'd RATHER get married this spring before the planting begins. He'd always be very good to you, I'm sure, and you know, Anne, I'd love to have you for a sister."

"I can't marry Billy," said Anne decidedly. She had recovered her wits, and was even feeling a little angry. It was all so ridiculous. "There is no use thinking of it, Jane. I don't care anything for him in that way, and you must tell him so."

"Well, I didn't suppose you would," said Jane with a resigned sigh, feeling that she had done her best. "I told Billy I didn't believe it was a bit of use to ask you, but he insisted. Well, you've made your decision, Anne, and I hope you won't regret it."

Jane spoke rather coldly. She had been perfectly sure that the enamored Billy had no chance at all of inducing Anne to marry him. Nevertheless, she felt a little resentment that Anne Shirley, who was, after all, merely an adopted orphan, without kith or kin, should refuse her brother—one of the Avonlea Andrews. Well, pride sometimes goes before a fall, Jane reflected ominously.

Anne permitted herself to smile in the darkness over the idea that she might ever regret not marrying Billy Andrews.

"I hope Billy won't feel very badly over it," she said nicely.

Jane made a movement as if she were tossing her head on her pillow.

"Oh, he won't break his heart. Billy has too much good sense for that. He likes Nettie Blewett pretty well, too, and mother would rather he married her than any one. She's such a good manager and saver. I think, when Billy is once sure you won't have him, he'll take Nettie. Please don't mention this to any one, will you, Anne?"

"Certainly not," said Anne, who had no desire whatever to publish abroad the fact that Billy Andrews wanted to marry her, preferring her, when all was said and done, to Nettie Blewett. Nettie Blewett!

"And now I suppose we'd better go to sleep," suggested Jane.

To sleep went Jane easily and speedily; but, though very unlike MacBeth in most respects, she had certainly contrived to murder sleep for Anne. That proposed-to damsel lay on a wakeful pillow until the wee sma's, but her meditations were far from being romantic. It was not, however, until the next morning that she had an opportunity to indulge in a good laugh over the whole affair. When Jane had gone home—still with a hint of frost in voice and manner because Anne had declined so ungratefully and decidedly the honor of an alliance with the House of Andrews—Anne retreated to the porch room, shut the door, and had her laugh out at last.

"If I could only share the joke with some one!" she thought. "But I can't. Diana is the only one I'd want to tell, and, even if I hadn't sworn secrecy to Jane, I can't tell Diana things now. She tells everything to Fred—I know she does. Well, I've had my first proposal. I supposed it would come some day—but I certainly never thought it would be by proxy. It's awfully funny—and yet there's a sting in it, too, somehow."

Anne knew quite well wherein the sting consisted, though she did not put it into words. She had had her secret dreams of the first time some one should ask her the great question. And it had, in those dreams, always been very romantic and beautiful: and the "some one" was to be very handsome and dark-eyed and distinguished-looking and eloquent, whether he were Prince Charming to be enraptured with "yes," or one to whom a regretful, beautifully worded, but hopeless refusal must be given. If the latter, the refusal was to be expressed so delicately that it would be next best thing to acceptance, and he would go away, after kissing her hand, assuring her of his unalterable, life-long devotion. And it would always be a beautiful memory, to be proud of and a little sad about, also.

And now, this thrilling experience had turned out to be merely grotesque. Billy Andrews had got his sister to propose for him because his father had given him the upper farm; and if Anne wouldn't "have him" Nettie Blewett would. There was romance for you, with a vengeance! Anne laughed—and then sighed. The bloom had been brushed from one little maiden dream. Would the painful process go on until everything became prosaic and hum-drum?

Chapter IX - An Unwelcome Lover and a Welcome Friend

The second term at Redmond sped as quickly as had the first—"actually whizzed away," Philippa said. Anne enjoyed it thoroughly in all its phases—the stimulating class rivalry, the making and deepening of new and helpful friendships, the gay little social stunts, the doings of the various societies of which she was a member, the widening of horizons and interests. She studied hard, for she had made up her mind to win the Thorburn Scholarship in English. This being won, meant that she could come back to Redmond the next year without trenching on Marilla's small savings—something Anne was determined she would not do.

Gilbert, too, was in full chase after a scholarship, but found plenty of time for frequent calls at Thirty-eight, St. John's. He was Anne's escort at nearly all the college affairs, and she knew that their names were coupled in Redmond gossip. Anne raged over this but was helpless; she could not cast an old friend like Gilbert aside, especially when he had grown suddenly wise and wary, as behooved him in the dangerous proximity of more than one Redmond youth who would gladly have taken his place by the side of the slender, red-haired coed, whose gray eyes were as alluring as stars of evening. Anne was never attended by the crowd of willing victims who hovered around Philippa's conquering march through her Freshman year; but there was a lanky, brainy Freshie, a jolly, little, round Sophomore, and a tall, learned Junior who all liked to call at Thirty-eight, St. John's, and talk over 'ologies and 'isms, as well as lighter subjects, with Anne, in the becushioned parlor of that domicile. Gilbert did not love any of them, and he was exceedingly careful to give none of them the advantage over him by any untimely display of his real feelings Anne-ward. To her he had become again the boy-comrade of Avonlea days, and as such could hold his own against any smitten swain who had so far entered the lists against him. As a companion, Anne honestly acknowledged nobody could be so satisfactory as Gilbert; she was very glad, so she told herself, that he had evidently dropped all nonsensical ideas—though she spent considerable time secretly wondering why.

Only one disagreeable incident marred that winter. Charlie Sloane, sitting bolt upright on Miss Ada's most dearly beloved cushion, asked Anne one night if she would promise "to become Mrs. Charlie Sloane some day." Coming after Billy

Andrews' proxy effort, this was not quite the shock to Anne's romantic sensibilities that it would otherwise have been; but it was certainly another heart-rending disillusion. She was angry, too, for she felt that she had never given Charlie the slightest encouragement to suppose such a thing possible. But what could you expect of a Sloane, as Mrs. Rachel Lynde would ask scornfully? Charlie's whole attitude, tone, air, words, fairly reeked with Sloanishness. "He was conferring a great honor—no doubt whatever about that. And when Anne, utterly insensible to the honor, refused him, as delicately and considerately as she could—for even a Sloane had feelings which ought not to be unduly lacerated—Sloanishness still further betrayed itself. Charlie certainly did not take his dismissal as Anne's imaginary rejected suitors did. Instead, he became angry, and showed it; he said two or three quite nasty things; Anne's temper flashed up mutinously and she retorted with a cutting little speech whose keenness pierced even Charlie's protective Sloanishness and reached the quick; he caught up his hat and flung himself out of the house with a very red face; Anne rushed upstairs, falling twice over Miss Ada's cushions on the way, and threw herself on her bed, in tears of humiliation and rage. Had she actually stooped to quarrel with a Sloane? Was it possible anything Charlie Sloane could say had power to make her angry? Oh, this was degradation, indeed—worse even than being the rival of Nettie Blewett!

"I wish I need never see the horrible creature again," she sobbed vindictively into her pillows.

She could not avoid seeing him again, but the outraged Charlie took care that it should not be at very close quarters. Miss Ada's cushions were henceforth safe from his depredations, and when he met Anne on the street, or in Redmond's halls, his bow was icy in the extreme. Relations between these two old schoolmates continued to be thus strained for nearly a year! Then Charlie transferred his blighted affections to a round, rosy, snub-nosed, blue-eyed, little Sophomore who appreciated them as they deserved, whereupon he forgave Anne and condescended to be civil to her again; in a patronizing manner intended to show her just what she had lost.

One day Anne scurried excitedly into Priscilla's room.

"Read that," she cried, tossing Priscilla a letter. "It's from Stella—and she's coming to Redmond next year—and what do you think of her idea? I think it's a perfectly splendid one, if we can only carry it out. Do you suppose we can, Pris?"

"I'll be better able to tell you when I find out what it is," said Priscilla, casting aside a Greek lexicon and taking up Stella's letter. Stella Maynard had been one of their chums at Queen's Academy and had been teaching school ever since.

"But I'm going to give it up, Anne dear," she wrote, "and go to college next year. As I took the third year at Queen's I can enter the Sophomore year. I'm tired of teaching in a back country school. Some day I'm going to write a treatise on 'The Trials of a Country Schoolmarm.' It will be a harrowing bit of realism. It seems to be the prevailing impression that we live in clover, and have nothing to do but draw our quarter's salary. My treatise shall tell the truth about us. Why, if a week should pass without some one telling me that I am doing easy work for big pay I would conclude that I might as well order my ascension robe 'immediately and to onct.' 'Well, you get your money easy,' some rate-payer will tell me, condescendingly. 'All you have to do is to sit there and hear lessons.' I used to argue the matter at first, but I'm wiser now. Facts are stubborn things, but as some one has wisely said, not half so stubborn as fallacies. So I only smile loftily now in eloquent silence. Why, I have nine grades in my school and I have to teach a little of everything, from investigating the interiors of earthworms to the study of the solar system. My youngest pupil is four—his mother sends him to school to 'get him out of the way'—and my oldest twenty—it 'suddenly struck him' that it would be easier to go to school and get an education than follow the plough any longer. In the wild effort to cram all sorts of research into six hours a day I don't wonder if the children feel like the little boy who was taken to see the biograph. 'I have to look for what's coming next before I know what went last,' he complained. I feel like that myself.

"And the letters I get, Anne! Tommy's mother writes me that Tommy is not coming on in arithmetic as fast as she would like. He is only in simple reduction yet, and Johnny Johnson is in fractions, and Johnny isn't half as smart as her Tommy, and she can't understand it. And Susy's father wants to know why Susy can't write a letter without misspelling half the words, and Dick's aunt wants me to change his seat, because that bad Brown boy he is sitting with is teaching him to say naughty words.

"As to the financial part—but I'll not begin on that. Those whom the gods wish to destroy they first make country schoolmarms!

"There, I feel better, after that growl. After all, I've enjoyed these past two years. But I'm coming to Redmond.

"And now, Anne, I've a little plan. You know how I loathe boarding. I've boarded for four years and I'm so tired of it. I don't feel like enduring three years more of it.

"Now, why can't you and Priscilla and I club together, rent a little house somewhere in Kingsport, and board ourselves? It would be cheaper than any other way. Of course, we would have to have a housekeeper and I have one ready on the spot. You've heard me speak of Aunt Jamesina? She's the sweetest aunt that ever lived, in spite of her name. She can't help that! She was called Jamesina because her father, whose name was James, was drowned at sea a month before she was born. I always call her Aunt Jimsie. Well, her only daughter has recently married and gone to the foreign mission field. Aunt Jamesina is left alone in a great big house, and she is horribly lonesome. She will come to Kingsport and keep house for us if we want her, and I know you'll both love her. The more I think of the plan the more I like it. We could have such good, independent times.

"Now, if you and Priscilla agree to it, wouldn't it be a good idea for you, who are on the spot, to look around and see if you can find a suitable house this spring? That would be better than leaving it till the fall. If you could get a furnished one so much the better, but if not, we can scare up a few sticks of finiture

441

between us and old family friends with attics. Anyhow, decide as soon as you can and write me, so that Aunt Jamesina will know what plans to make for next year."

"I think it's a good idea," said Priscilla.

"So do I," agreed Anne delightedly. "Of course, we have a nice boardinghouse here, but, when all's said and done, a boardinghouse isn't home. So let's go house-hunting at once, before exams come on."

"I'm afraid it will be hard enough to get a really suitable house," warned Priscilla. "Don't expect too much, Anne. Nice houses in nice localities will probably be away beyond our means. We'll likely have to content ourselves with a shabby little place on some street whereon live people whom to know is to be unknown, and make life inside compensate for the outside."

Accordingly they went house-hunting, but to find just what they wanted proved even harder than Priscilla had feared. Houses there were galore, furnished and unfurnished; but one was too big, another too small; this one too expensive, that one too far from Redmond. Exams were on and over; the last week of the term came and still their "house o'dreams," as Anne called it, remained a castle in the air.

"We shall have to give up and wait till the fall, I suppose," said Priscilla wearily, as they rambled through the park on one of April's darling days of breeze and blue, when the harbor was creaming and shimmering beneath the pearl-hued mists floating over it. "We may find some shack to shelter us then; and if not, boardinghouses we shall have always with us."

"I'm not going to worry about it just now, anyway, and spoil this lovely afternoon," said Anne, gazing around her with delight. The fresh chill air was faintly charged with the aroma of pine balsam, and the sky above was crystal clear and blue—a great inverted cup of blessing. "Spring is singing in my blood today, and the lure of April is abroad on the air. I'm seeing visions and dreaming dreams, Pris. That's because the wind is from the west. I do love the west wind. It sings of hope and gladness, doesn't it? When the east wind blows I always think of sorrowful rain on the eaves and sad waves on a gray shore. When I get old I shall have rheumatism when the wind is east."

"And isn't it jolly when you discard furs and winter garments for the first time and sally forth, like this, in spring attire?" laughed Priscilla. "Don't you feel as if you had been made over new?"

"Everything is new in the spring," said Anne. "Springs themselves are always so new, too. No spring is ever just like any other spring. It always has something of its own to be its own peculiar sweetness. See how green the grass is around that little pond, and how the willow buds are bursting."

"And exams are over and gone—the time of Convocation will come soon—next Wednesday. This day next week we'll be home."

"I'm glad," said Anne dreamily. "There are so many things I want to do. I want to sit on the back porch steps and feel the breeze blowing down over Mr. Harrison's fields. I want to hunt ferns in the Haunted Wood and gather violets in Violet Vale. Do you remember the day of our golden picnic, Priscilla? I want to hear the frogs singing and the poplars whispering. But I've learned to love Kingsport, too, and I'm glad I'm coming back next fall. If I hadn't won the Thorburn I don't believe I could have. I COULDN'T take any of Marilla's little hoard."

"If we could only find a house!" sighed Priscilla. "Look over there at Kingsport, Anne—houses, houses everywhere, and not one for us."

"Stop it, Pris. 'The best is yet to be.' Like the old Roman, we'll find a house or build one. On a day like this there's no such word as fail in my bright lexicon."

They lingered in the park until sunset, living in the amazing miracle and glory and wonder of the springtide; and they went home as usual, by way of Spofford Avenue, that they might have the delight of looking at Patty's Place.

"I feel as if something mysterious were going to happen right away—'by the pricking of my thumbs,'" said Anne, as they went up the slope. "It's a nice story-bookish feeling. Why—why—why! Priscilla Grant, look over there and tell me if it's true, or am I seein' things?"

Priscilla looked. Anne's thumbs and eyes had not deceived her. Over the arched gateway of Patty's Place dangled a little, modest sign. It said "To Let, Furnished. Inquire Within."

"Priscilla," said Anne, in a whisper, "do you suppose it's possible that we could rent Patty's Place?"

"No, I don't," averred Priscilla. "It would be too good to be true. Fairy tales don't happen nowadays. I won't hope, Anne. The disappointment would be too awful to bear. They're sure to want more for it than we can afford. Remember, it's on Spofford Avenue."

"We must find out anyhow," said Anne resolutely. "It's too late to call this evening, but we'll come tomorrow. Oh, Pris, if we can get this darling spot! I've always felt that my fortunes were linked with Patty's Place, ever since I saw it first."

Chapter X - Patty's Place

The next evening found them treading resolutely the herring-bone walk through the tiny garden. The April wind was filling the pine trees with its roundelay, and the grove was alive with robins—great, plump, saucy fellows, strutting along the paths. The girls rang rather timidly, and were admitted by a grim and ancient handmaiden. The door opened directly into a large living-room, where by a cheery little fire sat two other ladies, both of whom were also grim and ancient. Except that one looked to be about seventy and the other fifty, there seemed little difference between them. Each had amazingly big, light-blue eyes behind steel-rimmed spectacles; each wore a cap and a gray shawl; each was knitting without haste and without rest; each rocked placidly and looked at the girls without speaking; and just behind each sat a large white china dog, with round green spots all over it, a green nose and green ears. Those dogs captured Anne's fancy on the spot; they seemed like the twin guardian deities of Patty's Place.

For a few minutes nobody spoke. The girls were too nervous to find words, and neither the ancient ladies nor the china dogs seemed conversationally inclined. Anne glanced about the room. What a dear place it was! Another door opened out of it directly into the pine grove and the robins came boldly up on the very step. The floor was spotted with round, braided mats, such as Marilla made at Green Gables, but which were considered out of date everywhere else, even in Avonlea. And yet here they were on Spofford Avenue! A big, polished grandfather's clock ticked loudly and solemnly in a corner. There were delightful little cupboards over the mantelpiece, behind whose glass doors gleamed quaint bits of china. The walls were hung with old prints and silhouettes. In one corner the stairs went up, and at the first low turn was a long window with an inviting seat. It was all just as Anne had known it must be.

By this time the silence had grown too dreadful, and Priscilla nudged Anne to intimate that she must speak.

"We—we—saw by your sign that this house is to let," said Anne faintly, addressing the older lady, who was evidently Miss Patty Spofford.

"Oh, yes," said Miss Patty. "I intended to take that sign down today."

"Then—then we are too late," said Anne sorrowfully. "You've let it to some one else?"

"No, but we have decided not to let it at all."

"Oh, I'm so sorry," exclaimed Anne impulsively. "I love this place so. I did hope we could have got it."

Then did Miss Patty lay down her knitting, take off her specs, rub them, put them on again, and for the first time look at Anne as at a human being. The other lady followed her example so perfectly that she might as well have been a reflection in a mirror.

"You LOVE it," said Miss Patty with emphasis. "Does that mean that you really LOVE it? Or that you merely like the looks of it? The girls nowadays indulge in such exaggerated statements that one never can tell what they DO mean. It wasn't so in my young days. THEN a girl did not say she LOVED turnips, in just the same tone as she might have said she loved her mother or her Savior."

Anne's conscience bore her up.

"I really do love it," she said gently. "I've loved it ever since I saw it last fall. My two college chums and I want to keep house next year instead of boarding, so we are looking for a little place to rent; and when I saw that this house was to let I was so happy."

"If you love it, you can have it," said Miss Patty. "Maria and I decided today that we would not let it after all, because we did not like any of the people who have wanted it. We don't HAVE to let it. We can afford to go to Europe even if we don't let it. It would help us out, but not for gold will I let my home pass into the possession of such people as have come here and looked at it. YOU are different. I believe you do love it and will be good to it. You can have it."

"If—if we can afford to pay what you ask for it," hesitated Anne.

Miss Patty named the amount required. Anne and Priscilla looked at each other. Priscilla shook her head.

"I'm afraid we can't afford quite so much," said Anne, choking back her disappointment. "You see, we are only college girls and we are poor."

"What were you thinking you could afford?" demanded Miss Patty, ceasing not to knit.

Anne named her amount. Miss Patty nodded gravely.

"That will do. As I told you, it is not strictly necessary that we should let it at all. We are not rich, but we have enough to go to Europe on. I have never been in Europe in my life, and never expected or wanted to go. But my niece there, Maria Spofford, has taken a fancy to go. Now, you know a young person like Maria can't go globetrotting alone."

"No—I—I suppose not," murmured Anne, seeing that Miss Patty was quite solemnly in earnest.

"Of course not. So I have to go along to look after her. I expect to enjoy it, too; I'm seventy years old, but I'm not tired of living yet. I daresay I'd have gone to Europe before if the idea had occurred to me. We shall be away for two years, perhaps three. We sail in June and we shall send you the key, and leave all in order for you to take possession when you choose. We shall pack away a few things we prize especially, but all the rest will be left."

"Will you leave the china dogs?" asked Anne timidly.

"Would you like me to?"

"Oh, indeed, yes. They are delightful."

A pleased expression came into Miss Patty's face.

"I think a great deal of those dogs," she said proudly. "They are over a hundred years old, and they have sat on either side of this fireplace ever since my brother Aaron brought them from London fifty years ago. Spofford Avenue was called after my brother Aaron."

"A fine man he was," said Miss Maria, speaking for the first time. "Ah, you don't see the like of him nowadays."

"He was a good uncle to you, Maria," said Miss Patty, with evident emotion. "You do well to remember him."

"I shall always remember him," said Miss Maria solemnly. "I can see him, this minute, standing there before that fire, with his hands under his coat-tails, beaming on us."

Miss Maria took out her handkerchief and wiped her eyes; but Miss Patty came resolutely back from the regions of sentiment to those of business.

"I shall leave the dogs where they are, if you will promise to be very careful of them," she said. "Their names are Gog and Magog. Gog looks to the right and Magog to the left. And there's just one thing more. You don't object, I hope, to this house being called Patty's Place?"

"No, indeed. We think that is one of the nicest things about it."

"You have sense, I see," said Miss Patty in a tone of great satisfaction. "Would you believe it? All the people who came here to rent the house wanted to know if they couldn't take the name off the gate during their occupation of it. I told them roundly that the name went with the house. This has been Patty's Place ever since my brother Aaron left it to me in his will, and Patty's Place it shall remain until I die and Maria dies. After that happens the next possessor can call it any fool name he likes," concluded Miss Patty, much as she might have said, "After that—the deluge." "And now, wouldn't you like to go over the house and see it all before we consider the bargain made?"

Further exploration still further delighted the girls. Besides the big living-room, there was a kitchen and a small bedroom downstairs. Upstairs were three rooms, one large and two small. Anne took an especial fancy to one of the small ones, looking out into the big pines, and hoped it would be hers. It was papered in pale blue and had a little, old-timey toilet table with sconces for candles. There was a diamond-paned window with a seat under the blue muslin frills that would be a satisfying spot for studying or dreaming.

"It's all so delicious that I know we are going to wake up and find it a fleeting vision of the night," said Priscilla as they went away.

"Miss Patty and Miss Maria are hardly such stuff as dreams are made of," laughed Anne. "Can you fancy them 'globe-trotting'—especially in those shawls and caps?"

"I suppose they'll take them off when they really begin to trot," said Priscilla, "but I know they'll take their knitting with them everywhere. They simply couldn't be parted from it. They will walk about Westminster Abbey and knit, I feel sure. Meanwhile, Anne, we shall be living in Patty's Place—and on Spofford Avenue. I feel like a millionairess even now."

"I feel like one of the morning stars that sang for joy," said Anne.

Phil Gordon crept into Thirty-eight, St. John's, that night and flung herself on Anne's bed.

"Girls, dear, I'm tired to death. I feel like the man without a country—or was it without a shadow? I forget which. Anyway, I've been packing up."

"And I suppose you are worn out because you couldn't decide which things to pack first, or where to put them," laughed Priscilla.

"E-zackly. And when I had got everything jammed in somehow, and my landlady and her maid had both sat on it while I locked it, I discovered I had packed a whole lot of things I wanted for Convocation at the very bottom. I had to unlock the old thing and poke and dive into it for an hour before I fished out what I wanted. I would get hold of something that felt like what I was looking for, and I'd yank it up, and it would be something else. No, Anne, I did NOT swear."

"I didn't say you did."

"Well, you looked it. But I admit my thoughts verged on the profane. And I have such a cold in the head—I can do nothing but sniffle, sigh and sneeze. Isn't that alliterative agony for you? Queen Anne, do say something to cheer me up."

"Remember that next Thursday night, you'll be back in the land of Alec and Alonzo," suggested Anne.

Phil shook her head dolefully.

"More alliteration. No, I don't want Alec and Alonzo when I have a cold in the head. But what has happened you two? Now that I look at you closely you seem all lighted up with an internal iridescence. Why, you're actually SHINING! What's up?"

"We are going to live in Patty's Place next winter," said Anne triumphantly. "Live, mark you, not board! We've rented it, and Stella Maynard is coming, and her aunt is going to keep house for us."

Phil bounced up, wiped her nose, and fell on her knees before Anne.

"Girls—girls—let me come, too. Oh, I'll be so good. If there's no room for me I'll sleep in the little doghouse in the orchard—I've seen it. Only let me come."

"Get up, you goose."

"I won't stir off my marrow bones till you tell me I can live with you next winter."

Anne and Priscilla looked at each other. Then Anne said slowly, "Phil dear, we'd love to have you. But we may as well speak plainly. I'm poor—Pris is poor—Stella Maynard is poor—our housekeeping will have to be very simple and our table plain. You'd have to live as we would. Now, you are rich and your boardinghouse fare attests the fact."

"Oh, what do I care for that?" demanded Phil tragically. "Better a dinner of herbs where your chums are than a stalled ox in a lonely boardinghouse. Don't think I'm ALL stomach, girls. I'll be willing to live on bread and water—with just a LEETLE jam—if you'll let me come."

"And then," continued Anne, "there will be a good deal of work to be done. Stella's aunt can't do it all. We all expect to have our chores to do. Now, you—"

"Toil not, neither do I spin," finished Philippa. "But I'll learn to do things. You'll only have to show me once. I CAN make my own bed to begin with. And remember that, though I can't cook, I CAN keep my temper. That's something. And I NEVER growl about the weather. That's more. Oh, please, please! I never wanted anything so much in my life—and this floor is awfully hard."

"There's just one more thing," said Priscilla resolutely. "You, Phil, as all Redmond knows, entertain callers almost every evening. Now, at Patty's Place we can't do that. We have decided that we shall be at home to our friends on Friday evenings only. If you come with us you'll have to abide by that rule."

"Well, you don't think I'll mind that, do you? Why, I'm glad of it. I knew I should have had some such rule myself, but I hadn't enough decision to make it or stick to it. When I can shuffle off the responsibility on you it will be a real relief. If you won't let me cast in my lot with you I'll die of the disappointment and then I'll come back and haunt you. I'll camp on the very doorstep of Patty's Place and you won't be able to go out or come in without falling over my spook."

Again Anne and Priscilla exchanged eloquent looks.

"Well," said Anne, "of course we can't promise to take you until we've consulted with Stella; but I don't think she'll object, and, as far as we are concerned, you may come and glad welcome."

"If you get tired of our simple life you can leave us, and no questions asked," added Priscilla.

Phil sprang up, hugged them both jubilantly, and went on her way rejoicing.

"I hope things will go right," said Priscilla soberly.

"We must MAKE them go right," avowed Anne. "I think Phil will fit into our 'appy little 'ome very well."

"Oh, Phil's a dear to rattle round with and be chums. And, of course, the more there are of us the easier it will be on our slim purses. But how will she be to live with? You have to summer and winter with any one before you know if she's LIVABLE or not."

"Oh, well, we'll all be put to the test, as far as that goes. And we must quit us like sensible folk, living and let live. Phil isn't selfish, though she's a little thoughtless, and I believe we will all get on beautifully in Patty's Place."

Chapter XI - The Round of Life

Anne was back in Avonlea with the luster of the Thorburn Scholarship on her brow. People told her she hadn't changed much, in a tone which hinted they were surprised and a little disappointed she hadn't. Avonlea had not changed, either. At least, so it seemed at first. But as Anne sat in the Green Gables pew, on the first Sunday after her return, and looked over the congregation, she saw several little changes which, all coming home to her at once, made her realize that time did not quite stand still, even in Avonlea. A new minister was in the pulpit. In the pews more than one familiar face was missing forever. Old "Uncle Abe," his prophesying over and done with, Mrs. Peter Sloane, who had sighed, it was to be hoped, for the last time, Timothy Cotton, who, as Mrs. Rachel Lynde said "had actually managed to die at last after practicing at it for twenty years," and old Josiah Sloane, whom nobody knew in his coffin because he had his whiskers neatly trimmed, were all sleeping in the little graveyard behind the church. And Billy Andrews was married to Nettie Blewett! They "appeared out" that Sunday. When Billy, beaming with pride and happiness, showed his be-plumed and be-silked bride into the Harmon Andrews' pew, Anne dropped her lids to hide her dancing eyes. She recalled the stormy winter night of the Christmas holidays when Jane had proposed for Billy. He certainly had not broken his heart over his rejection. Anne wondered if Jane had also proposed to Nettie for him, or if he had mustered enough spunk to ask the fateful question himself. All the Andrews family seemed to share in his pride and pleasure, from Mrs. Harmon in the pew to Jane in the choir. Jane had resigned from the Avonlea school and intended to go West in the fall.

"Can't get a beau in Avonlea, that's what," said Mrs. Rachel Lynde scornfully. "SAYS she thinks she'll have better health out West. I never heard her health was poor before."

"Jane is a nice girl," Anne had said loyally. "She never tried to attract attention, as some did."

"Oh, she never chased the boys, if that's what you mean," said Mrs. Rachel. "But she'd like to be married, just as much as anybody, that's what. What else would take her out West to some forsaken place whose only recommendation is that men are plenty and women scarce? Don't you tell me!"

But it was not at Jane, Anne gazed that day in dismay and surprise. It was at Ruby Gillis, who sat beside her in the choir. What had happened to Ruby? She was even handsomer than ever; but her blue eyes were too bright and lustrous, and the color of her cheeks was hectically brilliant; besides, she was very thin; the hands that held her hymn-book were almost transparent in their delicacy.

"Is Ruby Gillis ill?" Anne asked of Mrs. Lynde, as they went home from church.

"Ruby Gillis is dying of galloping consumption," said Mrs. Lynde bluntly. "Everybody knows it except herself and her FAMILY. They won't give in. If you ask THEM, she's perfectly well. She hasn't been able to teach since she had that attack of congestion in the winter, but she says she's going to teach again in the fall, and she's after the White Sands school. She'll be in her grave, poor girl, when White Sands school opens, that's what."

Anne listened in shocked silence. Ruby Gillis, her old school-chum, dying? Could it be possible? Of late years they had grown apart; but the old tie of school-girl intimacy was there, and made itself felt sharply in the tug the news gave at Anne's heartstrings. Ruby, the brilliant, the merry, the coquettish! It was impossible to associate the thought of her with anything like death. She had greeted Anne with gay cordiality after church, and urged her to come up the next evening.

"I'll be away Tuesday and Wednesday evenings," she had whispered triumphantly. "There's a concert at Carmody and a party at White Sands. Herb Spencer's going to take me. He's my LATEST. Be sure to come up tomorrow. I'm dying for a good talk with you. I want to hear all about your doings at Redmond."

Anne knew that Ruby meant that she wanted to tell Anne all about her own recent flirtations, but she promised to go, and Diana offered to go with her.

"I've been wanting to go to see Ruby for a long while," she told Anne, when they left Green Gables the next evening, "but I really couldn't go alone. It's so awful to hear Ruby rattling on as she does, and pretending there is nothing the matter with her, even when she can hardly speak for coughing. She's fighting so hard for her life, and yet she hasn't any chance at all, they say."

The girls walked silently down the red, twilit road. The robins were singing vespers in the high treetops, filling the golden air with their jubilant voices. The silver fluting of the frogs came from marshes and ponds, over fields where seeds were beginning to stir with life and thrill to the sunshine and rain that had drifted over them. The air was fragrant with the wild, sweet, wholesome smell of young raspberry copses. White mists were hovering in the silent hollows and violet stars were shining bluely on the brooklands.

"What a beautiful sunset," said Diana. "Look, Anne, it's just like a land in itself, isn't it? That long, low back of purple cloud is the shore, and the clear sky further on is like a golden sea."

"If we could sail to it in the moonshine boat Paul wrote of in his old composition—you remember?—how nice it would be," said Anne, rousing from her reverie. "Do you think we could find all our yesterdays there, Diana—all our old springs and blossoms? The beds of flowers that Paul saw there are the roses that have bloomed for us in the past?"

"Don't!" said Diana. "You make me feel as if we were old women with everything in life behind us."

"I think I've almost felt as if we were since I heard about poor Ruby," said Anne. "If it is true that she is dying any other sad thing might be true, too."

"You don't mind calling in at Elisha Wright's for a moment, do you?" asked Diana. "Mother asked me to leave this little dish of jelly for Aunt Atossa."

"Who is Aunt Atossa?"

"Oh, haven't you heard? She's Mrs. Samson Coates of Spencervale—Mrs. Elisha Wright's aunt. She's father's aunt, too. Her husband died last winter and she was left very poor and lonely, so the Wrights took her to live with them. Mother thought we ought to take her, but father put his foot down. Live with Aunt Atossa he would not."

"Is she so terrible?" asked Anne absently.

"You'll probably see what she's like before we can get away," said Diana significantly. "Father says she has a face like a hatchet—it cuts the air. But her tongue is sharper still."

Late as it was Aunt Atossa was cutting potato sets in the Wright kitchen. She wore a faded old wrapper, and her gray hair was decidedly untidy. Aunt Atossa did not like being "caught in a kilter," so she went out of her way to be disagreeable.

"Oh, so you're Anne Shirley?" she said, when Diana introduced Anne. "I've heard of you." Her tone implied that she had heard nothing good. "Mrs. Andrews was telling me you were home. She said you had improved a good deal."

There was no doubt Aunt Atossa thought there was plenty of room for further improvement. She ceased not from cutting sets with much energy.

"Is it any use to ask you to sit down?" she inquired sarcastically. "Of course, there's nothing very entertaining here for you. The rest are all away."

"Mother sent you this little pot of rhubarb jelly," said Diana pleasantly. "She made it today and thought you might like some."

"Oh, thanks," said Aunt Atossa sourly. "I never fancy your mother's jelly—she always makes it too sweet. However, I'll try to worry some down. My appetite's been dreadful poor this spring. I'm far from well," continued Aunt Atossa solemnly, "but still I keep a-doing. People who can't work aren't wanted here. If it isn't too much trouble will you be condescending enough to set the jelly in the pantry? I'm in a hurry to get these spuds done tonight. I suppose you two LADIES never do anything like this. You'd be afraid of spoiling your hands."

"I used to cut potato sets before we rented the farm," smiled Anne.

"I do it yet," laughed Diana. "I cut sets three days last week. Of course," she added teasingly, "I did my hands up in lemon juice and kid gloves every night after it."

Aunt Atossa sniffed.

"I suppose you got that notion out of some of those silly magazines you read so many of. I wonder your mother allows you. But she always spoiled you. We all thought when George married her she wouldn't be a suitable wife for him."

Aunt Atossa sighed heavily, as if all forebodings upon the occasion of George Barry's marriage had been amply and darkly fulfilled.

"Going, are you?" she inquired, as the girls rose. "Well, I suppose you can't find much amusement talking to an old woman like me. It's such a pity the boys ain't home."

"We want to run in and see Ruby Gillis a little while," explained Diana.

"Oh, anything does for an excuse, of course," said Aunt Atossa, amiably. "Just whip in and whip out before you have time to say how-do decently. It's college airs, I s'pose. You'd be wiser to keep away from Ruby Gillis. The doctors say consumption's catching. I always knew Ruby'd get something, gadding off to Boston last fall for a visit. People who ain't content to stay home always catch something."

"People who don't go visiting catch things, too. Sometimes they even die," said Diana solemnly.

"Then they don't have themselves to blame for it," retorted Aunt Atossa triumphantly. "I hear you are to be married in June, Diana."

"There is no truth in that report," said Diana, blushing.

"Well, don't put it off too long," said Aunt Atossa significantly. "You'll fade soon—you're all complexion and hair. And the Wrights are terrible fickle. You ought to wear a hat, MISS SHIRLEY. Your nose is freckling scandalous. My, but you ARE redheaded! Well, I s'pose we're all as the Lord made us! Give Marilla Cuthbert my respects. She's never been to see me since I come to Avonlea, but I s'pose I oughtn't to complain. The Cuthberts always did think themselves a cut higher than any one else round here."

"Oh, isn't she dreadful?" gasped Diana, as they escaped down the lane.

"She's worse than Miss Eliza Andrews," said Anne. "But then think of living all your life with a name like Atossa! Wouldn't it sour almost any one? She should have tried to imagine her name was Cordelia. It might have helped her a great deal. It certainly helped me in the days when I didn't like ANNE."

"Josie Pye will be just like her when she grows up," said Diana. "Josie's mother and Aunt Atossa are cousins, you know. Oh, dear, I'm glad that's over. She's so malicious—she seems to put a bad flavor in everything. Father tells such a funny story about her. One time they had a minister in Spencervale who was a very good, spiritual man but very deaf. He couldn't hear any ordinary conversation at all. Well, they used to have a prayer meeting on Sunday evenings, and all the church members present would get up and pray in turn, or say a few words on some Bible verse. But one evening Aunt Atossa bounced up. She didn't either pray or preach. Instead, she lit into everybody else in the church and gave them a fearful raking down, calling them right out by name and telling them how they all had behaved, and casting up all the quarrels and scandals of the past ten years. Finally she wound up by saying that she was disgusted with Spencervale church and she never meant to darken its door again, and she hoped a fearful judgment would come upon it. Then she sat down out of breath, and the minister, who hadn't heard a word she said, immediately remarked, in a very devout voice, 'amen! The Lord grant our dear sister's prayer!' You ought to hear father tell the story."

"Speaking of stories, Diana," remarked Anne, in a significant, confidential tone, "do you know that lately I have been wondering if I could write a short story—a story that would be good enough to be published?"

"Why, of course you could," said Diana, after she had grasped the amazing suggestion. "You used to write perfectly thrilling stories years ago in our old Story Club."

"Well, I hardly meant one of that kind of stories," smiled Anne. "I've been thinking about it a little of late, but I'm almost afraid to try, for, if I should fail, it would be too humiliating."

"I heard Priscilla say once that all Mrs. Morgan's first stories were rejected. But I'm sure yours wouldn't be, Anne, for it's likely editors have more sense nowadays."

"Margaret Burton, one of the Junior girls at Redmond, wrote a story last winter and it was published in the Canadian Woman. I really do think I could write one at least as good."

"And will you have it published in the Canadian Woman?"

"I might try one of the bigger magazines first. It all depends on what kind of a story I write."

"What is it to be about?"

"I don't know yet. I want to get hold of a good plot. I believe this is very necessary from an editor's point of view. The only thing I've settled on is the heroine's name. It is to be AVERIL LESTER. Rather pretty, don't you think? Don't mention this to any one, Diana. I haven't told anybody but you and Mr. Harrison. HE wasn't very encouraging—he said there was far too much trash written nowadays as it was, and he'd expected something better of me, after a year at college."

"What does Mr. Harrison know about it?" demanded Diana scornfully.

They found the Gillis home gay with lights and callers. Leonard Kimball, of Spencervale, and Morgan Bell, of Carmody, were glaring at each other across the parlor. Several merry girls had dropped in. Ruby was dressed in white and her eyes and cheeks were very brilliant. She laughed and chattered incessantly, and after the other girls had gone she took Anne upstairs to display her new summer dresses.

"I've a blue silk to make up yet, but it's a little heavy for summer wear. I think I'll leave it until the fall. I'm going to teach in White Sands, you know. How do you like my hat? That one you had on in church yesterday was real dinky. But I like something brighter for myself. Did you notice those two ridiculous boys downstairs? They've both come determined to sit each other out. I don't care a single bit about either of them, you know. Herb Spencer is the one I like. Sometimes I really do think he's MR. RIGHT. At Christmas I thought the Spencervale schoolmaster was that. But I found out something about him that turned me against him. He nearly went insane when I turned him down. I wish those two boys hadn't come tonight. I wanted to have a nice good talk with you, Anne, and tell you such heaps of things. You and I were always good chums, weren't we?"

Ruby slipped her arm about Anne's waist with a shallow little laugh. But just for a moment their eyes met, and, behind all the luster of Ruby's, Anne saw something that made her heart ache.

"Come up often, won't you, Anne?" whispered Ruby. "Come alone—I want you."

"Are you feeling quite well, Ruby?"

"Me! Why, I'm perfectly well. I never felt better in my life. Of course, that congestion last winter pulled me down a little. But just see my color. I don't look much like an invalid, I'm sure."

Ruby's voice was almost sharp. She pulled her arm away from Anne, as if in resentment, and ran downstairs, where she was gayer than ever, apparently so much absorbed in bantering her two swains that Diana and Anne felt rather out of it and soon went away.

Chapter XII - "Averil's Atonement"

"What are you dreaming of, Anne?"

The two girls were loitering one evening in a fairy hollow of the brook. Ferns nodded in it, and little grasses were green, and wild pears hung finely-scented, white curtains around it.

Anne roused herself from her reverie with a happy sigh.

"I was thinking out my story, Diana."

"Oh, have you really begun it?" cried Diana, all alight with eager interest in a moment.

"Yes, I have only a few pages written, but I have it all pretty well thought out. I've had such a time to get a suitable plot. None of the plots that suggested themselves suited a girl named AVERIL."

"Couldn't you have changed her name?"

"No, the thing was impossible. I tried to, but I couldn't do it, any more than I could change yours. AVERIL was so real to me that no matter what other name I tried to give her I just thought of her as AVERIL behind it all. But finally I got a plot that matched her. Then came the excitement of choosing names for all my characters. You have no idea how fascinating that is. I've lain awake for hours thinking over those names. The hero's name is PERCEVAL DALRYMPLE."

"Have you named ALL the characters?" asked Diana wistfully. "If you hadn't I was going to ask you to let me name one—just some unimportant person. I'd feel as if I had a share in the story then."

"You may name the little hired boy who lived with the LESTERS," conceded Anne. "He is not very important, but he is the only one left unnamed."

"Call him RAYMOND FITZOSBORNE," suggested Diana, who had a store of such names laid away in her memory, relics of the old "Story Club," which she and Anne and Jane Andrews and Ruby Gillis had had in their schooldays.

Anne shook her head doubtfully.

"I'm afraid that is too aristocratic a name for a chore boy, Diana. I couldn't imagine a Fitzosborne feeding pigs and picking up chips, could you?"

Diana didn't see why, if you had an imagination at all, you couldn't stretch it to that extent; but probably Anne knew best, and the chore boy was finally christened ROBERT RAY, to be called BOBBY should occasion require.

"How much do you suppose you'll get for it?" asked Diana.

But Anne had not thought about this at all. She was in pursuit of fame, not filthy lucre, and her literary dreams were as yet untainted by mercenary considerations.

"You'll let me read it, won't you?" pleaded Diana.

"When it is finished I'll read it to you and Mr. Harrison, and I shall want you to criticize it SEVERELY. No one else shall see it until it is published."

"How are you going to end it—happily or unhappily?"

"I'm not sure. I'd like it to end unhappily, because that would be so much more romantic. But I understand editors have a prejudice against sad endings. I heard Professor Hamilton say once that nobody but a genius should try to write an unhappy ending. And," concluded Anne modestly, "I'm anything but a genius."

"Oh I like happy endings best. You'd better let him marry her," said Diana, who, especially since her engagement to Fred, thought this was how every story should end.

"But you like to cry over stories?"

"Oh, yes, in the middle of them. But I like everything to come right at last."

"I must have one pathetic scene in it," said Anne thoughtfully. "I might let ROBERT RAY be injured in an accident and have a death scene."

"No, you mustn't kill BOBBY off," declared Diana, laughing. "He belongs to me and I want him to live and flourish. Kill somebody else if you have to."

For the next fortnight Anne writhed or reveled, according to mood, in her literary pursuits. Now she would be jubilant over a brilliant idea, now despairing because some contrary character would NOT behave properly. Diana could not understand this.

"MAKE them do as you want them to," she said.

"I can't," mourned Anne. "Averil is such an unmanageable heroine. She WILL do and say things I never meant her to. Then that spoils everything that went before and I have to write it all over again."

Finally, however, the story was finished, and Anne read it to Diana in the seclusion of the porch gable. She had achieved her "pathetic scene" without sacrificing ROBERT RAY, and she kept a watchful eye on Diana as she read it. Diana rose to the occasion and cried properly; but, when the end came, she looked a little disappointed.

"Why did you kill MAURICE LENNOX?" she asked reproachfully.

"He was the villain," protested Anne. "He had to be punished."

"I like him best of them all," said unreasonable Diana.

"Well, he's dead, and he'll have to stay dead," said Anne, rather resentfully. "If I had let him live he'd have gone on persecuting AVERIL and PERCEVAL."

"Yes—unless you had reformed him."

"That wouldn't have been romantic, and, besides, it would have made the story too long."

"Well, anyway, it's a perfectly elegant story, Anne, and will make you famous, of that I'm sure. Have you got a title for it?"

"Oh, I decided on the title long ago. I call it AVERIL'S ATONEMENT. Doesn't that sound nice and alliterative? Now, Diana, tell me candidly, do you see any faults in my story?"

"Well," hesitated Diana, "that part where AVERIL makes the cake doesn't seem to me quite romantic enough to match the rest. It's just what anybody might do. Heroines shouldn't do cooking, *I* think."

"Why, that is where the humor comes in, and it's one of the best parts of the whole story," said Anne. And it may be stated that in this she was quite right.

Diana prudently refrained from any further criticism, but Mr. Harrison was much harder to please. First he told her there was entirely too much description in the story.

"Cut out all those flowery passages," he said unfeelingly.

Anne had an uncomfortable conviction that Mr. Harrison was right, and she forced herself to expunge most of her beloved descriptions, though it took three re-writings before the story could be pruned down to please the fastidious Mr. Harrison.

"I've left out ALL the descriptions but the sunset," she said at last. "I simply COULDN'T let it go. It was the best of them all."

"It hasn't anything to do with the story," said Mr. Harrison, "and you shouldn't have laid the scene among rich city people. What do you know of them? Why didn't you lay it right here in Avonlea—changing the name, of course, or else Mrs. Rachel Lynde would probably think she was the heroine."

"Oh, that would never have done," protested Anne. "Avonlea is the dearest place in the world, but it isn't quite romantic enough for the scene of a story."

"I daresay there's been many a romance in Avonlea—and many a tragedy, too," said Mr. Harrison drily. "But your folks ain't like real folks anywhere. They talk too much and use too high-flown language. There's one place where that DALRYMPLE chap talks even on for two pages, and never lets the girl get a word in edgewise. If he'd done that in real life she'd have pitched him."

"I don't believe it," said Anne flatly. In her secret soul she thought that the beautiful, poetical things said to AVERIL would win any girl's heart completely. Besides, it was gruesome to hear of AVERIL, the stately, queen-like AVERIL, "pitching" any one. AVERIL "declined her suitors."

"Anyhow," resumed the merciless Mr. Harrison, "I don't see why MAURICE LENNOX didn't get her. He was twice the man the other is. He did bad things, but he did them. Perceval hadn't time for anything but mooning."

"Mooning." That was even worse than "pitching!"

"MAURICE LENNOX was the villain," said Anne indignantly. "I don't see why every one likes him better than PERCEVAL."

"Perceval is too good. He's aggravating. Next time you write about a hero put a little spice of human nature in him."

"AVERIL couldn't have married MAURICE. He was bad."

"She'd have reformed him. You can reform a man; you can't reform a jelly-fish, of course. Your story isn't bad—it's kind of interesting, I'll admit. But you're too young to write a story that would be worth while. Wait ten years."

Anne made up her mind that the next time she wrote a story she wouldn't ask anybody to criticize it. It was too discouraging. She would not read the story to Gilbert, although she told him about it.

"If it is a success you'll see it when it is published, Gilbert, but if it is a failure nobody shall ever see it."

Marilla knew nothing about the venture. In imagination Anne saw herself reading a story out of a magazine to Marilla, entrapping her into praise of it—for in imagination all things are possible—and then triumphantly announcing herself the author.

One day Anne took to the Post Office a long, bulky envelope, addressed, with the delightful confidence of youth and inexperience, to the very biggest of the "big" magazines. Diana was as excited over it as Anne herself.

"How long do you suppose it will be before you hear from it?" she asked.

"It shouldn't be longer than a fortnight. Oh, how happy and proud I shall be if it is accepted!"

"Of course it will be accepted, and they will likely ask you to send them more. You may be as famous as Mrs. Morgan some day, Anne, and then how proud I'll be of knowing you," said Diana, who possessed, at least, the striking merit of an unselfish admiration of the gifts and graces of her friends.

A week of delightful dreaming followed, and then came a bitter awakening. One evening Diana found Anne in the porch gable, with suspicious-looking eyes. On the table lay a long envelope and a crumpled manuscript.

"Anne, your story hasn't come back?" cried Diana incredulously.

"Yes, it has," said Anne shortly.

"Well, that editor must be crazy. What reason did he give?"

"No reason at all. There is just a printed slip saying that it wasn't found ac-ceptable."

"I never thought much of that magazine, anyway," said Diana hotly. "The sto-ries in it are not half as interesting as those in the Canadian Woman, although it costs so much more. I suppose the editor is prejudiced against any one who isn't a Yankee. Don't be discouraged, Anne. Remember how Mrs. Morgan's stories came back. Send yours to the Canadian Woman."

"I believe I will," said Anne, plucking up heart. "And if it is published I'll send that American editor a marked copy. But I'll cut the sunset out. I believe Mr. Har-rison was right."

Out came the sunset; but in spite of this heroic mutilation the editor of the Ca-nadian Woman sent Averil's Atonement back so promptly that the indignant Diana declared that it couldn't have been read at all, and vowed she was going to stop her subscription immediately. Anne took this second rejection with the calm-ness of despair. She locked the story away in the garret trunk where the old Story Club tales reposed; but first she yielded to Diana's entreaties and gave her a copy.

"This is the end of my literary ambitions," she said bitterly.

She never mentioned the matter to Mr. Harrison, but one evening he asked her bluntly if her story had been accepted.

"No, the editor wouldn't take it," she answered briefly.

Mr. Harrison looked sidewise at the flushed, delicate profile.

"Well, I suppose you'll keep on writing them," he said encouragingly.

"No, I shall never try to write a story again," declared Anne, with the hopeless finality of nineteen when a door is shut in its face.

"I wouldn't give up altogether," said Mr. Harrison reflectively. "I'd write a story once in a while, but I wouldn't pester editors with it. I'd write of people and places like I knew, and I'd make my characters talk everyday English; and I'd let the sun rise and set in the usual quiet way without much fuss over the fact. If I had to have villains at all, I'd give them a chance, Anne—I'd give them a chance. There are some terrible bad men in the world, I suppose, but you'd have to go a long piece to find them—though Mrs. Lynde believes we're all bad. But most of us have got a little decency somewhere in us. Keep on writing, Anne."

"No. It was very foolish of me to attempt it. When I'm through Redmond I'll stick to teaching. I can teach. I can't write stories."

"It'll be time for you to be getting a husband when you're through Redmond," said Mr. Harrison. "I don't believe in putting marrying off too long—like I did."

Anne got up and marched home. There were times when Mr. Harrison was really intolerable. "Pitching," "mooning," and "getting a husband." Ow!!

Chapter XIII - The Way of Transgressors

Davy and Dora were ready for Sunday School. They were going alone, which did not often happen, for Mrs. Lynde always attended Sunday School. But Mrs. Lynde had twisted her ankle and was lame, so she was staying home this morning. The twins were also to represent the family at church, for Anne had gone away the evening before to spend Sunday with friends in Carmody, and Marilla had one of her headaches.

Davy came downstairs slowly. Dora was waiting in the hall for him, having been made ready by Mrs. Lynde. Davy had attended to his own preparations. He had a cent in his pocket for the Sunday School collection, and a five-cent piece for the church collection; he carried his Bible in one hand and his Sunday School quarterly in the other; he knew his lesson and his Golden Text and his catechism question perfectly. Had he not studied them—perforce—in Mrs. Lynde's kitchen, all last Sunday afternoon? Davy, therefore, should have been in a placid frame of mind. As a matter of fact, despite text and catechism, he was inwardly as a ravening wolf.

Mrs. Lynde limped out of her kitchen as he joined Dora.

"Are you clean?" she demanded severely.

"Yes—all of me that shows," Davy answered with a defiant scowl.

Mrs. Rachel sighed. She had her suspicions about Davy's neck and ears. But she knew that if she attempted to make a personal examination Davy would likely take to his heels and she could not pursue him today.

"Well, be sure you behave yourselves," she warned them. "Don't walk in the dust. Don't stop in the porch to talk to the other children. Don't squirm or wriggle in your places. Don't forget the Golden Text. Don't lose your collection or forget to put it in. Don't whisper at prayer time, and don't forget to pay attention to the sermon."

Davy deigned no response. He marched away down the lane, followed by the meek Dora. But his soul seethed within. Davy had suffered, or thought he had suffered, many things at the hands and tongue of Mrs. Rachel Lynde since she had come to Green Gables, for Mrs. Lynde could not live with anybody, whether they were nine or ninety, without trying to bring them up properly. And it was only the preceding afternoon that she had interfered to influence Marilla against allowing Davy to go fishing with the Timothy Cottons. Davy was still boiling over this.

As soon as he was out of the lane Davy stopped and twisted his countenance into such an unearthly and terrific contortion that Dora, although she knew his gifts in that respect, was honestly alarmed lest he should never in the world be able to get it straightened out again.

"Darn her," exploded Davy.

"Oh, Davy, don't swear," gasped Dora in dismay.

"'Darn' isn't swearing—not real swearing. And I don't care if it is," retorted Davy recklessly.

"Well, if you MUST say dreadful words don't say them on Sunday," pleaded Dora.

Davy was as yet far from repentance, but in his secret soul he felt that, perhaps, he had gone a little too far.

"I'm going to invent a swear word of my own," he declared.

"God will punish you if you do," said Dora solemnly.

"Then I think God is a mean old scamp," retorted Davy. "Doesn't He know a fellow must have some way of 'spressing his feelings?"

"Davy!!!" said Dora. She expected that Davy would be struck down dead on the spot. But nothing happened.

"Anyway, I ain't going to stand any more of Mrs. Lynde's bossing," spluttered Davy. "Anne and Marilla may have the right to boss me, but SHE hasn't. I'm going to do every single thing she told me not to do. You watch me."

In grim, deliberate silence, while Dora watched him with the fascination of horror, Davy stepped off the green grass of the roadside, ankle deep into the fine dust which four weeks of rainless weather had made on the road, and marched along in it, shuffling his feet viciously until he was enveloped in a hazy cloud.

"That's the beginning," he announced triumphantly. "And I'm going to stop in the porch and talk as long as there's anybody there to talk to. I'm going to squirm and wriggle and whisper, and I'm going to say I don't know the Golden Text. And I'm going to throw away both of my collections RIGHT NOW."

And Davy hurled cent and nickel over Mr. Barry's fence with fierce delight.

"Satan made you do that," said Dora reproachfully.

"He didn't," cried Davy indignantly. "I just thought it out for myself. And I've thought of something else. I'm not going to Sunday School or church at all. I'm going up to play with the Cottons. They told me yesterday they weren't going to Sunday School today, 'cause their mother was away and there was nobody to make them. Come along, Dora, we'll have a great time."

"I don't want to go," protested Dora.

"You've got to," said Davy. "If you don't come I'll tell Marilla that Frank Bell kissed you in school last Monday."

"I couldn't help it. I didn't know he was going to," cried Dora, blushing scarlet.

"Well, you didn't slap him or seem a bit cross," retorted Davy. "I'll tell her THAT, too, if you don't come. We'll take the short cut up this field."

"I'm afraid of those cows," protested poor Dora, seeing a prospect of escape.

"The very idea of your being scared of those cows," scoffed Davy. "Why, they're both younger than you."

"They're bigger," said Dora.

"They won't hurt you. Come along, now. This is great. When I grow up I ain't going to bother going to church at all. I believe I can get to heaven by myself."

"You'll go to the other place if you break the Sabbath day," said unhappy Dora, following him sorely against her will.

But Davy was not scared—yet. Hell was very far off, and the delights of a fishing expedition with the Cottons were very near. He wished Dora had more spunk. She kept looking back as if she were going to cry every minute, and that spoiled a fellow's fun. Hang girls, anyway. Davy did not say "darn" this time, even in thought. He was not sorry—yet—that he had said it once, but it might be as well not to tempt the Unknown Powers too far on one day.

The small Cottons were playing in their back yard, and hailed Davy's appearance with whoops of delight. Pete, Tommy, Adolphus, and Mirabel Cotton were all alone. Their mother and older sisters were away. Dora was thankful Mirabel was there, at least. She had been afraid she would be alone in a crowd of boys. Mirabel was almost as bad as a boy—she was so noisy and sunburned and reckless. But at least she wore dresses.

"We've come to go fishing," announced Davy.

"Whoop," yelled the Cottons. They rushed away to dig worms at once, Mirabel leading the van with a tin can. Dora could have sat down and cried. Oh, if only that hateful Frank Bell had never kissed her! Then she could have defied Davy, and gone to her beloved Sunday School.

They dared not, of course, go fishing on the pond, where they would be seen by people going to church. They had to resort to the brook in the woods behind the Cotton house. But it was full of trout, and they had a glorious time that morning—at least the Cottons certainly had, and Davy seemed to have it. Not being entirely bereft of prudence, he had discarded boots and stockings and borrowed Tommy Cotton's overalls. Thus accoutered, bog and marsh and undergrowth had no terrors for him. Dora was frankly and manifestly miserable. She followed the others in their peregrinations from pool to pool, clasping her Bible and quarterly tightly and thinking with bitterness of soul of her beloved class where she should be sitting that very moment, before a teacher she adored. Instead, here she was roaming the woods with those half-wild Cottons, trying to keep her boots clean and her pretty white dress free from rents and stains. Mirabel had offered the loan of an apron but Dora had scornfully refused.

The trout bit as they always do on Sundays. In an hour the transgressors had all the fish they wanted, so they returned to the house, much to Dora's relief. She sat primly on a hencoop in the yard while the others played an uproarious game of tag; and then they all climbed to the top of the pig-house roof and cut their initials on the saddleboard. The flat-roofed henhouse and a pile of straw beneath gave

Davy another inspiration. They spent a splendid half hour climbing on the roof and diving off into the straw with whoops and yells.

But even unlawful pleasures must come to an end. When the rumble of wheels over the pond bridge told that people were going home from church Davy knew they must go. He discarded Tommy's overalls, resumed his own rightful attire, and turned away from his string of trout with a sigh. No use to think of taking them home.

"Well, hadn't we a splendid time?" he demanded defiantly, as they went down the hill field.

"I hadn't," said Dora flatly. "And I don't believe you had—really—either," she added, with a flash of insight that was not to be expected of her.

"I had so," cried Davy, but in the voice of one who doth protest too much. "No wonder you hadn't—just sitting there like a—like a mule."

"I ain't going to, 'sociate with the Cottons," said Dora loftily.

"The Cottons are all right," retorted Davy. "And they have far better times than we have. They do just as they please and say just what they like before everybody. *I'm* going to do that, too, after this."

"There are lots of things you wouldn't dare say before everybody," averred Dora.

"No, there isn't."

"There is, too. Would you," demanded Dora gravely, "would you say 'tomcat' before the minister?"

This was a staggerer. Davy was not prepared for such a concrete example of the freedom of speech. But one did not have to be consistent with Dora.

"Of course not," he admitted sulkily.

"'Tomcat' isn't a holy word. I wouldn't mention such an animal before a minister at all."

"But if you had to?" persisted Dora.

"I'd call it a Thomas pussy," said Davy.

"*I* think 'gentleman cat' would be more polite," reflected Dora.

"YOU thinking!" retorted Davy with withering scorn.

Davy was not feeling comfortable, though he would have died before he admitted it to Dora. Now that the exhilaration of truant delights had died away, his conscience was beginning to give him salutary twinges. After all, perhaps it would have been better to have gone to Sunday School and church. Mrs. Lynde might be bossy; but there was always a box of cookies in her kitchen cupboard and she was not stingy. At this inconvenient moment Davy remembered that when he had torn his new school pants the week before, Mrs. Lynde had mended them beautifully and never said a word to Marilla about them.

But Davy's cup of iniquity was not yet full. He was to discover that one sin demands another to cover it. They had dinner with Mrs. Lynde that day, and the first thing she asked Davy was,

"Were all your class in Sunday School today?"

"Yes'm," said Davy with a gulp. "All were there—'cept one."

"Did you say your Golden Text and catechism?"

"Yes'm."

"Did you put your collection in?"

"Yes'm."

"Was Mrs. Malcolm MacPherson in church?"

"I don't know." This, at least, was the truth, thought wretched Davy.

"Was the Ladies' Aid announced for next week?"

"Yes'm"—quakingly.

"Was prayer-meeting?"

"I—I don't know."

"YOU should know. You should listen more attentively to the announcements. What was Mr. Harvey's text?"

Davy took a frantic gulp of water and swallowed it and the last protest of conscience together. He glibly recited an old Golden Text learned several weeks ago. Fortunately Mrs. Lynde now stopped questioning him; but Davy did not enjoy his dinner.

He could only eat one helping of pudding.

"What's the matter with you?" demanded justly astonished Mrs. Lynde. "Are you sick?"

"No," muttered Davy.

"You look pale. You'd better keep out of the sun this afternoon," admonished Mrs. Lynde.

"Do you know how many lies you told Mrs. Lynde?" asked Dora reproachfully, as soon as they were alone after dinner.

Davy, goaded to desperation, turned fiercely.

"I don't know and I don't care," he said. "You just shut up, Dora Keith."

Then poor Davy betook himself to a secluded retreat behind the woodpile to think over the way of transgressors.

Green Gables was wrapped in darkness and silence when Anne reached home. She lost no time going to bed, for she was very tired and sleepy. There had been several Avonlea jollifications the preceding week, involving rather late hours. Anne's head was hardly on her pillow before she was half asleep; but just then her door was softly opened and a pleading voice said, "Anne."

Anne sat up drowsily.

"Davy, is that you? What is the matter?"

A white-clad figure flung itself across the floor and on to the bed.

"Anne," sobbed Davy, getting his arms about her neck. "I'm awful glad you're home. I couldn't go to sleep till I'd told somebody."

"Told somebody what?"

"How mis'rubul I am."

"Why are you miserable, dear?"

"'Cause I was so bad today, Anne. Oh, I was awful bad—badder'n I've ever been yet."

"What did you do?"

"Oh, I'm afraid to tell you. You'll never like me again, Anne. I couldn't say my prayers tonight. I couldn't tell God what I'd done. I was 'shamed to have Him know."

"But He knew anyway, Davy."

"That's what Dora said. But I thought p'raps He mightn't have noticed just at the time. Anyway, I'd rather tell you first."

"WHAT is it you did?"

Out it all came in a rush.

"I run away from Sunday School—and went fishing with the Cottons—and I told ever so many whoppers to Mrs. Lynde—oh! 'most half a dozen—and—and—I—I said a swear word, Anne—a pretty near swear word, anyhow—and I called God names."

There was silence. Davy didn't know what to make of it. Was Anne so shocked that she never would speak to him again?

"Anne, what are you going to do to me?" he whispered.

"Nothing, dear. You've been punished already, I think."

"No, I haven't. Nothing's been done to me."

"You've been very unhappy ever since you did wrong, haven't you?"

"You bet!" said Davy emphatically.

"That was your conscience punishing you, Davy."

"What's my conscience? I want to know."

"It's something in you, Davy, that always tells you when you are doing wrong and makes you unhappy if you persist in doing it. Haven't you noticed that?"

"Yes, but I didn't know what it was. I wish I didn't have it. I'd have lots more fun. Where is my conscience, Anne? I want to know. Is it in my stomach?"

"No, it's in your soul," answered Anne, thankful for the darkness, since gravity must be preserved in serious matters.

"I s'pose I can't get clear of it then," said Davy with a sigh. "Are you going to tell Marilla and Mrs. Lynde on me, Anne?"

"No, dear, I'm not going to tell any one. You are sorry you were naughty, aren't you?"

"You bet!"

"And you'll never be bad like that again."

"No, but—" added Davy cautiously, "I might be bad some other way."

"You won't say naughty words, or run away on Sundays, or tell falsehoods to cover up your sins?"

"No. It doesn't pay," said Davy.

"Well, Davy, just tell God you are sorry and ask Him to forgive you."

"Have YOU forgiven me, Anne?"

"Yes, dear."

"Then," said Davy joyously, "I don't care much whether God does or not."

"Davy!"

"Oh—I'll ask Him—I'll ask Him," said Davy quickly, scrambling off the bed, convinced by Anne's tone that he must have said something dreadful. "I don't mind asking Him, Anne.—Please, God, I'm awful sorry I behaved bad today and I'll try to be good on Sundays always and please forgive me.—There now, Anne."

"Well, now, run off to bed like a good boy."

"All right. Say, I don't feel mis'rubul any more. I feel fine. Good night."

"Good night."

Anne slipped down on her pillows with a sigh of relief. Oh—how sleepy—she was! In another second—

"Anne!" Davy was back again by her bed. Anne dragged her eyes open.

"What is it now, dear?" she asked, trying to keep a note of impatience out of her voice.

"Anne, have you ever noticed how Mr. Harrison spits? Do you s'pose, if I practice hard, I can learn to spit just like him?"

Anne sat up.

"Davy Keith," she said, "go straight to your bed and don't let me catch you out of it again tonight! Go, now!"

Davy went, and stood not upon the order of his going.

Chapter XIV - The Summons

Anne was sitting with Ruby Gillis in the Gillis' garden after the day had crept lingeringly through it and was gone. It had been a warm, smoky summer afternoon. The world was in a splendor of out-flowering. The idle valleys were full of hazes. The woodways were pranked with shadows and the fields with the purple of the asters.

Anne had given up a moonlight drive to the White Sands beach that she might spend the evening with Ruby. She had so spent many evenings that summer, although she often wondered what good it did any one, and sometimes went home deciding that she could not go again.

Ruby grew paler as the summer waned; the White Sands school was given up—"her father thought it better that she shouldn't teach till New Year's"—and the fancy work she loved oftener and oftener fell from hands grown too weary for it. But she was always gay, always hopeful, always chattering and whispering of her beaux, and their rivalries and despairs. It was this that made Anne's visits hard for her. What had once been silly or amusing was gruesome, now; it was death peering through a wilful mask of life. Yet Ruby seemed to cling to her, and never let her go until she had promised to come again soon. Mrs. Lynde grumbled about Anne's frequent visits, and declared she would catch consumption; even Marilla was dubious.

"Every time you go to see Ruby you come home looking tired out," she said.

"It's so very sad and dreadful," said Anne in a low tone. "Ruby doesn't seem to realize her condition in the least. And yet I somehow feel she needs help—craves it—and I want to give it to her and can't. All the time I'm with her I feel as if I were watching her struggle with an invisible foe—trying to push it back with such feeble resistance as she has. That is why I come home tired."

But tonight Anne did not feel this so keenly. Ruby was strangely quiet. She said not a word about parties and drives and dresses and "fellows." She lay in the hammock, with her untouched work beside her, and a white shawl wrapped about her thin shoulders. Her long yellow braids of hair—how Anne had envied those beautiful braids in old schooldays!—lay on either side of her. She had taken the pins out—they made her head ache, she said. The hectic flush was gone for the time, leaving her pale and childlike.

The moon rose in the silvery sky, empearling the clouds around her. Below, the pond shimmered in its hazy radiance. Just beyond the Gillis homestead was the church, with the old graveyard beside it. The moonlight shone on the white stones, bringing them out in clear-cut relief against the dark trees behind.

"How strange the graveyard looks by moonlight!" said Ruby suddenly. "How ghostly!" she shuddered. "Anne, it won't be long now before I'll be lying over there. You and Diana and all the rest will be going about, full of life—and I'll be there—in the old graveyard—dead!"

The surprise of it bewildered Anne. For a few moments she could not speak.

"You know it's so, don't you?" said Ruby insistently.

"Yes, I know," answered Anne in a low tone. "Dear Ruby, I know."

"Everybody knows it," said Ruby bitterly. "I know it—I've known it all summer, though I wouldn't give in. And, oh, Anne"—she reached out and caught Anne's hand pleadingly, impulsively—"I don't want to die. I'm AFRAID to die."

"Why should you be afraid, Ruby?" asked Anne quietly.

"Because—because—oh, I'm not afraid but that I'll go to heaven, Anne. I'm a church member. But—it'll be all so different. I think—and think—and I get so frightened—and—and—homesick. Heaven must be very beautiful, of course, the Bible says so—but, Anne, IT WON'T BE WHAT I'VE BEEN USED TO."

Through Anne's mind drifted an intrusive recollection of a funny story she had heard Philippa Gordon tell—the story of some old man who had said very much the same thing about the world to come. It had sounded funny then—she remembered how she and Priscilla had laughed over it. But it did not seem in the least humorous now, coming from Ruby's pale, trembling lips. It was sad, tragic—and true! Heaven could not be what Ruby had been used to. There had been nothing in her gay, frivolous life, her shallow ideals and aspirations, to fit her for that great change, or make the life to come seem to her anything but alien and unreal and undesirable. Anne wondered helplessly what she could say that would help her. Could she say anything? "I think, Ruby," she began hesitatingly—for it was difficult for Anne to speak to any one of the deepest thoughts of her heart, or the new ideas that had vaguely begun to shape themselves in her mind, concerning the great mysteries of life here and hereafter, superseding her old childish conceptions, and it was hardest of all to speak of them to such as Ruby Gillis—"I think, perhaps, we have very mistaken ideas about heaven—what it is and what it holds for us. I don't think it can be so very different from life here as most people seem to think. I believe we'll just go on living, a good deal as we live here—and be OURSELVES just the same—only it will be easier to be good and to—follow the highest. All the hindrances and perplexities will be taken away, and we shall see clearly. Don't be afraid, Ruby."

"I can't help it," said Ruby pitifully. "Even if what you say about heaven is true—and you can't be sure—it may be only that imagination of yours—it won't be JUST the same. It CAN'T be. I want to go on living HERE. I'm so young, Anne. I haven't had my life. I've fought so hard to live—and it isn't any use—I have to die—and leave EVERYTHING I care for." Anne sat in a pain that was almost intolerable. She could not tell comforting falsehoods; and all that Ruby said was so horribly true. She WAS leaving everything she cared for. She had laid up her treasures on earth only; she had lived solely for the little things of life—the things that pass—forgetting the great things that go onward into eternity, bridging the gulf between the two lives and making of death a mere passing from one dwelling to the other—from twilight to unclouded day. God would take care of her there—Anne believed—she would learn—but now it was no wonder her soul clung, in blind helplessness, to the only things she knew and loved.

Ruby raised herself on her arm and lifted up her bright, beautiful blue eyes to the moonlit skies.

"I want to live," she said, in a trembling voice. "I want to live like other girls. I—I want to be married, Anne—and—and—have little children. You know I always loved babies, Anne. I couldn't say this to any one but you. I know you understand. And then poor Herb—he—he loves me and I love him, Anne. The others meant nothing to me, but HE does—and if I could live I would be his wife and be so happy. Oh, Anne, it's hard."

Ruby sank back on her pillows and sobbed convulsively. Anne pressed her hand in an agony of sympathy—silent sympathy, which perhaps helped Ruby more than broken, imperfect words could have done; for presently she grew calmer and her sobs ceased.

"I'm glad I've told you this, Anne," she whispered. "It has helped me just to say it all out. I've wanted to all summer—every time you came. I wanted to talk it over with you—but I COULDN'T. It seemed as if it would make death so SURE if I SAID I was going to die, or if any one else said it or hinted it. I wouldn't say it, or even think it. In the daytime, when people were around me and everything was cheerful, it wasn't so hard to keep from thinking of it. But in the night, when I couldn't sleep—it was so dreadful, Anne. I couldn't get away from it then. Death just came and stared me in the face, until I got so frightened I could have screamed.

"But you won't be frightened any more, Ruby, will you? You'll be brave, and believe that all is going to be well with you."

"I'll try. I'll think over what you have said, and try to believe it. And you'll come up as often as you can, won't you, Anne?"

"Yes, dear."

"It—it won't be very long now, Anne. I feel sure of that. And I'd rather have you than any one else. I always liked you best of all the girls I went to school with. You were never jealous, or mean, like some of them were. Poor Em White was up to see me yesterday. You remember Em and I were such chums for three years when we went to school? And then we quarrelled the time of the school concert. We've never spoken to each other since. Wasn't it silly? Anything like that seems silly NOW. But Em and I made up the old quarrel yesterday. She said she'd have spoken years ago, only she thought I wouldn't. And I never spoke to her because I was sure she wouldn't speak to me. Isn't it strange how people misunderstand each other, Anne?"

"Most of the trouble in life comes from misunderstanding, I think," said Anne. "I must go now, Ruby. It's getting late—and you shouldn't be out in the damp."

"You'll come up soon again."

"Yes, very soon. And if there's anything I can do to help you I'll be so glad."

"I know. You HAVE helped me already. Nothing seems quite so dreadful now. Good night, Anne."

"Good night, dear."

Anne walked home very slowly in the moonlight. The evening had changed something for her. Life held a different meaning, a deeper purpose. On the surface it would go on just the same; but the deeps had been stirred. It must not be with her as with poor butterfly Ruby. When she came to the end of one life it must not be to face the next with the shrinking terror of something wholly different— something for which accustomed thought and ideal and aspiration had unfitted her. The little things of life, sweet and excellent in their place, must not be the things lived for; the highest must be sought and followed; the life of heaven must be begun here on earth.

That good night in the garden was for all time. Anne never saw Ruby in life again. The next night the A.V.I.S. gave a farewell party to Jane Andrews before her departure for the West. And, while light feet danced and bright eyes laughed and merry tongues chattered, there came a summons to a soul in Avonlea that might not be disregarded or evaded. The next morning the word went from house to house that Ruby Gillis was dead. She had died in her sleep, painlessly and calmly, and on her face was a smile—as if, after all, death had come as a kindly friend to lead her over the threshold, instead of the grisly phantom she had dreaded.

Mrs. Rachel Lynde said emphatically after the funeral that Ruby Gillis was the handsomest corpse she ever laid eyes on. Her loveliness, as she lay, white-clad, among the delicate flowers that Anne had placed about her, was remembered and talked of for years in Avonlea. Ruby had always been beautiful; but her beauty had been of the earth, earthy; it had had a certain insolent quality in it, as if it flaunted itself in the beholder's eye; spirit had never shone through it, intellect had never refined it. But death had touched it and consecrated it, bringing out delicate modelings and purity of outline never seen before—doing what life and love and great sorrow and deep womanhood joys might have done for Ruby. Anne, looking down through a mist of tears, at her old playfellow, thought she saw the face God had meant Ruby to have, and remembered it so always.

Mrs. Gillis called Anne aside into a vacant room before the funeral procession left the house, and gave her a small packet.

"I want you to have this," she sobbed. "Ruby would have liked you to have it. It's the embroidered centerpiece she was working at. It isn't quite finished—the needle is sticking in it just where her poor little fingers put it the last time she laid it down, the afternoon before she died."

"There's always a piece of unfinished work left," said Mrs. Lynde, with tears in her eyes. "But I suppose there's always some one to finish it."

"How difficult it is to realize that one we have always known can really be dead," said Anne, as she and Diana walked home. "Ruby is the first of our schoolmates to go. One by one, sooner or later, all the rest of us must follow."

"Yes, I suppose so," said Diana uncomfortably. She did not want to talk of that. She would have preferred to have discussed the details of the funeral—the splendid white velvet casket Mr. Gillis had insisted on having for Ruby—"the Gillises must always make a splurge, even at funerals," quoth Mrs. Rachel Lynde—Herb Spencer's sad face, the uncontrolled, hysteric grief of one of Ruby's sisters—but Anne would not talk of these things. She seemed wrapped in a reverie in which Diana felt lonesomely that she had neither lot nor part.

"Ruby Gillis was a great girl to laugh," said Davy suddenly. "Will she laugh as much in heaven as she did in Avonlea, Anne? I want to know."

"Yes, I think she will," said Anne.

"Oh, Anne," protested Diana, with a rather shocked smile.

"Well, why not, Diana?" asked Anne seriously. "Do you think we'll never laugh in heaven?"

"Oh—I—I don't know" floundered Diana. "It doesn't seem just right, somehow. You know it's rather dreadful to laugh in church."

"But heaven won't be like church—all the time," said Anne.

"I hope it ain't," said Davy emphatically. "If it is I don't want to go. Church is awful dull. Anyway, I don't mean to go for ever so long. I mean to live to be a hundred years old, like Mr. Thomas Blewett of White Sands. He says he's lived so long 'cause he always smoked tobacco and it killed all the germs. Can I smoke tobacco pretty soon, Anne?"

"No, Davy, I hope you'll never use tobacco," said Anne absently.

"What'll you feel like if the germs kill me then?" demanded Davy.

Chapter XV - A Dream Turned Upside Down

"Just one more week and we go back to Redmond," said Anne. She was happy at the thought of returning to work, classes and Redmond friends. Pleasing visions were also being woven around Patty's Place. There was a warm pleasant sense of home in the thought of it, even though she had never lived there.

But the summer had been a very happy one, too—a time of glad living with summer suns and skies, a time of keen delight in wholesome things; a time of re-newing and deepening of old friendships; a time in which she had learned to live more nobly, to work more patiently, to play more heartily.

"All life lessons are not learned at college," she thought. "Life teaches them everywhere."

But alas, the final week of that pleasant vacation was spoiled for Anne, by one of those impish happenings which are like a dream turned upside down.

"Been writing any more stories lately?" inquired Mr. Harrison genially one evening when Anne was taking tea with him and Mrs. Harrison.

"No," answered Anne, rather crisply.

"Well, no offense meant. Mrs. Hiram Sloane told me the other day that a big envelope addressed to the Rollings Reliable Baking Powder Company of Montre-al had been dropped into the post office box a month ago, and she suspicioned that somebody was trying for the prize they'd offered for the best story that intro-duced the name of their baking powder. She said it wasn't addressed in your writing, but I thought maybe it was you."

"Indeed, no! I saw the prize offer, but I'd never dream of competing for it. I think it would be perfectly disgraceful to write a story to advertise a baking pow-der. It would be almost as bad as Judson Parker's patent medicine fence."

So spake Anne loftily, little dreaming of the valley of humiliation awaiting her. That very evening Diana popped into the porch gable, bright-eyed and rosy cheeked, carrying a letter.

"Oh, Anne, here's a letter for you. I was at the office, so I thought I'd bring it along. Do open it quick. If it is what I believe it is I shall just be wild with de-light." Anne, puzzled, opened the letter and glanced over the typewritten contents.

Miss Anne Shirley,
Green Gables,
Avonlea, P.E. Island.

"DEAR MADAM: We have much pleasure in informing you that your charming story 'Averil's Atonement' has won the prize of twenty-five dollars offered in our recent competition. We enclose the check herewith. We are arranging for the publication of the story in several prominent Canadian newspapers, and we also intend to have it printed in pamphlet form for distribution among our patrons. Thanking you for the interest you have shown in our enterprise, we remain,

"Yours very truly,

"THE ROLLINGS RELIABLE

"BAKING POWDER Co."

"I don't understand," said Anne, blankly.

Diana clapped her hands.

"Oh, I KNEW it would win the prize—I was sure of it. *I* sent your story into the competition, Anne."

"Diana—Barry!"

"Yes, I did," said Diana gleefully, perching herself on the bed. "When I saw the offer I thought of your story in a minute, and at first I thought I'd ask you to send it in. But then I was afraid you wouldn't—you had so little faith left in it. So I just decided I'd send the copy you gave me, and say nothing about it. Then, if it didn't win the prize, you'd never know and you wouldn't feel badly over it, because the stories that failed were not to be returned, and if it did you'd have such a delightful surprise."

Diana was not the most discerning of mortals, but just at this moment it struck her that Anne was not looking exactly overjoyed. The surprise was there, beyond doubt—but where was the delight?

"Why, Anne, you don't seem a bit pleased!" she exclaimed.

Anne instantly manufactured a smile and put it on.

"Of course I couldn't be anything but pleased over your unselfish wish to give me pleasure," she said slowly. "But you know—I'm so amazed—I can't realize it—and I don't understand. There wasn't a word in my story about—about—" Anne choked a little over the word—"baking powder."

"Oh, *I* put that in," said Diana, reassured. "It was as easy as wink—and of course my experience in our old Story Club helped me. You know the scene where Averil makes the cake? Well, I just stated that she used the Rollings Reliable in it, and that was why it turned out so well; and then, in the last paragraph, where PERCEVAL clasps AVERIL in his arms and says, 'Sweetheart, the beautiful coming years will bring us the fulfilment of our home of dreams,' I added, 'in which we will never use any baking powder except Rollings Reliable.'"

"Oh," gasped poor Anne, as if some one had dashed cold water on her.

"And you've won the twenty-five dollars," continued Diana jubilantly. "Why, I heard Priscilla say once that the Canadian Woman only pays five dollars for a story!"

Anne held out the hateful pink slip in shaking fingers.

"I can't take it—it's yours by right, Diana. You sent the story in and made the alterations. I—I would certainly never have sent it. So you must take the check."

"I'd like to see myself," said Diana scornfully. "Why, what I did wasn't any trouble. The honor of being a friend of the prizewinner is enough for me. Well, I must go. I should have gone straight home from the post office for we have company. But I simply had to come and hear the news. I'm so glad for your sake, Anne."

Anne suddenly bent forward, put her arms about Diana, and kissed her cheek.

"I think you are the sweetest and truest friend in the world, Diana," she said, with a little tremble in her voice, "and I assure you I appreciate the motive of what you've done."

Diana, pleased and embarrassed, got herself away, and poor Anne, after flinging the innocent check into her bureau drawer as if it were blood-money, cast herself on her bed and wept tears of shame and outraged sensibility. Oh, she could never live this down—never!

Gilbert arrived at dusk, brimming over with congratulations, for he had called at Orchard Slope and heard the news. But his congratulations died on his lips at sight of Anne's face.

"Why, Anne, what is the matter? I expected to find you radiant over winning Rollings Reliable prize. Good for you!"

"Oh, Gilbert, not you," implored Anne, in an ET-TU BRUTE tone. "I thought YOU would understand. Can't you see how awful it is?"

"I must confess I can't. WHAT is wrong?"

"Everything," moaned Anne. "I feel as if I were disgraced forever. What do you think a mother would feel like if she found her child tattooed over with a baking powder advertisement? I feel just the same. I loved my poor little story, and I wrote it out of the best that was in me. And it is SACRILEGE to have it degraded to the level of a baking powder advertisement. Don't you remember what Professor Hamilton used to tell us in the literature class at Queen's? He said we were never to write a word for a low or unworthy motive, but always to cling to the very highest ideals. What will he think when he hears I've written a story to advertise Rollings Reliable? And, oh, when it gets out at Redmond! Think how I'll be teased and laughed at!"

"That you won't," said Gilbert, wondering uneasily if it were that confounded Junior's opinion in particular over which Anne was worried. "The Reds will think just as I thought—that you, being like nine out of ten of us, not overburdened with worldly wealth, had taken this way of earning an honest penny to help yourself through the year. I don't see that there's anything low or unworthy about that, or anything ridiculous either. One would rather write masterpieces of literature no doubt—but meanwhile board and tuition fees have to be paid."

This commonsense, matter-of-fact view of the case cheered Anne a little. At least it removed her dread of being laughed at, though the deeper hurt of an outraged ideal remained.

Chapter XVI - Adjusted Relationships

"It's the homiest spot I ever saw—it's homier than home," avowed Philippa Gordon, looking about her with delighted eyes. They were all assembled at twilight in the big living-room at Patty's Place—Anne and Priscilla, Phil and Stella, Aunt Jamesina, Rusty, Joseph, the Sarah-Cat, and Gog and Magog. The firelight shadows were dancing over the walls; the cats were purring; and a huge bowl of hothouse chrysanthemums, sent to Phil by one of the victims, shone through the golden gloom like creamy moons.

It was three weeks since they had considered themselves settled, and already all believed the experiment would be a success. The first fortnight after their return had been a pleasantly exciting one; they had been busy setting up their household goods, organizing their little establishment, and adjusting different opinions.

Anne was not over-sorry to leave Avonlea when the time came to return to college. The last few days of her vacation had not been pleasant. Her prize story had been published in the Island papers; and Mr. William Blair had, upon the counter of his store, a huge pile of pink, green and yellow pamphlets, containing it, one of which he gave to every customer. He sent a complimentary bundle to Anne, who promptly dropped them all in the kitchen stove. Her humiliation was the consequence of her own ideals only, for Avonlea folks thought it quite splendid that she should have won the prize. Her many friends regarded her with honest admiration; her few foes with scornful envy. Josie Pye said she believed Anne Shirley had just copied the story; she was sure she remembered reading it in a paper years before. The Sloanes, who had found out or guessed that Charlie had been "turned down," said they didn't think it was much to be proud of; almost any one could have done it, if she tried. Aunt Atossa told Anne she was very sorry to hear she had taken to writing novels; nobody born and bred in Avonlea would do it; that was what came of adopting orphans from goodness knew where, with goodness knew what kind of parents. Even Mrs. Rachel Lynde was darkly dubious about the propriety of writing fiction, though she was almost reconciled to it by that twenty-five dollar check.

"It is perfectly amazing, the price they pay for such lies, that's what," she said, half-proudly, half-severely.

All things considered, it was a relief when going-away time came. And it was very jolly to be back at Redmond, a wise, experienced Soph with hosts of friends to greet on the merry opening day. Pris and Stella and Gilbert were there, Charlie Sloane, looking more important than ever a Sophomore looked before, Phil, with the Alec-and-Alonzo question still unsettled, and Moody Spurgeon MacPherson. Moody Spurgeon had been teaching school ever since leaving Queen's, but his mother had concluded it was high time he gave it up and turned his attention to learning how to be a minister. Poor Moody Spurgeon fell on hard luck at the very beginning of his college career. Half a dozen ruthless Sophs, who were among his fellow-boarders, swooped down upon him one night and shaved half of his head. In this guise the luckless Moody Spurgeon had to go about until his hair grew again. He told Anne bitterly that there were times when he had his doubts as to whether he was really called to be a minister.

Aunt Jamesina did not come until the girls had Patty's Place ready for her. Miss Patty had sent the key to Anne, with a letter in which she said Gog and Magog were packed in a box under the spare-room bed, but might be taken out when wanted; in a postscript she added that she hoped the girls would be careful about putting up pictures. The living room had been newly papered five years before and she and Miss Maria did not want any more holes made in that new paper than was absolutely necessary. For the rest she trusted everything to Anne.

How those girls enjoyed putting their nest in order! As Phil said, it was almost as good as getting married. You had the fun of homemaking without the bother of a husband. All brought something with them to adorn or make comfortable the little house. Pris and Phil and Stella had knick-knacks and pictures galore, which latter they proceeded to hang according to taste, in reckless disregard of Miss Patty's new paper.

"We'll putty the holes up when we leave, dear—she'll never know," they said to protesting Anne.

Diana had given Anne a pine needle cushion and Miss Ada had given both her and Priscilla a fearfully and wonderfully embroidered one. Marilla had sent a big box of preserves, and darkly hinted at a hamper for Thanksgiving, and Mrs. Lynde gave Anne a patchwork quilt and loaned her five more.

"You take them," she said authoritatively. "They might as well be in use as packed away in that trunk in the garret for moths to gnaw."

No moths would ever have ventured near those quilts, for they reeked of mothballs to such an extent that they had to be hung in the orchard of Patty's Place a full fortnight before they could be endured indoors. Verily, aristocratic Spofford Avenue had rarely beheld such a display. The gruff old millionaire who lived "next door" came over and wanted to buy the gorgeous red and yellow "tulip-pattern" one which Mrs. Rachel had given Anne. He said his mother used to make quilts like that, and by Jove, he wanted one to remind him of her. Anne would not sell it, much to his disappointment, but she wrote all about it to Mrs. Lynde. That highly-gratified lady sent word back that she had one just like it to spare, so the tobacco king got his quilt after all, and insisted on having it spread on his bed, to the disgust of his fashionable wife.

Mrs. Lynde's quilts served a very useful purpose that winter. Patty's Place for all its many virtues, had its faults also. It was really a rather cold house; and when the frosty nights came the girls were very glad to snuggle down under Mrs. Lynde's quilts, and hoped that the loan of them might be accounted unto her for righteousness. Anne had the blue room she had coveted at sight. Priscilla and Stella had the large one. Phil was blissfully content with the little one over the kitchen; and Aunt Jamesina was to have the downstairs one off the living-room. Rusty at first slept on the doorstep.

Anne, walking home from Redmond a few days after her return, became aware that the people that she met surveyed her with a covert, indulgent smile. Anne wondered uneasily what was the matter with her. Was her hat crooked? Was her belt loose? Craning her head to investigate, Anne, for the first time, saw Rusty.

Trotting along behind her, close to her heels, was quite the most forlorn specimen of the cat tribe she had ever beheld. The animal was well past kitten-hood, lank, thin, disreputable looking. Pieces of both ears were lacking, one eye was temporarily out of repair, and one jowl ludicrously swollen. As for color, if a once black cat had been well and thoroughly singed the result would have resembled the hue of this waif's thin, draggled, unsightly fur.

Anne "shooed," but the cat would not "shoo." As long as she stood he sat back on his haunches and gazed at her reproachfully out of his one good eye; when she resumed her walk he followed. Anne resigned herself to his company until she reached the gate of Patty's Place, which she coldly shut in his face, fondly supposing she had seen the last of him. But when, fifteen minutes later, Phil opened the door, there sat the rusty-brown cat on the step. More, he promptly darted in and sprang upon Anne's lap with a half-pleading, half-triumphant "miaow."

"Anne," said Stella severely, "do you own that animal?"

"No, I do NOT," protested disgusted Anne. "The creature followed me home from somewhere. I couldn't get rid of him. Ugh, get down. I like decent cats reasonably well; but I don't like beasties of your complexion."

Pussy, however, refused to get down. He coolly curled up in Anne's lap and began to purr.

"He has evidently adopted you," laughed Priscilla.

"I won't BE adopted," said Anne stubbornly.

"The poor creature is starving," said Phil pityingly. "Why, his bones are almost coming through his skin."

"Well, I'll give him a square meal and then he must return to whence he came," said Anne resolutely.

The cat was fed and put out. In the morning he was still on the doorstep. On the doorstep he continued to sit, bolting in whenever the door was opened. No coolness of welcome had the least effect on him; of nobody save Anne did he take the least notice. Out of compassion the girls fed him; but when a week had passed they decided that something must be done. The cat's appearance had improved.

His eye and cheek had resumed their normal appearance; he was not quite so thin; and he had been seen washing his face.

"But for all that we can't keep him," said Stella. "Aunt Jimsie is coming next week and she will bring the Sarah-cat with her. We can't keep two cats; and if we did this Rusty Coat would fight all the time with the Sarah-cat. He's a fighter by nature. He had a pitched battle last evening with the tobacco-king's cat and routed him, horse, foot and artillery."

"We must get rid of him," agreed Anne, looking darkly at the subject of their discussion, who was purring on the hearth rug with an air of lamb-like meekness. "But the question is—how? How can four unprotected females get rid of a cat who won't be got rid of?"

"We must chloroform him," said Phil briskly. "That is the most humane way."

"Who of us knows anything about chloroforming a cat?" demanded Anne gloomily.

"I do, honey. It's one of my few—sadly few—useful accomplishments. I've disposed of several at home. You take the cat in the morning and give him a good breakfast. Then you take an old burlap bag—there's one in the back porch—put the cat on it and turn over him a wooden box. Then take a two-ounce bottle of chloroform, uncork it, and slip it under the edge of the box. Put a heavy weight on top of the box and leave it till evening. The cat will be dead, curled up peacefully as if he were asleep. No pain—no struggle."

"It sounds easy," said Anne dubiously.

"It IS easy. Just leave it to me. I'll see to it," said Phil reassuringly.

Accordingly the chloroform was procured, and the next morning Rusty was lured to his doom. He ate his breakfast, licked his chops, and climbed into Anne's lap. Anne's heart misgave her. This poor creature loved her—trusted her. How could she be a party to this destruction?

"Here, take him," she said hastily to Phil. "I feel like a murderess."

"He won't suffer, you know," comforted Phil, but Anne had fled.

The fatal deed was done in the back porch. Nobody went near it that day. But at dusk Phil declared that Rusty must be buried.

"Pris and Stella must dig his grave in the orchard," declared Phil, "and Anne must come with me to lift the box off. That's the part I always hate."

The two conspirators tip-toed reluctantly to the back porch. Phil gingerly lifted the stone she had put on the box. Suddenly, faint but distinct, sounded an unmistakable mew under the box.

"He—he isn't dead," gasped Anne, sitting blankly down on the kitchen door-step.

"He must be," said Phil incredulously.

Another tiny mew proved that he wasn't. The two girls stared at each other.

"What will we do?" questioned Anne.

"Why in the world don't you come?" demanded Stella, appearing in the doorway. "We've got the grave ready. 'What silent still and silent all?'" she quoted teasingly.

"'Oh, no, the voices of the dead Sound like the distant torrent's fall,'" promptly counter-quoted Anne, pointing solemnly to the box.

A burst of laughter broke the tension.

"We must leave him here till morning," said Phil, replacing the stone. "He hasn't mewed for five minutes. Perhaps the mews we heard were his dying groan. Or perhaps we merely imagined them, under the strain of our guilty consciences."

But, when the box was lifted in the morning, Rusty bounded at one gay leap to Anne's shoulder where he began to lick her face affectionately. Never was there a cat more decidedly alive.

"Here's a knot hole in the box," groaned Phil. "I never saw it. That's why he didn't die. Now, we've got to do it all over again."

"No, we haven't," declared Anne suddenly. "Rusty isn't going to be killed again. He's my cat—and you've just got to make the best of it."

"Oh, well, if you'll settle with Aunt Jimsie and the Sarah-cat," said Stella, with the air of one washing her hands of the whole affair.

From that time Rusty was one of the family. He slept o'nights on the scrubbing cushion in the back porch and lived on the fat of the land. By the time Aunt Jamesina came he was plump and glossy and tolerably respectable. But, like Kipling's cat, he "walked by himself." His paw was against every cat, and every cat's paw against him. One by one he vanquished the aristocratic felines of Spofford Avenue. As for human beings, he loved Anne and Anne alone. Nobody else even dared stroke him. An angry spit and something that sounded much like very improper language greeted any one who did.

"The airs that cat puts on are perfectly intolerable," declared Stella.

"Him was a nice old pussens, him was," vowed Anne, cuddling her pet defiantly.

"Well, I don't know how he and the Sarah-cat will ever make out to live together," said Stella pessimistically. "Cat-fights in the orchard o'nights are bad enough. But cat-fights here in the livingroom are unthinkable." In due time Aunt Jamesina arrived. Anne and Priscilla and Phil had awaited her advent rather dubiously; but when Aunt Jamesina was enthroned in the rocking chair before the open fire they figuratively bowed down and worshipped her.

Aunt Jamesina was a tiny old woman with a little, softly-triangular face, and large, soft blue eyes that were alight with unquenchable youth, and as full of hopes as a girl's. She had pink cheeks and snow-white hair which she wore in quaint little puffs over her ears.

"It's a very old-fashioned way," she said, knitting industriously at something as dainty and pink as a sunset cloud. "But *I* am old-fashioned. My clothes are, and it stands to reason my opinions are, too. I don't say they're any the better of that, mind you. In fact, I daresay they're a good deal the worse. But they've worn nice and easy. New shoes are smarter than old ones, but the old ones are more comfortable. I'm old enough to indulge myself in the matter of shoes and opinions. I mean to take it real easy here. I know you expect me to look after you and keep you proper, but I'm not going to do it. You're old enough to know how to behave if you're ever going to be. So, as far as I am concerned," concluded Aunt Jamesina, with a twinkle in her young eyes, "you can all go to destruction in your own way."

"Oh, will somebody separate those cats?" pleaded Stella, shudderingly.

Aunt Jamesina had brought with her not only the Sarah-cat but Joseph. Joseph, she explained, had belonged to a dear friend of hers who had gone to live in Vancouver.

"She couldn't take Joseph with her so she begged me to take him. I really couldn't refuse. He's a beautiful cat—that is, his disposition is beautiful. She called him Joseph because his coat is of many colors."

It certainly was. Joseph, as the disgusted Stella said, looked like a walking rag-bag. It was impossible to say what his ground color was. His legs were white with black spots on them. His back was gray with a huge patch of yellow on one side and a black patch on the other. His tail was yellow with a gray tip. One ear was black and one yellow. A black patch over one eye gave him a fearfully rakish look. In reality he was meek and inoffensive, of a sociable disposition. In one respect, if in no other, Joseph was like a lily of the field. He toiled not neither did he spin or catch mice. Yet Solomon in all his glory slept not on softer cushions, or feasted more fully on fat things.

Joseph and the Sarah-cat arrived by express in separate boxes. After they had been released and fed, Joseph selected the cushion and corner which appealed to him, and the Sarah-cat gravely sat herself down before the fire and proceeded to wash her face. She was a large, sleek, gray-and-white cat, with an enormous dignity which was not at all impaired by any consciousness of her plebian origin. She had been given to Aunt Jamesina by her washerwoman.

"Her name was Sarah, so my husband always called puss the Sarah-cat," explained Aunt Jamesina. "She is eight years old, and a remarkable mouser. Don't worry, Stella. The Sarah-cat NEVER fights and Joseph rarely."

"They'll have to fight here in self-defense," said Stella.

At this juncture Rusty arrived on the scene. He bounded joyously half way across the room before he saw the intruders. Then he stopped short; his tail expanded until it was as big as three tails. The fur on his back rose up in a defiant arch; Rusty lowered his head, uttered a fearful shriek of hatred and defiance, and launched himself at the Sarah-cat.

The stately animal had stopped washing her face and was looking at him curiously. She met his onslaught with one contemptuous sweep of her capable paw. Rusty went rolling helplessly over on the rug; he picked himself up dazedly. What sort of a cat was this who had boxed his ears? He looked dubiously at the Sarah-cat. Would he or would he not? The Sarah-cat deliberately turned her back on him and resumed her toilet operations. Rusty decided that he would not. He never did. From that time on the Sarah-cat ruled the roost. Rusty never again interfered with her.

But Joseph rashly sat up and yawned. Rusty, burning to avenge his disgrace, swooped down upon him. Joseph, pacific by nature, could fight upon occasion and fight well. The result was a series of drawn battles. Every day Rusty and Joseph fought at sight. Anne took Rusty's part and detested Joseph. Stella was in despair. But Aunt Jamesina only laughed.

"Let them fight it out," she said tolerantly. "They'll make friends after a bit. Joseph needs some exercise—he was getting too fat. And Rusty has to learn he isn't the only cat in the world."

Eventually Joseph and Rusty accepted the situation and from sworn enemies became sworn friends. They slept on the same cushion with their paws about each other, and gravely washed each other's faces.

"We've all got used to each other," said Phil. "And I've learned how to wash dishes and sweep a floor."

"But you needn't try to make us believe you can chloroform a cat," laughed Anne.

"It was all the fault of the knothole," protested Phil.

"It was a good thing the knothole was there," said Aunt Jamesina rather severely. "Kittens HAVE to be drowned, I admit, or the world would be overrun. But no decent, grown-up cat should be done to death—unless he sucks eggs."

"You wouldn't have thought Rusty very decent if you'd seen him when he came here," said Stella. "He positively looked like the Old Nick."

"I don't believe Old Nick can be so very, ugly" said Aunt Jamesina reflectively. "He wouldn't do so much harm if he was. *I* always think of him as a rather handsome gentleman."

Chapter XVII - A Letter from Davy

"It's beginning to snow, girls," said Phil, coming in one November evening, "and there are the loveliest little stars and crosses all over the garden walk. I never noticed before what exquisite things snowflakes really are. One has time to notice things like that in the simple life. Bless you all for permitting me to live it. It's really delightful to feel worried because butter has gone up five cents a pound."

"Has it?" demanded Stella, who kept the household accounts.

"It has—and here's your butter. I'm getting quite expert at marketing. It's better fun than flirting," concluded Phil gravely.

"Everything is going up scandalously," sighed Stella.

"Never mind. Thank goodness air and salvation are still free," said Aunt Jamesina.

"And so is laughter," added Anne. "There's no tax on it yet and that is well, because you're all going to laugh presently. I'm going to read you Davy's letter. His spelling has improved immensely this past year, though he is not strong on apostrophes, and he certainly possesses the gift of writing an interesting letter. Listen and laugh, before we settle down to the evening's study-grind."

"Dear Anne," ran Davy's letter, "I take my pen to tell you that we are all pretty well and hope this will find you the same. It's snowing some today and Marilla says the old woman in the sky is shaking her feather beds. Is the old woman in the sky God's wife, Anne? I want to know.

"Mrs. Lynde has been real sick but she is better now. She fell down the cellar stairs last week. When she fell she grabbed hold of the shelf with all the milk pails and stewpans on it, and it gave way and went down with her and made a splendid crash. Marilla thought it was an earthquake at first.

"One of the stewpans was all dinged up and Mrs. Lynde straned her ribs. The doctor came and gave her medicine to rub on her ribs but she didn't under stand him and took it all inside instead. The doctor said it was a wonder it dident kill her but it dident and it cured her ribs and Mrs. Lynde says doctors dont know much anyhow. But we couldent fix up the stewpan. Marilla had to throw it out. Thanksgiving was last week. There was no school and we had a great dinner. I et mince pie and rost turkey and frut cake and donuts and cheese and jam and choklut cake. Marilla said I'd die but I dident. Dora had earake after it, only it wasent in her ears it was in her stummick. I dident have earake anywhere.

"Our new teacher is a man. He does things for jokes. Last week he made all us third-class boys write a composis] [shun on what kind of a wife we'd like to have and the girls on what kind of a husband. He laughed fit to kill when he read them. This was mine. I thought youd like to see it.

"'The kind of a wife I'd like to Have.

"'She must have good manners and get my meals on time and do what I tell her and always be very polite to me. She must be fifteen yers old. She must be good to the poor and keep her house tidy and be good tempered and go to church regularly. She must be very handsome and have curly hair. If I get a wife that is just what I like Ill be an awful good husband to her. I think a woman ought to be awful good to her husband. Some poor women haven't any husbands.

"'THE END.'"

"I was at Mrs. Isaac Wrights funeral at White Sands last week. The husband of the corpse felt real sorry. Mrs. Lynde says Mrs. Wrights grandfather stole a sheep but Marilla says we mustent speak ill of the dead. Why mustent we, Anne? I want to know. It's pretty safe, ain't it?

"Mrs. Lynde was awful mad the other day because I asked her if she was alive in Noah's time. I dident mean to hurt her feelings. I just wanted to know. Was she, Anne?

"Mr. Harrison wanted to get rid of his dog. So he hunged him once but he come to life and scooted for the barn while Mr. Harrison was digging the grave, so he hunged him again and he stayed dead that time. Mr. Harrison has a new man working for him. He's awful okward. Mr. Harrison says he is left handed in both his feet. Mr. Barry's hired man is lazy. Mrs. Barry says that but Mr. Barry says he aint lazy exactly only he thinks it easier to pray for things than to work for them.

"Mrs. Harmon Andrews prize pig that she talked so much of died in a fit. Mrs. Lynde says it was a judgment on her for pride. But I think it was hard on the pig. Milty Boulter has been sick. The doctor gave him medicine and it tasted horrid. I offered to take it for him for a quarter but the Boulters are so mean. Milty says he'd rather take it himself and save his money. I asked Mrs. Boulter how a person would go about catching a man and she got awful mad and said she dident know, shed never chased men.

"The A.V.I.S. is going to paint the hall again. They're tired of having it blue.

"The new minister was here to tea last night. He took three pieces of pie. If I did that Mrs. Lynde would call me piggy. And he et fast and took big bites and Marilla is always telling me not to do that. Why can ministers do what boys can't? I want to know.

"I haven't any more news. Here are six kisses. xxxxxx. Dora sends one. Heres hers. x.

"Your loving friend DAVID KEITH"

"P.S. Anne, who was the devils father? I want to know."

Chapter XVIII - Miss Josephine Remembers the Anne-girl

When Christmas holidays came the girls of Patty's Place scattered to their respective homes, but Aunt Jamesina elected to stay where she was.

"I couldn't go to any of the places I've been invited and take those three cats," she said. "And I'm not going to leave the poor creatures here alone for nearly three weeks. If we had any decent neighbors who would feed them I might, but there's nothing except millionaires on this street. So I'll stay here and keep Patty's Place warm for you."

Anne went home with the usual joyous anticipations—which were not wholly fulfilled. She found Avonlea in the grip of such an early, cold, and stormy winter as even the "oldest inhabitant" could not recall. Green Gables was literally hemmed in by huge drifts. Almost every day of that ill-starred vacation it stormed fiercely; and even on fine days it drifted unceasingly. No sooner were the roads broken than they filled in again. It was almost impossible to stir out. The A.V.I.S. tried, on three evenings, to have a party in honor of the college students, and on each evening the storm was so wild that nobody could go, so they gave up the attempt in despair. Anne, despite her love of and loyalty to Green Gables, could not help thinking longingly of Patty's Place, its cosy open fire, Aunt Jamesina's mirthful eyes, the three cats, the merry chatter of the girls, the pleasantness of Friday evenings when college friends dropped in to talk of grave and gay.

Anne was lonely; Diana, during the whole of the holidays, was imprisoned at home with a bad attack of bronchitis. She could not come to Green Gables and it was rarely Anne could get to Orchard Slope, for the old way through the Haunted Wood was impassable with drifts, and the long way over the frozen Lake of Shining Waters was almost as bad. Ruby Gillis was sleeping in the white-heaped graveyard; Jane Andrews was teaching a school on western prairies. Gilbert, to be sure, was still faithful, and waded up to Green Gables every possible evening. But Gilbert's visits were not what they once were. Anne almost dreaded them. It was very disconcerting to look up in the midst of a sudden silence and find Gilbert's hazel eyes fixed upon her with a quite unmistakable expression in their grave depths; and it was still more disconcerting to find herself blushing hotly and uncomfortably under his gaze, just as if—just as if—well, it was very embarrassing.

Anne wished herself back at Patty's Place, where there was always somebody else about to take the edge off a delicate situation. At Green Gables Marilla went promptly to Mrs. Lynde's domain when Gilbert came and insisted on taking the twins with her. The significance of this was unmistakable and Anne was in a helpless fury over it.

Davy, however, was perfectly happy. He reveled in getting out in the morning and shoveling out the paths to the well and henhouse. He gloried in the Christmas-tide delicacies which Marilla and Mrs. Lynde vied with each other in preparing for Anne, and he was reading an enthralling tale, in a school library book, of a wonderful hero who seemed blessed with a miraculous faculty for getting into scrapes from which he was usually delivered by an earthquake or a volcanic explosion, which blew him high and dry out of his troubles, landed him in a fortune, and closed the story with proper ECLAT.

"I tell you it's a bully story, Anne," he said ecstatically. "I'd ever so much rather read it than the Bible."

"Would you?" smiled Anne.

Davy peered curiously at her.

"You don't seem a bit shocked, Anne. Mrs. Lynde was awful shocked when I said it to her."

"No, I'm not shocked, Davy. I think it's quite natural that a nine-year-old boy would sooner read an adventure story than the Bible. But when you are older I hope and think that you will realize what a wonderful book the Bible is."

"Oh, I think some parts of it are fine," conceded Davy. "That story about Joseph now—it's bully. But if I'd been Joseph *I* wouldn't have forgive the brothers. No, siree, Anne. I'd have cut all their heads off. Mrs. Lynde was awful mad when I said that and shut the Bible up and said she'd never read me any more of it if I talked like that. So I don't talk now when she reads it Sunday afternoons; I just think things and say them to Milty Boulter next day in school. I told Milty the story about Elisha and the bears and it scared him so he's never made fun of Mr. Harrison's bald head once. Are there any bears on P.E. Island, Anne? I want to know."

"Not nowadays," said Anne, absently, as the wind blew a scud of snow against the window. "Oh, dear, will it ever stop storming."

"God knows," said Davy airily, preparing to resume his reading.

Anne WAS shocked this time.

"Davy!" she exclaimed reproachfully.

"Mrs. Lynde says that," protested Davy. "One night last week Marilla said 'Will Ludovic Speed and Theodora Dix EVER get married?' and Mrs. Lynde said, '''God knows'—just like that."

"Well, it wasn't right for her to say it," said Anne, promptly deciding upon which horn of this dilemma to empale herself. "It isn't right for anybody to take that name in vain or speak it lightly, Davy. Don't ever do it again."

"Not if I say it slow and solemn, like the minister?" queried Davy gravely.

"No, not even then."

"Well, I won't. Ludovic Speed and Theodora Dix live in Middle Grafton and Mrs. Rachel says he has been courting her for a hundred years. Won't they soon be too old to get married, Anne? I hope Gilbert won't court YOU that long. When are you going to be married, Anne? Mrs. Lynde says it's a sure thing."

"Mrs. Lynde is a—" began Anne hotly; then stopped. "Awful old gossip," completed Davy calmly. "That's what every one calls her. But is it a sure thing, Anne? I want to know."

"You're a very silly little boy, Davy," said Anne, stalking haughtily out of the room. The kitchen was deserted and she sat down by the window in the fast falling wintry twilight. The sun had set and the wind had died down. A pale chilly moon looked out behind a bank of purple clouds in the west. The sky faded out, but the strip of yellow along the western horizon grew brighter and fiercer, as if all the stray gleams of light were concentrating in one spot; the distant hills, rimmed with priest-like firs, stood out in dark distinctness against it. Anne looked across the still, white fields, cold and lifeless in the harsh light of that grim sunset, and sighed. She was very lonely; and she was sad at heart; for she was wondering if she would be able to return to Redmond next year. It did not seem likely. The only scholarship possible in the Sophomore year was a very small affair. She would not take Marilla's money; and there seemed little prospect of being able to earn enough in the summer vacation.

"I suppose I'll just have to drop out next year," she thought drearily, "and teach a district school again until I earn enough to finish my course. And by that time all my old class will have graduated and Patty's Place will be out of the question. But there! I'm not going to be a coward. I'm thankful I can earn my way through if necessary."

"Here's Mr. Harrison wading up the lane," announced Davy, running out. "I hope he's brought the mail. It's three days since we got it. I want to see what them pesky Grits are doing. I'm a Conservative, Anne. And I tell you, you have to keep your eye on them Grits."

Mr. Harrison had brought the mail, and merry letters from Stella and Priscilla and Phil soon dissipated Anne's blues. Aunt Jamesina, too, had written, saying that she was keeping the hearth-fire alight, and that the cats were all well, and the house plants doing fine.

"The weather has been real cold," she wrote, "so I let the cats sleep in the house—Rusty and Joseph on the sofa in the living-room, and the Sarah-cat on the foot of my bed. It's real company to hear her purring when I wake up in the night and think of my poor daughter in the foreign field. If it was anywhere but in India I wouldn't worry, but they say the snakes out there are terrible. It takes all the Sarah-cats's purring to drive away the thought of those snakes. I have enough faith for everything but the snakes. I can't think why Providence ever made them. Sometimes I don't think He did. I'm inclined to believe the Old Harry had a hand in making THEM."

Anne had left a thin, typewritten communication till the last, thinking it unimportant. When she had read it she sat very still, with tears in her eyes.

"What is the matter, Anne?" asked Marilla.

"Miss Josephine Barry is dead," said Anne, in a low tone.

"So she has gone at last," said Marilla. "Well, she has been sick for over a year, and the Barrys have been expecting to hear of her death any time. It is well she is at rest for she has suffered dreadfully, Anne. She was always kind to you."

"She has been kind to the last, Marilla. This letter is from her lawyer. She has left me a thousand dollars in her will."

"Gracious, ain't that an awful lot of money," exclaimed Davy. "She's the woman you and Diana lit on when you jumped into the spare room bed, ain't she? Diana told me that story. Is that why she left you so much?"

"Hush, Davy," said Anne gently. She slipped away to the porch gable with a full heart, leaving Marilla and Mrs. Lynde to talk over the news to their hearts' content.

"Do you s'pose Anne will ever get married now?" speculated Davy anxiously. "When Dorcas Sloane got married last summer she said if she'd had enough money to live on she'd never have been bothered with a man, but even a widower with eight children was better'n living with a sister-in-law."

"Davy Keith, do hold your tongue," said Mrs. Rachel severely. "The way you talk is scandalous for a small boy, that's what."

Chapter XIX - An Interlude

"To think that this is my twentieth birthday, and that I've left my teens behind me forever," said Anne, who was curled up on the hearth-rug with Rusty in her lap, to Aunt Jamesina who was reading in her pet chair. They were alone in the living room. Stella and Priscilla had gone to a committee meeting and Phil was upstairs adorning herself for a party.

"I suppose you feel kind of, sorry" said Aunt Jamesina. "The teens are such a nice part of life. I'm glad I've never gone out of them myself."

Anne laughed.

"You never will, Aunty. You'll be eighteen when you should be a hundred. Yes, I'm sorry, and a little dissatisfied as well. Miss Stacy told me long ago that by the time I was twenty my character would be formed, for good or evil. I don't feel that it's what it should be. It's full of flaws."

"So's everybody's," said Aunt Jamesina cheerfully. "Mine's cracked in a hundred places. Your Miss Stacy likely meant that when you are twenty your character would have got its permanent bent in one direction or 'tother, and would go on developing in that line. Don't worry over it, Anne. Do your duty by God and your neighbor and yourself, and have a good time. That's my philosophy and it's always worked pretty well. Where's Phil off to tonight?"

"She's going to a dance, and she's got the sweetest dress for it—creamy yellow silk and cobwebby lace. It just suits those brown tints of hers."

"There's magic in the words 'silk' and 'lace,' isn't there?" said Aunt Jamesina. "The very sound of them makes me feel like skipping off to a dance. And YELLOW silk. It makes one think of a dress of sunshine. I always wanted a yellow silk dress, but first my mother and then my husband wouldn't hear of it. The very first thing I'm going to do when I get to heaven is to get a yellow silk dress."

Amid Anne's peal of laughter Phil came downstairs, trailing clouds of glory, and surveyed herself in the long oval mirror on the wall.

"A flattering looking glass is a promoter of amiability," she said. "The one in my room does certainly make me green. Do I look pretty nice, Anne?"

"Do you really know how pretty you are, Phil?" asked Anne, in honest admiration.

"Of course I do. What are looking glasses and men for? That wasn't what I meant. Are all my ends tucked in? Is my skirt straight? And would this rose look better lower down? I'm afraid it's too high—it will make me look lop-sided. But I hate things tickling my ears."

"Everything is just right, and that southwest dimple of yours is lovely."

"Anne, there's one thing in particular I like about you—you're so ungrudging. There isn't a particle of envy in you."

"Why should she be envious?" demanded Aunt Jamesina. "She's not quite as goodlooking as you, maybe, but she's got a far handsomer nose."

"I know it," conceded Phil.

"My nose always has been a great comfort to me," confessed Anne.

"And I love the way your hair grows on your forehead, Anne. And that one wee curl, always looking as if it were going to drop, but never dropping, is delicious. But as for noses, mine is a dreadful worry to me. I know by the time I'm forty it will be Byrney. What do you think I'll look like when I'm forty, Anne?"

"Like an old, matronly, married woman," teased Anne.

"I won't," said Phil, sitting down comfortably to wait for her escort. "Joseph, you calico beastie, don't you dare jump on my lap. I won't go to a dance all over cat hairs. No, Anne, I WON'T look matronly. But no doubt I'll be married."

"To Alec or Alonzo?" asked Anne.

"To one of them, I suppose," sighed Phil, "if I can ever decide which."

"It shouldn't be hard to decide," scolded Aunt Jamesina.

"I was born a see-saw Aunty, and nothing can ever prevent me from teetering."

"You ought to be more levelheaded, Philippa."

"It's best to be levelheaded, of course," agreed Philippa, "but you miss lots of fun. As for Alec and Alonzo, if you knew them you'd understand why it's difficult to choose between them. They're equally nice."

"Then take somebody who is nicer" suggested Aunt Jamesina. "There's that Senior who is so devoted to you—Will Leslie. He has such nice, large, mild eyes."

"They're a little bit too large and too mild—like a cow's," said Phil cruelly.

"What do you say about George Parker?"

"There's nothing to say about him except that he always looks as if he had just been starched and ironed."

"Marr Holworthy then. You can't find a fault with him."

"No, he would do if he wasn't poor. I must marry a rich man, Aunt Jamesina. That—and good looks—is an indispensable qualification. I'd marry Gilbert Blythe if he were rich."

"Oh, would you?" said Anne, rather viciously.

"We don't like that idea a little bit, although we don't want Gilbert ourselves, oh, no," mocked Phil. "But don't let's talk of disagreeable subjects. I'll have to marry sometime, I suppose, but I shall put off the evil day as long as I can."

"You mustn't marry anybody you don't love, Phil, when all's said and done," said Aunt Jamesina.

> "'Oh, hearts that loved in the good old way
> Have been out o' the fashion this many a day.'"

trilled Phil mockingly. "There's the carriage. I fly—Bi-bi, you two old-fashioned darlings."

When Phil had gone Aunt Jamesina looked solemnly at Anne.

"That girl is pretty and sweet and goodhearted, but do you think she is quite right in her mind, by spells, Anne?"

"Oh, I don't think there's anything the matter with Phil's mind," said Anne, hiding a smile. "It's just her way of talking."

Aunt Jamesina shook her head.

"Well, I hope so, Anne. I do hope so, because I love her. But *I* can't understand her—she beats me. She isn't like any of the girls I ever knew, or any of the girls I was myself."

"How many girls were you, Aunt Jimsie?"

"About half a dozen, my dear."

Chapter XX - Gilbert Speaks

"This has been a dull, prosy day," yawned Phil, stretching herself idly on the sofa, having previously dispossessed two exceedingly indignant cats.

Anne looked up from Pickwick Papers. Now that spring examinations were over she was treating herself to Dickens.

"It has been a prosy day for us," she said thoughtfully, "but to some people it has been a wonderful day. Some one has been rapturously happy in it. Perhaps a great deed has been done somewhere today—or a great poem written—or a great man born. And some heart has been broken, Phil."

"Why did you spoil your pretty thought by tagging that last sentence on, honey?" grumbled Phil. "I don't like to think of broken hearts—or anything unpleasant."

"Do you think you'll be able to shirk unpleasant things all your life, Phil?"

"Dear me, no. Am I not up against them now? You don't call Alec and Alonzo pleasant things, do you, when they simply plague my life out?"

"You never take anything seriously, Phil."

"Why should I? There are enough folks who do. The world needs people like me, Anne, just to amuse it. It would be a terrible place if EVERYBODY were intellectual and serious and in deep, deadly earnest. MY mission is, as Josiah Allen says, 'to charm and allure.' Confess now. Hasn't life at Patty's Place been really much brighter and pleasanter this past winter because I've been here to leaven you?"

"Yes, it has," owned Anne.

"And you all love me—even Aunt Jamesina, who thinks I'm stark mad. So why should I try to be different? Oh, dear, I'm so sleepy. I was awake until one last night, reading a harrowing ghost story. I read it in bed, and after I had finished it do you suppose I could get out of bed to put the light out? No! And if Stella had not fortunately come in late that lamp would have burned good and bright till morning. When I heard Stella I called her in, explained my predicament, and got her to put out the light. If I had got out myself to do it I knew something would grab me by the feet when I was getting in again. By the way, Anne, has Aunt Jamesina decided what to do this summer?"

"Yes, she's going to stay here. I know she's doing it for the sake of those blessed cats, although she says it's too much trouble to open her own house, and she hates visiting."

"What are you reading?"

"Pickwick."

"That's a book that always makes me hungry," said Phil. "There's so much good eating in it. The characters seem always to be reveling on ham and eggs and milk punch. I generally go on a cupboard rummage after reading Pickwick. The mere thought reminds me that I'm starving. Is there any tidbit in the pantry, Queen Anne?"

"I made a lemon pie this morning. You may have a piece of it."

Phil dashed out to the pantry and Anne betook herself to the orchard in company with Rusty. It was a moist, pleasantly-odorous night in early spring. The snow was not quite all gone from the park; a little dingy bank of it yet lay under the pines of the harbor road, screened from the influence of April suns. It kept the harbor road muddy, and chilled the evening air. But grass was growing green in sheltered spots and Gilbert had found some pale, sweet arbutus in a hidden corner. He came up from the park, his hands full of it.

Anne was sitting on the big gray boulder in the orchard looking at the poem of a bare, birchen bough hanging against the pale red sunset with the very perfection of grace. She was building a castle in air—a wondrous mansion whose sunlit courts and stately halls were steeped in Araby's perfume, and where she reigned queen and chatelaine. She frowned as she saw Gilbert coming through the orchard. Of late she had managed not to be left alone with Gilbert. But he had caught her fairly now; and even Rusty had deserted her.

Gilbert sat down beside her on the boulder and held out his Mayflowers.

"Don't these remind you of home and our old schoolday picnics, Anne?"

Anne took them and buried her face in them.

"I'm in Mr. Silas Sloane's barrens this very minute," she said rapturously.

"I suppose you will be there in reality in a few days?"

"No, not for a fortnight. I'm going to visit with Phil in Bolingbroke before I go home. You'll be in Avonlea before I will."

"No, I shall not be in Avonlea at all this summer, Anne. I've been offered a job in the Daily News office and I'm going to take it."

"Oh," said Anne vaguely. She wondered what a whole Avonlea summer would be like without Gilbert. Somehow she did not like the prospect. "Well," she concluded flatly, "it is a good thing for you, of course."

"Yes, I've been hoping I would get it. It will help me out next year."

"You mustn't work too HARD," said Anne, without any very clear idea of what she was saying. She wished desperately that Phil would come out. "You've studied very constantly this winter. Isn't this a delightful evening? Do you know, I found a cluster of white violets under that old twisted tree over there today? I felt as if I had discovered a gold mine."

"You are always discovering gold mines," said Gilbert—also absently.

"Let us go and see if we can find some more," suggested Anne eagerly. "I'll call Phil and—"

"Never mind Phil and the violets just now, Anne," said Gilbert quietly, taking her hand in a clasp from which she could not free it. "There is something I want to say to you."

"Oh, don't say it," cried Anne, pleadingly. "Don't—PLEASE, Gilbert."

"I must. Things can't go on like this any longer. Anne, I love you. You know I do. I—I can't tell you how much. Will you promise me that some day you'll be my wife?"

"I—I can't," said Anne miserably. "Oh, Gilbert—you—you've spoiled everything."

"Don't you care for me at all?" Gilbert asked after a very dreadful pause, during which Anne had not dared to look up.

"Not—not in that way. I do care a great deal for you as a friend. But I don't love you, Gilbert."

"But can't you give me some hope that you will—yet?"

"No, I can't," exclaimed Anne desperately. "I never, never can love you—in that way—Gilbert. You must never speak of this to me again."

There was another pause—so long and so dreadful that Anne was driven at last to look up. Gilbert's face was white to the lips. And his eyes—but Anne shuddered and looked away. There was nothing romantic about this. Must proposals be either grotesque or—horrible? Could she ever forget Gilbert's face?

"Is there anybody else?" he asked at last in a low voice.

"No—no," said Anne eagerly. "I don't care for any one like THAT—and I LIKE you better than anybody else in the world, Gilbert. And we must—we must go on being friends, Gilbert."

Gilbert gave a bitter little laugh.

"Friends! Your friendship can't satisfy me, Anne. I want your love—and you tell me I can never have that."

"I'm sorry. Forgive me, Gilbert," was all Anne could say. Where, oh, where were all the gracious and graceful speeches wherewith, in imagination, she had been wont to dismiss rejected suitors?

Gilbert released her hand gently.

"There isn't anything to forgive. There have been times when I thought you did care. I've deceived myself, that's all. Goodbye, Anne."

Anne got herself to her room, sat down on her window seat behind the pines, and cried bitterly. She felt as if something incalculably precious had gone out of her life. It was Gilbert's friendship, of course. Oh, why must she lose it after this fashion?

"What is the matter, honey?" asked Phil, coming in through the moonlit gloom.

Anne did not answer. At that moment she wished Phil were a thousand miles away.

"I suppose you've gone and refused Gilbert Blythe. You are an idiot, Anne Shirley!"

"Do you call it idiotic to refuse to marry a man I don't love?" said Anne coldly, goaded to reply.

"You don't know love when you see it. You've tricked something out with your imagination that you think love, and you expect the real thing to look like that. There, that's the first sensible thing I've ever said in my life. I wonder how I managed it?"

"Phil," pleaded Anne, "please go away and leave me alone for a little while. My world has tumbled into pieces. I want to reconstruct it."

"Without any Gilbert in it?" said Phil, going.

A world without any Gilbert in it! Anne repeated the words drearily. Would it not be a very lonely, forlorn place? Well, it was all Gilbert's fault. He had spoiled their beautiful comradeship. She must just learn to live without it.

Chapter XXI - Roses of Yesterday

The fortnight Anne spent in Bolingbroke was a very pleasant one, with a little under current of vague pain and dissatisfaction running through it whenever she thought about Gilbert. There was not, however, much time to think about him. "Mount Holly," the beautiful old Gordon homestead, was a very gay place, over-run by Phil's friends of both sexes. There was quite a bewildering succession of drives, dances, picnics and boating parties, all expressively lumped together by Phil under the head of "jamborees"; Alec and Alonzo were so constantly on hand that Anne wondered if they ever did anything but dance attendance on that will-o'-the-wisp of a Phil. They were both nice, manly fellows, but Anne would not be drawn into any opinion as to which was the nicer.

"And I depended so on you to help me make up my mind which of them I should promise to marry," mourned Phil.

"You must do that for yourself. You are quite expert at making up your mind as to whom other people should marry," retorted Anne, rather caustically.

"Oh, that's a very different thing," said Phil, truly.

But the sweetest incident of Anne's sojourn in Bolingbroke was the visit to her birthplace—the little shabby yellow house in an out-of-the-way street she had so often dreamed about. She looked at it with delighted eyes, as she and Phil turned in at the gate.

"It's almost exactly as I've pictured it," she said. "There is no honeysuckle over the windows, but there is a lilac tree by the gate, and—yes, there are the muslin curtains in the windows. How glad I am it is still painted yellow."

A very tall, very thin woman opened the door.

"Yes, the Shirleys lived here twenty years ago," she said, in answer to Anne's question. "They had it rented. I remember 'em. They both died of fever at onct. It was turrible sad. They left a baby. I guess it's dead long ago. It was a sickly thing. Old Thomas and his wife took it—as if they hadn't enough of their own."

"It didn't die," said Anne, smiling. "I was that baby."

"You don't say so! Why, you have grown," exclaimed the woman, as if she were much surprised that Anne was not still a baby. "Come to look at you, I see the resemblance. You're complected like your pa. He had red hair. But you favor your ma in your eyes and mouth. She was a nice little thing. My darter went to school to her and was nigh crazy about her. They was buried in the one grave and the School Board put up a tombstone to them as a reward for faithful service. Will you come in?"

"Will you let me go all over the house?" asked Anne eagerly.

"Laws, yes, you can if you like. 'Twon't take you long—there ain't much of it. I keep at my man to build a new kitchen, but he ain't one of your hustlers. The parlor's in there and there's two rooms upstairs. Just prowl about yourselves. I've got to see to the baby. The east room was the one you were born in. I remember your ma saying she loved to see the sunrise; and I mind hearing that you was born just as the sun was rising and its light on your face was the first thing your ma saw."

Anne went up the narrow stairs and into that little east room with a full heart. It was as a shrine to her. Here her mother had dreamed the exquisite, happy dreams of anticipated motherhood; here that red sunrise light had fallen over them both in the sacred hour of birth; here her mother had died. Anne looked about her reverently, her eyes with tears. It was for her one of the jeweled hours of life that gleam out radiantly forever in memory.

"Just to think of it—mother was younger than I am now when I was born," she whispered.

When Anne went downstairs the lady of the house met her in the hall. She held out a dusty little packet tied with faded blue ribbon.

"Here's a bundle of old letters I found in that closet upstairs when I came here," she said. "I dunno what they are—I never bothered to look in 'em, but the address on the top one is 'Miss Bertha Willis,' and that was your ma's maiden name. You can take 'em if you'd keer to have 'em."

"Oh, thank you—thank you," cried Anne, clasping the packet rapturously.

"That was all that was in the house," said her hostess. "The furniture was all sold to pay the doctor bills, and Mrs. Thomas got your ma's clothes and little things. I reckon they didn't last long among that drove of Thomas youngsters. They was destructive young animals, as I mind 'em."

"I haven't one thing that belonged to my mother," said Anne, chokily. "I—I can never thank you enough for these letters."

"You're quite welcome. Laws, but your eyes is like your ma's. She could just about talk with hers. Your father was sorter homely but awful nice. I mind hearing folks say when they was married that there never was two people more in love with each other—Pore creatures, they didn't live much longer; but they was awful happy while they was alive, and I s'pose that counts for a good deal."

Anne longed to get home to read her precious letters; but she made one little pilgrimage first. She went alone to the green corner of the "old" Bolingbroke cemetery where her father and mother were buried, and left on their grave the white flowers she carried. Then she hastened back to Mount Holly, shut herself up in her room, and read the letters. Some were written by her father, some by her mother. There were not many—only a dozen in all—for Walter and Bertha Shirley had not been often separated during their courtship. The letters were yellow and faded and dim, blurred with the touch of passing years. No profound words of wisdom were traced on the stained and wrinkled pages, but only lines of love and trust. The sweetness of forgotten things clung to them—the far-off, fond imaginings of those long-dead lovers. Bertha Shirley had possessed the gift of writing letters which embodied the charming personality of the writer in words and thoughts that retained their beauty and fragrance after the lapse of time. The letters were tender, intimate, sacred. To Anne, the sweetest of all was the one written after her birth to the father on a brief absence. It was full of a proud young mother's accounts of "baby"—her cleverness, her brightness, her thousand sweet-nesses.

"I love her best when she is asleep and better still when she is awake," Bertha Shirley had written in the postscript. Probably it was the last sentence she had ever penned. The end was very near for her.

"This has been the most beautiful day of my life," Anne said to Phil that night. "I've FOUND my father and mother. Those letters have made them REAL to me. I'm not an orphan any longer. I feel as if I had opened a book and found roses of yesterday, sweet and beloved, between its leaves."

Chapter XXII - Spring and Anne Return to Green Gables

The firelight shadows were dancing over the kitchen walls at Green Gables, for the spring evening was chilly; through the open east window drifted in the subtly sweet voices of the night. Marilla was sitting by the fire—at least, in body. In spirit she was roaming olden ways, with feet grown young. Of late Marilla had thus spent many an hour, when she thought she should have been knitting for the twins.

"I suppose I'm growing old," she said.

Yet Marilla had changed but little in the past nine years, save to grow something thinner, and even more angular; there was a little more gray in the hair that was still twisted up in the same hard knot, with two hairpins—WERE they the same hairpins?—still stuck through it. But her expression was very different; the something about the mouth which had hinted at a sense of humor had developed wonderfully; her eyes were gentler and milder, her smile more frequent and tender.

Marilla was thinking of her whole past life, her cramped but not unhappy childhood, the jealously hidden dreams and the blighted hopes of her girlhood, the long, gray, narrow, monotonous years of dull middle life that followed. And the coming of Anne—the vivid, imaginative, impetuous child with her heart of love, and her world of fancy, bringing with her color and warmth and radiance, until the wilderness of existence had blossomed like the rose. Marilla felt that out of her sixty years she had lived only the nine that had followed the advent of Anne. And Anne would be home tomorrow night.

The kitchen door opened. Marilla looked up expecting to see Mrs. Lynde. Anne stood before her, tall and starry-eyed, with her hands full of Mayflowers and violets.

"Anne Shirley!" exclaimed Marilla. For once in her life she was surprised out of her reserve; she caught her girl in her arms and crushed her and her flowers against her heart, kissing the bright hair and sweet face warmly. "I never looked for you till tomorrow night. How did you get from Carmody?"

"Walked, dearest of Marillas. Haven't I done it a score of times in the Queen's days? The mailman is to bring my trunk tomorrow; I just got homesick all at once, and came a day earlier. And oh! I've had such a lovely walk in the May twilight; I stopped by the barrens and picked these Mayflowers; I came through Violet-Vale; it's just a big bowlful of violets now—the dear, sky-tinted things. Smell them, Marilla—drink them in."

Marilla sniffed obligingly, but she was more interested in Anne than in drinking violets.

"Sit down, child. You must be real tired. I'm going to get you some supper."

"There's a darling moonrise behind the hills tonight, Marilla, and oh, how the frogs sang me home from Carmody! I do love the music of the frogs. It seems bound up with all my happiest recollections of old spring evenings. And it always reminds me of the night I came here first. Do you remember it, Marilla?"

"Well, yes," said Marilla with emphasis. "I'm not likely to forget it ever."

"They used to sing so madly in the marsh and brook that year. I would listen to them at my window in the dusk, and wonder how they could seem so glad and so sad at the same time. Oh, but it's good to be home again! Redmond was splendid and Bolingbroke delightful—but Green Gables is HOME."

"Gilbert isn't coming home this summer, I hear," said Marilla.

"No." Something in Anne's tone made Marilla glance at her sharply, but Anne was apparently absorbed in arranging her violets in a bowl. "See, aren't they sweet?" she went on hurriedly. "The year is a book, isn't it, Marilla? Spring's pages are written in Mayflowers and violets, summer's in roses, autumn's in red maple leaves, and winter in holly and evergreen."

"Did Gilbert do well in his examinations?" persisted Marilla.

"Excellently well. He led his class. But where are the twins and Mrs. Lynde?"

"Rachel and Dora are over at Mr. Harrison's. Davy is down at Boulters'. I think I hear him coming now."

Davy burst in, saw Anne, stopped, and then hurled himself upon her with a joyful yell.

"Oh, Anne, ain't I glad to see you! Say, Anne, I've grown two inches since last fall. Mrs. Lynde measured me with her tape today, and say, Anne, see my front tooth. It's gone. Mrs. Lynde tied one end of a string to it and the other end to the door, and then shut the door, and then shut the door. I sold it to Milty for two cents. Milty's collecting teeth."

"What in the world does he want teeth for?" asked Marilla.

"To make a necklace for playing Indian Chief," explained Davy, climbing upon Anne's lap. "He's got fifteen already, and everybody's else's promised, so there's no use in the rest of us starting to collect, too. I tell you the Boulters are great business people."

"Were you a good boy at Mrs. Boulter's?" asked Marilla severely.

"Yes; but say, Marilla, I'm tired of being good."

"You'd get tired of being bad much sooner, Davy-boy," said Anne.

"Well, it'd be fun while it lasted, wouldn't it?" persisted Davy. "I could be sorry for it afterwards, couldn't I?"

"Being sorry wouldn't do away with the consequences of being bad, Davy. Don't you remember the Sunday last summer when you ran away from Sunday School? You told me then that being bad wasn't worth while. What were you and Milty doing today?"

"Oh, we fished and chased the cat, and hunted for eggs, and yelled at the echo. There's a great echo in the bush behind the Boulter barn. Say, what is echo, Anne; I want to know."

"Echo is a beautiful nymph, Davy, living far away in the woods, and laughing at the world from among the hills."

"What does she look like?"

"Her hair and eyes are dark, but her neck and arms are white as snow. No mortal can ever see how fair she is. She is fleeter than a deer, and that mocking voice of hers is all we can know of her. You can hear her calling at night; you can hear her laughing under the stars. But you can never see her. She flies afar if you follow her, and laughs at you always just over the next hill."

"Is that true, Anne? Or is it a whopper?" demanded Davy staring.

"Davy," said Anne despairingly, "haven't you sense enough to distinguish between a fairytale and a falsehood?"

"Then what is it that sasses back from the Boulter bush? I want to know," insisted Davy.

"When you are a little older, Davy, I'll explain it all to you."

The mention of age evidently gave a new turn to Davy's thoughts for after a few moments of reflection, he whispered solemnly:

"Anne, I'm going to be married."

"When?" asked Anne with equal solemnity.

"Oh, not until I'm grown-up, of course."

"Well, that's a relief, Davy. Who is the lady?"

"Stella Fletcher; she's in my class at school. And say, Anne, she's the prettiest girl you ever saw. If I die before I grow up you'll keep an eye on her, won't you?"

"Davy Keith, do stop talking such nonsense," said Marilla severely.

"'Tisn't nonsense," protested Davy in an injured tone. "She's my promised wife, and if I was to die she'd be my promised widow, wouldn't she? And she hasn't got a soul to look after her except her old grandmother."

"Come and have your supper, Anne," said Marilla, "and don't encourage that child in his absurd talk."

Chapter XXIII - Paul Cannot Find the Rock People

Life was very pleasant in Avonlea that summer, although Anne, amid all her vacation joys, was haunted by a sense of "something gone which should be there." She would not admit, even in her inmost reflections, that this was caused by Gilbert's absence. But when she had to walk home alone from prayer meetings and A.V.I.S. pow-wows, while Diana and Fred, and many other gay couples, loitered along the dusky, starlit country roads, there was a queer, lonely ache in her heart which she could not explain away. Gilbert did not even write to her, as she thought he might have done. She knew he wrote to Diana occasionally, but she would not inquire about him; and Diana, supposing that Anne heard from him, volunteered no information. Gilbert's mother, who was a gay, frank, light-hearted lady, but not overburdened with tact, had a very embarrassing habit of asking Anne, always in a painfully distinct voice and always in the presence of a crowd, if she had heard from Gilbert lately. Poor Anne could only blush horribly and murmur, "not very lately," which was taken by all, Mrs. Blythe included, to be merely a maidenly evasion.

Apart from this, Anne enjoyed her summer. Priscilla came for a merry visit in June; and, when she had gone, Mr. and Mrs. Irving, Paul and Charlotta the Fourth came "home" for July and August.

Echo Lodge was the scene of gaieties once more, and the echoes over the river were kept busy mimicking the laughter that rang in the old garden behind the spruces.

"Miss Lavendar" had not changed, except to grow even sweeter and prettier. Paul adored her, and the companionship between them was beautiful to see.

"But I don't call her 'mother' just by itself," he explained to Anne. "You see, THAT name belongs just to my own little mother, and I can't give it to any one else. You know, teacher. But I call her 'Mother Lavendar' and I love her next best to father. I—I even love her a LITTLE better than you, teacher."

"Which is just as it ought to be," answered Anne.

Paul was thirteen now and very tall for his years. His face and eyes were as beautiful as ever, and his fancy was still like a prism, separating everything that fell upon it into rainbows. He and Anne had delightful rambles to wood and field and shore. Never were there two more thoroughly "kindred spirits."

Charlotta the Fourth had blossomed out into young ladyhood. She wore her hair now in an enormous pompadour and had discarded the blue ribbon bows of auld lang syne, but her face was as freckled, her nose as snubbed, and her mouth and smiles as wide as ever.

"You don't think I talk with a Yankee accent, do you, Miss Shirley, ma'am?" she demanded anxiously.

"I don't notice it, Charlotta."

"I'm real glad of that. They said I did at home, but I thought likely they just wanted to aggravate me. I don't want no Yankee accent. Not that I've a word to say against the Yankees, Miss Shirley, ma'am. They're real civilized. But give me old P.E. Island every time."

Paul spent his first fortnight with his grandmother Irving in Avonlea. Anne was there to meet him when he came, and found him wild with eagerness to get to the shore—Nora and the Golden Lady and the Twin Sailors would be there. He could hardly wait to eat his supper. Could he not see Nora's elfin face peering around the point, watching for him wistfully? But it was a very sober Paul who came back from the shore in the twilight.

"Didn't you find your Rock People?" asked Anne.

Paul shook his chestnut curls sorrowfully.

"The Twin Sailors and the Golden Lady never came at all," he said. "Nora was there—but Nora is not the same, teacher. She is changed."

"Oh, Paul, it is you who are changed," said Anne. "You have grown too old for the Rock People. They like only children for playfellows. I am afraid the Twin Sailors will never again come to you in the pearly, enchanted boat with the sail of moonshine; and the Golden Lady will play no more for you on her golden harp. Even Nora will not meet you much longer. You must pay the penalty of growing-up, Paul. You must leave fairyland behind you."

"You two talk as much foolishness as ever you did," said old Mrs. Irving, half-indulgently, half-reprovingly.

"Oh, no, we don't," said Anne, shaking her head gravely. "We are getting very, very wise, and it is such a pity. We are never half so interesting when we have learned that language is given us to enable us to conceal our thoughts."

"But it isn't—it is given us to exchange our thoughts," said Mrs. Irving serious-ly. She had never heard of Tallyrand and did not understand epigrams.

Anne spent a fortnight of halcyon days at Echo Lodge in the golden prime of August. While there she incidentally contrived to hurry Ludovic Speed in his lei-surely courting of Theodora Dix, as related duly in another chronicle of her history[1]. Arnold Sherman, an elderly friend of the Irvings, was there at the same time, and added not a little to the general pleasantness of life.

"What a nice play-time this has been," said Anne. "I feel like a giant refreshed. And it's only a fortnight more till I go back to Kingsport, and Redmond and Pat-ty's Place. Patty's Place is the dearest spot, Miss Lavendar. I feel as if I had two

---

[1] Chronicles of Avonlea

homes—one at Green Gables and one at Patty's Place. But where has the summer gone? It doesn't seem a day since I came home that spring evening with the May-flowers. When I was little I couldn't see from one end of the summer to the other. It stretched before me like an unending season. Now, "tis a handbreadth, 'tis a tale.'"

"Anne, are you and Gilbert Blythe as good friends as you used to be?" asked Miss Lavendar quietly.

"I am just as much Gilbert's friend as ever I was, Miss Lavendar."

Miss Lavendar shook her head.

"I see something's gone wrong, Anne. I'm going to be impertinent and ask what. Have you quarrelled?"

"No; it's only that Gilbert wants more than friendship and I can't give him more."

"Are you sure of that, Anne?"

"Perfectly sure."

"I'm very, very sorry."

"I wonder why everybody seems to think I ought to marry Gilbert Blythe," said Anne petulantly.

"Because you were made and meant for each other, Anne—that is why. You needn't toss that young head of yours. It's a fact."

Chapter XXIV - Enter Jonas

"PROSPECT POINT, "August 20th.

"Dear Anne—spelled—with—an—E," wrote Phil, "I must prop my eyelids open long enough to write you. I've neglected you shamefully this summer, honey, but all my other correspondents have been neglected, too. I have a huge pile of letters to answer, so I must gird up the loins of my mind and hoe in. Excuse my mixed metaphors. I'm fearfully sleepy. Last night Cousin Emily and I were calling at a neighbor's. There were several other callers there, and as soon as those unfortunate creatures left, our hostess and her three daughters picked them all to pieces. I knew they would begin on Cousin Emily and me as soon as the door shut behind us. When we came home Mrs. Lilly informed us that the aforesaid neighbor's hired boy was supposed to be down with scarlet fever. You can always trust Mrs. Lilly to tell you cheerful things like that. I have a horror of scarlet fever. I couldn't sleep when I went to bed for thinking of it. I tossed and tumbled about, dreaming fearful dreams when I did snooze for a minute; and at three I wakened up with a high fever, a sore throat, and a raging headache. I knew I had scarlet fever; I got up in a panic and hunted up Cousin Emily's 'doctor book' to read up the symptoms. Anne, I had them all. So I went back to bed, and knowing the worst, slept like a top the rest of the night. Though why a top should sleep sounder than anything else I never could understand. But this morning I was quite well, so it couldn't have been the fever. I suppose if I did catch it last night it couldn't have developed so soon. I can remember that in daytime, but at three o'clock at night I never can be logical.

"I suppose you wonder what I'm doing at Prospect Point. Well, I always like to spend a month of summer at the shore, and father insists that I come to his second-cousin Emily's 'select boardinghouse' at Prospect Point. So a fortnight ago I came as usual. And as usual old 'Uncle Mark Miller' brought me from the station with his ancient buggy and what he calls his 'generous purpose' horse. He is a nice old man and gave me a handful of pink peppermints. Peppermints always seem to me such a religious sort of candy—I suppose because when I was a little girl Grandmother Gordon always gave them to me in church. Once I asked, referring to the smell of peppermints, 'Is that the odor of sanctity?' I didn't like to eat Uncle Mark's peppermints because he just fished them loose out of his pocket, and had to pick some rusty nails and other things from among them before he gave them to me. But I wouldn't hurt his dear old feelings for anything, so I carefully sowed them along the road at intervals. When the last one was gone, Uncle Mark said, a little rebukingly, 'Ye shouldn't a'et all them candies to onct, Miss Phil. You'll likely have the stummick-ache.'

"Cousin Emily has only five boarders besides myself—four old ladies and one young man. My right-hand neighbor is Mrs. Lilly. She is one of those people who seem to take a gruesome pleasure in detailing all their many aches and pains and sicknesses. You cannot mention any ailment but she says, shaking her head, 'Ah, I know too well what that is'—and then you get all the details. Jonas declares he once spoke of locomotor ataxia in hearing and she said she knew too well what that was. She suffered from it for ten years and was finally cured by a traveling doctor.

"Who is Jonas? Just wait, Anne Shirley. You'll hear all about Jonas in the proper time and place. He is not to be mixed up with estimable old ladies.

"My left-hand neighbor at the table is Mrs. Phinney. She always speaks with a wailing, dolorous voice—you are nervously expecting her to burst into tears every moment. She gives you the impression that life to her is indeed a vale of tears, and that a smile, never to speak of a laugh, is a frivolity truly reprehensible. She has a worse opinion of me than Aunt Jamesina, and she doesn't love me hard to atone for it, as Aunty J. does, either.

"Miss Maria Grimsby sits cati-corner from me. The first day I came I remarked to Miss Maria that it looked a little like rain—and Miss Maria laughed. I said the road from the station was very pretty—and Miss Maria laughed. I said there seemed to be a few mosquitoes left yet—and Miss Maria laughed. I said that Prospect Point was as beautiful as ever—and Miss Maria laughed. If I were to say to Miss Maria, 'My father has hanged himself, my mother has taken poison, my brother is in the penitentiary, and I am in the last stages of consumption,' Miss Maria would laugh. She can't help it—she was born so; but is very sad and awful.

"The fifth old lady is Mrs. Grant. She is a sweet old thing; but she never says anything but good of anybody and so she is a very uninteresting conversationalist.

"And now for Jonas, Anne.

"That first day I came I saw a young man sitting opposite me at the table, smiling at me as if he had known me from my cradle. I knew, for Uncle Mark had told me, that his name was Jonas Blake, that he was a Theological Student from St. Columbia, and that he had taken charge of the Point Prospect Mission Church for the summer.

"He is a very ugly young man—really, the ugliest young man I've ever seen. He has a big, loose-jointed figure with absurdly long legs. His hair is tow-color and lank, his eyes are green, and his mouth is big, and his ears—but I never think about his ears if I can help it.

"He has a lovely voice—if you shut your eyes he is adorable—and he certainly has a beautiful soul and disposition.

"We were good chums right way. Of course he is a graduate of Redmond, and that is a link between us. We fished and boated together; and we walked on the sands by moonlight. He didn't look so homely by moonlight and oh, he was nice. Niceness fairly exhaled from him. The old ladies—except Mrs. Grant—don't approve of Jonas, because he laughs and jokes—and because he evidently likes the society of frivolous me better than theirs.

"Somehow, Anne, I don't want him to think me frivolous. This is ridiculous. Why should I care what a tow-haired person called Jonas, whom I never saw before thinks of me?

"Last Sunday Jonas preached in the village church. I went, of course, but I couldn't realize that Jonas was going to preach. The fact that he was a minister— or going to be one—persisted in seeming a huge joke to me.

"Well, Jonas preached. And, by the time he had preached ten minutes, I felt so small and insignificant that I thought I must be invisible to the naked eye. Jonas never said a word about women and he never looked at me. But I realized then and there what a pitiful, frivolous, small-souled little butterfly I was, and how horribly different I must be from Jonas' ideal woman. SHE would be grand and strong and noble. He was so earnest and tender and true. He was everything a minister ought to be. I wondered how I could ever have thought him ugly—but he really is!—with those inspired eyes and that intellectual brow which the roughly-falling hair hid on week days.

"It was a splendid sermon and I could have listened to it forever, and it made me feel utterly wretched. Oh, I wish I was like YOU, Anne.

"He caught up with me on the road home, and grinned as cheerfully as usual. But his grin could never deceive me again. I had seen the REAL Jonas. I wondered if he could ever see the REAL PHIL—whom NOBODY, not even you, Anne, has ever seen yet.

"'Jonas,' I said—I forgot to call him Mr. Blake. Wasn't it dreadful? But there are times when things like that don't matter—'Jonas, you were born to be a minister. You COULDN'T be anything else.'

"'No, I couldn't,' he said soberly. 'I tried to be something else for a long time— I didn't want to be a minister. But I came to see at last that it was the work given me to do—and God helping me, I shall try to do it.'

"His voice was low and reverent. I thought that he would do his work and do it well and nobly; and happy the woman fitted by nature and training to help him do it. SHE would be no feather, blown about by every fickle wind of fancy. SHE would always know what hat to put on. Probably she would have only one. Ministers never have much money. But she wouldn't mind having one hat or none at all, because she would have Jonas.

"Anne Shirley, don't you dare to say or hint or think that I've fallen in love with Mr. Blake. Could I care for a lank, poor, ugly theologue—named Jonas? As Uncle Mark says, 'It's impossible, and what's more it's improbable.'

"Good night, PHIL."

"P.S. It is impossible—but I am horribly afraid it's true. I'm happy and wretched and scared. HE can NEVER care for me, I know. Do you think I could ever develop into a passable minister's wife, Anne? And WOULD they expect me to lead in prayer? P G."

Chapter XXV - Enter Prince Charming

"I'm contrasting the claims of indoors and out," said Anne, looking from the window of Patty's Place to the distant pines of the park.

"I've an afternoon to spend in sweet doing nothing, Aunt Jimsie. Shall I spend it here where there is a cosy fire, a plateful of delicious russets, three purring and harmonious cats, and two impeccable china dogs with green noses? Or shall I go to the park, where there is the lure of gray woods and of gray water lapping on the harbor rocks?"

"If I was as young as you, I'd decide in favor of the park," said Aunt Jamesina, tickling Joseph's yellow ear with a knitting needle.

"I thought that you claimed to be as young as any of us, Aunty," teased Anne.

"Yes, in my soul. But I'll admit my legs aren't as young as yours. You go and get some fresh air, Anne. You look pale lately."

"I think I'll go to the park," said Anne restlessly. "I don't feel like tame domestic joys today. I want to feel alone and free and wild. The park will be empty, for every one will be at the football match."

"Why didn't you go to it?"

"'Nobody axed me, sir, she said'—at least, nobody but that horrid little Dan Ranger. I wouldn't go anywhere with him; but rather than hurt his poor little tender feelings I said I wasn't going to the game at all. I don't mind. I'm not in the mood for football today somehow."

"You go and get some fresh air," repeated Aunt Jamesina, "but take your umbrella, for I believe it's going to rain. I've rheumatism in my leg."

"Only old people should have rheumatism, Aunty."

"Anybody is liable to rheumatism in her legs, Anne. It's only old people who should have rheumatism in their souls, though. Thank goodness, I never have. When you get rheumatism in your soul you might as well go and pick out your coffin."

It was November—the month of crimson sunsets, parting birds, deep, sad hymns of the sea, passionate wind-songs in the pines. Anne roamed through the pineland alleys in the park and, as she said, let that great sweeping wind blow the fogs out of her soul. Anne was not wont to be troubled with soul fog. But, somehow, since her return to Redmond for this third year, life had not mirrored her spirit back to her with its old, perfect, sparkling clearness.

Outwardly, existence at Patty's Place was the same pleasant round of work and study and recreation that it had always been. On Friday evenings the big, fire-lighted livingroom was crowded by callers and echoed to endless jest and laughter, while Aunt Jamesina smiled beamingly on them all. The "Jonas" of Phil's letter came often, running up from St. Columbia on the early train and departing on the late. He was a general favorite at Patty's Place, though Aunt Jamesina shook her head and opined that divinity students were not what they used to be.

"He's VERY nice, my dear," she told Phil, "but ministers ought to be graver and more dignified."

"Can't a man laugh and laugh and be a Christian still?" demanded Phil.

"Oh, MEN—yes. But I was speaking of MINISTERS, my dear," said Aunt Jamesina rebukingly. "And you shouldn't flirt so with Mr. Blake—you really shouldn't."

"I'm not flirting with him," protested Phil.

Nobody believed her, except Anne. The others thought she was amusing herself as usual, and told her roundly that she was behaving very badly.

"Mr. Blake isn't of the Alec-and-Alonzo type, Phil," said Stella severely. "He takes things seriously. You may break his heart."

"Do you really think I could?" asked Phil. "I'd love to think so."

"Philippa Gordon! I never thought you were utterly unfeeling. The idea of you saying you'd love to break a man's heart!"

"I didn't say so, honey. Quote me correctly. I said I'd like to think I COULD break it. I would like to know I had the POWER to do it."

"I don't understand you, Phil. You are leading that man on deliberately—and you know you don't mean anything by it."

"I mean to make him ask me to marry him if I can," said Phil calmly.

"I give you up," said Stella hopelessly.

Gilbert came occasionally on Friday evenings. He seemed always in good spirits, and held his own in the jests and repartee that flew about. He neither sought nor avoided Anne. When circumstances brought them in contact he talked to her pleasantly and courteously, as to any newly-made acquaintance. The old camaraderie was gone entirely. Anne felt it keenly; but she told herself she was very glad and thankful that Gilbert had got so completely over his disappointment in regard to her. She had really been afraid, that April evening in the orchard, that she had hurt him terribly and that the wound would be long in healing. Now she saw that she need not have worried. Men have died and the worms have eaten them but not for love. Gilbert evidently was in no danger of immediate dissolution. He was enjoying life, and he was full of ambition and zest. For him there was to be no wasting in despair because a woman was fair and cold. Anne, as she listened to the ceaseless badinage that went on between him and Phil, wondered if she had only imagined that look in his eyes when she had told him she could never care for him.

There were not lacking those who would gladly have stepped into Gilbert's vacant place. But Anne snubbed them without fear and without reproach. If the real

Prince Charming was never to come she would have none of a substitute. So she sternly told herself that gray day in the windy park.

Suddenly the rain of Aunt Jamesina's prophecy came with a swish and rush. Anne put up her umbrella and hurried down the slope. As she turned out on the harbor road a savage gust of wind tore along it. Instantly her umbrella turned wrong side out. Anne clutched at it in despair. And then—there came a voice close to her.

"Pardon me—may I offer you the shelter of my umbrella?"

Anne looked up. Tall and handsome and distinguished-looking—dark, melancholy, inscrutable eyes—melting, musical, sympathetic voice—yes, the very hero of her dreams stood before her in the flesh. He could not have more closely resembled her ideal if he had been made to order.

"Thank you," she said confusedly.

"We'd better hurry over to that little pavillion on the point," suggested the unknown. "We can wait there until this shower is over. It is not likely to rain so heavily very long."

The words were very commonplace, but oh, the tone! And the smile which accompanied them! Anne felt her heart beating strangely.

Together they scurried to the pavilion and sat breathlessly down under its friendly roof. Anne laughingly held up her false umbrella.

"It is when my umbrella turns inside out that I am convinced of the total depravity of inanimate things," she said gaily.

The raindrops sparkled on her shining hair; its loosened rings curled around her neck and forehead. Her cheeks were flushed, her eyes big and starry. Her companion looked down at her admiringly. She felt herself blushing under his gaze. Who could he be? Why, there was a bit of the Redmond white and scarlet pinned to his coat lapel. Yet she had thought she knew, by sight at least, all the Redmond students except the Freshmen. And this courtly youth surely was no Freshman.

"We are schoolmates, I see," he said, smiling at Anne's colors. "That ought to be sufficient introduction. My name is Royal Gardner. And you are the Miss Shirley who read the Tennyson paper at the Philomathic the other evening, aren't you?"

"Yes; but I cannot place you at all," said Anne, frankly. "Please, where DO you belong?"

"I feel as if I didn't belong anywhere yet. I put in my Freshman and Sophomore years at Redmond two years ago. I've been in Europe ever since. Now I've come back to finish my Arts course."

"This is my Junior year, too," said Anne.

"So we are classmates as well as collegemates. I am reconciled to the loss of the years that the locust has eaten," said her companion, with a world of meaning in those wonderful eyes of his.

The rain came steadily down for the best part of an hour. But the time seemed really very short. When the clouds parted and a burst of pale November sunshine fell athwart the harbor and the pines Anne and her companion walked home together. By the time they had reached the gate of Patty's Place he had asked permission to call, and had received it. Anne went in with cheeks of flame and her heart beating to her fingertips. Rusty, who climbed into her lap and tried to kiss her, found a very absent welcome. Anne, with her soul full of romantic thrills, had no attention to spare just then for a crop-eared pussy cat.

That evening a parcel was left at Patty's Place for Miss Shirley. It was a box containing a dozen magnificent roses. Phil pounced impertinently on the card that fell from it, read the name and the poetical quotation written on the back.

"Royal Gardner!" she exclaimed. "Why, Anne, I didn't know you were acquainted with Roy Gardner!"

"I met him in the park this afternoon in the rain," explained Anne hurriedly. "My umbrella turned inside out and he came to my rescue with his."

"Oh!" Phil peered curiously at Anne. "And is that exceedingly commonplace incident any reason why he should send us longstemmed roses by the dozen, with a very sentimental rhyme? Or why we should blush divinest rosy-red when we look at his card? Anne, thy face betrayeth thee."

"Don't talk nonsense, Phil. Do you know Mr. Gardner?"

"I've met his two sisters, and I know of him. So does everybody worthwhile in Kingsport. The Gardners are among the richest, bluest, of Bluenoses. Roy is adorably handsome and clever. Two years ago his mother's health failed and he had to leave college and go abroad with her—his father is dead. He must have been greatly disappointed to have to give up his class, but they say he was perfectly sweet about it. Fee—fi—fo—fum, Anne. I smell romance. Almost do I envy you, but not quite. After all, Roy Gardner isn't Jonas."

"You goose!" said Anne loftily. But she lay long awake that night, nor did she wish for sleep. Her waking fancies were more alluring than any vision of dreamland. Had the real Prince come at last? Recalling those glorious dark eyes which had gazed so deeply into her own, Anne was very strongly inclined to think he had.

Chapter XXVI - Enter Christine

The girls at Patty's Place were dressing for the reception which the Juniors were giving for the Seniors in February. Anne surveyed herself in the mirror of the blue room with girlish satisfaction. She had a particularly pretty gown on. Originally it had been only a simple little slip of cream silk with a chiffon over-dress. But Phil had insisted on taking it home with her in the Christmas holidays and embroidering tiny rosebuds all over the chiffon. Phil's fingers were deft, and the result was a dress which was the envy of every Redmond girl. Even Allie Boone, whose frocks came from Paris, was wont to look with longing eyes on that rosebud concoction as Anne trailed up the main staircase at Redmond in it.

Anne was trying the effect of a white orchid in her hair. Roy Gardner had sent her white orchids for the reception, and she knew no other Redmond girl would have them that night—when Phil came in with admiring gaze.

"Anne, this is certainly your night for looking handsome. Nine nights out of ten I can easily outshine you. The tenth you blossom out suddenly into something that eclipses me altogether. How do you manage it?"

"It's the dress, dear. Fine feathers."

"'Tisn't. The last evening you flamed out into beauty you wore your old blue flannel shirtwaist that Mrs. Lynde made you. If Roy hadn't already lost head and heart about you he certainly would tonight. But I don't like orchids on you, Anne. No; it isn't jealousy. Orchids don't seem to BELONG to you. They're too exotic—too tropical—too insolent. Don't put them in your hair, anyway."

"Well, I won't. I admit I'm not fond of orchids myself. I don't think they're related to me. Roy doesn't often send them—he knows I like flowers I can live with. Orchids are only things you can visit with."

"Jonas sent me some dear pink rosebuds for the evening—but—he isn't coming himself. He said he had to lead a prayer-meeting in the slums! I don't believe he wanted to come. Anne, I'm horribly afraid Jonas doesn't really care anything about me. And I'm trying to decide whether I'll pine away and die, or go on and get my B.A. and be sensible and useful."

"You couldn't possibly be sensible and useful, Phil, so you'd better pine away and die," said Anne cruelly.

"Heartless Anne!"

"Silly Phil! You know quite well that Jonas loves you."

"But—he won't TELL me so. And I can't MAKE him. He LOOKS it, I'll admit. But speak-to-me-only-with-thine-eyes isn't a really reliable reason for embroidering doilies and hemstitching tablecloths. I don't want to begin such work until I'm really engaged. It would be tempting Fate."

"Mr. Blake is afraid to ask you to marry him, Phil. He is poor and can't offer you a home such as you've always had. You know that is the only reason he hasn't spoken long ago."

"I suppose so," agreed Phil dolefully. "Well"—brightening up—"if he WON'T ask me to marry him I'll ask him, that's all. So it's bound to come right. I won't worry. By the way, Gilbert Blythe is going about constantly with Christine Stuart. Did you know?"

Anne was trying to fasten a little gold chain about her throat. She suddenly found the clasp difficult to manage. WHAT was the matter with it—or with her fingers?

"No," she said carelessly. "Who is Christine Stuart?"

"Ronald Stuart's sister. She's in Kingsport this winter studying music. I haven't seen her, but they say she's very pretty and that Gilbert is quite crazy over her. How angry I was when you refused Gilbert, Anne. But Roy Gardner was foreordained for you. I can see that now. You were right, after all."

Anne did not blush, as she usually did when the girls assumed that her eventual marriage to Roy Gardner was a settled thing. All at once she felt rather dull. Phil's chatter seemed trivial and the reception a bore. She boxed poor Rusty's ears.

"Get off that cushion instantly, you cat, you! Why don't you stay down where you belong?"

Anne picked up her orchids and went downstairs, where Aunt Jamesina was presiding over a row of coats hung before the fire to warm. Roy Gardner was waiting for Anne and teasing the Sarah-cat while he waited. The Sarah-cat did not approve of him. She always turned her back on him. But everybody else at Patty's Place liked him very much. Aunt Jamesina, carried away by his unfailing and deferential courtesy, and the pleading tones of his delightful voice, declared he was the nicest young man she ever knew, and that Anne was a very fortunate girl. Such remarks made Anne restive. Roy's wooing had certainly been as romantic as girlish heart could desire, but—she wished Aunt Jamesina and the girls would not take things so for granted. When Roy murmured a poetical compliment as he helped her on with her coat, she did not blush and thrill as usual; and he found her rather silent in their brief walk to Redmond. He thought she looked a little pale when she came out of the coeds' dressing room; but as they entered the reception room her color and sparkle suddenly returned to her. She turned to Roy with her gayest expression. He smiled back at her with what Phil called "his deep, black, velvety smile." Yet she really did not see Roy at all. She was acutely conscious that Gilbert was standing under the palms just across the room talking to a girl who must be Christine Stuart.

She was very handsome, in the stately style destined to become rather massive in middle life. A tall girl, with large dark-blue eyes, ivory outlines, and a gloss of darkness on her smooth hair.

"She looks just as I've always wanted to look," thought Anne miserably. "Rose-leaf complexion—starry violet eyes—raven hair—yes, she has them all. It's a wonder her name isn't Cordelia Fitzgerald into the bargain! But I don't believe her figure is as good as mine, and her nose certainly isn't."

Anne felt a little comforted by this conclusion.

Chapter XXVII - Mutual Confidences

March came in that winter like the meekest and mildest of lambs, bringing days that were crisp and golden and tingling, each followed by a frosty pink twilight which gradually lost itself in an elfland of moonshine.

Over the girls at Patty's Place was falling the shadow of April examinations. They were studying hard; even Phil had settled down to text and notebooks with a doggedness not to be expected of her.

"I'm going to take the Johnson Scholarship in Mathematics," she announced calmly. "I could take the one in Greek easily, but I'd rather take the mathematical one because I want to prove to Jonas that I'm really enormously clever."

"Jonas likes you better for your big brown eyes and your crooked smile than for all the brains you carry under your curls," said Anne.

"When I was a girl it wasn't considered lady-like to know anything about Mathematics," said Aunt Jamesina. "But times have changed. I don't know that it's all for the better. Can you cook, Phil?"

"No, I never cooked anything in my life except a gingerbread and it was a failure—flat in the middle and hilly round the edges. You know the kind. But, Aunty, when I begin in good earnest to learn to cook don't you think the brains that enable me to win a mathematical scholarship will also enable me to learn cooking just as well?"

"Maybe," said Aunt Jamesina cautiously. "I am not decrying the higher education of women. My daughter is an M.A. She can cook, too. But I taught her to cook BEFORE I let a college professor teach her Mathematics."

In mid-March came a letter from Miss Patty Spofford, saying that she and Miss Maria had decided to remain abroad for another year.

"So you may have Patty's Place next winter, too," she wrote. "Maria and I are going to run over Egypt. I want to see the Sphinx once before I die."

"Fancy those two dames 'running over Egypt'! I wonder if they'll look up at the Sphinx and knit," laughed Priscilla.

"I'm so glad we can keep Patty's Place for another year," said Stella. "I was afraid they'd come back. And then our jolly little nest here would be broken up—and we poor callow nestlings thrown out on the cruel world of boardinghouses again."

"I'm off for a tramp in the park," announced Phil, tossing her book aside. "I think when I am eighty I'll be glad I went for a walk in the park tonight."

"What do you mean?" asked Anne.

"Come with me and I'll tell you, honey."

They captured in their ramble all the mysteries and magics of a March evening. Very still and mild it was, wrapped in a great, white, brooding silence—a silence which was yet threaded through with many little silvery sounds which you could hear if you hearkened as much with your soul as your ears. The girls wandered down a long pineland aisle that seemed to lead right out into the heart of a deep-red, overflowing winter sunset.

"I'd go home and write a poem this blessed minute if I only knew how," declared Phil, pausing in an open space where a rosy light was staining the green tips of the pines. "It's all so wonderful here—this great, white stillness, and those dark trees that always seem to be thinking."

"'The woods were God's first temples,'" quoted Anne softly. "One can't help feeling reverent and adoring in such a place. I always feel so near Him when I walk among the pines."

"Anne, I'm the happiest girl in the world," confessed Phil suddenly.

"So Mr. Blake has asked you to marry him at last?" said Anne calmly.

"Yes. And I sneezed three times while he was asking me. Wasn't that horrid? But I said 'yes' almost before he finished—I was so afraid he might change his mind and stop. I'm besottedly happy. I couldn't really believe before that Jonas would ever care for frivolous me."

"Phil, you're not really frivolous," said Anne gravely. "'Way down underneath that frivolous exterior of yours you've got a dear, loyal, womanly little soul. Why do you hide it so?"

"I can't help it, Queen Anne. You are right—I'm not frivolous at heart. But there's a sort of frivolous skin over my soul and I can't take it off. As Mrs. Poyser says, I'd have to be hatched over again and hatched different before I could change it. But Jonas knows the real me and loves me, frivolity and all. And I love him. I never was so surprised in my life as I was when I found out I loved him. I'd never thought it possible to fall in love with an ugly man. Fancy me coming down to one solitary beau. And one named Jonas! But I mean to call him Jo. That's such a nice, crisp little name. I couldn't nickname Alonzo."

"What about Alec and Alonzo?"

"Oh, I told them at Christmas that I never could marry either of them. It seems so funny now to remember that I ever thought it possible that I might. They felt so badly I just cried over both of them—howled. But I knew there was only one man in the world I could ever marry. I had made up my own mind for once and it was real easy, too. It's very delightful to feel so sure, and know it's your own sureness and not somebody else's."

"Do you suppose you'll be able to keep it up?"

"Making up my mind, you mean? I don't know, but Jo has given me a splendid rule. He says, when I'm perplexed, just to do what I would wish I had done when I shall be eighty. Anyhow, Jo can make up his mind quickly enough, and it would be uncomfortable to have too much mind in the same house."

"What will your father and mother say?"

"Father won't say much. He thinks everything I do right. But mother WILL talk. Oh, her tongue will be as Byrney as her nose. But in the end it will be all right."

"You'll have to give up a good many things you've always had, when you marry Mr. Blake, Phil."

"But I'll have HIM. I won't miss the other things. We're to be married a year from next June. Jo graduates from St. Columbia this spring, you know. Then he's going to take a little mission church down on Patterson Street in the slums. Fancy me in the slums! But I'd go there or to Greenland's icy mountains with him."

"And this is the girl who would NEVER marry a man who wasn't rich," commented Anne to a young pine tree.

"Oh, don't cast up the follies of my youth to me. I shall be poor as gaily as I've been rich. You'll see. I'm going to learn how to cook and make over dresses. I've learned how to market since I've lived at Patty's Place; and once I taught a Sunday School class for a whole summer. Aunt Jamesina says I'll ruin Jo's career if I marry him. But I won't. I know I haven't much sense or sobriety, but I've got what is ever so much better—the knack of making people like me. There is a man in Bolingbroke who lisps and always testifies in prayer-meeting. He says, 'If you can't thine like an electric thtar thine like a candlethtick.' I'll be Jo's little candlestick."

"Phil, you're incorrigible. Well, I love you so much that I can't make nice, light, congratulatory little speeches. But I'm heart-glad of your happiness."

"I know. Those big gray eyes of yours are brimming over with real friendship, Anne. Some day I'll look the same way at you. You're going to marry Roy, aren't you, Anne?"

"My dear Philippa, did you ever hear of the famous Betty Baxter, who 'refused a man before he'd axed her'? I am not going to emulate that celebrated lady by either refusing or accepting any one before he 'axes' me."

"All Redmond knows that Roy is crazy about you," said Phil candidly. "And you DO love him, don't you, Anne?"

"I—I suppose so," said Anne reluctantly. She felt that she ought to be blushing while making such a confession; but she was not; on the other hand, she always blushed hotly when any one said anything about Gilbert Blythe or Christine Stuart in her hearing. Gilbert Blythe and Christine Stuart were nothing to her—absolutely nothing. But Anne had given up trying to analyze the reason of her blushes. As for Roy, of course she was in love with him—madly so. How could she help it? Was he not her ideal? Who could resist those glorious dark eyes, and that pleading voice? Were not half the Redmond girls wildly envious? And what a charming sonnet he had sent her, with a box of violets, on her birthday! Anne knew every word of it by heart. It was very good stuff of its kind, too. Not exactly up to the level of Keats or Shakespeare—even Anne was not so deeply in love as to think that. But it was very tolerable magazine verse. And it was addressed to

HER—not to Laura or Beatrice or the Maid of Athens, but to her, Anne Shirley. To be told in rhythmical cadences that her eyes were stars of the morning—that her cheek had the flush it stole from the sunrise—that her lips were redder than the roses of Paradise, was thrillingly romantic. Gilbert would never have dreamed of writing a sonnet to her eyebrows. But then, Gilbert could see a joke. She had once told Roy a funny story—and he had not seen the point of it. She recalled the chummy laugh she and Gilbert had had together over it, and wondered uneasily if life with a man who had no sense of humor might not be somewhat uninteresting in the long run. But who could expect a melancholy, inscrutable hero to see the humorous side of things? It would be flatly unreasonable.

Chapter XXVIII - A June Evening

"I wonder what it would be like to live in a world where it was always June," said Anne, as she came through the spice and bloom of the twilit orchard to the front door steps, where Marilla and Mrs. Rachel were sitting, talking over Mrs. Samson Coates' funeral, which they had attended that day. Dora sat between them, diligently studying her lessons; but Davy was sitting tailor-fashion on the grass, looking as gloomy and depressed as his single dimple would let him.

"You'd get tired of it," said Marilla, with a sigh.

"I daresay; but just now I feel that it would take me a long time to get tired of it, if it were all as charming as today. Everything loves June. Davy-boy, why this melancholy November face in blossom-time?"

"I'm just sick and tired of living," said the youthful pessimist.

"At ten years? Dear me, how sad!"

"I'm not making fun," said Davy with dignity. "I'm dis—dis—discouraged"—bringing out the big word with a valiant effort.

"Why and wherefore?" asked Anne, sitting down beside him.

"'Cause the new teacher that come when Mr. Holmes got sick give me ten sums to do for Monday. It'll take me all day tomorrow to do them. It isn't fair to have to work Saturdays. Milty Boulter said he wouldn't do them, but Marilla says I've got to. I don't like Miss Carson a bit."

"Don't talk like that about your teacher, Davy Keith," said Mrs. Rachel severely. "Miss Carson is a very fine girl. There is no nonsense about her."

"That doesn't sound very attractive," laughed Anne. "I like people to have a little nonsense about them. But I'm inclined to have a better opinion of Miss Carson than you have. I saw her in prayer-meeting last night, and she has a pair of eyes that can't always look sensible. Now, Davy-boy, take heart of grace. 'Tomorrow will bring another day' and I'll help you with the sums as far as in me lies. Don't waste this lovely hour 'twixt light and dark worrying over arithmetic."

"Well, I won't," said Davy, brightening up. "If you help me with the sums I'll have 'em done in time to go fishing with Milty. I wish old Aunt Atossa's funeral was tomorrow instead of today. I wanted to go to it 'cause Milty said his mother said Aunt Atossa would be sure to rise up in her coffin and say sarcastic things to the folks that come to see her buried. But Marilla said she didn't."

"Poor Atossa laid in her coffin peaceful enough," said Mrs. Lynde solemnly. "I never saw her look so pleasant before, that's what. Well, there weren't many tears shed over her, poor old soul. The Elisha Wrights are thankful to be rid of her, and I can't say I blame them a mite."

"It seems to me a most dreadful thing to go out of the world and not leave one person behind you who is sorry you are gone," said Anne, shuddering.

"Nobody except her parents ever loved poor Atossa, that's certain, not even her husband," averred Mrs. Lynde. "She was his fourth wife. He'd sort of got into the habit of marrying. He only lived a few years after he married her. The doctor said he died of dyspepsia, but I shall always maintain that he died of Atossa's tongue, that's what. Poor soul, she always knew everything about her neighbors, but she never was very well acquainted with herself. Well, she's gone anyhow; and I suppose the next excitement will be Diana's wedding."

"It seems funny and horrible to think of Diana's being married," sighed Anne, hugging her knees and looking through the gap in the Haunted Wood to the light that was shining in Diana's room.

"I don't see what's horrible about it, when she's doing so well," said Mrs. Lynde emphatically. "Fred Wright has a fine farm and he is a model young man."

"He certainly isn't the wild, dashing, wicked, young man Diana once wanted to marry," smiled Anne. "Fred is extremely good."

"That's just what he ought to be. Would you want Diana to marry a wicked man? Or marry one yourself?"

"Oh, no. I wouldn't want to marry anybody who was wicked, but I think I'd like it if he COULD be wicked and WOULDN'T. Now, Fred is HOPELESSLY good."

"You'll have more sense some day, I hope," said Marilla.

Marilla spoke rather bitterly. She was grievously disappointed. She knew Anne had refused Gilbert Blythe. Avonlea gossip buzzed over the fact, which had leaked out, nobody knew how. Perhaps Charlie Sloane had guessed and told his guesses for truth. Perhaps Diana had betrayed it to Fred and Fred had been indiscreet. At all events it was known; Mrs. Blythe no longer asked Anne, in public or private, if she had heard lately from Gilbert, but passed her by with a frosty bow. Anne, who had always liked Gilbert's merry, young-hearted mother, was grieved in secret over this. Marilla said nothing; but Mrs. Lynde gave Anne many exasperated digs about it, until fresh gossip reached that worthy lady, through the medium of Moody Spurgeon MacPherson's mother, that Anne had another "beau" at college, who was rich and handsome and good all in one. After that Mrs. Rachel held her tongue, though she still wished in her inmost heart that Anne had accepted Gilbert. Riches were all very well; but even Mrs. Rachel, practical soul though she was, did not consider them the one essential. If Anne "liked" the Handsome Unknown better than Gilbert there was nothing more to be said; but Mrs. Rachel was dreadfully afraid that Anne was going to make the mistake of marrying for money. Marilla knew Anne too well to fear this; but she felt that something in the universal scheme of things had gone sadly awry.

"What is to be, will be," said Mrs. Rachel gloomily, "and what isn't to be happens sometimes. I can't help believing it's going to happen in Anne's case, if Providence doesn't interfere, that's what." Mrs. Rachel sighed. She was afraid Providence wouldn't interfere; and she didn't dare to.

Anne had wandered down to the Dryad's Bubble and was curled up among the ferns at the root of the big white birch where she and Gilbert had so often sat in summers gone by. He had gone into the newspaper office again when college closed, and Avonlea seemed very dull without him. He never wrote to her, and Anne missed the letters that never came. To be sure, Roy wrote twice a week; his letters were exquisite compositions which would have read beautifully in a memoir or biography. Anne felt herself more deeply in love with him than ever when she read them; but her heart never gave the queer, quick, painful bound at sight of his letters which it had given one day when Mrs. Hiram Sloane had handed her out an envelope addressed in Gilbert's black, upright handwriting. Anne had hurried home to the east gable and opened it eagerly—to find a typewritten copy of some college society report—"only that and nothing more." Anne flung the harmless screed across her room and sat down to write an especially nice epistle to Roy.

Diana was to be married in five more days. The gray house at Orchard Slope was in a turmoil of baking and brewing and boiling and stewing, for there was to be a big, old-timey wedding. Anne, of course, was to be bridesmaid, as had been arranged when they were twelve years old, and Gilbert was coming from Kingsport to be best man. Anne was enjoying the excitement of the various preparations, but under it all she carried a little heartache. She was, in a sense, losing her dear old chum; Diana's new home would be two miles from Green Gables, and the old constant companionship could never be theirs again. Anne looked up at Diana's light and thought how it had beaconed to her for many years; but soon it would shine through the summer twilights no more. Two big, painful tears welled up in her gray eyes.

"Oh," she thought, "how horrible it is that people have to grow up—and marry—and CHANGE!"

Chapter XXIX - Diana's Wedding

"After all, the only real roses are the pink ones," said Anne, as she tied white ribbon around Diana's bouquet in the westward-looking gable at Orchard Slope. "They are the flowers of love and faith."

Diana was standing nervously in the middle of the room, arrayed in her bridal white, her black curls frosted over with the film of her wedding veil. Anne had draped that veil, in accordance with the sentimental compact of years before.

"It's all pretty much as I used to imagine it long ago, when I wept over your inevitable marriage and our consequent parting," she laughed. "You are the bride of my dreams, Diana, with the 'lovely misty veil'; and I am YOUR bridesmaid. But, alas! I haven't the puffed sleeves—though these short lace ones are even prettier. Neither is my heart wholly breaking nor do I exactly hate Fred."

"We are not really parting, Anne," protested Diana. "I'm not going far away. We'll love each other just as much as ever. We've always kept that 'oath' of friendship we swore long ago, haven't we?"

"Yes. We've kept it faithfully. We've had a beautiful friendship, Diana. We've never marred it by one quarrel or coolness or unkind word; and I hope it will always be so. But things can't be quite the same after this. You'll have other interests. I'll just be on the outside. But 'such is life' as Mrs. Rachel says. Mrs. Rachel has given you one of her beloved knitted quilts of the 'tobacco stripe' pattern, and she says when I am married she'll give me one, too."

"The mean thing about your getting married is that I won't be able to be your bridesmaid," lamented Diana.

"I'm to be Phil's bridesmaid next June, when she marries Mr. Blake, and then I must stop, for you know the proverb 'three times a bridesmaid, never a bride,'" said Anne, peeping through the window over the pink and snow of the blossoming orchard beneath. "Here comes the minister, Diana."

"Oh, Anne," gasped Diana, suddenly turning very pale and beginning to tremble. "Oh, Anne—I'm so nervous—I can't go through with it—Anne, I know I'm going to faint."

"If you do I'll drag you down to the rainwater hogshed and drop you in," said Anne unsympathetically. "Cheer up, dearest. Getting married can't be so very terrible when so many people survive the ceremony. See how cool and composed I am, and take courage."

"Wait till your turn comes, Miss Anne. Oh, Anne, I hear father coming upstairs. Give me my bouquet. Is my veil right? Am I very pale?"

"You look just lovely. Di, darling, kiss me good-bye for the last time. Diana Barry will never kiss me again."

"Diana Wright will, though. There, mother's calling. Come."

Following the simple, old-fashioned way in vogue then, Anne went down to the parlor on Gilbert's arm. They met at the top of the stairs for the first time since they had left Kingsport, for Gilbert had arrived only that day. Gilbert shook hands courteously. He was looking very well, though, as Anne instantly noted, rather thin. He was not pale; there was a flush on his cheek that had burned into it as Anne came along the hall towards him, in her soft, white dress with lilies-of-the-valley in the shining masses of her hair. As they entered the crowded parlor together a little murmur of admiration ran around the room. "What a fine-looking pair they are," whispered the impressible Mrs. Rachel to Marilla.

Fred ambled in alone, with a very red face, and then Diana swept in on her father's arm. She did not faint, and nothing untoward occurred to interrupt the ceremony. Feasting and merry-making followed; then, as the evening waned, Fred and Diana drove away through the moonlight to their new home, and Gilbert walked with Anne to Green Gables.

Something of their old comradeship had returned during the informal mirth of the evening. Oh, it was nice to be walking over that well-known road with Gilbert again!

The night was so very still that one should have been able to hear the whisper of roses in blossom—the laughter of daisies—the piping of grasses—many sweet sounds, all tangled up together. The beauty of moonlight on familiar fields irradiated the world.

"Can't we take a ramble up Lovers' Lane before you go in?" asked Gilbert as they crossed the bridge over the Lake of Shining Waters, in which the moon lay like a great, drowned blossom of gold.

Anne assented readily. Lovers' Lane was a veritable path in a fairyland that night—a shimmering, mysterious place, full of wizardry in the white-woven enchantment of moonlight. There had been a time when such a walk with Gilbert through Lovers' Lane would have been far too dangerous. But Roy and Christine had made it very safe now. Anne found herself thinking a good deal about Christine as she chatted lightly to Gilbert. She had met her several times before leaving Kingsport, and had been charmingly sweet to her. Christine had also been charmingly sweet. Indeed, they were a most cordial pair. But for all that, their acquaintance had not ripened into friendship. Evidently Christine was not a kindred spirit.

"Are you going to be in Avonlea all summer?" asked Gilbert.

"No. I'm going down east to Valley Road next week. Esther Haythorne wants me to teach for her through July and August. They have a summer term in that school, and Esther isn't feeling well. So I'm going to substitute for her. In one way I don't mind. Do you know, I'm beginning to feel a little bit like a stranger in

Avonlea now? It makes me sorry—but it's true. It's quite appalling to see the number of children who have shot up into big boys and girls—really young men and women—these past two years. Half of my pupils are grown up. It makes me feel awfully old to see them in the places you and I and our mates used to fill."

Anne laughed and sighed. She felt very old and mature and wise—which showed how young she was. She told herself that she longed greatly to go back to those dear merry days when life was seen through a rosy mist of hope and illusion, and possessed an indefinable something that had passed away forever. Where was it now—the glory and the dream?

"'So wags the world away,'" quoted Gilbert practically, and a trifle absently. Anne wondered if he were thinking of Christine. Oh, Avonlea was going to be so lonely now—with Diana gone!

Chapter XXX - Mrs. Skinner's Romance

Anne stepped off the train at Valley Road station and looked about to see if any one had come to meet her. She was to board with a certain Miss Janet Sweet, but she saw no one who answered in the least to her preconception of that lady, as formed from Esther's letter. The only person in sight was an elderly woman, sitting in a wagon with mail bags piled around her. Two hundred would have been a charitable guess at her weight; her face was as round and red as a harvest-moon and almost as featureless. She wore a tight, black, cashmere dress, made in the fashion of ten years ago, a little dusty black straw hat trimmed with bows of yellow ribbon, and faded black lace mits.

"Here, you," she called, waving her whip at Anne. "Are you the new Valley Road schoolma'am?"

"Yes."

"Well, I thought so. Valley Road is noted for its good-looking schoolma'ams, just as Millersville is noted for its humly ones. Janet Sweet asked me this morning if I could bring you out. I said, 'Sartin I kin, if she don't mind being scrunched up some. This rig of mine's kinder small for the mail bags and I'm some heftier than Thomas!' Just wait, miss, till I shift these bags a bit and I'll tuck you in somehow. It's only two miles to Janet's. Her next-door neighbor's hired boy is coming for your trunk tonight. My name is Skinner—Amelia Skinner."

Anne was eventually tucked in, exchanging amused smiles with herself during the process.

"Jog along, black mare," commanded Mrs. Skinner, gathering up the reins in her pudgy hands. "This is my first trip on the mail rowte. Thomas wanted to hoe his turnips today so he asked me to come. So I jest sot down and took a standing-up snack and started. I sorter like it. O' course it's rather tejus. Part of the time I sits and thinks and the rest I jest sits. Jog along, black mare. I want to git home airly. Thomas is terrible lonesome when I'm away. You see, we haven't been married very long."

"Oh!" said Anne politely.

"Just a month. Thomas courted me for quite a spell, though. It was real romantic." Anne tried to picture Mrs. Skinner on speaking terms with romance and failed.

"Oh?" she said again.

"Yes. Y'see, there was another man after me. Jog along, black mare. I'd been a widder so long folks had given up expecting me to marry again. But when my darter—she's a schoolma'am like you—went out West to teach I felt real lonesome and wasn't nowise sot against the idea. Bime-by Thomas began to come up and so did the other feller—William Obadiah Seaman, his name was. For a long time I couldn't make up my mind which of them to take, and they kep' coming and coming, and I kep' worrying. Y'see, W.O. was rich—he had a fine place and carried considerable style. He was by far the best match. Jog along, black mare."

"Why didn't you marry him?" asked Anne.

"Well, y'see, he didn't love me," answered Mrs. Skinner, solemnly.

Anne opened her eyes widely and looked at Mrs. Skinner. But there was not a glint of humor on that lady's face. Evidently Mrs. Skinner saw nothing amusing in her own case.

"He'd been a widder-man for three yers, and his sister kept house for him. Then she got married and he just wanted some one to look after his house. It was worth looking after, too, mind you that. It's a handsome house. Jog along, black mare. As for Thomas, he was poor, and if his house didn't leak in dry weather it was about all that could be said for it, though it looks kind of pictureaskew. But, y'see, I loved Thomas, and I didn't care one red cent for W.O. So I argued it out with myself. 'Sarah Crowe,' say I—my first was a Crowe—'you can marry your rich man if you like but you won't be happy. Folks can't get along together in this world without a little bit of love. You'd just better tie up to Thomas, for he loves you and you love him and nothing else ain't going to do you.' Jog along, black mare. So I told Thomas I'd take him. All the time I was getting ready I never dared drive past W.O.'s place for fear the sight of that fine house of his would put me in the swithers again. But now I never think of it at all, and I'm just that comfortable and happy with Thomas. Jog along, black mare."

"How did William Obadiah take it?" queried Anne.

"Oh, he rumpussed a bit. But he's going to see a skinny old maid in Millersville now, and I guess she'll take him fast enough. She'll make him a better wife than his first did. W.O. never wanted to marry her. He just asked her to marry him 'cause his father wanted him to, never dreaming but that she'd say 'no.' But mind you, she said 'yes.' There was a predicament for you. Jog along, black mare. She was a great housekeeper, but most awful mean. She wore the same bonnet for eighteen years. Then she got a new one and W.O. met her on the road and didn't know her. Jog along, black mare. I feel that I'd a narrer escape. I might have married him and been most awful miserable, like my poor cousin, Jane Ann. Jane Ann married a rich man she didn't care anything about, and she hasn't the life of a dog. She come to see me last week and says, says she, 'Sarah Skinner, I envy you. I'd rather live in a little hut on the side of the road with a man I was fond of than in my big house with the one I've got.' Jane Ann's man ain't such a bad sort, nuther, though he's so contrary that he wears his fur coat when the thermometer's at ninety. The only way to git him to do anything is to coax him to do the opposite. But there ain't any love to smooth things down and it's a poor way of living.

Jog along, black mare. There's Janet's place in the hollow—'Wayside,' she calls it. Quite pictureaskew, ain't it? I guess you'll be glad to git out of this, with all them mail bags jamming round you."

"Yes, but I have enjoyed my drive with you very much," said Anne sincerely.

"Git away now!" said Mrs. Skinner, highly flattered. "Wait till I tell Thomas that. He always feels dretful tickled when I git a compliment. Jog along, black mare. Well, here we are. I hope you'll git on well in the school, miss. There's a short cut to it through the ma'sh back of Janet's. If you take that way be awful keerful. If you once got stuck in that black mud you'd be sucked right down and never seen or heard tell of again till the day of judgment, like Adam Palmer's cow. Jog along, black mare."

Chapter XXXI - Anne to Philippa

"Anne Shirley to Philippa Gordon, greeting.

"Well-beloved, it's high time I was writing you. Here am I, installed once more as a country 'schoolma'am' at Valley Road, boarding at 'Wayside,' the home of Miss Janet Sweet. Janet is a dear soul and very nicelooking; tall, but not over-tall; stoutish, yet with a certain restraint of outline suggestive of a thrifty soul who is not going to be overlavish even in the matter of avoirdupois. She has a knot of soft, crimpy, brown hair with a thread of gray in it, a sunny face with rosy cheeks, and big, kind eyes as blue as forget-me-nots. Moreover, she is one of those delightful, old-fashioned cooks who don't care a bit if they ruin your digestion as long as they can give you feasts of fat things.

"I like her; and she likes me—principally, it seems, because she had a sister named Anne who died young.

"'I'm real glad to see you,' she said briskly, when I landed in her yard. 'My, you don't look a mite like I expected. I was sure you'd be dark—my sister Anne was dark. And here you're redheaded!'

"For a few minutes I thought I wasn't going to like Janet as much as I had expected at first sight. Then I reminded myself that I really must be more sensible than to be prejudiced against any one simply because she called my hair red. Probably the word 'auburn' was not in Janet's vocabulary at all.

"'Wayside' is a dear sort of little spot. The house is small and white, set down in a delightful little hollow that drops away from the road. Between road and house is an orchard and flower-garden all mixed up together. The front door walk is bordered with quahog clam-shells—'cow-hawks,' Janet calls them; there is Virginia Creeper over the porch and moss on the roof. My room is a neat little spot 'off the parlor'—just big enough for the bed and me. Over the head of my bed there is a picture of Robby Burns standing at Highland Mary's grave, shadowed by an enormous weeping willow tree. Robby's face is so lugubrious that it is no wonder I have bad dreams. Why, the first night I was here I dreamed I COULDN'T LAUGH.

"The parlor is tiny and neat. Its one window is so shaded by a huge willow that the room has a grotto-like effect of emerald gloom. There are wonderful tidies on the chairs, and gay mats on the floor, and books and cards carefully arranged on a round table, and vases of dried grass on the mantel-piece. Between the vases is a cheerful decoration of preserved coffin plates—five in all, pertaining respectively to Janet's father and mother, a brother, her sister Anne, and a hired man who died here once! If I go suddenly insane some of these days 'know all men by these presents' that those coffin-plates have caused it.

"But it's all delightful and I said so. Janet loved me for it, just as she detested poor Esther because Esther had said so much shade was unhygienic and had objected to sleeping on a feather bed. Now, I glory in feather-beds, and the more unhygienic and feathery they are the more I glory. Janet says it is such a comfort to see me eat; she had been so afraid I would be like Miss Haythorne, who wouldn't eat anything but fruit and hot water for breakfast and tried to make Janet give up frying things. Esther is really a dear girl, but she is rather given to fads. The trouble is that she hasn't enough imagination and HAS a tendency to indigestion.

"Janet told me I could have the use of the parlor when any young men called! I don't think there are many to call. I haven't seen a young man in Valley Road yet, except the next-door hired boy—Sam Toliver, a very tall, lank, tow-haired youth. He came over one evening recently and sat for an hour on the garden fence, near the front porch where Janet and I were doing fancy-work. The only remarks he volunteered in all that time were, 'Hev a peppermint, miss! Dew now-fine thing for carARRH, peppermints,' and, 'Powerful lot o' jump-grasses round here ternight. Yep.'

"But there is a love affair going on here. It seems to be my fortune to be mixed up, more or less actively, with elderly love affairs. Mr. and Mrs. Irving always say that I brought about their marriage. Mrs. Stephen Clark of Carmody persists in being most grateful to me for a suggestion which somebody else would probably have made if I hadn't. I do really think, though, that Ludovic Speed would never have got any further along than placid courtship if I had not helped him and Theodora Dix out.

"In the present affair I am only a passive spectator. I've tried once to help things along and made an awful mess of it. So I shall not meddle again. I'll tell you all about it when we meet."

Chapter XXXII - Tea with Mrs. Douglas

On the first Thursday night of Anne's sojourn in Valley Road Janet asked her to go to prayer-meeting. Janet blossomed out like a rose to attend that prayer-meeting. She wore a pale-blue, pansy-sprinkled muslin dress with more ruffles than one would ever have supposed economical Janet could be guilty of, and a white leghorn hat with pink roses and three ostrich feathers on it. Anne felt quite amazed. Later on, she found out Janet's motive in so arraying herself—a motive as old as Eden.

Valley Road prayer-meetings seemed to be essentially feminine. There were thirty-two women present, two half-grown boys, and one solitary man, beside the minister. Anne found herself studying this man. He was not handsome or young or graceful; he had remarkably long legs—so long that he had to keep them coiled up under his chair to dispose of them—and he was stoop-shouldered. His hands were big, his hair wanted barbering, and his moustache was unkempt. But Anne thought she liked his face; it was kind and honest and tender; there was something else in it, too—just what, Anne found it hard to define. She finally concluded that this man had suffered and been strong, and it had been made manifest in his face. There was a sort of patient, humorous endurance in his expression which indicated that he would go to the stake if need be, but would keep on looking pleasant until he really had to begin squirming.

When prayer-meeting was over this man came up to Janet and said,

"May I see you home, Janet?"

Janet took his arm—"as primly and shyly as if she were no more than sixteen, having her first escort home," Anne told the girls at Patty's Place later on.

"Miss Shirley, permit me to introduce Mr. Douglas," she said stiffly.

Mr. Douglas nodded and said, "I was looking at you in prayer-meeting, miss, and thinking what a nice little girl you were."

Such a speech from ninety-nine people out of a hundred would have annoyed Anne bitterly; but the way in which Mr. Douglas said it made her feel that she had received a very real and pleasing compliment. She smiled appreciatively at him and dropped obligingly behind on the moonlit road.

So Janet had a beau! Anne was delighted. Janet would make a paragon of a wife—cheery, economical, tolerant, and a very queen of cooks. It would be a flagrant waste on Nature's part to keep her a permanent old maid.

"John Douglas asked me to take you up to see his mother," said Janet the next day. "She's bed-rid a lot of the time and never goes out of the house. But she's powerful fond of company and always wants to see my boarders. Can you go up this evening?"

Anne assented; but later in the day Mr. Douglas called on his mother's behalf to invite them up to tea on Saturday evening.

"Oh, why didn't you put on your pretty pansy dress?" asked Anne, when they left home. It was a hot day, and poor Janet, between her excitement and her heavy black cashmere dress, looked as if she were being broiled alive.

"Old Mrs. Douglas would think it terrible frivolous and unsuitable, I'm afraid. John likes that dress, though," she added wistfully.

The old Douglas homestead was half a mile from "Wayside" cresting a windy hill. The house itself was large and comfortable, old enough to be dignified, and girdled with maple groves and orchards. There were big, trim barns behind it, and everything bespoke prosperity. Whatever the patient endurance in Mr. Douglas' face had meant it hadn't, so Anne reflected, meant debts and duns.

John Douglas met them at the door and took them into the sitting-room, where his mother was enthroned in an armchair.

Anne had expected old Mrs. Douglas to be tall and thin, because Mr. Douglas was. Instead, she was a tiny scrap of a woman, with soft pink cheeks, mild blue eyes, and a mouth like a baby's. Dressed in a beautiful, fashionably-made black silk dress, with a fluffy white shawl over her shoulders, and her snowy hair surmounted by a dainty lace cap, she might have posed as a grandmother doll.

"How do you do, Janet dear?" she said sweetly. "I am so glad to see you again, dear." She put up her pretty old face to be kissed. "And this is our new teacher. I'm delighted to meet you. My son has been singing your praises until I'm half jealous, and I'm sure Janet ought to be wholly so."

Poor Janet blushed, Anne said something polite and conventional, and then everybody sat down and made talk. It was hard work, even for Anne, for nobody seemed at ease except old Mrs. Douglas, who certainly did not find any difficulty in talking. She made Janet sit by her and stroked her hand occasionally. Janet sat and smiled, looking horribly uncomfortable in her hideous dress, and John Douglas sat without smiling.

At the tea table Mrs. Douglas gracefully asked Janet to pour the tea. Janet turned redder than ever but did it. Anne wrote a description of that meal to Stella.

"We had cold tongue and chicken and strawberry preserves, lemon pie and tarts and chocolate cake and raisin cookies and pound cake and fruit cake—and a few other things, including more pie—caramel pie, I think it was. After I had eaten twice as much as was good for me, Mrs. Douglas sighed and said she feared she had nothing to tempt my appetite.

"'I'm afraid dear Janet's cooking has spoiled you for any other,' she said sweetly. 'Of course nobody in Valley Road aspires to rival HER. WON'T you have another piece of pie, Miss Shirley? You haven't eaten ANYTHING.'

"Stella, I had eaten a helping of tongue and one of chicken, three biscuits, a generous allowance of preserves, a piece of pie, a tart, and a square of chocolate cake!"

After tea Mrs. Douglas smiled benevolently and told John to take "dear Janet" out into the garden and get her some roses. "Miss Shirley will keep me company while you are out—won't you?" she said plaintively. She settled down in her armchair with a sigh.

"I am a very frail old woman, Miss Shirley. For over twenty years I've been a great sufferer. For twenty long, weary years I've been dying by inches."

"How painful!" said Anne, trying to be sympathetic and succeeding only in feeling idiotic.

"There have been scores of nights when they've thought I could never live to see the dawn," went on Mrs. Douglas solemnly. "Nobody knows what I've gone through—nobody can know but myself. Well, it can't last very much longer now. My weary pilgrimage will soon be over, Miss Shirley. It is a great comfort to me that John will have such a good wife to look after him when his mother is gone— a great comfort, Miss Shirley."

"Janet is a lovely woman," said Anne warmly.

"Lovely! A beautiful character," assented Mrs. Douglas. "And a perfect house-keeper—something I never was. My health would not permit it, Miss Shirley. I am indeed thankful that John has made such a wise choice. I hope and believe that he will be happy. He is my only son, Miss Shirley, and his happiness lies very near my heart."

"Of course," said Anne stupidly. For the first time in her life she was stupid. Yet she could not imagine why. She seemed to have absolutely nothing to say to this sweet, smiling, angelic old lady who was patting her hand so kindly.

"Come and see me soon again, dear Janet," said Mrs. Douglas lovingly, when they left. "You don't come half often enough. But then I suppose John will be bringing you here to stay all the time one of these days." Anne, happening to glance at John Douglas, as his mother spoke, gave a positive start of dismay. He looked as a tortured man might look when his tormentors gave the rack the last turn of possible endurance. She felt sure he must be ill and hurried poor blushing Janet away.

"Isn't old Mrs. Douglas a sweet woman?" asked Janet, as they went down the road.

"M—m," answered Anne absently. She was wondering why John Douglas had looked so.

"She's been a terrible sufferer," said Janet feelingly. "She takes terrible spells. It keeps John all worried up. He's scared to leave home for fear his mother will take a spell and nobody there but the hired girl."

Chapter XXXIII - "He Just Kept Coming and Coming"

Three days later Anne came home from school and found Janet crying. Tears and Janet seemed so incongruous that Anne was honestly alarmed.

"Oh, what is the matter?" she cried anxiously.

"I'm—I'm forty today," sobbed Janet.

"Well, you were nearly that yesterday and it didn't hurt," comforted Anne, trying not to smile.

"But—but," went on Janet with a big gulp, "John Douglas won't ask me to marry him."

"Oh, but he will," said Anne lamely. "You must give him time, Janet

"Time!" said Janet with indescribable scorn. "He has had twenty years. How much time does he want?"

"Do you mean that John Douglas has been coming to see you for twenty years?"

"He has. And he has never so much as mentioned marriage to me. And I don't believe he ever will now. I've never said a word to a mortal about it, but it seems to me I've just got to talk it out with some one at last or go crazy. John Douglas begun to go with me twenty years ago, before mother died. Well, he kept coming and coming, and after a spell I begun making quilts and things; but he never said anything about getting married, only just kept coming and coming. There wasn't anything I could do. Mother died when we'd been going together for eight years. I thought he maybe would speak out then, seeing as I was left alone in the world. He was real kind and feeling, and did everything he could for me, but he never said marry. And that's the way it has been going on ever since. People blame ME for it. They say I won't marry him because his mother is so sickly and I don't want the bother of waiting on her. Why, I'd LOVE to wait on John's mother! But I let them think so. I'd rather they'd blame me than pity me! It's so dreadful humiliating that John won't ask me. And WHY won't he? Seems to me if I only knew his reason I wouldn't mind it so much."

"Perhaps his mother doesn't want him to marry anybody," suggested Anne.

"Oh, she does. She's told me time and again that she'd love to see John settled before her time comes. She's always giving him hints—you heard her yourself the other day. I thought I'd ha' gone through the floor."

"It's beyond me," said Anne helplessly. She thought of Ludovic Speed. But the cases were not parallel. John Douglas was not a man of Ludovic's type.

"You should show more spirit, Janet," she went on resolutely. "Why didn't you send him about his business long ago?"

"I couldn't," said poor Janet pathetically. "You see, Anne, I've always been awful fond of John. He might just as well keep coming as not, for there was never anybody else I'd want, so it didn't matter."

"But it might have made him speak out like a man," urged Anne.

Janet shook her head.

"No, I guess not. I was afraid to try, anyway, for fear he'd think I meant it and just go. I suppose I'm a poor-spirited creature, but that is how I feel. And I can't help it."

"Oh, you COULD help it, Janet. It isn't too late yet. Take a firm stand. Let that man know you are not going to endure his shillyshallying any longer. I'LL back you up."

"I dunno," said Janet hopelessly. "I dunno if I could ever get up enough spunk. Things have drifted so long. But I'll think it over."

Anne felt that she was disappointed in John Douglas. She had liked him so well, and she had not thought him the sort of man who would play fast and loose with a woman's feelings for twenty years. He certainly should be taught a lesson, and Anne felt vindictively that she would enjoy seeing the process. Therefore she was delighted when Janet told her, as they were going to prayer-meeting the next night, that she meant to show some "sperrit."

"I'll let John Douglas see I'm not going to be trodden on any longer."

"You are perfectly right," said Anne emphatically.

When prayer-meeting was over John Douglas came up with his usual request. Janet looked frightened but resolute.

"No, thank you," she said icily. "I know the road home pretty well alone. I ought to, seeing I've been traveling it for forty years. So you needn't trouble yourself, MR. Douglas."

Anne was looking at John Douglas; and, in that brilliant moonlight, she saw the last twist of the rack again. Without a word he turned and strode down the road.

"Stop! Stop!" Anne called wildly after him, not caring in the least for the other dumbfounded onlookers. "Mr. Douglas, stop! Come back."

John Douglas stopped but he did not come back. Anne flew down the road, caught his arm and fairly dragged him back to Janet.

"You must come back," she said imploringly. "It's all a mistake, Mr. Douglas—all my fault. I made Janet do it. She didn't want to—but it's all right now, isn't it, Janet?"

Without a word Janet took his arm and walked away. Anne followed them meekly home and slipped in by the back door.

"Well, you are a nice person to back me up," said Janet sarcastically.

"I couldn't help it, Janet," said Anne repentantly. "I just felt as if I had stood by and seen murder done. I HAD to run after him."

"Oh, I'm just as glad you did. When I saw John Douglas making off down that road I just felt as if every little bit of joy and happiness that was left in my life was going with him. It was an awful feeling."

"Did he ask you why you did it?" asked Anne.

"No, he never said a word about it," replied Janet dully.

Chapter XXXIV - John Douglas Speaks at Last

Anne was not without a feeble hope that something might come of it after all. But nothing did. John Douglas came and took Janet driving, and walked home from prayer-meeting with her, as he had been doing for twenty years, and as he seemed likely to do for twenty years more. The summer waned. Anne taught her school and wrote letters and studied a little. Her walks to and from school were pleasant. She always went by way of the swamp; it was a lovely place—a boggy soil, green with the greenest of mossy hillocks; a silvery brook meandered through it and spruces stood erectly, their boughs a-trail with gray-green mosses, their roots overgrown with all sorts of woodland lovelinesses.

Nevertheless, Anne found life in Valley Road a little monotonous. To be sure, there was one diverting incident.

She had not seen the lank, tow-headed Samuel of the peppermints since the evening of his call, save for chance meetings on the road. But one warm August night he appeared, and solemnly seated himself on the rustic bench by the porch. He wore his usual working habiliments, consisting of varipatched trousers, a blue jean shirt, out at the elbows, and a ragged straw hat. He was chewing a straw and he kept on chewing it while he looked solemnly at Anne. Anne laid her book aside with a sigh and took up her doily. Conversation with Sam was really out of the question.

After a long silence Sam suddenly spoke.

"I'm leaving over there," he said abruptly, waving his straw in the direction of the neighboring house.

"Oh, are you?" said Anne politely.

"Yep."

"And where are you going now?"

"Wall, I've been thinking some of gitting a place of my own. There's one that'd suit me over at Millersville. But ef I rents it I'll want a woman."

"I suppose so," said Anne vaguely.

"Yep."

There was another long silence. Finally Sam removed his straw again and said, "Will yeh hev me?"

"Wh—a—t!" gasped Anne.

"Will yeh hev me?"

"Do you mean—MARRY you?" queried poor Anne feebly.

"Yep."

"Why, I'm hardly acquainted with you," cried Anne indignantly.

"But yeh'd git acquainted with me after we was married," said Sam.

Anne gathered up her poor dignity.

"Certainly I won't marry you," she said haughtily.

"Wall, yeh might do worse," expostulated Sam. "I'm a good worker and I've got some money in the bank."

"Don't speak of this to me again. Whatever put such an idea into your head?" said Anne, her sense of humor getting the better of her wrath. It was such an absurd situation.

"Yeh're a likely-looking girl and hev a right-smart way o' stepping," said Sam. "I don't want no lazy woman. Think it over. I won't change my mind yit awhile. Wall, I must be gitting. Gotter milk the cows."

Anne's illusions concerning proposals had suffered so much of late years that there were few of them left. So she could laugh wholeheartedly over this one, not feeling any secret sting. She mimicked poor Sam to Janet that night, and both of them laughed immoderately over his plunge into sentiment.

One afternoon, when Anne's sojourn in Valley Road was drawing to a close, Alec Ward came driving down to "Wayside" in hot haste for Janet.

"They want you at the Douglas place quick," he said. "I really believe old Mrs. Douglas is going to die at last, after pretending to do it for twenty years."

Janet ran to get her hat. Anne asked if Mrs. Douglas was worse than usual.

"She's not half as bad," said Alec solemnly, "and that's what makes me think it's serious. Other times she'd be screaming and throwing herself all over the place. This time she's lying still and mum. When Mrs. Douglas is mum she is pretty sick, you bet."

"You don't like old Mrs. Douglas?" said Anne curiously.

"I like cats as IS cats. I don't like cats as is women," was Alec's cryptic reply.

Janet came home in the twilight.

"Mrs. Douglas is dead," she said wearily. "She died soon after I got there. She just spoke to me once—'I suppose you'll marry John now?' she said. It cut me to the heart, Anne. To think John's own mother thought I wouldn't marry him because of her! I couldn't say a word either—there were other women there. I was thankful John had gone out."

Janet began to cry drearily. But Anne brewed her a hot drink of ginger tea to her comforting. To be sure, Anne discovered later on that she had used white pepper instead of ginger; but Janet never knew the difference.

The evening after the funeral Janet and Anne were sitting on the front porch steps at sunset. The wind had fallen asleep in the pinelands and lurid sheets of heat-lightning flickered across the northern skies. Janet wore her ugly black dress and looked her very worst, her eyes and nose red from crying. They talked little, for Janet seemed faintly to resent Anne's efforts to cheer her up. She plainly preferred to be miserable.

Suddenly the gate-latch clicked and John Douglas strode into the garden. He walked towards them straight over the geranium bed. Janet stood up. So did Anne. Anne was a tall girl and wore a white dress; but John Douglas did not see her.

"Janet," he said, "will you marry me?"

The words burst out as if they had been wanting to be said for twenty years and MUST be uttered now, before anything else.

Janet's face was so red from crying that it couldn't turn any redder, so it turned a most unbecoming purple.

"Why didn't you ask me before?" she said slowly.

"I couldn't. She made me promise not to—mother made me promise not to. Nineteen years ago she took a terrible spell. We thought she couldn't live through it. She implored me to promise not to ask you to marry me while she was alive. I didn't want to promise such a thing, even though we all thought she couldn't live very long—the doctor only gave her six months. But she begged it on her knees, sick and suffering. I had to promise."

"What had your mother against me?" cried Janet.

"Nothing—nothing. She just didn't want another woman—ANY woman—there while she was living. She said if I didn't promise she'd die right there and I'd have killed her. So I promised. And she's held me to that promise ever since, though I've gone on my knees to her in my turn to beg her to let me off."

"Why didn't you tell me this?" asked Janet chokingly. "If I'd only KNOWN! Why didn't you just tell me?"

"She made me promise I wouldn't tell a soul," said John hoarsely. "She swore me to it on the Bible; Janet, I'd never have done it if I'd dreamed it was to be for so long. Janet, you'll never know what I've suffered these nineteen years. I know I've made you suffer, too, but you'll marry me for all, won't you, Janet? Oh, Janet, won't you? I've come as soon as I could to ask you."

At this moment the stupefied Anne came to her senses and realized that she had no business to be there. She slipped away and did not see Janet until the next morning, when the latter told her the rest of the story.

"That cruel, relentless, deceitful old woman!" cried Anne.

"Hush—she's dead," said Janet solemnly. "If she wasn't—but she IS. So we mustn't speak evil of her. But I'm happy at last, Anne. And I wouldn't have minded waiting so long a bit if I'd only known why."

"When are you to be married?"

"Next month. Of course it will be very quiet. I suppose people will talk terrible. They'll say I made enough haste to snap John up as soon as his poor mother was out of the way. John wanted to let them know the truth but I said, 'No, John; after all she was your mother, and we'll keep the secret between us, and not cast any shadow on her memory. I don't mind what people say, now that I know the truth myself. It don't matter a mite. Let it all be buried with the dead' says I to him. So I coaxed him round to agree with me."

"You're much more forgiving than I could ever be," Anne said, rather crossly.

"You'll feel differently about a good many things when you get to be my age," said Janet tolerantly. "That's one of the things we learn as we grow older—how to forgive. It comes easier at forty than it did at twenty."

Chapter XXXV - The Last Redmond Year Opens

"Here we are, all back again, nicely sunburned and rejoicing as a strong man to run a race," said Phil, sitting down on a suitcase with a sigh of pleasure. "Isn't it jolly to see this dear old Patty's Place again—and Aunty—and the cats? Rusty has lost another piece of ear, hasn't he?"

"Rusty would be the nicest cat in the world if he had no ears at all," declared Anne loyally from her trunk, while Rusty writhed about her lap in a frenzy of welcome.

"Aren't you glad to see us back, Aunty?" demanded Phil.

"Yes. But I wish you'd tidy things up," said Aunt Jamesina plaintively, looking at the wilderness of trunks and suitcases by which the four laughing, chattering girls were surrounded. "You can talk just as well later on. Work first and then play used to be my motto when I was a girl."

"Oh, we've just reversed that in this generation, Aunty. OUR motto is play your play and then dig in. You can do your work so much better if you've had a good bout of play first."

"If you are going to marry a minister," said Aunt Jamesina, picking up Joseph and her knitting and resigning herself to the inevitable with the charming grace that made her the queen of housemothers, "you will have to give up such expressions as 'dig in.'"

"Why?" moaned Phil. "Oh, why must a minister's wife be supposed to utter only prunes and prisms? I shan't. Everybody on Patterson Street uses slang—that is to say, metaphorical language—and if I didn't they would think me insufferably proud and stuck up."

"Have you broken the news to your family?" asked Priscilla, feeding the Sarah-cat bits from her lunchbasket.

Phil nodded.

"How did they take it?"

"Oh, mother rampaged. But I stood rockfirm—even I, Philippa Gordon, who never before could hold fast to anything. Father was calmer. Father's own daddy was a minister, so you see he has a soft spot in his heart for the cloth. I had Jo up to Mount Holly, after mother grew calm, and they both loved him. But mother gave him some frightful hints in every conversation regarding what she had hoped for me. Oh, my vacation pathway hasn't been exactly strewn with roses, girls dear. But—I've won out and I've got Jo. Nothing else matters."

"To you," said Aunt Jamesina darkly.

"Nor to Jo, either," retorted Phil. "You keep on pitying him. Why, pray? I think he's to be envied. He's getting brains, beauty, and a heart of gold in ME."

"It's well we know how to take your speeches," said Aunt Jamesina patiently. "I hope you don't talk like that before strangers. What would they think?"

"Oh, I don't want to know what they think. I don't want to see myself as others see me. I'm sure it would be horribly uncomfortable most of the time. I don't believe Burns was really sincere in that prayer, either."

"Oh, I daresay we all pray for some things that we really don't want, if we were only honest enough to look into our hearts," owned Aunt Jamesina candidly. "I've a notion that such prayers don't rise very far. *I* used to pray that I might be enabled to forgive a certain person, but I know now I really didn't want to forgive her. When I finally got that I DID want to I forgave her without having to pray about it."

"I can't picture you as being unforgiving for long," said Stella.

"Oh, I used to be. But holding spite doesn't seem worth while when you get along in years."

"That reminds me," said Anne, and told the tale of John and Janet.

"And now tell us about that romantic scene you hinted so darkly at in one of your letters," demanded Phil.

Anne acted out Samuel's proposal with great spirit. The girls shrieked with laughter and Aunt Jamesina smiled.

"It isn't in good taste to make fun of your beaux," she said severely; "but," she added calmly, "I always did it myself."

"Tell us about your beaux, Aunty," entreated Phil. "You must have had any number of them."

"They're not in the past tense," retorted Aunt Jamesina. "I've got them yet. There are three old widowers at home who have been casting sheep's eyes at me for some time. You children needn't think you own all the romance in the world."

"Widowers and sheep's eyes don't sound very romantic, Aunty."

"Well, no; but young folks aren't always romantic either. Some of my beaux certainly weren't. I used to laugh at them scandalous, poor boys. There was Jim Elwood—he was always in a sort of day-dream—never seemed to sense what was going on. He didn't wake up to the fact that I'd said 'no' till a year after I'd said it. When he did get married his wife fell out of the sleigh one night when they were driving home from church and he never missed her. Then there was Dan Winston. He knew too much. He knew everything in this world and most of what is in the next. He could give you an answer to any question, even if you asked him when the Judgment Day was to be. Milton Edwards was real nice and I liked him but I didn't marry him. For one thing, he took a week to get a joke through his head, and for another he never asked me. Horatio Reeve was the most interesting beau I ever had. But when he told a story he dressed it up so that you couldn't see it for frills. I never could decide whether he was lying or just letting his imagination run loose."

"And what about the others, Aunty?"

"Go away and unpack," said Aunt Jamesina, waving Joseph at them by mistake for a needle. "The others were too nice to make fun of. I shall respect their memory. There's a box of flowers in your room, Anne. They came about an hour ago."

After the first week the girls of Patty's Place settled down to a steady grind of study; for this was their last year at Redmond and graduation honors must be fought for persistently. Anne devoted herself to English, Priscilla pored over classics, and Philippa pounded away at Mathematics. Sometimes they grew tired, sometimes they felt discouraged, sometimes nothing seemed worth the struggle for it. In one such mood Stella wandered up to the blue room one rainy November evening. Anne sat on the floor in a little circle of light cast by the lamp beside her, amid a surrounding snow of crumpled manuscript.

"What in the world are you doing?"

"Just looking over some old Story Club yarns. I wanted something to cheer AND inebriate. I'd studied until the world seemed azure. So I came up here and dug these out of my trunk. They are so drenched in tears and tragedy that they are excruciatingly funny."

"I'm blue and discouraged myself," said Stella, throwing herself on the couch. "Nothing seems worthwhile. My very thoughts are old. I've thought them all before. What is the use of living after all, Anne?"

"Honey, it's just brain fag that makes us feel that way, and the weather. A pouring rainy night like this, coming after a hard day's grind, would squelch any one but a Mark Tapley. You know it IS worthwhile to live."

"Oh, I suppose so. But I can't prove it to myself just now."

"Just think of all the great and noble souls who have lived and worked in the world," said Anne dreamily. "Isn't it worthwhile to come after them and inherit what they won and taught? Isn't it worthwhile to think we can share their inspiration? And then, all the great souls that will come in the future? Isn't it worthwhile to work a little and prepare the way for them—make just one step in their path easier?"

"Oh, my mind agrees with you, Anne. But my soul remains doleful and uninspired. I'm always grubby and dingy on rainy nights."

"Some nights I like the rain—I like to lie in bed and hear it pattering on the roof and drifting through the pines."

"I like it when it stays on the roof," said Stella. "It doesn't always. I spent a gruesome night in an old country farmhouse last summer. The roof leaked and the rain came pattering down on my bed. There was no poetry in THAT. I had to get up in the 'mirk midnight' and chivy round to pull the bedstead out of the drip—and it was one of those solid, old-fashioned beds that weigh a ton—more or less. And then that drip-drop, drip-drop kept up all night until my nerves just went to pieces. You've no idea what an eerie noise a great drop of rain falling with a

---

mushy thud on a bare floor makes in the night. It sounds like ghostly footsteps and all that sort of thing. What are you laughing over, Anne?"

"These stories. As Phil would say they are killing—in more senses than one, for everybody died in them. What dazzlingly lovely heroines we had—and how we dressed them!

"Silks—satins—velvets—jewels—laces—they never wore anything else. Here is one of Jane Andrews' stories depicting her heroine as sleeping in a beautiful white satin nightdress trimmed with seed pearls."

"Go on," said Stella. "I begin to feel that life is worth living as long as there's a laugh in it."

"Here's one I wrote. My heroine is disporting herself at a ball 'glittering from head to foot with large diamonds of the first water.' But what booted beauty or rich attire? 'The paths of glory lead but to the grave.' They must either be murdered or die of a broken heart. There was no escape for them."

"Let me read some of your stories."

"Well, here's my masterpiece. Note its cheerful title—'My Graves.' I shed quarts of tears while writing it, and the other girls shed gallons while I read it. Jane Andrews' mother scolded her frightfully because she had so many handkerchiefs in the wash that week. It's a harrowing tale of the wanderings of a Methodist minister's wife. I made her a Methodist because it was necessary that she should wander. She buried a child every place she lived in. There were nine of them and their graves were severed far apart, ranging from Newfoundland to Vancouver. I described the children, pictured their several death beds, and detailed their tombstones and epitaphs. I had intended to bury the whole nine but when I had disposed of eight my invention of horrors gave out and I permitted the ninth to live as a hopeless cripple."

While Stella read My Graves, punctuating its tragic paragraphs with chuckles, and Rusty slept the sleep of a just cat who has been out all night curled up on a Jane Andrews tale of a beautiful maiden of fifteen who went to nurse in a leper colony—of course dying of the loathsome disease finally—Anne glanced over the other manuscripts and recalled the old days at Avonlea school when the members of the Story Club, sitting under the spruce trees or down among the ferns by the brook, had written them. What fun they had had! How the sunshine and mirth of those olden summers returned as she read. Not all the glory that was Greece or the grandeur that was Rome could weave such wizardry as those funny, tearful tales of the Story Club. Among the manuscripts Anne found one written on sheets of wrapping paper. A wave of laughter filled her gray eyes as she recalled the time and place of its genesis. It was the sketch she had written the day she fell through the roof of the Cobb duckhouse on the Tory Road.

Anne glanced over it, then fell to reading it intently. It was a little dialogue between asters and sweet-peas, wild canaries in the lilac bush, and the guardian spirit of the garden. After she had read it, she sat, staring into space; and when Stella had gone she smoothed out the crumpled manuscript.

"I believe I will," she said resolutely.

Chapter XXXVI - The Gardners'Call

"Here is a letter with an Indian stamp for you, Aunt Jimsie," said Phil. "Here are three for Stella, and two for Pris, and a glorious fat one for me from Jo. There's nothing for you, Anne, except a circular."

Nobody noticed Anne's flush as she took the thin letter Phil tossed her carelessly. But a few minutes later Phil looked up to see a transfigured Anne.

"Honey, what good thing has happened?"

"The Youth's Friend has accepted a little sketch I sent them a fortnight ago," said Anne, trying hard to speak as if she were accustomed to having sketches accepted every mail, but not quite succeeding.

"Anne Shirley! How glorious! What was it? When is it to be published? Did they pay you for it?"

"Yes; they've sent a check for ten dollars, and the editor writes that he would like to see more of my work. Dear man, he shall. It was an old sketch I found in my box. I re-wrote it and sent it in—but I never really thought it could be accepted because it had no plot," said Anne, recalling the bitter experience of Averil's Atonement.

"What are you going to do with that ten dollars, Anne? Let's all go up town and get drunk," suggested Phil.

"I AM going to squander it in a wild soulless revel of some sort," declared Anne gaily. "At all events it isn't tainted money—like the check I got for that horrible Reliable Baking Powder story. I spent IT usefully for clothes and hated them every time I put them on."

"Think of having a real live author at Patty's Place," said Priscilla.

"It's a great responsibility," said Aunt Jamesina solemnly.

"Indeed it is," agreed Pris with equal solemnity. "Authors are kittle cattle. You never know when or how they will break out. Anne may make copy of us."

"I meant that the ability to write for the Press was a great responsibility," said Aunt Jamesina severely, "and I hope Anne realizes, it. My daughter used to write stories before she went to the foreign field, but now she has turned her attention to higher things. She used to say her motto was 'Never write a line you would be ashamed to read at your own funeral.' You'd better take that for yours, Anne, if you are going to embark in literature. Though, to be sure," added Aunt Jamesina perplexedly, "Elizabeth always used to laugh when she said it. She always laughed so much that I don't know how she ever came to decide on being a missionary. I'm thankful she did—I prayed that she might—but—I wish she hadn't."

Then Aunt Jamesina wondered why those giddy girls all laughed.

Anne's eyes shone all that day; literary ambitions sprouted and budded in her brain; their exhilaration accompanied her to Jennie Cooper's walking party, and not even the sight of Gilbert and Christine, walking just ahead of her and Roy, could quite subdue the sparkle of her starry hopes. Nevertheless, she was not so rapt from things of earth as to be unable to notice that Christine's walk was decidedly ungraceful.

"But I suppose Gilbert looks only at her face. So like a man," thought Anne scornfully.

"Shall you be home Saturday afternoon?" asked Roy.

"Yes."

"My mother and sisters are coming to call on you," said Roy quietly.

Something went over Anne which might be described as a thrill, but it was hardly a pleasant one. She had never met any of Roy's family; she realized the significance of his statement; and it had, somehow, an irrevocableness about it that chilled her.

"I shall be glad to see them," she said flatly; and then wondered if she really would be glad. She ought to be, of course. But would it not be something of an ordeal? Gossip had filtered to Anne regarding the light in which the Gardners viewed the "infatuation" of son and brother. Roy must have brought pressure to bear in the matter of this call. Anne knew she would be weighed in the balance. From the fact that they had consented to call she understood that, willingly or unwillingly, they regarded her as a possible member of their clan.

"I shall just be myself. I shall not TRY to make a good impression," thought Anne loftily. But she was wondering what dress she would better wear Saturday afternoon, and if the new style of high hair-dressing would suit her better than the old; and the walking party was rather spoiled for her. By night she had decided that she would wear her brown chiffon on Saturday, but would do her hair low.

Friday afternoon none of the girls had classes at Redmond. Stella took the opportunity to write a paper for the Philomathic Society, and was sitting at the table in the corner of the living-room with an untidy litter of notes and manuscript on the floor around her. Stella always vowed she never could write anything unless she threw each sheet down as she completed it. Anne, in her flannel blouse and serge skirt, with her hair rather blown from her windy walk home, was sitting squarely in the middle of the floor, teasing the Sarah-cat with a wishbone. Joseph and Rusty were both curled up in her lap. A warm plummy odor filled the whole house, for Priscilla was cooking in the kitchen. Presently she came in, enshrouded in a huge work-apron, with a smudge of flour on her nose, to show Aunt Jamesina the chocolate cake she had just iced.

At this auspicious moment the knocker sounded. Nobody paid any attention to it save Phil, who sprang up and opened it, expecting a boy with the hat she had bought that morning. On the doorstep stood Mrs. Gardner and her daughters.

Anne scrambled to her feet somehow, emptying two indignant cats out of her lap as she did so, and mechanically shifting her wishbone from her right hand to her left. Priscilla, who would have had to cross the room to reach the kitchen door, lost her head, wildly plunged the chocolate cake under a cushion on the inglenook sofa, and dashed upstairs. Stella began feverishly gathering up her manuscript. Only Aunt Jamesina and Phil remained normal. Thanks to them, everybody was soon sitting at ease, even Anne. Priscilla came down, apronless and smudgeless, Stella reduced her corner to decency, and Phil saved the situation by a stream of ready small talk.

Mrs. Gardner was tall and thin and handsome, exquisitely gowned, cordial with a cordiality that seemed a trifle forced. Aline Gardner was a younger edition of her mother, lacking the cordiality. She endeavored to be nice, but succeeded only in being haughty and patronizing. Dorothy Gardner was slim and jolly and rather tomboyish. Anne knew she was Roy's favorite sister and warmed to her. She would have looked very much like Roy if she had had dreamy dark eyes instead of roguish hazel ones. Thanks to her and Phil, the call really went off very well, except for a slight sense of strain in the atmosphere and two rather untoward incidents. Rusty and Joseph, left to themselves, began a game of chase, and sprang madly into Mrs. Gardner's silken lap and out of it in their wild career. Mrs. Gardner lifted her lorgnette and gazed after their flying forms as if she had never seen cats before, and Anne, choking back slightly nervous laughter, apologized as best she could.

"You are fond of cats?" said Mrs. Gardner, with a slight intonation of tolerant wonder.

Anne, despite her affection for Rusty, was not especially fond of cats, but Mrs. Gardner's tone annoyed her. Inconsequently she remembered that Mrs. John Blythe was so fond of cats that she kept as many as her husband would allow.

"They ARE adorable animals, aren't they?" she said wickedly.

"I have never liked cats," said Mrs. Gardner remotely.

"I love them," said Dorothy. "They are so nice and selfish. Dogs are TOO good and unselfish. They make me feel uncomfortable. But cats are gloriously human."

"You have two delightful old china dogs there. May I look at them closely?" said Aline, crossing the room towards the fireplace and thereby becoming the unconscious cause of the other accident. Picking up Magog, she sat down on the cushion under which was secreted Priscilla's chocolate cake. Priscilla and Anne exchanged agonized glances but could do nothing. The stately Aline continued to sit on the cushion and discuss china dogs until the time of departure.

Dorothy lingered behind a moment to squeeze Anne's hand and whisper impulsively.

"I KNOW you and I are going to be chums. Oh, Roy has told me all about you. I'm the only one of the family he tells things to, poor boy—nobody COULD confide in mamma and Aline, you know. What glorious times you girls must have here! Won't you let me come often and have a share in them?"

"Come as often as you like," Anne responded heartily, thankful that one of Roy's sisters was likable. She would never like Aline, so much was certain; and Aline would never like her, though Mrs. Gardner might be won. Altogether, Anne sighed with relief when the ordeal was over.

> "'Of all sad words of tongue or pen   The saddest are it might have been,'"

quoted Priscilla tragically, lifting the cushion. "This cake is now what you might call a flat failure. And the cushion is likewise ruined. Never tell me that Friday isn't unlucky."

"People who send word they are coming on Saturday shouldn't come on Friday," said Aunt Jamesina.

"I fancy it was Roy's mistake," said Phil. "That boy isn't really responsible for what he says when he talks to Anne. Where IS Anne?"

Anne had gone upstairs. She felt oddly like crying. But she made herself laugh instead. Rusty and Joseph had been TOO awful! And Dorothy WAS a dear.

Chapter XXXVII - Full-fledged B.A.'s

"I wish I were dead, or that it were tomorrow night," groaned Phil.

"If you live long enough both wishes will come true," said Anne calmly.

"It's easy for you to be serene. You're at home in Philosophy. I'm not—and when I think of that horrible paper tomorrow I quail. If I should fail in it what would Jo say?"

"You won't fail. How did you get on in Greek today?"

"I don't know. Perhaps it was a good paper and perhaps it was bad enough to make Homer turn over in his grave. I've studied and mulled over notebooks until I'm incapable of forming an opinion of anything. How thankful little Phil will be when all this examining is over."

"Examining? I never heard such a word."

"Well, haven't I as good a right to make a word as any one else?" demanded Phil.

"Words aren't made—they grow," said Anne.

"Never mind—I begin faintly to discern clear water ahead where no examination breakers loom. Girls, do you—can you realize that our Redmond Life is almost over?"

"I can't," said Anne, sorrowfully. "It seems just yesterday that Pris and I were alone in that crowd of Freshmen at Redmond. And now we are Seniors in our final examinations."

"'Potent, wise, and reverend Seniors,'" quoted Phil. "Do you suppose we really are any wiser than when we came to Redmond?"

"You don't act as if you were by times," said Aunt Jamesina severely.

"Oh, Aunt Jimsie, haven't we been pretty good girls, take us by and large, these three winters you've mothered us?" pleaded Phil.

"You've been four of the dearest, sweetest, goodest girls that ever went together through college," averred Aunt Jamesina, who never spoiled a compliment by misplaced economy.

"But I mistrust you haven't any too much sense yet. It's not to be expected, of course. Experience teaches sense. You can't learn it in a college course. You've been to college four years and I never was, but I know heaps more than you do, young ladies."

"'There are lots of things that never go by rule,
There's a powerful pile o' knowledge
That you never get at college,
There are heaps of things you never learn at school,'"

quoted Stella.

"Have you learned anything at Redmond except dead languages and geometry and such trash?" queried Aunt Jamesina.

"Oh, yes. I think we have, Aunty," protested Anne.

"We've learned the truth of what Professor Woodleigh told us last Philomathic," said Phil. "He said, 'Humor is the spiciest condiment in the feast of existence. Laugh at your mistakes but learn from them, joke over your troubles but gather strength from them, make a jest of your difficulties but overcome them.' Isn't that worth learning, Aunt Jimsie?"

"Yes, it is, dearie. When you've learned to laugh at the things that should be laughed at, and not to laugh at those that shouldn't, you've got wisdom and understanding."

"What have you got out of your Redmond course, Anne?" murmured Priscilla aside.

"I think," said Anne slowly, "that I really have learned to look upon each little hindrance as a jest and each great one as the foreshadowing of victory. Summing up, I think that is what Redmond has given me."

"I shall have to fall back on another Professor Woodleigh quotation to express what it has done for me," said Priscilla. "You remember that he said in his address, 'There is so much in the world for us all if we only have the eyes to see it, and the heart to love it, and the hand to gather it to ourselves—so much in men and women, so much in art and literature, so much everywhere in which to delight, and for which to be thankful.' I think Redmond has taught me that in some measure, Anne."

"Judging from what you all, say" remarked Aunt Jamesina, "the sum and substance is that you can learn—if you've got natural gumption enough—in four years at college what it would take about twenty years of living to teach you. Well, that justifies higher education in my opinion. It's a matter I was always dubious about before."

"But what about people who haven't natural gumption, Aunt Jimsie?"

"People who haven't natural gumption never learn," retorted Aunt Jamesina, "neither in college nor life. If they live to be a hundred they really don't know anything more than when they were born. It's their misfortune not their fault, poor souls. But those of us who have some gumption should duly thank the Lord for it."

"Will you please define what gumption is, Aunt Jimsie?" asked Phil.

"No, I won't, young woman. Any one who has gumption knows what it is, and any one who hasn't can never know what it is. So there is no need of defining it."

The busy days flew by and examinations were over. Anne took High Honors in English. Priscilla took Honors in Classics, and Phil in Mathematics. Stella obtained a good all-round showing. Then came Convocation.

"This is what I would once have called an epoch in my life," said Anne, as she took Roy's violets out of their box and gazed at them thoughtfully. She meant to carry them, of course, but her eyes wandered to another box on her table. It was filled with lilies-of-the-valley, as fresh and fragrant as those which bloomed in the Green Gables yard when June came to Avonlea. Gilbert Blythe's card lay beside it.

Anne wondered why Gilbert should have sent her flowers for Convocation. She had seen very little of him during the past winter. He had come to Patty's Place only one Friday evening since the Christmas holidays, and they rarely met elsewhere. She knew he was studying very hard, aiming at High Honors and the Cooper Prize, and he took little part in the social doings of Redmond. Anne's own winter had been quite gay socially. She had seen a good deal of the Gardners; she and Dorothy were very intimate; college circles expected the announcement of her engagement to Roy any day. Anne expected it herself. Yet just before she left Patty's Place for Convocation she flung Roy's violets aside and put Gilbert's lilies-of-the-valley in their place. She could not have told why she did it. Somehow, old Avonlea days and dreams and friendships seemed very close to her in this attainment of her long-cherished ambitions. She and Gilbert had once pictured out merrily the day on which they should be capped and gowned graduates in Arts. The wonderful day had come and Roy's violets had no place in it. Only her old friend's flowers seemed to belong to this fruition of old-blossoming hopes which he had once shared.

For years this day had beckoned and allured to her; but when it came the one single, keen, abiding memory it left with her was not that of the breathless moment when the stately president of Redmond gave her cap and diploma and hailed her B.A.; it was not of the flash in Gilbert's eyes when he saw her lilies, nor the puzzled pained glance Roy gave her as he passed her on the platform. It was not of Aline Gardner's condescending congratulations, or Dorothy's ardent, impulsive good wishes. It was of one strange, unaccountable pang that spoiled this long-expected day for her and left in it a certain faint but enduring flavor of bitterness.

The Arts graduates gave a graduation dance that night. When Anne dressed for it she tossed aside the pearl beads she usually wore and took from her trunk the small box that had come to Green Gables on Christmas day. In it was a thread-like gold chain with a tiny pink enamel heart as a pendant. On the accompanying card was written, "With all good wishes from your old chum, Gilbert." Anne, laughing over the memory the enamel heart conjured up the fatal day when Gilbert had called her "Carrots" and vainly tried to make his peace with a pink candy heart, had written him a nice little note of thanks. But she had never worn the trinket. Tonight she fastened it about her white throat with a dreamy smile.

She and Phil walked to Redmond together. Anne walked in silence; Phil chattered of many things. Suddenly she said,

"I heard today that Gilbert Blythe's engagement to Christine Stuart was to be announced as soon as Convocation was over. Did you hear anything of it?"

"No," said Anne.

"I think it's true," said Phil lightly.

Anne did not speak. In the darkness she felt her face burning. She slipped her hand inside her collar and caught at the gold chain. One energetic twist and it gave way. Anne thrust the broken trinket into her pocket. Her hands were trembling and her eyes were smarting.

But she was the gayest of all the gay revellers that night, and told Gilbert unregretfully that her card was full when he came to ask her for a dance. Afterwards, when she sat with the girls before the dying embers at Patty's Place, removing the spring chilliness from their satin skins, none chatted more blithely than she of the day's events.

"Moody Spurgeon MacPherson called here tonight after you left," said Aunt Jamesina, who had sat up to keep the fire on. "He didn't know about the graduation dance. That boy ought to sleep with a rubber band around his head to train his ears not to stick out. I had a beau once who did that and it improved him immensely. It was I who suggested it to him and he took my advice, but he never forgave me for it."

"Moody Spurgeon is a very serious young man," yawned Priscilla. "He is concerned with graver matters than his ears. He is going to be a minister, you know."

"Well, I suppose the Lord doesn't regard the ears of a man," said Aunt Jamesina gravely, dropping all further criticism of Moody Spurgeon. Aunt Jamesina had a proper respect for the cloth even in the case of an unfledged parson.

Chapter XXXVIII - False Dawn

"Just imagine—this night week I'll be in Avonlea—delightful thought!" said Anne, bending over the box in which she was packing Mrs. Rachel Lynde's quilts. "But just imagine—this night week I'll be gone forever from Patty's Place—horrible thought!"

"I wonder if the ghost of all our laughter will echo through the maiden dreams of Miss Patty and Miss Maria," speculated Phil.

Miss Patty and Miss Maria were coming home, after having trotted over most of the habitable globe.

"We'll be back the second week in May" wrote Miss Patty. "I expect Patty's Place will seem rather small after the Hall of the Kings at Karnak, but I never did like big places to live in. And I'll be glad enough to be home again. When you start traveling late in life you're apt to do too much of it because you know you haven't much time left, and it's a thing that grows on you. I'm afraid Maria will never be contented again."

"I shall leave here my fancies and dreams to bless the next comer," said Anne, looking around the blue room wistfully—her pretty blue room where she had spent three such happy years. She had knelt at its window to pray and had bent from it to watch the sunset behind the pines. She had heard the autumn raindrops beating against it and had welcomed the spring robins at its sill. She wondered if old dreams could haunt rooms—if, when one left forever the room where she had joyed and suffered and laughed and wept, something of her, intangible and invisible, yet nonetheless real, did not remain behind like a voiceful memory.

"I think," said Phil, "that a room where one dreams and grieves and rejoices and lives becomes inseparably connected with those processes and acquires a personality of its own. I am sure if I came into this room fifty years from now it would say 'Anne, Anne' to me. What nice times we've had here, honey! What chats and jokes and good chummy jamborees! Oh, dear me! I'm to marry Jo in June and I know I will be rapturously happy. But just now I feel as if I wanted this lovely Redmond life to go on forever."

"I'm unreasonable enough just now to wish that, too," admitted Anne. "No matter what deeper joys may come to us later on we'll never again have just the same delightful, irresponsible existence we've had here. It's over forever, Phil."

"What are you going to do with Rusty?" asked Phil, as that privileged pussy padded into the room.

"I am going to take him home with me and Joseph and the Sarah-cat," announced Aunt Jamesina, following Rusty. "It would be a shame to separate those cats now that they have learned to live together. It's a hard lesson for cats and humans to learn."

"I'm sorry to part with Rusty," said Anne regretfully, "but it would be no use to take him to Green Gables. Marilla detests cats, and Davy would tease his life out. Besides, I don't suppose I'll be home very long. I've been offered the principalship of the Summerside High School."

"Are you going to accept it?" asked Phil.

"I—I haven't decided yet," answered Anne, with a confused flush.

Phil nodded understandingly. Naturally Anne's plans could not be settled until Roy had spoken. He would soon—there was no doubt of that. And there was no doubt that Anne would say "yes" when he said "Will you please?" Anne herself regarded the state of affairs with a seldom-ruffled complacency. She was deeply in love with Roy. True, it was not just what she had imagined love to be. But was anything in life, Anne asked herself wearily, like one's imagination of it? It was the old diamond disillusion of childhood repeated—the same disappointment she had felt when she had first seen the chill sparkle instead of the purple splendor she had anticipated. "That's not my idea of a diamond," she had said. But Roy was a dear fellow and they would be very happy together, even if some indefinable zest was missing out of life. When Roy came down that evening and asked Anne to walk in the park every one at Patty's Place knew what he had come to say; and every one knew, or thought they knew, what Anne's answer would be.

"Anne is a very fortunate girl," said Aunt Jamesina.

"I suppose so," said Stella, shrugging her shoulders. "Roy is a nice fellow and all that. But there's really nothing in him."

"That sounds very like a jealous remark, Stella Maynard," said Aunt Jamesina rebukingly.

"It does—but I am not jealous," said Stella calmly. "I love Anne and I like Roy. Everybody says she is making a brilliant match, and even Mrs. Gardner thinks her charming now. It all sounds as if it were made in heaven, but I have my doubts. Make the most of that, Aunt Jamesina."

Roy asked Anne to marry him in the little pavilion on the harbor shore where they had talked on the rainy day of their first meeting. Anne thought it very romantic that he should have chosen that spot. And his proposal was as beautifully worded as if he had copied it, as one of Ruby Gillis' lovers had done, out of a Deportment of Courtship and Marriage. The whole effect was quite flawless. And it was also sincere. There was no doubt that Roy meant what he said. There was no false note to jar the symphony. Anne felt that she ought to be thrilling from head to foot. But she wasn't; she was horribly cool. When Roy paused for his answer she opened her lips to say her fateful yes. And then—she found herself trembling as if she were reeling back from a precipice. To her came one of those moments when we realize, as by a blinding flash of illumination, more than all our previous years have taught us. She pulled her hand from Roy's.

"Oh, I can't marry you—I can't—I can't," she cried, wildly.

Roy turned pale—and also looked rather foolish. He had—small blame to him—felt very sure.

"What do you mean?" he stammered.

"I mean that I can't marry you," repeated Anne desperately. "I thought I could—but I can't."

"Why can't you?" Roy asked more calmly.

"Because—I don't care enough for you."

A crimson streak came into Roy's face.

"So you've just been amusing yourself these two years?" he said slowly.

"No, no, I haven't," gasped poor Anne. Oh, how could she explain? She COULDN'T explain. There are some things that cannot be explained. "I did think I cared—truly I did—but I know now I don't."

"You have ruined my life," said Roy bitterly.

"Forgive me," pleaded Anne miserably, with hot cheeks and stinging eyes.

Roy turned away and stood for a few minutes looking out seaward. When he came back to Anne, he was very pale again.

"You can give me no hope?" he said.

Anne shook her head mutely.

"Then—good-bye," said Roy. "I can't understand it—I can't believe you are not the woman I've believed you to be. But reproaches are idle between us. You are the only woman I can ever love. I thank you for your friendship, at least. Good-bye, Anne."

"Good-bye," faltered Anne. When Roy had gone she sat for a long time in the pavilion, watching a white mist creeping subtly and remorselessly landward up the harbor. It was her hour of humiliation and self-contempt and shame. Their waves went over her. And yet, underneath it all, was a queer sense of recovered freedom.

She slipped into Patty's Place in the dusk and escaped to her room. But Phil was there on the window seat.

"Wait," said Anne, flushing to anticipate the scene. "Wait til you hear what I have to say. Phil, Roy asked me to marry him-and I refused."

"You—you REFUSED him?" said Phil blankly.

"Yes."

"Anne Shirley, are you in your senses?"

"I think so," said Anne wearily. "Oh, Phil, don't scold me. You don't under-stand."

"I certainly don't understand. You've encouraged Roy Gardner in every way for two years—and now you tell me you've refused him. Then you've just been flirting scandalously with him. Anne, I couldn't have believed it of YOU."

"I WASN'T flirting with him—I honestly thought I cared up to the last minute—and then—well, I just knew I NEVER could marry him."

"I suppose," said Phil cruelly, "that you intended to marry him for his money, and then your better self rose up and prevented you."

"I DIDN'T. I never thought about his money. Oh, I can't explain it to you any more than I could to him."

"Well, I certainly think you have treated Roy shamefully," said Phil in exasperation. "He's handsome and clever and rich and good. What more do you want?"

"I want some one who BELONGS in my life. He doesn't. I was swept off my feet at first by his good looks and knack of paying romantic compliments; and later on I thought I MUST be in love because he was my dark-eyed ideal."

"I am bad enough for not knowing my own mind, but you are worse," said Phil.

"*I* DO know my own mind," protested Anne. "The trouble is, my mind changes and then I have to get acquainted with it all over again."

"Well, I suppose there is no use in saying anything to you."

"There is no need, Phil. I'm in the dust. This has spoiled everything backwards. I can never think of Redmond days without recalling the humiliation of this evening. Roy despises me—and you despise me—and I despise myself."

"You poor darling," said Phil, melting. "Just come here and let me comfort you. I've no right to scold you. I'd have married Alec or Alonzo if I hadn't met Jo. Oh, Anne, things are so mixed-up in real life. They aren't clear-cut and trimmed off, as they are in novels."

"I hope that NO one will ever again ask me to marry him as long as I live," sobbed poor Anne, devoutly believing that she meant it.

Chapter XXXIX - Deals with Weddings

Anne felt that life partook of the nature of an anticlimax during the first few weeks after her return to Green Gables. She missed the merry comradeship of Patty's Place. She had dreamed some brilliant dreams during the past winter and now they lay in the dust around her. In her present mood of self-disgust, she could not immediately begin dreaming again. And she discovered that, while solitude with dreams is glorious, solitude without them has few charms.

She had not seen Roy again after their painful parting in the park pavilion; but Dorothy came to see her before she left Kingsport.

"I'm awfully sorry you won't marry Roy," she said. "I did want you for a sister. But you are quite right. He would bore you to death. I love him, and he is a dear sweet boy, but really he isn't a bit interesting. He looks as if he ought to be, but he isn't."

"This won't spoil OUR friendship, will it, Dorothy?" Anne had asked wistfully.

"No, indeed. You're too good to lose. If I can't have you for a sister I mean to keep you as a chum anyway. And don't fret over Roy. He is feeling terribly just now—I have to listen to his outpourings every day—but he'll get over it. He always does."

"Oh—ALWAYS?" said Anne with a slight change of voice. "So he has 'got over it' before?"

"Dear me, yes," said Dorothy frankly. "Twice before. And he raved to me just the same both times. Not that the others actually refused him—they simply announced their engagements to some one else. Of course, when he met you he vowed to me that he had never really loved before—that the previous affairs had been merely boyish fancies. But I don't think you need worry."

Anne decided not to worry. Her feelings were a mixture of relief and resentment. Roy had certainly told her she was the only one he had ever loved. No doubt he believed it. But it was a comfort to feel that she had not, in all likelihood, ruined his life. There were other goddesses, and Roy, according to Dorothy, must needs be worshipping at some shrine. Nevertheless, life was stripped of several more illusions, and Anne began to think drearily that it seemed rather bare.

She came down from the porch gable on the evening of her return with a sorrowful face.

"What has happened to the old Snow Queen, Marilla?"

"Oh, I knew you'd feel bad over that," said Marilla. "I felt bad myself. That tree was there ever since I was a young girl. It blew down in the big gale we had in March. It was rotten at the core."

"I'll miss it so," grieved Anne. "The porch gable doesn't seem the same room without it. I'll never look from its window again without a sense of loss. And oh, I never came home to Green Gables before that Diana wasn't here to welcome me."

"Diana has something else to think of just now," said Mrs. Lynde significantly.

"Well, tell me all the Avonlea news," said Anne, sitting down on the porch steps, where the evening sunshine fell over her hair in a fine golden rain.

"There isn't much news except what we've wrote you," said Mrs. Lynde. "I suppose you haven't heard that Simon Fletcher broke his leg last week. It's a great thing for his family. They're getting a hundred things done that they've always wanted to do but couldn't as long as he was about, the old crank."

"He came of an aggravating family," remarked Marilla.

"Aggravating? Well, rather! His mother used to get up in prayer-meeting and tell all her children's shortcomings and ask prayers for them. 'Course it made them mad, and worse than ever."

"You haven't told Anne the news about Jane," suggested Marilla.

"Oh, Jane," sniffed Mrs. Lynde. "Well," she conceded grudgingly, "Jane Andrews is home from the West—came last week—and she's going to be married to a Winnipeg millionaire. You may be sure Mrs. Harmon lost no time in telling it far and wide."

"Dear old Jane—I'm so glad," said Anne heartily. "She deserves the good things of life."

"Oh, I ain't saying anything against Jane. She's a nice enough girl. But she isn't in the millionaire class, and you'll find there's not much to recommend that man but his money, that's what. Mrs. Harmon says he's an Englishman who has made money in mines but *I* believe he'll turn out to be a Yankee. He certainly must have money, for he has just showered Jane with jewelry. Her engagement ring is a diamond cluster so big that it looks like a plaster on Jane's fat paw."

Mrs. Lynde could not keep some bitterness out of her tone. Here was Jane Andrews, that plain little plodder, engaged to a millionaire, while Anne, it seemed, was not yet bespoken by any one, rich or poor. And Mrs. Harmon Andrews did brag insufferably.

"What has Gilbert Blythe been doing to at college?" asked Marilla. "I saw him when he came home last week, and he is so pale and thin I hardly knew him."

"He studied very hard last winter," said Anne. "You know he took High Honors in Classics and the Cooper Prize. It hasn't been taken for five years! So I think he's rather run down. We're all a little tired."

"Anyhow, you're a B.A. and Jane Andrews isn't and never will be," said Mrs. Lynde, with gloomy satisfaction.

A few evenings later Anne went down to see Jane, but the latter was away in Charlottetown—"getting sewing done," Mrs. Harmon informed Anne proudly. "Of course an Avonlea dressmaker wouldn't do for Jane under the circumstances."

"I've heard something very nice about Jane," said Anne.

"Yes, Jane has done pretty well, even if she isn't a B.A.," said Mrs. Harmon, with a slight toss of her head. "Mr. Inglis is worth millions, and they're going to Europe on their wedding tour. When they come back they'll live in a perfect mansion of marble in Winnipeg. Jane has only one trouble—she can cook so well and her husband won't let her cook. He is so rich he hires his cooking done. They're going to keep a cook and two other maids and a coachman and a man-of-all-work. But what about YOU, Anne? I don't hear anything of your being married, after all your college-going."

"Oh," laughed Anne, "I am going to be an old maid. I really can't find any one to suit me." It was rather wicked of her. She deliberately meant to remind Mrs. Andrews that if she became an old maid it was not because she had not had at least one chance of marriage. But Mrs. Harmon took swift revenge.

"Well, the over-particular girls generally get left, I notice. And what's this I hear about Gilbert Blythe being engaged to a Miss Stuart? Charlie Sloane tells me she is perfectly beautiful. Is it true?"

"I don't know if it is true that he is engaged to Miss Stuart," replied Anne, with Spartan composure, "but it is certainly true that she is very lovely."

"I once thought you and Gilbert would have made a match of it," said Mrs. Harmon. "If you don't take care, Anne, all of your beaux will slip through your fingers."

Anne decided not to continue her duel with Mrs. Harmon. You could not fence with an antagonist who met rapier thrust with blow of battle axe.

"Since Jane is away," she said, rising haughtily, "I don't think I can stay longer this morning. I'll come down when she comes home."

"Do," said Mrs. Harmon effusively. "Jane isn't a bit proud. She just means to associate with her old friends the same as ever. She'll be real glad to see you."

Jane's millionaire arrived the last of May and carried her off in a blaze of splendor. Mrs. Lynde was spitefully gratified to find that Mr. Inglis was every day of forty, and short and thin and grayish. Mrs. Lynde did not spare him in her enumeration of his shortcomings, you may be sure.

"It will take all his gold to gild a pill like him, that's what," said Mrs. Rachel solemnly.

"He looks kind and good-hearted," said Anne loyally, "and I'm sure he thinks the world of Jane."

"Humph!" said Mrs. Rachel.

Phil Gordon was married the next week and Anne went over to Bolingbroke to be her bridesmaid. Phil made a dainty fairy of a bride, and the Rev. Jo was so radiant in his happiness that nobody thought him plain.

"We're going for a lovers' saunter through the land of Evangeline," said Phil, "and then we'll settle down on Patterson Street. Mother thinks it is terrible—she thinks Jo might at least take a church in a decent place. But the wilderness of the Patterson slums will blossom like the rose for me if Jo is there. Oh, Anne, I'm so happy my heart aches with it."

Anne was always glad in the happiness of her friends; but it is sometimes a little lonely to be surrounded everywhere by a happiness that is not your own. And it was just the same when she went back to Avonlea. This time it was Diana who was bathed in the wonderful glory that comes to a woman when her first-born is laid beside her. Anne looked at the white young mother with a certain awe that had never entered into her feelings for Diana before. Could this pale woman with the rapture in her eyes be the little black-curled, rosy-cheeked Diana she had played with in vanished schooldays? It gave her a queer desolate feeling that she herself somehow belonged only in those past years and had no business in the present at all.

"Isn't he perfectly beautiful?" said Diana proudly.

The little fat fellow was absurdly like Fred—just as round, just as red. Anne really could not say conscientiously that she thought him beautiful, but she vowed sincerely that he was sweet and kissable and altogether delightful.

"Before he came I wanted a girl, so that I could call her ANNE," said Diana. "But now that little Fred is here I wouldn't exchange him for a million girls. He just COULDN'T have been anything but his own precious self."

"'Every little baby is the sweetest and the best,'" quoted Mrs. Allan gaily. "If little Anne HAD come you'd have felt just the same about her."

Mrs. Allan was visiting in Avonlea, for the first time since leaving it. She was as gay and sweet and sympathetic as ever. Her old girl friends had welcomed her back rapturously. The reigning minister's wife was an estimable lady, but she was not exactly a kindred spirit.

"I can hardly wait till he gets old enough to talk," sighed Diana. "I just long to hear him say 'mother.' And oh, I'm determined that his first memory of me shall be a nice one. The first memory I have of my mother is of her slapping me for something I had done. I am sure I deserved it, and mother was always a good mother and I love her dearly. But I do wish my first memory of her was nicer."

"I have just one memory of my mother and it is the sweetest of all my memories," said Mrs. Allan. "I was five years old, and I had been allowed to go to school one day with my two older sisters. When school came out my sisters went home in different groups, each supposing I was with the other. Instead I had run off with a little girl I had played with at recess. We went to her home, which was near the school, and began making mud pies. We were having a glorious time when my older sister arrived, breathless and angry.

"'You naughty girl' she cried, snatching my reluctant hand and dragging me along with her. 'Come home this minute. Oh, you're going to catch it! Mother is awful cross. She is going to give you a good whipping.'

"I had never been whipped. Dread and terror filled my poor little heart. I have never been so miserable in my life as I was on that walk home. I had not meant to be naughty. Phemy Cameron had asked me to go home with her and I had not known it was wrong to go. And now I was to be whipped for it. When we got home my sister dragged me into the kitchen where mother was sitting by the fire in the twilight. My poor wee legs were trembling so that I could hardly stand. And mother—mother just took me up in her arms, without one word of rebuke or harshness, kissed me and held me close to her heart. 'I was so frightened you were lost, darling,' she said tenderly. I could see the love shining in her eyes as she looked down on me. She never scolded or reproached me for what I had done— only told me I must never go away again without asking permission. She died very soon afterwards. That is the only memory I have of her. Isn't it a beautiful one?"

Anne felt lonelier than ever as she walked home, going by way of the Birch Path and Willowmere. She had not walked that way for many moons. It was a darkly-purple bloomy night. The air was heavy with blossom fragrance—almost too heavy. The cloyed senses recoiled from it as from an overfull cup. The birches of the path had grown from the fairy saplings of old to big trees. Everything had changed. Anne felt that she would be glad when the summer was over and she was away at work again. Perhaps life would not seem so empty then.

> "'I've tried the world—it wears no more
> The coloring of romance it wore,'"

sighed Anne—and was straightway much comforted by the romance in the idea of the world being denuded of romance!

Chapter XL - A Book of Revelation

The Irvings came back to Echo Lodge for the summer, and Anne spent a happy three weeks there in July. Miss Lavendar had not changed; Charlotta the Fourth was a very grown-up young lady now, but still adored Anne sincerely.

"When all's said and done, Miss Shirley, ma'am, I haven't seen any one in Boston that's equal to you," she said frankly.

Paul was almost grown up, too. He was sixteen, his chestnut curls had given place to close-cropped brown locks, and he was more interested in football than fairies. But the bond between him and his old teacher still held. Kindred spirits alone do not change with changing years.

It was a wet, bleak, cruel evening in July when Anne came back to Green Gables. One of the fierce summer storms which sometimes sweep over the gulf was ravaging the sea. As Anne came in the first raindrops dashed against the panes.

"Was that Paul who brought you home?" asked Marilla. "Why didn't you make him stay all night. It's going to be a wild evening."

"He'll reach Echo Lodge before the rain gets very heavy, I think. Anyway, he wanted to go back tonight. Well, I've had a splendid visit, but I'm glad to see you dear folks again. 'East, west, hame's best.' Davy, have you been growing again lately?"

"I've growed a whole inch since you left," said Davy proudly. "I'm as tall as Milty Boulter now. Ain't I glad. He'll have to stop crowing about being bigger. Say, Anne, did you know that Gilbert Blythe is dying?" Anne stood quite silent and motionless, looking at Davy. Her face had gone so white that Marilla thought she was going to faint.

"Davy, hold your tongue," said Mrs. Rachel angrily. "Anne, don't look like that—DON'T LOOK LIKE THAT! We didn't mean to tell you so suddenly."

"Is—it—true?" asked Anne in a voice that was not hers.

"Gilbert is very ill," said Mrs. Lynde gravely. "He took down with typhoid fever just after you left for Echo Lodge. Did you never hear of it?"

"No," said that unknown voice.

"It was a very bad case from the start. The doctor said he'd been terribly run down. They've a trained nurse and everything's been done. DON'T look like that, Anne. While there's life there's hope."

"Mr. Harrison was here this evening and he said they had no hope of him," re-iterated Davy.

Marilla, looking old and worn and tired, got up and marched Davy grimly out of the kitchen.

"Oh, DON'T look so, dear," said Mrs. Rachel, putting her kind old arms about the pallid girl. "I haven't given up hope, indeed I haven't. He's got the Blythe constitution in his favor, that's what."

Anne gently put Mrs. Lynde's arms away from her, walked blindly across the kitchen, through the hall, up the stairs to her old room. At its window she knelt down, staring out unseeingly. It was very dark. The rain was beating down over the shivering fields. The Haunted Woods was full of the groans of mighty trees wrung in the tempest, and the air throbbed with the thunderous crash of billows on the distant shore. And Gilbert was dying!

There is a book of Revelation in every one's life, as there is in the Bible. Anne read hers that bitter night, as she kept her agonized vigil through the hours of storm and darkness. She loved Gilbert—had always loved him! She knew that now. She knew that she could no more cast him out of her life without agony than she could have cut off her right hand and cast it from her. And the knowledge had come too late—too late even for the bitter solace of being with him at the last. If she had not been so blind—so foolish—she would have had the right to go to him now. But he would never know that she loved him—he would go away from this life thinking that she did not care. Oh, the black years of emptiness stretching before her! She could not live through them—she could not! She cowered down by her window and wished, for the first time in her gay young life, that she could die, too. If Gilbert went away from her, without one word or sign or message, she could not live. Nothing was of any value without him. She belonged to him and he to her. In her hour of supreme agony she had no doubt of that. He did not love Christine Stuart—never had loved Christine Stuart. Oh, what a fool she had been not to realize what the bond was that had held her to Gilbert—to think that the flattered fancy she had felt for Roy Gardner had been love. And now she must pay for her folly as for a crime.

Mrs. Lynde and Marilla crept to her door before they went to bed, shook their heads doubtfully at each other over the silence, and went away. The storm raged all night, but when the dawn came it was spent. Anne saw a fairy fringe of light on the skirts of darkness. Soon the eastern hilltops had a fire-shot ruby rim. The clouds rolled themselves away into great, soft, white masses on the horizon; the sky gleamed blue and silvery. A hush fell over the world.

Anne rose from her knees and crept downstairs. The freshness of the rain-wind blew against her white face as she went out into the yard, and cooled her dry, burning eyes. A merry rollicking whistle was lilting up the lane. A moment later Pacifique Buote came in sight.

Anne's physical strength suddenly failed her. If she had not clutched at a low willow bough she would have fallen. Pacifique was George Fletcher's hired man, and George Fletcher lived next door to the Blythes. Mrs. Fletcher was Gilbert's aunt. Pacifique would know if—if—Pacifique would know what there was to be known.

Pacifique strode sturdily on along the red lane, whistling. He did not see Anne. She made three futile attempts to call him. He was almost past before she succeeded in making her quivering lips call, "Pacifique!"

Pacifique turned with a grin and a cheerful good morning.

"Pacifique," said Anne faintly, "did you come from George Fletcher's this morning?"

"Sure," said Pacifique amiably. "I got de word las' night dat my fader, he was seeck. It was so stormy dat I couldn't go den, so I start vair early dis mornin'. I'm goin' troo de woods for short cut."

"Did you hear how Gilbert Blythe was this morning?" Anne's desperation drove her to the question. Even the worst would be more endurable than this hideous suspense.

"He's better," said Pacifique. "He got de turn las' night. De doctor say he'll be all right now dis soon while. Had close shave, dough! Dat boy, he jus' keel himself at college. Well, I mus' hurry. De old man, he'll be in hurry to see me."

Pacifique resumed his walk and his whistle. Anne gazed after him with eyes where joy was driving out the strained anguish of the night. He was a very lank, very ragged, very homely youth. But in her sight he was as beautiful as those who bring good tidings on the mountains. Never, as long as she lived, would Anne see Pacifique's brown, round, black-eyed face without a warm remembrance of the moment when he had given to her the oil of joy for mourning.

Long after Pacifique's gay whistle had faded into the phantom of music and then into silence far up under the maples of Lover's Lane Anne stood under the willows, tasting the poignant sweetness of life when some great dread has been removed from it. The morning was a cup filled with mist and glamor. In the corner near her was a rich surprise of new-blown, crystal-dewed roses. The trills and trickles of song from the birds in the big tree above her seemed in perfect accord with her mood. A sentence from a very old, very true, very wonderful Book came to her lips,

"Weeping may endure for a night but joy cometh in the morning."

XLI - Love Takes Up the Glass of Time

"I've come up to ask you to go for one of our old-time rambles through September woods and 'over hills where spices grow,' this afternoon," said Gilbert, coming suddenly around the porch corner. "Suppose we visit Hester Gray's garden."

Anne, sitting on the stone step with her lap full of a pale, filmy, green stuff, looked up rather blankly.

"Oh, I wish I could," she said slowly, "but I really can't, Gilbert. I'm going to Alice Penhallow's wedding this evening, you know. I've got to do something to this dress, and by the time it's finished I'll have to get ready. I'm so sorry. I'd love to go."

"Well, can you go tomorrow afternoon, then?" asked Gilbert, apparently not much disappointed.

"Yes, I think so."

"In that case I shall hie me home at once to do something I should otherwise have to do tomorrow. So Alice Penhallow is to be married tonight. Three weddings for you in one summer, Anne—Phil's, Alice's, and Jane's. I'll never forgive Jane for not inviting me to her wedding."

"You really can't blame her when you think of the tremendous Andrews connection who had to be invited. The house could hardly hold them all. I was only bidden by grace of being Jane's old chum—at least on Jane's part. I think Mrs. Harmon's motive for inviting me was to let me see Jane's surpassing gorgeousness."

"Is it true that she wore so many diamonds that you couldn't tell where the diamonds left off and Jane began?"

Anne laughed.

"She certainly wore a good many. What with all the diamonds and white satin and tulle and lace and roses and orange blossoms, prim little Jane was almost lost to sight. But she was VERY happy, and so was Mr. Inglis—and so was Mrs. Harmon."

"Is that the dress you're going to wear tonight?" asked Gilbert, looking down at the fluffs and frills.

"Yes. Isn't it pretty? And I shall wear starflowers in my hair. The Haunted Wood is full of them this summer."

Gilbert had a sudden vision of Anne, arrayed in a frilly green gown, with the virginal curves of arms and throat slipping out of it, and white stars shining against the coils of her ruddy hair. The vision made him catch his breath. But he turned lightly away.

"Well, I'll be up tomorrow. Hope you'll have a nice time tonight."

Anne looked after him as he strode away, and sighed. Gilbert was friendly—very friendly—far too friendly. He had come quite often to Green Gables after his recovery, and something of their old comradeship had returned. But Anne no longer found it satisfying. The rose of love made the blossom of friendship pale and scentless by contrast. And Anne had again begun to doubt if Gilbert now felt anything for her but friendship. In the common light of common day her radiant certainty of that rapt morning had faded. She was haunted by a miserable fear that her mistake could never be rectified. It was quite likely that it was Christine whom Gilbert loved after all. Perhaps he was even engaged to her. Anne tried to put all unsettling hopes out of her heart, and reconcile herself to a future where work and ambition must take the place of love. She could do good, if not noble, work as a teacher; and the success her little sketches were beginning to meet with in certain editorial sanctums augured well for her budding literary dreams. But—but—Anne picked up her green dress and sighed again.

When Gilbert came the next afternoon he found Anne waiting for him, fresh as the dawn and fair as a star, after all the gaiety of the preceding night. She wore a green dress—not the one she had worn to the wedding, but an old one which Gilbert had told her at a Redmond reception he liked especially. It was just the shade of green that brought out the rich tints of her hair, and the starry gray of her eyes and the iris-like delicacy of her skin. Gilbert, glancing at her sideways as they walked along a shadowy woodpath, thought she had never looked so lovely. Anne, glancing sideways at Gilbert, now and then, thought how much older he looked since his illness. It was as if he had put boyhood behind him forever.

The day was beautiful and the way was beautiful. Anne was almost sorry when they reached Hester Gray's garden, and sat down on the old bench. But it was beautiful there, too—as beautiful as it had been on the faraway day of the Golden Picnic, when Diana and Jane and Priscilla and she had found it. Then it had been lovely with narcissus and violets; now golden rod had kindled its fairy torches in the corners and asters dotted it bluely. The call of the brook came up through the woods from the valley of birches with all its old allurement; the mellow air was full of the purr of the sea; beyond were fields rimmed by fences bleached silvery gray in the suns of many summers, and long hills scarfed with the shadows of autumnal clouds; with the blowing of the west wind old dreams returned.

"I think," said Anne softly, "that 'the land where dreams come true' is in the blue haze yonder, over that little valley."

"Have you any unfulfilled dreams, Anne?" asked Gilbert.

Something in his tone—something she had not heard since that miserable evening in the orchard at Patty's Place—made Anne's heart beat wildly. But she made answer lightly.

"Of course. Everybody has. It wouldn't do for us to have all our dreams fulfilled. We would be as good as dead if we had nothing left to dream about. What a delicious aroma that low-descending sun is extracting from the asters and ferns. I wish we could see perfumes as well as smell them. I'm sure they would be very beautiful."

Gilbert was not to be thus sidetracked.

"I have a dream," he said slowly. "I persist in dreaming it, although it has often seemed to me that it could never come true. I dream of a home with a hearth-fire in it, a cat and dog, the footsteps of friends—and YOU!"

Anne wanted to speak but she could find no words. Happiness was breaking over her like a wave. It almost frightened her.

"I asked you a question over two years ago, Anne. If I ask it again today will you give me a different answer?"

Still Anne could not speak. But she lifted her eyes, shining with all the love-rapture of countless generations, and looked into his for a moment. He wanted no other answer.

They lingered in the old garden until twilight, sweet as dusk in Eden must have been, crept over it. There was so much to talk over and recall—things said and done and heard and thought and felt and misunderstood.

"I thought you loved Christine Stuart," Anne told him, as reproachfully as if she had not given him every reason to suppose that she loved Roy Gardner.

Gilbert laughed boyishly.

"Christine was engaged to somebody in her home town. I knew it and she knew I knew it. When her brother graduated he told me his sister was coming to Kingsport the next winter to take music, and asked me if I would look after her a bit, as she knew no one and would be very lonely. So I did. And then I liked Christine for her own sake. She is one of the nicest girls I've ever known. I knew college gossip credited us with being in love with each other. I didn't care. Nothing mattered much to me for a time there, after you told me you could never love me, Anne. There was nobody else—there never could be anybody else for me but you. I've loved you ever since that day you broke your slate over my head in school."

"I don't see how you could keep on loving me when I was such a little fool," said Anne.

"Well, I tried to stop," said Gilbert frankly, "not because I thought you what you call yourself, but because I felt sure there was no chance for me after Gardner came on the scene. But I couldn't—and I can't tell you, either, what it's meant to me these two years to believe you were going to marry him, and be told every week by some busybody that your engagement was on the point of being announced. I believed it until one blessed day when I was sitting up after the fever. I got a letter from Phil Gordon—Phil Blake, rather—in which she told me there was really nothing between you and Roy, and advised me to 'try again.' Well, the doctor was amazed at my rapid recovery after that."

Anne laughed—then shivered.

"I can never forget the night I thought you were dying, Gilbert. Oh, I knew—I KNEW then—and I thought it was too late."

"But it wasn't, sweetheart. Oh, Anne, this makes up for everything, doesn't it? Let's resolve to keep this day sacred to perfect beauty all our lives for the gift it has given us."

"It's the birthday of our happiness," said Anne softly. "I've always loved this old garden of Hester Gray's, and now it will be dearer than ever."

"But I'll have to ask you to wait a long time, Anne," said Gilbert sadly. "It will be three years before I'll finish my medical course. And even then there will be no diamond sunbursts and marble halls."

Anne laughed.

"I don't want sunbursts and marble halls. I just want YOU. You see I'm quite as shameless as Phil about it. Sunbursts and marble halls may be all very well, but there is more 'scope for imagination' without them. And as for the waiting, that doesn't matter. We'll just be happy, waiting and working for each other—and dreaming. Oh, dreams will be very sweet now."

Gilbert drew her close to him and kissed her. Then they walked home together in the dusk, crowned king and queen in the bridal realm of love, along winding paths fringed with the sweetest flowers that ever bloomed, and over haunted meadows where winds of hope and memory blew.

ANNE'S HOUSE OF DREAMS

"To Laura, in memory of the olden time."

CHAPTER 1 - IN THE GARRET OF GREEN GABLES

"Thanks be, I'm done with geometry, learning or teaching it," said Anne Shirley, a trifle vindictively, as she thumped a somewhat battered volume of Euclid into a big chest of books, banged the lid in triumph, and sat down upon it, looking at Diana Wright across the Green Gables garret, with gray eyes that were like a morning sky.

The garret was a shadowy, suggestive, delightful place, as all garrets should be. Through the open window, by which Anne sat, blew the sweet, scented, sun-warm air of the August afternoon; outside, poplar boughs rustled and tossed in the wind; beyond them were the woods, where Lover's Lane wound its enchanted path, and the old apple orchard which still bore its rosy harvests munificently. And, over all, was a great mountain range of snowy clouds in the blue southern sky. Through the other window was glimpsed a distant, white-capped, blue sea—the beautiful St. Lawrence Gulf, on which floats, like a jewel, Abegweit, whose softer, sweeter Indian name has long been forsaken for the more prosaic one of Prince Edward Island.

Diana Wright, three years older than when we last saw her, had grown somewhat matronly in the intervening time. But her eyes were as black and brilliant, her cheeks as rosy, and her dimples as enchanting, as in the long-ago days when she and Anne Shirley had vowed eternal friendship in the garden at Orchard Slope. In her arms she held a small, sleeping, black-curled creature, who for two happy years had been known to the world of Avonlea as "Small Anne Cordelia." Avonlea folks knew why Diana had called her Anne, of course, but Avonlea folks were puzzled by the Cordelia. There had never been a Cordelia in the Wright or Barry connections. Mrs. Harmon Andrews said she supposed Diana had found the name in some trashy novel, and wondered that Fred hadn't more sense than to allow it. But Diana and Anne smiled at each other. They knew how Small Anne Cordelia had come by her name.

"You always hated geometry," said Diana with a retrospective smile. "I should think you'd be real glad to be through with teaching, anyhow."

"Oh, I've always liked teaching, apart from geometry. These past three years in Summerside have been very pleasant ones. Mrs. Harmon Andrews told me when I came home that I wouldn't likely find married life as much better than teaching as I expected. Evidently Mrs. Harmon is of Hamlet's opinion that it may be better to bear the ills that we have than fly to others that we know not of."

Anne's laugh, as blithe and irresistible as of yore, with an added note of sweetness and maturity, rang through the garret. Marilla in the kitchen below, compounding blue plum preserve, heard it and smiled; then sighed to think how seldom that dear laugh would echo through Green Gables in the years to come. Nothing in her life had ever given Marilla so much happiness as the knowledge that Anne was going to marry Gilbert Blythe; but every joy must bring with it its little shadow of sorrow. During the three Summerside years Anne had been home often for vacations and weekends; but, after this, a bi-annual visit would be as much as could be hoped for.

"You needn't let what Mrs. Harmon says worry you," said Diana, with the calm assurance of the four-years matron. "Married life has its ups and downs, of course. You mustn't expect that everything will always go smoothly. But I can assure you, Anne, that it's a happy life, when you're married to the right man."

Anne smothered a smile. Diana's airs of vast experience always amused her a little.

"I daresay I'll be putting them on too, when I've been married four years," she thought. "Surely my sense of humor will preserve me from it, though."

"Is it settled yet where you are going to live?" asked Diana, cuddling Small Anne Cordelia with the inimitable gesture of motherhood which always sent through Anne's heart, filled with sweet, unuttered dreams and hopes, a thrill that was half pure pleasure and half a strange, ethereal pain.

"Yes. That was what I wanted to tell you when I 'phoned to you to come down today. By the way, I can't realize that we really have telephones in Avonlea now. It sounds so preposterously up-to-date and modernish for this darling, leisurely old place."

"We can thank the A. V. I. S. for them," said Diana. "We should never have got the line if they hadn't taken the matter up and carried it through. There was enough cold water thrown to discourage any society. But they stuck to it, nevertheless. You did a splendid thing for Avonlea when you founded that society, Anne. What fun we did have at our meetings! Will you ever forget the blue hall and Judson Parker's scheme for painting medicine advertisements on his fence?"

"I don't know that I'm wholly grateful to the A. V. I. S. in the matter of the telephone," said Anne. "Oh, I know it's most convenient—even more so than our old device of signalling to each other by flashes of candlelight! And, as Mrs. Rachel says, 'Avonlea must keep up with the procession, that's what.' But somehow I feel as if I didn't want Avonlea spoiled by what Mr. Harrison, when he wants to be witty, calls 'modern inconveniences.' I should like to have it kept always just as it was in the dear old years. That's foolish—and sentimental—and impossible. So I shall immediately become wise and practical and possible. The telephone, as Mr. Harrison concedes, is 'a buster of a good thing'—even if you do know that probably half a dozen interested people are listening along the line."

"That's the worst of it," sighed Diana. "It's so annoying to hear the receivers going down whenever you ring anyone up. They say Mrs. Harmon Andrews insisted that their 'phone should be put in their kitchen just so that she could listen whenever it rang and keep an eye on the dinner at the same time. Today, when you called me, I distinctly heard that queer clock of the Pyes' striking. So no doubt Josie or Gertie was listening."

"Oh, so that is why you said, 'You've got a new clock at Green Gables, haven't you?' I couldn't imagine what you meant. I heard a vicious click as soon as you had spoken. I suppose it was the Pye receiver being hung up with profane energy. Well, never mind the Pyes. As Mrs. Rachel says, 'Pyes they always were and Pyes they always will be, world without end, amen.' I want to talk of pleasanter things. It's all settled as to where my new home shall be."

"Oh, Anne, where? I do hope it's near here."

"No-o-o, that's the drawback. Gilbert is going to settle at Four Winds Harbor— sixty miles from here."

"Sixty! It might as well be six hundred," sighed Diana. "I never can get further from home now than Charlottetown."

"You'll have to come to Four Winds. It's the most beautiful harbor on the Island. There's a little village called Glen St. Mary at its head, and Dr. David Blythe has been practicing there for fifty years. He is Gilbert's great-uncle, you know. He is going to retire, and Gilbert is to take over his practice. Dr. Blythe is going to keep his house, though, so we shall have to find a habitation for ourselves. I don't know yet what it is, or where it will be in reality, but I have a little house o'dreams all furnished in my imagination—a tiny, delightful castle in Spain."

"Where are you going for your wedding tour?" asked Diana.

"Nowhere. Don't look horrified, Diana dearest. You suggest Mrs. Harmon Andrews. She, no doubt, will remark condescendingly that people who can't afford wedding 'towers' are real sensible not to take them; and then she'll remind me that Jane went to Europe for hers. I want to spend MY honeymoon at Four Winds in my own dear house of dreams."

"And you've decided not to have any bridesmaid?"

"There isn't any one to have. You and Phil and Priscilla and Jane all stole a march on me in the matter of marriage; and Stella is teaching in Vancouver. I have no other 'kindred soul' and I won't have a bridesmaid who isn't."

"But you are going to wear a veil, aren't you?" asked Diana, anxiously.

"Yes, indeedy. I shouldn't feel like a bride without one. I remember telling Matthew, that evening when he brought me to Green Gables, that I never expected to be a bride because I was so homely no one would ever want to marry me—unless some foreign missionary did. I had an idea then that foreign missionaries couldn't afford to be finicky in the matter of looks if they wanted a girl to risk her life among cannibals. You should have seen the foreign missionary Priscilla married. He was as handsome and inscrutable as those daydreams we once planned to marry ourselves, Diana; he was the best dressed man I ever met, and he raved over Priscilla's 'ethereal, golden beauty.' But of course there are no cannibals in Japan."

"Your wedding dress is a dream, anyhow," sighed Diana rapturously. "You'll look like a perfect queen in it—you're so tall and slender. How DO you keep so slim, Anne? I'm fatter than ever—I'll soon have no waist at all."

"Stoutness and slimness seem to be matters of predestination," said Anne. "At all events, Mrs. Harmon Andrews can't say to you what she said to me when I came home from Summerside, 'Well, Anne, you're just about as skinny as ever.' It sounds quite romantic to be 'slender,' but 'skinny' has a very different tang."

"Mrs. Harmon has been talking about your trousseau. She admits it's as nice as Jane's, although she says Jane married a millionaire and you are only marrying a 'poor young doctor without a cent to his name.'"

Anne laughed.

"My dresses ARE nice. I love pretty things. I remember the first pretty dress I ever had—the brown gloria Matthew gave me for our school concert. Before that everything I had was so ugly. It seemed to me that I stepped into a new world that night."

"That was the night Gilbert recited 'Bingen on the Rhine,' and looked at you when he said, 'There's another, NOT a sister.' And you were so furious because he put your pink tissue rose in his breast pocket! You didn't much imagine then that you would ever marry him."

"Oh, well, that's another instance of predestination," laughed Anne, as they went down the garret stairs.

CHAPTER 2 - THE HOUSE OF DREAMS

There was more excitement in the air of Green Gables than there had ever been before in all its history. Even Marilla was so excited that she couldn't help showing it—which was little short of being phenomenal.

"There's never been a wedding in this house," she said, half apologetically, to Mrs. Rachel Lynde. "When I was a child I heard an old minister say that a house was not a real home until it had been consecrated by a birth, a wedding and a death. We've had deaths here—my father and mother died here as well as Matthew; and we've even had a birth here. Long ago, just after we moved into this house, we had a married hired man for a little while, and his wife had a baby here. But there's never been a wedding before. It does seem so strange to think of Anne being married. In a way she just seems to me the little girl Matthew brought home here fourteen years ago. I can't realize that she's grown up. I shall never forget what I felt when I saw Matthew bringing in a GIRL. I wonder what became of the boy we would have got if there hadn't been a mistake. I wonder what HIS fate was."

"Well, it was a fortunate mistake," said Mrs. Rachel Lynde, "though, mind you, there was a time I didn't think so—that evening I came up to see Anne and she treated us to such a scene. Many things have changed since then, that's what."

Mrs. Rachel sighed, and then brisked up again. When weddings were in order Mrs. Rachel was ready to let the dead past bury its dead.

"I'm going to give Anne two of my cotton warp spreads," she resumed. "A tobacco-stripe one and an apple-leaf one. She tells me they're getting to be real fashionable again. Well, fashion or no fashion, I don't believe there's anything prettier for a spare-room bed than a nice apple-leaf spread, that's what. I must see about getting them bleached. I've had them sewed up in cotton bags ever since Thomas died, and no doubt they're an awful color. But there's a month yet, and dew-bleaching will work wonders."

Only a month! Marilla sighed and then said proudly:

"I'm giving Anne that half dozen braided rugs I have in the garret. I never supposed she'd want them—they're so old-fashioned, and nobody seems to want anything but hooked mats now. But she asked me for them—said she'd rather have them than anything else for her floors. They ARE pretty. I made them of the nicest rags, and braided them in stripes. It was such company these last few winters. And I'll make her enough blue plum preserve to stock her jam closet for a year. It seems real strange. Those blue plum trees hadn't even a blossom for three years, and I thought they might as well be cut down. And this last spring they were white, and such a crop of plums I never remember at Green Gables."

"Well, thank goodness that Anne and Gilbert really are going to be married after all. It's what I've always prayed for," said Mrs. Rachel, in the tone of one who is comfortably sure that her prayers have availed much. "It was a great relief to find out that she really didn't mean to take the Kingsport man. He was rich, to be sure, and Gilbert is poor—at least, to begin with; but then he's an Island boy."

"He's Gilbert Blythe," said Marilla contentedly. Marilla would have died the death before she would have put into words the thought that was always in the background of her mind whenever she had looked at Gilbert from his childhood up—the thought that, had it not been for her own wilful pride long, long ago, he might have been HER son. Marilla felt that, in some strange way, his marriage with Anne would put right that old mistake. Good had come out of the evil of the ancient bitterness.

As for Anne herself, she was so happy that she almost felt frightened. The gods, so says the old superstition, do not like to behold too happy mortals. It is certain, at least, that some human beings do not. Two of that ilk descended upon Anne one violet dusk and proceeded to do what in them lay to prick the rainbow bubble of her satisfaction. If she thought she was getting any particular prize in young Dr. Blythe, or if she imagined that he was still as infatuated with her as he might have been in his salad days, it was surely their duty to put the matter before her in another light. Yet these two worthy ladies were not enemies of Anne; on the contrary, they were really quite fond of her, and would have defended her as their own young had anyone else attacked her. Human nature is not obliged to be consistent.

Mrs. Inglis—nee Jane Andrews, to quote from the Daily Enterprise—came with her mother and Mrs. Jasper Bell. But in Jane the milk of human kindness had not been curdled by years of matrimonial bickerings. Her lines had fallen in pleasant places. In spite of the fact—as Mrs. Rachel Lynde would say—that she had married a millionaire, her marriage had been happy. Wealth had not spoiled her. She was still the placid, amiable, pink-cheeked Jane of the old quartette, sympathising with her old chum's happiness and as keenly interested in all the dainty details of Anne's trousseau as if it could rival her own silken and bejewelled splendors. Jane was not brilliant, and had probably never made a remark worth listening to in her life; but she never said anything that would hurt anyone's feelings—which may be a negative talent but is likewise a rare and enviable one.

"So Gilbert didn't go back on you after all," said Mrs. Harmon Andrews, contriving to convey an expression of surprise in her tone. "Well, the Blythes generally keep their word when they've once passed it, no matter what happens. Let me see—you're twenty-five, aren't you, Anne? When I was a girl twenty-five was the first corner. But you look quite young. Red-headed people always do."

"Red hair is very fashionable now," said Anne, trying to smile, but speaking rather coldly. Life had developed in her a sense of humor which helped her over many difficulties; but as yet nothing had availed to steel her against a reference to her hair.

"So it is—so it is," conceded Mrs. Harmon. "There's no telling what queer freaks fashion will take. Well, Anne, your things are very pretty, and very suitable to your position in life, aren't they, Jane? I hope you'll be very happy. You have my best wishes, I'm sure. A long engagement doesn't often turn out well. But, of course, in your case it couldn't be helped."

"Gilbert looks very young for a doctor. I'm afraid people won't have much confidence in him," said Mrs. Jasper Bell gloomily. Then she shut her mouth tightly, as if she had said what she considered it her duty to say and held her conscience clear. She belonged to the type which always has a stringy black feather in its hat and straggling locks of hair on its neck.

Anne's surface pleasure in her pretty bridal things was temporarily shadowed; but the deeps of happiness below could not thus be disturbed; and the little stings of Mesdames Bell and Andrews were forgotten when Gilbert came later, and they wandered down to the birches of the brook, which had been saplings when Anne had come to Green Gables, but were now tall, ivory columns in a fairy palace of twilight and stars. In their shadows Anne and Gilbert talked in lover-fashion of their new home and their new life together.

"I've found a nest for us, Anne."

"Oh, where? Not right in the village, I hope. I wouldn't like that altogether."

"No. There was no house to be had in the village. This is a little white house on the harbor shore, half way between Glen St. Mary and Four Winds Point. It's a little out of the way, but when we get a 'phone in that won't matter so much. The situation is beautiful. It looks to the sunset and has the great blue harbor before it. The sand-dunes aren't very far away—the sea winds blow over them and the sea spray drenches them."

"But the house itself, Gilbert,—OUR first home? What is it like?"

"Not very large, but large enough for us. There's a splendid living room with a fireplace in it downstairs, and a dining room that looks out on the harbor, and a little room that will do for my office. It is about sixty years old—the oldest house in Four Winds. But it has been kept in pretty good repair, and was all done over about fifteen years ago—shingled, plastered and re-floored. It was well built to begin with. I understand that there was some romantic story connected with its building, but the man I rented it from didn't know it."

"He said Captain Jim was the only one who could spin that old yarn now."

"Who is Captain Jim?"

"The keeper of the lighthouse on Four Winds Point. You'll love that Four Winds light, Anne. It's a revolving one, and it flashes like a magnificent star through the twilights. We can see it from our living room windows and our front door."

"Who owns the house?"

"Well, it's the property of the Glen St. Mary Presbyterian Church now, and I rented it from the trustees. But it belonged until lately to a very old lady, Miss Elizabeth Russell. She died last spring, and as she had no near relatives she left her property to the Glen St. Mary Church. Her furniture is still in the house, and I bought most of it—for a mere song you might say, because it was all so old-fashioned that the trustees despaired of selling it. Glen St. Mary folks prefer plush brocade and sideboards with mirrors and ornamentations, I fancy. But Miss Russell's furniture is very good and I feel sure you'll like it, Anne."

"So far, good," said Anne, nodding cautious approval. "But, Gilbert, people cannot live by furniture alone. You haven't yet mentioned one very important thing. Are there TREES about this house?"

"Heaps of them, oh, dryad! There is a big grove of fir trees behind it, two rows of Lombardy poplars down the lane, and a ring of white birches around a very delightful garden. Our front door opens right into the garden, but there is another entrance—a little gate hung between two firs. The hinges are on one trunk and the catch on the other. Their boughs form an arch overhead."

"Oh, I'm so glad! I couldn't live where there were no trees—something vital in me would starve. Well, after that, there's no use asking you if there's a brook anywhere near. THAT would be expecting too much."

"But there IS a brook—and it actually cuts across one corner of the garden."

"Then," said Anne, with a long sigh of supreme satisfaction, "this house you have found IS my house of dreams and none other."

CHAPTER 3 - THE LAND OF DREAMS AMONG

"Have you made up your mind who you're going to have to the wedding, Anne?" asked Mrs. Rachel Lynde, as she hemstitched table napkins industriously. "It's time your invitations were sent, even if they are to be only informal ones."

"I don't mean to have very many," said Anne. "We just want those we love best to see us married. Gilbert's people, and Mr. and Mrs. Allan, and Mr. and Mrs. Harrison."

"There was a time when you'd hardly have numbered Mr. Harrison among your dearest friends," said Marilla drily.

"Well, I wasn't VERY strongly attracted to him at our first meeting," acknowledged Anne, with a laugh over the recollection. "But Mr. Harrison has improved on acquaintance, and Mrs. Harrison is really a dear. Then, of course, there are Miss Lavendar and Paul."

"Have they decided to come to the Island this summer? I thought they were going to Europe."

"They changed their minds when I wrote them I was going to be married. I had a letter from Paul today. He says he MUST come to my wedding, no matter what happens to Europe."

"That child always idolised you," remarked Mrs. Rachel.

"That 'child' is a young man of nineteen now, Mrs. Lynde."

"How time does fly!" was Mrs. Lynde's brilliant and original response.

"Charlotta the Fourth may come with them. She sent word by Paul that she would come if her husband would let her. I wonder if she still wears those enormous blue bows, and whether her husband calls her Charlotta or Leonora. I should love to have Charlotta at my wedding. Charlotta and I were at a wedding long syne. They expect to be at Echo Lodge next week. Then there are Phil and the Reverend Jo——"

"It sounds awful to hear you speaking of a minister like that, Anne," said Mrs. Rachel severely.

"His wife calls him that."

"She should have more respect for his holy office, then," retorted Mrs. Rachel.

"I've heard you criticise ministers pretty sharply yourself," teased Anne.

"Yes, but I do it reverently," protested Mrs. Lynde. "You never heard me NICKNAME a minister."

Anne smothered a smile.

"Well, there are Diana and Fred and little Fred and Small Anne Cordelia—and Jane Andrews. I wish I could have Miss Stacey and Aunt Jamesina and Priscilla and Stella. But Stella is in Vancouver, and Pris is in Japan, and Miss Stacey is married in California, and Aunt Jamesina has gone to India to explore her daughter's mission field, in spite of her horror of snakes. It's really dreadful—the way people get scattered over the globe."

"The Lord never intended it, that's what," said Mrs. Rachel authoritatively. "In my young days people grew up and married and settled down where they were born, or pretty near it. Thank goodness you've stuck to the Island, Anne. I was afraid Gilbert would insist on rushing off to the ends of the earth when he got through college, and dragging you with him."

"If everybody stayed where he was born places would soon be filled up, Mrs. Lynde."

"Oh, I'm not going to argue with you, Anne. *I* am not a B.A. What time of the day is the ceremony to be?"

"We have decided on noon—high noon, as the society reporters say. That will give us time to catch the evening train to Glen St. Mary."

"And you'll be married in the parlor?"

"No—not unless it rains. We mean to be married in the orchard—with the blue sky over us and the sunshine around us. Do you know when and where I'd like to be married, if I could? It would be at dawn—a June dawn, with a glorious sunrise, and roses blooming in the gardens; and I would slip down and meet Gilbert and we would go together to the heart of the beech woods,—and there, under the green arches that would be like a splendid cathedral, we would be married."

Marilla sniffed scornfully and Mrs. Lynde looked shocked.

"But that would be terrible queer, Anne. Why, it wouldn't really seem legal. And what would Mrs. Harmon Andrews say?"

"Ah, there's the rub," sighed Anne. "There are so many things in life we cannot do because of the fear of what Mrs. Harmon Andrews would say. "Tis true, 'tis pity, and pity 'tis, 'tis true.' What delightful things we might do were it not for Mrs. Harmon Andrews!"

"By times, Anne, I don't feel quite sure that I understand you altogether," complained Mrs. Lynde.

"Anne was always romantic, you know," said Marilla apologetically.

"Well, married life will most likely cure her of that," Mrs. Rachel responded comfortingly.

Anne laughed and slipped away to Lover's Lane, where Gilbert found her; and neither of them seemed to entertain much fear, or hope, that their married life would cure them of romance.

The Echo Lodge people came over the next week, and Green Gables buzzed with the delight of them. Miss Lavendar had changed so little that the three years since her last Island visit might have been a watch in the night; but Anne gasped with amazement over Paul. Could this splendid six feet of manhood be the little Paul of Avonlea schooldays?

"You really make me feel old, Paul," said Anne. "Why, I have to look up to you!"

"You'll never grow old, Teacher," said Paul. "You are one of the fortunate mortals who have found and drunk from the Fountain of Youth,—you and Mother Lavendar. See here! When you're married I WON'T call you Mrs. Blythe. To me you'll always be 'Teacher'—the teacher of the best lessons I ever learned. I want to show you something."

The "something" was a pocketbook full of poems. Paul had put some of his beautiful fancies into verse, and magazine editors had not been as unappreciative as they are sometimes supposed to be. Anne read Paul's poems with real delight. They were full of charm and promise.

"You'll be famous yet, Paul. I always dreamed of having one famous pupil. He was to be a college president—but a great poet would be even better. Some day I'll be able to boast that I whipped the distinguished Paul Irving. But then I never did whip you, did I, Paul? What an opportunity lost! I think I kept you in at recess, however."

"You may be famous yourself, Teacher. I've seen a good deal of your work these last three years."

"No. I know what I can do. I can write pretty, fanciful little sketches that children love and editors send welcome cheques for. But I can do nothing big. My only chance for earthly immortality is a corner in your Memoirs."

Charlotta the Fourth had discarded the blue bows but her freckles were not noticeably less.

"I never did think I'd come down to marrying a Yankee, Miss Shirley, ma'am," she said. "But you never know what's before you, and it isn't his fault. He was born that way."

"You're a Yankee yourself, Charlotta, since you've married one."

"Miss Shirley, ma'am, I'm NOT! And I wouldn't be if I was to marry a dozen Yankees! Tom's kind of nice. And besides, I thought I'd better not be too hard to please, for I mightn't get another chance. Tom don't drink and he don't growl because he has to work between meals, and when all's said and done I'm satisfied, Miss Shirley, ma'am."

"Does he call you Leonora?" asked Anne.

"Goodness, no, Miss Shirley, ma'am. I wouldn't know who he meant if he did. Of course, when we got married he had to say, 'I take thee, Leonora,' and I declare to you, Miss Shirley, ma'am, I've had the most dreadful feeling ever since that it wasn't me he was talking to and I haven't been rightly married at all. And so you're going to be married yourself, Miss Shirley, ma'am? I always thought I'd like to marry a doctor. It would be so handy when the children had measles and croup. Tom is only a bricklayer, but he's real good-tempered. When I said to him, says I, 'Tom, can I go to Miss Shirley's wedding? I mean to go anyhow, but I'd like to have your consent,' he just says, 'Suit yourself, Charlotta, and you'll suit me.' That's a real pleasant kind of husband to have, Miss Shirley, ma'am."

Philippa and her Reverend Jo arrived at Green Gables the day before the wedding. Anne and Phil had a rapturous meeting which presently simmered down to a cosy, confidential chat over all that had been and was about to be.

"Queen Anne, you're as queenly as ever. I've got fearfully thin since the babies came. I'm not half so good-looking; but I think Jo likes it. There's not such a contrast between us, you see. And oh, it's perfectly magnificent that you're going to marry Gilbert. Roy Gardner wouldn't have done at all, at all. I can see that now, though I was horribly disappointed at the time. You know, Anne, you did treat Roy very badly."

"He has recovered, I understand," smiled Anne.

"Oh, yes. He is married and his wife is a sweet little thing and they're perfectly happy. Everything works together for good. Jo and the Bible say that, and they are pretty good authorities."

"Are Alec and Alonzo married yet?"

"Alec is, but Alonzo isn't. How those dear old days at Patty's Place come back when I'm talking to you, Anne! What fun we had!"

"Have you been to Patty's Place lately?"

"Oh, yes, I go often. Miss Patty and Miss Maria still sit by the fireplace and knit. And that reminds me—we've brought you a wedding gift from them, Anne. Guess what it is."

"I never could. How did they know I was going to be married?"

"Oh, I told them. I was there last week. And they were so interested. Two days ago Miss Patty wrote me a note asking me to call; and then she asked if I would take her gift to you. What would you wish most from Patty's Place, Anne?"

"You can't mean that Miss Patty has sent me her china dogs?"

"Go up head. They're in my trunk this very moment. And I've a letter for you. Wait a moment and I'll get it."

"Dear Miss Shirley," Miss Patty had written, "Maria and I were very much interested in hearing of your approaching nuptials. We send you our best wishes. Maria and I have never married, but we have no objection to other people doing so. We are sending you the china dogs. I intended to leave them to you in my will, because you seemed to have sincere affection for them. But Maria and I expect to live a good while yet (D.V.), so I have decided to give you the dogs while you are young. You will not have forgotten that Gog looks to the right and Magog to the left."

"Just fancy those lovely old dogs sitting by the fireplace in my house of dreams," said Anne rapturously. "I never expected anything so delightful."

That evening Green Gables hummed with preparations for the following day; but in the twilight Anne slipped away. She had a little pilgrimage to make on this last day of her girlhood and she must make it alone. She went to Matthew's grave, in the little poplar-shaded Avonlea graveyard, and there kept a silent tryst with old memories and immortal loves.

"How glad Matthew would be tomorrow if he were here," she whispered. "But I believe he does know and is glad of it—somewhere else. I've read somewhere that 'our dead are never dead until we have forgotten them.' Matthew will never be dead to me, for I can never forget him."

She left on his grave the flowers she had brought and walked slowly down the long hill. It was a gracious evening, full of delectable lights and shadows. In the west was a sky of mackerel clouds—crimson and amber-tinted, with long strips of apple-green sky between. Beyond was the glimmering radiance of a sunset sea, and the ceaseless voice of many waters came up from the tawny shore. All around her, lying in the fine, beautiful country silence, were the hills and fields and woods she had known and loved so long.

"History repeats itself," said Gilbert, joining her as she passed the Blythe gate. "Do you remember our first walk down this hill, Anne—our first walk together anywhere, for that matter?"

"I was coming home in the twilight from Matthew's grave—and you came out of the gate; and I swallowed the pride of years and spoke to you."

"And all heaven opened before me," supplemented Gilbert. "From that moment I looked forward to tomorrow. When I left you at your gate that night and walked home I was the happiest boy in the world. Anne had forgiven me."

"I think you had the most to forgive. I was an ungrateful little wretch—and after you had really saved my life that day on the pond, too. How I loathed that load of obligation at first! I don't deserve the happiness that has come to me."

Gilbert laughed and clasped tighter the girlish hand that wore his ring. Anne's engagement ring was a circlet of pearls. She had refused to wear a diamond.

"I've never really liked diamonds since I found out they weren't the lovely purple I had dreamed. They will always suggest my old disappointment."

"But pearls are for tears, the old legend says," Gilbert had objected.

"I'm not afraid of that. And tears can be happy as well as sad. My very happiest moments have been when I had tears in my eyes—when Marilla told me I might stay at Green Gables—when Matthew gave me the first pretty dress I ever had—when I heard that you were going to recover from the fever. So give me pearls for our troth ring, Gilbert, and I'll willingly accept the sorrow of life with its joy."

But tonight our lovers thought only of joy and never of sorrow. For the morrow was their wedding day, and their house of dreams awaited them on the misty, purple shore of Four Winds Harbor.

CHAPTER 4 - THE FIRST BRIDE OF GREEN GABLES

Anne wakened on the morning of her wedding day to find the sunshine winking in at the window of the little porch gable and a September breeze frolicking with her curtains.

"I'm so glad the sun will shine on me," she thought happily.

She recalled the first morning she had wakened in that little porch room, when the sunshine had crept in on her through the blossom-drift of the old Snow Queen. That had not been a happy wakening, for it brought with it the bitter disappointment of the preceding night. But since then the little room had been endeared and consecrated by years of happy childhood dreams and maiden visions. To it she had come back joyfully after all her absences; at its window she had knelt through that night of bitter agony when she believed Gilbert dying, and by it she had sat in speechless happiness the night of her betrothal. Many vigils of joy and some of sorrow had been kept there; and today she must leave it forever. Henceforth it would be hers no more; fifteen-year-old Dora was to inherit it when she had gone. Nor did Anne wish it otherwise; the little room was sacred to youth and girlhood—to the past that was to close today before the chapter of wifehood opened.

Green Gables was a busy and joyous house that forenoon. Diana arrived early, with little Fred and Small Anne Cordelia, to lend a hand. Davy and Dora, the Green Gables twins, whisked the babies off to the garden.

"Don't let Small Anne Cordelia spoil her clothes," warned Diana anxiously.

"You needn't be afraid to trust her with Dora," said Marilla. "That child is more sensible and careful than most of the mothers I've known. She's really a wonder in some ways. Not much like that other harum-scarum I brought up."

Marilla smiled across her chicken salad at Anne. It might even be suspected that she liked the harum-scarum best after all.

"Those twins are real nice children," said Mrs. Rachel, when she was sure they were out of earshot. "Dora is so womanly and helpful, and Davy is developing into a very smart boy. He isn't the holy terror for mischief he used to be."

"I never was so distracted in my life as I was the first six months he was here," acknowledged Marilla. "After that I suppose I got used to him. He's taken a great notion to farming lately, and wants me to let him try running the farm next year. I may, for Mr. Barry doesn't think he'll want to rent it much longer, and some new arrangement will have to be made."

"Well, you certainly have a lovely day for your wedding, Anne," said Diana, as she slipped a voluminous apron over her silken array. "You couldn't have had a finer one if you'd ordered it from Eaton's."

"Indeed, there's too much money going out of this Island to that same Eaton's," said Mrs. Lynde indignantly. She had strong views on the subject of octopus-like department stores, and never lost an opportunity of airing them. "And as for those catalogues of theirs, they're the Avonlea girls' Bible now, that's what. They pore over them on Sundays instead of studying the Holy Scriptures."

"Well, they're splendid to amuse children with," said Diana. "Fred and Small Anne look at the pictures by the hour."

"*I* amused ten children without the aid of Eaton's catalogue," said Mrs. Rachel severely.

"Come, you two, don't quarrel over Eaton's catalogue," said Anne gaily. "This is my day of days, you know. I'm so happy I want every one else to be happy, too."

"I'm sure I hope your happiness will last, child," sighed Mrs. Rachel. She did hope it truly, and believed it, but she was afraid it was in the nature of a challenge to Providence to flaunt your happiness too openly. Anne, for her own good, must be toned down a trifle.

But it was a happy and beautiful bride who came down the old, homespun-carpeted stairs that September noon—the first bride of Green Gables, slender and shining-eyed, in the mist of her maiden veil, with her arms full of roses. Gilbert, waiting for her in the hall below, looked up at her with adoring eyes. She was his at last, this evasive, long-sought Anne, won after years of patient waiting. It was to him she was coming in the sweet surrender of the bride. Was he worthy of her? Could he make her as happy as he hoped? If he failed her—if he could not measure up to her standard of manhood—then, as she held out her hand, their eyes met and all doubt was swept away in a glad certainty. They belonged to each other; and, no matter what life might hold for them, it could never alter that. Their happiness was in each other's keeping and both were unafraid.

They were married in the sunshine of the old orchard, circled by the loving and kindly faces of long-familiar friends. Mr. Allan married them, and the Reverend Jo made what Mrs. Rachel Lynde afterwards pronounced to be the "most beautiful wedding prayer" she had ever heard. Birds do not often sing in September, but one sang sweetly from some hidden bough while Gilbert and Anne repeated their deathless vows. Anne heard it and thrilled to it; Gilbert heard it, and wondered only that all the birds in the world had not burst into jubilant song; Paul heard it and later wrote a lyric about it which was one of the most admired in his first volume of verse; Charlotta the Fourth heard it and was blissfully sure it meant good luck for her adored Miss Shirley. The bird sang until the ceremony was ended and then it wound up with one mad little, glad little trill. Never had the old gray-green house among its enfolding orchards known a blither, merrier afternoon. All the

585

old jests and quips that must have done duty at weddings since Eden were served up, and seemed as new and brilliant and mirth-provoking as if they had never been uttered before. Laughter and joy had their way; and when Anne and Gilbert left to catch the Carmody train, with Paul as driver, the twins were ready with rice and old shoes, in the throwing of which Charlotta the Fourth and Mr. Harrison bore a valiant part. Marilla stood at the gate and watched the carriage out of sight down the long lane with its banks of goldenrod. Anne turned at its end to wave her last good-bye. She was gone—Green Gables was her home no more; Marilla's face looked very gray and old as she turned to the house which Anne had filled for fourteen years, and even in her absence, with light and life.

But Diana and her small fry, the Echo Lodge people and the Allans, had stayed to help the two old ladies over the loneliness of the first evening; and they contrived to have a quietly pleasant little supper time, sitting long around the table and chatting over all the details of the day. While they were sitting there Anne and Gilbert were alighting from the train at Glen St. Mary.

CHAPTER 5 - THE HOME COMING

Dr. David Blythe had sent his horse and buggy to meet them, and the urchin who had brought it slipped away with a sympathetic grin, leaving them to the delight of driving alone to their new home through the radiant evening.

Anne never forgot the loveliness of the view that broke upon them when they had driven over the hill behind the village. Her new home could not yet be seen; but before her lay Four Winds Harbor like a great, shining mirror of rose and silver. Far down, she saw its entrance between the bar of sand dunes on one side and a steep, high, grim, red sandstone cliff on the other. Beyond the bar the sea, calm and austere, dreamed in the afterlight. The little fishing village, nestled in the cove where the sand-dunes met the harbor shore, looked like a great opal in the haze. The sky over them was like a jewelled cup from which the dusk was pouring; the air was crisp with the compelling tang of the sea, and the whole landscape was infused with the subtleties of a sea evening. A few dim sails drifted along the darkening, fir-clad harbor shores. A bell was ringing from the tower of a little white church on the far side; mellowly and dreamily sweet, the chime floated across the water blent with the moan of the sea. The great revolving light on the cliff at the channel flashed warm and golden against the clear northern sky, a trembling, quivering star of good hope. Far out along the horizon was the crinkled gray ribbon of a passing steamer's smoke.

"Oh, beautiful, beautiful," murmured Anne. "I shall love Four Winds, Gilbert. Where is our house?"

"We can't see it yet—the belt of birch running up from that little cove hides it. It's about two miles from Glen St. Mary, and there's another mile between it and the light-house. We won't have many neighbors, Anne. There's only one house near us and I don't know who lives in it. Shall you be lonely when I'm away?"

"Not with that light and that loveliness for company. Who lives in that house, Gilbert?"

"I don't know. It doesn't look—exactly—as if the occupants would be kindred spirits, Anne, does it?"

The house was a large, substantial affair, painted such a vivid green that the landscape seemed quite faded by contrast. There was an orchard behind it, and a nicely kept lawn before it, but, somehow, there was a certain bareness about it.

Perhaps its neatness was responsible for this; the whole establishment, house, barns, orchard, garden, lawn and lane, was so starkly neat.

"It doesn't seem probable that anyone with that taste in paint could be VERY kindred," acknowledged Anne, "unless it were an accident—like our blue hall. I feel certain there are no children there, at least. It's even neater than the old Copp place on the Tory road, and I never expected to see anything neater than that."

They had not met anybody on the moist, red road that wound along the harbor shore. But just before they came to the belt of birch which hid their home, Anne saw a girl who was driving a flock of snow-white geese along the crest of a velvety green hill on the right. Great, scattered firs grew along it. Between their trunks one saw glimpses of yellow harvest fields, gleams of golden sand-hills, and bits of blue sea. The girl was tall and wore a dress of pale blue print. She walked with a certain springiness of step and erectness of bearing. She and her geese came out of the gate at the foot of the hill as Anne and Gilbert passed. She stood with her hand on the fastening of the gate, and looked steadily at them, with an expression that hardly attained to interest, but did not descend to curiosity. It seemed to Anne, for a fleeting moment, that there was even a veiled hint of hostility in it. But it was the girl's beauty which made Anne give a little gasp—a beauty so marked that it must have attracted attention anywhere. She was hatless, but heavy braids of burnished hair, the hue of ripe wheat, were twisted about her head like a coronet; her eyes were blue and star-like; her figure, in its plain print gown, was magnificent; and her lips were as crimson as the bunch of blood-red poppies she wore at her belt.

"Gilbert, who is the girl we have just passed?" asked Anne, in a low voice.

"I didn't notice any girl," said Gilbert, who had eyes only for his bride.

"She was standing by that gate—no, don't look back. She is still watching us. I never saw such a beautiful face."

"I don't remember seeing any very handsome girls while I was here. There are some pretty girls up at the Glen, but I hardly think they could be called beautiful."

"This girl is. You can't have seen her, or you would remember her. Nobody could forget her. I never saw such a face except in pictures. And her hair! It made me think of Browning's 'cord of gold' and 'gorgeous snake'!"

"Probably she's some visitor in Four Winds—likely some one from that big summer hotel over the harbor."

"She wore a white apron and she was driving geese."

"She might do that for amusement. Look, Anne—there's our house."

Anne looked and forgot for a time the girl with the splendid, resentful eyes. The first glimpse of her new home was a delight to eye and spirit—it looked so like a big, creamy seashell stranded on the harbor shore. The rows of tall Lombardy poplars down its lane stood out in stately, purple silhouette against the sky. Behind it, sheltering its garden from the too keen breath of sea winds, was a cloudy fir wood, in which the winds might make all kinds of weird and haunting music. Like all woods, it seemed to be holding and enfolding secrets in its recesses,—secrets whose charm is only to be won by entering in and patiently seeking. Outwardly, dark green arms keep them inviolate from curious or indifferent eyes.

The night winds were beginning their wild dances beyond the bar and the fishing hamlet across the harbor was gemmed with lights as Anne and Gilbert drove up the poplar lane. The door of the little house opened, and a warm glow of firelight flickered out into the dusk. Gilbert lifted Anne from the buggy and led her into the garden, through the little gate between the ruddy-tipped firs, up the trim, red path to the sandstone step.

"Welcome home," he whispered, and hand in hand they stepped over the threshold of their house of dreams.

CHAPTER 6 - CAPTAIN JIM

"Old Doctor Dave" and "Mrs. Doctor Dave" had come down to the little house to greet the bride and groom. Doctor Dave was a big, jolly, white-whiskered old fellow, and Mrs. Doctor was a trim rosy-cheeked, silver-haired little lady who took Anne at once to her heart, literally and figuratively.

"I'm so glad to see you, dear. You must be real tired. We've got a bite of supper ready, and Captain Jim brought up some trout for you. Captain Jim—where are you? Oh, he's slipped out to see to the horse, I suppose. Come upstairs and take your things off."

Anne looked about her with bright, appreciative eyes as she followed Mrs. Doctor Dave upstairs. She liked the appearance of her new home very much. It seemed to have the atmosphere of Green Gables and the flavor of her old traditions.

"I think I would have found Miss Elizabeth Russell a 'kindred spirit,'" she murmured when she was alone in her room. There were two windows in it; the dormer one looked out on the lower harbor and the sand-bar and the Four Winds light.

> "A magic casement opening on the foam
> Of perilous seas in fairy lands forlorn,"

quoted Anne softly. The gable window gave a view of a little harvest-hued valley through which a brook ran. Half a mile up the brook was the only house in sight—an old, rambling, gray one surrounded by huge willows through which its windows peered, like shy, seeking eyes, into the dusk. Anne wondered who lived there; they would be her nearest neighbors and she hoped they would be nice. She suddenly found herself thinking of the beautiful girl with the white geese.

"Gilbert thought she didn't belong here," mused Anne, "but I feel sure she does. There was something about her that made her part of the sea and the sky and the harbor. Four Winds is in her blood."

When Anne went downstairs Gilbert was standing before the fireplace talking to a stranger. Both turned as Anne entered.

"Anne, this is Captain Boyd. Captain Boyd, my wife."

It was the first time Gilbert had said "my wife" to anybody but Anne, and he narrowly escaped bursting with the pride of it. The old captain held out a sinewy hand to Anne; they smiled at each other and were friends from that moment. Kindred spirit flashed recognition to kindred spirit.

"I'm right down pleased to meet you, Mistress Blythe; and I hope you'll be as happy as the first bride was who came here. I can't wish you no better than THAT. But your husband doesn't introduce me jest exactly right. 'Captain Jim' is my week-a-day name and you might as well begin as you're sartain to end up—calling me that. You sartainly are a nice little bride, Mistress Blythe. Looking at you sorter makes me feel that I've jest been married myself."

Amid the laughter that followed Mrs. Doctor Dave urged Captain Jim to stay and have supper with them.

"Thank you kindly. 'Twill be a real treat, Mistress Doctor. I mostly has to eat my meals alone, with the reflection of my ugly old phiz in a looking-glass opposite for company. 'Tisn't often I have a chance to sit down with two such sweet, purty ladies."

Captain Jim's compliments may look very bald on paper, but he paid them with such a gracious, gentle deference of tone and look that the woman upon whom they were bestowed felt that she was being offered a queen's tribute in a kingly fashion.

Captain Jim was a high-souled, simple-minded old man, with eternal youth in his eyes and heart. He had a tall, rather ungainly figure, somewhat stooped, yet suggestive of great strength and endurance; a clean-shaven face deeply lined and bronzed; a thick mane of iron-gray hair falling quite to his shoulders, and a pair of remarkably blue, deep-set eyes, which sometimes twinkled and sometimes dreamed, and sometimes looked out seaward with a wistful quest in them, as of one seeking something precious and lost. Anne was to learn one day what it was for which Captain Jim looked.

It could not be denied that Captain Jim was a homely man. His spare jaws, rugged mouth, and square brow were not fashioned on the lines of beauty; and he had passed through many hardships and sorrows which had marked his body as well as his soul; but though at first sight Anne thought him plain she never thought anything more about it—the spirit shining through that rugged tenement beautified it so wholly.

They gathered gaily around the supper table. The hearth fire banished the chill of the September evening, but the window of the dining room was open and sea breezes entered at their own sweet will. The view was magnificent, taking in the harbor and the sweep of low, purple hills beyond. The table was heaped with Mrs. Doctor's delicacies but the piece de resistance was undoubtedly the big platter of sea trout.

"Thought they'd be sorter tasty after travelling," said Captain Jim. "They're fresh as trout can be, Mistress Blythe. Two hours ago they were swimming in the Glen Pond."

"Who is attending to the light tonight, Captain Jim?" asked Doctor Dave.

"Nephew Alec. He understands it as well as I do. Well, now, I'm real glad you asked me to stay to supper. I'm proper hungry—didn't have much of a dinner to-day."

"I believe you half starve yourself most of the time down at that light," said Mrs. Doctor Dave severely. "You won't take the trouble to get up a decent meal."

"Oh, I do, Mistress Doctor, I do," protested Captain Jim. "Why, I live like a king gen'rally. Last night I was up to the Glen and took home two pounds of steak. I meant to have a spanking good dinner today."

"And what happened to the steak?" asked Mrs. Doctor Dave. "Did you lose it on the way home?"

"No." Captain Jim looked sheepish. "Just at bedtime a poor, ornery sort of dog came along and asked for a night's lodging. Guess he belonged to some of the fishermen 'long shore. I couldn't turn the poor cur out—he had a sore foot. So I shut him in the porch, with an old bag to lie on, and went to bed. But somehow I couldn't sleep. Come to think it over, I sorter remembered that the dog looked hungry."

"And you got up and gave him that steak—ALL that steak," said Mrs. Doctor Dave, with a kind of triumphant reproof.

"Well, there wasn't anything else TO give him," said Captain Jim deprecatingly. "Nothing a dog'd care for, that is. I reckon he WAS hungry, for he made about two bites of it. I had a fine sleep the rest of the night but my dinner had to be sorter scanty—potatoes and point, as you might say. The dog, he lit out for home this morning. I reckon HE weren't a vegetarian."

"The idea of starving yourself for a worthless dog!" sniffed Mrs. Doctor.

"You don't know but he may be worth a lot to somebody," protested Captain Jim. "He didn't LOOK of much account, but you can't go by looks in jedging a dog. Like meself, he might be a real beauty inside. The First Mate didn't approve of him, I'll allow. His language was right down forcible. But the First Mate is prejudiced. No use in taking a cat's opinion of a dog. 'Tennyrate, I lost my dinner, so this nice spread in this dee-lightful company is real pleasant. It's a great thing to have good neighbors."

"Who lives in the house among the willows up the brook?" asked Anne.

"Mrs. Dick Moore," said Captain Jim—"and her husband," he added, as if by way of an afterthought.

Anne smiled, and deduced a mental picture of Mrs. Dick Moore from Captain Jim's way of putting it; evidently a second Mrs. Rachel Lynde.

"You haven't many neighbors, Mistress Blythe," Captain Jim went on. "This side of the harbor is mighty thinly settled. Most of the land belongs to Mr. Howard up yander past the Glen, and he rents it out for pasture. The other side of the harbor, now, is thick with folks—'specially MacAllisters. There's a whole colony of MacAllisters you can't throw a stone but you hit one. I was talking to old Leon Blacquiere the other day. He's been working on the harbor all summer. 'Dey're nearly all MacAllisters over thar,' he told me. 'Dare's Neil MacAllister and Sandy

MacAllister and William MacAllister and Alec MacAllister and Angus MacAllister—and I believe dare's de Devil MacAllister.'"

"There are nearly as many Elliotts and Crawfords," said Doctor Dave, after the laughter had subsided. "You know, Gilbert, we folk on this side of Four Winds have an old saying—'From the conceit of the Elliotts, the pride of the MacAllisters, and the vainglory of the Crawfords, good Lord deliver us.'"

"There's a plenty of fine people among them, though," said Captain Jim. "I sailed with William Crawford for many a year, and for courage and endurance and truth that man hadn't an equal. They've got brains over on that side of Four Winds. Mebbe that's why this side is sorter inclined to pick on 'em. Strange, ain't it, how folks seem to resent anyone being born a mite cleverer than they be."

Doctor Dave, who had a forty years' feud with the over-harbor people, laughed and subsided.

"Who lives in that brilliant emerald house about half a mile up the road?" asked Gilbert.

Captain Jim smiled delightedly.

"Miss Cornelia Bryant. She'll likely be over to see you soon, seeing you're Presbyterians. If you were Methodists she wouldn't come at all. Cornelia has a holy horror of Methodists."

"She's quite a character," chuckled Doctor Dave. "A most inveterate man-hater!"

"Sour grapes?" queried Gilbert, laughing.

"No, 'tisn't sour grapes," answered Captain Jim seriously. "Cornelia could have had her pick when she was young. Even yet she's only to say the word to see the old widowers jump. She jest seems to have been born with a sort of chronic spite agin men and Methodists. She's got the bitterest tongue and the kindest heart in Four Winds. Wherever there's any trouble, that woman is there, doing everything to help in the tenderest way. She never says a harsh word about another woman, and if she likes to card us poor scalawags of men down I reckon our tough old hides can stand it."

"She always speaks well of you, Captain Jim," said Mrs. Doctor.

"Yes, I'm afraid so. I don't half like it. It makes me feel as if there must be something sorter unnateral about me."

CHAPTER 7 - THE SCHOOLMASTER'S BRIDE

"Who was the first bride who came to this house, Captain Jim?" Anne asked, as they sat around the fireplace after supper.

"Was she a part of the story I've heard was connected with this house?" asked Gilbert. "Somebody told me you could tell it, Captain Jim."

"Well, yes, I know it. I reckon I'm the only person living in Four Winds now that can remember the schoolmaster's bride as she was when she come to the Island. She's been dead this thirty year, but she was one of them women you never forget."

"Tell us the story," pleaded Anne. "I want to find out all about the women who have lived in this house before me."

"Well, there's jest been three—Elizabeth Russell, and Mrs. Ned Russell, and the schoolmaster's bride. Elizabeth Russell was a nice, clever little critter, and Mrs. Ned was a nice woman, too. But they weren't ever like the schoolmaster's bride.

"The schoolmaster's name was John Selwyn. He came out from the Old Country to teach school at the Glen when I was a boy of sixteen. He wasn't much like the usual run of derelicts who used to come out to P.E.I. to teach school in them days. Most of them were clever, drunken critters who taught the children the three R's when they were sober, and lambasted them when they wasn't. But John Selwyn was a fine, handsome young fellow. He boarded at my father's, and he and me were cronies, though he was ten years older'n me. We read and walked and talked a heap together. He knew about all the poetry that was ever written, I reckon, and he used to quote it to me along shore in the evenings. Dad thought it an awful waste of time, but he sorter endured it, hoping it'd put me off the notion of going to sea. Well, nothing could do THAT—mother come of a race of sea-going folk and it was born in me. But I loved to hear John read and recite. It's almost sixty years ago, but I could repeat yards of poetry I learned from him. Nearly sixty years!"

Captain Jim was silent for a space, gazing into the glowing fire in a quest of the bygones. Then, with a sigh, he resumed his story.

"I remember one spring evening I met him on the sand-hills. He looked sorter uplifted—jest like you did, Dr. Blythe, when you brought Mistress Blythe in tonight. I thought of him the minute I seen you. And he told me that he had a sweetheart back home and that she was coming out to him. I wasn't more'n half pleased, ornery young lump of selfishness that I was; I thought he wouldn't be as much my friend after she came. But I'd enough decency not to let him see it. He told me all about her. Her name was Persis Leigh, and she would have come out with him if it hadn't been for her old uncle. He was sick, and he'd looked after her when her parents died and she wouldn't leave him. And now he was dead and she was coming out to marry John Selwyn. 'Twasn't no easy journey for a woman in them days. There weren't no steamers, you must ricollect.

"'When do you expect her?' says I.

"'She sails on the Royal William, the 20th of June,' says he, 'and so she should be here by mid-July. I must set Carpenter Johnson to building me a home for her. Her letter come today. I know before I opened it that it had good news for me. I saw her a few nights ago.'

"I didn't understand him, and then he explained—though I didn't understand THAT much better. He said he had a gift—or a curse. Them was his words, Mistress Blythe—a gift or a curse. He didn't know which it was. He said a great-great-grandmother of his had had it, and they burned her for a witch on account of it. He said queer spells—trances, I think was the name he give 'em—come over him now and again. Are there such things, Doctor?"

"There are people who are certainly subject to trances," answered Gilbert. "The matter is more in the line of psychical research than medical. What were the trances of this John Selwyn like?"

"Like dreams," said the old Doctor skeptically.

"He said he could see things in them," said Captain Jim slowly.

"Mind you, I'm telling you jest what HE said—things that were happening—things that were GOING to happen. He said they were sometimes a comfort to him and sometimes a horror. Four nights before this he'd been in one—went into it while he was sitting looking at the fire. And he saw an old room he knew well in England, and Persis Leigh in it, holding out her hands to him and looking glad and happy. So he knew he was going to hear good news of her."

"A dream—a dream," scoffed the old Doctor.

"Likely—likely," conceded Captain Jim. "That's what *I* said to him at the time. It was a vast more comfortable to think so. I didn't like the idea of him seeing things like that—it was real uncanny.

"'No,' says he, 'I didn't dream it. But we won't talk of this again. You won't be so much my friend if you think much about it.'

"I told him nothing could make me any less his friend. But he jest shook his head and says, says he:

"'Lad, I know. I've lost friends before because of this. I don't blame them. There are times when I feel hardly friendly to myself because of it. Such a power has a bit of divinity in it—whether of a good or an evil divinity who shall say? And we mortals all shrink from too close contact with God or devil.'

"Them was his words. I remember them as if 'twas yesterday, though I didn't know jest what he meant. What do you s'pose he DID mean, doctor?"

"I doubt if he knew what he meant himself," said Doctor Dave testily.

"I think I understand," whispered Anne. She was listening in her old attitude of clasped lips and shining eyes. Captain Jim treated himself to an admiring smile before he went on with his story.

"Well, purty soon all the Glen and Four Winds people knew the schoolmaster's bride was coming, and they were all glad because they thought so much of him. And everybody took an interest in his new house—THIS house. He picked this site for it, because you could see the harbor and hear the sea from it. He made the garden out there for his bride, but he didn't plant the Lombardies. Mrs. Ned Russell planted THEM. But there's a double row of rose-bushes in the garden that the little girls who went to the Glen school set out there for the schoolmaster's bride. He said they were pink for her cheeks and white for her brow and red for her lips. He'd quoted poetry so much that he sorter got into the habit of talking it, too, I reckon.

"Almost everybody sent him some little present to help out the furnishing of the house. When the Russells came into it they were well-to-do and furnished it real handsome, as you can see; but the first furniture that went into it was plain enough. This little house was rich in love, though. The women sent in quilts and tablecloths and towels, and one man made a chest for her, and another a table and so on. Even blind old Aunt Margaret Boyd wove a little basket for her out of the sweet-scented sand-hill grass. The schoolmaster's wife used it for years to keep her handkerchiefs in.

"Well, at last everything was ready—even to the logs in the big fireplace ready for lighting. 'Twasn't exactly THIS fireplace, though 'twas in the same place. Miss Elizabeth had this put in when she made the house over fifteen years ago. It was a big, old-fashioned fireplace where you could have roasted an ox. Many's the time I've sat here and spun yarns, same's I'm doing tonight."

Again there was a silence, while Captain Jim kept a passing tryst with visitants Anne and Gilbert could not see—the folks who had sat with him around that fireplace in the vanished years, with mirth and bridal joy shining in eyes long since closed forever under churchyard sod or heaving leagues of sea. Here on olden nights children had tossed laughter lightly to and fro. Here on winter evenings friends had gathered. Dance and music and jest had been here. Here youths and maidens had dreamed. For Captain Jim the little house was tenanted with shapes entreating remembrance.

"It was the first of July when the house was finished. The schoolmaster began to count the days then. We used to see him walking along the shore, and we'd say to each other, 'She'll soon be with him now.'

"She was expected the middle of July, but she didn't come then. Nobody felt anxious. Vessels were often delayed for days and mebbe weeks. The Royal William was a week overdue—and then two—and then three. And at last we began to be frightened, and it got worse and worse. Fin'lly I couldn't bear to look into John Selwyn's eyes. D'ye know, Mistress Blythe"—Captain Jim lowered his voice—"I used to think that they looked just like what his old great-great-grandmother's must have been when they were burning her to death. He never said much but he taught school like a man in a dream and then hurried to the shore. Many a night he walked there from dark to dawn. People said he was losing his mind. Everybody had given up hope—the Royal William was eight weeks overdue. It was the middle of September and the schoolmaster's bride hadn't come—never would come, we thought.

"There was a big storm then that lasted three days, and on the evening after it died away I went to the shore. I found the schoolmaster there, leaning with his arms folded against a big rock, gazing out to sea.

"I spoke to him but he didn't answer. His eyes seemed to be looking at something I couldn't see. His face was set, like a dead man's.

"'John—John,' I called out—jest like that—jest like a frightened child, 'wake up—wake up.'

"That strange, awful look seemed to sorter fade out of his eyes.

"He turned his head and looked at me. I've never forgot his face—never will forget it till I ships for my last voyage.

"'All is well, lad,' he says. 'I've seen the Royal William coming around East Point. She will be here by dawn. Tomorrow night I shall sit with my bride by my own hearth-fire.'

"Do you think he did see it?" demanded Captain Jim abruptly.

"God knows," said Gilbert softly. "Great love and great pain might compass we know not what marvels."

"I am sure he did see it," said Anne earnestly.

"Fol-de-rol," said Doctor Dave, but he spoke with less conviction than usual.

"Because, you know," said Captain Jim solemnly, "the Royal William came into Four Winds Harbor at daylight the next morning.

"Every soul in the Glen and along the shore was at the old wharf to meet her. The schoolmaster had been watching there all night. How we cheered as she sailed up the channel."

Captain Jim's eyes were shining. They were looking at the Four Winds Harbor of sixty years agone, with a battered old ship sailing through the sunrise splendor.

"And Persis Leigh was on board?" asked Anne.

"Yes—her and the captain's wife. They'd had an awful passage—storm after storm—and their provisions give out, too. But there they were at last. When Persis Leigh stepped onto the old wharf John Selwyn took her in his arms—and folks stopped cheering and begun to cry. I cried myself, though 'twas years, mind you, afore I'd admit it. Ain't it funny how ashamed boys are of tears?"

"Was Persis Leigh beautiful?" asked Anne.

"Well, I don't know that you'd call her beautiful exactly—I—don't—know," said Captain Jim slowly. "Somehow, you never got so far along as to wonder if she was handsome or not. It jest didn't matter. There was something so sweet and winsome about her that you had to love her, that was all. But she was pleasant to look at—big, clear, hazel eyes and heaps of glossy brown hair, and an English skin. John and her were married at our house that night at early candle-lighting;

everybody from far and near was there to see it and we all brought them down here afterwards. Mistress Selwyn lighted the fire, and we went away and left them sitting here, jest as John had seen in that vision of his. A strange thing—a strange thing! But I've seen a turrible lot of strange things in my time."

Captain Jim shook his head sagely.

"It's a dear story," said Anne, feeling that for once she had got enough romance to satisfy her. "How long did they live here?"

"Fifteen years. I ran off to sea soon after they were married, like the young scalawag I was. But every time I come back from a voyage I'd head for here, even before I went home, and tell Mistress Selwyn all about it. Fifteen happy years! They had a sort of talent for happiness, them two. Some folks are like that, if you've noticed. They COULDN'T be unhappy for long, no matter what happened. They quarrelled once or twice, for they was both high-sperrited. But Mistress Selwyn says to me once, says she, laughing in that pretty way of hers, 'I felt dreadful when John and I quarrelled, but underneath it all I was very happy because I had such a nice husband to quarrel with and make it up with.' Then they moved to Charlottetown, and Ned Russell bought this house and brought his bride here. They were a gay young pair, as I remember them. Miss Elizabeth Russell was Alec's sister. She came to live with them a year or so later, and she was a creature of mirth, too. The walls of this house must be sorter SOAKED with laughing and good times. You're the third bride I've seen come here, Mistress Blythe—and the handsomest."

Captain Jim contrived to give his sunflower compliment the delicacy of a violet, and Anne wore it proudly. She was looking her best that night, with the bridal rose on her cheeks and the love-light in her eyes; even gruff old Doctor Dave gave her an approving glance, and told his wife, as they drove home together, that that red-headed wife of the boy's was something of a beauty.

"I must be getting back to the light," announced Captain Jim. "I've enj'yed this evening something tremenjus."

"You must come often to see us," said Anne.

"I wonder if you'd give that invitation if you knew how likely I'll be to accept it," Captain Jim remarked whimsically.

"Which is another way of saying you wonder if I mean it," smiled Anne. "I do, 'cross my heart,' as we used to say at school."

"Then I'll come. You're likely to be pestered with me at any hour. And I'll be proud to have you drop down and visit me now and then, too. Gin'rally I haven't anyone to talk to but the First Mate, bless his sociable heart. He's a mighty good listener, and has forgot more'n any MacAllister of them all ever knew, but he isn't much of a conversationalist. You're young and I'm old, but our souls are about the same age, I reckon. We both belong to the race that knows Joseph, as Cornelia Bryant would say."

"The race that knows Joseph?" puzzled Anne.

"Yes. Cornelia divides all the folks in the world into two kinds—the race that knows Joseph and the race that don't. If a person sorter sees eye to eye with you, and has pretty much the same ideas about things, and the same taste in jokes—why, then he belongs to the race that knows Joseph."

"Oh, I understand," exclaimed Anne, light breaking in upon her.

"It's what I used to call—and still call in quotation marks 'kindred spirits.'"

"Jest so—jest so," agreed Captain Jim. "We're it, whatever IT is. When you come in tonight, Mistress Blythe, I says to myself, says I, 'Yes, she's of the race that knows Joseph.' And mighty glad I was, for if it wasn't so we couldn't have had any real satisfaction in each other's company. The race that knows Joseph is the salt of the airth, I reckon."

The moon had just risen when Anne and Gilbert went to the door with their guests. Four Winds Harbor was beginning to be a thing of dream and glamour and enchantment—a spellbound haven where no tempest might ever ravin. The Lombardies down the lane, tall and sombre as the priestly forms of some mystic band, were tipped with silver.

"Always liked Lombardies," said Captain Jim, waving a long arm at them. "They're the trees of princesses. They're out of fashion now. Folks complain that they die at the top and get ragged-looking. So they do—so they do, if you don't risk your neck every spring climbing up a light ladder to trim them out. I always did it for Miss Elizabeth, so her Lombardies never got out-at-elbows. She was especially fond of them. She liked their dignity and stand-offishness. THEY don't hobnob with every Tom, Dick and Harry. If it's maples for company, Mistress Blythe, it's Lombardies for society."

"What a beautiful night," said Mrs. Doctor Dave, as she climbed into the Doctor's buggy.

"Most nights are beautiful," said Captain Jim. "But I 'low that moonlight over Four Winds makes me sorter wonder what's left for heaven. The moon's a great friend of mine, Mistress Blythe. I've loved her ever since I can remember. When I was a little chap of eight I fell asleep in the garden one evening and wasn't missed. I woke up along in the night and I was most scared to death. What shadows and queer noises there was! I dursn't move. Jest crouched there quaking, poor small mite. Seemed 's if there weren't anyone in the world but meself and it was mighty big. Then all at once I saw the moon looking down at me through the apple boughs, jest like an old friend. I was comforted right off. Got up and walked to the house as brave as a lion, looking at her. Many's the night I've watched her from the deck of my vessel, on seas far away from here. Why don't you folks tell me to take in the slack of my jaw and go home?"

The laughter of the goodnights died away. Anne and Gilbert walked hand in hand around their garden. The brook that ran across the corner dimpled pellucidly in the shadows of the birches. The poppies along its banks were like shallow cups of moonlight. Flowers that had been planted by the hands of the schoolmaster's bride flung their sweetness on the shadowy air, like the beauty and blessing of sacred yesterdays. Anne paused in the gloom to gather a spray.

"I love to smell flowers in the dark," she said. "You get hold of their soul then. Oh, Gilbert, this little house is all I've dreamed it. And I'm so glad that we are not the first who have kept bridal tryst here!"

CHAPTER 8 - MISS CORNELIA BRYANT COMES TO CALL

That September was a month of golden mists and purple hazes at Four Winds Harbor—a month of sun-steeped days and of nights that were swimming in moonlight, or pulsating with stars. No storm marred it, no rough wind blew. Anne and Gilbert put their nest in order, rambled on the shores, sailed on the harbor, drove about Four Winds and the Glen, or through the ferny, sequestered roads of the woods around the harbor head; in short, had such a honeymoon as any lovers in the world might have envied them.

"If life were to stop short just now it would still have been richly worth while, just for the sake of these past four weeks, wouldn't it?" said Anne. "I don't suppose we will ever have four such perfect weeks again—but we've HAD them. Everything—wind, weather, folks, house of dreams—has conspired to make our honeymoon delightful. There hasn't even been a rainy day since we came here."

"And we haven't quarrelled once," teased Gilbert.

"Well, 'that's a pleasure all the greater for being deferred,'" quoted Anne. "I'm so glad we decided to spend our honeymoon here. Our memories of it will always belong here, in our house of dreams, instead of being scattered about in strange places."

There was a certain tang of romance and adventure in the atmosphere of their new home which Anne had never found in Avonlea. There, although she had lived in sight of the sea, it had not entered intimately into her life. In Four Winds it surrounded her and called to her constantly. From every window of her new home she saw some varying aspect of it. Its haunting murmur was ever in her ears. Vessels sailed up the harbor every day to the wharf at the Glen, or sailed out again through the sunset, bound for ports that might be half way round the globe. Fishing boats went white-winged down the channel in the mornings, and returned laden in the evenings. Sailors and fisher-folk travelled the red, winding harbor roads, light-hearted and content. There was always a certain sense of things going to happen—of adventures and farings-forth. The ways of Four Winds were less staid and settled and grooved than those of Avonlea; winds of change blew over them; the sea called ever to the dwellers on shore, and even those who might not answer its call felt the thrill and unrest and mystery and possibilities of it.

"I understand now why some men must go to sea," said Anne. "That desire which comes to us all at times—'to sail beyond the bourne of sunset'—must be very imperious when it is born in you. I don't wonder Captain Jim ran away because of it. I never see a ship sailing out of the channel, or a gull soaring over the sand-bar, without wishing I were on board the ship or had wings, not like a dove 'to fly away and be at rest,' but like a gull, to sweep out into the very heart of a storm."

"You'll stay right here with me, Anne-girl," said Gilbert lazily. "I won't have you flying away from me into the hearts of storms."

They were sitting on their red sand-stone doorstep in the late afternoon. Great tranquillities were all about them in land and sea and sky. Silvery gulls were soaring over them. The horizons were laced with long trails of frail, pinkish clouds. The hushed air was threaded with a murmurous refrain of minstrel winds and waves. Pale asters were blowing in the sere and misty meadows between them and the harbor.

"Doctors who have to be up all night waiting on sick folk don't feel very adventurous, I suppose," Anne said indulgently. "If you had had a good sleep last night, Gilbert, you'd be as ready as I am for a flight of imagination."

"I did good work last night, Anne," said Gilbert quietly. "Under God, I saved a life. This is the first time I could ever really claim that. In other cases I may have helped; but, Anne, if I had not stayed at Allonby's last night and fought death hand to hand, that woman would have died before morning. I tried an experiment that was certainly never tried in Four Winds before. I doubt if it was ever tried anywhere before outside of a hospital. It was a new thing in Kingsport hospital last winter. I could never have dared try it here if I had not been absolutely certain that there was no other chance. I risked it—and it succeeded. As a result, a good wife and mother is saved for long years of happiness and usefulness. As I drove home this morning, while the sun was rising over the harbor, I thanked God that I had chosen the profession I did. I had fought a good fight and won—think of it, Anne, WON, against the Great Destroyer. It's what I dreamed of doing long ago when we talked together of what we wanted to do in life. That dream of mine came true this morning."

"Was that the only one of your dreams that has come true?" asked Anne, who knew perfectly well what the substance of his answer would be, but wanted to hear it again.

"YOU know, Anne-girl," said Gilbert, smiling into her eyes. At that moment there were certainly two perfectly happy people sitting on the doorstep of a little white house on the Four Winds Harbor shore.

Presently Gilbert said, with a change of tone, "Do I or do I not see a full-rigged ship sailing up our lane?"

Anne looked and sprang up.

"That must be either Miss Cornelia Bryant or Mrs. Moore coming to call," she said.

"I'm going into the office, and if it is Miss Cornelia I warn you that I'll eaves-drop," said Gilbert. "From all I've heard regarding Miss Cornelia I conclude that her conversation will not be dull, to say the least."

"It may be Mrs. Moore."

"I don't think Mrs. Moore is built on those lines. I saw her working in her gar-den the other day, and, though I was too far away to see clearly, I thought she was rather slender. She doesn't seem very socially inclined when she has never called on you yet, although she's your nearest neighbor."

"She can't be like Mrs. Lynde, after all, or curiosity would have brought her," said Anne. "This caller is, I think, Miss Cornelia."

Miss Cornelia it was; moreover, Miss Cornelia had not come to make any brief and fashionable wedding call. She had her work under her arm in a substantial parcel, and when Anne asked her to stay she promptly took off her capacious sun-hat, which had been held on her head, despite irreverent September breezes, by a tight elastic band under her hard little knob of fair hair. No hat pins for Miss Cor-nelia, an it please ye! Elastic bands had been good enough for her mother and they were good enough for HER. She had a fresh, round, pink-and-white face, and jolly brown eyes. She did not look in the least like the traditional old maid, and there was something in her expression which won Anne instantly. With her old instinctive quickness to discern kindred spirits she knew she was going to like Miss Cornelia, in spite of uncertain oddities of opinion, and certain oddities of attire.

Nobody but Miss Cornelia would have come to make a call arrayed in a striped blue-and-white apron and a wrapper of chocolate print, with a design of huge, pink roses scattered over it. And nobody but Miss Cornelia could have looked dignified and suitably garbed in it. Had Miss Cornelia been entering a pal-ace to call on a prince's bride, she would have been just as dignified and just as wholly mistress of the situation. She would have trailed her rose-spattered flounce over the marble floors just as unconcernedly, and she would have proceeded just as calmly to disabuse the mind of the princess of any idea that the possession of a mere man, be he prince or peasant, was anything to brag of.

"I've brought my work, Mrs. Blythe, dearie," she remarked, unrolling some dainty material. "I'm in a hurry to get this done, and there isn't any time to lose."

Anne looked in some surprise at the white garment spread over Miss Cornel-ia's ample lap. It was certainly a baby's dress, and it was most beautifully made, with tiny frills and tucks. Miss Cornelia adjusted her glasses and fell to embroi-dering with exquisite stitches.

"This is for Mrs. Fred Proctor up at the Glen," she announced. "She's expect-ing her eighth baby any day now, and not a stitch has she ready for it. The other seven have wore out all she made for the first, and she's never had time or strength or spirit to make any more. That woman is a martyr, Mrs. Blythe, believe ME. When she married Fred Proctor *I* knew how it would turn out. He was one of your wicked, fascinating men. After he got married he left off being fascinating and just kept on being wicked. He drinks and he neglects his family. Isn't that like a man? I don't know how Mrs. Proctor would ever keep her children decently clothed if her neighbors didn't help her out."

As Anne was afterwards to learn, Miss Cornelia was the only neighbor who troubled herself much about the decency of the young Proctors.

"When I heard this eighth baby was coming I decided to make some things for it," Miss Cornelia went on. "This is the last and I want to finish it today."

"It's certainly very pretty," said Anne. "I'll get my sewing and we'll have a little thimble party of two. You are a beautiful sewer, Miss Bryant."

"Yes, I'm the best sewer in these parts," said Miss Cornelia in a matter-of-fact tone. "I ought to be! Lord, I've done more of it than if I'd had a hundred children of my own, believe ME! I s'pose I'm a fool, to be putting hand embroidery on this dress for an eighth baby. But, Lord, Mrs. Blythe, dearie, it isn't to blame for being the eighth, and I kind of wished it to have one real pretty dress, just as if it WAS wanted. Nobody's wanting the poor mite—so I put some extra fuss on its little things just on that account."

"Any baby might be proud of that dress," said Anne, feeling still more strongly that she was going to like Miss Cornelia.

"I s'pose you've been thinking I was never coming to call on you," resumed Miss Cornelia. "But this is harvest month, you know, and I've been busy—and a lot of extra hands hanging round, eating more'n they work, just like the men. I'd have come yesterday, but I went to Mrs. Roderick MacAllister's funeral. At first I thought my head was aching so badly I couldn't enjoy myself if I did go. But she was a hundred years old, and I'd always promised myself that I'd go to her funeral."

"Was it a successful function?" asked Anne, noticing that the office door was ajar.

"What's that? Oh, yes, it was a tremendous funeral. She had a very large connection. There was over one hundred and twenty carriages in the procession. There was one or two funny things happened. I thought that die I would to see old Joe Bradshaw, who is an infidel and never darkens the door of a church, singing 'Safe in the Arms of Jesus' with great gusto and fervor. He glories in singing— that's why he never misses a funeral. Poor Mrs. Bradshaw didn't look much like singing—all wore out slaving. Old Joe starts out once in a while to buy her a present and brings home some new kind of farm machinery. Isn't that like a man? But what else would you expect of a man who never goes to church, even a Methodist one? I was real thankful to see you and the young Doctor in the Presbyterian church your first Sunday. No doctor for me who isn't a Presbyterian."

"We were in the Methodist church last Sunday evening," said Anne wickedly.

"Oh, I s'pose Dr. Blythe has to go to the Methodist church once in a while or he wouldn't get the Methodist practice."

"We liked the sermon very much," declared Anne boldly. "And I thought the Methodist minster's prayer was one of the most beautiful I ever heard."

"Oh, I've no doubt he can pray. I never heard anyone make more beautiful prayers than old Simon Bentley, who was always drunk, or hoping to be, and the drunker he was the better he prayed."

"The Methodist minister is very fine looking," said Anne, for the benefit of the office door.

"Yes, he's quite ornamental," agreed Miss Cornelia. "Oh, and VERY ladylike. And he thinks that every girl who looks at him falls in love with him—as if a Methodist minister, wandering about like any Jew, was such a prize! If you and the young doctor take MY advice, you won't have much to do with the Methodists. My motto is—if you ARE a Presbyterian, BE a Presbyterian."

"Don't you think that Methodists go to heaven as well as Presbyterians?" asked Anne smilelessly.

"That isn't for US to decide. It's in higher hands than ours," said Miss Cornelia solemnly. "But I ain't going to associate with them on earth whatever I may have to do in heaven. THIS Methodist minister isn't married. The last one they had was, and his wife was the silliest, flightiest little thing I ever saw. I told her husband once that he should have waited till she was grown up before he married her. He said he wanted to have the training of her. Wasn't that like a man?"

"It's rather hard to decide just when people ARE grown up," laughed Anne.

"That's a true word, dearie. Some are grown up when they're born, and others ain't grown up when they're eighty, believe ME. That same Mrs. Roderick I was speaking of never grew up. She was as foolish when she was a hundred as when she was ten."

"Perhaps that was why she lived so long," suggested Anne.

"Maybe 'twas. I'd rather live fifty sensible years than a hundred foolish ones."

"But just think what a dull world it would be if everyone was sensible," pleaded Anne.

Miss Cornelia disdained any skirmish of flippant epigram.

"Mrs. Roderick was a Milgrave, and the Milgraves never had much sense. Her nephew, Ebenezer Milgrave, used to be insane for years. He believed he was dead and used to rage at his wife because she wouldn't bury him. I'd a-done it."

Miss Cornelia looked so grimly determined that Anne could almost see her with a spade in her hand.

"Don't you know ANY good husbands, Miss Bryant?"

"Oh, yes, lots of them—over yonder," said Miss Cornelia, waving her hand through the open window towards the little graveyard of the church across the harbor.

"But living—going about in the flesh?" persisted Anne.

"Oh, there's a few, just to show that with God all things are possible," acknowledged Miss Cornelia reluctantly. "I don't deny that an odd man here and there, if he's caught young and trained up proper, and if his mother has spanked him well beforehand, may turn out a decent being. YOUR husband, now, isn't so bad, as men go, from all I hear. I s'pose"—Miss Cornelia looked sharply at Anne over her glasses—"you think there's nobody like him in the world."

"There isn't," said Anne promptly.

"Ah, well, I heard another bride say that once," sighed Miss Cornelia. "Jennie Dean thought when she married that there wasn't anybody like HER husband in the world. And she was right—there wasn't! And a good thing, too, believe ME! He led her an awful life—and he was courting his second wife while Jennie was dying.

"Wasn't that like a man? However, I hope YOUR confidence will be better justified, dearie. The young doctor is taking real well. I was afraid at first he mightn't, for folks hereabouts have always thought old Doctor Dave the only doctor in the world. Doctor Dave hadn't much tact, to be sure—he was always talking of ropes in houses where someone had hanged himself. But folks forgot their hurt feelings when they had a pain in their stomachs. If he'd been a minister instead of a doctor they'd never have forgiven him. Soul-ache doesn't worry folks near as much as stomach-ache. Seeing as we're both Presbyterians and no Methodists around, will you tell me your candid opinion of OUR minister?"

"Why—really—I—well," hesitated Anne.

Miss Cornelia nodded.

"Exactly. I agree with you, dearie. We made a mistake when we called HIM. His face just looks like one of those long, narrow stones in the graveyard, doesn't it? 'Sacred to the memory' ought to be written on his forehead. I shall never forget the first sermon he preached after he came. It was on the subject of everyone doing what they were best fitted for—a very good subject, of course; but such illustrations as he used! He said, 'If you had a cow and an apple tree, and if you tied the apple tree in your stable and planted the cow in your orchard, with her legs up, how much milk would you get from the apple tree, or how many apples from the cow?' Did you ever hear the like in your born days, dearie? I was so thankful there were no Methodists there that day—they'd never have been done hooting over it. But what I dislike most in him is his habit of agreeing with everybody, no matter what is said. If you said to him, 'You're a scoundrel,' he'd say, with that smooth smile of his, 'Yes, that's so.' A minister should have more backbone. The long and the short of it is, I consider him a reverend jackass. But, of course, this is just between you and me. When there are Methodists in hearing I praise him to the skies. Some folks think his wife dresses too gay, but *I* say when she has to live with a face like that she needs something to cheer her up. You'll never hear ME condemning a woman for her dress. I'm only too thankful when her husband isn't too mean and miserly to allow it. Not that I bother much with dress myself. Women just dress to please the men, and I'd never stoop to THAT. I have had a real placid, comfortable life, dearie, and it's just because I never cared a cent what the men thought."

"Why do you hate the men so, Miss Bryant?"

"Lord, dearie, I don't hate them. They aren't worth it. I just sort of despise them. I think I'll like YOUR husband if he keeps on as he has begun. But apart from him about the only men in the world I've much use for are the old doctor and Captain Jim."

"Captain Jim is certainly splendid," agreed Anne cordially.

"Captain Jim is a good man, but he's kind of vexing in one way. You CAN'T make him mad. I've tried for twenty years and he just keeps on being placid. It does sort of rile me. And I s'pose the woman he should have married got a man who went into tantrums twice a day."

"Who was she?"

"Oh, I don't know, dearie. I never remember of Captain Jim making up to anybody. He was edging on old as far as my memory goes. He's seventy-six, you know. I never heard any reason for his staying a bachelor, but there must be one, believe ME. He sailed all his life till five years ago, and there's no corner of the earth he hasn't poked his nose into. He and Elizabeth Russell were great cronies, all their lives, but they never had any notion of sweet-hearting. Elizabeth never married, though she had plenty of chances. She was a great beauty when she was young. The year the Prince of Wales came to the Island she was visiting her uncle in Charlottetown and he was a Government official, and so she got invited to the great ball. She was the prettiest girl there, and the Prince danced with her, and all the other women he didn't dance with were furious about it, because their social standing was higher than hers and they said he shouldn't have passed them over. Elizabeth was always very proud of that dance. Mean folks said that was why she never married—she couldn't put up with an ordinary man after dancing with a prince. But that wasn't so. She told me the reason once—it was because she had such a temper that she was afraid she couldn't live peaceably with any man. She HAD an awful temper—she used to have to go upstairs and bite pieces out of her bureau to keep it down by times. But I told her that wasn't any reason for not marrying if she wanted to. There's no reason why we should let the men have a monopoly of temper, is there, Mrs. Blythe, dearie?"

"I've a bit of temper myself," sighed Anne.

"It's well you have, dearie. You won't be half so likely to be trodden on, believe ME! My, how that golden glow of yours is blooming! Your garden looks fine. Poor Elizabeth always took such care of it."

"I love it," said Anne. "I'm glad it's so full of old-fashioned flowers. Speaking of gardening, we want to get a man to dig up that little lot beyond the fir grove and set it out with strawberry plants for us. Gilbert is so busy he will never get time for it this fall. Do you know anyone we can get?"

"Well, Henry Hammond up at the Glen goes out doing jobs like that. He'll do, maybe. He's always a heap more interested in his wages than in his work, just like a man, and he's so slow in the uptake that he stands still for five minutes before it dawns on him that he's stopped. His father threw a stump at him when he was small.

"Nice gentle missile, wasn't it? So like a man! Course, the boy never got over it. But he's the only one I can recommend at all. He painted my house for me last spring. It looks real nice now, don't you think?"

Anne was saved by the clock striking five.

"Lord, is it that late?" exclaimed Miss Cornelia. "How time does slip by when you're enjoying yourself! Well, I must betake myself home."

"No, indeed! You are going to stay and have tea with us," said Anne eagerly.

"Are you asking me because you think you ought to, or because you really want to?" demanded Miss Cornelia.

"Because I really want to."

"Then I'll stay. YOU belong to the race that knows Joseph."

"I know we are going to be friends," said Anne, with the smile that only they of the household of faith ever saw.

"Yes, we are, dearie. Thank goodness, we can choose our friends. We have to take our relatives as they are, and be thankful if there are no penitentiary birds among them. Not that I've many—none nearer than second cousins. I'm a kind of lonely soul, Mrs. Blythe."

There was a wistful note in Miss Cornelia's voice.

"I wish you would call me Anne," exclaimed Anne impulsively. "It would seem more HOMEY. Everyone in Four Winds, except my husband, calls me Mrs. Blythe, and it makes me feel like a stranger. Do you know that your name is very near being the one I yearned after when I was a child. I hated 'Anne' and I called myself 'Cordelia' in imagination."

"I like Anne. It was my mother's name. Old-fashioned names are the best and sweetest in my opinion. If you're going to get tea you might send the young doctor to talk to me. He's been lying on the sofa in that office ever since I came, laughing fit to kill over what I've been saying."

"How did you know?" cried Anne, too aghast at this instance of Miss Cornelia's uncanny prescience to make a polite denial.

"I saw him sitting beside you when I came up the lane, and I know men's tricks," retorted Miss Cornelia. "There, I've finished my little dress, dearie, and the eighth baby can come as soon as it pleases."

CHAPTER 9 - AN EVENING AT FOUR WINDS POINT

It was late September when Anne and Gilbert were able to pay Four Winds light their promised visit. They had often planned to go, but something always occurred to prevent them. Captain Jim had "dropped in" several times at the little house.

"I don't stand on ceremony, Mistress Blythe," he told Anne. "It's a real pleasure to me to come here, and I'm not going to deny myself jest because you haven't got down to see me. There oughtn't to be no bargaining like that among the race that knows Joseph. I'll come when I can, and you come when you can, and so long's we have our pleasant little chat it don't matter a mite what roof's over us."

Captain Jim took a great fancy to Gog and Magog, who were presiding over the destinies of the hearth in the little house with as much dignity and aplomb as they had done at Patty's Place.

"Aren't they the cutest little cusses?" he would say delightedly; and he bade them greeting and farewell as gravely and invariably as he did his host and hostess. Captain Jim was not going to offend household deities by any lack of reverence and ceremony.

"You've made this little house just about perfect," he told Anne. "It never was so nice before. Mistress Selwyn had your taste and she did wonders; but folks in those days didn't have the pretty little curtains and pictures and nicknacks you have. As for Elizabeth, she lived in the past. You've kinder brought the future into it, so to speak. I'd be real happy even if we couldn't talk at all, when I come here—jest to sit and look at you and your pictures and your flowers would be enough of a treat. It's beautiful—beautiful."

Captain Jim was a passionate worshipper of beauty. Every lovely thing heard or seen gave him a deep, subtle, inner joy that irradiated his life. He was quite keenly aware of his own lack of outward comeliness and lamented it.

"Folks say I'm good," he remarked whimsically upon one occasion, "but I sometimes wish the Lord had made me only half as good and put the rest of it into looks. But there, I reckon He knew what He was about, as a good Captain should. Some of us have to be homely, or the purty ones—like Mistress Blythe here—wouldn't show up so well."

One evening Anne and Gilbert finally walked down to the Four Winds light. The day had begun sombrely in gray cloud and mist, but it had ended in a pomp of scarlet and gold. Over the western hills beyond the harbor were amber deeps and crystalline shallows, with the fire of sunset below. The north was a mackerel sky of little, fiery golden clouds. The red light flamed on the white sails of a vessel gliding down the channel, bound to a southern port in a land of palms. Beyond her, it smote upon and incarnadined the shining, white, grassless faces of the sand dunes. To the right, it fell on the old house among the willows up the brook, and gave it for a fleeting space casements more splendid than those of an old cathedral. They glowed out of its quiet and grayness like the throbbing, blood-red thoughts of a vivid soul imprisoned in a dull husk of environment.

"That old house up the brook always seems so lonely," said Anne. "I never see visitors there. Of course, its lane opens on the upper road—but I don't think there's much coming and going. It seems odd we've never met the Moores yet, when they live within fifteen minutes' walk of us. I may have seen them in church, of course, but if so I didn't know them. I'm sorry they are so unsociable, when they are our only near neighbors."

"Evidently they don't belong to the race that knows Joseph," laughed Gilbert. "Have you ever found out who that girl was whom you thought so beautiful?"

"No. Somehow I have never remembered to ask about her. But I've never seen her anywhere, so I suppose she must have been a stranger. Oh, the sun has just vanished—and there's the light."

As the dusk deepened, the great beacon cut swathes of light through it, sweeping in a circle over the fields and the harbor, the sandbar and the gulf.

"I feel as if it might catch me and whisk me leagues out to sea," said Anne, as one drenched them with radiance; and she felt rather relieved when they got so near the Point that they were inside the range of those dazzling, recurrent flashes.

As they turned into the little lane that led across the fields to the Point they met a man coming out of it—a man of such extraordinary appearance that for a moment they both frankly stared. He was a decidedly fine-looking person-tall, broad-shouldered, well-featured, with a Roman nose and frank gray eyes; he was dressed in a prosperous farmer's Sunday best; in so far he might have been any inhabitant of Four Winds or the Glen. But, flowing over his breast nearly to his knees, was a river of crinkly brown beard; and adown his back, beneath his commonplace felt hat, was a corresponding cascade of thick, wavy, brown hair.

"Anne," murmured Gilbert, when they were out of earshot, "you didn't put what Uncle Dave calls 'a little of the Scott Act' in that lemonade you gave me just before we left home, did you?"

"No, I didn't," said Anne, stifling her laughter, lest the retreating enigma should hear here. "Who in the world can he be?"

"I don't know; but if Captain Jim keeps apparitions like that down at this Point I'm going to carry cold iron in my pocket when I come here. He wasn't a sailor, or one might pardon his eccentricity of appearance; he must belong to the over-harbor clans. Uncle Dave says they have several freaks over there."

"Uncle Dave is a little prejudiced, I think. You know all the over-harbor people who come to the Glen Church seem very nice. Oh, Gilbert, isn't this beautiful?"

The Four Winds light was built on a spur of red sand-stone cliff jutting out into the gulf. On one side, across the channel, stretched the silvery sand shore of the bar; on the other, extended a long, curving beach of red cliffs, rising steeply from the pebbled coves. It was a shore that knew the magic and mystery of storm and star. There is a great solitude about such a shore. The woods are never solitary—they are full of whispering, beckoning, friendly life. But the sea is a mighty soul, forever moaning of some great, unshareable sorrow, which shuts it up into itself for all eternity. We can never pierce its infinite mystery—we may only wander, awed and spellbound, on the outer fringe of it. The woods call to us with a hundred voices, but the sea has one only—a mighty voice that drowns our souls in its majestic music. The woods are human, but the sea is of the company of the archangels.

Anne and Gilbert found Uncle Jim sitting on a bench outside the lighthouse, putting the finishing touches to a wonderful, full-rigged, toy schooner. He rose and welcomed them to his abode with the gentle, unconscious courtesy that became him so well.

"This has been a purty nice day all through, Mistress Blythe, and now, right at the last, it's brought its best. Would you like to sit down here outside a bit, while the light lasts? I've just finished this bit of a plaything for my little grand nephew, Joe, up at the Glen. After I promised to make it for him I was kinder sorry, for his mother was vexed. She's afraid he'll be wanting to go to sea later on and she doesn't want the notion encouraged in him. But what could I do, Mistress Blythe? I'd PROMISED him, and I think it's sorter real dastardly to break a promise you make to a child. Come, sit down. It won't take long to stay an hour."

The wind was off shore, and only broke the sea's surface into long, silvery ripples, and sent sheeny shadows flying out across it, from every point and headland, like transparent wings. The dusk was hanging a curtain of violet gloom over the sand dunes and the headlands where gulls were huddling. The sky was faintly filmed over with scarfs of silken vapor. Cloud fleets rode at anchor along the horizons. An evening star was watching over the bar.

"Isn't that a view worth looking at?" said Captain Jim, with a loving, proprietary pride. "Nice and far from the market-place, ain't it? No buying and selling and getting gain. You don't have to pay anything—all that sea and sky free—'without money and without price.' There's going to be a moonrise purty soon, too—I'm never tired of finding out what a moonrise can be over them rocks and sea and harbor. There's a surprise in it every time."

They had their moonrise, and watched its marvel and magic in a silence that asked nothing of the world or each other. Then they went up into the tower, and Captain Jim showed and explained the mechanism of the great light. Finally they found themselves in the dining room, where a fire of driftwood was weaving flames of wavering, elusive, sea-born hues in the open fireplace.

"I put this fireplace in myself," remarked Captain Jim. "The Government don't give lighthouse keepers such luxuries. Look at the colors that wood makes. If you'd like some driftwood for your fire, Mistress Blythe, I'll bring you up a load some day. Sit down. I'm going to make you a cup of tea."

Captain Jim placed a chair for Anne, having first removed therefrom a huge, orange-colored cat and a newspaper.

"Get down, Matey. The sofa is your place. I must put this paper away safe till I can find time to finish the story in it. It's called A Mad Love. 'Tisn't my favorite brand of fiction, but I'm reading it jest to see how long she can spin it out. It's at the sixty-second chapter now, and the wedding ain't any nearer than when it begun, far's I can see. When little Joe comes I have to read him pirate yarns. Ain't it strange how innocent little creatures like children like the blood-thirstiest stories?"

"Like my lad Davy at home," said Anne. "He wants tales that reek with gore."

Captain Jim's tea proved to be nectar. He was pleased as a child with Anne's compliments, but he affected a fine indifference.

"The secret is I don't skimp the cream," he remarked airily. Captain Jim had never heard of Oliver Wendell Holmes, but he evidently agreed with that writer's dictum that "big heart never liked little cream pot."

"We met an odd-looking personage coming out of your lane," said Gilbert as they sipped. "Who was he?"

Captain Jim grinned.

"That's Marshall Elliott—a mighty fine man with jest one streak of foolishness in him. I s'pose you wondered what his object was in turning himself into a sort of dime museum freak."

"Is he a modern Nazarite or a Hebrew prophet left over from olden times?" asked Anne.

"Neither of them. It's politics that's at the bottom of his freak. All those Elliotts and Crawfords and MacAllisters are dyed-in-the-wool politicians. They're born Grit or Tory, as the case may be, and they live Grit or Tory, and they die Grit or Tory; and what they're going to do in heaven, where there's probably no politics, is more than I can fathom. This Marshall Elliott was born a Grit. I'm a Grit myself in moderation, but there's no moderation about Marshall. Fifteen years ago there was a specially bitter general election. Marshall fought for his party tooth and nail. He was dead sure the Liberals would win—so sure that he got up at a public meeting and vowed that he wouldn't shave his face or cut his hair until the Grits were in power. Well, they didn't go in—and they've never got in yet—and you saw the result today for yourselves. Marshall stuck to his word."

"What does his wife think of it?" asked Anne.

"He's a bachelor. But if he had a wife I reckon she couldn't make him break that vow. That family of Elliotts has always been more stubborn than natteral. Marshall's brother Alexander had a dog he set great store by, and when it died the man actilly wanted to have it buried in the graveyard, 'along with the other Christians,' he said. Course, he wasn't allowed to; so he buried it just outside the graveyard fence, and never darkened the church door again. But Sundays he'd drive his family to church and sit by that dog's grave and read his Bible all the time service was going on. They say when he was dying he asked his wife to bury him beside the dog; she was a meek little soul but she fired up at THAT. She said SHE wasn't going to be buried beside no dog, and if he'd rather have his last resting place beside the dog than beside her, jest to say so. Alexander Elliott was a stubborn mule, but he was fond of his wife, so he give in and said, 'Well, durn it, bury me where you please. But when Gabriel's trump blows I expect my dog to rise with the rest of us, for he had as much soul as any durned Elliott or Crawford or MacAllister that ever strutted.' Them was HIS parting words. As for Marshall, we're all used to him, but he must strike strangers as right down peculiar-looking. I've known him ever since he was ten—he's about fifty now—and I like him. Him and me was out cod-fishing today. That's about all I'm good for now—catching trout and cod occasional. But 'tweren't always so—not by no manner of means. I used to do other things, as you'd admit if you saw my life-book."

Anne was just going to ask what his life-book was when the First Mate created a diversion by springing upon Captain Jim's knee. He was a gorgeous beastie, with a face as round as a full moon, vivid green eyes, and immense, white, double paws. Captain Jim stroked his velvet back gently.

"I never fancied cats much till I found the First Mate," he remarked, to the accompaniment of the Mate's tremendous purrs. "I saved his life, and when you've saved a creature's life you're bound to love it. It's next thing to giving life. There's some turrible thoughtless people in the world, Mistress Blythe. Some of them city folks who have summer homes over the harbor are so thoughtless that they're cruel. It's the worst kind of cruelty—the thoughtless kind. You can't cope with it. They keep cats there in the summer, and feed and pet 'em, and doll 'em up with ribbons and collars. And then in the fall they go off and leave 'em to starve or freeze. It makes my blood boil, Mistress Blythe. One day last winter I found a poor old mother cat dead on the shore, lying against the skin-and-bone bodies of her three little kittens. She'd died trying to shelter 'em. She had her poor stiff paws around 'em. Master, I cried. Then I swore. Then I carried them poor little kittens home and fed 'em up and found good homes for 'em. I knew the woman who left the cat and when she come back this summer I jest went over the harbor and told her my opinion of her. It was rank meddling, but I do love meddling in a good cause."

"How did she take it?" asked Gilbert.

"Cried and said she 'didn't think.' I says to her, says I, 'Do you s'pose that'll be held for a good excuse in the day of Jedgment, when you'll have to account for that poor old mother's life? The Lord'll ask you what He give you your brains for if it wasn't to think, I reckon.' I don't fancy she'll leave cats to starve another time."

"Was the First Mate one of the forsaken?" asked Anne, making advances to him which were responded to graciously, if condescendingly.

"Yes. I found HIM one bitter cold day in winter, caught in the branches of a tree by his durn-fool ribbon collar. He was almost starving. If you could have seen his eyes, Mistress Blythe! He was nothing but a kitten, and he'd got his living somehow since he'd been left until he got hung up. When I loosed him he gave my hand a pitiful swipe with his little red tongue. He wasn't the able seaman you see now. He was meek as Moses. That was nine years ago. His life has been long in the land for a cat. He's a good old pal, the First Mate is."

"I should have expected you to have a dog," said Gilbert.

Captain Jim shook his head.

"I had a dog once. I thought so much of him that when he died I couldn't bear the thought of getting another in his place. He was a FRIEND—you understand, Mistress Blythe? Matey's only a pal. I'm fond of Matey—all the fonder on account of the spice of devilment that's in him—like there is in all cats. But I LOVED my dog. I always had a sneaking sympathy for Alexander Elliott about HIS dog. There isn't any devil in a good dog. That's why they're more lovable than cats, I reckon. But I'm darned if they're as interesting. Here I am, talking too much. Why don't you check me? When I do get a chance to talk to anyone I run on turrible. If you've done your tea I've a few little things you might like to look at—picked 'em up in the queer corners I used to be poking my nose into."

Captain Jim's "few little things" turned out to be a most interesting collection of curios, hideous, quaint and beautiful. And almost every one had some striking story attached to it.

Anne never forgot the delight with which she listened to those old tales that moonlit evening by that enchanted driftwood fire, while the silver sea called to them through the open window and sobbed against the rocks below them.

Captain Jim never said a boastful word, but it was impossible to help seeing what a hero the man had been—brave, true, resourceful, unselfish. He sat there in his little room and made those things live again for his hearers. By a lift of the eyebrow, a twist of the lip, a gesture, a word, he painted a whole scene or character so that they saw it as it was.

Some of Captain Jim's adventures had such a marvellous edge that Anne and Gilbert secretly wondered if he were not drawing a rather long bow at their credulous expense. But in this, as they found later, they did him injustice. His tales were all literally true. Captain Jim had the gift of the born storyteller, whereby "unhappy, far-off things" can be brought vividly before the hearer in all their pristine poignancy.

Anne and Gilbert laughed and shivered over his tales, and once Anne found herself crying. Captain Jim surveyed her tears with pleasure shining from his face.

"I like to see folks cry that way," he remarked. "It's a compliment. But I can't do justice to the things I've seen or helped to do. I've 'em all jotted down in my life-book, but I haven't got the knack of writing them out properly. If I could hit on jest the right words and string 'em together proper on paper I could make a great book. It would beat A Mad Love holler, and I believe Joe'd like it as well as the pirate yarns. Yes, I've had some adventures in my time; and, do you know,

614

Mistress Blythe, I still lust after 'em. Yes, old and useless as I be, there's an awful longing sweeps over me at times to sail out—out—out there—forever and ever."

"Like Ulysses, you would

> 'Sail beyond the sunset and the baths
> Of all the western stars until you die,'"

said Anne dreamily.

"Ulysses? I've read of him. Yes, that's just how I feel—jest how all us old sailors feel, I reckon. I'll die on land after all, I s'pose. Well, what is to be will be. There was old William Ford at the Glen who never went on the water in his life, 'cause he was afraid of being drowned. A fortune-teller had predicted he would be. And one day he fainted and fell with his face in the barn trough and was drowned. Must you go? Well, come soon and come often. The doctor is to do the talking next time. He knows a heap of things I want to find out. I'm sorter lonesome here by times. It's been worse since Elizabeth Russell died. Her and me was such cronies."

Captain Jim spoke with the pathos of the aged, who see their old friends slipping from them one by one—friends whose place can never be quite filled by those of a younger generation, even of the race that knows Joseph. Anne and Gilbert promised to come soon and often.

"He's a rare old fellow, isn't he?" said Gilbert, as they walked home.

"Somehow, I can't reconcile his simple, kindly personality with the wild, adventurous life he has lived," mused Anne.

"You wouldn't find it so hard if you had seen him the other day down at the fishing village. One of the men of Peter Gautier's boat made a nasty remark about some girl along the shore. Captain Jim fairly scorched the wretched fellow with the lightning of his eyes. He seemed a man transformed. He didn't say much—but the way he said it! You'd have thought it would strip the flesh from the fellow's bones. I understand that Captain Jim will never allow a word against any woman to be said in his presence."

"I wonder why he never married," said Anne. "He should have sons with their ships at sea now, and grandchildren climbing over him to hear his stories—he's that kind of a man. Instead, he has nothing but a magnificent cat."

But Anne was mistaken. Captain Jim had more than that. He had a memory.

CHAPTER 10 - LESLIE MOORE

"I'm going for a walk to the outside shore tonight," Anne told Gog and Magog one October evening. There was no one else to tell, for Gilbert had gone over the harbor. Anne had her little domain in the speckless order one would expect of anyone brought up by Marilla Cuthbert, and felt that she could gad shoreward with a clear conscience. Many and delightful had been her shore rambles, sometimes with Gilbert, sometimes with Captain Jim, sometimes alone with her own thoughts and new, poignantly-sweet dreams that were beginning to span life with their rainbows. She loved the gentle, misty harbor shore and the silvery, wind-haunted sand shore, but best of all she loved the rock shore, with its cliffs and caves and piles of surf-worn boulders, and its coves where the pebbles glittered under the pools; and it was to this shore she hied herself tonight.

There had been an autumn storm of wind and rain, lasting for three days. Thunderous had been the crash of billows on the rocks, wild the white spray and spume that blew over the bar, troubled and misty and tempest-torn the erstwhile blue peace of Four Winds Harbor. Now it was over, and the shore lay clean-washed after the storm; not a wind stirred, but there was still a fine surf on, dashing on sand and rock in a splendid white turmoil—the only restless thing in the great, pervading stillness and peace.

"Oh, this is a moment worth living through weeks of storm and stress for," Anne exclaimed, delightedly sending her far gaze across the tossing waters from the top of the cliff where she stood. Presently she scrambled down the steep path to the little cove below, where she seemed shut in with rocks and sea and sky.

"I'm going to dance and sing," she said. "There's no one here to see me—the seagulls won't carry tales of the matter. I may be as crazy as I like."

She caught up her skirt and pirouetted along the hard strip of sand just out of reach of the waves that almost lapped her feet with their spent foam. Whirling round and round, laughing like a child, she reached the little headland that ran out to the east of the cove; then she stopped suddenly, blushing crimson; she was not alone; there had been a witness to her dance and laughter.

The girl of the golden hair and sea-blue eyes was sitting on a boulder of the headland, half-hidden by a jutting rock. She was looking straight at Anne with a strange expression—part wonder, part sympathy, part—could it be?—envy. She was bare-headed, and her splendid hair, more than ever like Browning's "gorgeous snake," was bound about her head with a crimson ribbon. She wore a dress of some dark material, very plainly made; but swathed about her waist, outlining its fine curves, was a vivid girdle of red silk. Her hands, clasped over her knee, were brown and somewhat work-hardened; but the skin of her throat and cheeks was as white as cream. A flying gleam of sunset broke through a low-lying western cloud and fell across her hair. For a moment she seemed the spirit of the sea personified—all its mystery, all its passion, all its elusive charm.

"You—you must think me crazy," stammered Anne, trying to recover her self-possession. To be seen by this stately girl in such an abandon of childishness—she, Mrs. Dr. Blythe, with all the dignity of the matron to keep up—it was too bad!

"No," said the girl, "I don't."

She said nothing more; her voice was expressionless; her manner slightly repellent; but there was something in her eyes—eager yet shy, defiant yet pleading—which turned Anne from her purpose of walking away. Instead, she sat down on the boulder beside the girl.

"Let's introduce ourselves," she said, with the smile that had never yet failed to win confidence and friendliness. "I am Mrs. Blythe—and I live in that little white house up the harbor shore."

"Yes, I know," said the girl. "I am Leslie Moore—Mrs. Dick Moore," she added stiffly.

Anne was silent for a moment from sheer amazement. It had not occurred to her that this girl was married—there seemed nothing of the wife about her. And that she should be the neighbor whom Anne had pictured as a commonplace Four Winds housewife! Anne could not quickly adjust her mental focus to this astonishing change.

"Then—then you live in that gray house up the brook," she stammered.

"Yes. I should have gone over to call on you long ago," said the other. She did not offer any explanation or excuse for not having gone.

"I wish you WOULD come," said Anne, recovering herself somewhat. "We're such near neighbors we ought to be friends. That is the sole fault of Four Winds—there aren't quite enough neighbors. Otherwise it is perfection."

"You like it?"

"LIKE it! I love it. It is the most beautiful place I ever saw."

"I've never seen many places," said Leslie Moore, slowly, "but I've always thought it was very lovely here. I—I love it, too."

She spoke, as she looked, shyly, yet eagerly. Anne had an odd impression that this strange girl—the word "girl" would persist—could say a good deal if she chose.

"I often come to the shore," she added.

"So do I," said Anne. "It's a wonder we haven't met here before."

"Probably you come earlier in the evening than I do. It is generally late—almost dark—when I come. And I love to come just after a storm—like this. I don't like the sea so well when it's calm and quiet. I like the struggle—and the crash—and the noise."

"I love it in all its moods," declared Anne. "The sea at Four Winds is to me what Lover's Lane was at home. Tonight it seemed so free—so untamed—something broke loose in me, too, out of sympathy. That was why I danced along the shore in that wild way. I didn't suppose anybody was looking, of course. If Miss Cornelia Bryant had seen me she would have forboded a gloomy prospect for poor young Dr. Blythe."

"You know Miss Cornelia?" said Leslie, laughing. She had an exquisite laugh; it bubbled up suddenly and unexpectedly with something of the delicious quality of a baby's. Anne laughed, too.

"Oh, yes. She has been down to my house of dreams several times."

"Your house of dreams?"

"Oh, that's a dear, foolish little name Gilbert and I have for our home. We just call it that between ourselves. It slipped out before I thought."

"So Miss Russell's little white house is YOUR house of dreams," said Leslie wonderingly. "*I* had a house of dreams once—but it was a palace," she added, with a laugh, the sweetness of which was marred by a little note of derision.

"Oh, I once dreamed of a palace, too," said Anne. "I suppose all girls do. And then we settle down contentedly in eight-room houses that seem to fulfill all the desires of our hearts—because our prince is there. YOU should have had your palace really, though—you are so beautiful. You MUST let me say it—it has to be said—I'm nearly bursting with admiration. You are the loveliest thing I ever saw, Mrs. Moore."

"If we are to be friends you must call me Leslie," said the other with an odd passion.

"Of course I will. And MY friends call me Anne."

"I suppose I am beautiful," Leslie went on, looking stormily out to sea. "I hate my beauty. I wish I had always been as brown and plain as the brownest and plainest girl at the fishing village over there. Well, what do you think of Miss Cornelia?"

The abrupt change of subject shut the door on any further confidences.

"Miss Cornelia is a darling, isn't she?" said Anne. "Gilbert and I were invited to her house to a state tea last week. You've heard of groaning tables."

"I seem to recall seeing the expression in the newspaper reports of weddings," said Leslie, smiling.

"Well, Miss Cornelia's groaned—at least, it creaked—positively. You couldn't have believed she would have cooked so much for two ordinary people. She had every kind of pie you could name, I think—except lemon pie. She said she had taken the prize for lemon pies at the Charlottetown Exhibition ten years ago and had never made any since for fear of losing her reputation for them."

"Were you able to eat enough pie to please her?"

"*I* wasn't. Gilbert won her heart by eating—I won't tell you how much. She said she never knew a man who didn't like pie better than his Bible. Do you know, I love Miss Cornelia."

"So do I," said Leslie. "She is the best friend I have in the world."

Anne wondered secretly why, if this were so, Miss Cornelia had never mentioned Mrs. Dick Moore to her. Miss Cornelia had certainly talked freely about every other individual in or near Four Winds.

"Isn't that beautiful?" said Leslie, after a brief silence, pointing to the exquisite effect of a shaft of light falling through a cleft in the rock behind them, across a dark green pool at its base. "If I had come here—and seen nothing but just that—I would go home satisfied."

"The effects of light and shadow all along these shores are wonderful," agreed Anne. "My little sewing room looks out on the harbor, and I sit at its window and feast my eyes. The colors and shadows are never the same two minutes together."

"And you are never lonely?" asked Leslie abruptly. "Never—when you are alone?"

"No. I don't think I've ever been really lonely in my life," answered Anne. "Even when I'm alone I have real good company—dreams and imaginations and pretendings. I LIKE to be alone now and then, just to think over things and TASTE them. But I love friendship—and nice, jolly little times with people. Oh, WON'T you come to see me—often? Please do. I believe," Anne added, laughing, "that you'd like me if you knew me."

"I wonder if YOU would like ME," said Leslie seriously. She was not fishing for a compliment. She looked out across the waves that were beginning to be garlanded with blossoms of moonlit foam, and her eyes filled with shadows.

"I'm sure I would," said Anne. "And please don't think I'm utterly irresponsible because you saw me dancing on the shore at sunset. No doubt I shall be dignified after a time. You see, I haven't been married very long. I feel like a girl, and sometimes like a child, yet."

"I have been married twelve years," said Leslie.

Here was another unbelievable thing.

"Why, you can't be as old as I am!" exclaimed Anne. "You must have been a child when you were married."

"I was sixteen," said Leslie, rising, and picking up the cap and jacket lying beside her. "I am twenty-eight now. Well, I must go back."

"So must I. Gilbert will probably be home. But I'm so glad we both came to the shore tonight and met each other."

Leslie said nothing, and Anne was a little chilled. She had offered friendship frankly but it had not been accepted very graciously, if it had not been absolutely repelled. In silence they climbed the cliffs and walked across a pasture-field of which the feathery, bleached, wild grasses were like a carpet of creamy velvet in the moonlight. When they reached the shore lane Leslie turned.

"I go this way, Mrs. Blythe. You will come over and see me some time, won't you?"

Anne felt as if the invitation had been thrown at her. She got the impression that Leslie Moore gave it reluctantly.

"I will come if you really want me to," she said a little coldly.

"Oh, I do—I do," exclaimed Leslie, with an eagerness which seemed to burst forth and beat down some restraint that had been imposed on it.

"Then I'll come. Good-night—Leslie."

"Good-night, Mrs. Blythe."

Anne walked home in a brown study and poured out her tale to Gilbert.

"So Mrs. Dick Moore isn't one of the race that knows Joseph?" said Gilbert teasingly.

"No—o—o, not exactly. And yet—I think she WAS one of them once, but has gone or got into exile," said Anne musingly. "She is certainly very different from the other women about here. You can't talk about eggs and butter to HER. To think I've been imagining her a second Mrs. Rachel Lynde! Have you ever seen Dick Moore, Gilbert?"

"No. I've seen several men working about the fields of the farm, but I don't know which was Moore."

"She never mentioned him. I KNOW she isn't happy."

"From what you tell me I suppose she was married before she was old enough to know her own mind or heart, and found out too late that she had made a mistake. It's a common tragedy enough, Anne.

"A fine woman would have made the best of it. Mrs. Moore has evidently let it make her bitter and resentful."

"Don't let us judge her till we know," pleaded Anne. "I don't believe her case is so ordinary. You will understand her fascination when you meet her, Gilbert. It is a thing quite apart from her beauty. I feel that she possesses a rich nature, into which a friend might enter as into a kingdom; but for some reason she bars every one out and shuts all her possibilities up in herself, so that they cannot develop and blossom. There, I've been struggling to define her to myself ever since I left her, and that is the nearest I can get to it. I'm going to ask Miss Cornelia about her."

CHAPTER 11 - THE STORY OF LESLIE MOORE

"Yes, the eighth baby arrived a fortnight ago," said Miss Cornelia, from a rocker before the fire of the little house one chilly October afternoon. "It's a girl. Fred was ranting mad—said he wanted a boy—when the truth is he didn't want it at all. If it had been a boy he'd have ranted because it wasn't a girl. They had four girls and three boys before, so I can't see that it made much difference what this one was, but of course he'd have to be cantankerous, just like a man. The baby is real pretty, dressed up in its nice little clothes. It has black eyes and the dearest, tiny hands."

"I must go and see it. I just love babies," said Anne, smiling to herself over a thought too dear and sacred to be put into words.

"I don't say but what they're nice," admitted Miss Cornelia. "But some folks seem to have more than they really need, believe ME. My poor cousin Flora up at the Glen had eleven, and such a slave as she is! Her husband suicided three years ago. Just like a man!"

"What made him do that?" asked Anne, rather shocked.

"Couldn't get his way over something, so he jumped into the well. A good riddance! He was a born tyrant. But of course it spoiled the well. Flora could never abide the thought of using it again, poor thing! So she had another dug and a frightful expense it was, and the water as hard as nails. If he HAD to drown himself there was plenty of water in the harbor, wasn't there? I've no patience with a man like that. We've only had two suicides in Four Winds in my recollection. The other was Frank West—Leslie Moore's father. By the way, has Leslie ever been over to call on you yet?"

"No, but I met her on the shore a few nights ago and we scraped an acquaintance," said Anne, pricking up her ears.

Miss Cornelia nodded.

"I'm glad, dearie. I was hoping you'd foregather with her. What do you think of her?"

"I thought her very beautiful."

"Oh, of course. There was never anybody about Four Winds could touch her for looks. Did you ever see her hair? It reaches to her feet when she lets it down. But I meant how did you like her?"

"I think I could like her very much if she'd let me," said Anne slowly.

"But she wouldn't let you—she pushed you off and kept you at arm's length. Poor Leslie! You wouldn't be much surprised if you knew what her life has been. It's been a tragedy—a tragedy!" repeated Miss Cornelia emphatically.

"I wish you would tell me all about her—that is, if you can do so without betraying any confidence."

"Lord, dearie, everybody in Four Winds knows poor Leslie's story. It's no secret—the OUTSIDE, that is. Nobody knows the INSIDE but Leslie herself, and she doesn't take folks into her confidence. I'm about the best friend she has on earth, I reckon, and she's never uttered a word of complaint to me. Have you ever seen Dick Moore?"

"No."

"Well, I may as well begin at the beginning and tell you everything straight through, so you'll understand it. As I said, Leslie's father was Frank West. He was clever and shiftless—just like a man. Oh, he had heaps of brains—and much good they did him! He started to go to college, and he went for two years, and then his health broke down. The Wests were all inclined to be consumptive. So Frank came home and started farming. He married Rose Elliott from over harbor. Rose was reckoned the beauty of Four Winds—Leslie takes her looks from her mother, but she has ten times the spirit and go that Rose had, and a far better figure. Now you know, Anne, I always take the ground that us women ought to stand by each other. We've got enough to endure at the hands of the men, the Lord knows, so I hold we hadn't ought to clapper-claw one another, and it isn't often you'll find me running down another woman. But I never had much use for Rose Elliott. She was spoiled to begin with, believe ME, and she was nothing but a lazy, selfish, whining creature. Frank was no hand to work, so they were poor as Job's turkey. Poor! They lived on potatoes and point, believe ME. They had two children—Leslie and Kenneth. Leslie had her mother's looks and her father's brains, and something she didn't get from either of them. She took after her Grandmother West—a splendid old lady. She was the brightest, friendliest, merriest thing when she was a child, Anne. Everybody liked her. She was her father's favorite and she was awful fond of him. They were 'chums,' as she used to say. She couldn't see any of his faults—and he WAS a taking sort of man in some ways.

"Well, when Leslie was twelve years old, the first dreadful thing happened. She worshipped little Kenneth—he was four years younger than her, and he WAS a dear little chap. And he was killed one day—fell off a big load of hay just as it was going into the barn, and the wheel went right over his little body and crushed the life out of it. And mind you, Anne, Leslie saw it. She was looking down from the loft. She gave one screech—the hired man said he never heard such a sound in all his life—he said it would ring in his ears till Gabriel's trump drove it out. But she never screeched or cried again about it. She jumped from the loft onto the load and from the load to the floor, and caught up the little bleeding, warm, dead body, Anne—they had to tear it from her before she would let it go. They sent for me—I can't talk of it."

Miss Cornelia wiped the tears from her kindly brown eyes and sewed in bitter silence for a few minutes.

"Well," she resumed, "it was all over—they buried little Kenneth in that graveyard over the harbor, and after a while Leslie went back to her school and her studies. She never mentioned Kenneth's name—I've never heard it cross her lips from that day to this. I reckon that old hurt still aches and burns at times; but she was only a child and time is real kind to children, Anne, dearie. After a while she began to laugh again—she had the prettiest laugh. You don't often hear it now."

"I heard it once the other night," said Anne. "It IS a beautiful laugh."

"Frank West began to go down after Kenneth's death. He wasn't strong and it was a shock to him, because he was real fond of the child, though, as I've said, Leslie was his favorite. He got mopy and melancholy, and couldn't or wouldn't work. And one day, when Leslie was fourteen years of age, he hanged himself— and in the parlor, too, mind you, Anne, right in the middle of the parlor from the lamp hook in the ceiling. Wasn't that like a man? It was the anniversary of his wedding day, too. Nice, tasty time to pick for it, wasn't it? And, of course, that poor Leslie had to be the one to find him. She went into the parlor that morning, singing, with some fresh flowers for the vases, and there she saw her father hanging from the ceiling, his face as black as a coal. It was something awful, believe ME!"

"Oh, how horrible!" said Anne, shuddering. "The poor, poor child!"

"Leslie didn't cry at her father's funeral any more then she had cried at Kenneth's. Rose whooped and howled for two, however, and Leslie had all she could do trying to calm and comfort her mother. I was disgusted with Rose and so was everyone else, but Leslie never got out of patience. She loved her mother. Leslie is clannish—her own could never do wrong in her eyes. Well, they buried Frank West beside Kenneth, and Rose put up a great big monument to him. It was bigger than his character, believe ME! Anyhow, it was bigger than Rose could afford, for the farm was mortgaged for more than its value. But not long after Leslie's old grandmother West died and she left Leslie a little money—enough to give her a year at Queen's Academy. Leslie had made up her mind to pass for a teacher if she could, and then earn enough to put herself through Redmond College. That had been her father's pet scheme—he wanted her to have what he had lost. Leslie was full of ambition and her head was chock full of brains. She went to Queen's, and she took two years' work in one year and got her First; and when she came home she got the Glen school. She was so happy and hopeful and full of life and eagerness. When I think of what she was then and what she is now, I say—drat the men!"

Miss Cornelia snipped her thread off as viciously as if, Nero-like, she was severing the neck of mankind by the stroke.

"Dick Moore came into her life that summer. His father, Abner Moore, kept store at the Glen, but Dick had a sea-going streak in him from his mother; he used to sail in summer and clerk in his father's store in winter. He was a big, handsome fellow, with a little ugly soul. He was always wanting something till he got it, and then he stopped wanting it—just like a man. Oh, he didn't growl at the weather when it was fine, and he was mostly real pleasant and agreeable when everything went right. But he drank a good deal, and there were some nasty stories told of him and a girl down at the fishing village. He wasn't fit for Leslie to wipe her feet on, that's the long and short of it. And he was a Methodist! But he was clean mad about her—because of her good looks in the first place, and because she wouldn't have anything to say to him in the second. He vowed he'd have her—and he got her!"

"How did he bring it about?"

"Oh, it was an iniquitous thing! I'll never forgive Rose West. You see, dearie, Abner Moore held the mortgage on the West farm, and the interest was overdue some years, and Dick just went and told Mrs. West that if Leslie wouldn't marry him he'd get his father to foreclose the mortgage. Rose carried on terrible—fainted and wept, and pleaded with Leslie not to let her be turned out of her home. She said it would break her heart to leave the home she'd come to as a bride. I wouldn't have blamed her for feeling dreadful bad over it—but you wouldn't have thought she'd be so selfish as to sacrifice her own flesh and blood because of it, would you? Well, she was.

"And Leslie gave in—she loved her mother so much she would have done anything to save her pain. She married Dick Moore. None of us knew why at the time. It wasn't till long afterward that I found out how her mother had worried her into it. I was sure there was something wrong, though, because I knew how she had snubbed him time and again, and it wasn't like Leslie to turn face—about like that. Besides, I knew that Dick Moore wasn't the kind of man Leslie could ever fancy, in spite of his good looks and dashing ways. Of course, there was no wedding, but Rose asked me to go and see them married. I went, but I was sorry I did. I'd seen Leslie's face at her brother's funeral and at her father's funeral—and now it seemed to me I was seeing it at her own funeral. But Rose was smiling as a basket of chips, believe ME!

"Leslie and Dick settled down on the West place—Rose couldn't bear to part with her dear daughter!—and lived there for the winter. In the spring Rose took pneumonia and died—a year too late! Leslie was heart-broken enough over it. Isn't it terrible the way some unworthy folks are loved, while others that deserve it far more, you'd think, never get much affection? As for Dick, he'd had enough of quiet married life—just like a man. He was for up and off. He went over to Nova Scotia to visit his relations—his father had come from Nova Scotia—and he wrote back to Leslie that his cousin, George Moore, was going on a voyage to Havana and he was going too. The name of the vessel was the Four Sisters and they were to be gone about nine weeks.

"It must have been a relief to Leslie. But she never said anything. From the day of her marriage she was just what she is now—cold and proud, and keeping everyone but me at a distance. I won't BE kept at a distance, believe ME! I've just stuck to Leslie as close as I knew how in spite of everything."

"She told me you were the best friend she had," said Anne.

"Did she?" exclaimed Miss Cornelia delightedly. "Well, I'm real thankful to hear it. Sometimes I've wondered if she really did want me around at all—she never let me think so. You must have thawed her out more than you think, or she wouldn't have said that much itself to you. Oh, that poor, heart-broken girl! I never see Dick Moore but I want to run a knife clean through him."

Miss Cornelia wiped her eyes again and having relieved her feelings by her blood-thirsty wish, took up her tale.

"Well, Leslie was left over there alone. Dick had put in the crop before he went, and old Abner looked after it. The summer went by and the Four Sisters didn't come back. The Nova Scotia Moores investigated, and found she had got to Havana and discharged her cargo and took on another and left for home; and that was all they ever found out about her. By degrees people began to talk of Dick Moore as one that was dead. Almost everyone believed that he was, though no one felt certain, for men have turned up here at the harbor after they'd been gone for years. Leslie never thought he was dead—and she was right. A thousand pities too! The next summer Captain Jim was in Havana—that was before he gave up the sea, of course. He thought he'd poke round a bit—Captain Jim was always meddlesome, just like a man—and he went to inquiring round among the sailors' boarding houses and places like that, to see if he could find out anything about the crew of the Four Sisters. He'd better have let sleeping dogs lie, in my opinion! Well, he went to one out-of-the-way place, and there he found a man he knew at first sight it was Dick Moore, though he had a big beard. Captain Jim got it shaved off and then there was no doubt—Dick Moore it was—his body at least. His mind wasn't there—as for his soul, in my opinion he never had one!"

"What had happened to him?"

"Nobody knows the rights of it. All the folks who kept the boarding house could tell was that about a year before they had found him lying on their doorstep one morning in an awful condition—his head battered to a jelly almost. They supposed he'd got hurt in some drunken row, and likely that's the truth of it. They took him in, never thinking he could live. But he did—and he was just like a child when he got well. He hadn't memory or intellect or reason. They tried to find out who he was but they never could. He couldn't even tell them his name—he could only say a few simple words. He had a letter on him beginning 'Dear Dick' and signed 'Leslie,' but there was no address on it and the envelope was gone. They let him stay on—he learned to do a few odd jobs about the place—and there Captain Jim found him. He brought him home—I've always said it was a bad day's work, though I s'pose there was nothing else he could do. He thought maybe when Dick got home and saw his old surroundings and familiar faces his memory would wake up. But it hadn't any effect. There he's been at the house up the brook ever since. He's just like a child, no more nor less. Takes fractious spells occasionally, but mostly he's just vacant and good humored and harmless. He's apt to run away if he isn't watched. That's the burden Leslie has had to carry for eleven years— and all alone. Old Abner Moore died soon after Dick was brought home and it was found he was almost bankrupt. When things were settled up there was nothing for Leslie and Dick but the old West farm. Leslie rented it to John Ward, and the rent is all she has to live on. Sometimes in summer she takes a boarder to help out. But most visitors prefer the other side of the harbor where the hotels and summer cottages are. Leslie's house is too far from the bathing shore. She's taken care of Dick and she's never been away from him for eleven years—she's tied to that imbecile for life. And after all the dreams and hopes she once had! You can imagine what it has been like for her, Anne, dearie—with her beauty and spirit and pride and cleverness. It's just been a living death."

"Poor, poor girl!" said Anne again. Her own happiness seemed to reproach her. What right had she to be so happy when another human soul must be so miserable?

"Will you tell me just what Leslie said and how she acted the night you met her on the shore?" asked Miss Cornelia.

She listened intently and nodded her satisfaction.

"YOU thought she was stiff and cold, Anne, dearie, but I can tell you she thawed out wonderful for her. She must have taken to you real strong. I'm so glad. You may be able to help her a good deal. I was thankful when I heard that a young couple was coming to this house, for I hoped it would mean some friends for Leslie; especially if you belonged to the race that knows Joseph. You WILL be her friend, won't you, Anne, dearie?"

"Indeed I will, if she'll let me," said Anne, with all her own sweet, impulsive earnestness.

"No, you must be her friend, whether she'll let you or not," said Miss Cornelia resolutely. "Don't you mind if she's stiff by times—don't notice it. Remember what her life has been—and is—and must always be, I suppose, for creatures like Dick Moore live forever, I understand. You should see how fat he's got since he came home. He used to be lean enough. Just MAKE her be friends—you can do it—you're one of those who have the knack. Only you mustn't be sensitive. And don't mind if she doesn't seem to want you to go over there much. She knows that some women don't like to be where Dick is—they complain he gives them the creeps. Just get her to come over here as often as she can. She can't get away so very much—she can't leave Dick long, for the Lord knows what he'd do—burn the house down most likely. At nights, after he's in bed and asleep, is about the only time she's free. He always goes to bed early and sleeps like the dead till next morning. That is how you came to meet her at the shore likely. She wanders there considerable."

"I will do everything I can for her," said Anne. Her interest in Leslie Moore, which had been vivid ever since she had seen her driving her geese down the hill, was intensified a thousand fold by Miss Cornelia's narration. The girl's beauty and sorrow and loneliness drew her with an irresistible fascination. She had never known anyone like her; her friends had hitherto been wholesome, normal, merry girls like herself, with only the average trials of human care and bereavement to shadow their girlish dreams. Leslie Moore stood apart, a tragic, appealing figure of thwarted womanhood. Anne resolved that she would win entrance into the kingdom of that lonely soul and find there the comradeship it could so richly give, were it not for the cruel fetters that held it in a prison not of its own making.

"And mind you this, Anne, dearie," said Miss Cornelia, who had not yet wholly relieved her mind, "You mustn't think Leslie is an infidel because she hardly ever goes to church—or even that she's a Methodist. She can't take Dick to church, of course—not that he ever troubled church much in his best days. But you just remember that she's a real strong Presbyterian at heart, Anne, dearie."

CHAPTER 12 - LESLIE COMES OVER

Leslie came over to the house of dreams one frosty October night, when moonlit mists were hanging over the harbor and curling like silver ribbons along the seaward glens. She looked as if she repented coming when Gilbert answered her knock; but Anne flew past him, pounced on her, and drew her in.

"I'm so glad you picked tonight for a call," she said gaily. "I made up a lot of extra good fudge this afternoon and we want someone to help us eat it—before the fire—while we tell stories. Perhaps Captain Jim will drop in, too. This is his night."

"No. Captain Jim is over home," said Leslie. "He—he made me come here," she added, half defiantly.

"I'll say a thank-you to him for that when I see him," said Anne, pulling easy chairs before the fire.

"Oh, I don't mean that I didn't want to come," protested Leslie, flushing a little. "I—I've been thinking of coming—but it isn't always easy for me to get away."

"Of course it must be hard for you to leave Mr. Moore," said Anne, in a matter-of-fact tone. She had decided that it would be best to mention Dick Moore occasionally as an accepted fact, and not give undue morbidness to the subject by avoiding it. She was right, for Leslie's air of constraint suddenly vanished. Evidently she had been wondering how much Anne knew of the conditions of her life and was relieved that no explanations were needed. She allowed her cap and jacket to be taken, and sat down with a girlish snuggle in the big armchair by Magog. She was dressed prettily and carefully, with the customary touch of color in the scarlet geranium at her white throat. Her beautiful hair gleamed like molten gold in the warm firelight. Her sea-blue eyes were full of soft laughter and allurement. For the moment, under the influence of the little house of dreams, she was a girl again—a girl forgetful of the past and its bitterness. The atmosphere of the many loves that had sanctified the little house was all about her; the companionship of two healthy, happy, young folks of her own generation encircled her; she felt and yielded to the magic of her surroundings—Miss Cornelia and Captain Jim would scarcely have recognized her; Anne found it hard to believe that this was the cold, unresponsive woman she had met on the shore—this animated girl who talked and listened with the eagerness of a starved soul. And how hungrily Leslie's eyes looked at the bookcases between the windows!

"Our library isn't very extensive," said Anne, "but every book in it is a FRIEND. We've picked our books up through the years, here and there, never buying one until we had first read it and knew that it belonged to the race of Joseph."

Leslie laughed—beautiful laughter that seemed akin to all the mirth that had echoed through the little house in the vanished years.

"I have a few books of father's—not many," she said. "I've read them until I know them almost by heart. I don't get many books. There's a circulating library at the Glen store—but I don't think the committee who pick the books for Mr. Parker know what books are of Joseph's race—or perhaps they don't care. It was so seldom I got one I really liked that I gave up getting any."

"I hope you'll look on our bookshelves as your own," said Anne.

"You are entirely and wholeheartedly welcome to the loan of any book on them."

"You are setting a feast of fat things before me," said Leslie, joyously. Then, as the clock struck ten, she rose, half unwillingly.

"I must go. I didn't realise it was so late. Captain Jim is always saying it doesn't take long to stay an hour. But I've stayed two—and oh, but I've enjoyed them," she added frankly.

"Come often," said Anne and Gilbert. They had risen and stood together in the firelight's glow. Leslie looked at them—youthful, hopeful, happy, typifying all she had missed and must forever miss. The light went out of her face and eyes; the girl vanished; it was the sorrowful, cheated woman who answered the invitation almost coldly and got herself away with a pitiful haste.

Anne watched her until she was lost in the shadows of the chill and misty night. Then she turned slowly back to the glow of her own radiant hearthstone.

"Isn't she lovely, Gilbert? Her hair fascinates me. Miss Cornelia says it reaches to her feet. Ruby Gillis had beautiful hair—but Leslie's is ALIVE—every thread of it is living gold."

"She is very beautiful," agreed Gilbert, so heartily that Anne almost wished he were a LITTLE less enthusiastic.

"Gilbert, would you like my hair better if it were like Leslie's?" she asked wistfully.

"I wouldn't have your hair any color but just what it is for the world," said Gilbert, with one or two convincing accompaniments.

You wouldn't be ANNE if you had golden hair—or hair of any color but"—

"Red," said Anne, with gloomy satisfaction.

"Yes, red—to give warmth to that milk-white skin and those shining gray-green eyes of yours. Golden hair wouldn't suit you at all Queen Anne—MY Queen Anne—queen of my heart and life and home."

"Then you may admire Leslie's all you like," said Anne magnanimously.

CHAPTER 13 - A GHOSTLY EVENING

One evening, a week later, Anne decided to run over the fields to the house up the brook for an informal call. It was an evening of gray fog that had crept in from the gulf, swathed the harbor, filled the glens and valleys, and clung heavily to the autumnal meadows. Through it the sea sobbed and shuddered. Anne saw Four Winds in a new aspect, and found it weird and mysterious and fascinating; but it also gave her a little feeling of loneliness. Gilbert was away and would be away until the morrow, attending a medical pow-wow in Charlottetown. Anne longed for an hour of fellowship with some girl friend. Captain Jim and Miss Cornelia were "good fellows" each, in their own way; but youth yearned to youth.

"If only Diana or Phil or Pris or Stella could drop in for a chat," she said to herself, "how delightful it would be! This is such a GHOSTLY night. I'm sure all the ships that ever sailed out of Four Winds to their doom could be seen tonight sailing up the harbor with their drowned crews on their decks, if that shrouding fog could suddenly be drawn aside. I feel as if it concealed innumerable mysteries—as if I were surrounded by the wraiths of old generations of Four Winds people peering at me through that gray veil. If ever the dear dead ladies of this little house came back to revisit it they would come on just such a night as this. If I sit here any longer I'll see one of them there opposite me in Gilbert's chair. This place isn't exactly canny tonight. Even Gog and Magog have an air of pricking up their ears to hear the footsteps of unseen guests. I'll run over to see Leslie before I frighten myself with my own fancies, as I did long ago in the matter of the Haunted Wood. I'll leave my house of dreams to welcome back its old inhabitants. My fire will give them my good-will and greeting—they will be gone before I come back, and my house will be mine once more. Tonight I am sure it is keeping a tryst with the past."

Laughing a little over her fancy, yet with something of a creepy sensation in the region of her spine, Anne kissed her hand to Gog and Magog and slipped out into the fog, with some of the new magazines under her arm for Leslie.

"Leslie's wild for books and magazines," Miss Cornelia had told her, "and she hardly ever sees one. She can't afford to buy them or subscribe for them. She's really pitifully poor, Anne. I don't see how she makes out to live at all on the little rent the farm brings in. She never even hints a complaint on the score of poverty, but I know what it must be. She's been handicapped by it all her life. She didn't mind it when she was free and ambitious, but it must gall now, believe ME. I'm glad she seemed so bright and merry the evening she spent with you. Captain Jim told me he had fairly to put her cap and coat on and push her out of the door. Don't be too long going to see her either. If you are she'll think it's because you don't like the sight of Dick, and she'll crawl into her shell again. Dick's a great, big, harmless baby, but that silly grin and chuckle of his do get on some people's nerves. Thank goodness, I've no nerves myself. I like Dick Moore better now than I ever did when he was in his right senses—though the Lord knows that isn't say-ing much. I was down there one day in housecleaning time helping Leslie a bit, and I was frying doughnuts. Dick was hanging round to get one, as usual, and all at once he picked up a scalding hot one I'd just fished out and dropped it on the back of my neck when I was bending over. Then he laughed and laughed. Believe ME, Anne, it took all the grace of God in my heart to keep me from just whisking up that stew-pan of boiling fat and pouring it over his head."

Anne laughed over Miss Cornelia's wrath as she sped through the darkness. But laughter accorded ill with that night. She was sober enough when she reached the house among the willows. Everything was very silent. The front part of the house seemed dark and deserted, so Anne slipped round to the side door, which opened from the veranda into a little sitting room. There she halted noiselessly.

The door was open. Beyond, in the dimly lighted room, sat Leslie Moore, with her arms flung out on the table and her head bent upon them. She was weeping horribly—with low, fierce, choking sobs, as if some agony in her soul were trying to tear itself out. An old black dog was sitting by her, his nose resting on his lap, his big doggish eyes full of mute, imploring sympathy and devotion. Anne drew back in dismay. She felt that she could not intermeddle with this bitterness. Her heart ached with a sympathy she might not utter. To go in now would be to shut the door forever on any possible help or friendship. Some instinct warned Anne that the proud, bitter girl would never forgive the one who thus surprised her in her abandonment of despair.

Anne slipped noiselessly from the veranda and found her way across the yard. Beyond, she heard voices in the gloom and saw the dim glow of a light. At the gate she met two men—Captain Jim with a lantern, and another who she knew must be Dick Moore—a big man, badly gone to fat, with a broad, round, red face, and vacant eyes. Even in the dull light Anne got the impression that there was something unusual about his eyes.

"Is this you, Mistress Blythe?" said Captain Jim. "Now, now, you hadn't oughter be roaming about alone on a night like this. You could get lost in this fog easier than not. Jest you wait till I see Dick safe inside the door and I'll come back and light you over the fields. I ain't going to have Dr. Blythe coming home and finding that you walked clean over Cape Leforce in the fog. A woman did that once, forty years ago.

"So you've been over to see Leslie," he said, when he rejoined her.

"I didn't go in," said Anne, and told what she had seen. Captain Jim sighed.

"Poor, poor, little girl! She don't cry often, Mistress Blythe—she's too brave for that. She must feel terrible when she does cry. A night like this is hard on poor women who have sorrows. There's something about it that kinder brings up all we've suffered—or feared."

"It's full of ghosts," said Anne, with a shiver. "That was why I came over—I wanted to clasp a human hand and hear a human voice.

"There seem to be so many INHUMAN presences about tonight. Even my own dear house was full of them. They fairly elbowed me out. So I fled over here for companionship of my kind."

"You were right not to go in, though, Mistress Blythe. Leslie wouldn't have liked it. She wouldn't have liked me going in with Dick, as I'd have done if I hadn't met you. I had Dick down with me all day. I keep him with me as much as I can to help Leslie a bit."

"Isn't there something odd about his eyes?" asked Anne.

"You noticed that? Yes, one is blue and t'other is hazel—his father had the same. It's a Moore peculiarity. That was what told me he was Dick Moore when I saw him first down in Cuby. If it hadn't a-bin for his eyes I mightn't a-known him, with his beard and fat. You know, I reckon, that it was me found him and brought him home. Miss Cornelia always says I shouldn't have done it, but I can't agree with her. It was the RIGHT thing to do—and so 'twas the only thing. There ain't no question in my mind about THAT. But my old heart aches for Leslie. She's only twenty-eight and she's eaten more bread with sorrow than most women do in eighty years."

They walked on in silence for a little while. Presently Anne said, "Do you know, Captain Jim, I never like walking with a lantern. I have always the strangest feeling that just outside the circle of light, just over its edge in the darkness, I am surrounded by a ring of furtive, sinister things, watching me from the shadows with hostile eyes. I've had that feeling from childhood. What is the reason? I never feel like that when I'm really in the darkness—when it is close all around me—I'm not the least frightened."

"I've something of that feeling myself," admitted Captain Jim. "I reckon when the darkness is close to us it is a friend. But when we sorter push it away from us—divorce ourselves from it, so to speak, with lantern light—it becomes an enemy. But the fog is lifting.

"There's a smart west wind rising, if you notice. The stars will be out when you get home."

They were out; and when Anne re-entered her house of dreams the red embers were still glowing on the hearth, and all the haunting presences were gone.

CHAPTER 14 - NOVEMBER DAYS

The splendor of color which had glowed for weeks along the shores of Four Winds Harbor had faded out into the soft gray-blue of late autumnal hills. There came many days when fields and shores were dim with misty rain, or shivering before the breath of a melancholy sea-wind—nights, too, of storm and tempest, when Anne sometimes wakened to pray that no ship might be beating up the grim north shore, for if it were so not even the great, faithful light whirling through the darkness unafraid, could avail to guide it into safe haven.

"In November I sometimes feel as if spring could never come again," she sighed, grieving over the hopeless unsightliness of her frosted and bedraggled flower-plots. The gay little garden of the schoolmaster's bride was rather a forlorn place now, and the Lombardies and birches were under bare poles, as Captain Jim said. But the fir-wood behind the little house was forever green and staunch; and even in November and December there came gracious days of sunshine and purple hazes, when the harbor danced and sparkled as blithely as in midsummer, and the gulf was so softly blue and tender that the storm and the wild wind seemed only things of a long-past dream.

Anne and Gilbert spent many an autumn evening at the lighthouse. It was always a cheery place. Even when the east wind sang in minor and the sea was dead and gray, hints of sunshine seemed to be lurking all about it. Perhaps this was because the First Mate always paraded it in panoply of gold. He was so large and effulgent that one hardly missed the sun, and his resounding purrs formed a pleasant accompaniment to the laughter and conversation which went on around Captain Jim's fireplace. Captain Jim and Gilbert had many long discussions and high converse on matters beyond the ken of cat or king.

"I like to ponder on all kinds of problems, though I can't solve 'em," said Captain Jim. "My father held that we should never talk of things we couldn't understand, but if we didn't, doctor, the subjects for conversation would be mighty few. I reckon the gods laugh many a time to hear us, but what matters so long as we remember that we're only men and don't take to fancying that we're gods ourselves, really, knowing good and evil. I reckon our pow-wows won't do us or anyone much harm, so let's have another whack at the whence, why and whither this evening, doctor."

While they "whacked," Anne listened or dreamed. Sometimes Leslie went to the lighthouse with them, and she and Anne wandered along the shore in the eerie twilight, or sat on the rocks below the lighthouse until the darkness drove them back to the cheer of the driftwood fire. Then Captain Jim would brew them tea and tell them

> "tales of land and sea
> And whatsoever might betide
> The great forgotten world outside."

Leslie seemed always to enjoy those lighthouse carousals very much, and bloomed out for the time being into ready wit and beautiful laughter, or glowing-eyed silence. There was a certain tang and savor in the conversation when Leslie was present which they missed when she was absent. Even when she did not talk she seemed to inspire others to brilliancy. Captain Jim told his stories better, Gilbert was quicker in argument and repartee, Anne felt little gushes and trickles of fancy and imagination bubbling to her lips under the influence of Leslie's personality.

"That girl was born to be a leader in social and intellectual circles, far away from Four Winds," she said to Gilbert as they walked home one night. "She's just wasted here—wasted."

"Weren't you listening to Captain Jim and yours truly the other night when we discussed that subject generally? We came to the comforting conclusion that the Creator probably knew how to run His universe quite as well as we do, and that, after all, there are no such things as 'wasted' lives, saving and except when an individual wilfully squanders and wastes his own life—which Leslie Moore certainly hasn't done. And some people might think that a Redmond B.A., whom editors were beginning to honor, was 'wasted' as the wife of a struggling country doctor in the rural community of Four Winds."

"Gilbert!"

"If you had married Roy Gardner, now," continued Gilbert mercilessly, "YOU could have been 'a leader in social and intellectual circles far away from Four Winds.'"

"Gilbert BLYTHE!"

"You KNOW you were in love with him at one time, Anne."

"Gilbert, that's mean—'pisen mean, just like all the men,' as Miss Cornelia says. I NEVER was in love with him. I only imagined I was. YOU know that. You KNOW I'd rather be your wife in our house of dreams and fulfillment than a queen in a palace."

Gilbert's answer was not in words; but I am afraid that both of them forgot poor Leslie speeding her lonely way across the fields to a house that was neither a palace nor the fulfillment of a dream.

The moon was rising over the sad, dark sea behind them and transfiguring it. Her light had not yet reached the harbor, the further side of which was shadowy and suggestive, with dim coves and rich glooms and jewelling lights.

"How the home lights shine out tonight through the dark!" said Anne. "That string of them over the harbor looks like a necklace. And what a coruscation there is up at the Glen! Oh, look, Gilbert; there is ours. I'm so glad we left it burning. I hate to come home to a dark house. OUR homelight, Gilbert! Isn't it lovely to see?"

"Just one of earth's many millions of homes, Anne—girl—but ours—OURS— our beacon in 'a naughty world.' When a fellow has a home and a dear, little, red-haired wife in it what more need he ask of life?"

"Well, he might ask ONE thing more," whispered Anne happily. "Oh, Gilbert, it seems as if I just COULDN'T wait for the spring."

CHAPTER 15 - CHRISTMAS AT FOUR WINDS

At first Anne and Gilbert talked of going home to Avonlea for Christmas; but eventually they decided to stay in Four Winds. "I want to spend the first Christmas of our life together in our own home," decreed Anne.

So it fell out that Marilla and Mrs. Rachel Lynde and the twins came to Four Winds for Christmas. Marilla had the face of a woman who had circumnavigated the globe. She had never been sixty miles away from home before; and she had never eaten a Christmas dinner anywhere save at Green Gables.

Mrs. Rachel had made and brought with her an enormous plum pudding. Nothing could have convinced Mrs. Rachel that a college graduate of the younger generation could make a Christmas plum pudding properly; but she bestowed approval on Anne's house.

"Anne's a good housekeeper," she said to Marilla in the spare room the night of their arrival. "I've looked into her bread box and her scrap pail. I always judge a housekeeper by those, that's what. There's nothing in the pail that shouldn't have been thrown away, and no stale pieces in the bread box. Of course, she was trained up with you—but, then, she went to college afterwards. I notice she's got my tobacco stripe quilt on the bed here, and that big round braided mat of yours before her living-room fire. It makes me feel right at home."

Anne's first Christmas in her own house was as delightful as she could have wished. The day was fine and bright; the first skim of snow had fallen on Christmas Eve and made the world beautiful; the harbor was still open and glittering.

Captain Jim and Miss Cornelia came to dinner. Leslie and Dick had been invited, but Leslie made excuse; they always went to her Uncle Isaac West's for Christmas, she said.

"She'd rather have it so," Miss Cornelia told Anne. "She can't bear taking Dick where there are strangers. Christmas is always a hard time for Leslie. She and her father used to make a lot of it."

Miss Cornelia and Mrs. Rachel did not take a very violent fancy to each other. "Two suns hold not their courses in one sphere." But they did not clash at all, for Mrs. Rachel was in the kitchen helping Anne and Marilla with the dinner, and it fell to Gilbert to entertain Captain Jim and Miss Cornelia,—or rather to be entertained by them, for a dialogue between those two old friends and antagonists was assuredly never dull.

"It's many a year since there was a Christmas dinner here, Mistress Blythe," said Captain Jim. "Miss Russell always went to her friends in town for Christmas. But I was here to the first Christmas dinner that was ever eaten in this house—and the schoolmaster's bride cooked it. That was sixty years ago today, Mistress Blythe—and a day very like this—just enough snow to make the hills white, and the harbor as blue as June. I was only a lad, and I'd never been invited out to dinner before, and I was too shy to eat enough. I've got all over THAT."

"Most men do," said Miss Cornelia, sewing furiously. Miss Cornelia was not going to sit with idle hands, even on Christmas.

Babies come without any consideration for holidays, and there was one expected in a poverty-stricken household at Glen St. Mary. Miss Cornelia had sent that household a substantial dinner for its little swarm, and so meant to eat her own with a comfortable conscience.

"Well, you know, the way to a man's heart is through his stomach, Cornelia," explained Captain Jim.

"I believe you—when he HAS a heart," retorted Miss Cornelia. "I suppose that's why so many women kill themselves cooking—just as poor Amelia Baxter did. She died last Christmas morning, and she said it was the first Christmas since she was married that she didn't have to cook a big, twenty-plate dinner. It must have been a real pleasant change for her. Well, she's been dead a year, so you'll soon hear of Horace Baxter taking notice."

"I heard he was taking notice already," said Captain Jim, winking at Gilbert. "Wasn't he up to your place one Sunday lately, with his funeral blacks on, and a boiled collar?"

"No, he wasn't. And he needn't come neither. I could have had him long ago when he was fresh. I don't want any second-hand goods, believe ME. As for Horace Baxter, he was in financial difficulties a year ago last summer, and he prayed to the Lord for help; and when his wife died and he got her life insurance he said he believed it was the answer to his prayer. Wasn't that like a man?"

"Have you really proof that he said that, Cornelia?"

"I have the Methodist minister's word for it—if you call THAT proof. Robert Baxter told me the same thing too, but I admit THAT isn't evidence. Robert Baxter isn't often known to tell the truth."

"Come, come, Cornelia, I think he generally tells the truth, but he changes his opinion so often it sometimes sounds as if he didn't."

"It sounds like it mighty often, believe ME. But trust one man to excuse another. I have no use for Robert Baxter. He turned Methodist just because the Presbyterian choir happened to be singing 'Behold the bridegroom cometh' for a collection piece when him and Margaret walked up the aisle the Sunday after they were married. Served him right for being late! He always insisted the choir did it on purpose to insult him, as if he was of that much importance. But that family always thought they were much bigger potatoes than they really were. His brother Eliphalet imagined the devil was always at his elbow—but *I* never believed the devil wasted that much time on him."

"I—don't—know," said Captain Jim thoughtfully. "Eliphalet Baxter lived too much alone—hadn't even a cat or dog to keep him human. When a man is alone he's mighty apt to be with the devil—if he ain't with God. He has to choose which company he'll keep, I reckon. If the devil always was at Life Baxter's elbow it must have been because Life liked to have him there."

"Man-like," said Miss Cornelia, and subsided into silence over a complicated arrangement of tucks until Captain Jim deliberately stirred her up again by remarking in a casual way:

"I was up to the Methodist church last Sunday morning."

"You'd better have been home reading your Bible," was Miss Cornelia's retort.

"Come, now, Cornelia, *I* can't see any harm in going to the Methodist church when there's no preaching in your own. I've been a Presbyterian for seventy-six years, and it isn't likely my theology will hoist anchor at this late day."

"It's setting a bad example," said Miss Cornelia grimly.

"Besides," continued wicked Captain Jim, "I wanted to hear some good singing. The Methodists have a good choir; and you can't deny, Cornelia, that the singing in our church is awful since the split in the choir."

"What if the singing isn't good? They're doing their best, and God sees no difference between the voice of a crow and the voice of a nightingale."

"Come, come, Cornelia," said Captain Jim mildly, "I've a better opinion of the Almighty's ear for music than THAT."

"What caused the trouble in our choir?" asked Gilbert, who was suffering from suppressed laughter.

"It dates back to the new church, three years ago," answered Captain Jim. "We had a fearful time over the building of that church—fell out over the question of a new site. The two sites wasn't more'n two hundred yards apart, but you'd have thought they was a thousand by the bitterness of that fight. We was split up into three factions—one wanted the east site and one the south, and one held to the old. It was fought out in bed and at board, and in church and at market. All the old scandals of three generations were dragged out of their graves and aired. Three matches was broken up by it. And the meetings we had to try to settle the question! Cornelia, will you ever forget the one when old Luther Burns got up and made a speech? HE stated his opinions forcibly."

"Call a spade a spade, Captain. You mean he got red-mad and raked them all, fore and aft. They deserved it too—a pack of incapables. But what would you expect of a committee of men? That building committee held twenty-seven meetings, and at the end of the twenty-seventh weren't no nearer having a church than when they begun—not so near, for a fact, for in one fit of hurrying things along they'd gone to work and tore the old church down, so there we were, without a church, and no place but the hall to worship in."

"The Methodists offered us their church, Cornelia."

"The Glen St. Mary church wouldn't have been built to this day," went on Miss Cornelia, ignoring Captain Jim, "if we women hadn't just started in and took charge. We said WE meant to have a church, if the men meant to quarrel till doomsday, and we were tired of being a laughing-stock for the Methodists. We held ONE meeting and elected a committee and canvassed for subscriptions. We got them, too. When any of the men tried to sass us we told them they'd tried for two years to build a church and it was our turn now. We shut them up close, believe ME, and in six months we had our church. Of course, when the men saw we were determined they stopped fighting and went to work, man-like, as soon as they saw they had to, or quit bossing. Oh, women can't preach or be elders; but they can build churches and scare up the money for them."

"The Methodists allow women to preach," said Captain Jim.

Miss Cornelia glared at him.

"I never said the Methodists hadn't common sense, Captain. What I say is, I doubt if they have much religion."

"I suppose you are in favor of votes for women, Miss Cornelia," said Gilbert.

"I'm not hankering after the vote, believe ME," said Miss Cornelia scornfully. "*I* know what it is to clean up after the men. But some of these days, when the men realize they've got the world into a mess they can't get it out of, they'll be glad to give us the vote, and shoulder their troubles over on us. That's THEIR scheme. Oh, it's well that women are patient, believe ME!"

"What about Job?" suggested Captain Jim.

"Job! It was such a rare thing to find a patient man that when one was really discovered they were determined he shouldn't be forgotten," retorted Miss Cornelia triumphantly. "Anyhow, the virtue doesn't go with the name. There never was such an impatient man born as old Job Taylor over harbor."

"Well, you know, he had a good deal to try him, Cornelia. Even you can't defend his wife. I always remember what old William MacAllister said of her at her funeral, 'There's nae doot she was a Chreestian wumman, but she had the de'il's own temper.'"

"I suppose she WAS trying," admitted Miss Cornelia reluctantly, "but that didn't justify what Job said when she died. He rode home from the graveyard the day of the funeral with my father. He never said a word till they got near home. Then he heaved a big sigh and said, 'You may not believe it, Stephen, but this is the happiest day of my life!' Wasn't that like a man?"

"I s'pose poor old Mrs. Job did make life kinder uneasy for him," reflected Captain Jim.

"Well, there's such a thing as decency, isn't there? Even if a man is rejoicing in his heart over his wife being dead, he needn't proclaim it to the four winds of heaven. And happy day or not, Job Taylor wasn't long in marrying again, you might notice. His second wife could manage him. She made him walk Spanish, believe me! The first thing she did was to make him hustle round and put up a tombstone to the first Mrs. Job—and she had a place left on it for her own name. She said there'd be nobody to make Job put up a monument to HER."

"Speaking of Taylors, how is Mrs. Lewis Taylor up at the Glen, doctor?" asked Captain Jim.

"She's getting better slowly—but she has to work too hard," replied Gilbert.

"Her husband works hard too—raising prize pigs," said Miss Cornelia. "He's noted for his beautiful pigs. He's a heap prouder of his pigs than of his children. But then, to be sure, his pigs are the best pigs possible, while his children don't amount to much. He picked a poor mother for them, and starved her while she was bearing and rearing them. His pigs got the cream and his children got the skim milk."

"There are times, Cornelia, when I have to agree with you, though it hurts me," said Captain Jim. "That's just exactly the truth about Lewis Taylor. When I see those poor, miserable children of his, robbed of all children ought to have, it p'isens my own bite and sup for days afterwards."

Gilbert went out to the kitchen in response to Anne's beckoning. Anne shut the door and gave him a connubial lecture.

"Gilbert, you and Captain Jim must stop baiting Miss Cornelia. Oh, I've been listening to you—and I just won't allow it."

'Anne, Miss Cornelia is enjoying herself hugely. You know she is.'

"Well, never mind. You two needn't egg her on like that. Dinner is ready now, and, Gilbert, DON'T let Mrs. Rachel carve the geese. I know she means to offer to do it because she doesn't think you can do it properly. Show her you can."

"I ought to be able to. I've been studying A-B-C-D diagrams of carving for the past month," said Gilbert. "Only don't talk to me while I'm doing it, Anne, for if you drive the letters out of my head I'll be in a worse predicament than you were in old geometry days when the teacher changed them."

Gilbert carved the geese beautifully. Even Mrs. Rachel had to admit that. And everybody ate of them and enjoyed them. Anne's first Christmas dinner was a great success and she beamed with housewifely pride. Merry was the feast and long; and when it was over they gathered around the cheer of the red hearth flame and Captain Jim told them stories until the red sun swung low over Four Winds Harbor, and the long blue shadows of the Lombardies fell across the snow in the lane.

"I must be getting back to the light," he said finally. "I'll jest have time to walk home before sundown. Thank you for a beautiful Christmas, Mistress Blythe. Bring Master Davy down to the light some night before he goes home."

"I want to see those stone gods," said Davy with a relish.

CHAPTER 16 - NEW YEAR'S EVE AT THE LIGHT

The Green Gables folk went home after Christmas, Marilla under solemn covenant to return for a month in the spring. More snow came before New Year's, and the harbor froze over, but the gulf still was free, beyond the white, imprisoned fields. The last day of the old year was one of those bright, cold, dazzling winter days, which bombard us with their brilliancy, and command our admiration but never our love. The sky was sharp and blue; the snow diamonds sparkled insistently; the stark trees were bare and shameless, with a kind of brazen beauty; the hills shot assaulting lances of crystal. Even the shadows were sharp and stiff and clear-cut, as no proper shadows should be. Everything that was handsome seemed ten times handsomer and less attractive in the glaring splendor; and everything that was ugly seemed ten times uglier, and everything was either handsome or ugly. There was no soft blending, or kind obscurity, or elusive mistiness in that searching glitter. The only things that held their own individuality were the firs— for the fir is the tree of mystery and shadow, and yields never to the encroachments of crude radiance.

But finally the day began to realise that she was growing old. Then a certain pensiveness fell over her beauty which dimmed yet intensified it; sharp angles, glittering points, melted away into curves and enticing gleams. The white harbor put on soft grays and pinks; the far-away hills turned amethyst.

"The old year is going away beautifully," said Anne.

She and Leslie and Gilbert were on their way to the Four Winds Point, having plotted with Captain Jim to watch the New Year in at the light. The sun had set and in the southwestern sky hung Venus, glorious and golden, having drawn as near to her earth-sister as is possible for her. For the first time Anne and Gilbert saw the shadow cast by that brilliant star of evening, that faint, mysterious shadow, never seen save when there is white snow to reveal it, and then only with averted vision, vanishing when you gaze at it directly.

"It's like the spirit of a shadow, isn't it?" whispered Anne. "You can see it so plainly haunting your side when you look ahead; but when you turn and look at it—it's gone."

"I have heard that you can see the shadow of Venus only once in a lifetime, and that within a year of seeing it your life's most wonderful gift will come to you," said Leslie. But she spoke rather hardly; perhaps she thought that even the shadow of Venus could bring her no gift of life. Anne smiled in the soft twilight; she felt quite sure what the mystic shadow promised her.

They found Marshall Elliott at the lighthouse. At first Anne felt inclined to resent the intrusion of this long-haired, long-bearded eccentric into the familiar little circle. But Marshall Elliott soon proved his legitimate claim to membership in the household of Joseph. He was a witty, intelligent, well-read man, rivalling Captain Jim himself in the knack of telling a good story. They were all glad when he agreed to watch the old year out with them.

Captain Jim's small nephew Joe had come down to spend New Year's with his great-uncle, and had fallen asleep on the sofa with the First Mate curled up in a huge golden ball at his feet.

"Ain't he a dear little man?" said Captain Jim gloatingly. "I do love to watch a little child asleep, Mistress Blythe. It's the most beautiful sight in the world, I reckon. Joe does love to get down here for a night, because I have him sleep with me. At home he has to sleep with the other two boys, and he doesn't like it. Why can't I sleep with father, Uncle Jim?" says he. 'Everybody in the Bible slept with their fathers.' As for the questions he asks, the minister himself couldn't answer them. They fair swamp me. 'Uncle Jim, if I wasn't ME who'd I be?' and, 'Uncle Jim, what would happen if God died?' He fired them two off at me tonight, afore he went to sleep. As for his imagination, it sails away from everything. He makes up the most remarkable yarns—and then his mother shuts him up in the closet for telling stories. And he sits down and makes up another one, and has it ready to relate to her when she lets him out. He had one for me when he come down tonight. 'Uncle Jim,' says he, solemn as a tombstone, 'I had a 'venture in the Glen today.' 'Yes, what was it?' says I, expecting something quite startling, but nowise prepared for what I really got. 'I met a wolf in the street,' says he, 'a 'normous wolf with a big, red mouf and AWFUL long teeth, Uncle Jim.' 'I didn't know there was any wolves up at the Glen,' says I. 'Oh, he comed there from far, far away,' says Joe, 'and I fought he was going to eat me up, Uncle Jim.' 'Were you scared?' says I. 'No, 'cause I had a big gun,' says Joe, 'and I shot the wolf dead, Uncle Jim,— solid dead—and then he went up to heaven and bit God,' says he. Well, I was fair staggered, Mistress Blythe."

The hours bloomed into mirth around the driftwood fire. Captain Jim told tales, and Marshall Elliott sang old Scotch ballads in a fine tenor voice; finally Captain Jim took down his old brown fiddle from the wall and began to play. He had a tolerable knack of fiddling, which all appreciated save the First Mate, who sprang from the sofa as if he had been shot, emitted a shriek of protest, and fled wildly up the stairs.

"Can't cultivate an ear for music in that cat nohow," said Captain Jim. "He won't stay long enough to learn to like it. When we got the organ up at the Glen church old Elder Richards bounced up from his seat the minute the organist began to play and scuttled down the aisle and out of the church at the rate of no-man's-business. It reminded me so strong of the First Mate tearing loose as soon as I begin to fiddle that I come nearer to laughing out loud in church than I ever did before or since."

There was something so infectious in the rollicking tunes which Captain Jim played that very soon Marshall Elliott's feet began to twitch. He had been a noted dancer in his youth. Presently he started up and held out his hands to Leslie. Instantly she responded. Round and round the firelit room they circled with a rhythmic grace that was wonderful. Leslie danced like one inspired; the wild, sweet abandon of the music seemed to have entered into and possessed her. Anne watched her in fascinated admiration. She had never seen her like this. All the innate richness and color and charm of her nature seemed to have broken loose and overflowed in crimson cheek and glowing eye and grace of motion. Even the aspect of Marshall Elliott, with his long beard and hair, could not spoil the picture. On the contrary, it seemed to enhance it. Marshall Elliott looked like a Viking of elder days, dancing with one of the blue-eyed, golden-haired daughters of the Northland.

"The purtiest dancing I ever saw, and I've seen some in my time," declared Captain Jim, when at last the bow fell from his tired hand. Leslie dropped into her chair, laughing, breathless.

"I love dancing," she said apart to Anne. "I haven't danced since I was sixteen—but I love it. The music seems to run through my veins like quicksilver and I forget everything—everything—except the delight of keeping time to it. There isn't any floor beneath me, or walls about me, or roof over me—I'm floating amid the stars."

Captain Jim hung his fiddle up in its place, beside a large frame enclosing several banknotes.

"Is there anybody else of your acquaintance who can afford to hang his walls with banknotes for pictures?" he asked. "There's twenty ten-dollar notes there, not worth the glass over them. They're old Bank of P. E. Island notes. Had them by me when the bank failed, and I had 'em framed and hung up, partly as a reminder not to put your trust in banks, and partly to give me a real luxurious, millionairy feeling. Hullo, Matey, don't be scared. You can come back now. The music and revelry is over for tonight. The old year has just another hour to stay with us. I've seen seventy-six New Years come in over that gulf yonder, Mistress Blythe."

"You'll see a hundred," said Marshall Elliott.

Captain Jim shook his head.

"No; and I don't want to—at least, I think I don't. Death grows friendlier as we grow older. Not that one of us really wants to die though, Marshall. Tennyson spoke truth when he said that. There's old Mrs. Wallace up at the Glen. She's had heaps of trouble all her life, poor soul, and she's lost almost everyone she cared about. She's always saying that she'll be glad when her time comes, and she doesn't want to sojourn any longer in this vale of tears. But when she takes a sick spell there's a fuss! Doctors from town, and a trained nurse, and enough medicine to kill a dog. Life may be a vale of tears, all right, but there are some folks who enjoy weeping, I reckon."

They spent the old year's last hour quietly around the fire. A few minutes before twelve Captain Jim rose and opened the door.

"We must let the New Year in," he said.

Outside was a fine blue night. A sparkling ribbon of moonlight garlanded the gulf. Inside the bar the harbor shone like a pavement of pearl. They stood before the door and waited—Captain Jim with his ripe, full experience, Marshall Elliott in his vigorous but empty middle life, Gilbert and Anne with their precious memories and exquisite hopes, Leslie with her record of starved years and her hopeless future. The clock on the little shelf above the fireplace struck twelve.

"Welcome, New Year," said Captain Jim, bowing low as the last stroke died away. "I wish you all the best year of your lives, mates. I reckon that whatever the New Year brings us will be the best the Great Captain has for us—and somehow or other we'll all make port in a good harbor."

CHAPTER 17 - A FOUR WINDS WINTER

Winter set in vigorously after New Year's. Big, white drifts heaped themselves about the little house, and palms of frost covered its windows. The harbor ice grew harder and thicker, until the Four Winds people began their usual winter travelling over it. The safe ways were "bushed" by a benevolent Government, and night and day the gay tinkle of the sleigh-bells sounded on it. On moonlit nights Anne heard them in her house of dreams like fairy chimes. The gulf froze over, and the Four Winds light flashed no more. During the months when navigation was closed Captain Jim's office was a sinecure.

"The First Mate and I will have nothing to do till spring except keep warm and amuse ourselves. The last lighthouse keeper used always to move up to the Glen in winter; but I'd rather stay at the Point. The First Mate might get poisoned or chewed up by dogs at the Glen. It's a mite lonely, to be sure, with neither the light nor the water for company, but if our friends come to see us often we'll weather it through."

Captain Jim had an ice boat, and many a wild, glorious spin Gilbert and Anne and Leslie had over the glib harbor ice with him. Anne and Leslie took long snowshoe tramps together, too, over the fields, or across the harbor after storms, or through the woods beyond the Glen. They were very good comrades in their rambles and their fireside communings. Each had something to give the other— each felt life the richer for friendly exchange of thought and friendly silence; each looked across the white fields between their homes with a pleasant consciousness of a friend beyond. But, in spite of all this, Anne felt that there was always a barrier between Leslie and herself—a constraint that never wholly vanished.

"I don't know why I can't get closer to her," Anne said one evening to Captain Jim. "I like her so much—I admire her so much—I WANT to take her right into my heart and creep right into hers. But I can never cross the barrier."

"You've been too happy all your life, Mistress Blythe," said Captain Jim thoughtfully. "I reckon that's why you and Leslie can't get real close together in your souls. The barrier between you is her experience of sorrow and trouble. She ain't responsible for it and you ain't; but it's there and neither of you can cross it."

"My childhood wasn't very happy before I came to Green Gables," said Anne, gazing soberly out of the window at the still, sad, dead beauty of the leafless tree-shadows on the moonlit snow.

"Mebbe not—but it was just the usual unhappiness of a child who hasn't any-one to look after it properly. There hasn't been any TRAGEDY in your life, Mistress Blythe. And poor Leslie's has been almost ALL tragedy. She feels, I reckon, though mebbe she hardly knows she feels it, that there's a vast deal in her life you can't enter nor understand—and so she has to keep you back from it—hold you off, so to speak, from hurting her. You know if we've got anything about us that hurts we shrink from anyone's touch on or near it. It holds good with our souls as well as our bodies, I reckon. Leslie's soul must be near raw—it's no won-der she hides it away."

"If that were really all, I wouldn't mind, Captain Jim. I would understand. But there are times—not always, but now and again—when I almost have to believe that Leslie doesn't—doesn't like me. Sometimes I surprise a look in her eyes that seems to show resentment and dislike—it goes so quickly—but I've seen it, I'm sure of that. And it hurts me, Captain Jim. I'm not used to being disliked—and I've tried so hard to win Leslie's friendship."

"You have won it, Mistress Blythe. Don't you go cherishing any foolish notion that Leslie don't like you. If she didn't she wouldn't have anything to do with you, much less chumming with you as she does. I know Leslie Moore too well not to be sure of that."

"The first time I ever saw her, driving her geese down the hill on the day I came to Four Winds, she looked at me with the same expression," persisted Anne. "I felt it, even in the midst of my admiration of her beauty. She looked at me re-sentfully—she did, indeed, Captain Jim."

"The resentment must have been about something else, Mistress Blythe, and you jest come in for a share of it because you happened past. Leslie DOES take sullen spells now and again, poor girl. I can't blame her, when I know what she has to put up with. I don't know why it's permitted. The doctor and I have talked a lot abut the origin of evil, but we haven't quite found out all about it yet. There's a vast of onunderstandable things in life, ain't there, Mistress Blythe? Sometimes things seem to work out real proper-like, same as with you and the doctor. And then again they all seem to go catawampus. There's Leslie, so clever and beautiful you'd think she was meant for a queen, and instead she's cooped up over there, robbed of almost everything a woman'd value, with no prospect except waiting on Dick Moore all her life. Though, mind you, Mistress Blythe, I daresay she'd choose her life now, such as it is, rather than the life she lived with Dick before he went away. THAT'S something a clumsy old sailor's tongue mustn't meddle with. But you've helped Leslie a lot—she's a different creature since you come to Four Winds. Us old friends see the difference in her, as you can't. Miss Cornelia and me was talking it over the other day, and it's one of the mighty few p'ints that we see eye to eye on. So jest you throw overboard any idea of her not liking you."

Anne could hardly discard it completely, for there were undoubtedly times when she felt, with an instinct that was not to be combated by reason, that Leslie harbored a queer, indefinable resentment towards her. At times, this secret con-sciousness marred the delight of their comradeship; at others it was almost forgotten; but Anne always felt the hidden thorn was there, and might prick her at any moment. She felt a cruel sting from it on the day when she told Leslie of what she hoped the spring would bring to the little house of dreams. Leslie looked at her with hard, bitter, unfriendly eyes.

"So you are to have THAT, too," she said in a choked voice. And without another word she had turned and gone across the fields homeward. Anne was deeply hurt; for the moment she felt as if she could never like Leslie again. But when Leslie came over a few evenings later she was so pleasant, so friendly, so frank, and witty, and winsome, that Anne was charmed into forgiveness and forgetfulness. Only, she never mentioned her darling hope to Leslie again; nor did Leslie ever refer to it. But one evening, when late winter was listening for the word of spring, she came over to the little house for a twilight chat; and when she went away she left a small, white box on the table. Anne found it after she was gone and opened it wonderingly. In it was a tiny white dress of exquisite workmanship—delicate embroidery, wonderful tucking, sheer loveliness. Every stitch in it was handwork; and the little frills of lace at neck and sleeves were of real Valenciennes. Lying on it was a card—"with Leslie's love."

"What hours of work she must have put on it," said Anne. "And the material must have cost more than she could really afford. It is very sweet of her."

But Leslie was brusque and curt when Anne thanked her, and again the latter felt thrown back upon herself.

Leslie's gift was not alone in the little house. Miss Cornelia had, for the time being, given up sewing for unwanted, unwelcome eighth babies, and fallen to sewing for a very much wanted first one, whose welcome would leave nothing to be desired. Philippa Blake and Diana Wright each sent a marvellous garment; and Mrs. Rachel Lynde sent several, in which good material and honest stitches took the place of embroidery and frills. Anne herself made many, desecrated by no touch of machinery, spending over them the happiest hours of the happy winter.

Captain Jim was the most frequent guest of the little house, and none was more welcome. Every day Anne loved the simple-souled, true-hearted old sailor more and more. He was as refreshing as a sea breeze, as interesting as some ancient chronicle. She was never tired of listening to his stories, and his quaint remarks and comments were a continual delight to her. Captain Jim was one of those rare and interesting people who "never speak but they say something." The milk of human kindness and the wisdom of the serpent were mingled in his composition in delightful proportions.

Nothing ever seemed to put Captain Jim out or depress him in any way.

"I've kind of contracted a habit of enj'ying things," he remarked once, when Anne had commented on his invariable cheerfulness. "It's got so chronic that I believe I even enj'y the disagreeable things. It's great fun thinking they can't last. 'Old rheumatiz,' says I, when it grips me hard, 'you've GOT to stop aching sometime. The worse you are the sooner you'll stop, mebbe. I'm bound to get the better of you in the long run, whether in the body or out of the body.'"

One night, by the fireside at the light Anne saw Captain Jim's "life-book." He needed no coaxing to show it and proudly gave it to her to read.

"I writ it to leave to little Joe," he said. "I don't like the idea of everything I've done and seen being clean forgot after I've shipped for my last v'yage. Joe, he'll remember it, and tell the yarns to his children."

It was an old leather-bound book filled with the record of his voyages and adventures. Anne thought what a treasure trove it would be to a writer. Every sentence was a nugget. In itself the book had no literary merit; Captain Jim's charm of storytelling failed him when he came to pen and ink; he could only jot roughly down the outline of his famous tales, and both spelling and grammar were sadly askew. But Anne felt that if anyone possessed of the gift could take that simple record of a brave, adventurous life, reading between the bald lines the tales of dangers staunchly faced and duty manfully done, a wonderful story might be made from it. Rich comedy and thrilling tragedy were both lying hidden in Captain Jim's "life-book," waiting for the touch of the master hand to waken the laughter and grief and horror of thousands.

Anne said something of this to Gilbert as they walked home.

"Why don't you try your hand at it yourself, Anne?"

Anne shook her head.

"No. I only wish I could. But it's not in the power of my gift. You know what my forte is, Gilbert—the fanciful, the fairylike, the pretty. To write Captain Jim's life-book as it should be written one should be a master of vigorous yet subtle style, a keen psychologist, a born humorist and a born tragedian. A rare combination of gifts is needed. Paul might do it if he were older. Anyhow, I'm going to ask him to come down next summer and meet Captain Jim."

"Come to this shore," wrote Anne to Paul. "I am afraid you cannot find here Nora or the Golden Lady or the Twin Sailors; but you will find one old sailor who can tell you wonderful stories."

Paul, however wrote back, saying regretfully that he could not come that year. He was going abroad for two year's study.

"When I return I'll come to Four Winds, dear Teacher," he wrote.

"But meanwhile, Captain Jim is growing old," said Anne, sorrowfully, "and there is nobody to write his life-book."

CHAPTER 18 - SPRING DAYS

The ice in the harbor grew black and rotten in the March suns; in April there were blue waters and a windy, white-capped gulf again; and again the Four Winds light begemmed the twilights.

"I'm so glad to see it once more," said Anne, on the first evening of its reappearance. "I've missed it so all winter. The northwestern sky has seemed blank and lonely without it."

The land was tender with brand-new, golden-green, baby leaves. There was an emerald mist on the woods beyond the Glen. The seaward valleys were full of fairy mists at dawn.

Vibrant winds came and went with salt foam in their breath. The sea laughed and flashed and preened and allured, like a beautiful, coquettish woman. The herring schooled and the fishing village woke to life. The harbor was alive with white sails making for the channel. The ships began to sail outward and inward again.

"On a spring day like this," said Anne, "I know exactly what my soul will feel like on the resurrection morning."

"There are times in spring when I sorter feel that I might have been a poet if I'd been caught young," remarked Captain Jim. "I catch myself conning over old lines and verses I heard the schoolmaster reciting sixty years ago. They don't trouble me at other times. Now I feel as if I had to get out on the rocks or the fields or the water and spout them."

Captain Jim had come up that afternoon to bring Anne a load of shells for her garden, and a little bunch of sweet-grass which he had found in a ramble over the sand dunes.

"It's getting real scarce along this shore now," he said. "When I was a boy there was a-plenty of it. But now it's only once in a while you'll find a plot—and never when you're looking for it. You jest have to stumble on it—you're walking along on the sand hills, never thinking of sweet-grass—and all at once the air is full of sweetness—and there's the grass under your feet. I favor the smell of sweet-grass. It always makes me think of my mother."

"She was fond of it?" asked Anne.

"Not that I knows on. Dunno's she ever saw any sweet-grass. No, it's because it has a kind of motherly perfume—not too young, you understand—something kind of seasoned and wholesome and dependable—jest like a mother. The schoolmaster's bride always kept it among her handkerchiefs. You might put that little bunch among yours, Mistress Blythe. I don't like these boughten scents—but a whiff of sweet-grass belongs anywhere a lady does."

Anne had not been especially enthusiastic over the idea of surrounding her flower beds with quahog shells; as a decoration they did not appeal to her on first thought. But she would not have hurt Captain Jim's feelings for anything; so she assumed a virtue she did not at first feel, and thanked him heartily. And when Captain Jim had proudly encircled every bed with a rim of the big, milk-white shells, Anne found to her surprise that she liked the effect. On a town lawn, or even up at the Glen, they would not have been in keeping, but here, in the old-fashioned, sea-bound garden of the little house of dreams, they BELONGED.

"They DO look nice," she said sincerely.

"The schoolmaster's bride always had cowhawks round her beds," said Captain Jim. "She was a master hand with flowers. She LOOKED at 'em—and touched 'em—SO—and they grew like mad. Some folks have that knack—I reckon you have it, too, Mistress Blythe."

"Oh, I don't know—but I love my garden, and I love working in it. To potter with green, growing things, watching each day to see the dear, new sprouts come up, is like taking a hand in creation, I think. Just now my garden is like faith—the substance of things hoped for. But bide a wee."

"It always amazes me to look at the little, wrinkled brown seeds and think of the rainbows in 'em," said Captain Jim. "When I ponder on them seeds I don't find it nowise hard to believe that we've got souls that'll live in other worlds. You couldn't hardly believe there was life in them tiny things, some no bigger than grains of dust, let alone color and scent, if you hadn't seen the miracle, could you?"

Anne, who was counting her days like silver beads on a rosary, could not now take the long walk to the lighthouse or up the Glen road. But Miss Cornelia and Captain Jim came very often to the little house. Miss Cornelia was the joy of Anne's and Gilbert's existence. They laughed side-splittingly over her speeches after every visit. When Captain Jim and she happened to visit the little house at the same time there was much sport for the listening. They waged wordy warfare, she attacking, he defending. Anne once reproached the Captain for his baiting of Miss Cornelia.

"Oh, I do love to set her going, Mistress Blythe," chuckled the unrepentant sinner. "It's the greatest amusement I have in life. That tongue of hers would blister a stone. And you and that young dog of a doctor enj'y listening to her as much as I do."

Captain Jim came along another evening to bring Anne some mayflowers. The garden was full of the moist, scented air of a maritime spring evening. There was a milk-white mist on the edge of the sea, with a young moon kissing it, and a silver gladness of stars over the Glen. The bell of the church across the harbor was ringing dreamily sweet. The mellow chime drifted through the dusk to mingle with the soft spring-moan of the sea. Captain Jim's mayflowers added the last completing touch to the charm of the night.

"I haven't seen any this spring, and I've missed them," said Anne, burying her face in them.

"They ain't to be found around Four Winds, only in the barrens away behind the Glen up yander. I took a little trip today to the Land-of-nothing-to-do, and hunted these up for you. I reckon they're the last you'll see this spring, for they're nearly done."

"How kind and thoughtful you are, Captain Jim. Nobody else—not even Gilbert"—with a shake of her head at him—"remembered that I always long for mayflowers in spring."

"Well, I had another errand, too—I wanted to take Mr. Howard back yander a mess of trout. He likes one occasional, and it's all I can do for a kindness he did me once. I stayed all the afternoon and talked to him. He likes to talk to me, though he's a highly eddicated man and I'm only an ignorant old sailor, because he's one of the folks that's GOT to talk or they're miserable, and he finds listeners scarce around here. The Glen folks fight shy of him because they think he's an infidel. He ain't that far gone exactly—few men is, I reckon—but he's what you might call a heretic. Heretics are wicked, but they're mighty int'resting. It's jest that they've got sorter lost looking for God, being under the impression that He's hard to find—which He ain't never. Most of 'em blunder to Him after awhile, I guess. I don't think listening to Mr. Howard's arguments is likely to do me much harm. Mind you, I believe what I was brought up to believe. It saves a vast of bother—and back of it all, God is good. The trouble with Mr. Howard is that he's a leetle TOO clever. He thinks that he's bound to live up to his cleverness, and that it's smarter to thrash out some new way of getting to heaven than to go by the old track the common, ignorant folks is travelling. But he'll get there sometime all right, and then he'll laugh at himself."

"Mr. Howard was a Methodist to begin with," said Miss Cornelia, as if she thought he had not far to go from that to heresy.

"Do you know, Cornelia," said Captain Jim gravely, "I've often thought that if I wasn't a Presbyterian I'd be a Methodist."

"Oh, well," conceded Miss Cornelia, "if you weren't a Presbyterian it wouldn't matter much what you were. Speaking of heresy, reminds me, doctor—I've brought back that book you lent me—that Natural Law in the Spiritual World—I didn't read more'n a third of it. I can read sense, and I can read nonsense, but that book is neither the one nor the other."

"It IS considered rather heretical in some quarters," admitted Gilbert, "but I told you that before you took it, Miss Cornelia."

"Oh, I wouldn't have minded its being heretical. I can stand wickedness, but I can't stand foolishness," said Miss Cornelia calmly, and with the air of having said the last thing there was to say about Natural Law.

"Speaking of books, A Mad Love come to an end at last two weeks ago," remarked Captain Jim musingly. "It run to one hundred and three chapters. When they got married the book stopped right off, so I reckon their troubles were all over. It's real nice that that's the way in books anyhow, isn't it, even if 'tistn't so anywhere else?"

"I never read novels," said Miss Cornelia. "Did you hear how Geordie Russell was today, Captain Jim?"

"Yes, I called in on my way home to see him. He's getting round all right—but stewing in a broth of trouble, as usual, poor man.

"'Course he brews up most of it for himself, but I reckon that don't make it any easier to bear."

"He's an awful pessimist," said Miss Cornelia.

"Well, no, he ain't a pessimist exactly, Cornelia. He only jest never finds anything that suits him."

"And isn't that a pessimist?"

"No, no. A pessimist is one who never expects to find anything to suit him. Geordie hain't got THAT far yet."

"You'd find something good to say of the devil himself, Jim Boyd."

"Well, you've heard the story of the old lady who said he was persevering. But no, Cornelia, I've nothing good to say of the devil."

"Do you believe in him at all?" asked Miss Cornelia seriously.

"How can you ask that when you know what a good Presbyterian I am, Cornelia? How could a Presbyterian get along without a devil?"

"DO you?" persisted Miss Cornelia.

Captain Jim suddenly became grave.

"I believe in what I heard a minister once call 'a mighty and malignant and INTELLIGENT power of evil working in the universe,'" he said solemnly. "I do THAT, Cornelia. You can call it the devil, or the 'principle of evil,' or the Old Scratch, or any name you like. It's THERE, and all the infidels and heretics in the world can't argue it away, any more'n they can argue God away. It's there, and it's working. But, mind you, Cornelia, I believe it's going to get the worst of it in the long run."

"I am sure I hope so," said Miss Cornelia, none too hopefully. "But speaking of the devil, I am positive that Billy Booth is possessed by him now. Have you heard of Billy's latest performance?"

"No, what was that?"

"He's gone and burned up his wife's new, brown broadcloth suit, that she paid twenty-five dollars for in Charlottetown, because he declares the men looked too admiring at her when she wore it to church the first time. Wasn't that like a man?"

"Mistress Booth IS mighty pretty, and brown's her color," said Captain Jim reflectively.

"Is that any good reason why he should poke her new suit into the kitchen stove? Billy Booth is a jealous fool, and he makes his wife's life miserable. She's cried all the week about her suit. Oh, Anne, I wish I could write like you, believe ME. Wouldn't I score some of the men round here!"

"Those Booths are all a mite queer," said Captain Jim. "Billy seemed the sanest of the lot till he got married and then this queer jealous streak cropped out in him. His brother Daniel, now, was always odd."

"Took tantrums every few days or so and wouldn't get out of bed," said Miss Cornelia with a relish. "His wife would have to do all the barn work till he got over his spell. When he died people wrote her letters of condolence; if I'd written anything it would have been one of congratulation. Their father, old Abram Booth, was a disgusting old sot. He was drunk at his wife's funeral, and kept reeling round and hiccuping 'I didn't dri—i—i—nk much but I feel a—a—awfully que—e—e—r.' I gave him a good jab in the back with my umbrella when he came near me, and it sobered him up until they got the casket out of the house. Young Johnny Booth was to have been married yesterday, but he couldn't be because he's gone and got the mumps. Wasn't that like a man?"

"How could he help getting the mumps, poor fellow?"

"I'd poor fellow him, believe ME, if I was Kate Sterns. I don't know how he could help getting the mumps, but I DO know the wedding supper was all prepared and everything will be spoiled before he's well again. Such a waste! He should have had the mumps when he was a boy."

"Come, come, Cornelia, don't you think you're a mite unreasonable?"

Miss Cornelia disdained to reply and turned instead to Susan Baker, a grim-faced, kind-hearted elderly spinster of the Glen, who had been installed as maid-of-all-work at the little house for some weeks. Susan had been up to the Glen to make a sick call, and had just returned.

"How is poor old Aunt Mandy tonight?" asked Miss Cornelia.

Susan sighed.

"Very poorly—very poorly, Cornelia. I am afraid she will soon be in heaven, poor thing!"

"Oh, surely, it's not so bad as that!" exclaimed Miss Cornelia, sympathetically.

Captain Jim and Gilbert looked at each other. Then they suddenly rose and went out.

"There are times," said Captain Jim, between spasms, "when it would be a sin NOT to laugh. Them two excellent women!"

CHAPTER 19 - DAWN AND DUSK

In early June, when the sand hills were a great glory of pink wild roses, and the Glen was smothered in apple blossoms, Marilla arrived at the little house, accompanied by a black horsehair trunk, patterned with brass nails, which had reposed undisturbed in the Green Gables garret for half a century. Susan Baker, who, during her few weeks' sojourn in the little house, had come to worship "young Mrs. Doctor," as she called Anne, with blind fervor, looked rather jealously askance at Marilla at first. But as Marilla did not try to interfere in kitchen matters, and showed no desire to interrupt Susan's ministrations to young Mrs. Doctor, the good handmaiden became reconciled to her presence, and told her cronies at the Glen that Miss Cuthbert was a fine old lady and knew her place.

One evening, when the sky's limpid bowl was filled with a red glory, and the robins were thrilling the golden twilight with jubilant hymns to the stars of evening, there was a sudden commotion in the little house of dreams. Telephone messages were sent up to the Glen, Doctor Dave and a white-capped nurse came hastily down, Marilla paced the garden walks between the quahog shells, murmuring prayers between her set lips, and Susan sat in the kitchen with cotton wool in her ears and her apron over her head.

Leslie, looking out from the house up the brook, saw that every window of the little house was alight, and did not sleep that night.

The June night was short; but it seemed an eternity to those who waited and watched.

"Oh, will it NEVER end?" said Marilla; then she saw how grave the nurse and Doctor Dave looked, and she dared ask no more questions. Suppose Anne—but Marilla could not suppose it.

"Do not tell me," said Susan fiercely, answering the anguish in Marilla's eyes, "that God could be so cruel as to take that darling lamb from us when we all love her so much."

"He has taken others as well beloved," said Marilla hoarsely.

But at dawn, when the rising sun rent apart the mists hanging over the sandbar, and made rainbows of them, joy came to the little house. Anne was safe, and a wee, white lady, with her mother's big eyes, was lying beside her. Gilbert, his face gray and haggard from his night's agony, came down to tell Marilla and Susan.

"Thank God," shuddered Marilla.

Susan got up and took the cotton wool out of her ears.

"Now for breakfast," she said briskly. "I am of the opinion that we will all be glad of a bite and sup. You tell young Mrs. Doctor not to worry about a single thing—Susan is at the helm. You tell her just to think of her baby."

Gilbert smiled rather sadly as he went away. Anne, her pale face blanched with its baptism of pain, her eyes aglow with the holy passion of motherhood, did not need to be told to think of her baby. She thought of nothing else. For a few hours she tasted of happiness so rare and exquisite that she wondered if the angels in heaven did not envy her.

"Little Joyce," she murmured, when Marilla came in to see the baby. "We planned to call her that if she were a girlie. There were so many we would have liked to name her for; we couldn't choose between them, so we decided on Joyce—we can call her Joy for short—Joy—it suits so well. Oh, Marilla, I thought I was happy before. Now I know that I just dreamed a pleasant dream of happiness. THIS is the reality."

"You mustn't talk, Anne—wait till you're stronger," said Marilla warningly.

"You know how hard it is for me NOT to talk," smiled Anne.

At first she was too weak and too happy to notice that Gilbert and the nurse looked grave and Marilla sorrowful. Then, as subtly, and coldly, and remorselessly as a sea-fog stealing landward, fear crept into her heart. Why was not Gilbert gladder? Why would he not talk about the baby? Why would they not let her have it with her after that first heavenly—happy hour? Was—was there anything wrong?

"Gilbert," whispered Anne imploringly, "the baby—is all right—isn't she? Tell me—tell me."

Gilbert was a long while in turning round; then he bent over Anne and looked in her eyes. Marilla, listening fearfully outside the door, heard a pitiful, heartbroken moan, and fled to the kitchen where Susan was weeping.

"Oh, the poor lamb—the poor lamb! How can she bear it, Miss Cuthbert? I am afraid it will kill her. She has been that built up and happy, longing for that baby, and planning for it. Cannot anything be done nohow, Miss Cuthbert?"

"I'm afraid not, Susan. Gilbert says there is no hope. He knew from the first the little thing couldn't live."

"And it is such a sweet baby," sobbed Susan. "I never saw one so white—they are mostly red or yellow. And it opened its big eyes as if it was months old. The little, little thing! Oh, the poor, young Mrs. Doctor!"

At sunset the little soul that had come with the dawning went away, leaving heartbreak behind it. Miss Cornelia took the wee, white lady from the kindly but stranger hands of the nurse, and dressed the tiny waxen form in the beautiful dress Leslie had made for it. Leslie had asked her to do that. Then she took it back and laid it beside the poor, broken, tear-blinded little mother.

"The Lord has given and the Lord has taken away, dearie," she said through her own tears. "Blessed be the name of the Lord."

Then she went away, leaving Anne and Gilbert alone together with their dead.

The next day, the small white Joy was laid in a velvet casket which Leslie had lined with apple-blossoms, and taken to the graveyard of the church across the harbor. Miss Cornelia and Marilla put all the little love-made garments away, together with the ruffled basket which had been befrilled and belaced for dimpled limbs and downy head. Little Joy was never to sleep there; she had found a colder, narrower bed.

"This has been an awful disappointment to me," sighed Miss Cornelia. "I've looked forward to this baby—and I did want it to be a girl, too."

"I can only be thankful that Anne's life was spared," said Marilla, with a shiver, recalling those hours of darkness when the girl she loved was passing through the valley of the shadow.

"Poor, poor lamb! Her heart is broken," said Susan.

"I ENVY Anne," said Leslie suddenly and fiercely, "and I'd envy her even if she had died! She was a mother for one beautiful day. I'd gladly give my life for THAT!"

"I wouldn't talk like that, Leslie, dearie," said Miss Cornelia deprecatingly. She was afraid that the dignified Miss Cuthbert would think Leslie quite terrible.

Anne's convalescence was long, and made bitter for her by many things. The bloom and sunshine of the Four Winds world grated harshly on her; and yet, when the rain fell heavily, she pictured it beating so mercilessly down on that little grave across the harbor; and when the wind blew around the eaves she heard sad voices in it she had never heard before.

Kindly callers hurt her, too, with the well-meant platitudes with which they strove to cover the nakedness of bereavement. A letter from Phil Blake was an added sting. Phil had heard of the baby's birth, but not of its death, and she wrote Anne a congratulatory letter of sweet mirth which hurt her horribly.

"I would have laughed over it so happily if I had my baby," she sobbed to Marilla. "But when I haven't it just seems like wanton cruelty—though I know Phil wouldn't hurt me for the world. Oh, Marilla, I don't see how I can EVER be happy again—EVERYTHING will hurt me all the rest of my life."

"Time will help you," said Marilla, who was racked with sympathy but could never learn to express it in other than age-worn formulas.

"It doesn't seem FAIR," said Anne rebelliously. "Babies are born and live where they are not wanted—where they will be neglected—where they will have no chance. I would have loved my baby so—and cared for it so tenderly—and tried to give her every chance for good. And yet I wasn't allowed to keep her."

"It was God's will, Anne," said Marilla, helpless before the riddle of the universe—the WHY of undeserved pain. "And little Joy is better off."

"I can't believe THAT," cried Anne bitterly. Then, seeing that Marilla looked shocked, she added passionately, "Why should she be born at all—why should any one be born at all—if she's better off dead? I DON'T believe it is better for a child to die at birth than to live its life out—and love and be loved—and enjoy and suffer—and do its work—and develop a character that would give it a personality in eternity. And how do you know it was God's will? Perhaps it was just a

656

thwarting of His purpose by the Power of Evil. We can't be expected to be re-signed to THAT."

"Oh, Anne, don't talk so," said Marilla, genuinely alarmed lest Anne were drifting into deep and dangerous waters. "We can't understand—but we must have faith—we MUST believe that all is for the best. I know you find it hard to think so, just now. But try to be brave—for Gilbert's sake. He's so worried about you. You aren't getting strong as fast as you should."

"Oh, I know I've been very selfish," sighed Anne. "I love Gilbert more than ever—and I want to live for his sake. But it seems as if part of me was buried over there in that little harbor graveyard—and it hurts so much that I'm afraid of life."

"It won't hurt so much always, Anne."

"The thought that it may stop hurting sometimes hurts me worse than all else, Marilla."

"Yes, I know, I've felt that too, about other things. But we all love you, Anne. Captain Jim has been up every day to ask for you—and Mrs. Moore haunts the place—and Miss Bryant spends most of her time, I think, cooking up nice things for you. Susan doesn't like it very well. She thinks she can cook as well as Miss Bryant."

"Dear Susan! Oh, everybody has been so dear and good and lovely to me, Marilla. I'm not ungrateful—and perhaps—when this horrible ache grows a little less—I'll find that I can go on living."

CHAPTER 20 - LOST MARGARET

Anne found that she could go on living; the day came when she even smiled again over one of Miss Cornelia's speeches. But there was something in the smile that had never been in Anne's smile before and would never be absent from it again.

On the first day she was able to go for a drive Gilbert took her down to Four Winds Point, and left her there while he rowed over the channel to see a patient at the fishing village. A rollicking wind was scudding across the harbor and the dunes, whipping the water into white-caps and washing the sandshore with long lines of silvery breakers.

"I'm real proud to see you here again, Mistress Blythe," said Captain Jim. "Sit down—sit down. I'm afeared it's mighty dusty here today—but there's no need of looking at dust when you can look at such scenery, is there?"

"I don't mind the dust," said Anne, "but Gilbert says I must keep in the open air. I think I'll go and sit on the rocks down there."

"Would you like company or would you rather be alone?"

"If by company you mean yours I'd much rather have it than be alone," said Anne, smiling. Then she sighed. She had never before minded being alone. Now she dreaded it. When she was alone now she felt so dreadfully alone.

"Here's a nice little spot where the wind can't get at you," said Captain Jim, when they reached the rocks. "I often sit here. It's a great place jest to sit and dream."

"Oh—dreams," sighed Anne. "I can't dream now, Captain Jim—I'm done with dreams."

"Oh, no, you're not, Mistress Blythe—oh, no, you're not," said Captain Jim meditatively. "I know how you feel jest now—but if you keep on living you'll get glad again, and the first thing you know you'll be dreaming again—thank the good Lord for it! If it wasn't for our dreams they might as well bury us. How'd we stand living if it wasn't for our dream of immortality? And that's a dream that's BOUND to come true, Mistress Blythe. You'll see your little Joyce again some day."

"But she won't be my baby," said Anne, with trembling lips. "Oh, she may be, as Longfellow says, 'a fair maiden clothed with celestial grace'—but she'll be a stranger to me."

"God will manage better'n THAT, I believe," said Captain Jim.

They were both silent for a little time. Then Captain Jim said very softly:

"Mistress Blythe, may I tell you about lost Margaret?"

"Of course," said Anne gently. She did not know who "lost Margaret" was, but she felt that she was going to hear the romance of Captain Jim's life.

"I've often wanted to tell you about her," Captain Jim went on.

"Do you know why, Mistress Blythe? It's because I want somebody to remember and think of her sometime after I'm gone. I can't bear that her name should be forgotten by all living souls. And now nobody remembers lost Margaret but me."

Then Captain Jim told the story—an old, old forgotten story, for it was over fifty years since Margaret had fallen asleep one day in her father's dory and drifted—or so it was supposed, for nothing was ever certainly known as to her fate—out of the channel, beyond the bar, to perish in the black thundersquall which had come up so suddenly that long-ago summer afternoon. But to Captain Jim those fifty years were but as yesterday when it is past.

"I walked the shore for months after that," he said sadly, "looking to find her dear, sweet little body; but the sea never give her back to me. But I'll find her sometime, Mistress Blythe—I'll find her sometime. She's waiting for me. I wish I could tell you jest how she looked, but I can't. I've seen a fine, silvery mist hanging over the bar at sunrise that seemed like her—and then again I've seen a white birch in the woods back yander that made me think of her. She had pale, brown hair and a little white, sweet face, and long slender fingers like yours, Mistress Blythe, only browner, for she was a shore girl. Sometimes I wake up in the night and hear the sea calling to me in the old way, and it seems as if lost Margaret called in it. And when there's a storm and the waves are sobbing and moaning I hear her lamenting among them. And when they laugh on a gay day it's HER laugh—lost Margaret's sweet, roguish, little laugh. The sea took her from me, but some day I'll find her. Mistress Blythe. It can't keep us apart forever."

"I am glad you have told me about her," said Anne. "I have often wondered why you had lived all your life alone."

"I couldn't ever care for anyone else. Lost Margaret took my heart with her—out there," said the old lover, who had been faithful for fifty years to his drowned sweetheart. "You won't mind if I talk a good deal about her, will you, Mistress Blythe? It's a pleasure to me—for all the pain went out of her memory years ago and jest left its blessing. I know you'll never forget her, Mistress Blythe. And if the years, as I hope, bring other little folks to your home, I want you to promise me that you'll tell THEM the story of lost Margaret, so that her name won't be forgotten among humankind."

CHAPTER 21 - BARRIERS SWEPT AWAY

"Anne," said Leslie, breaking abruptly a short
silence, "you don't know how GOOD it is to be sitting here with you again—
working—and talking—and being silent together."

They were sitting among the blue-eyed grasses on the bank of the brook in
Anne's garden. The water sparkled and crooned past them; the birches threw dappled shadows over them; roses bloomed along the walks. The sun was beginning
to be low, and the air was full of woven music. There was one music of the wind
in the firs behind the house, and another of the waves on the bar, and still another
from the distant bell of the church near which the wee, white lady slept. Anne
loved that bell, though it brought sorrowful thoughts now.

She looked curiously at Leslie, who had thrown down her sewing and spoken
with a lack of restraint that was very unusual with her.

"On that horrible night when you were so ill," Leslie went on, "I kept thinking
that perhaps we'd have no more talks and walks and WORKS together. And I realised just what your friendship had come to mean to me—just what YOU
meant—and just what a hateful little beast I had been."

"Leslie! Leslie! I never allow anyone to call my friends names."

"It's true. That's exactly what I am—a hateful little beast. There's something
I've GOT to tell you, Anne. I suppose it will make you despise me, but I MUST
confess it. Anne, there have been times this past winter and spring when I have
HATED you."

"I KNEW it," said Anne calmly.

"You KNEW it?"

"Yes, I saw it in your eyes."

"And yet you went on liking me and being my friend."

"Well, it was only now and then you hated me, Leslie. Between times you
loved me, I think."

"I certainly did. But that other horrid feeling was always there, spoiling it,
back in my heart. I kept it down—sometimes I forgot it—but sometimes it would
surge up and take possession of me. I hated you because I ENVIED you—oh, I
was sick with envy of you at times. You had a dear little home—and love—and
happiness—and glad dreams—everything I wanted—and never had—and never
could have. Oh, never could have! THAT was what stung. I wouldn't have envied

you, if I had had any HOPE that life would ever be different for me. But I hadn't—I hadn't—and it didn't seem FAIR. It made me rebellious—and it hurt me—and so I hated you at times. Oh, I was so ashamed of it—I'm dying of shame now—but I couldn't conquer it.

"That night, when I was afraid you mightn't live—I thought I was going to be punished for my wickedness—and I loved you so then. Anne, Anne, I never had anything to love since my mother died, except Dick's old dog—and it's so dreadful to have nothing to love—life is so EMPTY—and there's NOTHING worse than emptiness—and I might have loved you so much—and that horrible thing had spoiled it—"

Leslie was trembling and growing almost incoherent with the violence of her emotion.

"Don't, Leslie," implored Anne, "oh, don't. I understand—don't talk of it any more."

"I must—I must. When I knew you were going to live I vowed that I would tell you as soon as you were well—that I wouldn't go on accepting your friendship and companionship without telling you how unworthy I was of it. And I've been so afraid—it would turn you against me."

"You needn't fear that, Leslie."

"Oh, I'm so glad—so glad, Anne." Leslie clasped her brown, work-hardened hands tightly together to still their shaking. "But I want to tell you everything, now I've begun. You don't remember the first time I saw you, I suppose—it wasn't that night on the shore—"

"No, it was the night Gilbert and I came home. You were driving your geese down the hill. I should think I DO remember it! I thought you were so beautiful—I longed for weeks after to find out who you were."

"I knew who YOU were, although I had never seen either of you before. I had heard of the new doctor and his bride who were coming to live in Miss Russell's little house. I—I hated you that very moment, Anne."

"I felt the resentment in your eyes—then I doubted—I thought I must be mistaken—because WHY should it be?"

"It was because you looked so happy. Oh, you'll agree with me now that I AM a hateful beast—to hate another woman just because she was happy,—and when her happiness didn't take anything from me! That was why I never went to see you. I knew quite well I ought to go—even our simple Four Winds customs demanded that. But I couldn't. I used to watch you from my window—I could see you and your husband strolling about your garden in the evening—or you running down the poplar lane to meet him. And it hurt me. And yet in another way I wanted to go over. I felt that, if I were not so miserable, I could have liked you and found in you what I've never had in my life—an intimate, REAL friend of my own age. And then you remember that night at the shore? You were afraid I would think you crazy. You must have thought *I* was."

"No, but I couldn't understand you, Leslie. One moment you drew me to you—the next you pushed me back."

"I was very unhappy that evening. I had had a hard day. Dick had been very—very hard to manage that day. Generally he is quite good-natured and easily controlled, you know, Anne. But some days he is very different. I was so heartsick—I ran away to the shore as soon as he went to sleep. It was my only refuge. I sat there thinking of how my poor father had ended his life, and wondering if I wouldn't be driven to it some day. Oh, my heart was full of black thoughts! And then you came dancing along the cove like a glad, light-hearted child. I—I hated you more then than I've ever done since. And yet I craved your friendship. The one feeling swayed me one moment; the other feeling the next. When I got home that night I cried for shame of what you must think of me. But it's always been just the same when I came over here. Sometimes I'd be happy and enjoy my visit. And at other times that hideous feeling would mar it all. There were times when everything about you and your house hurt me. You had so many dear little things I couldn't have. Do you know—it's ridiculous—but I had an especial spite at those china dogs of yours. There were times when I wanted to catch up Gog and Magog and bang their pert black noses together! Oh, you smile, Anne—but it was never funny to me. I would come here and see you and Gilbert with your books and your flowers, and your household gods, and your little family jokes—and your love for each other showing in every look and word, even when you didn't know it—and I would go home to—you know what I went home to! Oh, Anne, I don't believe I'm jealous and envious by nature. When I was a girl I lacked many things my schoolmates had, but I never cared—I never disliked them for it. But I seem to have grown so hateful—"

"Leslie, dearest, stop blaming yourself. You are NOT hateful or jealous or envious. The life you have to live has warped you a little, perhaps-but it would have ruined a nature less fine and noble than yours. I'm letting you tell me all this because I believe it's better for you to talk it out and rid your soul of it. But don't blame yourself any more."

"Well, I won't. I just wanted you to know me as I am. That time you told me of your darling hope for the spring was the worst of all, Anne. I shall never forgive myself for the way I behaved then. I repented it with tears. And I DID put many a tender and loving thought of you into the little dress I made. But I might have known that anything I made could only be a shroud in the end."

"Now, Leslie, that IS bitter and morbid—put such thoughts away.

"I was so glad when you brought the little dress; and since I had to lose little Joyce I like to think that the dress she wore was the one you made for her when you let yourself love me."

"Anne, do you know, I believe I shall always love you after this. I don't think I'll ever feel that dreadful way about you again. Talking it all out seems to have done away with it, somehow. It's very strange—and I thought it so real and bitter. It's like opening the door of a dark room to show some hideous creature you've believed to be there—and when the light streams in your monster turns out to have been just a shadow, vanishing when the light comes. It will never come between us again."

"No, we are real friends now, Leslie, and I am very glad."

"I hope you won't misunderstand me if I say something else. Anne, I was grieved to the core of my heart when you lost your baby; and if I could have saved her for you by cutting off one of my hands I would have done it. But your sorrow has brought us closer together. Your perfect happiness isn't a barrier any longer. Oh, don't misunderstand, dearest—I'm NOT glad that your happiness isn't perfect any longer—I can say that sincerely; but since it isn't, there isn't such a gulf between us."

"I DO understand that, too, Leslie. Now, we'll just shut up the past and forget what was unpleasant in it. It's all going to be different. We're both of the race of Joseph now. I think you've been wonderful—wonderful. And, Leslie, I can't help believing that life has something good and beautiful for you yet."

Leslie shook her head.

"No," she said dully. "There isn't any hope. Dick will never be better—and even if his memory were to come back—oh, Anne, it would be worse, even worse, than it is now. This is something you can't understand, you happy bride. Anne, did Miss Cornelia ever tell you how I came to marry Dick?"

"Yes."

"I'm glad—I wanted you to know—but I couldn't bring myself to talk of it if you hadn't known. Anne, it seems to me that ever since I was twelve years old life has been bitter. Before that I had a happy childhood. We were very poor—but we didn't mind. Father was so splendid—so clever and loving and sympathetic. We were chums as far back as I can remember. And mother was so sweet. She was very, very beautiful. I look like her, but I am not so beautiful as she was."

"Miss Cornelia says you are far more beautiful."

"She is mistaken—or prejudiced. I think my figure IS better—mother was slight and bent by hard work—but she had the face of an angel. I used just to look up at her in worship. We all worshipped her,—father and Kenneth and I."

Anne remembered that Miss Cornelia had given her a very different impression of Leslie's mother. But had not love the truer vision? Still, it WAS selfish of Rose West to make her daughter marry Dick Moore.

"Kenneth was my brother," went on Leslie. "Oh, I can't tell you how I loved him. And he was cruelly killed. Do you know how?"

"Yes."

"Anne, I saw his little face as the wheel went over him. He fell on his back. Anne—Anne—I can see it now. I shall always see it. Anne, all I ask of heaven is that that recollection shall be blotted out of my memory. O my God!"

"Leslie, don't speak of it. I know the story—don't go into details that only harrow your soul up unavailingly. It WILL be blotted out."

After a moment's struggle, Leslie regained a measure of self-control.

"Then father's health got worse and he grew despondent—his mind became unbalanced—you've heard all that, too?"

"Yes."

"After that I had just mother to live for. But I was very ambitious. I meant to teach and earn my way through college. I meant to climb to the very top—oh, I won't talk of that either. It's no use. You know what happened. I couldn't see my dear little heart-broken mother, who had been such a slave all her life, turned out of her home. Of course, I could have earned enough for us to live on. But mother COULDN'T leave her home. She had come there as a bride—and she had loved father so—and all her memories were there. Even yet, Anne, when I think that I made her last year happy I'm not sorry for what I did. As for Dick—I didn't hate him when I married him—I just felt for him the indifferent, friendly feeling I had for most of my schoolmates. I knew he drank some—but I had never heard the story of the girl down at the fishing cove. If I had, I COULDN'T have married him, even for mother's sake. Afterwards—I DID hate him—but mother never knew. She died—and then I was alone. I was only seventeen and I was alone. Dick had gone off in the Four Sisters. I hoped he wouldn't be home very much more. The sea had always been in his blood. I had no other hope. Well, Captain Jim brought him home, as you know—and that's all there is to say. You know me now, Anne—the worst of me—the barriers are all down. And you still want to be my friend?"

Anne looked up through the birches, at the white paper-lantern of a half moon drifting downwards to the gulf of sunset. Her face was very sweet.

"I am your friend and you are mine, for always," she said. "Such a friend as I never had before. I have had many dear and beloved friends—but there is a something in you, Leslie, that I never found in anyone else. You have more to offer me in that rich nature of yours, and I have more to give you than I had in my careless girlhood. We are both women—and friends forever."

They clasped hands and smiled at each other through the tears that filled the gray eyes and the blue.

CHAPTER 22 - MISS CORNELIA ARRANGES MATTERS

Gilbert insisted that Susan should be kept on at the little house for the summer. Anne protested at first.

"Life here with just the two of us is so sweet, Gilbert. It spoils it a little to have anyone else. Susan is a dear soul, but she is an outsider. It won't hurt me to do the work here."

"You must take your doctor's advice," said Gilbert. "There's an old proverb to the effect that shoemakers' wives go barefoot and doctors' wives die young. I don't mean that it shall be true in my household. You will keep Susan until the old spring comes back into your step, and those little hollows on your cheeks fill out."

"You just take it easy, Mrs. Doctor, dear," said Susan, coming abruptly in. "Have a good time and do not worry about the pantry. Susan is at the helm. There is no use in keeping a dog and doing your own barking. I am going to take your breakfast up to you every morning."

"Indeed you are not," laughed Anne. "I agree with Miss Cornelia that it's a scandal for a woman who isn't sick to eat her breakfast in bed, and almost justifies the men in any enormities."

"Oh, Cornelia!" said Susan, with ineffable contempt. "I think you have better sense, Mrs. Doctor, dear, than to heed what Cornelia Bryant says. I cannot see why she must be always running down the men, even if she is an old maid. *I* am an old maid, but you never hear ME abusing the men. I like 'em. I would have married one if I could. Is it not funny nobody ever asked me to marry him, Mrs. Doctor, dear? I am no beauty, but I am as good-looking as most of the married women you see. But I never had a beau. What do you suppose is the reason?"

"It may be predestination," suggested Anne, with unearthly solemnity.

Susan nodded.

"That is what I have often thought, Mrs. Doctor, dear, and a great comfort it is. I do not mind nobody wanting me if the Almighty decreed it so for His own wise purposes. But sometimes doubt creeps in, Mrs. Doctor, dear, and I wonder if maybe the Old Scratch has not more to do with it than anyone else. I cannot feel resigned THEN. But maybe," added Susan, brightening up, "I will have a chance to get married yet. I often and often think of the old verse my aunt used to repeat:

There never was a goose so gray but sometime soon or late
Some honest gander came her way and took her for his mate!

A woman cannot ever be sure of not being married till she is buried, Mrs. Doctor, dear, and meanwhile I will make a batch of cherry pies. I notice the doctor favors 'em, and I DO like cooking for a man who appreciates his victuals."

Miss Cornelia dropped in that afternoon, puffing a little.

"I don't mind the world or the devil much, but the flesh DOES rather bother me," she admitted. "You always look as cool as a cucumber, Anne, dearie. Do I smell cherry pie? If I do, ask me to stay to tea. Haven't tasted a cherry pie this summer. My cherries have all been stolen by those scamps of Gilman boys from the Glen."

"Now, now, Cornelia," remonstrated Captain Jim, who had been reading a sea novel in a corner of the living room, "you shouldn't say that about those two poor, motherless Gilman boys, unless you've got certain proof. Jest because their father ain't none too honest isn't any reason for calling them thieves. It's more likely it's been the robins took your cherries. They're turrible thick this year."

"Robins!" said Miss Cornelia disdainfully. "Humph! Two-legged robins, believe ME!"

"Well, most of the Four Winds robins ARE constructed on that principle," said Captain Jim gravely.

Miss Cornelia stared at him for a moment. Then she leaned back in her rocker and laughed long and ungrudgingly.

"Well, you HAVE got one on me at last, Jim Boyd, I'll admit. Just look how pleased he is, Anne, dearie, grinning like a Chessy-cat. As for the robins' legs if robins have great, big, bare, sunburned legs, with ragged trousers hanging on 'em, such as I saw up in my cherry tree one morning at sunrise last week, I'll beg the Gilman boys' pardon. By the time I got down they were gone. I couldn't understand how they had disappeared so quick, but Captain Jim has enlightened me. They flew away, of course."

Captain Jim laughed and went away, regretfully declining an invitation to stay to supper and partake of cherry pie.

"I'm on my way to see Leslie and ask her if she'll take a boarder," Miss Cornelia resumed. "I'd a letter yesterday from a Mrs. Daly in Toronto, who boarded a spell with me two years ago. She wanted me to take a friend of hers for the summer. His name is Owen Ford, and he's a newspaper man, and it seems he's a grandson of the schoolmaster who built this house. John Selwyn's oldest daughter married an Ontario man named Ford, and this is her son. He wants to see the old place his grandparents lived in. He had a bad spell of typhoid in the spring and hasn't got rightly over it, so his doctor has ordered him to the sea. He doesn't want to go to the hotel—he just wants a quiet home place. I can't take him, for I have to be away in August. I've been appointed a delegate to the W.F.M.S. convention in Kingsport and I'm going. I don't know whether Leslie'll want to be bothered with him, either, but there's no one else. If she can't take him he'll have to go over the harbor."

"When you've seen her come back and help us eat our cherry pies," said Anne. "Bring Leslie and Dick, too, if they can come. And so you're going to Kingsport? What a nice time you will have. I must give you a letter to a friend of mine there—Mrs. Jonas Blake."

"I've prevailed on Mrs. Thomas Holt to go with me," said Miss Cornelia complacently. "It's time she had a little holiday, believe ME. She has just about worked herself to death. Tom Holt can crochet beautifully, but he can't make a living for his family. He never seems to be able to get up early enough to do any work, but I notice he can always get up early to go fishing. Isn't that like a man?"

Anne smiled. She had learned to discount largely Miss Cornelia's opinions of the Four Winds men. Otherwise she must have believed them the most hopeless assortment of reprobates and ne'er-do-wells in the world, with veritable slaves and martyrs for wives. This particular Tom Holt, for example, she knew to be a kind husband, a much loved father, and an excellent neighbor. If he were rather inclined to be lazy, liking better the fishing he had been born for than the farming he had not, and if he had a harmless eccentricity for doing fancy work, nobody save Miss Cornelia seemed to hold it against him. His wife was a "hustler," who gloried in hustling; his family got a comfortable living off the farm; and his strapping sons and daughters, inheriting their mother's energy, were all in a fair way to do well in the world. There was not a happier household in Glen St. Mary than the Holts'.

Miss Cornelia returned satisfied from the house up the brook.

"Leslie's going to take him," she announced. "She jumped at the chance. She wants to make a little money to shingle the roof of her house this fall, and she didn't know how she was going to manage it. I expect Captain Jim'll be more than interested when he hears that a grandson of the Selwyns' is coming here. Leslie said to tell you she hankered after cherry pie, but she couldn't come to tea because she has to go and hunt up her turkeys. They've strayed away. But she said, if there was a piece left, for you to put it in the pantry and she'd run over in the cat's light, when prowling's in order, to get it. You don't know, Anne, dearie, what good it did my heart to hear Leslie send you a message like that, laughing like she used to long ago.

"There's a great change come over her lately. She laughs and jokes like a girl, and from her talk I gather she's here real often."

"Every day—or else I'm over there," said Anne. "I don't know what I'd do without Leslie, especially just now when Gilbert is so busy. He's hardly ever home except for a few hours in the wee sma's. He's really working himself to death. So many of the over-harbor people send for him now."

"They might better be content with their own doctor," said Miss Cornelia. "Though to be sure I can't blame them, for he's a Methodist. Ever since Dr. Blythe brought Mrs. Allonby round folks think he can raise the dead. I believe Dr. Dave is a mite jealous—just like a man. He thinks Dr. Blythe has too many newfangled notions! 'Well,' I says to him, 'it was a new-fangled notion saved Rhoda Allonby. If YOU'D been attending her she'd have died, and had a tombstone saying it had pleased God to take her away.' Oh, I DO like to speak my mind to Dr. Dave! He's bossed the Glen for years, and he thinks he's forgotten more than other people ever knew. Speaking of doctors, I wish Dr. Blythe'd run over and see to that boil on Dick Moore's neck. It's getting past Leslie's skill. I'm sure I don't know what Dick Moore wants to start in having boils for—as if he wasn't enough trouble without that!"

"Do you know, Dick has taken quite a fancy to me," said Anne. "He follows me round like a dog, and smiles like a pleased child when I notice him."

"Does it make you creepy?"

"Not at all. I rather like poor Dick Moore. He seems so pitiful and appealing, somehow."

"You wouldn't think him very appealing if you'd see him on his cantankerous days, believe ME. But I'm glad you don't mind him—it's all the nicer for Leslie. She'll have more to do when her boarder comes. I hope he'll be a decent creature. You'll probably like him—he's a writer."

"I wonder why people so commonly suppose that if two individuals are both writers they must therefore be hugely congenial," said Anne, rather scornfully. "Nobody would expect two blacksmiths to be violently attracted toward each other merely because they were both blacksmiths."

Nevertheless, she looked forward to the advent of Owen Ford with a pleasant sense of expectation. If he were young and likeable he might prove a very pleasant addition to society in Four Winds. The latch-string of the little house was always out for the race of Joseph.

CHAPTER 23 - OWEN FORD COMES

One evening Miss Cornelia telephoned down to Anne.

"The writer man has just arrived here. I'm going to drive him down to your place, and you can show him the way over to Leslie's. It's shorter than driving round by the other road, and I'm in a mortal hurry. The Reese baby has gone and fallen into a pail of hot water at the Glen, and got nearly scalded to death and they want me right off—to put a new skin on the child, I presume. Mrs. Reese is always so careless, and then expects other people to mend her mistakes. You won't mind, will you, dearie? His trunk can go down tomorrow."

"Very well," said Anne. "What is he like, Miss Cornelia?"

"You'll see what he's like outside when I take him down. As for what he's like inside only the Lord who made him knows THAT. I'm not going to say another word, for every receiver in the Glen is down."

"Miss Cornelia evidently can't find much fault with Mr. Ford's looks, or she would find it in spite of the receivers," said Anne. "I conclude therefore, Susan, that Mr. Ford is rather handsome than otherwise."

"Well, Mrs. Doctor, dear, I DO enjoy seeing a well-looking man," said Susan candidly. "Had I not better get up a snack for him? There is a strawberry pie that would melt in your mouth."

"No, Leslie is expecting him and has his supper ready. Besides, I want that strawberry pie for my own poor man. He won't be home till late, so leave the pie and a glass of milk out for him, Susan."

"That I will, Mrs. Doctor, dear. Susan is at the helm. After all, it is better to give pie to your own men than to strangers, who may be only seeking to devour, and the doctor himself is as well-looking a man as you often come across."

When Owen Ford came Anne secretly admitted, as Miss Cornelia towed him in, that he was very "well-looking" indeed. He was tall and broad-shouldered, with thick, brown hair, finely-cut nose and chin, large and brilliant dark-gray eyes.

"And did you notice his ears and his teeth, Mrs. Doctor, dear?" queried Susan later on. "He has got the nicest-shaped ears I ever saw on a man's head. I am choice about ears. When I was young I was scared that I might have to marry a man with ears like flaps. But I need not have worried, for never a chance did I have with any kind of ears."

Anne had not noticed Owen Ford's ears, but she did see his teeth, as his lips parted over them in a frank and friendly smile. Unsmiling, his face was rather sad and absent in expression, not unlike the melancholy, inscrutable hero of Anne's own early dreams; but mirth and humor and charm lighted it up when he smiled. Certainly, on the outside, as Miss Cornelia said, Owen Ford was a very presentable fellow.

"You cannot realise how delighted I am to be here, Mrs. Blythe," he said, looking around him with eager, interested eyes. "I have an odd feeling of coming home. My mother was born and spent her childhood here, you know. She used to talk a great deal to me of her old home. I know the geography of it as well as of the one I lived in, and, of course, she told me the story of the building of the house, and of my grandfather's agonised watch for the Royal William. I had thought that so old a house must have vanished years ago, or I should have come to see it before this."

"Old houses don't vanish easily on this enchanted coast," smiled Anne. "This is a 'land where all things always seem the same'—nearly always, at least. John Selwyn's house hasn't even been much changed, and outside the rose-bushes your grandfather planted for his bride are blooming this very minute."

"How the thought links me with them! With your leave I must explore the whole place soon."

"Our latch-string will always be out for you," promised Anne. "And do you know that the old sea captain who keeps the Four Winds light knew John Selwyn and his bride well in his boyhood? He told me their story the night I came here— the third bride of the old house."

"Can it be possible? This IS a discovery. I must hunt him up."

"It won't be difficult; we are all cronies of Captain Jim. He will be as eager to see you as you could be to see him. Your grandmother shines like a star in his memory. But I think Mrs. Moore is expecting you. I'll show you our 'cross-lots' road."

Anne walked with him to the house up the brook, over a field that was as white as snow with daisies. A boat-load of people were singing far across the harbor. The sound drifted over the water like faint, unearthly music wind-blown across a starlit sea. The big light flashed and beaconed. Owen Ford looked around him with satisfaction.

"And so this is Four Winds," he said. "I wasn't prepared to find it quite so beautiful, in spite of all mother's praises. What colors—what scenery—what charm! I shall get as strong as a horse in no time. And if inspiration comes from beauty, I should certainly be able to begin my great Canadian novel here."

"You haven't begun it yet?" asked Anne.

"Alack-a-day, no. I've never been able to get the right central idea for it. It lurks beyond me—it allures—and beckons—and recedes—I almost grasp it and it is gone. Perhaps amid this peace and loveliness, I shall be able to capture it. Miss Bryant tells me that you write."

"Oh, I do little things for children. I haven't done much since I was married. And—I have no designs on a great Canadian novel," laughed Anne. "That is quite beyond me."

Owen Ford laughed too.

"I dare say it is beyond me as well. All the same I mean to have a try at it some day, if I can ever get time. A newspaper man doesn't have much chance for that sort of thing. I've done a good deal of short story writing for the magazines, but I've never had the leisure that seems to be necessary for the writing of a book. With three months of liberty I ought to make a start, though—if I could only get the necessary motif for it—the SOUL of the book."

An idea whisked through Anne's brain with a suddenness that made her jump. But she did not utter it, for they had reached the Moore house. As they entered the yard Leslie came out on the veranda from the side door, peering through the gloom for some sign of her expected guest. She stood just where the warm yellow light flooded her from the open door. She wore a plain dress of cheap, cream-tinted cotton voile, with the usual girdle of crimson. Leslie was never without her touch of crimson. She had told Anne that she never felt satisfied without a gleam of red somewhere about her, if it were only a flower. To Anne, it always seemed to symbolise Leslie's glowing, pent-up personality, denied all expression save in that flaming glint. Leslie's dress was cut a little away at the neck and had short sleeves. Her arms gleamed like ivory-tinted marble. Every exquisite curve of her form was outlined in soft darkness against the light. Her hair shone in it like flame. Beyond her was a purple sky, flowering with stars over the harbor.

Anne heard her companion give a gasp. Even in the dusk she could see the amazement and admiration on his face.

"Who is that beautiful creature?" he asked.

"That is Mrs. Moore," said Anne. "She is very lovely, isn't she?"

"I—I never saw anything like her," he answered, rather dazedly. "I wasn't prepared—I didn't expect—good heavens, one DOESN'T expect a goddess for a landlady! Why, if she were clothed in a gown of sea-purple, with a rope of amethysts in her hair, she would be a veritable sea-queen. And she takes in boarders!"

"Even goddesses must live," said Anne. "And Leslie isn't a goddess. She's just a very beautiful woman, as human as the rest of us. Did Miss Bryant tell you about Mr. Moore?"

"Yes,—he's mentally deficient, or something of the sort, isn't he? But she said nothing about Mrs. Moore, and I supposed she'd be the usual hustling country housewife who takes in boarders to earn an honest penny."

"Well, that's just what Leslie is doing," said Anne crisply. "And it isn't altogether pleasant for her, either. I hope you won't mind Dick. If you do, please don't let Leslie see it. It would hurt her horribly. He's just a big baby, and sometimes a rather annoying one."

"Oh, I won't mind him. I don't suppose I'll be much in the house anyhow, except for meals. But what a shame it all is! Her life must be a hard one."

"It is. But she doesn't like to be pitied."

Leslie had gone back into the house and now met them at the front door. She greeted Owen Ford with cold civility, and told him in a business-like tone that his room and his supper were ready for him. Dick, with a pleased grin, shambled upstairs with the valise, and Owen Ford was installed as an inmate of the old house among the willows.

CHAPTER 24 - THE LIFE-BOOK OF CAPTAIN JIM

"I have a little brown cocoon of an idea that may possibly expand into a magnificent moth of fulfilment," Anne told Gilbert when she reached home. He had returned earlier than she had expected, and was enjoying Susan's cherry pie. Susan herself hovered in the background, like a rather grim but beneficent guardian spirit, and found as much pleasure in watching Gilbert eat pie as he did in eating it.

"What is your idea?" he asked.

"I sha'n't tell you just yet—not till I see if I can bring the thing about."

"What sort of a chap is Ford?"

"Oh, very nice, and quite good-looking."

"Such beautiful ears, doctor, dear," interjected Susan with a relish.

"He is about thirty or thirty-five, I think, and he meditates writing a novel. His voice is pleasant and his smile delightful, and he knows how to dress. He looks as if life hadn't been altogether easy for him, somehow."

Owen Ford came over the next evening with a note to Anne from Leslie; they spent the sunset time in the garden and then went for a moonlit sail on the harbor, in the little boat Gilbert had set up for summer outings. They liked Owen immensely and had that feeling of having known him for many years which distinguishes the freemasonry of the house of Joseph. "He is as nice as his ears, Mrs. Doctor, dear," said Susan, when he had gone. He had told Susan that he had never tasted anything like her strawberry shortcake and Susan's susceptible heart was his forever.

"He has got a way with him," she reflected, as she cleared up the relics of the supper. "It is real queer he is not married, for a man like that could have anybody for the asking. Well, maybe he is like me, and has not met the right one yet."

Susan really grew quite romantic in her musings as she washed the supper dishes.

Two nights later Anne took Owen Ford down to Four Winds Point to introduce him to Captain Jim. The clover fields along the harbor shore were whitening in the western wind, and Captain Jim had one of his finest sunsets on exhibition. He himself had just returned from a trip over the harbor.

"I had to go over and tell Henry Pollack he was dying. Everybody else was afraid to tell him. They expected he'd take on turrible, for he's been dreadful determined to live, and been making no end of plans for the fall. His wife thought he oughter be told and that I'd be the best one to break it to him that he couldn't get better. Henry and me are old cronies—we sailed in the Gray Gull for years together. Well, I went over and sat down by Henry's bed and I says to him, says I, jest right out plain and simple, for if a thing's got to be told it may as well be told first as last, says I, 'Mate, I reckon you've got your sailing orders this time,' I was sorter quaking inside, for it's an awful thing to have to tell a man who hain't any idea he's dying that he is. But lo and behold, Mistress Blythe, Henry looks up at me, with those bright old black eyes of his in his wizened face and says, says he, 'Tell me something I don't know, Jim Boyd, if you want to give me information. I've known THAT for a week.' I was too astonished to speak, and Henry, he chuckled. 'To see you coming in here,' says he, 'with your face as solemn as a tombstone and sitting down there with your hands clasped over your stomach, and passing me out a blue-mouldy old item of news like that! It'd make a cat laugh, Jim Boyd,' says he. 'Who told you?' says I, stupid like. 'Nobody,' says he. 'A week ago Tuesday night I was lying here awake—and I jest knew. I'd suspicioned it before, but then I KNEW. I've been keeping up for the wife's sake. And I'd LIKE to have got that barn built, for Eben'll never get it right. But anyhow, now that you've eased your mind, Jim, put on a smile and tell me something interesting,' Well, there it was. They'd been so scared to tell him and he knew it all the time. Strange how nature looks out for us, ain't it, and lets us know what we should know when the time comes? Did I never tell you the yarn about Henry getting the fish hook in his nose, Mistress Blythe?"

"No."

"Well, him and me had a laugh over it today. It happened nigh unto thirty years ago. Him and me and several more was out mackerel fishing one day. It was a great day—never saw such a school of mackerel in the gulf—and in the general excitement Henry got quite wild and contrived to stick a fish hook clean through one side of his nose. Well, there he was; there was barb on one end and a big piece of lead on the other, so it couldn't be pulled out. We wanted to take him ashore at once, but Henry was game; he said he'd be jiggered if he'd leave a school like that for anything short of lockjaw; then he kept fishing away, hauling in hand over fist and groaning between times. Fin'lly the school passed and we come in with a load; I got a file and begun to try to file through that hook. I tried to be as easy as I could, but you should have heard Henry—no, you shouldn't either. It was well no ladies were around. Henry wasn't a swearing man, but he'd heard some few matters of that sort along shore in his time, and he fished 'em all out of his recollection and hurled 'em at me. Fin'lly he declared he couldn't stand it and I had no bowels of compassion. So we hitched up and I drove him to a doctor in Charlottetown, thirty-five miles—there weren't none nearer in them days—with that blessed hook still hanging from his nose. When we got there old Dr.

Crabb jest took a file and filed that hook jest the same as I'd tried to do, only he weren't a mite particular about doing it easy!"

Captain Jim's visit to his old friend had revived many recollections and he was now in the full tide of reminiscences.

"Henry was asking me today if I remembered the time old Father Chiniquy blessed Alexander MacAllister's boat. Another odd yarn—and true as gospel. I was in the boat myself. We went out, him and me, in Alexander MacAllister's boat one morning at sunrise. Besides, there was a French boy in the boat— Catholic of course. You know old Father Chiniquy had turned Protestant, so the Catholics hadn't much use for him. Well, we sat out in the gulf in the broiling sun till noon, and not a bite did we get. When we went ashore old Father Chiniquy had to go, so he said in that polite way of his, 'I'm very sorry I cannot go out with you dis afternoon, Mr. MacAllister, but I leave you my blessing. You will catch a t'ousand dis afternoon. 'Well, we did not catch a thousand, but we caught exactly nine hundred and ninety-nine—the biggest catch for a small boat on the whole north shore that summer. Curious, wasn't it? Alexander MacAllister, he says to Andrew Peters, 'Well, and what do you think of Father Chiniquy now?' 'Vell,' growled Andrew, 'I t'ink de old devil has got a blessing left yet.' Laws, how Henry did laugh over that today!"

"Do you know who Mr. Ford is, Captain Jim?" asked Anne, seeing that Captain Jim's fountain of reminiscence had run out for the present. "I want you to guess."

Captain Jim shook his head.

"I never was any hand at guessing, Mistress Blythe, and yet somehow when I come in I thought, 'Where have I seen them eyes before?'—for I HAVE seen 'em."

"Think of a September morning many years ago," said Anne, softly. "Think of a ship sailing up the harbor—a ship long waited for and despaired of. Think of the day the Royal William came in and the first look you had at the schoolmaster's bride."

Captain Jim sprang up.

"They're Persis Selwyn's eyes," he almost shouted. "You can't be her son—you must be her—"

"Grandson; yes, I am Alice Selwyn's son."

Captain Jim swooped down on Owen Ford and shook his hand over again.

"Alice Selwyn's son! Lord, but you're welcome! Many's the time I've wondered where the descendants of the schoolmaster were living. I knew there was none on the Island. Alice—Alice—the first baby ever born in that little house. No baby ever brought more joy! I've dandled her a hundred times. It was from my knee she took her first steps alone. Can't I see her mother's face watching her— and it was near sixty years ago. Is she living yet?"

"No, she died when I was only a boy."

"Oh, it doesn't seem right that I should be living to hear that," sighed Captain Jim. "But I'm heart-glad to see you. It's brought back my youth for a little while.

You don't know yet what a boon THAT is. Mistress Blythe here has the trick—she does it quite often for me."

Captain Jim was still more excited when he discovered that Owen Ford was what he called a "real writing man." He gazed at him as at a superior being. Captain Jim knew that Anne wrote, but he had never taken that fact very seriously. Captain Jim thought women were delightful creatures, who ought to have the vote, and everything else they wanted, bless their hearts; but he did not believe they could write.

"Jest look at A Mad Love," he would protest. "A woman wrote that and jest look at it—one hundred and three chapters when it could all have been told in ten. A writing woman never knows when to stop; that's the trouble. The p'int of good writing is to know when to stop."

"Mr. Ford wants to hear some of your stories, Captain Jim" said Anne. "Tell him the one about the captain who went crazy and imagined he was the Flying Dutchman."

This was Captain Jim's best story. It was a compound of horror and humor, and though Anne had heard it several times she laughed as heartily and shivered as fearsomely over it as Mr. Ford did. Other tales followed, for Captain Jim had an audience after his own heart. He told how his vessel had been run down by a steamer; how he had been boarded by Malay pirates; how his ship had caught fire; how he helped a political prisoner escape from a South African republic; how he had been wrecked one fall on the Magdalens and stranded there for the winter; how a tiger had broken loose on board ship; how his crew had mutinied and marooned him on a barren island—these and many other tales, tragic or humorous or grotesque, did Captain Jim relate. The mystery of the sea, the fascination of far lands, the lure of adventure, the laughter of the world—his hearers felt and realised them all. Owen Ford listened, with his head on his hand, and the First Mate purring on his knee, his brilliant eyes fastened on Captain Jim's rugged, eloquent face.

"Won't you let Mr. Ford see your life-book, Captain Jim?" asked Anne, when Captain Jim finally declared that yarn-spinning must end for the time.

"Oh, he don't want to be bothered with THAT," protested Captain Jim, who was secretly dying to show it.

"I should like nothing better than to see it, Captain Boyd," said Owen. "If it is half as wonderful as your tales it will be worth seeing."

With pretended reluctance Captain Jim dug his life-book out of his old chest and handed it to Owen.

"I reckon you won't care to wrastle long with my old hand o' write. I never had much schooling," he observed carelessly. "Just wrote that there to amuse my nephew Joe. He's always wanting stories. Comes here yesterday and says to me, reproachful-like, as I was lifting a twenty-pound codfish out of my boat, 'Uncle Jim, ain't a codfish a dumb animal?' I'd been a-telling him, you see, that he must be real kind to dumb animals, and never hurt 'em in any way. I got out of the scrape by saying a codfish was dumb enough but it wasn't an animal, but Joe didn't look satisfied, and I wasn't satisfied myself. You've got to be mighty careful what you tell them little critters. THEY can see through you."

While talking, Captain Jim watched Owen Ford from the corner of his eye as the latter examined the life-book; and presently observing that his guest was lost in its pages, he turned smilingly to his cupboard and proceeded to make a pot of tea. Owen Ford separated himself from the life-book, with as much reluctance as a miser wrenches himself from his gold, long enough to drink his tea, and then returned to it hungrily.

"Oh, you can take that thing home with you if you want to," said Captain Jim, as if the "thing" were not his most treasured possession. "I must go down and pull my boat up a bit on the skids. There's a wind coming. Did you notice the sky to-night?

> Mackerel skies and mares' tails
> Make tall ships carry short sails."

Owen Ford accepted the offer of the life-book gladly. On their way home Anne told him the story of lost Margaret.

"That old captain is a wonderful old fellow," he said. "What a life he has led! Why, the man had more adventures in one week of his life than most of us have in a lifetime. Do you really think his tales are all true?"

"I certainly do. I am sure Captain Jim could not tell a lie; and besides, all the people about here say that everything happened as he relates it. There used to be plenty of his old shipmates alive to corroborate him. He's one of the last of the old type of P.E. Island sea-captains. They are almost extinct now."

CHAPTER 25 - THE WRITING OF THE BOOK

Owen Ford came over to the little house the next morning in a state of great excitement. "Mrs. Blythe, this is a wonderful book—absolutely wonderful. If I could take it and use the material for a book I feel certain I could make the novel of the year out of it. Do you suppose Captain Jim would let me do it?"

"Let you! I'm sure he would be delighted," cried Anne. "I admit that it was what was in my head when I took you down last night. Captain Jim has always been wishing he could get somebody to write his life-book properly for him."

"Will you go down to the Point with me this evening, Mrs. Blythe? I'll ask him about that life-book myself, but I want you to tell him that you told me the story of lost Margaret and ask him if he will let me use it as a thread of romance with which to weave the stories of the life-book into a harmonious whole."

Captain Jim was more excited than ever when Owen Ford told him of his plan. At last his cherished dream was to be realized and his "life-book" given to the world. He was also pleased that the story of lost Margaret should be woven into it.

"It will keep her name from being forgotten," he said wistfully.

"That's why I want it put in."

"We'll collaborate," cried Owen delightedly. "You will give the soul and I the body. Oh, we'll write a famous book between us, Captain Jim. And we'll get right to work."

"And to think my book is to be writ by the schoolmaster's grandson!" exclaimed Captain Jim. "Lad, your grandfather was my dearest friend. I thought there was nobody like him. I see now why I had to wait so long. It couldn't be writ till the right man come. You BELONG here—you've got the soul of this old north shore in you—you're the only one who COULD write it."

It was arranged that the tiny room off the living room at the lighthouse should be given over to Owen for a workshop. It was necessary that Captain Jim should be near him as he wrote, for consultation upon many matters of sea-faring and gulf lore of which Owen was quite ignorant.

He began work on the book the very next morning, and flung himself into it heart and soul. As for Captain Jim, he was a happy man that summer. He looked upon the little room where Owen worked as a sacred shrine. Owen talked everything over with Captain Jim, but he would not let him see the manuscript.

"You must wait until it is published," he said. "Then you'll get it all at once in its best shape."

He delved into the treasures of the life-book and used them freely. He dreamed and brooded over lost Margaret until she became a vivid reality to him and lived in his pages. As the book progressed it took possession of him and he worked at it with feverish eagerness. He let Anne and Leslie read the manuscript and criticise it; and the concluding chapter of the book, which the critics, later on, were pleased to call idyllic, was modelled upon a suggestion of Leslie's.

Anne fairly hugged herself with delight over the success of her idea.

"I knew when I looked at Owen Ford that he was the very man for it," she told Gilbert. "Both humor and passion were in his face, and that, together with the art of expression, was just what was necessary for the writing of such a book. As Mrs. Rachel would say, he was predestined for the part."

Owen Ford wrote in the mornings. The afternoons were generally spent in some merry outing with the Blythes. Leslie often went, too, for Captain Jim took charge of Dick frequently, in order to set her free. They went boating on the harbor and up the three pretty rivers that flowed into it; they had clambakes on the bar and mussel-bakes on the rocks; they picked strawberries on the sand-dunes; they went out cod-fishing with Captain Jim; they shot plover in the shore fields and wild ducks in the cove—at least, the men did. In the evenings they rambled in the low-lying, daisied, shore fields under a golden moon, or they sat in the living room at the little house where often the coolness of the sea breeze justified a driftwood fire, and talked of the thousand and one things which happy, eager, clever young people can find to talk about.

Ever since the day on which she had made her confession to Anne Leslie had been a changed creature. There was no trace of her old coldness and reserve, no shadow of her old bitterness. The girlhood of which she had been cheated seemed to come back to her with the ripeness of womanhood; she expanded like a flower of flame and perfume; no laugh was readier than hers, no wit quicker, in the twilight circles of that enchanted summer. When she could not be with them all felt that some exquisite savor was lacking in their intercourse. Her beauty was illumined by the awakened soul within, as some rosy lamp might shine through a flawless vase of alabaster. There were hours when Anne's eyes seemed to ache with the splendor of her. As for Owen Ford, the "Margaret" of his book, although she had the soft brown hair and elfin face of the real girl who had vanished so long ago, "pillowed where lost Atlantis sleeps," had the personality of Leslie Moore, as it was revealed to him in those halcyon days at Four Winds Harbor.

All in all, it was a never-to-be-forgotten summer—one of those summers which come seldom into any life, but leave a rich heritage of beautiful memories in their going—one of those summers which, in a fortunate combination of delightful weather, delightful friends and delightful doings, come as near to perfection as anything can come in this world.

"Too good to last," Anne told herself with a little sigh, on the September day when a certain nip in the wind and a certain shade of intense blue on the gulf water said that autumn was hard by.

That evening Owen Ford told them that he had finished his book and that his vacation must come to an end.

"I have a good deal to do to it yet—revising and pruning and so forth," he said, "but in the main it's done. I wrote the last sentence this morning. If I can find a publisher for it it will probably be out next summer or fall."

Owen had not much doubt that he would find a publisher. He knew that he had written a great book—a book that would score a wonderful success—a book that would LIVE. He knew that it would bring him both fame and fortune; but when he had written the last line of it he had bowed his head on the manuscript and so sat for a long time. And his thoughts were not of the good work he had done.

CHAPTER 26 - OWEN FORD'S CONFESSION

"I'm so sorry Gilbert is away," said Anne. "He had to go—Allan Lyons at the Glen has met with a serious accident. He will not likely be home till very late. But he told me to tell you he'd be up and over early enough in the morning to see you before you left. It's too provoking. Susan and I had planned such a nice little jamboree for your last night here."

She was sitting beside the garden brook on the little rustic seat Gilbert had built. Owen Ford stood before her, leaning against the bronze column of a yellow birch. He was very pale and his face bore the marks of the preceding sleepless night. Anne, glancing up at him, wondered if, after all, his summer had brought him the strength it should. Had he worked too hard over his book? She remembered that for a week he had not been looking well.

"I'm rather glad the doctor is away," said Owen slowly. "I wanted to see you alone, Mrs. Blythe. There is something I must tell somebody, or I think it will drive me mad. I've been trying for a week to look it in the face—and I can't. I know I can trust you—and, besides, you will understand. A woman with eyes like yours always understands. You are one of the folks people instinctively tell things to. Mrs. Blythe, I love Leslie. LOVE her! That seems too weak a word!"

His voice suddenly broke with the suppressed passion of his utterance. He turned his head away and hid his face on his arm. His whole form shook. Anne sat looking at him, pale and aghast. She had never thought of this! And yet—how was it she had never thought of it? It now seemed a natural and inevitable thing. She wondered at her own blindness. But—but—things like this did not happen in Four Winds. Elsewhere in the world human passions might set at defiance human conventions and laws—but not HERE, surely. Leslie had kept summer boarders off and on for ten years, and nothing like this had happened. But perhaps they had not been like Owen Ford; and the vivid, LIVING Leslie of this summer was not the cold, sullen girl of other years. Oh, SOMEBODY should have thought of this! Why hadn't Miss Cornelia thought of it? Miss Cornelia was always ready enough to sound the alarm where men were concerned. Anne felt an unreasonable resentment against Miss Cornelia. Then she gave a little inward groan. No matter who was to blame the mischief was done. And Leslie—what of Leslie? It was for Leslie Anne felt most concerned.

"Does Leslie know this, Mr. Ford?" she asked quietly.

"No—no,—unless she has guessed it. You surely don't think I'd be cad and scoundrel enough to tell her, Mrs. Blythe. I couldn't help loving her—that's all—and my misery is greater than I can bear."

"Does SHE care?" asked Anne. The moment the question crossed her lips she felt that she should not have asked it. Owen Ford answered it with overeager protest.

"No—no, of course not. But I could make her care if she were free—I know I could."

"She does care—and he knows it," thought Anne. Aloud she said, sympathetically but decidedly:

"But she is not free, Mr. Ford. And the only thing you can do is to go away in silence and leave her to her own life."

"I know—I know," groaned Owen. He sat down on the grassy bank and stared moodily into the amber water beneath him. "I know there's nothing to do—nothing but to say conventionally, 'Good-bye, Mrs. Moore. Thank you for all your kindness to me this summer,' just as I would have said it to the sonsy, bustling, keen-eyed housewife I expected her to be when I came. Then I'll pay my board money like any honest boarder and go! Oh, it's very simple. No doubt—no perplexity—a straight road to the end of the world!

"And I'll walk it—you needn't fear that I won't, Mrs. Blythe. But it would be easier to walk over red-hot ploughshares."

Anne flinched with the pain of his voice. And there was so little she could say that would be adequate to the situation. Blame was out of the question—advice was not needed—sympathy was mocked by the man's stark agony. She could only feel with him in a maze of compassion and regret. Her heart ached for Leslie! Had not that poor girl suffered enough without this?

"It wouldn't be so hard to go and leave her if she were only happy," resumed Owen passionately. "But to think of her living death—to realise what it is to which I do leave her! THAT is the worst of all. I would give my life to make her happy—and I can do nothing even to help her—nothing. She is bound forever to that poor wretch—with nothing to look forward to but growing old in a succession of empty, meaningless, barren years. It drives me mad to think of it. But I must go through my life, never seeing her, but always knowing what she is enduring. It's hideous—hideous!"

"It is very hard," said Anne sorrowfully. "We—her friends here—all know how hard it is for her."

"And she is so richly fitted for life," said Owen rebelliously.

"Her beauty is the least of her dower—and she is the most beautiful woman I've ever known. That laugh of hers! I've angled all summer to evoke that laugh, just for the delight of hearing it. And her eyes—they are as deep and blue as the gulf out there. I never saw such blueness—and gold! Did you ever see her hair down, Mrs. Blythe?"

"No."

"I did—once. I had gone down to the Point to go fishing with Captain Jim but it was too rough to go out, so I came back. She had taken the opportunity of what she expected to be an afternoon alone to wash her hair, and she was standing on the veranda in the sunshine to dry it. It fell all about her to her feet in a fountain of living gold. When she saw me she hurried in, and the wind caught her hair and swirled it all around her—Danae in her cloud. Somehow, just then the knowledge that I loved her came home to me—and realised that I had loved her from the moment I first saw her standing against the darkness in that glow of light. And she must live on here—petting and soothing Dick, pinching and saving for a mere existence, while I spend my life longing vainly for her, and debarred, by that very fact, from even giving her the little help a friend might. I walked the shore last night, almost till dawn, and thrashed it all out over and over again. And yet, in spite of everything, I can't find it in my heart to be sorry that I came to Four Winds. It seems to me that, bad as everything is, it would be still worse never to have known Leslie. It's burning, searing pain to love her and leave her—but not to have loved her is unthinkable. I suppose all this sounds very crazy—all these terrible emotions always do sound foolish when we put them into our inadequate words. They are not meant to be spoken—only felt and endured. I shouldn't have spoken—but it has helped—some. At least, it has given me strength to go away respectably tomorrow morning, without making a scene. You'll write me now and then, won't you, Mrs. Blythe, and give me what news there is to give of her?"

"Yes," said Anne. "Oh, I'm so sorry you are going—we'll miss you so—we've all been such friends! If it were not for this you could come back other summers. Perhaps, even yet—by-and-by—when you've forgotten, perhaps—"

"I shall never forget—and I shall never come back to Four Winds," said Owen briefly.

Silence and twilight fell over the garden. Far away the sea was lapping gently and monotonously on the bar. The wind of evening in the poplars sounded like some sad, weird, old rune—some broken dream of old memories. A slender shapely young aspen rose up before them against the fine maize and emerald and paling rose of the western sky, which brought out every leaf and twig in dark, tremulous, elfin loveliness.

"Isn't that beautiful?" said Owen, pointing to it with the air of a man who puts a certain conversation behind him.

"It's so beautiful that it hurts me," said Anne softly. "Perfect things like that always did hurt me—I remember I called it 'the queer ache' when I was a child. What is the reason that pain like this seems inseparable from perfection? Is it the pain of finality—when we realise that there can be nothing beyond but retrogression?"

"Perhaps," said Owen dreamily, "it is the prisoned infinite in us calling out to its kindred infinite as expressed in that visible perfection."

"You seem to have a cold in the head. Better rub some tallow on your nose when you go to bed," said Miss Cornelia, who had come in through the little gate between the firs in time to catch Owen's last remark. Miss Cornelia liked Owen;

but it was a matter of principle with her to visit any "high-falutin" language from a man with a snub.

Miss Cornelia personated the comedy that ever peeps around the corner at the tragedy of life. Anne, whose nerves had been rather strained, laughed hysterically, and even Owen smiled. Certainly, sentiment and passion had a way of shrinking out of sight in Miss Cornelia's presence. And yet to Anne nothing seemed quite as hopeless and dark and painful as it had seemed a few moments before. But sleep was far from her eyes that night.

CHAPTER 27 - ON THE SAND BAR

Owen Ford left Four Winds the next morning. In the evening Anne went over to see Leslie, but found nobody. The house was locked and there was no light in any window. It looked like a home left soulless. Leslie did not run over on the following day—which Anne thought a bad sign.

Gilbert having occasion to go in the evening to the fishing cove, Anne drove with him to the Point, intending to stay awhile with Captain Jim. But the great light, cutting its swathes through the fog of the autumn evening, was in care of Alec Boyd and Captain Jim was away.

"What will you do?" asked Gilbert. "Come with me?"

"I don't want to go to the cove—but I'll go over the channel with you, and roam about on the sand shore till you come back. The rock shore is too slippery and grim tonight."

Alone on the sands of the bar Anne gave herself up to the eerie charm of the night. It was warm for September, and the late afternoon had been very foggy; but a full moon had in part lessened the fog and transformed the harbor and the gulf and the surrounding shores into a strange, fantastic, unreal world of pale silver mist, through which everything loomed phantom-like. Captain Josiah Crawford's black schooner sailing down the channel, laden with potatoes for Bluenose ports, was a spectral ship bound for a far uncharted land, ever receding, never to be reached. The calls of unseen gulls overhead were the cries of the souls of doomed seamen. The little curls of foam that blew across the sand were elfin things stealing up from the sea-caves. The big, round-shouldered sand-dunes were the sleeping giants of some old northern tale. The lights that glimmered palely across the harbor were the delusive beacons on some coast of fairyland. Anne pleased herself with a hundred fancies as she wandered through the mist. It was delightful—romantic—mysterious to be roaming here alone on this enchanted shore.

But was she alone? Something loomed in the mist before her—took shape and form—suddenly moved towards her across the wave-rippled sand.

"Leslie!" exclaimed Anne in amazement. "Whatever are you doing—HERE—tonight?"

"If it comes to that, whatever are YOU doing here?" said Leslie, trying to laugh. The effort was a failure. She looked very pale and tired; but the love locks under her scarlet cap were curling about her face and eyes like little sparkling rings of gold.

"I'm waiting for Gilbert—he's over at the Cove. I intended to stay at the light, but Captain Jim is away."

"Well, *I* came here because I wanted to walk—and walk—and WALK," said Leslie restlessly. "I couldn't on the rock shore—the tide was too high and the rocks prisoned me. I had to come here—or I should have gone mad, I think. I rowed myself over the channel in Captain Jim's flat. I've been here for an hour. Come—come—let us walk. I can't stand still. Oh, Anne!"

"Leslie, dearest, what is the trouble?" asked Anne, though she knew too well already.

"I can't tell you—don't ask me. I wouldn't mind your knowing—I wish you did know—but I can't tell you—I can't tell anyone. I've been such a fool, Anne—and oh, it hurts so terribly to be a fool. There's nothing so painful in the world."

She laughed bitterly. Anne slipped her arm around her.

"Leslie, is it that you have learned to care for Mr. Ford?"

Leslie turned herself about passionately.

"How did you know?" she cried. "Anne, how did you know? Oh, is it written in my face for everyone to see? Is it as plain as that?"

"No, no. I—I can't tell you how I knew. It just came into my mind, somehow. Leslie, don't look at me like that!"

"Do you despise me?" demanded Leslie in a fierce, low tone. "Do you think I'm wicked—unwomanly? Or do you think I'm just plain fool?"

"I don't think you any of those things. Come, dear, let's just talk it over sensibly, as we might talk over any other of the great crises of life. You've been brooding over it and let yourself drift into a morbid view of it. You know you have a little tendency to do that about everything that goes wrong, and you promised me that you would fight against it."

"But—oh, it's so—so shameful," murmured Leslie. "To love him—unsought—and when I'm not free to love anybody."

"There's nothing shameful about it. But I'm very sorry that you have learned to care for Owen, because, as things are, it will only make you more unhappy."

"I didn't LEARN to care," said Leslie, walking on and speaking passionately. "If it had been like that I could have prevented it. I never dreamed of such a thing until that day, a week ago, when he told me he had finished his book and must soon go away. Then—then I knew. I felt as if someone had struck me a terrible blow. I didn't say anything—I couldn't speak—but I don't know what I looked like. I'm so afraid my face betrayed me. Oh, I would die of shame if I thought he knew—or suspected."

Anne was miserably silent, hampered by her deductions from her conversation with Owen. Leslie went on feverishly, as if she found relief in speech.

"I was so happy all this summer, Anne—happier than I ever was in my life. I thought it was because everything had been made clear between you and me, and that it was our friendship which made life seem so beautiful and full once more.

And it WAS, in part—but not all—oh, not nearly all. I know now why everything was so different. And now it's all over—and he has gone. How can I live, Anne? When I turned back into the house this morning after he had gone the solitude struck me like a blow in the face."

"It won't seem so hard by and by, dear," said Anne, who always felt the pain of her friends so keenly that she could not speak easy, fluent words of comforting. Besides, she remembered how well-meant speeches had hurt her in her own sorrow and was afraid.

"Oh, it seems to me it will grow harder all the time," said Leslie miserably. "I've nothing to look forward to. Morning will come after morning—and he will not come back—he will never come back. Oh, when I think that I will never see him again I feel as if a great brutal hand had twisted itself among my heartstrings, and was wrenching them. Once, long ago, I dreamed of love—and I thought it must be beautiful—and NOW—its like THIS. When he went away yesterday morning he was so cold and indifferent. He said 'Good-bye, Mrs. Moore' in the coldest tone in the world—as if we had not even been friends—as if I meant absolutely nothing to him. I know I don't—I didn't want him to care—but he MIGHT have been a little kinder."

"Oh, I wish Gilbert would come," thought Anne. She was racked between her sympathy for Leslie and the necessity of avoiding anything that would betray Owen's confidence. She knew why his good-bye had been so cold—why it could not have the cordiality that their good-comradeship demanded—but she could not tell Leslie.

"I couldn't help it, Anne—I couldn't help it," said poor Leslie.

"I know that."

"Do you blame me so very much?"

"I don't blame you at all."

"And you won't—you won't tell Gilbert?"

"Leslie! Do you think I would do such a thing?"

"Oh, I don't know—you and Gilbert are such CHUMS. I don't see how you could help telling him everything."

"Everything about my own concerns—yes. But not my friends' secrets."

"I couldn't have HIM know. But I'm glad YOU know. I would feel guilty if there were anything I was ashamed to tell you. I hope Miss Cornelia won't find out. Sometimes I feel as if those terrible, kind brown eyes of hers read my very soul. Oh, I wish this mist would never lift—I wish I could just stay in it forever, hidden away from every living being. I don't see how I can go on with life. This summer has been so full. I never was lonely for a moment. Before Owen came there used to be horrible moments—when I had been with you and Gilbert—and then had to leave you. You two would walk away together and I would walk away ALONE. After Owen came he was always there to walk home with me—we would laugh and talk as you and Gilbert were doing—there were no more lonely, envious moments for me. And NOW! Oh, yes, I've been a fool. Let's have done talking about my folly. I'll never bore you with it again."

"Here is Gilbert, and you are coming back with us," said Anne, who had no intention of leaving Leslie to wander alone on the sand-bar on such a night and in such a mood. "There's plenty of room in our boat for three, and we'll tie the flat on behind."

"Oh, I suppose I must reconcile myself to being the odd one again," said poor Leslie with another bitter laugh. "Forgive me, Anne—that was hateful. I ought to be thankful—and I AM—that I have two good friends who are glad to count me in as a third. Don't mind my hateful speeches. I just seem to be one great pain all over and everything hurts me."

"Leslie seemed very quiet tonight, didn't she?" said Gilbert, when he and Anne reached home. "What in the world was she doing over there on the bar alone?"

"Oh, she was tired—and you know she likes to go to the shore after one of Dick's bad days."

"What a pity she hadn't met and married a fellow like Ford long ago," ruminated Gilbert. "They'd have made an ideal couple, wouldn't they?"

"For pity's sake, Gilbert, don't develop into a match-maker. It's an abominable profession for a man," cried Anne rather sharply, afraid that Gilbert might blunder on the truth if he kept on in this strain.

"Bless us, Anne-girl, I'm not matchmaking," protested Gilbert, rather surprised at her tone. "I was only thinking of one of the might-have-beens."

"Well, don't. It's a waste of time," said Anne. Then she added suddenly:

"Oh, Gilbert, I wish everybody could be as happy as we are."

CHAPTER 28 - ODDS AND ENDS

"I've been reading obituary notices," said Miss Cornelia, laying down the Daily Enterprise and taking up her sewing.

The harbor was lying black and sullen under a dour November sky; the wet, dead leaves clung drenched and sodden to the window sills; but the little house was gay with firelight and spring-like with Anne's ferns and geraniums.

"It's always summer here, Anne," Leslie had said one day; and all who were the guests of that house of dreams felt the same.

"The Enterprise seems to run to obituaries these days," quoth Miss Cornelia. "It always has a couple of columns of them, and I read every line. It's one of my forms of recreation, especially when there's some original poetry attached to them. Here's a choice sample for you:

> She's gone to be with her Maker,
> Never more to roam.
> She used to play and sing with joy
> The song of Home, Sweet Home.

Who says we haven't any poetical talent on the Island! Have you ever noticed what heaps of good people die, Anne, dearie? It's kind of pitiful. Here's ten obituaries, and every one of them saints and models, even the men. Here's old Peter Stimson, who has 'left a large circle of friends to mourn his untimely loss.' Lord, Anne, dearie, that man was eighty, and everybody who knew him had been wishing him dead these thirty years. Read obituaries when you're blue, Anne, dearie—especially the ones of folks you know. If you've any sense of humor at all they'll cheer you up, believe ME. I just wish *I* had the writing of the obituaries of some people. Isn't 'obituary' an awful ugly word? This very Peter I've been speaking of had a face exactly like one. I never saw it but I thought of the word OBITUARY then and there. There's only one uglier word that I know of, and that's RELICT. Lord, Anne, dearie, I may be an old maid, but there's this comfort in it—I'll never be any man's 'relict.'"

"It IS an ugly word," said Anne, laughing. "Avonlea graveyard was full of old tombstones 'sacred to the memory of So-and-So, RELICT of the late So-and-So.' It always made me think of something worn out and moth eaten. Why is it that so many of the words connected with death are so disagreeable? I do wish that the custom of calling a dead body 'the remains' could be abolished. I positively shiver when I hear the undertaker say at a funeral, 'All who wish to see the remains please step this way.' It always gives me the horrible impression that I am about to view the scene of a cannibal feast."

"Well, all I hope," said Miss Cornelia calmly, "is that when I'm dead nobody will call me 'our departed sister.' I took a scunner at this sister-and-brothering business five years ago when there was a travelling evangelist holding meetings at the Glen. I hadn't any use for him from the start. I felt in my bones that there was something wrong with him. And there was. Mind you, he was pretending to be a Presbyterian—PresbyTARian, HE called it—and all the time he was a Methodist. He brothered and sistered everybody. He had a large circle of relations, that man had. He clutched my hand fervently one night, and said imploringly, 'My DEAR sister Bryant, are you a Christian?' I just looked him over a bit, and then I said calmly, 'The only brother I ever had, MR. Fiske, was buried fifteen years ago, and I haven't adopted any since. As for being a Christian, I was that, I hope and believe, when you were crawling about the floor in petticoats.' THAT squelched him, believe ME. Mind you, Anne dearie, I'm not down on all evangelists. We've had some real fine, earnest men, who did a lot of good and made the old sinners squirm. But this Fiske-man wasn't one of them. I had a good laugh all to myself one evening. Fiske had asked all who were Christians to stand up. *I* didn't, believe me! I never had any use for that sort of thing. But most of them did, and then he asked all who wanted to be Christians to stand up. Nobody stirred for a spell, so Fiske started up a hymn at the top of his voice. Just in front of me poor little Ikey Baker was sitting in the Millison pew. He was a home boy, ten years old, and Millison just about worked him to death. The poor little creature was always so tired he fell asleep right off whenever he went to church or anywhere he could sit still for a few minutes. He'd been sleeping all through the meeting, and I was thankful to see the poor child getting a rest, believe ME. Well, when Fiske's voice went soaring skyward and the rest joined in, poor Ikey wakened with a start. He thought it was just an ordinary singing and that everybody ought to stand up, so he scrambled to his feet mighty quick, knowing he'd get a combing down from Maria Millison for sleeping in meeting. Fiske saw him, stopped and shouted, 'Another soul saved! Glory Hallelujah!' And there was poor, frightened Ikey, only half awake and yawning, never thinking about his soul at all. Poor child, he never had time to think of anything but his tired, overworked little body.

"Leslie went one night and the Fiske-man got right after her—oh, he was especially anxious about the souls of the nice-looking girls, believe me!—and he hurt her feelings so she never went again. And then he prayed every night after that, right in public, that the Lord would soften her hard heart. Finally I went to Mr. Leavitt, our minister then, and told him if he didn't make Fiske stop that I'd just rise up the next night and throw my hymn book at him when he mentioned that 'beautiful but unrepentant young woman.' I'd have done it too, believe ME. Mr. Leavitt did put a stop to it, but Fiske kept on with his meetings until Charley Douglas put an end to his career in the Glen. Mrs. Charley had been out in California all winter. She'd been real melancholy in the fall—religious melancholy—it ran in her family. Her father worried so much over believing that he had committed the unpardonable sin that he died in the asylum. So when Rose Douglas got that way Charley packed her off to visit her sister in Los Angeles. She got perfectly well and came home just when the Fiske revival was in full swing. She stepped off the train at the Glen, real smiling and chipper, and the first thing she saw staring her in the face on the black, gable-end of the freight shed, was the question, in big white letters, two feet high, 'Whither goest thou—to heaven or hell?' That had been one of Fiske's ideas, and he had got Henry Hammond to paint it. Rose just gave a shriek and fainted; and when they got her home she was worse than ever. Charley Douglas went to Mr. Leavitt and told him that every Douglas would leave the church if Fiske was kept there any longer. Mr. Leavitt had to give in, for the Douglases paid half his salary, so Fiske departed, and we had to depend on our Bibles once more for instructions on how to get to heaven. After he was gone Mr. Leavitt found out he was just a masquerading Methodist, and he felt pretty sick, believe ME. Mr. Leavitt fell short in some ways, but he was a good, sound Presbyterian."

"By the way, I had a letter from Mr. Ford yesterday," said Anne. "He asked me to remember him kindly to you."

"I don't want his remembrances," said Miss Cornelia, curtly.

"Why?" said Anne, in astonishment. "I thought you liked him."

"Well, so I did, in a kind of way. But I'll never forgive him for what he done to Leslie. There's that poor child eating her heart out about him—as if she hadn't had trouble enough—and him ranting round Toronto, I've no doubt, enjoying himself same as ever. Just like a man."

"Oh, Miss Cornelia, how did you find out?"

"Lord, Anne, dearie, I've got eyes, haven't I? And I've known Leslie since she was a baby. There's been a new kind of heartbreak in her eyes all the fall, and I know that writer-man was behind it somehow. I'll never forgive myself for being the means of bringing him here. But I never expected he'd be like he was. I thought he'd just be like the other men Leslie had boarded—conceited young asses, every one of them, that she never had any use for. One of them did try to flirt with her once and she froze him out—so bad, I feel sure he's never got himself thawed since. So I never thought of any danger."

"Don't let Leslie suspect you know her secret," said Anne hurriedly. "I think it would hurt her."

"Trust me, Anne, dearie. *I* wasn't born yesterday. Oh, a plague on all the men! One of them ruined Leslie's life to begin with, and now another of the tribe comes and makes her still more wretched. Anne, this world is an awful place, believe me."

> "There's something in the world amiss
> Will be unriddled by and by,"

quoted Anne dreamily.

"If it is, it'll be in a world where there aren't any men," said Miss Cornelia gloomily.

"What have the men been doing now?" asked Gilbert, entering.

"Mischief—mischief! What else did they ever do?"

"It was Eve ate the apple, Miss Cornelia."

"'Twas a he-creature tempted her," retorted Miss Cornelia triumphantly.

Leslie, after her first anguish was over, found it possible to go on with life after all, as most of us do, no matter what our particular form of torment has been. It is even possible that she enjoyed moments of it, when she was one of the gay circle in the little house of dreams. But if Anne ever hoped that she was forgetting Owen Ford she would have been undeceived by the furtive hunger in Leslie's eyes whenever his name was mentioned. Pitiful to that hunger, Anne always contrived to tell Captain Jim or Gilbert bits of news from Owen's letters when Leslie was with them. The girl's flush and pallor at such moments spoke all too eloquently of the emotion that filled her being. But she never spoke of him to Anne, or mentioned that night on the sand-bar.

One day her old dog died and she grieved bitterly over him.

"He's been my friend so long," she said sorrowfully to Anne. "He was Dick's old dog, you know—Dick had him for a year or so before we were married. He left him with me when he sailed on the Four Sisters. Carlo got very fond of me—and his dog-love helped me through that first dreadful year after mother died, when I was alone. When I heard that Dick was coming back I was afraid Carlo wouldn't be so much mine. But he never seemed to care for Dick, though he had been so fond of him once. He would snap and growl at him as if he were a stranger. I was glad. It was nice to have one thing whose love was all mine. That old dog has been such a comfort to me, Anne. He got so feeble in the fall that I was afraid he couldn't live long—but I hoped I could nurse him through the winter. He seemed pretty well this morning. He was lying on the rug before the fire; then, all at once, he got up and crept over to me; he put his head on my lap and gave me one loving look out of his big, soft, dog eyes—and then he just shivered and died. I shall miss him so."

"Let me give you another dog, Leslie," said Anne. "I'm getting a lovely Gordon setter for a Christmas present for Gilbert. Let me give you one too."

Leslie shook her head.

"Not just now, thank you, Anne. I don't feel like having another dog yet. I don't seem to have any affection left for another. Perhaps—in time—I'll let you give me one. I really need one as a kind of protection. But there was something almost human about Carlo—it wouldn't be DECENT to fill his place too hurriedly, dear old fellow."

Anne went to Avonlea a week before Christmas and stayed until after the holidays. Gilbert came up for her, and there was a glad New Year celebration at Green Gables, when Barrys and Blythes and Wrights assembled to devour a dinner which had cost Mrs. Rachel and Marilla much careful thought and preparation. When they went back to Four Winds the little house was almost drifted over, for the third storm of a winter that was to prove phenomenally stormy had whirled up the harbor and heaped huge snow mountains about everything it encountered. But Captain Jim had shovelled out doors and paths, and Miss Cornelia had come down and kindled the hearth-fire.

"It's good to see you back, Anne, dearie! But did you ever see such drifts? You can't see the Moore place at all unless you go upstairs. Leslie'll be so glad you're back. She's almost buried alive over there. Fortunately Dick can shovel snow, and thinks it's great fun. Susan sent me word to tell you she would be on hand tomorrow. Where are you off to now, Captain?"

"I reckon I'll plough up to the Glen and sit a bit with old Martin Strong. He's not far from his end and he's lonesome. He hasn't many friends—been too busy all his life to make any. He's made heaps of money, though."

"Well, he thought that since he couldn't serve God and Mammon he'd better stick to Mammon," said Miss Cornelia crisply. "So he shouldn't complain if he doesn't find Mammon very good company now."

Captain Jim went out, but remembered something in the yard and turned back for a moment.

"I'd a letter from Mr. Ford, Mistress Blythe, and he says the life-book is accepted and is going to be published next fall. I felt fair uplifted when I got the news. To think that I'm to see it in print at last."

"That man is clean crazy on the subject of his life-book," said Miss Cornelia compassionately. "For my part, I think there's far too many books in the world now."

CHAPTER 29 - GILBERT AND ANNE DISAGREE

Gilbert laid down the ponderous medical tome over which he had been poring until the increasing dusk of the March evening made him desist. He leaned back in his chair and gazed meditatively out of the window. It was early spring— probably the ugliest time of the year. Not even the sunset could redeem the dead, sodden landscape and rotten black harbor ice upon which he looked. No sign of life was visible, save a big black crow winging his solitary way across a leaden field. Gilbert speculated idly concerning that crow. Was he a family crow, with a black but comely crow wife awaiting him in the woods beyond the Glen? Or was he a glossy young buck of a crow on courting thoughts intent? Or was he a cynical bachelor crow, believing that he travels the fastest who travels alone? Whatever he was, he soon disappeared in congenial gloom and Gilbert turned to the cheerier view indoors.

The firelight flickered from point to point, gleaming on the white and green coats of Gog and Magog, on the sleek, brown head of the beautiful setter basking on the rug, on the picture frames on the walls, on the vaseful of daffodils from the window garden, on Anne herself, sitting by her little table, with her sewing beside her and her hands clasped over her knee while she traced out pictures in the fire— Castles in Spain whose airy turrets pierced moonlit cloud and sunset bar-ships sailing from the Haven of Good Hopes straight to Four Winds Harbor with precious burthen. For Anne was again a dreamer of dreams, albeit a grim shape of fear went with her night and day to shadow and darken her visions.

Gilbert was accustomed to refer to himself as "an old married man." But he still looked upon Anne with the incredulous eyes of a lover. He couldn't wholly believe yet that she was really his. It MIGHT be only a dream after all, part and parcel of this magic house of dreams. His soul still went on tip-toe before her, lest the charm be shattered and the dream dispelled.

"Anne," he said slowly, "lend me your ears. I want to talk with you about something."

Anne looked across at him through the fire-lit gloom.

"What is it?" she asked gaily. "You look fearfully solemn, Gilbert. I really haven't done anything naughty today. Ask Susan."

"It's not of you—or ourselves—I want to talk. It's about Dick Moore."

"Dick Moore?" echoed Anne, sitting up alertly. "Why, what in the world have you to say about Dick Moore?"

"I've been thinking a great deal about him lately. Do you remember that time last summer I treated him for those carbuncles on his neck?"

"Yes—yes."

"I took the opportunity to examine the scars on his head thoroughly. I've always thought Dick was a very interesting case from a medical point of view. Lately I've been studying the history of trephining and the cases where it has been employed. Anne, I have come to the conclusion that if Dick Moore were taken to a good hospital and the operation of trephining performed on several places in his skull, his memory and faculties might be restored."

"Gilbert!" Anne's voice was full of protest. "Surely you don't mean it!"

"I do, indeed. And I have decided that it is my duty to broach the subject to Leslie."

"Gilbert Blythe, you shall NOT do any such thing," cried Anne vehemently. "Oh, Gilbert, you won't—you won't. You couldn't be so cruel. Promise me you won't."

"Why, Anne-girl, I didn't suppose you would take it like this. Be reasonable—"

"I won't be reasonable—I can't be reasonable—I AM reasonable. It is you who are unreasonable. Gilbert, have you ever once thought what it would mean for Leslie if Dick Moore were to be restored to his right senses? Just stop and think! She's unhappy enough now; but life as Dick's nurse and attendant is a thousand times easier for her than life as Dick's wife. I know—I KNOW! It's unthinkable. Don't you meddle with the matter. Leave well enough alone."

"I HAVE thought over that aspect of the case thoroughly, Anne. But I believe that a doctor is bound to set the sanctity of a patient's mind and body above all other considerations, no matter what the consequences may be. I believe it his duty to endeavor to restore health and sanity, if there is any hope whatever of it."

"But Dick isn't your patient in that respect," cried Anne, taking another tack. "If Leslie had asked you if anything could be done for him, THEN it might be your duty to tell her what you really thought. But you've no right to meddle."

"I don't call it meddling. Uncle Dave told Leslie twelve years ago that nothing could be done for Dick. She believes that, of course."

"And why did Uncle Dave tell her that, if it wasn't true?" cried Anne, triumphantly. "Doesn't he know as much about it as you?"

"I think not—though it may sound conceited and presumptuous to say it. And you know as well as I that he is rather prejudiced against what he calls 'these new-fangled notions of cutting and carving.' He's even opposed to operating for appendicitis."

"He's right," exclaimed Anne, with a complete change of front. 'I believe myself that you modern doctors are entirely too fond of making experiments with human flesh and blood."

695

"Rhoda Allonby would not be a living woman today if I had been afraid of making a certain experiment," argued Gilbert. "I took the risk—and saved her life."

"I'm sick and tired of hearing about Rhoda Allonby," cried Anne—most unjustly, for Gilbert had never mentioned Mrs. Allonby's name since the day he had told Anne of his success in regard to her. And he could not be blamed for other people's discussion of it.

Gilbert felt rather hurt.

"I had not expected you to look at the matter as you do, Anne," he said a little stiffly, getting up and moving towards the office door. It was their first approach to a quarrel.

But Anne flew after him and dragged him back.

"Now, Gilbert, you are not 'going off mad.' Sit down here and I'll apologise bee-YEW-ti-fully, I shouldn't have said that. But—oh, if you knew—"

Anne checked herself just in time. She had been on the very verge of betraying Leslie's secret.

"Knew what a woman feels about it," she concluded lamely.

"I think I do know. I've looked at the matter from every point of view—and I've been driven to the conclusion that it is my duty to tell Leslie that I believe it is possible that Dick can be restored to himself; there my responsibility ends. It will be for her to decide what she will do."

"I don't think you've any right to put such a responsibility on her. She has enough to bear. She is poor—how could she afford such an operation?"

"That is for her to decide," persisted Gilbert stubbornly.

"You say you think that Dick can be cured. But are you SURE of it?"

"Certainly not. Nobody could be sure of such a thing. There may have been lesions of the brain itself, the effect of which can never be removed. But if, as I believe, his loss of memory and other faculties is due merely to the pressure on the brain centers of certain depressed areas of bone, then he can be cured."

"But it's only a possibility!" insisted Anne. "Now, suppose you tell Leslie and she decides to have the operation. It will cost a great deal. She will have to borrow the money, or sell her little property. And suppose the operation is a failure and Dick remains the same.

"How will she be able to pay back the money she borrows, or make a living for herself and that big helpless creature if she sells the farm?"

"Oh, I know—I know. But it is my duty to tell her. I can't get away from that conviction."

"Oh, I know the Blythe stubbornness," groaned Anne. "But don't do this solely on your own responsibility. Consult Doctor Dave."

"I HAVE done so," said Gilbert reluctantly.

"And what did he say?"

"In brief—as you say—leave well enough alone. Apart from his prejudice against new-fangled surgery, I'm afraid he looks at the case from your point of view—don't do it, for Leslie's sake."

"There now," cried Anne triumphantly. "I do think, Gilbert, that you ought to abide by the judgment of a man nearly eighty, who has seen a great deal and saved scores of lives himself—surely his opinion ought to weigh more than a mere boy's."

"Thank you."

"Don't laugh. It's too serious."

"That's just my point. It IS serious. Here is a man who is a helpless burden. He may be restored to reason and usefulness—"

"He was so very useful before," interjected Anne witheringly.

"He may be given a chance to make good and redeem the past. His wife doesn't know this. I do. It is therefore my duty to tell her that there is such a possibility. That, boiled down, is my decision."

"Don't say 'decision' yet, Gilbert. Consult somebody else. Ask Captain Jim what he thinks about it."

"Very well. But I'll not promise to abide by his opinion, Anne.

"This is something a man must decide for himself. My conscience would never be easy if I kept silent on the subject."

"Oh, your conscience!" moaned Anne. "I suppose that Uncle Dave has a conscience too, hasn't he?"

"Yes. But I am not the keeper of his conscience. Come, Anne, if this affair did not concern Leslie—if it were a purely abstract case, you would agree with me,—you know you would."

"I wouldn't," vowed Anne, trying to believe it herself. "Oh, you can argue all night, Gilbert, but you won't convince me. Just you ask Miss Cornelia what she thinks of it."

"You're driven to the last ditch, Anne, when you bring up Miss Cornelia as a reinforcement. She will say, 'Just like a man,' and rage furiously. No matter. This is no affair for Miss Cornelia to settle. Leslie alone must decide it."

"You know very well how she will decide it," said Anne, almost in tears. "She has ideals of duty, too. I don't see how you can take such a responsibility on your shoulders. *I* couldn't."

> "'Because right is right to follow right
> Were wisdom in the scorn of consequence,'"

quoted Gilbert.

"Oh, you think a couplet of poetry a convincing argument!" scoffed Anne. "That is so like a man."

And then she laughed in spite of herself. It sounded so like an echo of Miss Cornelia.

"Well, if you won't accept Tennyson as an authority, perhaps you will believe the words of a Greater than he," said Gilbert seriously. "'Ye shall know the truth and the truth shall make you free.' I believe that, Anne, with all my heart. It's the greatest and grandest verse in the Bible—or in any literature—and the TRUEST, if there are comparative degrees of trueness. And it's the first duty of a man to tell the truth, as he sees it and believes it."

"In this case the truth won't make poor Leslie free," sighed Anne. "It will probably end in still more bitter bondage for her. Oh, Gilbert, I CAN'T think you are right."

CHAPTER 30 - LESLIE DECIDES

A sudden outbreak of a virulent type of influenza at the Glen and down at the fishing village kept Gilbert so busy for the next fortnight that he had no time to pay the promised visit to Captain Jim. Anne hoped against hope that he had abandoned the idea about Dick Moore, and, resolving to let sleeping dogs lie, she said no more about the subject. But she thought of it incessantly.

"I wonder if it would be right for me to tell him that Leslie cares for Owen," she thought. "He would never let her suspect that he knew, so her pride would not suffer, and it MIGHT convince him that he should let Dick Moore alone. Shall I—shall I? No, after all, I cannot. A promise is sacred, and I've no right to betray Leslie's secret. But oh, I never felt so worried over anything in my life as I do over this. It's spoiling the spring—it's spoiling everything."

One evening Gilbert abruptly proposed that they go down and see Captain Jim. With a sinking heart Anne agreed, and they set forth. Two weeks of kind sunshine had wrought a miracle in the bleak landscape over which Gilbert's crow had flown. The hills and fields were dry and brown and warm, ready to break into bud and blossom; the harbor was laughter-shaken again; the long harbor road was like a gleaming red ribbon; down on the dunes a crowd of boys, who were out smelt fishing, were burning the thick, dry sandhill grass of the preceding summer. The flames swept over the dunes rosily, flinging their cardinal banners against the dark gulf beyond, and illuminating the channel and the fishing village. It was a picturesque scene which would at other times have delighted Anne's eyes; but she was not enjoying this walk. Neither was Gilbert. Their usual good-comradeship and Josephian community of taste and viewpoint were sadly lacking. Anne's disapproval of the whole project showed itself in the haughty uplift of her head and the studied politeness of her remarks. Gilbert's mouth was set in all the Blythe obstinacy, but his eyes were troubled. He meant to do what he believed to be his duty; but to be at outs with Anne was a high price to pay. Altogether, both were glad when they reached the light—and remorseful that they should be glad.

Captain Jim put away the fishing net upon which he was working, and welcomed them joyfully. In the searching light of the spring evening he looked older than Anne had ever seen him. His hair had grown much grayer, and the strong old hand shook a little. But his blue eyes were clear and steady, and the staunch soul looked out through them gallant and unafraid.

Captain Jim listened in amazed silence while Gilbert said what he had come to say. Anne, who knew how the old man worshipped Leslie, felt quite sure that he would side with her, although she had not much hope that this would influence Gilbert. She was therefore surprised beyond measure when Captain Jim, slowly and sorrowfully, but unhesitatingly, gave it as his opinion that Leslie should be told.

"Oh, Captain Jim, I didn't think you'd say that," she exclaimed reproachfully. "I thought you wouldn't want to make more trouble for her."

Captain Jim shook his head.

"I don't want to. I know how you feel about it, Mistress Blythe—just as I feel meself. But it ain't our feelings we have to steer by through life—no, no, we'd make shipwreck mighty often if we did that. There's only the one safe compass and we've got to set our course by that—what it's right to do. I agree with the doctor. If there's a chance for Dick, Leslie should be told of it. There's no two sides to that, in my opinion."

"Well," said Anne, giving up in despair, "wait until Miss Cornelia gets after you two men."

"Cornelia'll rake us fore and aft, no doubt," assented Captain Jim. "You women are lovely critters, Mistress Blythe, but you're just a mite illogical. You're a highly eddicated lady and Cornelia isn't, but you're like as two peas when it comes to that. I dunno's you're any the worse for it. Logic is a sort of hard, merciless thing, I reckon. Now, I'll brew a cup of tea and we'll drink it and talk of pleasant things, jest to calm our minds a bit."

At least, Captain Jim's tea and conversation calmed Anne's mind to such an extent that she did not make Gilbert suffer so acutely on the way home as she had deliberately intended to do. She did not refer to the burning question at all, but she chatted amiably of other matters, and Gilbert understood that he was forgiven under protest.

"Captain Jim seems very frail and bent this spring. The winter has aged him," said Anne sadly. "I am afraid that he will soon be going to seek lost Margaret. I can't bear to think of it."

"Four Winds won't be the same place when Captain Jim 'sets out to sea,'" agreed Gilbert.

The following evening he went to the house up the brook. Anne wandered dismally around until his return.

"Well, what did Leslie say?" she demanded when he came in.

"Very little. I think she felt rather dazed."

"And is she going to have the operation?"

"She is going to think it over and decide very soon."

Gilbert flung himself wearily into the easy chair before the fire. He looked tired. It had not been an easy thing for him to tell Leslie. And the terror that had sprung into her eyes when the meaning of what he told her came home to her was not a pleasant thing to remember. Now, when the die was cast, he was beset with doubts of his own wisdom.

Anne looked at him remorsefully; then she slipped down on the rug beside him and laid her glossy red head on his arm.

"Gilbert, I've been rather hateful over this. I won't be any more. Please just call me red-headed and forgive me."

By which Gilbert understood that, no matter what came of it, there would be no I-told-you-so's. But he was not wholly comforted. Duty in the abstract is one thing; duty in the concrete is quite another, especially when the doer is confronted by a woman's stricken eyes.

Some instinct made Anne keep away from Leslie for the next three days. On the third evening Leslie came down to the little house and told Gilbert that she had made up her mind; she would take Dick to Montreal and have the operation.

She was very pale and seemed to have wrapped herself in her old mantle of aloofness. But her eyes had lost the look which had haunted Gilbert; they were cold and bright; and she proceeded to discuss details with him in a crisp, business-like way. There were plans to be made and many things to be thought over. When Leslie had got the information she wanted she went home. Anne wanted to walk part of the way with her.

"Better not," said Leslie curtly. "Today's rain has made the ground damp. Good-night."

"Have I lost my friend?" said Anne with a sigh. "If the operation is successful and Dick Moore finds himself again Leslie will retreat into some remote fastness of her soul where none of us can ever find her."

"Perhaps she will leave him," said Gilbert.

"Leslie would never do that, Gilbert. Her sense of duty is very strong. She told me once that her Grandmother West always impressed upon her the fact that when she assumed any responsibility she must never shirk it, no matter what the consequences might be. That is one of her cardinal rules. I suppose it's very old-fashioned."

"Don't be bitter, Anne-girl. You know you don't think it old-fashioned—you know you have the very same idea of sacredness of assumed responsibilities yourself. And you are right. Shirking responsibilities is the curse of our modern life—the secret of all the unrest and discontent that is seething in the world."

"Thus saith the preacher," mocked Anne. But under the mockery she felt that he was right; and she was very sick at heart for Leslie.

A week later Miss Cornelia descended like an avalanche upon the little house. Gilbert was away and Anne was compelled to bear the shock of the impact alone.

Miss Cornelia hardly waited to get her hat off before she began.

"Anne, do you mean to tell me it's true what I've heard—that Dr. Blythe has told Leslie Dick can be cured, and that she is going to take him to Montreal to have him operated on?"

"Yes, it is quite true, Miss Cornelia," said Anne bravely.

"Well, it's inhuman cruelty, that's what it is," said Miss Cornelia, violently agitated. "I did think Dr. Blythe was a decent man. I didn't think he could have been guilty of this."

"Dr. Blythe thought it was his duty to tell Leslie that there was a chance for Dick," said Anne with spirit, "and," she added, loyalty to Gilbert getting the better of her, "I agree with him."

"Oh, no, you don't, dearie," said Miss Cornelia. "No person with any bowels of compassion could."

"Captain Jim does."

"Don't quote that old ninny to me," cried Miss Cornelia. "And I don't care who agrees with him. Think—THINK what it means to that poor hunted, harried girl."

"We DO think of it. But Gilbert believes that a doctor should put the welfare of a patient's mind and body before all other considerations."

"That's just like a man. But I expected better things of you, Anne," said Miss Cornelia, more in sorrow than in wrath; then she proceeded to bombard Anne with precisely the same arguments with which the latter had attacked Gilbert; and Anne valiantly defended her husband with the weapons he had used for his own protection. Long was the fray, but Miss Cornelia made an end at last.

"It's an iniquitous shame," she declared, almost in tears. "That's just what it is—an iniquitous shame. Poor, poor Leslie!"

"Don't you think Dick should be considered a little too?" pleaded Anne.

"Dick! Dick Moore! HE'S happy enough. He's a better behaved and more reputable member of society now than he ever was before.

"Why, he was a drunkard and perhaps worse. Are you going to set him loose again to roar and to devour?"

"He may reform," said poor Anne, beset by foe without and traitor within.

"Reform your grandmother!" retorted Miss Cornelia. "Dick Moore got the injuries that left him as he is in a drunken brawl. He DESERVES his fate. It was sent on him for a punishment. I don't believe the doctor has any business to tamper with the visitations of God."

"Nobody knows how Dick was hurt, Miss Cornelia. It may not have been in a drunken brawl at all. He may have been waylaid and robbed."

"Pigs MAY whistle, but they've poor mouths for it," said Miss Cornelia. "Well, the gist of what you tell me is that the thing is settled and there's no use in talking. If that's so I'll hold my tongue. I don't propose to wear MY teeth out gnawing files. When a thing has to be I give in to it. But I like to make mighty sure first that it HAS to be. Now, I'll devote MY energies to comforting and sustaining Leslie. And after all," added Miss Cornelia, brightening up hopefully, "perhaps nothing can be done for Dick."

CHAPTER 31 - THE TRUTH MAKES FREE

Leslie, having once made up her mind what to do, proceeded to do it with characteristic resolution and speed. House-cleaning must be finished with first, whatever issues of life and death might await beyond. The gray house up the brook was put into flawless order and cleanliness, with Miss Cornelia's ready assistance. Miss Cornelia, having said her say to Anne, and later on to Gilbert and Captain Jim—sparing neither of them, let it be assured—never spoke of the matter to Leslie. She accepted the fact of Dick's operation, referred to it when necessary in a business-like way, and ignored it when it was not. Leslie never attempted to discuss it. She was very cold and quiet during these beautiful spring days. She seldom visited Anne, and though she was invariably courteous and friendly, that very courtesy was as an icy barrier between her and the people of the little house. The old jokes and laughter and chumminess of common things could not reach her over it. Anne refused to feel hurt. She knew that Leslie was in the grip of a hideous dread—a dread that wrapped her away from all little glimpses of happiness and hours of pleasure. When one great passion seizes possession of the soul all other feelings are crowded aside. Never in all her life had Leslie Moore shuddered away from the future with more intolerable terror. But she went forward as unswervingly in the path she had elected as the martyrs of old walked their chosen way, knowing the end of it to be the fiery agony of the stake.

The financial question was settled with greater ease than Anne had feared. Leslie borrowed the necessary money from Captain Jim, and, at her insistence, he took a mortgage on the little farm.

"So that is one thing off the poor girl's mind," Miss Cornelia told Anne, "and off mine too. Now, if Dick gets well enough to work again he'll be able to earn enough to pay the interest on it; and if he doesn't I know Captain Jim'll manage someway that Leslie won't have to. He said as much to me. 'I'm getting old, Cornelia,' he said, 'and I've no chick or child of my own. Leslie won't take a gift from a living man, but mebbe she will from a dead one.' So it will be all right as far as THAT goes. I wish everything else might be settled as satisfactorily. As for that wretch of a Dick, he's been awful these last few days. The devil was in him, believe ME! Leslie and I couldn't get on with our work for the tricks he'd play. He chased all her ducks one day around the yard till most of them died. And not one thing would he do for us. Sometimes, you know, he'll make himself quite handy, bringing in pails of water and wood. But this week if we sent him to the well he'd try to climb down into it. I thought once, 'If you'd only shoot down there head-first everything would be nicely settled.'"

"Oh, Miss Cornelia!"

"Now, you needn't Miss Cornelia me, Anne, dearie. ANYBODY would have thought the same. If the Montreal doctors can make a rational creature out of Dick Moore they're wonders."

Leslie took Dick to Montreal early in May. Gilbert went with her, to help her, and make the necessary arrangements for her. He came home with the report that the Montreal surgeon whom they had consulted agreed with him that there was a good chance of Dick's restoration.

"Very comforting," was Miss Cornelia's sarcastic comment.

Anne only sighed. Leslie had been very distant at their parting.

But she had promised to write. Ten days after Gilbert's return the letter came. Leslie wrote that the operation had been successfully performed and that Dick was making a good recovery.

"What does she mean by 'successfully?'" asked Anne. "Does she mean that Dick's memory is really restored?"

"Not likely—since she says nothing of it," said Gilbert. "She uses the word 'successfully' from the surgeon's point of view. The operation has been performed and followed by normal results. But it is too soon to know whether Dick's faculties will be eventually restored, wholly or in part. His memory would not be likely to return to him all at once. The process will be gradual, if it occurs at all. Is that all she says?"

"Yes—there's her letter. It's very short. Poor girl, she must be under a terrible strain. Gilbert Blythe, there are heaps of things I long to say to you, only it would be mean."

"Miss Cornelia says them for you," said Gilbert with a rueful smile. "She combs me down every time I encounter her. She makes it plain to me that she regards me as little better than a murderer, and that she thinks it a great pity that Dr. Dave ever let me step into his shoes. She even told me that the Methodist doctor over the harbor was to be preferred before me. With Miss Cornelia the force of condemnation can no further go."

"If Cornelia Bryant was sick, it would not be Doctor Dave or the Methodist doctor she would send for," sniffed Susan. "She would have you out of your hard-earned bed in the middle of the night, doctor, dear, if she took a spell of misery, that she would. And then she would likely say your bill was past all reason. But do not mind her, doctor, dear. It takes all kinds of people to make a world."

No further word came from Leslie for some time. The May days crept away in a sweet succession and the shores of Four Winds Harbor greened and bloomed and purpled. One day in late May Gilbert came home to be met by Susan in the stable yard.

"I am afraid something has upset Mrs. Doctor, doctor, dear," she said mysteriously. "She got a letter this afternoon and since then she has just been walking round the garden and talking to herself. You know it is not good for her to be on her feet so much, doctor, dear. She did not see fit to tell me what her news was, and I am no pry, doctor, dear, and never was, but it is plain something has upset her. And it is not good for her to be upset."

Gilbert hurried rather anxiously to the garden. Had anything happened at Green Gables? But Anne, sitting on the rustic seat by the brook, did not look troubled, though she was certainly much excited. Her eyes were their grayest, and scarlet spots burned on her cheeks.

"What has happened, Anne?"

Anne gave a queer little laugh.

"I think you'll hardly believe it when I tell you, Gilbert. *I* can't believe it yet. As Susan said the other day, 'I feel like a fly coming to live in the sun—dazed-like.' It's all so incredible. I've read the letter a score of times and every time it's just the same—I can't believe my own eyes. Oh, Gilbert, you were right—so right. I can see that clearly enough now—and I'm so ashamed of myself—and will you ever really forgive me?"

"Anne, I'll shake you if you don't grow coherent. Redmond would be ashamed of you. WHAT has happened?"

"You won't believe it—you won't believe it—"

"I'm going to phone for Uncle Dave," said Gilbert, pretending to start for the house.

"Sit down, Gilbert. I'll try to tell you. I've had a letter, and oh, Gilbert, it's all so amazing—so incredibly amazing—we never thought—not one of us ever dreamed—"

"I suppose," said Gilbert, sitting down with a resigned air, "the only thing to do in a case of this kind is to have patience and go at the matter categorically. Whom is your letter from?"

"Leslie—and, oh, Gilbert—"

"Leslie! Whew! What has she to say? What's the news about Dick?"

Anne lifted the letter and held it out, calmly dramatic in a moment.

"There is NO Dick! The man we have thought Dick Moore—whom everybody in Four Winds has believed for twelve years to be Dick Moore—is his cousin, George Moore, of Nova Scotia, who, it seems, always resembled him very strikingly. Dick Moore died of yellow fever thirteen years ago in Cuba."

CHAPTER 32 - MISS CORNELIA DISCUSSES THE AFFAIR

"And do you mean to tell me, Anne, dearie, that Dick Moore has turned out not to be Dick Moore at all but somebody else? Is THAT what you phoned up to me today?"

"Yes, Miss Cornelia. It is very amazing, isn't it?"

"It's—it's—just like a man," said Miss Cornelia helplessly. She took off her hat with trembling fingers. For once in her life Miss Cornelia was undeniably staggered.

"I can't seem to sense it, Anne," she said. "I've heard you say it—and I believe you—but I can't take it in. Dick Moore is dead—has been dead all these years—and Leslie is free?"

"Yes. The truth has made her free. Gilbert was right when he said that verse was the grandest in the Bible."

"Tell me everything, Anne, dearie. Since I got your phone I've been in a regular muddle, believe ME. Cornelia Bryant was never so kerflummuxed before."

"There isn't a very great deal to tell. Leslie's letter was short. She didn't go into particulars. This man—George Moore—has recovered his memory and knows who he is. He says Dick took yellow fever in Cuba, and the Four Sisters had to sail without him. George stayed behind to nurse him. But he died very shortly afterwards.

"George did not write Leslie because he intended to come right home and tell her himself."

"And why didn't he?"

"I suppose his accident must have intervened. Gilbert says it is quite likely that George Moore remembers nothing of his accident, or what led to it, and may never remember it. It probably happened very soon after Dick's death. We may find out more particulars when Leslie writes again."

"Does she say what she is going to do? When is she coming home?"

"She says she will stay with George Moore until he can leave the hospital. She has written to his people in Nova Scotia. It seems that George's only near relative is a married sister much older than himself. She was living when George sailed on the Four Sisters, but of course we do not know what may have happened since. Did you ever see George Moore, Miss Cornelia?"

"I did. It is all coming back to me. He was here visiting his Uncle Abner eighteen years ago, when he and Dick would be about seventeen. They were double cousins, you see. Their fathers were brothers and their mothers were twin sisters, and they did look a terrible lot alike. Of course," added Miss Cornelia scornfully, "it wasn't one of those freak resemblances you read of in novels where two people are so much alike that they can fill each other's places and their nearest and dearest can't tell between them. In those days you could tell easy enough which was George and which was Dick, if you saw them together and near at hand. Apart, or some distance away, it wasn't so easy. They played lots of tricks on people and thought it great fun, the two scamps. George Moore was a little taller and a good deal fatter than Dick—though neither of them was what you would call fat—they were both of the lean kind. Dick had higher color than George, and his hair was a shade lighter. But their features were just alike, and they both had that queer freak of eyes—one blue and one hazel. They weren't much alike in any other way, though. George was a real nice fellow, though he was a scalawag for mischief, and some said he had a liking for a glass even then. But everybody liked him better than Dick. He spent about a month here. Leslie never saw him; she was only about eight or nine then and I remember now that she spent that whole winter over harbor with her grandmother West. Captain Jim was away, too—that was the winter he was wrecked on the Magdalens. I don't suppose either he or Leslie had ever heard about the Nova Scotia cousin looking so much like Dick. Nobody ever thought of him when Captain Jim brought Dick—George, I should say—home. Of course, we all thought Dick had changed considerable—he'd got so lumpish and fat. But we put that down to what had happened to him, and no doubt that was the reason, for, as I've said, George wasn't fat to begin with either. And there was no other way we could have guessed, for the man's senses were clean gone. I can't see that it is any wonder we were all deceived. But it's a staggering thing. And Leslie has sacrificed the best years of her life to nursing a man who hadn't any claim on her! Oh, drat the men! No matter what they do, it's the wrong thing. And no matter who they are, it's somebody they shouldn't be. They do exasperate me."

"Gilbert and Captain Jim are men, and it is through them that the truth has been discovered at last," said Anne.

"Well, I admit that," conceded Miss Cornelia reluctantly. "I'm sorry I raked the doctor off so. It's the first time in my life I've ever felt ashamed of anything I said to a man. I don't know as I shall tell him so, though. He'll just have to take it for granted. Well, Anne, dearie, it's a mercy the Lord doesn't answer all our prayers. I've been praying hard right along that the operation wouldn't cure Dick. Of course I didn't put it just quite so plain. But that was what was in the back of my mind, and I have no doubt the Lord knew it."

"Well, He has answered the spirit of your prayer. You really wished that things shouldn't be made any harder for Leslie. I'm afraid that in my secret heart I've been hoping the operation wouldn't succeed, and I am wholesomely ashamed of it."

"How does Leslie seem to take it?"

"She writes like one dazed. I think that, like ourselves, she hardly realises it yet. She says, 'It all seems like a strange dream to me, Anne.' That is the only reference she makes to herself."

"Poor child! I suppose when the chains are struck off a prisoner he'd feel queer and lost without them for a while. Anne, dearie, here's a thought keeps coming into my mind. What about Owen Ford? We both know Leslie was fond of him. Did it ever occur to you that he was fond of her?"

"It—did—once," admitted Anne, feeling that she might say so much.

"Well, I hadn't any reason to think he was, but it just appeared to me he MUST be. Now, Anne, dearie, the Lord knows I'm not a match-maker, and I scorn all such doings. But if I were you and writing to that Ford man I'd just mention, casual-like, what has happened. That is what *I*'d do."

"Of course I will mention it when I write him," said Anne, a trifle distantly. Somehow, this was a thing she could not discuss with Miss Cornelia. And yet, she had to admit that the same thought had been lurking in her mind ever since she had heard of Leslie's freedom. But she would not desecrate it by free speech.

"Of course there is no great rush, dearie. But Dick Moore's been dead for thirteen years and Leslie has wasted enough of her life for him. We'll just see what comes of it. As for this George Moore, who's gone and come back to life when everyone thought he was dead and done for, just like a man, I'm real sorry for him. He won't seem to fit in anywhere."

"He is still a young man, and if he recovers completely, as seems likely, he will be able to make a place for himself again. It must be very strange for him, poor fellow. I suppose all these years since his accident will not exist for him."

CHAPTER 33 - LESLIE RETURNS

A fortnight later Leslie Moore came home alone to the old house where she had spent so many bitter years. In the June twilight she went over the fields to Anne's, and appeared with ghost-like suddenness in the scented garden.

"Leslie!" cried Anne in amazement. "Where have you sprung from? We never knew you were coming. Why didn't you write? We would have met you."

"I couldn't write somehow, Anne. It seemed so futile to try to say anything with pen and ink. And I wanted to get back quietly and unobserved."

Anne put her arms about Leslie and kissed her. Leslie returned the kiss warmly. She looked pale and tired, and she gave a little sigh as she dropped down on the grasses beside a great bed of daffodils that were gleaming through the pale, silvery twilight like golden stars.

"And you have come home alone, Leslie?"

"Yes. George Moore's sister came to Montreal and took him home with her. Poor fellow, he was sorry to part with me—though I was a stranger to him when his memory first came back. He clung to me in those first hard days when he was trying to realise that Dick's death was not the thing of yesterday that it seemed to him. It was all very hard for him. I helped him all I could. When his sister came it was easier for him, because it seemed to him only the other day that he had seen her last. Fortunately she had not changed much, and that helped him, too."

"It is all so strange and wonderful, Leslie. I think we none of us realise it yet."

"I cannot. When I went into the house over there an hour ago, I felt that it MUST be a dream—that Dick must be there, with his childish smile, as he had been for so long. Anne, I seem stunned yet. I'm not glad or sorry—or ANYTHING. I feel as if something had been torn suddenly out of my life and left a terrible hole. I feel as if I couldn't be *I*—as if I must have changed into somebody else and couldn't get used to it. It gives me a horrible lonely, dazed, helpless feeling. It's good to see you again—it seems as if you were a sort of anchor for my drifting soul. Oh, Anne, I dread it all—the gossip and wonderment and questioning. When I think of that, I wish that I need not have come home at all. Dr. Dave was at the station when I came off the train—he brought me home. Poor old man, he feels very badly because he told me years ago that nothing could be done for Dick. 'I honestly thought so, Leslie,' he said to me today. 'But I should have told you not to depend on my opinion—I should have told you to go to a specialist. If I had, you would have been saved many bitter years, and poor George Moore many wasted ones. I blame myself very much, Leslie.' I told him not to do that—he had done what he thought right. He has always been so kind to me—I couldn't bear to see him worrying over it."

"And Dick—George, I mean? Is his memory fully restored?"

"Practically. Of course, there are a great many details he can't recall yet—but he remembers more and more every day. He went out for a walk on the evening after Dick was buried. He had Dick's money and watch on him; he meant to bring them home to me, along with my letter. He admits he went to a place where the sailors resorted—and he remembers drinking—and nothing else. Anne, I shall never forget the moment he remembered his own name. I saw him looking at me with an intelligent but puzzled expression. I said, 'Do you know me, Dick?' He answered, 'I never saw you before. Who are you? And my name is not Dick. I am George Moore, and Dick died of yellow fever yesterday! Where am I? What has happened to me?' I—I fainted, Anne. And ever since I have felt as if I were in a dream."

"You will soon adjust yourself to this new state of things, Leslie. And you are young—life is before you—you will have many beautiful years yet."

"Perhaps I shall be able to look at it in that way after a while, Anne. Just now I feel too tired and indifferent to think about the future. I'm—I'm—Anne, I'm lonely. I miss Dick. Isn't it all very strange? Do you know, I was really fond of poor Dick—George, I suppose I should say—just as I would have been fond of a helpless child who depended on me for everything. I would never have admitted it—I was really ashamed of it—because, you see, I had hated and despised Dick so much before he went away. When I heard that Captain Jim was bringing him home I expected I would just feel the same to him. But I never did—although I continued to loathe him as I remembered him before. From the time he came home I felt only pity—a pity that hurt and wrung me. I supposed then that it was just because his accident had made him so helpless and changed. But now I believe it was because there was really a different personality there. Carlo knew it, Anne—I know now that Carlo knew it. I always thought it strange that Carlo shouldn't have known Dick. Dogs are usually so faithful. But HE knew it was not his master who had come back, although none of the rest of us did. I had never seen George Moore, you know. I remember now that Dick once mentioned casually that he had a cousin in Nova Scotia who looked as much like him as a twin; but the thing had gone out of my memory, and in any case I would never have thought it of any importance. You see, it never occurred to me to question Dick's identity. Any change in him seemed to me just the result of the accident.

"Oh, Anne, that night in April when Gilbert told me he thought Dick might be cured! I can never forget it. It seemed to me that I had once been a prisoner in a hideous cage of torture, and then the door had been opened and I could get out. I was still chained to the cage but I was not in it. And that night I felt that a merciless hand was drawing me back into the cage—back to a torture even more terrible than it had once been. I didn't blame Gilbert. I felt he was right. And he

710

had been very good—he said that if, in view of the expense and uncertainty of the operation, I should decide not to risk it, he would not blame me in the least. But I knew how I ought to decide—and I couldn't face it. All night I walked the floor like a mad woman, trying to compel myself to face it. I couldn't, Anne—I thought I couldn't—and when morning broke I set my teeth and resolved that I WOULDN'T. I would let things remain as they were. It was very wicked, I know. It would have been just punishment for such wickedness if I had just been left to abide by that decision. I kept to it all day. That afternoon I had to go up to the Glen to do some shopping. It was one of Dick's quiet, drowsy days, so I left him alone. I was gone a little longer than I had expected, and he missed me. He felt lonely. And when I got home, he ran to meet me just like a child, with such a pleased smile on his face. Somehow, Anne, I just gave way then. That smile on his poor vacant face was more than I could endure. I felt as if I were denying a child the chance to grow and develop. I knew that I must give him his chance, no matter what the consequences might be. So I came over and told Gilbert. Oh, Anne, you must have thought me hateful in those weeks before I went away. I didn't mean to be—but I couldn't think of anything except what I had to do, and everything and everybody about me were like shadows."

"I know—I understood, Leslie. And now it is all over—your chain is broken—there is no cage."

"There is no cage," repeated Leslie absently, plucking at the fringing grasses with her slender, brown hands. "But—it doesn't seem as if there were anything else, Anne. You—you remember what I told you of my folly that night on the sand-bar? I find one doesn't get over being a fool very quickly. Sometimes I think there are people who are fools forever. And to be a fool—of that kind—is almost as bad as being a—a dog on a chain."

"You will feel very differently after you get over being tired and bewildered," said Anne, who, knowing a certain thing that Leslie did not know, did not feel herself called upon to waste overmuch sympathy.

Leslie laid her splendid golden head against Anne's knee.

"Anyhow, I have YOU," she said. "Life can't be altogether empty with such a friend. Anne, pat my head—just as if I were a little girl—MOTHER me a bit—and let me tell you while my stubborn tongue is loosed a little just what you and your comradeship have meant to me since that night I met you on the rock shore."

CHAPTER 34 - THE SHIP O'DREAMS COMES TO HARBOR

One morning, when a windy golden sunrise was billowing over the gulf in waves of light, a certain weary stork flew over the bar of Four Winds Harbor on his way from the Land of Evening Stars. Under his wing was tucked a sleepy, starry-eyed, little creature. The stork was tired, and he looked wistfully about him. He knew he was somewhere near his destination, but he could not yet see it. The big, white light-house on the red sandstone cliff had its good points; but no stork possessed of any gumption would leave a new, velvet baby there. An old gray house, surrounded by willows, in a blossomy brook valley, looked more promising, but did not seem quite the thing either. The staring green abode further on was manifestly out of the question. Then the stork brightened up. He had caught sight of the very place—a little white house nestled against a big, whispering fir-wood, with a spiral of blue smoke winding up from its kitchen chimney—a house which just looked as if it were meant for babies. The stork gave a sigh of satisfaction, and softly alighted on the ridge-pole.

Half an hour later Gilbert ran down the hall and tapped on the spare-room door. A drowsy voice answered him and in a moment Marilla's pale, scared face peeped out from behind the door.

"Marilla, Anne has sent me to tell you that a certain young gentleman has arrived here. He hasn't brought much luggage with him, but he evidently means to stay."

"For pity's sake!" said Marilla blankly. "You don't mean to tell me, Gilbert, that it's all over. Why wasn't I called?"

"Anne wouldn't let us disturb you when there was no need. Nobody was called until about two hours ago. There was no 'passage perilous' this time."

"And—and—Gilbert—will this baby live?"

"He certainly will. He weighs ten pounds and—why, listen to him. Nothing wrong with his lungs, is there? The nurse says his hair will be red. Anne is furious with her, and I'm tickled to death."

That was a wonderful day in the little house of dreams.

"The best dream of all has come true," said Anne, pale and rapturous. "Oh, Marilla, I hardly dare believe it, after that horrible day last summer. I have had a heartache ever since then—but it is gone now."

"This baby will take Joy's place," said Marilla.

"Oh, no, no, NO, Marilla. He can't—nothing can ever do that. He has his own place, my dear, wee man-child. But little Joy has hers, and always will have it. If she had lived she would have been over a year old. She would have been toddling around on her tiny feet and lisping a few words. I can see her so plainly, Marilla. Oh, I know now that Captain Jim was right when he said God would manage better than that my baby would seem a stranger to me when I found her Beyond. I've learned THAT this past year. I've followed her development day by day and week by week—I always shall. I shall know just how she grows from year to year—and when I meet her again I'll know her—she won't be a stranger. Oh, Marilla, LOOK at his dear, darling toes! Isn't it strange they should be so perfect?"

"It would be stranger if they weren't," said Marilla crisply. Now that all was safely over, Marilla was herself again.

"Oh, I know—but it seems as if they couldn't be quite FINISHED, you know—and they are, even to the tiny nails. And his hands—JUST look at his hands, Marilla."

"They appear to be a good deal like hands," Marilla conceded.

"See how he clings to my finger. I'm sure he knows me already. He cries when the nurse takes him away. Oh, Marilla, do you think—you don't think, do you— that his hair is going to be red?"

"I don't see much hair of any color," said Marilla. "I wouldn't worry about it, if I were you, until it becomes visible."

"Marilla, he HAS hair—look at that fine little down all over his head. Anyway, nurse says his eyes will be hazel and his forehead is exactly like Gilbert's."

"And he has the nicest little ears, Mrs. Doctor, dear," said Susan. "The first thing I did was to look at his ears. Hair is deceitful and noses and eyes change, and you cannot tell what is going to come of them, but ears is ears from start to finish, and you always know where you are with them. Just look at their shape— and they are set right back against his precious head. You will never need to be ashamed of his ears, Mrs. Doctor, dear."

Anne's convalescence was rapid and happy. Folks came and worshipped the baby, as people have bowed before the kingship of the new-born since long before the Wise Men of the East knelt in homage to the Royal Babe of the Bethlehem manger. Leslie, slowly finding herself amid the new conditions of her life, hovered over it, like a beautiful, golden-crowned Madonna. Miss Cornelia nursed it as knackily as could any mother in Israel. Captain Jim held the small creature in his big brown hands and gazed tenderly at it, with eyes that saw the children who had never been born to him.

"What are you going to call him?" asked Miss Cornelia.

"Anne has settled his name," answered Gilbert.

"James Matthew—after the two finest gentlemen I've ever known—not even saving your presence," said Anne with a saucy glance at Gilbert.

Gilbert smiled.

"I never knew Matthew very well; he was so shy we boys couldn't get acquainted with him—but I quite agree with you that Captain Jim is one of the rarest and finest souls God ever clothed in clay. He is so delighted over the fact that we have given his name to our small lad. It seems he has no other namesake."

"Well, James Matthew is a name that will wear well and not fade in the washing," said Miss Cornelia. "I'm glad you didn't load him down with some highfalutin, romantic name that he'd be ashamed of when he gets to be a grandfather. Mrs. William Drew at the Glen has called her baby Bertie Shakespeare. Quite a combination, isn't it? And I'm glad you haven't had much trouble picking on a name. Some folks have an awful time. When the Stanley Flaggs' first boy was born there was so much rivalry as to who the child should be named for that the poor little soul had to go for two years without a name. Then a brother came along and there it was—'Big Baby' and 'Little Baby.' Finally they called Big Baby Peter and Little Baby Isaac, after the two grandfathers, and had them both christened together. And each tried to see if it couldn't howl the other down. You know that Highland Scotch family of MacNabs back of the Glen? They've got twelve boys and the oldest and the youngest are both called Neil—Big Neil and Little Neil in the same family. Well, I s'pose they ran out of names."

"I have read somewhere," laughed Anne, "that the first child is a poem but the tenth is very prosy prose. Perhaps Mrs. MacNab thought that the twelfth was merely an old tale re-told."

"Well, there's something to be said for large families," said Miss Cornelia, with a sigh. "I was an only child for eight years and I did long for a brother and sister. Mother told me to pray for one—and pray I did, believe ME. Well, one day Aunt Nellie came to me and said, 'Cornelia, there is a little brother for you upstairs in your ma's room. You can go up and see him.' I was so excited and delighted I just flew upstairs. And old Mrs. Flagg lifted up the baby for me to see. Lord, Anne, dearie, I never was so disappointed in my life. You see, I'd been praying for A BROTHER TWO YEARS OLDER THAN MYSELF."

"How long did it take you to get over your disappointment?" asked Anne, amid her laughter.

"Well, I had a spite at Providence for a good spell, and for weeks I wouldn't even look at the baby. Nobody knew why, for I never told. Then he began to get real cute, and held out his wee hands to me and I began to get fond of him. But I didn't get really reconciled to him until one day a school chum came to see him and said she thought he was awful small for his age. I just got boiling mad, and I sailed right into her, and told her she didn't know a nice baby when she saw one, and ours was the nicest baby in the world. And after that I just worshipped him. Mother died before he was three years old and I was sister and mother to him both. Poor little lad, he was never strong, and he died when he wasn't much over twenty. Seems to me I'd have given anything on earth, Anne, dearie, if he'd only lived."

Miss Cornelia sighed. Gilbert had gone down and Leslie, who had been crooning over the small James Matthew in the dormer window, laid him asleep in his basket and went her way. As soon as she was safely out of earshot, Miss Cornelia bent forward and said in a conspirator's whisper:

"Anne, dearie, I'd a letter from Owen Ford yesterday. He's in Vancouver just now, but he wants to know if I can board him for a month later on. YOU know what that means. Well, I hope we're doing right."

"We've nothing to do with it—we couldn't prevent him from coming to Four Winds if he wanted to," said Anne quickly. She did not like the feeling of matchmaking Miss Cornelia's whispers gave her; and then she weakly succumbed herself.

"Don't let Leslie know he is coming until he is here," she said. "If she found out I feel sure she would go away at once. She intends to go in the fall anyhow—she told me so the other day. She is going to Montreal to take up nursing and make what she can of her life."

"Oh, well, Anne, dearie," said Miss Cornelia, nodding sagely "that is all as it may be. You and I have done our part and we must leave the rest to Higher Hands."

CHAPTER 35 - POLITICS AT FOUR WINDS

When Anne came downstairs again, the Island, as well as all Canada, was in the throes of a campaign preceding a general election. Gilbert, who was an ardent Conservative, found himself caught in the vortex, being much in demand for speech-making at the various county rallies. Miss Cornelia did not approve of his mixing up in politics and told Anne so.

"Dr. Dave never did it. Dr. Blythe will find he is making a mistake, believe ME. Politics is something no decent man should meddle with."

"Is the government of the country to be left solely to the rogues then?" asked Anne.

"Yes—so long as it's Conservative rogues," said Miss Cornelia, marching off with the honors of war. "Men and politicians are all tarred with the same brush. The Grits have it laid on thicker than the Conservatives, that's all— CONSIDERABLY thicker. But Grit or Tory, my advice to Dr. Blythe is to steer clear of politics. First thing you know, he'll be running an election himself, and going off to Ottawa for half the year and leaving his practice to go to the dogs."

"Ah, well, let's not borrow trouble," said Anne. "The rate of interest is too high. Instead, let's look at Little Jem. It should be spelled with a G. Isn't he perfectly beautiful? Just see the dimples in his elbows. We'll bring him up to be a good Conservative, you and I, Miss Cornelia."

"Bring him up to be a good man," said Miss Cornelia. "They're scarce and valuable; though, mind you, I wouldn't like to see him a Grit. As for the election, you and I may be thankful we don't live over harbor. The air there is blue these days. Every Elliott and Crawford and MacAllister is on the warpath, loaded for bear. This side is peaceful and calm, seeing there's so few men. Captain Jim's a Grit, but it's my opinion he's ashamed of it, for he never talks politics. There isn't any earthly doubt that the Conservatives will be returned with a big majority again."

Miss Cornelia was mistaken. On the morning after the election Captain Jim dropped in at the little house to tell the news. So virulent is the microbe of party politics, even in a peaceable old man, that Captain Jim's cheeks were flushed and his eyes were flashing with all his old-time fire.

"Mistress Blythe, the Liberals are in with a sweeping majority. After eighteen years of Tory mismanagement this down-trodden country is going to have a chance at last."

"I never heard you make such a bitter partisan speech before, Captain Jim. I didn't think you had so much political venom in you," laughed Anne, who was not much excited over the tidings. Little Jem had said "Wow-ga" that morning. What were principalities and powers, the rise and fall of dynasties, the overthrow of Grit or Tory, compared with that miraculous occurrence?

"It's been accumulating for a long while," said Captain Jim, with a deprecating smile. "I thought I was only a moderate Grit, but when the news came that we were in I found out how Gritty I really was."

"You know the doctor and I are Conservatives."

"Ah, well, it's the only bad thing I know of either of you, Mistress Blythe. Cornelia is a Tory, too. I called in on my way from the Glen to tell her the news."

"Didn't you know you took your life in your hands?"

"Yes, but I couldn't resist the temptation."

"How did she take it?"

"Comparatively calm, Mistress Blythe, comparatively calm. She says, says she, 'Well, Providence sends seasons of humiliation to a country, same as to individuals. You Grits have been cold and hungry for many a year. Make haste to get warmed and fed, for you won't be in long.' 'Well, now Cornelia,' I says, 'mebbe Providence thinks Canada needs a real long spell of humiliation.' Ah, Susan, have YOU heard the news? The Liberals are in."

Susan had just come in from the kitchen, attended by the odor of delectable dishes which always seemed to hover around her.

"Now, are they?" she said, with beautiful unconcern. "Well, I never could see but that my bread rose just as light when Grits were in as when they were not. And if any party, Mrs. Doctor, dear, will make it rain before the week is out, and save our kitchen garden from entire ruination, that is the party Susan will vote for. In the meantime, will you just step out and give me your opinion on the meat for dinner? I am fearing that it is very tough, and I think that we had better change our butcher as well as our government."

One evening, a week later, Anne walked down to the Point, to see if she could get some fresh fish from Captain Jim, leaving Little Jem for the first time. It was quite a tragedy. Suppose he cried? Suppose Susan did not know just exactly what to do for him? Susan was calm and serene.

"I have had as much experience with him as you, Mrs. Doctor, dear, have I not?"

"Yes, with him—but not with other babies. Why, I looked after three pairs of twins, when I was a child, Susan. When they cried, I gave them peppermint or castor oil quite coolly. It's quite curious now to recall how lightly I took all those babies and their woes."

"Oh, well, if Little Jem cries, I will just clap a hot water bag on his little stomach," said Susan.

"Not too hot, you know," said Anne anxiously. Oh, was it really wise to go?

"Do not you fret, Mrs. Doctor, dear. Susan is not the woman to burn a wee man. Bless him, he has no notion of crying."

Anne tore herself away finally and enjoyed her walk to the Point after all, through the long shadows of the sun-setting. Captain Jim was not in the living room of the lighthouse, but another man was—a handsome, middle-aged man, with a strong, clean-shaven chin, who was unknown to Anne. Nevertheless, when she sat down, he began to talk to her with all the assurance of an old acquaintance. There was nothing amiss in what he said or the way he said it, but Anne rather resented such a cool taking-for-granted in a complete stranger. Her replies were frosty, and as few as decency required. Nothing daunted, her companion talked on for several minutes, then excused himself and went away. Anne could have sworn there was a twinkle in his eye and it annoyed her. Who was the creature? There was something vaguely familiar about him but she was certain she had never seen him before.

"Captain Jim, who was that who just went out?" she asked, as Captain Jim came in.

"Marshall Elliott," answered the captain.

"Marshall Elliott!" cried Anne. "Oh, Captain Jim—it wasn't—yes, it WAS his voice—oh, Captain Jim, I didn't know him—and I was quite insulting to him! WHY didn't he tell me? He must have seen I didn't know him."

"He wouldn't say a word about it—he'd just enjoy the joke. Don't worry over snubbing him—he'll think it fun. Yes, Marshall's shaved off his beard at last and cut his hair. His party is in, you know. I didn't know him myself first time I saw him. He was up in Carter Flagg's store at the Glen the night after election day, along with a crowd of others, waiting for the news. About twelve the 'phone came through—the Liberals were in. Marshall just got up and walked out—he didn't cheer or shout—he left the others to do that, and they nearly lifted the roof off Carter's store, I reckon. Of course, all the Tories were over in Raymond Russell's store. Not much cheering THERE. Marshall went straight down the street to the side door of Augustus Palmer's barber shop. Augustus was in bed asleep, but Marhall hammered on the door until he got up and come down, wanting to know what all the racket was about.

"Come into your shop and do the best job you ever did in your life, Gus,' said Marshall. 'The Liberals are in and you're going to barber a good Grit before the sun rises.'

"Gus was mad as hops—partly because he'd been dragged out of bed, but more because he's a Tory. He vowed he wouldn't shave any man after twelve at night.

"'You'll do what I want you to do, sonny,' said Marshall, 'or I'll jest turn you over my knee and give you one of those spankings your mother forgot.'

"He'd have done it, too, and Gus knew it, for Marshall is as strong as an ox and Gus is only a midget of a man. So he gave in and towed Marshall in to the shop and went to work. 'Now,' says he, 'I'll barber you up, but if you say one word to me about the Grits getting in while I'm doing it I'll cut your throat with this razor,' says he. You wouldn't have thought mild little Gus could be so bloodthirsty, would you? Shows what party politics will do for a man. Marshall kept quiet and got his hair and beard disposed of and went home. When his old housekeeper heard him come upstairs she peeked out of her bedroom door to see whether 'twas him or the hired boy. And when she saw a strange man striding down the hall with a candle in his hand she screamed blue murder and fainted dead away. They had to send for the doctor before they could bring her to, and it was several days before she could look at Marshall without shaking all over."

Captain Jim had no fish. He seldom went out in his boat that summer, and his long tramping expeditions were over. He spent a great deal of his time sitting by his seaward window, looking out over the gulf, with his swiftly-whitening head leaning on his hand. He sat there tonight for many silent minutes, keeping some tryst with the past which Anne would not disturb. Presently he pointed to the iris of the West:

"That's beautiful, isn't, it, Mistress Blythe? But I wish you could have seen the sunrise this morning. It was a wonderful thing—wonderful. I've seen all kinds of sunrises come over that gulf. I've been all over the world, Mistress Blythe, and take it all in all, I've never seen a finer sight than a summer sunrise over the gulf. A man can't pick his time for dying, Mistress Blythe—jest got to go when the Great Captain gives His sailing orders. But if I could I'd go out when the morning comes across that water. I've watched it many a time and thought what a thing it would be to pass out through that great white glory to whatever was waiting bey-ant, on a sea that ain't mapped out on any airthly chart. I think, Mistress Blythe, that I'd find lost Margaret there."

Captain Jim had often talked to Anne of lost Margaret since he had told her the old story. His love for her trembled in every tone—that love that had never grown faint or forgetful.

"Anyway, I hope when my time comes I'll go quick and easy. I don't think I'm a coward, Mistress Blythe—I've looked an ugly death in the face more than once without blenching. But the thought of a lingering death does give me a queer, sick feeling of horror."

"Don't talk about leaving us, dear, DEAR Captain, Jim," pleaded Anne, in a choked voice, patting the old brown hand, once so strong, but now grown very feeble. "What would we do without you?"

Captain Jim smiled beautifully.

"Oh, you'd get along nicely—nicely—but you wouldn't forget the old man al-together, Mistress Blythe—no, I don't think you'll ever quite forget him. The race of Joseph always remembers one another. But it'll be a memory that won't hurt—I like to think that my memory won't hurt my friends—it'll always be kind of pleas-ant to them, I hope and believe. It won't be very long now before lost Margaret calls me, for the last time. I'll be all ready to answer. I jest spoke of this because there's a little favor I want to ask you. Here's this poor old Matey of mine"—Captain Jim reached out a hand and poked the big, warm, velvety, golden ball on the sofa. The First Mate uncoiled himself like a spring with a nice, throaty, com-fortable sound, half purr, half meow, stretched his paws in air, turned over and coiled himself up again. "HE'll miss me when I start on the V'yage. I can't bear to think of leaving the poor critter to starve, like he was left before. If anything happens to me will you give Matey a bite and a corner, Mistress Blythe?"

"Indeed I will."

"Then that is all I had on my mind. Your Little Jem is to have the few curious things I picked up—I've seen to that. And now I don't like to see tears in those pretty eyes, Mistress Blythe. I'll mebbe hang on for quite a spell yet. I heard you reading a piece of poetry one day last winter—one of Tennyson's pieces. I'd sorter like to hear it again, if you could recite it for me."

Softly and clearly, while the seawind blew in on them, Anne repeated the beautiful lines of Tennyson's wonderful swan song—"Crossing the Bar." The old captain kept time gently with his sinewy hand.

"Yes, yes, Mistress Blythe," he said, when she had finished, "that's it, that's it. He wasn't a sailor, you tell me—I dunno how he could have put an old sailor's feelings into words like that, if he wasn't one. He didn't want any 'sadness o' farewells' and neither do I, Mistress Blythe—for all will be well with me and mine beyant the bar."

CHAPTER 36 - BEAUTY FOR ASHES

"Any news from Green Gables, Anne?"

"Nothing very especial," replied Anne, folding up Marilla's letter. "Jake Donnell has been there shingling the roof. He is a full-fledged carpenter now, so it seems he has had his own way in regard to the choice of a life-work. You remember his mother wanted him to be a college professor. I shall never forget the day she came to the school and rated me for failing to call him St. Clair."

"Does anyone ever call him that now?"

"Evidently not. It seems that he has completely lived it down. Even his mother has succumbed. I always thought that a boy with Jake's chin and mouth would get his own way in the end. Diana writes me that Dora has a beau. Just think of it—that child!"

"Dora is seventeen," said Gilbert. "Charlie Sloane and I were both mad about you when you were seventeen, Anne."

"Really, Gilbert, we must be getting on in years," said Anne, with a half-rueful smile, "when children who were six when we thought ourselves grown up are old enough now to have beaux. Dora's is Ralph Andrews—Jane's brother. I remember him as a little, round, fat, white-headed fellow who was always at the foot of his class. But I understand he is quite a fine-looking young man now."

"Dora will probably marry young. She's of the same type as Charlotta the Fourth—she'll never miss her first chance for fear she might not get another."

"Well; if she marries Ralph I hope he will be a little more up-and-coming than his brother Billy," mused Anne.

"For instance," said Gilbert, laughing, "let us hope he will be able to propose on his own account. Anne, would you have married Billy if he had asked you himself, instead of getting Jane to do it for him?"

"I might have." Anne went off into a shriek of laughter over the recollection of her first proposal. "The shock of the whole thing might have hypnotized me into some such rash and foolish act. Let us be thankful he did it by proxy."

"I had a letter from George Moore yesterday," said Leslie, from the corner where she was reading.

"Oh, how is he?" asked Anne interestedly, yet with an unreal feeling that she was inquiring about some one whom she did not know.

"He is well, but he finds it very hard to adapt himself to all the changes in his old home and friends. He is going to sea again in the spring. It's in his blood, he says, and he longs for it. But he told me something that made me glad for him, poor fellow. Before he sailed on the Four Sisters he was engaged to a girl at home. He did not tell me anything about her in Montreal, because he said he supposed she would have forgotten him and married someone else long ago, and with him, you see, his engagement and love was still a thing of the present. It was pretty hard on him, but when he got home he found she had never married and still cared for him. They are to be married this fall. I'm going to ask him to bring her over here for a little trip; he says he wants to come and see the place where he lived so many years without knowing it."

"What a nice little romance," said Anne, whose love for the romantic was immortal. "And to think," she added with a sigh of self-reproach, "that if I had had my way George Moore would never have come up from the grave in which his identity was buried. How I did fight against Gilbert's suggestion! Well, I am punished: I shall never be able to have a different opinion from Gilbert's again! If I try to have, he will squelch me by casting George Moore's case up to me!"

"As if even that would squelch a woman!" mocked Gilbert. "At least do not become my echo, Anne. A little opposition gives spice to life. I do not want a wife like John MacAllister's over the harbor. No matter what he says, she at once remarks in that drab, lifeless little voice of hers, 'That is very true, John, dear me!'"

Anne and Leslie laughed. Anne's laughter was silver and Leslie's golden, and the combination of the two was as satisfactory as a perfect chord in music.

Susan, coming in on the heels of the laughter, echoed it with a resounding sigh.

"Why, Susan, what is the matter?" asked Gilbert.

"There's nothing wrong with little Jem, is there, Susan?" cried Anne, starting up in alarm.

"No, no, calm yourself, Mrs. Doctor, dear. Something has happened, though. Dear me, everything has gone catawampus with me this week. I spoiled the bread, as you know too well—and I scorched the doctor's best shirt bosom—and I broke your big platter. And now, on the top of all this, comes word that my sister Matilda has broken her leg and wants me to go and stay with her for a spell."

"Oh, I'm very sorry—sorry that your sister has met with such an accident, I mean," exclaimed Anne.

"Ah, well, man was made to mourn, Mrs. Doctor, dear. That sounds as if it ought to be in the Bible, but they tell me a person named Burns wrote it. And there is no doubt that we are born to trouble as the sparks fly upward. As for Matilda, I do not know what to think of her. None of our family ever broke their legs before. But whatever she has done she is still my sister, and I feel that it is my duty to go and wait on her, if you can spare me for a few weeks, Mrs. Doctor, dear."

"Of course, Susan, of course. I can get someone to help me while you are gone."

"If you cannot I will not go, Mrs. Doctor, dear, Matilda's leg to the contrary notwithstanding. I will not have you worried, and that blessed child upset in consequence, for any number of legs."

"Oh, you must go to your sister at once, Susan. I can get a girl from the cove, who will do for a time."

"Anne, will you let me come and stay with you while Susan is away?" exclaimed Leslie. "Do! I'd love to—and it would be an act of charity on your part. I'm so horribly lonely over there in that big barn of a house. There's so little to do—and at night I'm worse than lonely—I'm frightened and nervous in spite of locked doors. There was a tramp around two days ago."

Anne joyfully agreed, and next day Leslie was installed as an inmate of the little house of dreams. Miss Cornelia warmly approved of the arrangement.

"It seems Providential," she told Anne in confidence. "I'm sorry for Matilda Clow, but since she had to break her leg it couldn't have happened at a better time. Leslie will be here while Owen Ford is in Four Winds, and those old cats up at the Glen won't get the chance to meow, as they would if she was living over there alone and Owen going to see her. They are doing enough of it as it is, because she doesn't put on mourning. I said to one of them, 'If you mean she should put on mourning for George Moore, it seems to me more like his resurrection than his funeral; and if it's Dick you mean, I confess *I* can't see the propriety of going into weeds for a man who died thirteen years ago and good riddance then!' And when old Louisa Baldwin remarked to me that she thought it very strange that Leslie should never have suspected it wasn't her own husband *I* said, 'YOU never suspected it wasn't Dick Moore, and you were next-door neighbor to him all his life, and by nature you're ten times as suspicious as Leslie.' But you can't stop some people's tongues, Anne, dearie, and I'm real thankful Leslie will be under your roof while Owen is courting her."

Owen Ford came to the little house one August evening when Leslie and Anne were absorbed in worshipping the baby. He paused at the open door of the living room, unseen by the two within, gazing with greedy eyes at the beautiful picture. Leslie sat on the floor with the baby in her lap, making ecstatic dabs at his fat little hands as he fluttered them in the air.

"Oh, you dear, beautiful, beloved baby," she mumbled, catching one wee hand and covering it with kisses.

"Isn't him ze darlingest itty sing," crooned Anne, hanging over the arm of her chair adoringly. "Dem itty wee pads are ze very tweetest handies in ze whole big world, isn't dey, you darling itty man."

Anne, in the months before Little Jem's coming, had pored diligently over several wise volumes, and pinned her faith to one in especial, "Sir Oracle on the Care and Training of Children." Sir Oracle implored parents by all they held sacred never to talk "baby talk" to their children. Infants should invariably be addressed in classical language from the moment of their birth. So should they learn to speak English undefiled from their earliest utterance. "How," demanded Sir Oracle, "can a mother reasonably expect her child to learn correct speech, when she continually accustoms its impressionable gray matter to such absurd expressions and distortions of our noble tongue as thoughtless mothers inflict every day on the helpless creatures committed to their care? Can a child who is constantly called 'tweet itty wee singie' ever attain to any proper conception of his own being and possibilities and destiny?"

Anne was vastly impressed with this, and informed Gilbert that she meant to make it an inflexible rule never, under any circumstances, to talk "baby talk" to her children. Gilbert agreed with her, and they made a solemn compact on the subject—a compact which Anne shamelessly violated the very first moment Little Jem was laid in her arms. "Oh, the darling itty wee sing!" she had exclaimed. And she had continued to violate it ever since. When Gilbert teased her she laughed Sir Oracle to scorn.

"He never had any children of his own, Gilbert—I am positive he hadn't or he would never have written such rubbish. You just can't help talking baby talk to a baby. It comes natural—and it's RIGHT. It would be inhuman to talk to those tiny, soft, velvety little creatures as we do to great big boys and girls. Babies want love and cuddling and all the sweet baby talk they can get, and Little Jem is going to have it, bless his dear itty heartums."

"But you're the worst I ever heard, Anne," protested Gilbert, who, not being a mother but only a father, was not wholly convinced yet that Sir Oracle was wrong. "I never heard anything like the way you talk to that child."

"Very likely you never did. Go away—go away. Didn't I bring up three pairs of Hammond twins before I was eleven? You and Sir Oracle are nothing but cold-blooded theorists. Gilbert, JUST look at him! He's smiling at me—he knows what we're talking about. And oo dest agwees wif evy word muzzer says, don't oo, angel-lover?"

Gilbert put his arm about them. "Oh you mothers!" he said. "You mothers! God knew what He was about when He made you."

So Little Jem was talked to and loved and cuddled; and he throve as became a child of the house of dreams. Leslie was quite as foolish over him as Anne was. When their work was done and Gilbert was out of the way, they gave themselves over to shameless orgies of love-making and ecstasies of adoration, such as that in which Owen Ford had surprised them.

Leslie was the first to become aware of him. Even in the twilight Anne could see the sudden whiteness that swept over her beautiful face, blotting out the crimson of lip and cheeks.

Owen came forward, eagerly, blind for a moment to Anne.

"Leslie!" he said, holding out his hand. It was the first time he had ever called her by her name; but the hand Leslie gave him was cold; and she was very quiet all the evening, while Anne and Gilbert and Owen laughed and talked together. Before his call ended she excused herself and went upstairs. Owen's gay spirits flagged and he went away soon after with a downcast air.

Gilbert looked at Anne.

"Anne, what are you up to? There's something going on that I don't understand. The whole air here tonight has been charged with electricity. Leslie sits like the muse of tragedy; Owen Ford jokes and laughs on the surface, and watches Leslie with the eyes of his soul. You seem all the time to be bursting with some suppressed excitement. Own up. What secret have you been keeping from your deceived husband?"

"Don't be a goose, Gilbert," was Anne's conjugal reply. "As for Leslie, she is absurd and I'm going up to tell her so."

Anne found Leslie at the dormer window of her room. The little place was filled with the rhythmic thunder of the sea. Leslie sat with locked hands in the misty moonshine—a beautiful, accusing presence.

"Anne," she said in a low, reproachful voice, "did you know Owen Ford was coming to Four Winds?"

"I did," said Anne brazenly.

"Oh, you should have told me, Anne," Leslie cried passionately. "If I had known I would have gone away—I wouldn't have stayed here to meet him. You should have told me. It wasn't fair of you, Anne—oh, it wasn't fair!"

Leslie's lips were trembling and her whole form was tense with emotion. But Anne laughed heartlessly. She bent over and kissed Leslie's upturned reproachful face.

"Leslie, you are an adorable goose. Owen Ford didn't rush from the Pacific to the Atlantic from a burning desire to see ME. Neither do I believe that he was inspired by any wild and frenzied passion for Miss Cornelia. Take off your tragic airs, my dear friend, and fold them up and put them away in lavender. You'll never need them again. There are some people who can see through a grindstone when there is a hole in it, even if you cannot. I am not a prophetess, but I shall venture on a prediction. The bitterness of life is over for you. After this you are going to have the joys and hopes—and I daresay the sorrows, too—of a happy woman. The omen of the shadow of Venus did come true for you, Leslie. The year in which you saw it brought your life's best gift for you—your love for Owen Ford. Now, go right to bed and have a good sleep."

Leslie obeyed orders in so far that she went to bed: but it may be questioned if she slept much. I do not think she dared to dream wakingly; life had been so hard for this poor Leslie, the path on which she had had to walk had been so strait, that she could not whisper to her own heart the hopes that might wait on the future. But she watched the great revolving light bestarring the short hours of the summer night, and her eyes grew soft and bright and young once more. Nor, when Owen Ford came next day, to ask her to go with him to the shore, did she say him nay.

CHAPTER 37 - MISS CORNELIA MAKES A STARTLING ANNOUNCEMENT

Miss Cornelia sailed down to the little house one drowsy afternoon, when the gulf was the faint, bleached blue of the August seas, and the orange lilies at the gate of Anne's garden held up their imperial cups to be filled with the molten gold of August sunshine. Not that Miss Cornelia concerned herself with painted oceans or sun-thirsty lilies. She sat in her favorite rocker in unusual idleness. She sewed not, neither did she spin. Nor did she say a single derogatory word concerning any portion of mankind. In short, Miss Cornelia's conversation was singularly devoid of spice that day, and Gilbert, who had stayed home to listen to her, instead of going a-fishing, as he had intended, felt himself aggrieved. What had come over Miss Cornelia? She did not look cast down or worried. On the contrary, there was a certain air of nervous exultation about her.

"Where is Leslie?" she asked—not as if it mattered much either.

"Owen and she went raspberrying in the woods back of her farm," answered Anne. "They won't be back before supper time—if then."

"They don't seem to have any idea that there is such a thing as a clock," said Gilbert. "I can't get to the bottom of that affair. I'm certain you women pulled strings. But Anne, undutiful wife, won't tell me. Will you, Miss Cornelia?"

"No, I shall not. But," said Miss Cornelia, with the air of one determined to take the plunge and have it over, "I will tell you something else. I came today on purpose to tell it. I am going to be married."

Anne and Gilbert were silent. If Miss Cornelia had announced her intention of going out to the channel and drowning herself the thing might have been believable. This was not. So they waited. Of course Miss Cornelia had made a mistake.

"Well, you both look sort of kerflummexed," said Miss Cornelia, with a twinkle in her eyes. Now that the awkward moment of revelation was over, Miss Cornelia was her own woman again. "Do you think I'm too young and inexperienced for matrimony?"

"You know—it IS rather staggering," said Gilbert, trying to gather his wits together. "I've heard you say a score of times that you wouldn't marry the best man in the world."

"I'm not going to marry the best man in the world," retorted Miss Cornelia. "Marshall Elliott is a long way from being the best."

"Are you going to marry Marshall Elliott?" exclaimed Anne, recovering her power of speech under this second shock.

"Yes. I could have had him any time these twenty years if I'd lifted my finger. But do you suppose I was going to walk into church beside a perambulating haystack like that?"

"I am sure we are very glad—and we wish you all possible happiness," said Anne, very flatly and inadequately, as she felt. She was not prepared for such an occasion. She had never imagined herself offering betrothal felicitations to Miss Cornelia.

"Thanks, I knew you would," said Miss Cornelia. "You are the first of my friends to know it."

"We shall be so sorry to lose you, though, dear Miss Cornelia," said Anne, beginning to be a little sad and sentimental.

"Oh, you won't lose me," said Miss Cornelia unsentimentally. "You don't suppose I would live over harbor with all those MacAllisters and Elliotts and Crawfords, do you? 'From the conceit of the Elliotts, the pride of the MacAllisters and the vain-glory of the Crawfords, good Lord deliver us.' Marshall is coming to live at my place. I'm sick and tired of hired men. That Jim Hastings I've got this summer is positively the worst of the species. He would drive anyone to getting married. What do you think? He upset the churn yesterday and spilled a big churning of cream over the yard. And not one whit concerned about it was he! Just gave a foolish laugh and said cream was good for the land. Wasn't that like a man? I told him I wasn't in the habit of fertilising my back yard with cream."

"Well, I wish you all manner of happiness too, Miss Cornelia," said Gilbert, solemnly; "but," he added, unable to resist the temptation to tease Miss Cornelia, despite Anne's imploring eyes, "I fear your day of independence is done. As you know, Marshall Elliott is a very determined man."

"I like a man who can stick to a thing," retorted Miss Cornelia. "Amos Grant, who used to be after me long ago, couldn't. You never saw such a weather-vane. He jumped into the pond to drown himself once and then changed his mind and swum out again. Wasn't that like a man? Marshall would have stuck to it and drowned."

"And he has a bit of a temper, they tell me," persisted Gilbert.

"He wouldn't be an Elliott if he hadn't. I'm thankful he has. It will be real fun to make him mad. And you can generally do something with a tempery man when it comes to repenting time. But you can't do anything with a man who just keeps placid and aggravating."

"You know he's a Grit, Miss Cornelia."

"Yes, he IS," admitted Miss Cornelia rather sadly. "And of course there is no hope of making a Conservative of him. But at least he is a Presbyterian. So I suppose I shall have to be satisfied with that."

"Would you marry him if he were a Methodist, Miss Cornelia?"

"No, I would not. Politics is for this world, but religion is for both."

"And you may be a 'relict' after all, Miss Cornelia."

"Not I. Marshall will live me out. The Elliotts are long-lived, and the Bryants are not."

"When are you to be married?" asked Anne.

"In about a month's time. My wedding dress is to be navy blue silk. And I want to ask you, Anne, dearie, if you think it would be all right to wear a veil with a navy blue dress. I've always thought I'd like to wear a veil if I ever got married. Marshall says to have it if I want to. Isn't that like a man?"

"Why shouldn't you wear it if you want to?" asked Anne.

"Well, one doesn't want to be different from other people," said Miss Cornelia, who was not noticeably like anyone else on the face of the earth. "As I say, I do fancy a veil. But maybe it shouldn't be worn with any dress but a white one. Please tell me, Anne, dearie, what you really think. I'll go by your advice."

"I don't think veils are usually worn with any but white dresses," admitted Anne, "but that is merely a convention; and I am like Mr. Elliott, Miss Cornelia. I don't see any good reason why you shouldn't have a veil if you want one."

But Miss Cornelia, who made her calls in calico wrappers, shook her head.

"If it isn't the proper thing I won't wear it," she said, with a sigh of regret for a lost dream.

"Since you are determined to be married, Miss Cornelia," said Gilbert solemnly, "I shall give you the excellent rules for the management of a husband which my grandmother gave my mother when she married my father."

"Well, I reckon I can manage Marshall Elliott," said Miss Cornelia placidly. "But let us hear your rules."

"The first one is, catch him."

"He's caught. Go on."

"The second one is, feed him well."

"With enough pie. What next?"

"The third and fourth are—keep your eye on him."

"I believe you," said Miss Cornelia emphatically.

CHAPTER 38 - RED ROSES

The garden of the little house was a haunt beloved of bees and reddened by late roses that August. The little house folk lived much in it, and were given to taking picnic suppers in the grassy corner beyond the brook and sitting about in it through the twilights when great night moths sailed athwart the velvet gloom. One evening Owen Ford found Leslie alone in it. Anne and Gilbert were away, and Susan, who was expected back that night, had not yet returned.

The northern sky was amber and pale green over the fir tops. The air was cool, for August was nearing September, and Leslie wore a crimson scarf over her white dress. Together they wandered through the little, friendly, flower-crowded paths in silence. Owen must go soon. His holiday was nearly over. Leslie found her heart beating wildly. She knew that this beloved garden was to be the scene of the binding words that must seal their as yet unworded understanding.

"Some evenings a strange odor blows down the air of this garden, like a phantom perfume," said Owen. "I have never been able to discover from just what flower it comes. It is elusive and haunting and wonderfully sweet. I like to fancy it is the soul of Grandmother Selwyn passing on a little visit to the old spot she loved so well. There should be a lot of friendly ghosts about this little old house."

"I have lived under its roof only a month," said Leslie, "but I love it as I never loved the house over there where I have lived all my life."

"This house was builded and consecrated by love," said Owen. "Such houses, MUST exert an influence over those who live in them. And this garden—it is over sixty years old and the history of a thousand hopes and joys is written in its blossoms. Some of those flowers were actually set out by the schoolmaster's bride, and she has been dead for thirty years. Yet they bloom on every summer. Look at those red roses, Leslie—how they queen it over everything else!"

"I love the red roses," said Leslie. "Anne likes the pink ones best, and Gilbert likes the white. But I want the crimson ones. They satisfy some craving in me as no other flower does."

"These roses are very late—they bloom after all the others have gone—and they hold all the warmth and soul of the summer come to fruition," said Owen, plucking some of the glowing, half-opened buds.

"The rose is the flower of love—the world has acclaimed it so for centuries. The pink roses are love hopeful and expectant—the white roses are love dead or forsaken—but the red roses—ah, Leslie, what are the red roses?"

"Love triumphant," said Leslie in a low voice.

"Yes—love triumphant and perfect. Leslie, you know—you understand. I have loved you from the first. And I KNOW you love me—I don't need to ask you. But I want to hear you say it—my darling—my darling!"

Leslie said something in a very low and tremulous voice. Their hands and lips met; it was life's supreme moment for them and as they stood there in the old garden, with its many years of love and delight and sorrow and glory, he crowned her shining hair with the red, red rose of a love triumphant.

Anne and Gilbert returned presently, accompanied by Captain Jim. Anne lighted a few sticks of driftwood in the fireplace, for love of the pixy flames, and they sat around it for an hour of good fellowship.

"When I sit looking at a driftwood fire it's easy to believe I'm young again," said Captain Jim.

"Can you read futures in the fire, Captain Jim?" asked Owen.

Captain Jim looked at them all affectionately and then back again at Leslie's vivid face and glowing eyes.

"I don't need the fire to read your futures," he said. "I see happiness for all of you—all of you—for Leslie and Mr. Ford—and the doctor here and Mistress Blythe—and Little Jem—and children that ain't born yet but will be. Happiness for you all—though, mind you, I reckon you'll have your troubles and worries and sorrows, too. They're bound to come—and no house, whether it's a palace or a little house of dreams, can bar 'em out. But they won't get the better of you if you face 'em TOGETHER with love and trust. You can weather any storm with them two for compass and pilot."

The old man rose suddenly and placed one hand on Leslie's head and one on Anne's.

"Two good, sweet women," he said. "True and faithful and to be depended on. Your husbands will have honor in the gates because of you—your children will rise up and call you blessed in the years to come."

There was a strange solemnity about the little scene. Anne and Leslie bowed as those receiving a benediction. Gilbert suddenly brushed his hand over his eyes; Owen Ford was rapt as one who can see visions. All were silent for a space. The little house of dreams added another poignant and unforgettable moment to its store of memories.

"I must be going now," said Captain Jim slowly at last. He took up his hat and looked lingeringly about the room.

"Good night, all of you," he said, as he went out.

Anne, pierced by the unusual wistfulness of his farewell, ran to the door after him.

"Come back soon, Captain Jim," she called, as he passed through the little gate hung between the firs.

"Ay, ay," he called cheerily back to her. But Captain Jim had sat by the old fireside of the house of dreams for the last time.

Anne went slowly back to the others.

"It's so—so pitiful to think of him going all alone down to that lonely Point," she said. "And there is no one to welcome him there."

"Captain Jim is such good company for others that one can't imagine him being anything but good company for himself," said Owen. "But he must often be lonely. There was a touch of the seer about him tonight—he spoke as one to whom it had been given to speak. Well, I must be going, too."

Anne and Gilbert discreetly melted away; but when Owen had gone Anne returned, to find Leslie standing by the hearth.

"Oh, Leslie—I know—and I'm so glad, dear," she said, putting her arms about her.

"Anne, my happiness frightens me," whispered Leslie. "It seems too great to be real—I'm afraid to speak of it—to think of it. It seems to me that it must just be another dream of this house of dreams and it will vanish when I leave here."

"Well, you are not going to leave here—until Owen takes you. You are going to stay with me until that times comes. Do you think I'd let you go over to that lonely, sad place again?"

"Thank you, dear. I meant to ask you if I might stay with you. I didn't want to go back there—it would seem like going back into the chill and dreariness of the old life again. Anne, Anne, what a friend you've been to me—'a good, sweet woman—true and faithful and to be depended on'—Captain Jim summed you up."

"He said 'women,' not 'woman,'" smiled Anne. "Perhaps Captain Jim sees us both through the rose-colored spectacles of his love for us. But we can try to live up to his belief in us, at least."

"Do you remember, Anne," said Leslie slowly, "that I once said—that night we met on the shore—that I hated my good looks? I did—then. It always seemed to me that if I had been homely Dick would never have thought of me. I hated my beauty because it had attracted him, but now—oh, I'm glad that I have it. It's all I have to offer Owen,—his artist soul delights in it. I feel as if I do not come to him quite empty-handed."

"Owen loves your beauty, Leslie. Who would not? But it's foolish of you to say or think that that is all you bring him. HE will tell you that—I needn't. And now I must lock up. I expected Susan back tonight, but she has not come."

"Oh, yes, here I am, Mrs. Doctor, dear," said Susan, entering unexpectedly from the kitchen, "and puffing like a hen drawing rails at that! It's quite a walk from the Glen down here."

"I'm glad to see you back, Susan. How is your sister?"

"She is able to sit up, but of course she cannot walk yet. However, she is very well able to get on without me now, for her daughter has come home for her vacation. And I am thankful to be back, Mrs. Doctor, dear. Matilda's leg was broken and no mistake, but her tongue was not. She would talk the legs off an iron pot, that she would, Mrs. Doctor, dear, though I grieve to say it of my own sister. She was always a great talker and yet she was the first of our family to get married. She really did not care much about marrying James Clow, but she could not bear to disoblige him. Not but what James is a good man—the only fault I have to find with him is that he always starts in to say grace with such an unearthly groan, Mrs. Doctor, dear. It always frightens my appetite clear away. And speaking of getting married, Mrs. Doctor, dear, is it true that Cornelia Bryant is going to be married to Marshall Elliott?"

"Yes, quite true, Susan."

"Well, Mrs. Doctor, dear, it does NOT seem to me fair. Here is me, who never said a word against the men, and I cannot get married nohow. And there is Cornelia Bryant, who is never done abusing them, and all she has to do is to reach out her hand and pick one up, as it were. It is a very strange world, Mrs. Doctor, dear."

"There's another world, you know, Susan."

"Yes," said Susan with a heavy sigh, "but, Mrs. Doctor, dear, there is neither marrying nor giving in marriage there."

CHAPTER 39 - CAPTAIN JIM CROSSES THE BAR

One day in late September Owen Ford's book came at last. Captain Jim had gone faithfully to the Glen post office every day for a month, expecting it. This day he had not gone, and Leslie brought his copy home with hers and Anne's.

"We'll take it down to him this evening," said Anne, excited as a schoolgirl.

The long walk to the Point on that clear, beguiling evening along the red harbor road was very pleasant. Then the sun dropped down behind the western hills into some valley that must have been full of lost sunsets, and at the same instant the big light flashed out on the white tower of the point.

"Captain Jim is never late by the fraction of a second," said Leslie.

Neither Anne nor Leslie ever forgot Captain Jim's face when they gave him the book—HIS book, transfigured and glorified. The cheeks that had been blanched of late suddenly flamed with the color of boyhood; his eyes glowed with all the fire of youth; but his hands trembled as he opened it.

It was called simply The Life-Book of Captain Jim, and on the title page the names of Owen Ford and James Boyd were printed as collaborators. The frontispiece was a photograph of Captain Jim himself, standing at the door of the lighthouse, looking across the gulf. Owen Ford had "snapped" him one day while the book was being written. Captain Jim had known this, but he had not known that the picture was to be in the book.

"Just think of it," he said, "the old sailor right there in a real printed book. This is the proudest day of my life. I'm like to bust, girls. There'll be no sleep for me tonight. I'll read my book clean through before sun-up."

"We'll go right away and leave you free to begin it," said Anne.

Captain Jim had been handling the book in a kind of reverent rapture. Now he decidedly closed it and laid it aside.

"No, no, you're not going away before you take a cup of tea with the old man," he protested. "I couldn't hear to that—could you, Matey? The life-book will keep, I reckon. I've waited for it this many a year. I can wait a little longer while I'm enjoying my friends."

Captain Jim moved about getting his kettle on to boil, and setting out his bread and butter. Despite his excitement he did not move with his old briskness. His movements were slow and halting. But the girls did not offer to help him. They knew it would hurt his feelings.

"You just picked the right evening to visit me," he said, producing a cake from his cupboard. "Leetle Joe's mother sent me down a big basket full of cakes and pies today. A blessing on all good cooks, says I. Look at this purty cake, all frosting and nuts. 'Tain't often I can entertain in such style. Set in, girls, set in! We'll 'tak a cup o' kindness yet for auld lang syne.'"

The girls "set in" right merrily. The tea was up to Captain Jim's best brewing. Little Joe's mother's cake was the last word in cakes; Captain Jim was the prince of gracious hosts, never even permitting his eyes to wander to the corner where the life-book lay, in all its bravery of green and gold. But when his door finally closed behind Anne and Leslie they knew that he went straight to it, and as they walked home they pictured the delight of the old man poring over the printed pages wherein his own life was portrayed with all the charm and color of reality itself.

"I wonder how he will like the ending—the ending I suggested," said Leslie.

She was never to know. Early the next morning Anne awakened to find Gilbert bending over her, fully dressed, and with an expression of anxiety on his face.

"Are you called out?" she asked drowsily.

"No. Anne, I'm afraid there's something wrong at the Point. It's an hour after sunrise now, and the light is still burning. You know it has always been a matter of pride with Captain Jim to start the light the moment the sun sets, and put it out the moment it rises."

Anne sat up in dismay. Through her window she saw the light blinking palely against the blue skies of dawn.

"Perhaps he has fallen asleep over his life-book," she said anxiously, "or become so absorbed in it that he has forgotten the light."

Gilbert shook his head.

"That wouldn't be like Captain Jim. Anyway, I'm going down to see."

"Wait a minute and I'll go with you," exclaimed Anne. "Oh, yes, I must—Little Jem will sleep for an hour yet, and I'll call Susan. You may need a woman's help if Captain Jim is ill."

It was an exquisite morning, full of tints and sounds at once ripe and delicate. The harbor was sparkling and dimpling like a girl; white gulls were soaring over the dunes; beyond the bar was a shining, wonderful sea. The long fields by the shore were dewy and fresh in that first fine, purely-tinted light. The wind came dancing and whistling up the channel to replace the beautiful silence with a music more beautiful still. Had it not been for the baleful star on the white tower that early walk would have been a delight to Anne and Gilbert. But they went softly with fear.

Their knock was not responded to. Gilbert opened the door and they went in.

The old room was very quiet. On the table were the remnants of the little evening feast. The lamp still burned on the corner stand. The First Mate was asleep in a square of sunshine by the sofa.

CHAPTER 39 - CAPTAIN JIM CROSSES THE BAR

Captain Jim lay on the sofa, with his hands clasped over the life-book, open at the last page, lying on his breast. His eyes were closed and on his face was a look of the most perfect peace and happiness—the look of one who has long sought and found at last.

"He is asleep?" whispered Anne tremulously.

Gilbert went to the sofa and bent over him for a few moments. Then he straightened up.

"Yes, he sleeps—well," he added quietly. "Anne, Captain Jim has crossed the bar."

They could not know precisely at what hour he had died, but Anne always believed that he had had his wish, and went out when the morning came across the gulf. Out on that shining tide his spirit drifted, over the sunrise sea of pearl and silver, to the haven where lost Margaret waited, beyond the storms and calms.

CHAPTER 40 - FAREWELL TO THE HOUSE OF DREAMS

Captain Jim was buried in the little over-harbor graveyard, very near to the spot where the wee white lady slept. His relatives put up a very expensive, very ugly "monument"—a monument at which he would have poked sly fun had he seen it in life. But his real monument was in the hearts of those who knew him, and in the book that was to live for generations.

Leslie mourned that Captain Jim had not lived to see the amazing success of it.

"How he would have delighted in the reviews—they are almost all so kindly. And to have seen his life-book heading the lists of the best sellers—oh, if he could just have lived to see it, Anne!"

But Anne, despite her grief, was wiser.

"It was the book itself he cared for, Leslie—not what might be said of it—and he had it. He had read it all through. That last night must have been one of the greatest happiness for him—with the quick, painless ending he had hoped for in the morning. I am glad for Owen's sake and yours that the book is such a success—but Captain Jim was satisfied—I KNOW."

The lighthouse star still kept a nightly vigil; a substitute keeper had been sent to the Point, until such time as an all-wise government could decide which of many applicants was best fitted for the place—or had the strongest pull. The First Mate was at home in the little house, beloved by Anne and Gilbert and Leslie, and tolerated by a Susan who had small liking for cats.

"I can put up with him for the sake of Captain Jim, Mrs. Doctor, dear, for I liked the old man. And I will see that he gets bite and sup, and every mouse the traps account for. But do not ask me to do more than that, Mrs. Doctor, dear. Cats is cats, and take my word for it, they will never be anything else. And at least, Mrs. Doctor, dear, do keep him away from the blessed wee man. Picture to yourself how awful it would be if he was to suck the darling's breath."

"That might be fitly called a CAT-astrophe," said Gilbert.

"Oh, you may laugh, doctor, dear, but it would be no laughing matter."

"Cats never suck babies' breaths," said Gilbert. "That is only an old superstition, Susan."

"Oh, well, it may be a superstition or it may not, doctor, dear. All that I know is, it has happened. My sister's husband's nephew's wife's cat sucked their baby's breath, and the poor innocent was all but gone when they found it. And superstition or not, if I find that yellow beast lurking near our baby I will whack him with the poker, Mrs. Doctor, dear."

Mr. and Mrs. Marshall Elliott were living comfortably and harmoniously in the green house. Leslie was busy with sewing, for she and Owen were to be married at Christmas. Anne wondered what she would do when Leslie was gone.

"Changes come all the time. Just as soon as things get really nice they change," she said with a sigh.

"The old Morgan place up at the Glen is for sale," said Gilbert, apropos of nothing in especial.

"Is it?" asked Anne indifferently.

"Yes. Now that Mr. Morgan has gone, Mrs. Morgan wants to go to live with her children in Vancouver. She will sell cheaply, for a big place like that in a small village like the Glen will not be very easy to dispose of."

"Well, it's certainly a beautiful place, so it is likely she will find a purchaser," said Anne, absently, wondering whether she should hemstitch or feather-stitch little Jem's "short" dresses. He was to be shortened the next week, and Anne felt ready to cry at the thought of it.

"Suppose we buy it, Anne?" remarked Gilbert quietly.

Anne dropped her sewing and stared at him.

"You're not in earnest, Gilbert?"

"Indeed I am, dear."

"And leave this darling spot—our house of dreams?" said Anne incredulously. "Oh, Gilbert, it's—it's unthinkable!"

"Listen patiently to me, dear. I know just how you feel about it. I feel the same. But we've always known we would have to move some day."

"Oh, but not so soon, Gilbert—not just yet."

"We may never get such a chance again. If we don't buy the Morgan place someone else will—and there is no other house in the Glen we would care to have, and no other really good site on which to build. This little house is—well, it is and has been what no other house can ever be to us, I admit, but you know it is out-of-the-way down here for a doctor. We have felt the inconvenience, though we've made the best of it. And it's a tight fit for us now. Perhaps, in a few years, when Jem wants a room of his own, it will be entirely too small."

"Oh, I know—I know," said Anne, tears filling her eyes. "I know all that can be said against it, but I love it so—and it's so beautiful here."

"You would find it very lonely here after Leslie goes—and Captain Jim has gone too. The Morgan place is beautiful, and in time we would love it. You know you have always admired it, Anne."

"Oh, yes, but—but—this has all seemed to come up so suddenly, Gilbert. I'm dizzy. Ten minutes ago I had no thought of leaving this dear spot. I was planning what I meant to do for it in the spring—what I meant to do in the garden. And if we leave this place who will get it? It IS out-of-the-way, so it's likely some poor, shiftless, wandering family will rent it—and over-run it—and oh, that would be desecration. It would hurt me horribly."

"I know. But we cannot sacrifice our own interests to such considerations, Anne-girl. The Morgan place will suit us in every essential particular—we really can't afford to miss such a chance. Think of that big lawn with those magnificent old trees; and of that splendid hardwood grove behind it—twelve acres of it. What a play place for our children! There's a fine orchard, too, and you've always admired that high brick wall around the garden with the door in it—you've thought it was so like a story-book garden. And there is almost as fine a view of the harbor and the dunes from the Morgan place as from here."

"You can't see the lighthouse star from it."

"Yes, You can see it from the attic window. THERE'S another advantage, Anne-girl—you love big garrets."

"There's no brook in the garden."

"Well, no, but there is one running through the maple grove into the Glen pond. And the pond itself isn't far away. You'll be able to fancy you have your own Lake of Shining Waters again."

"Well, don't say anything more about it just now, Gilbert. Give me time to think—to get used to the idea."

"All right. There is no great hurry, of course. Only—if we decide to buy, it would be well to be moved in and settled before winter."

Gilbert went out, and Anne put away Little Jem's short dresses with trembling hands. She could not sew any more that day. With tear-wet eyes she wandered over the little domain where she had reigned so happy a queen. The Morgan place was all that Gilbert claimed. The grounds were beautiful, the house old enough to have dignity and repose and traditions, and new enough to be comfortable and up-to-date. Anne had always admired it; but admiring is not loving; and she loved this house of dreams so much. She loved EVERYTHING about it—the garden she had tended, and which so many women had tended before her—the gleam and sparkle of the little brook that crept so roguishly across the corner—the gate between the creaking fir trees—the old red sandstone step—the stately Lombardies—the two tiny quaint glass cupboards over the chimney-piece in the living-room—the crooked pantry door in the kitchen—the two funny dormer windows upstairs—the little jog in the staircase—why, these things were a part of her! How could she leave them?

And how this little house, consecrated aforetime by love and joy, had been re-consecrated for her by her happiness and sorrow! Here she had spent her bridal moon; here wee Joyce had lived her one brief day; here the sweetness of motherhood had come again with Little Jem; here she had heard the exquisite music of her baby's cooing laughter; here beloved friends had sat by her fireside. Joy and grief, birth and death, had made sacred forever this little house of dreams.

And now she must leave it. She knew that, even while she had contended against the idea to Gilbert. The little house was outgrown. Gilbert's interests made the change necessary; his work, successful though it had been, was hampered by his location. Anne realised that the end of their life in this dear place drew nigh, and that she must face the fact bravely. But how her heart ached!

"It will be just like tearing something out of my life," she sobbed. "And oh, if I could hope that some nice folk would come here in our place—or even that it would be left vacant. That itself would be better than having it overrun with some horde who know nothing of the geography of dreamland, and nothing of the history that has given this house its soul and its identity. And if such a tribe come here the place will go to rack and ruin in no time—an old place goes down so quickly if it is not carefully attended to. They'll tear up my garden—and let the Lombardies get ragged—and the paling will come to look like a mouth with half the teeth missing—and the roof will leak—and the plaster fall—and they'll stuff pillows and rags in broken window panes—and everything will be out-at-elbows."

Anne's imagination pictured forth so vividly the coming degeneration of her dear little house that it hurt her as severely as if it had already been an accomplished fact. She sat down on the stairs and had a long, bitter cry. Susan found her there and enquired with much concern what the trouble was.

"You have not quarrelled with the doctor, have you now, Mrs. Doctor, dear? But if you have, do not worry. It is a thing quite likely to happen to married couples, I am told, although I have had no experience that way myself. He will be sorry, and you can soon make it up."

"No, no, Susan, we haven't quarrelled. It's only—Gilbert is going to buy the Morgan place, and we'll have to go and live at the Glen. And it will break my heart."

Susan did not enter into Anne's feelings at all. She was, indeed, quite rejoiced over the prospect of living at the Glen. Her one grievance against her place in the little house was its lonesome location.

"Why, Mrs. Doctor, dear, it will be splendid. The Morgan house is such a fine, big one."

"I hate big houses," sobbed Anne.

"Oh, well, you will not hate them by the time you have half a dozen children," remarked Susan calmly. "And this house is too small already for us. We have no spare room, since Mrs. Moore is here, and that pantry is the most aggravating place I ever tried to work in. There is a corner every way you turn. Besides, it is out-of-the-world down here. There is really nothing at all but scenery."

"Out of your world perhaps, Susan—but not out of mine," said Anne with a faint smile.

"I do not quite understand you, Mrs. Doctor, dear, but of course I am not well educated. But if Dr. Blythe buys the Morgan place he will make no mistake, and that you may tie to. They have water in it, and the pantries and closets are beautiful, and there is not another such cellar in P. E. Island, so I have been told. Why, the cellar here, Mrs. Doctor, dear, has been a heart-break to me, as well you know."

"Oh, go away, Susan, go away," said Anne forlornly. "Cellars and pantries and closets don't make a HOME. Why don't you weep with those who weep?"

"Well, I never was much hand for weeping, Mrs. Doctor, dear. I would rather fall to and cheer people up than weep with them. Now, do not you cry and spoil your pretty eyes. This house is very well and has served your turn, but it is high time you had a better."

Susan's point of view seemed to be that of most people. Leslie was the only one who sympathised understandingly with Anne. She had a good cry, too, when she heard the news. Then they both dried their tears and went to work at the preparations for moving.

"Since we must go let us go as soon as we can and have it over," said poor Anne with bitter resignation.

"You know you will like that lovely old place at the Glen after you have lived in it long enough to have dear memories woven about it," said Leslie. "Friends will come there, as they have come here—happiness will glorify it for you. Now, it's just a house to you—but the years will make it a home."

Anne and Leslie had another cry the next week when they shortened Little Jem. Anne felt the tragedy of it until evening when in his long nightie she found her own dear baby again.

"But it will be rompers next—and then trousers—and in no time he will be grown-up," she sighed.

"Well, you would not want him to stay a baby always, Mrs. Doctor, dear, would you?" said Susan. "Bless his innocent heart, he looks too sweet for anything in his little short dresses, with his dear feet sticking out. And think of the save in the ironing, Mrs. Doctor, dear."

"Anne, I have just had a letter from Owen," said Leslie, entering with a bright face. "And, oh! I have such good news. He writes me that he is going to buy this place from the church trustees and keep it to spend our summer vacations in. Anne, are you not glad?"

"Oh, Leslie, 'glad' isn't the word for it! It seems almost too good to be true. I sha'n't feel half so badly now that I know this dear spot will never be desecrated by a vandal tribe, or left to tumble down in decay. Why, it's lovely! It's lovely!"

One October morning Anne wakened to the realisation that she had slept for the last time under the roof of her little house. The day was too busy to indulge regret and when evening came the house was stripped and bare. Anne and Gilbert were alone in it to say farewell. Leslie and Susan and Little Jem had gone to the Glen with the last load of furniture. The sunset light streamed in through the curtainless windows.

"It has all such a heart-broken, reproachful look, hasn't it?" said Anne. "Oh, I shall be so homesick at the Glen tonight!"

"We have been very happy here, haven't we, Anne-girl?" said Gilbert, his voice full of feeling.

Anne choked, unable to answer. Gilbert waited for her at the fir-tree gate, while she went over the house and said farewell to every room. She was going away; but the old house would still be there, looking seaward through its quaint windows. The autumn winds would blow around it mournfully, and the gray rain would beat upon it and the white mists would come in from the sea to enfold it; and the moonlight would fall over it and light up the old paths where the school-master and his bride had walked. There on that old harbor shore the charm of story would linger; the wind would still whistle alluringly over the silver sand-dunes; the waves would still call from the red rock-coves.

"But we will be gone," said Anne through her tears.

She went out, closing and locking the door behind her. Gilbert was waiting for her with a smile. The lighthouse star was gleaming northward. The little garden, where only marigolds still bloomed, was already hooding itself in shadows.

Anne knelt down and kissed the worn old step which she had crossed as a bride.

"Good-bye, dear little house of dreams," she said.

RAINBOW VALLEY

"The thoughts of youth are long, long thoughts."
—LONGFELLOW

TO THE MEMORY OF
GOLDWIN LAPP, ROBERT BROOKES
AND MORLEY SHIER
WHO MADE THE SUPREME
SACRIFICE THAT THE HAPPY
VALLEYS OF THEIR HOME LAND
MIGHT BE KEPT SACRED FROM THE
RAVAGE OF THE INVADER

CHAPTER I. HOME AGAIN

It was a clear, apple-green evening in May, and Four Winds Harbour was mirroring back the clouds of the golden west between its softly dark shores. The sea moaned eerily on the sand-bar, sorrowful even in spring, but a sly, jovial wind came piping down the red harbour road along which Miss Cornelia's comfortable, matronly figure was making its way towards the village of Glen St. Mary. Miss Cornelia was rightfully Mrs. Marshall Elliott, and had been Mrs. Marshall Elliott for thirteen years, but even yet more people referred to her as Miss Cornelia than as Mrs. Elliott. The old name was dear to her old friends, only one of them contemptuously dropped it. Susan Baker, the gray and grim and faithful handmaiden of the Blythe family at Ingleside, never lost an opportunity of calling her "Mrs. Marshall Elliott," with the most killing and pointed emphasis, as if to say "You wanted to be Mrs. and Mrs. you shall be with a vengeance as far as I am concerned."

Miss Cornelia was going up to Ingleside to see Dr. and Mrs. Blythe, who were just home from Europe. They had been away for three months, having left in February to attend a famous medical congress in London; and certain things, which Miss Cornelia was anxious to discuss, had taken place in the Glen during their absence. For one thing, there was a new family in the manse. And such a family! Miss Cornelia shook her head over them several times as she walked briskly along.

Susan Baker and the Anne Shirley of other days saw her coming, as they sat on the big veranda at Ingleside, enjoying the charm of the cat's light, the sweetness of sleepy robins whistling among the twilit maples, and the dance of a gusty group of daffodils blowing against the old, mellow, red brick wall of the lawn.

Anne was sitting on the steps, her hands clasped over her knee, looking, in the kind dusk, as girlish as a mother of many has any right to be; and the beautiful gray-green eyes, gazing down the harbour road, were as full of unquenchable sparkle and dream as ever. Behind her, in the hammock, Rilla Blythe was curled up, a fat, roly-poly little creature of six years, the youngest of the Ingleside children. She had curly red hair and hazel eyes that were now buttoned up after the funny, wrinkled fashion in which Rilla always went to sleep.

Shirley, "the little brown boy," as he was known in the family "Who's Who," was asleep in Susan's arms. He was brown-haired, brown-eyed and brown-skinned, with very rosy cheeks, and he was Susan's especial love. After his birth Anne had been very ill for a long time, and Susan "mothered" the baby with a passionate tenderness which none of the other children, dear as they were to her, had ever called out. Dr. Blythe had said that but for her he would never have lived.

"I gave him life just as much as you did, Mrs. Dr. dear," Susan was wont to say. "He is just as much my baby as he is yours." And, indeed, it was always to Susan that Shirley ran, to be kissed for bumps, and rocked to sleep, and protected from well-deserved spankings. Susan had conscientiously spanked all the other Blythe children when she thought they needed it for their souls' good, but she would not spank Shirley nor allow his mother to do it. Once, Dr. Blythe had spanked him and Susan had been stormily indignant.

"That man would spank an angel, Mrs. Dr. dear, that he would," she had declared bitterly; and she would not make the poor doctor a pie for weeks.

She had taken Shirley with her to her brother's home during his parents' absence, while all the other children had gone to Avonlea, and she had three blessed months of him all to herself. Nevertheless, Susan was very glad to find herself back at Ingleside, with all her darlings around her again. Ingleside was her world and in it she reigned supreme. Even Anne seldom questioned her decisions, much to the disgust of Mrs. Rachel Lynde of Green Gables, who gloomily told Anne, whenever she visited Four Winds, that she was letting Susan get to be entirely too much of a boss and would live to rue it.

"Here is Cornelia Bryant coming up the harbour road, Mrs. Dr. dear," said Susan. "She will be coming up to unload three months' gossip on us."

"I hope so," said Anne, hugging her knees. "I'm starving for Glen St. Mary gossip, Susan. I hope Miss Cornelia can tell me everything that has happened while we've been away—EVERYTHING— who has got born, or married, or drunk; who has died, or gone away, or come, or fought, or lost a cow, or found a beau. It's so delightful to be home again with all the dear Glen folks, and I want to know all about them. Why, I remember wondering, as I walked through Westminster Abbey which of her two especial beaux Millicent Drew would finally marry. Do you know, Susan, I have a dreadful suspicion that I love gossip."

"Well, of course, Mrs. Dr. dear," admitted Susan, "every proper woman likes to hear the news. I am rather interested in Millicent Drew's case myself. I never had a beau, much less two, and I do not mind now, for being an old maid does not hurt when you get used to it. Millicent's hair always looks to me as if she had swept it up with a broom. But the men do not seem to mind that."

"They see only her pretty, piquant, mocking, little face, Susan."

"That may very well be, Mrs. Dr. dear. The Good Book says that favour is deceitful and beauty is vain, but I should not have minded finding that out for myself, if it had been so ordained. I have no doubt we will all be beautiful when we are angels, but what good will it do us then? Speaking of gossip, however, they do say that poor Mrs. Harrison Miller over harbour tried to hang herself last week."

CHAPTER I. HOME AGAIN

"Oh, Susan!"

"Calm yourself, Mrs. Dr. dear. She did not succeed. But I really do not blame her for trying, for her husband is a terrible man. But she was very foolish to think of hanging herself and leaving the way clear for him to marry some other woman. If I had been in her shoes, Mrs. Dr. dear, I would have gone to work to worry him so that he would try to hang himself instead of me. Not that I hold with people hanging themselves under any circumstances, Mrs. Dr. dear."

"What is the matter with Harrison Miller, anyway?" said Anne impatiently. "He is always driving some one to extremes."

"Well, some people call it religion and some call it cussedness, begging your pardon, Mrs. Dr. dear, for using such a word. It seems they cannot make out which it is in Harrison's case. There are days when he growls at everybody because he thinks he is fore-ordained to eternal punishment. And then there are days when he says he does not care and goes and gets drunk. My own opinion is that he is not sound in his intellect, for none of that branch of the Millers were. His grandfather went out of his mind. He thought he was surrounded by big black spiders. They crawled over him and floated in the air about him. I hope I shall never go insane, Mrs. Dr. dear, and I do not think I will, because it is not a habit of the Bakers. But, if an all-wise Providence should decree it, I hope it will not take the form of big black spiders, for I loathe the animals. As for Mrs. Miller, I do not know whether she really deserves pity or not. There are some who say she just married Harrison to spite Richard Taylor, which seems to me a very peculiar reason for getting married. But then, of course, *I* am no judge of things matrimonial, Mrs. Dr. dear. And there is Cornelia Bryant at the gate, so I will put this blessed brown baby on his bed and get my knitting."

CHAPTER II. SHEER GOSSIP

"Where are the other children?" asked Miss Cornelia, when the first greetings—cordial on her side, rapturous on Anne's, and dignified on Susan's—were over.

"Shirley is in bed and Jem and Walter and the twins are down in their beloved Rainbow Valley," said Anne. "They just came home this afternoon, you know, and they could hardly wait until supper was over before rushing down to the valley. They love it above every spot on earth. Even the maple grove doesn't rival it in their affections."

"I am afraid they love it too well," said Susan gloomily. "Little Jem said once he would rather go to Rainbow Valley than to heaven when he died, and that was not a proper remark."

"I suppose they had a great time in Avonlea?" said Miss Cornelia.

"Enormous. Marilla does spoil them terribly. Jem, in particular, can do no wrong in her eyes."

"Miss Cuthbert must be an old lady now," said Miss Cornelia, getting out her knitting, so that she could hold her own with Susan. Miss Cornelia held that the woman whose hands were employed always had the advantage over the woman whose hands were not.

"Marilla is eighty-five," said Anne with a sigh. "Her hair is snow-white. But, strange to say, her eyesight is better than it was when she was sixty."

"Well, dearie, I'm real glad you're all back. I've been dreadful lonesome. But we haven't been dull in the Glen, believe ME. There hasn't been such an exciting spring in my time, as far as church matters go. We've got settled with a minister at last, Anne dearie."

"The Reverend John Knox Meredith, Mrs. Dr. dear," said Susan, resolved not to let Miss Cornelia tell all the news.

"Is he nice?" asked Anne interestedly.

Miss Cornelia sighed and Susan groaned.

"Yes, he's nice enough if that were all," said the former. "He is VERY nice—and very learned—and very spiritual. But, oh Anne dearie, he has no common sense!

"How was it you called him, then?"

"Well, there's no doubt he is by far the best preacher we ever had in Glen St. Mary church," said Miss Cornelia, veering a tack or two. "I suppose it is because he is so moony and absent-minded that he never got a town call. His trial sermon was simply wonderful, believe ME. Every one went mad about it— and his looks."

"He is VERY comely, Mrs. Dr. dear, and when all is said and done,

I DO like to see a well-looking man in the pulpit," broke in

Susan, thinking it was time she asserted herself again.

"Besides," said Miss Cornelia, "we were anxious to get settled. And Mr. Meredith was the first candidate we were all agreed on. Somebody had some objection to all the others. There was some talk of calling Mr. Folsom. He was a good preacher, too, but somehow people didn't care for his appearance. He was too dark and sleek."

"He looked exactly like a great black tomcat, that he did, Mrs. Dr. dear," said Susan. "I never could abide such a man in the pulpit every Sunday."

"Then Mr. Rogers came and he was like a chip in porridge—neither harm nor good," resumed Miss Cornelia. "But if he had preached like Peter and Paul it would have profited him nothing, for that was the day old Caleb Ramsay's sheep strayed into church and gave a loud 'ba-a-a' just as he announced his text. Everybody laughed, and poor Rogers had no chance after that. Some thought we ought to call Mr. Stewart, because he was so well educated. He could read the New Testament in five languages."

"But I do not think he was any surer than other men of getting to heaven because of that," interjected Susan.

"Most of us didn't like his delivery," said Miss Cornelia, ignoring Susan. "He talked in grunts, so to speak. And Mr. Arnett couldn't preach AT ALL. And he picked about the worst candidating text there is in the Bible—'Curse ye Meroz.'"

"Whenever he got stuck for an idea, he would bang the Bible and shout very bitterly, 'Curse ye Meroz.' Poor Meroz got thoroughly cursed that day, whoever he was, Mrs. Dr. dear," said Susan.

"The minister who is candidating can't be too careful what text he chooses," said Miss Cornelia solemnly. "I believe Mr. Pierson would have got the call if he had picked a different text. But when he announced 'I will lift my eyes to the hills' HE was done for. Every one grinned, for every one knew that those two Hill girls from the Harbour Head have been setting their caps for every single minister who came to the Glen for the last fifteen years. And Mr. Newman had too large a family."

"He stayed with my brother-in-law, James Clow," said Susan. "'How many children have you got?' I asked him. 'Nine boys and a sister for each of them,' he said. 'Eighteen!' said I. 'Dear me, what a family!' And then he laughed and laughed. But I do not know why, Mrs. Dr. dear, and I am certain that eighteen children would be too many for any manse."

"He had only ten children, Susan," explained Miss Cornelia, with contemptuous patience. "And ten good children would not be much worse for the manse and congregation than the four who are there now. Though I wouldn't say, Anne dearie, that they are so bad, either. I like them—everybody likes them. It's impossible to help liking them. They would be real nice little souls if there was anyone to look after their manners and teach them what is right and proper. For instance, at school the teacher says they are model children. But at home they simply run wild."

"What about Mrs. Meredith?" asked Anne.

"There's NO Mrs. Meredith. That is just the trouble. Mr. Meredith is a widower. His wife died four years ago. If we had known that I don't suppose we would have called him, for a widower is even worse in a congregation than a single man. But he was heard to speak of his children and we all supposed there was a mother, too. And when they came there was nobody but old Aunt Martha, as they call her. She's a cousin of Mr. Meredith's mother, I believe, and he took her in to save her from the poorhouse. She is seventy-five years old, half blind, and very deaf and very cranky."

"And a very poor cook, Mrs. Dr. dear."

"The worst possible manager for a manse," said Miss Cornelia bitterly. "Mr. Meredith won't get any other housekeeper because he says it would hurt Aunt Martha's feelings. Anne dearie, believe me, the state of that manse is something terrible. Everything is thick with dust and nothing is ever in its place. And we had painted and papered it all so nice before they came."

"There are four children, you say?" asked Anne, beginning to mother them already in her heart.

"Yes. They run up just like the steps of a stair. Gerald's the oldest. He's twelve and they call him Jerry. He's a clever boy. Faith is eleven. She is a regular tomboy but pretty as a picture, I must say."

"She looks like an angel but she is a holy terror for mischief, Mrs. Dr. dear," said Susan solemnly. "I was at the manse one night last week and Mrs. James Millison was there, too. She had brought them up a dozen eggs and a little pail of milk—a VERY little pail, Mrs. Dr. dear. Faith took them and whisked down the cellar with them. Near the bottom of the stairs she caught her toe and fell the rest of the way, milk and eggs and all. You can imagine the result, Mrs. Dr. dear. But that child came up laughing. 'I don't know whether I'm myself or a custard pie,' she said. And Mrs. James Millison was very angry. She said she would never take another thing to the manse if it was to be wasted and destroyed in that fashion."

"Maria Millison never hurt herself taking things to the manse," sniffed Miss Cornelia. "She just took them that night as an excuse for curiosity. But poor Faith is always getting into scrapes. She is so heedless and impulsive."

"Just like me. I'm going to like your Faith," said Anne decidedly.

"She is full of spunk—and I do like spunk, Mrs. Dr. dear," admitted Susan.

"There's something taking about her," conceded Miss Cornelia. "You never see her but she's laughing, and somehow it always makes you want to laugh too. She can't even keep a straight face in church. Una is ten—she's a sweet little thing—

not pretty, but sweet. And Thomas Carlyle is nine. They call him Carl, and he has a regular mania for collecting toads and bugs and frogs and bringing them into the house."

"I suppose he was responsible for the dead rat that was lying on a chair in the parlour the afternoon Mrs. Grant called. It gave her a turn," said Susan, "and I do not wonder, for manse parlours are no places for dead rats. To be sure it may have been the cat who left it, there. HE is as full of the old Nick as he can be stuffed, Mrs. Dr. dear. A manse cat should at least LOOK respectable, in my opinion, whatever he really is. But I never saw such a rakish-looking beast. And he walks along the ridgepole of the manse almost every evening at sunset, Mrs. Dr. dear, and waves his tail, and that is not becoming."

"The worst of it is, they are NEVER decently dressed," sighed Miss Cornelia. "And since the snow went they go to school barefooted. Now, you know Anne dearie, that isn't the right thing for manse children—especially when the Methodist minister's little girl always wears such nice buttoned boots. And I DO wish they wouldn't play in the old Methodist graveyard."

"It's very tempting, when it's right beside the manse," said Anne. "I've always thought graveyards must be delightful places to play in."

"Oh, no, you did not, Mrs. Dr. dear," said loyal Susan, determined to protect Anne from herself. "You have too much good sense and decorum."

"Why did they ever build that manse beside the graveyard in the first place?" asked Anne. "Their lawn is so small there is no place for them to play except in the graveyard."

"It WAS a mistake," admitted Miss Cornelia. "But they got the lot cheap. And no other manse children ever thought of playing there. Mr. Meredith shouldn't allow it. But he has always got his nose buried in a book, when he is home. He reads and reads, or walks about in his study in a day-dream. So far he hasn't forgotten to be in church on Sundays, but twice he has forgotten about the prayer-meeting and one of the elders had to go over to the manse and remind him. And he forgot about Fanny Cooper's wedding. They rang him up on the 'phone and then he rushed right over, just as he was, carpet slippers and all. One wouldn't mind if the Methodists didn't laugh so about it. But there's one comfort—they can't criticize his sermons. He wakes up when he's in the pulpit, believe ME. And the Methodist minister can't preach at all—so they tell me. *I* have never heard him, thank goodness."

Miss Cornelia's scorn of men had abated somewhat since her marriage, but her scorn of Methodists remained untinged of charity. Susan smiled slyly.

"They do say, Mrs. Marshall Elliott, that the Methodists and Presbyterians are talking of uniting," she said.

"Well, all I hope is that I'll be under the sod if that ever comes to pass," retorted Miss Cornelia. "I shall never have truck or trade with Methodists, and Mr. Meredith will find that he'd better steer clear of them, too. He is entirely too sociable with them, believe ME. Why, he went to the Jacob Drews' silver-wedding supper and got into a nice scrape as a result."

"What was it?"

"Mrs. Drew asked him to carve the roast goose—for Jacob Drew never did or could carve. Well, Mr. Meredith tackled it, and in the process he knocked it clean off the platter into Mrs. Reese's lap, who was sitting next him. And he just said dreamily. 'Mrs. Reese, will you kindly return me that goose?' Mrs. Reese 're-turned' it, as meek as Moses, but she must have been furious, for she had on her new silk dress. The worst of it is, she was a Methodist."

"But I think that is better than if she was a Presbyterian," interjected Susan. "If she had been a Presbyterian she would mostly likely have left the church and we cannot afford to lose our members. And Mrs. Reese is not liked in her own church, because she gives herself such great airs, so that the Methodists would be rather pleased that Mr. Meredith spoiled her dress."

"The point is, he made himself ridiculous, and *I*, for one, do not like to see my minister made ridiculous in the eyes of the Methodists," said Miss Cornelia stiffly. "If he had had a wife it would not have happened."

"I do not see if he had a dozen wives how they could have prevented Mrs. Drew from using up her tough old gander for the wedding-feast," said Susan stubbornly.

"They say that was her husband's doing," said Miss Cornelia.

"Jacob Drew is a conceited, stingy, domineering creature."

"And they do say he and his wife detest each other—which does not seem to me the proper way for married folks to get along. But then, of course, I have had no experience along that line," said Susan, tossing her head. "And *I* am not one to blame everything on the men. Mrs. Drew is mean enough herself. They say that the only thing she was ever known to give away was a crock of butter made out of cream a rat had fell into. She contributed it to a church social. Nobody found out about the rat until afterwards."

"Fortunately, all the people the Merediths have offended so far are Methodists," said Miss Cornelia. "That Jerry went to the Methodist prayer-meeting one night about a fortnight ago and sat beside old William Marsh who got up as usual and testified with fearful groans. 'Do you feel any better now?" whispered Jerry when William sat down. Poor Jerry meant to be sympathetic, but Mr. Marsh thought he was impertinent and is furious at him. Of course, Jerry had no business to be in a Methodist prayer-meeting at all. But they go where they like."

"I hope they will not offend Mrs. Alec Davis of the Harbour Head," said Susan. "She is a very touchy woman, I understand, but she is very well off and pays the most of any one to the salary. I have heard that she says the Merediths are the worst brought up children she ever saw."

"Every word you say convinces me more and more that the Merediths belong to the race that knows Joseph," said Mistress Anne decidedly.

"When all is said and done, they DO," admitted Miss Cornelia. "And that balances everything. Anyway, we've got them now and we must just do the best we can by them and stick up for them to the Methodists. Well, I suppose I must be getting down harbour. Marshall will soon be home—he went over-harbour today—and wanting his super, man-like. I'm sorry I haven't seen the other children. And where's the doctor?"

"Up at the Harbour Head. We've only been home three days and in that time he has spent three hours in his own bed and eaten two meals in his own house."

"Well, everybody who has been sick for the last six weeks has been waiting for him to come home—and I don't blame them. When that over-harbour doctor married the undertaker's daughter at Lowbridge people felt suspicious of him. It didn't look well. You and the doctor must come down soon and tell us all about your trip. I suppose you've had a splendid time."

"We had," agreed Anne. "It was the fulfilment of years of dreams. The old world is very lovely and very wonderful. But we have come back very well satisfied with our own land. Canada is the finest country in the world, Miss Cornelia."

"Nobody ever doubted that," said Miss Cornelia, complacently.

"And old P.E.I. is the loveliest province in it and Four Winds the loveliest spot in P.E.I.," laughed Anne, looking adoringly out over the sunset splendour of glen and harbour and gulf. She waved her hand at it. "I saw nothing more beautiful than that in Europe, Miss Cornelia. Must you go? The children will be sorry to have missed you."

"They must come and see me soon. Tell them the doughnut jar is always full."

"Oh, at supper they were planning a descent on you. They'll go soon; but they must settle down to school again now. And the twins are going to take music lessons."

"Not from the Methodist minister's wife, I hope?" said Miss
Cornelia anxiously.

"No—from Rosemary West. I was up last evening to arrange it with her. What a pretty girl she is!"

"Rosemary holds her own well. She isn't as young as she once was."

"I thought her very charming. I've never had any real acquaintance with her, you know. Their house is so out of the way, and I've seldom ever seen her except at church."

"People always have liked Rosemary West, though they don't understand her," said Miss Cornelia, quite unconscious of the high tribute she was paying to Rosemary's charm. "Ellen has always kept her down, so to speak. She has tyrannized over her, and yet she has always indulged her in a good many ways. Rosemary was engaged once, you know—to young Martin Crawford. His ship was wrecked on the Magdalens and all the crew were drowned. Rosemary was just a child—only seventeen. But she was never the same afterwards. She and Ellen have stayed very close at home since their mother's death. They don't often get to their own church at Lowbridge and I understand Ellen doesn't approve of going too often to a Presbyterian church. To the Methodist she NEVER goes, I'll say that much for her. That family of Wests have always been strong Episcopalians. Rosemary and Ellen are pretty well off. Rosemary doesn't really need to give music lessons. She does it because she likes to. They are distantly related to Leslie, you know. Are the Fords coming to the harbour this summer?"

"No. They are going on a trip to Japan and will probably be away for a year. Owen's new novel is to have a Japanese setting. This will be the first summer that the dear old House of Dreams will be empty since we left it."

"I should think Owen Ford might find enough to write about in Canada without dragging his wife and his innocent children off to a heathen country like Japan," grumbled Miss Cornelia. "*The Life Book* was the best book he's ever written and he got the material for that right here in Four Winds."

"Captain Jim gave him the most of that, you know. And he collected it all over the world. But Owen's books are all delightful, I think."

"Oh, they're well enough as far as they go. I make it a point to read every one he writes, though I've always held, Anne dearie, that reading novels is a sinful waste of time. I shall write and tell him my opinion of this Japanese business, believe ME. Does he want Kenneth and Persis to be converted into pagans?"

With which unanswerable conundrum Miss Cornelia took her departure. Susan proceeded to put Rilla in bed and Anne sat on the veranda steps under the early stars and dreamed her incorrigible dreams and learned all over again for the hundredth happy time what a moonrise splendour and sheen could be on Four Winds Harbour.

CHAPTER III. THE INGLESIDE CHILDREN

In daytime the Blythe children liked very well to play in the rich, soft greens and glooms of the big maple grove between Ingleside and the Glen St. Mary pond; but for evening revels there was no place like the little valley behind the maple grove. It was a fairy realm of romance to them. Once, looking from the attic windows of Ingleside, through the mist and aftermath of a summer thunderstorm, they had seen the beloved spot arched by a glorious rainbow, one end of which seemed to dip straight down to where a corner of the pond ran up into the lower end of the valley.

"Let us call it Rainbow Valley," said Walter delightedly, and
Rainbow Valley thenceforth it was.

Outside of Rainbow Valley the wind might be rollicking and boisterous. Here it always went gently. Little, winding, fairy paths ran here and there over spruce roots cushioned with moss. Wild cherry trees, that in blossom time would be misty white, were scattered all over the valley, mingling with the dark spruces. A little brook with amber waters ran through it from the Glen village. The houses of the village were comfortably far away; only at the upper end of the valley was a little tumble-down, deserted cottage, referred to as "the old Bailey house." It had not been occupied for many years, but a grass-grown dyke surrounded it and inside was an ancient garden where the Ingleside children could find violets and daisies and June lilies still blooming in season. For the rest, the garden was overgrown with caraway that swayed and foamed in the moonshine of summer eves like seas of silver.

To the sought lay the pond and beyond it the ripened distance lost itself in purple woods, save where, on a high hill, a solitary old gray homestead looked down on glen and harbour. There was a certain wild woodsiness and solitude about Rainbow Valley, in spite of its nearness to the village, which endeared it to the children of Ingleside.

The valley was full of dear, friendly hollows and the largest of these was their favourite stamping ground. Here they were assembled on this particular evening. There was a grove of young spruces in this hollow, with a tiny, grassy glade in its heart, opening on the bank of the brook. By the brook grew a silver birch-tree, a young, incredibly straight thing which Walter had named the "White Lady." In this glade, too, were the "Tree Lovers," as Walter called a spruce and maple which grew so closely together that their boughs were inextricably intertwined. Jem had hung an old string of sleigh-bells, given him by the Glen blacksmith, on the Tree Lovers, and every visitant breeze called out sudden fairy tinkles from it.

"How nice it is to be back!" said Nan. "After all, none of the Avonlea places are quite as nice as Rainbow Valley."

But they were very fond of the Avonlea places for all that. A visit to Green Gables was always considered a great treat. Aunt Marilla was very good to them, and so was Mrs. Rachel Lynde, who was spending the leisure of her old age in knitting cotton-warp quilts against the day when Anne's daughters should need a "setting-out." There were jolly playmates there, too—"Uncle" Davy's children and "Aunt" Diana's children. They knew all the spots their mother had loved so well in her girlhood at old Green Gables—the long Lover's Lane, that was pink-hedged in wild-rose time, the always neat yard, with its willows and poplars, the Dryad's Bubble, lucent and lovely as of yore, the Lake of Shining Waters, and Willowmere. The twins had their mother's old porch-gable room, and Aunt Marilla used to come in at night, when she thought they were asleep, to gloat over them. But they all knew she loved Jem the best.

Jem was at present busily occupied in frying a mess of small trout which he had just caught in the pond. His stove consisted of a circle of red stones, with a fire kindled in it, and his culinary utensils were an old tin can, hammered out flat, and a fork with only one tine left. Nevertheless, ripping good meals had before now been thus prepared.

Jem was the child of the House of Dreams. All the others had been born at Ingleside. He had curly red hair, like his mother's, and frank hazel eyes, like his father's; he had his mother's fine nose and his father's steady, humorous mouth. And he was the only one of the family who had ears nice enough to please Susan. But he had a standing feud with Susan because she would not give up calling him Little Jem. It was outrageous, thought thirteen-year-old Jem. Mother had more sense.

"I'm NOT little any more, Mother," he had cried indignantly, on his eighth birthday. "I'm AWFUL big."

Mother had sighed and laughed and sighed again; and she never called him Little Jem again—in his hearing at least.

He was and always had been a sturdy, reliable little chap. He never broke a promise. He was not a great talker. His teachers did not think him brilliant, but he was a good, all-round student. He never took things on faith; he always liked to investigate the truth of a statement for himself. Once Susan had told him that if he touched his tongue to a frosty latch all the skin would tear off it. Jem had promptly done it, "just to see if it was so." He found it was "so," at the cost of a very sore tongue for several days. But Jem did not grudge suffering in the interests of science. By constant experiment and observation he learned a great deal and his brothers and sisters thought his extensive knowledge of their little world quite wonderful. Jem always knew where the first and ripest berries grew, where the first pale violets shyly wakened from their winter's sleep, and how many blue eggs were in a given robin's nest in the maple grove. He could tell fortunes from daisy petals and suck honey from red clovers, and grub up all sorts of edible roots on the banks of the pond, while Susan went in daily fear that they would all be poisoned. He knew where the finest spruce-gum was to be found, in pale amber knots on the lichened bark, he knew where the nuts grew thickest in the bee-chwoods around the Harbour Head, and where the best trouting places up the brooks were. He could mimic the call of any wild bird or beast in Four Winds and he knew the haunt of every wild flower from spring to autumn.

Walter Blythe was sitting under the White Lady, with a volume of poems lying beside him, but he was not reading. He was gazing now at the emerald-misted willows by the pond, and now at a flock of clouds, like little silver sheep, herded by the wind, that were drifting over Rainbow Valley, with rapture in his wide splendid eyes. Walter's eyes were very wonderful. All the joy and sorrow and laughter and loyalty and aspiration of many generations lying under the sod looked out of their dark gray depths.

Walter was a "hop out of kin," as far as looks went. He did not resemble any known relative. He was quite the handsomest of the Ingleside children, with straight black hair and finely modelled features. But he had all his mother's vivid imagination and passionate love of beauty. Frost of winter, invitation of spring, dream of summer and glamour of autumn, all meant much to Walter.

In school, where Jem was a chieftain, Walter was not thought highly of. He was supposed to be "girly" and milk-soppish, because he never fought and seldom joined in the school sports, preferring to herd by himself in out of the way corners and read books—especially "po'try books." Walter loved the poets and pored over their pages from the time he could first read. Their music was woven into his growing soul—the music of the immortals. Walter cherished the ambition to be a poet himself some day. The thing could be done. A certain Uncle Paul—so called out of courtesy—who lived now in that mysterious realm called "the States," was Walter's model. Uncle Paul had once been a little school boy in Avonlea and now his poetry was read everywhere. But the Glen schoolboys did not know of Walter's dreams and would not have been greatly impressed if they had. In spite of his lack of physical prowess, however, he commanded a certain unwilling respect because of his power of "talking book talk." Nobody in Glen St. Mary school could talk like him. He "sounded like a preacher," one boy said; and for this reason he was generally left alone and not persecuted, as most boys were who were suspected of disliking or fearing fisticuffs.

The ten year old Ingleside twins violated twin tradition by not looking in the least alike. Anne, who was always called Nan, was very pretty, with velvety nut-brown eyes and silky nut-brown hair. She was a very blithe and dainty little maiden—Blythe by name and blithe by nature, one of her teachers had said. Her complexion was quite faultless, much to her mother's satisfaction.

"I'm so glad I have one daughter who can wear pink," Mrs. Blythe was wont to say jubilantly.

Diana Blythe, known as Di, was very like her mother, with gray-green eyes that always shone with a peculiar lustre and brilliancy in the dusk, and red hair. Perhaps this was why she was her father's favourite. She and Walter were especial chums; Di was the only one to whom he would ever read the verses he wrote himself—the only one who knew that he was secretly hard at work on an epic, strikingly resembling "Marmion" in some things, if not in others. She kept all his secrets, even from Nan, and told him all hers.

"Won't you soon have those fish ready, Jem?" said Nan, sniffing with her dainty nose. "The smell makes me awfully hungry."

"They're nearly ready," said Jem, giving one a dexterous turn.

"Get out the bread and the plates, girls. Walter, wake up."

"How the air shines to-night," said Walter dreamily. Not that he despised fried trout either, by any means; but with Walter food for the soul always took first place. "The flower angel has been walking over the world to-day, calling to the flowers. I can see his blue wings on that hill by the woods."

"Any angels' wings I ever saw were white," said Nan.

"The flower angel's aren't. They are a pale misty blue, just like the haze in the valley. Oh, how I wish I could fly. It must be glorious."

"One does fly in dreams sometimes," said Di.

"I never dream that I'm flying exactly," said Walter. "But I often dream that I just rise up from the ground and float over the fences and the trees. It's delightful—and I always think, 'This ISN'T a dream like it's always been before. THIS is real'—and then I wake up after all, and it's heart-breaking."

"Hurry up, Nan," ordered Jem.

Nan had produced the banquet-board—a board literally as well as figuratively—from which many a feast, seasoned as no viands were elsewhere, had been eaten in Rainbow Valley. It was converted into a table by propping it on two large, mossy stones. Newspapers served as tablecloth, and broken plates and handleless cups from Susan's discard furnished the dishes. From a tin box secreted at the root of a spruce tree Nan brought forth bread and salt. The brook gave Adam's ale of unsurpassed crystal. For the rest, there was a certain sauce, compounded of fresh air and appetite of youth, which gave to everything a divine flavour. To sit in Rainbow Valley, steeped in a twilight half gold, half amethyst, rife with the odours of balsam-fir and woodsy growing things in their springtime prime, with the pale stars of wild strawberry blossoms all around you, and with the sough of the wind and tinkle of bells in the shaking tree tops, and eat fried trout and dry bread, was something which the mighty of earth might have envied them.

"Sit in," invited Nan, as Jem placed his sizzling tin platter of trout on the table. "It's your turn to say grace, Jem."

"I've done my part frying the trout," protested Jem, who hated saying grace. "Let Walter say it. He LIKES saying grace. And cut it short, too, Walt. I'm starving."

But Walter said no grace, short or long, just then. An interruption occurred.

CHAPTER III. THE INGLESIDE CHILDREN

"Who's coming down from the manse hill?" said Di.

CHAPTER IV. THE MANSE CHILDREN

Aunt Martha might be, and was, a very poor housekeeper; the Rev. John Knox Meredith might be, and was, a very absent-minded, indulgent man. But it could not be denied that there was something very homelike and lovable about the Glen St. Mary manse in spite of its untidiness. Even the critical housewives of the Glen felt it, and were unconsciously mellowed in judgment because of it. Perhaps its charm was in part due to accidental circumstances—the luxuriant vines clustering over its gray, clap-boarded walls, the friendly acacias and balm-of-gileads that crowded about it with the freedom of old acquaintance, and the beautiful views of harbour and sand-dunes from its front windows. But these things had been there in the reign of Mr. Meredith's predecessor, when the manse had been the primmest, neatest, and dreariest house in the Glen. So much of the credit must be given to the personality of its new inmates. There was an atmosphere of laughter and comradeship about it; the doors were always open; and inner and outer worlds joined hands. Love was the only law in Glen St. Mary manse.

The people of his congregation said that Mr. Meredith spoiled his children. Very likely he did. It is certain that he could not bear to scold them. "They have no mother," he used to say to himself, with a sigh, when some unusually glaring peccadillo forced itself upon his notice. But he did not know the half of their goings-on. He belonged to the sect of dreamers. The windows of his study looked out on the graveyard but, as he paced up and down the room, reflecting deeply on the immortality of the soul, he was quite unaware that Jerry and Carl were playing leap-frog hilariously over the flat stones in that abode of dead Methodists. Mr. Meredith had occasional acute realizations that his children were not so well looked after, physically or morally, as they had been before his wife died, and he had always a dim sub-consciousness that house and meals were very different under Aunt Martha's management from what they had been under Cecilia's. For the rest, he lived in a world of books and abstractions; and, therefore, although his clothes were seldom brushed, and although the Glen housewives concluded, from the ivory-like pallor of his clear-cut features and slender hands, that he never got enough to eat, he was not an unhappy man.

If ever a graveyard could be called a cheerful place, the old Methodist graveyard at Glen St. Mary might be so called. The new graveyard, at the other side of the Methodist church, was a neat and proper and doleful spot; but the old one had been left so long to Nature's kindly and gracious ministries that it had become very pleasant.

It was surrounded on three sides by a dyke of stones and sod, topped by a gray and uncertain paling. Outside the dyke grew a row of tall fir trees with thick, balsamic boughs. The dyke, which had been built by the first settlers of the Glen, was old enough to be beautiful, with mosses and green things growing out of its crevices, violets purpling at its base in the early spring days, and asters and golden-rod making an autumnal glory in its corners. Little ferns clustered companionably between its stones, and here and there a big bracken grew.

On the eastern side there was neither fence nor dyke. The graveyard there straggled off into a young fir plantation, ever pushing nearer to the graves and deepening eastward into a thick wood. The air was always full of the harp-like voices of the sea, and the music of gray old trees, and in the spring mornings the choruses of birds in the elms around the two churches sang of life and not of death. The Meredith children loved the old graveyard.

Blue-eyed ivy, "garden-spruce," and mint ran riot over the sunken graves. Blueberry bushes grew lavishly in the sandy corner next to the fir wood. The varying fashions of tombstones for three generations were to be found there, from the flat, oblong, red sandstone slabs of old settlers, down through the days of weeping willows and clasped hands, to the latest monstrosities of tall "monuments" and draped urns. One of the latter, the biggest and ugliest in the graveyard, was sacred to the memory of a certain Alec Davis who had been born a Methodist but had taken to himself a Presbyterian bride of the Douglas clan. She had made him turn Presbyterian and kept him toeing the Presbyterian mark all his life. But when he died she did not dare to doom him to a lonely grave in the Presbyterian graveyard over-harbour. His people were all buried in the Methodist cemetery; so Alec Davis went back to his own in death and his widow consoled herself by erecting a monument which cost more than any of the Methodists could afford. The Meredith children hated it, without just knowing why, but they loved the old, flat, bench-like stones with the tall grasses growing rankly about them. They made jolly seats for one thing. They were all sitting on one now. Jerry, tired of leap frog, was playing on a jew's-harp. Carl was lovingly poring over a strange beetle he had found; Una was trying to make a doll's dress, and Faith, leaning back on her slender brown wrists, was swinging her bare feet in lively time to the jew's-harp.

Jerry had his father's black hair and large black eyes, but in him the latter were flashing instead of dreamy. Faith, who came next to him, wore her beauty like a rose, careless and glowing. She had golden-brown eyes, golden-brown curls and crimson cheeks. She laughed too much to please her father's congregation and had shocked old Mrs. Taylor, the disconsolate spouse of several departed husbands, by saucily declaring—in the church-porch at that—"The world ISN'T a vale of tears, Mrs. Taylor. It's a world of laughter."

Little dreamy Una was not given to laughter. Her braids of straight, dead-black hair betrayed no lawless kinks, and her almond-shaped, dark-blue eyes had something wistful and sorrowful in them. Her mouth had a trick of falling open over her tiny white teeth, and a shy, meditative smile occasionally crept over her small face. She was much more sensitive to public opinion than Faith, and had an uneasy consciousness that there was something askew in their way of living. She longed to put it right, but did not know how. Now and then she dusted the furniture—but it was so seldom she could find the duster because it was never in the same place twice. And when the clothes-brush was to be found she tried to brush her father's best suit on Saturdays, and once sewed on a missing button with coarse white thread. When Mr. Meredith went to church next day every female eye saw that button and the peace of the Ladies' Aid was upset for weeks.

Carl had the clear, bright, dark-blue eyes, fearless and direct, of his dead mother, and her brown hair with its glints of gold. He knew the secrets of bugs and had a sort of freemasonry with bees and beetles. Una never liked to sit near him because she never knew what uncanny creature might be secreted about him. Jerry refused to sleep with him because Carl had once taken a young garter snake to bed with him; so Carl slept in his old cot, which was so short that he could never stretch out, and had strange bed-fellows. Perhaps it was just as well that Aunt Martha was half blind when she made that bed. Altogether they were a jolly, lovable little crew, and Cecilia Meredith's heart must have ached bitterly when she faced the knowledge that she must leave them.

"Where would you like to be buried if you were a Methodist?" asked Faith cheerfully.

This opened up an interesting field of speculation.

"There isn't much choice. The place is full," said Jerry. "I'D like that corner near the road, I guess. I could hear the teams going past and the people talking."

"I'd like that little hollow under the weeping birch," said Una. "That birch is such a place for birds and they sing like mad in the mornings."

"I'd take the Porter lot where there's so many children buried. *I* like lots of company," said Faith. "Carl, where'd you?"

"I'd rather not be buried at all," said Carl, "but if I had to be

I'd like the ant-bed. Ants are AWF'LY int'resting."

"How very good all the people who are buried here must have been," said Una, who had been reading the laudatory old epitaphs. "There doesn't seem to be a single bad person in the whole graveyard. Methodists must be better than Presbyterians after all."

"Maybe the Methodists bury their bad people just like they do cats," suggested Carl. "Maybe they don't bother bringing them to the graveyard at all."

"Nonsense," said Faith. "The people that are buried here weren't any better than other folks, Una. But when anyone is dead you mustn't say anything of him but good or he'll come back and ha'nt you. Aunt Martha told me that. I asked father if it was true and he just looked through me and muttered, 'True? True? What is truth? What IS truth, O jesting Pilate?' I concluded from that it must be true."

"I wonder if Mr. Alec Davis would come back and ha'nt me if I threw a stone at the urn on top of his tombstone," said Jerry.

"Mrs. Davis would," giggled Faith. "She just watches us in church like a cat watching mice. Last Sunday I made a face at her nephew and he made one back at me and you should have seen her glare. I'll bet she boxed HIS ears when they got out. Mrs. Marshall Elliott told me we mustn't offend her on any account or I'd have made a face at her, too!"

"They say Jem Blythe stuck out his tongue at her once and she would never have his father again, even when her husband was dying," said Jerry. "I wonder what the Blythe gang will be like."

"I liked their looks," said Faith. The manse children had been at the station that afternoon when the Blythe small fry had arrived. "I liked Jem's looks ESPECIALLY."

"They say in school that Walter's a sissy," said Jerry.

"I don't believe it," said Una, who had thought Walter very handsome.

"Well, he writes poetry, anyhow. He won the prize the teacher offered last year for writing a poem, Bertie Shakespeare Drew told me. Bertie's mother thought HE should have got the prize because of his name, but Bertie said he couldn't write poetry to save his soul, name or no name."

"I suppose we'll get acquainted with them as soon as they begin going to school," mused Faith. "I hope the girls are nice. I don't like most of the girls round here. Even the nice ones are poky. But the Blythe twins look jolly. I thought twins always looked alike, but they don't. I think the red-haired one is the nicest."

"I liked their mother's looks," said Una with a little sigh. Una envied all children their mothers. She had been only six when her mother died, but she had some very precious memories, treasured in her soul like jewels, of twilight cuddlings and morning frolics, of loving eyes, a tender voice, and the sweetest, gayest laugh.

"They say she isn't like other people," said Jerry.

"Mrs. Elliot says that is because she never really grew up," said Faith.

"She's taller than Mrs. Elliott."

"Yes, yes, but it is inside—Mrs. Elliot says Mrs. Blythe just stayed a little girl inside."

"What do I smell?" interrupted Carl, sniffing.

They all smelled it now. A most delectable odour came floating up on the still evening air from the direction of the little woodsy dell below the manse hill.

"That makes me hungry," said Jerry.

"We had only bread and molasses for supper and cold ditto for dinner," said Una plaintively.

Aunt Martha's habit was to boil a large slab of mutton early in the week and serve it up every day, cold and greasy, as long as it lasted. To this Faith, in a moment of inspiration, had give the name of "ditto", and by this it was invariably known at the manse.

"Let's go and see where that smell is coming from," said Jerry.

They all sprang up, frolicked over the lawn with the abandon of young puppies, climbed a fence, and tore down the mossy slope, guided by the savory lure that ever grew stronger. A few minutes later they arrived breathlessly in the sanctum sanctorum of Rainbow Valley where the Blythe children were just about to give thanks and eat.

They halted shyly. Una wished they had not been so precipitate: but Di Blythe was equal to that and any occasion. She stepped forward, with a comrade's smile.

"I guess I know who you are," she said. "You belong to the manse, don't you?"

Faith nodded, her face creased by dimples.

"We smelled your trout cooking and wondered what it was."

"You must sit down and help us eat them," said Di.

"Maybe you haven't more than you want yourselves," said Jerry, looking hungrily at the tin platter.

"We've heaps—three apiece," said Jem. "Sit down."

No more ceremony was necessary. Down they all sat on mossy stones. Merry was that feast and long. Nan and Di would probably have died of horror had they known what Faith and Una knew perfectly well—that Carl had two young mice in his jacket pocket. But they never knew it, so it never hurt them. Where can folks get better acquainted than over a meal table? When the last trout had vanished, the manse children and the Ingleside children were sworn friends and allies. They had always known each other and always would. The race of Joseph recognized its own.

They poured out the history of their little pasts. The manse children heard of Avonlea and Green Gables, of Rainbow Valley traditions, and of the little house by the harbour shore where Jem had been born. The Ingleside children heard of Maywater, where the Merediths had lived before coming to the Glen, of Una's beloved, one-eyed doll and Faith's pet rooster.

Faith was inclined to resent the fact that people laughed at her for petting a rooster. She liked the Blythes because they accepted it without question.

"A handsome rooster like Adam is just as nice a pet as a dog or cat, *I* think," she said. "If he was a canary nobody would wonder. And I brought him up from a little, wee, yellow chicken. Mrs. Johnson at Maywater gave him to me. A weasel had killed all his brothers and sisters. I called him after her husband. I never liked dolls or cats. Cats are too sneaky and dolls are DEAD."

"Who lives in that house away up there?" asked Jerry.

"The Miss Wests—Rosemary and Ellen," answered Nan. "Di and I are going to take music lessons from Miss Rosemary this summer."

Una gazed at the lucky twins with eyes whose longing was too gentle for envy. Oh, if she could only have music lessons! It was one of the dreams of her little hidden life. But nobody ever thought of such a thing.

"Miss Rosemary is so sweet and she always dresses so pretty," said Di. "Her hair is just the colour of new molasses taffy," she added wistfully—for Di, like her mother before her, was not resigned to her own ruddy tresses.

"I like Miss Ellen, too," said Nan. "She always used to give me candies when she came to church. But Di is afraid of her."

"Her brows are so black and she has such a great deep voice," said Di. "Oh, how scared of her Kenneth Ford used to be when he was little! Mother says the first Sunday Mrs. Ford brought him to church Miss Ellen happened to be there, sitting right behind them. And the minute Kenneth saw her he just screamed and screamed until Mrs. Ford had to carry him out."

"Who is Mrs. Ford?" asked Una wonderingly.

"Oh, the Fords don't live here. They only come here in the summer. And they're not coming this summer. They live in that little house 'way, 'way down on the harbour shore where father and mother used to lie. I wish you could see Persis Ford. She is just like a picture."

"I've heard of Mrs. Ford," broke in Faith. "Bertie Shakespeare Drew told me about her. She was married fourteen years to a dead man and then he came to life."

"Nonsense," said Nan. "That isn't the way it goes at all. Bertie Shakespeare can never get anything straight. I know the whole story and I'll tell it to you some time, but not now, for it's too long and it's time for us to go home. Mother doesn't like us to be out late these damp evenings."

Nobody cared whether the manse children were out in the damp or not. Aunt Martha was already in bed and the minister was still too deeply lost in speculations concerning the immortality of the soul to remember the mortality of the body. But they went home, too, with visions of good times coming in their heads.

"I think Rainbow Valley is even nicer than the graveyard," said Una. "And I just love those dear Blythes. It's SO nice when you can love people because so often you CAN'T. Father said in his sermon last Sunday that we should love everybody. But how can we? How could we love Mrs. Alec Davis?"

"Oh, father only said that in the pulpit," said Faith airily.

"He has more sense than to really think it outside."

The Blythe children went up to Ingleside, except Jem, who slipped away for a few moments on a solitary expedition to a remote corner of Rainbow Valley. Mayflowers grew there and Jem never forgot to take his mother a bouquet as long as they lasted.

CHAPTER V. THE ADVENT OF MARY VANCE

"This is just the sort of day you feel as if things might happen," said Faith, responsive to the lure of crystal air and blue hills. She hugged herself with delight and danced a hornpipe on old Hezekiah Pollock's bench tombstone, much to the horror of two ancient maidens who happened to be driving past just as Faith hopped on one foot around the stone, waving the other and her arms in the air.

"And that," groaned one ancient maiden, "is our minister's daughter."

"What else could you expect of a widower's family?" groaned the other ancient maiden. And then they both shook their heads.

It was early on Saturday morning and the Merediths were out in the dew-drenched world with a delightful consciousness of the holiday. They had never had anything to do on a holiday. Even Nan and Di Blythe had certain household tasks for Saturday mornings, but the daughters of the manse were free to roam from blushing morn to dewy eve if so it pleased them. It DID please Faith, but Una felt a secret, bitter humiliation because they never learned to do anything. The other girls in her class at school could cook and sew and knit; she only was a little ignoramus.

Jerry suggested that they go exploring; so they went lingeringly through the fir grove, picking up Carl on the way, who was on his knees in the dripping grass studying his darling ants. Beyond the grove they came out in Mr. Taylor's pasture field, sprinkled over with the white ghosts of dandelions; in a remote corner was an old tumbledown barn, where Mr. Taylor sometimes stored his surplus hay crop but which was never used for any other purpose. Thither the Meredith children trooped, and prowled about the ground floor for several minutes.

"What was that?" whispered Una suddenly.

They all listened. There was a faint but distinct rustle in the hayloft above. The Merediths looked at each other.

"There's something up there," breathed Faith.

"I'm going up to see what it is," said Jerry resolutely.

"Oh, don't," begged Una, catching his arm.

"I'm going."

"We'll all go, too, then," said Faith.

CHAPTER V. THE ADVENT OF MARY VANCE

The whole four climbed the shaky ladder, Jerry and Faith quite dauntless, Una pale from fright, and Carl rather absent-mindedly speculating on the possibility of finding a bat up in the loft. He longed to see a bat in daylight.

When they stepped off the ladder they saw what had made the rustle and the sight struck them dumb for a few moments.

In a little nest in the hay a girl was curled up, looking as if she had just wakened from sleep. When she saw them she stood up, rather shakily, as it seemed, and in the bright sunlight that streamed through the cobwebbed window behind her, they saw that her thin, sunburned face was very pale under its tan. She had two braids of lank, thick, tow-coloured hair and very odd eyes—"white eyes," the manse children thought, as she stared at them half defiantly, half piteously. They were really of so pale a blue that they did seem almost white, especially when contrasted with the narrow black ring that circled the iris. She was barefooted and bareheaded, and was clad in a faded, ragged, old plaid dress, much too short and tight for her. As for years, she might have been almost any age, judging from her wizened little face, but her height seemed to be somewhere in the neighbourhood of twelve.

"Who are you?" asked Jerry.

The girl looked about her as if seeking a way of escape. Then she seemed to give in with a little shiver of despair.

"I'm Mary Vance," she said.

"Where'd you come from?" pursued Jerry.

Mary, instead of replying, suddenly sat, or fell, down on the hay and began to cry. Instantly Faith had flung herself down beside her and put her arm around the thin, shaking shoulders.

"You stop bothering her," she commanded Jerry. Then she hugged the waif. "Don't cry, dear. Just tell us what's the matter. WE'RE friends."

"I'm so—so—hungry," wailed Mary. "I—I hain't had a thing to eat since Thursday morning, 'cept a little water from the brook out there."

The manse children gazed at each other in horror. Faith sprang up.

"You come right up to the manse and get something to eat before you say another word."

Mary shrank.

"Oh—I can't. What will your pa and ma say? Besides, they'd send me back."

"We've no mother, and father won't bother about you. Neither will Aunt Martha. Come, I say." Faith stamped her foot impatiently. Was this queer girl going to insist on starving to death almost at their very door?

Mary yielded. She was so weak that she could hardly climb down the ladder, but somehow they got her down and over the field and into the manse kitchen. Aunt Martha, muddling through her Saturday cooking, took no notice of her. Faith and Una flew to the pantry and ransacked it for such eatables as it contained—some "ditto," bread, butter, milk and a doubtful pie. Mary Vance attacked the food ravenously and uncritically, while the manse children stood around and watched her. Jerry noticed that she had a pretty mouth and very nice, even, white teeth. Faith decided, with secret horror, that Mary had not one stitch on her except that ragged, faded dress. Una was full of pure pity, Carl of amused wonder, and all of them of curiosity.

"Now come out to the graveyard and tell us about yourself," ordered Faith, when Mary's appetite showed signs of failing her. Mary was now nothing loath. Food had restored her natural vivacity and unloosed her by no means reluctant tongue.

"You won't tell your pa or anybody if I tell you?" she stipulated, when she was enthroned on Mr. Pollock's tombstone. Opposite her the manse children lined up on another. Here was spice and mystery and adventure. Something HAD happened.

"No, we won't."

"Cross your hearts?"

"Cross our hearts."

"Well, I've run away. I was living with Mrs. Wiley over-harbour.
Do you know Mrs. Wiley?"

"No."

"Well, you don't want to know her. She's an awful woman. My, how I hate her! She worked me to death and wouldn't give me half enough to eat, and she used to larrup me 'most every day. Look a-here."

Mary rolled up her ragged sleeves, and held up her scrawny arms and thin hands, chapped almost to rawness. They were black with bruises. The manse children shivered. Faith flushed crimson with indignation. Una's blue eyes filled with tears.

"She licked me Wednesday night with a stick," said Mary, indifferently. "It was 'cause I let the cow kick over a pail of milk. How'd I know the darn old cow was going to kick?"

A not unpleasant thrill ran over her listeners. They would never dream of using such dubious words, but it was rather titivating to hear someone else use them—and a girl, at that. Certainly this Mary Vance was an interesting creature.

"I don't blame you for running away," said Faith.

"Oh, I didn't run away 'cause she licked me. A licking was all in the day's work with me. I was darn well used to it. Nope, I'd meant to run away for a week 'cause I'd found out that Mrs. Wiley was going to rent her farm and go to Lowbridge to live and give me to a cousin of hers up Charlottetown way. I wasn't going to stand for THAT. She was a worse sort than Mrs. Wiley even. Mrs. Wiley lent me to her for a month last summer and I'd rather live with the devil himself."

Sensation number two. But Una looked doubtful.

"So I made up my mind I'd beat it. I had seventy cents saved up that Mrs. John Crawford give me in the spring for planting potatoes for her. Mrs. Wiley didn't know about it. She was away visiting her cousin when I planted them. I thought I'd sneak up here to the Glen and buy a ticket to Charlottetown and try to get work there. I'm a hustler, let me tell you. There ain't a lazy bone in MY body. So I lit out Thursday morning 'fore Mrs. Wiley was up and walked to the Glen—six miles. And when I got to the station I found I'd lost my money. Dunno how—dunno where. Anyhow, it was gone. I didn't know what to do. If I went back to old Lady Wiley she'd take the hide off me. So I went and hid in that old barn."

"And what will you do now?" asked Jerry.

"Dunno. I s'pose I'll have to go back and take my medicine. Now that I've got some grub in my stomach I guess I can stand it."

But there was fear behind the bravado in Mary's eyes. Una suddenly slipped from the one tombstone to the other and put her arm about Mary.

"Don't go back. Just stay here with us."

"Oh, Mrs. Wiley'll hunt me up," said Mary. "It's likely she's on my trail before this. I might stay here till she finds me, I s'pose, if your folks don't mind. I was a darn fool ever to think of skipping out. She'd run a weasel to earth. But I was so misrebul."

Mary's voice quivered, but she was ashamed of showing her weakness.

"I hain't had the life of a dog for these four years," she explained defiantly.

"You've been four years with Mrs. Wiley?"

"Yip. She took me out of the asylum over in Hopetown when I was eight."

"That's the same place Mrs. Blythe came from," exclaimed Faith.

"I was two years in the asylum. I was put there when I was six.
My ma had hung herself and my pa had cut his throat."

"Holy cats! Why?" said Jerry.

"Booze," said Mary laconically.

"And you've no relations?"

"Not a darn one that I know of. Must have had some once, though. I was called after half a dozen of them. My full name is Mary Martha Lucilla Moore Ball Vance. Can you beat that? My grandfather was a rich man. I'll bet he was richer than YOUR grandfather. But pa drunk it all up and ma, she did her part. THEY used to beat me, too. Laws, I've been licked so much I kind of like it."

Mary tossed her head. She divined that the manse children were pitying her for her many stripes and she did not want pity. She wanted to be envied. She looked gaily about her. Her strange eyes, now that the dullness of famine was removed from them, were brilliant. She would show these youngsters what a personage she was.

"I've been sick an awful lot," she said proudly. "There's not many kids could have come through what I have. I've had scarlet fever and measles and ersipelas and mumps and whooping cough and pewmonia."

"Were you ever fatally sick?" asked Una.

"I don't know," said Mary doubtfully.

"Of course she wasn't," scoffed Jerry. "If you're fatally sick you die."

"Oh, well, I never died exactly," said Mary, "but I come blamed near it once. They thought I was dead and they were getting ready to lay me out when I up and come to."

"What is it like to be half dead?" asked Jerry curiously.

"Like nothing. I didn't know it for days afterwards. It was when I had the pewmonia. Mrs. Wiley wouldn't have the doctor—said she wasn't going to no such expense for a home girl. Old Aunt Christina MacAllister nursed me with poultices. She brung me round. But sometimes I wish I'd just died the other half and done with it. I'd been better off."

"If you went to heaven I s'pose you would," said Faith, rather doubtfully.

"Well, what other place is there to go to?" demanded Mary in a puzzled voice.

"There's hell, you know," said Una, dropping her voice and hugging Mary to lessen the awfulness of the suggestion.

"Hell? What's that?"

"Why, it's where the devil lives," said Jerry. "You've heard of him—you spoke about him."

"Oh, yes, but I didn't know he lived anywhere. I thought he just roamed round. Mr. Wiley used to mention hell when he was alive. He was always telling folks to go there. I thought it was some place over in New Brunswick where he come from."

"Hell is an awful place," said Faith, with the dramatic enjoyment that is born of telling dreadful things. "Bad people go there when they die and burn in fire for ever and ever and ever."

"Who told you that?" demanded Mary incredulously.

"It's in the Bible. And Mr. Isaac Crothers at Maywater told us, too, in Sunday School. He was an elder and a pillar in the church and knew all about it. But you needn't worry. If you're good you'll go to heaven and if you're bad I guess you'd rather go to hell."

"I wouldn't," said Mary positively. "No matter how bad I was I wouldn't want to be burned and burned. _I_ know what it's like. I picked up a red hot poker once by accident. What must you do to be good?"

"You must go to church and Sunday School and read your Bible and pray every night and give to missions," said Una.

"It sounds like a large order," said Mary. "Anything else?"

"You must ask God to forgive the sins you've committed."

"But I've never com—committed any," said Mary. "What's a sin any way?"

"Oh, Mary, you must have. Everybody does. Did you never tell a lie?"

"Heaps of 'em," said Mary.

"That's a dreadful sin," said Una solemnly.

"Do you mean to tell me," demanded Mary, "that I'd be sent to hell for telling a lie now and then? Why, I HAD to. Mr. Wiley would have broken every bone in my body one time if I hadn't told him a lie. Lies have saved me many a whack, I can tell you."

Una sighed. Here were too many difficulties for her to solve. She shuddered as she thought of being cruelly whipped. Very likely she would have lied too. She squeezed Mary's little calloused hand.

"Is that the only dress you've got?" asked Faith, whose joyous nature refused to dwell on disagreeable subjects.

CHAPTER V. THE ADVENT OF MARY VANCE

"I just put on this dress because it was no good," cried Mary flushing. "Mrs. Wiley'd bought my clothes and I wasn't going to be beholden to her for anything. And I'm honest. If I was going to run away I wasn't going to take what belong to HER that was worth anything. When I grow up I'm going to have a blue sating dress. Your own clothes don't look so stylish. I thought ministers' children were always dressed up."

It was plain that Mary had a temper and was sensitive on some points. But there was a queer, wild charm about her which captivated them all. She was taken to Rainbow Valley that afternoon and introduced to the Blythes as "a friend of ours from over-harbour who is visiting us." The Blythes accepted her unquestioningly, perhaps because she was fairly respectable now. After dinner—through which Aunt Martha had mumbled and Mr. Meredith had been in a state of semi-unconsciousness while brooding his Sunday sermon—Faith had prevailed on Mary to put on one of her dresses, as well as certain other articles of clothing. With her hair neatly braided Mary passed muster tolerably well. She was an acceptable playmate, for she knew several new and exciting games, and her conversation lacked not spice. In fact, some of her expressions made Nan and Di look at her rather askance. They were not quite sure what their mother would have thought of her, but they knew quite well what Susan would. However, she was a visitor at the manse, so she must be all right.

When bedtime came there was the problem of where Mary should sleep.

"We can't put her in the spare room, you know," said Faith perplexedly to Una.

"I haven't got anything in my head," cried Mary in an injured tone.

"Oh, I didn't mean THAT," protested Faith. "The spare room is all torn up. The mice have gnawed a big hole in the feather tick and made a nest in it. We never found it out till Aunt Martha put the Rev. Mr. Fisher from Charlottetown there to sleep last week. HE soon found it out. Then father had to give him his bed and sleep on the study lounge. Aunt Martha hasn't had time to fix the spare room bed up yet, so she says; so NOBODY can sleep there, no matter how clean their heads are. And our room is so small, and the bed so small you can't sleep with us."

"I can go back to the hay in the old barn for the night if you'll lend me a quilt," said Mary philosophically. "It was kind of chilly last night, but 'cept for that I've had worse beds."

"Oh, no, no, you mustn't do that," said Una. "I've thought of a plan, Faith. You know that little trestle bed in the garret room, with the old mattress on it, that the last minister left there? Let's take up the spare room bedclothes and make Mary a bed there. You won't mind sleeping in the garret, will you, Mary? It's just above our room."

"Any place'll do me. Laws, I never had a decent place to sleep in my life. I slept in the loft over the kitchen at Mrs. Wiley's. The roof leaked rain in the summer and the snow druv in in winter. My bed was a straw tick on the floor. You won't find me a mite huffy about where *I* sleep."

The manse garret was a long, low, shadowy place, with one gable end partitioned off. Here a bed was made up for Mary of the dainty hemstitched sheets and embroidered spread which Cecilia Meredith had once so proudly made for her spare-room, and which still survived Aunt Martha's uncertain washings. The good nights were said and silence fell over the manse. Una was just falling asleep when she heard a sound in the room just above that made her sit up suddenly.

"Listen, Faith—Mary's crying," she whispered. Faith replied not, being already asleep. Una slipped out of bed, and made her way in her little white gown down the hall and up the garret stairs. The creaking floor gave ample notice of her coming, and when she reached the corner room all was moonlit silence and the trestle bed showed only a hump in the middle.

"Mary," whispered Una.

There was no response.

Una crept close to the bed and pulled at the spread. "Mary, I know you are crying. I heard you. Are you lonesome?"

Mary suddenly appeared to view but said nothing.

"Let me in beside you. I'm cold," said Una shivering in the chilly air, for the little garret window was open and the keen breath of the north shore at night blew in.

Mary moved over and Una snuggled down beside her.

"NOW you won't be lonesome. We shouldn't have left you here alone the first night."

"I wasn't lonesome," sniffed Mary.

"What were you crying for then?"

"Oh, I just got to thinking of things when I was here alone. I thought of having to go back to Mrs. Wiley—and of being licked for running away—and—and—and of going to hell for telling lies. It all worried me something scandalous."

"Oh, Mary," said poor Una in distress. "I don't believe God will send you to hell for telling lies when you didn't know it was wrong. He COULDN'T. Why, He's kind and good. Of course, you mustn't tell any more now that you know it's wrong."

"If I can't tell lies what's to become of me?" said Mary with a sob. "YOU don't understand. You don't know anything about it. You've got a home and a kind father—though it does seem to me that he isn't more'n about half there. But anyway he doesn't lick you, and you get enough to eat such as it is—though that old aunt of yours doesn't know ANYTHING about cooking. Why, this is the first day I ever remember of feeling 'sif I'd enough to eat. I've been knocked about all of my life, 'cept for the two years I was at the asylum. They didn't lick me there and it wasn't too bad, though the matron was cross. She always looked ready to bite my head off a nail. But Mrs. Wiley is a holy terror, that's what SHE is, and I'm just scared stiff when I think of going back to her."

"Perhaps you won't have to. Perhaps we'll be able to think of a way out. Let's both ask God to keep you from having to go back to Mrs. Wiley. You say your prayers, don't you Mary?"

"Oh, yes, I always go over an old rhyme 'fore I get into bed," said Mary indifferently. "I never thought of asking for anything in particular though. Nobody in this world ever bothered themselves about me so I didn't s'pose God would. He MIGHT take more trouble for you, seeing you're a minister's daughter."

"He'd take every bit as much trouble for you, Mary, I'm sure," said Una. "It doesn't matter whose child you are. You just ask Him—and I will, too."

"All right," agreed Mary. "It won't do any harm if it doesn't do much good. If you knew Mrs. Wiley as well as I do you wouldn't think God would want to meddle with her. Anyhow, I won't cry any more about it. This is a big sight better'n last night down in that old barn, with the mice running about. Look at the Four Winds light. Ain't it pretty?"

"This is the only window we can see it from," said Una. "I love to watch it."

"Do you? So do I. I could see it from the Wiley loft and it was the only comfort I had. When I was all sore from being licked I'd watch it and forget about the places that hurt. I'd think of the ships sailing away and away from it and wish I was on one of them sailing far away too—away from everything. On winter nights when it didn't shine, I just felt real lonesome. Say, Una, what makes all you folks so kind to me when I'm just a stranger?"

"Because it's right to be. The bible tells us to be kind to everybody."

"Does it? Well, I guess most folks don't mind it much then. I never remember of any one being kind to me before—true's you live I don't. Say, Una, ain't them shadows on the walls pretty? They look just like a flock of little dancing birds. And say, Una, I like all you folks and them Blythe boys and Di, but I don't like that Nan. She's a proud one."

"Oh, no, Mary, she isn't a bit proud," said Una eagerly. "Not a single bit."

"Don't tell me. Any one that holds her head like that IS proud. I don't like her."

"WE all like her very much."

"Oh, I s'pose you like her better'n me?" said Mary jealously.

"Do you?"

"Why, Mary—we've known her for weeks and we've only known you a few hours," stammered Una.

"So you do like her better then?" said Mary in a rage. "All right! Like her all you want to. *I* don't care. *I* can get along without you."

She flung herself over against the wall of the garret with a slam.

"Oh, Mary," said Una, pushing a tender arm over Mary's uncompromising back, "don't talk like that. I DO like you ever so much. And you make me feel so bad."

No answer. Presently Una gave a sob. Instantly Mary squirmed around again and engulfed Una in a bear's hug.

"Hush up," she ordered. "Don't go crying over what I said. I was as mean as the devil to talk that way. I orter to be skinned alive—and you all so good to me. I should think you WOULD like any one better'n me. I deserve every licking I ever got. Hush, now. If you cry any more I'll go and walk right down to the harbour in this night-dress and drown myself."

This terrible threat made Una choke back her sobs. Her tears were wiped away by Mary with the lace frill of the spare-room pillow and forgiver and forgiven cuddled down together again, harmony restored, to watch the shadows of the vine leaves on the moonlit wall until they fell asleep.

And in the study below Rev. John Meredith walked the floor with rapt face and shining eyes, thinking out his message of the morrow, and knew not that under his own roof there was a little forlorn soul, stumbling in darkness and ignorance, beset by terror and compassed about with difficulties too great for it to grapple in its unequal struggle with a big indifferent world.

CHAPTER VI. MARY STAYS AT THE MANSE

The manse children took Mary Vance to church with them the next day. At first Mary objected to the idea.

"Didn't you go to church over-harbour?" asked Una.

"You bet. Mrs. Wiley never troubled church much, but I went every Sunday I could get off. I was mighty thankful to go to some place where I could sit down for a spell. But I can't go to church in this old ragged dress."

This difficulty was removed by Faith offering the loan of her second best dress.

"It's faded a little and two of the buttons are off, but I guess it'll do."

"I'll sew the buttons on in a jiffy," said Mary.

"Not on Sunday," said Una, shocked.

"Sure. The better the day the better the deed. You just gimme a needle and thread and look the other way if you're squeamish."

Faith's school boots, and an old black velvet cap that had once been Cecilia Meredith's, completed Mary's costume, and to church she went. Her behaviour was quite conventional, and though some wondered who the shabby little girl with the manse children was she did not attract much attention. She listened to the sermon with outward decorum and joined lustily in the singing. She had, it appeared, a clear, strong voice and a good ear.

"His blood can make the VIOLETS clean," carolled Mary blithely. Mrs. Jimmy Milgrave, whose pew was just in front of the manse pew, turned suddenly and looked the child over from top to toe. Mary, in a mere superfluity of naughtiness, stuck out her tongue at Mrs. Milgrave, much to Una's horror.

"I couldn't help it," she declared after church. "What'd she want to stare at me like that for? Such manners! I'm GLAD stuck my tongue out at her. I wish I'd stuck it farther out. Say, I saw Rob MacAllister from over-harbour there. Wonder if he'll tell Mrs. Wiley on me."

No Mrs. Wiley appeared, however, and in a few day the children forgot to look for her. Mary was apparently a fixture at the manse. But she refused to go to school with the others.

"Nope. I've finished my education," she said, when Faith urged her to go. "I went to school four winters since I come to Mrs. Wiley's and I've had all I want of

THAT. I'm sick and tired of being everlastingly jawed at 'cause I didn't get my home-lessons done. I'D no time to do home-lessons."

"Our teacher won't jaw you. He is awfully nice," said Faith.

"Well, I ain't going. I can read and write and cipher up to fractions. That's all I want. You fellows go and I'll stay home. You needn't be scared I'll steal anything. I swear I'm honest."

Mary employed herself while the others were at school in cleaning up the manse. In a few days it was a different place. Floors were swept, furniture dusted, everything straightened out. She mended the spare-room bed-tick, she sewed on missing buttons, she patched clothes neatly, she even invaded the study with broom and dustpan and ordered Mr. Meredith out while she put it to rights. But there was one department with which Aunt Martha refused to let her interfere. Aunt Martha might be deaf and half blind and very childish, but she was resolved to keep the commissariat in her own hands, in spite of all Mary's wiles and stratagems.

"I can tell you if old Martha'd let ME cook you'd have some decent meals," she told the manse children indignantly. "There'd be no more 'ditto'—and no more lumpy porridge and blue milk either. What DOES she do with all the cream?"

"She gives it to the cat. He's hers, you know," said Faith.

"I'd like to CAT her, "exclaimed Mary bitterly. "I've no use for cats anyhow. They belong to the old Nick. You can tell that by their eyes. Well, if old Martha won't, she won't, I s'pose. But it gits on my nerves to see good vittles spoiled."

When school came out they always went to Rainbow Valley. Mary refused to play in the graveyard. She declared she was afraid of ghosts.

"There's no such thing as ghosts," declared Jem Blythe.

"Oh, ain't there?"

"Did you ever see any?"

"Hundreds of 'em," said Mary promptly.

"What are they like?" said Carl.

"Awful-looking. Dressed all in white with skellington hands and heads," said Mary.

"What did you do?" asked Una.

"Run like the devil," said Mary. Then she caught Walter's eyes and blushed. Mary was a good deal in awe of Walter. She declared to the manse girls that his eyes made her nervous.

"I think of all the lies I've ever told when I look into them," she said, "and I wish I hadn't."

Jem was Mary's favourite. When he took her to the attic at Ingleside and showed her the museum of curios that Captain Jim Boyd had bequeathed to him she was immensely pleased and flattered. She also won Carl's heart entirely by her interest in his beetles and ants. It could not be denied that Mary got on rather better with the boys than with the girls. She quarrelled bitterly with Nan Blythe the second day.

"Your mother is a witch," she told Nan scornfully. "Red-haired women are always witches." Then she and Faith fell out about the rooster. Mary said its tail was too short. Faith angrily retorted that she guessed God know what length to make a rooster's tail. They did not "speak" for a day over this. Mary treated Una's hairless, one-eyed doll with consideration; but when Una showed her other prized treasure—a picture of an angel carrying a baby, presumably to heaven, Mary declared that it looked too much like a ghost for her. Una crept away to her room and cried over this, but Mary hunted her out, hugged her repentantly and implored forgiveness. No one could keep up a quarrel long with Mary—not even Nan, who was rather prone to hold grudges and never quite forgave the insult to her mother. Mary was jolly. She could and did tell the most thrilling ghost stories. Rainbow Valley seances were undeniably more exciting after Mary came. She learned to play on the jew's-harp and soon eclipsed Jerry.

"Never struck anything yet I couldn't do if I put my mind to it," she declared. Mary seldom lost a chance of tooting her own horn. She taught them how to make "blow-bags" out of the thick leaves of the "live-forever" that flourished in the old Bailey garden, she initiated them into the toothsome qualities of the "sours" that grew in the niches of the graveyard dyke, and she could make the most wonderful shadow pictures on the walls with her long, flexible fingers. And when they all went picking gum in Rainbow Valley Mary always got "the biggest chew" and bragged about it. There were times when they hated her and times when they loved her. But at all times they found her interesting. So they submitted quite meekly to her bossing, and by the end of a fortnight had come to feel that she must always have been with them.

"It's the queerest thing that Mrs. Wiley hain't been after me," said Mary. "I can't understand it."

"Maybe she isn't going to bother about you at all," said Una.

"Then you can just go on staying here."

"This house ain't hardly big enough for me and old Martha," said Mary darkly. "It's a very fine thing to have enough to eat—I've often wondered what it would be like—but I'm p'ticler about my cooking. And Mrs. Wiley'll be here yet. SHE'S got a rod in pickle for me all right. I don't think about it so much in daytime but say, girls, up there in that garret at night I git to thinking and thinking of it, till I just almost wish she'd come and have it over with. I dunno's one real good whipping would be much worse'n all the dozen I've lived through in my mind ever since I run away. Were any of you ever licked?"

"No, of course not," said Faith indignantly. "Father would never do such a thing."

"You don't know you're alive," said Mary with a sigh half of envy, half of superiority. "You don't know what I've come through. And I s'pose the Blythes were never licked either?"

"No-o-o, I guess not. But I THINK they were sometimes spanked when they were small."

"A spanking doesn't amount to anything," said Mary contemptuously. "If my folks had just spanked me I'd have thought they were petting me. Well, it ain't a fair world. I wouldn't mind taking my share of wallopings but I've had a darn sight too many."

"It isn't right to say that word, Mary," said Una reproachfully.

"You promised me you wouldn't say it."

"G'way," responded Mary. "If you knew some of the words I COULD say if I liked you wouldn't make such a fuss over darn. And you know very well I hain't ever told any lies since I come here."

"What about all those ghosts you said you saw?" asked Faith.

Mary blushed.

"That was diff'runt," she said defiantly. "I knew you wouldn't believe them yarns and I didn't intend you to. And I really did see something queer one night when I was passing the over-harbour graveyard, true's you live. I dunno whether 'twas a ghost or Sandy Crawford's old white nag, but it looked blamed queer and I tell you I scooted at the rate of no man's business."

CHAPTER VII. A FISHY EPISODE

Rilla Blythe walked proudly, and perhaps a little primly, through the main "street" of the Glen and up the manse hill, carefully carrying a small basketful of early strawberries, which Susan had coaxed into lusciousness in one of the sunny nooks of Ingleside. Susan had charged Rilla to give the basket to nobody except Aunt Martha or Mr. Meredith, and Rilla, very proud of being entrusted with such an errand, was resolved to carry out her instructions to the letter.

Susan had dressed her daintily in a white, starched, and embroidered dress, with sash of blue and beaded slippers. Her long ruddy curls were sleek and round, and Susan had let her put on her best hat, out of compliment to the manse. It was a somewhat elaborate affair, wherein Susan's taste had had more to say than Anne's, and Rilla's small soul gloried in its splendours of silk and lace and flowers. She was very conscious of her hat, and I am afraid she strutted up the manse hill. The strut, or the hat, or both, got on the nerves of Mary Vance, who was swinging on the lawn gate. Mary's temper was somewhat ruffled just then, into the bargain. Aunt Martha had refused to let her peel the potatoes and had ordered her out of the kitchen.

"Yah! You'll bring the potatoes to the table with strips of skin hanging to them and half boiled as usual! My, but it'll be nice to go to your funeral," shrieked Mary. She went out of the kitchen, giving the door such a bang that even Aunt Martha heard it, and Mr. Meredith in his study felt the vibration and thought absently that there must have been a slight earthquake shock. Then he went on with his sermon.

Mary slipped from the gate and confronted the spick-and-span damsel of Ingleside.

"What you got there?" she demanded, trying to take the basket.

Rilla resisted. "It'th for Mithter Meredith," she lisped.

"Give it to me. I'LL give it to him," said Mary.

"No. Thuthan thaid that I wathn't to give it to anybody but Mithter Mer'dith or Aunt Martha," insisted Rilla.

Mary eyed her sourly.

"You think you're something, don't you, all dressed up like a doll! Look at me. My dress is all rags and *I* don't care! I'd rather be ragged than a doll baby. Go home and tell them to put you in a glass case. Look at me—look at me—look at me!"

Mary executed a wild dance around the dismayed and bewildered Rilla, flirting her ragged skirt and vociferating "Look at me—look at me" until poor Rilla was dizzy. But as the latter tried to edge away towards the gate Mary pounced on her again.

"You give me that basket," she ordered with a grimace. Mary was past mistress in the art of "making faces." She could give her countenance a most grotesque and unearthly appearance out of which her strange, brilliant, white eyes gleamed with weird effect.

"I won't," gasped Rilla, frightened but staunch. "You let me go, Mary Vanth."

Mary let go for a minute and looked around here. Just inside the gate was a small "flake," on which a half a dozen large codfish were drying. One of Mr. Meredith's parishioners had presented him with them one day, perhaps in lieu of the subscription he was supposed to pay to the stipend and never did. Mr. Meredith had thanked him and then forgotten all about the fish, which would have promptly spoiled had not the indefatigable Mary prepared them for drying and rigged up the "flake" herself on which to dry them.

Mary had a diabolical inspiration. She flew to the "flake" and seized the largest fish there—a huge, flat thing, nearly as big as herself. With a whoop she swooped down on the terrified Rilla, brandishing her weird missile. Rilla's courage gave way. To be lambasted with a dried codfish was such an unheard-of thing that Rilla could not face it. With a shriek she dropped her basket and fled. The beautiful berries, which Susan had so tenderly selected for the minister, rolled in a rosy torrent over the dusty road and were trodden on by the flying feet of pursuer and pursued. The basket and contents were no longer in Mary's mind. She thought only of the delight of giving Rilla Blythe the scare of her life. She would teach HER to come giving herself airs because of her fine clothes.

Rilla flew down the hill and along the street. Terror lent wings to her feet, and she just managed to keep ahead of Mary, who was somewhat hampered by her own laughter, but who had breath enough to give occasional blood-curdling whoops as she ran, flourishing her codfish in the air. Through the Glen street they swept, while everybody ran to the windows and gates to see them. Mary felt she was making a tremendous sensation and enjoyed it. Rilla, blind with terror and spent of breath, felt that she could run no longer. In another instant that terrible girl would be on her with the codfish. At this point the poor mite stumbled and fell into the mud-puddle at the end of the street just as Miss Cornelia came out of Carter Flagg's store.

Miss Cornelia took the whole situation in at a glance. So did Mary. The latter stopped short in her mad career and before Miss Cornelia could speak she had whirled around and was running up as fast as she had run down. Miss Cornelia's lips tightened ominously, but she knew it was no use to think of chasing her. So she picked up poor, sobbing, dishevelled Rilla instead and took her home. Rilla was heart-broken. Her dress and slippers and hat were ruined and her six year old pride had received terrible bruises.

Susan, white with indignation, heard Miss Cornelia's story of Mary Vance's exploit.

"Oh, the hussy—oh, the littly hussy!" she said, as she carried Rilla away for purification and comfort.

"This thing has gone far enough, Anne dearie," said Miss Cornelia resolutely. "Something must be done. WHO is this creature who is staying at the manse and where does she come from?"

"I understood she was a little girl from over-harbour who was visiting at the manse," answered Anne, who saw the comical side of the codfish chase and secretly thought Rilla was rather vain and needed a lesson or two.

"I know all the over-harbour families who come to our church and that imp doesn't belong to any of them," retorted Miss Cornelia. "She is almost in rags and when she goes to church she wears Faith Meredith's old clothes. There's some mystery here, and I'm going to investigate it, since it seems nobody else will. I believe she was at the bottom of their goings-on in Warren Mead's spruce bush the other day. Did you hear of their frightening his mother into a fit?"

"No. I knew Gilbert had been called to see her, but I did not hear what the trouble was."

"Well, you know she has a weak heart. And one day last week, when she was all alone on the veranda, she heard the most awful shrieks of 'murder' and 'help' coming from the bush—positively frightful sounds, Anne dearie. Her heart gave out at once. Warren heard them himself at the barn, and went straight to the bush to investigate, and there he found all the manse children sitting on a fallen tree and screaming 'murder' at the top of their lungs. They told him they were only in fun and didn't think anyone would hear them. They were just playing Indian ambush. Warren went back to the house and found his poor mother unconscious on the veranda."

Susan, who had returned, sniffed contemptuously.

"I think she was very far from being unconscious, Mrs. Marshall Elliott, and that you may tie to. I have been hearing of Amelia Warren's weak heart for forty years. She had it when she was twenty. She enjoys making a fuss and having the doctor, and any excuse will do."

"I don't think Gilbert thought her attack very serious," said Anne.

"Oh, that may very well be," said Miss Cornelia. "But the matter has made an awful lot of talk and the Meads being Methodists makes it that much worse. What is going to become of those children? Sometimes I can't sleep at nights for thinking about them, Anne dearie. I really do question if they get enough to eat, even, for their father is so lost in dreams that he doesn't often remember he has a stomach, and that lazy old woman doesn't bother cooking what she ought. They are just running wild and now that school is closing they'll be worse than ever."

"They do have jolly times," said Anne, laughing over the recollections of some Rainbow Valley happenings that had come to her ears. "And they are all brave and frank and loyal and truthful."

"That's a true word, Anne dearie, and when you come to think of all the trouble in the church those two tattling, deceitful youngsters of the last minister's made, I'm inclined to overlook a good deal in the Merediths."

"When all is said and done, Mrs. Dr. dear, they are very nice children," said Susan. "They have got plenty of original sin in them and that I will admit, but maybe it is just as well, for if they had not they might spoil from over-sweetness. Only I do think it is not proper for them to play in a graveyard and that I will maintain."

"But they really play quite quietly there," excused Anne. "They don't run and yell as they do elsewhere. Such howls as drift up here from Rainbow Valley sometimes! Though I fancy my own small fry bear a valiant part in them. They had a sham battle there last night and had to 'roar' themselves, because they had no artillery to do it, so Jem says. Jem is passing through the stage where all boys hanker to be soldiers."

"Well, thank goodness, he'll never be a soldier," said Miss Cornelia. "I never approved of our boys going to that South African fracas. But it's over, and not likely anything of the kind will ever happen again. I think the world is getting more sensible. As for the Merediths, I've said many a time and I say it again, if Mr. Meredith had a wife all would be well."

"He called twice at the Kirks' last week, so I am told," said Susan.

"Well," said Miss Cornelia thoughtfully, "as a rule, I don't approve of a minister marrying in his congregation. It generally spoils him. But in this case it would do no harm, for every one likes Elizabeth Kirk and nobody else is hankering for the job of stepmothering those youngsters. Even the Hill girls balk at that. They haven't been found laying traps for Mr. Meredith. Elizabeth would make him a good wife if he only thought so. But the trouble is, she really is homely and, Anne dearie, Mr. Meredith, abstracted as he is, has an eye for a good-looking woman, man-like. He isn't SO other-worldly when it comes to that, believe ME."

"Elizabeth Kirk is a very nice person, but they do say that people have nearly frozen to death in her mother's spare-room bed before now, Mrs. Dr. dear," said Susan darkly. "If I felt I had any right to express an opinion concerning such a solemn matter as a minister's marriage I would say that I think Elizabeth's cousin Sarah, over-harbour, would make Mr. Meredith a better wife."

"Why, Sarah Kirk is a Methodist," said Miss Cornelia, much as if Susan had suggested a Hottentot as a manse bride.

"She would likely turn Presbyterian if she married Mr. Meredith," retorted Susan.

Miss Cornelia shook her head. Evidently with her it was, once a Methodist, always a Methodist.

"Sarah Kirk is entirely out of the question," she said positively. "And so is Emmeline Drew—though the Drews are all trying to make the match. They are literally throwing poor Emmeline at his head, and he hasn't the least idea of it."

"Emmeline Drew has no gumption, I must allow," said Susan. "She is the kind of woman, Mrs. Dr. dear, who would put a hot-water bottle in your bed on a dog-night and then have her feelings hurt because you were not grateful. And her mother was a very poor housekeeper. Did you ever hear the story of her dish-cloth? She lost her dishcloth one day. But the next day she found it. Oh, yes, Mrs. Dr. dear, she found it, in the goose at the dinner-table, mixed up with the stuffing. Do you think a woman like that would do for a minister's mother-in-law? I do not. But no doubt I would be better employed in mending little Jem's trousers than in talking gossip about my neighbours. He tore them something scandalous last night in Rainbow Valley."

"Where is Walter?" asked Anne.

"He is up to no good, I fear, Mrs. Dr. dear. He is in the attic writing something in an exercise book. And he has not done as well in arithmetic this term as he should, so the teacher tells me. Too well I know the reason why. He has been writing silly rhymes when he should have been doing his sums. I am afraid that boy is going to be a poet, Mrs. Dr. dear."

"He is a poet now, Susan."

"Well, you take it real calm, Mrs. Dr. dear. I suppose it is the best way, when a person has the strength. I had an uncle who began by being a poet and ended up by being a tramp. Our family were dreadfully ashamed of him."

"You don't seem to think very highly of poets, Susan," said Anne, laughing.

"Who does, Mrs. Dr. dear?" asked Susan in genuine astonishment.

"What about Milton and Shakespeare? And the poets of the Bible?"

"They tell me Milton could not get along with his wife, and Shakespeare was no more than respectable by times. As for the Bible, of course things were different in those sacred days— although I never had a high opinion of King David, say what you will. I never knew any good to come of writing poetry, and I hope and pray that blessed boy will outgrow the tendency. If he does not—we must see what emulsion of cod-liver oil will do."

CHAPTER VIII. MISS CORNELIA INTERVENES

Miss Cornelia descended upon the manse the next day and cross-questioned Mary, who, being a young person of considerable discernment and astuteness, told her story simple and truthfully, with an entire absence of complaint or bravado. Miss Cornelia was more favourably impressed than she had expected to be, but deemed it her duty to be severe.

"Do you think," she said sternly, "that you showed your gratitude to this family, who have been far too kind to you, by insulting and chasing one of their little friends as you did yesterday?"

"Say, it was rotten mean of me," admitted Mary easily. "I dunno what possessed me. That old codfish seemed to come in so blamed handy. But I was awful sorry—I cried last night after I went to bed about it, honest I did. You ask Una if I didn't. I wouldn't tell her what for 'cause I was ashamed of it, and then she cried, too, because she was afraid someone had hurt my feelings. Laws, *I* ain't got any feelings to hurt worth speaking of. What worries me is why Mrs. Wiley hain't been hunting for me. It ain't like her."

Miss Cornelia herself thought it rather peculiar, but she merely admonished Mary sharply not to take any further liberties with the minister's codfish, and went to report progress at Ingleside.

"If the child's story is true the matter ought to be looked into," she said. "I know something about that Wiley woman, believe ME. Marshall used to be well acquainted with her when he lived over-harbour. I heard him say something last summer about her and a home child she had—likely this very Mary-creature. He said some one told him she was working the child to death and not half feeding and clothing it. You know, Anne dearie, it has always been my habit neither to make nor meddle with those over-harbour folks. But I shall send Marshall over to-morrow to find out the rights of this if he can. And THEN I'll speak to the minister. Mind you, Anne dearie, the Merediths found this girl literally starving in James Taylor's old hay barn. She had been there all night, cold and hungry and alone. And us sleeping warm in our beds after good suppers."

"The poor little thing," said Anne, picturing one of her own dear babies, cold and hungry and alone in such circumstances. "If she has been ill-used, Miss Cornelia, she mustn't be taken back to such a place. *I* was an orphan once in a very similar situation."

"We'll have to consult the Hopetown asylum folks," said Miss Cornelia. "Anyway, she can't be left at the manse. Dear knows what those poor children might learn from her. I understand that she has been known to swear. But just think of her being there two whole weeks and Mr Meredith never waking up to it! What business has a man like that to have a family? Why, Anne dearie, he ought to be a monk."

Two evenings later Miss Cornelia was back at Ingleside.

"It's the most amazing thing!" she said. "Mrs. Wiley was found dead in her bed the very morning after this Mary-creature ran away. She has had a bad heart for years and the doctor had warned her it might happen at any time. She had sent away her hired man and there was nobody in the house. Some neighbours found her the next day. They missed the child, it seems, but supposed Mrs. Wiley had sent her to her cousin near Charlottetown as she had said she was going to do. The cousin didn't come to the funeral and so nobody ever knew that Mary wasn't with her. The people Marshall talked to told him some things about the way Mrs. Wiley used this Mary that made his blood boil, so he declares. You know, it puts Marshall in a regular fury to hear of a child being ill-used. They said she whipped her mercilessly for every little fault or mistake. Some folks talked of writing to the asylum authorities but everybody's business is nobody's business and it was never done."

"I am sorry that Wiley person is dead," said Susan fiercely. "I should like to go over-harbour and give her a piece of my mind. Starving and beating a child, Mrs. Dr. dear! As you know, I hold with lawful spanking, but I go no further. And what is to become of this poor child now, Mrs. Marshall Elliott?"

"I suppose she must be sent back to Hopetown," said Miss Cornelia. "I think every one hereabouts who wants a home child has one. I'll see Mr. Meredith to-morrow and tell him my opinion of the whole affair."

"And no doubt she will, Mrs. Dr. dear," said Susan, after Miss Cornelia had gone. "She would stick at nothing, not even at shingling the church spire if she took it into her head. But I cannot understand how even Cornelia Bryant can talk to a minister as she does. You would think he was just any common person."

When Miss Cornelia had gone, Nan Blythe uncurled herself from the hammock where she had been studying her lessons and slipped away to Rainbow Valley. The others were already there. Jem and Jerry were playing quoits with old horseshoes borrowed from the Glen blacksmith. Carl was stalking ants on a sunny hillock. Walter, lying on his stomach among the fern, was reading aloud to Mary and Di and Faith and Una from a wonderful book of myths wherein were fascinating accounts of Prester John and the Wandering Jew, divining rods and tailed men, of Schamir, the worm that split rocks and opened the way to golden treasure, of Fortunate Isles and swan-maidens. It was a great shock to Walter to learn that William Tell and Gelert were myths also; and the story of Bishop Hatto was to keep him awake all that night; but best of all he loved the stories of the Pied Piper and the San Greal. He read them thrillingly, while the bells on the

Tree Lovers tinkled in the summer wind and the coolness of the evening shadows crept across the valley.

"Say, ain't them in'resting lies?" said Mary admiringly when Walter had closed the book.

"They aren't lies," said Di indignantly.

"You don't mean they're true?" asked Mary incredulously.

"No—not exactly. They're like those ghost-stories of yours. They weren't true—but you didn't expect us to believe them, so they weren't lies."

"That yarn about the divining rod is no lie, anyhow," said Mary. "Old Jake Crawford over-harbour can work it. They send for him from everywhere when they want to dig a well. And I believe I know the Wandering Jew."

"Oh, Mary," said Una, awe-struck.

"I do—true's you're alive. There was an old man at Mrs. Wiley's one day last fall. He looked old enough to be ANYTHING. She was asking him about cedar posts, if he thought they'd last well. And he said, 'Last well? They'll last a thousand years. I know, for I've tried them twice.' Now, if he was two thousand years old who was he but your Wandering Jew?"

"I don't believe the Wandering Jew would associate with a person like Mrs. Wiley," said Faith decidedly.

"I love the Pied Piper story," said Di, "and so does mother. I always feel so sorry for the poor little lame boy who couldn't keep up with the others and got shut out of the mountain. He must have been so disappointed. I think all the rest of his life he'd be wondering what wonderful thing he had missed and wishing he could have got in with the others."

"But how glad his mother must have been," said Una softly. "I think she had been sorry all her life that he was lame. Perhaps she even used to cry about it. But she would never be sorry again—never. She would be glad he was lame because that was why she hadn't lost him."

"Some day," said Walter dreamily, looking afar into the sky, "the Pied Piper will come over the hill up there and down Rainbow Valley, piping merrily and sweetly. And I will follow him—follow him down to the shore—down to the sea—away from you all. I don't think I'll want to go—Jem will want to go—it will be such an adventure—but I won't. Only I'll HAVE to—the music will call and call and call me until I MUST follow."

"We'll all go," cried Di, catching fire at the flame of Walter's fancy, and half-believing she could see the mocking, retreating figure of the mystic piper in the far, dim end of the valley.

"No. You'll sit here and wait," said Walter, his great, splendid eyes full of strange glamour. "You'll wait for us to come back. And we may not come—for we cannot come as long as the Piper plays. He may pipe us round the world. And still you'll sit here and wait—and WAIT."

"Oh, dry up," said Mary, shivering. "Don't look like that, Walter Blythe. You give me the creeps. Do you want to set me bawling? I could just see that horrid old Piper going away on, and you boys following him, and us girls sitting here waiting all alone. I dunno why it is—I never was one of the blubbering kind—but as soon as you start your spieling I always want to cry."

Walter smiled in triumph. He liked to exercise this power of his over his companions—to play on their feelings, waken their fears, thrill their souls. It satisfied some dramatic instinct in him. But under his triumph was a queer little chill of some mysterious dread. The Pied Piper had seemed very real to him—as if the fluttering veil that hid the future had for a moment been blown aside in the starlit dusk of Rainbow Valley and some dim glimpse of coming years granted to him.

Carl, coming up to their group with a report of the doings in ant-land, brought them all back to the realm of facts.

"Ants ARE darned in'resting," exclaimed Mary, glad to escape the shadowy Piper's thrall. "Carl and me watched that bed in the graveyard all Saturday afternoon. I never thought there was so much in bugs. Say, but they're quarrelsome little cusses—some of 'em like to start a fight 'thout any reason, far's we could see. And some of 'em are cowards. They got so scared they just doubled theirselves up into a ball and let the other fellows bang 'em. They wouldn't put up a fight at all. Some of 'em are lazy and won't work. We watched 'em shirking. And there was one ant died of grief 'cause another ant got killed—wouldn't work— wouldn't eat—just died—it did, honest to Go—oodness."

A shocked silence prevailed. Every one knew that Mary had not started out to say "goodness." Faith and Di exchanged glances that would have done credit to Miss Cornelia herself. Walter and Carl looked uncomfortable and Una's lip trembled.

Mary squirmed uncomfortably.

"That slipped out 'fore I thought—it did, honest to—I mean, true's you live, and I swallowed half of it. You folks over here are mighty squeamish seems to me. Wish you could have heard the Wileys when they had a fight."

"Ladies don't say such things," said Faith, very primly for her.

"It isn't right," whispered Una.

"I ain't a lady," said Mary. "What chance've I ever had of being a lady? But I won't say that again if I can help it. I promise you."

"Besides," said Una, "you can't expect God to answer your prayers if you take His name in vain, Mary."

"I don't expect Him to answer 'em anyhow," said Mary of little faith. "I've been asking Him for a week to clear up this Wiley affair and He hasn't done a thing. I'm going to give up."

At this juncture Nan arrived breathless.

"Oh, Mary, I've news for you. Mrs. Elliott has been over-harbour and what do you think she found out? Mrs. Wiley is dead—she was found dead in bed the morning after you ran away. So you'll never have to go back to her."

"Dead!" said Mary stupefied. Then she shivered.

"Do you s'pose my praying had anything to do with that?" she cried imploringly to Una. "If it had I'll never pray again as long as I live. Why, she may come back and ha'nt me."

"No, no, Mary," said Una comfortingly, "it hadn't. Why, Mrs.
Wiley died long before you ever began to pray about it at all."

"That's so," said Mary recovering from her panic. "But I tell you it gave me a start. I wouldn't like to think I'd prayed anybody to death. I never thought of such a thing as her dying when I was praying. She didn't seem much like the dying kind. Did Mrs. Elliott say anything about me?"

"She said you would likely have to go back to the asylum."

"I thought as much," said Mary drearily. "And then they'll give me out again—likely to some one just like Mrs. Wiley. Well, I s'pose I can stand it. I'm tough."

"I'm going to pray that you won't have to go back," whispered

Una, as she and Mary walked home to the manse.

"You can do as you like," said Mary decidedly, "but I vow *I* won't. I'm good and scared of this praying business. See what's come of it. If Mrs. Wiley HAD died after I started praying it would have been my doings."

"Oh, no, it wouldn't," said Una. "I wish I could explain things better—father could, I know, if you'd talk to him, Mary."

"Catch me! I don't know what to make of your father, that's the long and short of it. He goes by me and never sees me in broad daylight. I ain't proud—but I ain't a door-mat, neither!"

"Oh, Mary, it's just father's way. Most of the time he never sees us, either. He is thinking deeply, that is all. And I AM going to pray that God will keep you in Four Winds—because I like you, Mary."

"All right. Only don't let me hear of any more people dying on account of it," said Mary. "I'd like to stay in Four Winds fine. I like it and I like the harbour and the light house—and you and the Blythes. You're the only friends I ever had and I'd hate to leave you."

CHAPTER IX. UNA INTERVENES

Miss Cornelia had an interview with Mr. Meredith which proved something of a shock to that abstracted gentleman. She pointed out to him, none too respectfully, his dereliction of duty in allowing a waif like Mary Vance to come into his family and associate with his children without knowing or learning anything about her.

"I don't say there is much harm done, of course," she concluded. "This Mary-creature isn't what you might call bad, when all is said and done. I've been questioning your children and the Blythes, and from what I can make out there's nothing much to be said against the child except that she's slangy and doesn't use very refined language. But think what might have happened if she'd been like some of those home children we know of. You know yourself what that poor little creature the Jim Flaggs' had, taught and told the Flagg children."

Mr. Meredith did know and was honestly shocked over his own carelessness in the matter.

"But what is to be done, Mrs. Elliott?" he asked helplessly. "We can't turn the poor child out. She must be cared for."

"Of course. We'd better write to the Hopetown authorities at once. Meanwhile, I suppose she might as well stay here for a few more days till we hear from them. But keep your eyes and ears open, Mr. Meredith."

Susan would have died of horror on the spot if she had heard Miss Cornelia so admonishing a minister. But Miss Cornelia departed in a warm glow of satisfaction over duty done, and that night Mr. Meredith asked Mary to come into his study with him. Mary obeyed, looking literally ghastly with fright. But she got the surprise of her poor, battered little life. This man, of whom she had stood so terribly in awe, was the kindest, gentlest soul she had ever met. Before she knew what happened Mary found herself pouring all her troubles into his ear and receiving in return such sympathy and tender understanding as it had never occurred to her to imagine. Mary left the study with her face and eyes so softened that Una hardly knew her.

"Your father's all right, when he does wake up," she said with a sniff that just escaped being a sob. "It's a pity he doesn't wake up oftener. He said I wasn't to blame for Mrs. Wiley dying, but that I must try to think of her good points and not of her bad ones. I dunno what good points she had, unless it was keeping her house clean and making first-class butter. I know I 'most wore my arms out scrubbing her old kitchen floor with the knots in it. But anything your father says goes with me after this."

Mary proved a rather dull companion in the following days, however. She confided to Una that the more she thought of going back to the asylum the more she hated it. Una racked her small brains for some way of averting it, but it was Nan Blythe who came to the rescue with a somewhat startling suggestion.

"Mrs. Elliott might take Mary herself. She has a great big house and Mr. Elliott is always wanting her to have help. It would be just a splendid place for Mary. Only she'd have to behave herself."

"Oh, Nan, do you think Mrs. Elliott would take her?"

"It wouldn't do any harm if you asked her," said Nan. At first Una did not think she could. She was so shy that to ask a favour of anybody was agony to her. And she was very much in awe of the bustling, energetic Mrs. Elliott. She liked her very much and always enjoyed a visit to her house; but to go and ask her to adopt Mary Vance seemed such a height of presumption that Una's timid spirit quailed.

When the Hopetown authorities wrote to Mr. Meredith to send Mary to them without delay Mary cried herself to sleep in the manse attic that night and Una found a desperate courage. The next evening she slipped away from the manse to the harbour road. Far down in Rainbow Valley she heard joyous laughter but her way lay not there. She was terribly pale and terribly in earnest—so much so that she took no notice of the people she met—and old Mrs. Stanley Flagg was quite huffed and said Una Meredith would be as absentminded as her father when she grew up.

Miss Cornelia lived half way between the Glen and Four Winds Point, in a house whose original glaring green hue had mellowed down to an agreeable greenish gray. Marshall Elliott had planted trees about it and set out a rose garden and a spruce hedge. It was quite a different place from what it had been in years agone. The manse children and the Ingleside children liked to go there. It was a beautiful walk down the old harbour road, and there was always a well-filled cooky jar at the end.

The misty sea was lapping softly far down on the sands. Three big boats were skimming down the harbour like great white sea-birds. A schooner was coming up the channel. The world of Four Winds was steeped in glowing colour, and subtle music, and strange glamour, and everybody should have been happy in it. But when Una turned in at Miss Cornelia's gate her very legs had almost refused to carry her.

Miss Cornelia was alone on the veranda. Una had hoped Mr. Elliott would be there. He was so big and hearty and twinkly that there would be encouragement in his presence. She sat on the little stool Miss Cornelia brought out and tried to eat the doughnut Miss Cornelia gave her. It stuck in her throat, but she swallowed desperately lest Miss Cornelia be offended. She could not talk; she was still pale;

and her big, dark-blue eyes looked so piteous that Miss Cornelia concluded the child was in some trouble.

"What's on your mind, dearie?" she asked. "There's something, that's plain to be seen."

Una swallowed the last twist of doughnut with a desperate gulp.

"Mrs. Elliott, won't you take Mary Vance?" she said beseechingly.

Miss Cornelia stared blankly.

"Me! Take Mary Vance! Do you mean keep her?"

"Yes—keep her—adopt her," said Una eagerly, gaining courage now that the ice was broken. "Oh, Mrs. Elliott, PLEASE do. She doesn't want to go back to the asylum—she cries every night about it. She's so afraid of being sent to another hard place. And she's SO smart—there isn't anything she can't do. I know you wouldn't be sorry if you took her."

"I never thought of such a thing," said Miss Cornelia rather helplessly.

"WON'T you think of it?" implored Una.

"But, dearie, I don't want help. I'm quite able to do all the work here. And I never thought I'd like to have a home girl if I did need help."

The light went out of Una's eyes. Her lips trembled. She sat down on her stool again, a pathetic little figure of disappointment, and began to cry.

"Don't—dearie—don't," exclaimed Miss Cornelia in distress. She could never bear to hurt a child. "I don't say I WON'T take her—but the idea is so new it has just kerflummuxed me. I must think it over."

"Mary is SO smart," said Una again.

"Humph! So I've heard. I've heard she swears, too. Is that true?"

"I've never heard her swear EXACTLY," faltered Una uncomfortably.

"But I'm afraid she COULD."

"I believe you! Does she always tell the truth?"

"I think she does, except when she's afraid of a whipping."

"And yet you want me to take her!"

"SOME ONE has to take her," sobbed Una. "SOME ONE has to look after her, Mrs. Elliott."

"That's true. Perhaps it IS my duty to do it," said Miss Cornelia with a sigh. "Well, I'll have to talk it over with Mr. Elliott. So don't say anything about it just yet. Take another doughnut, dearie."

Una took it and ate it with a better appetite.

"I'm very fond of doughnuts," she confessed "Aunt Martha never makes any. But Miss Susan at Ingleside does, and sometimes she lets us have a plateful in Rainbow Valley. Do you know what I do when I'm hungry for doughnuts and can't get any, Mrs. Elliott?"

"No, dearie. What?"

"I get out mother's old cook book and read the doughnut recipe—and the other recipes. They sound SO nice. I always do that when I'm hungry—especially after we've had ditto for dinner. THEN I read the fried chicken and the roast goose recipes. Mother could make all those nice things."

"Those manse children will starve to death yet if Mr. Meredith doesn't get married," Miss Cornelia told her husband indignantly after Una had gone. "And he won't—and what's to be done? And SHALL we take this Mary-creature, Marshall?"

"Yes, take her," said Marshall laconically.

"Just like a man," said his wife, despairingly." 'Take her'—as if that was all. There are a hundred things to be considered, believe ME."

"Take her—and we'll consider them afterwards, Cornelia," said her husband.

In the end Miss Cornelia did take her and went up to announce her decision to the Ingleside people first.

"Splendid!" said Anne delightedly. "I've been hoping you would do that very thing, Miss Cornelia. I want that poor child to get a good home. I was a homeless little orphan just like her once."

"I don't think this Mary-creature is or ever will be much like you," retorted Miss Cornelia gloomily. "She's a cat of another colour. But she's also a human being with an immortal soul to save. I've got a shorter catechism and a small tooth comb and I'm going to do my duty by her, now that I've set my hand to the plough, believe me."

Mary received the news with chastened satisfaction.

"It's better luck than I expected," she said.

"You'll have to mind your p's and q's with Mrs. Elliott," said Nan.

"Well, I can do that," flashed Mary. "I know how to behave when I want to just as well as you, Nan Blythe."

"You mustn't use bad words, you know, Mary," said Una anxiously.

"I s'pose she'd die of horror if I did," grinned Mary, her white eyes shining with unholy glee over the idea. "But you needn't worry, Una. Butter won't melt in my mouth after this. I'll be all prunes and prisms."

"Nor tell lies," added Faith.

"Not even to get off from a whipping?" pleaded Mary.

"Mrs. Elliott will NEVER whip you—NEVER," exclaimed Di.

"Won't she?" said Mary skeptically. "If I ever find myself in a place where I ain't licked I'll think it's heaven all right. No fear of me telling lies then. I ain't fond of telling 'em—I'd ruther not, if it comes to that."

The day before Mary's departure from the manse they had a picnic in her honour in Rainbow Valley, and that evening all the manse children gave her something from their scanty store of treasured things for a keepsake. Carl gave her his Noah's ark and Jerry his second best jew's-harp. Faith gave her a little hairbrush with a mirror in the back of it, which Mary had always considered very wonderful. Una hesitated between an old beaded purse and a gay picture of Daniel in the lion's den, and finally offered Mary her choice. Mary really hankered after the beaded purse, but she knew Una loved it, so she said,

"Give me Daniel. I'd rusher have it 'cause I'm partial to lions. Only I wish they'd et Daniel up. It would have been more exciting."

At bedtime Mary coaxed Una to sleep with her.

"It's for the last time," she said, "and it's raining tonight, and I hate sleeping up there alone when it's raining on account of that graveyard. I don't mind it on fine nights, but a night like this I can't see anything but the rain pouring down on them old white stones, and the wind round the window sounds as if them dead people were trying to get in and crying 'cause they couldn't."

"I like rainy nights," said Una, when they were cuddled down together in the little attic room, "and so do the Blythe girls."

"I don't mind 'em when I'm not handy to graveyards," said Mary. "If I was alone here I'd cry my eyes out I'd be so lonesome. I feel awful bad to be leaving you all."

"Mrs. Elliott will let you come up and play in Rainbow Valley quite often I'm sure," said Una. "And you WILL be a good girl, won't you, Mary?"

"Oh, I'll try," sighed Mary. "But it won't be as easy for me to be good—inside, I mean, as well as outside—as it is for you. You hadn't such scalawags of relations as I had."

"But your people must have had some good qualities as well as bad ones," argued Una. "You must live up to them and never mind their bad ones."

"I don't believe they had any good qualities," said Mary gloomily. "I never heard of any. My grandfather had money, but they say he was a rascal. No, I'll just have to start out on my own hook and do the best I can."

"And God will help you, you know, Mary, if you ask Him."

"I don't know about that."

"Oh, Mary. You know we asked God to get a home for you and He did."

"I don't see what He had to do with it," retorted Mary. "It was you put it into Mrs. Elliott's head."

"But God put it into her HEART to take you. All my putting it into her HEAD wouldn't have done any good if He hadn't."

"Well, there may be something in that," admitted Mary. "Mind you, I haven't got anything against God, Una. I'm willing to give Him a chance. But, honest, I think He's an awful lot like your father—just absent-minded and never taking any notice of a body most of the time, but sometimes waking up all of a sudden and being awful good and kind and sensible."

"Oh, Mary, no!" exclaimed horrified Una. "God isn't a bit like father—I mean He's a thousand times better and kinder."

"If He's as good as your father He'll do for me," said Mary. "When your father was talking to me I felt as if I never could be bad any more."

"I wish you'd talk to father about Him," sighed Una. "He can explain it all so much better than I can."

"Why, so I will, next time he wakes up," promised Mary. "That night he talked to me in the study he showed me real clear that my praying didn't kill Mrs. Wiley. My mind's been easy since, but I'm real cautious about praying. I guess the old rhyme is the safest. Say, Una, it seems to me if one has to pray to any-body it'd be better to pray to the devil than to God. God's good, anyhow so you say, so He won't do you any harm, but from all I can make out the devil needs to be pacified. I think the sensible way would be to say to HIM, 'Good devil, please don't tempt me. Just leave me alone, please.' Now, don't you?"

"Oh, no, no, Mary. I'm sure it couldn't be right to pray to the devil. And it wouldn't do any good because he's bad. It might aggravate him and he'd be worse than ever."

"Well, as to this God-matter," said Mary stubbornly, "since you and I can't set-tle it, there ain't no use in talking more about it until we've a chanct to find out the rights of it. I'll do the best I can alone till then."

"If mother was alive she could tell us everything," said Una with a sigh.

"I wisht she was alive," said Mary. "I don't know what's going to become of you youngsters when I'm gone. Anyhow, DO try and keep the house a little tidy. The way people talks about it is scandalous. And the first thing you know your father will be getting married again and then your noses will be out of joint."

Una was startled. The idea of her father marrying again had never presented itself to her before. She did not like it and she lay silent under the chill of it.

"Stepmothers are AWFUL creatures," Mary went on. "I could make your blood run cold if I was to tell you all I know about 'em. The Wilson kids across the road from Wiley's had a stepmother. She was just as bad to 'em as Mrs. Wiley was to me. It'll be awful if you get a stepmother."

"I'm sure we won't," said Una tremulously. "Father won't marry anybody else."

"He'll be hounded into it, I expect," said Mary darkly. "All the old maids in the settlement are after him. There's no being up to them. And the worst of step-mothers is, they always set your father against you. He'd never care anything about you again. He'd always take her part and her children's part. You see, she'd make him believe you were all bad."

"I wish you hadn't told me this, Mary," cried Una. "It makes me feel so un-happy."

"I only wanted to warn you," said Mary, rather repentantly. "Of course, your father's so absent-minded he mightn't happen to think of getting married again. But it's better to be prepared."

Long after Mary slept serenely little Una lay awake, her eyes smarting with tears. On, how dreadful it would be if her father should marry somebody who would make him hate her and Jerry and Faith and Carl! She couldn't bear it—she couldn't!

Mary had not instilled any poison of the kind Miss Cornelia had feared into the manse children's minds. Yet she had certainly contrived to do a little mischief with the best of intentions. But she slept dreamlessly, while Una lay awake and the rain fell and the wind wailed around the old gray manse. And the Rev. John Meredith forgot to go to bed at all because he was absorbed in reading a life of St. Augustine. It was gray dawn when he finished it and went upstairs, wrestling with the problems of two thousand years ago. The door of the girls' room was open and he saw Faith lying asleep, rosy and beautiful. He wondered where Una was. Perhaps she had gone over to "stay all night" with the Blythe girls. She did this occasionally, deeming it a great treat. John Meredith sighed. He felt that Una's whereabouts ought not to be a mystery to him. Cecelia would have looked after her better than that.

If only Cecelia were still with him! How pretty and gay she had been! How the old manse up at Maywater had echoed to her songs! And she had gone away so suddenly, taking her laughter and music and leaving silence—so suddenly that he had never quite got over his feeling of amazement. How could SHE, the beautiful and vivid, have died?

The idea of a second marriage had never presented itself seriously to John Meredith. He had loved his wife so deeply that he believed he could never care for any woman again. He had a vague idea that before very long Faith would be old enough to take her mother's place. Until then, he must do the best he could alone. He sighed and went to his room, where the bed was still unmade. Aunt Martha had forgotten it, and Mary had not dared to make it because Aunt Martha had forbidden her to meddle with anything in the minister's room. But Mr. Meredith did not notice that it was unmade. His last thoughts were of St. Augustine.

CHAPTER X. THE MANSE GIRLS CLEAN HOUSE

"Ugh," said Faith, sitting up in bed with a shiver. "It's raining. I do hate a rainy Sunday. Sunday is dull enough even when it's fine."

"We oughtn't to find Sunday dull," said Una sleepily, trying to pull her drowsy wits together with an uneasy conviction that they had overslept.

"But we DO, you know," said Faith candidly. "Mary Vance says most Sundays are so dull she could hang herself."

"We ought to like Sunday better than Mary Vance," said Una remorsefully. "We're the minister's children."

"I wish we were a blacksmith's children," protested Faith angrily, hunting for her stockings. "THEN people wouldn't expect us to be better than other children. JUST look at the holes in my heels. Mary darned them all up before she went away, but they're as bad as ever now. Una, get up. I can't get the breakfast alone. Oh, dear. I wish father and Jerry were home. You wouldn't think we'd miss father much—we don't see much of him when he is home. And yet EVERYTHING seems gone. I must run in and see how Aunt Martha is."

"Is she any better?" asked Una, when Faith returned.

"No, she isn't. She's groaning with the misery still. Maybe we ought to tell Dr. Blythe. But she says not—she never had a doctor in her life and she isn't going to begin now. She says doctors just live by poisoning people. Do you suppose they do?"

"No, of course not," said Una indignantly. "I'm sure Dr. Blythe wouldn't poison anybody."

"Well, we'll have to rub Aunt Martha's back again after breakfast. We'd better not make the flannels as hot as we did yesterday."

Faith giggled over the remembrance. They had nearly scalded the skin off poor Aunt Martha's back. Una sighed. Mary Vance would have known just what the precise temperature of flannels for a misery back should be. Mary knew everything. They knew nothing. And how could they learn, save by bitter experience for which, in this instance, unfortunate Aunt Martha had paid?

The preceding Monday Mr. Meredith had left for Nova Scotia to spend his short vacation, taking Jerry with him. On Wednesday Aunt Martha was suddenly seized with a recurring and mysterious ailment which she always called "the misery," and which was tolerably certain to attack her at the most inconvenient times. She could not rise from her bed, any movement causing agony. A doctor she flatly refused to have. Faith and Una cooked the meals and waited on her. The less said about the meals the better—yet they were not much worse than Aunt Martha's had been. There were many women in the village who would have been glad to come and help, but Aunt Martha refused to let her plight be known.

"You must worry on till I kin git around," she groaned. "Thank goodness, John isn't here. There's a plenty o' cold biled meat and bread and you kin try your hand at making porridge."

The girls had tried their hand, but so far without much success. The first day it had been too thin. The next day so thick that you could cut it in slices. And both days it had been burned.

"I hate porridge," said Faith viciously. "When I have a house of my own I'm NEVER going to have a single bit of porridge in it."

"What'll your children do then?" asked Una. "Children have to have porridge or they won't grow. Everybody says so."

"They'll have to get along without it or stay runts," retorted Faith stubbornly. "Here, Una, you stir it while I set the table. If I leave it for a minute the horrid stuff will burn. It's half past nine. We'll be late for Sunday School."

"I haven't seen anyone going past yet," said Una. "There won't likely be many out. Just see how it's pouring. And when there's no preaching the folks won't come from a distance to bring the children."

"Go and call Carl," said Faith.

Carl, it appeared, had a sore throat, induced by getting wet in the Rainbow Valley marsh the previous evening while pursuing dragon-flies. He had come home with dripping stockings and boots and had sat out the evening in them. He could not eat any breakfast and Faith made him go back to bed again. She and Una left the table as it was and went to Sunday School. There was no one in the school room when they got there and no one came. They waited until eleven and then went home.

"There doesn't seem to be anybody at the Methodist Sunday School either," said Una.

"I'm GLAD," said Faith. "I'd hate to think the Methodists were better at going to Sunday School on rainy Sundays than the Presbyterians. But there's no preaching in their Church to-day, either, so likely their Sunday School is in the afternoon."

Una washed the dishes, doing them quite nicely, for so much had she learned from Mary Vance. Faith swept the floor after a fashion and peeled the potatoes for dinner, cutting her finger in the process.

"I wish we had something for dinner besides ditto," sighed Una. "I'm so tired of it. The Blythe children don't know what ditto is. And we NEVER have any pudding. Nan says Susan would faint if they had no pudding on Sundays. Why aren't we like other people, Faith?"

"I don't want to be like other people," laughed Faith, tying up her bleeding finger. "I like being myself. It's more interesting. Jessie Drew is as good a housekeeper as her mother, but would you want to be as stupid as she is?"

"But our house isn't right. Mary Vance says so. She says people talk about it being so untidy."

Faith had an inspiration.

"We'll clean it all up," she cried. "We'll go right to work to-morrow. It's a real good chance when Aunt Martha is laid up and can't interfere with us. We'll have it all lovely and clean when father comes home, just like it was when Mary went away. ANY ONE can sweep and dust and wash windows. People won't be able to talk about us any more. Jem Blythe says it's only old cats that talk, but their talk hurts just as much as anybody's."

"I hope it will be fine to-morrow," said Una, fired with enthusiasm. "Oh, Faith, it will be splendid to be all cleaned up and like other people."

"I hope Aunt Martha's misery will last over to-morrow," said Faith. "If it doesn't we won't get a single thing done."

Faith's amiable wish was fulfilled. The next day found Aunt Martha still unable to rise. Carl, too, was still sick and easily prevailed on to stay in bed. Neither Faith nor Una had any idea how sick the boy really was; a watchful mother would have had a doctor without delay; but there was no mother, and poor little Carl, with his sore throat and aching head and crimson cheeks, rolled himself up in his twisted bedclothes and suffered alone, somewhat comforted by the companionship of a small green lizard in the pocket of his ragged nighty.

The world was full of summer sunshine after the rain. It was a peerless day for house-cleaning and Faith and Una went gaily to work.

"We'll clean the dining-room and the parlour," said Faith. "It wouldn't do to meddle with the study, and it doesn't matter much about the upstairs. The first thing is to take everything out."

Accordingly, everything was taken out. The furniture was piled on the veranda and lawn and the Methodist graveyard fence was gaily draped with rugs. An orgy of sweeping followed, with an attempt at dusting on Una's part, while Faith washed the windows of the dining-room, breaking one pane and cracking two in the process. Una surveyed the streaked result dubiously.

"They don't look right, somehow," she said. "Mrs. Elliott's and Susan's windows just shine and sparkle."

"Never mind. They let the sunshine through just as well," said Faith cheerfully. "They MUST be clean after all the soap and water I've used, and that's the main thing. Now, it's past eleven, so I'll wipe up this mess on the floor and we'll go outside. You dust the furniture and I'll shake the rugs. I'm going to do it in the graveyard. I don't want to send dust flying all over the lawn.

Faith enjoyed the rug shaking. To stand on Hezekiah Pollock's tombstone, flapping and shaking rugs, was real fun. To be sure, Elder Abraham Clow and his wife, driving past in their capacious double-seated buggy, seemed to gaze at her in grim disapproval.

"Isn't that a terrible sight?" said Elder Abraham solemnly.

"I would never have believed it if I hadn't seen it with my own eyes," said Mrs. Elder Abraham, more solemnly still.

Faith waved a door mat cheerily at the Clow party. It did not worry her that the elder and his wife did not return her greeting. Everybody knew that Elder Abraham had never been known to smile since he had been appointed Superintendent of the Sunday School fourteen years previously. But it hurt her that Minnie and Adella Clow did not wave back. Faith liked Minnie and Adella. Next to the Blythes, they were her best friends in school and she always helped Adella with her sums. This was gratitude for you. Her friends cut her because she was shaking rugs in an old graveyard where, as Mary Vance said, not a living soul had been buried for years. Faith flounced around to the veranda, where she found Una grieved in spirit because the Clow girls had not waved to her, either.

"I suppose they're mad over something," said Faith. "Perhaps they're jealous because we play so much in Rainbow Valley with the Blythes. Well, just wait till school opens and Adella wants me to show her how to do her sums! We'll get square then. Come on, let's put the things back in. I'm tired to death and I don't believe the rooms will look much better than before we started— though I shook out pecks of dust in the graveyard. I HATE house-cleaning."

It was two o'clock before the tired girls finished the two rooms. They got a dreary bite in the kitchen and intended to wash the dishes at once. But Faith happened to pick up a new story-book Di Blythe had lent her and was lost to the world until sunset. Una took a cup of rank tea up to Carl but found him asleep; so she curled herself up on Jerry's bed and went to sleep too. Meanwhile, a weird story flew through Glen St. Mary and folks asked each other seriously what was to be done with those manse youngsters.

"That is past laughing at, believe ME," said Miss Cornelia to her husband, with a heavy sigh. "I couldn't believe it at first. Miranda Drew brought the story home from the Methodist Sunday School this afternoon and I simply scoffed at it. But Mrs. Elder Abraham says she and the Elder saw it with their own eyes."

"Saw what?" asked Marshall.

"Faith and Una Meredith stayed home from Sunday School this morning and CLEANED HOUSE," said Miss Cornelia, in accents of despair. "When Elder Abraham went home from the church—he had stayed behind to straighten out the library books—he saw them shaking rugs in the Methodist graveyard. I can never look a Methodist in the face again. Just think what a scandal it will make!"

A scandal it assuredly did make, growing more scandalous as it spread, until the over-harbour people heard that the manse children had not only cleaned house and put out a washing on Sunday, but had wound up with an afternoon picnic in the graveyard while the Methodist Sunday School was going on. The only household which remained in blissful ignorance of the terrible thing was the manse itself; on what Faith and Una fondly believed to be Tuesday it rained again; for the next three days it rained; nobody came near the manse; the manse folk went nowhere; they might have waded through the misty Rainbow Valley up to Ingleside, but all the Blythe family, save Susan and the doctor, were away on a visit to Avonlea.

"This is the last of our bread," said Faith, "and the ditto is done. If Aunt Martha doesn't get better soon WHAT will we do?"

"We can buy some bread in the village and there's the codfish

Mary dried," said Una. "But we don't know how to cook it."

"Oh, that's easy," laughed Faith. "You just boil it."

Boil it they did; but as it did not occur to them to soak it beforehand it was too salty to eat. That night they were very hungry; but by the following day their troubles were over. Sunshine returned to the world; Carl was well and Aunt Martha's misery left her as suddenly as it had come; the butcher called at the manse and chased famine away. To crown all, the Blythes returned home, and that evening they and the manse children and Mary Vance kept sunset tryst once more in Rainbow Valley, where the daisies were floating upon the grass like spirits of the dew and the bells on the Tree Lovers rang like fairy chimes in the scented twilight.

CHAPTER XI. A DREADFUL DISCOVERY

"Well, you kids have gone and done it now," was Mary's greeting, as she joined them in the Valley. Miss Cornelia was up at Ingleside, holding agonized conclave with Anne and Susan, and Mary hoped that the session might be a long one, for it was all of two weeks since she had been allowed to revel with her chums in the dear valley of rainbows.

"Done what?" demanded everybody but Walter, who was day-dreaming as usual.

"It's you manse young ones, I mean," said Mary. "It was just awful of you. *I* wouldn't have done such a thing for the world, and *I* weren't brought up in a manse—weren't brought up ANYWHERE—just COME up."

"What have WE done?" asked Faith blankly.

"Done! You'd BETTER ask! The talk is something terrible. I expect it's ruined your father in this congregation. He'll never be able to live it down, poor man! Everybody blames him for it, and that isn't fair. But nothing IS fair in this world. You ought to be ashamed of yourselves."

"What HAVE we done?" asked Una again, despairingly. Faith said nothing, but her eyes flashed golden-brown scorn at Mary.

"Oh, don't pretend innocence," said Mary, witheringly.

"Everybody knows what you have done."

"*I* don't," interjected Jem Blythe indignantly. "Don't let me catch you making Una cry, Mary Vance. What are you talking about?"

"I s'pose you don't know, since you're just back from up west," said Mary, somewhat subdued. Jem could always manage her. "But everybody else knows, you'd better believe."

"Knows what?"

"That Faith and Una stayed home from Sunday School last Sunday and CLEANED HOUSE."

"We didn't," cried Faith and Una, in passionate denial.

Mary looked haughtily at them.

"I didn't suppose you'd deny it, after the way you've combed ME down for lying," she said. "What's the good of saying you didn't? Everybody knows you DID. Elder Clow and his wife saw you. Some people say it will break up the church, but *I* don't go that far. You ARE nice ones."

Nan Blythe stood up and put her arms around the dazed Faith and Una.

"They were nice enough to take you in and feed you and clothe you when you were starving in Mr. Taylor's barn, Mary Vance," she said. "You are VERY grateful, I must say."

"I AM grateful," retorted Mary. "You'd know it if you'd heard me standing up for Mr. Meredith through thick and thin. I've blistered my tongue talking for him this week. I've said again and again that he isn't to blame if his young ones did clean house on Sunday. He was away—and they knew better."

"But we didn't," protested Una. "It was MONDAY we cleaned house. Wasn't it, Faith?"

"Of course it was," said Faith, with flashing eyes. "We went to Sunday School in spite of the rain—and no one came—not even Elder Abraham, for all his talk about fair-weather Christians."

"It was Saturday it rained," said Mary. "Sunday was as fine as silk. I wasn't at Sunday School because I had toothache, but every one else was and they saw all your stuff out on the lawn. And Elder Abraham and Mrs. Elder Abraham saw you shaking rugs in the graveyard."

Una sat down among the daisies and began to cry.

"Look here," said Jem resolutely, "this thing must be cleared up. SOMEBODY has made a mistake. Sunday WAS fine, Faith. How could you have thought Saturday was Sunday?"

"Prayer-meeting was Thursday night," cried Faith, "and Adam flew into the soup-pot on Friday when Aunt Martha's cat chased him, and spoiled our dinner; and Saturday there was a snake in the cellar and Carl caught it with a forked stick and carried it out, and Sunday it rained. So there!"

"Prayer-meeting was Wednesday night," said Mary. "Elder Baxter was to lead and he couldn't go Thursday night and it was changed to Wednesday. You were just a day out, Faith Meredith, and you DID work on Sunday."

Suddenly Faith burst into a peal of laughter.

"I suppose we did. What a joke!"

"It isn't much of a joke for your father," said Mary sourly.

"It'll be all right when people find out it was just a mistake," said Faith carelessly. "We'll explain."

"You can explain till you're black in the face," said Mary, "but a lie like that'll travel faster'n further than you ever will. I'VE seen more of the world than you and *I* know. Besides, there are plenty of folks won't believe it was a mistake."

"They will if I tell them," said Faith.

"You can't tell everybody," said Mary. "No, I tell you you've disgraced your father."

Una's evening was spoiled by this dire reflection, but Faith refused to be made uncomfortable. Besides, she had a plan that would put everything right. So she put the past with its mistake behind her and gave herself over to enjoyment of the present. Jem went away to fish and Walter came out of his reverie and proceeded to describe the woods of heaven. Mary pricked up her ears and listened respect-fully. Despite her awe of Walter she revelled in his "book talk." It always gave her a delightful sensation. Walter had been reading his Coleridge that day, and he pictured a heaven where

"There were gardens bright with sinuous rills
    Where blossomed many an incense bearing tree,
And there were forests ancient as the hills
    Enfolding sunny spots of greenery."

"I didn't know there was any woods in heaven," said Mary, with a long breath. "I thought it was all streets—and streets—AND streets."

"Of course there are woods," said Nan. "Mother can't live without trees and I can't, so what would be the use of going to heaven if there weren't any trees?"

"There are cities, too," said the young dreamer, "splendid cities—coloured just like the sunset, with sapphire towers and rainbow domes. They are built of gold and diamonds—whole streets of diamonds, flashing like the sun. In the squares there are crystal fountains kissed by the light, and everywhere the asphodel blooms—the flower of heaven."

"Fancy!" said Mary. "I saw the main street in Charlottetown once and I thought it was real grand, but I s'pose it's nothing to heaven. Well, it all sounds gorgeous the way you tell it, but won't it be kind of dull, too?"

"Oh, I guess we can have some fun when the angels' backs are turned," said Faith comfortably.

"Heaven is ALL fun," declared Di.

"The Bible doesn't say so," cried Mary, who had read so much of the Bible on Sunday afternoons under Miss Cornelia's eye that she now considered herself quite an authority on it.

"Mother says the Bible language is figurative," said Nan.

"Does that mean that it isn't true?" asked Mary hopefully.

"No—not exactly—but I think it means that heaven will be just like what you'd like it to be."

"I'd like it to be just like Rainbow Valley," said Mary, "with all you kids to gas and play with. THAT'S good enough for me. Anyhow, we can't go to heaven till we're dead and maybe not then, so what's the use of worrying? Here's Jem with a string of trout and it's my turn to fry them."

"We ought to know more about heaven than Walter does when we're the min-ister's family," said Una, as they walked home that night.

"We KNOW just as much, but Walter can IMAGINE," said Faith.

"Mrs. Elliott says he gets it from his mother."

"I do wish we hadn't made that mistake about Sunday," sighed Una.

"Don't worry over that. I've thought of a great plan to explain so that every-body will know," said Faith. "Just wait till to-morrow night."

CHAPTER XII. AN EXPLANATION AND A DARE

The Rev. Dr. Cooper preached in Glen St. Mary the next evening and the Presbyterian Church was crowded with people from near and far. The Reverend Doctor was reputed to be a very eloquent speaker; and, bearing in mind the old dictum that a minister should take his best clothes to the city and his best sermons to the country, he delivered a very scholarly and impressive discourse. But when the folks went home that night it was not of Dr. Cooper's sermon they talked. They had completely forgotten all about it.

Dr. Cooper had concluded with a fervent appeal, had wiped the perspiration from his massive brow, had said "Let us pray" as he was famed for saying it, and had duly prayed. There was a slight pause. In Glen St. Mary church the old fashion of taking the collection after the sermon instead of before still held—mainly because the Methodists had adopted the new fashion first, and Miss Cornelia and Elder Clow would not hear of following where Methodists had led. Charles Baxter and Thomas Douglas, whose duty it was to pass the plates, were on the point of rising to their feet. The organist had got out the music of her anthem and the choir had cleared its throat. Suddenly Faith Meredith rose in the manse pew, walked up to the pulpit platform, and faced the amazed audience.

Miss Cornelia half rose in her seat and then sat down again. Her pew was far back and it occurred to her that whatever Faith meant to do or say would be half done or said before she could reach her. There was no use making the exhibition worse than it had to be. With an anguished glance at Mrs. Dr. Blythe, and another at Deacon Warren of the Methodist Church, Miss Cornelia resigned herself to another scandal.

"If the child was only dressed decently itself," she groaned in spirit.

Faith, having spilled ink on her good dress, had serenely put on an old one of faded pink print. A caticornered rent in the skirt had been darned with scarlet tracing cotton and the hem had been let down, showing a bright strip of unfaded pink around the skirt. But Faith was not thinking of her clothes at all. She was feeling suddenly nervous. What had seemed easy in imagination was rather hard in reality. Confronted by all those staring questioning eyes Faith's courage almost failed her. The lights were so bright, the silence so awesome. She thought she could not speak after all. But she MUST—her father MUST be cleared of suspicion. Only—the words would NOT come.

Una's little pearl-pure face gleamed up at her beseechingly from the manse pew. The Blythe children were lost in amazement. Back under the gallery Faith saw the sweet graciousness of Miss Rosemary West's smile and the amusement of Miss Ellen's. But none of these helped her. It was Bertie Shakespeare Drew who saved the situation. Bertie Shakespeare sat in the front seat of the gallery and he made a derisive face at Faith. Faith promptly made a dreadful one back at him, and, in her anger over being grimaced at by Bertie Shakespeare, forgot her stage fright. She found her voice and spoke out clearly and bravely.

"I want to explain something," she said, "and I want to do it now because everybody will hear it that heard the other. People are saying that Una and I stayed home last Sunday and cleaned house instead of going to Sunday School. Well, we did—but we didn't mean to. We got mixed up in the days of the week. It was all Elder Baxter's fault"—sensation in Baxter's pew—"because he went and changed the prayer-meeting to Wednesday night and then we thought Thursday was Friday and so on till we thought Saturday was Sunday. Carl was laid up sick and so was Aunt Martha, so they couldn't put us right. We went to Sunday School in all that rain on Saturday and nobody came. And then we thought we'd clean house on Monday and stop old cats from talking about how dirty the manse was"—general sensation all over the church—"and we did. I shook the rugs in the Methodist graveyard because it was such a convenient place and not because I meant to be disrespectful of the dead. It isn't the dead folks who have made the fuss over this—it's the living folks. And it isn't right for any of you to blame my father for this, because he was away and didn't know, and anyhow we thought it was Monday. He's just the best father that ever lived in the world and we love him with all our hearts."

Faith's bravado ebbed out in a sob. She ran down the steps and flashed out of the side door of the church. There the friendly starlit, summer night comforted her and the ache went out of her eyes and throat. She felt very happy. The dreadful explanation was over and everybody knew now that her father wasn't to blame and that she and Una were not so wicked as to have cleaned house knowingly on Sunday.

Inside the church people gazed blankly at each other, but Thomas Douglas rose and walked up the aisle with a set face. HIS duty was clear; the collection must be taken if the skies fell. Taken it was; the choir sang the anthem, with a dismal conviction that it fell terribly flat, and Dr. Cooper gave out the concluding hymn and pronounced the benediction with considerably less unction than usual. The Reverend Doctor had a sense of humour and Faith's performance tickled him. Besides, John Meredith was well known in Presbyterian circles.

Mr. Meredith returned home the next afternoon, but before his coming Faith contrived to scandalize Glen St. Mary again. In the reaction from Sunday evening's intensity and strain she was especially full of what Miss Cornelia would have called "devilment" on Monday. This led her to dare Walter Blythe to ride through Main Street on a pig, while she rode another one.

The pigs in question were two tall, lank animals, supposed to belong to Bertie Shakespeare Drew's father, which had been haunting the roadside by the manse for a couple of weeks. Walter did not want to ride a pig through Glen St. Mary, but whatever Faith Meredith dared him to do must be done. They tore down the hill and through the village, Faith bent double with laughter over her terrified courser, Walter crimson with shame. They tore past the minister himself, just coming home from the station; he, being a little less dreamy and abstracted than usual—owing to having had a talk on the train with Miss Cornelia who always wakened him up temporarily—noticed them, and thought he really must speak to Faith about it and tell her that such conduct was not seemly. But he had forgotten the trifling incident by the time he reached home. They passed Mrs. Alec Davis, who shrieked in horror, and they passed Miss Rosemary West who laughed and sighed. Finally, just before the pigs swooped into Bertie Shakespeare Drew's back yard, never to emerge therefrom again, so great had been the shock to their nerves—Faith and Walter jumped off, as Dr. and Mrs. Blythe drove swiftly by.

"So that is how you bring up your boys," said Gilbert with mock severity.

"Perhaps I do spoil them a little," said Anne contritely, "but, oh, Gilbert, when I think of my own childhood before I came to Green Gables I haven't the heart to be very strict. How hungry for love and fun I was—an unloved little drudge with never a chance to play! They do have such good times with the manse children."

"What about the poor pigs?" asked Gilbert.

Anne tried to look sober and failed.

"Do you really think it hurt them?" she said. "I don't think anything could hurt those animals. They've been the plague of the neighbourhood this summer and the Drews WON'T shut them up. But I'll talk to Walter—if I can keep from laughing when I do it."

Miss Cornelia came up to Ingleside that evening to relieve her feelings over Sunday night. To her surprise she found that Anne did not view Faith's performance in quite the same light as she did.

"I thought there was something brave and pathetic in her getting up there before that churchful of people, to confess," she said. "You could see she was frightened to death—yet she was bound to clear her father. I loved her for it."

"Oh, of course, the poor child meant well," sighed Miss Cornelia, "but just the same it was a terrible thing to do, and is making more talk than the house-cleaning on Sunday. THAT had begun to die away, and this has started it all up again. Rosemary West is like you—she said last night as she left the church that it was a plucky thing for Faith to do, but it made her feel sorry for the child, too. Miss Ellen thought it all a good joke, and said she hadn't had as much fun in church for years. Of course THEY don't care—they are Episcopalians. But we Presbyterians feel it. And there were so many hotel people there that night and scores of Methodists. Mrs. Leander Crawford cried, she felt so bad. And Mrs. Alec Davis said the little hussy ought to be spanked."

CHAPTER XII. AN EXPLANATION AND A DARE

"Mrs. Leander Crawford is always crying in church," said Susan contemptuously. "She cries over every affecting thing the minister says. But you do not often see her name on a subscription list, Mrs. Dr. dear. Tears come cheaper. She tried to talk to me one day about Aunt Martha being such a dirty housekeeper; and I wanted to say, 'Every one knows that YOU have been seen mixing up cakes in the kitchen wash-pan, Mrs. Leander Crawford!' But I did not say it, Mrs. Dr. dear, because I have too much respect for myself to condescend to argue with the likes of her. But I could tell worse things than THAT of Mrs. Leander Crawford, if I was disposed to gossip. And as for Mrs. Alec Davis, if she had said that to me, Mrs. Dr. dear, do you know what I would have said? I would have said, 'I have no doubt you would like to spank Faith, Mrs. Davis, but you will never have the chance to spank a minister's daughter either in this world or in that which is to come.'"

"If poor Faith had only been decently dressed," lamented Miss Cornelia again, "it wouldn't have been quite that bad. But that dress looked dreadful, as she stood there upon the platform."

"It was clean, though, Mrs. Dr. dear," said Susan. "They ARE clean children. They may be very heedless and reckless, Mrs. Dr. dear, and I am not saying they are not, but they NEVER forget to wash behind their ears."

"The idea of Faith forgetting what day was Sunday," persisted Miss Cornelia. "She will grow up just as careless and impractical as her father, believe ME. I suppose Carl would have known better if he hadn't been sick. I don't know what was wrong with him, but I think it very likely he had been eating those blueberries that grew in the graveyard. No wonder they made him sick. If I was a Methodist I'd try to keep my graveyard cleaned up at least."

"I am of the opinion that Carl only ate the sours that grow on the dyke," said Susan hopefully. "I do not think ANY minister's son would eat blueberries that grew on the graves of dead people. You know it would not be so bad, Mrs. Dr. dear, to eat things that grew on the dyke."

"The worst of last night's performance was the face Faith made made at somebody in the congregation before she started in," said Miss Cornelia. "Elder Clow declares she made it at him. And DID you hear that she was seen riding on a pig to-day?"

"I saw her. Walter was with her. I gave him a little—a VERY little—scolding about it. He did not say much, but he gave me the impression that it had been his idea and that Faith was not to blame."

"I do not not believe THAT, Mrs. Dr. dear," cried Susan, up in arms. "That is just Walter's way—to take the blame on himself. But you know as well as I do, Mrs. Dr. dear, that that blessed child would never have thought of riding on a pig, even if he does write poetry."

"Oh, there's no doubt the notion was hatched in Faith Meredith's brain," said Miss Cornelia. "And I don't say that I'm sorry that Amos Drew's old pigs did get their come-uppance for once. But the minister's daughter!"

"AND the doctor's son!" said Anne, mimicking Miss Cornelia's tone. Then she laughed. "Dear Miss Cornelia, they're only little children. And you KNOW they've never yet done anything bad—they're just heedless and impulsive—as I was myself once. They'll grow sedate and sober—as I've done."

Miss Cornelia laughed, too.

"There are times, Anne dearie, when I know by your eyes that YOUR sober-ness is put on like a garment and you're really aching to do something wild and young again. Well, I feel encouraged. Somehow, a talk with you always does have that effect on me. Now, when I go to see Barbara Samson, it's just the oppo-site. She makes me feel that everything's wrong and always will be. But of course living all your life with a man like Joe Samson wouldn't be exactly cheering."

"It is a very strange thing to think that she married Joe Samson after all her chances," remarked Susan. "She was much sought after when she was a girl. She used to boast to me that she had twenty-one beaus and Mr. Pethick."

"What was Mr. Pethick?"

"Well, he was a sort of hanger-on, Mrs. Dr. dear, but you could not exactly call him a beau. He did not really have any intentions. Twenty-one beaus—and me that never had one! But Barbara went through the woods and picked up the crooked stick after all. And yet they say her husband can make better baking powder biscuits than she can, and she always gets him to make them when com-pany comes to tea."

"Which reminds ME that I have company coming to tea to-morrow and I must go home and set my bread," said Miss Cornelia. "Mary said she could set it and no doubt she could. But while I live and move and have my being *I* set my own bread, believe me."

"How is Mary getting on?" asked Anne.

"I've no fault to find with Mary," said Miss Cornelia rather gloomily. "She's getting some flesh on her bones and she's clean and respectful—though there's more in her than *I* can fathom. She's a sly puss. If you dug for a thousand years you couldn't get to the bottom of that child's mind, believe ME! As for work, I never saw anything like her. She EATS it up. Mrs. Wiley may have been cruel to her, but folks needn't say she made Mary work. Mary's a born worker. Some-times I wonder which will wear out first—her legs or her tongue. I don't have enough to do to keep me out of mischief these days. I'll be real glad when school opens, for then I'll have something to do again. Mary doesn't want to go to school, but I put my foot down and said that go she must. I shall NOT have the Methodists saying that I kept her out of school while I lolled in idleness."

CHAPTER XIII. THE HOUSE ON THE HILL

There was a little unfailing spring, always icy cold and crystal pure, in a certain birch-screened hollow of Rainbow Valley in the lower corner near the marsh. Not a great many people knew of its existence. The manse and Ingleside children knew, of course, as they knew everything else about the magic valley. Occasionally they went there to get a drink, and it figured in many of their plays as a fountain of old romance. Anne knew of it and loved it because it somehow reminded her of the beloved Dryad's Bubble at Green Gables. Rosemary West knew of it; it was her fountain of romance, too. Eighteen years ago she had sat behind it one spring twilight and heard young Martin Crawford stammer out a confession of fervent, boyish love. She had whispered her own secret in return, and they had kissed and promised by the wild wood spring. They had never stood together by it again—Martin had sailed on his fatal voyage soon after; but to Rosemary West it was always a sacred spot, hallowed by that immortal hour of youth and love. Whenever she passed near it she turned aside to hold a secret tryst with an old dream—a dream from which the pain had long gone, leaving only its unforgettable sweetness.

The spring was a hidden thing. You might have passed within ten feet of it and never have suspected its existence. Two generations past a huge old pine had fallen almost across it. Nothing was left of the tree but its crumbling trunk out of which the ferns grew thickly, making a green roof and a lacy screen for the water. A maple-tree grew beside it with a curiously gnarled and twisted trunk, creeping along the ground for a little way before shooting up into the air, and so forming a quaint seat; and September had flung a scarf of pale smoke-blue asters around the hollow.

John Meredith, taking the cross-lots road through Rainbow Valley on his way home from some pastoral visitations around the Harbour head one evening, turned aside to drink of the little spring. Walter Blythe had shown it to him one afternoon only a few days before, and they had had a long talk together on the maple seat. John Meredith, under all his shyness and aloofness, had the heart of a boy. He had been called Jack in his youth, though nobody in Glen St. Mary would ever have believed it. Walter and he had taken to each other and had talked unreservedly. Mr. Meredith found his way into some sealed and sacred chambers of the lad's soul wherein not even Di had ever looked. They were to be chums from that friendly hour and Walter knew that he would never be frightened of the minister again.

"I never believed before that it was possible to get really acquainted with a minister," he told his mother that night.

John Meredith drank from his slender white hand, whose grip of steel always surprised people who were unacquainted with it, and then sat down on the maple seat. He was in no hurry to go home; this was a beautiful spot and he was mentally weary after a round of rather uninspiring conversations with many good and stupid people. The moon was rising. Rainbow Valley was wind-haunted and star-sentinelled only where he was, but afar from the upper end came the gay notes of children's laughter and voices.

The ethereal beauty of the asters in the moonlight, the glimmer of the little spring, the soft croon of the brook, the wavering grace of the brackens all wove a white magic round John Meredith. He forgot congregational worries and spiritual problems; the years slipped away from him; he was a young divinity student again and the roses of June were blooming red and fragrant on the dark, queenly head of his Cecilia. He sat there and dreamed like any boy. And it was at this propitious moment that Rosemary West stepped aside from the by-path and stood beside him in that dangerous, spell-weaving place. John Meredith stood up as she came in and saw her—REALLY saw her—for the first time.

He had met her in his church once or twice and shaken hands with her abstractedly as he did with anyone he happened to encounter on his way down the aisle. He had never met her elsewhere, for the Wests were Episcopalians, with church affinities in Lowbridge, and no occasion for calling upon them had ever arisen. Before to-night, if anyone had asked John Meredith what Rosemary West looked like he would not have had the slightest notion. But he was never to forget her, as she appeared to him in the glamour of kind moonlight by the spring.

She was certainly not in the least like Cecilia, who had always been his ideal of womanly beauty. Cecilia had been small and dark and vivacious—Rosemary West was tall and fair and placid, yet John Meredith thought he had never seen so beautiful a woman.

She was bareheaded and her golden hair—hair of a warm gold, "molasses taffy" colour as Di Blythe had said—was pinned in sleek, close coils over her head; she had large, tranquil, blue eyes that always seemed full of friendliness, a high white forehead and a finely shaped face.

Rosemary West was always called a "sweet woman." She was so sweet that even her high-bred, stately air had never gained for her the reputation of being "stuck-up," which it would inevitably have done in the case of anyone else in Glen St. Mary. Life had taught her to be brave, to be patient, to love, to forgive. She had watched the ship on which her lover went sailing out of Four Winds Harbour into the sunset. But, though she watched long, she had never seen it coming sailing back. That vigil had taken girlhood from her eyes, yet she kept her youth to a marvellous degree. Perhaps this was because she always seemed to preserve that attitude of delighted surprise towards life which most of us leave behind in childhood—an attitude which not only made Rosemary herself seem young, but flung a pleasing illusion of youth over the consciousness of every one who talked to her.

John Meredith was startled by her loveliness and Rosemary was startled by his presence. She had never thought she would find anyone by that remote spring, least of all the recluse of Glen St. Mary manse. She almost dropped the heavy armful of books she was carrying home from the Glen lending library, and then, to cover her confusion, she told one of those small fibs which even the best of women do tell at times.

"I—I came for a drink," she said, stammering a little, in answer to Mr. Meredith's grave "good evening, Miss West." She felt that she was an unpardonable goose and she longed to shake herself. But John Meredith was not a vain man and he knew she would likely have been as much startled had she met old Elder Clow in that unexpected fashion. Her confusion put him at ease and he forgot to be shy; besides, even the shyest of men can sometimes be quite audacious in moonlight.

"Let me get you a cup," he said smiling. There was a cup near by, if he had only known it, a cracked, handleless blue cup secreted under the maple by the Rainbow Valley children; but he did not know it, so he stepped out to one of the birch-trees and stripped a bit of its white skin away. Deftly he fashioned this into a three-cornered cup, filled it from the spring, and handed it to Rosemary.

Rosemary took it and drank every drop to punish herself for her fib, for she was not in the least thirsty, and to drink a fairly large cupful of water when you are not thirsty is somewhat of an ordeal. Yet the memory of that draught was to be very pleasant to Rosemary. In after years it seemed to her that there was something sacramental about it. Perhaps this was because of what the minister did when she handed him back the cup. He stooped again and filled it and drank of it himself. It was only by accident that he put his lips just where Rosemary had put hers, and Rosemary knew it. Nevertheless, it had a curious significance for her. They two had drunk of the same cup. She remembered idly that an old aunt of hers used to say that when two people did this their after-lives would be linked in some fashion, whether for good or ill.

John Meredith held the cup uncertainly. He did not know what to do with it. The logical thing would have been to toss it away, but somehow he was disinclined to do this. Rosemary held out her hand for it.

"Will you let me have it?" she said. "You made it so knackily. I never saw anyone make a birch cup so since my little brother used to make them long ago—before he died."

"I learned how to make them when *I* was a boy, camping out one summer. An old hunter taught me," said Mr. Meredith. "Let me carry your books, Miss West."

Rosemary was startled into another fib and said oh, they were not heavy. But the minister took them from her with quite a masterful air and they walked away together. It was the first time Rosemary had stood by the valley spring without thinking of Martin Crawford. The mystic tryst had been broken.

The little by-path wound around the marsh and then struck up the long wooded hill on the top of which Rosemary lived. Beyond, through the trees, they could see the moonlight shining across the level summer fields. But the little path was shadowy and narrow. Trees crowded over it, and trees are never quite as friendly to human beings after nightfall as they are in daylight. They wrap themselves away from us. They whisper and plot furtively. If they reach out a hand to us it has a hostile, tentative touch. People walking amid trees after night always draw closer together instinctively and involuntarily, making an alliance, physical and mental, against certain alien powers around them. Rosemary's dress brushed against John Meredith as they walked. Not even an absent-minded minister, who was after all a young man still, though he firmly believed he had outlived romance, could be insensible to the charm of the night and the path and the companion.

It is never quite safe to think we have done with life. When we imagine we have finished our story fate has a trick of turning the page and showing us yet another chapter. These two people each thought their hearts belonged irrevocably to the past; but they both found their walk up that hill very pleasant. Rosemary thought the Glen minister was by no means as shy and tongue-tied as he had been represented. He seemed to find no difficulty in talking easily and freely. Glen housewives would have been amazed had they heard him. But then so many Glen housewives talked only gossip and the price of eggs, and John Meredith was not interested in either. He talked to Rosemary of books and music and wide-world doings and something of his own history, and found that she could understand and respond. Rosemary, it appeared, possessed a book which Mr. Meredith had not read and wished to read. She offered to lend it to him and when they reached the old homestead on the hill he went in to get it.

The house itself was an old-fashioned gray one, hung with vines, through which the light in the sitting-room winked in friendly fashion. It looked down the Glen, over the harbour, silvered in the moonlight, to the sand-dunes and the moaning ocean. They walked in through a garden that always seemed to smell of roses, even when no roses were in bloom. There was a sisterhood of lilies at the gate and a ribbon of asters on either side of the broad walk, and a lacery of fir trees on the hill's edge beyond the house.

"You have the whole world at your doorstep here," said John Meredith, with a long breath. "What a view—what an outlook! At times I feel stifled down there in the Glen. You can breathe up here."

"It is calm to-night," said Rosemary laughing. "If there were a wind it would blow your breath away. We get 'a' the airts the wind can blow' up here. This place should be called Four Winds instead of the Harbour."

"I like wind," he said. "A day when there is no wind seems to me DEAD. A windy day wakes me up." He gave a conscious laugh. "On a calm day I fall into day dreams. No doubt you know my reputation, Miss West. If I cut you dead the next time we meet don't put it down to bad manners. Please understand that it is only abstraction and forgive me—and speak to me."

CHAPTER XIII. THE HOUSE ON THE HILL

They found Ellen West in the sitting room when they went in. She laid her glasses down on the book she had been reading and looked at them in amazement tinctured with something else. But she shook hands amiably with Mr. Meredith and he sat down and talked to her, while Rosemary hunted out his book.

Ellen West was ten years older than Rosemary, and so different from her that it was hard to believe they were sisters. She was dark and massive, with black hair, thick, black eyebrows and eyes of the clear, slaty blue of the gulf water in a north wind. She had a rather stern, forbidding look, but she was in reality very jolly, with a hearty, gurgling laugh and a deep, mellow, pleasant voice with a suggestion of masculinity about it. She had once remarked to Rosemary that she would really like to have a talk with that Presbyterian minister at the Glen, to see if he could find a word to say to a woman when he was cornered. She had her chance now and she tackled him on world politics. Miss Ellen, who was a great reader, had been devouring a book on the Kaiser of Germany, and she demanded Mr. Meredith's opinion of him.

"A dangerous man," was his answer.

"I believe you!" Miss Ellen nodded. "Mark my words, Mr. Meredith, that man is going to fight somebody yet. He's ACHING to. He is going to set the world on fire."

"If you mean that he will wantonly precipitate a great war I hardly think so," said Mr. Meredith. "The day has gone by for that sort of thing."

"Bless you, it hasn't," rumbled Ellen. "The day never goes by for men and nations to make asses of themselves and take to the fists. The millenniun isn't THAT near, Mr. Meredith, and YOU don't think it is any more than I do. As for this Kaiser, mark my words, he is going to make a heap of trouble"—and Miss Ellen prodded her book emphatically with her long finger. "Yes, if he isn't nipped in the bud he's going to make trouble. WE'LL live to see it—you and I will live to see it, Mr. Meredith. And who is going to nip him? England should, but she won't. WHO is going to nip him? Tell me that, Mr. Meredith."

Mr. Meredith couldn't tell her, but they plunged into a discussion of German militarism that lasted long after Rosemary had found the book. Rosemary said nothing, but sat in a little rocker behind Ellen and stroked an important black cat meditatively. John Meredith hunted big game in Europe with Ellen, but he looked oftener at Rosemary than at Ellen, and Ellen noticed it. After Rosemary had gone to the door with him and come back Ellen rose and looked at her accusingly.

"Rosemary West, that man has a notion of courting you."

Rosemary quivered. Ellen's speech was like a blow to her. It rubbed all the bloom off the pleasant evening. But she would not let Ellen see how it hurt her.

"Nonsense," she said, and laughed, a little too carelessly. "You see a beau for me in every bush, Ellen. Why he told me all about his wife to-night—how much she was to him—how empty her death had left the world."

"Well, that may be HIS way of courting," retorted Ellen. "Men have all kinds of ways, I understand. But don't forget your promise, Rosemary."

"There is no need of my either forgetting or remembering it," said Rosemary, a little wearily. "YOU forget that I'm an old maid, Ellen. It is only your sisterly delusion that I am still young and blooming and dangerous. Mr. Meredith merely wants to be a friend—if he wants that much itself. He'll forget us both long before he gets back to the manse."

"I've no objection to your being friends with him," conceded Ellen, "but it musn't go beyond friendship, remember. I'm always suspicious of widowers. They are not given to romantic ideas about friendship. They're apt to mean business. As for this Presbyterian man, what do they call him shy for? He's not a bit shy, though he may be absent-minded—so absent-minded that he forgot to say goodnight to ME when you started to go to the door with him. He's got brains, too. There's so few men round here that can talk sense to a body. I've enjoyed the evening. I wouldn't mind seeing more of him. But no philandering, Rosemary, mind you—no philandering."

Rosemary was quite used to being warned by Ellen from philandering if she so much as talked five minutes to any marriageable man under eighty or over eighteen. She had always laughed at the warning with unfeigned amusement. This time it did not amuse her—it irritated her a little. Who wanted to philander?

"Don't be such a goose, Ellen," she said with unaccustomed shortness as she took her lamp. She went upstairs without saying goodnight.

Ellen shook her head dubiously and looked at the black cat.

"What is she so cross about, St. George?" she asked. "When you howl you're hit, I've always heard, George. But she promised, Saint—she promised, and we Wests always keep our word. So it won't matter if he does want to philander, George. She promised. I won't worry."

Upstairs, in her room, Rosemary sat for a long while looking out of the window across the moonlit garden to the distant, shining harbour. She felt vaguely upset and unsettled. She was suddenly tired of outworn dreams. And in the garden the petals of the last red rose were scattered by a sudden little wind. Summer was over—it was autumn.

CHAPTER XIV. MRS. ALEC DAVIS MAKES A CALL

John Meredith walked slowly home. At first he thought a little about Rosemary, but by the time he reached Rainbow Valley he had forgotten all about her and was meditating on a point regarding German theology which Ellen had raised. He passed through Rainbow Valley and knew it not. The charm of Rainbow Valley had no potency against German theology. When he reached the manse he went to his study and took down a bulky volume in order to see which had been right, he or Ellen. He remained immersed in its mazes until dawn, struck a new trail of speculation and pursued it like a sleuth hound for the next week, utterly lost to the world, his parish and his family. He read day and night; he forgot to go to his meals when Una was not there to drag him to them; he never thought about Rosemary or Ellen again. Old Mrs. Marshall, over-harbour, was very ill and sent for him, but the message lay unheeded on his desk and gathered dust. Mrs. Marshall recovered but never forgave him. A young couple came to the manse to be married and Mr. Meredith, with unbrushed hair, in carpet slippers and faded dressing gown, married them. To be sure, he began by reading the funeral service to them and got along as far as "ashes to ashes and dust to dust" before he vaguely suspected that something was wrong.

"Dear me," he said absently, "that is strange—very strange."

The bride, who was very nervous, began to cry. The bridegroom, who was not in the least nervous, giggled.

"Please, sir, I think you're burying us instead of marrying us," he said.

"Excuse me," said Mr. Meredith, as it it did not matter much. He turned up the marriage service and got through with it, but the bride never felt quite properly married for the rest of her life.

He forgot his prayer-meeting again—but that did not matter, for it was a wet night and nobody came. He might even have forgotten his Sunday service if it had not been for Mrs. Alec Davis. Aunt Martha came in on Saturday afternoon and told him that Mrs. Davis was in the parlour and wanted to see him. Mr. Meredith sighed. Mrs. Davis was the only woman in Glen St. Mary church whom he positively detested. Unfortunately, she was also the richest, and his board of managers had warned Mr. Meredith against offending her. Mr. Meredith seldom thought of such a worldly matter as his stipend; but the managers were more practical. Also, they were astute. Without mentioning money, they contrived to instil into Mr. Meredith's mind a conviction that he should not offend Mrs. Davis. Otherwise, he would likely have forgotten all about her as soon as Aunt Martha had gone out. As it was, he turned down his Ewald with a feeling of annoyance and went across the hall to the parlour.

Mrs. Davis was sitting on the sofa, looking about her with an air of scornful disapproval.

What a scandalous room! There were no curtains on the window. Mrs. Davis did not know that Faith and Una had taken them down the day before to use as court trains in one of their plays and had forgotten to put them up again, but she could not have accused those windows more fiercely if she had known. The blinds were cracked and torn. The pictures on the walls were crooked; the rugs were awry; the vases were full of faded flowers; the dust lay in heaps—literally in heaps.

"What are we coming to?" Mrs. Davis asked herself, and then primmed up her unbeautiful mouth.

Jerry and Carl had been whooping and sliding down the banisters as she came through the hall. They did not see her and continued whooping and sliding, and Mrs. Davis was convinced they did it on purpose. Faith's pet rooster ambled through the hall, stood in the parlour doorway and looked at her. Not liking her looks, he did not venture in. Mrs. Davis gave a scornful sniff. A pretty manse, indeed, where roosters paraded the halls and stared people out of countenance.

"Shoo, there," commanded Mrs. Davis, poking her flounced, changeable-silk parasol at him.

Adam shooed. He was a wise rooster and Mrs. Davis had wrung the necks of so many roosters with her own fair hands in the course of her fifty years that an air of the executioner seemed to hang around her. Adam scuttled through the hall as the minister came in.

Mr. Meredith still wore slippers and dressing gown, and his dark hair still fell in uncared-for locks over his high brow. But he looked the gentleman he was; and Mrs. Alec Davis, in her silk dress and beplumed bonnet, and kid gloves and gold chain looked the vulgar, coarse-souled woman she was. Each felt the antagonism of the other's personality. Mr. Meredith shrank, but Mrs. Davis girded up her loins for the fray. She had come to the manse to propose a certain thing to the minister and she meant to lose no time in proposing it. She was going to do him a favour— a great favour—and the sooner he was made aware of it the better. She had been thinking about it all summer and had come to a decision at last. This was all that mattered, Mrs. Davis thought. When she decided a thing it WAS decided. Nobody else had any say in the matter. That had always been her attitude. When she had made her mind up to marry Alec Davis she had married him and that was the end to it. Alec had never known how it happened, but what odds? So in this case—Mrs. Davis had arranged everything to her own satisfaction. Now it only remained to inform Mr. Meredith.

"Will you please shut that door?" said Mrs. Davis, unprimming her mouth slightly to say it, but speaking with asperity. "I have something important to say, and I can't say it with that racket in the hall."

Mr. Meredith shut the door meekly. Then he sat down before Mrs. Davis. He was not wholly aware of her yet. His mind was still wrestling with Ewald's arguments. Mrs. Davis sensed this detachment and it annoyed her.

"I have come to tell you, Mr. Meredith," she said aggressively, "that I have decided to adopt Una."

"To—adopt—Una!" Mr. Meredith gazed at her blankly, not understanding in the least.

"Yes. I've been thinking it over for some time. I have often thought of adopting a child, since my husband's death. But it seemed so hard to get a suitable one. It is very few children I would want to take into MY home. I wouldn't think of taking a home child—some outcast of the slums in all probability. And there is hardly ever any other child to be got. One of the fishermen down at the harbour died last fall and left six youngsters. They tried to get me to take one, but I soon gave them to understand that I had no idea of adopting trash like that. Their grandfather stole a horse. Besides, they were all boys and I wanted a girl—a quiet, obedient girl that I could train up to be a lady. Una will suit me exactly. She would be a nice little thing if she was properly looked after—so different from Faith. I would never dream of adopting Faith. But I'll take Una and I'll give her a good home, and up-bringing, Mr. Meredith, and if she behaves herself I'll leave her all my money when I die. Not one of my own relatives shall have a cent of it in any case, I'm determined on that. It was the idea of aggravating them that set me to thinking of adopting a child as much as anything in the first place. Una shall be well dressed and educated and trained, Mr. Meredith, and I shall give her music and painting lessons and treat her as if she was my own."

Mr. Meredith was wide enough awake by this time. There was a faint flush in his pale cheek and a dangerous light in his fine dark eyes. Was this woman, whose vulgarity and consciousness of money oozed out of her at every pore, actually asking him to give her Una—his dear little wistful Una with Cecilia's own dark-blue eyes—the child whom the dying mother had clasped to her heart after the other children had been led weeping from the room. Cecilia had clung to her baby until the gates of death had shut between them. She had looked over the little dark head to her husband.

"Take good care of her, John," she had entreated. "She is so small—and sensitive. The others can fight their way—but the world will hurt HER. Oh, John, I don't know what you and she are going to do. You both need me so much. But keep her close to you—keep her close to you."

These had been almost her last words except a few unforgettable ones for him alone. And it was this child whom Mrs. Davis had coolly announced her intention of taking from him. He sat up straight and looked at Mrs. Davis. In spite of the worn dressing gown and the frayed slippers there was something about him that made Mrs. Davis feel a little of the old reverence for "the cloth" in which she had been brought up. After all, there WAS a certain divinity hedging a minister, even a poor, unworldly, abstracted one.

"I thank you for your kind intentions, Mrs. Davis," said Mr. Meredith with a gentle, final, quite awful courtesy, "but I cannot give you my child."

Mrs. Davis looked blank. She had never dreamed of his refusing.

"Why, Mr. Meredith," she said in astonishment. "You must be cr—you can't mean it. You must think it over—think of all the advantages I can give her."

"There is no need to think it over, Mrs. Davis. It is entirely out of the question. All the worldly advantages it is in your power to bestow on her could not compensate for the loss of a father's love and care. I thank you again—but it is not to be thought of."

Disappointment angered Mrs. Davis beyond the power of old habit to control. Her broad red face turned purple and her voice trembled.

"I thought you'd be only too glad to let me have her," she sneered.

"Why did you think that?" asked Mr. Meredith quietly.

"Because nobody ever supposed you cared anything about any of your children," retorted Mrs. Davis contemptuously. "You neglect them scandalously. It is the talk of the place. They aren't fed and dressed properly, and they're not trained at all. They have no more manners than a pack of wild Indians. You never think of doing your duty as a father. You let a stray child come here among them for a fortnight and never took any notice of her—a child that swore like a trooper I'm told. YOU wouldn't have cared if they'd caught small-pox from her. And Faith made an exhibition of herself getting up in preaching and making that speech! And she rid a pig down the street—under your very eyes I understand. The way they act is past belief and you never lift a finger to stop them or try to teach them anything. And now when I offer one of them a good home and good prospects you refuse it and insult me. A pretty father you, to talk of loving and caring for your children!"

"That will do, woman!" said Mr. Meredith. He stood up and looked at Mrs. Davis with eyes that made her quail. "That will do," he repeated. "I desire to hear no more, Mrs. Davis. You have said too much. It may be that I have been remiss in some respects in my duty as a parent, but it is not for you to remind me of it in such terms as you have used. Let us say good afternoon."

Mrs. Davis did not say anything half so amiable as good afternoon, but she took her departure. As she swept past the minister a large, plump toad, which Carl had secreted under the lounge, hopped out almost under her feet. Mrs. Davis gave a shriek and in trying to avoid treading on the awful thing, lost her balance and her parasol. She did not exactly fall, but she staggered and reeled across the room in a very undignified fashion and brought up against the door with a thud that jarred her from head to foot. Mr. Meredith, who had not seen the toad, wondered if she had been attacked with some kind of apoplectic or paralytic seizure, and ran in alarm to her assistance. But Mrs. Davis, recovering her feet, waved him back furiously.

"Don't you dare to touch me," she almost shouted. "This is some more of your children's doings, I suppose. This is no fit place for a decent woman. Give me my umbrella and let me go. I'll never darken the doors of your manse or your church again."

Mr. Meredith picked up the gorgeous parasol meekly enough and gave it to her. Mrs. Davis seized it and marched out. Jerry and Carl had given up banister sliding and were sitting on the edge of the veranda with Faith. Unfortunately, all three were singing at the tops of their healthy young voices "There'll be a hot time in the old town to-night." Mrs. Davis believed the song was meant for her and her only. She stopped and shook her parasol at them.

"Your father is a fool," she said, "and you are three young varmints that ought to be whipped within an inch of your lives."

"He isn't," cried Faith. "We're not," cried the boys. But Mrs.

Davis was gone.

"Goodness, isn't she mad!" said Jerry. "And what is a 'varmint' anyhow?"

John Meredith paced up and down the parlour for a few minutes; then he went back to his study and sat down. But he did not return to his German theology. He was too grievously disturbed for that. Mrs. Davis had wakened him up with a vengeance. WAS he such a remiss, careless father as she had accused him of being? HAD he so scandalously neglected the bodily and spiritual welfare of the four little motherless creatures dependent on him? WERE his people talking of it as harshly as Mrs. Davis had declared? It must be so, since Mrs. Davis had come to ask for Una in the full and confident belief that he would hand the child over to her as unconcernedly and gladly as one might hand over a strayed, unwelcome kitten. And, if so, what then?

John Meredith groaned and resumed his pacing up and down the dusty, disordered room. What could he do? He loved his children as deeply as any father could and he knew, past the power of Mrs. Davis or any of her ilk, to disturb his conviction, that they loved him devotedly. But WAS he fit to have charge of them? He knew—none better—his weaknesses and limitations. What was needed was a good woman's presence and influence and common sense. But how could that be arranged? Even were he able to get such a housekeeper it would cut Aunt Martha to the quick. She believed she could still do all that was meet and necessary. He could not so hurt and insult the poor old woman who had been so kind to him and his. How devoted she had been to Cecilia! And Cecilia had asked him to be very considerate of Aunt Martha. To be sure, he suddenly remembered that Aunt Martha had once hinted that he ought to marry again. He felt she would not resent a wife as she would a housekeeper. But that was out of the question. He did not wish to marry—he did not and could not care for anyone. Then what could he do? It suddenly occurred to him that he would go over to Ingleside and talk over his difficulties with Mrs. Blythe. Mrs. Blythe was one of the few women he never felt shy or tongue-tied with. She was always so sympathetic and refreshing. It might be that she could suggest some solution of his problems. And even if she could not Mr. Meredith felt that he needed a little decent human companionship after his dose of Mrs. Davis—something to take the taste of her out of his soul.

He dressed hurriedly and ate his supper less abstractedly than usual. It occurred to him that it was a poor meal. He looked at his children; they were rosy and healthy looking enough—except Una, and she had never been very strong even when her mother was alive. They were all laughing and talking—certainly they seemed happy. Carl was especially happy because he had two most beautiful spiders crawling around his supper plate. Their voices were pleasant, their manners did not seem bad, they were considerate of and gentle to one another. Yet Mrs. Davis had said their behaviour was the talk of the congregation.

As Mr. Meredith went through his gate Dr. Blythe and Mrs. Blythe drove past on the road that led to Lowbridge. The minister's face fell. Mrs. Blythe was going away—there was no use in going to Ingleside. And he craved a little companionship more than ever. As he gazed rather hopelessly over the landscape the sunset light struck on a window of the old West homestead on the hill. It flared out rosily like a beacon of good hope. He suddenly remembered Rosemary and Ellen West. He thought that he would relish some of Ellen's pungent conversation. He thought it would be pleasant to see Rosemary's slow, sweet smile and calm, heavenly blue eyes again. What did that old poem of Sir Philip Sidney's say?—"continual comfort in a face"—that just suited her. And he needed comfort. Why not go and call? He remembered that Ellen had asked him to drop in sometimes and there was Rosemary's book to take back—he ought to take it back before he forgot. He had an uneasy suspicion that there were a great many books in his library which he had borrowed at sundry times and in divers places and had forgotten to take back. It was surely his duty to guard against that in this case. He went back into his study, got the book, and plunged downward into Rainbow Valley.

CHAPTER XV. MORE GOSSIP

On the evening after Mrs. Myra Murray of the over-harbour section had been buried Miss Cornelia and Mary Vance came up to Ingleside. There were several things concerning which Miss Cornelia wished to unburden her soul. The funeral had to be all talked over, of course. Susan and Miss Cornelia thrashed this out between them; Anne took no part or delight in such goulish conversations. She sat a little apart and watched the autumnal flame of dahlias in the garden, and the dreaming, glamorous harbour of the September sunset. Mary Vance sat beside her, knitting meekly. Mary's heart was down in the Rainbow Valley, whence came sweet, distance-softened sounds of children's laughter, but her fingers were under Miss Cornelia's eye. She had to knit so many rounds of her stocking before she might go to the valley. Mary knit and held her tongue, but used her ears.

"I never saw a nicer looking corpse," said Miss Cornelia judicially. "Myra Murray was always a pretty woman—she was a Corey from Lowbridge and the Coreys were noted for their good looks."

"I said to the corpse as I passed it, 'poor woman. I hope you are as happy as you look.'" sighed Susan. "She had not changed much. That dress she wore was the black satin she got for her daughter's wedding fourteen years ago. Her Aunt told her then to keep it for her funeral, but Myra laughed and said, 'I may wear it to my funeral, Aunty, but I will have a good time out of it first.' And I may say she did. Myra Murray was not a woman to attend her own funeral before she died. Many a time afterwards when I saw her enjoying herself out in company I thought to myself, 'You are a handsome woman, Myra Murray, and that dress becomes you, but it will likely be your shroud at last.' And you see my words have come true, Mrs. Marshall Elliott."

Susan sighed again heavily. She was enjoying herself hugely. A funeral was really a delightful subject of conversation.

"I always liked to meet Myra," said Miss Cornelia. "She was always so gay and cheerful—she made you feel better just by her handshake. Myra always made the best of things."

"That is true," asserted Susan. "Her sister-in-law told me that when the doctor told her at last that he could do nothing for her and she would never rise from that bed again, Myra said quite cheerfully, 'Well, if that is so, I'm thankful the preserving is all done, and I will not have to face the fall house-cleaning. I always liked house-cleaning in spring,' she says, 'but I always hated it in the fall. I will get clear of it this year, thank goodness.' There are people who would call that levity, Mrs. Marshall Elliott, and I think her sister-in-law was a little ashamed of it. She said perhaps her sickness had made Myra a little light-headed. But I said, 'No, Mrs. Murray, do not worry over it. It was just Myra's way of looking at the bright side.'"

"Her sister Luella was just the opposite," said Miss Cornelia. "There was no bright side for Luella—there was just black and shades of gray. For years she used always to be declaring she was going to die in a week or so. 'I won't be here to burden you long,' she would tell her family with a groan. And if any of them ventured to talk about their little future plans she'd groan also and say, 'Ah, *I* won't be here then.' When I went to see her I always agreed with her and it made her so mad that she was always quite a lot better for several days afterwards. She has better health now but no more cheerfulness. Myra was so different. She was always doing or saying something to make some one feel good. Perhaps the men they married had something to do with it. Luella's man was a Tartar, believe ME, while Jim Murray was decent, as men go. He looked heart-broken to-day. It isn't often I feel sorry for a man at his wife's funeral, but I did feel for Jim Murray."

"No wonder he looked sad. He will not get a wife like Myra again in a hurry," said Susan. "Maybe he will not try, since his children are all grown up and Mirabel is able to keep house. But there is no predicting what a widower may or may not do and I, for one, will not try."

"We'll miss Myra terrible in church," said Miss Cornelia. "She was such a worker. Nothing ever stumped HER. If she couldn't get over a difficulty she'd get around it, and if she couldn't get around it she'd pretend it wasn't there—and generally it wasn't. 'I'll keep a stiff upper lip to my journey's end,' said she to me once. Well, she has ended her journey."

"Do you think so?" asked Anne suddenly, coming back from dreamland. "I can't picture HER journey as being ended. Can YOU think of her sitting down and folding her hands—that eager, asking spirit of hers, with its fine adventurous outlook? No, I think in death she just opened a gate and went through—on—on— to new, shining adventures."

"Maybe—maybe," assented Miss Cornelia. "Do you know, Anne dearie, I never was much taken with this everlasting rest doctrine myself—though I hope it isn't heresy to say so. I want to bustle round in heaven the same as here. And I hope there'll be a celestial substitute for pies and doughnuts—something that has to be MADE. Of course, one does get awful tired at times—and the older you are the tireder you get. But the very tiredest could get rested in something short of eternity, you'd think—except, perhaps, a lazy man."

"When I meet Myra Murray again," said Anne, "I want to see her coming towards me, brisk and laughing, just as she always did here."

"Oh, Mrs. Dr. dear," said Susan, in a shocked tone, "you surely do not think that Myra will be laughing in the world to come?"

"Why not, Susan? Do you think we will be crying there?"

"No, no, Mrs. Dr. dear, do not misunderstand me. I do not think we shall be either crying or laughing."

"What then?"

"Well," said Susan, driven to it. "it is my opinion, Mrs. Dr. dear, that we shall just look solemn and holy."

"And do you really think, Susan," said Anne, looking solemn enough, "that either Myra Murray or I could look solemn and holy all the time—ALL the time, Susan?"

"Well," admitted Susan reluctantly, "I might go so far as to say that you both would have to smile now and again, but I can never admit that there will be laughing in heaven. The idea seems really irreverent, Mrs. Dr. dear."

"Well, to come back to earth," said Miss Cornelia, "who can we get to take Myra's class in Sunday School? Julia Clow has been teaching it since Myra took ill, but she's going to town for the winter and we'll have to get somebody else."

"I heard that Mrs. Laurie Jamieson wanted it," said Anne. "The Jamiesons have come to church very regularly since they moved to the Glen from Lowbridge."

"New brooms!" said Miss Cornelia dubiously. "Wait till they've gone regularly for a year."

"You cannot depend on Mrs. Jamieson a bit, Mrs. Dr. dear," said Susan solemnly. "She died once and when they were measuring her for her coffin, after laying her out just beautiful, did she not go and come back to life! Now, Mrs. Dr. dear, you know you CANNOT depend on a woman like that."

"She might turn Methodist at any moment," said Miss Cornelia. "They tell me they went to the Methodist Church at Lowbridge quite as often as to the Presbyterian. I haven't caught them at it here yet, but I would not approve of taking Mrs. Jamieson into the Sunday School. Yet we must not offend them. We are losing too many people, by death or bad temper. Mrs. Alec Davis has left the church, no one knows why. She told the managers that she would never pay another cent to Mr. Meredith's salary. Of course, most people say that the children offended her, but somehow I don't think so. I tried to pump Faith, but all I could get out of her was that Mrs. Davis had come, seemingly in high good humour, to see her father, and had left in an awful rage, calling them all 'varmints!'"

"Varmints, indeed!" said Susan furiously. "Does Mrs. Alec Davis forget that her uncle on her mother's side was suspected of poisoning his wife? Not that it was ever proved, Mrs. Dr. dear, and it does not do to believe all you hear. But if *I* had an uncle whose wife died without any satisfactory reason, *I* would not go about the country calling innocent children varmints."

"The point is," said Miss Cornelia, "that Mrs. Davis paid a large subscription, and how its loss is going to be made up is a problem. And if she turns the other Douglases against Mr. Meredith, as she will certainly try to do, he will just have to go."

"I do not think Mrs. Alec Davis is very well liked by the rest of the clan," said Susan. "It is not likely she will be able to influence them."

"But those Douglases all hang together so. If you touch one, you touch all. We can't do without them, so much is certain. They pay half the salary. They are not mean, whatever else may be said of them. Norman Douglas used to give a hundred a year long ago before he left."

"What did he leave for?" asked Anne.

"He declared a member of the session cheated him in a cow deal. He hasn't come to church for twenty years. His wife used to come regular while she was alive, poor thing, but he never would let her pay anything, except one red cent every Sunday. She felt dreadfully humiliated. I don't know that he was any too good a husband to her, though she was never heard to complain. But she always had a cowed look. Norman Douglas didn't get the woman he wanted thirty years ago and the Douglases never liked to put up with second best."

"Who was the woman he did want."

"Ellen West. They weren't engaged exactly, I believe, but they went about together for two years. And then they just broke off—nobody ever know why. Just some silly quarrel, I suppose. And Norman went and married Hester Reese before his temper had time to cool—married her just to spite Ellen, I haven't a doubt. So like a man! Hester was a nice little thing, but she never had much spirit and he broke what little she had. She was too meek for Norman. He needed a woman who could stand up to him. Ellen would have kept him in fine order and he would have liked her all the better for it. He despised Hester, that is the truth, just because she always gave in to him. I used to hear him say many a time, long ago when he was a young fellow 'Give me a spunky woman—spunk for me every time.' And then he went and married a girl who couldn't say boo to a goose—man-like. That family of Reeses were just vegetables. They went through the motions of living, but they didn't LIVE."

"Russell Reese used his first wife's wedding-ring to marry his second," said Susan reminiscently. "That was TOO economical in my opinion, Mrs. Dr. dear. And his brother John has his own tombstone put up in the over-harbour grave-yard, with everything on it but the date of death, and he goes and looks at it every Sunday. Most folks would not consider that much fun, but it is plain he does. People do have such different ideas of enjoyment. As for Norman Douglas, he is a perfect heathen. When the last minister asked him why he never went to church he said "Too many ugly women there, parson—too many ugly women!" I should like to go to such a man, Mrs. Dr. dear, and say to him solemnly, 'There is a hell!'"

"Oh, Norman doesn't believe there is such a place," said Miss Cornelia. "I hope he'll find out his mistake when he comes to die. There, Mary, you've knit your three inches and you can go and play with the children for half an hour."

Mary needed no second bidding. She flew to Rainbow Valley with a heart as light as her heels, and in the course of conversation told Faith Meredith all about Mrs. Alec Davis.

"And Mrs. Elliott says that she'll turn all the Douglases against your father and then he'll have to leave the Glen because his salary won't be paid," concluded

Mary. "*I* don't know what is to be done, honest to goodness. If only old Norman Douglas would come back to church and pay, it wouldn't be so bad. But he won't—and the Douglases will leave—and you all will have to go."

Faith carried a heavy heart to bed with her that night. The thought of leaving the Glen was unbearable. Nowhere else in the world were there such chums as the Blythes. Her little heart had been wrung when they had left Maywater—she had shed many bitter tears when she parted with Maywater chums and the old manse there where her mother had lived and died. She could not contemplate calmly the thought of such another and harder wrench. She COULDN'T leave Glen St. Mary and dear Rainbow Valley and that delicious graveyard.

"It's awful to be minister's family," groaned Faith into her pillow. "Just as soon as you get fond of a place you are torn up by the roots. I'll never, never, NEVER marry a minister, no matter how nice he is."

Faith sat up in bed and looked out of the little vine-hung window. The night was very still, the silence broken only by Una's soft breathing. Faith felt terribly alone in the world. She could see Glen St. Mary lying under the starry blue meadows of the autumn night. Over the valley a light shone from the girls' room at Ingleside, and another from Walter's room. Faith wondered if poor Walter had toothache again. Then she sighed, with a little passing sigh of envy of Nan and Di. They had a mother and a settled home—THEY were not at the mercy of people who got angry without any reason and called you a varmint. Away beyond the Glen, amid fields that were very quiet with sleep, another light was burning. Faith knew it shone in the house where Norman Douglas lived. He was reputed to sit up all hours of the night reading. Mary had said if he could only be induced to return to the church all would be well. And why not? Faith looked at a big, low star hanging over the tall, pointed spruce at the gate of the Methodist Church and had an inspiration. She knew what ought to be done and she, Faith Meredith, would do it. She would make everything right. With a sigh of satisfaction, she turned from the lonely, dark world and cuddled down beside Una.

CHAPTER XVI. TIT FOR TAT

With Faith, to decide was to act. She lost no time in carrying out the idea. As soon as she came home from school the next day she left the manse and made her way down the Glen. Walter Blythe joined her as she passed the post office.

"I'm going to Mrs. Elliott's on an errand for mother," he said. "Where are you going, Faith?"

"I am going somewhere on church business," said Faith loftily. She did not volunteer any further information and Walter felt rather snubbed. They walked on in silence for a little while. It was a warm, windy evening with a sweet, resinous air. Beyond the sand dunes were gray seas, soft and beautiful. The Glen brook bore down a freight of gold and crimson leaves, like fairy shallops. In Mr. James Reese's buckwheat stubble-land, with its beautiful tones of red and brown, a crow parliament was being held, whereat solemn deliberations regarding the welfare of crowland were in progress. Faith cruelly broke up the august assembly by climbing up on the fence and hurling a broken rail at it. Instantly the air was filled with flapping black wings and indignant caws.

"Why did you do that?" said Walter reproachfully. "They were having such a good time."

"Oh, I hate crows," said Faith airily. "They are so black and sly I feel sure they're hypocrites. They steal little birds' eggs out of their nests, you know. I saw one do it on our lawn last spring. Walter, what makes you so pale to-day? Did you have the toothache again last night?"

Walter shivered.

"Yes—a raging one. I couldn't sleep a wink—so I just paced up and down the floor and imagined I was an early Christian martyr being tortured at the command of Nero. That helped ever so much for a while—and then I got so bad I couldn't imagine anything."

"Did you cry?" asked Faith anxiously.

"No—but I lay down on the floor and groaned," admitted Walter. "Then the girls came in and Nan put cayenne pepper in it—and that made it worse—Di made me hold a swallow of cold water in my mouth—and I couldn't stand it, so they called Susan. Susan said it served me right for sitting up in the cold garret yesterday writing poetry trash. But she started up the kitchen fire and got me a hot-water bottle and it stopped the toothache. As soon as I felt better I told Susan

my poetry wasn't trash and she wasn't any judge. And she said no, thank goodness she was not and she did not know anything about poetry except that it was
mostly a lot of lies. Now you know, Faith, that isn't so. That is one reason why I
like writing poetry—you can say so many things in it that are true in poetry but
wouldn't be true in prose. I told Susan so, but she said to stop my jawing and go
to sleep before the water got cold, or she'd leave me to see if rhyming would cure
toothache, and she hoped it would be a lesson to me."

"Why don't you go to the dentist at Lowbridge and get the tooth out?"

Walter shivered again.

"They want me to—but I can't. It would hurt so."

"Are you afraid of a little pain?" asked Faith contemptuously.

Walter flushed.

"It would be a BIG pain. I hate being hurt. Father said he wouldn't insist on
my going—he'd wait until I'd made up my own mind to go."

"It wouldn't hurt as long as the toothache," argued Faith, "You've had five
spells of toothache. If you'd just go and have it out there'd be no more bad nights.
I had a tooth out once. I yelled for a moment, but it was all over then—only the
bleeding."

"The bleeding is worst of all—it's so ugly," cried Walter. "It just made me
sick when Jem cut his foot last summer. Susan said I looked more like fainting
than Jem did. But I couldn't hear to see Jem hurt, either. Somebody is always
getting hurt, Faith— and it's awful. I just can't BEAR to see things hurt. It makes
me just want to run—and run—and run—till I can't hear or see them."

"There's no use making a fuss over anyone getting hurt," said Faith, tossing her
curls. "Of course, if you've hurt yourself very bad, you have to yell—and blood
IS messy—and I don't like seeing other people hurt, either. But I don't want to
run—I want to go to work and help them. Your father HAS to hurt people lots of
times to cure them. What would they do if HE ran away?"

"I didn't say I WOULD run. I said I WANTED to run. That's a different
thing. I want to help people, too. But oh, I wish there weren't any ugly, dreadful
things in the world. I wish everything was glad and beautiful."

"Well, don't let's think of what isn't," said Faith. "After all, there's lots of fun
in being alive. You wouldn't have toothache if you were dead, but still, wouldn't
you lots rather be alive than dead? I would, a hundred times. Oh, here's Dan
Reese. He's been down to the harbour for fish."

"I hate Dan Reese," said Walter.

"So do I. All us girls do. I'm just going to walk past and never take the least
notice of him. You watch me!"

Faith accordingly stalked past Dan with her chin out and an expression of
scorn that bit into his soul. He turned and shouted after her.

"Pig-girl! Pig-girl!! Pig-girl!!!" in a crescendo of insult.

Faith walked on, seemingly oblivious. But her lip trembled slightly with a
sense of outrage. She knew she was no match for Dan Reese when it came to an
exchange of epithets. She wished Jem Blythe had been with her instead of Wal-

ter. If Dan Reese had dared to call her a pig-girl in Jem's hearing, Jem would have wiped up the dust with him. But it never occurred to Faith to expect Walter to do it, or blame him for not doing it. Walter, she knew, never fought other boys. Neither did Charlie Clow of the north road. The strange part was that, while she despised Charlie for a coward, it never occurred to her to disdain Walter. It was simply that he seemed to her an inhabitant of a world of his own, where different traditions prevailed. Faith would as soon have expected a starry-eyed young angel to pummel dirty, freckled Dan Reese for her as Walter Blythe. She would not have blamed the angel and she did not blame Walter Blythe. But she wished that sturdy Jem or Jerry had been there and Dan's insult continued to rankle in her soul.

Walter was pale no longer. He had flushed crimson and his beautiful eyes were clouded with shame and anger. He knew that he ought to have avenged Faith. Jem would have sailed right in and made Dan eat his words with bitter sauce. Ritchie Warren would have overwhelmed Dan with worse "names" than Dan had called Faith. But Walter could not—simply could not—"call names." He knew he would get the worst of it. He could never conceive or utter the vulgar, ribald insults of which Dan Reese had unlimited command. And as for the trial by fist, Walter couldn't fight. He hated the idea. It was rough and painful—and, worst of all, it was ugly. He never could understand Jem's exultation in an occasional conflict. But he wished he COULD fight Dan Reese. He was horribly ashamed because Faith Meredith had been insulted in his presence and he had not tried to punish her insulter. He felt sure she must despise him. She had not even spoken to him since Dan had called her pig-girl. He was glad when they came to the parting of the ways.

Faith, too, was relieved, though for a different reason. She wanted to be alone because she suddenly felt rather nervous about her errand. Impulse had cooled, especially since Dan had bruised her self-respect. She must go through with it, but she no longer had enthusiasm to sustain her. She was going to see Norman Douglas and ask him to come back to church, and she began to be afraid of him. What had seemed so easy and simple up at the Glen seemed very different down here. She had heard a good deal about Norman Douglas, and she knew that even the biggest boys in school were afraid of him. Suppose he called her something nasty—she had heard he was given to that. Faith could not endure being called names—they subdued her far more quickly than a physical blow. But she would go on—Faith Meredith always went on. If she did not her father might have to leave the Glen.

At the end of the long lane Faith came to the house—a big, old-fashioned one with a row of soldierly Lombardies marching past it. On the back veranda Norman Douglas himself was sitting, reading a newspaper. His big dog was beside him. Behind, in the kitchen, where his housekeeper, Mrs. Wilson, was getting supper, there was a clatter of dishes—an angry clatter, for Norman Douglas had just had a quarrel with Mrs. Wilson, and both were in a very bad temper over it.

Consequently, when Faith stepped on the veranda and Norman Douglas lowered his newspaper she found herself looking into the choleric eyes of an irritated man.

Norman Douglas was rather a fine-looking personage in his way. He had a sweep of long red beard over his broad chest and a mane of red hair, ungrizzled by the years, on his massive head. His high, white forehead was unwrinkled and his blue eyes could flash still with all the fire of his tempestuous youth. He could be very amiable when he liked, and he could be very terrible. Poor Faith, so anxiously bent on retrieving the situation in regard to the church, had caught him in one of his terrible moods.

He did not know who she was and he gazed at her with disfavour. Norman Douglas liked girls of spirit and flame and laughter. At this moment Faith was very pale. She was of the type to which colour means everything. Lacking her crimson cheeks she seemed meek and even insignificant. She looked apologetic and afraid, and the bully in Norman Douglas's heart stirred.

"Who the dickens are you? And what do you want here?" he demanded in his great resounding voice, with a fierce scowl.

For once in her life Faith had nothing to say. She had never supposed Norman Douglas was like THIS. She was paralyzed with terror of him. He saw it and it made him worse.

"What's the matter with you?" he boomed. "You look as if you wanted to say something and was scared to say it. What's troubling you? Confound it, speak up, can't you?"

No. Faith could not speak up. No words would come. But her lips began to tremble.

"For heaven's sake, don't cry," shouted Norman. "I can't stand snivelling. If you've anything to say, say it and have done. Great Kitty, is the girl possessed of a dumb spirit? Don't look at me like that—I'm human—I haven't got a tail! Who are you—who are you, I say?"

Norman's voice could have been heard at the harbour. Operations in the kitchen were suspended. Mrs. Wilson was listening open-eared and eyed. Norman put his huge brown hands on his knees and leaned forward, staring into Faith's pallid, shrinking face. He seemed to loom over her like some evil giant out of a fairy tale. She felt as if he would eat her up next thing, body and bones.

"I—am—Faith—Meredith," she said, in little more than a whisper.

"Meredith, hey? One of the parson's youngsters, hey? I've heard of you—I've heard of you! Riding on pigs and breaking the Sabbath! A nice lot! What do you want here, hey? What do you want of the old pagan, hey? *I* don't ask favours of parsons—and I don't give any. What do you want, I say?"

Faith wished herself a thousand miles away. She stammered out her thought in its naked simplicity.

"I came—to ask you—to go to church—and pay—to the salary."

Norman glared at her. Then he burst forth again.

"You impudent hussy—you! Who put you up to it, jade? Who put you up to it?"

"Nobody," said poor Faith.

"That's a lie. Don't lie to me! Who sent you here? It wasn't your father—he hasn't the smeddum of a flea—but he wouldn't send you to do what he dassn't do himself. I suppose it was some of them confounded old maids at the Glen, was it—was it, hey?"

"No—I—I just came myself."

"Do you take me for a fool?" shouted Norman.

"No—I thought you were a gentleman," said Faith faintly, and certainly without any thought of being sarcastic.

Norman bounced up.

"Mind your own business. I don't want to hear another word from you. If you wasn't such a kid I'd teach you to interfere in what doesn't concern you. When I want parsons or pill-dosers I'll send for them. Till I do I'll have no truck with them. Do you understand? Now, get out, cheese-face."

Faith got out. She stumbled blindly down the steps, out of the yard gate and into the lane. Half way up the lane her daze of fear passed away and a reaction of tingling anger possessed her. By the time she reached the end of the lane she was in such a furious temper as she had never experienced before. Norman Douglas' insults burned in her soul, kindling a scorching flame. Go home! Not she! She would go straight back and tell that old ogre just what she thought of him—she would show him—oh, wouldn't she! Cheese-face, indeed!

Unhesitatingly she turned and walked back. The veranda was deserted and the kitchen door shut. Faith opened the door without knocking, and went in. Norman Douglas had just sat down at the supper table, but he still held his newspaper. Faith walked inflexibly across the room, caught the paper from his hand, flung it on the floor and stamped on it. Then she faced him, with her flashing eyes and scarlet cheeks. She was such a handsome young fury that Norman Douglas hardly recognized her.

"What's brought you back?" he growled, but more in bewilderment than rage.

Unquailingly she glared back into the angry eyes against which so few people could hold their own.

"I have come back to tell you exactly what I think of you," said Faith in clear, ringing tones. "I am not afraid of you. You are a rude, unjust, tyrannical, disagreeable old man. Susan says you are sure to go to hell, and I was sorry for you, but I am not now. Your wife never had a new hat for ten years—no wonder she died. I am going to make faces at you whenever I see you after this. Every time I am behind you you will know what is happening. Father has a picture of the devil in a book in his study, and I mean to go home and write your name under it. You are an old vampire and I hope you'll have the Scotch fiddle!"

Faith did not know what a vampire meant any more than she knew what the Scotch fiddle was. She had heard Susan use the expressions and gathered from her tone that both were dire things. But Norman Douglas knew what the latter meant at least. He had listened in absolute silence to Faith's tirade. When she paused for breath, with a stamp of her foot, he suddenly burst into loud laughter. With a mighty slap of hand on knee he exclaimed,

"I vow you've got spunk, after all—I like spunk. Come, sit down—sit down!"

"I will not." Faith's eyes flashed more passionately. She thought she was being made fun of—treated contemptuously. She would have enjoyed another explosion of rage, but this cut deep. "I will not sit down in your house. I am going home. But I am glad I came back here and told you exactly what my opinion of you is."

"So am I—so am I," chuckled Norman. "I like you—you're fine—you're great. Such roses—such vim! Did I call her cheese-face? Why, she never smelt a cheese. Sit down. If you'd looked like that at the first, girl! So you'll write my name under the devil's picture, will you? But he's black, girl, he's black—and I'm red. It won't do—it won't do! And you hope I'll have the Scotch fiddle, do you? Lord love you, girl, I had IT when I was a boy. Don't wish it on me again. Sit down—sit in. We'll tak' a cup o' kindness."

"No, thank you," said Faith haughtily.

"Oh, yes, you will. Come, come now, I apologize, girl—I apologize. I made a fool of myself and I'm sorry. Man can't say fairer. Forget and forgive. Shake hands, girl—shake hands. She won't—no, she won't! But she must! Look-a-here, girl, if you'll shake hands and break bread with me I'll pay what I used to to the salary and I'll go to church the first Sunday in every month and I'll make Kitty Alec hold her jaw. I'm the only one in the clan can do it. Is it a bargain, girl?"

It seemed a bargain. Faith found herself shaking hands with the ogre and then sitting at his board. Her temper was over—Faith's tempers never lasted very long—but its excitement still sparkled in her eyes and crimsoned her cheeks. Norman Douglas looked at her admiringly.

"Go, get some of your best preserves, Wilson," he ordered, "and stop sulking, woman, stop sulking. What if we did have a quarrel, woman? A good squall clears the air and briskens things up. But no drizzling and fogging afterwards— no drizzling and fogging, woman. I can't stand that. Temper in a woman but no tears for me. Here, girl, is some messed up meat and potatoes for you. Begin on that. Wilson has some fancy name for it, but I call lit macanaccady. Anything I can't analyze in the eating line I call macanaccady and anything wet that puzzles me I call shallamagouslem. Wilson's tea is shallamagouslem. I swear she makes it out of burdocks. Don't take any of the ungodly black liquid—here's some milk for you. What did you say your name was?"

"Faith."

"No name that—no name that! I can't stomach such a name. Got any other?"

"No, sir."

"Don't like the name, don't like it. There's no smeddum to it. Besides, it makes me think of my Aunt Jinny. She called her three girls Faith, Hope, and Charity. Faith didn't believe in anything—Hope was a born pessimist—and Charity was a miser. You ought to be called Red Rose—you look like one when you're mad. I'LL call you Red Rose. And you've roped me into promising to go to church?

But only once a month, remember—only once a month. Come now, girl, will you let me off? I used to pay a hundred to the salary every year and go to church. If I promise to pay two hundred a year will you let me off going to church? Come now!"

"No, no, sir," said Faith, dimpling roguishly. "I want you to go to church, too."

"Well, a bargain is a bargain. I reckon I can stand it twelve times a year. What a sensation it'll make the first Sunday I go! And old Susan Baker says I'm going to hell, hey? Do you believe I'll go there—come, now, do you?"

"I hope not, sir," stammered Faith in some confusion.

"WHY do you hope not? Come, now, WHY do you hope not? Give us a reason, girl—give us a reason."

"It—it must be a very—uncomfortable place, sir."

"Uncomfortable? All depends on your taste in comfortable, girl. I'd soon get tired of angels. Fancy old Susan in a halo, now!"

Faith did fancy it, and it tickled her so much that she had to laugh. Norman eyed her approvingly.

"See the fun of it, hey? Oh, I like you—you're great. About this church business, now—can your father preach?"

"He is a splendid preacher," said loyal Faith.

"He is, hey? I'll see—I'll watch out for flaws. He'd better be careful what he says before ME. I'll catch him—I'll trip him up—I'll keep tabs on his arguments. I'm bound to have some fun out of this church going business. Does he ever preach hell?"

"No—o—o—I don't think so."

"Too bad. I like sermons on that subject. You tell him that if he wants to keep me in good humour to preach a good rip-roaring sermon on hell once every six months—and the more brimstone the better. I like 'em smoking. And think of all the pleasure he'd give the old maids, too. They'd all keep looking at old Norman Douglas and thinking, 'That's for you, you old reprobate. That's what's in store for YOU!' I'll give an extra ten dollars every time you get your father to preach on hell. Here's Wilson and the jam. Like that, hey? IT isn't macanaccady. Taste!"

Faith obediently swallowed the big spoonful Norman held out to her. Luckily it WAS good.

"Best plum jam in the world," said Norman, filling a large saucer and plumping it down before her. "Glad you like it. I'll give you a couple of jars to take home with you. There's nothing mean about me—never was. The devil can't catch me at THAT corner, anyhow. It wasn't my fault that Hester didn't have a new hat for ten years. It was her own—she pinched on hats to save money to give yellow fellows over in China. *I* never gave a cent to missions in my life—never will. Never you try to bamboozle me into that! A hundred a year to the salary and church once a month—but no spoiling good heathens to make poor Christians! Why, girl, they wouldn't be fit for heaven or hell—clean spoiled for either place—clean spoiled. Hey, Wilson, haven't you got a smile on yet? Beats all how you women can sulk! *I* never sulked in my life—it's just one big flash and crash with me and then—pouf—the squall's over and the sun is out and you could eat out of my hand."

Norman insisted on driving Faith home after supper and he filled the buggy up with apples, cabbages, potatoes and pumpkins and jars of jam.

"There's a nice little tom-pussy out in the barn. I'll give you that too, if you'd like it. Say the word," he said.

"No, thank you," said Faith decidedly. "I don't like cats, and besides, I have a rooster."

"Listen to her. You can't cuddle a rooster as you can a kitten. Who ever heard of petting a rooster? Better take little Tom. I want to find a good home for him."

"No. Aunt Martha has a cat and he would kill a strange kitten."

Norman yielded the point rather reluctantly. He gave Faith an exciting drive home, behind his wild two-year old, and when he had let her out at the kitchen door of the manse and dumped his cargo on the back veranda he drove away shouting,

"It's only once a month—only once a month, mind!"

Faith went up to bed, feeling a little dizzy and breathless, as if she had just escaped from the grasp of a genial whirlwind. She was happy and thankful. No fear now that they would have to leave the Glen and the graveyard and Rainbow Valley. But she fell asleep troubled by a disagreeable subconsciousness that Dan Reese had called her pig-girl and that, having stumbled on such a congenial epithet, he would continue to call her so whenever opportunity offered.

CHAPTER XVII. A DOUBLE VICTORY

Norman Douglas came to church the first Sunday in November and made all the sensation he desired. Mr. Meredith shook hands with him absently on the church steps and hoped dreamily that Mrs. Douglas was well.

"She wasn't very well just before I buried her ten years ago, but I reckon she has better health now," boomed Norman, to the horror and amusement of every one except Mr. Meredith, who was absorbed in wondering if he had made the last head of his sermon as clear as he might have, and hadn't the least idea what Norman had said to him or he to Norman.

Norman intercepted Faith at the gate.

"Kept my word, you see—kept my word, Red Rose. I'm free now till the first Sunday in December. Fine sermon, girl—fine sermon. Your father has more in his head than he carries on his face. But he contradicted himself once—tell him he contradicted himself. And tell him I want that brimstone sermon in December. Great way to wind up the old year—with a taste of hell, you know. And what's the matter with a nice tasty discourse on heaven for New Year's? Though it wouldn't be half as interesting as hell, girl—not half. Only I'd like to know what your father thinks about heaven—he CAN think—rarest thing in the world—a person who can think. But he DID contradict himself. Ha, ha! Here's a question you might ask him sometime when he's awake, girl. 'Can God make a stone so big He couldn't lift it Himself?' Don't forget now. I want to hear his opinion on it. I've stumped many a minister with that, girl."

Faith was glad to escape him and run home. Dan Reese, standing among the crowd of boys at the gate,

looked at her and shaped his mouth into "pig-girl," but dared not utter it aloud just there. Next day in school was a different matter. At noon recess Faith encountered Dan in the little spruce plantation behind the school and Dan shouted once more,

"Pig-girl! Pig-girl! ROOSTER-GIRL!"

Walter Blythe suddenly rose from a mossy cushion behind a little clump of firs where he had been reading. He was very pale, but his eyes blazed.

"You hold your tongue, Dan Reese!" he said.

"Oh, hello, Miss Walter," retorted Dan, not at all abashed. He vaulted airily to the top of the rail fence and chanted insultingly,

"Cowardy, cowardy-custard
Stole a pot of mustard,
Cowardy, cowardy-custard!"

"You are a coincidence!" said Walter scornfully, turning still whiter. He had only a very hazy idea what a coincidence was, but Dan had none at all and thought it must be something peculiarly opprobrious.

"Yah! Cowardy!" he yelled gain. "Your mother writes lies—lies—lies! And Faith Meredith is a pig-girl—a—pig-girl—a pig-girl! And she's a rooster-girl—a rooster-girl—a rooster-girl! Yah! Cowardy—cowardy—cust—"

Dan got no further. Walter had hurled himself across the intervening space and knocked Dan off the fence backward with one well-directed blow. Dan's sudden inglorious sprawl was greeted with a burst of laughter and a clapping of hands from Faith. Dan sprang up, purple with rage, and began to climb the fence. But just then the school-bell rang and Dan knew what happened to boys who were late during Mr. Hazard's regime.

"We'll fight this out," he howled. "Cowardy!"

"Any time you like," said Walter.

"Oh, no, no, Walter," protested Faith. "Don't fight him. *I* don't mind what he says—I wouldn't condescend to mind the like of HIM."

"He insulted you and he insulted my mother," said Walter, with the same deadly calm. "Tonight after school, Dan."

"I've got to go right home from school to pick taters after the harrows, dad says," answered Dan sulkily. "But to-morrow night'll do."

"All right—here to-morrow night," agreed Walter.

"And I'll smash your sissy-face for you," promised Dan.

Walter shuddered—not so much from fear of the threat as from repulsion over the ugliness and vulgarity of it. But he held his head high and marched into school. Faith followed in a conflict of emotions. She hated to think of Walter fighting that little sneak, but oh, he had been splendid! And he was going to fight for HER—Faith Meredith—to punish her insulter! Of course he would win—such eyes spelled victory.

Faith's confidence in her champion had dimmed a little by evening, however. Walter had seemed so very quiet and dull the rest of the day in school.

"If it were only Jem," she sighed to Una, as they sat on Hezekiah Pollock's tombstone in the graveyard. "HE is such a fighter—he could finish Dan off in no time. But Walter doesn't know much about fighting."

"I'm so afraid he'll be hurt," sighed Una, who hated fighting and couldn't understand the subtle, secret exultation she divined in Faith.

"He oughtn't to be," said Faith uncomfortably. "He's every bit as big as Dan."

"But Dan's so much older," said Una. "Why, he's nearly a year older."

"Dan hasn't done much fighting when you come to count up," said Faith. "I believe he's really a coward. He didn't think Walter would fight, or he wouldn't have called names before him. Oh, if you could just have seen Walter's face when he looked at him, Una! It made me shiver—with a nice shiver. He looked just like Sir Galahad in that poem father read us on Saturday."

"I hate the thought of them fighting and I wish it could be stopped," said Una.

"Oh, it's got to go on now," cried Faith. "It's a matter of honour. Don't you DARE tell anyone, Una. If you do I'll never tell you secrets again!"

"I won't tell," agreed Una. "But I won't stay to-morrow to watch the fight. I'm coming right home."

"Oh, all right. *I* have to be there—it would be mean not to, when Walter is fighting for me. I'm going to tie my colours on his arm—that's the thing to do when he's my knight. How lucky Mrs. Blythe gave me that pretty blue hair-ribbon for my birthday! I've only worn it twice so it will be almost new. But I wish I was sure Walter would win. It will be so—so HUMILIATING if he doesn't."

Faith would have been yet more dubious if she could have seen her champion just then. Walter had gone home from school with all his righteous anger at a low ebb and a very nasty feeling in its place. He had to fight Dan Reese the next night—and he didn't want to—he hated the thought of it. And he kept thinking of it all the time. Not for a minute could he get away from the thought. Would it hurt much? He was terribly afraid that it would hurt. And would he be defeated and shamed?

He could not eat any supper worth speaking of. Susan had made a big batch of his favourite monkey-faces, but he could choke only one down. Jem ate four. Walter wondered how he could. How could ANYBODY eat? And how could they all talk gaily as they were doing? There was mother, with her shining eyes and pink cheeks. SHE didn't know her son had to fight next day. Would she be so gay if she knew, Walter wondered darkly. Jem had taken Susan's picture with his new camera and the result was passed around the table and Susan was terribly indignant over it.

"I am no beauty, Mrs. Dr. dear, and well I know it, and have always known it," she said in an aggrieved tone, "but that I am as ugly as that picture makes me out I will never, no, never believe."

Jem laughed over this and Anne laughed again with him. Walter couldn't endure it. He got up and fled to his room.

"That child has got something on his mind, Mrs. Dr. dear," said Susan. "He has et next to nothing. Do you suppose he is plotting another poem?"

Poor Walter was very far removed in spirit from the starry realms of poesy just then. He propped his elbow on his open window-sill and leaned his head drearily on his hands.

"Come on down to the shore, Walter," cried Jem, busting in. "The boys are going to burn the sand-hill grass to-night. Father says we can go. Come on."

At any other time Walter would have been delighted. He gloried in the burning of the sand-hill grass. But now he flatly refused to go, and no arguments or entreaties could move him. Disappointed Jem, who did not care for the long dark walk to Four Winds Point alone, retreated to his museum in the garret and buried himself in a book. He soon forgot his disappointment, revelling with the heroes of old romance, and pausing occasionally to picture himself a famous general, leading his troops to victory on some great battlefield.

Walter sat at his window until bedtime. Di crept in, hoping to be told what was wrong, but Walter could not talk of it, even to Di. Talking of it seemed to give it a reality from which he shrank. It was torture enough to think of it. The crisp, withered leaves rustled on the maple trees outside his window. The glow of rose and flame had died out of the hollow, silvery sky, and the full moon was rising gloriously over Rainbow Valley. Afar off, a ruddy woodfire was painting a page of glory on the horizon beyond the hills. It was a sharp, clear evening when far-away sounds were heard distinctly. A fox was barking across the pond; an engine was puffing down at the Glen station; a blue-jay was screaming madly in the maple grove; there was laughter over on the manse lawn. How could people laugh? How could foxes and blue-jays and engines behave as if nothing were going to happen on the morrow?

"Oh, I wish it was over," groaned Walter.

He slept very little that night and had hard work choking down his porridge in the morning. Susan WAS rather lavish in her platefuls. Mr. Hazard found him an unsatisfactory pupil that day. Faith Meredith's wits seemed to be wool-gathering, too. Dan Reese kept drawing surreptitious pictures of girls, with pig or rooster heads, on his slate and holding them up for all to see. The news of the coming battle had leaked out and most of the boys and many of the girls were in the spruce plantation when Dan and Walter sought it after school. Una had gone home, but Faith was there, having tied her blue ribbon around Walter's arm. Walter was thankful that neither Jem nor Di nor Nan were among the crowd of spectators. Somehow they had not heard of what was in the wind and had gone home, too. Walter faced Dan quite undauntedly now. At the last moment all his fear had vanished, but he still felt disgust at the idea of fighting. Dan, it was noted, was really paler under his freckles than Walter was. One of the older boys gave the word and Dan struck Walter in the face.

Walter reeled a little. The pain of the blow tingled through all his sensitive frame for a moment. Then he felt pain no longer. Something, such as he had never experienced before, seemed to roll over him like a flood. His face flushed crimson, his eyes burned like flame. The scholars of Glen St. Mary school had never dreamed that "Miss Walter" could look like that. He hurled himself forward and closed with Dan like a young wildcat.

There were no particular rules in the fights of the Glen school boys. It was catch-as-catch can, and get your blows in anyhow. Walter fought with a savage fury and a joy in the struggle against which Dan could not hold his ground. It was all over very speedily. Walter had no clear consciousness of what he was doing until suddenly the red mist cleared from his sight and he found himself kneeling on the body of the prostrate Dan whose nose—oh, horror!—was spouting blood.

"Have you had enough?" demanded Walter through his clenched teeth.

Dan sulkily admitted that he had.

"My mother doesn't write lies?"

"No."

"Faith Meredith isn't a pig-girl?"

"No."

"Nor a rooster-girl?"

"No."

"And I'm not a coward?"

"No."

Walter had intended to ask, "And you are a liar?" but pity intervened and he did not humiliate Dan further. Besides, that blood was so horrible.

"You can go, then," he said contemptuously.

There was a loud clapping from the boys who were perched on the rail fence, but some of the girls were crying. They were frightened. They had seen schoolboy fights before, but nothing like Walter as he had grappled with Dan. There had been something terrifying about him. They thought he would kill Dan. Now that all was over they sobbed hysterically—except Faith, who still stood tense and crimson cheeked.

Walter did not stay for any conqueror's meed. He sprang over the fence and rushed down the spruce hill to Rainbow Valley. He felt none of the victor's joy, but he felt a certain calm satisfaction in duty done and honour avenged—mingled with a sickish qualm when he thought of Dan's gory nose. It had been so ugly, and Walter hated ugliness.

Also, he began to realize that he himself was somewhat sore and battered up. His lip was cut and swollen and one eye felt very strange. In Rainbow Valley he encountered Mr. Meredith, who was coming home from an afternoon call on the Miss Wests. That reverend gentleman looked gravely at him.

"It seems to me that you have been fighting, Walter?"

"Yes, sir," said Walter, expecting a scolding.

"What was it about?"

"Dan Reese said my mother wrote lies and that that Faith was a pig-girl," answered Walter bluntly.

"Oh—h! Then you were certainly justified, Walter."

"Do you think it's right to fight, sir?" asked Walter curiously.

"Not always—and not often—but sometimes—yes, sometimes," said John Meredith. "When womenkind are insulted for instance—as in your case. My motto, Walter, is, don't fight till you're sure you ought to, and THEN put every ounce of you into it. In spite of sundry discolorations I infer that you came off best."

"Yes. I made him take it all back."

"Very good—very good, indeed. I didn't think you were such a fighter, Walter."

"I never fought before—and I didn't want to right up to the last—and then," said Walter, determined to make a clean breast of it, "I liked it while I was at it."

The Rev. John's eyes twinkled.

"You were—a little frightened—at first?"

"I was a whole lot frightened," said honest Walter. "But I'm not going to be frightened any more, sir. Being frightened of things is worse than the things themselves. I'm going to ask father to take me over to Lowbridge to-morrow to get my tooth out."

"Right again. 'Fear is more pain than is the pain it fears.' Do you know who wrote that, Walter? It was Shakespeare. Was there any feeling or emotion or experience of the human heart that that wonderful man did not know? When you go home tell your mother I am proud of you."

Walter did not tell her that, however; but he told her all the rest, and she sympathized with him and told him she was glad he had stood up for her and Faith, and she anointed his sore spots and rubbed cologne on his aching head.

"Are all mothers as nice as you?" asked Walter, hugging her.

"You're WORTH standing up for."

Miss Cornelia and Susan were in the living room when Anne came downstairs, and listened to the story with much enjoyment. Susan in particular was highly gratified.

"I am real glad to hear he has had a good fight, Mrs. Dr. dear.

Perhaps it may knock that poetry nonsense out of him. And I

never, no, never could bear that little viper of a Dan Reese.

Will you not sit nearer to the fire, Mrs. Marshall Elliott?

These November evenings are very chilly."

"Thank you, Susan, I'm not cold. I called at the manse before I came here and got quite warm—though I had to go to the kitchen to do it, for there was no fire anywhere else. The kitchen looked as if it had been stirred up with a stick, believe ME. Mr. Meredith wasn't home. I couldn't find out where he was, but I have an idea that he was up at the Wests'. Do you know, Anne dearie, they say he has been going there frequently all the fall and people are beginning to think he is going to see Rosemary."

"He would get a very charming wife if he married Rosemary," said

Anne, piling driftwood on the fire. "She is one of the most

delightful girls I've ever known—truly one of the race of

Joseph."

"Ye—s—only she is an Episcopalian," said Miss Cornelia doubtfully. "Of course, that is better than if she was a Methodist—but I do think Mr. Meredith could find a good enough wife in his own denomination. However, very likely there is nothing in it. It's only a month ago that I said to him, 'You ought to marry again, Mr. Meredith.' He looked as shocked as if I had suggested something improper. 'My wife is in her grave, Mrs. Elliott,' he said, in that gentle, saintly way of his. 'I suppose so,' I said, 'or I wouldn't be advising you to marry again.' Then he looked more shocked than ever. So I doubt if there is much in this Rosemary story. If a single minister calls twice at a house where there is a single woman all the gossips have it he is courting her."

"It seems to me—if I may presume to say so—that Mr. Meredith is too shy to go courting a second wife," said Susan solemnly.

"He ISN'T shy, believe ME," retorted Miss Cornelia. "Absent-minded,—yes—but shy, no. And for all he is so abstracted and dreamy he has a very good opinion of himself, man-like, and when he is really awake he wouldn't think it much of a chore to ask any woman to have him. No, the trouble is, he's deluding himself into believing that his heart is buried, while all the time it's beating away inside of him just like anybody else's. He may have a notion of Rosemary West and he may not. If he has, we must make the best of it. She is a sweet girl and a fine housekeeper, and would make a good mother for those poor, neglected children. And," concluded Miss Cornelia resignedly, "my own grandmother was an Episcopalian."

CHAPTER XVIII. MARY BRINGS EVIL TIDINGS

Mary Vance, whom Mrs. Elliott had sent up to the manse on an errand, came tripping down Rainbow Valley on her way to Ingleside where she was to spend the afternoon with Nan and Di as a Saturday treat. Nan and Di had been picking spruce gum with Faith and Una in the manse woods and the four of them were now sitting on a fallen pine by the brook, all, it must be admitted, chewing rather vigorously. The Ingleside twins were not allowed to chew spruce gum anywhere but in the seclusion of Rainbow Valley, but Faith and Una were unrestricted by such rules of etiquette and cheerfully chewed it everywhere, at home and abroad, to the very proper horror of the Glen. Faith had been chewing it in church one day; but Jerry had realized the enormity of THAT, and had given her such an older-brotherly scolding that she never did it again.

"I was so hungry I just felt as if I had to chew something," she protested. "You know well enough what breakfast was like, Jerry Meredith. I COULDN'T eat scorched porridge and my stomach just felt so queer and empty. The gum helped a lot—and I didn't chew VERY hard. I didn't make any noise and I never cracked the gum once."

"You mustn't chew gum in church, anyhow," insisted Jerry. "Don't let me catch you at it again."

"You chewed yourself in prayer-meeting last week," cried Faith.

"THAT'S different," said Jerry loftily. "Prayer-meeting isn't on Sunday. Besides, I sat away at the back in a dark seat and nobody saw me. You were sitting right up front where every one saw you. And I took the gum out of my mouth for the last hymn and stuck it on the back of the pew right up in front where every one saw you. And I took the gum out of my mouth for the last hymn and stuck it on the back of the pew in front of me. Then I came away and forgot it. I went back to get it next morning, but it was gone. I suppose Rod Warren swiped it. And it was a dandy chew."

Mary Vance walked down the Valley with her head held high. She had on a new blue velvet cap with a scarlet rosette in it, a coat of navy blue cloth and a little squirrel-fur muff. She was very conscious of her new clothes and very well pleased with herself. Her hair was elaborately crimped, her face was quite plump, her cheeks rosy, her white eyes shining. She did not look much like the forlorn and ragged waif the Merediths had found in the old Taylor barn. Una tried not to feel envious. Here was Mary with a new velvet cap, but she and Faith had to wear their shabby old gray tams again this winter. Nobody ever thought of getting them new ones and they were afraid to ask their father for them for fear that he might be short of money and then he would feel badly. Mary had told them once that ministers were always short of money, and found it "awful hard" to make ends meet. Since then Faith and Una would have gone in rags rather than ask their father for anything if they could help it. They did not worry a great deal over their shabbiness; but it was rather trying to see Mary Vance coming out in such style and putting on such airs about it, too. The new squirrel muff was really the last straw. Neither Faith nor Una had ever had a muff, counting themselves lucky if they could compass mittens without holes in them. Aunt Martha could not see to darn holes and though Una tried to, she made sad cobbling. Somehow, they could not make their greeting of Mary very cordial. But Mary did not mind or notice that; she was not overly sensitive. She vaulted lightly to a seat on the pine tree, and laid the offending muff on a bough. Una saw that it was lined with shirred red satin and had red tassels. She looked down at her own rather purple, chapped, little hands and wondered if she would ever, EVER be able to put them into a muff like that.

"Give us a chew," said Mary companionably. Nan, Di and Faith all produced an amber-hued knot or two from their pockets and passed them to Mary. Una sat very still. She had four lovely big knots in the pocket of her tight, thread-bare little jacket, but she wasn't going to give one of them to Mary Vance—not one Let Mary pick her own gum! People with squirrel muffs needn't expect to get everything in the world.

"Great day, isn't it?" said Mary, swinging her legs, the better, perhaps, to display new boots with very smart cloth tops. Una tucked HER feet under her. There was a hole in the toe of one of her boots and both laces were much knotted. But they were the best she had. Oh, this Mary Vance! Why hadn't they left her in the old barn?

Una never felt badly because the Ingleside twins were better dressed than she and Faith were. THEY wore their pretty clothes with careless grace and never seemed to think about them at all. Somehow, they did not make other people feel shabby. But when Mary Vance was dressed up she seemed fairly to exude clothes—to walk in an atmosphere of clothes—to make everybody else feel and think clothes. Una, as she sat there in the honey-tinted sunshine of the gracious December afternoon, was acutely and miserably conscious of everything she had on—the faded tam, which was yet her best, the skimpy jacket she had worn for three winters, the holes in her skirt and her boots, the shivering insufficiency of her poor little undergarments. Of course, Mary was going out for a visit and she was not. But even if she had been she had nothing better to put on and in this lay the sting.

"Say, this is great gum. Listen to me cracking it. There ain't any gum spruces down at Four Winds," said Mary. "Sometimes I just hanker after a chew. Mrs. Elliott won't let me chew gum if she sees me. She says it ain't lady-like. This lady-business puzzles me. I can't get on to all its kinks. Say, Una, what's the matter with you? Cat got your tongue?"

"No," said Una, who could not drag her fascinated eyes from that squirrel muff. Mary leaned past her, picked it up and thrust it into Una's hands.

"Stick your paws in that for a while," she ordered. "They look sorter pinched. Ain't that a dandy muff? Mrs. Elliott give it to me last week for a birthday present. I'm to get the collar at Christmas. I heard her telling Mr. Elliott that."

"Mrs. Elliott is very good to you," said Faith.

"You bet she is. And I'M good to her, too," retorted Mary. "I work like a nigger to make it easy for her and have everything just as she likes it. We was made for each other. 'Tisn't every one could get along with her as well as I do. She's pizen neat, but so am I, and so we agree fine."

"I told you she would never whip you."

"So you did. She's never tried to lay a finger on me and I ain't never told a lie to her—not one, true's you live. She combs me down with her tongue sometimes though, but that just slips off ME like water off a duck's back. Say, Una, why didn't you hang on to the muff?"

Una had put it back on the bough.

"My hands aren't cold, thank you," she said stiffly.

"Well, if you're satisfied, *I* am. Say, old Kitty Alec has come back to church as meek as Moses and nobody knows why. But everybody is saying it was Faith brought Norman Douglas out. His housekeeper says you went there and gave him an awful tongue-lashing. Did you?"

"I went and asked him to come to church," said Faith uncomfortably.

"Fancy your spunk!" said Mary admiringly. "*I* wouldn't have dared do that and I'm not so slow. Mrs. Wilson says the two of you jawed something scandalous, but you come off best and then he just turned round and like to eat you up. Say, is your father going to preach here to-morrow?"

"No. He's going to exchange with Mr. Perry from Charlottetown. Father went to town this morning and Mr. Perry is coming out to-night."

"I THOUGHT there was something in the wind, though old Martha wouldn't give me any satisfaction. But I felt sure she wouldn't have been killing that rooster for nothing."

"What rooster? What do you mean?" cried Faith, turning pale.

"*I* don't know what rooster. I didn't see it. When she took the butter Mrs. Elliott sent up she said she'd been out to the barn killing a rooster for dinner tomorrow."

Faith sprang down from the pine.

"It's Adam—we have no other rooster—she has killed Adam."

"Now, don't fly off the handle. Martha said the butcher at the Glen had no meat this week and she had to have something and the hens were all laying and too poor."

"If she has killed Adam—" Faith began to run up the hill.

Mary shrugged her shoulders.

"She'll go crazy now. She was so fond of that Adam. He ought to have been in the pot long ago—he'll be as tough as sole leather. But *I* wouldn't like to be in Martha's shoes. Faith's just white with rage; Una, you'd better go after her and try to peacify her."

Mary had gone a few steps with the Blythe girls when Una suddenly turned and ran after her.

"Here's some gum for you, Mary," she said, with a little repentant catch in her voice, thrusting all her four knots into Mary's hands, "and I'm glad you have such a pretty muff."

"Why, thanks," said Mary, rather taken by surprise. To the Blythe girls, after Una had gone, she said, "Ain't she a queer little mite? But I've always said she had a good heart."

CHAPTER XIX. POOR ADAM!

When Una got home Faith was lying face downwards on her bed, utterly refusing to be comforted. Aunt Martha had killed Adam. He was reposing on a platter in the pantry that very minute, trussed and dressed, encircled by his liver and heart and gizzard. Aunt Martha heeded Faith's passion of grief and anger not a whit.

"We had to have something for the strange minister's dinner," she said. "You're too big a girl to make such a fuss over an old rooster. You knew he'd have to be killed sometime."

"I'll tell father when he comes home what you've done," sobbed Faith.

"Don't you go bothering your poor father. He has troubles enough. And I'M housekeeper here."

"Adam was MINE—Mrs. Johnson gave him to me. You had no business to touch him," stormed Faith.

"Don't you get sassy now. The rooster's killed and there's an end of it. I ain't going to set no strange minister down to a dinner of cold b'iled mutton. I was brought up to know better than that, if I have come down in the world."

Faith would not go down to supper that night and she would not go to church the next morning. But at dinner time she went to the table, her eyes swollen with crying, her face sullen.

The Rev. James Perry was a sleek, rubicund man, with a bristling white moustache, bushy white eyebrows, and a shining bald head. He was certainly not handsome and he was a very tiresome, pompous sort of person. But if he had looked like the Archangel Michael and talked with the tongues of men and angels Faith would still have utterly detested him. He carved Adam up dexterously, showing off his plump white hands and very handsome diamond ring. Also, he made jovial remarks all through the performance. Jerry and Carl giggled, and even Una smiled wanly, because she thought politeness demanded it. But Faith only scowled darkly. The Rev. James thought her manners shockingly bad. Once, when he was delivering himself of an unctuous remark to Jerry, Faith broke in rudely with a flat contradiction. The Rev. James drew his bushy eyebrows together at her.

"Little girls should not interrupt," he said, "and they should not contradict people who know far more than they do."

This put Faith in a worse temper than ever. To be called "little girl" as if she were no bigger than chubby Rilla Blythe over at Ingleside! It was insufferable. And how that abominable Mr. Perry did eat! He even picked poor Adam's bones. Neither Faith nor Una would touch a mouthful, and looked upon the boys as little better than cannibals. Faith felt that if that awful repast did not soon come to an end she would wind it up by throwing something at Mr. Perry's gleaming head. Fortunately, Mr. Perry found Aunt Martha's leathery apple pie too much even for his powers of mastication and the meal came to an end, after a long grace in which Mr. Perry offered up devout thanks for the food which a kind and beneficent Providence had provided for sustenance and temperate pleasure.

"God hadn't a single thing to do with providing Adam for you," muttered Faith rebelliously under her breath.

The boys gladly made their escape to outdoors, Una went to help Aunt Martha with the dishes—though that rather grumpy old dame never welcomed her timid assistance—and Faith betook herself to the study where a cheerful wood fire was burning in the grate. She thought she would thereby escape from the hated Mr. Perry, who had announced his intention of taking a nap in his room during the afternoon. But scarcely had Faith settled herself in a corner, with a book, when he walked in and, standing before the fire, proceeded to survey the disorderly study with an air of disapproval.

"You father's books seem to be in somewhat deplorable confusion, my little girl," he said severely.

Faith darkled in her corner and said not a word. She would NOT talk to this—this creature.

"You should try to put them in order," Mr. Perry went on, playing with his handsome watch chain and smiling patronizingly on Faith. "You are quite old enough to attend to such duties. MY little daughter at home is only ten and she is already an excellent little housekeeper and the greatest help and comfort to her mother. She is a very sweet child. I wish you had the privilege of her acquaintance. She could help you in many ways. Of course, you have not had the inestimable privilege of a good mother's care and training. A sad lack—a very sad lack. I have spoken more than once to your father in this connection and pointed out his duty to him faithfully, but so far with no effect. I trust he may awaken to a realization of his responsibility before it is too late. In the meantime, it is your duty and privilege to endeavour to take your sainted mother's place. You might exercise a great influence over your brothers and your little sister— you might be a true mother to them. I fear that you do not think of these things as you should. My dear child, allow me to open your eyes in regard to them."

Mr. Perry's oily, complacent voice trickled on. He was in his element. Nothing suited him better than to lay down the law, patronize and exhort. He had no idea of stopping, and he did not stop. He stood before the fire, his feet planted firmly on the rug, and poured out a flood of pompous platitudes. Faith heard not a word. She was really not listening to him at all. But she was watching his long black coat-tails with impish delight growing in her brown eyes. Mr. Perry was standing VERY near the fire. His coat-tails began to scorch—his coat-tails began to smoke. He still prosed on, wrapped up in his own eloquence. The coat-tails smoked worse. A tiny spark flew up from the burning wood and alighted in the middle of one. It clung and caught and spread into a smouldering flame. Faith could restrain herself no longer and broke into a stifled giggle.

Mr. Perry stopped short, angered over this impertinence. Suddenly he became conscious that a reek of burning cloth filled the room. He whirled round and saw nothing. Then he clapped his hands to his coat-tails and brought them around in front of him. There was already quite a hole in one of them—and this was his new suit. Faith shook with helpless laughter over his pose and expression.

"Did you see my coat-tails burning?" he demanded angrily.

"Yes, sir," said Faith demurely.

"Why didn't you tell me?" he demanded, glaring at her.

"You said it wasn't good manners to interrupt, sir," said Faith, more demurely still.

"If—if I was your father, I would give you a spanking that you would remember all your life, Miss," said a very angry reverend gentleman, as he stalked out of the study. The coat of Mr. Meredith's second best suit would not fit Mr. Perry, so he had to go to the evening service with his singed coat-tail. But he did not walk up the aisle with his usual consciousness of the honour he was conferring on the building. He never would agree to an exchange of pulpits with Mr. Meredith again, and he was barely civil to the latter when they met for a few minutes at the station the next morning. But Faith felt a certain gloomy satisfaction. Adam was partially avenged.

CHAPTER XX. FAITH MAKES A FRIEND

Next day in school was a hard one for Faith. Mary Vance had told the tale of Adam, and all the scholars, except the Blythes, thought it quite a joke. The girls told Faith, between giggles, that it was too bad, and the boys wrote sardonic notes of condolence to her. Poor Faith went home from school feeling her very soul raw and smarting within her.

"I'm going over to Ingleside to have a talk with Mrs. Blythe," she sobbed. "SHE won't laugh at me, as everybody else does. I've just GOT to talk to somebody who understands how bad I feel."

She ran down through Rainbow Valley. Enchantment had been at work the night before. A light snow had fallen and the powdered firs were dreaming of a spring to come and a joy to be. The long hill beyond was richly purple with leafless beeches. The rosy light of sunset lay over the world like a pink kiss. Of all the airy, fairy places, full of weird, elfin grace, Rainbow Valley that winter evening was the most beautiful. But all its dreamlike loveliness was lost on poor, sore-hearted little Faith.

By the brook she came suddenly upon Rosemary West, who was sitting on the old pine tree. She was on her way home from Ingleside, where she had been giving the girls their music lesson. She had been lingering in Rainbow Valley quite a little time, looking across its white beauty and roaming some by-ways of dream. Judging from the expression of her face, her thoughts were pleasant ones. Perhaps the faint, occasional tinkle from the bells on the Tree Lovers brought the little lurking smile to her lips. Or perhaps it was occasioned by the consciousness that John Meredith seldom failed to spend Monday evening in the gray house on the white wind-swept hill.

Into Rosemary's dreams burst Faith Meredith full of rebellious bitterness. Faith stopped abruptly when she saw Miss West. She did not know her very well—just well enough to speak to when they met. And she did not want to see any one just then—except Mrs. Blythe. She knew her eyes and nose were red and swollen and she hated to have a stranger know she had been crying.

"Good evening, Miss West," she said uncomfortably.

"What is the matter, Faith?" asked Rosemary gently.

"Nothing," said Faith rather shortly.

"Oh!" Rosemary smiled. "You mean nothing that you can tell to outsiders, don't you?"

Faith looked at Miss West with sudden interest. Here was a person who understood things. And how pretty she was! How golden her hair was under her plumy hat! How pink her cheeks were over her velvet coat! How blue and companionable her eyes were! Faith felt that Miss West could be a lovely friend—if only she were a friend instead of a stranger!

"I—I'm going up to tell Mrs. Blythe," said Faith. "She always understands—she never laughs at us. I always talk things over with her. It helps."

"Dear girlie, I'm sorry to have to tell you that Mrs. Blythe isn't home," said Miss West, sympathetically. "She went to Avonlea to-day and isn't coming back till the last of the week."

Faith's lip quivered.

"Then I might as well go home again," she said miserably.

"I suppose so—unless you think you could bring yourself to talk it over with me instead," said Miss Rosemary gently. "It IS such a help to talk things over. *I* know. I don't suppose I can be as good at understanding as Mrs. Blythe—but I promise you that I won't laugh."

"You wouldn't laugh outside," hesitated Faith. "But you might—inside."

"No, I wouldn't laugh inside, either. Why should I? Something has hurt you—it never amuses me to see anybody hurt, no matter what hurts them. If you feel that you'd like to tell me what has hurt you I'll be glad to listen. But if you think you'd rather not—that's all right, too, dear."

Faith took another long, earnest look into Miss West's eyes. They were very serious—there was no laughter in them, not even far, far back. With a little sigh she sat down on the old pine beside her new friend and told her all about Adam and his cruel fate.

Rosemary did not laugh or feel like laughing. She understood and sympathized—really, she was almost as good as Mrs. Blythe—yes, quite as good.

"Mr. Perry is a minister, but he should have been a BUTCHER," said Faith bitterly. "He is so fond of carving things up. He ENJOYED cutting poor Adam to pieces. He just sliced into him as if he were any common rooster."

"Between you and me, Faith, *I* don't like Mr. Perry very well myself," said Rosemary, laughing a little—but at Mr. Perry, not at Adam, as Faith clearly understood. "I never did like him. I went to school with him—he was a Glen boy, you know—and he was a most detestable little prig even then. Oh, how we girls used to hate holding his fat, clammy hands in the ring-around games. But we must remember, dear, that he didn't know that Adam had been a pet of yours. He thought he WAS just a common rooster. We must be just, even when we are terribly hurt."

"I suppose so," admitted Faith. "But why does everybody seem to think it funny that I should have loved Adam so much, Miss West? If it had been a horrid old cat nobody would have thought it queer. When Lottie Warren's kitten had its legs cut off by the binder everybody was sorry for her. She cried two days in school and nobody laughed at her, not even Dan Reese. And all her chums went to the kitten's funeral and helped her bury it—only they couldn't bury its poor little paws with it, because they couldn't find them. It was a horrid thing to have happen, of course, but I don't think it was as dreadful as seeing your pet EATEN UP. Yet everybody laughs at ME."

"I think it is because the name 'rooster' seems rather a funny one," said Rosemary gravely. "There IS something in it that is comical. Now, 'chicken' is different. It doesn't sound so funny to talk of loving a chicken."

"Adam was the dearest little chicken, Miss West. He was just a little golden ball. He would run up to me and peck out of my hand. And he was handsome when he grew up, too—white as snow, with such a beautiful curving white tail, though Mary Vance said it was too short. He knew his name and always came when I called him—he was a very intelligent rooster. And Aunt Martha had no right to kill him. He was mine. It wasn't fair, was it, Miss West?"

"No, it wasn't," said Rosemary decidedly. "Not a bit fair. I remember I had a pet hen when I was a little girl. She was such a pretty little thing—all golden brown and speckly. I loved her as much as I ever loved any pet. She was never killed—she died of old age. Mother wouldn't have her killed because she was my pet."

"If MY mother had been living she wouldn't have let Adam be killed," said Faith. "For that matter, father wouldn't have either, if he'd been home and known of it. I'm SURE he wouldn't, Miss West."

"I'm sure, too," said Rosemary. There was a little added flush on her face. She looked rather conscious but Faith noticed nothing.

"Was it VERY wicked of me not to tell Mr. Perry his coat-tails were scorching?" she asked anxiously.

"Oh, terribly wicked," answered Rosemary, with dancing eyes. "But *I* would have been just as naughty, Faith—*I* wouldn't have told him they were scorching—and I don't believe I would ever have been a bit sorry for my wickedness, either."

"Una thought I should have told him because he was a minister."

"Dearest, if a minister doesn't behave as a gentleman we are not bound to respect his coat-tails. I know *I* would just have loved to see Jimmy Perry's coat-tails burning up. It must have been fun."

Both laughed; but Faith ended with a bitter little sigh.

"Well, anyway, Adam is dead and I am NEVER going to love anything again."

"Don't say that, dear. We miss so much out of life if we don't love. The more we love the richer life is—even if it is only some little furry or feathery pet. Would you like a canary, Faith—a little golden bit of a canary? If you would I'll give you one. We have two up home."

"Oh, I WOULD like that," cried Faith. "I love birds. Only—would Aunt Martha's cat eat it? It's so TRAGIC to have your pets eaten. I don't think I could endure it a second time."

"If you hang the cage far enough from the wall I don't think the cat could harm it. I'll tell you just how to take care of it and I'll bring it to Ingleside for you the next time I come down."

To herself, Rosemary was thinking,

"It will give every gossip in the Glen something to talk of, but

I WILL not care. I want to comfort this poor little heart."

Faith was comforted. Sympathy and understanding were very sweet. She and Miss Rosemary sat on the old pine until the twilight crept softly down over the white valley and the evening star shone over the gray maple grove. Faith told Rosemary all her small history and hopes, her likes and dislikes, the ins and outs of life at the manse, the ups and downs of school society. Finally they parted firm friends.

Mr. Meredith was, as usual, lost in dreams when supper began that evening, but presently a name pierced his abstraction and brought him back to reality. Faith was telling Una of her meeting with Rosemary.

"She is just lovely, I think," said Faith. "Just as nice as Mrs. Blythe—but different. I felt as if I wanted to hug her. She did hug ME—such a nice, velvety hug. And she called me 'dearest.' It THRILLED me. I could tell her ANYTHING."

"So you liked Miss West, Faith?" Mr. Meredith asked, with a rather odd intonation.

"I love her," cried Faith.

"Ah!" said Mr. Meredith. "Ah!"

CHAPTER XXI. THE IMPOSSIBLE WORD

John Meredith walked meditatively through the clear crispness of a winter night in Rainbow Valley. The hills beyond glistened with the chill splendid lustre of moonlight on snow. Every little fir tree in the long valley sang its own wild song to the harp of wind and frost. His children and the Blythe lads and lasses were coasting down the eastern slope and whizzing over the glassy pond. They were having a glorious time and their gay voices and gayer laughter echoed up and down the valley, dying away in elfin cadences among the trees. On the right the lights of Ingleside gleamed through the maple grove with the genial lure and invitation which seems always to glow in the beacons of a home where we know there is love and good-cheer and a welcome for all kin, whether of flesh or spirit. Mr. Meredith liked very well on occasion to spend an evening arguing with the doctor by the drift wood fire, where the famous china dogs of Ingleside kept ceaseless watch and ward, as became deities of the hearth, but to-night he did not look that way. Far on the western hill gleamed a paler but more alluring star. Mr. Meredith was on his way to see Rosemary West, and he meant to tell her something which had been slowly blossoming in his heart since their first meeting and had sprung into full flower on the evening when Faith had so warmly voiced her admiration for Rosemary.

He had come to realize that he had learned to care for Rosemary. Not as he had cared for Cecilia, of course. THAT was entirely different. That love of romance and dream and glamour could never, he thought, return. But Rosemary was beautiful and sweet and dear—very dear. She was the best of companions. He was happier in her company than he had ever expected to be again. She would be an ideal mistress for his home, a good mother to his children.

During the years of his widowhood Mr. Meredith had received innumerable hints from brother members of Presbytery and from many parishioners who could not be suspected of any ulterior motive, as well as from some who could, that he ought to marry again: But these hints never made any impression on him. It was commonly thought he was never aware of them. But he was quite acutely aware of them. And in his own occasional visitations of common sense he knew that the common sensible thing for him to do was to marry. But common sense was not the strong point of John Meredith, and to choose out, deliberately and cold-bloodedly, some "suitable" woman, as one might choose a housekeeper or a business partner, was something he was quite incapable of doing. How he hated that word "suitable." It reminded him so strongly of James Perry. "A SUIT able woman of SUIT able age," that unctuous brother of the cloth had said, in his far from subtle hint. For the moment John Meredith had had a perfectly unbelievable desire to rush madly away and propose marriage to the youngest, most unsuitable woman it was possible to discover.

Mrs. Marshall Elliott was his good friend and he liked her. But when she had bluntly told him he should marry again he felt as if she had torn away the veil that hung before some sacred shrine of his innermost life, and he had been more or less afraid of her ever since. He knew there were women in his congregation "of suitable age" who would marry him quite readily. That fact had seeped through all his abstraction very early in his ministry in Glen St. Mary. They were good, substantial, uninteresting women, one or two fairly comely, the others not exactly so and John Meredith would as soon have thought of marrying any one of them as of hanging himself. He had some ideals to which no seeming necessity could make him false. He could ask no woman to fill Cecilia's place in his home unless he could offer her at least some of the affection and homage he had given to his girlish bride. And where, in his limited feminine acquaintance, was such a woman to be found?

Rosemary West had come into his life on that autumn evening bringing with her an atmosphere in which his spirit recognized native air. Across the gulf of strangerhood they clasped hands of friendship. He knew her better in that ten minutes by the hidden spring than he knew Emmeline Drew or Elizabeth Kirk or Amy Annetta Douglas in a year, or could know them, in a century. He had fled to her for comfort when Mrs. Alec Davis had outraged his mind and soul and had found it. Since then he had gone often to the house on the hill, slipping through the shadowy paths of night in Rainbow Valley so astutely that Glen gossip could never be absolutely certain that he DID go to see Rosemary West. Once or twice he had been caught in the West living room by other visitors; that was all the Ladies' Aid had to go by. But when Elizabeth Kirk heard it she put away a secret hope she had allowed herself to cherish, without a change of expression on her kind plain face, and Emmeline Drew resolved that the next time she saw a certain old bachelor of Lowbridge she would not snub him as she had done at a previous meeting. Of course, if Rosemary West was out to catch the minister she would catch him; she looked younger than she was and MEN thought her pretty; besides, the West girls had money!

"It is to be hoped that he won't be so absent-minded as to propose to Ellen by mistake," was the only malicious thing she allowed herself to say to a sympathetic sister Drew. Emmeline bore no further grudge towards Rosemary. When all was said and done, an unencumbered bachelor was far better than a widower with four children. It had been only the glamour of the manse that had temporarily blinded Emmeline's eyes to the better part.

A sled with three shrieking occupants sped past Mr. Meredith to the pond. Faith's long curls streamed in the wind and her laughter rang above that of the others. John Meredith looked after them kindly and longingly. He was glad that his children had such chums as the Blythes—glad that they had so wise and gay and tender a friend as Mrs. Blythe. But they needed something more, and that something would be supplied when he brought Rosemary West as a bride to the old manse. There was in her a quality essentially maternal.

It was Saturday night and he did not often go calling on Saturday night, which was supposed to be dedicated to a thoughtful revision of Sunday's sermon. But he had chosen this night because he had learned that Ellen West was going to be away and Rosemary would be alone. Often as he had spent pleasant evenings in the house on the hill he had never, since that first meeting at the spring, seen Rosemary alone. Ellen had always been there.

He did not precisely object to Ellen being there. He liked Ellen West very much and they were the best of friends. Ellen had an almost masculine understanding and a sense of humour which his own shy, hidden appreciation of fun found very agreeable. He liked her interest in politics and world events. There was no man in the Glen, not even excepting Dr. Blythe, who had a better grasp of such things.

"I think it is just as well to be interested in things as long as you live," she had said. "If you're not, it doesn't seem to me that there's much difference between the quick and the dead."

He liked her pleasant, deep, rumbly voice; he liked the hearty laugh with which she always ended up some jolly and well-told story. She never gave him digs about his children as other Glen women did; she never bored him with local gossip; she had no malice and no pettiness. She was always splendidly sincere. Mr. Meredith, who had picked up Miss Cornelia's way of classifying people, considered that Ellen belonged to the race of Joseph. Altogether, an admirable woman for a sister-in-law. Nevertheless, a man did not want even the most admirable of women around when he was proposing to another woman. And Ellen was always around. She did not insist on talking to Mr. Meredith herself all the time. She let Rosemary have a fair share of him. Many evenings, indeed, Ellen effaced herself almost totally, sitting back in the corner with St. George in her lap, and letting Mr. Meredith and Rosemary talk and sing and read books together. Sometimes they quite forgot her presence. But if their conversation or choice of duets ever betrayed the least tendency to what Ellen considered philandering, Ellen promptly nipped that tendency in the bud and blotted Rosemary out for the rest of the evening. But not even the grimmest of amiable dragons can altogether prevent a certain subtle language of eye and smile and eloquent silence; and so the minister's courtship progressed after a fashion.

But if it was ever to reach a climax that climax must come when Ellen was away. And Ellen was so seldom away, especially in winter. She found her own fireside the pleasantest place in the world, she vowed. Gadding had no attraction for her. She was fond of company but she wanted it at home. Mr. Meredith had almost been driven to the conclusion that he must write to Rosemary what he wanted to say, when Ellen casually announced one evening that she was going to a silver wedding next Saturday night. She had been bridesmaid when the principals were married. Only old guests were invited, so Rosemary was not included. Mr. Meredith pricked up his ears a trifle and a gleam flashed into his dreamy dark eyes. Both Ellen and Rosemary saw it; and both Ellen and Rosemary felt, with a tingling shock, that Mr. Meredith would certainly come up the hill next Saturday night.

"Might as well have it over with, St. George," Ellen sternly told the black cat, after Mr. Meredith had gone home and Rosemary had silently gone upstairs. "He means to ask her, St. George—I'm perfectly sure of that. So he might as well have his chance to do it and find out he can't get her, George. She'd rather like to take him, Saint. I know that—but she promised, and she's got to keep her promise. I'm rather sorry in some ways, St. George. I don't know of a man I'd sooner have for a brother-in-law if a brother-in-law was convenient. I haven't a thing against him, Saint—not a thing except that he won't see and can't be made to see that the Kaiser is a menace to the peace of Europe. That's HIS blind spot. But he's good company and I like him. A woman can say anything she likes to a man with a mouth like John Meredith's and be sure of not being misunderstood. Such a man is more precious than rubies, Saint—and much rarer, George. But he can't have Rosemary—and I suppose when he finds out he can't have her he'll drop us both. And we'll miss him, Saint—we'll miss him something scandalous, George. But she promised, and I'll see that she keeps her promise!"

Ellen's face looked almost ugly in its lowering resolution.

Upstairs Rosemary was crying into her pillow.

So Mr. Meredith found his lady alone and looking very beautiful. Rosemary had not made any special toilet for the occasion; she wanted to, but she thought it would be absurd to dress up for a man you meant to refuse. So she wore her plain dark afternoon dress and looked like a queen in it. Her suppressed excitement coloured her face to brilliancy, her great blue eyes were pools of light less placid than usual.

She wished the interview were over. She had looked forward to it all day with dread. She felt quite sure that John Meredith cared a great deal for her after a fashion—and she felt just as sure that he did not care for her as he had cared for his first love. She felt that her refusal would disappoint him considerably, but she did not think it would altogether overwhelm him. Yet she hated to make it; hated for his sake and—Rosemary was quite honest with herself—for her own. She knew she could have loved John Meredith if—if it had been permissible. She knew that life would be a blank thing if, rejected as lover, he refused longer to be a friend. She knew that she could be very happy with him and that she could make him happy. But between her and happiness stood the prison gate of the promise she had made to Ellen years ago. Rosemary could not remember her father. He had died when she was only three years old. Ellen, who had been thirteen, remembered him, but with no special tenderness. He had been a stern, reserved man many years older than his fair, pretty wife. Five years later their brother of twelve died also; since his death the two girls had always lived alone with their mother. They had never mingled very freely in the social life of the Glen or Lowbridge, though where they went the wit and spirit of Ellen and the sweetness and beauty of Rosemary made them welcome guests. Both had what was called "a disappointment" in their girlhood. The sea had not given up Rosemary's lover; and Norman Douglas, then a handsome, red-haired young giant, noted for wild driving and noisy though harmless escapades, had quarrelled with Ellen and left her in a fit of pique.

There were not lacking candidates for both Martin's and Norman's places, but none seemed to find favour in the eyes of the West girls, who drifted slowly out of youth and bellehood without any seeming regret. They were devoted to their mother, who was a chronic invalid. The three had a little circle of home interests—books and pets and flowers—which made them happy and contented.

Mrs. West's death, which occurred on Rosemary's twenty-fifth birthday, was a bitter grief to them. At first they were intolerably lonely. Ellen, especially, continued to grieve and brood, her long, moody musings broken only by fits of stormy, passionate weeping. The old Lowbridge doctor told Rosemary that he feared permanent melancholy or worse.

Once, when Ellen had sat all day, refusing either to speak or eat, Rosemary had flung herself on her knees by her sister's side.

"Oh, Ellen, you have me yet," she said imploringly. "Am I nothing to you? We have always loved each other so."

"I won't have you always," Ellen had said, breaking her silence with harsh intensity. "You will marry and leave me. I shall be left all alone. I cannot bear the thought—I CANNOT. I would rather die."

"I will never marry," said Rosemary, "never, Ellen."

Ellen bent forward and looked searchingly into Rosemary's eyes.

"Will you promise me that solemnly?" she said. "Promise it on mother's Bible."

Rosemary assented at once, quite willing to humour Ellen. What did it matter? She knew quite well she would never want to marry any one. Her love had gone down with Martin Crawford to the deeps of the sea; and without love she could not marry any one. So she promised readily, though Ellen made rather a fearsome rite of it. They clasped hands over the Bible, in their mother's vacant room, and both vowed to each other that they would never marry and would always live together.

Ellen's condition improved from that hour. She soon regained her normal cheery poise. For ten years she and Rosemary lived in the old house happily, undisturbed by any thought of marrying or giving in marriage. Their promise sat very lightly on them. Ellen never failed to remind her sister of it whenever any eligible male creature crossed their paths, but she had never been really alarmed until John Meredith came home that night with Rosemary. As for Rosemary, Ellen's obsession regarding that promise had always been a little matter of mirth to her—until lately. Now, it was a merciless fetter, self-imposed but never to be shaken off. Because of it to-night she must turn her face from happiness.

It was true that the shy, sweet, rosebud love she had given to her boy-lover she could never give to another. But she knew now that she could give to John Meredith a love richer and more womanly. She knew that he touched deeps in her nature that Martin had never touched—that had not, perhaps, been in the girl of seventeen to touch. And she must send him away to-night—send him back to his lonely hearth and his empty life and his heart-breaking problems, because she had promised Ellen, ten years before, on their mother's Bible, that she would never marry.

John Meredith did not immediately grasp his opportunity. On the contrary, he talked for two good hours on the least lover-like of subjects. He even tried politics, though politics always bored Rosemary. The later began to think that she had been altogether mistaken, and her fears and expectations suddenly seemed to her grotesque. She felt flat and foolish. The glow went out of her face and the lustre out of her eyes. John Meredith had not the slightest intention of asking her to marry him.

And then, quite suddenly, he rose, came across the room, and standing by her chair, he asked it. The room had grown terribly still. Even St. George ceased to purr. Rosemary heard her own heart beating and was sure John Meredith must hear it too.

Now was the time for her to say no, gently but firmly. She had been ready for days with her stilted, regretful little formula. And now the words of it had completely vanished from her mind. She had to say no—and she suddenly found she could not say it. It was the impossible word. She knew now that it was not that she COULD have loved John Meredith, but that she DID love him. The thought of putting him from her life was agony.

She must say SOMETHING; she lifted her bowed golden head and asked him stammeringly to give her a few days for—for consideration.

John Meredith was a little surprised. He was not vainer than any man has a right to be, but he had expected that Rosemary West would say yes. He had been tolerably sure she cared for him. Then why this doubt—this hesitation? She was not a school girl to be uncertain as to her own mind. He felt an ugly shock of disappointment and dismay. But he assented to her request with his unfailing gentle courtesy and went away at once.

"I will tell you in a few days," said Rosemary, with downcast eyes and burning face.

When the door shut behind him she went back into the room and wrung her hands.

CHAPTER XXII. ST. GEORGE KNOWS ALL ABOUT IT

At midnight Ellen West was walking home from the Pollock silver wedding. She had stayed a little while after the other guests had gone, to help the gray-haired bride wash the dishes. The distance between the two houses was not far and the road good, so that Ellen was enjoying the walk back home in the moonlight.

The evening had been a pleasant one. Ellen, who had not been to a party for years, found it very pleasant. All the guests had been members of her old set and there was no intrusive youth to spoil the flavour, for the only son of the bride and groom was far away at college and could not be present. Norman Douglas had been there and they had met socially for the first time in years, though she had seen him once or twice in church that winter. Not the least sentiment was awakened in Ellen's heart by their meeting. She was accustomed to wonder, when she thought about it at all, how she could ever have fancied him or felt so badly over his sudden marriage. But she had rather liked meeting him again. She had forgotten how bracing and stimulating he could be. No gathering was ever stagnant when Norman Douglas was present. Everybody had been surprised when Norman came. It was well known he never went anywhere. The Pollocks had invited him because he had been one of the original guests, but they never thought he would come. He had taken his second cousin, Amy Annetta Douglas, out to supper and seemed rather attentive to her. But Ellen sat across the table from him and had a spirited argument with him—an argument during which all his shouting and banter could not fluster her and in which she came off best, flooring Norman so composedly and so completely that he was silent for ten minutes. At the end of which time he had muttered in his ruddy beard—"spunky as ever—spunky as ever"—and began to hector Amy Annetta, who giggled foolishly over his sallies where Ellen would have retorted bitingly.

Ellen thought these things over as she walked home, tasting them with reminiscent relish. The moonlit air sparkled with frost. The snow crisped under her feet. Below her lay the Glen with the white harbour beyond. There was a light in the manse study. So John Meredith had gone home. Had he asked Rosemary to marry him? And after what fashion had she made her refusal known? Ellen felt that she would never know this, though she was quite curious. She was sure Rosemary would never tell her anything about it and she would not dare to ask. She must just be content with the fact of the refusal. After all, that was the only thing that really mattered.

"I hope he'll have sense enough to come back once in a while and be friendly," she said to herself. She disliked so much to be alone that thinking aloud was one of her devices for circumventing unwelcome solitude. "It's awful never to have a man-body with some brains to talk to once in a while. And like as not he'll never come near the house again. There's Norman Douglas, too—I like that man, and I'd like to have a good rousing argument with him now and then. But he'd never dare come up for fear people would think he was courting me again—for fear I'D think it, too, most likely—though he's more a stranger to me now than John Meredith. It seems like a dream that we could ever have been beaus. But there it is— there's only two men in the Glen I'd ever want to talk to—and what with gossip and this wretched love-making business it's not likely I'll ever see either of them again. I could," said Ellen, addressing the unmoved stars with a spiteful emphasis, "I could have made a better world myself."

She paused at her gate with a sudden vague feeling of alarm. There was still a light in the living-room and to and fro across the window-shades went the shadow of a woman walking restlessly up and down. What was Rosemary doing up at this hour of the night? And why was she striding about like a lunatic?

Ellen went softly in. As she opened the hall door Rosemary came out of the room. She was flushed and breathless. An atmosphere of stress and passion hung about her like a garment.

"Why aren't you in bed, Rosemary?" demanded Ellen.

"Come in here," said Rosemary intensely. "I want to tell you something."

Ellen composedly removed her wraps and overshoes, and followed her sister into the warm, fire-lighted room. She stood with her hand on the table and waited. She was looking very handsome herself, in her own grim, black-browed style. The new black velvet dress, with its train and V-neck, which she had made purposely for the party, became her stately, massive figure. She wore coiled around her neck the rich heavy necklace of amber beads which was a family heirloom. Her walk in the frosty air had stung her cheeks into a glowing scarlet. But her steel-blue eyes were as icy and unyielding as the sky of the winter night. She stood waiting in a silence which Rosemary could break only by a convulsive effort.

"Ellen, Mr. Meredith was here this evening."

"Yes?"

"And—and—he asked me to marry him."

"So I expected. Of course, you refused him?"

"No."

"Rosemary." Ellen clenched her hands and took an involuntary step forward. "Do you mean to tell me that you accepted him?"

"No—no."

859

Ellen recovered her self-command.

"What DID you do then?"

"I—I asked him to give me a few days to think it over."

"I hardly see why that was necessary," said Ellen, coldly contemptuous, "when there is only the one answer you can make him."

Rosemary held out her hands beseechingly.

"Ellen," she said desperately, "I love John Meredith—I want to be his wife. Will you set me free from that promise?"

"No," said Ellen, merciless, because she was sick from fear.

"Ellen—Ellen—"

"Listen," interrupted Ellen. "I did not ask you for that promise. You offered it."

"I know—I know. But I did not think then that I could ever care for anyone again."

"You offered it," went on Ellen unmovably. "You promised it over our mother's Bible. It was more than a promise—it was an oath. Now you want to break it."

"I only asked you to set me free from it, Ellen."

"I will not do it. A promise is a promise in my eyes. I will not do it. Break your promise—be forsworn if you will—but it shall not be with any assent of mine."

"You are very hard on me, Ellen."

"Hard on you! And what of me? Have you ever given a thought to what my loneliness would be here if you left me? I could not bear it—I would go crazy. I CANNOT live alone. Haven't I been a good sister to you? Have I ever opposed any wish of yours? Haven't I indulged you in everything?"

"Yes—yes."

"Then why do you want to leave me for this man whom you hadn't seen a year ago?"

"I love him, Ellen."

"Love! You talk like a school miss instead of a middle-aged woman. He doesn't love you. He wants a housekeeper and a governess. You don't love him. You want to be 'Mrs.'—you are one of those weak-minded women who think it's a disgrace to be ranked as an old maid. That's all there is to it."

Rosemary quivered. Ellen could not, or would not, understand.

There was no use arguing with her.

"So you won't release me, Ellen?"

"No, I won't. And I won't talk of it again. You promised and you've got to keep your word. That's all. Go to bed. Look at the time! You're all romantic and worked up. To-morrow you'll be more sensible. At any rate, don't let me hear any more of this nonsense. Go."

Rosemary went without another word, pale and spiritless. Ellen walked stormily about the room for a few minutes, then paused before the chair where St. George had been calmly sleeping through the whole evening. A reluctant smile overspread her dark face. There had been only one time in her life—the time of her mother's death—when Ellen had not been able to temper tragedy with comedy. Even in that long ago bitterness, when Norman Douglas had, after a fashion, jilted her, she had laughed at herself quite as often as she had cried.

"I expect there'll be some sulking, St. George. Yes, Saint, I expect we are in for a few unpleasant foggy days. Well, we'll weather them through, George. We've dealt with foolish children before, Saint. Rosemary'll sulk a while—and then she'll get over it—and all will be as before, George. She promised—and she's got to keep her promise. And that's the last word on the subject I'll say to you or her or anyone, Saint."

But Ellen lay savagely awake till morning.

There was no sulking, however. Rosemary was pale and quiet the next day, but beyond that Ellen could detect no difference in her. Certainly, she seemed to bear Ellen no grudge. It was stormy, so no mention was made of going to church. In the afternoon Rosemary shut herself in her room and wrote a note to John Meredith. She could not trust herself to say "no" in person. She felt quite sure that if he suspected she was saying "no" reluctantly he would not take it for an answer, and she could not face pleading or entreaty. She must make him think she cared nothing at all for him and she could do that only by letter. She wrote him the stiffest, coolest little refusal imaginable. It was barely courteous; it certainly left no loophole of hope for the boldest lover—and John Meredith was anything but that. He shrank into himself, hurt and mortified, when he read Rosemary's letter next day in his dusty study. But under his mortification a dreadful realization presently made itself felt. He had thought he did not love Rosemary as deeply as he had loved Cecilia. Now, when he had lost her, he knew that he did. She was everything to him—everything! And he must put her out of his life completely. Even friendship was impossible now. Life stretched before him in intolerable dreariness. He must go on—there was his work—his children—but the heart had gone out of him. He sat alone all that evening in his dark, cold, comfortless study with his head bowed on his hands. Up on the hill Rosemary had a headache and went early to bed, while Ellen remarked to St. George, purring his disdain of foolish humankind, who did not know that a soft cushion was the only thing that really mattered,

"What would women do if headaches had never been invented, St.
George? But never mind, Saint. We'll just wink the other eye
for a few weeks. I admit I don't feel comfortable myself,
George. I feel as if I had drowned a kitten. But she promised,
Saint—and she was the one to offer it, George. Bismillah!"

CHAPTER XXIII. THE GOOD-CONDUCT CLUB

A light rain had been falling all day—a little, delicate, beautiful spring rain, that somehow seemed to hint and whisper of mayflowers and wakening violets. The harbour and the gulf and the low-lying shore fields had been dim with pearl-gray mists. But now in the evening the rain had ceased and the mists had blown out to sea. Clouds sprinkled the sky over the harbour like little fiery roses. Beyond it the hills were dark against a spendthrift splendour of daffodil and crimson. A great silvery evening star was watching over the bar. A brisk, dancing, new-sprung wind was blowing up from Rainbow Valley, resinous with the odours of fir and damp mosses. It crooned in the old spruces around the graveyard and ruffled Faith's splendid curls as she sat on Hezekiah Pollock's tombstone with her arms round Mary Vance and Una. Carl and Jerry were sitting opposite them on another tombstone and all were rather full of mischief after being cooped up all day.

"The air just SHINES to-night, doesn't it? It's been washed so clean, you see," said Faith happily.

Mary Vance eyed her gloomily. Knowing what she knew, or fancied she knew, Mary considered that Faith was far too light-hearted. Mary had something on her mind to say and she meant to say it before she went home. Mrs. Elliott had sent her up to the manse with some new-laid eggs, and had told her not to stay longer than half an hour. The half hour was nearly up, so Mary uncurled her cramped legs from under her and said abruptly,

"Never mind about the air. Just you listen to me. You manse young ones have just got to behave yourselves better than you've been doing this spring—that's all there is to it. I just come up to-night a-purpose to tell you so. The way people are talking about you is awful."

"What have we been doing now?" cried Faith in amazement, pulling her arm away from Mary. Una's lips trembled and her sensitive little soul shrank within her. Mary was always so brutally frank. Jerry began to whistle out of bravado. He meant to let Mary see he didn't care for HER tirades. Their behaviour was no business of HERS anyway. What right had SHE to lecture them on their conduct?

"Doing now! You're doing ALL the time," retorted Mary. "Just as soon as the talk about one of your didos fades away you do something else to start it up again. It seems to me you haven't any idea of how manse children ought to behave!"

"Maybe YOU can tell us," said Jerry, killingly sarcastic.

Sarcasm was quite thrown away on Mary.

"*I* can tell you what will happen if you don't learn to behave yourselves. The session will ask your father to resign. There now, Master Jerry-know-it-all. Mrs. Alec Davis said so to Mrs. Elliott. I heard her. I always have my ears pricked up when Mrs. Alec Davis comes to tea. She said you were all going from bad to worse and that though it was only what was to be expected when you had nobody to bring you up, still the congregation couldn't be expected to put up with it much longer, and something would have to be done. The Methodists just laugh and laugh at you, and that hurts the Presbyterian feelings. SHE says you all need a good dose of birch tonic. Lor', if that would make folks good *I* oughter be a young saint. I'm not telling you this because I want to hurt YOUR feelings. I'm sorry for you"—Mary was past mistress of the gentle art of condescension." *I* understand that you haven't much chance, the way things are. But other people don't make as much allowance as *I* do. Miss Drew says Carl had a frog in his pocket in Sunday School last Sunday and it hopped out while she was hearing the lesson. She says she's going to give up the class. Why don't you keep your in-secks home?"

"I popped it right back in again," said Carl. "It didn't hurt anybody—a poor little frog! And I wish old Jane Drew WOULD give up our class. I hate her. Her own nephew had a dirty plug of tobacco in his pocket and offered us fellows a chew when Elder Clow was praying. I guess that's worse than a frog."

"No, 'cause frogs are more unexpected-like. They make more of a sensation. 'Sides, he wasn't caught at it. And then that praying competition you had last week has made a fearful scandal. Everybody is talking about it."

"Why, the Blythes were in that as well as us," cried Faith, indignantly. "It was Nan Blythe who suggested it in the first place. And Walter took the prize."

"Well, you get the credit of it any way. It wouldn't have been so bad if you hadn't had it in the graveyard."

"I should think a graveyard was a very good place to pray in," retorted Jerry.

"Deacon Hazard drove past when YOU were praying," said Mary, "and he saw and heard you, with your hands folded over your stomach, and groaning after every sentence. He thought you were making fun of HIM."

"So I was," declared unabashed Jerry. "Only I didn't know he was going by, of course. That was just a mean accident. *I* wasn't praying in real earnest—I knew I had no chance of winning the prize. So I was just getting what fun I could out of it. Walter Blythe can pray bully. Why, he can pray as well as dad."

"Una is the only one of US who really likes praying," said Faith pensively.

"Well, if praying scandalizes people so much we mustn't do it any more," sighed Una.

"Shucks, you can pray all you want to, only not in the graveyard—and don't make a game of it. That was what made it so bad—that, and having a tea-party on the tombstones."

"We hadn't."

"Well, a soap-bubble party then. You had SOMETHING. The over-harbour people swear you had a tea-party, but I'm willing to take your word. And you used this tombstone as a table."

"Well, Martha wouldn't let us blow bubbles in the house. She was awful cross that day," explained Jerry. "And this old slab made such a jolly table."

"Weren't they pretty?" cried Faith, her eyes sparkling over the remembrance. "They reflected the trees and the hills and the harbour like little fairy worlds, and when we shook them loose they floated away down to Rainbow Valley."

"All but one and it went over and bust up on the Methodist spire," said Carl.

"I'm glad we did it once, anyhow, before we found out it was wrong," said Faith.

"It wouldn't have been wrong to blow them on the lawn," said Mary impatiently. "Seems like I can't knock any sense into your heads. You've been told often enough you shouldn't play in the graveyard. The Methodists are sensitive about it."

"We forget," said Faith dolefully. "And the lawn is so small—and so caterpillary—and so full of shrubs and things. We can't be in Rainbow Valley all the time—and where are we to go?"

"It's the things you DO in the graveyard. It wouldn't matter if you just sat here and talked quiet, same as we're doing now. Well, I don't know what is going to come of it all, but I DO know that Elder Warren is going to speak to your pa about it. Deacon Hazard is his cousin."

"I wish they wouldn't bother father about us," said Una.

"Well, people think he ought to bother himself about you a little more. *I* don't—*I* understand him. He's a child in some ways himself—that's what he is, and needs some one to look after him as bad as you do. Well, perhaps he'll have some one before long, if all tales is true."

"What do you mean?" asked Faith.

"Haven't you got any idea—honest?" demanded Mary.

"No, no. What DO you mean?"

"Well, you are a lot of innocents, upon my word. Why, EVERYbody is talking of it. Your pa goes to see Rosemary West. SHE is going to be your step-ma."

"I don't believe it," cried Una, flushing crimson.

"Well, *I* dunno. I just go by what folks say. *I* don't give it for a fact. But it would be a good thing. Rosemary West'd make you toe the mark if she came here, I'll bet a cent, for all she's so sweet and smiley on the face of her. They're always that way till they've caught them. But you need some one to bring you up. You're disgracing your pa and I feel for him. I've always thought an awful lot of your pa ever since that night he talked to me so nice. I've never said a single swear word since, or told a lie. And I'd like to see him happy and comfortable, with his buttons on and his meals decent, and you young ones licked into shape, and that old cat of a Martha put in HER proper place. The way she looked at the eggs I brought her to-night. 'I hope they're fresh,' says she. I just wished they WAS rotten. But you just mind that she gives you all one for breakfast, including your pa. Make a fuss if she doesn't. That was what they was sent up for—but I don't trust old Martha. She's quite capable of feeding 'em to her cat."

Mary's tongue being temporarily tired, a brief silence fell over the graveyard. The manse children did not feel like talking. They were digesting the new and not altogether palatable ideas Mary had suggested to them. Jerry and Carl were somewhat startled. But, after all, what did it matter? And it wasn't likely there was a word of truth in it. Faith, on the whole, was pleased. Only Una was seriously upset. She felt that she would like to get away and cry.

"Will there be any stars in my crown?" sang the Methodist choir, beginning to practise in the Methodist church.

"*I* want just three," said Mary, whose theological knowledge had increased notably since her residence with Mrs. Elliott. "Just three—setting up on my head, like a corownet, a big one in the middle and a small one each side."

"Are there different sizes in souls?" asked Carl.

"Of course. Why, little babies must have smaller ones than big men. Well, it's getting dark and I must scoot home. Mrs. Elliott doesn't like me to be out after dark. Laws, when I lived with Mrs. Wiley the dark was just the same as the daylight to me. I didn't mind it no more'n a gray cat. Them days seem a hundred years ago. Now, you mind what I've said and try to behave yourselves, for you pa's sake. I'LL always back you up and defend you—you can be dead sure of that. Mrs. Elliott says she never saw the like of me for sticking up for my friends. I was real sassy to Mrs. Alec Davis about you and Mrs. Elliott combed me down for it afterwards. The fair Cornelia has a tongue of her own and no mistake. But she was pleased underneath for all, 'cause she hates old Kitty Alec and she's real fond of you. *I* can see through folks."

Mary sailed off, excellently well pleased with herself, leaving a rather depressed little group behind her.

"Mary Vance always says something that makes us feel bad when she comes up," said Una resentfully.

"I wish we'd left her to starve in the old barn," said Jerry vindictively.

"Oh, that's wicked, Jerry," rebuked Una.

"May as well have the game as the name," retorted unrepentant Jerry. "If people say we're so bad let's BE bad."

"But not if it hurts father," pleaded Faith.

Jerry squirmed uncomfortably. He adored his father. Through the unshaded study window they could see Mr. Meredith at his desk. He did not seem to be either reading or writing. His head was in his hands and there was something in his whole attitude that spoke of weariness and dejection. The children suddenly felt it.

"I dare say somebody's been worrying him about us to-day," said Faith. "I wish we COULD get along without making people talk. Oh—Jem Blythe! How you scared me!"

Jem Blythe had slipped into the graveyard and sat down beside the girls. He had been prowling about Rainbow Valley and had succeeded in finding the first little star-white cluster of arbutus for his mother. The manse children were rather silent after his coming. Jem was beginning to grow away from them somewhat this spring. He was studying for the entrance examination of Queen's Academy and stayed after school with the older pupils for extra lessons. Also, his evenings were so full of work that he seldom joined the others in Rainbow Valley now. He seemed to be drifting away into grown-up land.

"What is the matter with you all to-night?" he asked. "There's no fun in you."

"Not much," agreed Faith dolefully. "There wouldn't be much fun in you either if YOU knew you were disgracing your father and making people talk about you."

"Who's been talking about you now?"

"Everybody—so Mary Vance says." And Faith poured out her troubles to sympathetic Jem. "You see," she concluded dolefully, "we've nobody to bring us up. And so we get into scrapes and people think we're bad."

"Why don't you bring yourselves up?" suggested Jem. "I'll tell you what to do. Form a Good-Conduct Club and punish yourselves every time you do anything that's not right."

"That's a good idea," said Faith, struck by it. "But," she added doubtfully, "things that don't seem a bit of harm to US seem simply dreadful to other people. How can we tell? We can't be bothering father all the time—and he has to be away a lot, anyhow."

"You could mostly tell if you stopped to think a thing over before doing it and ask yourselves what the congregation would say about it," said Jem. "The trouble is you just rush into things and don't think them over at all. Mother says you're all too impulsive, just as she used to be. The Good-Conduct Club would help you to think, if you were fair and honest about punishing yourselves when you broke the rules. You'd have to punish in some way that really HURT, or it wouldn't do any good."

"Whip each other?"

"Not exactly. You'd have to think up different ways of punishment to suit the person. You wouldn't punish each other—you'd punish YOURSELVES. I read all about such a club in a story-book. You try it and see how it works."

"Let's," said Faith; and when Jem was gone they agreed they would. "If things aren't right we've just got to make them right," said Faith, resolutely.

"We've got to be fair and square, as Jem says," said Jerry. "This is a club to bring ourselves up, seeing there's nobody else to do it. There's no use in having many rules. Let's just have one and any of us that breaks it has got to be punished hard."

"But HOW."

"We'll think that up as we go along. We'll hold a session of the club here in the graveyard every night and talk over what we've done through the day, and if we think we've done anything that isn't right or that would disgrace dad the one that does it, or is responsible for it, must be punished. That's the rule. We'll all decide on the kind of punishment—it must be made to fit the crime, as Mr. Flagg says. And the one that's, guilty will be bound to carry it out and no shirking. There's going to be fun in this," concluded Jerry, with a relish.

"You suggested the soap-bubble party," said Faith.

"But that was before we'd formed the club," said Jerry hastily. "Everything starts from to-night."

"But what if we can't agree on what's right, or what the punishment ought to be? S'pose two of us thought of one thing and two another. There ought to be five in a club like this."

"We can ask Jem Blythe to be umpire. He is the squarest boy in Glen St. Mary. But I guess we can settle our own affairs mostly. We want to keep this as much of a secret as we can. Don't breathe a word to Mary Vance. She'd want to join and do the bringing up."

"*I* think," said Faith, "that there's no use in spoiling every day by dragging punishments in. Let's have a punishment day."

"We'd better choose Saturday because there is no school to interfere," suggested Una.

"And spoil the one holiday in the week," cried Faith. "Not much! No, let's take Friday. That's fish day, anyhow, and we all hate fish. We may as well have all the disagreeable things in one day. Then other days we can go ahead and have a good time."

"Nonsense," said Jerry authoritatively. "Such a scheme wouldn't work at all. We'll just punish ourselves as we go along and keep a clear slate. Now, we all understand, don't we? This is a Good-Conduct Club, for the purpose of bringing ourselves up. We agree to punish ourselves for bad conduct, and always to stop before we do anything, no matter what, and ask ourselves if it is likely to hurt dad in any way, and any one who shirks is to be cast out of the club and never allowed to play with the rest of us in Rainbow Valley again. Jem Blythe to be umpire in case of disputes. No more taking bugs to Sunday School, Carl, and no more chewing gum in public, if you please, Miss Faith."

"No more making fun of elders praying or going to the Methodist prayer meeting," retorted Faith.

"Why, it isn't any harm to go to the Methodist prayer meeting," protested Jerry in amazement.

"Mrs. Elliott says it is, She says manse children have no business to go anywhere but to Presbyterian things."

"Darn it, I won't give up going to the Methodist prayer meeting," cried Jerry. "It's ten times more fun than ours is."

"You said a naughty word," cried Faith. "NOW, you've got to punish yourself."

"Not till it's all down in black and white. We're only talking the club over. It isn't really formed until we've written it out and signed it. There's got to be a constitution and by-laws. And you KNOW there's nothing wrong in going to a prayer meeting."

"But it's not only the wrong things we're to punish ourselves for, but anything that might hurt father."

"It won't hurt anybody. You know Mrs. Elliott is cracked on the subject of Methodists. Nobody else makes any fuss about my going. I always behave myself. You ask Jem or Mrs. Blythe and see what they say. I'll abide by their opinion. I'm going for the paper now and I'll bring out the lantern and we'll all sign."

Fifteen minutes later the document was solemnly signed on Hezekiah Pollock's tombstone, on the centre of which stood the smoky manse lantern, while the children knelt around it. Mrs. Elder Clow was going past at the moment and next day all the Glen heard that the manse children had been having another praying competition and had wound it up by chasing each other all over the graves with a lantern. This piece of embroidery was probably suggested by the fact that, after the signing and sealing was completed, Carl had taken the lantern and had walked circumspectly to the little hollow to examine his ant-hill. The others had gone quietly into the manse and to bed.

"Do you think it is true that father is going to marry Miss West?" Una had tremulously asked of Faith, after their prayers had been said.

"I don't know, but I'd like it," said Faith.

"Oh, I wouldn't," said Una, chokingly. "She is nice the way she is. But Mary Vance says it changes people ALTOGETHER to be made stepmothers. They get horrid cross and mean and hateful then, and turn your father against you. She says they're sure to do that. She never knew it to fail in a single case."

"I don't believe Miss West would EVER try to do that," cried Faith.

"Mary says ANYBODY would. She knows ALL about stepmothers, Faith—she says she's seen hundreds of them—and you've never seen one. Oh, Mary has told me blood-curdling things about them. She says she knew of one who whipped her husband's little girls on their bare shoulders till they bled, and then shut them up in a cold, dark coal cellar all night. She says they're ALL aching to do things like that."

"I don't believe Miss West would. You don't know her as well as I do, Una. Just think of that sweet little bird she sent me. I love it far more even than Adam."

"It's just being a stepmother changes them. Mary says they can't help it. I wouldn't mind the whippings so much as having father hate us."

"You know nothing could make father hate us. Don't be silly, Una. I dare say there's nothing to worry over. Likely if we run our club right and bring ourselves up properly father won't think of marrying any one. And if he does, I KNOW Miss West will be lovely to us."

But Una had no such conviction and she cried herself to sleep.

CHAPTER XXIV. A CHARITABLE IMPULSE

For a fortnight things ran smoothly in the Good-Conduct Club. It seemed to work admirably. Not once was Jem Blythe called in as umpire. Not once did any of the manse children set the Glen gossips by the ears. As for their minor peccadilloes at home, they kept sharp tabs on each other and gamely underwent their self-imposed punishment—generally a voluntary absence from some gay Friday night frolic in Rainbow Valley, or a sojourn in bed on some spring evening when all young bones ached to be out and away. Faith, for whispering in Sunday School, condemned herself to pass a whole day without speaking a single word, unless it was absolutely necessary, and accomplished it. It was rather unfortunate that Mr. Baker from over-harbour should have chosen that evening for calling at the manse, and that Faith should have happened to go to the door. Not one word did she reply to his genial greeting, but went silently away to call her father briefly. Mr. Baker was slightly offended and told his wife when he went home that that the biggest Meredith girl seemed a very shy, sulky little thing, without manners enough to speak when she was spoken to. But nothing worse came of it, and generally their penances did no harm to themselves or anybody else. All of them were beginning to feel quite cocksure that after all, it was a very easy matter to bring yourself up.

"I guess people will soon see that we can behave ourselves properly as well as anybody," said Faith jubilantly. "It isn't hard when we put our minds to it."

She and Una were sitting on the Pollock tombstone. It had been a cold, raw, wet day of spring storm and Rainbow Valley was out of the question for girls, though the manse and the Ingleside boys were down there fishing. The rain had held up, but the east wind blew mercilessly in from the sea, cutting to bone and marrow. Spring was late in spite of its early promise, and there was even yet a hard drift of old snow and ice in the northern corner of the graveyard. Lida Marsh, who had come up to bring the manse a mess of herring, slipped in through the gate shivering. She belonged to the fishing village at the harbour mouth and her father had, for thirty years, made a practice of sending a mess from his first spring catch to the manse. He never darkened a church door; he was a hard drinker and a reckless man, but as long as he sent those herring up to the manse every spring, as his father had done before him, he felt comfortably sure that his account with the Powers That Govern was squared for the year. He would not have expected a good mackerel catch if he had not so sent the first fruits of the season.

Lida was a mite of ten and looked younger, because she was such a small, wizened little creature. To-night, as she sidled boldly enough up to the manse girls, she looked as if she had never been warm since she was born. Her face was purple and her pale-blue, bold little eyes were red and watery. She wore a tattered print dress and a ragged woollen comforter, tied across her thin shoulders and under her arms. She had walked the three miles from the harbour mouth barefooted, over a road where there was still snow and slush and mud. Her feet and legs were as purple as her face. But Lida did not mind this much. She was used to being cold, and she had been going barefooted for a month already, like all the other swarming young fry of the fishing village. There was no self-pity in her heart as she sat down on the tombstone and grinned cheerfully at Faith and Una. Faith and Una grinned cheerfully back. They knew Lida slightly, having met her once or twice the preceding summer when they had gone down the harbour with the Blythes.

"Hello!" said Lida, "ain't this a fierce kind of a night?

"T'ain't fit for a dog to be out, is it?"

"Then why are you out?" asked Faith.

"Pa made me bring you up some herring," returned Lida. She shivered, coughed, and stuck out her bare feet. Lida was not thinking about herself or her feet, and was making no bid for sympathy. She held her feet out instinctively to keep them from the wet grass around the tombstone. But Faith and Una were instantly swamped with a wave of pity for her. She looked so cold—so miserable.

"Oh, why are you barefooted on such a cold night?" cried Faith.

"Your feet must be almost frozen."

"Pretty near," said Lida proudly. "I tell you it was fierce walking up that harbour road."

"Why didn't you put on your shoes and stockings?" asked Una.

"Hain't none to put on. All I had was wore out by the time winter was over," said Lida indifferently.

For a moment Faith stated in horror. This was terrible. Here was a little girl, almost a neighbour, half frozen because she had no shoes or stockings in this cruel spring weather. Impulsive Faith thought of nothing but the dreadfulness of it. In a moment she was pulling off her own shoes and stockings.

"Here, take these and put them right on," she said, forcing them into the hands of the astonished Lida. "Quick now. You'll catch your death of cold. I've got others. Put them right on."

Lida, recovering her wits, snatched at the offered gift, with a sparkle in her dull eyes. Sure she would put them on, and that mighty quick, before any one appeared with authority to recall them. In a minute she had pulled the stockings over her scrawny little legs and slipped Faith's shoes over her thick little ankles.

"I'm obliged to you," she said, "but won't your folks be cross?"

"No—and I don't care if they are," said Faith. "Do you think I could see any one freezing to death without helping them if I could? It wouldn't be right, especially when my father's a minister."

"Will you want them back? It's awful cold down at the harbour mouth—long after it's warm up here," said Lida slyly.

"No, you're to keep them, of course. That is what I meant when I gave them. I have another pair of shoes and plenty of stockings."

Lida had meant to stay awhile and talk to the girls about many things. But now she thought she had better get away before somebody came and made her yield up her booty. So she shuffled off through the bitter twilight, in the noiseless, shadowy way she had slipped in. As soon as she was out of sight of the manse she sat down, took off the shoes and stockings, and put them in her herring basket. She had no intention of keeping them on down that dirty harbour road. They were to be kept good for gala occasions. Not another little girl down at the harbour mouth had such fine black cashmere stockings and such smart, almost new shoes. Lida was furnished forth for the summer. She had no qualms in the matter. In her eyes the manse people were quite fabulously rich, and no doubt those girls had slathers of shoes and stockings. Then Lida ran down to the Glen village and played for an hour with the boys before Mr. Flagg's store, splashing about in a pool of slush with the maddest of them, until Mrs. Elliott came along and bade her begone home.

"I don't think, Faith, that you should have done that," said Una, a little reproachfully, after Lida had gone. "You'll have to wear your good boots every day now and they'll soon scuff out."

"I don't care," cried Faith, still in the fine glow of having done a kindness to a fellow creature. "It isn't fair that I should have two pairs of shoes and poor little Lida Marsh not have any. NOW we both have a pair. You know perfectly well, Una, that father said in his sermon last Sunday that there was no real happiness in getting or having—only in giving. And it's true. I feel FAR happier now than I ever did in my whole life before. Just think of Lida walking home this very minute with her poor little feet all nice and warm and comfy."

"You know you haven't another pair of black cashmere stockings," said Una. "Your other pair were so full of holes that Aunt Martha said she couldn't darn them any more and she cut the legs up for stove dusters. You've nothing but those two pairs of striped stockings you hate so."

All the glow and uplift went out of Faith. Her gladness collapsed like a pricked balloon. She sat for a few dismal minutes in silence, facing the consequences of her rash act.

"Oh, Una, I never thought of that," she said dolefully. "I didn't stop to think at all."

The striped stockings were thick, heavy, coarse, ribbed stockings of blue and red which Aunt Martha had knit for Faith in the winter. They were undoubtedly hideous. Faith loathed them as she had never loathed anything before. Wear them she certainly would not. They were still unworn in her bureau drawer.

"You'll have to wear the striped stockings after this," said Una. "Just think how the boys in school will laugh at you. You know how they laugh at Mamie Warren for her striped stockings and call her barber pole and yours are far worse."

"I won't wear them," said Faith. "I'll go barefooted first, cold as it is."

"You can't go barefooted to church to-morrow. Think what people would say."

"Then I'll stay home."

"You can't. You know very well Aunt Martha will make you go."

Faith did know this. The one thing on which Aunt Martha troubled herself to insist was that they must all go to church, rain or shine. How they were dressed, or if they were dressed at all, never concerned her. But go they must. That was how Aunt Martha had been brought up seventy years ago, and that was how she meant to bring them up.

"Haven't you got a pair you can lend me, Una?" said poor Faith piteously.

Una shook her head. "No, you know I only have the one black pair. And they're so tight I can hardly get them on. They wouldn't go on you. Neither would my gray ones. Besides, the legs of THEM are all darned AND darned."

"I won't wear those striped stockings," said Faith stubbornly.

"The feel of them is even worse than the looks. They make me feel as if my legs were as big as barrels and they're so SCRATCHY."

"Well, I don't know what you're going to do."

"If father was home I'd go and ask him to get me a new pair before the store closes. But he won't be home till too late. I'll ask him Monday—and I won't go to church tomorrow. I'll pretend I'm sick and Aunt Martha'll HAVE to let me stay home."

"That would be acting a lie, Faith," cried Una. "You CAN'T do that. You know it would be dreadful. What would father say if he knew? Don't you re-member how he talked to us after mother died and told us we must always be TRUE, no matter what else we failed in. He said we must never tell or act a lie— he said he'd TRUST us not to. You CAN'T do it, Faith. Just wear the striped stockings. It'll only be for once. Nobody will notice them in church. It isn't like school. And your new brown dress is so long they won't show much. Wasn't it lucky Aunt Martha made it big, so you'd have room to grow in it, for all you hated it so when she finished it?"

"I won't wear those stockings," repeated Faith. She uncoiled her bare, white legs from the tombstone and deliberately walked through the wet, cold grass to the bank of snow. Setting her teeth, she stepped upon it and stood there.

"What are you doing?" cried Una aghast. "You'll catch your death of cold, Faith Meredith."

"I'm trying to," answered Faith. "I hope I'll catch a fearful cold and be AWFUL sick to-morrow. Then I won't be acting a lie. I'm going to stand here as long as I can bear it."

"But, Faith, you might really die. You might get pneumonia.

Please, Faith don't. Let's go into the house and get SOMETHING for your feet. Oh, here's Jerry. I'm so thankful. Jerry, MAKE Faith get off that snow. Look at her feet."

"Holy cats! Faith, what ARE you doing?" demanded Jerry. "Are you crazy?"

"No. Go away!" snapped Faith.

"Then are you punishing yourself for something? It isn't right, if you are. You'll be sick."

"I want to be sick. I'm not punishing myself. Go away."

"Where's her shoes and stockings?" asked Jerry of Una.

"She gave them to Lida Marsh."

"Lida Marsh? What for?"

"Because Lida had none—and her feet were so cold. And now she wants to be sick so that she won't have to go to church to-morrow and wear her striped stockings. But, Jerry, she may die."

"Faith," said Jerry, "get off that ice-bank or I'll pull you off."

"Pull away," dared Faith.

Jerry sprang at her and caught her arms. He pulled one way and Faith pulled another. Una ran behind Faith and pushed. Faith stormed at Jerry to leave her alone. Jerry stormed back at her not to be a dizzy idiot; and Una cried. They made no end of noise and they were close to the road fence of the graveyard. Henry Warren and his wife drove by and heard and saw them. Very soon the Glen heard that the manse children had been having an awful fight in the graveyard and using most improper language. Meanwhile, Faith had allowed herself to be pulled off the ice because her feet were aching so sharply that she was ready to get off any way. They all went in amiably and went to bed. Faith slept like a cherub and woke in the morning without a trace of a cold. She felt that she couldn't feign sickness and act a lie, after remembering that long-ago talk with her father. But she was still as fully determined as ever that she would not wear those abominable stockings to church.

CHAPTER XXV. ANOTHER SCANDAL AND ANOTHER "EXPLANATION"

Faith went early to Sunday School and was seated in the corner of her class pew before any one came. Therefore, the dreadful truth did not burst upon any one until Faith left the class pew near the door to walk up to the manse pew after Sunday School. The church was already half filled and all who were sitting near the aisle saw that the minister's daughter had boots on but no stockings!

Faith's new brown dress, which Aunt Martha had made from an ancient pattern, was absurdly long for her, but even so it did not meet her boot-tops. Two good inches of bare white leg showed plainly.

Faith and Carl sat alone in the manse pew. Jerry had gone into the gallery to sit with a chum and the Blythe girls had taken Una with them. The Meredith children were given to "sitting all over the church" in this fashion and a great many people thought it very improper. The gallery especially, where irresponsible lads congregated and were known to whisper and suspected of chewing tobacco during service, was no place, for a son of the manse. But Jerry hated the manse pew at the very top of the church, under the eyes of Elder Clow and his family. He escaped from it whenever he could.

Carl, absorbed in watching a spider spinning its web at the window, did not notice Faith's legs. She walked home with her father after church and he never noticed them. She got on the hated striped stockings before Jerry and Una arrived, so that for the time being none of the occupants of the manse knew what she had done. But nobody else in Glen St. Mary was ignorant of it. The few who had not seen soon heard. Nothing else was talked of on the way home from church. Mrs. Alec Davis said it was only what she expected, and the next thing you would see some of those young ones coming to church with no clothes on at all. The president of the Ladies' Aid decided that she would bring the matter up at the next Aid meeting, and suggest that they wait in a body on the minister and protest. Miss Cornelia said that she, for her part, gave up. There was no use worrying over the manse fry any longer. Even Mrs. Dr. Blythe felt a little shocked, though she attributed the occurrence solely to Faith's forgetfulness. Susan could not immediately begin knitting stockings for Faith because it was Sunday, but she had one set up before any one else was out of bed at Ingleside the next morning.

XXV. ANOTHER SCANDAL AND ANOTHER "EXPLANATION"

CHAPTER XXV. ANOTHER SCANDAL AND ANOTHER "EXPLANATION"

"You need not tell me anything but that it was old Martha's fault, Mrs. Dr. dear." she told Anne. "I suppose that poor little child had no decent stockings to wear. I suppose every stocking she had was in holes, as you know very well they generally are. And *I* think, Mrs. Dr. dear, that the Ladies' Aid would be better employed in knitting some for them than in fighting over the new carpet for the pulpit platform. *I* am not a Ladies' Aider, but I shall knit Faith two pairs of stockings, out of this nice black yarn, as fast as my fingers can move and that you may tie to. Never shall I forget my sensations, Mrs. Dr. dear, when I saw a minister's child walking up the aisle of our church with no stockings on. I really did not know what way to look."

"And the church was just full of Methodists yesterday, too," groaned Miss Cornelia, who had come up to the Glen to do some shopping and run into Ingleside to talk the affair over. "I don't know how it is, but just as sure as those manse children do something especially awful the church is sure to be crowded with Methodists. I thought Mrs. Deacon Hazard's eyes would drop out of her head. When she came out of church she said, 'Well, that exhibition was no more than decent. I do pity the Presbyterians.' And we just had to TAKE it. There was nothing one could say."

"There was something *I* could have said, Mrs. Dr. dear, if I had heard her," said Susan grimly. "I would have said, for one thing, that in my opinion clean bare legs were quite as decent as holes. And I would have said, for another, that the Presbyterians did not feel greatly in need of pity seeing that they had a minister who could PREACH and the Methodists had NOT. I could have squelched Mrs. Deacon Hazard, Mrs. Dr dear, and that you may tie to."

"I wish Mr. Meredith didn't preach quite so well and looked after his family a little better," retorted Miss Cornelia. "He could at least glance over his children before they went to church and see that they were quite properly clothed. I'm tired making excuses for him, believe ME."

Meanwhile, Faith's soul was being harrowed up in Rainbow Valley. Mary Vance was there and, as usual, in a lecturing mood. She gave Faith to understand that she had disgraced herself and her father beyond redemption and that she, Mary Vance, was done with her. "Everybody" was talking, and "everybody" said the same thing.

"I simply feel that I can't associate with you any longer," she concluded.

"WE are going to associate with her then," cried Nan Blythe. Nan secretly thought Faith HAD done a awful thing, but she wasn't going to let Mary Vance run matters in this high-handed fashion. "And if YOU are not you needn't come any more to Rainbow Valley, MISS Vance."

Nan and Di both put their arms around Faith and glared defiance at Mary. The latter suddenly crumpled up, sat down on a stump and began to cry.

"It ain't that I don't want to," she wailed. "But if I keep in with Faith people'll be saying I put her up to doing things. Some are saying it now, true's you live. I can't afford to have such things said of me, now that I'm in a respectable place and trying to be a lady. And *I* never went bare-legged in church in my toughest days.

I'd never have thought of doing such a thing. But that hateful old Kitty Alec says Faith has never been the same girl since that time I stayed in the manse. She says Cornelia Elliott will live to rue the day she took me in. It hurts my feelings, I tell you. But it's Mr. Meredith I'm really worried over."

"I think you needn't worry about him," said Di scornfully. "It isn't likely necessary. Now, Faith darling, stop crying and tell us why you did it."

Faith explained tearfully. The Blythe girls sympathized with her, and even Mary Vance agreed that it was a hard position to be in. But Jerry, on whom the thing came like a thunderbolt, refused to be placated. So THIS was what some mysterious hints he had got in school that day meant! He marched Faith and Una home without ceremony, and the Good-Conduct Club held an immediate session in the graveyard to sit in judgment on Faith's case.

"I don't see that it was any harm," said Faith defiantly. "Not MUCH of my legs showed. It wasn't WRONG and it didn't hurt anybody."

"It will hurt Dad. You KNOW it will. You know people blame him whenever we do anything queer."

"I didn't think of that," muttered Faith.

"That's just the trouble. You didn't think and you SHOULD have thought. That's what our Club is for—to bring us up and MAKE us think. We promised we'd always stop and think before doing things. You didn't and you've got to be punished, Faith—and real hard, too. You'll wear those striped stockings to school for a week for punishment."

"Oh, Jerry, won't a day do—two days? Not a whole week!"

"Yes, a whole week," said inexorable Jerry. "It is fair—ask Jem Blythe if it isn't."

Faith felt she would rather submit then ask Jem Blythe about such a matter. She was beginning to realize that her offence was a quite shameful one.

"I'll do it, then," she muttered, a little sulkily.

"You're getting off easy," said, Jerry severely. "And no matter how we punish you it won't help father. People will always think you just did it for mischief, and they'll blame father for not stopping it. We can never explain it to everybody."

This aspect of the case weighed on Faith's mind. Her own condemnation she could bear, but it tortured her that her father should be blamed. If people knew the true facts of the case they would not blame him. But how could she make them known to all the world? Getting up in church, as she had once done, and explaining the matter was out of the question. Faith had heard from Mary Vance how the congregation had looked upon that performance and realized that she must not repeat it. Faith worried over the problem for half a week. Then she had an inspiration and promptly acted upon it. She spent that evening in the garret, with a lamp and an exercise book, writing busily, with flushed cheeks and shining eyes. It was the very thing! How clever she was to have thought of it! It would put everything right and explain everything and yet cause no scandal. It was eleven o'clock when she had finished to her satisfaction and crept down to bed, dreadfully tired, but perfectly happy.

In a few days the little weekly published in the Glen under the name of *The Journal* came out as usual, and the Glen had another sensation. A letter signed "Faith Meredith" occupied a prominent place on the front page and ran as follows:—

"TO WHOM IT MAY CONCERN:

I want to explain to everybody how it was I came to go to church without stockings on, so that everybody will know that father was not to blame one bit for it, and the old gossips need not say he is, because it is not true. I gave my only pair of black stockings to Lida Marsh, because she hadn't any and her poor little feet were awful cold and I was so sorry for her. No child ought to have to go without shoes and stockings in a Christian community before the snow is all gone, and I think the W. F. M. S. ought to have given her stockings. Of course, I know they are sending things to the little heathen children, and that is all right and a kind thing to do. But the little heathen children have lots more warm weather than we have, and I think the women of our church ought to look after Lida and not leave it all to me. When I gave her my stockings I forgot they were the only black pair I had without holes, but I am glad I did give them to her, because my conscience would have been uncomfortable if I hadn't. When she had gone away, looking so proud and happy, the poor little thing, I remembered that all I had to wear were the horrid red and blue things Aunt Martha knit last winter for me out of some yarn that Mrs. Joseph Burr of Upper Glen sent us. It was dreadfully coarse yarn and all knots, and I never saw any of Mrs. Burr's own children wearing things made of such yarn. But Mary Vance says Mrs. Burr gives the minister stuff that she can't use or eat herself, and thinks it ought to go as part of the salary her husband signed to pay, but never does.

I just couldn't bear to wear those hateful stockings. They were so ugly and rough and felt so scratchy. Everybody would have made fun of me. I thought at first I'd pretend to be sick and not go to church next day, but I decided I couldn't do that, because it would be acting a lie, and father told us after mother died that was something we must never, never do. It is just as bad to act a lie as to tell one, though I know some people, right here in the Glen, who act them, and never seem to feel a bit bad about it. I will not mention any names, but I know who they are and so does father.

Then I tried my best to catch cold and really be sick by standing on the snowbank in the Methodist graveyard with my bare feet until Jerry pulled me off. But it didn't hurt me a bit and so I couldn't get out of going to church. So I just decided I would put my boots on and go that way. I can't see why it was so wrong and I was so careful to wash my legs just as clean as my face, but, anyway, father wasn't to blame for it. He was in the study thinking of his sermon and other heavenly things, and I kept out of his way before I went to Sunday School. Father does not look at people's legs in church, so of course he did not notice mine, but all the gossips did and talked about it, and that is why I am writing this letter to the *Journal* to explain. I suppose I did very wrong, since everybody says so, and I am sorry and I am wearing those awful stockings to punish myself, although father bought me two nice new black pairs as soon as Mr. Flagg's store opened on Monday morning. But it was all my fault, and if people blame father for it after they read this they are not Christians and so I do not mind what they say.

There is another thing I want to explain about before I stop. Mary Vance told me that Mr. Evan Boyd is blaming the Lew Baxters for stealing potatoes out of his field last fall. They did not touch his potatoes. They are very poor, but they are honest. It was us did it—Jerry and Carl and I. Una was not with us at the time. We never thought it was stealing. We just wanted a few potatoes to cook over a fire in Rainbow Valley one evening to eat with our fried trout. Mr. Boyd's field was the nearest, just between the valley and the village, so we climbed over his fence and pulled up some stalks. The potatoes were awful small, because Mr. Boyd did not put enough fertilizer on them and we had to pull up a lot of stalks before we got enough, and then they were not much bigger than marbles. Walter and Di Blythe helped us eat them, but they did not come along until we had them cooked and did not know where we got them, so they were not to blame at all, only us. We didn't mean any harm, but if it was stealing we are very sorry and we will pay Mr. Boyd for them if he will wait until we grow up. We never have any money now because we are not big enough to earn any, and Aunt Martha says it takes every cent of poor father's salary, even when it is paid up regularly—and it isn't often—to run this house. But Mr. Boyd must not blame the Lew Baxters any more, when they were quite innocent, and give them a bad name. Yours respectfully, FAITH MEREDITH."

CHAPTER XXVI. MISS CORNELIA GETS A NEW POINT OF VIEW

"Susan, after I'm dead I'm going to come back to earth every time when the daffodils blow in this garden," said Anne rapturously. "Nobody may see me, but I'll be here. If anybody is in the garden at the time—I THINK I'll come on an evening just like this, but it MIGHT be just at dawn—a lovely, pale-pinky spring dawn—they'll just see the daffodils nodding wildly as if an extra gust of wind had blown past them, but it will be *I*."

"Indeed, Mrs. Dr. dear, you will not be thinking of flaunting worldly things like daffies after you are dead," said Susan. "And I do NOT believe in ghosts, seen or unseen."

"Oh, Susan, I shall not be a ghost! That has such a horrible sound. I shall just be ME. And I shall run around in the twilight, whether it is morn or eve, and see all the spots I love. Do you remember how badly I felt when I left our little House of Dreams, Susan? I thought I could never love Ingleside so well. But I do. I love every inch of the ground and every stick and stone on it."

"I am rather fond of the place myself," said Susan, who would have died if she had been removed from it, "but we must not set our affections too much on earthly things, Mrs. Dr. dear. There are such things as fires and earthquakes. We should always be prepared. The Tom MacAllisters over-harbour were burned out three nights ago. Some say Tom MacAllister set the house on fire himself to get the insurance. That may or may not be. But I advise the doctor to have our chimneys seen to at once. An ounce of prevention is worth a pound of cure. But I see Mrs. Marshall Elliott coming in at the gate, looking as if she had been sent for and couldn't go."

"Anne dearie, have you seen the *Journal* to-day?"

Miss Cornelia's voice was trembling, partly from emotion, partly from the fact that she had hurried up from the store too fast and lost her breath.

Anne bent over the daffodils to hide a smile. She and Gilbert had laughed heartily and heartlessly over the front page of the *Journal* that day, but she knew that to dear Miss Cornelia it was almost a tragedy, and she must not wound her feelings by any display of levity.

"Isn't it dreadful? What IS to be done?" asked Miss Cornelia despairingly. Miss Cornelia had vowed that she was done with worrying over the pranks of the manse children, but she went on worrying just the same.

Anne led the way to the veranda, where Susan was knitting, with Shirley and Rilla conning their primers on either side. Susan was already on her second pair of stockings for Faith. Susan never worried over poor humanity. She did what in her lay for its betterment and serenely left the rest to the Higher Powers.

"Cornelia Elliott thinks she was born to run this world, Mrs. Dr. dear," she had once said to Anne, "and so she is always in a stew over something. I have never thought *I* was, and so I go calmly along. Not but what it has sometimes occurred to me that things might be run a little better than they are. But it is not for us poor worms to nourish such thoughts. They only make us uncomfortable and do not get us anywhere."

"I don't see that anything can be done—now—" said Anne, pulling out a nice, cushiony chair for Miss Cornelia. "But how in the world did Mr. Vickers allow that letter to be printed? Surely he should have known better."

"Why, he's away, Anne dearie—he's been away to New Brunswick for a week. And that young scalawag of a Joe Vickers is editing the *Journal* in his absence. Of course, Mr. Vickers would never have put it in, even if he is a Methodist, but Joe would just think it a good joke. As you say, I don't suppose there is anything to be done now, only live it down. But if I ever get Joe Vickers cornered somewhere I'll give him a talking to he won't forget in a hurry. I wanted Marshall to stop our subscription to the *Journal* instantly, but he only laughed and said that to-day's issue was the only one that had had anything readable in it for a year. Marshall never will take anything seriously—just like a man. Fortunately, Evan Boyd is like that, too. He takes it as a joke and is laughing all over the place about it. And he's another Methodist! As for Mrs. Burr of Upper Glen, of course she will be furious and they will leave the church. Not that it will be a great loss from any point of view. The Methodists are quite welcome to THEM."

"It serves Mrs. Burr right," said Susan, who had an old feud with the lady in question and had been hugely tickled over the reference to her in Faith's letter. "She will find that she will not be able to cheat the Methodist parson out of HIS salary with bad yarn."

"The worst of it is, there's not much hope of things getting any better," said Miss Cornelia gloomily. "As long as Mr. Meredith was going to see Rosemary West I did hope the manse would soon have a proper mistress. But that is all off. I suppose she wouldn't have him on account of the children—at least, everybody seems to think so."

"I do not believe that he ever asked her," said Susan, who could not conceive of any one refusing a minister.

"Well, nobody knows anything about THAT. But one thing is certain, he doesn't go there any longer. And Rosemary didn't look well all the spring. I hope her visit to Kingsport will do her good. She's been gone for a month and will stay another month, I understand. I can't remember when Rosemary was away from home before. She and Ellen could never bear to be parted. But I understand Ellen insisted on her going this time. And meanwhile Ellen and Norman Douglas are warming up the old soup."

"Is that really so?" asked Anne, laughing. "I heard a rumour of it, but I hardly believed it."

"Believe it! You may believe it all right, Anne, dearie. Nobody is in ignorance of it. Norman Douglas never left anybody in doubt as to his intentions in regard to anything. He always did his courting before the public. He told Marshall that he hadn't thought about Ellen for years, but the first time he went to church last fall he saw her and fell in love with her all over again. He said he'd clean forgot how handsome she was. He hadn't seen her for twenty years, if you can believe it. Of course he never went to church, and Ellen never went anywhere else round here. Oh, we all know what Norman means, but what Ellen means is a different matter. I shan't take it upon me to predict whether it will be a match or not."

"He jilted her once—but it seems that does not count with some people, Mrs. Dr. dear," Susan remarked rather acidly.

"He jilted her in a fit of temper and repented it all his life," said Miss Cornelia. "That is different from a cold-blooded jilting. For my part, I never detested Norman as some folks do. He could never over-crow ME. I DO wonder what started him coming to church. I have never been able to believe Mrs. Wilsons's story that Faith Meredith went there and bullied him into it. I've always intended to ask Faith herself, but I've never happened to think of it just when I saw her. What influence could SHE have over Norman Douglas? He was in the store when I left, bellowing with laughter over that scandalous letter. You could have heard him at Four Winds Point. 'The greatest girl in the world,' he was shouting. 'She's that full of spunk she's bursting with it. And all the old grannies want to tame her, darn them. But they'll never be able to do it—never! They might as well try to drown a fish. Boyd, see that you put more fertilizer on your potatoes next year. Ho, ho, ho!' And then he laughed till the roof shook."

"Mr. Douglas pays well to the salary, at least," remarked Susan.

"Oh, Norman isn't mean in some ways. He'd give a thousand without blinking a lash, and roar like a Bull of Bashan if he had to pay five cents too much for anything. Besides, he likes Mr. Meredith's sermons, and Norman Douglas was always willing to shell out if he got his brains tickled up. There is no more Christianity about him than there is about a black, naked heathen in Africa and never will be. But he's clever and well read and he judges sermons as he would lectures. Anyhow, it's well he backs up Mr. Meredith and the children as he does, for they'll need friends more than ever after this. I am tired of making excuses for them, believe ME."

"Do you know, dear Miss Cornelia," said Anne seriously, "I think we have all been making too many excuses. It is very foolish and we ought to stop it. I am going to tell you what I'd LIKE to do. I shan't do it, of course"—Anne had noted a glint of alarm in Susan's eye—"it would be too unconventional, and we must be conventional or die, after we reach what is supposed to be a dignified age. But I'd LIKE to do it. I'd like to call a meeting of the Ladies Aid and W.M.S. and the Girls Sewing Society, and include in the audience all and any Methodists who have been criticizing the Merediths—although I do think if we Presbyterians stopped criticizing and excusing we would find that other denominations would trouble themselves very little about our manse folks. I would say to them, 'Dear Christian friends'—with marked emphasis on 'Christian'—I have something to say to you and I want to say it good and hard, that you may take it home and repeat it to your families. You Methodists need not pity us, and we Presbyterians need not pity ourselves. We are not going to do it any more. And we are going to say, boldly and truthfully, to all critics and sympathizers, 'We are PROUD of our minister and his family. Mr. Meredith is the best preacher Glen St. Mary church ever had. Moreover, he is a sincere, earnest teacher of truth and Christian charity. He is a faithful friend, a judicious pastor in all essentials, and a refined, scholarly, well-bred man. His family are worthy of him. Gerald Meredith is the cleverest pupil in the Glen school, and Mr. Hazard says that he is destined to a brilliant career. He is a manly, honourable, truthful little fellow. Faith Meredith is a beauty, and as inspiring and original as she is beautiful. There is nothing commonplace about her. All the other girls in the Glen put together haven't the vim, and wit, and joyousness and 'spunk' she has. She has not an enemy in the world. Every one who knows her loves her. Of how many, children or grown-ups, can that be said? Una Meredith is sweetness personified. She will make a most lovable woman. Carl Meredith, with his love for ants and frogs and spiders, will some day be a naturalist whom all Canada—nay, all the world, will delight to honour. Do you know of any other family in the Glen, or out of it, of whom all these things can be said? Away with shamefaced excuses and apologies. We REJOICE in our minister and his splendid boys and girls!"

Anne stopped, partly because she was out of breath after her vehement speech and partly because she could not trust herself to speak further in view of Miss Cornelia's face. That good lady was staring helplessly at Anne, apparently engulfed in billows of new ideas. But she came up with a gasp and struck out for shore gallantly.

"Anne Blythe, I wish you WOULD call that meeting and say just that! You've made me ashamed of myself, for one, and far be it from me to refuse to admit it. OF COURSE, that is how we should have talked—especially to the Methodists. And it's every word of it true—every word. We've just been shutting our eyes to the big worth-while things and squinting them on the little things that don't really matter a pin's worth. Oh, Anne dearie, I can see a thing when it's hammered into my head. No more apologizing for Cornelia Marshall! *I* shall hold MY head up after this, believe ME—though I MAY talk things over with you as usual just to relieve my feelings if the Merediths do any more startling stunts. Even that letter I felt so bad about—why, it's only a good joke after all, as Norman says. Not many girls would have been cute enough to think of writing it—and all punctuated so nicely and not one word misspelled. Just let me hear any Methodist say one word about it—though all the same I'll never forgive Joe Vickers—believe ME! Where are the rest of your small fry to-night?"

"Walter and the twins are in Rainbow Valley. Jem is studying in the garret."

"They are all crazy about Rainbow Valley. Mary Vance thinks it's the only place in the world. She'd be off up here every evening if I'd let her. But I don't encourage her in gadding. Besides, I miss the creature when she isn't around, Anne dearie. I never thought I'd get so fond of her. Not but what I see her faults and try to correct them. But she has never said one saucy word to me since she came to my house and she is a GREAT help—for when all is said and done, Anne dearie, I am not so young as I once was, and there is no sense denying it. I was fifty-nine my last birthday. I don't FEEL it, but there is no gainsaying the Family Bible."

CHAPTER XXVII. A SACRED CONCERT

In spite of Miss Cornelia's new point of view she could not help feeling a little disturbed over the next performance of the manse children. In public she carried off the situation splendidly, saying to all the gossips the substance of what Anne had said in daffodil time, and saying it so pointedly and forcibly that her hearers found themselves feeling rather foolish and began to think that, after all, they were making too much of a childish prank. But in private Miss Cornelia allowed herself the relief of bemoaning it to Anne.

"Anne dearie, they had a CONCERT IN THE GRAVEYARD last Thursday evening, while the Methodist prayer meeting was going on. There they sat, on Hezekiah Pollock's tombstone, and sang for a solid hour. Of course, I understand it was mostly hymns they sang, and it wouldn't have been quite so bad if they'd done nothing else. But I'm told they finished up with *Polly Wolly Doodle* at full length—and that just when Deacon Baxter was praying."

"I was there that night," said Susan," and, although I did not say anything about it to you, Mrs. Dr. dear, I could not help thinking that it was a great pity they picked that particular evening. It was truly blood-curdling to hear them sitting there in that abode of the dead, shouting that frivolous song at the tops of their lungs."

"I don't know what YOU were doing in a Methodist prayer meeting," said Miss Cornelia acidly.

"I have never found that Methodism was catching," retorted Susan stiffly. "And, as I was going to say when I was interrupted, badly as I felt, I did NOT give in to the Methodists. When Mrs. Deacon Baxter said, as we came out, 'What a disgraceful exhibition!' *I* said, looking her fairly in the eye, 'They are all beautiful singers, and none of YOUR choir, Mrs. Baxter, ever bother themselves coming out to your prayer meeting, it seems. Their voices appear to be in tune only on Sundays!' She was quite meek and I felt that I had snubbed her properly. But I could have done it much more thoroughly, Mrs. Dr. dear, if only they had left out *Polly Wolly Doodle*. It is truly terrible to think of that being sung in a graveyard."

"Some of those dead folks sang *Polly Wolly Doodle* when they were living, Susan. Perhaps they like to hear it yet," suggested Gilbert.

Miss Cornelia looked at him reproachfully and made up her mind that, on some future occasion, she would hint to Anne that the doctor should be admonished not to say such things. They might injure his practice. People might get it into their heads that he wasn't orthodox. To be sure, Marshall said even worse things habitually, but then HE was not a public man.

"I understand that their father was in his study all the time, with his windows open, but never noticed them at all. Of course, he was lost in a book as usual. But I spoke to him about it yesterday, when he called."

"How could you dare, Mrs. Marshall Elliott?" asked Susan rebukingly.

"Dare! It's time somebody dared something. Why, they say he knows nothing about that letter of Faith's to the JOURNAL because nobody liked to mention it to him. He never looks at a JOURNAL of course. But I thought he ought to know of this to prevent any such performances in future. He said he would 'discuss it with them.' But of course he'd never think of it again after he got out of our gate. That man has no sense of humour, Anne, believe ME. He preached last Sunday on 'How to Bring up Children.' A beautiful sermon it was, too—and everybody in church thinking 'what a pity you can't practise what you preach.'"

Miss Cornelia did Mr. Meredith an injustice in thinking he would soon forget what she had told him. He went home much disturbed and when the children came from Rainbow Valley that night, at a much later hour than they should have been prowling in it, he called them into his study.

They went in, somewhat awed. It was such an unusual thing for their father to do. What could he be going to say to them? They racked their memories for any recent transgression of sufficient importance, but could not recall any. Carl had spilled a saucerful of jam on Mrs. Peter Flagg's silk dress two evenings before, when, at Aunt Martha's invitation, she had stayed to supper. But Mr. Meredith had not noticed it, and Mrs. Flagg, who was a kindly soul, had made no fuss. Besides, Carl had been punished by having to wear Una's dress all the rest of the evening.

Una suddenly thought that perhaps her father meant to tell them that he was going to marry Miss West. Her heart began to beat violently and her legs trembled. Then she saw that Mr. Meredith looked very stern and sorrowful. No, it could not be that.

"Children," said Mr. Meredith, "I have heard something that has pained me very much. Is it true that you sat out in the graveyard all last Thursday evening and sang ribald songs while a prayer meeting was being held in the Methodist church?"

"Great Caesar, Dad, we forgot all about it being their prayer meeting night," exclaimed Jerry in dismay.

"Then it is true—you did do this thing?"

"Why, Dad, I don't know what you mean by ribald songs. We sang hymns—it was a sacred concert, you know. What harm was that? I tell you we never thought about it's being Methodist prayer meeting night. They used to have their meeting Tuesday nights and since they've changed to Thursdays it's hard to remember."

"Did you sing nothing but hymns?"

"Why," said Jerry, turning red, "we DID sing *Polly Wolly Doodle* at the last. Faith said, 'Let's have something cheerful to wind up with.' But we didn't mean any harm, Father—truly we didn't."

"The concert was my idea, Father," said Faith, afraid that Mr. Meredith might blame Jerry too much. "You know the Methodists themselves had a sacred concert in their church three Sunday nights ago. I thought it would be good fun to get one up in imitation of it. Only they had prayers at theirs, and we left that part out, because we heard that people thought it awful for us to pray in a graveyard. YOU were sitting in here all the time," she added, "and never said a word to us."

"I did not notice what you were doing. That is no excuse for me, of course. I am more to blame than you—I realize that. But why did you sing that foolish song at the end?"

"We didn't think," muttered Jerry, feeling that it was a very lame excuse, seeing that he had lectured Faith so strongly in the Good-Conduct Club sessions for her lack of thought. "We're sorry, Father—truly, we are. Pitch into us hard—we deserve a regular combing down."

But Mr. Meredith did no combing down or pitching into. He sat down and gathered his small culprits close to him and talked a little to them, tenderly and wisely. They were overcome with remorse and shame, and felt that they could never be so silly and thoughtless again.

"We've just got to punish ourselves good and hard for this," whispered Jerry as they crept upstairs. "We'll have a session of the Club first thing tomorrow and decide how we'll do it. I never saw father so cut up. But I wish to goodness the Methodists would stick to one night for their prayer meeting and not wander all over the week."

"Anyhow, I'm glad it wasn't what I was afraid it was," murmured Una to herself.

Behind them, in the study, Mr. Meredith had sat down at his desk and buried his face in his arms.

"God help me!" he said. "I'm a poor sort of father. Oh, Rosemary! If you had only cared!"

CHAPTER XXVIII. A FAST DAY

The Good-Conduct Club had a special session the next morning before school. After various suggestions, it was decided that a fast day would be an appropriate punishment.

"We won't eat a single thing for a whole day," said Jerry. "I'm kind of curious to see what fasting is like, anyhow. This will be a good chance to find out."

"What day will we choose for it?" asked Una, who thought it would be quite an easy punishment and rather wondered that Jerry and Faith had not devised something harder.

"Let's pick Monday," said Faith. "We mostly have a pretty FILLING dinner on Sundays, and Mondays meals never amount to much anyhow."

"But that's just the point," exclaimed Jerry. "We mustn't take the easiest day to fast, but the hardest—and that's Sunday, because, as you say, we mostly have roast beef that day instead of cold ditto. It wouldn't be much punishment to fast from ditto. Let's take next Sunday. It will be a good day, for father is going to exchange for the morning service with the Upper Lowbridge minister. Father will be away till evening. If Aunt Martha wonders what's got into us, we'll tell her right up that we're fasting for the good of our souls, and it is in the Bible and she is not to interfere, and I guess she won't."

Aunt Martha did not. She merely said in her fretful mumbling way, "What foolishness are you young rips up to now?" and thought no more about it. Mr. Meredith had gone away early in the morning before any one was up. He went without his breakfast, too, but that was, of course, of common occurrence. Half of the time he forgot it and there was no one to remind him of it. Breakfast—Aunt Martha's breakfast—was not a hard meal to miss. Even the hungry "young rips" did not feel it any great deprivation to abstain from the "lumpy porridge and blue milk" which had aroused the scorn of Mary Vance. But it was different at dinner time. They were furiously hungry then, and the odor of roast beef which pervaded the manse, and which was wholly delightful in spite of the fact that the roast beef was badly underdone, was almost more than they could stand. In desperation they rushed to the graveyard where they couldn't smell it. But Una could not keep her eyes from the dining room window, through which the Upper Lowbridge minister could be seen, placidly eating.

"If I could only have just a weeny, teeny piece," she sighed.

"Now, you stop that," commanded Jerry. "Of course it's hard—but that's the punishment of it. I could eat a graven image this very minute, but am I complaining? Let's think of something else. We've just got to rise above our stomachs."

At supper time they did not feel the pangs of hunger which they had suffered earlier in the day.

"I suppose we're getting used to it," said Faith. "I feel an awfully queer all-gone sort of feeling, but I can't say I'm hungry."

"My head is funny," said Una. "It goes round and round sometimes."

But she went gamely to church with the others. If Mr. Meredith had not been so wholly wrapped up in and carried away with his subject he might have noticed the pale little face and hollow eyes in the manse pew beneath. But he noticed nothing and his sermon was something longer than usual. Then, just before be gave out the final hymn, Una Meredith tumbled off the seat of the manse pew and lay in a dead faint on the floor.

Mrs. Elder Clow was the first to reach her. She caught the thin little body from the arms of white-faced, terrified Faith and carried it into the vestry. Mr. Meredith forgot the hymn and everything else and rushed madly after her. The congregation dismissed itself as best it could.

"Oh, Mrs. Clow," gasped Faith, "is Una dead? Have we killed her?"

"What is the matter with my child?" demanded the pale father.

"She has just fainted, I think," said Mrs. Clow. "Oh, here's the doctor, thank goodness."

Gilbert did not find it a very easy thing to bring Una back to consciousness. He worked over her for a long time before her eyes opened. Then he carried her over to the manse, followed by Faith, sobbing hysterically in her relief.

"She is just hungry, you know—she didn't eat a thing to-day— none of us did—we were all fasting."

"Fasting!" said Mr. Meredith, and "Fasting?" said the doctor.

"Yes—to punish ourselves for singing *Polly Wolly* in the graveyard," said Faith.

"My child, I don't want you to punish yourselves for that," said Mr. Meredith in distress. "I gave you your little scolding—and you were all penitent—and I forgave you."

"Yes, but we had to be punished," explained Faith. "It's our rule—in our Good-Conduct Club, you know—if we do anything wrong, or anything that is likely to hurt father in the congregation, we HAVE to punish ourselves. We are bringing ourselves up, you know, because there is nobody to do it."

Mr. Meredith groaned, but the doctor got up from Una's side with an air of relief.

"Then this child simply fainted from lack of food and all she needs is a good square meal," he said. "Mrs. Clow, will you be kind enough to see she gets it? And I think from Faith's story that they all would be the better for something to eat, or we shall have more faintings."

"I suppose we shouldn't have made Una fast," said Faith remorsefully. "When I think of it, only Jerry and I should have been punished. WE got up the concert and we were the oldest."

"I sang *Polly Wolly* just the same as the rest of you," said

Una's weak little voice, "so I had to be punished, too."

Mrs. Clow came with a glass of milk, Faith and Jerry and Carl sneaked off to the pantry, and John Meredith went into his study, where he sat in the darkness for a long time, alone with his bitter thoughts. So his children were bringing themselves up because there was "nobody to do it"—struggling along amid their little perplexities without a hand to guide or a voice to counsel. Faith's innocently uttered phrase rankled in her father's mind like a barbed shaft. There was "nobody" to look after them—to comfort their little souls and care for their little bodies. How frail Una had looked, lying there on the vestry sofa in that long faint! How thin were her tiny hands, how pallid her little face! She looked as if she might slip away from him in a breath—sweet little Una, of whom Cecilia had begged him to take such special care. Since his wife's death he had not felt such an agony of dread as when he had hung over his little girl in her unconsciousness. He must do something—but what? Should he ask Elizabeth Kirk to marry him? She was a good woman—she would be kind to his children. He might bring himself to do it if it were not for his love for Rosemary West. But until he had crushed that out he could not seek another woman in marriage. And he could not crush it out—he had tried and he could not. Rosemary had been in church that evening, for the first time since her return from Kingsport. He had caught a glimpse of her face in the back of the crowded church, just as he had finished his sermon. His heart had given a fierce throb. He sat while the choir sang the "collection piece," with his bent head and tingling pulses. He had not seen her since the evening upon which he had asked her to marry him. When he had risen to give out the hymn his hands were trembling and his pale face was flushed. Then Una's fainting spell had banished everything from his mind for a time. Now, in the darkness and solitude of the study it rushed back. Rosemary was the only woman in the world for him. It was of no use for him to think of marrying any other. He could not commit such a sacrilege even for his children's sake. He must take up his burden alone—he must try to be a better, a more watchful father—he must tell his children not to be afraid to come to him with all their little problems. Then he lighted his lamp and took up a bulky new book which was setting the theological world by the ears. He would read just one chapter to compose his mind. Five minutes later he was lost to the world and the troubles of the world.

CHAPTER XXIX. A WEIRD TALE

On an early June evening Rainbow Valley was an entirely delightful place and the children felt it to be so, as they sat in the open glade where the bells rang elfishly on the Tree Lovers, and the White Lady shook her green tresses. The wind was laughing and whistling about them like a leal, glad-hearted comrade. The young ferns were spicy in the hollow. The wild cherry trees scattered over the valley, among the dark firs, were mistily white. The robins were whistling over in the maples behind Ingleside. Beyond, on the slopes of the Glen, were blossoming orchards, sweet and mystic and wonderful, veiled in dusk. It was spring, and young things MUST be glad in spring. Everybody was glad in Rainbow Valley that evening—until Mary Vance froze their blood with the story of Henry Warren's ghost.

Jem was not there. Jem spent his evenings now studying for his entrance examination in the Ingleside garret. Jerry was down near the pond, trouting. Walter had been reading Longfellow's sea poems to the others and they were steeped in the beauty and mystery of the ships. Then they talked of what they would do when they were grown up—where they would travel—the far, fair shores they would see. Nan and Di meant to go to Europe. Walter longed for the Nile moaning past its Egyptian sands, and a glimpse of the sphinx. Faith opined rather dismally that she supposed she would have to be a missionary—old Mrs. Taylor told her she ought to be—and then she would at least see India or China, those mysterious lands of the Orient. Carl's heart was set on African jungles. Una said nothing. She thought she would just like to stay at home. It was prettier here than anywhere else. It would be dreadful when they were all grown up and had to scatter over the world. The very idea made Una feel lonesome and homesick. But the others dreamed on delightedly until Mary Vance arrived and vanished poesy and dreams at one fell swoop.

"Laws, but I'm out of puff," she exclaimed. "I've run down that hill like sixty. I got an awful scare up there at the old Bailey place."

"What frightened you?" asked Di.

"I dunno. I was poking about under them lilacs in the old garden, trying to see if there was any lilies-of-the-valley out yet. It was dark as a pocket there—and all at once I seen something stirring and rustling round at the other side of the garden, in those cherry bushes. It was WHITE. I tell you I didn't stop for a second look. I flew over the dyke quicker than quick. I was sure it was Henry Warren's ghost."

"Who was Henry Warren?" asked Di.

"And why should he have a ghost?" asked Nan.

"Laws, did you never hear the story? And you brought up in the Glen. Well, wait a minute till I get by breath all back and I'll tell you."

Walter shivered delightsomely. He loved ghost stories. Their mystery, their dramatic climaxes, their eeriness gave him a fearful, exquisite pleasure. Longfellow instantly grew tame and commonplace. He threw the book aside and stretched himself out, propped upon his elbows to listen whole-heartedly, fixing his great luminous eyes on Mary's face. Mary wished he wouldn't look at her so. She felt she could make a better job of the ghost story if Walter were not looking at her. She could put on several frills and invent a few artistic details to enhance the horror. As it was, she had to stick to the bare truth—or what had been told her for the truth.

"Well," she began, "you know old Tom Bailey and his wife used to live in that house up there thirty years ago. He was an awful old rip, they say, and his wife wasn't much better. They'd no children of their own, but a sister of old Tom's died and left a little boy—this Henry Warren—and they took him. He was about twelve when he came to them, and kind of undersized and delicate. They say Tom and his wife used him awful from the start—whipped him and starved him. Folks said they wanted him to die so's they could get the little bit of money his mother had left for him. Henry didn't die right off, but he begun having fits—epileps, they called 'em—and he grew up kind of simple, till he was about eighteen. His uncle used to thrash him in that garden up there 'cause it was back of the house where no one could see him. But folks could hear, and they say it was awful sometimes hearing poor Henry plead with his uncle not to kill him. But nobody dared interfere 'cause old Tom was such a reprobate he'd have been sure to get square with 'em some way. He burned the barns of a man at Harbour Head who offended him. At last Henry died and his uncle and aunt give out he died in one of his fits and that was all anybody ever knowed, but everybody said Tom had just up and killed him for keeps at last. And it wasn't long till it got around that Henry WALKED. That old garden was HA'NTED. He was heard there at nights, moaning and crying. Old Tom and his wife got out—went out West and never came back. The place got such a bad name nobody'd buy or rent it. That's why it's all gone to ruin. That was thirty years ago, but Henry Warren's ghost ha'nts it yet."

"Do you believe that?" asked Nan scornfully. "*I* don't."

"Well, GOOD people have seen him—and heard him." retorted Mary. "They say he appears and grovels on the ground and holds you by the legs and gibbers and moans like he did when he was alive. I thought of that as soon as I seen that white thing in the bushes and thought if it caught me like that and moaned I'd drop down dead on the spot. So I cut and run. It MIGHTN'T have been his ghost, but I wasn't going to take any chances with a ha'nt."

"It was likely old Mrs. Stimson's white calf," laughed Di. "It pastures in that garden—I've seen it."

"Maybe so. But I'M not going home through the Bailey garden any more. Here's Jerry with a big string of trout and it's my turn to cook them. Jem and Jerry both say I'm the best cook in the Glen. And Cornelia told me I could bring up this batch of cookies. I all but dropped them when I saw Henry's ghost."

Jerry hooted when he heard the ghost story—which Mary repeated as she fried the fish, touching it up a trifle or so, since Walter had gone to help Faith to set the table. It made no impression on Jerry, but Faith and Una and Carl had been secretly much frightened, though they would never have given in to it. It was all right as long as the others were with them in the valley: but when the feast was over and the shadows fell they quaked with remembrance. Jerry went up to Ingleside with the Blythes to see Jem about something, and Mary Vance went around that way home. So Faith and Una and Carl had to go back to the manse alone. They walked very close together and gave the old Bailey garden a wide berth. They did not believe that it was haunted, of course, but they would not go near it for all that.

CHAPTER XXX. THE GHOST ON THE DYKE

Somehow, Faith and Carl and Una could not shake off the hold which the story of Henry Warren's ghost had taken upon their imaginations. They had never believed in ghosts. Ghost tales they had heard a-plenty—Mary Vance had told some far more blood-curdling than this; but those tales were all of places and people and spooks far away and unknown. After the first half-awful, half-pleasant thrill of awe and terror they thought of them no more. But this story came home to them. The old Bailey garden was almost at their very door—almost in their beloved Rainbow Valley. They had passed and repassed it constantly; they had hunted for flowers in it; they had made short cuts through it when they wished to go straight from the village to the valley. But never again! After the night when Mary Vance told them its gruesome tale they would not have gone through or near it on pain of death. Death! What was death compared to the unearthly possibility of falling into the clutches of Henry Warren's grovelling ghost?

One warm July evening the three of them were sitting under the Tree Lovers, feeling a little lonely. Nobody else had come near the valley that evening. Jem Blythe was away in Charlottetown, writing on his entrance examinations. Jerry and Walter Blythe were off for a sail on the harbour with old Captain Crawford. Nan and Di and Rilla and Shirley had gone down the harbour road to visit Kenneth and Persis Ford, who had come with their parents for a flying visit to the little old House of Dreams. Nan had asked Faith to go with them, but Faith had declined. She would never have admitted it, but she felt a little secret jealousy of Persis Ford, concerning whose wonderful beauty and city glamour she had heard a great deal. No, she wasn't going to go down there and play second fiddle to anybody. She and Una took their story books to Rainbow Valley and read, while Carl investigated bugs along the banks of the brook, and all three were happy until they suddenly realized that it was twilight and that the old Bailey garden was uncomfortably near by. Carl came and sat down close to the girls. They all wished they had gone home a little sooner, but nobody said anything.

Great, velvety, purple clouds heaped up in the west and spread over the valley. There was no wind and everything was suddenly, strangely, dreadfully still. The marsh was full of thousands of fire-flies. Surely some fairy parliament was being convened that night. Altogether, Rainbow Valley was not a canny place just then.

Faith looked fearfully up the valley to the old Bailey garden. Then, if anybody's blood ever did freeze, Faith Meredith's certainly froze at that moment. The eyes of Carl and Una followed her entranced gaze and chills began gallopading up and down their spines also. For there, under the big tamarack tree on the tumbledown, grass-grown dyke of the Bailey garden, was something white—shapelessly white in the gathering gloom. The three Merediths sat and gazed as if turned to stone.

"It's—it's the—calf," whispered Una at last.

"It's—too—big—for the calf," whispered Faith. Her mouth and lips were so dry she could hardly articulate the words.

Suddenly Carl gasped,

"It's coming here."

The girls gave one last agonized glance. Yes, it was creeping down over the dyke, as no calf ever did or could creep. Reason fled before sudden, overmastering panic. For the moment every one of the trio was firmly convinced that what they saw was Henry Warren's ghost. Carl sprang to his feet and bolted blindly. With a simultaneous shriek the girls followed him. Like mad creatures they tore up the hill, across the road and into the manse. They had left Aunt Martha sewing in the kitchen. She was not there. They rushed to the study. It was dark and tenantless. As with one impulse, they swung around and made for Ingleside—but not across Rainbow Valley. Down the hill and through the Glen street they flew on the wings of their wild terror, Carl in the lead, Una bringing up the rear. Nobody tried to stop them, though everybody who saw them wondered what fresh devilment those manse youngsters were up to now. But at the gate of Ingleside they ran into Rosemary West, who had just been in for a moment to return some borrowed books.

She saw their ghastly faces and staring eyes. She realized that their poor little souls were wrung with some awful and real fear, whatever its cause. She caught Carl with one arm and Faith with the other. Una stumbled against her and held on desperately.

"Children, dear, what has happened?" she said. "What has frightened you?"

"Henry Warren's ghost," answered Carl, through his chattering teeth.

"Henry—Warren's—ghost!" said amazed Rosemary, who had never heard the story.

"Yes," sobbed Faith hysterically. "It's there—on the Bailey dyke—we saw it—and it started to—chase us."

Rosemary herded the three distracted creatures to the Ingleside veranda. Gilbert and Anne were both away, having also gone to the House of Dreams, but Susan appeared in the doorway, gaunt and practical and unghostlike.

"What is all this rumpus about?" she inquired.

Again the children gasped out their awful tale, while Rosemary held them close to her and soothed them with wordless comfort.

"Likely it was an owl," said Susan, unstirred.

An owl! The Meredith children never had any opinion of Susan's intelligence after that!

"It was bigger than a million owls," said Carl, sobbing—oh, how ashamed Carl was of that sobbing in after days—"and it—it GROVELLED just as Mary said—and it was crawling down over the dyke to get at us. Do owls CRAWL?"

Rosemary looked at Susan.

"They must have seen something to frighten them so," she said.

"I will go and see," said Susan coolly. "Now, children, calm yourselves. Whatever you have seen, it was not a ghost. As for poor Henry Warren, I feel sure he would be only too glad to rest quietly in his peaceful grave once he got there. No fear of HIM venturing back, and that you may tie to. If you can make them see reason, Miss West, I will find out the truth of the matter."

Susan departed for Rainbow Valley, valiantly grasping a pitchfork which she found leaning against the back fence where the doctor had been working in his little hay-field. A pitchfork might not be of much use against "ha'nts," but it was a comforting sort of weapon. There was nothing to be seen in Rainbow Valley when Susan reached it. No white visitants appeared to be lurking in the shadowy, tangled old Bailey garden. Susan marched boldly through it and beyond it, and rapped with her pitchfork on the door of the little cottage on the other side, where Mrs. Stimson lived with her two daughters.

Back at Ingleside Rosemary had succeeded in calming the children. They still sobbed a little from shock, but they were beginning to feel a lurking and salutary suspicion that they had made dreadful geese of themselves. This suspicion became a certainty when Susan finally returned.

"I have found out what your ghost was," she said, with a grim smile, sitting down on a rocker and fanning herself. "Old Mrs. Stimson has had a pair of factory cotton sheets bleaching in the Bailey garden for a week. She spread them on the dyke under the tamarack tree because the grass was clean and short there. This evening she went out to take them in. She had her knitting in her hands so she hung the sheets over her shoulders by way of carrying them. And then she must have dropped one of her needles and find it she could not and has not yet. But she went down on her knees and crept about to hunt for it, and she was at that when she heard awful yells down in the valley and saw the three children tearing up the hill past her. She thought they had been bit by something and it gave her poor old heart such a turn that she could not move or speak, but just crouched there till they disappeared. Then she staggered back home and they have been applying stimulants to her ever since, and her heart is in a terrible condition and she says she will not get over this fright all summer."

The Merediths sat, crimson with a shame that even Rosemary's understanding sympathy could not remove. They sneaked off home, met Jerry at the manse gate and made remorseful confession. A session of the Good-Conduct Club was arranged for next morning.

"Wasn't Miss West sweet to us to-night?" whispered Faith in bed.

"Yes," admitted Una. "It is such a pity it changes people so much to be made stepmothers."

"I don't believe it does," said Faith loyally.

CHAPTER XXXI. CARL DOES PENANCE

"I don't see why we should be punished at all," said Faith, rather sulkily. "We didn't do anything wrong. We couldn't help being frightened. And it won't do father any harm. It was just an accident."

"You were cowards," said Jerry with judicial scorn, "and you gave way to your cowardice. That is why you should be punished. Everybody will laugh at you about this, and that is a disgrace to the family."

"If you knew how awful the whole thing was," said Faith with a shiver, "you would think we had been punished enough already. I wouldn't go through it again for anything in the whole world."

"I believe you'd have run yourself if you'd been there," muttered Carl.

"From an old woman in a cotton sheet," mocked Jerry. "Ho, ho, ho!"

"It didn't look a bit like an old woman," cried Faith. "It was just a great, big, white thing crawling about in the grass just as Mary Vance said Henry Warren did. It's all very fine for you to laugh, Jerry Meredith, but you'd have laughed on the other side of your mouth if you'd been there. And how are we to be punished? *I* don't think it's fair, but let's know what we have to do, Judge Meredith!"

"The way I look at it," said Jerry, frowning, "is that Carl was the most to blame. He bolted first, as I understand it. Besides, he was a boy, so he should have stood his ground to protect you girls, whatever the danger was. You know that, Carl, don't you?"

"I s'pose so," growled Carl shamefacedly.

"Very well. This is to be your punishment. To-night you'll sit on Mr. Hezekiah Pollock's tombstone in the graveyard alone, until twelve o'clock."

Carl gave a little shudder. The graveyard was not so very far from the old Bailey garden. It would be a trying ordeal, but Carl was anxious to wipe out his disgrace and prove that he was not a coward after all.

"All right," he said sturdily. "But how'll I know when it is twelve?"

"The study windows are open and you'll hear the clock striking. And mind you that you are not to budge out of that graveyard until the last stroke. As for you girls, you've got to go without jam at supper for a week."

Faith and Una looked rather blank. They were inclined to think that even Carl's comparatively short though sharp agony was lighter punishment than this long drawn-out ordeal. A whole week of soggy bread without the saving grace of jam! But no shirking was permitted in the club. The girls accepted their lot with such philosophy as they could summon up.

That night they all went to bed at nine, except Carl, who was already keeping vigil on the tombstone. Una slipped in to bid him good night. Her tender heart was wrung with sympathy.

"Oh, Carl, are you much scared?" she whispered.

"Not a bit," said Carl airily.

"I won't sleep a wink till after twelve," said Una. "If you get lonesome just look up at our window and remember that I'm inside, awake, and thinking about you. That will be a little company, won't it?"

"I'll be all right. Don't you worry about me," said Carl.

But in spite of his dauntless words Carl was a pretty lonely boy when the lights went out in the manse. He had hoped his father would be in the study as he so often was. He would not feel alone then. But that night Mr. Meredith had been summoned to the fishing village at the harbour mouth to see a dying man. He would not likely be back until after midnight. Carl must dree his weird alone.

A Glen man went past carrying a lantern. The mysterious shadows caused by the lantern-light went hurtling madly over the graveyard like a dance of demons or witches. Then they passed and darkness fell again. One by one the lights in the Glen went out. It was a very dark night, with a cloudy sky, and a raw east wind that was cold in spite of the calendar. Far away on the horizon was the low dim lustre of the Charlottetown lights. The wind wailed and sighed in the old fir-trees. Mr. Alec Davis' tall monument gleamed whitely through the gloom. The willow beside it tossed long, writhing arms spectrally. At times, the gyrations of its boughs made it seem as if the monument were moving, too.

Carl curled himself up on the tombstone with his legs tucked under him. It wasn't precisely pleasant to hang them over the edge of the stone. Just suppose—just suppose—bony hands should reach up out of Mr. Pollock's grave under it and clutch him by the ankles. That had been one of Mary Vance's cheerful speculations one time when they had all been sitting there. It returned to haunt Carl now. He didn't believe those things; he didn't even really believe in Henry Warren's ghost. As for Mr. Pollock, he had been dead sixty years, so it wasn't likely he cared who sat on his tombstone now. But there is something very strange and terrible in being awake when all the rest of the world is asleep. You are alone then with nothing but your own feeble personality to pit against the mighty principalities and powers of darkness. Carl was only ten and the dead were all around him—and he wished, oh, he wished that the clock would strike twelve. Would it NEVER strike twelve? Surely Aunt Martha must have forgotten to wind it.

And then it struck eleven—only eleven! He must stay yet another hour in that grim place. If only there were a few friendly stars to be seen! The darkness was so thick it seemed to press against his face. There was a sound as of stealthy passing footsteps all over the graveyard. Carl shivered, partly with prickling terror, partly with real cold.

Then it began to rain—a chill, penetrating drizzle. Carl's thin little cotton blouse and shirt were soon wet through. He felt chilled to the bone. He forgot mental terrors in his physical discomfort. But he must stay there till twelve—he was punishing himself and he was on his honour. Nothing had been said about rain—but it did not make any difference. When the study clock finally struck twelve a drenched little figure crept stiffly down off Mr. Pollock's tombstone, made its way into the manse and upstairs to bed. Carl's teeth were chattering. He thought he would never get warm again.

He was warm enough when morning came. Jerry gave one startled look at his crimson face and then rushed to call his father. Mr. Meredith came hurriedly, his own face ivory white from the pallor of his long night vigil by a death bed. He had not got home until daylight. He bent over his little lad anxiously.

"Carl, are you sick?" he said.

"That—tombstone—over here," said Carl, "it's—moving—about— it's com-ing—at—me—keep it—away—please."

Mr. Meredith rushed to the telephone. In ten minutes Dr. Blythe was at the manse. Half an hour later a wire was sent to town for a trained nurse, and all the Glen knew that Carl Meredith was very ill with pneumonia and that Dr. Blythe had been seen to shake his head.

Gilbert shook his head more than once in the fortnight that followed. Carl de-veloped double pneumonia. There was one night when Mr. Meredith paced his study floor, and Faith and Una huddled in their bedroom and cried, and Jerry, wild with remorse, refused to budge from the floor of the hall outside Carl's door. Dr. Blythe and the nurse never left the bedside. They fought death gallantly until the red dawn and they won the victory. Carl rallied and passed the crisis in safety. The news was phoned about the waiting Glen and people found out how much they really loved their minister and his children.

"I haven't had one decent night's sleep since I heard the child was sick," Miss Cornelia told Anne, "and Mary Vance has cried until those queer eyes of hers looked like burnt holes in a blanket. Is it true that Carl got pneumonia from stray-ing out in the graveyard that wet night for a dare?"

"No. He was staying there to punish himself for cowardice in that affair of the Warren ghost. It seems they have a club for bringing themselves up, and they punish themselves when they do wrong. Jerry told Mr. Meredith all about it."

"The poor little souls," said Miss Cornelia.

Carl got better rapidly, for the congregation took enough nourishing things to the manse to furnish forth a hospital. Norman Douglas drove up every evening with a dozen fresh eggs and a jar of Jersey cream. Sometimes he stayed an hour and bellowed arguments on predestination with Mr. Meredith in the study; oftener he drove on up to the hill that overlooked the Glen.

When Carl was able to go again to Rainbow Valley they had a special feast in his honour and the doctor came down and helped them with the fireworks. Mary Vance was there, too, but she did not tell any ghost stories. Miss Cornelia had given her a talking on that subject which Mary would not forget in a hurry.

CHAPTER XXXII. TWO STUBBORN PEOPLE

Rosemary West, on her way home from a music lesson at Ingleside, turned aside to the hidden spring in Rainbow Valley. She had not been there all summer; the beautiful little spot had no longer any allurement for her. The spirit of her young lover never came to the tryst now; and the memories connected with John Meredith were too painful and poignant. But she had happened to glance backward up the valley and had seen Norman Douglas vaulting as airily as a stripling over the old stone dyke of the Bailey garden and thought he was on his way up the hill. If he overtook her she would have to walk home with him and she was not going to do that. So she slipped at once behind the maples of the spring, hoping he had not seen her and would pass on.

But Norman had seen her and, what was more, was in pursuit of her. He had been wanting for some time to have talk with Rosemary, but she had always, so it seemed, avoided him. Rosemary had never, at any time, liked Norman Douglas very well. His bluster, his temper, his noisy hilarity, had always antagonized her. Long ago she had often wondered how Ellen could possibly be attracted to him. Norman Douglas was perfectly aware of her dislike and he chuckled over it. It never worried Norman if people did not like him. It did not even make him dislike them in return, for he took it as a kind of extorted compliment. He thought Rosemary a fine girl, and he meant to be an excellent, generous brother-in-law to her. But before he could be her brother-in-law he had to have a talk with her, so, having seen her leaving Ingleside as he stood in the doorway of a Glen store, he had straightway plunged into the valley to overtake her.

Rosemary was sitting pensively on the maple seat where John Meredith had been sitting on that evening nearly a year ago. The tiny spring shimmered and dimpled under its fringe of ferns. Ruby-red gleams of sunset fell through the arching boughs. A tall clump of perfect asters grew at her side. The little spot was as dreamy and witching and evasive as any retreat of fairies and dryads in ancient forests. Into it Norman Douglas bounced, scattering and annihilating its charm in a moment. His personality seemed to swallow the place up. There was simply nothing there but Norman Douglas, big, red-bearded, complacent.

"Good evening," said Rosemary coldly, standing up.

"'Evening, girl. Sit down again—sit down again. I want to have a talk with you. Bless the girl, what's she looking at me like that for? I don't want to eat you—I've had my supper. Sit down and be civil."

"I can hear what you have to say quite as well here," said Rosemary.

"So you can, girl, if you use your ears. I only wanted you to be comfortable. You look so durned uncomfortable, standing there. Well, I'LL sit anyway."

Norman accordingly sat down in the very place John Meredith had once sat. The contrast was so ludicrous that Rosemary was afraid she would go off into a peal of hysterical laughter over it. Norman cast his hat aside, placed his huge, red hands on his knees, and looked up at her with his eyes a-twinkle.

"Come, girl, don't be so stiff," he said, ingratiatingly. When he liked he could be very ingratiating. "Let's have a reasonable, sensible, friendly chat. There's something I want to ask you. Ellen says she won't, so it's up to me to do it."

Rosemary looked down at the spring, which seemed to have shrunk to the size of a dewdrop. Norman gazed at her in despair.

"Durn it all, you might help a fellow out a bit," he burst forth.

"What is it you want me to help you say?" asked Rosemary scornfully.

"You know as well as I do, girl. Don't be putting on your tragedy airs. No wonder Ellen was scared to ask you. Look here, girl, Ellen and I want to marry each other. That's plain English, isn't it? Got that? And Ellen says she can't unless you give her back some tom-fool promise she made. Come now, will you do it? Will you do it?"

"Yes," said Rosemary.

Norman bounced up and seized her reluctant hand.

"Good! I knew you would—I told Ellen you would. I knew it would only take a minute. Now, girl, you go home and tell Ellen, and we'll have a wedding in a fortnight and you'll come and live with us. We shan't leave you to roost on that hill-top like a lonely crow—don't you worry. I know you hate me, but, Lord, it'll be great fun living with some one that hates me. Life'll have some spice in it after this. Ellen will roast me and you'll freeze me. I won't have a dull moment."

Rosemary did not condescend to tell him that nothing would ever induce her to live in his house. She let him go striding back to the Glen, oozing delight and complacency, and she walked slowly up the hill home. She had known this was coming ever since she had returned from Kingsport, and found Norman Douglas established as a frequent evening caller. His name was never mentioned between her and Ellen, but the very avoidance of it was significant. It was not in Rosemary's nature to feel bitter, or she would have felt very bitter. She was coldly civil to Norman, and she made no difference in any way with Ellen. But Ellen had not found much comfort in her second courtship.

She was in the garden, attended by St. George, when Rosemary came home. The two sisters met in the dahlia walk. St. George sat down on the gravel walk between them and folded his glossy black tail gracefully around his white paws, with all the indifference of a well-fed, well-bred, well-groomed cat.

"Did you ever see such dahlias?" demanded Ellen proudly. "They are just the finest we've ever had."

Rosemary had never cared for dahlias. Their presence in the garden was her concession to Ellen's taste. She noticed one huge mottled one of crimson and yellow that lorded it over all the others.

"That dahlia," she said, pointing to it, "is exactly like Norman Douglas. It might easily be his twin brother."

Ellen's dark-browed face flushed. She admired the dahlia in question, but she knew Rosemary did not, and that no compliment was intended. But she dared not resent Rosemary's speech—poor Ellen dared not resent anything just then. And it was the first time Rosemary had ever mentioned Norman's name to her. She felt that this portended something.

"I met Norman Douglas in the valley," said Rosemary, looking straight at her sister, "and he told me you and he wanted to be married—if I would give you permission."

"Yes? What did you say?" asked Ellen, trying to speak naturally and off-handedly, and failing completely. She could not meet Rosemary's eyes. She looked down at St. George's sleek back and felt horribly afraid. Rosemary had either said she would or she wouldn't. If she would Ellen would feel so ashamed and remorseful that she would be a very uncomfortable bride-elect; and if she wouldn't—well, Ellen had once learned to live without Norman Douglas, but she had forgotten the lesson and felt that she could never learn it again.

"I said that as far as I was concerned you were at full liberty to marry each other as soon as you liked," said Rosemary.

"Thank you," said Ellen, still looking at St. George.

Rosemary's face softened.

"I hope you'll be happy, Ellen," she said gently.

"Oh, Rosemary," Ellen looked up in distress, "I'm so ashamed—I don't deserve it—after all I said to you—"

"We won't speak about that," said Rosemary hurriedly and decidedly.

"But—but," persisted Ellen, "you are free now, too—and it's not too late—John Meredith—"

"Ellen West!" Rosemary had a little spark of temper under all her sweetness and it flashed forth now in her blue eyes. "Have you quite lost your senses in EVERY respect? Do you suppose for an instant that *I* am going to go to John Meredith and say meekly, 'Please, sir, I've changed my mind and please, sir, I hope you haven't changed yours.' Is that what you want me to do?"

"No—no—but a little—encouragement—he would come back—"

"Never. He despises me—and rightly. No more of this, Ellen. I bear you no grudge—marry whom you like. But no meddling in my affairs."

"Then you must come and live with me," said Ellen. "I shall not leave you here alone."

"Do you really think that I would go and live in Norman Douglas's house?"

"Why not?" cried Ellen, half angrily, despite her humiliation.

Rosemary began to laugh.

"Ellen, I thought you had a sense of humour. Can you see me doing it?"

"I don't see why you wouldn't. His house is big enough—you'd have your share of it to yourself—he wouldn't interfere."

"Ellen, the thing is not to be thought of. Don't bring this up again."

"Then," said Ellen coldly, and determinedly, "I shall not marry him. I shall not leave you here alone. That is all there is to be said about it."

"Nonsense, Ellen."

"It is not nonsense. It is my firm decision. It would be absurd for you to think of living here by yourself—a mile from any other house. If you won't come with me I'll stay with you. Now, we won't argue the matter, so don't try"

"I shall leave Norman to do the arguing," said Rosemary.

"I'LL deal with Norman. I can manage HIM. I would never have asked you to give me back my promise—never—but I had to tell Norman why I couldn't marry him and he said HE would ask you. I couldn't prevent him. You need not suppose you are the only person in the world who possesses self-respect. I never dreamed of marrying and leaving you here alone. And you'll find I can be as determined as yourself."

Rosemary turned away and went into the house, with a shrug of her shoulders. Ellen looked down at St. George, who had never blinked an eyelash or stirred a whisker during the whole interview.

"St. George, this world would be a dull place without the men, I'll admit, but I'm almost tempted to wish there wasn't one of 'em in it. Look at the trouble and bother they've made right here, George—torn our happy old life completely up by the roots, Saint. John Meredith began it and Norman Douglas has finished it. And now both of them have to go into limbo. Norman is the only man I ever met who agrees with me that the Kaiser of Germany is the most dangerous creature alive on this earth—and I can't marry this sensible person because my sister is stubborn and I'm stubborner. Mark my words, St. George, the minister would come back if she raised her little finger. But she won't George— she'll never do it—she won't even crook it—and I don't dare meddle, Saint. I won't sulk, George; Rosemary didn't sulk, so I'm determined I won't either, Saint; Norman will tear up the turf, but the long and short of it is, St. George, that all of us old fools must just stop thinking of marrying. Well, well, 'despair is a free man, hope is a slave,' Saint. So now come into the house, George, and I'll solace you with a saucerful of cream. Then there will be one happy and contented creature on this hill at least."

CHAPTER XXXIII. CARL IS—NOT—WHIPPED

"There is something I think I ought to tell you," said Mary Vance mysteriously.

She and Faith and Una were walking arm in arm through the village, having foregathered at Mr. Flagg's store. Una and Faith exchanged looks which said, "NOW something disagreeable is coming." When Mary Vance thought she ought to tell them things there was seldom much pleasure in the hearing. They often wondered why they kept on liking Mary Vance—for like her they did, in spite of everything. To be sure, she was generally a stimulating and agreeable companion. If only she would not have those convictions that it was her duty to tell them things!

"Do you know that Rosemary West won't marry your pa because she thinks you are such a wild lot? She's afraid she couldn't bring you up right and so she turned him down."

Una's heart thrilled with secret exultation. She was very glad to hear that Miss West would not marry her father. But Faith was rather disappointed.

"How do you know?" she asked.

"Oh, everybody's saying it. I heard Mrs. Elliott talking it over with Mrs. Doctor. They thought I was too far away to hear, but I've got ears like a cat's. Mrs. Elliott said she hadn't a doubt that Rosemary was afraid to try stepmothering you because you'd got such a reputation. Your pa never goes up the hill now. Neither does Norman Douglas. Folks say Ellen has jilted him just to get square with him for jilting her ages ago. But Norman is going about declaring he'll get her yet. And I think you ought to know you've spoiled your pa's match and *I* think it's a pity, for he's bound to marry somebody before long, and Rosemary West would have been the best wife *I* know of for him."

"You told me all stepmothers were cruel and wicked," said Una.

"Oh—well," said Mary rather confusedly, "they're mostly awful cranky, I know. But Rosemary West couldn't be very mean to any one. I tell you if your pa turns round and marries Emmeline Drew you'll wish you'd behaved yourselves better and not frightened Rosemary out of it. It's awful that you've got such a reputation that no decent woman'll marry your pa on account of you. Of course, *I* know that half the yarns that are told about you ain't true. But give a dog a bad name. Why, some folks are saying that it was Jerry and Carl that threw the stones through Mrs. Stimson's window the other night when it was really them two Boyd boys. But I'm afraid it was Carl that put the eel in old Mrs. Carr's buggy, though I said at first I wouldn't believe it until I'd better proof than old Kitty Alec's word. I told Mrs. Elliott so right to her face."

"What did Carl do?" cried Faith.

"Well, they say—now, mind, I'm only telling you what people say—so there's no use in your blaming me for it—that Carl and a lot of other boys were fishing eels over the bridge one evening last week. Mrs. Carr drove past in that old rattle-trap buggy of hers with the open back. And Carl he just up and threw a big eel into the back. When poor old Mrs. Carr was driving up the hill by Ingleside that eel came squirming out between her feet. She thought it was a snake and she just give one awful screech and stood up and jumped clean over the wheels. The horse bolted, but it went home and no damage was done. But Mrs. Carr jarred her legs most terrible, and has had nervous spasms ever since whenever she thinks of the eel. Say, it was a rotten trick to play on the poor old soul. She's a decent body, if she is as queer as Dick's hat band."

Faith and Una looked at each other again. This was a matter for the Good-Conduct Club. They would not talk it over with Mary.

"There goes your pa," said Mary as Mr. Meredith passed them, "and never seeing us no more'n if we weren't here. Well, I'm getting so's I don't mind it. But there are folks who do."

Mr. Meredith had not seen them, but he was not walking along in his usual dreamy and abstracted fashion. He strode up the hill in agitation and distress. Mrs. Alec Davis had just told him the story of Carl and the eel. She had been very indignant about it. Old Mrs. Carr was her third cousin. Mr. Meredith was more than indignant. He was hurt and shocked. He had not thought Carl would do anything like this. He was not inclined to be hard on pranks of heedlessness or forgetfulness, but THIS was different. THIS had a nasty tang in it. When he reached home he found Carl on the lawn, patiently studying the habits and customs of a colony of wasps. Calling him into the study Mr. Meredith confronted him, with a sterner face than any of his children had ever seen before, and asked him if the story were true.

"Yes," said Carl, flushing, but meeting his father's eyes bravely.

Mr. Meredith groaned. He had hoped that there had been at least exaggeration.

"Tell me the whole matter," he said.

"The boys were fishing for eels over the bridge," said Carl. "Link Drew had caught a whopper—I mean an awful big one—the biggest eel I ever saw. He caught it right at the start and it had been lying in his basket a long time, still as still. I thought it was dead, honest I did. Then old Mrs. Carr drove over the bridge and she called us all young varmints and told us to go home. And we hadn't said a word to her, father, truly. So when she drove back again, after going to the store, the boys dared me to put Link's eel in her buggy. I thought it was so dead it couldn't hurt her and I threw it in. Then the eel came to life on the hill and we heard her scream and saw her jump out. I was awful sorry. That's all, father."

It was not quite as bad as Mr. Meredith had feared, but it was quite bad enough. "I must punish you, Carl," he said sorrowfully.

"Yes, I know, father."

"I—I must whip you."

Carl winced. He had never been whipped. Then, seeing how badly his father felt, he said cheerfully,

"All right, father."

Mr. Meredith misunderstood his cheerfulness and thought him insensible. He told Carl to come to the study after supper, and when the boy had gone out he flung himself into his chair and groaned again. He dreaded the evening sevenfold more than Carl did. The poor minister did not even know what he should whip his boy with. What was used to whip boys? Rods? Canes? No, that would be too brutal. A timber switch, then? And he, John Meredith, must hie him to the woods and cut one. It was an abominable thought. Then a picture presented itself unbidden to his mind. He saw Mrs. Carr's wizened, nut-cracker little face at the appearance of that reviving eel—he saw her sailing witch-like over the buggy wheels. Before he could prevent himself the minister laughed. Then he was angry with himself and angrier still with Carl. He would get that switch at once—and it must not be too limber, after all.

Carl was talking the matter over in the graveyard with Faith and Una, who had just come home. They were horrified at the idea of his being whipped—and by father, who had never done such a thing! But they agreed soberly that it was just.

"You know it was a dreadful thing to do," sighed Faith. "And you never owned up in the club."

"I forgot," said Carl. "Besides, I didn't think any harm came of it. I didn't know she jarred her legs. But I'm to be whipped and that will make things square."

"Will it hurt—very much?" said Una, slipping her hand into Carl's.

"Oh, not so much, I guess," said Carl gamely. "Anyhow, I'm not going to cry, no matter how much it hurts. It would make father feel so bad, if I did. He's all cut up now. I wish I could whip myself hard enough and save him doing it."

After supper, at which Carl had eaten little and Mr. Meredith nothing at all, both went silently into the study. The switch lay on the table. Mr. Meredith had had a bad time getting a switch to suit him. He cut one, then felt it was too slender. Carl had done a really indefensible thing. Then he cut another—it was far too thick. After all, Carl had thought the eel was dead. The third one suited him better; but as he picked it up from the table it seemed very thick and heavy—more like a stick than a switch.

"Hold out your hand," he said to Carl.

Carl threw back his head and held out his hand unflinchingly. But he was not very old and he could not quite keep a little fear out of his eyes. Mr. Meredith looked down into those eyes—why, they were Cecilia's eyes—her very eyes—and in them was the selfsame expression he had once seen in Cecilia's eyes when she had come to him to tell him something she had been a little afraid to tell him. Here were her eyes in Carl's little, white face—and six weeks ago he had thought, through one endless, terrible night, that his little lad was dying.

John Meredith threw down the switch.

"Go," he said, "I cannot whip you."

Carl fled to the graveyard, feeling that the look on his father's face was worse than any whipping.

"Is it over so soon?" asked Faith. She and Una had been holding hands and setting teeth on the Pollock tombstone.

"He—he didn't whip me at all," said Carl with a sob, "and—I wish he had—and he's in there, feeling just awful."

Una slipped away. Her heart yearned to comfort her father. As noiselessly as a little gray mouse she opened the study door and crept in. The room was dark with twilight. Her father was sitting at his desk. His back was towards her—his head was in his hands. He was talking to himself—broken, anguished words—but Una heard—heard and understood, with the sudden illumination that comes to sensitive, unmothered children. As silently as she had come in she slipped out and closed the door. John Meredith went on talking out his pain in what he deemed his undisturbed solitude.

CHAPTER XXXIV. UNA VISITS THE HILL

Una went upstairs. Carl and Faith were already on their way through the early moonlight to Rainbow Valley, having heard therefrom the elfin lilt of Jerry's jews-harp and having guessed that the Blythes were there and fun afoot. Una had no wish to go. She sought her own room first where she sat down on her bed and had a little cry. She did not want anybody to come in her dear mother's place. She did not want a stepmother who would hate her and make her father hate her. But father was so desperately unhappy—and if she could do any anything to make him happier she MUST do it. There was only one thing she could do—and she had known the moment she had left the study that she must do it. But it was a very hard thing to do.

After Una cried her heart out she wiped her eyes and went to the spare room. It was dark and rather musty, for the blind had not been drawn up nor the window opened for a long time. Aunt Martha was no fresh-air fiend. But as nobody ever thought of shutting a door in the manse this did not matter so much, save when some unfortunate minister came to stay all night and was compelled to breathe the spare room atmosphere.

There was a closet in the spare room and far back in the closet a gray silk dress was hanging. Una went into the closet and shut the door, went down on her knees and pressed her face against the soft silken folds. It had been her mother's wedding-dress. It was still full of a sweet, faint, haunting perfume, like lingering love. Una always felt very close to her mother there—as if she were kneeling at her feet with head in her lap. She went there once in a long while when life was TOO hard.

"Mother," she whispered to the gray silk gown, "*I* will never forget you, mother, and I'll ALWAYS love you best. But I have to do it, mother, because father is so very unhappy. I know you wouldn't want him to be unhappy. And I will be very good to her, mother, and try to love her, even if she is like Mary Vance said stepmothers always were."

Una carried some fine, spiritual strength away from her secret shrine. She slept peacefully that night with the tear stains still glistening on her sweet, serious, little face.

The next afternoon she put on her best dress and hat. They were shabby enough. Every other little girl in the Glen had new clothes that summer except

Faith and Una. Mary Vance had a lovely dress of white embroidered lawn, with scarlet silk sash and shoulder bows. But to-day Una did not mind her shabbiness. She only wanted to be very neat. She washed her face carefully. She brushed her black hair until it was as smooth as satin. She tied her shoelaces carefully, having first sewed up two runs in her one pair of good stockings. She would have liked to black her shoes, but she could not find any blacking. Finally, she slipped away from the manse, down through Rainbow Valley, up through the whispering woods, and out to the road that ran past the house on the hill. It was quite a long walk and Una was tired and warm when she got there.

She saw Rosemary West sitting under a tree in the garden and stole past the dahlia beds to her. Rosemary had a book in her lap, but she was gazing afar across the harbour and her thoughts were sorrowful enough. Life had not been pleasant lately in the house on the hill. Ellen had not sulked—Ellen had been a brick. But things can be felt that are never said and at times the silence between the two women was intolerably eloquent. All the many familiar things that had once made life sweet had a flavour of bitterness now. Norman Douglas made periodical irruptions also, bullying and coaxing Ellen by turns. It would end, Rosemary believed, by his dragging Ellen off with him some day, and Rosemary felt that she would be almost glad when it happened. Existence would be horribly lonely then, but it would be no longer charged with dynamite.

She was roused from her unpleasant reverie by a timid little touch on her shoulder. Turning, she saw Una Meredith.

"Why, Una, dear, did you walk up here in all this heat?"

"Yes," said Una, "I came to—I came to—"

But she found it very hard to say what she had come to do. Her voice failed—her eyes filled with tears.

"Why, Una, little girl, what is the trouble? Don't be afraid to tell me."

Rosemary put her arm around the thin little form and drew the child close to her. Her eyes were very beautiful—her touch so tender that Una found courage.

"I came—to ask you—to marry father," she gasped.

Rosemary was silent for a moment from sheer dumbfounderment. She stared at Una blankly.

"Oh, don't be angry, please, dear Miss West," said Una, pleadingly. "You see, everybody is saying that you wouldn't marry father because we are so bad. He is VERY unhappy about it. So I thought I would come and tell you that we are never bad ON PURPOSE. And if you will only marry father we will all try to be good and do just what you tell us. I'm SURE you won't have any trouble with us. PLEASE, Miss West."

Rosemary had been thinking rapidly. Gossiping surmise, she saw, had put this mistaken idea into Una's mind. She must be perfectly frank and sincere with the child.

"Una, dear," she said softly. "It isn't because of you poor little souls that I cannot be your father's wife. I never thought of such a thing. You are not bad—I never supposed you were. There—there was another reason altogether, Una."

"Don't you like father?" asked Una, lifting reproachful eyes. "Oh, Miss West, you don't know how nice he is. I'm sure he'd make you a GOOD husband."

Even in the midst of her perplexity and distress Rosemary couldn't help a twisted, little smile.

"Oh, don't laugh, Miss West," Una cried passionately. "Father feels DREADFUL about it."

"I think you're mistaken, dear," said Rosemary.

"I'm not. I'm SURE I'm not. Oh, Miss West, father was going to whip Carl yesterday—Carl had been naughty—and father couldn't do it because you see he had no PRACTICE in whipping. So when Carl came out and told us father felt so bad, I slipped into the study to see if I could help him—he LIKES me to comfort him, Miss West—and he didn't hear me come in and I heard what he was saying. I'll tell you, Miss West, if you'll let me whisper it in your ear."

Una whispered earnestly. Rosemary's face turned crimson. So John Meredith still cared. HE hadn't changed his mind. And he must care intensely if he had said that—care more than she had ever supposed he did. She sat still for a moment, stroking Una's hair. Then she said,

"Will you take a little letter from me to your father, Una?"

"Oh, are you going to marry him, Miss West?" asked Una eagerly.

"Perhaps—if he really wants me to," said Rosemary, blushing again.

"I'm glad—I'm glad," said Una bravely. Then she looked up, with quivering lips. "Oh, Miss West, you won't turn father against us—you won't make him hate us, will you?" she said beseechingly.

Rosemary stared again.

"Una Meredith! Do you think I would do such a thing? Whatever put such an idea into your head?"

"Mary Vance said stepmothers were all like that—and that they all hated their stepchildren and made their father hate them—she said they just couldn't help it—just being stepmothers made them like that"—

"You poor child! And yet you came up here and asked me to marry your father because you wanted to make him happy? You're a darling—a heroine—as Ellen would say, you're a brick. Now listen to me, very closely, dearest. Mary Vance is a silly little girl who doesn't know very much and she is dreadfully mistaken about some things. I would never dream of trying to turn your father against you. I would love you all dearly. I don't want to take your own mother's place—she must always have that in your hearts. But neither have I any intention of being a stepmother. I want to be your friend and helper and CHUM. Don't you think that would be nice, Una—if you and Faith and Carl and Jerry could just think of me as a good jolly chum—a big older sister?"

"Oh, it would be lovely," cried Una, with a transfigured face. She flung her arms impulsively round Rosemary's neck. She was so happy that she felt as if she could fly on wings.

"Do the others—do Faith and the boys have the same idea you had about stepmothers?"

"No. Faith never believed Mary Vance. I was dreadfully foolish to believe her, either. Faith loves you already—she has loved you ever since poor Adam was eaten. And Jerry and Carl will think it is jolly. Oh, Miss West, when you come to live with us, will you—could you—teach me to cook—a little—and sew—and— and—and do things? I don't know anything. I won't be much trouble—I'll try to learn fast."

"Darling, I'll teach you and help you all I can. Now, you won't say a word to anybody about this, will you—not even to Faith, until your father himself tells you you may? And you'll stay and have tea with me?"

"Oh, thank you—but—but—I think I'd rather go right back and take the letter to father," faltered Una. "You see, he'll be glad that much SOONER, Miss West."

"I see," said Rosemary. She went to the house, wrote a note and gave it to Una. When that small damsel had run off, a palpitating bundle of happiness, Rosemary went to Ellen, who was shelling peas on the back porch.

"Ellen," she said, "Una Meredith has just been here to ask me to marry her father."

Ellen looked up and read her sister's face.

"And you're going to?" she said.

"It's quite likely."

Ellen went on shelling peas for a few minutes. Then she suddenly put her hands up to her own face. There were tears in her black-browed eyes.

"I—I hope we'll all be happy," she said between a sob and a laugh.

Down at the manse Una Meredith, warm, rosy, triumphant, marched boldly into her father's study and laid a letter on the desk before him. His pale face flushed as he saw the clear, fine handwriting he knew so well. He opened the letter. It was very short—but he shed twenty years as he read it. Rosemary asked him if he could meet her that evening at sunset by the spring in Rainbow Valley.

CHAPTER XXXV. "LET THE PIPER COME"

"And so," said Miss Cornelia, "the double wedding is to be sometime about the middle of this month."

There was a faint chill in the air of the early September evening, so Anne had lighted her ever ready fire of driftwood in the big living room, and she and Miss Cornelia basked in its fairy flicker.

"It is so delightful—especially in regard to Mr. Meredith and Rosemary," said Anne. "I'm as happy in the thought of it, as I was when I was getting married myself. I felt exactly like a bride again last evening when I was up on the hill seeing Rosemary's trousseau."

"They tell me her things are fine enough for a princess," said Susan from a shadowy corner where she was cuddling her brown boy. "I have been invited up to see them also and I intend to go some evening. I understand that Rosemary is to wear white silk and a veil, but Ellen is to be married in navy blue. I have no doubt, Mrs. Dr. dear, that that is very sensible of her, but for my own part I have always felt that if I were ever married *I* would prefer the white and the veil, as being more bride-like."

A vision of Susan in "white and a veil" presented itself before

Anne's inner vision and was almost too much for her.

"As for Mr. Meredith," said Miss Cornelia, "even his engagement has made a different man of him. He isn't half so dreamy and absent-minded, believe me. I was so relieved when I heard that he had decided to close the manse and let the children visit round while he was away on his honeymoon. If he had left them and old Aunt Martha there alone for a month I should have expected to wake every morning and see the place burned down."

"Aunt Martha and Jerry are coming here," said Anne. "Carl is going to Elder Clow's. I haven't heard where the girls are going."

"Oh, I'm going to take them," said Miss Cornelia. "Of course, I was glad to, but Mary would have given me no peace till I asked them any way. The Ladies' Aid is going to clean the manse from top to bottom before the bride and groom come back, and Norman Douglas has arranged to fill the cellar with vegetables. Nobody ever saw or heard anything quite like Norman Douglas these days, believe ME. He's so tickled that he's going to marry Ellen West after wanting her all his life. If *I* was Ellen—but then, I'm not, and if she is satisfied I can very well be. I heard her say years ago when she was a schoolgirl that she didn't want a tame puppy for a husband. There's nothing tame about Norman, believe ME."

The sun was setting over Rainbow Valley. The pond was wearing a wonderful tissue of purple and gold and green and crimson. A faint blue haze rested on the eastern hill, over which a great, pale, round moon was just floating up like a silver bubble.

They were all there, squatted in the little open glade—Faith and Una, Jerry and Carl, Jem and Walter, Nan and Di, and Mary Vance. They had been having a special celebration, for it would be Jem's last evening in Rainbow Valley. On the morrow he would leave for Charlottetown to attend Queen's Academy. Their charmed circle would be broken; and, in spite of the jollity of their little festival, there was a hint of sorrow in every gay young heart.

"See—there is a great golden palace over there in the sunset," said Walter, pointing. "Look at the shining tower—and the crimson banners streaming from them. Perhaps a conqueror is riding home from battle—and they are hanging them out to do honour to him."

"Oh, I wish we had the old days back again," exclaimed Jem. "I'd love to be a soldier—a great, triumphant general. I'd give EVERYTHING to see a big battle."

Well, Jem was to be a soldier and see a greater battle than had ever been fought in the world; but that was as yet far in the future; and the mother, whose first-born son he was, was wont to look on her boys and thank God that the "brave days of old," which Jem longed for, were gone for ever, and that never would it be necessary for the sons of Canada to ride forth to battle "for the ashes of their fathers and the temples of their gods."

The shadow of the Great Conflict had not yet made felt any forerunner of its chill. The lads who were to fight, and perhaps fall, on the fields of France and Flanders, Gallipoli and Palestine, were still roguish schoolboys with a fair life in prospect before them: the girls whose hearts were to be wrung were yet fair little maidens a-star with hopes and dreams.

Slowly the banners of the sunset city gave up their crimson and gold; slowly the conqueror's pageant faded out. Twilight crept over the valley and the little group grew silent. Walter had been reading again that day in his beloved book of myths and he remembered how he had once fancied the Pied Piper coming down the valley on an evening just like this.

He began to speak dreamily, partly because he wanted to thrill his companions a little, partly because something apart from him seemed to be speaking through his lips.

"The Piper is coming nearer," he said, "he is nearer than he was that evening I saw him before. His long, shadowy cloak is blowing around him. He pipes—he pipes—and we must follow—Jem and Carl and Jerry and I—round and round the world. Listen— listen—can't you hear his wild music?"

The girls shivered.

"You know you're only pretending," protested Mary Vance, "and I wish you wouldn't. You make it too real. I hate that old Piper of yours."

But Jem sprang up with a gay laugh. He stood up on a little hillock, tall and splendid, with his open brow and his fearless eyes. There were thousands like him all over the land of the maple.

"Let the Piper come and welcome," he cried, waving his hand.

"I'LL follow him gladly round and round the world."

THE END

RILLA OF INGLESIDE

CHAPTER I - GLEN "NOTES" AND OTHER MATTERS

It was a warm, golden-cloudy, lovable afternoon. In the big living-room at In-gleside Susan Baker sat down with a certain grim satisfaction hovering about her like an aura; it was four o'clock and Susan, who had been working incessantly since six that morning, felt that she had fairly earned an hour of repose and gos-sip. Susan just then was perfectly happy; everything had gone almost uncannily well in the kitchen that day. Dr. Jekyll had not been Mr. Hyde and so had not grated on her nerves; from where she sat she could see the pride of her heart—the bed of peonies of her own planting and culture, blooming as no other peony plot in Glen St. Mary ever did or could bloom, with peonies crimson, peonies silvery pink, peonies white as drifts of winter snow.

Susan had on a new black silk blouse, quite as elaborate as anything Mrs. Mar-shall Elliott ever wore, and a white starched apron, trimmed with complicated crocheted lace fully five inches wide, not to mention insertion to match. Therefore Susan had all the comfortable consciousness of a well-dressed woman as she opened her copy of the Daily Enterprise and prepared to read the Glen "Notes" which, as Miss Cornelia had just informed her, filled half a column of it and men-tioned almost everybody at Ingleside. There was a big, black headline on the front page of the Enterprise, stating that some Archduke Ferdinand or other had been assassinated at a place bearing the weird name of Sarajevo, but Susan tarried not over uninteresting, immaterial stuff like that; she was in quest of something really vital. Oh, here it was—"Jottings from Glen St. Mary." Susan settled down keenly, reading each one over aloud to extract all possible gratification from it.

Mrs. Blythe and her visitor, Miss Cornelia—alias Mrs. Marshall Elliott—were chatting together near the open door that led to the veranda, through which a cool, delicious breeze was blowing, bringing whiffs of phantom perfume from the gar-den, and charming gay echoes from the vine-hung corner where Rilla and Miss Oliver and Walter were laughing and talking. Wherever Rilla Blythe was, there was laughter.

There was another occupant of the living-room, curled up on a couch, who must not be overlooked, since he was a creature of marked individuality, and, moreover, had the distinction of being the only living thing whom Susan really hated.

All cats are mysterious but Dr. Jekyll-and-Mr. Hyde—"Doc" for short—was trebly so. He was a cat of double personality—or else, as Susan vowed, he was possessed by the devil. To begin with, there had been something uncanny about the very dawn of his existence. Four years previously Rilla Blythe had had a treasured darling of a kitten, white as snow, with a saucy black tip to its tail, which she called Jack Frost. Susan disliked Jack Frost, though she could not or would not give any valid reason therefor.

"Take my word for it, Mrs. Dr. dear," she was wont to say ominously, "that cat will come to no good."

"But why do you think so?" Mrs. Blythe would ask.

"I do not think—I know," was all the answer Susan would vouchsafe.

With the rest of the Ingleside folk Jack Frost was a favourite; he was so very clean and well groomed, and never allowed a spot or stain to be seen on his beautiful white suit; he had endearing ways of purring and snuggling; he was scrupulously honest.

And then a domestic tragedy took place at Ingleside. Jack Frost had kittens!

It would be vain to try to picture Susan's triumph. Had she not always insisted that that cat would turn out to be a delusion and a snare? Now they could see for themselves!

Rilla kept one of the kittens, a very pretty one, with peculiarly sleek glossy fur of a dark yellow crossed by orange stripes, and large, satiny, golden ears. She called it Goldie and the name seemed appropriate enough to the little frolicsome creature which, during its kittenhood, gave no indication of the sinister nature it really possessed. Susan, of course, warned the family that no good could be expected from any offspring of that diabolical Jack Frost; but Susan's Cassandra-like croakings were unheeded.

The Blythes had been so accustomed to regard Jack Frost as a member of the male sex that they could not get out of the habit. So they continually used the masculine pronoun, although the result was ludicrous. Visitors used to be quite electrified when Rilla referred casually to "Jack and his kitten," or told Goldie sternly, "Go to your mother and get him to wash your fur."

"It is not decent, Mrs. Dr. dear," poor Susan would say bitterly. She herself compromised by always referring to Jack as "it" or "the white beast," and one heart at least did not ache when "it" was accidentally poisoned the following winter.

In a year's time "Goldie" became so manifestly an inadequate name for the orange kitten that Walter, who was just then reading Stevenson's story, changed it to Dr. Jekyll-and-Mr. Hyde. In his Dr. Jekyll mood the cat was a drowsy, affectionate, domestic, cushion-loving puss, who liked petting and gloried in being nursed and patted. Especially did he love to lie on his back and have his sleek, cream-coloured throat stroked gently while he purred in somnolent satisfaction. He was a notable purrer; never had there been an Ingleside cat who purred so constantly and so ecstatically.

"The only thing I envy a cat is its purr," remarked Dr. Blythe once, listening to Doc's resonant melody. "It is the most contented sound in the world."

Doc was very handsome; his every movement was grace; his poses magnificent. When he folded his long, dusky-ringed tail about his feet and sat him down on the veranda to gaze steadily into space for long intervals the Blythes felt that an Egyptian sphinx could not have made a more fitting Deity of the Portal.

When the Mr. Hyde mood came upon him—which it invariably did before rain, or wind—he was a wild thing with changed eyes. The transformation always came suddenly. He would spring fiercely from a reverie with a savage snarl and bite at any restraining or caressing hand. His fur seemed to grow darker and his eyes gleamed with a diabolical light. There was really an unearthly beauty about him. If the change happened in the twilight all the Ingleside folk felt a certain terror of him. At such times he was a fearsome beast and only Rilla defended him, asserting that he was "such a nice prowly cat." Certainly he prowled.

Dr. Jekyll loved new milk; Mr. Hyde would not touch milk and growled over his meat. Dr. Jekyll came down the stairs so silently that no one could hear him. Mr. Hyde made his tread as heavy as a man's. Several evenings, when Susan was alone in the house, he "scared her stiff," as she declared, by doing this. He would sit in the middle of the kitchen floor, with his terrible eyes fixed unwinkingly upon hers for an hour at a time. This played havoc with her nerves, but poor Susan really held him in too much awe to try to drive him out. Once she had dared to throw a stick at him and he had promptly made a savage leap towards her. Susan rushed out of doors and never attempted to meddle with Mr. Hyde again—though she visited his misdeeds upon the innocent Dr. Jekyll, chasing him ignominiously out of her domain whenever he dared to poke his nose in and denying him certain savoury tidbits for which he yearned.

"'The many friends of Miss Faith Meredith, Gerald Meredith and James Blythe,'" read Susan, rolling the names like sweet morsels under her tongue, "'were very much pleased to welcome them home a few weeks ago from Redmond College. James Blythe, who was graduated in Arts in 1913, had just completed his first year in medicine.'"

"Faith Meredith has really got to be the most handsomest creature I ever saw," commented Miss Cornelia above her filet crochet. "It's amazing how those children came on after Rosemary West went to the manse. People have almost forgotten what imps of mischief they were once. Anne, dearie, will you ever forget the way they used to carry on? It's really surprising how well Rosemary got on with them. She's more like a chum than a step-mother. They all love her and Una adores her. As for that little Bruce, Una just makes a perfect slave of herself to him. Of course, he is a darling. But did you ever see any child look as much like an aunt as he looks like his Aunt Ellen? He's just as dark and just as emphatic. I can't see a feature of Rosemary in him. Norman Douglas always vows at the top of his voice that the stork meant Bruce for him and Ellen and took him to the manse by mistake."

"Bruce adores Jem," said Mrs Blythe. "When he comes over here he follows Jem about silently like a faithful little dog, looking up at him from under his black brows. He would do anything for Jem, I verily believe."

"Are Jem and Faith going to make a match of it?"

Mrs. Blythe smiled. It was well known that Miss Cornelia, who had been such a virulent man-hater at one time, had actually taken to match-making in her declining years.

"They are only good friends yet, Miss Cornelia."

"Very good friends, believe me," said Miss Cornelia emphatically. "I hear all about the doings of the young fry."

"I have no doubt that Mary Vance sees that you do, Mrs. Marshall Elliott," said Susan significantly, "but I think it is a shame to talk about children making matches."

"Children! Jem is twenty-one and Faith is nineteen," retorted Miss Cornelia. "You must not forget, Susan, that we old folks are not the only grown-up people in the world."

Outraged Susan, who detested any reference to her age—not from vanity but from a haunting dread that people might come to think her too old to work—returned to her "Notes."

"'Carl Meredith and Shirley Blythe came home last Friday evening from Queen's Academy. We understand that Carl will be in charge of the school at Harbour Head next year and we are sure he will be a popular and successful teacher.'"

"He will teach the children all there is to know about bugs, anyhow," said Miss Cornelia. "He is through with Queen's now and Mr. Meredith and Rosemary wanted him to go right on to Redmond in the fall, but Carl has a very independent streak in him and means to earn part of his own way through college. He'll be all the better for it."

"'Walter Blythe, who has been teaching for the past two years at Lowbridge, has resigned,'" read Susan. "'He intends going to Redmond this fall.'"

"Is Walter quite strong enough for Redmond yet?" queried Miss Cornelia anxiously.

"We hope that he will be by the fall," said Mrs. Blythe. "An idle summer in the open air and sunshine will do a great deal for him."

"Typhoid is a hard thing to get over," said Miss Cornelia emphatically, "especially when one has had such a close shave as Walter had. I think he'd do well to stay out of college another year. But then he's so ambitious. Are Di and Nan going too?"

"Yes. They both wanted to teach another year but Gilbert thinks they had better go to Redmond this fall."

"I'm glad of that. They'll keep an eye on Walter and see that he doesn't study too hard. I suppose," continued Miss Cornelia, with a side glance at Susan, "that after the snub I got a few minutes ago it will not be safe for me to suggest that Jerry Meredith is making sheep's eyes at Nan."

Susan ignored this and Mrs. Blythe laughed again.

"Dear Miss Cornelia, I have my hands full, haven't I?—with all these boys and girls sweethearting around me? If I took it seriously it would quite crush me. But I don't—it is too hard yet to realize that they're grown up. When I look at those two tall sons of mine I wonder if they can possibly be the fat, sweet, dimpled babies I kissed and cuddled and sang to slumber the other day—only the other day, Miss Cornelia. Wasn't Jem the dearest baby in the old House of Dreams? and now he's a B.A. and accused of courting."

"We're all growing older," sighed Miss Cornelia.

"The only part of me that feels old," said Mrs. Blythe, "is the ankle I broke when Josie Pye dared me to walk the Barry ridge-pole in the Green Gables days. I have an ache in it when the wind is east. I won't admit that it is rheumatism, but it does ache. As for the children, they and the Merediths are planning a gay summer before they have to go back to studies in the fall. They are such a fun-loving little crowd. They keep this house in a perpetual whirl of merriment."

"Is Rilla going to Queen's when Shirley goes back?"

"It isn't decided yet. I rather fancy not. Her father thinks she is not quite strong enough—she has rather outgrown her strength—she's really absurdly tall for a girl not yet fifteen. I am not anxious to have her go—why, it would be terrible not to have a single one of my babies home with me next winter. Susan and I would fall to fighting with each other to break the monotony."

Susan smiled at this pleasantry. The idea of her fighting with "Mrs. Dr. dear!"

"Does Rilla herself want to go?" asked Miss Cornelia.

"No. The truth is, Rilla is the only one of my flock who isn't ambitious. I really wish she had a little more ambition. She has no serious ideals at all—her sole aspiration seems to be to have a good time."

"And why should she not have it, Mrs. Dr. dear?" cried Susan, who could not bear to hear a single word against anyone of the Ingleside folk, even from one of themselves. "A young girl should have a good time, and that I will maintain. There will be time enough for her to think of Latin and Greek."

"I should like to see a little sense of responsibility in her, Susan. And you know yourself that she is abominably vain."

"She has something to be vain about," retorted Susan. "She is the prettiest girl in Glen St. Mary. Do you think that all those over-harbour MacAllisters and Crawfords and Elliotts could scare up a skin like Rilla's in four generations? They could not. No, Mrs. Dr. dear, I know my place but I cannot allow you to run down Rilla. Listen to this, Mrs. Marshall Elliott."

Susan had found a chance to get square with Miss Cornelia for her digs at the children's love affairs. She read the item with gusto.

"'Miller Douglas has decided not to go West. He says old P.E.I. is good enough for him and he will continue to farm for his aunt, Mrs. Alec Davis.'"

Susan looked keenly at Miss Cornelia.

"I have heard, Mrs. Marshall Elliott, that Miller is courting Mary Vance."

This shot pierced Miss Cornelia's armour. Her sonsy face flushed.

"I won't have Miller Douglas hanging round Mary," she said crisply. "He comes of a low family. His father was a sort of outcast from the Douglases—they never really counted him in—and his mother was one of those terrible Dillons from the Harbour Head."

"I think I have heard, Mrs. Marshall Elliott, that Mary Vance's own parents were not what you could call aristocratic."

"Mary Vance has had a good bringing up and she is a smart, clever, capable girl," retorted Miss Cornelia. "She is not going to throw herself away on Miller Douglas, believe me! She knows my opinion on the matter and Mary has never disobeyed me yet."

"Well, I do not think you need worry, Mrs. Marshall Elliott, for Mrs. Alec Davis is as much against it as you could be, and says no nephew of hers is ever going to marry a nameless nobody like Mary Vance."

Susan returned to her mutton, feeling that she had got the best of it in this passage of arms, and read another "note."

"'We are pleased to hear that Miss Oliver has been engaged as teacher for another year. Miss Oliver will spend her well-earned vacation at her home in Lowbridge.'"

"I'm so glad Gertrude is going to stay," said Mrs. Blythe. "We would miss her horribly. And she has an excellent influence over Rilla who worships her. They are chums, in spite of the difference in their ages."

"I thought I heard she was going to be married?"

"I believe it was talked of but I understand it is postponed for a year."

"Who is the young man?"

"Robert Grant. He is a young lawyer in Charlottetown. I hope Gertrude will be happy. She has had a sad life, with much bitterness in it, and she feels things with a terrible keenness. Her first youth is gone and she is practically alone in the world. This new love that has come into her life seems such a wonderful thing to her that I think she hardly dares believe in its permanence. When her marriage had to be put off she was quite in despair—though it certainly wasn't Mr. Grant's fault. There were complications in the settlement of his father's estate—his father died last winter—and he could not marry till the tangles were unravelled. But I think Gertrude felt it was a bad omen and that her happiness would somehow elude her yet."

"It does not do, Mrs. Dr. dear, to set your affections too much on a man," remarked Susan solemnly.

"Mr. Grant is quite as much in love with Gertrude as she is with him, Susan. It is not he whom she distrusts—it is fate. She has a little mystic streak in her—I suppose some people would call her superstitious. She has an odd belief in dreams and we have not been able to laugh it out of her. I must own, too, that some of her dreams—but there, it would not do to let Gilbert hear me hinting such heresy. What have you found of much interest, Susan?"

Susan had given an exclamation.

"Listen to this, Mrs. Dr. dear. 'Mrs. Sophia Crawford has given up her house at Lowbridge and will make her home in future with her niece, Mrs. Albert Crawford.' Why that is my own cousin Sophia, Mrs. Dr. dear. We quarrelled when we were children over who should get a Sunday-school card with the words 'God is Love,' wreathed in rosebuds, on it, and have never spoken to each other since. And now she is coming to live right across the road from us."

"You will have to make up the old quarrel, Susan. It will never do to be at outs with your neighbours."

"Cousin Sophia began the quarrel, so she can begin the making up also, Mrs. Dr. dear," said Susan loftily. "If she does I hope I am a good enough Christian to meet her half-way. She is not a cheerful person and has been a wet blanket all her life. The last time I saw her, her face had a thousand wrinkles—maybe more, maybe less—from worrying and foreboding. She howled dreadful at her first husband's funeral but she married again in less than a year. The next note, I see, describes the special service in our church last Sunday night and says the decorations were very beautiful."

"Speaking of that reminds me that Mr. Pryor strongly disapproves of flowers in church," said Miss Cornelia. "I always said there would be trouble when that man moved here from Lowbridge. He should never have been put in as elder—it was a mistake and we shall live to rue it, believe me! I have heard that he has said that if the girls continue to 'mess up the pulpit with weeds' that he will not go to church."

"The church got on very well before old Whiskers-on-the-moon came to the Glen and it is my opinion it will get on without him after he is gone," said Susan.

"Who in the world ever gave him that ridiculous nickname?" asked Mrs. Blythe.

"Why, the Lowbridge boys have called him that ever since I can remember, Mrs. Dr. dear—I suppose because his face is so round and red, with that fringe of sandy whisker about it. It does not do for anyone to call him that in his hearing, though, and that you may tie to. But worse than his whiskers, Mrs. Dr. dear, he is a very unreasonable man and has a great many queer ideas. He is an elder now and they say he is very religious; but I can well remember the time, Mrs. Dr. dear, twenty years ago, when he was caught pasturing his cow in the Lowbridge graveyard. Yes, indeed, I have not forgotten that, and I always think of it when he is praying in meeting. Well, that is all the notes and there is not much else in the paper of any importance. I never take much interest in foreign parts. Who is this Archduke man who has been murdered?"

"What does it matter to us?" asked Miss Cornelia, unaware of the hideous answer to her question which destiny was even then preparing. "Somebody is always murdering or being murdered in those Balkan States. It's their normal condition and I don't really think that our papers ought to print such shocking things. The Enterprise is getting far too sensational with its big headlines. Well, I must be getting home. No, Anne dearie, it's no use asking me to stay to supper. Marshall has got to thinking that if I'm not home for a meal it's not worth eating—just like a man. So off I go. Merciful goodness, Anne dearie, what is the matter with that cat? Is he having a fit?"—this, as Doc suddenly bounded to the rug at Miss Cornelia's feet, laid back his ears, swore at her, and then disappeared with one fierce leap through the window.

"Oh, no. He's merely turning into Mr. Hyde—which means that we shall have rain or high wind before morning. Doc is as good as a barometer."

"Well, I am thankful he has gone on the rampage outside this time and not into my kitchen," said Susan. "And I am going out to see about supper. With such a crowd as we have at Ingleside now it behooves us to think about our meals betimes."

CHAPTER II - DEW OF MORNING

Outside, the Ingleside lawn was full of golden pools of sunshine and plots of alluring shadows. Rilla Blythe was swinging in the hammock under the big Scotch pine, Gertrude Oliver sat at its roots beside her, and Walter was stretched at full length on the grass, lost in a romance of chivalry wherein old heroes and beauties of dead and gone centuries lived vividly again for him.

Rilla was the "baby" of the Blythe family and was in a chronic state of secret indignation because nobody believed she was grown up. She was so nearly fifteen that she called herself that, and she was quite as tall as Di and Nan; also, she was nearly as pretty as Susan believed her to be. She had great, dreamy, hazel eyes, a milky skin dappled with little golden freckles, and delicately arched eyebrows, giving her a demure, questioning look which made people, especially lads in their teens, want to answer it. Her hair was ripely, ruddily brown and a little dent in her upper lip looked as if some good fairy had pressed it in with her finger at Rilla's christening. Rilla, whose best friends could not deny her share of vanity, thought her face would do very well, but worried over her figure, and wished her mother could be prevailed upon to let her wear longer dresses. She, who had been so plump and roly-poly in the old Rainbow Valley days, was incredibly slim now, in the arms-and-legs period. Jem and Shirley harrowed her soul by calling her "Spider." Yet she somehow escaped awkwardness. There was something in her movements that made you think she never walked but always danced. She had been much petted and was a wee bit spoiled, but still the general opinion was that Rilla Blythe was a very sweet girl, even if she were not so clever as Nan and Di.

Miss Oliver, who was going home that night for vacation, had boarded for a year at Ingleside. The Blythes had taken her to please Rilla who was fathoms deep in love with her teacher and was even willing to share her room, since no other was available. Gertrude Oliver was twenty-eight and life had been a struggle for her. She was a striking-looking girl, with rather sad, almond-shaped brown eyes, a clever, rather mocking mouth, and enormous masses of black hair twisted about her head. She was not pretty but there was a certain charm of interest and mystery in her face, and Rilla found her fascinating. Even her occasional moods of gloom and cynicism had allurement for Rilla. These moods came only when Miss Oliver was tired. At all other times she was a stimulating companion, and the gay set at Ingleside never remembered that she was so much older than themselves. Walter and Rilla were her favourites and she was the confidante of the secret wishes and aspirations of both. She knew that Rilla longed to be "out"—to go to parties as Nan and Di did, and to have dainty evening dresses and—yes, there is no mincing matters—beaux! In the plural, at that! As for Walter, Miss Oliver knew that he had written a sequence of sonnets "to Rosamond"—i.e., Faith Meredith—and that he aimed at a Professorship of English literature in some big college. She knew his passionate love of beauty and his equally passionate hatred of ugliness; she knew his strength and his weakness.

Walter was, as ever, the handsomest of the Ingleside boys. Miss Oliver found pleasure in looking at him for his good looks—he was so exactly like what she would have liked her own son to be. Glossy black hair, brilliant dark grey eyes, faultless features. And a poet to his fingertips! That sonnet sequence was really a remarkable thing for a lad of twenty to write. Miss Oliver was no partial critic and she knew that Walter Blythe had a wonderful gift.

Rilla loved Walter with all her heart. He never teased her as Jem and Shirley did. He never called her "Spider." His pet name for her was "Rilla-my-Rilla"—a little pun on her real name, Marilla. She had been named after Aunt Marilla of Green Gables, but Aunt Marilla had died before Rilla was old enough to know her very well, and Rilla detested the name as being horribly old-fashioned and prim. Why couldn't they have called her by her first name, Bertha, which was beautiful and dignified, instead of that silly "Rilla"? She did not mind Walter's version, but nobody else was allowed to call her that, except Miss Oliver now and then. "Rilla-my-Rilla" in Walter's musical voice sounded very beautiful to her—like the lilt and ripple of some silvery brook. She would have died for Walter if it would have done him any good, so she told Miss Oliver. Rilla was as fond of italics as most girls of fifteen are—and the bitterest drop in her cup was her suspicion that he told Di more of his secrets than he told her.

"He thinks I'm not grown up enough to understand," she had once lamented rebelliously to Miss Oliver, "but I am! And I would never tell them to a single soul—not even to you, Miss Oliver. I tell you all my own—I just couldn't be happy if I had any secret from you, dearest—but I would never betray his. I tell him everything—I even show him my diary. And it hurts me dreadfully when he doesn't tell me things. He shows me all his poems, though—they are marvellous, Miss Oliver. Oh, I just live in the hope that some day I shall be to Walter what Wordsworth's sister Dorothy was to him. Wordsworth never wrote anything like Walter's poems—nor Tennyson, either."

"I wouldn't say just that. Both of them wrote a great deal of trash," said Miss Oliver dryly. Then, repenting, as she saw a hurt look in Rilla's eye, she added hastily,

"But I believe Walter will be a great poet, too—some day—and you will have more of his confidence as you grow older."

"When Walter was in the hospital with typhoid last year I was almost crazy," sighed Rilla, a little importantly. "They never told me how ill he really was until it was all over—father wouldn't let them. I'm glad I didn't know—I couldn't have

926

borne it. I cried myself to sleep every night as it was. But sometimes," concluded Rilla bitterly—she liked to speak bitterly now and then in imitation of Miss Oliver—"sometimes I think Walter cares more for Dog Monday than he does for me."

Dog Monday was the Ingleside dog, so called because he had come into the family on a Monday when Walter had been reading Robinson Crusoe. He really belonged to Jem but was much attached to Walter also. He was lying beside Walter now with nose snuggled against his arm, thumping his tail rapturously whenever Walter gave him an absent pat. Monday was not a collie or a setter or a hound or a Newfoundland. He was just, as Jem said, "plain dog"—very plain dog, uncharitable people added. Certainly, Monday's looks were not his strong point. Black spots were scattered at random over his yellow carcass, one of them, apparently, blotting out an eye. His ears were in tatters, for Monday was never successful in affairs of honour. But he possessed one talisman. He knew that not all dogs could be handsome or eloquent or victorious, but that every dog could love. Inside his homely hide beat the most affectionate, loyal, faithful heart of any dog since dogs were; and something looked out of his brown eyes that was nearer akin to a soul than any theologian would allow. Everybody at Ingleside was fond of him, even Susan, although his one unfortunate propensity of sneaking into the spare room and going to sleep on the bed tried her affection sorely.

On this particular afternoon Rilla had no quarrel on hand with existing conditions.

"Hasn't June been a delightful month?" she asked, looking dreamily afar at the little quiet silvery clouds hanging so peacefully over Rainbow Valley. "We've had such lovely times—and such lovely weather. It has just been perfect every way."

"I don't half like that," said Miss Oliver, with a sigh. "It's ominous—somehow. A perfect thing is a gift of the gods—a sort of compensation for what is coming afterwards. I've seen that so often that I don't care to hear people say they've had a perfect time. June has been delightful, though."

"Of course, it hasn't been very exciting," said Rilla. "The only exciting thing that has happened in the Glen for a year was old Miss Mead fainting in Church. Sometimes I wish something dramatic would happen once in a while."

"Don't wish it. Dramatic things always have a bitterness for some one. What a nice summer all you gay creatures will have! And me moping at Lowbridge!"

"You'll be over often, won't you? I think there's going to be lots of fun this summer, though I'll just be on the fringe of things as usual, I suppose. Isn't it horrid when people think you're a little girl when you're not?"

"There's plenty of time for you to be grown up, Rilla. Don't wish your youth away. It goes too quickly. You'll begin to taste life soon enough."

"Taste life! I want to eat it," cried Rilla, laughing. "I want everything—everything a girl can have. I'll be fifteen in another month, and then nobody can say I'm a child any longer. I heard someone say once that the years from fifteen to nineteen are the best years in a girl's life. I'm going to make them perfectly splendid—just fill them with fun."

"There's no use thinking about what you're going to do—you are tolerably sure not to do it."

"Oh, but you do get a lot of fun out of the thinking," cried Rilla.

"You think of nothing but fun, you monkey," said Miss Oliver indulgently, reflecting that Rilla's chin was really the last word in chins. "Well, what else is fifteen for? But have you any notion of going to college this fall?"

"No—nor any other fall. I don't want to. I never cared for all those ologies and isms Nan and Di are so crazy about. And there's five of us going to college already. Surely that's enough. There's bound to be one dunce in every family. I'm quite willing to be a dunce if I can be a pretty, popular, delightful one. I can't be clever. I have no talent at all, and you can't imagine how comfortable it is. Nobody expects me to do anything so I'm never pestered to do it. And I can't be a housewifely, cookly creature, either. I hate sewing and dusting, and when Susan couldn't teach me to make biscuits nobody could. Father says I toil not neither do I spin. Therefore, I must be a lily of the field," concluded Rilla, with another laugh.

"You are too young to give up your studies altogether, Rilla."

"Oh, mother will put me through a course of reading next winter. It will polish up her B.A. degree. Luckily I like reading. Don't look at me so sorrowfully and so disapprovingly, dearest. I can't be sober and serious—everything looks so rosy and rainbowy to me. Next month I'll be fifteen—and next year sixteen—and the year after that seventeen. Could anything be more enchanting?"

"Rap wood," said Gertrude Oliver, half laughingly, half seriously. "Rap wood, Rilla-my-Rilla."

CHAPTER III - MOONLIT MIRTH

Rilla, who still buttoned up her eyes when she went to sleep so that she always looked as if she were laughing in her slumber, yawned, stretched, and smiled at Gertrude Oliver. The latter had come over from Lowbridge the previous evening and had been prevailed upon to remain for the dance at the Four Winds lighthouse the next night.

"The new day is knocking at the window. What will it bring us, I wonder."

Miss Oliver shivered a little. She never greeted the days with Rilla's enthusiasm. She had lived long enough to know that a day may bring a terrible thing.

"I think the nicest thing about days is their unexpectedness," went on Rilla. "It's jolly to wake up like this on a golden-fine morning and wonder what surprise packet the day will hand you. I always day-dream for ten minutes before I get up, imagining the heaps of splendid things that may happen before night."

"I hope something very unexpected will happen today," said Gertrude. "I hope the mail will bring us news that war has been averted between Germany and France."

"Oh—yes," said Rilla vaguely. "It will be dreadful if it isn't, I suppose. But it won't really matter much to us, will it? I think a war would be so exciting. The Boer war was, they say, but I don't remember anything about it, of course. Miss Oliver, shall I wear my white dress tonight or my new green one? The green one is by far the prettier, of course, but I'm almost afraid to wear it to a shore dance for fear something will happen to it. And will you do my hair the new way? None of the other girls in the Glen wear it yet and it will make such a sensation."

"How did you induce your mother to let you go to the dance?"

"Oh, Walter coaxed her over. He knew I would be heart-broken if I didn't go. It's my first really-truly grown-up party, Miss Oliver, and I've just lain awake at nights for a week thinking it over. When I saw the sun shining this morning I wanted to whoop for joy. It would be simply terrible if it rained tonight. I think I'll wear the green dress and risk it. I want to look my nicest at my first party. Besides, it's an inch longer than my white one. And I'll wear my silver slippers too. Mrs. Ford sent them to me last Christmas and I've never had a chance to wear them yet. They're the dearest things. Oh, Miss Oliver, I do hope some of the boys will ask me to dance. I shall die of mortification—truly I will, if nobody does and I have to sit stuck up against the wall all the evening. Of course Carl and Jerry can't dance because they're the minister's sons, or else I could depend on them to save me from utter disgrace."

"You'll have plenty of partners—all the over-harbour boys are coming—there'll be far more boys than girls."

"I'm glad I'm not a minister's daughter," laughed Rilla. "Poor Faith is so furious because she won't dare to dance tonight. Una doesn't care, of course. She has never hankered after dancing. Somebody told Faith there would be a taffy-pull in the kitchen for those who didn't dance and you should have seen the face she made. She and Jem will sit out on the rocks most of the evening, I suppose. Did you know that we are all to walk down as far as that little creek below the old House of Dreams and then sail to the lighthouse? Won't it just be absolutely divine?"

"When I was fifteen I talked in italics and superlatives too," said Miss Oliver sarcastically. "I think the party promises to be pleasant for young fry. I expect to be bored. None of those boys will bother dancing with an old maid like me. Jem and Walter will take me out once out of charity. So you can't expect me to look forward to it with your touching young rapture."

"Didn't you have a good time at your first party, though, Miss Oliver?"

"No. I had a hateful time. I was shabby and homely and nobody asked me to dance except one boy, homelier and shabbier than myself. He was so awkward I hated him—and even he didn't ask me again. I had no real girlhood, Rilla. It's a sad loss. That's why I want you to have a splendid, happy girlhood. And I hope your first party will be one you'll remember all your life with pleasure."

"I dreamed last night I was at the dance and right in the middle of things I discovered I was dressed in my kimono and bedroom shoes," sighed Rilla. "I woke up with a gasp of horror."

"Speaking of dreams—I had an odd one," said Miss Oliver absently. "It was one of those vivid dreams I sometimes have—they are not the vague jumble of ordinary dreams—they are as clear cut and real as life."

"What was your dream?"

"I was standing on the veranda steps, here at Ingleside, looking down over the fields of the Glen. All at once, far in the distance, I saw a long, silvery, glistening wave breaking over them. It came nearer and nearer—just a succession of little white waves like those that break on the sandshore sometimes. The Glen was being swallowed up. I thought, 'Surely the waves will not come near Ingleside'—but they came nearer and nearer—so rapidly—before I could move or call they were breaking right at my feet—and everything was gone—there was nothing but a waste of stormy water where the Glen had been. I tried to draw back—and I saw that the edge of my dress was wet with blood—and I woke—shivering. I don't like the dream. There was some sinister significance in it. That kind of vivid dream always 'comes true' with me."

"I hope it doesn't mean there's a storm coming up from the east to spoil the party," murmured Rilla.

"Incorrigible fifteen!" said Miss Oliver dryly. "No, Rilla-my-Rilla, I don't think there is any danger that it foretells anything so awful as that."

There had been an undercurrent of tension in the Ingleside existence for several days. Only Rilla, absorbed in her own budding life, was unaware of it. Dr. Blythe had taken to looking grave and saying little over the daily paper. Jem and Walter were keenly interested in the news it brought. Jem sought Walter out in excitement that evening.

"Oh, boy, Germany has declared war on France. This means that England will fight too, probably—and if she does—well, the Piper of your old fancy will have come at last."

"It wasn't a fancy," said Walter slowly. "It was a presentiment—a vision— Jem, I really saw him for a moment that evening long ago. Suppose England does fight?"

"Why, we'll all have to turn in and help her," cried Jem gaily. "We couldn't let the 'old grey mother of the northern sea' fight it out alone, could we? But you can't go—the typhoid has done you out of that. Sort of a shame, eh?"

Walter did not say whether it was a shame or not. He looked silently over the Glen to the dimpling blue harbour beyond.

"We're the cubs—we've got to pitch in tooth and claw if it comes to a family row," Jem went on cheerfully, rumpling up his red curls with a strong, lean, sensitive brown hand—the hand of the born surgeon, his father often thought. "What an adventure it would be! But I suppose Grey or some of those wary old chaps will patch matters up at the eleventh hour. It'll be a rotten shame if they leave France in the lurch, though. If they don't, we'll see some fun. Well, I suppose it's time to get ready for the spree at the light."

Jem departed whistling "Wi' a hundred pipers and a' and a'," and Walter stood for a long time where he was. There was a little frown on his forehead. This had all come up with the blackness and suddenness of a thundercloud. A few days ago nobody had even thought of such a thing. It was absurd to think of it now. Some way out would be found. War was a hellish, horrible, hideous thing—too horrible and hideous to happen in the twentieth century between civilized nations. The mere thought of it was hideous, and made Walter unhappy in its threat to the beauty of life. He would not think of it—he would resolutely put it out of his mind. How beautiful the old Glen was, in its August ripeness, with its chain of bowery old homesteads, tilled meadows and quiet gardens. The western sky was like a great golden pearl. Far down the harbour was frosted with a dawning moonlight. The air was full of exquisite sounds—sleepy robin whistles, wonderful, mournful, soft murmurs of wind in the twilit trees, rustle of aspen poplars talking in silvery whispers and shaking their dainty, heart-shaped leaves, lilting young laughter from the windows of rooms where the girls were making ready for the dance. The world was steeped in maddening loveliness of sound and colour. He would think only of these things and of the deep, subtle joy they gave him. "Anyhow, no one will expect me to go," he thought. "As Jem says, typhoid has seen to that."

Rilla was leaning out of her room window, dressed for the dance. A yellow pansy slipped from her hair and fell out over the sill like a falling star of gold. She caught at it vainly—but there were enough left. Miss Oliver had woven a little wreath of them for her pet's hair.

"It's so beautifully calm—isn't that splendid? We'll have a perfect night. Listen, Miss Oliver—I can hear those old bells in Rainbow Valley quite clearly. They've been hanging there for over ten years."

"Their wind chime always makes me think of the aerial, celestial music Adam and Eve heard in Milton's Eden," responded Miss Oliver.

"We used to have such fun in Rainbow Valley when we were children," said Rilla dreamily.

Nobody ever played in Rainbow Valley now. It was very silent on summer evenings. Walter liked to go there to read. Jem and Faith trysted there considerably; Jerry and Nan went there to pursue uninterruptedly the ceaseless wrangles and arguments on profound subjects that seemed to be their preferred method of sweethearting. And Rilla had a beloved little sylvan dell of her own there where she liked to sit and dream.

"I must run down to the kitchen before I go and show myself off to Susan. She would never forgive me if I didn't."

Rilla whirled into the shadowy kitchen at Ingleside, where Susan was prosaically darning socks, and lighted it up with her beauty. She wore her green dress with its little pink daisy garlands, her silk stockings and silver slippers. She had golden pansies in her hair and at her creamy throat. She was so pretty and young and glowing that even Cousin Sophia Crawford was compelled to admire her— and Cousin Sophia Crawford admired few transient earthly things. Cousin Sophia and Susan had made up, or ignored, their old feud since the former had come to live in the Glen, and Cousin Sophia often came across in the evenings to make a neighbourly call. Susan did not always welcome her rapturously for Cousin Sophia was not what could be called an exhilarating companion. "Some calls are visits and some are visitations, Mrs. Dr. dear," Susan said once, and left it to be inferred that Cousin Sophia's were the latter.

Cousin Sophia had a long, pale, wrinkled face, a long, thin nose, a long, thin mouth, and very long, thin, pale hands, generally folded resignedly on her black calico lap. Everything about her seemed long and thin and pale. She looked mournfully upon Rilla Blythe and said sadly,

"Is your hair all your own?"

"Of course it is," cried Rilla indignantly.

"Ah, well!" Cousin Sophia sighed. "It might be better for you if it wasn't! Such a lot of hair takes from a person's strength. It's a sign of consumption, I've heard, but I hope it won't turn out like that in your case. I s'pose you'll all be dancing tonight—even the minister's boys most likely. I s'pose his girls won't go that far. Ah, well, I never held with dancing. I knew a girl once who dropped dead while she was dancing. How any one could ever dance aga' after a judgment like that I cannot comprehend."

"Did she ever dance again?" asked Rilla pertly.

"I told you she dropped dead. Of course she never danced again, poor creature. She was a Kirke from Lowbridge. You ain't a-going off like that with nothing on your bare neck, are you?"

"It's a hot evening," protested Rilla. "But I'll put on a scarf when we go on the water."

"I knew of a boat load of young folks who went sailing on that harbour forty years ago just such a night as this—just exactly such a night as this," said Cousin Sophia lugubriously, "and they were upset and drowned—every last one of them. I hope nothing like that'll happen to you tonight. Do you ever try anything for the freckles? I used to find plantain juice real good."

"You certainly should be a judge of freckles, Cousin Sophia," said Susan, rushing to Rilla's defence. "You were more speckled than any toad when you was a girl. Rilla's only come in summer but yours stayed put, season in and season out; and you had not a ground colour like hers behind them neither. You look real nice, Rilla, and that way of fixing your hair is becoming. But you are not going to walk to the harbour in those slippers, are you?"

"Oh, no. We'll all wear our old shoes to the harbour and carry our slippers. Do you like my dress, Susan?"

"It minds me of a dress I wore when I was a girl," sighed Cousin Sophia before Susan could reply. "It was green with pink posies on it, too, and it was flounced from the waist to the hem. We didn't wear the skimpy things girls wear nowadays. Ah me, times has changed and not for the better I'm afraid. I tore a big hole in it that night and someone spilled a cup of tea all over it. Ruined it completely. But I hope nothing will happen to your dress. It orter to be a bit longer I'm thinking—your legs are so terrible long and thin."

"Mrs. Dr. Blythe does not approve of little girls dressing like grown-up ones," said Susan stiffly, intending merely a snub to Cousin Sophia. But Rilla felt insulted. A little girl indeed! She whisked out of the kitchen in high dudgeon. Another time she wouldn't go down to show herself off to Susan—Susan, who thought nobody was grown up until she was sixty! And that horrid Cousin Sophia with her digs about freckles and legs! What business had an old—an old beanpole like that to talk of anybody else being long and thin? Rilla felt all her pleasure in herself and her evening clouded and spoiled. The very teeth of her soul were set on edge and she could have sat down and cried.

But later on her spirits rose again when she found herself one of the gay crowd bound for the Four Winds light.

The Blythes left Ingleside to the melancholy music of howls from Dog Monday, who was locked up in the barn lest he make an uninvited guest at the light. They picked up the Merediths in the village, and others joined them as they walked down the old harbour road. Mary Vance, resplendent in blue crepe, with lace overdress, came out of Miss Cornelia's gate and attached herself to Rilla and Miss Oliver who were walking together and who did not welcome her over-warmly. Rilla was not very fond of Mary Vance. She had never forgotten the humiliating day when Mary had chased her through the village with a dried codfish. Mary Vance, to tell the truth, was not exactly popular with any of her set. Still, they enjoyed her society—she had such a biting tongue that it was stimulating. "Mary Vance is a habit of ours—we can't do without her even when we are furious with her," Di Blythe had once said.

Most of the little crowd were paired off after a fashion. Jem walked with Faith Meredith, of course, and Jerry Meredith with Nan Blythe. Di and Walter were together, deep in confidential conversation which Rilla envied.

Carl Meredith was walking with Miranda Pryor, more to torment Joe Milgrave than for any other reason. Joe was known to have a strong hankering for the said Miranda, which shyness prevented him from indulging on all occasions. Joe might summon enough courage to amble up beside Miranda if the night were dark, but here, in this moonlit dusk, he simply could not do it. So he trailed along after the procession and thought things not lawful to be uttered of Carl Meredith. Miranda was the daughter of Whiskers-on-the-moon; she did not share her father's unpopularity but she was not much run after, being a pale, neutral little creature, somewhat addicted to nervous giggling. She had silvery blonde hair and her eyes were big china blue orbs that looked as if she had been badly frightened when she was little and had never got over it. She would much rather have walked with Joe than with Carl, with whom she did not feel in the least at home. Yet it was something of an honour, too, to have a college boy beside her, and a son of the manse at that.

Shirley Blythe was with Una Meredith and both were rather silent because such was their nature. Shirley was a lad of sixteen, sedate, sensible, thoughtful, full of a quiet humour. He was Susan's "little brown boy" yet, with his brown hair, brown eyes, and clear brown skin. He liked to walk with Una Meredith because she never tried to make him talk or badgered him with chatter. Una was as sweet and shy as she had been in the Rainbow Valley days, and her large, dark-blue eyes were as dreamy and wistful. She had a secret, carefully-hidden fancy for Walter Blythe that nobody but Rilla ever suspected. Rilla sympathized with it and wished Walter would return it. She liked Una better than Faith, whose beauty and aplomb rather overshadowed other girls—and Rilla did not enjoy being overshadowed.

But just now she was very happy. It was so delightful to be tripping with her friends down that dark, gleaming road sprinkled with its little spruces and firs, whose balsam made all the air resinous around them. Meadows of sunset afterlight were behind the westering hills. Before them was the shining harbour. A bell was ringing in the little church over-harbour and the lingering dream-notes died around the dim, amethystine points. The gulf beyond was still silvery blue in the afterlight. Oh, it was all glorious—the clear air with its salt tang, the balsam of the firs, the laughter of her friends. Rilla loved life—its bloom and brilliance; she loved the ripple of music, the hum of merry conversation; she wanted to walk on forever over this road of silver and shadow. It was her first party and she was going to have a splendid time. There was nothing in the world to worry about—not even freckles and over-long legs—nothing except one little haunting fear that no-body would ask her to dance. It was beautiful and satisfying just to be alive—to be fifteen—to be pretty. Rilla drew a long breath of rapture—and caught it mid-way rather sharply. Jem was telling some story to Faith—something that had happened in the Balkan War.

"The doctor lost both his legs—they were smashed to pulp—and he was left on the field to die. And he crawled about from man to man, to all the wounded men round him, as long as he could, and did everything possible to relieve their sufferings—never thinking of himself—he was tying a bit of bandage round an-other man's leg when he went under. They found them there, the doctor's dead hands still held the bandage tight, the bleeding was stopped and the other man's life was saved. Some hero, wasn't he, Faith? I tell you when I read that—"

Jem and Faith moved on out of hearing. Gertrude Oliver suddenly shivered. Rilla pressed her arm sympathetically.

"Wasn't it dreadful, Miss Oliver? I don't know why Jem tells such gruesome things at a time like this when we're all out for fun."

"Do you think it dreadful, Rilla? I thought it wonderful—beautiful. Such a sto-ry makes one ashamed of ever doubting human nature. That man's action was godlike. And how humanity responds to the ideal of self-sacrifice. As for my shiver, I don't know what caused it. The evening is certainly warm enough. Per-haps someone is walking over the dark, starshiny spot that is to be my grave. That is the explanation the old superstition would give. Well, I won't think of that on this lovely night. Do you know, Rilla, that when night-time comes I'm always glad I live in the country. We know the real charm of night here as town dwellers never do. Every night is beautiful in the country—even the stormy ones. I love a wild night storm on this old gulf shore. As for a night like this, it is almost too beautiful—it belongs to youth and dreamland and I'm half afraid of it."

"I feel as if I were part of it," said Rilla.

"Ah yes, you're young enough not to be afraid of perfect things. Well, here we are at the House of Dreams. It seems lonely this summer. The Fords didn't come?"

"Mr. and Mrs. Ford and Persis didn't. Kenneth did—but he stayed with his mother's people over-harbour. We haven't seen a great deal of him this summer. He's a little lame, so didn't go about very much."

"Lame? What happened to him?"

"He broke his ankle in a football game last fall and was laid up most of the winter. He has limped a little ever since but it is getting better all the time and he expects it will be all right before long. He has been up to Ingleside only twice."

"Ethel Reese is simply crazy about him," said Mary Vance. "She hasn't got the sense she was born with where he is concerned. He walked home with her from the over-harbour church last prayer-meeting night and the airs she has put on since would really make you weary of life. As if a Toronto boy like Ken Ford would ever really think of a country girl like Ethel!"

Rilla flushed. It did not matter to her if Kenneth Ford walked home with Ethel Reese a dozen times—it did not! Nothing that he did mattered to her. He was ages older than she was. He chummed with Nan and Di and Faith, and looked upon her, Rilla, as a child whom he never noticed except to tease. And she detested Ethel Reese and Ethel Reese hated her—always had hated her since Walter had pummelled Dan so notoriously in Rainbow Valley days; but why need she be thought beneath Kenneth Ford's notice because she was a country girl, pray? As for Mary Vance, she was getting to be an out-and-out gossip and thought of nothing but who walked home with people!

There was a little pier on the harbour shore below the House of Dreams, and two boats were moored there. One boat was skippered by Jem Blythe, the other by Joe Milgrave, who knew all about boats and was nothing loth to let Miranda Pryor see it. They raced down the harbour and Joe's boat won. More boats were coming down from the Harbour Head and across the harbour from the western side. Everywhere there was laughter. The big white tower on Four Winds Point was overflowing with light, while its revolving beacon flashed overhead. A family from Charlottetown, relatives of the light's keeper, were summering at the light, and they were giving the party to which all the young people of Four Winds and Glen St. Mary and over-harbour had been invited. As Jem's boat swung in below the lighthouse Rilla desperately snatched off her shoes and donned her silver slippers behind Miss Oliver's screening back. A glance had told her that the rock-cut steps climbing up to the light were lined with boys, and lighted by Chinese lanterns, and she was determined she would not walk up those steps in the heavy shoes her mother had insisted on her wearing for the road. The slippers pinched abominably, but nobody would have suspected it as Rilla tripped smilingly up the steps, her soft dark eyes glowing and questioning, her colour deepening richly on her round, creamy cheeks. The very minute she reached the top of the steps an over-harbour boy asked her to dance and the next moment they were in the pavilion that had been built seaward of the lighthouse for dances. It was a delightful spot, roofed over with fir-boughs and hung with lanterns. Beyond was the sea in a radiance that glowed and shimmered, to the left the moonlit crests and hollows of the sand-dunes, to the right the rocky shore with its inky shadows and its crystalline coves. Rilla and her partner swung in among the dancers; she drew a long breath of delight; what witching music Ned Burr of the Upper Glen was coaxing from his fiddle—it was really like the magical pipes of the old tale which compelled all who heard them to dance. How cool and fresh the gulf breeze blew; how white and wonderful the moonlight was over everything! This was life—enchanting life. Rilla felt as if her feet and her soul both had wings.

CHAPTER IV - THE PIPER PIPES

Rilla's first party was a triumph—or so it seemed at first. She had so many partners that she had to split her dances. Her silver slippers seemed verily to dance of themselves and though they continued to pinch her toes and blister her heels that did not interfere with her enjoyment in the least. Ethel Reese gave her a bad ten minutes by beckoning her mysteriously out of the pavilion and whispering, with a Reese-like smirk, that her dress gaped behind and that there was a stain on the flounce. Rilla rushed miserably to the room in the lighthouse which was fitted up for a temporary ladies' dressing-room, and discovered that the stain was merely a tiny grass smear and that the gap was equally tiny where a hook had pulled loose. Irene Howard fastened it up for her and gave her some over-sweet, condescending compliments. Rilla felt flattered by Irene's condescension. She was an Upper Glen girl of nineteen who seemed to like the society of the younger girls—spiteful friends said because she could queen it over them without rivalry. But Rilla thought Irene quite wonderful and loved her for her patronage. Irene was pretty and stylish; she sang divinely and spent every winter in Charlottetown taking music lessons. She had an aunt in Montreal who sent her wonderful things to wear; she was reported to have had a sad love affair—nobody knew just what, but its very mystery allured. Rilla felt that Irene's compliments crowned her evening. She ran gaily back to the pavilion and lingered for a moment in the glow of the lanterns at the entrance looking at the dancers. A momentary break in the whirling throng gave her a glimpse of Kenneth Ford standing at the other side.

Rilla's heart skipped a beat—or, if that be a physiological impossibility, she thought it did. So he was here, after all. She had concluded he was not coming—not that it mattered in the least. Would he see her? Would he take any notice of her? Of course, he wouldn't ask her to dance—that couldn't be hoped for. He thought her just a mere child. He had called her "Spider" not three weeks ago when he had been at Ingleside one evening. She had cried about it upstairs afterwards and hated him. But her heart skipped a beat when she saw that he was edging his way round the side of the pavilion towards her. Was he coming to her—was he?—was he?—yes, he was! He was looking for her—he was here beside her—he was gazing down at her with something in his dark grey eyes that Rilla had never seen in them. Oh, it was almost too much to bear! and everything was going on as before—the dancers were spinning round, the boys who couldn't get partners were hanging about the pavilion, canoodling couples were sitting out on the rocks—nobody seemed to realize what a stupendous thing had happened.

Kenneth was a tall lad, very good looking, with a certain careless grace of bearing that somehow made all the other boys seem stiff and awkward by contrast. He was reported to be awesomely clever, with the glamour of a far-away city and a big university hanging around him. He had also the reputation of being a bit of a lady-killer. But that probably accrued to him from his possession of a laughing, velvety voice which no girl could hear without a heartbeat, and a dangerous way of listening as if she were saying something that he had longed all his life to hear.

"Is this Rilla-my-Rilla?" he asked in a low tone.

"Yeth," said Rilla, and immediately wished she could throw herself headlong down the lighthouse rock or otherwise vanish from a jeering world.

Rilla had lisped in early childhood; but she had grown out of it. Only on occasions of stress and strain did the tendency re-assert itself. She hadn't lisped for a year; and now at this very moment, when she was so especially desirous of appearing grown up and sophisticated, she must go and lisp like a baby! It was too mortifying; she felt as if tears were going to come into her eyes; the next minute she would be—blubbering—yes, just blubbering—she wished Kenneth would go away—she wished he had never come. The party was spoiled. Everything had turned to dust and ashes.

And he had called her "Rilla-my-Rilla"—not "Spider" or "Kid" or "Puss," as he had been used to call her when he took any notice whatever of her. She did not at all resent his using Walter's pet name for her; it sounded beautifully in his low caressing tones, with just the faintest suggestion of emphasis on the "my." It would have been so nice if she had not made a fool of herself. She dared not look up lest she should see laughter in his eyes. So she looked down; and as her lashes were very long and dark and her lids very thick and creamy, the effect was quite charming and provocative, and Kenneth reflected that Rilla Blythe was going to be the beauty of the Ingleside girls after all. He wanted to make her look up—to catch again that little, demure, questioning glance. She was the prettiest thing at the party, there was no doubt of that.

What was he saying? Rilla could hardly believe her ears.

"Can we have a dance?"

"Yes," said Rilla. She said it with such a fierce determination not to lisp that she fairly blurted the word out. Then she writhed in spirit again. It sounded so bold—so eager—as if she were fairly jumping at him! What would he think of her? Oh, why did dreadful things like this happen, just when a girl wanted to appear at her best?

Kenneth drew her in among the dancers.

"I think this game ankle of mine is good for one hop around, at least," he said.

"How is your ankle?" said Rilla. Oh, why couldn't she think of something else to say? She knew he was sick of inquiries about his ankle. She had heard him say so at Ingleside—heard him tell Di he was going to wear a placard on his breast announcing to all and sundry that the ankle was improving, etc. And now she must go and ask this stale question again.

Kenneth was tired of inquiries about his ankle. But then he had not often been asked about it by lips with such an adorable kissable dent just above them. Perhaps that was why he answered very patiently that it was getting on well and didn't trouble him much, if he didn't walk or stand too long at a time.

"They tell me it will be as strong as ever in time, but I'll have to cut football out this fall."

They danced together and Rilla knew every girl in sight envied her. After the dance they went down the rock steps and Kenneth found a little flat and they rowed across the moonlit channel to the sand-shore; they walked on the sand till Kenneth's ankle made protest and then they sat down among the dunes. Kenneth talked to her as he had talked to Nan and Di. Rilla, overcome with a shyness she did not understand, could not talk much, and thought he would think her frightfully stupid; but in spite of this it was all very wonderful—the exquisite moonlit night, the shining sea, the tiny little wavelets swishing on the sand, the cool and freakish wind of night crooning in the stiff grasses on the crest of the dunes, the music sounding faintly and sweetly over the channel.

"'A merry lilt o' moonlight for mermaiden revelry,'" quoted Kenneth softly from one of Walter's poems.

And just he and she alone together in the glamour of sound and sight! If only her slippers didn't bite so! and if only she could talk cleverly like Miss Oliver—nay, if she could only talk as she did herself to other boys! But words would not come, she could only listen and murmur little commonplace sentences now and again. But perhaps her dreamy eyes and her dented lip and her slender throat talked eloquently for her. At any rate Kenneth seemed in no hurry to suggest going back and when they did go back supper was in progress. He found a seat for her near the window of the lighthouse kitchen and sat on the sill beside her while she ate her ices and cake. Rilla looked about her and thought how lovely her first party had been. She would never forget it. The room re-echoed to laughter and jest. Beautiful young eyes sparkled and shone. From the pavilion outside came the lilt of the fiddle and the rhythmic steps of the dancers.

There was a little disturbance among a group of boys crowded about the door; a young fellow pushed through and halted on the threshold, looking about him rather sombrely. It was Jack Elliott from over-harbour—a McGill medical student, a quiet chap not much addicted to social doings. He had been invited to the party but had not been expected to come since he had to go to Charlottetown that day and could not be back until late. Yet here he was—and he carried a folded paper in his hand.

Gertrude Oliver looked at him from her corner and shivered again. She had enjoyed the party herself, after all, for she had foregathered with a Charlottetown acquaintance who, being a stranger and much older than most of the guests, felt himself rather out of it, and had been glad to fall in with this clever girl who could talk of world doings and outside events with the zest and vigour of a man. In the pleasure of his society she had forgotten some of her misgivings of the day. Now they suddenly returned to her. What news did Jack Elliott bring? Lines from an old poem flashed unbidden into her mind—"there was a sound of revelry by night"—"Hush! Hark! A deep sound strikes like a rising knell"—why should she think of that now? Why didn't Jack Elliott speak—if he had anything to tell? Why did he just stand there, glowering importantly?

"Ask him—ask him," she said feverishly to Allan Daly. But somebody else had already asked him. The room grew very silent all at once. Outside the fiddler had stopped for a rest and there was silence there too. Afar off they heard the low moan of the gulf—the presage of a storm already on its way up the Atlantic. A girl's laugh drifted up from the rocks and died away as if frightened out of existence by the sudden stillness.

"England declared war on Germany today," said Jack Elliott slowly. "The news came by wire just as I left town."

"God help us," whispered Gertrude Oliver under her breath. "My dream—my dream! The first wave has broken." She looked at Allan Daly and tried to smile.

"Is this Armageddon?" she asked.

"I am afraid so," he said gravely.

A chorus of exclamations had arisen round them—light surprise and idle interest for the most part. Few there realized the import of the message—fewer still realized that it meant anything to them. Before long the dancing was on again and the hum of pleasure was as loud as ever. Gertrude and Allan Daly talked the news over in low, troubled tones. Walter Blythe had turned pale and left the room. Outside he met Jem, hurrying up the rock steps.

"Have you heard the news, Jem?"

"Yes. The Piper has come. Hurrah! I knew England wouldn't leave France in the lurch. I've been trying to get Captain Josiah to hoist the flag but he says it isn't the proper caper till sunrise. Jack says they'll be calling for volunteers tomorrow."

"What a fuss to make over nothing," said Mary Vance disdainfully as Jem dashed off. She was sitting out with Miller Douglas on a lobster trap which was not only an unromantic but an uncomfortable seat. But Mary and Miller were both supremely happy on it. Miller Douglas was a big, strapping, uncouth lad, who thought Mary Vance's tongue uncommonly gifted and Mary Vance's white eyes stars of the first magnitude; and neither of them had the least inkling why Jem Blythe wanted to hoist the lighthouse flag. "What does it matter if there's going to be a war over there in Europe? I'm sure it doesn't concern us."

Walter looked at her and had one of his odd visitations of prophecy.

"Before this war is over," he said—or something said through his lips—"every man and woman and child in Canada will feel it—you, Mary, will feel it—feel it to your heart's core. You will weep tears of blood over it. The Piper has come—and he will pipe until every corner of the world has heard his awful and irresistible music. It will be years before the dance of death is over—years, Mary. And in those years millions of hearts will break."

"Fancy now!" said Mary who always said that when she couldn't think of anything else to say. She didn't know what Walter meant but she felt uncomfortable. Walter Blythe was always saying odd things. That old Piper of his—she hadn't heard anything about him since their playdays in Rainbow Valley—and now here he was bobbing up again. She didn't like it, and that was the long and short of it.

"Aren't you painting it rather strong, Walter?" asked Harvey Crawford, coming up just then. "This war won't last for years—it'll be over in a month or two. England will just wipe Germany off the map in no time."

"Do you think a war for which Germany has been preparing for twenty years will be over in a few weeks?" said Walter passionately. "This isn't a paltry struggle in a Balkan corner, Harvey. It is a death grapple. Germany comes to conquer or to die. And do you know what will happen if she conquers? Canada will be a German colony."

"Well, I guess a few things will happen before that," said Harvey shrugging his shoulders. "The British navy would have to be licked for one; and for another, Miller here, now, and I, we'd raise a dust, wouldn't we, Miller? No Germans need apply for this old country, eh?"

Harvey ran down the steps laughing.

"I declare, I think all you boys talk the craziest stuff," said Mary Vance in disgust. She got up and dragged Miller off to the rock-shore. It didn't happen often that they had a chance for a talk together; Mary was determined that this one shouldn't be spoiled by Walter Blythe's silly blather about Pipers and Germans and such like absurd things. They left Walter standing alone on the rock steps, looking out over the beauty of Four Winds with brooding eyes that saw it not.

The best of the evening was over for Rilla, too. Ever since Jack Elliott's announcement, she had sensed that Kenneth was no longer thinking about her. She felt suddenly lonely and unhappy. It was worse than if he had never noticed her at all. Was life like this—something delightful happening and then, just as you were revelling in it, slipping away from you? Rilla told herself pathetically that she felt years older than when she had left home that evening. Perhaps she did—perhaps she was. Who knows? It does not do to laugh at the pangs of youth. They are very terrible because youth has not yet learned that "this, too, will pass away." Rilla sighed and wished she were home, in bed, crying into her pillow.

"Tired?" said Kenneth, gently but absently—oh, so absently. He really didn't care a bit whether she were tired or not, she thought.

"Kenneth," she ventured timidly, "you don't think this war will matter much to us in Canada, do you?"

"Matter? Of course it will matter to the lucky fellows who will be able to take a hand. I won't—thanks to this confounded ankle. Rotten luck, I call it."

"I don't see why we should fight England's battles," cried Rilla. "She's quite able to fight them herself."

"That isn't the point. We are part of the British Empire. It's a family affair. We've got to stand by each other. The worst of it is, it will be over before I can be of any use."

"Do you mean that you would really volunteer to go if it wasn't for your ankle? asked Rilla incredulously.

"Sure I would. You see they'll go by thousands. Jem'll be off, I'll bet a cent—Walter won't be strong enough yet, I suppose. And Jerry Meredith—he'll go! And I was worrying about being out of football this year!"

Rilla was too startled to say anything. Jem—and Jerry! Nonsense! Why father and Mr. Meredith wouldn't allow it. They weren't through college. Oh, why hadn't Jack Elliott kept his horrid news to himself?

Mark Warren came up and asked her to dance. Rilla went, knowing Kenneth didn't care whether she went or stayed. An hour ago on the sand-shore he had been looking at her as if she were the only being of any importance in the world. And now she was nobody. His thoughts were full of this Great Game which was to be played out on bloodstained fields with empires for stakes—a Game in which womenkind could have no part. Women, thought Rilla miserably, just had to sit and cry at home. But all this was foolishness. Kenneth couldn't go—he admitted that himself—and Walter couldn't—thank goodness for that—and Jem and Jerry would have more sense. She wouldn't worry—she would enjoy herself. But how awkward Mark Warren was! How he bungled his steps! Why, for mercy's sake, did boys try to dance who didn't know the first thing about dancing; and who had feet as big as boats? There, he had bumped her into somebody! She would never dance with him again!

She danced with others, though the zest was gone out of the performance and she had begun to realize that her slippers hurt her badly. Kenneth seemed to have gone—at least nothing was to be seen of him. Her first party was spoiled, though it had seemed so beautiful at one time. Her head ached—her toes burned. And worse was yet to come. She had gone down with some over-harbour friends to the rock-shore where they all lingered as dance after dance went on above them. It was cool and pleasant and they were tired. Rilla sat silent, taking no part in the gay conversation. She was glad when someone called down that the over-harbour boats were leaving. A laughing scramble up the lighthouse rock followed. A few couples still whirled about in the pavilion but the crowd had thinned out. Rilla looked about her for the Glen group. She could not see one of them. She ran into the lighthouse. Still, no sign of anybody. In dismay she ran to the rock steps, down which the over-harbour guests were hurrying. She could see the boats below—where was Jem's—where was Joe's?

"Why, Rilla Blythe, I thought you'd be gone home long ago," said Mary Vance, who was waving her scarf at a boat skimming up the channel, skippered by Miller Douglas.

"Where are the rest?" gasped Rilla.

"Why, they're gone—Jem went an hour ago—Una had a headache. And the rest went with Joe about fifteen minutes ago. See—they're just going around Birch Point. I didn't go because it's getting rough and I knew I'd be seasick. I don't mind walking home from here. It's only a mile and a half. I s'posed you'd gone. Where were you?"

"Down on the rocks with Jem and Mollie Crawford. Oh, why didn't they look for me?"

"They did—but you couldn't be found. Then they concluded you must have gone in the other boat. Don't worry. You can stay all night with me and we'll 'phone up to Ingleside where you are."

Rilla realized that there was nothing else to do. Her lips trembled and tears came into her eyes. She blinked savagely—she would not let Mary Vance see her crying. But to be forgotten like this! To think nobody had thought it worth while to make sure where she was—not even Walter. Then she had a sudden dismayed recollection.

"My shoes," she exclaimed. "I left them in the boat."

"Well, I never," said Mary. "You're the most thoughtless kid I ever saw. You'll have to ask Hazel Lewison to lend you a pair of shoes."

"I won't." cried Rilla, who didn't like the said Hazel. "I'll go barefoot first."

Mary shrugged her shoulders.

"Just as you like. Pride must suffer pain. It'll teach you to be more careful. Well, let's hike."

Accordingly they hiked. But to "hike" along a deep-rutted, pebbly lane in frail, silver-hued slippers with high French heels, is not an exhilarating performance. Rilla managed to limp and totter along until they reached the harbour road; but she could go no farther in those detestable slippers. She took them and her dear silk stockings off and started barefoot. That was not pleasant either; her feet were very tender and the pebbles and ruts of the road hurt them. Her blistered heels smarted. But physical pain was almost forgotten in the sting of humiliation. This was a nice predicament! If Kenneth Ford could see her now, limping along like a little girl with a stone bruise! Oh, what a horrid way for her lovely party to end! She just had to cry—it was too terrible. Nobody cared for her—nobody bothered about her at all. Well, if she caught cold from walking home barefoot on a dew-wet road and went into a decline perhaps they would be sorry. She furtively wiped her tears away with her scarf—handkerchiefs seemed to have vanished like shoes!—but she could not help sniffling. Worse and worse!

"You've got a cold, I see," said Mary. "You ought to have known you would, sitting down in the wind on those rocks. Your mother won't let you go out again in a hurry I can tell you. It's certainly been something of a party. The Lewisons know how to do things, I'll say that for them, though Hazel Lewison is no choice of mine. My, how black she looked when she saw you dancing with Ken Ford. And so did that little hussy of an Ethel Reese. What a flirt he is!"

"I don't think he's a flirt," said Rilla as defiantly as two desperate sniffs would let her.

"You'll know more about men when you're as old as I am," said Mary patronizingly. "Mind you, it doesn't do to believe all they tell you. Don't let Ken Ford think that all he has to do to get you on a string is to drop his handkerchief. Have more spirit than that, child."

To be thus hectored and patronized by Mary Vance was unendurable! And it was unendurable to walk on stony roads with blistered heels and bare feet! And it was unendurable to be crying and have no handkerchief and not to be able to stop crying!

"I'm not thinking"—sniff—"about Kenneth"—sniff—"Ford"—two sniffs—"at all," cried tortured Rilla.

"There's no need to fly off the handle, child. You ought to be willing to take advice from older people. I saw how you slipped over to the sands with Ken and stayed there ever so long with him. Your mother wouldn't like it if she knew."

"I'll tell my mother all about it—and Miss Oliver—and Walter," Rilla gasped between sniffs. "You sat for hours with Miller Douglas on that lobster trap, Mary Vance! What would Mrs. Elliott say to that if she knew?"

"Oh, I'm not going to quarrel with you," said Mary, suddenly retreating to high and lofty ground. "All I say is, you should wait until you're grown-up before you do things like that."

Rilla gave up trying to hide the fact that she was crying. Everything was spoiled—even that beautiful, dreamy, romantic, moonlit hour with Kenneth on the sands was vulgarized and cheapened. She loathed Mary Vance.

"Why, whatever's wrong?" cried mystified Mary. "What are you crying for?"

"My feet—hurt so—" sobbed Rilla clinging to the last shred of her pride. It was less humiliating to admit crying because of your feet than because—because somebody had been amusing himself with you, and your friends had forgotten you, and other people patronized you.

"I daresay they do," said Mary, not unkindly. "Never mind. I know where there's a pot of goose-grease in Cornelia's tidy pantry and it beats all the fancy cold creams in the world. I'll put some on your heels before you go to bed."

Goose-grease on your heels! So this was what your first party and your first beau and your first moonlit romance ended in!

Rilla gave over crying in sheer disgust at the futility of tears and went to sleep in Mary Vance's bed in the calm of despair. Outside, the dawn came greyly in on wings of storm; Captain Josiah, true to his word, ran up the Union Jack at the Four Winds Light and it streamed on the fierce wind against the clouded sky like a gallant unquenchable beacon.

CHAPTER V - "THE SOUND OF A GOING"

Rilla ran down through the sunlit glory of the maple grove behind Ingleside, to her favourite nook in Rainbow Valley. She sat down on a green-mossed stone among the fern, propped her chin on her hands and stared unseeingly at the dazzling blue sky of the August afternoon—so blue, so peaceful, so unchanged, just as it had arched over the valley in the mellow days of late summer ever since she could remember.

She wanted to be alone—to think things out—to adjust herself, if it were possible, to the new world into which she seemed to have been transplanted with a suddenness and completeness that left her half bewildered as to her own identity. Was she—could she be—the same Rilla Blythe who had danced at Four Winds Light six days ago—only six days ago? It seemed to Rilla that she had lived as much in those six days as in all her previous life—and if it be true that we should count time by heart-throbs she had. That evening, with its hopes and fears and triumphs and humiliations, seemed like ancient history now. Could she really ever have cried just because she had been forgotten and had to walk home with Mary Vance? Ah, thought Rilla sadly, how trivial and absurd such a cause of tears now appeared to her. She could cry now with a right good will—but she would not—she must not. What was it mother had said, looking, with her white lips and stricken eyes, as Rilla had never seen her mother look before,

> "When our women fail in courage,
> Shall our men be fearless still?"

Yes, that was it. She must be brave—like mother—and Nan—and Faith—Faith, who had cried with flashing eyes, "Oh, if I were only a man, to go too!" Only, when her eyes ached and her throat burned like this she had to hide herself in Rainbow Valley for a little, just to think things out and remember that she wasn't a child any longer—she was grown-up and women had to face things like this. But it was—nice—to get away alone now and then, where nobody could see her and where she needn't feel that people thought her a little coward if some tears came in spite of her.

How sweet and woodsey the ferns smelled! How softly the great feathery boughs of the firs waved and murmured over her! How elfinly rang the bells of the "Tree Lovers"—just a tinkle now and then as the breeze swept by! How purple and elusive the haze where incense was being offered on many an altar of the hills! How the maple leaves whitened in the wind until the grove seemed covered with pale silvery blossoms! Everything was just the same as she had seen it hundreds of times; and yet the whole face of the world seemed changed.

"How wicked I was to wish that something dramatic would happen!" she thought. "Oh, if we could only have those dear, monotonous, pleasant days back again! I would never, never grumble about them again."

Rilla's world had tumbled to pieces the very day after the party. As they lingered around the dinner table at Ingleside, talking of the war, the telephone had rung. It was a long-distance call from Charlottetown for Jem. When he had finished talking he hung up the receiver and turned around, with a flushed face and glowing eyes. Before he had said a word his mother and Nan and Di had turned pale. As for Rilla, for the first time in her life she felt that every one must hear her heart beating and that something had clutched at her throat.

"They are calling for volunteers in town, father," said Jem. "Scores have joined up already. I'm going in tonight to enlist."

"Oh—Little Jem," cried Mrs. Blythe brokenly. She had not called him that for many years—not since the day he had rebelled against it. "Oh—no—no—Little Jem."

"I must, mother. I'm right—am I not, father?" said Jem.

Dr. Blythe had risen. He was very pale, too, and his voice was husky. But he did not hesitate.

"Yes, Jem, yes—if you feel that way, yes—"

Mrs. Blythe covered her face. Walter stared moodily at his plate. Nan and Di clasped each others' hands. Shirley tried to look unconcerned. Susan sat as if paralysed, her piece of pie half-eaten on her plate. Susan never did finish that piece of pie—a fact which bore eloquent testimony to the upheaval in her inner woman for Susan considered it a cardinal offence against civilized society to begin to eat anything and not finish it. That was wilful waste, hens to the contrary notwithstanding.

Jem turned to the phone again. "I must ring the manse. Jerry will want to go, too."

At this Nan had cried out "Oh!" as if a knife had been thrust into her, and rushed from the room. Di followed her. Rilla turned to Walter for comfort but Walter was lost to her in some reverie she could not share.

"All right," Jem was saying, as coolly as if he were arranging the details of a picnic. "I thought you would—yes, tonight—the seven o'clock—meet me at the station. So long."

"Mrs. Dr. dear," said Susan. "I wish you would wake me up. Am I dreaming—or am I awake? Does that blessed boy realize what he is saying? Does he mean that he is going to enlist as a soldier? You do not mean to tell me that they want children like him! It is an outrage. Surely you and the doctor will not permit it."

"We can't stop him," said Mrs. Blythe, chokingly. "Oh, Gilbert!"

CHAPTER V - "THE SOUND OF A GOING"

Dr. Blythe came up behind his wife and took her hand gently, looking down into the sweet grey eyes that he had only once before seen filled with such imploring anguish as now. They both thought of that other time—the day years ago in the House of Dreams when little Joyce had died.

"Would you have him stay, Anne—when the others are going—when he thinks it his duty—would you have him so selfish and small-souled?"

"No—no! But—oh—our first-born son—he's only a lad—Gilbert—I'll try to be brave after a while—just now I can't. It's all come so suddenly. Give me time."

The doctor and his wife went out of the room. Jem had gone—Walter had gone—Shirley got up to go. Rilla and Susan remained staring at each other across the deserted table. Rilla had not yet cried—she was too stunned for tears. Then she saw that Susan was crying—Susan, whom she had never seen shed a tear before.

"Oh, Susan, will he really go?" she asked.

"It—it—it is just ridiculous, that is what it is," said Susan.

She wiped away her tears, gulped resolutely and got up.

"I am going to wash the dishes. That has to be done, even if everybody has gone crazy. There now, dearie, do not you cry. Jem will go, most likely—but the war will be over long before he gets anywhere near it. Let us take a brace and not worry your poor mother."

"In the Enterprise today it was reported that Lord Kitchener says the war will last three years," said Rilla dubiously.

"I am not acquainted with Lord Kitchener," said Susan, composedly, "but I dare say he makes mistakes as often as other people. Your father says it will be over in a few months and I have as much faith in his opinion as I have in Lord Anybody's. So just let us be calm and trust in the Almighty and get this place tidied up. I am done with crying which is a waste of time and discourages everybody."

Jem and Jerry went to Charlottetown that night and two days later they came back in khaki. The Glen hummed with excitement over it. Life at Ingleside had suddenly become a tense, strained, thrilling thing. Mrs. Blythe and Nan were brave and smiling and wonderful. Already Mrs. Blythe and Miss Cornelia were organizing a Red Cross. The doctor and Mr. Meredith were rounding up the men for a Patriotic Society. Rilla, after the first shock, reacted to the romance of it all, in spite of her heartache. Jem certainly looked magnificent in his uniform. It was splendid to think of the lads of Canada answering so speedily and fearlessly and uncalculatingly to the call of their country. Rilla carried her head high among the girls whose brothers had not so responded. In her diary she wrote:

"He goes to do what I had done
Had Douglas's daughter been his son,"

and was sure she meant it. If she were a boy of course she would go, too! She hadn't the least doubt of that.

She wondered if it was very dreadful of her to feel glad that Walter hadn't got strong as soon as they had wished after the fever.

"I couldn't bear to have Walter go," she wrote. "I love Jem ever so much but Walter means more to me than anyone in the world and I would die if he had to go. He seems so changed these days. He hardly ever talks to me. I suppose he wants to go, too, and feels badly because he can't. He doesn't go about with Jem and Jerry at all. I shall never forget Susan's face when Jem came home in his khaki. It worked and twisted as if she were going to cry, but all she said was, 'You look almost like a man in that, Jem.' Jem laughed. He never minds because Susan thinks him just a child still. Everybody seems busy but me. I wish there was something I could do but there doesn't seem to be anything. Mother and Nan and Di are busy all the time and I just wander about like a lonely ghost. What hurts me terribly, though, is that mother's smiles, and Nan's, just seem put on from the outside. Mother's eyes never laugh now. It makes me feel that I shouldn't laugh either—that it's wicked to feel laughy. And it's so hard for me to keep from laughing, even if Jem is going to be a soldier. But when I laugh I don't enjoy it either, as I used to do. There's something behind it all that keeps hurting me—especially when I wake up in the night. Then I cry because I am afraid that Kitchener of Khartoum is right and the war will last for years and Jem may be—but no, I won't write it. It would make me feel as if it were really going to happen. The other day Nan said, 'Nothing can ever be quite the same for any of us again.' It made me feel rebellious. Why shouldn't things be the same again—when everything is over and Jem and Jerry are back? We'll all be happy and jolly again and these days will seem just like a bad dream.

"The coming of the mail is the most exciting event of every day now. Father just snatches the paper—I never saw father snatch before—and the rest of us crowd round and look at the headlines over his shoulder. Susan vows she does not and will not believe a word the papers say but she always comes to the kitchen door, and listens and then goes back, shaking her head. She is terribly indignant all the time, but she cooks up all the things Jem likes especially, and she did not make a single bit of fuss when she found Monday asleep on the spare-room bed yesterday right on top of Mrs. Rachel Lynde's apple-leaf spread. 'The Almighty only knows where your master will be having to sleep before long, you poor dumb beast,' she said as she put him quite gently out. But she never relents towards Doc. She says the minute he saw Jem in khaki he turned into Mr. Hyde then and there and she thinks that ought to be proof enough of what he really is. Susan is funny, but she is an old dear. Shirley says she is one half angel and the other half good cook. But then Shirley is the only one of us she never scolds.

"Faith Meredith is wonderful. I think she and Jem are really engaged now. She goes about with a shining light in her eyes, but her smiles are a little stiff and starched, just like mother's. I wonder if I could be as brave as she is if I had a lover and he was going to the war. It is bad enough when it is your brother. Bruce Meredith cried all night, Mrs. Meredith says, when he heard Jem and Jerry were going. And he wanted to know if the 'K. of K.' his father talked about was the King of Kings. He is the dearest kiddy. I just love him—though I don't really care much for children. I don't like babies one bit—though when I say so people look at me as if I had said something perfectly shocking. Well, I don't, and I've got to be honest about it. I don't mind looking at a nice clean baby if somebody else holds it—but I wouldn't touch it for anything and I don't feel a single real spark of interest in it. Gertrude Oliver says she just feels the same. (She is the most honest person I know. She never pretends anything.) She says babies bore her until they are old enough to talk and then she likes them—but still a good ways off. Mother and Nan and Di all adore babies and seem to think I'm unnatural because I don't.

"I haven't seen Kenneth since the night of the party. He was here one evening after Jem came back but I happened to be away. I don't think he mentioned me at all—at least nobody told me he did and I was determined I wouldn't ask—but I don't care in the least. All that matters absolutely nothing to me now. The only thing that does matter is that Jem has volunteered for active service and will be going to Valcartier in a few more days—my big, splendid brother Jem. Oh, I'm so proud of him!

"I suppose Kenneth would enlist too if it weren't for his ankle. I think that is quite providential. He is his mother's only son and how dreadful she would feel if he went. Only sons should never think of going!"

Walter came wandering through the valley as Rilla sat there, with his head bent and his hands clasped behind him. When he saw Rilla he turned abruptly away; then as abruptly he turned and came back to her.

"Rilla-my-Rilla, what are you thinking of?"

"Everything is so changed, Walter," said Rilla wistfully. "Even you—you're changed. A week ago we were all so happy—and—and—now I just can't find myself at all. I'm lost."

Walter sat down on a neighbouring stone and took Rilla's little appealing hand.

"I'm afraid our old world has come to an end, Rilla. We've got to face that fact."

"It's so terrible to think of Jem," pleaded Rilla. "Sometimes I forget for a little while what it really means and feel excited and proud—and then it comes over me again like a cold wind."

"I envy Jem!" said Walter moodily.

"Envy Jem! Oh, Walter you—you don't want to go too."

"No," said Walter, gazing straight before him down the emerald vistas of the valley, "no, I don't want to go. That's just the trouble. Rilla, I'm afraid to go. I'm a coward."

"You're not!" Rilla burst out angrily. "Why, anybody would be afraid to go. You might be—why, you might be killed."

"I wouldn't mind that if it didn't hurt," muttered Walter. "I don't think I'm afraid of death itself—it's of the pain that might come before death—it wouldn't be so bad to die and have it over—but to keep on dying! Rilla, I've always been afraid of pain—you know that. I can't help it—I shudder when I think of the possibility of being mangled or—or blinded. Rilla, I cannot face that thought. To be blind—never to see the beauty of the world again—moonlight on Four Winds—

the stars twinkling through the fir-trees—mist on the gulf. I ought to go—I ought to want to go—but I don't—I hate the thought of it—I'm ashamed—ashamed."

"But, Walter, you couldn't go anyhow," said Rilla piteously. She was sick with a new terror that Walter would go after all. "You're not strong enough."

"I am. I've felt as fit as ever I did this last month. I'd pass any examination—I know it. Everybody thinks I'm not strong yet—and I'm skulking behind that belief. I—I should have been a girl," Walter concluded in a burst of passionate bitterness.

"Even if you were strong enough, you oughtn't to go," sobbed Rilla. "What would mother do? She's breaking her heart over Jem. It would kill her to see you both go."

"Oh, I'm not going—don't worry. I tell you I'm afraid to go—afraid. I don't mince the matter to myself. It's a relief to own up even to you, Rilla. I wouldn't confess it to anybody else—Nan and Di would despise me. But I hate the whole thing—the horror, the pain, the ugliness. War isn't a khaki uniform or a drill parade—everything I've read in old histories haunts me. I lie awake at night and see things that have happened—see the blood and filth and misery of it all. And a bayonet charge! If I could face the other things I could never face that. It turns me sick to think of it—sicker even to think of giving it than receiving it—to think of thrusting a bayonet through another man." Walter writhed and shuddered. "I think of these things all the time—and it doesn't seem to me that Jem and Jerry ever think of them. They laugh and talk about 'potting Huns'! But it maddens me to see them in the khaki. And they think I'm grumpy because I'm not fit to go."

Walter laughed bitterly. "It is not a nice thing to feel yourself a coward." But Rilla got her arms about him and cuddled her head on his shoulder. She was so glad he didn't want to go—for just one minute she had been horribly frightened. And it was so nice to have Walter confiding his troubles to her—to her, not Di. She didn't feel so lonely and superfluous any longer.

"Don't you despise me, Rilla-my-Rilla?" asked Walter wistfully. Somehow, it hurt him to think Rilla might despise him—hurt him as much as if it had been Di. He realized suddenly how very fond he was of this adoring kid sister with her appealing eyes and troubled, girlish face.

"No, I don't. Why, Walter, hundreds of people feel just as you do. You know what that verse of Shakespeare in the old Fifth Reader says—'the brave man is not he who feels no fear.'"

"No—but it is 'he whose noble soul its fear subdues.' I don't do that. We can't gloss it over, Rilla. I'm a coward."

"You're not. Think of how you fought Dan Reese long ago."

"One spurt of courage isn't enough for a lifetime."

"Walter, one time I heard father say that the trouble with you was a sensitive nature and a vivid imagination. You feel things before they really come—feel them all alone when there isn't anything to help you bear them—to take away from them. It isn't anything to be ashamed of. When you and Jem got your hands burned when the grass was fired on the sand-hills two years ago Jem made twice the fuss over the pain that you did. As for this horrid old war, there'll be plenty to go without you. It won't last long."

"I wish I could believe it. Well, it's supper-time, Rilla. You'd better run. I don't want anything."

"Neither do I. I couldn't eat a mouthful. Let me stay here with you, Walter. It's such a comfort to talk things over with someone. The rest all think that I'm too much of a baby to understand."

So they two sat there in the old valley until the evening star shone through a pale-grey, gauzy cloud over the maple grove, and a fragrant dewy darkness filled their little sylvan dell. It was one of the evenings Rilla was to treasure in remembrance all her life—the first one on which Walter had ever talked to her as if she were a woman and not a child. They comforted and strengthened each other. Walter felt, for the time being at least, that it was not such a despicable thing after all to dread the horror of war; and Rilla was glad to be made the confidante of his struggles—to sympathize with and encourage him. She was of importance to somebody.

When they went back to Ingleside they found callers sitting on the veranda. Mr. and Mrs. Meredith had come over from the manse, and Mr. and Mrs. Norman Douglas had come up from the farm. Cousin Sophia was there also, sitting with Susan in the shadowy background. Mrs. Blythe and Nan and Di were away, but Dr. Blythe was home and so was Dr. Jekyll, sitting in golden majesty on the top step. And of course they were all talking of the war, except Dr. Jekyll who kept his own counsel and looked contempt as only a cat can. When two people foregathered in those days they talked of the war; and old Highland Sandy of the Harbour Head talked of it when he was alone and hurled anathemas at the Kaiser across all the acres of his farm. Walter slipped away, not caring to see or be seen, but Rilla sat down on the steps, where the garden mint was dewy and pungent. It was a very calm evening with a dim, golden afterlight irradiating the glen. She felt happier than at any time in the dreadful week that had passed. She was no longer haunted by the fear that Walter would go.

"I'd go myself if I was twenty years younger," Norman Douglas was shouting. Norman always shouted when he was excited. "I'd show the Kaiser a thing or two! Did I ever say there wasn't a hell? Of course there's a hell—dozens of hells—hundreds of hells—where the Kaiser and all his brood are bound for."

"I knew this war was coming," said Mrs. Norman triumphantly. "I saw it coming right along. I could have told all those stupid Englishmen what was ahead of them. I told you, John Meredith, years ago what the Kaiser was up to but you wouldn't believe it. You said he would never plunge the world in war. Who was right about the Kaiser, John? You—or I? Tell me that."

"You were, I admit," said Mr. Meredith.

"It's too late to admit it now," said Mrs. Norman, shaking her head, as if to intimate that if John Meredith had admitted it sooner there might have been no war.

"Thank God, England's navy is ready," said the doctor.

"Amen to that," nodded Mrs. Norman. "Bat-blind as most of them were somebody had foresight enough to see to that."

"Maybe England'll manage not to get into trouble over it," said Cousin Sophia plaintively. "I dunno. But I'm much afraid."

"One would suppose that England was in trouble over it already, up to her neck, Sophia Crawford," said Susan. "But your ways of thinking are beyond me and always were. It is my opinion that the British Navy will settle Germany in a jiffy and that we are all getting worked up over nothing."

Susan spat out the words as if she wanted to convince herself more than anybody else. She had her little store of homely philosophies to guide her through life, but she had nothing to buckler her against the thunderbolts of the week that had just passed. What had an honest, hard-working, Presbyterian old maid of Glen St. Mary to do with a war thousands of miles away? Susan felt that it was indecent that she should have to be disturbed by it.

"The British army will settle Germany," shouted Norman. "Just wait till it gets into line and the Kaiser will find that real war is a different thing from parading round Berlin with your moustaches cocked up."

"Britain hasn't got an army," said Mrs. Norman emphatically. "You needn't glare at me, Norman. Glaring won't make soldiers out of timothy stalks. A hundred thousand men will just be a mouthful for Germany's millions."

"There'll be some tough chewing in the mouthful, I reckon," persisted Norman valiantly. "Germany'll break her teeth on it. Don't you tell me one Britisher isn't a match for ten foreigners. I could polish off a dozen of 'em myself with both hands tied behind my back!"

"I am told," said Susan, "that old Mr. Pryor does not believe in this war. I am told that he says England went into it just because she was jealous of Germany and that she did not really care in the least what happened to Belgium."

"I believe he's been talking some such rot," said Norman. "I haven't heard him. When I do, Whiskers-on-the-moon won't know what happened to him. That precious relative of mine, Kitty Alec, holds forth to the same effect, I understand. Not before me, though—somehow, folks don't indulge in that kind of conversation in my presence. Lord love you, they've a kind of presentiment, so to speak, that it wouldn't be healthy for their complaint."

"I am much afraid that this war has been sent as a punishment for our sins," said Cousin Sophia, unclasping her pale hands from her lap and reclasping them solemnly over her stomach. "'The world is very evil—the times are waxing late.'"

"Parson here's got something of the same idea," chuckled Norman. "Haven't you, Parson? That's why you preached t'other night on the text 'Without shedding of blood there is no remission of sins.' I didn't agree with you—wanted to get up in the pew and shout out that there wasn't a word of sense in what you were saying, but Ellen, here, she held me down. I never have any fun sassing parsons since I got married."

"Without shedding of blood there is no anything," said Mr. Meredith, in the gentle dreamy way which had an unexpected trick of convincing his hearers.

"Everything, it seems to me, has to be purchased by self-sacrifice. Our race has marked every step of its painful ascent with blood. And now torrents of it must flow again. No, Mrs. Crawford, I don't think the war has been sent as a punishment for sin. I think it is the price humanity must pay for some blessing—some advance great enough to be worth the price—which we may not live to see but which our children's children will inherit."

"If Jerry is killed will you feel so fine about it?" demanded Norman, who had been saying things like that all his life and never could be made to see any reason why he shouldn't. "Now, never mind kicking me in the shins, Ellen. I want to see if Parson meant what he said or if it was just a pulpit frill."

Mr. Meredith's face quivered. He had had a terrible hour alone in his study on the night Jem and Jerry had gone to town. But he answered quietly.

"Whatever I felt, it could not alter my belief—my assurance that a country whose sons are ready to lay down their lives in her defence will win a new vision because of their sacrifice."

"You do mean it, Parson. I can always tell when people mean what they say. It's a gift that was born in me. Makes me a terror to most parsons, that! But I've never caught you yet saying anything you didn't mean. I'm always hoping I will—that's what reconciles me to going to church. It'd be such a comfort to me—such a weapon to batter Ellen here with when she tries to civilize me. Well, I'm off over the road to see Ab. Crawford a minute. The gods be good to you all."

"The old pagan!" muttered Susan, as Norman strode away. She did not care if Ellen Douglas did hear her. Susan could never understand why fire did not descend from heaven upon Norman Douglas when he insulted ministers the way he did. But the astonishing thing was Mr. Meredith seemed really to like his brother-in-law.

Rilla wished they would talk of something besides war. She had heard nothing else for a week and she was really a little tired of it. Now that she was relieved from her haunting fear that Walter would want to go it made her quite impatient. But she supposed—with a sigh—that there would be three or four months of it yet.

CHAPTER VI - SUSAN, RILLA, AND DOG MONTDAY MAKE A RESOLUTION

The big living-room at Ingleside was snowed over with drifts of white cotton. Word had come from Red Cross headquarters that sheets and bandages would be required. Nan and Di and Rilla were hard at work. Mrs. Blythe and Susan were upstairs in the boys' room, engaged in a more personal task. With dry, anguished eyes they were packing up Jem's belongings. He must leave for Valcartier the next morning. They had been expecting the word but it was none the less dreadful when it came.

Rilla was basting the hem of a sheet for the first time in her life. When the word had come that Jem must go she had her cry out among the pines in Rainbow Valley and then she had gone to her mother.

"Mother, I want to do something. I'm only a girl—I can't do anything to win the war—but I must do something to help at home."

"The cotton has come up for the sheets," said Mrs. Blythe. "You can help Nan and Di make them up. And Rilla, don't you think you could organize a Junior Red Cross among the young girls? I think they would like it better and do better work by themselves than if mixed up with the older people."

"But, mother—I've never done anything like that."

"We will all have to do a great many things in the months ahead of us that we have never done before, Rilla."

"Well"—Rilla took the plunge—"I'll try, mother—if you'll tell me how to begin. I have been thinking it all over and I have decided that I must be as brave and heroic and unselfish as I can possibly be."

Mrs. Blythe did not smile at Rilla's italics. Perhaps she did not feel like smiling or perhaps she detected a real grain of serious purpose behind Rilla's romantic pose. So here was Rilla hemming sheets and organizing a Junior Red Cross in her thoughts as she hemmed; moreover, she was enjoying it—the organizing that is, not the hemming. It was interesting and Rilla discovered a certain aptitude in herself for it that surprised her. Who would be president? Not she. The older girls would not like that. Irene Howard? No, somehow Irene was not quite as popular as she deserved to be. Marjorie Drew? No, Marjorie hadn't enough backbone. She was too prone to agree with the last speaker. Betty Mead—calm, capable, tactful

Betty—the very one! And Una Meredith for treasurer; and, if they were very insistent, they might make her, Rilla, secretary. As for the various committees, they must be chosen after the Juniors were organized, but Rilla knew just who should be put on which. They would meet around—and there must be no eats—Rilla knew she would have a pitched battle with Olive Kirk over that—and everything should be strictly business-like and constitutional. Her minute book should be covered in white with a Red Cross on the cover—and wouldn't it be nice to have some kind of uniform which they could all wear at the concerts they would have to get up to raise money—something simple but smart?

"You have basted the top hem of that sheet on one side and the bottom hem on the other," said Di.

Rilla picked out her stitches and reflected that she hated sewing. Running the Junior Reds would be much more interesting.

Mrs. Blythe was saying upstairs, "Susan, do you remember that first day Jem lifted up his little arms to me and called me 'mo'er'—the very first word he ever tried to say?"

"You could not mention anything about that blessed baby that I do not and will not remember till my dying day," said Susan drearily.

"Susan, I keep thinking today of once when he cried for me in the night. He was just a few months old. Gilbert didn't want me to go to him—he said the child was well and warm and that it would be fostering bad habits in him. But I went—and took him up—I can feel that tight clinging of his little arms round my neck yet. Susan, if I hadn't gone that night, twenty-one years ago, and taken my baby up when he cried for me I couldn't face tomorrow morning."

"I do not know how we are going to face it anyhow, Mrs. Dr. dear. But do not tell me that it will be the final farewell. He will be back on leave before he goes overseas, will he not?"

"We hope so but we are not very sure. I am making up my mind that he will not, so that there will be no disappointment to bear. Susan, I am determined that I will send my boy off tomorrow with a smile. He shall not carry away with him the remembrance of a weak mother who had not the courage to send when he had the courage to go. I hope none of us will cry."

"I am not going to cry, Mrs. Dr. dear, and that you may tie to, but whether I shall manage to smile or not will be as Providence ordains and as the pit of my stomach feels. Have you room there for this fruit-cake? And the shortbread? And the mince-pie? That blessed boy shall not starve, whether they have anything to eat in that Quebec place or not. Everything seems to be changing all at once, does it not? Even the old cat at the manse has passed away. He breathed his last at a quarter to ten last night and Bruce is quite heart-broken, they tell me."

"It's time that pussy went where good cats go. He must be at least fifteen years old. He has seemed so lonely since Aunt Martha died."

"I should not have lamented, Mrs. Dr. dear, if that Hyde-beast had died also. He has been Mr. Hyde most of the time since Jem came home in khaki, and that has a meaning I will maintain. I do not know what Monday will do when Jem is gone. The creature just goes about with a human look in his eyes that takes all the good out of me when I see it. Ellen West used to be always railing at the Kaiser and we thought her crazy, but now I see that there was a method in her madness. This tray is packed, Mrs. Dr. dear, and I will go down and put in my best licks preparing supper. I wish I knew when I would cook another supper for Jem but such things are hidden from our eyes."

Jem Blythe and Jerry Meredith left next morning. It was a dull day, threatening rain, and the clouds lay in heavy grey rolls over the sky; but almost everybody in the Glen and Four Winds and Harbour Head and Upper Glen and over-harbour—except Whiskers-on-the-moon—was there to see them off. The Blythe family and the Meredith family were all smiling. Even Susan, as Providence did ordain, wore a smile, though the effect was somewhat more painful than tears would have been. Faith and Nan were very pale and very gallant. Rilla thought she would get on very well if something in her throat didn't choke her, and if her lips didn't take such spells of trembling. Dog Monday was there, too. Jem had tried to say good-bye to him at Ingleside but Monday implored so eloquently that Jem relented and let him go to the station. He kept close to Jem's legs and watched every movement of his beloved master.

"I can't bear that dog's eyes," said Mrs. Meredith.

"The beast has more sense than most humans," said Mary Vance. "Well, did we any of us ever think we'd live to see this day? I bawled all night to think of Jem and Jerry going like this. I think they're plumb deranged. Miller got a maggot in his head about going but I soon talked him out of it—likewise his aunt said a few touching things. For once in our lives Kitty Alec and I agree. It's a miracle that isn't likely to happen again. There's Ken, Rilla."

Rilla knew Kenneth was there. She had been acutely conscious of it from the moment he had sprung from Leo West's buggy. Now he came up to her smiling.

"Doing the brave-smiling-sister-stunt, I see. What a crowd for the Glen to muster! Well, I'm off home in a few days myself."

A queer little wind of desolation that even Jem's going had not caused blew over Rilla's spirit.

"Why? You have another month of vacation."

"Yes—but I can't hang around Four Winds and enjoy myself when the world's on fire like this. It's me for little old Toronto where I'll find some way of helping in spite of this bally ankle. I'm not looking at Jem and Jerry—makes me too sick with envy. You girls are great—no crying, no grim endurance. The boys'll go off with a good taste in their mouths. I hope Persis and mother will be as game when my turn comes."

"Oh, Kenneth—the war will be over before your turn cometh."

There! She had lisped again. Another great moment of life spoiled! Well, it was her fate. And anyhow, nothing mattered. Kenneth was off already—he was talking to Ethel Reese, who was dressed, at seven in the morning, in the gown she had worn to the dance, and was crying. What on earth had Ethel to cry about? None of the Reeses were in khaki. Rilla wanted to cry, too—but she would not.

What was that horrid old Mrs. Drew saying to mother, in that melancholy whine of hers? "I don't know how you can stand this, Mrs. Blythe. I couldn't if it was my pore boy." And mother—oh, mother could always be depended on! How her grey eyes flashed in her pale face. "It might have been worse, Mrs. Drew. I might have had to urge him to go." Mrs. Drew did not understand but Rilla did. She flung up her head. Her brother did not have to be urged to go.

Rilla found herself standing alone and listening to disconnected scraps of talk as people walked up and down past her.

"I told Mark to wait and see if they asked for a second lot of men. If they did I'd let him go—but they won't," said Mrs. Palmer Burr.

"I think I'll have it made with a crush girdle of velvet," said Bessie Clow.

"I'm frightened to look at my husband's face for fear I'll see in it that he wants to go too," said a little over-harbour bride.

"I'm scared stiff," said whimsical Mrs. Jim Howard. "I'm scared Jim will enlist—and I'm scared he won't."

"The war will be over by Christmas," said Joe Vickers.

"Let them European nations fight it out between them," said Abner Reese.

"When he was a boy I gave him many a good trouncing," shouted Norman Douglas, who seemed to be referring to some one high in military circles in Charlottetown. "Yes, sir, I walloped him well, big gun as he is now."

"The existence of the British Empire is at stake," said the Methodist minister.

"There's certainly something about uniforms," sighed Irene Howard.

"It's a commercial war when all is said and done and not worth one drop of good Canadian blood," said a stranger from the shore hotel.

"The Blythe family are taking it easy," said Kate Drew.

"Them young fools are just going for adventure," growled Nathan Crawford.

"I have absolute confidence in Kitchener," said the over-harbour doctor.

In these ten minutes Rilla passed through a dizzying succession of anger, laughter, contempt, depression and inspiration. Oh, people were—funny! How little they understood. "Taking it easy," indeed—when even Susan hadn't slept a wink all night! Kate Drew always was a minx.

Rilla felt as if she were in some fantastic nightmare. Were these the people who, three weeks ago, were talking of crops and prices and local gossip?

There—the train was coming—mother was holding Jem's hand—Dog Monday was licking it—everybody was saying good-bye—the train was in! Jem kissed Faith before everybody—old Mrs. Drew whooped hysterically—the men, led by Kenneth, cheered—Rilla felt Jem seize her hand—"Good-bye, Spider"—somebody kissed her cheek—she believed it was Jerry but never was sure—they were off—the train was pulling out—Jem and Jerry were waving to everybody—everybody was waving back—mother and Nan were smiling still, but as if they had just forgotten to take the smile off—Monday was howling dismally and being forcibly restrained by the Methodist minister from tearing after the train—Susan was waving her best bonnet and hurrahing like a man—had she gone crazy?—the train rounded a curve. They had gone.

Rilla came to herself with a gasp. There was a sudden quiet. Nothing to do now but to go home—and wait. The doctor and Mrs. Blythe walked off together—so did Nan and Faith—so did John Meredith and Rosemary. Walter and Una and Shirley and Di and Carl and Rilla went in a group. Susan had put her bonnet back on her head, hindside foremost, and stalked grimly off alone. Nobody missed Dog Monday at first. When they did Shirley went back for him. He found Dog Monday curled up in one of the shipping-sheds near the station and tried to coax him home. Dog Monday would not move. He wagged his tail to show he had no hard feelings but no blandishments availed to budge him.

"Guess Monday has made up his mind to wait there till Jem comes back," said Shirley, trying to laugh as he rejoined the rest. This was exactly what Dog Monday had done. His dear master had gone—he, Monday, had been deliberately and of malice aforethought prevented from going with him by a demon disguised in the garb of a Methodist minister. Wherefore, he, Monday, would wait there until the smoking, snorting monster, which had carried his hero off, carried him back.

Ay, wait there, little faithful dog with the soft, wistful, puzzled eyes. But it will be many a long bitter day before your boyish comrade comes back to you.

The doctor was away on a case that night and Susan stalked into Mrs. Blythe's room on her way to bed to see if her adored Mrs. Dr. dear were "comfortable and composed." She paused solemnly at the foot of the bed and solemnly declared,

"Mrs. Dr. dear, I have made up my mind to be a heroine."

"Mrs. Dr. dear" found herself violently inclined to laugh—which was manifestly unfair, since she had not laughed when Rilla had announced a similar heroic determination. To be sure, Rilla was a slim, white-robed thing, with a flower-like face and starry young eyes aglow with feeling; whereas Susan was arrayed in a grey flannel nightgown of strait simplicity, and had a strip of red woollen worsted tied around her grey hair as a charm against neuralgia. But that should not make any vital difference. Was it not the spirit that counted? Yet Mrs. Blythe was hard put to it not to laugh.

"I am not," proceeded Susan firmly, "going to lament or whine or question the wisdom of the Almighty any more as I have been doing lately. Whining and shirking and blaming Providence do not get us anywhere. We have just got to grapple with whatever we have to do whether it is weeding the onion patch, or running the Government. I shall grapple. Those blessed boys have gone to war; and we women, Mrs. Dr. dear, must tarry by the stuff and keep a stiff upper lip."

CHAPTER VII - A WAR-BABY AND A SOUP TUREEN

"Liege and Namur—and now Brussels!" The doctor shook his head. "I don't like it—I don't like it."

"Do not you lose heart, Dr. dear; they were just defended by foreigners," said Susan superbly. "Wait you till the Germans come against the British; there will be a very different story to tell and that you may tie to."

The doctor shook his head again, but a little less gravely; perhaps they all shared subconsciously in Susan's belief that "the thin grey line" was unbreakable, even by the victorious rush of Germany's ready millions. At any rate, when the terrible day came—the first of many terrible days—with the news that the British army was driven back they stared at each other in blank dismay.

"It—it can't be true," gasped Nan, taking a brief refuge in temporary incredulity.

"I felt that there was to be bad news today," said Susan, "for that cat-creature turned into Mr. Hyde this morning without rhyme or reason for it, and that was no good omen."

"'A broken, a beaten, but not a demoralized, army,'" muttered the doctor, from a London dispatch. "Can it be England's army of which such a thing is said?"

"It will be a long time now before the war is ended," said Mrs. Blythe despairingly.

Susan's faith, which had for a moment been temporarily submerged, now reappeared triumphantly.

"Remember, Mrs. Dr. dear, that the British army is not the British navy. Never forget that. And the Russians are on their way, too, though Russians are people I do not know much about and consequently will not tie to."

"The Russians will not be in time to save Paris," said Walter gloomily. "Paris is the heart of France—and the road to it is open. Oh, I wish"—he stopped abruptly and went out.

After a paralysed day the Ingleside folk found it was possible to "carry on" even in the face of ever-darkening bad news. Susan worked fiercely in her kitchen, the doctor went out on his round of visits, Nan and Di returned to their Red Cross activities; Mrs. Blythe went to Charlottetown to attend a Red Cross Convention; Rilla after relieving her feelings by a stormy fit of tears in Rainbow Valley and an outburst in her diary, remembered that she had elected to be brave and heroic. And, she thought, it really was heroic to volunteer to drive about the Glen and Four Winds one day, collecting promised Red Cross supplies with Abner Crawford's old grey horse. One of the Ingleside horses was lame and the doctor needed the other, so there was nothing for it but the Crawford nag, a placid, unhasting, thick-skinned creature with an amiable habit of stopping every few yards to kick a fly off one leg with the foot of the other. Rilla felt that this, coupled with the fact that the Germans were only fifty miles from Paris, was hardly to be endured. But she started off gallantly on an errand fraught with amazing results.

Late in the afternoon she found herself, with a buggy full of parcels, at the entrance to a grassy, deep-rutted lane leading to the harbour shore, wondering whether it was worth while to call down at the Anderson house. The Andersons were desperately poor and it was not likely Mrs. Anderson had anything to give. On the other hand, her husband, who was an Englishman by birth and who had been working in Kingsport when the war broke out, had promptly sailed for England to enlist there, without, it may be said, coming home or sending much hard cash to represent him. So possibly Mrs. Anderson might feel hurt if she were overlooked. Rilla decided to call. There were times afterwards when she wished she hadn't, but in the long run she was very thankful that she did.

The Anderson house was a small and tumbledown affair, crouching in a grove of battered spruces near the shore as if rather ashamed of itself and anxious to hide. Rilla tied her grey nag to the rickety fence and went to the door. It was open; and the sight she saw bereft her temporarily of the power of speech or motion.

Through the open door of the small bedroom opposite her, Rilla saw Mrs. Anderson lying on the untidy bed; and Mrs. Anderson was dead. There was no doubt of that; neither was there any doubt that the big, frowzy, red-headed, red-faced, over-fat woman sitting near the door-way, smoking a pipe quite comfortably, was very much alive. She rocked idly back and forth amid her surroundings of squalid disorder, and paid no attention whatever to the piercing wails proceeding from a cradle in the middle of the room.

Rilla knew the woman by sight and reputation. Her name was Mrs. Conover; she lived down at the fishing village; she was a great-aunt of Mrs. Anderson; and she drank as well as smoked.

Rilla's first impulse was to turn and flee. But that would never do. Perhaps this woman, repulsive as she was, needed help—though she certainly did not look as if she were worrying over the lack of it.

"Come in," said Mrs. Conover, removing her pipe and staring at Rilla with her little, rat-like eyes.

"Is—is Mrs. Anderson really dead?" asked Rilla timidly, as she stepped over the sill.

"Dead as a door nail," responded Mrs. Conover cheerfully. "Kicked the bucket half an hour ago. I've sent Jen Conover to 'phone for the undertaker and get some help up from the shore. You're the doctor's miss, ain't ye? Have a cheer?"

Rilla did not see any chair which was not cluttered with something. She remained standing.

"Wasn't it—very sudden?"

"Well, she's been a-pining ever since that worthless Jim lit out for England—which I say it's a pity as he ever left. It's my belief she was took for death when she heard the news. That young un there was born a fortnight ago and since then she's just gone down and today she up and died, without a soul expecting it."

"Is there anything I can do to—to help?" hesitated Rilla.

"Bless yez, no—unless ye've a knack with kids. I haven't. That young un there never lets up squalling, day or night. I've just got that I take no notice of it."

Rilla tiptoed gingerly over to the cradle and more gingerly still pulled down the dirty blanket. She had no intention of touching the baby—she had no "knack with kids" either. She saw an ugly midget with a red, distorted little face, rolled up in a piece of dingy old flannel. She had never seen an uglier baby. Yet a feeling of pity for the desolate, orphaned mite which had "come out of the everywhere" into such a dubious "here", took sudden possession of her.

"What is going to become of the baby?" she asked.

"Lord knows," said Mrs. Conover candidly. "Min worried awful over that before she died. She kept on a-saying 'Oh, what will become of my pore baby' till it really got on my nerves. I ain't a-going to trouble myself with it, I can tell yez. I brung up a boy that my sister left and he skinned out as soon as he got to be some good and won't give me a mite o' help in my old age, ungrateful whelp as he is. I told Min it'd have to be sent to an orphan asylum till we'd see if Jim ever came back to look after it. Would yez believe it, she didn't relish the idee. But that's the long and short of it."

"But who will look after it until it can be taken to the asylum?" persisted Rilla. Somehow the baby's fate worried her.

"S'pose I'll have to," grunted Mrs. Conover. She put away her pipe and took an unblushing swig from a black bottle she produced from a shelf near her. "It's my opinion the kid won't live long. It's sickly. Min never had no gimp and I guess it hain't either. Likely it won't trouble any one long and good riddance, sez I."

Rilla drew the blanket down a little farther.

"Why, the baby isn't dressed!" she exclaimed, in a shocked tone.

"Who was to dress him I'd like to know," demanded Mrs. Conover truculently. "I hadn't time—took me all the time there was looking after Min. 'Sides, as I told yez, I don't know nithing about kids. Old Mrs. Billy Crawford, she was here when it was born and she washed it and rolled it up in that flannel, and Jen she's tended it a bit since. The critter is warm enough. This weather would melt a brass monkey."

Rilla was silent, looking down at the crying baby. She had never encountered any of the tragedies of life before and this one smote her to the core of her heart. The thought of the poor mother going down into the valley of the shadow alone, fretting about her baby, with no one near but this abominable old woman, hurt her terribly. If she had only come a little sooner! Yet what could she have done—

what could she do now? She didn't know, but she must do something. She hated babies—but she simply could not go away and leave that poor little creature with Mrs. Conover—who was applying herself again to her black bottle and would probably be helplessly drunk before anybody came.

"I can't stay," thought Rilla. "Mr. Crawford said I must be home by supper-time because he wanted the pony this evening himself. Oh, what can I do?"

She made a sudden, desperate, impulsive resolution.

"I'll take the baby home with me," she said. "Can I?"

"Sure, if yez wants to," said Mrs. Conover amiably. "I hain't any objection. Take it and welcome."

"I—I can't carry it," said Rilla. "I have to drive the horse and I'd be afraid I'd drop it. Is there a—a basket anywhere that I could put it in?"

"Not as I knows on. There ain't much here of anything, I kin tell yez. Min was pore and as shiftless as Jim. Ef ye opens that drawer over there yez'll find a few baby clo'es. Best take them along."

Rilla got the clothes—the cheap, sleazy garments the poor mother had made ready as best she could. But this did not solve the pressing problem of the baby's transportation. Rilla looked helplessly round. Oh, for mother—or Susan! Her eyes fell on an enormous blue soup tureen at the back of the dresser.

"May I have this to—to lay him in?" she asked.

"Well, 'tain't mine but I guess yez kin take it. Don't smash it if yez can help—Jim might make a fuss about it if he comes back alive—which he sure will, seein' he ain't any good. He brung that old tureen out from England with him—said it'd always been in the family. Him and Min never used it—never had enough soup to put in it—but Jim thought the world of it. He was mighty perticuler about some things but didn't worry him none that there weren't much in the way o' eatables to put in the dishes."

For the first time in her life Rilla Blythe touched a baby—lifted it—rolled it in a blanket, trembling with nervousness lest she drop it or—or—break it. Then she put it in the soup tureen.

"Is there any fear of it smothering?" she asked anxiously.

"Not much odds if it do," said Mrs. Conover.

Horrified Rilla loosened the blanket round the baby's face a little. The mite had stopped crying and was blinking up at her. It had big dark eyes in its ugly little face.

"Better not let the wind blow on it," admonished Mrs. Conover. "Take its breath if it do."

Rilla wrapped the tattered little quilt around the soup tureen.

"Will you hand this to me after I get into the buggy, please?"

"Sure I will," said Mrs. Conover, getting up with a grunt.

And so it was that Rilla Blythe, who had driven to the Anderson house a self-confessed hater of babies, drove away from it carrying one in a soup tureen on her lap!

CHAPTER VII - A WAR-BABY AND A SOUP TUREEN

Rilla thought she would never get to Ingleside. In the soup tureen there was an uncanny silence. In one way she was thankful the baby did not cry but she wished it would give an occasional squeak to prove that it was alive. Suppose it were smothered! Rilla dared not unwrap it to see, lest the wind, which was now blowing a hurricane, should "take its breath," whatever dreadful thing that might be. She was a thankful girl when at last she reached harbour at Ingleside.

Rilla carried the soup tureen to the kitchen, and set it on the table under Susan's eyes. Susan looked into the tureen and for once in her life was so completely floored that she had not a word to say.

"What in the world is this?" asked the doctor, coming in.

Rilla poured out her story. "I just had to bring it, father," she concluded. "I couldn't leave it there."

"What are you going to do with it?" asked the doctor coolly.

Rilla hadn't exactly expected this kind of question.

"We—we can keep it here for awhile—can't we—until something can be arranged?" she stammered confusedly.

Dr. Blythe walked up and down the kitchen for a moment or two while the baby stared at the white walls of the soup tureen and Susan showed signs of returning animation.

Presently the doctor confronted Rilla.

"A young baby means a great deal of additional work and trouble in a household, Rilla. Nan and Di are leaving for Redmond next week and neither your mother nor Susan is able to assume so much extra care under present conditions. If you want to keep that baby here you must attend to it yourself."

"Me!" Rilla was dismayed into being ungrammatical. "Why—father—I—I couldn't!"

"Younger girls than you have had to look after babies. My advice and Susan's is at your disposal. If you cannot, then the baby must go back to Meg Conover. Its lease of life will be short if it does for it is evident that it is a delicate child and requires particular care. I doubt if it would survive even if sent to an orphans' home. But I cannot have your mother and Susan over-taxed."

The doctor walked out of the kitchen, looking very stern and immovable. In his heart he knew quite well that the small inhabitant of the big soup tureen would remain at Ingleside, but he meant to see if Rilla could not be induced to rise to the occasion.

Rilla sat looking blankly at the baby. It was absurd to think she could take care of it. But—that poor little, frail, dead mother who had worried about it—that dreadful old Meg Conover.

"Susan, what must be done for a baby?" she asked dolefully.

"You must keep it warm and dry and wash it every day, and be sure the water is neither too hot nor too cold, and feed it every two hours. If it has colic, you put hot things on its stomach," said Susan, rather feebly and flatly for her.

The baby began to cry again.

"It must be hungry—it has to be fed anyhow," said Rilla desperately. "Tell me what to get for it, Susan, and I'll get it."

Under Susan's directions a ration of milk and water was prepared, and a bottle obtained from the doctor's office. Then Rilla lifted the baby out of the soup tureen and fed it. She brought down the old basket of her own infancy from the attic and laid the now sleeping baby in it. She put the soup tureen away in the pantry. Then she sat down to think things over.

The result of her thinking things over was that she went to Susan when the baby woke.

"I'm going to see what I can do, Susan. I can't let that poor little thing go back to Mrs. Conover. Tell me how to wash and dress it."

Under Susan's supervision Rilla bathed the baby. Susan dared not help, other than by suggestion, for the doctor was in the living-room and might pop in at any moment. Susan had learned by experience that when Dr. Blythe put his foot down and said a thing must be, that thing was. Rilla set her teeth and went ahead. In the name of goodness, how many wrinkles and kinks did a baby have? Why, there wasn't enough of it to take hold of. Oh, suppose she let it slip into the water—it was so wobbly! If it would only stop howling like that! How could such a tiny morsel make such an enormous noise. Its shrieks could be heard over Ingleside from cellar to attic.

"Am I really hurting it much, Susan, do you suppose?" she asked piteously.

"No, dearie. Most new babies hate like poison to be washed. You are real knacky for a beginner. Keep your hand under its back, whatever you do, and keep cool."

Keep cool! Rilla was oozing perspiration at every pore. When the baby was dried and dressed and temporarily quieted with another bottle she was as limp as a rag.

"What must I do with it tonight, Susan?"

A baby by day was dreadful enough; a baby by night was unthinkable.

"Set the basket on a chair by your bed and keep it covered. You will have to feed it once or twice in the night, so you would better take the oil heater upstairs. If you cannot manage it call me and I will go, doctor or no doctor."

"But, Susan, if it cries?"

The baby, however, did not cry. It was surprisingly good—perhaps because its poor little stomach was filled with proper food. It slept most of the night but Rilla did not. She was afraid to go to sleep for fear something would happen to the baby. She prepared its three o'clock ration with a grim determination that she would not call Susan. Oh, was she dreaming? Was it really she, Rilla Blythe, who had got into this absurd predicament? She did not care if the Germans were near Paris—she did not care if they were in Paris—if only the baby wouldn't cry or choke or smother or have convulsions. Babies did have convulsions, didn't they? Oh, why had she forgotten to ask Susan what she must do if the baby had convulsions? She reflected rather bitterly that father was very considerate of mother's and Susan's health, but what about hers? Did he think she could continue to exist

964

if she never got any sleep? But she was not going to back down now—not she. She would look after this detestable little animal if it killed her. She would get a book on baby hygiene and be beholden to nobody. She would never go to father for advice—she wouldn't bother mother—and she would only condescend to Susan in dire extremity. They would all see!

Thus it came about that Mrs. Blythe, when she returned home two nights later and asked Susan where Rilla was, was electrified by Susan's composed reply.

"She's upstairs, Mrs. Dr. dear, putting her baby to bed."

CHAPTER VIII - RILLA DECIDES

Families and individuals alike soon become used to new conditions and accept them unquestioningly. By the time a week had elapsed it seemed as if the Anderson baby had always been at Ingleside. After the first three distracted nights Rilla began to sleep again, waking automatically to attend to her charge on schedule time. She bathed and fed and dressed it as skilfully as if she had been doing it all her life. She liked neither her job nor the baby any the better; she still handled it as gingerly as if it were some kind of a small lizard, and a breakable lizard at that; but she did her work thoroughly and there was not a cleaner, better-cared-for infant in Glen St. Mary. She even took to weighing the creature every day and jotting the result down in her diary; but sometimes she asked herself pathetically why unkind destiny had ever led her down the Anderson lane on that fatal day. Shirley, Nan, and Di did not tease her as much as she had expected. They all seemed rather stunned by the mere fact of Rilla adopting a war-baby; perhaps, too, the doctor had issued instructions. Walter, of course, never had teased her over anything; one day he told her she was a brick.

"It took more courage for you to tackle that five pounds of new infant, Rilla-my-Rilla, than it would be for Jem to face a mile of Germans. I wish I had half your pluck," he said ruefully.

Rilla was very proud of Walter's approval; nevertheless, she wrote gloomily in her diary that night:—

"I wish I could like the baby a little bit. It would make things easier. But I don't. I've heard people say that when you took care of a baby you got fond of it—but you don't—I don't, anyway. And it's a nuisance—it interferes with everything. It just ties me down—and now of all times when I'm trying to get the Junior Reds started. And I couldn't go to Alice Clow's party last night and I was just dying to. Of course father isn't really unreasonable and I can always get an hour or two off in the evening when it's necessary; but I knew he wouldn't stand for my being out half the night and leaving Susan or mother to see to the baby. I suppose it was just as well, because the thing did take colic—or something—about one o'clock. It didn't kick or stiffen out, so I knew that, according to Morgan, it wasn't crying for temper; and it wasn't hungry and no pins were sticking in it. It screamed till it was black in the face; I got up and heated water and put the hot-water bottle on its stomach, and it howled worse than ever and drew up its poor wee thin legs. I was

CHAPTER VIII - RILLA DECIDES

afraid I had burnt it but I don't believe I did. Then I walked the floor with it although 'Morgan on Infants' says that should never be done. I walked miles, and oh, I was so tired and discouraged and mad—yes, I was. I could have shaken the creature if it had been big enough to shake, but it wasn't. Father was out on a case, and mother had had a headache and Susan is squiffy because when she and Morgan differ I insist upon going by what Morgan says, so I was determined I wouldn't call her unless I had to.

"Finally, Miss Oliver came in. She has rooms with Nan now, not me, all because of the baby, and I am broken-hearted about it. I miss our long talks after we went to bed, so much. It was the only time I ever had her to myself. I hated to think the baby's yells had wakened her up, for she has so much to bear now. Mr. Grant is at Valcartier, too, and Miss Oliver feels it dreadfully, though she is splendid about it. She thinks he will never come back and her eyes just break my heart—they are so tragic. She said it wasn't the baby that woke her—she hadn't been able to sleep because the Germans are so near Paris; she took the little wretch and laid it flat on its stomach across her knee and thumped its back gently a few times, and it stopped shrieking and went right off to sleep and slept like a lamb the rest of the night. I didn't—I was too worn out.

"I'm having a perfectly dreadful time getting the Junior Reds started. I succeeded in getting Betty Mead as president, and I am secretary, but they put Jen Vickers in as treasurer and I despise her. She is the sort of girl who calls any clever, handsome, or distinguished people she knows slightly by their first names—behind their backs. And she is sly and two-faced. Una doesn't mind, of course. She is willing to do anything that comes to hand and never minds whether she has an office or not. She is just a perfect angel, while I am only angelic in spots and demonic in other spots. I wish Walter would take a fancy to her, but he never seems to think about her in that way, although I heard him say once she was like a tea rose. She is too. And she gets imposed upon, just because she is so sweet and willing; but I don't allow people to impose on Rilla Blythe and 'that you may tie to,' as Susan says.

"Just as I expected, Olive was determined we should have lunch served at our meetings. We had a battle royal over it. The majority was against eats and now the minority is sulking. Irene Howard was on the eats side and she has been very cool to me ever since and it makes me feel miserable. I wonder if mother and Mrs. Elliott have problems in the Senior Society too. I suppose they have, but they just go on calmly in spite of everything. I go on—but not calmly—I rage and cry—but I do it all in private and blow off steam in this diary; and when it's over I vow I'll show them. I never sulk. I detest people who sulk. Anyhow, we've got the society started and we're to meet once a week, and we're all going to learn to knit.

"Shirley and I went down to the station again to try to induce Dog Monday to come home but we failed. All the family have tried and failed. Three days after Jem had gone Walter went down and brought Monday home by main force in the buggy and shut him up for three days. Then Monday went on a hunger strike and howled like a Banshee night and day. We had to let him out or he would have starved to death.

"So we have decided to let him alone and father has arranged with the butcher near the station to feed him with bones and scraps. Besides, one of us goes down nearly every day to take him something. He just lies curled up in the shipping-shed, and every time a train comes in he will rush over to the platform, wagging his tail expectantly, and tear around to every one who comes off the train. And then, when the train goes and he realizes that Jem has not come, he creeps deject-edly back to his shed, with his disappointed eyes, and lies down patiently to wait for the next train. Mr. Gray, the station master, says there are times when he can hardly help crying from sheer sympathy. One day some boys threw stones at Monday and old Johnny Mead, who never was known to take notice of anything before, snatched up a meat axe in the butcher's shop and chased them through the village. Nobody has molested Monday since.

"Kenneth Ford has gone back to Toronto. He came up two evenings ago to say good-bye. I wasn't home—some clothes had to be made for the baby and Mrs. Meredith offered to help me, so I was over at the manse, and I didn't see Kenneth. Not that it matters; he told Nan to say good-bye to Spider for him and tell me not to forget him wholly in my absorbing maternal duties. If he could leave such a frivolous, insulting message as that for me it shows plainly that our beautiful hour on the sandshore meant nothing to him and I am not going to think about him or it again.

"Fred Arnold was at the manse and walked home with me. He is the new Methodist minister's son and very nice and clever, and would be quite handsome if it were not for his nose. It is a really dreadful nose. When he talks of common-place things it does not matter so much, but when he talks of poetry and ideals the contrast between his nose and his conversation is too much for me and I want to shriek with laughter. It is really not fair, because everything he said was perfectly charming and if somebody like Kenneth had said it I would have been enraptured. When I listened to him with my eyes cast down I was quite fascinated; but as soon as I looked up and saw his nose the spell was broken. He wants to enlist, too, but can't because he is only seventeen. Mrs. Elliott met us as we were walking through the village and could not have looked more horrified if she caught me walking with the Kaiser himself. Mrs. Elliott detests the Methodists and all their works. Father says it is an obsession with her."

About 1st September there was an exodus from Ingleside and the manse. Faith, Nan, Di and Walter left for Redmond; Carl betook himself to his Harbour Head school and Shirley was off to Queen's. Rilla was left alone at Ingleside and would have been very lonely if she had had time to be. She missed Walter keenly; since their talk in Rainbow Valley they had grown very near together and Rilla dis-cussed problems with Walter which she never mentioned to others. But she was so busy with the Junior Reds and her baby that there was rarely a spare minute for loneliness; sometimes, after she went to bed, she cried a little in her pillow over

Walter's absence and Jem at Valcartier and Kenneth's unromantic farewell message, but she was generally asleep before the tears got fairly started.

"Shall I make arrangements to have the baby sent to Hopetown?" the doctor asked one day two weeks after the baby's arrival at Ingleside.

For a moment Rilla was tempted to say "Yes." The baby could be sent to Hopetown—it would be decently looked after—she could have her free days and untrammelled nights back again. But—but—that poor young mother who hadn't wanted it to go to the asylum! Rilla couldn't get that out of her thoughts. And that very morning she discovered that the baby had gained eight ounces since its coming to Ingleside. Rilla had felt such a thrill of pride over this.

"You—you said it mightn't live if it went to Hopetown," she said.

"It mightn't. Somehow, institutional care, no matter how good it may be, doesn't always succeed with delicate babies. But you know what it means if you want it kept here, Rilla."

"I've taken care of it for a fortnight—and it has gained half a pound," cried Rilla. "I think we'd better wait until we hear from its father anyhow. He mightn't want to have it sent to an orphan asylum, when he is fighting the battles of his country."

The doctor and Mrs. Blythe exchanged amused, satisfied smiles behind Rilla's back; and nothing more was said about Hopetown.

Then the smile faded from the doctor's face; the Germans were twenty miles from Paris. Horrible tales were beginning to appear in the papers of deeds done in martyred Belgium. Life was very tense at Ingleside for the older people.

"We eat up the war news," Gertrude Oliver told Mrs. Meredith, trying to laugh and failing. "We study the maps and nip the whole Hun army in a few well-directed strategic moves. But Papa Joffre hasn't the benefit of our advice—and so Paris—must—fall."

"Will they reach it—will not some mighty hand yet intervene?" murmured John Meredith.

"I teach school like one in a dream," continued Gertrude; "then I come home and shut myself in my room and walk the floor. I am wearing a path right across Nan's carpet. We are so horribly near this war."

"Them German men are at Senlis. Nothing nor nobody can save Paris now," wailed Cousin Sophia. Cousin Sophia had taken to reading the newspapers and had learned more about the geography of northern France, if not about the pronunciation of French names, in her seventy-first year than she had ever known in her schooldays.

"I have not such a poor opinion of the Almighty, or of Kitchener," said Susan stubbornly. "I see there is a Bernstoff man in the States who says that the war is over and Germany has won—and they tell me Whiskers-on-the-moon says the same thing and is quite pleased about it, but I could tell them both that it is chancy work counting chickens even the day before they are hatched, and bears have been known to live long after their skins were sold."

"Why ain't the British navy doing more?" persisted Cousin Sophia.

"Even the British navy cannot sail on dry land, Sophia Crawford. I have not given up hope, and I shall not, Tomascow and Mobbage and all such barbarous names to the contrary notwithstanding. Mrs. Dr. dear, can you tell me if R-h-e-i-m-s is Rimes or Reems or Rames or Rems?"

"I believe it's really more like 'Rhangs,' Susan."

"Oh, those French names," groaned Susan.

"They tell me the Germans has about ruined the church there," sighed Cousin Sophia. "I always thought the Germans was Christians."

"A church is bad enough but their doings in Belgium are far worse," said Susan grimly. "When I heard the doctor reading about them bayonetting the babies, Mrs. Dr. dear, I just thought, 'Oh, what if it were our little Jem!' I was stirring the soup when that thought came to me and I just felt that if I could have lifted that saucepan full of that boiling soup and thrown it at the Kaiser I would not have lived in vain."

"Tomorrow—tomorrow—will bring the news that the Germans are in Paris," said Gertrude Oliver, through her tense lips. She had one of those souls that are always tied to the stake, burning in the suffering of the world around them. Apart from her own personal interest in the war, she was racked by the thought of Paris falling into the ruthless hands of the hordes who had burned Louvain and ruined the wonder of Rheims.

But on the morrow and the next morrow came the news of the miracle of the Marne. Rilla rushed madly home from the office waving the Enterprise with its big red headlines. Susan ran out with trembling hands to hoist the flag. The doctor stalked about muttering "Thank God." Mrs. Blythe cried and laughed and cried again.

"God just put out His hand and touched them—'thus far—no farther'," said Mr. Meredith that evening.

Rilla was singing upstairs as she put the baby to bed. Paris was saved—the war was over—Germany had lost—there would soon be an end now—Jem and Jerry would be back. The black clouds had rolled by.

"Don't you dare have colic this joyful night," she told the baby. "If you do I'll clap you back into your soup tureen and ship you off to Hopetown—by freight—on the early train. You have got beautiful eyes—and you're not quite as red and wrinkled as you were—but you haven't a speck of hair—and your hands are like little claws—and I don't like you a bit better than I ever did. But I hope your poor little white mother knows that you're tucked in a soft basket with a bottle of milk as rich as Morgan allows instead of perishing by inches with old Meg Conover. And I hope she doesn't know that I nearly drowned you that first morning when Susan wasn't there and I let you slip right out of my hands into the water. Why will you be so slippery? No, I don't like you and I never will but for all that I'm going to make a decent, upstanding infant of you. You are going to get as fat as a self-respecting child should be, for one thing. I am not going to have people saying 'what a puny little thing that baby of Rilla Blythe's is' as old Mrs. Drew said at the senior Red Cross yesterday. If I can't love you I mean to be proud of you at least."

CHAPTER IX - DOC HAS A MISADVENTURE

"The war will not be over before next spring now," said Dr. Blythe, when it became apparent that the long battle of the Aisne had resulted in a stalemate.

Rilla was murmuring "knit four, purl one" under her breath, and rocking the baby's cradle with one foot. Morgan disapproved of cradles for babies but Susan did not, and it was worth while to make some slight sacrifice of principle to keep Susan in good humour. She laid down her knitting for a moment and said, "Oh, how can we bear it so long?"—then picked up her sock and went on. The Rilla of two months before would have rushed off to Rainbow Valley and cried.

Miss Oliver sighed and Mrs. Blythe clasped her hands for a moment. Then Susan said briskly, "Well, we must just gird up our loins and pitch in. Business as usual is England's motto, they tell me, Mrs. Dr. dear, and I have taken it for mine, not thinking I could easily find a better. I shall make the same kind of pudding today I always make on Saturday. It is a good deal of trouble to make, and that is well, for it will employ my thoughts. I will remember that Kitchener is at the helm and Joffer is doing very well for a Frenchman. I shall get that box of cake off to little Jem and finish that pair of socks today likewise. A sock a day is my allowance. Old Mrs. Albert Mead of Harbour Head manages a pair and a half a day but she has nothing to do but knit. You know, Mrs. Dr. dear, she has been bed-rid for years and she has been worrying terrible because she was no good to anybody and a dreadful expense, and yet could not die and be out of the way. And now they tell me she is quite chirked up and resigned to living because there is something she can do, and she knits for the soldiers from daylight to dark. Even Cousin Sophia has taken to knitting, Mrs. Dr. dear, and it is a good thing, for she cannot think of quite so many doleful speeches to make when her hands are busy with her needles instead of being folded on her stomach. She thinks we will all be Germans this time next year but I tell her it will take more than a year to make a German out of me. Do you know that Rick MacAllister has enlisted, Mrs. Dr. dear? And they say Joe Milgrave would too, only he is afraid that if he does that Whiskers-on-the-moon will not let him have Miranda. Whiskers says that he will believe the stories of German atrocities when he sees them, and that it is a good thing that Rangs Cathedral has been destroyed because it was a Roman Catholic church. Now, I am not a Roman Catholic, Mrs. Dr. dear, being born and bred a good Presbyterian and meaning to live and die one, but I maintain that the Catholics have as good a right to their churches as we have to ours and that the Huns had no kind of business to destroy them. Just think, Mrs. Dr. dear," concluded Susan pathetically, "how we would feel if a German shell knocked down the spire of our church here in the glen, and I'm sure it is every bit as bad to think of Rangs cathedral being hammered to pieces."

And, meanwhile, everywhere, the lads of the world rich and poor, low and high, white and brown, were following the Piper's call.

"Even Billy Andrews' boy is going—and Jane's only son—and Diana's little Jack," said Mrs. Blythe. "Priscilla's son has gone from Japan and Stella's from Vancouver—and both the Rev. Jo's boys. Philippa writes that her boys 'went right away, not being afflicted with her indecision.'"

"Jem says that he thinks they will be leaving very soon now, and that he will not be able to get leave to come so far before they go, as they will have to start at a few hours' notice," said the doctor, passing the letter to his wife.

"That is not fair," said Susan indignantly. "Has Sir Sam Hughes no regard for our feelings? The idea of whisking that blessed boy away to Europe without letting us even have a last glimpse of him! If I were you, doctor dear, I would write to the papers about it."

"Perhaps it is as well," said the disappointed mother. "I don't believe I could bear another parting from him—now that I know the war will not be over as soon as we hoped when he left first. Oh, if only—but no, I won't say it! Like Susan and Rilla," concluded Mrs. Blythe, achieving a laugh, "I am determined to be a heroine."

"You're all good stuff," said the doctor, "I'm proud of my women folk. Even Rilla here, my 'lily of the field,' is running a Red Cross Society full blast and saving a little life for Canada. That's a good piece of work. Rilla, daughter of Anne, what are you going to call your war-baby?"

"I'm waiting to hear from Jim Anderson," said Rilla. "He may want to name his own child."

But as the autumn weeks went by no word came from Jim Anderson, who had never been heard from since he sailed from Halifax, and to whom the fate of wife and child seemed a matter of indifference. Eventually Rilla decided to call the baby James, and Susan opined that Kitchener should be added thereto. So James Kitchener Anderson became the possessor of a name somewhat more imposing than himself. The Ingleside family promptly shortened it to Jims, but Susan obstinately called him "Little Kitchener" and nothing else.

"Jims is no name for a Christian child, Mrs. Dr. dear," she said disapprovingly. "Cousin Sophia says it is too flippant, and for once I consider she utters sense, though I would not please her by openly agreeing with her. As for the child, he is beginning to look something like a baby, and I must admit that Rilla is wonderful with him, though I would not pamper pride by saying so to her face. Mrs. Dr. dear, I shall never, no never, forget the first sight I had of that infant, lying in that big soup tureen, rolled up in dirty flannel. It is not often that Susan Baker is flabbergasted, but flabbergasted I was then, and that you may tie to. For one awful moment I thought my mind had given way and that I was seeing visions. Then thinks I, 'No, I never heard of anyone having a vision of a soup tureen, so it must be real at least,' and I plucked up confidence. When I heard the doctor tell Rilla that she must take care of the baby I thought he was joking, for I did not believe for a minute she would or could do it. But you see what has happened and it is making a woman of her. When we have to do a thing, Mrs. Dr. dear, we can do it."

Susan added another proof to this concluding dictum of hers one day in October. The doctor and his wife were away. Rilla was presiding over Jims' afternoon siesta upstairs, purling four and knitting one with ceaseless vim. Susan was seated on the back veranda, shelling beans, and Cousin Sophia was helping her. Peace and tranquility brooded over the Glen; the sky was fleeced over with silvery, shining clouds. Rainbow Valley lay in a soft, autumnal haze of fairy purple. The maple grove was a burning bush of colour and the hedge of sweet-briar around the kitchen yard was a thing of wonder in its subtle tintings. It did not seem that strife could be in the world, and Susan's faithful heart was lulled into a brief forgetfulness, although she had lain awake most of the preceding night thinking of little Jem far out on the Atlantic, where the great fleet was carrying Canada's first army across the ocean. Even Cousin Sophia looked less melancholy than usual and admitted that there was not much fault to be found in the day, although there was no doubt it was a weather-breeder and there would be an awful storm on its heels.

"Things is too calm to last," she said.

As if in confirmation of her assertion, a most unearthly din suddenly arose behind them. It was quite impossible to describe the confused medley of bangs and rattles and muffled shrieks and yowls that proceeded from the kitchen, accompanied by occasional crashes. Susan and Cousin Sophia stared at each other in dismay.

"What upon airth has bruk loose in there?" gasped Cousin Sophia.

"It must be that Hyde-cat gone clean mad at last," muttered Susan. "I have always expected it."

Rilla came flying out of the side door of the living-room.

"What has happened?" she demanded.

"It is beyond me to say, but that possessed beast of yours is evidently at the bottom of it," said Susan. "Do not go near him, at least. I will open the door and peep in. There goes some more of the crockery. I have always said that the devil was in him and that I will tie to."

"It is my opinion that the cat has hydrophobia," said Cousin Sophia solemnly. "I once heard of a cat that went mad and bit three people—and they all died a most terrible death, and turned black as ink."

Undismayed by this, Susan opened the door and looked in. The floor was littered with fragments of broken dishes, for it seemed that the fatal tragedy had taken place on the long dresser where Susan's array of cooking bowls had been marshalled in shining state. Around the kitchen tore a frantic cat, with his head wedged tightly in an old salmon can. Blindly he careered about with shrieks and profanity commingled, now banging the can madly against anything he encountered, now trying vainly to wrench it off with his paws.

The sight was so funny that Rilla doubled up with laughter. Susan looked at her reproachfully.

"I see nothing to laugh at. That beast has broken your ma's big blue mixing-bowl that she brought from Green Gables when she was married. That is no small calamity, in my opinion. But the thing to consider now is how to get that can off Hyde's head."

"Don't you dast go touching it," exclaimed Cousin Sophia, galvanized into animation. "It might be your death. Shut the kitchen up and send for Albert."

"I am not in the habit of sending for Albert during family difficulties," said Susan loftily. "That beast is in torment, and whatever my opinion of him may be, I cannot endure to see him suffering pain. You keep away, Rilla, for little Kitchener's sake, and I will see what I can do."

Susan stalked undauntedly into the kitchen, seized an old storm coat of the doctor's and after a wild pursuit and several fruitless dashes and pounces, managed to throw it over the cat and can. Then she proceeded to saw the can loose with a can-opener, while Rilla held the squirming animal, rolled in the coat. Anything like Doc's shrieks while the process was going on was never heard at Ingleside. Susan was in mortal dread that the Albert Crawfords would hear it and conclude she was torturing the creature to death. Doc was a wrathful and indignant cat when he was freed. Evidently he thought the whole thing was a put-up job to bring him low. He gave Susan a baleful glance by way of gratitude and rushed out of the kitchen to take sanctuary in the jungle of the sweet-briar hedge, where he sulked for the rest of the day. Susan swept up her broken dishes grimly.

"The Huns themselves couldn't have worked more havoc here," she said bitterly. "But when people will keep a Satanic animal like that, in spite of all warnings, they cannot complain when their wedding bowls get broken. Things have come to a pretty pass when an honest woman cannot leave her kitchen for a few minutes without a fiend of a cat rampaging through it with his head in a salmon can."

CHAPTER X - THE TROUBLES OF RILLA

October passed out and the dreary days of November and December dragged by. The world shook with the thunder of contending armies; Antwerp fell—Turkey declared war—gallant little Serbia gathered herself together and struck a deadly blow at her oppressor; and in quiet, hill-girdled Glen St. Mary, thousands of miles away, hearts beat with hope and fear over the varying dispatches from day to day.

"A few months ago," said Miss Oliver, "we thought and talked in terms of Glen St. Mary. Now, we think and talk in terms of military tactics and diplomatic intrigue."

There was just one great event every day—the coming of the mail. Even Susan admitted that from the time the mail-courier's buggy rumbled over the little bridge between the station and the village until the papers were brought home and read, she could not work properly.

"I must take up my knitting then and knit hard till the papers come, Mrs. Dr. dear. Knitting is something you can do, even when your heart is going like a trip-hammer and the pit of your stomach feels all gone and your thoughts are ca-tawampus. Then when I see the headlines, be they good or be they bad, I calm down and am able to go about my business again. It is an unfortunate thing that the mail comes in just when our dinner rush is on, and I think the Government could arrange things better. But the drive on Calais has failed, as I felt perfectly sure it would, and the Kaiser will not eat his Christmas dinner in London this year. Do you know, Mrs. Dr. dear,"—Susan's voice lowered as a token that she was going to impart a very shocking piece of information,—"I have been told on good authority—or else you may be sure I would not be repeating it when it con-cerns a minster—that the Rev. Mr. Arnold goes to Charlottetown every week and takes a Turkish bath for his rheumatism. The idea of him doing that when we are at war with Turkey? One of his own deacons has always insisted that Mr. Arnold's theology was not sound and I am beginning to believe that there is some reason to fear it. Well, I must bestir myself this afternoon and get little Jem's Christmas cake packed up for him. He will enjoy it, if the blessed boy is not drowned in mud before that time."

Jem was in camp on Salisbury Plain and was writing gay, cheery letters home in spite of the mud. Walter was at Redmond and his letters to Rilla were anything but cheerful. She never opened one without a dread tugging at her heart that it would tell her he had enlisted. His unhappiness made her unhappy. She wanted to put her arm round him and comfort him, as she had done that day in Rainbow Valley. She hated everybody who was responsible for Walter's unhappiness.

"He will go yet," she murmured miserably to herself one afternoon, as she sat alone in Rainbow Valley, reading a letter from him, "he will go yet—and if he does I just can't bear it."

Walter wrote that some one had sent him an envelope containing a white feather.

"I deserved it, Rilla. I felt that I ought to put it on and wear it—proclaiming myself to all Redmond the coward I know I am. The boys of my year are going— going. Every day two or three of them join up. Some days I almost make up my mind to do it—and then I see myself thrusting a bayonet through another man— some woman's husband or sweetheart or son—perhaps the father of little children—I see myself lying alone torn and mangled, burning with thirst on a cold, wet field, surrounded by dead and dying men—and I know I never can. I can't face even the thought of it. How could I face the reality? There are times when I wish I had never been born. Life has always seemed such a beautiful thing to me—and now it is a hideous thing. Rilla-my-Rilla, if it weren't for your letters— your dear, bright, merry, funny, comical, believing letters—I think I'd give up. And Una's! Una is really a little brick, isn't she? There's a wonderful fineness and firmness under all that shy, wistful girlishness of her. She hasn't your knack of writing laugh-provoking epistles, but there's something in her letters—I don't know what—that makes me feel at least while I'm reading them, that I could even go to the front. Not that she ever says a word about my going—or hints that I ought to go—she isn't that kind. It's just the spirit of them—the personality that is in them. Well, I can't go. You have a brother and Una has a friend who is a coward."

"Oh, I wish Walter wouldn't write such things," sighed Rilla. "It hurts me. He isn't a coward—he isn't—he isn't!"

She looked wistfully about her—at the little woodland valley and the grey, lonely fallows beyond. How everything reminded her of Walter! The red leaves still clung to the wild sweet-briars that overhung a curve of the brook; their stems were gemmed with the pearls of the gentle rain that had fallen a little while before. Walter had once written a poem describing them. The wind was sighing and rustling among the frosted brown bracken ferns, then lessening sorrowfully away down the brook. Walter had said once that he loved the melancholy of the autumn wind on a November day. The old Tree Lovers still clasped each other in a faithful embrace, and the White Lady, now a great white-branched tree, stood out beautifully fine, against the grey velvet sky. Walter had named them long ago; and last November, when he had walked with her and Miss Oliver in the Valley, he had said, looking at the leafless Lady, with a young silver moon hanging over her, "A white birch is a beautiful Pagan maiden who has never lost the Eden secret of being naked and unashamed." Miss Oliver had said, "Put that into a poem,

Walter," and he had done so, and read it to them the next day—just a short thing with goblin imagination in every line of it. Oh, how happy they had been then!

Well—Rilla scrambled to her feet—time was up. Jims would soon be awake—his lunch had to be prepared—his little slips had to be ironed—there was a committee meeting of the Junior Reds that night—there was her new knitting bag to finish—it would be the handsomest bag in the Junior Society—handsomer even than Irene Howard's—she must get home and get to work. She was busy these days from morning till night. That little monkey of a Jims took so much time. But he was growing—he was certainly growing. And there were times when Rilla felt sure that it was not merely a pious hope but an absolute fact that he was getting decidedly better looking. Sometimes she felt quite proud of him; and sometimes she yearned to spank him. But she never kissed him or wanted to kiss him.

"The Germans captured Lodz today," said Miss Oliver, one December evening, when she, Mrs. Blythe, and Susan were busy sewing or knitting in the cosy living-room. "This war is at least extending my knowledge of geography. Schoolma'am though I am, three months ago I didn't know there was such a place in the world such as Lodz. Had I heard it mentioned I would have known nothing about it and cared as little. I know all about it now—its size, its standing, its military significance. Yesterday the news that the Germans have captured it in their second rush to Warsaw made my heart sink into my boots. I woke up in the night and worried over it. I don't wonder babies always cry when they wake up in the night. Everything presses on my soul then and no cloud has a silver lining."

"When I wake up in the night and cannot go to sleep again," remarked Susan, who was knitting and reading at the same time, "I pass the moments by torturing the Kaiser to death. Last night I fried him in boiling oil and a great comfort it was to me, remembering those Belgian babies."

"If the Kaiser were here and had a pain in his shoulder you'd be the first to run for the liniment bottle to rub him down," laughed Miss Oliver.

"Would I?" cried outraged Susan. "Would I, Miss Oliver? I would rub him down with coal oil, Miss Oliver—and leave it to blister. That is what I would do and that you may tie to. A pain in his shoulder, indeed! He will have pains all over him before he is through with what he has started."

"We are told to love our enemies, Susan," said the doctor solemnly.

"Yes, our enemies, but not King George's enemies, doctor dear," retorted Susan crushingly. She was so well pleased with herself over this flattening out of the doctor completely that she even smiled as she polished her glasses. Susan had never given in to glasses before, but she had done so at last in order to be able to read the war news—and not a dispatch got by her. "Can you tell me, Miss Oliver, how to pronounce M-l-a-w-a and B-z-u-r-a and P-r-z-e-m-y-s-l?"

"That last is a conundrum which nobody seems to have solved yet, Susan. And I can make only a guess at the others."

"These foreign names are far from being decent, in my opinion," said disgusted Susan.

"I dare say the Austrians and Russians would think Saskatchewan and Mus-quodoboit about as bad, Susan," said Miss Oliver. "The Serbians have done wonderfully of late. They have captured Belgrade."

"And sent the Austrian creatures packing across the Danube with a flea in their ear," said Susan with a relish, as she settled down to examine a map of Eastern Europe, prodding each locality with the knitting needle to brand it on her memory. "Cousin Sophia said awhile ago that Serbia was done for, but I told her there was still such a thing as an over-ruling Providence, doubt it who might. It says here that the slaughter was terrible. For all they were foreigners it is awful to think of so many men being killed, Mrs. Dr. dear—for they are scarce enough as it is."

Rilla was upstairs relieving her over-charged feelings by writing in her diary.

"Things have all 'gone catawampus,' as Susan says, with me this week. Part of it was my own fault and part of it wasn't, and I seem to be equally unhappy over both parts.

"I went to town the other day to buy a new winter hat. It was the first time no-body insisted on coming with me to help me select it, and I felt that mother had really given up thinking of me as a child. And I found the dearest hat—it was simply bewitching. It was a velvet hat, of the very shade of rich green that was made for me. It just goes with my hair and complexion beautifully, bringing out the red-brown shades and what Miss Oliver calls my 'creaminess' so well. Only once before in my life have I come across that precise shade of green. When I was twelve I had a little beaver hat of it, and all the girls in school were wild over it. Well, as soon as I saw this hat I felt that I simply must have it—and have it I did. The price was dreadful. I will not put it down here because I don't want my de-scendants to know I was guilty of paying so much for a hat, in war-time, too, when everybody is—or should be—trying to be economical.

"When I got home and tried on the hat again in my room I was assailed by qualms. Of course, it was very becoming; but somehow it seemed too elaborate and fussy for church going and our quiet little doings in the Glen—too conspicu-ous, in short. It hadn't seemed so at the milliner's but here in my little white room it did. And that dreadful price tag! And the starving Belgians! When mother saw the hat and the tag she just looked at me. Mother is some expert at looking. Father says she looked him into love with her years ago in Avonlea school and I can well believe it—though I have heard a weird tale of her banging him over the head with a slate at the very beginning of their acquaintance. Mother was a limb when she was a little girl, I understand, and even up to the time when Jem went away she was full of ginger. But let me return to my mutton—that is to say, my new green velvet hat.

"'Do you think, Rilla,' mother said quietly—far too quietly—'that it was right to spend so much for a hat, especially when the need of the world is so great?'

"'I paid for it out of my own allowance, mother,' I exclaimed.

"'That is not the point. Your allowance is based on the principle of a reasona-ble amount for each thing you need. If you pay too much for one thing you must cut off somewhere else and that is not satisfactory. But if you think you did right, Rilla, I have no more to say. I leave it to your conscience.'

"I wish mother would not leave things to my conscience! And anyway, what was I to do? I couldn't take that hat back—I had worn it to a concert in town—I had to keep it! I was so uncomfortable that I flew into a temper—a cold, calm, deadly temper.

"'Mother,' I said haughtily, 'I am sorry you disapprove of my hat—'

"'Not of the hat exactly,' said mother, 'though I consider it in doubtful taste for so young a girl—but of the price you paid for it.'

"Being interrupted didn't improve my temper, so I went on, colder and calmer and deadlier than ever, just as if mother had not spoken.

"'—but I have to keep it now. However, I promise you that I will not get another hat for three years or for the duration of the war, if it lasts longer than that. Even you'—oh, the sarcasm I put into the 'you'—'cannot say that what I paid was too much when spread over at least three years.'

"'You will be very tired of that hat before three years, Rilla,' said mother, with a provoking grin, which, being interpreted, meant that I wouldn't stick it out.

"'Tired or not, I will wear it that long,' I said: and then I marched upstairs and cried to think that I had been sarcastic to mother.

"I hate that hat already. But three years or the duration of the war, I said, and three years or the duration of the war it shall be. I vowed and I shall keep my vow, cost what it will.

"That is one of the 'catawampus' things. The other is that I have quarrelled with Irene Howard—or she quarrelled with me—or, no, we both quarrelled.

"The Junior Red Cross met here yesterday. The hour of meeting was half-past two but Irene came at half-past one, because she got the chance of a drive down from the Upper Glen. Irene hasn't been a bit nice to me since the fuss about the eats; and besides I feel sure she resents not being president. But I have been determined that things should go smoothly, so I have never taken any notice, and when she came yesterday she seemed so nice and sweet again that I hoped she had got over her huffiness and we could be the chums we used to be.

"But as soon as we sat down Irene began to rub me the wrong way. I saw her cast a look at my new knitting-bag. All the girls have always said Irene was jealous-minded and I would never believe them before. But now I feel that perhaps she is.

"The first thing she did was to pounce on Jims—Irene pretends to adore babies—pick him out of his cradle and kiss him all over his face. Now, Irene knows perfectly well that I don't like to have Jims kissed like that. It is not hygienic. After she had worried him till he began to fuss, she looked at me and gave quite a nasty little laugh but she said, oh, so sweetly,

"'Why, Rilla, darling, you look as if you thought I was poisoning the baby.'

"'Oh, no, I don't, Irene,' I said—every bit as sweetly, 'but you know Morgan says that the only place a baby should be kissed is on its forehead, for fear of germs, and that is my rule with Jims.'

"'Dear me, am I so full of germs?' said Irene plaintively. I knew she was making fun of me and I began to boil inside—but outside no sign of a simmer. I was determined I would not scrap with Irene.

"Then she began to bounce Jims. Now, Morgan says bouncing is almost the worst thing that can be done to a baby. I never allow Jims to be bounced. But Irene bounced him and that exasperating child liked it. He smiled—for the very first time. He is four months old and he has never smiled once before. Not even mother or Susan have been able to coax that thing to smile, try as they would. And here he was smiling because Irene Howard bounced him! Talk of gratitude!

"I admit that smile made a big difference in him. Two of the dearest dimples came out in his cheeks and his big brown eyes seemed full of laughter. The way Irene raved over those dimples was silly, I consider. You would have supposed she thought she had really brought them into existence. But I sewed steadily and did not enthuse, and soon Irene got tired of bouncing Jims and put him back in his cradle. He did not like that after being played with, and he began to cry and was fussy the rest of the afternoon, whereas if Irene had only left him alone he would not have been a bit of trouble.

"Irene looked at him and said, 'Does he often cry like that?' as if she had never heard a baby crying before.

"I explained patiently that children have to cry so many minutes per day in order to expand their lungs. Morgan says so.

"'If Jims didn't cry at all I'd have to make him cry for at least twenty minutes,' I said.

"'Oh, indeed!' said Irene, laughing as if she didn't believe me. 'Morgan on the Care of Infants' was upstairs or I would soon have convinced her. Then she said Jims didn't have much hair—she had never seen a four months' old baby so bald.

"Of course, I knew Jims hadn't much hair—yet; but Irene said it in a tone that seemed to imply it was my fault that he hadn't any hair. I said I had seen dozens of babies every bit as bald as Jims, and Irene said, Oh very well, she hadn't meant to offend me—when I wasn't offended.

"It went on like that the rest of the hour—Irene kept giving me little digs all the time. The girls have always said she was revengeful like that if she were peeved about anything; but I never believed it before; I used to think Irene just perfect, and it hurt me dreadfully to find she could stoop to this. But I corked up my feelings and sewed away for dear life on a Belgian child's nightgown.

"Then Irene told me the meanest, most contemptible thing that someone had said about Walter. I won't write it down—I can't. Of course, she said it made her furious to hear it and all that—but there was no need for her to tell me such a thing even if she did hear it. She simply did it to hurt me.

"I just exploded. 'How dare you come here and repeat such a thing about my brother, Irene Howard?' I exclaimed. 'I shall never forgive you—never. Your brother hasn't enlisted—hasn't any idea of enlisting.'

"'Why Rilla, dear, I didn't say it,' said Irene. 'I told you it was Mrs. George Burr. And I told her—'

"'I don't want to hear what you told her. Don't you ever speak to me again, Irene Howard.'

"Oh course, I shouldn't have said that. But it just seemed to say itself. Then the other girls all came in a bunch and I had to calm down and act the hostess' part as well as I could. Irene paired off with Olive Kirk all the rest of the afternoon and went away without so much as a look. So I suppose she means to take me at my word and I don't care, for I do not want to be friends with a girl who could repeat such a falsehood about Walter. But I feel unhappy over it for all that. We've always been such good chums and until lately Irene was lovely to me; and now another illusion has been stripped from my eyes and I feel as if there wasn't such a thing as real true friendship in the world.

"Father got old Joe Mead to build a kennel for Dog Monday in the corner of the shipping-shed today. We thought perhaps Monday would come home when the cold weather came but he wouldn't. No earthly influence can coax Monday away from that shed even for a few minutes. There he stays and meets every train. So we had to do something to make him comfortable. Joe built the kennel so that Monday could lie in it and still see the platform, so we hope he will occupy it.

"Monday has become quite famous. A reporter of the Enterprise came out from town and photographed him and wrote up the whole story of his faithful vigil. It was published in the Enterprise and copied all over Canada. But that doesn't matter to poor little Monday, Jem has gone away—Monday doesn't know where or why—but he will wait until he comes back. Somehow it comforts me: it's foolish, I suppose, but it gives me a feeling that Jem will come back or else Monday wouldn't keep on waiting for him.

"Jims is snoring beside me in his cradle. It is just a cold that makes him snore—not adenoids. Irene had a cold yesterday and I know she gave it to him, kissing him. He is not quite such a nuisance as he was; he has got some backbone and can sit up quite nicely, and he loves his bath now and splashes unsmilingly in the water instead of twisting and shrieking. Oh, shall I ever forget those first two months! I don't know how I lived through them. But here I am and here is Jims and we both are going to 'carry on.' I tickled him a little bit tonight when I undressed him—I wouldn't bounce him but Morgan doesn't mention tickling—just to see if he would smile for me as well as Irene. And he did—and out popped the dimples. What a pity his mother couldn't have seen them!

"I finished my sixth pair of socks today. With the first three I got Susan to set the heel for me. Then I thought that was a bit of shirking, so I learned to do it myself. I hate it—but I have done so many things I hate since 4th of August that one more or less doesn't matter. I just think of Jem joking about the mud on Salisbury Plain and I go at them."

CHAPTER XI - DARK AND BRIGHT

At Christmas the college boys and girls came home and for a little while Ingleside was gay again. But all were not there—for the first time one was missing from the circle round the Christmas table. Jem, of the steady lips and fearless eyes, was far away, and Rilla felt that the sight of his vacant chair was more than she could endure. Susan had taken a stubborn freak and insisted on setting out Jem's place for him as usual, with the twisted little napkin ring he had always had since a boy, and the odd, high Green Gables goblet that Aunt Marilla had once given him and from which he always insisted on drinking.

"That blessed boy shall have his place, Mrs. Dr. dear," said Susan firmly, "and do not you feel over it, for you may be sure he is here in spirit and next Christmas he will be here in the body. Wait you till the Big Push comes in the spring and the war will be over in a jiffy."

They tried to think so, but a shadow stalked in the background of their determined merrymaking. Walter, too, was quiet and dull, all through the holidays. He showed Rilla a cruel, anonymous letter he had received at Redmond—a letter far more conspicuous for malice than for patriotic indignation.

"Nevertheless, all it says is true, Rilla."

Rilla had caught it from him and thrown it into the fire.

"There isn't one word of truth in it," she declared hotly. "Walter, you've got morbid—as Miss Oliver says she gets when she broods too long over one thing."

"I can't get away from it at Redmond, Rilla. The whole college is aflame over the war. A perfectly fit fellow, of military age, who doesn't join up is looked upon as a shirker and treated accordingly. Dr. Milne, the English professor, who has always made a special pet of me, has two sons in khaki; and I can feel the change in his manner towards me."

"It's not fair—you're not fit."

"Physically I am. Sound as a bell. The unfitness is in the soul and it's a taint and a disgrace. There, don't cry, Rilla. I'm not going if that's what you're afraid of. The Piper's music rings in my ears day and night—but I cannot follow."

"You would break mother's heart and mine if you did," sobbed Rilla. "Oh, Walter, one is enough for any family."

The holidays were an unhappy time for her. Still, having Nan and Di and Walter and Shirley home helped in the enduring of things. A letter and book came for her from Kenneth Ford, too; some sentences in the letter made her cheeks burn and her heart beat—until the last paragraph, which sent an icy chill over everything.

"My ankle is about as good as new. I'll be fit to join up in a couple of months more, Rilla-my-Rilla. It will be some feeling to get into khaki all right. Little Ken will be able to look the whole world in the face then and owe not any man. It's been rotten lately, since I've been able to walk without limping. People who don't know look at me as much as to say 'Slacker!' Well, they won't have the chance to look it much longer."

"I hate this war," said Rilla bitterly, as she gazed out into the maple grove that was a chill glory of pink and gold in the winter sunset.

"Nineteen-fourteen has gone," said Dr. Blythe on New Year's Day. "Its sun, which rose fairly, has set in blood. What will nineteen-fifteen bring?"

"Victory!" said Susan, for once laconic.

"Do you really believe we'll win the war, Susan?" said Miss Oliver drearily. She had come over from Lowbridge to spend the day and see Walter and the girls before they went back to Redmond. She was in a rather blue and cynical mood and inclined to look on the dark side.

"'Believe' we'll win the war!" exclaimed Susan. "No, Miss Oliver, dear, I do not believe—I know. That does not worry me. What does worry me is the trouble and expense of it all. But then you cannot make omelets without breaking eggs, so we must just trust in God and make big guns."

"Sometimes I think the big guns are better to trust in than God," said Miss Oliver defiantly.

"No, no, dear, you do not. The Germans had the big guns at the Marne, had they not? But Providence settled them. Do not ever forget that. Just hold on to that when you feel inclined to doubt. Clutch hold of the sides of your chair and sit tight and keep saying, 'Big guns are good but the Almighty is better, and He is on our side, no matter what the Kaiser says about it.' I would have gone crazy many a day lately, Miss Oliver, dear, if I had not sat tight and repeated that to myself. My cousin Sophia is, like you, somewhat inclined to despond. 'Oh, dear me, what will we do if the Germans ever get here,' she wailed to me yesterday. 'Bury them,' said I, just as off-hand as that. 'There is plenty of room for the graves.' Cousin Sophia said that I was flippant but I was not flippant, Miss Oliver, dear, only calm and confident in the British navy and our Canadian boys. I am like old Mr. William Pollock of the Harbour Head. He is very old and has been ill for a long time, and one night last week he was so low that his daughter-in-law whispered to some one that she thought he was dead. 'Darn it, I ain't,' he called right out—only, Miss Oliver, dear, he did not use so mild a word as 'darn'—'darn it, I ain't, and I don't mean to die until the Kaiser is well licked.' Now, that, Miss Oliver, dear," concluded Susan, "is the kind of spirit I admire."

"I admire it but I can't emulate it," sighed Gertrude. "Before this, I have always been able to escape from the hard things of life for a little while by going into dreamland, and coming back like a giant refreshed. But I can't escape from this."

"Nor I," said Mrs. Blythe. "I hate going to bed now. All my life I've liked going to bed, to have a gay, mad, splendid half-hour of imagining things before sleeping. Now I imagine them still. But such different things."

"I am rather glad when the time comes to go to bed," said Miss Oliver. "I like the darkness because I can be myself in it—I needn't smile or talk bravely. But sometimes my imagination gets out of hand, too, and I see what you do—terrible things—terrible years to come."

"I am very thankful that I never had any imagination to speak of," said Susan. "I have been spared that. I see by this paper that the Crown Prince is killed again. Do you suppose there is any hope of his staying dead this time? And I also see that Woodrow Wilson is going to write another note. I wonder," concluded Susan, with the bitter irony she had of late begun to use when referring to the poor President, "if that man's schoolmaster is alive."

In January Jims was five months old and Rilla celebrated the anniversary by shortening him.

"He weighs fourteen pounds," she announced jubilantly. "Just exactly what he should weigh at five months, according to Morgan."

There was no longer any doubt in anybody's mind that Jims was getting positively pretty. His little cheeks were round and firm and faintly pink, his eyes were big and bright, his tiny paws had dimples at the root of every finger. He had even begun to grow hair, much to Rilla's unspoken relief. There was a pale golden fuzz all over his head that was distinctly visible in some lights. He was a good infant, generally sleeping and digesting as Morgan decreed. Occasionally he smiled but he had never laughed, in spite of all efforts to make him. This worried Rilla also, because Morgan said that babies usually laughed aloud from the third to the fifth month. Jims was five months and had no notion of laughing. Why hadn't he? Wasn't he normal?

One night Rilla came home late from a recruiting meeting at the Glen where she had been giving patriotic recitations. Rilla had never been willing to recite in public before. She was afraid of her tendency to lisp, which had a habit of reviving if she were doing anything that made her nervous. When she had first been asked to recite at the Upper Glen meeting she had refused. Then she began to worry over her refusal. Was it cowardly? What would Jem think if he knew? After two days of worry Rilla phoned to the president of the Patriotic Society that she would recite. She did, and lisped several times, and lay awake most of the night in an agony of wounded vanity. Then two nights after she recited again at Harbour Head. She had been at Lowbridge and over-harbour since then and had become resigned to an occasional lisp. Nobody except herself seemed to mind it. And she was so earnest and appealing and shining-eyed! More than one recruit joined up because Rilla's eyes seemed to look right at him when she passionately demanded how could men die better than fighting for the ashes of their fathers and the temples of their gods, or assured her audience with thrilling intensity that one crowded hour of glorious life was worth an age without a name. Even stolid Miller Douglas was so fired one night that it took Mary Vance a good hour to talk him back to sense. Mary Vance said bitterly that if Rilla Blythe felt as bad as she had pretended to feel over Jem's going to the front she wouldn't be urging other girls' brothers and friends to go.

On this particular night Rilla was tired and cold and very thankful to creep into her warm nest and cuddle down between her blankets, though as usual with a sorrowful wonder how Jem and Jerry were faring. She was just getting warm and drowsy when Jims suddenly began to cry—and kept on crying.

Rilla curled herself up in her bed and determined she would let him cry. She had Morgan behind her for justification. Jims was warm, physically comfortable—his cry wasn't the cry of pain—and had his little tummy as full as was good for him. Under such circumstances it would be simply spoiling him to fuss over him, and she wasn't going to do it. He could cry until he got good and tired and ready to go to sleep again.

Then Rilla's imagination began to torment her. Suppose, she thought, I was a tiny, helpless creature only five months old, with my father somewhere in France and my poor little mother, who had been so worried about me, in the graveyard. Suppose I was lying in a basket in a big, black room, without one speck of light, and nobody within miles of me, for all I could see or know. Suppose there wasn't a human being anywhere who loved me—for a father who had never seen me couldn't love me very much, especially when he had never written a word to or about me. Wouldn't I cry, too? Wouldn't I feel just so lonely and forsaken and frightened that I'd have to cry?

Rilla hopped out. She picked Jims out of his basket and took him into her own bed. His hands were cold, poor mite. But he had promptly ceased to cry. And then, as she held him close to her in the darkness, suddenly Jims laughed—a real, gurgly, chuckly, delighted, delightful laugh.

"Oh, you dear little thing!" exclaimed Rilla. "Are you so pleased at finding you're not all alone, lost in a huge, big, black room?" Then she knew she wanted to kiss him and she did. She kissed his silky, scented little head, she kissed his chubby little cheek, she kissed his little cold hands. She wanted to squeeze him—to cuddle him, just as she used to squeeze and cuddle her kittens. Something delightful and yearning and brooding seemed to have taken possession of her. She had never felt like this before.

In a few minutes Jims was sound asleep; and, as Rilla listened to his soft, regular breathing and felt the little body warm and contented against her, she realized that—at last—she loved her war-baby.

"He has got to be—such—a—darling," she thought drowsily, as she drifted off to slumberland herself.

In February Jem and Jerry and Robert Grant were in the trenches and a little more tension and dread was added to the Ingleside life. In March "Yiprez," as Susan called it, had come to have a bitter significance. The daily list of casualties had begun to appear in the papers and no one at Ingleside ever answered the telephone without a horrible cold shrinking—for it might be the station-master phoning up to say a telegram had come from overseas. No one at Ingleside ever got up in the morning without a sudden piercing wonder over what the day might bring.

"And I used to welcome the mornings so," thought Rilla.

Yet the round of life and duty went steadily on and every week or so one of the Glen lads who had just the other day been a rollicking schoolboy went into khaki.

"It is bitter cold out tonight, Mrs. Dr. dear," said Susan, coming in out of the clear starlit crispness of the Canadian winter twilight. "I wonder if the boys in the trenches are warm."

"How everything comes back to this war," cried Gertrude Oliver. "We can't get away from it—not even when we talk of the weather. I never go out these dark cold nights myself without thinking of the men in the trenches—not only our men but everybody's men. I would feel the same if there were nobody I knew at the front. When I snuggle down in my comfortable bed I am ashamed of being comfortable. It seems as if it were wicked of me to be so when many are not."

"I saw Mrs. Meredith down at the store," said Susan, "and she tells me that they are really troubled over Bruce, he takes things so much to heart. He has cried himself to sleep for a week, over the starving Belgians. 'Oh, mother,' he will say to her, so beseeching-like, 'surely the babies are never hungry—oh, not the babies, mother! Just say the babies are not hungry, mother.' And she cannot say it because it would not be true, and she is at her wits' end. They try to keep such things from him but he finds them out and then they cannot comfort him. It breaks my heart to read about them myself, Mrs. Dr. dear, and I cannot console myself with the thought that the tales are not true. When I read a novel that makes me want to weep I just say severely to myself, 'Now, Susan Baker, you know that is all a pack of lies.' But we must carry on. Jack Crawford says he is going to the war because he is tired of farming. I hope he will find it a pleasant change. And Mrs. Richard Elliott over-harbour is worrying herself sick because she used to be always scolding her husband about smoking up the parlour curtains. Now that he has enlisted she wishes she had never said a word to him. You know Josiah Cooper and William Daley, Mrs. Dr. dear. They used to be fast friends but they quarrelled twenty years ago and have never spoken since. Well, the other day Josiah went to William and said right out, 'Let us be friends. 'Tain't any time to be holding grudges.' William was real glad and held out his hand, and they sat down for a good talk. And in less than half an hour they had quarrelled again, over how the war ought to be fought, Josiah holding that the Dardanelles expedition was rank folly and William maintaining that it was the one sensible thing the Allies had done. And now they are madder at each other than ever and William says Josiah is as bad a pro-German as Whiskers-on-the-Moon. Whiskers-on-the-moon vows he is no pro-German but calls himself a pacifist, whatever that may be. It is nothing proper or Whiskers would not be it and that you may tie to. He says that the big British victory at New Chapelle cost more than it was worth and he has forbid Joe Milgrave to come near the house because Joe ran up his father's flag when the news came. Have you noticed, Mrs. Dr. dear, that the Czar has changed that Prish name to Premysl, which proves that the man had good sense, Russian though he is? Joe

Vickers told me in the store that he saw a very queer looking thing in the sky to-night over Lowbridge way. Do you suppose it could have been a Zeppelin, Mrs. Dr. dear?"

"I do not think it very likely, Susan."

"Well, I would feel easier about it if Whiskers-on-the-moon were not living in the Glen. They say he was seen going through strange manoeuvres with a lantern in his back yard one night lately. Some people think he was signalling."

"To whom—or what?"

"Ah, that is the mystery, Mrs. Dr. dear. In my opinion the Government would do well to keep an eye on that man if it does not want us to be all murdered in our beds some night. Now I shall just look over the papers a minute before going to write a letter to little Jem. Two things I never did, Mrs. Dr. dear, were write letters and read politics. Yet here I am doing both regular and I find there is something in politics after all. Whatever Woodrow Wilson means I cannot fathom but I am hoping I will puzzle it out yet."

Susan, in her pursuit of Wilson and politics, presently came upon something that disturbed her and exclaimed in a tone of bitter disappointment,

"That devilish Kaiser has only a boil after all."

"Don't swear, Susan," said Dr. Blythe, pulling a long face.

"'Devilish' is not swearing, doctor, dear. I have always understood that swearing was taking the name of the Almighty in vain?"

"Well, it isn't—ahem—refined," said the doctor, winking at Miss Oliver.

"No, doctor, dear, the devil and the Kaiser—if so be that they are really two different people—are not refined. And you cannot refer to them in a refined way. So I abide by what I said, although you may notice that I am careful not to use such expressions when young Rilla is about. And I maintain that the papers have no right to say that the Kaiser has pneumonia and raise people's hopes, and then come out and say he has nothing but a boil. A boil, indeed! I wish he was covered with them."

Susan stalked out to the kitchen and settled down to write to Jem; deeming him in need of some home comfort from certain passages in his letter that day.

"We're in an old wine cellar tonight, dad," he wrote, "in water to our knees. Rats everywhere—no fire—a drizzling rain coming down—rather dismal. But it might be worse. I got Susan's box today and everything was in tip-top order and we had a feast. Jerry is up the line somewhere and he says the rations are rather worse than Aunt Martha's ditto used to be. But here they're not bad—only monotonous. Tell Susan I'd give a year's pay for a good batch of her monkey-faces; but don't let that inspire her to send any for they wouldn't keep.

"We have been under fire since the last week in February. One boy—he was a Nova Scotian—was killed right beside me yesterday. A shell burst near us and when the mess cleared away he was lying dead—not mangled at all—he just looked a little startled. It was the first time I'd been close to anything like that and it was a nasty sensation, but one soon gets used to horrors here. We're in an absolutely different world. The only things that are the same are the stars—and they are never in their right places, somehow.

"Tell mother not to worry—I'm all right—fit as a fiddle—and glad I came. There's something across from us here that has got to be wiped out of the world, that's all—an emanation of evil that would otherwise poison life for ever. It's got to be done, dad, however long it takes, and whatever it costs, and you tell the Glen people this for me. They don't realize yet what it is has broken loose—I didn't when I first joined up. I thought it was fun. Well, it isn't! But I'm in the right place all right—make no mistake about that. When I saw what had been done here to homes and gardens and people—well, dad, I seemed to see a gang of Huns marching through Rainbow Valley and the Glen, and the garden at Ingleside. There were gardens over here—beautiful gardens with the beauty of centuries— and what are they now? Mangled, desecrated things! We are fighting to make those dear old places where we had played as children, safe for other boys and girls—fighting for the preservation and safety of all sweet, wholesome things.

"Whenever any of you go to the station be sure to give Dog Monday a double pat for me. Fancy the faithful little beggar waiting there for me like that! Honestly, dad, on some of these dark cold nights in the trenches, it heartens and braces me up no end to think that thousands of miles away at the old Glen station there is a small spotted dog sharing my vigil.

"Tell Rilla I'm glad her war-baby is turning out so well, and tell Susan that I'm fighting a good fight against both Huns and cooties."

"Mrs. Dr. dear," whispered Susan solemnly, "what are cooties?"

Mrs. Blythe whispered back and then said in reply to Susan's horrified ejaculations, "It's always like that in the trenches, Susan."

Susan shook her head and went away in grim silence to re-open a parcel she had sewed up for Jem and slip in a fine tooth comb.

CHAPTER XII - IN THE DAYS OF LANGEMARCK

"How can spring come and be beautiful in such a horror," wrote Rilla in her diary. "When the sun shines and the fluffy yellow catkins are coming out on the willow-trees down by the brook, and the garden is beginning to be beautiful I can't realize that such dreadful things are happening in Flanders. But they are!

"This past week has been terrible for us all, since the news came of the fighting around Ypres and the battles of Langemarck and St. Julien. Our Canadian boys have done splendidly—General French says they 'saved the situation,' when the Germans had all but broken through. But I can't feel pride or exultation or anything but a gnawing anxiety over Jem and Jerry and Mr. Grant. The casualty lists are coming out in the papers every day—oh, there are so many of them. I can't bear to read them for fear I'd find Jem's name—for there have been cases where people have seen their boys' names in the casualty lists before the official telegram came. As for the telephone, for a day or two I just refused to answer it, because I thought I could not endure the horrible moment that came between saying 'Hello' and hearing the response. That moment seemed a hundred years long, for I was always dreading to hear 'There is a telegram for Dr. Blythe.' Then, when I had shirked for a while, I was ashamed of leaving it all for mother or Susan, and now I make myself go. But it never gets any easier. Gertrude teaches school and reads compositions and sets examination papers just as she always has done, but I know her thoughts are over in Flanders all the time. Her eyes haunt me.

"And Kenneth is in khaki now, too. He has got a lieutenant's commission and expects to go overseas in midsummer, so he wrote me. There wasn't much else in the letter—he seemed to be thinking of nothing but going overseas. I shall not see him again before he goes—perhaps I will never see him again. Sometimes I ask myself if that evening at Four Winds was all a dream. It might as well be—it seems as if it happened in another life lived years ago—and everybody has forgotten it but me.

"Walter and Nan and Di came home last night from Redmond. When Walter stepped off the train Dog Monday rushed to meet him, frantic with joy. I suppose he thought Jem would be there, too. After the first moment, he paid no attention to Walter and his pats, but just stood there, wagging his tail nervously and looking past Walter at the other people coming out, with eyes that made me choke up, for I couldn't help thinking that, for all we knew, Monday might never see Jem come off that train again. Then, when all the people were out, Monday looked up at Walter, gave his hand a little lick as if to say, 'I know it isn't your fault he didn't come—excuse me for feeling disappointed,' and then he trotted back to his shed, with that funny little sidelong waggle of his that always makes it seem that his hind legs are travelling directly away from the point at which his forelegs are aiming.

"We tried to coax him home with us—Di even got down and kissed him between the eyes and said, 'Monday, old duck, won't you come up with us just for the evening?' And Monday said—he did!—'I am very sorry but I can't. I've got a date to meet Jem here, you know, and there's a train goes through at eight.'

"It's lovely to have Walter back again though he seems quiet and sad, just as he was at Christmas. But I'm going to love him hard and cheer him up and make him laugh as he used to. It seems to me that every day of my life Walter means more to me.

"The other evening Susan happened to say that the mayflowers were out in Rainbow Valley. I chanced to be looking at mother when Susan spoke. Her face changed and she gave a queer little choked cry. Most of the time mother is so spunky and gay you would never guess what she feels inside; but now and then some little thing is too much for her and we see under the surface. 'Mayflowers!' she said. 'Jem brought me mayflowers last year!' and she got up and went out of the room. I would have rushed off to Rainbow Valley and brought her an armful of mayflowers, but I knew that wasn't what she wanted. And after Walter got home last night he slipped away to the valley and brought mother home all the mayflowers he could find. Nobody had said a word to him about it—he just remembered himself that Jem used to bring mother the first mayflowers and so he brought them in Jem's place. It shows how tender and thoughtful he is. And yet there are people who send him cruel letters!

"It seems strange that we can go in with ordinary life just as if nothing were happening overseas that concerned us, just as if any day might not bring us awful news. But we can and do. Susan is putting in the garden, and mother and she are housecleaning, and we Junior Reds are getting up a concert in aid of the Belgians. We have been practising for a month and having no end of trouble and bother with cranky people. Miranda Pryor promised to help with a dialogue and when she had her part all learnt her father put his foot down and refused to allow her to help at all. I am not blaming Miranda exactly, but I do think she might have a little more spunk sometimes. If she put her foot down once in a while she might bring her father to terms, for she is all the housekeeper he has and what would he do if she 'struck'? If I were in Miranda's shoes I'd find some way of managing Whiskers-on-the-moon. I would horse-whip him, or bite him, if nothing else would serve. But Miranda is a meek and obedient daughter whose days should be long in the land.

"I couldn't get anyone else to take the part, because nobody liked it, so finally I had to take it myself. Olive Kirk is on the concert committee and goes against me in every single thing. But I got my way in asking Mrs. Channing to come out from town and sing for us, anyhow. She is a beautiful singer and will draw such a crowd that we will make more than we will have to pay her. Olive Kirk thought our local talent good enough and Minnie Clow won't sing at all now in the choruses because she would be so nervous before Mrs. Channing. And Minnie is the only good alto we have! There are times when I am so exasperated that I feel tempted to wash my hands of the whole affair; but after I dance round my room a few times in sheer rage I cool down and have another whack at it. Just at present I am racked with worry for fear the Isaac Reeses are taking whooping-cough. They have all got a dreadful cold and there are five of them who have important parts in the programme and if they go and develop whooping-cough what shall I do? Dick Reese's violin solo is to be one of our titbits and Kit Reese is in every tableau and the three small girls have the cutest flag-drill. I've been toiling for weeks to train them in it, and now it seems likely that all my trouble will go for nothing.

"Jims cut his first tooth today. I am very glad, for he is nearly nine months old and Mary Vance has been insinuating that he is awfully backward about cutting his teeth. He has begun to creep but doesn't crawl as most babies do. He trots about on all fours and carries things in his mouth like a little dog. Nobody can say he isn't up to schedule time in the matter of creeping anyway—away ahead of it indeed, since ten months is Morgan's average for creeping. He is so cute, it will be a shame if his dad never sees him. His hair is coming on nicely too, and I am not without hope that it will be curly.

"Just for a few minutes, while I've been writing of Jims and the concert, I've forgotten Ypres and the poison gas and the casualty lists. Now it all rushes back, worse than ever. Oh, if we could just know that Jem is all right! I used to be so furious with Jem when he called me Spider. And now, if he would just come whistling through the hall and call out, 'Hello, Spider,' as he used to do, I would think it the loveliest name in the world."

Rilla put away her diary and went out to the garden. The spring evening was very lovely. The long, green, seaward-looking glen was filled with dusk, and beyond it were meadows of sunset. The harbour was radiant, purple here, azure there, opal elsewhere. The maple grove was beginning to be misty green. Rilla looked about her with wistful eyes. Who said that spring was the joy of the year? It was the heart-break of the year. And the pale-purply mornings and the daffodil stars and the wind in the old pine were so many separate pangs of the heart-break. Would life ever be free from dread again?

"It's good to see P.E.I. twilight once more," said Walter, joining her. "I didn't really remember that the sea was so blue and the roads so red and the wood nooks so wild and fairy haunted. Yes, the fairies still abide here. I vow I could find scores of them under the violets in Rainbow Valley."

Rilla was momentarily happy. This sounded like the Walter of yore. She hoped he was forgetting certain things that had troubled him.

"And isn't the sky blue over Rainbow Valley?" she said, responding to his mood. "Blue—blue—you'd have to say 'blue' a hundred times before you could express how blue it is."

Susan wandered by, her head tied up with a shawl, her hands full of garden implements. Doc, stealthy and wild-eyed, was shadowing her steps among the spirea bushes.

"The sky may be blue," said Susan, "but that cat has been Hyde all day so we will likely have rain tonight and by the same token I have rheumatism in my shoulder."

"It may rain—but don't think rheumatism, Susan—think violets," said Walter gaily—rather too gaily, Rilla thought.

Susan considered him unsympathetic.

"Indeed, Walter dear, I do not know what you mean by thinking violets," she responded stiffly, "and rheumatism is not a thing to be joked about, as you may some day realize for yourself. I hope I am not of the kind that is always complaining of their aches and pains, especially now when the news is so terrible. Rheumatism is bad enough but I realize, and none better, that it is not to be compared to being gassed by the Huns."

"Oh, my God, no!" exclaimed Walter passionately. He turned and went back to the house.

Susan shook her head. She disapproved entirely of such ejaculations. "I hope he will not let his mother hear him talking like that," she thought as she stacked the hoes and rake away.

Rilla was standing among the budding daffodils with tear-filled eyes. Her evening was spoiled; she detested Susan, who had somehow hurt Walter; and Jem—had Jem been gassed? Had he died in torture?

"I can't endure this suspense any longer," said Rilla desperately.

But she endured it as the others did for another week. Then a letter came from Jem. He was all right.

"I've come through without a scratch, dad. Don't know how I or any of us did it. You'll have seen all about it in the papers—I can't write of it. But the Huns haven't got through—they won't get through. Jerry was knocked stiff by a shell one time, but it was only the shock. He was all right in a few days. Grant is safe, too."

Nan had a letter from Jerry Meredith. "I came back to consciousness at dawn," he wrote. "Couldn't tell what had happened to me but thought that I was done for. I was all alone and afraid—terribly afraid. Dead men were all around me, lying on the horrible grey, slimy fields. I was woefully thirsty—and I thought of David and the Bethlehem water—and of the old spring in Rainbow Valley under the maples. I seemed to see it just before me—and you standing laughing on the other side of it—and I thought it was all over with me. And I didn't care. Honestly, I didn't care. I just felt a dreadful childish fear of loneliness and of those dead men around me, and a sort of wonder how this could have happened to me. Then they found me and carted me off and before long I discovered that there wasn't really anything wrong with me. I'm going back to the trenches tomorrow. Every man is needed there that can be got."

"Laughter is gone out of the world," said Faith Meredith, who had come over to report on her letters. "I remember telling old Mrs. Taylor long ago that the world was a world of laughter. But it isn't so any longer."

"It's a shriek of anguish," said Gertrude Oliver.

"We must keep a little laughter, girls," said Mrs. Blythe. "A good laugh is as good as a prayer sometimes—only sometimes," she added under her breath. She had found it very hard to laugh during the three weeks she had just lived through—she, Anne Blythe, to whom laughter had always come so easily and freshly. And what hurt most was that Rilla's laughter had grown so rare—Rilla whom she used to think laughed over-much. Was all the child's girlhood to be so clouded? Yet how strong and clever and womanly she was growing! How patiently she knitted and sewed and manipulated those uncertain Junior Reds! And how wonderful she was with Jims.

"She really could not do better for that child than if she had raised a baker's dozen, Mrs. Dr. dear," Susan had avowed solemnly. "Little did I ever expect it of her on the day she landed here with that soup tureen."

CHAPTER XIII - A SLICE OF HUMBLE PIE

"I am very much afraid, Mrs. Dr. dear," said Susan, who had been on a pilgrimage to the station with some choice bones for Dog Monday, "that something terrible has happened. Whiskers-on-the-moon came off the train from Charlottetown and he was looking pleased. I do not remember that I ever saw him with a smile on in public before. Of course he may have just been getting the better of somebody in a cattle deal but I have an awful presentiment that the Huns have broken through somewhere."

Perhaps Susan was unjust in connecting Mr. Pryor's smile with the sinking of the Lusitania, news of which circulated an hour later when the mail was distributed. But the Glen boys turned out that night in a body and broke all his windows in a fine frenzy of indignation over the Kaiser's doings.

"I do not say they did right and I do not say they did wrong," said Susan, when she heard of it. "But I will say that I wouldn't have minded throwing a few stones myself. One thing is certain—Whiskers-on-the-moon said in the post office the day the news came, in the presence of witnesses, that folks who could not stay home after they had been warned deserved no better fate. Norman Douglas is fairly foaming at the mouth over it all. 'If the devil doesn't get those men who sunk the Lusitania then there is no use in there being a devil,' he was shouting in Carter's store last night. Norman Douglas always has believed that anybody who opposed him was on the side of the devil, but a man like that is bound to be right once in a while. Bruce Meredith is worrying over the babies who were drowned. And it seems he prayed for something very special last Friday night and didn't get it, and was feeling quite disgruntled over it. But when he heard about the Lusitania he told his mother that he understood now why God didn't answer his prayer—He was too busy attending to the souls of all the people who went down on the Lusitania. That child's brain is a hundred years older than his body, Mrs. Dr. dear. As for the Lusitania, it is an awful occurrence, whatever way you look at it. But Woodrow Wilson is going to write a note about it, so why worry? A pretty president!" and Susan banged her pots about wrathfully. President Wilson was rapidly becoming anathema in Susan's kitchen.

Mary Vance dropped in one evening to tell the Ingleside folks that she had withdrawn all opposition to Miller Douglas's enlisting.

"This Lusitania business was too much for me," said Mary brusquely. "When the Kaiser takes to drowning innocent babies it's high time somebody told him where he gets off at. This thing must be fought to a finish. It's been soaking into my mind slow but I'm on now. So I up and told Miller he could go as far as I was concerned. Old Kitty Alec won't be converted though. If every ship in the world was submarined and every baby drowned, Kitty wouldn't turn a hair. But I flatter myself that it was me kept Miller back all along and not the fair Kitty. I may have deceived myself—but we shall see."

They did see. The next Sunday Miller Douglas walked into the Glen Church beside Mary Vance in khaki. And Mary was so proud of him that her white eyes fairly blazed. Joe Milgrave, back under the gallery, looked at Miller and Mary and then at Miranda Pryor, and sighed so heavily that every one within a radius of three pews heard him and knew what his trouble was. Walter Blythe did not sigh. But Rilla, scanning his face anxiously, saw a look that cut into her heart. It haunted her for the next week and made an undercurrent of soreness in her soul, which was externally being harrowed up by the near approach of the Red Cross concert and the worries connected therewith. The Reese cold had not developed into whooping-cough, so that tangle was straightened out. But other things were hanging in the balance; and on the very day before the concert came a regretful letter from Mrs. Channing saying that she could not come to sing. Her son, who was in Kingsport with his regiment, was seriously ill with pneumonia, and she must go to him at once.

The members of the concert committee looked at each other in blank dismay. What was to be done?

"This comes of depending on outside help," said Olive Kirk, disagreeably.

"We must do something," said Rilla, too desperate to care for Olive's manner. "We've advertised the concert everywhere—and crowds are coming—there's even a big party coming out from town—and we were short enough of music as it was. We must get some one to sing in Mrs. Channing's place."

"I don't know who you can get at this late date," said Olive. "Irene Howard could do it; but it is not likely she will after the way she was insulted by our society."

"How did our society insult her?" asked Rilla, in what she called her 'cold-pale tone.' Its coldness and pallor did not daunt Olive.

"You insulted her," she answered sharply. "Irene told me all about it—she was literally heart-broken. You told her never to speak to you again—and Irene told me she simply could not imagine what she had said or done to deserve such treatment. That was why she never came to our meetings again but joined in with the Lowbridge Red Cross. I do not blame her in the least, and I, for one, will not ask her to lower herself by helping us out of this scrape."

"You don't expect me to ask her?" giggled Amy MacAllister, the other member of the committee. "Irene and I haven't spoken for a hundred years. Irene is always getting 'insulted' by somebody. But she is a lovely singer, I'll admit that, and people would just as soon hear her as Mrs. Channing."

"It wouldn't do any good if you did ask her," said Olive significantly. "Soon after we began planning this concert, back in April, I met Irene in town one day and asked her if she wouldn't help us out. She said she'd love to but she really didn't see how she could when Rilla Blythe was running the programme, after the strange way Rilla had behaved to her. So there it is and here we are, and a nice failure our concert will be."

Rilla went home and shut herself up in her room, her soul in a turmoil. She would not humiliate herself by apologizing to Irene Howard! Irene had been as much in the wrong as she had been; and she had told such mean, distorted versions of their quarrel everywhere, posing as a puzzled, injured martyr. Rilla could never bring herself to tell her side of it. The fact that a slur at Walter was mixed up in it tied her tongue. So most people believed that Irene had been badly used, except a few girls who had never liked her and sided with Rilla. And yet—the concert over which she had worked so hard was going to be a failure. Mrs. Channing's four solos were the feature of the whole programme.

"Miss Oliver, what do you think about it?" she asked in desperation.

"I think Irene is the one who should apologize," said Miss Oliver. "But unfortunately my opinion will not fill the blanks in your programme."

"If I went and apologized meekly to Irene she would sing, I am sure," sighed Rilla. "She really loves to sing in public. But I know she'll be nasty about it—I feel I'd rather do anything than go. I suppose I should go—if Jem and Jerry can face the Huns surely I can face Irene Howard, and swallow my pride to ask a favour of her for the good of the Belgians. Just at present I feel that I cannot do it but for all that I have a presentiment that after supper you'll see me meekly trotting through Rainbow Valley on my way to the Upper Glen Road."

Rilla's presentiment proved correct. After supper she dressed herself carefully in her blue, beaded crepe—for vanity is harder to quell than pride and Irene always saw any flaw or shortcoming in another girl's appearance. Besides, as Rilla had told her mother one day when she was nine years old, "It is easier to behave nicely when you have your good clothes on."

Rilla did her hair very becomingly and donned a long raincoat for fear of a shower. But all the while her thoughts were concerned with the coming distasteful interview, and she kept rehearsing mentally her part in it. She wished it were over—she wished she had never tried to get up a Belgian Relief concert—she wished she had not quarreled with Irene. After all, disdainful silence would have been much more effective in meeting the slur upon Walter. It was foolish and childish to fly out as she had done—well, she would be wiser in the future, but meanwhile a large and very unpalatable slice of humble pie had to be eaten, and Rilla Blythe was no fonder of that wholesome article of diet than the rest of us.

By sunset she was at the door of the Howard house—a pretentious abode, with white scroll-work round the eaves and an eruption of bay-windows on all its sides. Mrs. Howard, a plump, voluble dame, met Rilla gushingly and left her in the parlour while she went to call Irene. Rilla threw off her rain-coat and looked at herself critically in the mirror over the mantel. Hair, hat, and dress were satisfactory—nothing there for Miss Irene to make fun of. Rilla remembered how clever and amusing she used to think Irene's biting little comments about other girls. Well, it had come home to her now.

Presently, Irene skimmed down, elegantly gowned, with her pale, straw-coloured hair done in the latest and most extreme fashion, and an over-luscious atmosphere of perfume enveloping her.

"Why how do you do, Miss Blythe?" she said sweetly. "This is a very unexpected pleasure."

Rilla had risen to take Irene's chilly finger-tips and now, as she sat down again, she saw something that temporarily stunned her. Irene saw it too, as she sat down, and a little amused, impertinent smile appeared on her lips and hovered there during the rest of the interview.

On one of Rilla's feet was a smart little steel-buckled shoe and a filmy blue silk stocking. The other was clad in a stout and rather shabby boot and black lisle!

Poor Rilla! She had changed, or begun to change her boots and stockings after she had put on her dress. This was the result of doing one thing with your hands and another with your brain. Oh, what a ridiculous position to be in—and before Irene Howard of all people—Irene, who was staring at Rilla's feet as if she had never seen feet before! And once she had thought Irene's manner perfection! Everything that Rilla had prepared to say vanished from her memory. Vainly trying to tuck her unlucky foot under her chair, she blurted out a blunt statement.

"I have come to athk a favour of you, Irene."

There—lisping! Oh, she had been prepared for humiliation but not to this extent! Really, there were limits!

"Yes?" said Irene in a cool, questioning tone, lifting her shallowly-set, insolent eyes to Rilla's crimson face for a moment and then dropping them again as if she could not tear them from their fascinated gaze at the shabby boot and the gallant shoe.

Rilla gathered herself together. She would not lisp—she would be calm and composed.

"Mrs. Channing cannot come because her son is ill in Kingsport, and I have come on behalf of the committee to ask you if you will be so kind as to sing for us in her place." Rilla enunciated every word so precisely and carefully that she seemed to be reciting a lesson.

"It's something of a fiddler's invitation, isn't it?" said Irene, with one of her disagreeable smiles.

"Olive Kirk asked you to help when we first thought of the concert and you refused," said Rilla.

"Why, I could hardly help—then—could I?" asked Irene plaintively. "After you ordered me never to speak to you again? It would have been very awkward for us both, don't you think?"

Now for the humble pie.

"I want to apologize to you for saying that, Irene." said Rilla steadily. "I should not have said it and I have been very sorry ever since. Will you forgive me?"

"And sing at your concert?" said Irene sweetly and insultingly.

"If you mean," said Rilla miserably, "that I would not be apologizing to you if it were not for the concert perhaps that is true. But it is also true that I have felt ever since it happened that I should not have said what I did and that I have been sorry for it all winter. That is all I can say. If you feel you can't forgive me I suppose there is nothing more to be said."

"Oh, Rilla dear, don't snap me up like that," pleaded Irene. "Of course I'll forgive you—though I did feel awfully about it—how awfully I hope you'll never know. I cried for weeks over it. And I hadn't said or done a thing!"

Rilla choked back a retort. After all, there was no use in arguing with Irene, and the Belgians were starving.

"Don't you think you can help us with the concert," she forced herself to say. Oh, if only Irene would stop looking at that boot! Rilla could just hear her giving Olive Kirk an account of it.

"I don't see how I really can at the last moment like this," protested Irene. "There isn't time to learn anything new."

"Oh, you have lots of lovely songs that nobody in the Glen ever heard before," said Rilla, who knew Irene had been going to town all winter for lessons and that this was only a pretext. "They will all be new down there."

"But I have no accompanist," protested Irene.

"Una Meredith can accompany you," said Rilla.

"Oh, I couldn't ask her," sighed Irene. "We haven't spoken since last fall. She was so hateful to me the time of our Sunday-school concert that I simply had to give her up."

Dear, dear, was Irene at feud with everybody? As for Una Meredith being hateful to anybody, the idea was so farcical that Rilla had much ado to keep from laughing in Irene's very face.

"Miss Oliver is a beautiful pianist and can play any accompaniment at sight," said Rilla desperately. "She will play for you and you could run over your songs easily tomorrow evening at Ingleside before the concert."

"But I haven't anything to wear. My new evening-dress isn't home from Charlottetown yet, and I simply cannot wear my old one at such a big affair. It is too shabby and old-fashioned."

"Our concert," said Rilla slowly, "is in aid of Belgian children who are starving to death. Don't you think you could wear a shabby dress once for their sake, Irene?"

"Oh, don't you think those accounts we get of the conditions of the Belgians are very much exaggerated?" said Irene. "I'm sure they can't be actually starving you know, in the twentieth century. The newspapers always colour things so highly."

Rilla concluded that she had humiliated herself enough. There was such a thing as self-respect. No more coaxing, concert or no concert. She got up, boot and all.

"I am sorry you can't help us, Irene, but since you cannot we must do the best we can."

Now this did not suit Irene at all. She desired exceedingly to sing at that concert, and all her hesitations were merely by way of enhancing the boon of her final consent. Besides, she really wanted to be friends with Rilla again. Rilla's whole-hearted, ungrudging adoration had been very sweet incense to her. And Ingleside was a very charming house to visit, especially when a handsome college student like Walter was home. She stopped looking at Rilla's feet.

"Rilla, darling, don't be so abrupt. I really want to help you, if I can manage it. Just sit down and let's talk it over."

"I'm sorry, but I can't. I have to be home soon—Jims has to be settled for the night, you know."

"Oh, yes—the baby you are bringing up by the book. It's perfectly sweet of you to do it when you hate children so. How cross you were just because I kissed him! But we'll forget all that and be chums again, won't we? Now, about the concert—I dare say I can run into town on the morning train after my dress, and out again on the afternoon one in plenty of time for the concert, if you'll ask Miss Oliver to play for me. I couldn't—she's so dreadfully haughty and supercilious that she simply paralyses poor little me."

Rilla did not waste time or breath defending Miss Oliver. She coolly thanked Irene, who had suddenly become very amiable and gushing, and got away. She was very thankful the interview was over. But she knew now that she and Irene could never be the friends they had been. Friendly, yes—but friends, no. Nor did she wish it. All winter she had felt under her other and more serious worries, a little feeling of regret for her lost chum. Now it was suddenly gone. Irene was not as Mrs. Elliott would say, of the race that knew Joseph. Rilla did not say or think that she had outgrown Irene. Had the thought occurred to her she would have considered it absurd when she was not yet seventeen and Irene was twenty. But it was the truth. Irene was just what she had been a year ago—just what she would always be. Rilla Blythe's nature in that year had changed and matured and deepened. She found herself seeing through Irene with a disconcerting clearness—discerning under all her superficial sweetness, her pettiness, her vindictiveness, her insincerity, her essential cheapness. Irene had lost for ever her faithful worshipper.

But not until Rilla had traversed the Upper Glen Road and found herself in the moon-dappled solitude of Rainbow Valley did she fully recover her composure of spirit. Then she stopped under a tall wild plum that was ghostly white and fair in its misty spring bloom and laughed.

"There is only one thing of importance just now—and that is that the Allies win the war," she said aloud. "Therefore, it follows without dispute that the fact that I went to see Irene Howard with odd shoes and stockings on is of no importance whatever. Nevertheless, I, Bertha Marilla Blythe, swear solemnly with the moon as witness"—Rilla lifted her hand dramatically to the said moon—"that I will never leave my room again without looking carefully at both my feet."

CHAPTER XIV - THE VALLEY OF DECISION

Susan kept the flag flying at Ingleside all the next day, in honour of Italy's declaration of war.

"And not before it was time, Mrs. Dr. dear, considering the way things have begun to go on the Russian front. Say what you will, those Russians are kittle cattle, the grand duke Nicholas to the contrary notwithstanding. It is a fortunate thing for Italy that she has come in on the right side, but whether it is as fortunate for the Allies I will not predict until I know more about Italians than I do now. However, she will give that old reprobate of a Francis Joseph something to think about. A pretty Emperor indeed—with one foot in the grave and yet plotting wholesale murder"—and Susan thumped and kneaded her bread with as much vicious energy as she could have expended in punching Francis Joseph himself if he had been so unlucky as to fall into her clutches.

Walter had gone to town on the early train, and Nan offered to look after Jims for the day and so set Rilla free. Rilla was wildly busy all day, helping to decorate the Glen hall and seeing to a hundred last things. The evening was beautiful, in spite of the fact that Mr. Pryor was reported to have said that he "hoped it would rain pitch forks points down," and to have wantonly kicked Miranda's dog as he said it. Rilla, rushing home from the hall, dressed hurriedly. Everything had gone surprisingly well at the last; Irene was even then downstairs practising her songs with Miss Oliver; Rilla was excited and happy, forgetful even of the Western front for the moment. It gave her a sense of achievement and victory to have brought her efforts of weeks to such a successful conclusion. She knew that there had not lacked people who thought and hinted that Rilla Blythe had not the tact or patience to engineer a concert programme. She had shown them! Little snatches of song bubbled up from her lips as she dressed. She thought she was looking very well. Excitement brought a faint, becoming pink into her round creamy cheeks, quite drowning out her few freckles, and her hair gleamed with red-brown lustre. Should she wear crab-apple blossoms in it, or her little fillet of pearls? After some agonised wavering she decided on the crab-apple blossoms and tucked the white waxen cluster behind her left ear. Now for a final look at her feet. Yes, both slippers were on. She gave the sleeping Jims a kiss—what a dear little warm, rosy, satin face he had—and hurried down the hill to the hall. Already it was filling—soon it was crowded. Her concert was going to be a brilliant success.

The first three numbers were successfully over. Rilla was in the little dressing-room behind the platform, looking out on the moonlit harbour and rehearsing her own recitations. She was alone, the rest of the performers being in the larger room on the other side. Suddenly she felt two soft bare arms slipping round her waist, then Irene Howard dropped a light kiss on her cheek.

"Rilla, you sweet thing, you're looking simply angelic to-night. You have spunk—I thought you would feel so badly over Walter's enlisting that you'd hardly be able to bear up at all, and here you are as cool as a cucumber. I wish I had half your nerve."

Rilla stood perfectly still. She felt no emotion whatever—she felt nothing. The world of feeling had just gone blank.

"Walter—enlisting"—she heard herself saying—then she heard Irene's affected little laugh.

"Why, didn't you know? I thought you did of course, or I wouldn't have mentioned it. I am always putting my foot in it, aren't I? Yes, that is what he went to town for to-day—he told me coming out on the train to-night, I was the first person he told. He isn't in khaki yet—they were out of uniforms—but he will be in a day or two. I always said Walter had as much pluck as anybody. I assure you I felt proud of him, Rilla, when he told me what he'd done. Oh, there's an end of Rick MacAllister's reading. I must fly. I promised I'd play for the next chorus—Alice Clow has such a headache."

She was gone—oh, thank God, she was gone! Rilla was alone again, staring out at the unchanged, dream-like beauty of moonlit Four Winds. Feeling was coming back to her—a pang of agony so acute as to be almost physical seemed to rend her apart.

"I cannot bear it," she said. And then came the awful thought that perhaps she could bear it and that there might be years of this hideous suffering before her.

She must get away—she must rush home—she must be alone. She could not go out there and play for drills and give readings and take part in dialogues now. It would spoil half the concert; but that did not matter—nothing mattered. Was this she, Rilla Blythe—this tortured thing, who had been quite happy a few minutes ago? Outside, a quartette was singing "We'll never let the old flag fall"—the music seemed to be coming from some remote distance. Why couldn't she cry, as she had cried when Jem told them he must go? If she could cry perhaps this horrible something that seemed to have seized on her very life might let go. But no tears came! Where were her scarf and coat? She must get away and hide herself like an animal hurt to the death.

Was it a coward's part to run away like this? The question came to her suddenly as if someone else had asked it. She thought of the shambles of the Flanders front—she thought of her brother and her playmate helping to hold those fire-swept trenches. What would they think of her if she shirked her little duty here—the humble duty of carrying the programme through for her Red Cross? But she couldn't stay—she couldn't—yet what was it mother had said when Jem went:

"When our women fail in courage shall our men be fearless still?" But this—this was unbearable.

Still, she stopped half-way to the door and went back to the window. Irene was singing now; her beautiful voice—the only real thing about her—soared clear and sweet through the building. Rilla knew that the girls' Fairy Drill came next. Could she go out there and play for it? Her head was aching now—her throat was burning. Oh, why had Irene told her just then, when telling could do no good? Irene had been very cruel. Rilla remembered now that more than once that day she had caught her mother looking at her with an odd expression. She had been too busy to wonder what it meant. She understood now. Mother had known why Walter went to town but wouldn't tell her until the concert was over. What spirit and endurance mother had!

"I must stay here and see things through," said Rilla, clasping her cold hands together.

The rest of the evening always seemed like a fevered dream to her. Her body was crowded by people but her soul was alone in a torture-chamber of its own. Yet she played steadily for the drills and gave her readings without faltering. She even put on a grotesque old Irish woman's costume and acted the part in the dialogue which Miranda Pryor had not taken. But she did not give her "brogue" the inimitable twist she had given it in the practices, and her readings lacked their usual fire and appeal. As she stood before the audience she saw one face only—that of the handsome, dark-haired lad sitting beside her mother—and she saw that same face in the trenches—saw it lying cold and dead under the stars—saw it pining in prison—saw the light of its eyes blotted out—saw a hundred horrible things as she stood there on the beflagged platform of the Glen hall with her own face whiter than the milky crab-blossoms in her hair. Between her numbers she walked restlessly up and down the little dressing-room. Would the concert never end!

It ended at last. Olive Kirk rushed up and told her exultantly that they had made a hundred dollars. "That's good," Rilla said mechanically. Then she was away from them all—oh, thank God, she was away from them all—Walter was waiting for her at the door. He put his arm through hers silently and they went together down the moonlit road. The frogs were singing in the marshes, the dim, ensilvered fields of home lay all around them. The spring night was lovely and appealing. Rilla felt that its beauty was an insult to her pain. She would hate moonlight for ever.

"You know?" said Walter.

"Yes. Irene told me," answered Rilla chokingly.

"We didn't want you to know till the evening was over. I knew when you came out for the drill that you had heard. Little sister, I had to do it. I couldn't live any longer on such terms with myself as I have been since the Lusitania was sunk. When I pictured those dead women and children floating about in that pitiless, ice-cold water—well, at first I just felt a sort of nausea with life. I wanted to get out of the world where such a thing could happen—shake its accursed dust from my feet for ever. Then I knew I had to go."

"There are—plenty—without you."

"That isn't the point, Rilla-my-Rilla. I'm going for my own sake—to save my soul alive. It will shrink to something small and mean and lifeless if I don't go. That would be worse than blindness or mutilation or any of the things I've feared."

"You may—be—killed," Rilla hated herself for saying it—she knew it was a weak and cowardly thing to say—but she had rather gone to pieces after the tension of the evening.

> "'Comes he slow or comes he fast
> It is but death who comes at last.'"

quoted Walter. "It's not death I fear—I told you that long ago. One can pay too high a price for mere life, little sister. There's so much hideousness in this war—I've got to go and help wipe it out of the world. I'm going to fight for the beauty of life, Rilla-my-Rilla—that is my duty. There may be a higher duty, perhaps—but that is mine. I owe life and Canada that, and I've got to pay it. Rilla, tonight for the first time since Jem left I've got back my self-respect. I could write poetry," Walter laughed. "I've never been able to write a line since last August. Tonight I'm full of it. Little sister, be brave—you were so plucky when Jem went."

"This—is—different," Rilla had to stop after every word to fight down a wild outburst of sobs. "I loved—Jem—of course—but—when—he went—away—we thought—the war—would soon—be over—and you are—everything to me, Walter."

"You must be brave to help me, Rilla-my-Rilla. I'm exalted tonight—drunk with the excitement of victory over myself—but there will be other times when it won't be like this—I'll need your help then."

"When—do—you—go?" She must know the worst at once.

"Not for a week—then we go to Kingsport for training. I suppose we'll go overseas about the middle of July—we don't know."

One week—only one week more with Walter! The eyes of youth did not see how she was to go on living.

When they turned in at the Ingleside gate Walter stopped in the shadows of the old pines and drew Rilla close to him.

"Rilla-my-Rilla, there were girls as sweet and pure as you in Belgium and Flanders. You—even you—know what their fate was. We must make it impossible for such things to happen again while the world lasts. You'll help me, won't you?"

"I'll try, Walter," she said. "Oh, I will try."

As she clung to him with her face pressed against his shoulder she knew that it had to be. She accepted the fact then and there. He must go—her beautiful Walter with his beautiful soul and dreams and ideals. And she had known all along that it would come sooner or later. She had seen it coming to her—coming—coming—as one sees the shadow of a cloud drawing near over a sunny field, swiftly and inescapably. Amid all her pain she was conscious of an odd feeling of relief in some hidden part of her soul, where a little dull, unacknowledged soreness had been lurking all winter. No one—no one could ever call Walter a slacker now.

Rilla did not sleep that night. Perhaps no one at Ingleside did except Jims. The body grows slowly and steadily, but the soul grows by leaps and bounds. It may come to its full stature in an hour. From that night Rilla Blythe's soul was the soul of a woman in its capacity for suffering, for strength, for endurance.

When the bitter dawn came she rose and went to her window. Below her was a big apple-tree, a great swelling cone of rosy blossom. Walter had planted it years ago when he was a little boy. Beyond Rainbow Valley there was a cloudy shore of morning with little ripples of sunrise breaking over it. The far, cold beauty of a lingering star shone above it. Why, in this world of springtime loveliness, must hearts break?

Rilla felt arms go about her lovingly, protectingly. It was mother—pale, large-eyed mother.

"Oh, mother, how can you bear it?" she cried wildly. "Rilla, dear, I've known for several days that Walter meant to go. I've had time to—to rebel and grow reconciled. We must give him up. There is a Call greater and more insistent than the call of our love—he has listened to it. We must not add to the bitterness of his sacrifice."

"Our sacrifice is greater than his," cried Rilla passionately. "Our boys give only themselves. We give them."

Before Mrs. Blythe could reply Susan stuck her head in at the door, never troubling over such frills of etiquette as knocking. Her eyes were suspiciously red but all she said was,

"Will I bring up your breakfast, Mrs. Dr. dear."

"No, no, Susan. We will all be down presently. Do you know—that Walter has joined up."

"Yes, Mrs. Dr. dear. The doctor told me last night. I suppose the Almighty has His own reasons for allowing such things. We must submit and endeavour to look on the bright side. It may cure him of being a poet, at least"—Susan still persisted in thinking that poets and tramps were tarred with the same brush—"and that would be something. But thank God," she muttered in a lower tone, "that Shirley is not old enough to go."

"Isn't that the same thing as thanking Him that some other woman's son has to go in Shirley's place?" asked the doctor, pausing on the threshold.

"No, it is not, doctor dear," said Susan defiantly, as she picked up Jims, who was opening his big dark eyes and stretching up his dimpled paws. "Do not you put words in my mouth that I would never dream of uttering. I am a plain woman and cannot argue with you, but I do not thank God that anybody has to go. I only know that it seems they do have to go, unless we all want to be Kaiserised—for I can assure you that the Monroe doctrine, whatever it is, is nothing to tie to, with Woodrow Wilson behind it. The Huns, Dr. dear, will never be brought to book by notes. And now," concluded Susan, tucking Jims in the crook of her gaunt arms and marching downstairs, "having cried my cry and said my say I shall take a brace, and if I cannot look pleasant I will look as pleasant as I can."

CHAPTER XV - UNTIL THE DAY BREAK

"The Germans have recaptured Premysl," said Susan despairingly, looking up from her newspaper, "and now I suppose we will have to begin calling it by that uncivilised name again. Cousin Sophia was in when the mail came and when she heard the news she hove a sigh up from the depths of her stomach, Mrs. Dr. dear, and said, 'Ah yes, and they will get Petrograd next I have no doubt.' I said to her, 'My knowledge of geography is not so profound as I wish it was but I have an idea that it is quite a walk from Premysl to Petrograd.' Cousin Sophia sighed again and said, 'The Grand Duke Nicholas is not the man I took him to be.' 'Do not let him know that,' said I. 'It might hurt his feelings and he has likely enough to worry him as it is. But you cannot cheer Cousin Sophia up, no matter how sarcastic you are, Mrs. Dr. dear. She sighed for the third time and groaned out, 'But the Russians are retreating fast,' and I said, 'Well, what of it? They have plenty of room for retreating, have they not?' But all the same, Mrs. Dr. dear, though I would never admit it to Cousin Sophia, I do not like the situation on the eastern front."

Nobody else liked it either; but all summer the Russian retreat went on—a long-drawn-out agony.

"I wonder if I shall ever again be able to await the coming of the mail with feelings of composure—never to speak of pleasure," said Gertrude Oliver. "The thought that haunts me night and day is—will the Germans smash Russia completely and then hurl their eastern army, flushed with victory, against the western front?"

"They will not, Miss Oliver dear," said Susan, assuming the role of prophetess.

"In the first place, the Almighty will not allow it, in the second, Grand Duke Nicholas, though he may have been a disappointment to us in some respects, knows how to run away decently and in order, and that is a very useful knowledge when Germans are chasing you. Norman Douglas declares he is just luring them on and killing ten of them to one he loses. But I am of the opinion he cannot help himself and is just doing the best he can under the circumstances, the same as the rest of us. So do not go so far afield to borrow trouble, Miss Oliver dear, when there is plenty of it already camping on our very doorstep."

Walter had gone to Kingsport the first of June. Nan, Di and Faith had gone also to do Red Cross work in their vacation. In mid-July Walter came home for a week's leave before going overseas. Rilla had lived through the days of his absence on the hope of that week, and now that it had come she drank every minute of it thirstily, hating even the hours she had to spend in sleep, they seemed such a waste of precious moments. In spite of its sadness, it was a beautiful week, full of poignant, unforgettable hours, when she and Walter had long walks and talks and silences together. He was all her own and she knew that he found strength and comfort in her sympathy and understanding. It was very wonderful to know she meant so much to him—the knowledge helped her through moments that would otherwise have been unendurable, and gave her power to smile—and even to laugh a little. When Walter had gone she might indulge in the comfort of tears, but not while he was here. She would not even let herself cry at night, lest her eyes should betray her to him in the morning.

On his last evening at home they went together to Rainbow Valley and sat down on the bank of the brook, under the White Lady, where the gay revels of olden days had been held in the cloudless years. Rainbow Valley was roofed over with a sunset of unusual splendour that night; a wonderful grey dusk just touched with starlight followed it; and then came moonshine, hinting, hiding, revealing, lighting up little dells and hollows here, leaving others in dark, velvet shadow.

"When I am 'somewhere in France,'" said Walter, looking around him with eager eyes on all the beauty his soul loved, "I shall remember these still, dewy, moon-drenched places. The balsam of the fir-trees; the peace of those white pools of moonshine; the 'strength of the hills'—what a beautiful old Biblical phrase that is. Rilla! Look at those old hills around us—the hills we looked up at as children, wondering what lay for us in the great world beyond them. How calm and strong they are—how patient and changeless—like the heart of a good woman. Rilla-my-Rilla, do you know what you have been to me the past year? I want to tell you before I go. I could not have lived through it if it had not been for you, little loving, believing heart."

Rilla dared not try to speak. She slipped her hand into Walter's and pressed it hard.

"And when I'm over there, Rilla, in that hell upon earth which men who have forgotten God have made, it will be the thought of you that will help me most. I know you'll be as plucky and patient as you have shown yourself to be this past year—I'm not afraid for you. I know that no matter what happens, you'll be Rilla-my-Rilla—no matter what happens."

Rilla repressed tear and sigh, but she could not repress a little shiver, and Walter knew that he had said enough. After a moment of silence, in which each made an unworded promise to each other, he said, "Now we won't be sober any more. We'll look beyond the years—to the time when the war will be over and Jem and Jerry and I will come marching home and we'll all be happy again."

"We won't be—happy—in the same way," said Rilla.

"No, not in the same way. Nobody whom this war has touched will ever be happy again in quite the same way. But it will be a better happiness, I think, little sister—a happiness we've earned. We were very happy before the war, weren't we? With a home like Ingleside, and a father and mother like ours we couldn't help being happy. But that happiness was a gift from life and love; it wasn't really ours—life could take it back at any time. It can never take away the happiness we win for ourselves in the way of duty. I've realised that since I went into khaki. In spite of my occasional funks, when I fall to living over things beforehand, I've been happy since that night in May. Rilla, be awfully good to mother while I'm away. It must be a horrible thing to be a mother in this war—the mothers and sisters and wives and sweethearts have the hardest times. Rilla, you beautiful little thing, are you anybody's sweetheart? If you are, tell me before I go."

"No," said Rilla. Then, impelled by a wish to be absolutely frank with Walter in this talk that might be the last they would ever have, she added, blushing wildly in the moonlight, "but if—Kenneth Ford—wanted me to be—"

"I see," said Walter. "And Ken's in khaki, too. Poor little girlie, it's a bit hard for you all round. Well, I'm not leaving any girl to break her heart about me— thank God for that."

Rilla glanced up at the Manse on the hill. She could see a light in Una Meredith's window. She felt tempted to say something—then she knew she must not. It was not her secret: and, anyway, she did not know—she only suspected.

Walter looked about him lingeringly and lovingly. This spot had always been so dear to him. What fun they all had had here lang syne. Phantoms of memory seemed to pace the dappled paths and peep merrily through the swinging boughs—Jem and Jerry, bare-legged, sunburned schoolboys, fishing in the brook and frying trout over the old stone fireplace; Nan and Di and Faith, in their dimpled, fresh-eyed childish beauty; Una the sweet and shy, Carl, poring over ants and bugs, little slangy, sharp-tongued, good-hearted Mary Vance—the old Walter that had been himself lying on the grass reading poetry or wandering through palaces of fancy. They were all there around him—he could see them almost as plainly as he saw Rilla—as plainly as he had once seen the Pied Piper piping down the valley in a vanished twilight. And they said to him, those gay little ghosts of other days, "We were the children of yesterday, Walter—fight a good fight for the children of to-day and to-morrow."

"Where are you, Walter," cried Rilla, laughing a little. "Come back—come back."

Walter came back with a long breath. He stood up and looked about him at the beautiful valley of moonlight, as if to impress on his mind and heart every charm it possessed—the great dark plumes of the firs against the silvery sky, the stately White Lady, the old magic of the dancing brook, the faithful Tree Lovers, the beckoning, tricksy paths.

"I shall see it so in my dreams," he said, as he turned away.

They went back to Ingleside. Mr. and Mrs. Meredith were there, with Gertrude Oliver, who had come from Lowbridge to say good-bye. Everybody was quite cheerful and bright, but nobody said much about the war being soon over, as they had said when Jem went away. They did not talk about the war at all—and they thought of nothing else. At last they gathered around the piano and sang the grand old hymn:

> "Oh God, our help in ages past
>   Our hope for years to come.
> Our shelter from the stormy blast
>   And our eternal home."

"We all come back to God in these days of soul-sifting," said Gertrude to John Meredith. "There have been many days in the past when I didn't believe in God— not as God—only as the impersonal Great First Cause of the scientists. I believe in Him now—I have to—there's nothing else to fall back on but God—humbly, starkly, unconditionally."

"'Our help in ages past'—'the same yesterday, to-day and for ever,'" said the minister gently. "When we forget God—He remembers us."

There was no crowd at the Glen Station the next morning to see Walter off. It was becoming a commonplace for a khaki clad boy to board that early morning train after his last leave. Besides his own, only the Manse folk were there, and Mary Vance. Mary had sent her Miller off the week before, with a determined grin, and now considered herself entitled to give expert opinion on how such partings should be conducted.

"The main thing is to smile and act as if nothing was happening," she informed the Ingleside group. "The boys all hate the sob act like poison. Miller told me I wasn't to come near the station if I couldn't keep from bawling. So I got through with my crying beforehand, and at the last I said to him, 'Good luck, Miller, and if you come back you'll find I haven't changed any, and if you don't come back I'll always be proud you went, and in any case don't fall in love with a French girl.' Miller swore he wouldn't, but you never can tell about those fascinating foreign hussies. Anyhow, the last sight he had of me I was smiling to my limit. Gee, all the rest of the day my face felt as if it had been starched and ironed into a smile."

In spite of Mary's advice and example Mrs. Blythe, who had sent Jem off with a smile, could not quite manage one for Walter. But at least no one cried. Dog Monday came out of his lair in the shipping-shed and sat down close to Walter, thumping his tail vigorously on the boards of the platform whenever Walter spoke to him, and looking up with confident eyes, as if to say, "I know you'll find Jem and bring him back to me."

"So long, old fellow," said Carl Meredith cheerfully, when the good-byes had to be said. "Tell them over there to keep their spirits up—I am coming along presently."

"Me too," said Shirley laconically, proffering a brown paw. Susan heard him and her face turned very grey.

Una shook hands quietly, looking at him with wistful, sorrowful, dark-blue eyes. But then Una's eyes had always been wistful. Walter bent his handsome black head in its khaki cap and kissed her with the warm, comradely kiss of a brother. He had never kissed her before, and for a fleeting moment Una's face betrayed her, if anyone had noticed. But nobody did; the conductor was shouting "all aboard"; everybody was trying to look very cheerful. Walter turned to Rilla; she held his hands and looked up at him. She would not see him again until the day broke and the shadows vanished—and she knew not if that daybreak would be on this side of the grave or beyond it.

"Good-bye," she said.

On her lips it lost all the bitterness it had won through the ages of parting and bore instead all the sweetness of the old loves of all the women who had ever loved and prayed for the beloved.

"Write me often and bring Jims up faithfully, according to the gospel of Morgan," Walter said lightly, having said all his serious things the night before in Rainbow Valley. But at the last moment he took her face between his hands and looked deep into her gallant eyes. "God bless you, Rilla-my-Rilla," he said softly and tenderly. After all it was not a hard thing to fight for a land that bore daughters like this.

He stood on the rear platform and waved to them as the train pulled out. Rilla was standing by herself, but Una Meredith came to her and the two girls who loved him most stood together and held each other's cold hands as the train rounded the curve of the wooded hill.

Rilla spent an hour in Rainbow Valley that morning about which she never said a word to anyone; she did not even write in her diary about it; when it was over she went home and made rompers for Jims. In the evening she went to a Junior Red Cross committee meeting and was severely businesslike.

"You would never suppose," said Irene Howard to Olive Kirk afterwards, "that Walter had left for the front only this morning. But some people really have no depth of feeling. I often wish I could take things as lightly as Rilla Blythe."

CHAPTER XVI - REALISM AND ROMANCE

"Warsaw has fallen," said Dr. Blythe with a resigned air, as he brought the mail in one warm August day.

Gertrude and Mrs. Blythe looked dismally at each other, and Rilla, who was feeding Jims a Morganized diet from a carefully sterilized spoon, laid the said spoon down on his tray, utterly regardless of germs, and said, "Oh, dear me," in as tragic a tone as if the news had come as a thunderbolt instead of being a foregone conclusion from the preceding week's dispatches. They had thought they were quite resigned to Warsaw's fall but now they knew they had, as always, hoped against hope.

"Now, let us take a brace," said Susan. "It is not the terrible thing we have been thinking. I read a dispatch three columns long in the Montreal Herald yesterday that proved that Warsaw was not important from a military point of view at all. So let us take the military point of view, doctor dear."

"I read that dispatch, too, and it has encouraged me immensely," said Gertrude. "I knew then and I know now that it was a lie from beginning to end. But I am in that state of mind where even a lie is a comfort, providing it is a cheerful lie."

"In that case, Miss Oliver dear, the German official reports ought to be all you need," said Susan sarcastically. "I never read them now because they make me so mad I cannot put my thoughts properly on my work after a dose of them. Even this news about Warsaw has taken the edge off my afternoon's plans. Misfortunes never come singly. I spoiled my baking of bread today—and now Warsaw has fallen—and here is little Kitchener bent on choking himself to death."

Jims was evidently trying to swallow his spoon, germs and all. Rilla rescued him mechanically and was about to resume the operation of feeding him when a casual remark of her father's sent such a shock and thrill over her that for the second time she dropped that doomed spoon.

"Kenneth Ford is down at Martin West's over-harbour," the doctor was saying. "His regiment was on its way to the front but was held up in Kingsport for some reason, and Ken got leave of absence to come over to the Island."

"I hope he will come up to see us," exclaimed Mrs. Blythe.

"He only has a day or two off, I believe," said the doctor absently.

Nobody noticed Rilla's flushed face and trembling hands. Even the most thoughtful and watchful of parents do not see everything that goes on under their very noses. Rilla made a third attempt to give the long-suffering Jims his dinner, but all she could think of was the question—Would Ken come to see her before he went away? She had not heard from him for a long while. Had he forgotten her completely? If he did not come she would know that he had. Perhaps there was even—some other girl back there in Toronto. Of course there was. She was a little fool to be thinking about him at all. She would not think about him. If he came, well and good. It would only be courteous of him to make a farewell call at Ingleside where he had often been a guest. If he did not come—well and good, too. It did not matter very much. Nobody was going to fret. That was all settled comfortably—she was quite indifferent—but meanwhile Jims was being fed with a haste and recklessness that would have filled the soul of Morgan with horror. Jims himself didn't like it, being a methodical baby, accustomed to swallowing spoonfuls with a decent interval for breath between each. He protested, but his protests availed him nothing. Rilla, as far as the care and feeding of infants was concerned, was utterly demoralized.

Then the telephone-bell rang. There was nothing unusual about the telephone ringing. It rang on an average every ten minutes at Ingleside. But Rilla dropped Jims' spoon again—on the carpet this time—and flew to the 'phone as if life depended on her getting there before anybody else. Jims, his patience exhausted, lifted up his voice and wept.

"Hello, is this Ingleside?"

"Yes."

"That you, Rilla?" "Yeth—yeth." Oh, why couldn't Jims stop howling for just one little minute? Why didn't somebody come in and choke him?

"Know who's speaking?"

Oh, didn't she know! Wouldn't she know that voice anywhere—at any time?

"It's Ken—isn't it?"

"Sure thing. I'm here for a look-in. Can I come up to Ingleside tonight and see you?"

"Of courthe."

Had he used "you" in the singular or plural sense? Presently she would wring Jims' neck—oh, what was Ken saying?

"See here, Rilla, can you arrange that there won't be more than a few dozen people round? Understand? I can't make my meaning clearer over this bally rural line. There are a dozen receivers down."

Did she understand! Yes, she understood.

"I'll try," she said.

"I'll be up about eight then. By-by."

Rilla hung up the 'phone and flew to Jims. But she did not wring that injured infant's neck. Instead she snatched him bodily out of his chair, crushed him against her face, kissed him rapturously on his milky mouth, and danced wildly around the room with him in her arms. After this Jims was relieved to find that she returned to sanity, gave him the rest of his dinner properly, and tucked him away for his afternoon nap with the little lullaby he loved best of all. She sewed at

Red Cross shirts for the rest of the afternoon and built a crystal castle of dreams, all a-quiver with rainbows. Ken wanted to see her—to see her alone. That could be easily managed. Shirley wouldn't bother them, father and mother were going to the Manse, Miss Oliver never played gooseberry, and Jims always slept the clock round from seven to seven. She would entertain Ken on the veranda—it would be moonlight—she would wear her white georgette dress and do her hair up—yes, she would—at least in a low knot at the nape of her neck. Mother couldn't object to that, surely. Oh, how wonderful and romantic it would be! Would Ken say any-thing—he must mean to say something or why should he be so particular about seeing her alone? What if it rained—Susan had been complaining about Mr. Hyde that morning! What if some officious Junior Red called to discuss Belgians and shirts? Or, worst of all, what if Fred Arnold dropped in? He did occasionally.

The evening came at last and was all that could be desired in an evening. The doctor and his wife went to the Manse, Shirley and Miss Oliver went they alone knew where, Susan went to the store for household supplies, and Jims went to Dreamland. Rilla put on her georgette gown, knotted up her hair and bound a little double string of pearls around it. Then she tucked a cluster of pale pink baby ros-es at her belt. Would Ken ask her for a rose for a keepsake? She knew that Jem had carried to the trenches in Flanders a faded rose that Faith Meredith had kissed and given him the night before he left.

Rilla looked very sweet when she met Ken in the mingled moonlight and vine shadows of the big veranda. The hand she gave him was cold and she was so des-perately anxious not to lisp that her greeting was prim and precise. How handsome and tall Kenneth looked in his lieutenant's uniform! It made him seem older, too—so much so that Rilla felt rather foolish. Hadn't it been the height of absurdity for her to suppose that this splendid young officer had anything special to say to her, little Rilla Blythe of Glen St. Mary? Likely she hadn't understood him after all—he had only meant that he didn't want a mob of folks around mak-ing a fuss over him and trying to lionize him, as they had probably done over-harbour. Yes, of course, that was all he meant—and she, little idiot, had gone and vainly imagined that he didn't want anybody but her. And he would think she had manoeuvred everybody away so that they could be alone together, and he would laugh to himself at her.

"This is better luck than I hoped for," said Ken, leaning back in his chair and looking at her with very unconcealed admiration in his eloquent eyes. "I was sure someone would be hanging about and it was just you I wanted to see, Rilla-my-Rilla."

Rilla's dream castle flashed into the landscape again. This was unmistakable enough certainly—not much doubt as to his meaning here.

"There aren't—so many of us—to poke around as there used to be," she said softly.

"No, that's so," said Ken gently. "Jem and Walter and the girls away—it makes a big blank, doesn't it? But—" he leaned forward until his dark curls almost brushed her hair—"doesn't Fred Arnold try to fill the blank occasionally. I've been told so."

At this moment, before Rilla could make any reply, Jims began to cry at the top of his voice in the room whose open window was just above them—Jims, who hardly ever cried in the evening. Moreover, he was crying, as Rilla knew from experience, with a vim and energy that betokened that he had been already whimpering softly unheard for some time and was thoroughly exasperated. When Jims started in crying like that he made a thorough job of it. Rilla knew that there was no use to sit still and pretend to ignore him. He wouldn't stop; and conversation of any kind was out of the question when such shrieks and howls were floating over your head. Besides, she was afraid Kenneth would think she was utterly unfeeling if she sat still and let a baby cry like that. He was not likely acquainted with Morgan's invaluable volume.

She got up. "Jims has had a nightmare, I think. He sometimes has one and he is always badly frightened by it. Excuse me for a moment."

Rilla flew upstairs, wishing quite frankly that soup tureens had never been invented. But when Jims, at sight of her, lifted his little arms entreatingly and swallowed several sobs, with tears rolling down his cheeks, resentment went out of her heart. After all, the poor darling was frightened. She picked him up gently and rocked him soothingly until his sobs ceased and his eyes closed. Then she essayed to lay him down in his crib. Jims opened his eyes and shrieked a protest. This performance was repeated twice. Rilla grew desperate. She couldn't leave Ken down there alone any longer—she had been away nearly half an hour already. With a resigned air she marched downstairs, carrying Jims, and sat down on the veranda. It was, no doubt, a ridiculous thing to sit and cuddle a contrary war-baby when your best young man was making his farewell call, but there was nothing else to be done.

Jims was supremely happy. He kicked his little pink-soled feet rapturously out under his white nighty and gave one of his rare laughs. He was beginning to be a very pretty baby; his golden hair curled in silken ringlets all over his little round head and his eyes were beautiful.

"He's a decorative kiddy all right, isn't he?" said Ken.

"His looks are very well," said Rilla, bitterly, as if to imply that they were much the best of him. Jims, being an astute infant, sensed trouble in the atmosphere and realized that it was up to him to clear it away. He turned his face up to Rilla, smiled adorably and said, clearly and beguilingly, "Will—Will."

It was the very first time he had spoken a word or tried to speak. Rilla was so delighted that she forgot her grudge against him. She forgave him with a hug and kiss. Jims, understanding that he was restored to favour, cuddled down against her just where a gleam of light from the lamp in the living-room struck across his hair and turned it into a halo of gold against her breast.

Kenneth sat very still and silent, looking at Rilla—at the delicate, girlish silhouette of her, her long lashes, her dented lip, her adorable chin. In the dim moonlight, as she sat with her head bent a little over Jims, the lamplight glinting on her pearls until they glistened like a slender nimbus, he thought she looked exactly like the Madonna that hung over his mother's desk at home. He carried that picture of her in his heart to the horror of the battlefields of France. He had had a strong fancy for Rilla Blythe ever since the night of the Four Winds dance; but it was when he saw her there, with little Jims in her arms, that he loved her and realized it. And all the while, poor Rilla was sitting, disappointed and humiliated, feeling that her last evening with Ken was spoiled and wondering why things always had to go so contrarily outside of books. She felt too absurd to try to talk. Evidently Ken was completely disgusted, too, since he was sitting there in such stony silence.

Hope revived momentarily when Jims went so thoroughly asleep that she thought it would be safe to lay him down on the couch in the living-room. But when she came out again Susan was sitting on the veranda, loosening her bonnet strings with the air of one who meant to stay where she was for some time.

"Have you got your baby to sleep?" she asked kindly.

Your baby! Really, Susan might have more tact.

"Yes," said Rilla shortly.

Susan laid her parcels on the reed table, as one determined to do her duty. She was very tired but she must help Rilla out. Here was Kenneth Ford who had come to call on the family and they were all unfortunately out, and "the poor child" had had to entertain him alone. But Susan had come to her rescue—Susan would do her part no matter how tired she was.

"Dear me, how you have grown up," she said, looking at Ken's six feet of khaki uniform without the least awe. Susan had grown used to khaki now, and at sixty-four even a lieutenant's uniform is just clothes and nothing else. "It is an amazing thing how fast children do grow up. Rilla here, now, is almost fifteen."

"I'm going on seventeen, Susan," cried Rilla almost passionately. She was a whole month past sixteen. It was intolerable of Susan.

"It seems just the other day that you were all babies," said Susan, ignoring Rilla's protest. "You were really the prettiest baby I ever saw, Ken, though your mother had an awful time trying to cure you of sucking your thumb. Do you remember the day I spanked you?"

"No," said Ken.

"Oh well, I suppose you would be too young—you were only about four and you were here with your mother and you insisted on teasing Nan until she cried. I had tried several ways of stopping you but none availed, and I saw that a spanking was the only thing that would serve. So I picked you up and laid you across my knee and lambasted you well. You howled at the top of your voice but you left Nan alone after that."

Rilla was writhing. Hadn't Susan any realization that she was addressing an officer of the Canadian Army? Apparently she had not. Oh, what would Ken think? "I suppose you do not remember the time your mother spanked you either," continued Susan, who seemed to be bent on reviving tender reminiscences that evening. "I shall never, no never, forget it. She was up here one night with you when you were about three, and you and Walter were playing out in the kitchen yard with a kitten. I had a big puncheon of rainwater by the spout which I was reserving for making soap. And you and Walter began quarrelling over the kitten. Walter was at one side of the puncheon standing on a chair, holding the kitten, and you were standing on a chair at the other side. You leaned across that puncheon and grabbed the kitten and pulled. You were always a great hand for taking what you wanted without too much ceremony. Walter held on tight and the poor kitten yelled but you dragged Walter and the kitten half over and then you both lost your balance and tumbled into that puncheon, kitten and all. If I had not been on the spot you would both have been drowned. I flew to the rescue and hauled you all three out before much harm was done, and your mother, who had seen it all from the upstairs window, came down and picked you up, dripping as you were, and gave you a beautiful spanking. Ah," said Susan with a sigh, "those were happy old days at Ingleside."

"Must have been," said Ken. His voice sounded queer and stiff. Rilla supposed he was hopelessly enraged. The truth was he dared not trust his voice lest it betray his frantic desire to laugh.

"Rilla here, now," said Susan, looking affectionately at that unhappy damsel, "never was much spanked. She was a real well-behaved child for the most part. But her father did spank her once. She got two bottles of pills out of his office and dared Alice Clow to see which of them could swallow all the pills first, and if her father had not happened in the nick of time those two children would have been corpses by night. As it was, they were both sick enough shortly after. But the doctor spanked Rilla then and there and he made such a thorough job of it that she never meddled with anything in his office afterwards. We hear a great deal nowadays of something that is called 'moral persuasion,' but in my opinion a good spanking and no nagging afterwards is a much better thing."

Rilla wondered viciously whether Susan meant to relate all the family spankings. But Susan had finished with the subject and branched off to another cheerful one.

"I remember little Tod MacAllister over-harbour killed himself that very way, eating up a whole box of fruitatives because he thought they were candy. It was a very sad affair. He was," said Susan earnestly, "the very cutest little corpse I ever laid my eyes on. It was very careless of his mother to leave the fruitatives where he could get them, but she was well-known to be a heedless creature. One day she found a nest of five eggs as she was going across the fields to church with a brand new blue silk dress on. So she put them in the pocket of her petticoat and when she got to church she forgot all about them and sat down on them and her dress was ruined, not to speak of the petticoat. Let me see—would not Tod be some relation of yours? Your great grandmother West was a MacAllister. Her brother Amos was a MacDonaldite in religion. I am told he used to take the jerks something fearful. But you look more like your great grandfather West than the MacAllisters. He died of a paralytic stroke quite early in life."

"Did you see anybody at the store?" asked Rilla desperately, in the faint hope of directing Susan's conversation into more agreeable channels.

"Nobody except Mary Vance," said Susan, "and she was stepping round as brisk as the Irishman's flea."

What terrible similes Susan used! Would Kenneth think she acquired them from the family!

"To hear Mary talk about Miller Douglas you would think he was the only Glen boy who had enlisted," Susan went on. "But of course she always did brag and she has some good qualities I am willing to admit, though I did not think so that time she chased Rilla here through the village with a dried codfish till the poor child fell, heels over head, into the puddle before Carter Flagg's store."

Rilla went cold all over with wrath and shame. Were there any more disgraceful scenes in her past that Susan could rake up? As for Ken, he could have howled over Susan's speeches, but he would not so insult the duenna of his lady, so he sat with a preternaturally solemn face which seemed to poor Rilla a haughty and offended one.

"I paid eleven cents for a bottle of ink tonight," complained Susan. "Ink is twice as high as it was last year. Perhaps it is because Woodrow Wilson has been writing so many notes. It must cost him considerable. My cousin Sophia says Woodrow Wilson is not the man she expected him to be—but then no man ever was. Being an old maid, I do not know much about men and have never pretended to, but my cousin Sophia is very hard on them, although she married two of them, which you might think was a fair share. Albert Crawford's chimney blew down in that big gale we had last week, and when Sophia heard the bricks clattering on the roof she thought it was a Zeppelin raid and went into hysterics. And Mrs. Albert Crawford says that of the two things she would have preferred the Zeppelin raid."

Rilla sat limply in her chair like one hypnotized. She knew Susan would stop talking when she was ready to stop and that no earthly power could make her stop any sooner. As a rule, she was very fond of Susan but just now she hated her with a deadly hatred. It was ten o'clock. Ken would soon have to go—the others would soon be home—and she had not even had a chance to explain to Ken that Fred Arnold filled no blank in her life nor ever could. Her rainbow castle lay in ruins round her.

Kenneth got up at last. He realized that Susan was there to stay as long as he did, and it was a three mile walk to Martin West's over-harbour. He wondered if Rilla had put Susan up to this, not wanting to be left alone with him, lest he say something Fred Arnold's sweetheart did not want to hear. Rilla got up, too, and walked silently the length of the veranda with him. They stood there for a moment, Ken on the lower step. The step was half sunk into the earth and mint grew thickly about and over its edge. Often crushed by so many passing feet it gave out its essence freely, and the spicy odour hung round them like a soundless, invisible benediction. Ken looked up at Rilla, whose hair was shining in the moonlight and whose eyes were pools of allurement. All at once he felt sure there was nothing in that gossip about Fred Arnold.

"Rilla," he said in a sudden, intense whisper, "you are the sweetest thing."

Rilla flushed and looked at Susan. Ken looked, too, and saw that Susan's back was turned. He put his arm about Rilla and kissed her. It was the first time Rilla had ever been kissed. She thought perhaps she ought to resent it but she didn't. Instead, she glanced timidly into Kenneth's seeking eyes and her glance was a kiss.

"Rilla-my-Rilla," said Ken, "will you promise that you won't let anyone else kiss you until I come back?"

"Yes," said Rilla, trembling and thrilling.

Susan was turning round. Ken loosened his hold and stepped to the walk.

"Good-bye," he said casually. Rilla heard herself saying it just as casually. She stood and watched him down the walk, out of the gate, and down the road. When the fir wood hid him from her sight she suddenly said "Oh," in a choked way and ran down to the gate, sweet blossomy things catching at her skirts as she ran. Leaning over the gate she saw Kenneth walking briskly down the road, over the bars of tree shadows and moonlight, his tall, erect figure grey in the white radiance. As he reached the turn he stopped and looked back and saw her standing amid the tall white lilies by the gate. He waved his hand—she waved hers—he was gone around the turn.

Rilla stood there for a little while, gazing across the fields of mist and silver. She had heard her mother say that she loved turns in roads—they were so provocative and alluring. Rilla thought she hated them. She had seen Jem and Jerry vanish from her around a bend in the road—then Walter—and now Ken. Brothers and playmate and sweetheart—they were all gone, never, it might be, to return. Yet still the Piper piped and the dance of death went on.

When Rilla walked slowly back to the house Susan was still sitting by the veranda table and Susan was sniffing suspiciously.

"I have been thinking, Rilla dear, of the old days in the House of Dreams, when Kenneth's mother and father were courting and Jem was a little baby and you were not born or thought of. It was a very romantic affair and she and your mother were such chums. To think I should have lived to see her son going to the front. As if she had not had enough trouble in her early life without this coming upon her! But we must take a brace and see it through."

All Rilla's anger against Susan had evaporated. With Ken's kiss still burning on her lips, and the wonderful significance of the promise he had asked thrilling heart and soul, she could not be angry with anyone. She put her slim white hand into Susan's brown, work-hardened one and gave it a squeeze. Susan was a faithful old dear and would lay down her life for any one of them.

"You are tired, Rilla dear, and had better go to bed," Susan said, patting her hand. "I noticed you were too tired to talk tonight. I am glad I came home in time to help you out. It is very tiresome trying to entertain young men when you are not accustomed to it."

Rilla carried Jims upstairs and went to bed, but not before she had sat for a long time at her window reconstructing her rainbow castle, with several added domes and turrets.

"I wonder," she said to herself, "if I am, or am not, engaged to Kenneth Ford."

CHAPTER XVII - THE WEEKS WEAR BY

Rilla read her first love letter in her Rainbow Valley fir-shadowed nook, and a girl's first love letter, whatever blase, older people may think of it, is an event of tremendous importance in the teens. After Kenneth's regiment had left Kingsport there came a fortnight of dully-aching anxiety and when the congregation sang in Church on Sunday evenings,

"Oh, hear us when we cry to Thee

For those in peril on the sea,"

Rilla's voice always failed her; for with the words came a horribly vivid mind picture of a submarined ship sinking beneath pitiless waves amid the struggles and cries of drowning men. Then word came that Kenneth's regiment had arrived safely in England; and now, at last, here was his letter. It began with something that made Rilla supremely happy for the moment and ended with a paragraph that crimsoned her cheeks with the wonder and thrill and delight of it. Between beginning and ending the letter was just such a jolly, newsy epistle as Ken might have written to anyone; but for the sake of that beginning and ending Rilla slept with the letter under her pillow for weeks, sometimes waking in the night to slip her fingers under and just touch it, and looked with secret pity on other girls whose sweethearts could never have written them anything half so wonderful and exquisite. Kenneth was not the son of a famous novelist for nothing. He "had a way" of expressing things in a few poignant, significant words that seemed to suggest far more than they uttered, and never grew stale or flat or foolish with ever so many scores of readings. Rilla went home from Rainbow Valley as if she flew rather than walked.

But such moments of uplift were rare that autumn. To be sure, there was one day in September when great news came of a big Allied victory in the west and Susan ran out to hoist the flag—the first time she had hoisted it since the Russian line broke and the last time she was to hoist it for many dismal moons.

"Likely the Big Push has begun at last, Mrs. Dr. dear," she exclaimed, "and we will soon see the finish of the Huns. Our boys will be home by Christmas now. Hurrah!"

Susan was ashamed of herself for hurrahing the minute she had done it, and apologized meekly for such an outburst of juvenility. "But indeed, Mrs. Dr. dear, this good news has gone to my head after this awful summer of Russian slumps and Gallipoli setbacks."

"Good news!" said Miss Oliver bitterly. "I wonder if the women whose men have been killed for it will call it good news. Just because our own men are not on that part of the front we are rejoicing as if the victory had cost no lives."

"Now, Miss Oliver dear, do not take that view of it," deprecated Susan. "We have not had much to rejoice over of late and yet men were being killed just the same. Do not let yourself slump like poor Cousin Sophia. She said, when the word came, 'Ah, it is nothing but a rift in the clouds. We are up this week but we will be down the next.' 'Well, Sophia Crawford,' said I,—for I will never give in to her, Mrs. Dr. dear—'God himself cannot make two hills without a hollow between them, as I have heard it said, but that is no reason why we should not take the good of the hills when we are on them.' But Cousin Sophia moaned on. 'Here is the Gallipolly expedition a failure and the Grand Duke Nicholas sent off, and everyone knows the Czar of Rooshia is a pro-German and the Allies have no ammunition and Bulgaria is going against us. And the end is not yet, for England and France must be punished for their deadly sins until they repent in sackcloth and ashes.' 'I think myself,' I said, 'that they will do their repenting in khaki and trench mud, and it seems to me that the Huns should have a few sins to repent of also.' 'They are instruments in the hands of the Almighty, to purge the garner,' said Sophia. And then I got mad, Mrs. Dr. dear, and told her I did not and never would believe that the Almighty ever took such dirty instruments in hand for any purpose whatever, and that I did not consider it decent for her to be using the words of Holy Writ as glibly as she was doing in ordinary conversation. She was not, I told her, a minister or even an elder. And for the time being I squelched her, Mrs. Dr. dear. Cousin Sophia has no spirit. She is very different from her niece, Mrs. Dean Crawford over-harbour. You know the Dean Crawfords had five boys and now the new baby is another boy. All the connection and especially Dean Crawford were much disappointed because their hearts had been set on a girl; but Mrs. Dean just laughed and said, 'Everywhere I went this summer I saw the sign "MEN WANTED" staring me in the face. Do you think I could go and have a girl under such circumstances?' There is spirit for you, Mrs. Dr. dear. But Cousin Sophia would say the child was just so much more cannon fodder."

Cousin Sophia had full range for her pessimism that gloomy autumn, and even Susan, incorrigible old optimist as she was, was hard put to it for cheer. When Bulgaria lined up with Germany Susan only remarked scornfully, "One more nation anxious for a licking," but the Greek tangle worried her beyond her powers of philosophy to endure calmly.

"Constantine of Greece has a German wife, Mrs. Dr. dear, and that fact squelches hope. To think that I should have lived to care what kind of a wife Constantine of Greece had! The miserable creature is under his wife's thumb and that is a bad place for any man to be. I am an old maid and an old maid has to be independent or she will be squashed out. But if I had been a married woman, Mrs. Dr.

dear, I would have been meek and humble. It is my opinion that this Sophia of Greece is a minx."

Susan was furious when the news came that Venizelos had met with defeat. "I could spank Constantine and skin him alive afterwards, that I could," she exclaimed bitterly.

"Oh, Susan, I'm surprised at you," said the doctor, pulling a long face. "Have you no regard for the proprieties? Skin him alive by all means but omit the spanking."

"If he had been well spanked in his younger days he might have more sense now," retorted Susan. "But I suppose princes are never spanked, more is the pity. I see the Allies have sent him an ultimatum. I could tell them that it will take more than ultimatums to skin a snake like Constantine. Perhaps the Allied blockade will hammer sense into his head; but that will take some time I am thinking, and in the meantime what is to become of poor Serbia?"

They saw what became of Serbia, and during the process Susan was hardly to be lived with. In her exasperation she abused everything and everybody except Kitchener, and she fell upon poor President Wilson tooth and claw.

"If he had done his duty and gone into the war long ago we should not have seen this mess in Serbia," she avowed.

"It would be a serious thing to plunge a great country like the United States, with its mixed population, into the war, Susan," said the doctor, who sometimes came to the defence of the President, not because he thought Wilson needed it especially, but from an unholy love of baiting Susan.

"Maybe, doctor dear—maybe! But that makes me think of the old story of the girl who told her grandmother she was going to be married. 'It is a solemn thing to be married,' said the old lady. 'Yes, but it is a solemner thing not to be,' said the girl. And I can testify to that out of my own experience, doctor dear. And I think it is a solemner thing for the Yankees that they have kept out of the war than it would have been if they had gone into it. However, though I do not know much about them, I am of the opinion that we will see them starting something yet, Woodrow Wilson or no Woodrow Wilson, when they get it into their heads that this war is not a correspondence school. They will not," said Susan, energetically waving a saucepan with one hand and a soup ladle with the other, "be too proud to fight then."

On a pale-yellow, windy evening in October Carl Meredith went away. He had enlisted on his eighteenth birthday. John Meredith saw him off with a set face. His two boys were gone—there was only little Bruce left now. He loved Bruce and Bruce's mother dearly; but Jerry and Carl were the sons of the bride of his youth and Carl was the only one of all his children who had Cecilia's very eyes. As they looked lovingly out at him above Carl's uniform the pale minister suddenly remembered the day when for the first and last time he had tried to whip Carl for his prank with the eel. That was the first time he had realised how much Carl's eyes were like Cecilia's. Now he realised it again once more. Would he ever again see his dead wife's eyes looking at him from his son's face? What a bonny, clean, handsome lad he was! It was—hard—to see him go. John Meredith seemed to be looking at a torn plain strewed with the bodies of "able-bodied men between the ages of eighteen and forty-five." Only the other day Carl had been a little scrap of a boy, hunting bugs in Rainbow Valley, taking lizards to bed with him, and scandalizing the Glen by carrying frogs to Sunday School. It seemed hardly—right— somehow that he should be an "able-bodied man" in khaki. Yet John Meredith had said no word to dissuade him when Carl had told him he must go.

Rilla felt Carl's going keenly. They had always been cronies and playmates. He was only a little older than she was and they had been children in Rainbow Valley together. She recalled all their old pranks and escapades as she walked slowly home alone. The full moon peeped through the scudding clouds with sudden floods of weird illumination, the telephone wires sang a shrill weird song in the wind, and the tall spikes of withered, grey-headed golden-rod in the fence corners swayed and beckoned wildly to her like groups of old witches weaving unholy spells. On such a night as this, long ago, Carl would come over to Ingleside and whistle her out to the gate. "Let's go on a moon-spree, Rilla," he would say, and the two of them would scamper off to Rainbow Valley. Rilla had never been afraid of his beetles and bugs, though she drew a hard and fast line at snakes. They used to talk together of almost everything and were teased about each other at school; but one evening when they were about ten years of age they had solemnly promised, by the old spring in Rainbow Valley, that they would never marry each other. Alice Clow had "crossed out" their names on her slate in school that day, and it came out that "both married." They did not like the idea at all, hence the mutual vow in Rainbow Valley. There was nothing like an ounce of prevention. Rilla laughed over the old memory—and then sighed. That very day a dispatch from some London paper had contained the cheerful announcement that "the present moment is the darkest since the war began." It was dark enough, and Rilla wished desperately that she could do something besides waiting and serving at home, as day after day the Glen boys she had known went away. If she were only a boy, speeding in khaki by Carl's side to the Western front! She had wished that in a burst of romance when Jem had gone, without, perhaps, really meaning it. She meant it now. There were moments when waiting at home, in safety and comfort, seemed an unendurable thing.

The moon burst triumphantly through an especially dark cloud and shadow and silver chased each other in waves over the Glen. Rilla remembered one moonlit evening of childhood when she had said to her mother, "The moon just looks like a sorry, sorry face." She thought it looked like that still—an agonised, care-worn face, as though it looked down on dreadful sights. What did it see on the Western front? In broken Serbia? On shell-swept Gallipoli?

"I am tired," Miss Oliver had said that day, in a rare outburst of impatience, "of this horrible rack of strained emotions, when every day brings a new horror or the dread of it. No, don't look reproachfully at me, Mrs. Blythe. There's nothing heroic about me today. I've slumped. I wish England had left Belgium to her fate—I wish Canada had never sent a man—I wish we'd tied our boys to our apron strings and not let one of them go. Oh—I shall be ashamed of myself in half an hour—but at this very minute I mean every word of it. Will the Allies never strike?"

"Patience is a tired mare but she jogs on," said Susan.

"While the steeds of Armageddon thunder, trampling over our hearts," retorted Miss Oliver. "Susan, tell me—don't you ever—didn't you ever—take spells of feeling that you must scream—or swear—or smash something—just because your torture reaches a point when it becomes unbearable?"

"I have never sworn or desired to swear, Miss Oliver dear, but I will admit," said Susan, with the air of one determined to make a clean breast of it once and for all, "that I have experienced occasions when it was a relief to do considerable banging."

"Don't you think that is a kind of swearing, Susan? What is the difference between slamming a door viciously and saying d——"

"Miss Oliver dear," interrupted Susan, desperately determined to save Gertrude from herself, if human power could do it, "you are all tired out and unstrung—and no wonder, teaching those obstreperous youngsters all day and coming home to bad war news. But just you go upstairs and lie down and I will bring you up a cup of hot tea and a bite of toast and very soon you will not want to slam doors or swear."

"Susan, you're a good soul—a very pearl of Susans! But, Susan, it would be such a relief—to say just one soft, low, little tiny d——"

"I will bring you a hot-water bottle for the soles of your feet, also," interposed Susan resolutely, "and it would not be any relief to say that word you are thinking of, Miss Oliver, and that you may tie to."

"Well, I'll try the hot-water bottle first," said Miss Oliver, repenting herself on teasing Susan and vanishing upstairs, to Susan's intense relief. Susan shook her head ominously as she filled the hot-water bottle. The war was certainly relaxing the standards of behaviour woefully. Here was Miss Oliver admittedly on the point of profanity.

"We must draw the blood from her brain," said Susan, "and if this bottle is not effective I will see what can be done with a mustard plaster."

Gertrude rallied and carried on. Lord Kitchener went to Greece, whereat Susan foretold that Constantine would soon experience a change of heart. Lloyd George began to heckle the Allies regarding equipment and guns and Susan said you would hear more of Lloyd George yet. The gallant Anzacs withdrew from Gallipoli and Susan approved the step, with reservations. The siege of Kut-El-Amara began and Susan pored over maps of Mesopotamia and abused the Turks. Henry Ford started for Europe and Susan flayed him with sarcasm. Sir John French was superseded by Sir Douglas Haig and Susan dubiously opined that it was poor policy to swap horses crossing a stream, "though, to be sure, Haig was a good name and French had a foreign sound, say what you might." Not a move on the great chess-board of king or bishop or pawn escaped Susan, who had once read only Glen St. Mary notes. "There was a time," she said sorrowfully, "when I did not

care what happened outside of P.E. Island, and now a king cannot have a toothache in Russia or China but it worries me. It may be broadening to the mind, as
the doctor said, but it is very painful to the feelings."

When Christmas came again Susan did not set any vacant places at the festive
board. Two empty chairs were too much even for Susan who had thought in September that there would not be one.

"This is the first Christmas that Walter was not home," Rilla wrote in her diary
that night. "Jem used to be away for Christmases up in Avonlea, but Walter never
was. I had letters from Ken and him today. They are still in England but expect to
be in the trenches very soon. And then—but I suppose we'll be able to endure it
somehow. To me, the strangest of all the strange things since 1914 is how we
have all learned to accept things we never thought we could—to go on with life as
a matter of course. I know that Jem and Jerry are in the trenches—that Ken and
Walter will be soon—that if one of them does not come back my heart will
break—yet I go on and work and plan—yes, and even enjoy life by times. There
are moments when we have real fun because, just for the moment, we don't think
about things and then—we remember—and the remembering is worse than thinking of it all the time would have been.

"Today was dark and cloudy and tonight is wild enough, as Gertrude says, to
please any novelist in search of suitable matter for a murder or elopement. The
raindrops streaming over the panes look like tears running down a face, and the
wind is shrieking through the maple grove.

"This hasn't been a nice Christmas Day in any way. Nan had toothache and
Susan had red eyes, and assumed a weird and gruesome flippancy of manner to
deceive us into thinking she hadn't; and Jims had a bad cold all day and I'm afraid
of croup. He has had croup twice since October. The first time I was nearly
frightened to death, for father and mother were both away—father always is
away, it seems to me, when any of this household gets sick. But Susan was cool
as a fish and knew just what to do, and by morning Jims was all right. That child
is a cross between a duck and an imp. He's a year and four months old, trots about
everywhere, and says quite a few words. He has the cutest little way of calling me
"Willa-will." It always brings back that dreadful, ridiculous, delightful night when
Ken came to say good-bye, and I was so furious and happy. Jims is pink and
white and big-eyed and curly-haired and every now and then I discover a new
dimple in him. I can never quite believe he is really the same creature as that
scrawny, yellow, ugly little changeling I brought home in the soup tureen. Nobody has ever heard a word from Jim Anderson. If he never comes back I shall
keep Jims always. Everybody here worships and spoils him—or would spoil him
if Morgan and I didn't stand remorselessly in the way. Susan says Jims is the
cleverest child she ever saw and can recognize Old Nick when he sees him—this
because Jims threw poor Doc out of an upstairs window one day. Doc turned into
Mr. Hyde on his way down and landed in a currant bush, spitting and swearing. I
tried to console his inner cat with a saucer of milk but he would have none of it,
and remained Mr. Hyde the rest of the day. Jims's latest exploit was to paint the

cushion of the big arm-chair in the sun parlour with molasses; and before anybody found it out Mrs. Fred Clow came in on Red Cross business and sat down on it. Her new silk dress was ruined and nobody could blame her for being vexed. But she went into one of her tempers and said nasty things and gave me such slams about 'spoiling' Jims that I nearly boiled over, too. But I kept the lid on till she had waddled away and then I exploded.

"'The fat, clumsy, horrid old thing,' I said—and oh, what a satisfaction it was to say it.

"'She has three sons at the front,' mother said rebukingly.

"'I suppose that covers all her shortcomings in manners,' I retorted. But I was ashamed—for it is true that all her boys have gone and she was very plucky and loyal about it too; and she is a perfect tower of strength in the Red Cross. It's a little hard to remember all the heroines. Just the same, it was her second new silk dress in one year and that when everybody is—or should be—trying to 'save and serve.'

"I had to bring out my green velvet hat again lately and begin wearing it. I hung on to my blue straw sailor as long as I could. How I hate the green velvet hat! It is so elaborate and conspicuous. I don't see how I could ever have liked it. But I vowed to wear it and wear it I will.

"Shirley and I went down to the station this morning to take Little Dog Monday a bang-up Christmas dinner. Dog Monday waits and watches there still, with just as much hope and confidence as ever. Sometimes he hangs around the station house and talks to people and the rest of his time he sits at his little kennel door and watches the track unwinkingly. We never try to coax him home now: we know it is of no use. When Jem comes back, Monday will come home with him; and if Jem—never comes back—Monday will wait there for him as long as his dear dog heart goes on beating.

"Fred Arnold was here last night. He was eighteen in November and is going to enlist just as soon as his mother is over an operation she has to have. He has been coming here very often lately and though I like him so much it makes me uncomfortable, because I am afraid he is thinking that perhaps I could care something for him. I can't tell him about Ken—because, after all, what is there to tell? And yet I don't like to behave coldly and distantly when he will be going away so soon. It is very perplexing. I remember I used to think it would be such fun to have dozens of beaux—and now I'm worried to death because two are too many.

"I am learning to cook. Susan is teaching me. I tried to learn long ago—but no, let me be honest—Susan tried to teach me, which is a very different thing. I never seemed to succeed with anything and I got discouraged. But since the boys have gone away I wanted to be able to make cake and things for them myself and so I started in again and this time I'm getting on surprisingly well. Susan says it is all in the way I hold my mouth and father says my subconscious mind is desirous of learning now, and I dare say they're both right. Anyhow, I can make dandy short-bread and fruitcake. I got ambitious last week and attempted cream puffs, but made an awful failure of them. They came out of the oven flat as flukes. I thought maybe the cream would fill them up again and make them plump but it didn't. I think Susan was secretly pleased. She is past mistress in the art of making cream puffs and it would break her heart if anyone else here could make them as well. I wonder if Susan tampered—but no, I won't suspect her of such a thing.

"Miranda Pryor spent an afternoon here a few days ago, helping me cut out certain Red Cross garments known by the charming name of 'vermin shirts.' Susan thinks that name is not quite decent, so I suggested she call them 'cootie sarks,' which is old Highland Sandy's version of it. But she shook her head and I heard her telling mother later that, in her opinion, 'cooties' and 'sarks' were not proper subjects for young girls to talk about. She was especially horrified when Jem wrote in his last letter to mother, 'Tell Susan I had a fine cootie hunt this morning and caught fifty-three!' Susan positively turned pea-green. 'Mrs. Dr. dear,' she said, 'when I was young, if decent people were so unfortunate as to get—those insects—they kept it a secret if possible. I do not want to be narrow-minded, Mrs. Dr. dear, but I still think it is better not to mention such things.'

"Miranda grew confidential over our vermin shirts and told me all her troubles. She is desperately unhappy. She is engaged to Joe Milgrave and Joe joined up in October and has been training in Charlottetown ever since. Her father was furious when he joined and forbade Miranda ever to have any dealing or communication with him again. Poor Joe expects to go overseas any day and wants Miranda to marry him before he goes, which shows that there have been 'communications' in spite of Whiskers-on-the-moon. Miranda wants to marry him but cannot, and she declares it will break her heart.

"'Why don't you run away and marry him?' I said. It didn't go against my conscience in the least to give her such advice. Joe Milgrave is a splendid fellow and Mr. Pryor fairly beamed on him until the war broke out and I know Mr. Pryor would forgive Miranda very quickly, once it was over and he wanted his housekeeper back. But Miranda shook her silvery head dolefully.

"'Joe wants me to but I can't. Mother's last words to me, as she lay on her dying-bed, were, "Never, never run away, Miranda," and I promised.'

"Miranda's mother died two years ago, and it seems, according to Miranda, that her mother and father actually ran away to be married themselves. To picture Whiskers-on-the-moon as the hero of an elopement is beyond my power. But such was the case and Mrs. Pryor at least lived to repent it. She had a hard life of it with Mr. Pryor, and she thought it was a punishment on her for running away. So she made Miranda promise she would never, for any reason whatever, do it.

"Of course, you cannot urge a girl to break a promise made to a dying mother, so I did not see what Miranda could do unless she got Joe to come to the house when her father was away and marry her there. But Miranda said that couldn't be managed. Her father seemed to suspect she might be up to something of the sort and he never went away for long at a time, and, of course, Joe couldn't get leave of absence at an hour's notice.

"'No, I shall just have to let Joe go, and he will be killed—I know he will be killed—and my heart will break,' said Miranda, her tears running down and copiously bedewing the vermin shirts!

"I am not writing like this for lack of any real sympathy with poor Miranda. I've just got into the habit of giving things a comical twist if I can, when I'm writing to Jem and Walter and Ken, to make them laugh. I really felt sorry for Miranda who is as much in love with Joe as a china-blue girl can be with anyone and who is dreadfully ashamed of her father's pro-German sentiments. I think she understood that I did, for she said she had wanted to tell me all about her worries because I had grown so sympathetic this past year. I wonder if I have. I know I used to be a selfish, thoughtless creature—how selfish and thoughtless I am ashamed to remember now, so I can't be quite so bad as I was.

"I wish I could help Miranda. It would be very romantic to contrive a war-wedding and I should dearly love to get the better of Whiskers-on-the-moon. But at present the oracle has not spoken."

CHAPTER XVIII - A WAR-WEDDING

"I can tell you this Dr. dear," said Susan, pale with wrath, "that Germany is getting to be perfectly ridiculous."

They were all in the big Ingleside kitchen. Susan was mixing biscuits for supper. Mrs. Blythe was making shortbread for Jem, and Rilla was compounding candy for Ken and Walter—it had once been "Walter and Ken" in her thoughts but somehow, quite unconsciously, this had changed until Ken's name came naturally first. Cousin Sophia was also there, knitting. All the boys were going to be killed in the long run, so Cousin Sophia felt in her bones, but they might better die with warm feet than cold ones, so Cousin Sophia knitted faithfully and gloomily.

Into this peaceful scene erupted the doctor, wrathful and excited over the burning of the Parliament Buildings in Ottawa. And Susan became automatically quite as wrathful and excited.

"What will those Huns do next?" she demanded. "Coming over here and burning our Parliament building! Did anyone ever hear of such an outrage?"

"We don't know that the Germans are responsible for this," said the doctor—much as if he felt quite sure they were. "Fires do start without their agency sometimes. And Uncle Mark MacAllister's barn was burnt last week. You can hardly accuse the Germans of that, Susan."

"Indeed, Dr. dear, I do not know." Susan nodded slowly and portentously. "Whiskers-on-the-moon was there that very day. The fire broke out half an hour after he was gone. So much is a fact—but I shall not accuse a Presbyterian elder of burning anybody's barn until I have proof. However, everybody knows, Dr. dear, that both Uncle Mark's boys have enlisted, and that Uncle Mark himself makes speeches at all the recruiting meetings. So no doubt Germany is anxious to get square with him."

"I could never speak at a recruiting meeting," said Cousin Sophia solemnly. "I could never reconcile it to my conscience to ask another woman's son to go, to murder and be murdered."

"Could you not?" said Susan. "Well, Sophia Crawford, I felt as if I could ask anyone to go when I read last night that there were no children under eight years of age left alive in Poland. Think of that, Sophia Crawford"—Susan shook a floury finger at Sophia—"not—one—child—under—eight—years—of—age!"

"I suppose the Germans has et 'em all," sighed Cousin Sophia.

"Well, no-o-o," said Susan reluctantly, as if she hated to admit that there was any crime the Huns couldn't be accused of. "The Germans have not turned cannibal yet—as far as I know. They have died of starvation and exposure, the poor little creatures. There is murdering for you, Cousin Sophia Crawford. The thought of it poisons every bite and sup I take."

"I see that Fred Carson of Lowbridge has been awarded a Distinguished Conduct Medal," remarked the doctor, over his local paper.

"I heard that last week," said Susan. "He is a battalion runner and he did something extra brave and daring. His letter, telling his folks about it, came when his old Grandmother Carson was on her dying-bed. She had only a few minutes more to live and the Episcopal minister, who was there, asked her if she would not like him to pray. 'Oh yes, yes, you can pray,' she said impatient-like—she was a Dean, Dr. dear, and the Deans were always high-spirited—'you can pray, but for pity's sake pray low and don't disturb me. I want to think over this splendid news and I have not much time left to do it.' That was Almira Carson all over. Fred was the apple of her eye. She was seventy-five years of age and had not a grey hair in her head, they tell me."

"By the way, that reminds me—I found a grey hair this morning—my very first," said Mrs. Blythe.

"I have noticed that grey hair for some time, Mrs. Dr. dear, but I did not speak of it. Thought I to myself, 'She has enough to bear.' But now that you have discovered it let me remind you that grey hairs are honourable."

"I must be getting old, Gilbert." Mrs. Blythe laughed a trifle ruefully. "People are beginning to tell me I look so young. They never tell you that when you are young. But I shall not worry over my silver thread. I never liked red hair. Gilbert, did I ever tell you of that time, years ago at Green Gables, when I dyed my hair? Nobody but Marilla and I knew about it."

"Was that the reason you came out once with your hair shingled to the bone?"

"Yes. I bought a bottle of dye from a German Jew pedlar. I fondly expected it would turn my hair black—and it turned it green. So it had to be cut off."

"You had a narrow escape, Mrs. Dr. dear," exclaimed Susan. "Of course you were too young then to know what a German was. It was a special mercy of Providence that it was only green dye and not poison."

"It seems hundreds of years since those Green Gables days," sighed Mrs. Blythe. "They belonged to another world altogether. Life has been cut in two by the chasm of war. What is ahead I don't know—but it can't be a bit like the past. I wonder if those of us who have lived half our lives in the old world will ever feel wholly at home in the new."

"Have you noticed," asked Miss Oliver, glancing up from her book, "how everything written before the war seems so far away now, too? One feels as if one was reading something as ancient as the Iliad. This poem of Wordsworth's—the Senior class have it in their entrance work—I've been glancing over it. Its classic calm and repose and the beauty of the lines seem to belong to another planet, and to have as little to do with the present world-welter as the evening star."

"The only thing that I find much comfort in reading nowadays is the Bible," remarked Susan, whisking her biscuits into the oven. "There are so many passages in it that seem to me exactly descriptive of the Huns. Old Highland Sandy declares that there is no doubt that the Kaiser is the Anti-Christ spoken of in Revelations, but I do not go as far as that. It would, in my humble opinion, Mrs. Dr. dear, be too great an honour for him."

Early one morning, several days later, Miranda Pryor slipped up to Ingleside, ostensibly to get some Red Cross sewing, but in reality to talk over with sympathetic Rilla troubles that were past bearing alone. She brought her dog with her—an over-fed, bandy-legged little animal very dear to her heart because Joe Milgrave had given it to her when it was a puppy. Mr. Pryor regarded all dogs with disfavour; but in those days he had looked kindly upon Joe as a suitor for Miranda's hand and so he had allowed her to keep the puppy. Miranda was so grateful that she endeavoured to please her father by naming her dog after his political idol, the great Liberal chieftain, Sir Wilfrid Laurier—though his title was soon abbreviated to Wilfy. Sir Wilfrid grew and flourished and waxed fat; but Miranda spoiled him absurdly and nobody else liked him. Rilla especially hated him because of his detestable trick of lying flat on his back and entreating you with waving paws to tickle his sleek stomach. When she saw that Miranda's pale eyes bore unmistakable testimony of her having cried all night, Rilla asked her to come up to her room, knowing Miranda had a tale of woe to tell, but she ordered Sir Wilfrid to remain below.

"Oh, can't he come, too?" said Miranda wistfully. "Poor Wilfy won't be any bother—and I wiped his paws so carefully before I brought him in. He is always so lonesome in a strange place without me—and very soon he'll be—all—I'll have left—to remind me—of Joe."

Rilla yielded, and Sir Wilfrid, with his tail curled at a saucy angle over his brindled back, trotted triumphantly up the stairs before them.

"Oh, Rilla," sobbed Miranda, when they had reached sanctuary. "I'm so unhappy. I can't begin to tell you how unhappy I am. Truly, my heart is breaking."

Rilla sat down on the lounge beside her. Sir Wilfrid squatted on his haunches before them, with his impertinent pink tongue stuck out, and listened. "What is the trouble, Miranda?"

"Joe is coming home tonight on his last leave. I had a letter from him on Saturday—he sends my letters in care of Bob Crawford, you know, because of father—and, oh, Rilla, he will only have four days—he has to go away Friday morning—and I may never see him again."

"Does he still want you to marry him?" asked Rilla.

"Oh, yes. He implored me in his letter to run away and be married. But I cannot do that, Rilla, not even for Joe. My only comfort is that I will be able to see him for a little while tomorrow afternoon. Father has to go to Charlottetown on business. At least we will have one good farewell talk. But oh—afterwards—why, Rilla, I know father won't even let me go to the station Friday morning to see Joe off."

"Why in the world don't you and Joe get married tomorrow afternoon at home?" demanded Rilla.

Miranda swallowed a sob in such amazement that she almost choked.

"Why—why—that is impossible, Rilla."

"Why?" briefly demanded the organizer of the Junior Red Cross and the transporter of babies in soup tureens.

"Why—why—we never thought of such a thing—Joe hasn't a license—I have no dress—I couldn't be married in black—I—I—we—you—you—" Miranda lost herself altogether and Sir Wilfrid, seeing that she was in dire distress threw back his head and emitted a melancholy yelp.

Rilla Blythe thought hard and rapidly for a few minutes. Then she said, "Miranda, if you will put yourself into my hands I'll have you married to Joe before four o'clock tomorrow afternoon."

"Oh, you couldn't."

"I can and I will. But you'll have to do exactly as I tell you."

"Oh—I—don't think—oh, father will kill me—"

"Nonsense. He'll be very angry I suppose. But are you more afraid of your father's anger than you are of Joe's never coming back to you?"

"No," said Miranda, with sudden firmness, "I'm not."

"Will you do as I tell you then?"

"Yes, I will."

"Then get Joe on the long-distance at once and tell him to bring out a license and ring tonight."

"Oh, I couldn't," wailed the aghast Miranda, "it—it would be so—so indelicate."

Rilla shut her little white teeth together with a snap. "Heaven grant me patience," she said under her breath. "I'll do it then," she said aloud, "and meanwhile, you go home and make what preparations you can. When I 'phone down to you to come up and help me sew come at once."

As soon as Miranda, pallid, scared, but desperately resolved, had gone, Rilla flew to the telephone and put in a long-distance call for Charlottetown. She got through with such surprising quickness that she was convinced Providence approved of her undertaking, but it was a good hour before she could get in touch with Joe Milgrave at his camp. Meanwhile, she paced impatiently about, and prayed that when she did get Joe there would be no listeners on the line to carry news to Whiskers-on-the-moon.

"Is that you, Joe? Rilla Blythe is speaking—Rilla—Rilla—oh, never mind. Listen to this. Before you come home tonight get a marriage license—a marriage license—yes, a marriage license—and a wedding-ring. Did you get that? And will you do it? Very well, be sure you do it—it is your only chance."

Flushed with triumph—for her only fear was that she might not be able to locate Joe in time—Rilla rang the Pryor ring. This time she had not such good luck for she drew Whiskers-on-the-moon.

"Is that Miranda? Oh—Mr. Pryor! Well, Mr. Pryor, will you kindly ask Miranda if she can come up this afternoon and help me with some sewing. It is very important, or I would not trouble her. Oh—thank you."

Mr. Pryor had consented somewhat grumpily, but he had consented—he did not want to offend Dr. Blythe, and he knew that if he refused to allow Miranda to do any Red Cross work public opinion would make the Glen too hot for comfort. Rilla went out to the kitchen, shut all the doors with a mysterious expression which alarmed Susan, and then said solemnly, "Susan can you make a wedding-cake this afternoon?"

"A wedding-cake!" Susan stared. Rilla had, without any warning, brought her a war-baby once upon a time. Was she now, with equal suddenness, going to produce a husband?

"Yes, a wedding-cake—a scrumptious wedding-cake, Susan—a beautiful, plummy, eggy, citron-peely wedding-cake. And we must make other things too. I'll help you in the morning. But I can't help you in the afternoon for I have to make a wedding-dress and time is the essence of the contract, Susan."

Susan felt that she was really too old to be subjected to such shocks.

"Who are you going to marry, Rilla?" she asked feebly.

"Susan, darling, I am not the happy bride. Miranda Pryor is going to marry Joe Milgrave tomorrow afternoon while her father is away in town. A war-wedding, Susan—isn't that thrilling and romantic? I never was so excited in my life."

The excitement soon spread over Ingleside, infecting even Mrs. Blythe and Susan.

"I'll go to work on that cake at once," vowed Susan, with a glance at the clock. "Mrs. Dr. dear, will you pick over the fruit and beat up the eggs? If you will I can have that cake ready for the oven by the evening. Tomorrow morning we can make salads and other things. I will work all night if necessary to get the better of Whiskers-on-the-moon."

Miranda arrived, tearful and breathless.

"We must fix over my white dress for you to wear," said Rilla. "It will fit you very nicely with a little alteration."

To work went the two girls, ripping, fitting, basting, sewing for dear life. By dint of unceasing effort they got the dress done by seven o'clock and Miranda tried it on in Rilla's room.

"It's very pretty—but oh, if I could just have a veil," sighed Miranda. "I've always dreamed of being married in a lovely white veil."

Some good fairy evidently waits on the wishes of war-brides. The door opened and Mrs. Blythe came in, her arms full of a filmy burden.

"Miranda dear," she said, "I want you to wear my wedding-veil tomorrow. It is twenty-four years since I was a bride at old Green Gables—the happiest bride that ever was—and the wedding-veil of a happy bride brings good luck, they say."

"Oh, how sweet of you, Mrs. Blythe," said Miranda, the ready tears starting to her eyes.

CHAPTER XVIII - A WAR-WEDDING

The veil was tried on and draped. Susan dropped in to approve but dared not linger.

"I've got that cake in the oven," she said, "and I am pursuing a policy of watchful waiting. The evening news is that the Grand Duke has captured Erzerum. That is a pill for the Turks. I wish I had a chance to tell the Czar just what a mistake he made when he turned Nicholas down."

Susan disappeared downstairs to the kitchen, whence a dreadful thud and a piercing shriek presently sounded. Everybody rushed to the kitchen—the doctor and Miss Oliver, Mrs. Blythe, Rilla, Miranda in her wedding-veil. Susan was sitting flatly in the middle of the kitchen floor with a dazed, bewildered look on her face, while Doc, evidently in his Hyde incarnation, was standing on the dresser, with his back up, his eyes blazing, and his tail the size of three tails.

"Susan, what has happened?" cried Mrs. Blythe in alarm. "Did you fall? Are you hurt?"

Susan picked herself up.

"No," she said grimly, "I am not hurt, though I am jarred all over. Do not be alarmed. As for what has happened—I tried to kick that darned cat with both feet, that is what happened."

Everybody shrieked with laughter. The doctor was quite helpless.

"Oh, Susan, Susan," he gasped. "That I should live to hear you swear."

"I am sorry," said Susan in real distress, "that I used such an expression before two young girls. But I said that beast was darned, and darned it is. It belongs to Old Nick."

"Do you expect it will vanish some of these days with a bang and the odour of brimstone, Susan?"

"It will go to its own place in due time and that you may tie to," said Susan dourly, shaking out her raddled bones and going to her oven. "I suppose my plunking down like that has shaken my cake so that it will be as heavy as lead."

But the cake was not heavy. It was all a bride's cake should be, and Susan iced it beautifully. Next day she and Rilla worked all the forenoon, making delicacies for the wedding-feast, and as soon as Miranda phoned up that her father was safely off everything was packed in a big hamper and taken down to the Pryor house. Joe soon arrived in his uniform and a state of violent excitement, accompanied by his best man, Sergeant Malcolm Crawford. There were quite a few guests, for all the Manse and Ingleside folk were there, and a dozen or so of Joe's relatives, including his mother, "Mrs. Dead Angus Milgrave," so called, cheerfully, to distinguish her from another lady whose Angus was living. Mrs. Dead Angus wore a rather disapproving expression, not caring over-much for this alliance with the house of Whiskers-on-the-moon.

So Miranda Pryor was married to Private Joseph Milgrave on his last leave. It should have been a romantic wedding but it was not. There were too many factors working against romance, as even Rilla had to admit. In the first place, Miranda, in spite of her dress and veil, was such a flat-faced, commonplace, uninteresting little bride. In the second place, Joe cried bitterly all through the ceremony, and this vexed Miranda unreasonably. Long afterwards she told Rilla, "I just felt like saying to him then and there, 'If you feel so bad over having to marry me you don't have to.' But it was just because he was thinking all the time of how soon he would have to leave me."

In the third place, Jims, who was usually so well-behaved in public, took a fit of shyness and contrariness combined and began to cry at the top of his voice for "Willa." Nobody wanted to take him out, because everybody wanted to see the marriage, so Rilla who was a bridesmaid, had to take him and hold him during the ceremony.

In the fourth place, Sir Wilfrid Laurier took a fit.

Sir Wilfrid was entrenched in a corner of the room behind Miranda's piano. During his seizure he made the weirdest, most unearthly noises. He would begin with a series of choking, spasmodic sounds, continuing into a gruesome gurgle, and ending up with a strangled howl. Nobody could hear a word Mr. Meredith was saying, except now and then, when Sir Wilfrid stopped for breath. Nobody looked at the bride except Susan, who never dragged her fascinated eyes from Miranda's face—all the others were gazing at the dog. Miranda had been trembling with nervousness but as soon as Sir Wilfrid began his performance she forgot it. All that she could think of was that her dear dog was dying and she could not go to him. She never remembered a word of the ceremony.

Rilla, who in spite of Jims, had been trying her best to look rapt and romantic, as beseemed a war bridesmaid, gave up the hopeless attempt, and devoted her energies to choking down untimely merriment. She dared not look at anybody in the room, especially Mrs. Dead Angus, for fear all her suppressed mirth should suddenly explode in a most un-young-ladylike yell of laughter.

But married they were, and then they had a wedding-supper in the dining-room which was so lavish and bountiful that you would have thought it was the product of a month's labour. Everybody had brought something. Mrs. Dead Angus had brought a large apple-pie, which she placed on a chair in the dining-room and then absently sat down on it. Neither her temper nor her black silk wedding garment was improved thereby, but the pie was never missed at the gay bridal feast. Mrs. Dead Angus eventually took it home with her again. Whiskers-on-the-moon's pacifist pig should not get it, anyhow.

That evening Mr. and Mrs. Joe, accompanied by the recovered Sir Wilfrid, departed for the Four Winds Lighthouse, which was kept by Joe's uncle and in which they meant to spend their brief honeymoon. Una Meredith and Rilla and Susan washed the dishes, tidied up, left a cold supper and Miranda's pitiful little note on the table for Mr. Pryor, and walked home, while the mystic veil of dreamy, haunted winter twilight wrapped itself over the Glen.

"I would really not have minded being a war-bride myself," remarked Susan sentimentally.

But Rilla felt rather flat—perhaps as a reaction to all the excitement and rush of the past thirty-six hours. She was disappointed somehow—the whole affair had been so ludicrous, and Miranda and Joe so lachrymose and commonplace.

"If Miranda hadn't given that wretched dog such an enormous dinner he wouldn't have had that fit," she said crossly. "I warned her—but she said she couldn't starve the poor dog—he would soon be all she had left, etc. I could have shaken her."

"The best man was more excited than Joe was," said Susan. "He wished Miranda many happy returns of the day. She did not look very happy, but perhaps you could not expect that under the circumstances."

"Anyhow," thought Rilla, "I can write a perfectly killing account of it all to the boys. How Jem will howl over Sir Wilfrid's part in it!"

But if Rilla was rather disappointed in the war wedding she found nothing lacking on Friday morning when Miranda said good-bye to her bridegroom at the Glen station. The dawn was white as a pearl, clear as a diamond. Behind the station the balsamy copse of young firs was frost-misted. The cold moon of dawn hung over the westering snow fields but the golden fleeces of sunrise shone above the maples up at Ingleside. Joe took his pale little bride in his arms and she lifted her face to his. Rilla choked suddenly. It did not matter that Miranda was insignificant and commonplace and flat-featured. It did not matter that she was the daughter of Whiskers-on-the-moon. All that mattered was that rapt, sacrificial look in her eyes—that ever-burning, sacred fire of devotion and loyalty and fine courage that she was mutely promising Joe she and thousands of other women would keep alive at home while their men held the Western front. Rilla walked away, realising that she must not spy on such a moment. She went down to the end of the platform where Sir Wilfrid and Dog Monday were sitting, looking at each other.

Sir Wilfrid remarked condescendingly: "Why do you haunt this old shed when you might lie on the hearthrug at Ingleside and live on the fat of the land? Is it a pose? Or a fixed idea?"

Whereat Dog Monday, laconically: "I have a tryst to keep."

When the train had gone Rilla rejoined the little trembling Miranda. "Well, he's gone," said Miranda, "and he may never come back—but I'm his wife, and I'm going to be worthy of him. I'm going home."

"Don't you think you had better come with me now?" asked Rilla doubtfully. Nobody knew yet how Mr. Pryor had taken the matter.

"No. If Joe can face the Huns I guess I can face father," said Miranda daringly. "A soldier's wife can't be a coward. Come on, Wilfy. I'll go straight home and meet the worst."

There was nothing very dreadful to face, however. Perhaps Mr. Pryor had reflected that housekeepers were hard to get and that there were many Milgrave homes open to Miranda—also, that there was such a thing as a separation allowance. At all events, though he told her grumpily that she had made a nice fool of herself, and would live to regret it, he said nothing worse, and Mrs. Joe put on her apron and went to work as usual, while Sir Wilfrid Laurier, who had a poor opinion of lighthouses for winter residences, went to sleep in his pet nook behind the woodbox, a thankful dog that he was done with war-weddings.

CHAPTER XIX - "THEY SHALL NOT PASS"

One cold grey morning in February Gertrude Oliver wakened with a shiver, slipped into Rilla's room, and crept in beside her.

"Rilla—I'm frightened—frightened as a baby—I've had another of my strange dreams. Something terrible is before us—I know."

"What was it?" asked Rilla.

"I was standing again on the veranda steps—just as I stood in that dream on the night before the lighthouse dance, and in the sky a huge black, menacing thunder cloud rolled up from the east. I could see its shadow racing before it and when it enveloped me I shivered with icy cold. Then the storm broke—and it was a dreadful storm—blinding flash after flash and deafening peal after peal, driving torrents of rain. I turned in panic and tried to run for shelter, and as I did so a man—a soldier in the uniform of a French army officer—dashed up the steps and stood beside me on the threshold of the door. His clothes were soaked with blood from a wound in his breast, he seemed spent and exhausted; but his white face was set and his eyes blazed in his hollow face. 'They shall not pass,' he said, in low, passionate tones which I heard distinctly amid all the turmoil of the storm. Then I awakened. Rilla, I'm frightened—the spring will not bring the Big Push we've all been hoping for—instead it is going to bring some dreadful blow to France. I am sure of it. The Germans will try to smash through somewhere."

"But he told you that they would not pass," said Rilla, seriously. She never laughed at Gertrude's dreams as the doctor did.

"I do not know if that was prophecy or desperation, Rilla, the horror of that dream holds me yet in an icy grip. We shall need all our courage before long."

Dr. Blythe did laugh at the breakfast table—but he never laughed at Miss Oliver's dreams again; for that day brought news of the opening of the Verdun offensive, and thereafter through all the beautiful weeks of spring the Ingleside family, one and all, lived in a trance of dread. There were days when they waited in despair for the end as foot by foot the Germans crept nearer and nearer to the grim barrier of desperate France.

Susan's deeds were in her spotless kitchen at Ingleside, but her thoughts were on the hills around Verdun. "Mrs. Dr. dear," she would stick her head in at Mrs. Blythe's door the last thing at night to remark, "I do hope the French have hung onto the Crow's Wood today," and she woke at dawn to wonder if Dead Man's

Hill—surely named by some prophet—was still held by the "poyloos." Susan could have drawn a map of the country around Verdun that would have satisfied a chief of staff.

"If the Germans capture Verdun the spirit of France will be broken," Miss Oliver said bitterly.

"But they will not capture it," staunchly said Susan, who could not eat her dinner that day for fear lest they do that very thing. "In the first place, you dreamed they would not—you dreamed the very thing the French are saying before they ever said it—'they shall not pass.' I declare to you, Miss Oliver, dear, when I read that in the paper, and remembered your dream, I went cold all over with awe. It seemed to me like Biblical times when people dreamed things like that quite frequently.

"I know—I know," said Gertrude, walking restlessly about. "I cling to a persistent faith in my dream, too—but every time bad news comes it fails me. Then I tell myself 'mere coincidence'—'subconscious memory' and so forth."

"I do not see how any memory could remember a thing before it was ever said at all," persisted Susan, "though of course I am not educated like you and the doctor. I would rather not be, if it makes anything as simple as that so hard to believe. But in any case we need not worry over Verdun, even if the Huns get it. Joffre says it has no military significance."

"That old sop of comfort has been served up too often already when reverses came," retorted Gertrude. "It has lost its power to charm."

"Was there ever a battle like this in the world before?" said Mr. Meredith, one evening in mid-April.

"It's such a titanic thing we can't grasp it," said the doctor. "What were the scraps of a few Homeric handfuls compared to this? The whole Trojan war might be fought around a Verdun fort and a newspaper correspondent would give it no more than a sentence. I am not in the confidence of the occult powers"—the doctor threw Gertrude a twinkle—"but I have a hunch that the fate of the whole war hangs on the issue of Verdun. As Susan and Joffre say, it has no real military significance; but it has the tremendous significance of an Idea. If Germany wins there she will win the war. If she loses, the tide will set against her."

"Lose she will," said Mr. Meredith: emphatically. "The Idea cannot be conquered. France is certainly very wonderful. It seems to me that in her I see the white form of civilization making a determined stand against the black powers of barbarism. I think our whole world realizes this and that is why we all await the issue so breathlessly. It isn't merely the question of a few forts changing hands or a few miles of blood-soaked ground lost and won."

"I wonder," said Gertrude dreamily, "if some great blessing, great enough for the price, will be the meed of all our pain? Is the agony in which the world is shuddering the birth-pang of some wondrous new era? Or is it merely a futile

> struggle of ants
> In the gleam of a million million of suns?

We think very lightly, Mr. Meredith, of a calamity which destroys an ant-hill and half its inhabitants. Does the Power that runs the universe think us of more importance than we think ants?"

"You forget," said Mr. Meredith, with a flash of his dark eyes, "that an infinite Power must be infinitely little as well as infinitely great. We are neither, therefore there are things too little as well as too great for us to apprehend. To the infinitely little an ant is of as much importance as a mastodon. We are witnessing the birth-pangs of a new era—but it will be born a feeble, wailing life like everything else. I am not one of those who expect a new heaven and a new earth as the immediate result of this war. That is not the way God works. But work He does, Miss Oliver, and in the end His purpose will be fulfilled."

"Sound and orthodox—sound and orthodox," muttered Susan approvingly in the kitchen. Susan liked to see Miss Oliver sat upon by the minister now and then. Susan was very fond of her but she thought Miss Oliver liked saying heretical things to ministers far too well, and deserved an occasional reminder that these matters were quite beyond her province.

In May Walter wrote home that he had been awarded a D.C. Medal. He did not say what for, but the other boys took care that the Glen should know the brave thing Walter had done. "In any war but this," wrote Jerry Meredith, "it would have meant a V.C. But they can't make V.C.'s as common as the brave things done every day here."

"He should have had the V.C.," said Susan, and was very indignant over it. She was not quite sure who was to blame for his not getting it, but if it were General Haig she began for the first time to entertain serious doubts as to his fitness for being Commander-in-Chief.

Rilla was beside herself with delight. It was her dear Walter who had done this thing—Walter, to whom someone had sent a white feather at Redmond—it was Walter who had dashed back from the safety of the trench to drag in a wounded comrade who had fallen on No-man's-land. Oh, she could see his white beautiful face and wonderful eyes as he did it! What a thing to be the sister of such a hero! And he hadn't thought it worth while writing about. His letter was full of other things—little intimate things that they two had known and loved together in the dear old cloudless days of a century ago.

"I've been thinking of the daffodils in the garden at Ingleside," he wrote. "By the time you get this they will be out, blowing there under that lovely rosy sky. Are they really as bright and golden as ever, Rilla? It seems to me that they must be dyed red with blood—like our poppies here. And every whisper of spring will be falling as a violet in Rainbow Valley.

"There is a young moon tonight—a slender, silver, lovely thing hanging over these pits of torment. Will you see it tonight over the maple grove?

"I'm enclosing a little scrap of verse, Rilla. I wrote it one evening in my trench dug-out by the light of a bit of candle—or rather it came to me there—I didn't feel as if I were writing it—something seemed to use me as an instrument. I've had that feeling once or twice before, but very rarely and never so strongly as this time. That was why I sent it over to the London Spectator. It printed it and the copy came today. I hope you'll like it. It's the only poem I've written since I came overseas."

The poem was a short, poignant little thing. In a month it had carried Walter's name to every corner of the globe. Everywhere it was copied—in metropolitan dailies and little village weeklies—in profound reviews and "agony columns," in Red Cross appeals and Government recruiting propaganda. Mothers and sisters wept over it, young lads thrilled to it, the whole great heart of humanity caught it up as an epitome of all the pain and hope and pity and purpose of the mighty conflict, crystallized in three brief immortal verses. A Canadian lad in the Flanders trenches had written the one great poem of the war. "The Piper," by Pte. Walter Blythe, was a classic from its first printing.

Rilla copied it in her diary at the beginning of an entry in which she poured out the story of the hard week that had just passed.

"It has been such a dreadful week," she wrote, "and even though it is over and we know that it was all a mistake that does not seem to do away with the bruises left by it. And yet it has in some ways been a very wonderful week and I have had some glimpses of things I never realized before—of how fine and brave people can be even in the midst of horrible suffering. I am sure I could never be as splendid as Miss Oliver was.

"Just a week ago today she had a letter from Mr. Grant's mother in Charlottetown. And it told her that a cable had just come saying that Major Robert Grant had been killed in action a few days before.

"Oh, poor Gertrude! At first she was crushed. Then after just a day she pulled herself together and went back to her school. She did not cry—I never saw her shed a tear—but oh, her face and her eyes!

"'I must go on with my work,' she said. 'That is my duty just now.'

"I could never have risen to such a height.

"She never spoke bitterly except once, when Susan said something about spring being here at last, and Gertrude said,

"'Can the spring really come this year?'

"Then she laughed—such a dreadful little laugh, just as one might laugh in the face of death, I think, and said,

"'Observe my egotism. Because I, Gertrude Oliver, have lost a friend, it is incredible that the spring can come as usual. The spring does not fail because of the million agonies of others—but for mine—oh, can the universe go on?'

"'Don't feel bitter with yourself, dear,' mother said gently. 'It is a very natural thing to feel as if things couldn't go on just the same when some great blow has changed the world for us. We all feel like that.'

"Then that horrid old Cousin Sophia of Susan's piped up. She was sitting there, knitting and croaking like an old 'raven of bode and woe' as Walter used to call her.

"'You ain't as bad off as some, Miss Oliver,' she said, 'and you shouldn't take it so hard. There's some as has lost their husbands; that's a hard blow; and there's some as has lost their sons. You haven't lost either husband or son.'

"'No,' said Gertrude, more bitterly still. 'It's true I haven't lost a husband—I have only lost the man who would have been my husband. I have lost no son—only the sons and daughters who might have been born to me—who will never be born to me now.'

"'It isn't ladylike to talk like that,' said Cousin Sophia in a shocked tone; and then Gertrude laughed right out, so wildly that Cousin Sophia was really frightened. And when poor tortured Gertrude, unable to endure it any longer, hurried out of the room, Cousin Sophia asked mother if the blow hadn't affected Miss Oliver's mind.

"'I suffered the loss of two good kind partners,' she said, 'but it did not affect me like that.'

"I should think it wouldn't! Those poor men must have been thankful to die.

"I heard Gertrude walking up and down her room most of the night. She walked like that every night. But never so long as that night. And once I heard her give a dreadful sudden little cry as if she had been stabbed. I couldn't sleep for suffering with her; and I couldn't help her. I thought the night would never end. But it did; and then 'joy came in the morning' as the Bible says. Only it didn't come exactly in the morning but well along in the afternoon. The telephone rang and I answered it. It was old Mrs. Grant speaking from Charlottetown, and her news was that it was all a mistake—Robert wasn't killed at all; he had only been slightly wounded in the arm and was safe in the hospital out of harm's way for a time anyhow. They hadn't learned yet how the mistake had happened but supposed there must have been another Robert Grant.

"I hung up the telephone and flew to Rainbow Valley. I'm sure I did fly—I can't remember my feet ever touching the ground. I met Gertrude on her way home from school in the glade of spruces where we used to play, and I just gasped out the news to her. I ought to have had more sense, of course. But I was so crazy with joy and excitement that I never stopped to think. Gertrude just dropped there among the golden young ferns as if she had been shot. The fright it gave me ought to make me sensible—in this respect at least—for the rest of my life. I thought I had killed her—I remembered that her mother had died very suddenly from heart failure when quite a young woman. It seemed years to me before I discovered that her heart was still beating. A pretty time I had! I never saw anybody faint before, and I knew there was nobody up at the house to help, because everybody else had gone to the station to meet Di and Nan coming home from Redmond. But I knew—theoretically—how people in a faint should be treated, and now I know it practically. Luckily the brook was handy, and after I had worked frantically over her for a while Gertrude came back to life. She never said one word about my news and I didn't dare to refer to it again. I helped her walk up through the maple grove and up to her room, and then she said, 'Rob—is—living,' as if the words were torn out of her, and flung herself on her bed and cried and cried and cried. I never saw anyone cry so before. All the tears that she hadn't shed all that week came then. She cried most of last night, I think, but her face this morning looked as if she had seen a vision of some kind, and we were all so happy that we were almost afraid.

"Di and Nan are home for a couple of weeks. Then they go back to Red Cross work in the training camp at Kingsport. I envy them. Father says I'm doing just as good work here, with Jims and my Junior Reds. But it lacks the romance theirs must have.

"Kut has fallen. It was almost a relief when it did fall, we had been dreading it so long. It crushed us flat for a day and then we picked up and put it behind us. Cousin Sophia was as gloomy as usual and came over and groaned that the British were losing everywhere.

"'They're good losers,' said Susan grimly. 'When they lose a thing they keep on looking till they find it again! Anyhow, my king and country need me now to cut potato sets for the back garden, so get you a knife and help me, Sophia Crawford. It will divert your thoughts and keep you from worrying over a campaign that you are not called upon to run.'

"Susan is an old brick, and the way she flattens out poor Cousin Sophia is beautiful to behold.

"As for Verdun, the battle goes on and on, and we see-saw between hope and fear. But I know that strange dream of Miss Oliver's foretold the victory of France. 'They shall not pass.'"

CHAPTER XX - NORMAN DOUGLAS SPEAKS OUT IN MEETING

"Where are you wandering, Anne o' mine?" asked the doctor, who even yet, after twenty-four years of marriage, occasionally addressed his wife thus when nobody was about. Anne was sitting on the veranda steps, gazing absently over the wonderful bridal world of spring blossom, Beyond the white orchard was a copse of dark young firs and creamy wild cherries, where the robins were whistling madly; for it was evening and the fire of early stars was burning over the maple grove.

Anne came back with a little sigh.

"I was just taking relief from intolerable realities in a dream, Gilbert—a dream that all our children were home again—and all small again—playing in Rainbow Valley. It is always so silent now—but I was imagining I heard clear voices and gay, childish sounds coming up as I used to. I could hear Jem's whistle and Walter's yodel, and the twins' laughter, and for just a few blessed minutes I forgot about the guns on the Western front, and had a little false, sweet happiness."

The doctor did not answer. Sometimes his work tricked him into forgetting for a few moments the Western front, but not often. There was a good deal of grey now in his still thick curls that had not been there two years ago. Yet he smiled down into the starry eyes he loved—the eyes that had once been so full of laughter, and now seemed always full of unshed tears.

Susan wandered by with a hoe in her hand and her second best bonnet on her head.

"I have just finished reading a piece in the Enterprise which told of a couple being married in an aeroplane. Do you think it would be legal, doctor dear?" she inquired anxiously.

"I think so," said the doctor gravely.

"Well," said Susan dubiously, "it seems to me that a wedding is too solemn for anything so giddy as an aeroplane. But nothing is the same as it used to be. Well, it is half an hour yet before prayer-meeting time, so I am going around to the kitchen garden to have a little evening hate with the weeds. But all the time I am strafing them I will be thinking about this new worry in the Trentino. I do not like this Austrian caper, Mrs. Dr. dear."

"Nor I," said Mrs. Blythe ruefully. "All the forenoon I preserved rhubarb with my hands and waited for the war news with my soul. When it came I shrivelled. Well, I suppose I must go and get ready for the prayer-meeting, too."

Every village has its own little unwritten history, handed down from lip to lip through the generations, of tragic, comic, and dramatic events. They are told at weddings and festivals, and rehearsed around winter firesides. And in these oral annals of Glen St. Mary the tale of the union prayer-meeting held that night in the Methodist Church was destined to fill an imperishable place.

The union prayer-meeting was Mr. Arnold's idea. The county battalion, which had been training all winter in Charlottetown, was to leave shortly for overseas. The Four Winds Harbour boys belonging to it from the Glen and over-harbour and Harbour Head and Upper Glen were all home on their last leave, and Mr. Arnold thought, properly enough, that it would be a fitting thing to hold a union prayer-meeting for them before they went away. Mr. Meredith having agreed, the meeting was announced to be held in the Methodist Church. Glen prayer-meetings were not apt to be too well attended, but on this particular evening the Methodist Church was crowded. Everybody who could go was there. Even Miss Cornelia came—and it was the first time in her life that Miss Cornelia had ever set foot inside a Methodist Church. It took no less than a world conflict to bring that about.

"I used to hate Methodists," said Miss Cornelia calmly, when her husband expressed surprise over her going, "but I don't hate them now. There is no sense in hating Methodists when there is a Kaiser or a Hindenburg in the world."

So Miss Cornelia went. Norman Douglas and his wife went too. And Whiskers-on-the-moon strutted up the aisle to a front pew, as if he fully realized what a distinction he conferred upon the building. People were somewhat surprised that he should be there, since he usually avoided all assemblages connected in any way with the war. But Mr. Meredith had said that he hoped his session would be well represented, and Mr. Pryor had evidently taken the request to heart. He wore his best black suit and white tie, his thick, tight, iron-grey curls were neatly arranged, and his broad, red round face looked, as Susan most uncharitably thought, more "sanctimonious" than ever.

"The minute I saw that man coming into the Church, looking like that, I felt that mischief was brewing, Mrs. Dr. dear," she said afterwards. "What form it would take I could not tell, but I knew from face of him that he had come there for no good."

The prayer-meeting opened conventionally and continued quietly. Mr. Meredith spoke first with his usual eloquence and feeling. Mr. Arnold followed with an address which even Miss Cornelia had to confess was irreproachable in taste and subject-matter.

And then Mr. Arnold asked Mr. Pryor to lead in prayer.

Miss Cornelia had always averred that Mr. Arnold had no gumption. Miss Cornelia was not apt to err on the side of charity in her judgment of Methodist ministers, but in this case she did not greatly overshoot the mark. The Rev. Mr.

Arnold certainly did not have much of that desirable, indefinable quality known as gumption, or he would never have asked Whiskers-on-the-moon to lead in prayer at a khaki prayer-meeting. He thought he was returning the compliment to Mr. Meredith, who, at the conclusion of his address, had asked a Methodist deacon to lead.

Some people expected Mr. Pryor to refuse grumpily—and that would have made enough scandal. But Mr. Pryor bounded briskly to his feet, unctuously said, "Let us pray," and forthwith prayed. In a sonorous voice which penetrated to every corner of the crowded building Mr. Pryor poured forth a flood of fluent words, and was well on in his prayer before his dazed and horrified audience awakened to the fact that they were listening to a pacifist appeal of the rankest sort. Mr. Pryor had at least the courage of his convictions; or perhaps, as people afterwards said, he thought he was safe in a church and that it was an excellent chance to air certain opinions he dared not voice elsewhere, for fear of being mobbed. He prayed that the unholy war might cease—that the deluded armies being driven to slaughter on the Western front might have their eyes opened to their iniquity and repent while yet there was time—that the poor young men present in khaki, who had been hounded into a path of murder and militarism, should yet be rescued—

Mr. Pryor had got this far without let or hindrance; and so paralysed were his hearers, and so deeply imbued with their born-and-bred conviction that no disturbance must ever be made in a church, no matter what the provocation, that it seemed likely that he would continue unchecked to the end. But one man at least in that audience was not hampered by inherited or acquired reverence for the sacred edifice. Norman Douglas was, as Susan had often vowed crisply, nothing more or less than a "pagan." But he was a rampantly patriotic pagan, and when the significance of what Mr. Pryor was saying fully dawned on him, Norman Douglas suddenly went berserk. With a positive roar he bounded to his feet in his side pew, facing the audience, and shouted in tones of thunder:

"Stop—stop—STOP that abominable prayer! What an abominable prayer!"

Every head in the church flew up. A boy in khaki at the back gave a faint cheer. Mr. Meredith raised a deprecating hand, but Norman was past caring for anything like that. Eluding his wife's restraining grasp, he gave one mad spring over the front of the pew and caught the unfortunate Whiskers-on-the-moon by his coat collar. Mr. Pryor had not "stopped" when so bidden, but he stopped now, perforce, for Norman, his long red beard literally bristling with fury, was shaking him until his bones fairly rattled, and punctuating his shakes with a lurid assortment of abusive epithets.

"You blatant beast!"—shake—"You malignant carrion"—shake—"You pigheaded varmint!"—shake—"you putrid pup"—shake—"you pestilential parasite"—shake—"you—Hunnish scum"—shake—"you indecent reptile—you—you—" Norman choked for a moment. Everybody believed that the next thing he would say, church or no church, would be something that would have to be spelt with asterisks; but at that moment Norman encountered his wife's eye and he fell back with a thud on Holy Writ. "You whited sepulchre!" he bellowed, with a final shake, and cast Whiskers-on-the-moon from him with a vigour which impelled that unhappy pacifist to the very verge of the choir entrance door. Mr. Pryor's once ruddy face was ashen. But he turned at bay. "I'll have the law on you for this," he gasped.

"Do—do," roared Norman, making another rush. But Mr. Pryor was gone. He had no desire to fall a second time into the hands of an avenging militarist. Norman turned to the platform for one graceless, triumphant moment.

"Don't look so flabbergasted, parsons," he boomed. "You couldn't do it—nobody would expect it of the cloth—but somebody had to do it. You know you're glad I threw him out—he couldn't be let go on yammering and yodelling and yawping sedition and treason. Sedition and treason—somebody had to deal with it. I was born for this hour—I've had my innings in church at last. I can sit quiet for another sixty years now! Go ahead with your meeting, parsons. I reckon you won't be troubled with any more pacifist prayers."

But the spirit of devotion and reverence had fled. Both ministers realized it and realized that the only thing to do was to close the meeting quietly and let the excited people go. Mr. Meredith addressed a few earnest words to the boys in khaki—which probably saved Mr. Pryor's windows from a second onslaught—and Mr. Arnold pronounced an incongruous benediction, at least he felt it was incongruous, for he could not at once banish from his memory the sight of gigantic Norman Douglas shaking the fat, pompous little Whiskers-on-the-moon as a huge mastiff might shake an overgrown puppy. And he knew that the same picture was in everybody's mind. Altogether the union prayer-meeting could hardly be called an unqualified success. But it was remembered in Glen St. Mary when scores of orthodox and undisturbed assemblies were totally forgotten.

"You will never, no, never, Mrs. Dr. dear, hear me call Norman Douglas a pagan again," said Susan when she reached home. "If Ellen Douglas is not a proud woman this night she should be."

"Norman Douglas did a wholly indefensible thing," said the doctor. "Pryor should have been let severely alone until the meeting was over. Then later on, his own minister and session should deal with him. That would have been the proper procedure. Norman's performance was utterly improper and scandalous and outrageous; but, by George,"—the doctor threw back his head and chuckled, "by George, Anne-girl, it was satisfying."

CHAPTER XXI - "LOVE AFFAIRS ARE HORRIBLE"

Ingleside
20th June 1916

"We have been so busy, and day after day has brought such exciting news, good and bad, that I haven't had time and composure to write in my diary for weeks. I like to keep it up regularly, for father says a diary of the years of the war should be a very interesting thing to hand down to one's children. The trouble is, I like to write a few personal things in this blessed old book that might not be exactly what I'd want my children to read. I feel that I shall be a far greater stickler for propriety in regard to them than I am for myself!

"The first week in June was another dreadful one. The Austrians seemed just on the point of overrunning Italy: and then came the first awful news of the Battle of Jutland, which the Germans claimed as a great victory. Susan was the only one who carried on. 'You need never tell me that the Kaiser has defeated the British Navy,' she said, with a contemptuous sniff. 'It is all a German lie and that you may tie to.' And when a couple of days later we found out that she was right and that it had been a British victory instead of a British defeat, we had to put up with a great many 'I told you so's,' but we endured them very comfortably.

"It took Kitchener's death to finish Susan. For the first time I saw her down and out. We all felt the shock of it but Susan plumbed the depths of despair. The news came at night by 'phone but Susan wouldn't believe it until she saw the Enterprise headline the next day. She did not cry or faint or go into hysterics; but she forgot to put salt in the soup, and that is something Susan never did in my recollection. Mother and Miss Oliver and I cried but Susan looked at us in stony sarcasm and said, 'The Kaiser and his six sons are all alive and thriving. So the world is not left wholly desolate. Why cry, Mrs. Dr. dear?' Susan continued in this stony, hopeless condition for twenty-four hours, and then Cousin Sophia appeared and began to condole with her.

"'This is terrible news, ain't it, Susan? We might as well prepare for the worst for it is bound to come. You said once—and well do I remember the words, Susan Baker—that you had complete confidence in God and Kitchener. Ah well, Susan Baker, there is only God left now.'

"Whereat Cousin Sophia put her handkerchief to her eyes pathetically as if the world were indeed in terrible straits. As for Susan, Cousin Sophia was the salvation of her. She came to life with a jerk.

"'Sophia Crawford, hold your peace!' she said sternly. 'You may be an idiot but you need not be an irreverent idiot. It is no more than decent to be weeping and wailing because the Almighty is the sole stay of the Allies now. As for Kitchener, his death is a great loss and I do not dispute it. But the outcome of this war does not depend on one man's life and now that the Russians are coming on again you will soon see a change for the better.'

"Susan said this so energetically that she convinced herself and cheered up immediately. But Cousin Sophia shook her head.

"'Albert's wife wants to call the baby after Brusiloff,' she said, 'but I told her to wait and see what becomes of him first. Them Russians has such a habit of petering out.'

"The Russians are doing splendidly, however, and they have saved Italy. But even when the daily news of their sweeping advance comes we don't feel like running up the flag as we used to do. As Gertrude says, Verdun has slain all exultation. We would all feel more like rejoicing if the victories were on the western front. 'When will the British strike?' Gertrude sighed this morning. 'We have waited so long—so long.'

"Our greatest local event in recent weeks was the route march the county battalion made through the county before it left for overseas. They marched from Charlottetown to Lowbridge, then round the Harbour Head and through the Upper Glen and so down to the St. Mary station. Everybody turned out to see them, except old Aunt Fannie Clow, who is bedridden and Mr. Pryor, who hadn't been seen out even in church since the night of the Union Prayer Meeting the previous week.

"It was wonderful and heartbreaking to see that battalion marching past. There were young men and middle-aged men in it. There was Laurie McAllister from over-harbour who is only sixteen but swore he was eighteen, so that he could enlist; and there was Angus Mackenzie, from the Upper Glen who is fifty-five if he is a day and swore he was forty-four. There were two South African veterans from Lowbridge, and the three eighteen-year-old Baxter triplets from Harbour Head. Everybody cheered as they went by, and they cheered Foster Booth, who is forty, walking side by side with his son Charley who is twenty. Charley's mother died when he was born, and when Charley enlisted Foster said he'd never yet let Charley go anywhere he daren't go himself, and he didn't mean to begin with the Flanders trenches. At the station Dog Monday nearly went out of his head. He tore about and sent messages to Jem by them all. Mr. Meredith read an address and Reta Crawford recited 'The Piper.' The soldiers cheered her like mad and cried 'We'll follow—we'll follow—we won't break faith,' and I felt so proud to think that it was my dear brother who had written such a wonderful, heart-stirring thing. And then I looked at the khaki ranks and wondered if those tall fellows in uniform could be the boys I've laughed with and played with and danced with and teased all my life. Something seems to have touched them and set them apart. They have heard the Piper's call.

"Fred Arnold was in the battalion and I felt dreadfully about him, for I realized that it was because of me that he was going away with such a sorrowful expression. I couldn't help it but I felt as badly as if I could.

"The last evening of his leave Fred came up to Ingleside and told me he loved me and asked me if I would promise to marry him some day, if he ever came back. He was desperately in earnest and I felt more wretched than I ever did in my life. I couldn't promise him that—why, even if there was no question of Ken, I don't care for Fred that way and never could—but it seemed so cruel and heartless to send him away to the front without any hope of comfort. I cried like a baby; and yet—oh, I am afraid that there must be something incurably frivolous about me, because, right in the middle of it all, with me crying and Fred looking so wild and tragic, the thought popped into my head that it would be an unendurable thing to see that nose across from me at the breakfast table every morning of my life. There, that is one of the entries I wouldn't want my descendants to read in this journal. But it is the humiliating truth; and perhaps it's just as well that thought did come or I might have been tricked by pity and remorse into giving him some rash assurance. If Fred's nose were as handsome as his eyes and mouth some such thing might have happened. And then what an unthinkable predicament I should have been in!

"When poor Fred became convinced that I couldn't promise him, he behaved beautifully—though that rather made things worse. If he had been nasty about it I wouldn't have felt so heartbroken and remorseful—though why I should feel remorseful I don't know, for I never encouraged Fred to think I cared a bit about him. Yet feel remorseful I did—and do. If Fred Arnold never comes back from overseas, this will haunt me all my life.

"Then Fred said if he couldn't take my love with him to the trenches at least he wanted to feel that he had my friendship, and would I kiss him just once in good-bye before he went—perhaps for ever?

"I don't know how I could ever had imagined that love affairs were delightful, interesting things. They are horrible. I couldn't even give poor heartbroken Fred one little kiss, because of my promise to Ken. It seemed so brutal. I had to tell Fred that of course he would have my friendship, but that I couldn't kiss him because I had promised somebody else I wouldn't.

"He said, 'It is—is it—Ken Ford?'

"I nodded. It seemed dreadful to have to tell it—it was such a sacred little secret just between me and Ken.

"When Fred went away I came up here to my room and cried so long and so bitterly that mother came up and insisted on knowing what was the matter. I told her. She listened to my tale with an expression that clearly said, 'Can it be possible that anyone has been wanting to marry this baby?' But she was so nice and understanding and sympathetic, oh, just so race-of-Josephy—that I felt indescribably comforted. Mothers are the dearest things.

"'But oh, mother,' I sobbed, 'he wanted me to kiss him good-bye—and I couldn't—and that hurt me worse than all the rest.'

"'Well, why didn't you kiss him?' asked mother coolly. 'Considering the circumstances, I think you might have.'

"'But I couldn't, mother—I promised Ken when he went away that I wouldn't kiss anybody else until he came back.'

"This was another high explosive for poor mother. She exclaimed, with the queerest little catch in her voice, 'Rilla, are you engaged to Kenneth Ford?'

"'I—don't—know,' I sobbed.

"'You—don't—know?' repeated mother.

"Then I had to tell her the whole story, too; and every time I tell it it seems sillier and sillier to imagine that Ken meant anything serious. I felt idiotic and ashamed by the time I got through.

"Mother sat a little while in silence. Then she came over, sat down beside me, and took me in her arms.

"'Don't cry, dear little Rilla-my-Rilla. You have nothing to reproach yourself with in regard to Fred; and if Leslie West's son asked you to keep your lips for him, I think you may consider yourself engaged to him. But—oh, my baby—my last little baby—I have lost you—the war has made a woman of you too soon.'

"I shall never be too much of a woman to find comfort in mother's hugs. Nevertheless, when I saw Fred marching by two days later in the parade, my heart ached unbearably.

"But I'm glad mother thinks I'm really engaged to Ken!"

CHAPTER XXII - LITTLE DOG MONDAY KNOWS

"It is two years tonight since the dance at the light, when Jack Elliott brought us news of the war. Do you remember, Miss Oliver?"

Cousin Sophia answered for Miss Oliver. "Oh, indeed, Rilla, I remember that evening only too well, and you a-prancing down here to show off your party clothes. Didn't I warn you that we could not tell what was before us? Little did you think that night what was before you."

"Little did any of us think that," said Susan sharply, "not being gifted with the power of prophecy. It does not require any great foresight, Sophia Crawford, to tell a body that she will have some trouble before her life is over. I could do as much myself."

"We all thought the war would be over in a few months then," said Rilla wistfully. "When I look back it seems so ridiculous that we ever could have supposed it."

"And now, two years later, it is no nearer the end than it was then," said Miss Oliver gloomily.

Susan clicked her knitting-needles briskly.

"Now, Miss Oliver, dear, you know that is not a reasonable remark. You know we are just two years nearer the end, whenever the end is appointed to be."

"Albert read in a Montreal paper today that a war expert gives it as his opinion that it will last five years more," was Cousin Sophia's cheerful contribution.

"It can't," cried Rilla; then she added with a sigh, "Two years ago we would have said 'It can't last two years.' But five more years of this!"

"If Rumania comes in, as I have strong hopes now of her doing, you will see the end in five months instead of five years," said Susan.

"I've no faith in furriners," sighed Cousin Sophia.

"The French are foreigners," retorted Susan, "and look at Verdun. And think of all the Somme victories this blessed summer. The Big Push is on and the Russians are still going well. Why, General Haig says that the German officers he has captured admit that they have lost the war."

"You can't believe a word the Germans say," protested Cousin Sophia. "There is no sense in believing a thing just because you'd like to believe it, Susan Baker.

The British have lost millions of men at the Somme and how far have they got? Look facts in the face, Susan Baker, look facts in the face."

"They are wearing the Germans out and so long as that happens it does not matter whether it is done a few miles east or a few miles west. I am not," admitted Susan in tremendous humility, "I am not a military expert, Sophia Crawford, but even I can see that, and so could you if you were not determined to take a gloomy view of everything. The Huns have not got all the cleverness in the world. Have you not heard the story of Alistair MacCallum's son Roderick, from the Upper Glen? He is a prisoner in Germany and his mother got a letter from him last week. He wrote that he was being very kindly treated and that all the prisoners had plenty of food and so on, till you would have supposed everything was lovely. But when he signed his name, right in between Roderick and MacCallum, he wrote two Gaelic words that meant 'all lies' and the German censor did not understand Gaelic and thought it was all part of Roddy's name. So he let it pass, never dreaming how he was diddled. Well, I am going to leave the war to Haig for the rest of the day and make a frosting for my chocolate cake. And when it is made I shall put it on the top shelf. The last one I made I left it on the lower shelf and little Kitchener sneaked in and clawed all the icing off and ate it. We had company for tea that night and when I went to get my cake what a sight did I behold!"

"Has that pore orphan's father never been heerd from yet?" asked Cousin Sophia.

"Yes, I had a letter from him in July," said Rilla. "He said that when he got word of his wife's death and of my taking the baby—Mr. Meredith wrote him, you know—he wrote right away, but as he never got any answer he had begun to think his letter must have been lost."

"It took him two years to begin to think it," said Susan scornfully. "Some people think very slow. Jim Anderson has not got a scratch, for all he has been two years in the trenches. A fool for luck, as the old proverb says."

"He wrote very nicely about Jims and said he'd like to see him," said Rilla. "So I wrote and told him all about the wee man, and sent him snapshots. Jims will be two years old next week and he is a perfect duck."

"You didn't used to be very fond of babies," said Cousin Sophia.

"I'm not a bit fonder of babies in the abstract than ever I was," said Rilla, frankly. "But I do love Jims, and I'm afraid I wasn't really half as glad as I should have been when Jim Anderson's letter proved that he was safe and sound."

"You wasn't hoping the man would be killed!" cried Cousin Sophia in horrified accents.

"No—no—no! I just hoped he would go on forgetting about Jims, Mrs. Crawford."

"And then your pa would have the expense of raising him," said Cousin Sophia reprovingly. "You young creeturs are terrible thoughtless."

Jims himself ran in at this juncture, so rosy and curly and kissable, that he extorted a qualified compliment even from Cousin Sophia.

"He's a reel healthy-looking child now, though mebbee his colour is a mite too high—sorter consumptive looking, as you might say. I never thought you'd raise him when I saw him the day after you brung him home. I reely did not think it was in you and I told Albert's wife so when I got home. Albert's wife says, says she, 'There's more in Rilla Blythe than you'd think for, Aunt Sophia.' Them was her very words. 'More in Rilla Blythe than you'd think for.' Albert's wife always had a good opinion of you."

Cousin Sophia sighed, as if to imply that Albert's wife stood alone in this against the world. But Cousin Sophia really did not mean that. She was quite fond of Rilla in her own melancholy way; but young creeturs had to be kept down. If they were not kept down society would be demoralized.

"Do you remember your walk home from the light two years ago tonight?" whispered Gertrude Oliver to Rilla, teasingly.

"I should think I do," smiled Rilla; and then her smile grew dreamy and absent; she was remembering something else—that hour with Kenneth on the sandshore. Where would Ken be tonight? And Jem and Jerry and Walter and all the other boys who had danced and moonlighted on the old Four Winds Point that evening of mirth and laughter—their last joyous unclouded evening. In the filthy trenches of the Somme front, with the roar of the guns and the groans of stricken men for the music of Ned Burr's violin, and the flash of star shells for the silver sparkles on the old blue gulf. Two of them were sleeping under the Flanders poppies—Alec Burr from the Upper Glen, and Clark Manley of Lowbridge. Others were wounded in the hospitals. But so far nothing had touched the manse and the Ingleside boys. They seemed to bear charmed lives. Yet the suspense never grew any easier to bear as the weeks and months of war went by.

"It isn't as if it were some sort of fever to which you might conclude they were immune when they hadn't taken it for two years," sighed Rilla. "The danger is just as great and just as real as it was the first day they went into the trenches. I know this, and it tortures me every day. And yet I can't help hoping that since they've come this far unhurt they'll come through. Oh, Miss Oliver, what would it be like not to wake up in the morning feeling afraid of the news the day would bring? I can't picture such a state of things somehow. And two years ago this morning I woke wondering what delightful gift the new day would give me. These are the two years I thought would be filled with fun."

"Would you exchange them—now—for two years filled with fun?"

"No," said Rilla slowly. "I wouldn't. It's strange—isn't it?—They have been two terrible years—and yet I have a queer feeling of thankfulness for them—as if they had brought me something very precious, with all their pain. I wouldn't want to go back and be the girl I was two years ago, not even if I could. Not that I think I've made any wonderful progress—but I'm not quite the selfish, frivolous little doll I was then. I suppose I had a soul then, Miss Oliver—but I didn't know it. I know it now—and that is worth a great deal—worth all the suffering of the past two years. And still"—Rilla gave a little apologetic laugh, "I don't want to suffer any more—not even for the sake of more soul growth. At the end of two more years I might look back and be thankful for the development they had brought me, too; but I don't want it now."

"We never do," said Miss Oliver. "That is why we are not left to choose our own means and measure of development, I suppose. No matter how much we value what our lessons have brought us we don't want to go on with the bitter schooling. Well, let us hope for the best, as Susan says; things are really going well now and if Rumania lines up, the end may come with a suddenness that will surprise us all."

Rumania did come in—and Susan remarked approvingly that its king and queen were the finest looking royal couple she had seen pictures of. So the summer passed away. Early in September word came that the Canadians had been shifted to the Somme front and anxiety grew tenser and deeper. For the first time Mrs. Blythe's spirit failed her a little, and as the days of suspense wore on the doctor began to look gravely at her, and veto this or that special effort in Red Cross work.

"Oh, let me work—let me work, Gilbert," she entreated feverishly. "While I'm working I don't think so much. If I'm idle I imagine everything—rest is only torture for me. My two boys are on the frightful Somme front—and Shirley pores day and night over aviation literature and says nothing. But I see the purpose growing in his eyes. No, I cannot rest—don't ask it of me, Gilbert."

But the doctor was inexorable.

"I can't let you kill yourself, Anne-girl," he said. "When the boys come back I want a mother here to welcome them. Why, you're getting transparent. It won't do—ask Susan there if it will do."

"Oh, if Susan and you are both banded together against me!" said Anne helplessly.

One day the glorious news came that the Canadians had taken Courcelette and Martenpuich, with many prisoners and guns. Susan ran up the flag and said it was plain to be seen that Haig knew what soldiers to pick for a hard job. The others dared not feel exultant. Who knew what price had been paid?

Rilla woke that morning when the dawn was beginning to break and went to her window to look out, her thick creamy eyelids heavy with sleep. Just at dawn the world looks as it never looks at any other time. The air was cold with dew and the orchard and grove and Rainbow Valley were full of mystery and wonder. Over the eastern hill were golden deeps and silvery-pink shallows. There was no wind, and Rilla heard distinctly a dog howling in a melancholy way down in the direction of the station. Was it Dog Monday? And if it were, why was he howling like that? Rilla shivered; the sound had something boding and grievous in it. She remembered that Miss Oliver said once, when they were coming home in the darkness and heard a dog howl, "When a dog cries like that the Angel of Death is passing." Rilla listened with a curdling fear at her heart. It was Dog Monday—she felt sure of it. Whose dirge was he howling—to whose spirit was he sending that anguished greeting and farewell?

Rilla went back to bed but she could not sleep. All day she watched and waited in a dread of which she did not speak to anyone. She went down to see Dog Monday and the station-master said, "That dog of yours howled from midnight to sunrise something weird. I dunno what got into him. I got up once and went out and hollered at him but he paid no 'tention to me. He was sitting all alone in the moonlight out there at the end of the platform, and every few minutes the poor lonely little beggar'd lift his nose and howl as if his heart was breaking. He never did it afore—always slept in his kennel real quiet and canny from train to train. But he sure had something on his mind last night."

Dog Monday was lying in his kennel. He wagged his tail and licked Rilla's hand. But he would not touch the food she brought for him.

"I'm afraid he's sick," she said anxiously. She hated to go away and leave him. But no bad news came that day—nor the next—nor the next. Rilla's fear lifted. Dog Monday howled no more and resumed his routine of train meeting and watching. When five days had passed the Ingleside people began to feel that they might be cheerful again. Rilla dashed about the kitchen helping Susan with the breakfast and singing so sweetly and clearly that Cousin Sophia across the road heard her and croaked out to Mrs. Albert,

"'Sing before eating, cry before sleeping,' I've always heard."

But Rilla Blythe shed no tears before the nightfall. When her father, his face grey and drawn and old, came to her that afternoon and told her that Walter had been killed in action at Courcelette she crumpled up in a pitiful little heap of merciful unconsciousness in his arms. Nor did she waken to her pain for many hours.

CHAPTER XXIII - "AND SO, GOODNIGHT"

The fierce flame of agony had burned itself out and the grey dust of its ashes was over all the world. Rilla's younger life recovered physically sooner than her mother. For weeks Mrs. Blythe lay ill from grief and shock. Rilla found it was possible to go on with existence, since existence had still to be reckoned with. There was work to be done, for Susan could not do all. For her mother's sake she had to put on calmness and endurance as a garment in the day; but night after night she lay in her bed, weeping the bitter rebellious tears of youth until at last tears were all wept out and the little patient ache that was to be in her heart until she died took their place.

She clung to Miss Oliver, who knew what to say and what not to say. So few people did. Kind, well-meaning callers and comforters gave Rilla some terrible moments.

"You'll get over it in time," Mrs. William Reese said, cheerfully. Mrs. Reese had three stalwart sons, not one of whom had gone to the front.

"It's such a blessing it was Walter who was taken and not Jem," said Miss Sarah Clow. "Walter was a member of the church, and Jem wasn't. I've told Mr. Meredith many a time that he should have spoken seriously to Jem about it before he went away."

"Pore, pore Walter," sighed Mrs. Reese.

"Do not you come here calling him poor Walter," said Susan indignantly, appearing in the kitchen door, much to the relief of Rilla, who felt that she could endure no more just then. "He was not poor. He was richer than any of you. It is you who stay at home and will not let your sons go who are poor—poor and naked and mean and small—pisen poor, and so are your sons, with all their prosperous farms and fat cattle and their souls no bigger than a flea's—if as big."

"I came here to comfort the afflicted and not to be insulted," said Mrs. Reese, taking her departure, unregretted by anyone. Then the fire went out of Susan and she retreated to her kitchen, laid her faithful old head on the table and wept bitterly for a time. Then she went to work and ironed Jims's little rompers. Rilla scolded her gently for it when she herself came in to do it.

"I am not going to have you kill yourself working for any war-baby," Susan said obstinately.

"Oh, I wish I could just keep on working all the time, Susan," cried poor Rilla. "And I wish I didn't have to go to sleep. It is hideous to go to sleep and forget it for a little while, and wake up and have it all rush over me anew the next morning. Do people ever get used to things like this, Susan? And oh, Susan, I can't get away from what Mrs. Reese said. Did Walter suffer much—he was always so sensitive to pain. Oh, Susan, if I knew that he didn't I think I could gather up a little courage and strength."

This merciful knowledge was given to Rilla. A letter came from Walter's commanding officer, telling them that he had been killed instantly by a bullet during a charge at Courcelette. The same day there was a letter for Rilla from Walter himself.

Rilla carried it unopened to Rainbow Valley and read it there, in the spot where she had had her last talk with him. It is a strange thing to read a letter after the writer is dead—a bitter-sweet thing, in which pain and comfort are strangely mingled. For the first time since the blow had fallen Rilla felt—a different thing from tremulous hope and faith—that Walter, of the glorious gift and the splendid ideals, still lived, with just the same gift and just the same ideals. That could not be destroyed—these could suffer no eclipse. The personality that had expressed itself in that last letter, written on the eve of Courcelette, could not be snuffed out by a German bullet. It must carry on, though the earthly link with things of earth were broken.

"We're going over the top tomorrow, Rilla-my-Rilla," wrote Walter. "I wrote mother and Di yesterday, but somehow I feel as if I must write you tonight. I hadn't intended to do any writing tonight—but I've got to. Do you remember old Mrs. Tom Crawford over-harbour, who was always saying that it was 'laid on her' to do such and such a thing? Well, that is just how I feel. It's 'laid on me' to write you tonight—you, sister and chum of mine. There are some things I want to say before—well, before tomorrow.

"You and Ingleside seem strangely near me tonight. It's the first time I've felt this since I came. Always home has seemed so far away—so hopelessly far away from this hideous welter of filth and blood. But tonight it is quite close to me—it seems to me I can almost see you—hear you speak. And I can see the moonlight shining white and still on the old hills of home. It has seemed to me ever since I came here that it was impossible that there could be calm gentle nights and unshattered moonlight anywhere in the world. But tonight somehow, all the beautiful things I have always loved seem to have become possible again—and this is good, and makes me feel a deep, certain, exquisite happiness. It must be autumn at home now—the harbour is a-dream and the old Glen hills blue with haze, and Rainbow Valley a haunt of delight with wild asters blowing all over it—our old "farewell-summers." I always liked that name better than 'aster'—it was a poem in itself.

"Rilla, you know I've always had premonitions. You remember the Pied Piper—but no, of course you wouldn't—you were too young. One evening long ago when Nan and Di and Jem and the Merediths and I were together in Rainbow Valley I had a queer vision or presentiment—whatever you like to call it. Rilla, I saw the Piper coming down the Valley with a shadowy host behind him. The others thought I was only pretending—but I saw him for just one moment. And Rilla, last night I saw him again. I was doing sentry-go and I saw him marching across No-man's-land from our trenches to the German trenches—the same tall shadowy form, piping weirdly—and behind him followed boys in khaki. Rilla, I tell you I saw him—it was no fancy—no illusion. I heard his music, and then—he was gone. But I had seen him—and I knew what it meant—I knew that I was among those who followed him.

"Rilla, the Piper will pipe me 'west' tomorrow. I feel sure of this. And Rilla, I'm not afraid. When you hear the news, remember that. I've won my own freedom here—freedom from all fear. I shall never be afraid of anything again—not of death—nor of life, if after all, I am to go on living. And life, I think, would be the harder of the two to face—for it could never be beautiful for me again. There would always be such horrible things to remember—things that would make life ugly and painful always for me. I could never forget them. But whether it's life or death, I'm not afraid, Rilla-my-Rilla, and I am not sorry that I came. I'm satisfied. I'll never write the poems I once dreamed of writing—but I've helped to make Canada safe for the poets of the future—for the workers of the future—ay, and the dreamers, too—for if no man dreams, there will be nothing for the workers to fulfil—the future, not of Canada only but of the world—when the 'red rain' of Langemarck and Verdun shall have brought forth a golden harvest—not in a year or two, as some foolishly think, but a generation later, when the seed sown now shall have had time to germinate and grow. Yes, I'm glad I came, Rilla. It isn't only the fate of the little sea-born island I love that is in the balance—nor of Canada nor of England. It's the fate of mankind. That is what we're fighting for. And we shall win—never for a moment doubt that, Rilla. For it isn't only the living who are fighting—the dead are fighting too. Such an army cannot be defeated.

"Is there laughter in your face yet, Rilla? I hope so. The world will need laughter and courage more than ever in the years that will come next. I don't want to preach—this isn't any time for it. But I just want to say something that may help you over the worst when you hear that I've gone 'west.' I've a premonition about you, Rilla, as well as about myself. I think Ken will go back to you—and that there are long years of happiness for you by-and-by. And you will tell your children of the Idea we fought and died for—teach them it must be lived for as well as died for, else the price paid for it will have been given for nought. This will be part of your work, Rilla. And if you—all you girls back in the homeland—do it, then we who don't come back will know that you have not 'broken faith' with us.

"I meant to write to Una tonight, too, but I won't have time now. Read this letter to her and tell her it's really meant for you both—you two dear, fine loyal girls. Tomorrow, when we go over the top—I'll think of you both—of your laughter, Rilla-my-Rilla, and the steadfastness in Una's blue eyes—somehow I see those eyes very plainly tonight, too. Yes, you'll both keep faith—I'm sure of that—you and Una. And so—goodnight. We go over the top at dawn."

Rilla read her letter over many times. There was a new light on her pale young face when she finally stood up, amid the asters Walter had loved, with the sunshine of autumn around her. For the moment at least, she was lifted above pain and loneliness.

"I will keep faith, Walter," she said steadily. "I will work—and teach—and learn—and laugh, yes, I will even laugh—through all my years, because of you and because of what you gave when you followed the call."

Rilla meant to keep Walter's letter as a sacred treasure. But, seeing the look on Una Meredith's face when Una had read it and held it back to her, she thought of something. Could she do it? Oh, no, she could not give up Walter's letter—his last letter. Surely it was not selfishness to keep it. A copy would be such a soulless thing. But Una—Una had so little—and her eyes were the eyes of a woman stricken to the heart, who yet must not cry out or ask for sympathy.

"Una, would you like to have this letter—to keep?" she asked slowly.

"Yes—if you can give it to me," Una said dully.

"Then—you may have it," said Rilla hurriedly.

"Thank you," said Una. It was all she said, but there was something in her voice which repaid Rilla for her bit of sacrifice.

Una took the letter and when Rilla had gone she pressed it against her lonely lips. Una knew that love would never come into her life now—it was buried for ever under the blood-stained soil "Somewhere in France." No one but herself—and perhaps Rilla—knew it—would ever know it. She had no right in the eyes of her world to grieve. She must hide and bear her long pain as best she could—alone. But she, too, would keep faith.

CHAPTER XXIV - MARY IS JUST IN TIME

The autumn of 1916 was a bitter season for Ingleside. Mrs. Blythe's return to health was slow, and sorrow and loneliness were in all hearts. Every one tried to hide it from the others and "carry on" cheerfully. Rilla laughed a good deal. Nobody at Ingleside was deceived by her laughter; it came from her lips only, never from her heart. But outsiders said some people got over trouble very easily, and Irene Howard remarked that she was surprised to find how shallow Rilla Blythe really was. "Why, after all her pose of being so devoted to Walter, she doesn't seem to mind his death at all. Nobody has ever seen her shed a tear or heard her mention his name. She has evidently quite forgotten him. Poor fellow—you'd really think his family would feel it more. I spoke of him to Rilla at the last Junior Red meeting—of how fine and brave and splendid he was—and I said life could never be just the same to me again, now that Walter had gone—we were such friends, you know—why I was the very first person he told about having enlisted—and Rilla answered, as coolly and indifferently as if she were speaking of an entire stranger, 'He was just one of many fine and splendid boys who have given everything for their country.' Well, I wish I could take things as calmly—but I'm not made like that. I'm so sensitive—things hurt me terribly—I really never get over them. I asked Rilla right out why she didn't put on mourning for Walter. She said her mother didn't wish it. But every one is talking about it."

"Rilla doesn't wear colours—nothing but white," protested Betty Mead.

"White becomes her better than anything else," said Irene significantly. "And we all know black doesn't suit her complexion at all. But of course I'm not saying that is the reason she doesn't wear it. Only, it's funny. If my brother had died I'd have gone into deep mourning. I wouldn't have had the heart for anything else. I confess I'm disappointed in Rilla Blythe."

"I am not, then," cried Betty Meade, loyally, "I think Rilla is just a wonderful girl. A few years ago I admit I did think she was rather too vain and gigglesome; but now she is nothing of the sort. I don't think there is a girl in the Glen who is so unselfish and plucky as Rilla, or who has done her bit as thoroughly and patiently. Our Junior Red Cross would have gone on the rocks a dozen times if it hadn't been for her tact and perseverance and enthusiasm—you know that perfectly well, Irene."

"Why, I am not running Rilla down," said Irene, opening her eyes widely. "It was only her lack of feeling I was criticizing. I suppose she can't help it. Of course, she's a born manager—everyone knows that. She's very fond of managing, too—and people like that are very necessary I admit. So don't look at me as if I'd said something perfectly dreadful, Betty, please. I'm quite willing to agree that Rilla Blythe is the embodiment of all the virtues, if that will please you. And no doubt it is a virtue to be quite unmoved by things that would crush most people."

Some of Irene's remarks were reported to Rilla; but they did not hurt her as they would once have done. They didn't matter, that was all. Life was too big to leave room for pettiness. She had a pact to keep and a work to do; and through the long hard days and weeks of that disastrous autumn she was faithful to her task. The war news was consistently bad, for Germany marched from victory to victory over poor Rumania. "Foreigners—foreigners," Susan muttered dubiously. "Russians or Rumanians or whatever they may be, they are foreigners and you cannot tie to them. But after Verdun I shall not give up hope. And can you tell me, Mrs. Dr. dear, if the Dobruja is a river or a mountain range, or a condition of the atmosphere?"

The Presidential election in the United States came off in November, and Susan was red-hot over that—and quite apologetic for her excitement.

"I never thought I would live to see the day when I would be interested in a Yankee election, Mrs. Dr. dear. It only goes to show we can never know what we will come to in this world, and therefore we should not be proud."

Susan stayed up late on the evening of the eleventh, ostensibly to finish a pair of socks. But she 'phoned down to Carter Flagg's store at intervals, and when the first report came through that Hughes had been elected she stalked solemnly upstairs to Mrs. Blythe's room and announced it in a thrilling whisper from the foot of the bed.

"I thought if you were not asleep you would be interested in knowing it. I believe it is for the best. Perhaps he will just fall to writing notes, too, Mrs. Dr. dear, but I hope for better things. I never was very partial to whiskers, but one cannot have everything."

When news came in the morning that after all Wilson was re-elected, Susan tacked to catch another breeze of optimism.

"Well, better a fool you know than a fool you do not know, as the old proverb has it," she remarked cheerfully. "Not that I hold Woodrow to be a fool by any means, though by times you would not think he has the sense he was born with. But he is a good letter writer at least, and we do not know if the Hughes man is even that. All things being considered I commend the Yankees. They have shown good sense and I do not mind admitting it. Cousin Sophia wanted them to elect Roosevelt, and is much disgruntled because they would not give him a chance. I had a hankering for him myself, but we must believe that Providence over-rules these matters and be satisfied—though what the Almighty means in this affair of Rumania I cannot fathom—saying it with all reverence."

Susan fathomed it—or thought she did—when the Asquith ministry went down and Lloyd George became Premier.

"Mrs. Dr. dear, Lloyd George is at the helm at last. I have been praying for this for many a day. Now we shall soon see a blessed change. It took the Rumanian disaster to bring it about, no less, and that is the meaning of it, though I could not see it before. There will be no more shilly-shallying. I consider that the war is as good as won, and that I shall tie to, whether Bucharest falls or not."

Bucharest did fall—and Germany proposed peace negotiations. Whereat Susan scornfully turned a deaf ear and absolutely refused to listen to such proposals. When President Wilson sent his famous December peace note Susan waxed violently sarcastic.

"Woodrow Wilson is going to make peace, I understand. First Henry Ford had a try at it and now comes Wilson. But peace is not made with ink, Woodrow, and that you may tie to," said Susan, apostrophizing the unlucky President out of the kitchen window nearest the United States. "Lloyd George's speech will tell the Kaiser what is what, and you may keep your peace screeds at home and save postage."

"What a pity President Wilson can't hear you, Susan," said Rilla slyly.

"Indeed, Rilla dear, it is a pity that he has no one near him to give him good advice, as it is clear he has not, in all those Democrats and Republicans," retorted Susan. "I do not know the difference between them, for the politics of the Yankees is a puzzle I cannot solve, study it as I may. But as far as seeing through a grindstone goes, I am afraid—" Susan shook her head dubiously, "that they are all tarred with the same brush."

"I am thankful Christmas is over," Rilla wrote in her diary during the last week of a stormy December. "We had dreaded it so—the first Christmas since Courcelette. But we had all the Merediths down for dinner and nobody tried to be gay or cheerful. We were all just quiet and friendly, and that helped. Then, too, I was so thankful that Jims had got better—so thankful that I almost felt glad—almost but not quite. I wonder if I shall ever feel really glad over anything again. It seems as if gladness were killed in me—shot down by the same bullet that pierced Walter's heart. Perhaps some day a new kind of gladness will be born in my soul—but the old kind will never live again.

"Winter set in awfully early this year. Ten days before Christmas we had a big snowstorm—at least we thought it big at the time. As it happened, it was only a prelude to the real performance. It was fine the next day, and Ingleside and Rainbow Valley were wonderful, with the trees all covered with snow, and big drifts everywhere, carved into the most fantastic shapes by the chisel of the northeast wind. Father and mother went up to Avonlea. Father thought the change would do mother good, and they wanted to see poor Aunt Diana, whose son Jock had been seriously wounded a short time before. They left Susan and me to keep house, and father expected to be back the next day. But he never got back for a week. That night it began to storm again, and it stormed unbrokenly for four days. It was the worst and longest storm that Prince Edward Island has known for years. Everything was disorganized—the roads were completely choked up, the trains block-aded, and the telephone wires put entirely out of commission.

"And then Jims took ill.

"He had a little cold when father and mother went away, and he kept getting worse for a couple of days, but it didn't occur to me that there was danger of any-thing serious. I never even took his temperature, and I can't forgive myself, because it was sheer carelessness. The truth is I had slumped just then. Mother was away, so I let myself go. All at once I was tired of keeping up and pretending to be brave and cheerful, and I just gave up for a few days and spent most of the time lying on my face on my bed, crying. I neglected Jims—that is the hateful truth—I was cowardly and false to what I promised Walter—and if Jims had died I could never have forgiven myself.

"Then, the third night after father and mother went away, Jims suddenly got worse—oh, so much worse—all at once. Susan and I were all alone. Gertrude had been at Lowbridge when the storm began and had never got back. At first we were not much alarmed. Jims has had several bouts of croup and Susan and Mor-gan and I have always brought him through without much trouble. But it wasn't very long before we were dreadfully alarmed.

"'I never saw croup like this before,' said Susan.

"As for me, I knew, when it was too late, what kind of croup it was. I knew it was not the ordinary croup—'false croup' as doctors call it—but the 'true croup'—and I knew that it was a deadly and dangerous thing. And father was away and there was no doctor nearer than Lowbridge—and we could not 'phone and neither horse nor man could get through the drifts that night.

"Gallant little Jims put up a good fight for his life,—Susan and I tried every remedy we could think of or find in father's books, but he continued to grow worse. It was heart-rending to see and hear him. He gasped so horribly for breath—the poor little soul—and his face turned a dreadful bluish colour and had such an agonized expression, and he kept struggling with his little hands, as if he were appealing to us to help him somehow. I found myself thinking that the boys who had been gassed at the front must have looked like that, and the thought haunted me amid all my dread and misery over Jims. And all the time the fatal membrane in his wee throat grew and thickened and he couldn't get it up.

"Oh, I was just wild! I never realized how dear Jims was to me until that mo-ment. And I felt so utterly helpless."

"And then Susan gave up. 'We cannot save him! Oh, if your father was here—look at him, the poor little fellow! I know not what to do.'

"I looked at Jims and I thought he was dying. Susan was holding him up in his crib to give him a better chance for breath, but it didn't seem as if he could breathe at all. My little war-baby, with his dear ways and sweet roguish face, was choking to death before my very eyes, and I couldn't help him. I threw down the hot poul-tice I had ready in despair. Of what use was it? Jims was dying, and it was my fault—I hadn't been careful enough!

"Just then—at eleven o'clock at night—the door bell rang. Such a ring—it pealed all over the house above the roar of the storm. Susan couldn't go—she dared not lay Jims down—so I rushed downstairs. In the hall I paused just a minute—I was suddenly overcome by an absurd dread. I thought of a weird story Gertrude had told me once. An aunt of hers was alone in a house one night with her sick husband. She heard a knock at the door. And when she went and opened it there was nothing there—nothing that could be seen, at least. But when she opened the door a deadly cold wind blew in and seemed to sweep past her right up the stairs, although it was a calm, warm summer night outside. Immediately she heard a cry. She ran upstairs—and her husband was dead. And she always believed, so Gertrude said, that when she opened that door she let Death in.

"It was so ridiculous of me to feel so frightened. But I was distracted and worn out, and I simply felt for a moment that I dared not open the door—that death was waiting outside. Then I remembered that I had no time to waste—must not be so foolish—I sprang forward and opened the door.

"Certainly a cold wind did blow in and filled the hall with a whirl of snow. But there on the threshold stood a form of flesh and blood—Mary Vance, coated from head to foot with snow—and she brought Life, not Death, with her, though I didn't know that then. I just stared at her.

"'I haven't been turned out,' grinned Mary, as she stepped in and shut the door. 'I came up to Carter Flagg's two days ago and I've been stormed-stayed there ever since. But old Abbie Flagg got on my nerves at last, and tonight I just made up my mind to come up here. I thought I could wade this far, but I can tell you it was as much as a bargain. Once I thought I was stuck for keeps. Ain't it an awful night?'

"I came to myself and knew I must hurry upstairs. I explained as quickly as I could to Mary, and left her trying to brush the snow off. Upstairs I found that Jims was over that paroxysm, but almost as soon as I got back to the room he was in the grip of another. I couldn't do anything but moan and cry—oh, how ashamed I am when I think of it; and yet what could I do—we had tried everything we knew—and then all at once I heard Mary Vance saying loudly behind me, 'Why, that child is dying!'

"I whirled around. Didn't I know he was dying—my little Jims! I could have thrown Mary Vance out of the door or the window—anywhere—at that moment. There she stood, cool and composed, looking down at my baby, with those, weird white eyes of hers, as she might look at a choking kitten. I had always disliked Mary Vance—and just then I hated her.

"'We have tried everything,' said poor Susan dully. 'It is not ordinary croup.'

"'No, it's the dipthery croup,' said Mary briskly, snatching up an apron. 'And there's mighty little time to lose—but I know what to do. When I lived over-harbour with Mrs. Wiley, years ago, Will Crawford's kid died of dipthery croup, in spite of two doctors. And when old Aunt Christina MacAllister heard of it—she was the one brought me round when I nearly died of pneumonia you know—she was a wonder—no doctor was a patch on her—they don't hatch her breed of cats nowadays, let me tell you—she said she could have saved him with her grandmother's remedy if she'd been there. She told Mrs. Wiley what it was and I've never forgot it. I've the greatest memory ever—a thing just lies in the back of my head till the time comes to use it. Got any sulphur in the house, Susan?'

"Yes, we had sulphur. Susan went down with Mary to get it, and I held Jims. I hadn't any hope—not the least. Mary Vance might brag as she liked—she was always bragging—but I didn't believe any grandmother's remedy could save Jims now. Presently Mary came back. She had tied a piece of thick flannel over her mouth and nose, and she carried Susan's old tin chip pan, half full of burning coals.

"'You watch me,' she said boastfully. 'I've never done this, but it's kill or cure that child is dying anyway.'

"She sprinkled a spoonful of sulphur over the coals; and then she picked up Jims, turned him over, and held him face downward, right over those choking, blinding fumes. I don't know why I didn't spring forward and snatch him away. Susan says it was because it was fore-ordained that I shouldn't, and I think she is right, because it did really seem that I was powerless to move. Susan herself seemed transfixed, watching Mary from the doorway. Jims writhed in those big, firm, capable hands of Mary—oh yes, she is capable all right—and choked and wheezed—and choked and wheezed—and I felt that he was being tortured to death—and then all at once, after what seemed to me an hour, though it really wasn't long, he coughed up the membrane that was killing him. Mary turned him over and laid him back on his bed. He was white as marble and the tears were pouring out of his brown eyes—but that awful livid look was gone from his face and he could breathe quite easily.

"'Wasn't that some trick?' said Mary gaily. 'I hadn't any idea how it would work, but I just took a chance. I'll smoke his throat out again once or twice before morning, just to kill all the germs, but you'll see he'll be all right now.'

"Jims went right to sleep—real sleep, not coma, as I feared at first. Mary 'smoked him,' as she called it, twice through the night, and at daylight his throat was perfectly clear and his temperature was almost normal. When I made sure of that I turned and looked at Mary Vance. She was sitting on the lounge laying down the law to Susan on some subject about which Susan must have known forty times as much as she did. But I didn't mind how much law she laid down or how much she bragged. She had a right to brag—she had dared to do what I would never have dared, and had saved Jims from a horrible death. It didn't matter any more that she had once chased me through the Glen with a codfish; it didn't matter that she had smeared goose-grease all over my dream of romance the night of the lighthouse dance; it didn't matter that she thought she knew more than anybody else and always rubbed it in—I would never dislike Mary Vance again. I went over to her and kissed her.

"'What's up now?' she said.

"'Nothing—only I'm so grateful to you, Mary.'

"'Well, I think you ought to be, that's a fact. You two would have let that baby die on your hands if I hadn't happened along,' said Mary, just beaming with complacency. She got Susan and me a tip-top breakfast and made us eat it, and 'bossed the life out of us,' as Susan says, for two days, until the roads were opened so that she could get home. Jims was almost well by that time, and father turned up. He heard our tale without saying much. Father is rather scornful generally about what he calls 'old wives' remedies.' He laughed a little and said, 'After this, Mary Vance will expect me to call her in for consultation in all my serious cases.'

"So Christmas was not so hard as I expected it to be; and now the New Year is coming—and we are still hoping for the 'Big Push' that will end the war—and Little Dog Monday is getting stiff and rheumatic from his cold vigils, but still he 'carries on,' and Shirley continues to read the exploits of the aces. Oh, nineteen-seventeen, what will you bring?"

CHAPTER XXV - SHIRLEY GOES

"No, Woodrow, there will be no peace without victory," said Susan, sticking her knitting needle viciously through President Wilson's name in the newspaper column. "We Canadians mean to have peace and victory, too. You, if it pleases you, Woodrow, can have the peace without the victory"—and Susan stalked off to bed with the comfortable consciousness of having got the better of the argument with the President. But a few days later she rushed to Mrs. Blythe in red-hot excitement.

"Mrs. Dr. dear, what do you think? A 'phone message has just come through from Charlottetown that Woodrow Wilson has sent that German ambassador man to the right about at last. They tell me that means war. So I begin to think that Woodrow's heart is in the right place after all, wherever his head may be, and I am going to commandeer a little sugar and celebrate the occasion with some fudge, despite the howls of the Food Board. I thought that submarine business would bring things to a crisis. I told Cousin Sophia so when she said it was the beginning of the end for the Allies."

"Don't let the doctor hear of the fudge, Susan," said Anne, with a smile. "You know he has laid down very strict rules for us along the lines of economy the government has asked for."

"Yes, Mrs. Dr. dear, and a man should be master in his own household, and his women folk should bow to his decrees. I flatter myself that I am becoming quite efficient in economizing"—Susan had taken to using certain German terms with killing effect—"but one can exercise a little gumption on the quiet now and then. Shirley was wishing for some of my fudge the other day—the Susan brand, as he called it—and I said 'The first victory there is to celebrate I shall make you some.' I consider this news quite equal to a victory, and what the doctor does not know will never grieve him. I take the whole responsibility, Mrs. Dr. dear, so do not you vex your conscience."

Susan spoiled Shirley shamelessly that winter. He came home from Queen's every week-end, and Susan had all his favourite dishes for him, in so far as she could evade or wheedle the doctor, and waited on him hand and foot. Though she talked war constantly to everyone else she never mentioned it to him or before him, but she watched him like a cat watching a mouse; and when the German retreat from the Bapaume salient began and continued, Susan's exultation was linked up with something deeper than anything she expressed. Surely the end was in sight—would come now before—anyone else—could go.

"Things are coming our way at last. We have got the Germans on the run," she boasted. "The United States has declared war at last, as I always believed they would, in spite of Woodrow's gift for letter writing, and you will see they will go into it with a vim since I understand that is their habit, when they do start. And we have got the Germans on the run, too."

"The States mean well," moaned Cousin Sophia, "but all the vim in the world cannot put them on the fighting line this spring, and the Allies will be finished before that. The Germans are just luring them on. That man Simonds says their retreat has put the Allies in a hole."

"That man Simonds has said more than he will ever live to make good," retorted Susan. "I do not worry myself about his opinion as long as Lloyd George is Premier of England. He will not be bamboozled and that you may tie to. Things look good to me. The U. S. is in the war, and we have got Kut and Bagdad back— and I would not be surprised to see the Allies in Berlin by June—and the Russians, too, since they have got rid of the Czar. That, in my opinion was a good piece of work."

"Time will show if it is," said Cousin Sophia, who would have been very indignant if anyone had told her that she would rather see Susan put to shame as a seer, than a successful overthrow of tyranny, or even the march of the Allies down Unter den Linden. But then the woes of the Russian people were quite unknown to Cousin Sophia, while this aggravating, optimistic Susan was an ever-present thorn in her side.

Just at that moment Shirley was sitting on the edge of the table in the living-room, swinging his legs—a brown, ruddy, wholesome lad, from top to toe, every inch of him—and saying coolly, "Mother and dad, I was eighteen last Monday. Don't you think it's about time I joined up?"

The pale mother looked at him.

"Two of my sons have gone and one will never return. Must I give you too, Shirley?"

The age-old cry—"Joseph is not and Simeon is not; and ye will take Benjamin away." How the mothers of the Great War echoed the old Patriarch's moan of so many centuries agone!

"You wouldn't have me a slacker, mother? I can get into the flying-corps. What say, dad?"

The doctor's hands were not quite steady as he folded up the powders he was concocting for Abbie Flagg's rheumatism. He had known this moment was coming, yet he was not altogether prepared for it. He answered slowly, "I won't try to hold you back from what you believe to be your duty. But you must not go unless your mother says you may."

Shirley said nothing more. He was not a lad of many words. Anne did not say anything more just then, either. She was thinking of little Joyce's grave in the old burying-ground over-harbour—little Joyce who would have been a woman now, had she lived—of the white cross in France and the splendid grey eyes of the little boy who had been taught his first lessons of duty and loyalty at her knee—of Jem in the terrible trenches—of Nan and Di and Rilla, waiting—waiting—waiting, while the golden years of youth passed by—and she wondered if she could bear any more. She thought not; surely she had given enough.

Yet that night she told Shirley that he might go.

They did not tell Susan right away. She did not know it until, a few days later, Shirley presented himself in her kitchen in his aviation uniform. Susan didn't make half the fuss she had made when Jem and Walter had gone. She said stonily, "So they're going to take you, too."

"Take me? No. I'm going, Susan—got to."

Susan sat down by the table, folded her knotted old hands, that had grown warped and twisted working for the Ingleside children to still their shaking, and said:

"Yes, you must go. I did not see once why such things must be, but I can see now."

"You're a brick, Susan," said Shirley. He was relieved that she took it so cooly—he had been a little afraid, with a boy's horror of "a scene." He went out whistling gaily; but half an hour later, when pale Anne Blythe came in, Susan was still sitting there.

"Mrs. Dr. dear," said Susan, making an admission she would once have died rather than make, "I feel very old. Jem and Walter were yours but Shirley is mine. And I cannot bear to think of him flying—his machine crashing down—the life crushed out of his body—the dear little body I nursed and cuddled when he was a wee baby."

"Susan—don't," cried Anne.

"Oh, Mrs. Dr. dear, I beg your pardon. I ought not to have said anything like that out loud. I sometimes forget that I resolved to be a heroine. This—this has shaken me a little. But I will not forget myself again. Only if things do not go as smoothly in the kitchen for a few days I hope you will make due allowance for me. At least," said poor Susan, forcing a grim smile in a desperate effort to recover lost standing, "at least flying is a clean job. He will not get so dirty and messed up as he would in the trenches, and that is well, for he has always been a tidy child."

So Shirley went—not radiantly, as to a high adventure, like Jem, not in a white flame of sacrifice, like Walter, but in a cool, business-like mood, as of one doing something, rather dirty and disagreeable, that had just got to be done. He kissed Susan for the first time since he was five years old, and said, "Good-bye, Susan— mother Susan."

"My little brown boy—my little brown boy," said Susan. "I wonder," she thought bitterly, as she looked at the doctor's sorrowful face, "if you remember how you spanked him once when he was a baby. I am thankful I have nothing like that on my conscience now."

The doctor did not remember the old discipline. But before he put on his hat to go out on his round of calls he stood for a moment in the great silent living-room that had once been full of children's laughter.

"Our last son—our last son," he said aloud. "A good, sturdy, sensible lad, too. Always reminded me of my father. I suppose I ought to be proud that he wanted to go—I was proud when Jem went—even when Walter went—but 'our house is left us desolate.'"

"I have been thinking, doctor," old Sandy of the Upper Glen said to him that afternoon, "that your house will be seeming very big the day."

Highland Sandy's quaint phrase struck the doctor as perfectly expressive. Ingleside did seem very big and empty that night. Yet Shirley had been away all winter except for week-ends, and had always been a quiet fellow even when home. Was it because he had been the only one left that his going seemed to leave such a huge blank—that every room seemed vacant and deserted—that the very trees on the lawn seemed to be trying to comfort each other with caresses of freshly-budding boughs for the loss of the last of the little lads who had romped under them in childhood?

Susan worked very hard all day and late into the night. When she had wound the kitchen clock and put Dr. Jekyll out, none too gently, she stood for a little while on the doorstep, looking down the Glen, which lay tranced in faint, silvery light from a sinking young moon. But Susan did not see the familiar hills and harbour. She was looking at the aviation camp in Kingsport where Shirley was that night.

"He called me 'Mother Susan,'" she was thinking. "Well, all our men folk have gone now—Jem and Walter and Shirley and Jerry and Carl. And none of them had to be driven to it. So we have a right to be proud. But pride—" Susan sighed bitterly—"pride is cold company and that there is no gainsaying."

The moon sank lower into a black cloud in the west, the Glen went out in an eclipse of sudden shadow—and thousands of miles away the Canadian boys in khaki—the living and the dead—were in possession of Vimy Ridge.

Vimy Ridge is a name written in crimson and gold on the Canadian annals of the Great War. "The British couldn't take it and the French couldn't take it," said a German prisoner to his captors, "but you Canadians are such fools that you don't know when a place can't be taken!"

So the "fools" took it—and paid the price.

Jerry Meredith was seriously wounded at Vimy Ridge—shot in the back, the telegram said.

"Poor Nan," said Mrs. Blythe, when the news came. She thought of her own happy girlhood at old Green Gables. There had been no tragedy like this in it. How the girls of to-day had to suffer! When Nan came home from Redmond two weeks later her face showed what those weeks had meant to her. John Meredith, too, seemed to have grown old suddenly in them. Faith did not come home; she was on her way across the Atlantic as a V.A.D. Di had tried to wring from her father consent to her going also, but had been told that for her mother's sake it could not be given. So Di, after a flying visit home, went back to her Red Cross work in Kingsport.

The mayflowers bloomed in the secret nooks of Rainbow Valley. Rilla was watching for them. Jem had once taken his mother the earliest mayflowers; Walter brought them to her when Jem was gone; last spring Shirley had sought them out for her; now, Rilla thought she must take the boys' place in this. But before she had discovered any, Bruce Meredith came to Ingleside one twilight with his hands full of delicate pink sprays. He stalked up the steps of the veranda and laid them on Mrs. Blythe's lap.

"Because Shirley isn't here to bring them," he said in his funny, shy, blunt way.

"And you thought of this, you darling," said Anne, her lips quivering, as she looked at the stocky, black-browed little chap, standing before her, with his hands thrust into his pockets.

"I wrote Jem to-day and told him not to worry 'bout you not getting your mayflowers," said Bruce seriously, "'cause I'd see to that. And I told him I would be ten pretty soon now, so it won't be very long before I'll be eighteen, and then I'll go to help him fight, and maybe let him come home for a rest while I took his place. I wrote Jerry, too. Jerry's getting better, you know."

"Is he? Have you had any good news about him?"

"Yes. Mother had a letter to-day, and it said he was out of danger."

"Oh, thank God," murmured Mrs. Blythe, in a half-whisper.

Bruce looked at her curiously.

"That is what father said when mother told him. But when I said it the other day when I found out Mr. Mead's dog hadn't hurt my kitten—I thought he had shooken it to death, you know—father looked awful solemn and said I must never say that again about a kitten. But I couldn't understand why, Mrs. Blythe. I felt awful thankful, and it must have been God that saved Stripey, because that Mead dog had 'normous jaws, and oh, how it shook poor Stripey. And so why couldn't I thank Him? 'Course," added Bruce reminiscently, "maybe I said it too loud— 'cause I was awful glad and excited when I found Stripey was all right. I 'most shouted it, Mrs. Blythe. Maybe if I'd said it sort of whispery like you and father it would have been all right. Do you know, Mrs. Blythe"—Bruce dropped to a "whispery" tone, edging a little nearer to Anne—"what I would like to do to the Kaiser if I could?"

"What would you like to do, laddie?"

"Norman Reese said in school to-day that he would like to tie the Kaiser to a tree and set cross dogs to worrying him," said Bruce gravely. "And Emily Flagg said she would like to put him in a cage and poke sharp things into him. And they all said things like that. But Mrs. Blythe"—Bruce took a little square paw out of his pocket and put it earnestly on Anne's knee—"I would like to turn the Kaiser into a good man—a very good man—all at once if I could. That is what I would do. Don't you think, Mrs. Blythe, that would be the very worstest punishment of all?"

"Bless the child," said Susan, "how do you make out that would be any kind of a punishment for that wicked fiend?"

"Don't you see," said Bruce, looking levelly at Susan, out of his blackly blue eyes, "if he was turned into a good man he would understand how dreadful the things he has done are, and he would feel so terrible about it that he would be more unhappy and miserable than he could ever be in any other way. He would feel just awful—and he would go on feeling like that forever. Yes"—Bruce clenched his hands and nodded his head emphatically, "yes, I would make the Kaiser a good man—that is what I would do—it would serve him 'zackly right."

CHAPTER XXVI - SUSAN HAS A PROPOSAL OF MARRIAGE

An aeroplane was flying over Glen St. Mary, like a great bird poised against the western sky—a sky so clear and of such a pale, silvery yellow, that it gave an impression of a vast, wind-freshened space of freedom. The little group on the Ingleside lawn looked up at it with fascinated eyes, although it was by no means an unusual thing to see an occasional hovering plane that summer. Susan was always intensely excited. Who knew but that it might be Shirley away up there in the clouds, flying over to the Island from Kingsport? But Shirley had gone overseas now, so Susan was not so keenly interested in this particular aeroplane and its pilot. Nevertheless, she looked at it with awe.

"I wonder, Mrs. Dr. dear," she said solemnly, "what the old folks down there in the graveyard would think if they could rise out of their graves for one moment and behold that sight. I am sure my father would disapprove of it, for he was a man who did not believe in new-fangled ideas of any sort. He always cut his grain with a reaping hook to the day of his death. A mower he would not have. What was good enough for his father was good enough for him, he used to say. I hope it is not unfilial to say that I think he was wrong in that point of view, but I am not sure I go so far as to approve of aeroplanes, though they may be a military necessity. If the Almighty had meant us to fly he would have provided us with wings. Since He did not it is plain He meant us to stick to the solid earth. At any rate, you will never see me, Mrs. Dr. dear, cavorting through the sky in an aeroplane."

"But you won't refuse to cavort a bit in father's new automobile when it comes, will you, Susan?" teased Rilla.

"I do not expect to trust my old bones in automobiles, either," retorted Susan. "But I do not look upon them as some narrow-minded people do. Whiskers-on-the-moon says the Government should be turned out of office for permitting them to run on the Island at all. He foams at the mouth, they tell me, when he sees one. The other day he saw one coming along that narrow side-road by his wheatfield, and Whiskers bounded over the fence and stood right in the middle of the road, with his pitchfork. The man in the machine was an agent of some kind, and Whiskers hates agents as much as he hates automobiles. He made the car come to a halt, because there was not room to pass him on either side, and the agent could not actually run over him. Then he raised his pitchfork and shouted, 'Get out of this with your devil-machine or I will run this pitchfork clean through you.' And Mrs. Dr. dear, if you will believe me, that poor agent had to back his car clean out to the Lowbridge road, nearly a mile, Whiskers following him every step, shaking his pitchfork and bellowing insults. Now, Mrs. Dr. dear, I call such conduct unreasonable; but all the same," added Susan, with a sigh, "what with aeroplanes and automobiles and all the rest of it, this Island is not what it used to be."

The aeroplane soared and dipped and circled, and soared again, until it became a mere speck far over the sunset hills.

"'With the majesty of pinion Which the Theban eagles bear Sailing with supreme dominion Through the azure fields of air.'"

quoted Anne Blythe dreamily.

"I wonder," said Miss Oliver, "if humanity will be any happier because of aeroplanes. It seems to me that the sum of human happiness remains much the same from age to age, no matter how it may vary in distribution, and that all the 'many inventions' neither lessen nor increase it."

"After all, the 'kingdom of heaven is within you,'" said Mr. Meredith, gazing after the vanishing speck which symbolized man's latest victory in a world-old struggle. "It does not depend on material achievements and triumphs."

"Nevertheless, an aeroplane is a fascinating thing," said the doctor. "It has always been one of humanity's favourite dreams—the dream of flying. Dream after dream comes true—or rather is made true by persevering effort. I should like to have a flight in an aeroplane myself."

"Shirley wrote me that he was dreadfully disappointed in his first flight," said Rilla. "He had expected to experience the sensation of soaring up from the earth like a bird—and instead he just had the feeling that he wasn't moving at all, but that the earth was dropping away under him. And the first time he went up alone he suddenly felt terribly homesick. He had never felt like that before; but all at once, he said, he felt as if he were adrift in space—and he had a wild desire to get back home to the old planet and the companionship of fellow creatures. He soon got over that feeling, but he says his first flight alone was a nightmare to him because of that dreadful sensation of ghastly loneliness."

The aeroplane disappeared. The doctor threw back his head with a sigh.

"When I have watched one of those bird-men out of sight I come back to earth with an odd feeling of being merely a crawling insect. Anne," he said, turning to his wife, "do you remember the first time I took you for a buggy ride in Avonlea—that night we went to the Carmody concert, the first fall you taught in Avonlea? I had out little black mare with the white star on her forehead, and a shining brand-new buggy—and I was the proudest fellow in the world, barring none. I suppose our grandson will be taking his sweetheart out quite casually for an evening 'fly' in his aeroplane."

"An aeroplane won't be as nice as little Silverspot was," said Anne. "A machine is simply a machine—but Silverspot, why she was a personality, Gilbert. A drive behind her had something in it that not even a flight among sunset clouds could have. No, I don't envy my grandson's sweetheart, after all. Mr. Meredith is right. 'The kingdom of Heaven'—and of love—and of happiness—doesn't depend on externals."

"Besides," said the doctor gravely, "our said grandson will have to give most of his attention to the aeroplane—he won't be able to let the reins lie on its back while he gazes into his lady's eyes. And I have an awful suspicion that you can't run an aeroplane with one arm. No"—the doctor shook his head—"I believe I'd still prefer Silverspot after all."

The Russian line broke again that summer and Susan said bitterly that she had expected it ever since Kerensky had gone and got married.

"Far be it from me to decry the holy state of matrimony, Mrs. Dr. dear, but I felt that when a man was running a revolution he had his hands full and should have postponed marriage until a more fitting season. The Russians are done for this time and there would be no sense in shutting our eyes to the fact. But have you seen Woodrow Wilson's reply to the Pope's peace proposals? It is magnificent. I really could not have expressed the rights of the matter better myself. I feel that I can forgive Wilson everything for it. He knows the meaning of words and that you may tie to. Speaking of meanings, have you heard the latest story about Whiskers-on-the-moon, Mrs. Dr. dear? It seems he was over at the Lowbridge Road school the other day and took a notion to examine the fourth class in spelling. They have the summer term there yet, you know, with the spring and fall vacations, being rather backward people on that road. My niece, Ella Baker, goes to that school and she it was who told me the story. The teacher was not feeling well, having a dreadful headache, and she went out to get a little fresh air while Mr. Pryor was examining the class. The children got along all right with the spelling but when Whiskers began to question them about the meanings of the words they were all at sea, because they had not learned them. Ella and the other big scholars felt terrible over it. They love their teacher so, and it seems Mr. Pryor's brother, Abel Pryor, who is trustee of that school, is against her and has been trying to turn the other trustees over to his way of thinking. And Ella and the rest were afraid that if the fourth class couldn't tell Whiskers the meanings of the words he would think the teacher was no good and tell Abel so, and Abel would have a fine handle. But little Sandy Logan saved the situation. He is a Home boy, but he is as smart as a steel trap, and he sized up Whiskers-on-the-moon right off. 'What does "anatomy" mean?' Whiskers demanded. 'A pain in your stomach,' Sandy replied, quick as a flash and never batting an eyelid. Whiskers-on-the-moon is a very ignorant man, Mrs. Dr. dear; he didn't know the meaning of the words himself, and he said 'Very good—very good.' The class caught right on—at least three or four of the brighter ones did—and they kept up the fun. Jean Blane said that 'acoustic' meant 'a religious squabble,' and Muriel Baker said that an 'agnostic' was 'a man who had indigestion,' and Jim Carter said that 'acerbity' meant that 'you ate nothing but vegetable food,' and so on all down the list. Whiskers swallowed it all, and kept saying 'Very good—very good' until Ella thought that die she would trying to keep a straight face. When the teacher came in, Whiskers complimented her on the splendid understanding the children had of their lesson and said he meant to tell the trustees what a jewel they had. It was 'very unusual,' he said, to find a fourth class who could answer up so prompt when it came to explaining what words meant. He went off beaming. But Ella told me this as a great secret, Mrs. Dr. dear, and we must keep it as such, for the sake of the Low-bridge Road teacher. It would likely be the ruin of her chances of keeping the school if Whiskers should ever find out how he had been bamboozled."

Mary Vance came up to Ingleside that same afternoon to tell them that Miller Douglas, who had been wounded when the Canadians took Hill 70, had had to have his leg amputated. The Ingleside folk sympathized with Mary, whose zeal and patriotism had taken some time to kindle but now burned with a glow as steady and bright as any one's.

"Some folks have been twitting me about having a husband with only one leg. But," said Mary, rising to a lofty height, "I would rather Miller with only one leg than any other man in the world with a dozen—unless," she added as an after-thought, "unless it was Lloyd George. Well, I must be going. I thought you'd be interested in hearing about Miller so I ran up from the store, but I must hustle home for I promised Luke MacAllister I'd help him build his grain stack this evening. It's up to us girls to see that the harvest is got in, since the boys are so scarce. I've got overalls and I can tell you they're real becoming. Mrs. Alec Doug-las says they're indecent and shouldn't be allowed, and even Mrs. Elliott kinder looks askance at them. But bless you, the world moves, and anyhow there's no fun for me like shocking Kitty Alec."

"By the way, father," said Rilla, "I'm going to take Jack Flagg's place in his fa-ther's store for a month. I promised him today that I would, if you didn't object. Then he can help the farmers get the harvest in. I don't think I'd be much use in a harvest myself—though lots of the girls are—but I can set Jack free while I do his work. Jims isn't much bother in the daytime now, and I'll always be home at night."

"Do you think you'll like weighing out sugar and beans, and trafficking in but-ter and eggs?" said the doctor, twinkling.

"Probably not. That isn't the question. It's just one way of doing my bit." So Rilla went behind Mr. Flagg's counter for a month; and Susan went into Albert Crawford's oat-fields.

"I am as good as any of them yet," she said proudly. "Not a man of them can beat me when it comes to building a stack. When I offered to help Albert looked doubtful. 'I am afraid the work will be too hard for you,' he said. 'Try me for a day and see,' said I. 'I will do my darnedest.'"

None of the Ingleside folks spoke for just a moment. Their silence meant that they thought Susan's pluck in "working out" quite wonderful. But Susan mistook their meaning and her sun-burned face grew red.

"This habit of swearing seems to be growing on me, Mrs. Dr. dear," she said apologetically. "To think that I should be acquiring it at my age! It is such a dreadful example to the young girls. I am of the opinion it comes of reading the newspapers so much. They are so full of profanity and they do not spell it with stars either, as used to be done in my young days. This war is demoralizing everybody."

Susan, standing on a load of grain, her grey hair whipping in the breeze and her skirt kilted up to her knees for safety and convenience—no overalls for Susan, if you please—neither a beautiful nor a romantic figure; but the spirit that animated her gaunt arms was the self-same one that captured Vimy Ridge and held the German legions back from Verdun.

It is not the least likely, however, that this consideration was the one which appealed most strongly to Mr. Pryor when he drove past one afternoon and saw Susan pitching sheaves gamely.

"Smart woman that," he reflected. "Worth two of many a younger one yet. I might do worse—I might do worse. If Milgrave comes home alive I'll lose Miranda and hired housekeepers cost more than a wife and are liable to leave a man in the lurch any time. I'll think it over."

A week later Mrs. Blythe, coming up from the village late in the afternoon, paused at the gate of Ingleside in an amazement which temporarily bereft her of the power of motion. An extraordinary sight met her eyes. Round the end of the kitchen burst Mr. Pryor, running as stout, pompous Mr. Pryor had not run in years, with terror imprinted on every lineament—a terror quite justifiable, for behind him, like an avenging fate, came Susan, with a huge, smoking iron pot grasped in her hands, and an expression in her eye that boded ill to the object of her indignation, if she should overtake him. Pursuer and pursued tore across the lawn. Mr. Pryor reached the gate a few feet ahead of Susan, wrenched it open, and fled down the road, without a glance at the transfixed lady of Ingleside.

"Susan," gasped Anne.

Susan halted in her mad career, set down her pot, and shook her fist after Mr. Pryor, who had not ceased to run, evidently believing that Susan was still full cry after him.

"Susan, what does this mean?" demanded Anne, a little severely.

"You may well ask that, Mrs. Dr. dear," Susan replied wrathfully. "I have not been so upset in years. That—that—that pacifist has actually had the audacity to come up here and, in my own kitchen, to ask me to marry him. HIM!"

Anne choked back a laugh.

"But—Susan! Couldn't you have found a—well, a less spectacular method of refusing him? Think what a gossip this would have made if anyone had been going past and had seen such a performance."

"Indeed, Mrs. Dr. dear, you are quite right. I did not think of it because I was quite past thinking rationally. I was just clean mad. Come in the house and I will tell you all about it."

Susan picked up her pot and marched into the kitchen, still trembling with wrathful excitement. She set her pot on the stove with a vicious thud. "Wait a moment until I open all the windows to air this kitchen well, Mrs. Dr. dear. There, that is better. And I must wash my hands, too, because I shook hands with Whiskers-on-the-moon when he came in—not that I wanted to, but when he stuck out his fat, oily hand I did not know just what else to do at the moment. I had just finished my afternoon cleaning and thanks be, everything was shining and spotless; and thought I 'now that dye is boiling and I will get my rug rags and have them nicely out of the way before supper.'

"Just then a shadow fell over the floor and looking up I saw Whiskers-on-the-moon, standing in the doorway, dressed up and looking as if he had just been starched and ironed. I shook hands with him, as aforesaid, Mrs. Dr. dear, and told him you and the doctor were both away. But he said,

"I have come to see you, Miss Baker.'

"I asked him to sit down, for the sake of my own manners, and then I stood there right in the middle of the floor and gazed at him as contemptuously as I could. In spite of his brazen assurance this seemed to rattle him a little; but he began trying to look sentimental at me out of his little piggy eyes, and all at once an awful suspicion flashed into my mind. Something told me, Mrs. Dr. dear, that I was about to receive my first proposal. I have always thought that I would like to have just one offer of marriage to reject, so that I might be able to look other women in the face, but you will not hear me bragging of this. I consider it an insult and if I could have thought of any way of preventing it I would. But just then, Mrs. Dr. dear, you will see I was at a disadvantage, being taken so completely by surprise. Some men, I am told, consider a little preliminary courting the proper thing before a proposal, if only to give fair warning of their intentions; but Whiskers-on-the-moon probably thought it was any port in a storm for me and that I would jump at him. Well, he is undeceived—yes, he is undeceived, Mrs. Dr. dear. I wonder if he has stopped running yet."

"I understand that you don't feel flattered, Susan. But couldn't you have refused him a little more delicately than by chasing him off the premises in such a fashion?"

"Well, maybe I might have, Mrs. Dr. dear, and I intended to, but one remark he made aggravated me beyond my powers of endurance. If it had not been for that I would not have chased him with my dye-pot. I will tell you the whole interview. Whiskers sat down, as I have said, and right beside him on another chair Doc was lying. The animal was pretending to be asleep but I knew very well he was not, for he has been Hyde all day and Hyde never sleeps. By the way, Mrs. Dr. dear, have you noticed that that cat is far oftener Hyde than Jekyll now? The more victories Germany wins the Hyder he becomes. I leave you to draw your own conclusions from that. I suppose Whiskers thought he might curry favour with me by praising the creature, little dreaming what my real sentiments towards it were, so he stuck out his pudgy hand and stroked Mr. Hyde's back. 'What a nice cat,' he said. The nice cat flew at him and bit him. Then it gave a fearful yowl, and bounded out of the door. Whiskers looked after it quite amazed. 'That is a queer kind of a varmint,' he said. I agreed with him on that point, but I was not going to let him see it. Besides, what business had he to call our cat a varmint? 'It may be a varmint or it may not,' I said, 'but it knows the difference between a Canadian and a Hun.' You would have thought, would you not, Mrs. Dr. dear, that a hint like that would have been enough for him! But it went no deeper than his skin. I saw him settling back quite comfortable, as if for a good talk, and thought I, 'If there is anything coming it may as well come soon and be done with, for with all these rags to dye before supper I have no time to waste in flirting,' so I spoke right out. 'If you have anything particular to discuss with me, Mr. Pryor, I would feel obliged if you would mention it without loss of time, because I am very busy this afternoon.' He fairly beamed at me out of that circle of red whisker, and said, 'You are a business-like woman and I agree with you. There is no use in wasting time beating around the bush. I came up here today to ask you to marry me.' So there it was, Mrs. Dr. dear. I had a proposal at last, after waiting sixty-four years for one.

"I just glared at that presumptuous creature and I said, 'I would not marry you if you were the last man on earth, Josiah Pryor. So there you have my answer and you can take it away forthwith.' You never saw a man so taken aback as he was, Mrs. Dr. dear. He was so flabbergasted that he just blurted out the truth. 'Why, I thought you'd be only too glad to get a chance to be married,' he said. That was when I lost my head, Mrs. Dr. dear. Do you think I had a good excuse, when a Hun and a pacifist made such an insulting remark to me? 'Go,' I thundered, and I just caught up that iron pot. I could see that he thought I had suddenly gone insane, and I suppose he considered an iron pot full of boiling dye was a dangerous weapon in the hands of a lunatic. At any rate he went, and stood not upon the order of his going, as you saw for yourself. And I do not think we will see him back here proposing to us again in a hurry. No, I think he has learned that there is at least one single woman in Glen St. Mary who has no hankering to become Mrs. Whiskers-on-the-moon."

CHAPTER XXVII - WAITING

Ingleside,
1st November 1917

"It is November—and the Glen is all grey and brown, except where the Lombardy poplars stand up here and there like great golden torches in the sombre landscape, although every other tree has shed its leaves. It has been very hard to keep our courage alight of late. The Caporetto disaster is a dreadful thing and not even Susan can extract much consolation out of the present state of affairs. The rest of us don't try. Gertrude keeps saying desperately, 'They must not get Venice—they must not get Venice,' as if by saying it often enough she can prevent them. But what is to prevent them from getting Venice I cannot see. Yet, as Susan fails not to point out, there was seemingly nothing to prevent them from getting to Paris in 1914, yet they did not get it, and she affirms they shall not get Venice either. Oh, how I hope and pray they will not—Venice the beautiful Queen of the Adriatic. Although I've never seen it I feel about it just as Byron did—I've always loved it—it has always been to me 'a fairy city of the heart.' Perhaps I caught my love of it from Walter, who worshipped it. It was always one of his dreams to see Venice. I remember we planned once—down in Rainbow Valley one evening just before the war broke out—that some time we would go together to see it and float in a gondola through its moonlit streets.

"Every fall since the war began there has been some terrible blow to our troops—Antwerp in 1914, Serbia in 1915; last fall, Rumania, and now Italy, the worst of all. I think I would give up in despair if it were not for what Walter said in his dear last letter—that 'the dead as well as the living were fighting on our side and such an army cannot be defeated.' No it cannot. We will win in the end. I will not doubt it for one moment. To let myself doubt would be to 'break faith.'

"We have all been campaigning furiously of late for the new Victory Loan. We Junior Reds canvassed diligently and landed several tough old customers who had at first flatly refused to invest. I—even I—tackled Whiskers-on-the-moon. I expected a bad time and a refusal. But to my amazement he was quite agreeable and promised on the spot to take a thousand dollar bond. He may be a pacifist, but he knows a good investment when it is handed out to him. Five and a half per cent is five and a half per cent, even when a militaristic government pays it.

"Father, to tease Susan, says it was her speech at the Victory Loan Campaign meeting that converted Mr. Pryor. I don't think that at all likely, since Mr. Pryor has been publicly very bitter against Susan ever since her quite unmistakable rejection of his lover-like advances. But Susan did make a speech—and the best one made at the meeting, too. It was the first time she ever did such a thing and she vows it will be the last. Everybody in the Glen was at the meeting, and quite a number of speeches were made, but somehow things were a little flat and no especial enthusiasm could be worked up. Susan was quite dismayed at the lack of zeal, because she had been burningly anxious that the Island should go over the top in regard to its quota. She kept whispering viciously to Gertrude and me that there was 'no ginger' in the speeches; and when nobody went forward to subscribe to the loan at the close Susan 'lost her head.' At least, that is how she describes it herself. She bounded to her feet, her face grim and set under her bonnet—Susan is the only woman in Glen St. Mary who still wears a bonnet—and said sarcastically and loudly, 'No doubt it is much cheaper to talk patriotism than it is to pay for it. And we are asking charity, of course—we are asking you to lend us your money for nothing! No doubt the Kaiser will feel quite downcast when he hears of this meeting!'

"Susan has an unshaken belief that the Kaiser's spies—presumably represented by Mr. Pryor—promptly inform him of every happening in our Glen.

"Norman Douglas shouted out 'Hear! Hear!' and some boy at the back said, 'What about Lloyd George?' in a tone Susan didn't like. Lloyd George is her pet hero, now that Kitchener is gone.

"'I stand behind Lloyd George every time,' retorted Susan.

"'I suppose that will hearten him up greatly,' said Warren Mead, with one of his disagreeable 'haw-haws.'

"Warren's remark was spark to powder. Susan just 'sailed in' as she puts it, and 'said her say.' She said it remarkably well, too. There was no lack of 'ginger' in her speech, anyhow. When Susan is warmed up she has no mean powers of oratory, and the way she trimmed those men down was funny and wonderful and effective all at once. She said it was the likes of her, millions of her, that did stand behind Lloyd George, and did hearten him up. That was the key-note of her speech. Dear old Susan! She is a perfect dynamo of patriotism and loyalty and contempt for slackers of all kinds, and when she let it loose on that audience in her one grand outburst she electrified it. Susan always vows she is no suffragette, but she gave womanhood its due that night, and she literally made those men cringe. When she finished with them they were ready to eat out of her hand. She wound up by ordering them—yes, ordering them—to march up to the platform forthwith and subscribe for Victory Bonds. And after wild applause most of them did it, even Warren Mead. When the total amount subscribed came out in the Charlottetown dailies the next day we found that the Glen led every district on the Island—and certainly Susan has the credit for it. She, herself, after she came home that night was quite ashamed and evidently feared that she had been guilty of unbecoming conduct: she confessed to mother that she had been 'rather unladylike.'

"We were all—except Susan—out for a trial ride in father's new automobile tonight. A very good one we had, too, though we did get ingloriously ditched at the end, owing to a certain grim old dame—to wit, Miss Elizabeth Carr of the Upper Glen—who wouldn't rein her horse out to let us pass, honk as we might. Father was quite furious; but in my heart I believe I sympathized with Miss Elizabeth. If I had been a spinster lady, driving along behind my own old nag, in maiden meditation fancy free, I wouldn't have lifted a rein when an obstreperous car hooted blatantly behind me. I should just have sat up as dourly as she did and said 'Take the ditch if you are determined to pass.'

"We did take the ditch—and got up to our axles in sand—and sat foolishly there while Miss Elizabeth clucked up her horse and rattled victoriously away.

"Jem will have a laugh when I write him this. He knows Miss Elizabeth of old.

"But—will—Venice—be—saved?"

19th November 1917

"It is not saved yet—it is still in great danger. But the Italians are making a stand at last on the Piave line. To be sure military critics say they cannot possibly hold it and must retreat to the Adige. But Susan and Gertrude and I say they must hold it, because Venice must be saved, so what are the military critics to do?

"Oh, if I could only believe that they can hold it!

"Our Canadian troops have won another great victory—they have stormed the Passchendaele Ridge and held it in the face of all counter attacks. None of our boys were in the battle—but oh, the casualty list of other people's boys! Joe Milgrave was in it but came through safe. Miranda had some bad days until she got word from him. But it is wonderful how Miranda has bloomed out since her marriage. She isn't the same girl at all. Even her eyes seem to have darkened and deepened—though I suppose that is just because they glow with the greater intensity that has come to her. She makes her father stand round in a perfectly amazing fashion; she runs up the flag whenever a yard of trench on the western front is taken; and she comes up regularly to our Junior Red Cross; and she does—yes, she does—put on funny little 'married woman' airs that are quite killing. But she is the only war-bride in the Glen and surely nobody need grudge her the satisfaction she gets out of it.

"The Russian news is bad, too—Kerensky's government has fallen and Lenin is dictator of Russia. Somehow, it is very hard to keep up courage in the dull hopelessness of these grey autumn days of suspense and boding news. But we are beginning to 'get in a low,' as old Highland Sandy says, over the approaching election. Conscription is the real issue at stake and it will be the most exciting election we ever had. All the women 'who have got de age'—to quote Jo Poirier, and who have husbands, sons, and brothers at the front, can vote. Oh, if I were only twenty-one! Gertrude and Susan are both furious because they can't vote.

"'It is not fair,' Gertrude says passionately. 'There is Agnes Carr who can vote because her husband went. She did everything she could to prevent him from going, and now she is going to vote against the Union Government. Yet I have no vote, because my man at the front is only my sweetheart and not my husband!"

"As for Susan, when she reflects that she cannot vote, while a rank old pacifist like Mr. Pryor can—and will—her comments are sulphurous.

"I really feel sorry for the Elliotts and Crawfords and MacAllisters over-harbour. They have always lined up in clearly divided camps of Liberal and Conservative, and now they are torn from their moorings—I know I'm mixing my metaphors dreadfully—and set hopelessly adrift. It will kill some of those old Grits to vote for Sir Robert Borden's side—and yet they have to because they believe the time has come when we must have conscription. And some poor Conservatives who are against conscription must vote for Laurier, who always has been anathema to them. Some of them are taking it terribly hard. Others seem to be in much the same attitude as Mrs. Marshall Elliott has come to be regarding Church Union.

"She was up here last night. She doesn't come as often as she used to. She is growing too old to walk this far—dear old 'Miss Cornelia.' I hate to think of her growing old—we have always loved her so and she has always been so good to us Ingleside young fry.

"She used to be so bitterly opposed to Church Union. But last night, when father told her it was practically decided, she said in a resigned tone, 'Well, in a world where everything is being rent and torn what matters one more rending and tearing? Anyhow, compared with Germans even Methodists seem attractive to me.'

"Our Junior R.C. goes on quite smoothly, in spite of the fact that Irene has come back to it—having fallen out with the Lowbridge society, I understand. She gave me a sweet little jab last meeting—about knowing me across the square in Charlottetown 'by my green velvet hat.' Everybody knows me by that detestable and detested hat. This will be my fourth season for it. Even mother wanted me to get a new one this fall; but I said, 'No.' As long as the war lasts so long do I wear that velvet hat in winter."

23rd November 1917

"The Piave line still holds—and General Byng has won a splendid victory at Cambrai. I did run up the flag for that—but Susan only said 'I shall set a kettle of water on the kitchen range tonight. I notice little Kitchener always has an attack of croup after any British victory. I do hope he has no pro-German blood in his veins. Nobody knows much about his father's people.'

"Jims has had a few attacks of croup this fall—just the ordinary croup—not that terrible thing he had last year. But whatever blood runs in his little veins it is good, healthy blood. He is rosy and plump and curly and cute; and he says such funny things and asks such comical questions. He likes very much to sit in a special chair in the kitchen; but that is Susan's favourite chair, too, and when she wants it, out Jims must go. The last time she put him out of it he turned around and asked solemnly, 'When you are dead, Susan, can I sit in that chair?' Susan thought it quite dreadful, and I think that was when she began to feel anxiety about his possible ancestry. The other night I took Jims with me for a walk down to the store. It was the first time he had ever been out so late at night, and when he saw the stars he exclaimed, 'Oh, Willa, see the big moon and all the little moons!' And last Wednesday morning, when he woke up, my little alarm clock had stopped because I had forgotten to wind it up. Jims bounded out of his crib and ran across to me, his face quite aghast above his little blue flannel pyjamas. 'The clock is dead,' he gasped, 'oh Willa, the clock is dead.'

"One night he was quite angry with both Susan and me because we would not give him something he wanted very much. When he said his prayers he plumped down wrathfully, and when he came to the petition 'Make me a good boy' he tacked on emphatically, 'and please make Willa and Susan good, 'cause they're not.'

"I don't go about quoting Jims's speeches to all I meet. That always bores me when other people do it! I just enshrine them in this old hotch-potch of a journal!

"This very evening as I put Jims to bed he looked up and asked me gravely, 'Why can't yesterday come back, Willa?'

"Oh, why can't it, Jims? That beautiful 'yesterday' of dreams and laughter— when our boys were home—when Walter and I read and rambled and watched new moons and sunsets together in Rainbow Valley. If it could just come back! But yesterdays never come back, little Jims—and the todays are dark with clouds—and we dare not think about the tomorrows."

11th December 1917

"Wonderful news came today. The British troops captured Jerusalem yesterday. We ran up the flag and some of Gertrude's old sparkle came back to her for a moment.

"'After all,' she said, 'it is worth while to live in the days which see the object of the Crusades attained. The ghosts of all the Crusaders must have crowded the walls of Jerusalem last night, with Coeur-de-lion at their head.'

"Susan had cause for satisfaction also.

"'I am so thankful I can pronounce Jerusalem and Hebron,' she said. 'They give me a real comfortable feeling after Przemysl and Brest-Litovsk! Well, we have got the Turks on the run, at least, and Venice is safe and Lord Lansdowne is not to be taken seriously; and I see no reason why we should be downhearted.'

"Jerusalem! The 'meteor flag of England!' floats over you—the Crescent is gone. How Walter would have thrilled over that!"

18th December 1917

"Yesterday the election came off. In the evening mother and Susan and Gertrude and I forgathered in the living-room and waited in breathless suspense, father having gone down to the village. We had no way of hearing the news, for Carter Flagg's store is not on our line, and when we tried to get it Central always answered that the line 'was busy'—as no doubt it was, for everybody for miles around was trying to get Carter's store for the same reason we were.

"About ten o'clock Gertrude went to the 'phone and happened to catch someone from over-harbour talking to Carter Flagg. Gertrude shamelessly listened in and got for her comforting what eavesdroppers are proverbially supposed to get— to wit, unpleasant hearing; the Union Government had 'done nothing' in the West.

"We looked at each other in dismay. If the Government had failed to carry the West, it was defeated.

"'Canada is disgraced in the eyes of the world,' said Gertrude bitterly.

"'If everybody was like the Mark Crawfords over-harbour this would not have happened,' groaned Susan. 'They locked their Uncle up in the barn this morning and would not let him out until he promised to vote Union. That is what I call effective argument, Mrs. Dr. dear.'

"Gertrude and I couldn't rest after all that. We walked the floor until our legs gave out and we had to sit down perforce. Mother knitted away as steadily as clockwork and pretended to be calm and serene—pretended so well that we were all deceived and envious until the next day, when I caught her ravelling out four inches of her sock. She had knit that far past where the heel should have begun!

"It was twelve before father came home. He stood in the doorway and looked at us and we looked at him. We did not dare ask him what the news was. Then he said that it was Laurier who had 'done nothing' in the West, and that the Union Government was in with a big majority. Gertrude clapped her hands. I wanted to laugh and cry, mother's eyes flashed with their old-time starriness and Susan emitted a queer sound between a gasp and a whoop.

"This will not comfort the Kaiser much,' she said.

"Then we went to bed, but were too excited to sleep. Really, as Susan said solemnly this morning, 'Mrs. Dr. dear, I think politics are too strenuous for women.'"
31st December 1917

"Our fourth War Christmas is over. We are trying to gather up some courage wherewith to face another year of it. Germany has, for the most part, been victorious all summer. And now they say she has all her troops from the Russian front ready for a 'big push' in the spring. Sometimes it seems to me that we just cannot live through the winter waiting for that.

"I had a great batch of letters from overseas this week. Shirley is at the front now, too, and writes about it all as coolly and matter-of-factly as he used to write of football at Queen's. Carl wrote that it had been raining for weeks and that nights in the trenches always made him think of the night of long ago when he did penance in the graveyard for running away from Henry Warren's ghost. Carl's letters are always full of jokes and bits of fun. They had a great rat-hunt the night before he wrote—spearing rats with their bayonets—and he got the best bag and won the prize. He has a tame rat that knows him and sleeps in his pocket at night. Rats don't worry Carl as they do some people—he was always chummy with all little beasts. He says he is making a study of the habits of the trench rat and means to write a treatise on it some day that will make him famous.

"Ken wrote a short letter. His letters are all rather short now—and he doesn't often slip in those dear little sudden sentences I love so much. Sometimes I think he has forgotten all about the night he was here to say goodbye—and then there will be just a line or a word that makes me think he remembers and always will remember. For instance to-day's letter hadn't a thing in it that mightn't have been written to any girl, except that he signed himself 'Your Kenneth,' instead of

'Yours, Kenneth,' as he usually does. Now, did he leave that 's' off intentionally or was it only carelessness? I shall lie awake half the night wondering. He is a captain now. I am glad and proud—and yet Captain Ford sounds so horribly far away and high up. Ken and Captain Ford seem like two different persons. I may be practically engaged to Ken—mother's opinion on that point is my stay and bulwark—but I can't be to Captain Ford!

"And Jem is a lieutenant now—won his promotion on the field. He sent me a snap-shot, taken in his new uniform. He looked thin and old—old—my boy-brother Jem. I can't forget mother's face when I showed it to her. 'That—my little Jem—the baby of the old House of Dreams?' was all she said.

"There was a letter from Faith, too. She is doing V.A.D. work in England and writes hopefully and brightly. I think she is almost happy—she saw Jem on his last leave and she is so near him she could go to him, if he were wounded. That means so much to her. Oh, if I were only with her! But my work is here at home. I know Walter wouldn't have wanted me to leave mother and in everything I try to 'keep faith' with him, even to the little details of daily life. Walter died for Canada—I must live for her. That is what he asked me to do."

28th January 1918

"'I shall anchor my storm-tossed soul to the British fleet and make a batch of bran biscuits,' said Susan today to Cousin Sophia, who had come in with some weird tale of a new and all-conquering submarine, just launched by Germany. But Susan is a somewhat disgruntled woman at present, owing to the regulations regarding cookery. Her loyalty to the Union Government is being sorely tried. It surmounted the first strain gallantly. When the order about flour came Susan said, quite cheerfully, 'I am an old dog to be learning new tricks, but I shall learn to make war bread if it will help defeat the Huns.'

"But the later suggestions went against Susan's grain. Had it not been for father's decree I think she would have snapped her fingers at Sir Robert Borden.

"'Talk about trying to make bricks without straw, Mrs. Dr. dear! How am I to make a cake without butter or sugar? It cannot be done—not cake that is cake. Of course one can make a slab, Mrs. Dr. dear. And we cannot even camooflash it with a little icing! To think that I should have lived to see the day when a government at Ottawa should step into my kitchen and put me on rations!'

"Susan would give the last drop of her blood for her 'king and country,' but to surrender her beloved recipes is a very different and much more serious matter.

"I had letters from Nan and Di too—or rather notes. They are too busy to write letters, for exams are looming up. They will graduate in Arts this spring. I am evidently to be the dunce of the family. But somehow I never had any hankering for a college course, and even now it doesn't appeal to me. I'm afraid I'm rather devoid of ambition. There is only one thing I really want to be—and I don't know if I'll be it or not. If not—I don't want to be anything. But I shan't write it down. It is all right to think it; but, as Cousin Sophia would say, it might be brazen to write it down.

"I will write it down. I won't be cowed by the conventions and Cousin Sophia! I want to be Kenneth Ford's wife! There now!

"I've just looked in the glass, and I hadn't the sign of a blush on my face. I suppose I'm not a properly constructed damsel at all.

"I was down to see little Dog Monday today. He has grown quite stiff and rheumatic but there he sat, waiting for the train. He thumped his tail and looked pleadingly into my eyes. 'When will Jem come?' he seemed to say. Oh, Dog Monday, there is no answer to that question; and there is, as yet, no answer to the other which we are all constantly asking 'What will happen when Germany strikes again on the western front—her one great, last blow for victory!"

1st March 1918

"'What will spring bring?' Gertrude said today. 'I dread it as I never dreaded spring before. Do you suppose there will ever again come a time when life will be free from fear? For almost four years we have lain down with fear and risen up with it. It has been the unbidden guest at every meal, the unwelcome companion at every gathering.'

"'Hindenburg says he will be in Paris on 1st April,' sighed Cousin Sophia.

"'Hindenburg!' There is no power in pen and ink to express the contempt which Susan infused into that name. 'Has he forgotten what day the first of April is?'

"'Hindenburg has kept his word hitherto,' said Gertrude, as gloomily as Cousin Sophia herself could have said it.

"'Yes, fighting against the Russians and Rumanians,' retorted Susan. 'Wait you till he comes up against the British and French, not to speak of the Yankees, who are getting there as fast as they can and will no doubt give a good account of themselves.'

"'You said just the same thing before Mons, Susan,' I reminded her.

"'Hindenburg says he will spend a million lives to break the Allied front,' said Gertrude. 'At such a price he must purchase some successes and how can we live through them, even if he is baffled in the end. These past two months when we have been crouching and waiting for the blow to fall have seemed as long as all the preceding months of the war put together. I work all day feverishly and waken at three o'clock at night to wonder if the iron legions have struck at last. It is then I see Hindenburg in Paris and Germany triumphant. I never see her so at any other time than that accursed hour.'

"Susan looked dubious over Gertrude's adjective, but evidently concluded that the 'a' saved the situation.

"'I wish it were possible to take some magic draught and go to sleep for the next three months—and then waken to find Armageddon over,' said mother, almost impatiently.

"It is not often that mother slumps into a wish like that—or at least the verbal expression of it. Mother has changed a great deal since that terrible day in September when we knew that Walter would not come back; but she has always been brave and patient. Now it seemed as if even she had reached the limit of her endurance.

"Susan went over to mother and touched her shoulder.

"'Do not you be frightened or downhearted, Mrs. Dr. dear,' she said gently. 'I felt somewhat that way myself last night, and I rose from my bed and lighted my lamp and opened my Bible; and what do you think was the first verse my eyes lighted upon? It was 'And they shall fight against thee but they shall not prevail against thee, for I am with thee, saith the Lord of Hosts, to deliver thee.' I am not gifted in the way of dreaming, as Miss Oliver is, but I knew then and there, Mrs. Dr. dear, that it was a manifest leading, and that Hindenburg will never see Paris. So I read no further but went back to my bed and I did not waken at three o'clock or at any other hour before morning.'

"I say that verse Susan read over and over again to myself. The Lord of Hosts is with us—and the spirits of all just men made perfect—and even the legions and guns that Germany is massing on the western front must break against such a barrier. This is in certain uplifted moments; but when other moments come I feel, like Gertrude, that I cannot endure any longer this awful and ominous hush before the coming storm."

23rd March 1918

"Armageddon has begun!—'the last great fight of all!' Is it, I wonder? Yesterday I went down to the post office for the mail. It was a dull, bitter day. The snow was gone but the grey, lifeless ground was frozen hard and a biting wind was blowing. The whole Glen landscape was ugly and hopeless.

"Then I got the paper with its big black headlines. Germany struck on the twenty-first. She makes big claims of guns and prisoners taken. General Haig reports that 'severe fighting continues.' I don't like the sound of that last expression.

"We all find we cannot do any work that requires concentration of thought. So we all knit furiously, because we can do that mechanically. At least the dreadful waiting is over—the horrible wondering where and when the blow will fall. It has fallen—but they shall not prevail against us!

"Oh, what is happening on the western front tonight as I write this, sitting here in my room with my journal before me? Jims is asleep in his crib and the wind is wailing around the window; over my desk hangs Walter's picture, looking at me with his beautiful deep eyes; the Mona Lisa he gave me the last Christmas he was home hangs on one side of it, and on the other a framed copy of "The Piper." It seems to me that I can hear Walter's voice repeating it—that little poem into which he put his soul, and which will therefore live for ever, carrying Walter's name on through the future of our land. Everything about me is calm and peaceful and 'homey.' Walter seems very near me—if I could just sweep aside the thin wavering little veil that hangs between, I could see him—just as he saw the Pied Piper the night before Courcelette.

"Over there in France tonight—does the line hold?"

CHAPTER XXVIII - BLACK SUNDAY

In March of the year of grace 1918 there was one week into which must have crowded more of searing human agony than any seven days had ever held before in the history of the world. And in that week there was one day when all humanity seemed nailed to the cross; on that day the whole planet must have been agroan with universal convulsion; everywhere the hearts of men were failing them for fear.

It dawned calmly and coldly and greyly at Ingleside. Mrs. Blythe and Rilla and Miss Oliver made ready for church in a suspense tempered by hope and confidence. The doctor was away, having been summoned during the wee sma's to the Marwood household in Upper Glen, where a little war-bride was fighting gallantly on her own battleground to give life, not death, to the world. Susan announced that she meant to stay home that morning—a rare decision for Susan.

"But I would rather not go to church this morning, Mrs. Dr. dear," she explained. "If Whiskers-on-the-moon were there and I saw him looking holy and pleased, as he always looks when he thinks the Huns are winning, I fear I would lose my patience and my sense of decorum and hurl a Bible or hymn-book at him, thereby disgracing myself and the sacred edifice. No, Mrs. Dr. dear, I shall stay home from church till the tide turns and pray hard here."

"I think I might as well stay home, too, for all the good church will do me to-day," Miss Oliver said to Rilla, as they walked down the hard-frozen red road to the church. "I can think of nothing but the question, 'Does the line still hold?'"

"Next Sunday will be Easter," said Rilla. "Will it herald death or life to our cause?"

Mr. Meredith preached that morning from the text, "He that endureth to the end shall be saved," and hope and confidence rang through his inspiring sentences. Rilla, looking up at the memorial tablet on the wall above their pew, "sacred to the memory of Walter Cuthbert Blythe," felt herself lifted out of her dread and filled anew with courage. Walter could not have laid down his life for naught. His had been the gift of prophetic vision and he had foreseen victory. She would cling to that belief—the line would hold.

In this renewed mood she walked home from church almost gaily. The others, too, were hopeful, and all went smiling into Ingleside. There was no one in the living-room, save Jims, who had fallen asleep on the sofa, and Doc, who sat "hushed in grim repose" on the hearth-rug, looking very Hydeish indeed. No one was in the dining-room either—and, stranger still, no dinner was on the table, which was not even set. Where was Susan?

"Can she have taken ill?" exclaimed Mrs. Blythe anxiously. "I thought it strange that she did not want to go to church this morning."

The kitchen door opened and Susan appeared on the threshold with such a ghastly face that Mrs. Blythe cried out in sudden panic.

"Susan, what is it?"

"The British line is broken and the German shells are falling on Paris," said Susan dully.

The three women stared at each other, stricken.

"It's not true—it's not," gasped Rilla.

"The thing would be—ridiculous," said Gertrude Oliver—and then she laughed horribly.

"Susan, who told you this—when did the news come?" asked Mrs. Blythe.

"I got it over the long-distance phone from Charlottetown half an hour ago," said Susan. "The news came to town late last night. It was Dr. Holland phoned it out and he said it was only too true. Since then I have done nothing, Mrs. Dr. dear. I am very sorry dinner is not ready. It is the first time I have been so remiss. If you will be patient I will soon have something for you to eat. But I am afraid I let the potatoes burn."

"Dinner! Nobody wants any dinner, Susan," said Mrs. Blythe wildly. "Oh, this thing is unbelievable—it must be a nightmare."

"Paris is lost—France is lost—the war is lost," gasped Rilla, amid the utter ruins of hope and confidence and belief.

"Oh God—Oh God," moaned Gertrude Oliver, walking about the room and wringing her hands, "Oh—God!"

Nothing else—no other words—nothing but that age old plea—the old, old cry of supreme agony and appeal, from the human heart whose every human staff has failed it.

"Is God dead?" asked a startled little voice from the doorway of the living-room. Jims stood there, flushed from sleep, his big brown eyes filled with dread, "Oh Willa—oh, Willa, is God dead?"

Miss Oliver stopped walking and exclaiming, and stared at Jims, in whose eyes tears of fright were beginning to gather. Rilla ran to his comforting, while Susan bounded up from the chair upon which she had dropped.

"No," she said briskly, with a sudden return of her real self. "No, God isn't dead—nor Lloyd George either. We were forgetting that, Mrs. Dr. dear. Don't cry, little Kitchener. Bad as things are, they might be worse. The British line may be broken but the British navy is not. Let us tie to that. I will take a brace and get up a bite to eat, for strength we must have."

They made a pretence of eating Susan's "bite," but it was only a pretence. Nobody at Ingleside ever forgot that black afternoon. Gertrude Oliver walked the floor—they all walked the floor; except Susan, who got out her grey war sock.

"Mrs. Dr. dear, I must knit on Sunday at last. I have never dreamed of doing it before for, say what might be said, I have considered it was a violation of the third commandment. But whether it is or whether it is not I must knit today or I shall go mad."

"Knit if you can, Susan," said Mrs. Blythe restlessly. "I would knit if I could—but I cannot—I cannot."

"If we could only get fuller information," moaned Rilla. "There might be something to encourage us—if we knew all."

"We know that the Germans are shelling Paris," said Miss Oliver bitterly. "In that case they must have smashed through everywhere and be at the very gates. No, we have lost—let us face the fact as other peoples in the past have had to face it. Other nations, with right on their side, have given their best and bravest—and gone down to defeat in spite of it. Ours is 'but one more To baffled millions who have gone before.'"

"I won't give up like that," cried Rilla, her pale face suddenly flushing. "I won't despair. We are not conquered—no, if Germany overruns all France we are not conquered. I am ashamed of myself for this hour of despair. You won't see me slump again like that, I'm going to ring up town at once and ask for particulars."

But town could not be got. The long-distance operator there was submerged by similar calls from every part of the distracted country. Rilla finally gave up and slipped away to Rainbow Valley. There she knelt down on the withered grey grasses in the little nook where she and Walter had had their last talk together, with her head bowed against the mossy trunk of a fallen tree. The sun had broken through the black clouds and drenched the valley with a pale golden splendour. The bells on the Tree Lovers twinkled elfinly and fitfully in the gusty March wind.

"Oh God, give me strength," Rilla whispered. "Just strength—and courage." Then like a child she clasped her hands together and said, as simply as Jims could have done, "Please send us better news tomorrow."

She knelt there a long time, and when she went back to Ingleside she was calm and resolute. The doctor had arrived home, tired but triumphant, little Douglas Haig Marwood having made a safe landing on the shores of time. Gertrude was still pacing restlessly but Mrs. Blythe and Susan had reacted from the shock, and Susan was already planning a new line of defence for the channel ports.

"As long as we can hold them," she declared, "the situation is saved. Paris has really no military significance."

"Don't," said Gertrude sharply, as if Susan had run something into her. She thought the old worn phrase 'no military significance' nothing short of ghastly mockery under the circumstances, and more terrible to endure than the voice of despair would have been.

"I heard up at Marwood's of the line being broken," said the doctor, "but this story of the Germans shelling Paris seems to be rather incredible. Even if they broke through they were fifty miles from Paris at the nearest point and how could they get their artillery close enough to shell it in so short a time? Depend upon it, girls, that part of the message can't be true. I'm going to try to try a long-distance call to town myself."

The doctor was no more successful than Rilla had been, but his point of view cheered them all a little, and helped them through the evening. And at nine o'clock a long-distance message came through at last, that helped them through the night.

"The line broke only in one place, before St. Quentin," said the doctor, as he hung up the receiver, "and the British troops are retreating in good order. That's not so bad. As for the shells that are falling on Paris, they are coming from a distance of seventy miles—from some amazing long-range gun the Germans have invented and sprung with the opening offensive. That is all the news to date, and Dr. Holland says it is reliable."

"It would have been dreadful news yesterday," said Gertrude, "but compared to what we heard this morning it is almost like good news. But still," she added, trying to smile, "I am afraid I will not sleep much tonight."

"There is one thing to be thankful for at any rate, Miss Oliver, dear," said Susan, "and that is that Cousin Sophia did not come in today. I really could not have endured her on top of all the rest."

CHAPTER XXIX - "WOUNDED AND MISSING"

"Battered but Not Broken" was the headline in Monday's paper, and Susan repeated it over and over to herself as she went about her work. The gap caused by the St. Quentin disaster had been patched up in time, but the Allied line was being pushed relentlessly back from the territory they had purchased in 1917 with half a million lives. On Wednesday the headline was "British and French Check Germans"; but still the retreat went on. Back—and back—and back! Where would it end? Would the line break again—this time disastrously?

On Saturday the headline was "Even Berlin Admits Offensive Checked," and for the first time in that terrible week the Ingleside folk dared to draw a long breath.

"Well, we have got one week over—now for the next," said Susan staunchly.

"I feel like a prisoner on the rack when they stopped turning it," Miss Oliver said to Rilla, as they went to church on Easter morning. "But I am not off the rack. The torture may begin again at any time."

"I doubted God last Sunday," said Rilla, "but I don't doubt him today. Evil cannot win. Spirit is on our side and it is bound to outlast flesh."

Nevertheless her faith was often tried in the dark spring that followed. Armageddon was not, as they had hoped, a matter of a few days. It stretched out into weeks and months. Again and again Hindenburg struck his savage, sudden blows, with alarming, though futile success. Again and again the military critics declared the situation extremely perilous. Again and again Cousin Sophia agreed with the military critics.

"If the Allies go back three miles more the war is lost," she wailed.

"Is the British navy anchored in those three miles?" demanded Susan scornfully.

"It is the opinion of a man who knows all about it," said Cousin Sophia solemnly.

"There is no such person," retorted Susan. "As for the military critics, they do not know one blessed thing about it, any more than you or I. They have been mistaken times out of number. Why do you always look on the dark side, Sophia Crawford?"

"Because there ain't any bright side, Susan Baker."

"Oh, is there not? It is the twentieth of April, and Hindy is not in Paris yet, although he said he would be there by April first. Is that not a bright spot at least?"

"It is my opinion that the Germans will be in Paris before very long and more than that, Susan Baker, they will be in Canada."

"Not in this part of it. The Huns shall never set foot in Prince Edward Island as long as I can handle a pitchfork," declared Susan, looking, and feeling quite equal to routing the entire German army single-handed. "No, Sophia Crawford, to tell you the plain truth I am sick and tired of your gloomy predictions. I do not deny that some mistakes have been made. The Germans would never have got back Passchendaele if the Canadians had been left there; and it was bad business trusting to those Portuguese at the Lys River. But that is no reason why you or anyone should go about proclaiming the war is lost. I do not want to quarrel with you, least of all at such a time as this, but our morale must be kept up, and I am going to speak my mind out plainly and tell you that if you cannot keep from such croaking your room is better than your company."

Cousin Sophia marched home in high dudgeon to digest her affront, and did not reappear in Susan's kitchen for many weeks. Perhaps it was just as well, for they were hard weeks, when the Germans continued to strike, now here, now there, and seemingly vital points fell to them at every blow. And one day in early May, when wind and sunshine frolicked in Rainbow Valley and the maple grove was golden-green and the harbour all blue and dimpled and white-capped, the news came about Jem.

There had been a trench raid on the Canadian front—a little trench raid so insignificant that it was never even mentioned in the dispatches and when it was over Lieutenant James Blythe was reported "wounded and missing."

"I think this is even worse than the news of his death would have been," moaned Rilla through her white lips, that night.

"No—no—'missing' leaves a little hope, Rilla," urged Gertrude Oliver.

"Yes—torturing, agonized hope that keeps you from ever becoming quite resigned to the worst," said Rilla. "Oh, Miss Oliver—must we go for weeks and months—not knowing whether Jem is alive or dead? Perhaps we will never know. I—I cannot bear it—I cannot. Walter—and now Jem. This will kill mother—look at her face, Miss Oliver, and you will see that. And Faith—poor Faith—how can she bear it?"

Gertrude shivered with pain. She looked up at the pictures hanging over Rilla's desk and felt a sudden hatred of Mona Lisa's endless smile.

"Will not even this blot it off your face?" she thought savagely.

But she said gently, "No, it won't kill your mother. She's made of finer mettle than that. Besides, she refuses to believe Jem is dead; she will cling to hope and we must all do that. Faith, you may be sure, will do it."

"I cannot," moaned Rilla, "Jem was wounded—what chance would he have? Even if the Germans found him—we know how they have treated wounded prisoners. I wish I could hope, Miss Oliver—it would help, I suppose. But hope seems dead in me. I can't hope without some reason for it—and there is no reason."

When Miss Oliver had gone to her own room and Rilla was lying on her bed in the moonlight, praying desperately for a little strength, Susan stepped in like a gaunt shadow and sat down beside her.

"Rilla, dear, do not you worry. Little Jem is not dead."

"Oh, how can you believe that, Susan?"

"Because I know. Listen you to me. When that word came this morning the first thing I thought of was Dog Monday. And tonight, as soon as I got the supper dishes washed and the bread set, I went down to the station. There was Dog Monday, waiting for the train, just as patient as usual. Now, Rilla, dear, that trench raid was four days ago—last Monday—and I said to the station-agent, 'Can you tell me if that dog howled or made any kind of a fuss last Monday night?' He thought it over a bit, and then he said, 'No, he did not.' 'Are you sure?' I said. 'There's more depends on it than you think!' 'Dead sure,' he said. 'I was up all night last Monday night because my mare was sick, and there was never a sound out of him. I would have heard if there had been, for the stable door was open all the time and his kennel is right across from it!' Now Rilla dear, those were the man's very words. And you know how that poor little dog howled all night after the battle of Courcelette. Yet he did not love Walter as much as he loved Jem. If he mourned for Walter like that, do you suppose he would sleep sound in his kennel the night after Jem had been killed? No, Rilla dear, little Jem is not dead, and that you may tie to. If he were, Dog Monday would have known, just as he knew before, and he would not be still waiting for the trains."

It was absurd—and irrational—and impossible. But Rilla believed it, for all that; and Mrs. Blythe believed it; and the doctor, though he smiled faintly in pretended derision, felt an odd confidence replace his first despair; and foolish and absurd or not, they all plucked up heart and courage to carry on, just because a faithful little dog at the Glen station was still watching with unbroken faith for his master to come home. Common sense might scorn—incredulity might mutter "Mere superstition"—but in their hearts the folk of Ingleside stood by their belief that Dog Monday knew.

CHAPTER XXX - THE TURNING OF THE TIDE

Susan was very sorrowful when she saw the beautiful old lawn of Ingleside ploughed up that spring and planted with potatoes. Yet she made no protest, even when her beloved peony bed was sacrificed. But when the Government passed the Daylight Saving law Susan balked. There was a Higher Power than the Union Government, to which Susan owed allegiance.

"Do you think it right to meddle with the arrangements of the Almighty?" she demanded indignantly of the doctor. The doctor, quite unmoved, responded that the law must be observed, and the Ingleside clocks were moved on accordingly. But the doctor had no power over Susan's little alarm.

"I bought that with my own money, Mrs. Dr. dear," she said firmly, "and it shall go on God's time and not Borden's time."

Susan got up and went to bed by "God's time," and regulated her own goings and comings by it. She served the meals, under protest, by Borden's time, and she had to go to church by it, which was the crowning injury. But she said her prayers by her own clock, and fed the hens by it; so that there was always a furtive triumph in her eye when she looked at the doctor. She had got the better of him by so much at least.

"Whiskers-on-the-moon is very much delighted with this daylight saving business," she told him one evening. "Of course he naturally would be, since I understand that the Germans invented it. I hear he came near losing his entire wheat-crop lately. Warren Mead's cows broke into the field one day last week—it was the very day the Germans captured the Chemang-de-dam, which may have been a coincidence or may not—and were making fine havoc of it when Mrs. Dick Clow happened to see them from her attic window. At first she had no intention of letting Mr. Pryor know. She told me she had just gloated over the sight of those cows pasturing on his wheat. She felt it served him exactly right. But presently she reflected that the wheat-crop was a matter of great importance and that 'save and serve' meant that those cows must be routed out as much as it meant anything. So she went down and phoned over to Whiskers about the matter. All the thanks she got was that he said something queer right out to her. She is not prepared to state that it was actually swearing for you cannot be sure just what you hear over the phone; but she has her own opinion, and so have I, but I will not express it for here comes Mr. Meredith, and Whiskers is one of his elders, so we must be discreet."

"Are you looking for the new star?" asked Mr. Meredith, joining Miss Oliver and Rilla, who were standing among the blossoming potatoes gazing skyward.

"Yes—we have found it—see, it is just above the tip of the tallest old pine."

"It's wonderful to be looking at something that happened three thousand years ago, isn't it?" said Rilla. "That is when astronomers think the collision took place which produced this new star. It makes me feel horribly insignificant," she added under her breath.

"Even this event cannot dwarf into what may be the proper perspective in star systems the fact that the Germans are again only one leap from Paris," said Gertrude restlessly.

"I think I would like to have been an astronomer," said Mr. Meredith dreamily, gazing at the star.

"There must be a strange pleasure in it," agreed Miss Oliver, "an unearthly pleasure, in more senses than one. I would like to have a few astronomers for my friends."

"Fancy talking the gossip of the hosts of heaven," laughed Rilla.

"I wonder if astronomers feel a very deep interest in earthly affairs?" said the doctor. "Perhaps students of the canals of Mars would not be so keenly sensitive to the significance of a few yards of trenches lost or won on the western front."

"I have read somewhere," said Mr. Meredith, "that Ernest Renan wrote one of his books during the siege of Paris in 1870 and 'enjoyed the writing of it very much.' I suppose one would call him a philosopher."

"I have read also," said Miss Oliver, "that shortly before his death he said that his only regret in dying was that he must die before he had seen what that 'extremely interesting young man, the German Emperor,' would do in his life. If Ernest Renan 'walked' today and saw what that interesting young man had done to his beloved France, not to speak of the world, I wonder if his mental detachment would be as complete as it was in 1870."

"I wonder where Jem is tonight," thought Rilla, in a sudden bitter inrush of remembrance.

It was over a month since the news had come about Jem. Nothing had been discovered concerning him, in spite of all efforts. Two or three letters had come from him, written before the trench raid, and since then there had been only unbroken silence. Now the Germans were again at the Marne, pressing nearer and nearer Paris; now rumours were coming of another Austrian offensive against the Piave line. Rilla turned away from the new star, sick at heart. It was one of the moments when hope and courage failed her utterly—when it seemed impossible to go on even one more day. If only they knew what had happened to Jem—you can face anything you know. But a beleaguerment of fear and doubt and suspense is a hard thing for the morale. Surely, if Jem were alive, some word would have come through. He must be dead. Only—they would never know—they could never be quite sure; and Dog Monday would wait for the train until he died of old age. Monday was only a poor, faithful, rheumatic little dog, who knew nothing more of his master's fate than they did.

Rilla had a "white night" and did not fall asleep until late. When she wakened Gertrude Oliver was sitting at her window leaning out to meet the silver mystery of the dawn. Her clever, striking profile, with the masses of black hair behind it, came out clearly against the pallid gold of the eastern sky. Rilla remembered Jem's admiration of the curve of Miss Oliver's brow and chin, and she shuddered. Everything that reminded her of Jem was beginning to give intolerable pain. Walter's death had inflicted on her heart a terrible wound. But it had been a clean wound and had healed slowly, as such wounds do, though the scar must remain for ever. But the torture of Jem's disappearance was another thing: there was a poison in it that kept it from healing. The alternations of hope and despair, the endless watching each day for the letter that never came—that might never come—the newspaper tales of ill-usage of prisoners—the bitter wonder as to Jem's wound—all were increasingly hard to bear.

Gertrude Oliver turned her head. There was an odd brilliancy in her eyes.

"Rilla, I've had another dream."

"Oh, no—no," cried Rilla, shrinking. Miss Oliver's dreams had always foretold coming disaster.

"Rilla, it was a good dream. Listen—I dreamed just as I did four years ago, that I stood on the veranda steps and looked down the Glen. And it was still covered by waves that lapped about my feet. But as I looked the waves began to ebb—and they ebbed as swiftly as, four years ago, they rolled in—ebbed out and out, to the gulf; and the Glen lay before me, beautiful and green, with a rainbow spanning Rainbow Valley—a rainbow of such splendid colour that it dazzled me—and I woke. Rilla—Rilla Blythe—the tide has turned."

"I wish I could believe it," sighed Rilla.

> "Sooth was my prophecy of fear
> Believe it when it augurs cheer,"

quoted Gertrude, almost gaily. "I tell you I have no doubt."

Yet, in spite of the great Italian victory at the Piave that came a few days later, she had doubt many a time in the hard month that followed; and when in mid-July the Germans crossed the Marne again despair came sickeningly. It was idle, they all felt, to hope that the miracle of the Marne would be repeated. But it was: again, as in 1914, the tide turned at the Marne. The French and the American troops struck their sudden smashing blow on the exposed flank of the enemy and, with the almost inconceivable rapidity of a dream, the whole aspect of the war changed.

"The Allies have won two tremendous victories," said the doctor on 20th July.

"It is the beginning of the end—I feel it—I feel it," said Mrs. Blythe.

"Thank God," said Susan, folding her trembling old hands, Then she added, under her breath, "but it won't bring our boys back."

Nevertheless she went out and ran up the flag, for the first time since the fall of Jerusalem. As it caught the breeze and swelled gallantly out above her, Susan lifted her hand and saluted it, as she had seen Shirley do. "We've all given something to keep you flying," she said. "Four hundred thousand of our boys gone overseas—fifty thousand of them killed. But—you are worth it!" The wind whipped her grey hair about her face and the gingham apron that shrouded her from head to foot was cut on lines of economy, not of grace; yet, somehow, just then Susan made an imposing figure. She was one of the women—courageous, unquailing, patient, heroic—who had made victory possible. In her, they all saluted the symbol for which their dearest had fought. Something of this was in the doctor's mind as he watched her from the door.

"Susan," he said, when she turned to come in, "from first to last of this business you have been a brick!"

CHAPTER XXXI - MRS. MATILDA PITTMAN

Rilla and Jims were standing on the rear platform of their car when the train stopped at the little Millward siding. The August evening was so hot and close that the crowded cars were stifling. Nobody ever knew just why trains stopped at Millward siding. Nobody was ever known to get off there or get on. There was only one house nearer to it than four miles, and it was surrounded by acres of blueberry barrens and scrub spruce-trees.

Rilla was on her way into Charlottetown to spend the night with a friend and the next day in Red Cross shopping; she had taken Jims with her, partly because she did not want Susan or her mother to be bothered with his care, partly because of a hungry desire in her heart to have as much of him as she could before she might have to give him up forever. James Anderson had written to her not long before this; he was wounded and in the hospital; he would not be able to go back to the front and as soon as he was able he would be coming home for Jims.

Rilla was heavy-hearted over this, and worried also. She loved Jims dearly and would feel deeply giving him up in any case; but if Jim Anderson were a different sort of a man, with a proper home for the child, it would not be so bad. But to give Jims up to a roving, shiftless, irresponsible father, however kind and good-hearted he might be—and she knew Jim Anderson was kind and good-hearted enough—was a bitter prospect to Rilla. It was not even likely Anderson would stay in the Glen; he had no ties there now; he might even go back to England. She might never see her dear, sunshiny, carefully brought-up little Jims again. With such a father what might his fate be? Rilla meant to beg Jim Anderson to leave him with her, but, from his letter, she had not much hope that he would.

"If he would only stay in the Glen, where I could keep an eye on Jims and have him often with me I wouldn't feel so worried over it," she reflected. "But I feel sure he won't—and Jims will never have any chance. And he is such a bright little chap—he has ambition, wherever he got it—and he isn't lazy. But his father will never have a cent to give him any education or start in life. Jims, my little war-baby, whatever is going to become of you?"

Jims was not in the least concerned over what was to become of him. He was gleefully watching the antics of a striped chipmunk that was frisking over the roof of the little siding. As the train pulled out Jims leaned eagerly forward for a last look at Chippy, pulling his hand from Rilla's. Rilla was so engrossed in wondering what was to become of Jims in the future that she forgot to take notice of what was happening to him in the present. What did happen was that Jims lost his balance, shot headlong down the steps, hurtled across the little siding platform, and landed in a clump of bracken fern on the other side.

Rilla shrieked and lost her head. She sprang down the steps and jumped off the train.

Fortunately, the train was still going at a comparatively slow speed; fortunately also, Rilla retained enough sense to jump the way it was going; nevertheless, she fell and sprawled helplessly down the embankment, landing in a ditch full of a rank growth of golden-rod and fireweed.

Nobody had seen what had happened and the train whisked briskly away round a curve in the barrens. Rilla picked herself up, dizzy but unhurt, scrambled out of the ditch, and flew wildly across the platform, expecting to find Jims dead or broken in pieces. But Jims, except for a few bruises, and a big fright, was quite uninjured. He was so badly scared that he didn't even cry, but Rilla, when she found that he was safe and sound, burst into tears and sobbed wildly.

"Nasty old twain," remarked Jims in disgust. "And nasty old God," he added, with a scowl at the heavens.

A laugh broke into Rilla's sobbing, producing something very like what her father would have called hysterics. But she caught herself up before the hysteria could conquer her.

"Rilla Blythe, I'm ashamed of you. Pull yourself together immediately. Jims, you shouldn't have said anything like that."

"God frew me off the twain," declared Jims defiantly. "Somebody frew me; you didn't frow me; so it was God."

"No, it wasn't. You fell because you let go of my hand and bent too far forward. I told you not to do that. So that it was your own fault."

Jims looked to see if she meant it; then glanced up at the sky again.

"Excuse me, then, God," he remarked airily.

Rilla scanned the sky also; she did not like its appearance; a heavy thundercloud was appearing in the northwest. What in the world was to be done? There was no other train that night, since the nine o'clock special ran only on Saturdays. Would it be possible for them to reach Hannah Brewster's house, two miles away, before the storm broke? Rilla thought she could do it alone easily enough, but with Jims it was another matter. Were his little legs good for it?

"We've got to try it," said Rilla desperately. "We might stay in the siding until the thunderstorm is over; but it may keep on raining all night and anyway it will be pitch dark. If we can get to Hannah's she will keep us all night."

Hannah Brewster, when she had been Hannah Crawford, had lived in the Glen and gone to school with Rilla. They had been good friends then, though Hannah had been three years the older. She had married very young and had gone to live in Millward. What with hard work and babies and a ne'er-do-well husband, her life had not been an easy one, and Hannah seldom revisited her old home. Rilla had visited her once soon after her marriage, but had not seen her or even heard of her for years; she knew, however, that she and Jims would find welcome and harbourage in any house where rosy-faced, open-hearted, generous Hannah lived.

For the first mile they got on very well but the second one was harder. The road, seldom used, was rough and deep-rutted. Jims grew so tired that Rilla had to carry him for the last quarter. She reached the Brewster house, almost exhausted, and dropped Jims on the walk with a sigh of thankfulness. The sky was black with clouds; the first heavy drops were beginning to fall; and the rumble of thunder was growing very loud. Then she made an unpleasant discovery. The blinds were all down and the doors locked. Evidently the Brewsters were not at home. Rilla ran to the little barn. It, too, was locked. No other refuge presented itself. The bare whitewashed little house had not even a veranda or porch.

It was almost dark now and her plight seemed desperate.

"I'm going to get in if I have to break a window," said Rilla resolutely. "Hannah would want me to do that. She'd never get over it if she heard I came to her house for refuge in a thunderstorm and couldn't get in."

Luckily she did not have to go to the length of actual housebreaking. The kitchen window went up quite easily. Rilla lifted Jims in and scrambled through herself, just as the storm broke in good earnest.

"Oh, see all the little pieces of thunder," cried Jims in delight, as the hail danced in after them. Rilla shut the window and with some difficulty found and lighted a lamp. They were in a very snug little kitchen. Opening off it on one side was a trim, nicely furnished parlour, and on the other a pantry, which proved to be well stocked.

"I'm going to make myself at home," said Rilla. "I know that is just what Hannah would want me to do. I'll get a little snack for Jims and me, and then if the rain continues and nobody comes home I'll just go upstairs to the spare room and go to bed. There is nothing like acting sensibly in an emergency. If I had not been a goose when I saw Jims fall off the train I'd have rushed back into the car and got some one to stop it. Then I wouldn't have been in this scrape. Since I am in it I'll make the best of it.

"This house," she added, looking around, "is fixed up much nicer than when I was here before. Of course Hannah and Ted were just beginning housekeeping then. But somehow I've had the idea that Ted hasn't been very prosperous. He must have done better than I've been led to believe, when they can afford furniture like this. I'm awfully glad for Hannah's sake."

The thunderstorm passed, but the rain continued to fall heavily. At eleven o'clock Rilla decided that nobody was coming home. Jims had fallen asleep on the sofa; she carried him up to the spare room and put him to bed. Then she undressed, put on a nightgown she found in the washstand drawer, and scrambled sleepily in between very nice lavender-scented sheets. She was so tired, after her adventures and exertions, that not even the oddity of her situation could keep her awake; she was sound asleep in a few minutes.

Rilla slept until eight o'clock the next morning and then wakened with startling suddenness. Somebody was saying in a harsh, gruff voice, "Here, you two, wake up. I want to know what this means."

Rilla did wake up, promptly and effectually. She had never in all her life wakened up so thoroughly before. Standing in the room were three people, one of them a man, who were absolute strangers to her. The man was a big fellow with a bushy black beard and an angry scowl. Beside him was a woman—a tall, thin, angular person, with violently red hair and an indescribable hat. She looked even crosser and more amazed than the man, if that were possible. In the background was another woman—a tiny old lady who must have been at least eighty. She was, in spite of her tinyness, a very striking-looking personage; she was dressed in unrelieved black, had snow-white hair, a dead-white face, and snapping, vivid, coal-black eyes. She looked as amazed as the other two, but Rilla realized that she didn't look cross.

Rilla also was realizing that something was wrong—fearfully wrong. Then the man said, more gruffly than ever, "Come now. Who are you and what business have you here?"

Rilla raised herself on one elbow, looking and feeling hopelessly bewildered and foolish. She heard the old black-and-white lady in the background chuckle to herself. "She must be real," Rilla thought. "I can't be dreaming her." Aloud she gasped,

"Isn't this Theodore Brewster's place?"

"No," said the big woman, speaking for the first time, "this place belongs to us. We bought it from the Brewsters last fall. They moved to Greenvale. Our name is Chapley."

Poor Rilla fell back on her pillow, quite overcome.

"I beg your pardon," she said. "I—I—thought the Brewsters lived here. Mrs. Brewster is a friend of mine. I am Rilla Blythe—Dr. Blythe's daughter from Glen St. Mary. I—I was going to town with my—my—this little boy—and he fell off the train—and I jumped off after him—and nobody knew of it. I knew we couldn't get home last night and a storm was coming up—so we came here and when we found nobody at home—we—we—just got in through the window and—and—made ourselves at home."

"So it seems," said the woman sarcastically.

"A likely story," said the man.

"We weren't born yesterday," added the woman.

Madam Black-and-White didn't say anything; but when the other two made their pretty speeches she doubled up in a silent convulsion of mirth, shaking her head from side to side and beating the air with her hands.

Rilla, stung by the disagreeable attitude of the Chapleys, regained her self-possession and lost her temper. She sat up in bed and said in her haughtiest voice, "I do not know when you were born, or where, but it must have been somewhere where very peculiar manners were taught. If you will have the decency to leave my room—er—this room—until I can get up and dress I shall not transgress upon your hospitality"—Rilla was killingly sarcastic—"any longer. And I shall pay you amply for the food we have eaten and the night's lodging I have taken."

The black-and-white apparition went through the motion of clapping her hands, but not a sound did she make. Perhaps Mr. Chapley was cowed by Rilla's tone—or perhaps he was appeased at the prospect of payment; at all events, he spoke more civilly.

"Well, that's fair. If you pay up it's all right."

"She shall do no such thing as pay you," said Madam Black-and-White in a surprisingly clear, resolute, authoritative tone of voice. "If you haven't got any shame for yourself, Robert Chapley, you've got a mother-in-law who can be ashamed for you. No strangers shall be charged for room and lodging in any house where Mrs. Matilda Pitman lives. Remember that, though I may have come down in the world, I haven't quite forgot all decency for all that. I knew you was a skinflint when Amelia married you, and you've made her as bad as yourself. But Mrs. Matilda Pitman has been boss for a long time, and Mrs. Matilda Pitman will remain boss. Here you, Robert Chapley, take yourself out of here and let that girl get dressed. And you, Amelia, go downstairs and cook a breakfast for her."

Never, in all her life, had Rilla seen anything like the abject meekness with which those two big people obeyed that mite. They went without word or look of protest. As the door closed behind them Mrs. Matilda Pitman laughed silently, and rocked from side to side in her merriment.

"Ain't it funny?" she said. "I mostly lets them run the length of their tether, but sometimes I has to pull them up, and then I does it with a jerk. They don't dast aggravate me, because I've got considerable hard cash, and they're afraid I won't leave it all to them. Neither I will. I'll leave 'em some, but some I won't, just to vex 'em. I haven't made up my mind where I will leave it but I'll have to, soon, for at eighty a body is living on borrowed time. Now, you can take your time about dressing, my dear, and I'll go down and keep them mean scallawags in order. That's a handsome child you have there. Is he your brother?"

"No, he's a little war-baby I've been taking care of, because his mother died and his father was overseas," answered Rilla in a subdued tone.

"War-baby! Humph! Well, I'd better skin out before he wakes up or he'll likely start crying. Children don't like me—never did. I can't recollect any youngster ever coming near me of its own accord. Never had any of my own. Amelia was my step-daughter. Well, it's saved me a world of bother. If kids don't like me I don't like them, so that's an even score. But that certainly is a handsome child."

Jims chose this moment for waking up. He opened his big brown eyes and looked at Mrs. Matilda Pitman unblinkingly. Then he sat up, dimpled deliciously, pointed to her and said solemnly to Rilla, "Pwitty lady, Willa, pwitty lady."

Mrs. Matilda Pitman smiled. Even eighty-odd is sometimes vulnerable in vanity. "I've heard that children and fools tell the truth," she said. "I was used to compliments when I was young—but they're scarcer when you get as far along as I am. I haven't had one for years. It tastes good. I s'pose now, you monkey, you wouldn't give me a kiss."

Then Jims did a quite surprising thing. He was not a demonstrative youngster and was chary with kisses even to the Ingleside people. But without a word he stood up in bed, his plump little body encased only in his undershirt, ran to the footboard, flung his arms about Mrs. Matilda Pitman's neck, and gave her a bear hug, accompanied by three or four hearty, ungrudging smacks.

"Jims," protested Rilla, aghast at this liberty.

"You leave him be," ordered Mrs. Matilda Pitman, setting her bonnet straight.

"Laws I like to see some one that isn't skeered of me. Everybody is—you are, though you're trying to hide it. And why? Of course Robert and Amelia are because I make 'em skeered on purpose. But folks always are—no matter how civil I be to them. Are you going to keep this child?"

"I'm afraid not. His father is coming home before long."

"Is he any good—the father, I mean?"

"Well—he's kind and nice—but he's poor—and I'm afraid he always will be," faltered Rilla.

"I see—shiftless—can't make or keep. Well, I'll see—I'll see. I have an idea. It's a good idea, and besides it will make Robert and Amelia squirm. That's its main merit in my eyes, though I like that child, mind you, because he ain't skeered of me. He's worth some bother. Now, you get dressed, as I said before, and come down when you're good and ready."

Rilla was stiff and sore after her tumble and walk of the night before but she was not long in dressing herself and Jims. When she went down to the kitchen she found a smoking hot breakfast on the table. Mr. Chapley was nowhere in sight and Mrs. Chapley was cutting bread with a sulky air. Mrs. Matilda Pitman was sitting in an armchair, knitting a grey army sock. She still wore her bonnet and her triumphant expression.

"Set right in, dears, and make a good breakfast," she said.

"I am not hungry," said Rilla almost pleadingly. "I don't think I can eat anything. And it is time I was starting for the station. The morning train will soon be along. Please excuse me and let us go—I'll take a piece of bread and butter for Jims."

Mrs. Matilda Pitman shook a knitting-needle playfully at Rilla.

"Sit down and take your breakfast," she said. "Mrs. Matilda Pitman commands you. Everybody obeys Mrs. Matilda Pitman—even Robert and Amelia. You must obey her too."

Rilla did obey her. She sat down and, such was the influence of Mrs. Matilda Pitman's mesmeric eye, she ate a tolerable breakfast. The obedient Amelia never spoke; Mrs. Matilda Pitman did not speak either; but she knitted furiously and chuckled. When Rilla had finished, Mrs. Matilda Pitman rolled up her sock.

"Now you can go if you want to," she said, "but you don't have to go. You can stay here as long as you want to and I'll make Amelia cook your meals for you."

The independent Miss Blythe, whom a certain clique of Junior Red Cross girls accused of being domineering and "bossy," was thoroughly cowed.

"Thank you," she said meekly, "but we must really go."

"Well, then," said Mrs. Matilda Pitman, throwing open the door, "your conveyance is ready for you. I told Robert he must hitch up and drive you to the station. I enjoy making Robert do things. It's almost the only sport I have left. I'm over eighty and most things have lost their flavour except bossing Robert."

Robert sat before the door on the front seat of a trim, double-seated, rubber-tired buggy. He must have heard every word his mother-in-law said but he gave no sign.

"I do wish," said Rilla, plucking up what little spirit she had left, "that you would let me—oh—ah—" then she quailed again before Mrs. Matilda Pitman's eye—"recompense you for—for—"

"Mrs. Matilda Pitman said before—and meant it—that she doesn't take pay for entertaining strangers, nor let other people where she lives do it, much as their natural meanness would like to do it. You go along to town and don't forget to call the next time you come this way. Don't be scared. Not that you are scared of much, I reckon, considering the way you sassed Robert back this morning. I like your spunk. Most girls nowadays are such timid, skeery creeturs. When I was a girl I wasn't afraid of nothing nor nobody. Mind you take good care of that boy. He ain't any common child. And make Robert drive round all the puddles in the road. I won't have that new buggy splashed."

As they drove away Jims threw kisses at Mrs. Matilda Pitman as long as he could see her, and Mrs. Matilda Pitman waved her sock back at him. Robert spoke no word, either good or bad, all the way to the station, but he remembered the puddles. When Rilla got out at the siding she thanked him courteously. The only response she got was a grunt as Robert turned his horse and started for home.

"Well"—Rilla drew a long breath—"I must try to get back into Rilla Blythe again. I've been somebody else these past few hours—I don't know just who—some creation of that extraordinary old person's. I believe she hypnotized me. What an adventure this will be to write the boys."

And then she sighed. Bitter remembrance came that there were only Jerry, Ken, Carl and Shirley to write it to now. Jem—who would have appreciated Mrs. Matilda Pitman keenly—where was Jem?

CHAPTER XXXII - WORD FROM JEM

4th August 1918

"It is four years tonight since the dance at the lighthouse—four years of war. It seems like three times four. I was fifteen then. I am nineteen now. I expected that these past four years would be the most delightful years of my life and they have been years of war—years of fear and grief and worry—but I humbly hope, of a little growth in strength and character as well.

"Today I was going through the hall and I heard mother saying something to father about me. I didn't mean to listen—I couldn't help hearing her as I went along the hall and upstairs—so perhaps that is why I heard what listeners are said never to hear—something good of myself. And because it was mother who said it I'm going to write it here in my journal, for my comforting when days of discouragement come upon me, in which I feel that I am vain and selfish and weak and that there is no good thing in me.

"'Rilla has developed in a wonderful fashion these past four years. She used to be such an irresponsible young creature. She has changed into a capable, womanly girl and she is such a comfort to me. Nan and Di have grown a little away from me—they have been so little at home—but Rilla has grown closer and closer to me. We are chums. I don't see how I could have got through these terrible years without her, Gilbert.'

"There, that is just what mother said—and I feel glad—and sorry—and proud—and humble! It's beautiful to have my mother think that about me—but I don't deserve it quite. I'm not as good and strong as all that. There are heaps of times when I have felt cross and impatient and woeful and despairing. It is mother and Susan who have been this family's backbone. But I have helped a little, I believe, and I am so glad and thankful.

"The war news has been good right along. The French and Americans are pushing the Germans back and back and back. Sometimes I am afraid it is too good to last—after nearly four years of disasters one has a feeling that this constant success is unbelievable. We don't rejoice noisily over it. Susan keeps the flag up but we go softly. The price paid has been too high for jubilation. We are just thankful that it has not been paid in vain.

"No word has come from Jem. We hope—because we dare not do anything else. But there are hours when we all feel—though we never say so—that such hoping is foolishness. These hours come more and more frequently as the weeks go by. And we may never know. That is the most terrible thought of all. I wonder how Faith is bearing it. To judge from her letters she has never for a moment given up hope, but she must have had her dark hours of doubt like the rest of us."

20th August 1918

"The Canadians have been in action again and Mr. Meredith had a cable today saying that Carl had been slightly wounded and is in the hospital. It did not say where the wound was, which is unusual, and we all feel worried. There is news of a fresh victory every day now."

30th August 1918

"The Merediths had a letter from Carl today. His wound was "only a slight one"—but it was in his right eye and the sight is gone for ever!

"'One eye is enough to watch bugs with,' Carl writes cheerfully. And we know it might have been oh so much worse! If it had been both eyes! But I cried all the afternoon after I saw Carl's letter. Those beautiful, fearless blue eyes of his!

"There is one comfort—he will not have to go back to the front. He is coming home as soon as he is out of the hospital—the first of our boys to return. When will the others come?

"And there is one who will never come. At least we will not see him if he does. But, oh, I think he will be there—when our Canadian soldiers return there will be a shadow army with them—the army of the fallen. We will not see them—but they will be there!"

1st September 1918

"Mother and I went into Charlottetown yesterday to see the moving picture, "Hearts of the World." I made an awful goose of myself—father will never stop teasing me about it for the rest of my life. But it all seemed so horribly real—and I was so intensely interested that I forgot everything but the scenes I saw enacted before my eyes. And then, quite near the last came a terribly exciting one. The heroine was struggling with a horrible German soldier who was trying to drag her away. I knew she had a knife—I had seen her hide it, to have it in readiness—and I couldn't understand why she didn't produce it and finish the brute. I thought she must have forgotten it, and just at the tensest moment of the scene I lost my head altogether. I just stood right up on my feet in that crowded house and shrieked at the top of my voice—'The knife is in your stocking—the knife is in your stocking!'

"I created a sensation!

"The funny part was, that just as I said it, the girl did snatch out the knife and stab the soldier with it!

"Everybody in the house laughed. I came to my senses and fell back in my seat, overcome with mortification. Mother was shaking with laughter. I could have shaken her. Why hadn't she pulled me down and choked me before I had made such an idiot of myself. She protests that there wasn't time.

"Fortunately the house was dark, and I don't believe there was anybody there who knew me. And I thought I was becoming sensible and self-controlled and womanly! It is plain I have some distance to go yet before I attain that devoutly desired consummation."

20th September 1918

"In the east Bulgaria has asked for peace, and in the west the British have smashed the Hindenburg line; and right here in Glen St. Mary little Bruce Meredith has done something that I think wonderful—wonderful because of the love behind it. Mrs. Meredith was here tonight and told us about it—and mother and I cried, and Susan got up and clattered the things about the stove.

"Bruce always loved Jem very devotedly, and the child has never forgotten him in all these years. He has been as faithful in his way as Dog Monday was in his. We have always told him that Jem would come back. But it seems that he was in Carter Flagg's store last night and he heard his Uncle Norman flatly declaring that Jem Blythe would never come back and that the Ingleside folk might as well give up hoping he would. Bruce went home and cried himself to sleep. This morning his mother saw him going out of the yard, with a very sorrowful and determined look, carrying his pet kitten. She didn't think much more about it until later on he came in, with the most tragic little face, and told her, his little body shaking with sobs, that he had drowned Stripey.

"'Why did you do that?' Mrs. Meredith exclaimed.

"'To bring Jem back,' sobbed Bruce. 'I thought if I sacrificed Stripey God would send Jem back. So I drownded him—and, oh mother, it was awful hard—but surely God will send Jem back now, 'cause Stripey was the dearest thing I had. I just told God I would give Him Stripey if He would send Jem back. And He will, won't He, mother?'

"Mrs. Meredith didn't know what to say to the poor child. She just could not tell him that perhaps his sacrifice wouldn't bring Jem back—that God didn't work that way. She told him that he mustn't expect it right away—that perhaps it would be quite a long time yet before Jem came back.

"But Bruce said, 'It oughtn't to take longer'n a week, mother. Oh, mother, Stripey was such a nice little cat. He purred so pretty. Don't you think God ought to like him enough to let us have Jem?"

"Mr. Meredith is worried about the effect on Bruce's faith in God, and Mrs. Meredith is worried about the effect on Bruce himself if his hope isn't fulfilled. And I feel as if I must cry every time I think of it. It was so splendid—and sad—and beautiful. The dear devoted little fellow! He worshipped that kitten. And if it all goes for nothing—as so many sacrifices seem to go for nothing—he will be brokenhearted, for he isn't old enough to understand that God doesn't answer our prayers just as we hope—and doesn't make bargains with us when we yield something we love up to Him."

24th September 1918

"I have been kneeling at my window in the moonshine for a long time, just thanking God over and over again. The joy of last night and today has been so great that it seemed half pain—as if our hearts weren't big enough to hold it.

"Last night I was sitting here in my room at eleven o'clock writing a letter to Shirley. Every one else was in bed, except father, who was out. I heard the telephone ring and I ran out to the hall to answer it, before it should waken mother. It was long-distance calling, and when I answered it said 'This is the telegraph Company's office in Charlottetown. There is an overseas cable for Dr. Blythe.'

"I thought of Shirley—my heart stood still—and then I heard him saying, 'It's from Holland.'

"The message was,

'Just arrived. Escaped from Germany. Quite well. Writing.
James Blythe.'

"I didn't faint or fall or scream. I didn't feel glad or surprised. I didn't feel anything. I felt numb, just as I did when I heard Walter had enlisted. I hung up the receiver and turned round. Mother was standing in her doorway. She wore her old rose kimono, and her hair was hanging down her back in a long thick braid, and her eyes were shining. She looked just like a young girl.

"'There is word from Jem?' she said.

"How did she know? I hadn't said a word at the phone except 'Yes—yes—yes.' She says she doesn't know how she knew, but she did know. She was awake and she heard the ring and she knew that there was word from Jem.

"'He's alive—he's well—he's in Holland,' I said.

"Mother came out into the hall and said, 'I must get your father on the 'phone and tell him. He is in the Upper Glen.'

"She was very calm and quiet—not a bit like I would have expected her to be. But then I wasn't either. I went and woke up Gertrude and Susan and told them. Susan said 'Thank God,' firstly, and secondly she said 'Did I not tell you Dog Monday knew?' and thirdly, 'I'll go down and make a cup of tea'—and she stalked down in her nightdress to make it. She did make it—and made mother and Gertrude drink it—but I went back to my room and shut my door and locked it, and I knelt by my window and cried—just as Gertrude did when her great news came.

"I think I know at last exactly what I shall feel like on the resurrection morning."

4th October 1918

"Today Jem's letter came. It has been in the house only six hours and it is almost read to pieces. The post-mistress told everybody in the Glen it had come, and everybody came up to hear the news.

"Jem was badly wounded in the thigh—and he was picked up and taken to prison, so delirious with fever that he didn't know what was happening to him or where he was. It was weeks before he came to his senses and was able to write. Then he did write—but it never came. He wasn't treated at all badly at his camp—only the food was poor. He had nothing to eat but a little black bread and boiled turnips and now and then a little soup with black peas in it. And we sat down every one of those days to three good square luxurious meals! He wrote us as often as he could but he was afraid we were not getting his letters because no reply came. As soon as he was strong enough he tried to escape, but was caught and brought

1111

back; a month later he and a comrade made another attempt and succeeded in reaching Holland.

"Jem can't come home right away. He isn't quite so well as his cable said, for his wound has not healed properly and he has to go into a hospital in England for further treatment. But he says he will be all right eventually, and we know he is safe and will be back home sometime, and oh, the difference it makes in everything!

"I had a letter from Jim Anderson today, too. He has married an English girl, got his discharge, and is coming right home to Canada with his bride. I don't know whether to be glad or sorry. It will depend on what kind of a woman she is. I had a second letter also of a somewhat mysterious tenor. It is from a Charlottetown lawyer, asking me to go in to see him at my earliest convenience in regard to a certain matter connected with the estate of the 'late Mrs. Matilda Pitman.'

"I read a notice of Mrs. Pitman's death—from heart failure—in the Enterprise a few weeks ago. I wonder if this summons has anything to do with Jims."
5th October 1918

"I went into town this morning and had an interview with Mrs. Pitman's lawyer—a little thin, wispy man, who spoke of his late client with such a profound respect that it is evident that he as was much under her thumb as Robert and Amelia were. He drew up a new will for her a short time before her death. She was worth thirty thousand dollars, the bulk of which was left to Amelia Chapley. But she left five thousand to me in trust for Jims. The interest is to be used as I see fit for his education, and the principal is to be paid over to him on his twentieth birthday. Certainly Jims was born lucky. I saved him from slow extinction at the hands of Mrs. Conover—Mary Vance saved him from death by diptheritic croup—his star saved him when he fell off the train. And he tumbled not only into a clump of bracken, but right into this nice little legacy.

"Evidently, as Mrs. Matilda Pitman said, and as I have always believed, he is no common child and he has no common destiny in store for him.

"At all events he is provided for, and in such a fashion that Jim Anderson can't squander his inheritance if he wanted to. Now, if the new English stepmother is only a good sort I shall feel quite easy about the future of my war-baby.

"I wonder what Robert and Amelia think of it. I fancy they will nail down their windows when they leave home after this!"

CHAPTER XXXIII - VICTORY!

"A day 'of chilling winds and gloomy skies,'" Rilla quoted one Sunday afternoon—the sixth of October to be exact. It was so cold that they had lighted a fire in the living-room and the merry little flames were doing their best to counteract the outside dourness. "It's more like November than October—November is such an ugly month."

Cousin Sophia was there, having again forgiven Susan, and Mrs. Martin Clow, who was not visiting on Sunday but had dropped in to borrow Susan's cure for rheumatism—that being cheaper than getting one from the doctor. "I'm afeared we're going to have an airly winter," foreboded Cousin Sophia. "The muskrats are building awful big houses round the pond, and that's a sign that never fails. Dear me, how that child has grown!" Cousin Sophia sighed again, as if it were an unhappy circumstance that a child should grow. "When do you expect his father?"

"Next week," said Rilla.

"Well, I hope the stepmother won't abuse the pore child," sighed Cousin Sophia, "but I have my doubts—I have my doubts. Anyhow, he'll be sure to feel the difference between his usage here and what he'll get anywhere else. You've spoiled him so, Rilla, waiting on him hand and foot the way you've always done."

Rilla smiled and pressed her cheek to Jims' curls. She knew sweet-tempered, sunny, little Jims was not spoiled. Nevertheless her heart was anxious behind her smile. She, too, thought much about the new Mrs. Anderson and wondered uneasily what she would be like.

"I can't give Jims up to a woman who won't love him," she thought rebelliously.

"I b'lieve it's going to rain," said Cousin Sophia. "We have had an awful lot of rain this fall already. It's going to make it awful hard for people to get their roots in. It wasn't so in my young days. We gin'rally had beautiful Octobers then. But the seasons is altogether different now from what they used to be." Clear across Cousin Sophia's doleful voice cut the telephone bell. Gertrude Oliver answered it. "Yes—what? What? Is it true—is it official? Thank you—thank you."

Gertrude turned and faced the room dramatically, her dark eyes flashing, her dark face flushed with feeling. All at once the sun broke through the thick clouds and poured through the big crimson maple outside the window. Its reflected glow enveloped her in a weird immaterial flame. She looked like a priestess performing some mystic, splendid rite.

"Germany and Austria are suing for peace," she said.

Rilla went crazy for a few minutes. She sprang up and danced around the room, clapping her hands, laughing, crying.

"Sit down, child," said Mrs. Clow, who never got excited over anything, and so had missed a tremendous amount of trouble and delight in her journey through life.

"Oh," cried Rilla, "I have walked the floor for hours in despair and anxiety in these past four years. Now let me walk in joy. It was worth living long dreary years for this minute, and it would be worth living them again just to look back to it. Susan, let's run up the flag—and we must phone the news to every one in the Glen."

"Can we have as much sugar as we want to now?" asked Jims eagerly.

It was a never-to-be-forgotten afternoon. As the news spread excited people ran about the village and dashed up to Ingleside. The Merediths came over and stayed to supper and everybody talked and nobody listened. Cousin Sophia tried to protest that Germany and Austria were not to be trusted and it was all part of a plot, but nobody paid the least attention to her.

"This Sunday makes up for that one in March," said Susan.

"I wonder," said Gertrude dreamily, apart to Rilla, "if things won't seem rather flat and insipid when peace really comes. After being fed for four years on horrors and fears, terrible reverses, amazing victories, won't anything less be tame and uninteresting? How strange—and blessed—and dull it will be not to dread the coming of the mail every day."

"We must dread it for a little while yet, I suppose," said Rilla. "Peace won't come—can't come—for some weeks yet. And in those weeks dreadful things may happen. My excitement is over. We have won the victory—but oh, what a price we have paid!"

"Not too high a price for freedom," said Gertrude softly. "Do you think it was, Rilla?"

"No," said Rilla, under her breath. She was seeing a little white cross on a battlefield of France. "No—not if those of us who live will show ourselves worthy of it—if we 'keep faith.'"

"We will keep faith," said Gertrude. She rose suddenly. A silence fell around the table, and in the silence Gertrude repeated Walter's famous poem "The Piper." When she finished Mr. Meredith stood up and held up his glass. "Let us drink," he said, "to the silent army—to the boys who followed when the Piper summoned. 'For our tomorrow they gave their today'—theirs is the victory!"

CHAPTER XXXIV - MR. HYDE GOES TO HIS OWN PLACE AND SUSAN TAKES A HONEYMOON

Early in November Jims left Ingleside. Rilla saw him go with many tears but a heart free from boding. Mrs. Jim Anderson, Number Two, was such a nice little woman that one was rather inclined to wonder at the luck which bestowed her on Jim. She was rosy-faced and blue-eyed and wholesome, with the roundness and trigness of a geranium leaf. Rilla saw at first glance that she was to be trusted with Jims.

"I'm fond of children, miss," she said heartily. "I'm used to them—I've left six little brothers and sisters behind me. Jims is a dear child and I must say you've done wonders in bringing him up so healthy and handsome. I'll be as good to him as if he was my own, miss. And I'll make Jim toe the line all right. He's a good worker—all he needs is some one to keep him at it, and to take charge of his money. We've rented a little farm just out of the village, and we're going to settle down there. Jim wanted to stay in England but I says 'No.' I hankered to try a new country and I've always thought Canada would suit me."

"I'm so glad you are going to live near us. You'll let Jims come here often, won't you? I love him dearly."

"No doubt you do, miss, for a lovabler child I never did see. We understand, Jim and me, what you've done for him, and you won't find us ungrateful. He can come here whenever you want him and I'll always be glad of any advice from you about his bringing up. He is more your baby than anyone else's I should say, and I'll see that you get your fair share of him, miss."

So Jims went away—with the soup tureen, though not in it. Then the news of the Armistice came, and even Glen St. Mary went mad. That night the village had a bonfire, and burned the Kaiser in effigy. The fishing village boys turned out and burned all the sandhills off in one grand glorious conflagration that extended for seven miles. Up at Ingleside Rilla ran laughing to her room.

"Now I'm going to do a most unladylike and inexcusable thing," she said, as she pulled her green velvet hat out of its box. "I'm going to kick this hat about the room until it is without form and void; and I shall never as long as I live wear anything of that shade of green again."

"You've certainly kept your vow pluckily," laughed Miss Oliver.

"It wasn't pluck—it was sheer obstinacy—I'm rather ashamed of it," said Rilla, kicking joyously. "I wanted to show mother. It's mean to want to show your own mother—most unfilial conduct! But I have shown her. And I've shown myself a few things! Oh, Miss Oliver, just for one moment I'm really feeling quite young again—young and frivolous and silly. Did I ever say November was an ugly month? Why it's the most beautiful month in the whole year. Listen to the bells ringing in Rainbow Valley! I never heard them so clearly. They're ringing for peace—and new happiness—and all the dear, sweet, sane, homey things that we can have again now, Miss Oliver. Not that I am sane just now—I don't pretend to be. The whole world is having a little crazy spell today. Soon we'll sober down—and 'keep faith'—and begin to build up our new world. But just for today let's be mad and glad."

Susan came in from the outdoor sunlight looking supremely satisfied.

"Mr. Hyde is gone," she announced.

"Gone! Do you mean he is dead, Susan?"

"No, Mrs. Dr. dear, that beast is not dead. But you will never see him again. I feel sure of that."

"Don't be so mysterious, Susan. What has happened to him?"

"Well, Mrs. Dr. dear, he was sitting out on the back steps this afternoon. It was just after the news came that the Armistice had been signed and he was looking his Hydest. I can assure you he was an awesome looking beast. All at once, Mrs. Dr. dear, Bruce Meredith came around the corner of the kitchen walking on his stilts. He has been learning to walk on them lately and came over to show me how well he could do it. Mr. Hyde just took a look and one bound carried him over the yard fence. Then he went tearing through the maple grove in great leaps with his ears laid back. You never saw a creature so terrified, Mrs. Dr. dear. He has never returned."

"Oh, he'll come back, Susan, probably chastened in spirit by his fright."

"We will see, Mrs. Dr. dear—we will see. Remember, the Armistice has been signed. And that reminds me that Whiskers-on-the-moon had a paralytic stroke last night. I am not saying it is a judgment on him, because I am not in the counsels of the Almighty, but one can have one's own thoughts about it. Neither Whiskers-on-the-moon or Mr. Hyde will be much more heard of in Glen St. Mary, Mrs. Dr. dear, and that you may tie to."

Mr. Hyde certainly was heard of no more. As it could hardly have been his fright that kept him away the Ingleside folk decided that some dark fate of shot or poison had descended on him—except Susan, who believed and continued to affirm that he had merely "gone to his own place." Rilla lamented him, for she had been very fond of her stately golden pussy, and had liked him quite as well in his weird Hyde moods as in his tame Jekyll ones.

"And now, Mrs. Dr. dear," said Susan, "since the fall house-cleaning is over and the garden truck is all safe in cellar, I am going to take a honeymoon to celebrate the peace."

"A honeymoon, Susan?"

"Yes, Mrs. Dr. dear, a honeymoon," repeated Susan firmly. "I shall never be able to get a husband but I am not going to be cheated out of everything and a honeymoon I intend to have. I am going to Charlottetown to visit my married brother and his family. His wife has been ailing all the fall, but nobody knows whether she is going to die not. She never did tell anyone what she was going to do until she did it. That is the main reason why she was never liked in our family. But to be on the safe side I feel that I should visit her. I have not been in town for over a day for twenty years and I have a feeling that I might as well see one of those moving pictures there is so much talk of, so as not to be wholly out of the swim. But have no fear that I shall be carried away with them, Mrs. Dr. dear. I shall be away a fortnight if you can spare me so long."

"You certainly deserve a good holiday, Susan. Better take a month—that is the proper length for a honeymoon."

"No, Mrs. Dr. dear, a fortnight is all I require. Besides, I must be home for at least three weeks before Christmas to make the proper preparations. We will have a Christmas that is a Christmas this year, Mrs. Dr. dear. Do you think there is any chance of our boys being home for it?"

"No, I think not, Susan. Both Jem and Shirley write that they don't expect to be home before spring—it may be even midsummer before Shirley comes. But Carl Meredith will be home, and Nan and Di, and we will have a grand celebration once more. We'll set chairs for all, Susan, as you did our first war Christmas—yes, for all—for my dear lad whose chair must always be vacant, as well as for the others, Susan."

"It is not likely I would forget to set his place, Mrs. Dr. dear," said Susan, wiping her eyes as she departed to pack up for her "honeymoon."

CHAPTER XXXV - "RILLA-MY-RILLA!"

Carl Meredith and Miller Douglas came home just before Christmas and Glen St. Mary met them at the station with a brass band borrowed from Lowbridge and speeches of home manufacture. Miller was brisk and beaming in spite of his wooden leg; he had developed into a broad-shouldered, imposing looking fellow and the D. C. Medal he wore reconciled Miss Cornelia to the shortcomings of his pedigree to such a degree that she tacitly recognized his engagement to Mary.

The latter put on a few airs—especially when Carter Flagg took Miller into his store as head clerk—but nobody grudged them to her.

"Of course farming's out of the question for us now," she told Rilla, "but Miller thinks he'll like storekeeping fine once he gets used to a quiet life again, and Carter Flagg will be a more agreeable boss than old Kitty. We're going to be married in the fall and live in the old Mead house with the bay windows and the mansard roof. I've always thought that the handsomest house in the Glen, but never did I dream I'd ever live there. We're only renting it, of course, but if things go as we expect and Carter Flagg takes Miller into partnership we'll own it some day. Say, I've got on some in society, haven't I, considering what I come from? I never aspired to being a storekeeper's wife. But Miller's real ambitious and he'll have a wife that'll back him up. He says he never saw a French girl worth looking at twice and that his heart beat true to me every moment he was away."

Jerry Meredith and Joe Milgrave came back in January, and all winter the boys from the Glen and its environs came home by twos and threes. None of them came back just as they went away, not even those who had been so fortunate as to escape injury.

One spring day, when the daffodils were blowing on the Ingleside lawn, and the banks of the brook in Rainbow Valley were sweet with white and purple violets, the little, lazy afternoon accommodation train pulled into the Glen station. It was very seldom that passengers for the Glen came by that train, so nobody was there to meet it except the new station agent and a small black-and-yellow dog, who for four and a half years had met every train that had steamed into Glen St. Mary. Thousands of trains had Dog Monday met and never had the boy he waited and watched for returned. Yet still Dog Monday watched on with eyes that never quite lost hope. Perhaps his dog-heart failed him at times; he was growing old and rheumatic; when he walked back to his kennel after each train had gone his gait was very sober now—he never trotted but went slowly with a drooping head and a depressed tail that had quite lost its old saucy uplift.

One passenger stepped off the train—a tall fellow in a faded lieutenant's uniform, who walked with a barely perceptible limp. He had a bronzed face and there were some grey hairs in the ruddy curls that clustered around his forehead. The new station agent looked at him anxiously. He was used to seeing the khaki-clad figures come off the train, some met by a tumultuous crowd, others, who had sent no word of their coming, stepping off quietly like this one. But there was a certain distinction of bearing and features in this soldier that caught his attention and made him wonder a little more interestedly who he was.

A black-and-yellow streak shot past the station agent. Dog Monday stiff? Dog Monday rheumatic? Dog Monday old? Never believe it. Dog Monday was a young pup, gone clean mad with rejuvenating joy.

He flung himself against the tall soldier, with a bark that choked in his throat from sheer rapture. He flung himself on the ground and writhed in a frenzy of welcome. He tried to climb the soldier's khaki legs and slipped down and groveled in an ecstasy that seemed as if it must tear his little body in pieces. He licked his boots and when the lieutenant had, with laughter on his lips and tears in his eyes, succeeded in gathering the little creature up in his arms Dog Monday laid his head on the khaki shoulder and licked the sunburned neck, making queer sounds between barks and sobs.

The station agent had heard the story of Dog Monday. He knew now who the returned soldier was. Dog Monday's long vigil was ended. Jem Blythe had come home.

"We are all very happy—and sad—and thankful," wrote Rilla in her diary a week later, "though Susan has not yet recovered—never will recover, I believe—from the shock of having Jem come home the very night she had, owing to a strenuous day, prepared a 'pick up' supper. I shall never forget the sight of her, tearing madly about from pantry to cellar, hunting out stored away goodies. Just as if anybody cared what was on the table—none of us could eat, anyway. It was meat and drink just to look at Jem. Mother seemed afraid to take her eyes off him lest he vanish out of her sight. It is wonderful to have Jem back—and little Dog Monday. Monday refuses to be separated from Jem for a moment. He sleeps on the foot of his bed and squats beside him at meal-times. And on Sunday he went to church with him and insisted on going right into our pew, where he went to sleep on Jem's feet. In the middle of the sermon he woke up and seemed to think he must welcome Jem all over again, for he bounded up with a series of barks and wouldn't quiet down until Jem took him up in his arms. But nobody seemed to mind, and Mr. Meredith came and patted his head after the service and said, "'Faith and affection and loyalty are precious things wherever they are found. That little dog's love is a treasure, Jem.'

"One night when Jem and I were talking things over in Rainbow Valley, I asked him if he had ever felt afraid at the front.

"Jem laughed.

"'Afraid! I was afraid scores of times—sick with fear—I who used to laugh at Walter when he was frightened. Do you know, Walter was never frightened after he got to the front. Realities never scared him—only his imagination could do that. His colonel told me that Walter was the bravest man in the regiment. Rilla, I never realized that Walter was dead till I came back home. You don't know how I miss him now—you folks here have got used to it in a sense—but it's all fresh to me. Walter and I grew up together—we were chums as well as brothers—and now here, in this old valley we loved when we were children, it has come home to me that I'm not to see him again.'

"Jem is going back to college in the fall and so are Jerry and Carl. I suppose Shirley will, too. He expects to be home in July. Nan and Di will go on teaching. Faith doesn't expect to be home before September. I suppose she will teach then too, for she and Jem can't be married until he gets through his course in medicine. Una Meredith has decided, I think, to take a course in Household Science at Kingsport—and Gertrude is to be married to her Major and is frankly happy about it—'shamelessly happy' she says; but I think her attitude is very beautiful. They are all talking of their plans and hopes—more soberly than they used to do long ago, but still with interest, and a determination to carry on and make good in spite of lost years.

"'We're in a new world,' Jem says, 'and we've got to make it a better one than the old. That isn't done yet, though some folks seem to think it ought to be. The job isn't finished—it isn't really begun. The old world is destroyed and we must build up the new one. It will be the task of years. I've seen enough of war to realize that we've got to make a world where wars can't happen. We've given Prussianism its mortal wound but it isn't dead yet and it isn't confined to Germany either. It isn't enough to drive out the old spirit—we've got to bring in the new.'

"I'm writing down those words of Jem's in my diary so that I can read them over occasionally and get courage from them, when moods come when I find it not so easy to 'keep faith.'"

Rilla closed her journal with a little sigh. Just then she was not finding it easy to keep faith. All the rest seemed to have some special aim or ambition about which to build up their lives—she had none. And she was very lonely, horribly lonely. Jem had come back—but he was not the laughing boy-brother who had gone away in 1914 and he belonged to Faith. Walter would never come back. She had not even Jims left. All at once her world seemed wide and empty—that is, it had seemed wide and empty from the moment yesterday when she had read in a Montreal paper a fortnight-old list of returned soldiers in which was the name of Captain Kenneth Ford.

So Ken was home—and he had not even written her that he was coming. He had been in Canada two weeks and she had not had a line from him. Of course he had forgotten—if there was ever anything to forget—a handclasp—a kiss—a look—a promise asked under the influence of a passing emotion. It was all absurd—she had been a silly, romantic, inexperienced goose. Well, she would be wiser in the future—very wise—and very discreet—and very contemptuous of men and their ways.

"I suppose I'd better go with Una and take up Household Science too," she thought, as she stood by her window and looked down through a delicate emerald tangle of young vines on Rainbow Valley, lying in a wonderful lilac light of sunset. There did not seem anything very attractive just then about Household Science, but, with a whole new world waiting to be built, a girl must do something.

The door bell rang, Rilla turned reluctantly stairwards. She must answer it—there was no one else in the house; but she hated the idea of callers just then. She went downstairs slowly, and opened the front door.

A man in khaki was standing on the steps—a tall fellow, with dark eyes and hair, and a narrow white scar running across his brown cheek. Rilla stared at him foolishly for a moment. Who was it?

She ought to know him—there was certainly something very familiar about him—"Rilla-my-Rilla," he said.

"Ken," gasped Rilla. Of course, it was Ken—but he looked so much older—he was so much changed—that scar—the lines about his eyes and lips—her thoughts went whirling helplessly.

Ken took the uncertain hand she held out, and looked at her. The slim Rilla of four years ago had rounded out into symmetry. He had left a school girl, and he found a woman—a woman with wonderful eyes and a dented lip, and rose-bloom cheek—a woman altogether beautiful and desirable—the woman of his dreams.

"Is it Rilla-my-Rilla?" he asked, meaningly.

Emotion shook Rilla from head to foot. Joy—happiness—sorrow—fear—every passion that had wrung her heart in those four long years seemed to surge up in her soul for a moment as the deeps of being were stirred. She had tried to speak; at first voice would not come. Then—"Yeth," said Rilla.

Lucy Maud Montgomery - Collected Short Stories
Lucy Maud Montgomery
Oxford City Press, 2012
984 pages
ISBN: 978-1-78139-239-3

Available from www.amazon.com,
www.amazon.co.uk

Lucy Maud Montgomery was a Canadian author and
is best known for her novels, the first of which was Anne of Green Gables,
published in 1908. She also published over 500 short stories, and 142 of
these are available in this collected short stories. The stories in this volume
show L.M. Montgomery's early talent as a writer. The characters are interesting, the Canadian settings are described beautifully and a plot with dramatic
tension is introduced quickly. The stories vary in style from romantic to funny to sinister. This book offers a fascinating series of stories to read.

Also
  Lucy Maud Montgomery Short Stories 1896 to 1901   978-1-84902-279-8
  Lucy Maud Montgomery Short Stories 1902-1903   978-1-78139-240-9
  Lucy Maud Montgomery Short Stories 1904   978-1-78139-241-6
  Lucy Maud Montgomery Short Stories 1905-1906   978-1-78139-242-3
  Lucy Maud Montgomery Short Stories 1907-1908   978-1-78139-243-0
  Lucy Maud Montgomery Short Stories 1909-1922   978-1-78139-244-7

**The Complete Little Women - Little Women, Good
Wives, Little Men, Jo's Boys**
Louisa May Alcott
Benediction Classics, 2012
804 pages
ISBN: 978-1-78139-233-1

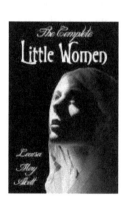

Available from www.amazon.com, www.amazon.co.uk

Little Women, Good Wives, Little Men and Jo's Boys are
a series of novels by American author Louisa May Alcott
(1832-1888). The books are loosely based on the author's childhood experiences with her three sisters. The novels are classics - the publisher unable to
keep up with the demand when the first book in the series was published.
Themes of romance, family drama, gender constraints and the validation of
virtue over wealth are explored in these timeless stories.

**Penny Nichols Omnibus - Finds a Clue, Mystery of the
Lost Key, Black Imp, & Knob Hill Mystery**
Joan Clark
Oxford City Press, 2012
484 pages
ISBN: 978-1-78139-158-7

Available from www.amazon.com, www.amazon.co.uk

The Penny Nichols series consists of four titles: 1. Penny
Nichols Finds a Clue (1936) 2. Penny Nichols and the Mystery of the Lost Key
(1936) 3. Penny Nichols and the Black Imp (1936) 4. Penny Nichols and the
Knob Hill Mystery (1939) Penny Nichols is the daughter of Christopher Nichols, an eminent detective. Penny's dad often disregards her ideas, but time
and again she is proved right and he has to recognise that she is also a good
detective. Penny is often accompanied in her adventures by her best friend,
Susan Altman. These books have fabulous plots and are page turners for children of any age. Enjoy!

**Frances Hodgson Burnett Children's Stories Omnibus
(unabridged) The Secret Garden, A Little Princess, Lit-
tle Lord Fauntleroy, Racketty-Packetty House, The
Lost Prince, Little Saint Elizabeth and other stories,
Land of the Blue Flower, Sara Crewe or What Hap-
pened At Miss Minchin's Boarding School**
Frances Hodgson Burnett
Benediction Classics, 2012
786 pages
ISBN: 978-1-78139-253-9

Available from www.amazon.com, www.amazon.co.uk

Frances Hodgson Burnett is considered to be one of the greatest writers of
Children's stories. This volume contains her three most well known stories:
The Secret Garden, A Little Princess and Little Lord Fauntleroy, with The Lost
Prince and a number of short stories. The contents are: The Secret Garden, A
Little Princess, Little Lord Fauntleroy, Racketty-Packetty House, The Lost
Prince, Little Saint Elizabeth and other stories, Land of the Blue Flower, Sara
Crewe or What Happened At Miss Minchin's Boarding School.

Also from Benediction Books …
Wandering Between Two Worlds: Essays on Faith and Art
Anita Mathias
Benediction Books, 2007
152 pages
ISBN: 0955373700

Available from www.amazon.com, www.amazon.co.uk

In these wide-ranging lyrical essays, Anita Mathias writes, in lush, lovely prose, of her naughty Catholic childhood in Jamshedpur, India; her large, eccentric family in Mangalore, a sea-coast town converted by the Portuguese in the sixteenth century; her rebellion and atheism as a teenager in her Himalayan boarding school, run by German missionary nuns, St. Mary's Convent, Nainital; and her abrupt religious conversion after which she entered Mother Teresa's convent in Calcutta as a novice. Later rich, elegant essays explore the dualities of her life as a writer, mother, and Christian in the United States-- Domesticity and Art, Writing and Prayer, and the experience of being "an alien and stranger" as an immigrant in America, sensing the need for roots.

About the Author

Anita Mathias is the author of *Wandering Between Two Worlds: Essays on Faith and Art.* She has a B.A. and M.A. in English from Somerville College, Oxford University, and an M.A. in Creative Writing from the Ohio State University, USA. Anita won a National Endowment of the Arts fellowship in Creative Non-fiction in 1997. She lives in Oxford, England with her husband, Roy, and her daughters, Zoe and Irene.

Anita's website:
    http://www.anitamathias.com, and
Anita's blog Dreaming Beneath the Spires:
    http://dreamingbeneaththespires.blogspot.com

The Church That Had Too Much
Anita Mathias
Benediction Books, 2010
52 pages
ISBN: 9781849026567

Available from www.amazon.com, www.amazon.co.uk

The Church That Had Too Much was very well-intentioned. She wanted to love God, she wanted to love people, but she was both hampered by her muchness and the abundance of her possessions, and beset by ambition, power struggles and snobbery. Read about the surprising way The Church That Had Too Much began to resolve her problems in this deceptively simple and enchanting fable.

About the Author

Anita Mathias is the author of *Wandering Between Two Worlds: Essays on Faith and Art*. She has a B.A. and M.A. in English from Somerville College, Oxford University, and an M.A. in Creative Writing from the Ohio State University, USA. Anita won a National Endowment of the Arts fellowship in Creative Non-fiction in 1997. She lives in Oxford, England with her husband, Roy, and her daughters, Zoe and Irene.

Anita's website:
    http://www.anitamathias.com, and
Anita's blog Dreaming Beneath the Spires:
    http://dreamingbeneaththespires.blogspot.com

CPSIA information can be obtained
at www.ICGtesting.com
Printed in the USA
BVHW08*2307161018
530209BV00025B/544/P